THE ENCYCLOPEDIA
OF THE
NEW YORK STAGE,
1920–1930

THE ENCYCLOPEDIA OF THE NEW YORK STAGE, 1920–1930

A-M

SAMUEL L. LEITER, *Editor-in-Chief*

Holly Hill, *Associate Editor*

Greenwood Press
Westport, Connecticut • London, England

Library of Congress Cataloging in Publication Data

Leiter, Samuel L.
  The encyclopedia of the New York stage, 1920-1930.

  Bibliography: p.
  Includes indexes.
  1. Theater—New York (N.Y.)—Dictionaries. I. Hill,
Holly. II. Title.
PN2277.N5L36 1985   792.9'5'097471   84-6558
ISBN 0-313-23615-1 (lib. bdg.)
ISBN 0-313-25037-5 (lib. bdg.: v. 1)
ISBN 0-313-25038-3 (lib. bdg.: v. 2)

Library of Congress Catalog Card Number: 84-6558
ISBN: 0-313-23615-1 (set)
ISBN: 0-313-25037-5 (v. 1)
ISBN: 0-313-25038-3 (v. 2)

First published in 1985

Greenwood Press
A division of Congressional Information Service, Inc.
88 Post Road West
Westport, Connecticut 06881

Printed in the United States of America

10 9 8 7 6 5 4 3 2 1

To the loving memory of my friends and teachers Wilson Lehr
and "Skipper" Jo Davidson

Contents

Preface

This book, the first of a planned multivolume series, is an attempt to provide a description of every legitimate theatre production—play, musical, revue, revival—given in the New York professional theatre during the decade of the 1920s. Since the conventional computation of a theatre season is from June 16 of one year to June 15 of the next, the book covers all works staged between June 16, 1920, and June 15, 1930.[1] Only works produced in Manhattan are given, and these works are restricted to the theatres of Broadway and what would today be called Off Broadway. One or two out-of-the-way theatres in Manhattan, such as the Shubert-Riviera, functioned as road-show houses, getting productions that had already played their regular engagement and were now being toured; such theatres are not covered here. There was considerable theatre activity in the other boroughs, especially in Brooklyn, but to have included that activity here would have made this volume unmanageable.

The listings are not restricted to English-language productions; every known foreign-language production visiting the city and reviewed in the English-language press has been chronicled. In fewer than a half-dozen of such shows, the titles, dates, and company names only have been given, since critical coverage was nil. However, because English-language reviews and other press coverage often overlooked foreign actors and companies playing for local ethnic audiences, it should not be assumed that the present volume is comprehensive for such productions.

Ethnic theatre offerings were extensive, with many New York-based companies offering plays regularly in Italian, Yiddish, Spanish, German, and other languages. Many of these productions were amateur and thus are not included here; however, a lot of professional activity, especially in Italian and Yiddish, was carried on. The most extensive and highly developed ethnic theatre activity was in the Yiddish language. The *Encyclopedia of the New York Stage* treats local ethnic theatre productions selectively (based largely on their coverage in the English-language press).

Often, it was difficult to determine whether a given production was amateur or professional. A few of the works entered here might loosely be defined as "semiprofessional.''[2] In two or three cases they were included because a famous actor played the leading role. In other cases they were included because the company involved was recognized sufficiently to receive regular critical coverage. The Provincetown Players, for example, liked to consider itself as an amateur group in its early years, but to ignore it would leave a serious gap in this work. Similarly, the productions of the American Laboratory Theatre and those of the Theatre Guild's students have been included because of the ultimate importance these companies and/or their participants have had on the American stage. These works were reviewed fairly extensively by the major critics and were, in most cases, treated on the same level as those of the better recognized professionals. Only when the critics made it perfectly clear that a specific company was made up of amateurs have their productions been omitted.

There are approximately 2,500 production entries here, arranged alphabetically. There are not that many titles, however, since some plays were given multiple presentations. By turning to *The Merchant of Venice*, for instance, you will find a chronological listing of all stagings of that play during the decade. Titles that begin with the abbreviations *Mr., Mrs., Mme., Mlle.*, and *Dr.* are considered as if these words were fully spelled out: *Mister, Mistress, Madame, Mademoiselle*, and *Doctor*. Titles beginning with contractions such as *It's, Don't*, and *I'll* are considered as if they were spelled without the apostrophe. Titles that begin with articles such as *A, An, The, Il, Le, Les*, and *Los* have these words placed at their ends, for example, *Dice of the Gods, The*.

Each listing is headed by specific information concerning the respective offering. Contemporary credits were not always complete, nor were they 100 percent reliable; thus in some cases certain pieces of information are not provided, usually because they were unavailable.

The following are typical examples of entry headings:

ACCUSED (L'Avocat)

[Drama/Law/Crime/Romance/French] A: Eugene Brieux; TR: George Middleton; D/P: David Belasco; S: Joseph Wickes; T: Belasco Theatre; 9/29/25 (95)

HOMME ET SES FANTÔMES, L' (Man and His Phantoms)

[Drama/Spiritualism/Romance/French/French Language] A: H. R. Lenormand; D: Firmin Gémier; T: Jolson's Fifty-ninth Street Theatre; 11/13/24 (3)

CAPTAIN JINKS

[Musical/Romance/Military/Show Business] B/P: Frank Mandel and Laurence Schwab; M: Lewis E. Gensler and Stephen Jones; LY: B. G. De Sylva; SC: Clyde Fitch's play *Captain Jinks of the Horse Marines*; D: Edgar J. MacGregor;

CH: Sammy Lee; S: Frederick Jones III; C: Kiviette; T: Martin Beck Theatre; 9/8/25 (167)

The types of data included in the entry headings and their respective abbreviations (where applicable) are noted below:

1. *Title*: Most works are listed under the title by which they were advertised or reviewed; in some cases this title was in a foreign language but the work, being well known in English, may be entered under its English name with the foreign title in parentheses. If the play is entered under the foreign title, an English version follows in parentheses. When the same play was given under different titles during the period, all discussions of the play will be found under whichever title is considered the best known. (See, for example, *Candle Light*.) When known, earlier titles by which a play may have been known before its New York production are given in the text of the specific entry. Any question about a title may be resolved by checking the Index of Titles. All entries in the text are arranged alphabetically. When there is more than one entry (production) for a title, the entries are arranged chronologically.

2. *Categories*: Following the title, and placed within brackets, are the categories to which the play has been found to correspond. Each new work (works determined not to be revivals) has been designated, for the sake of simplicity, as a comedy, drama, comedy-drama, musical, pantomime, or revue. The genre words *tragedy, melodrama, farce, operetta, comic opera, musical comedy*, and so on have not been used in the category listings but will often be found within the text entries. Following the genre designation are various categories appropriate to the work. Terms such as those given in the above examples should provide a bird's-eye view of the nature of the play. This subject categorization is as thorough as possible, although these categories are meant as a guide and should not always be accepted literally. A play may only be indirectly related to war, for example, but the word *war* in the heading may signal that this is indeed a "war play." Perusal of the specific entry should make clearer the reason for inclusion of the word. As in the second example given above, some plays are also categorized by the language in which they were presented, if other than English. Appendix 2, where all such categorizations are compiled into lists, provides further background on the category listings. In most cases, the category listings are self-explanatory. Titles designated as "Dramatic Revivals" or "Musical Revivals" have not been further categorized, aside from whether they were presented in a specific foreign tongue. This is also true for "Revues," which are further categorized only if they are of foreign origin or were given by black performers.

3. *Author* (A): The name of the playwright(s) of a straight (nonmusical)

play. When the author serves in other capacities as well, such as director, producer, and so on, a slash (/) signifies this, for example, A/D. When the same individual functions alone in one capacity and with someone else in another, the slash is not used and the name is given separately according to the specific function. This holds true for all of the artists listed below.

4. *Translator* (TR) or *Adaptor* (AD): The name of the person who translated or adapted the work into English.

5. *Revised By* (REV): The person who revised a script before it was produced; only rarely credited.

6. *Book* (B): The name of the librettist(s) of a musical or review. The credit for adding material to the book is ADD.B.

7. *Conceived By* (CN): The person responsible for conceptualizing a show; used mainly for revues.

8. *Music* (M): The name of the composer(s) of a musical or revue. Also, the person who composes incidental music for a straight play.

9. *Lyricist* (LY): The name of the lyricist(s) of a musical or revue.

10. *Additional Music* (ADD. M.): Used when a composer is credited with providing material in addition to that which is composed by the main composer; this was a frequent practice when many songs were interpolated into musicals by individuals other than those responsible for most of the score.

11. *Additional Lyrics* (ADD. L.): See no. 9.

12. *Source* (SC): The source—novel, short story, poem, and so on—upon which the work is based.

13. *Director* (D): The name of the director, where known.

14. *Choreographer* (CH): This term was barely used during the period but is now the word by which the artist who creates dances for musicals (and some straight plays) is known. It was not always clear who the choreographer was, so these listings are not as complete as others.

15. *Set Designer* (S): This category, too, was not always credited. Set designers often provided costume designs; when they did, the designation *DS* has been used for overall designer.

16. *Costume Designer* (C): Another not well-credited department; see no. 15.

17. *Designer* (DS): See no. 15.

18. *Producer* (P): The name of the producer(s), not always credited. When multiple producers were credited, their participation was often described with a designation such as "by arrangement with," "by special arrangement with," or "in association with." Here, such arrangements are abbreviated to *b/a/w*, *b/s/a/w*, and *i/a/w*.

19. *Theatre* (T): The name of the theatre where the production opened. In one or two cases the theatre named is that where the work had its regular run, after a trial performance elsewhere. In these instances the name of the original theatre is given in the entry. When the name of the playhouse is followed by (OB), it means that the theatre was what would today be considered an Off-Broadway theatre, either because of size or location. When there is no (OB), the theatre should be considered a part of Broadway. During the 1920s all professional theatre in New York was loosely called "Broadway," the term *Off-Broadway* not being originated until the 1930s and not coming into general public acceptance until the early 1950s. Whenever known, the theatre(s) to which a production moved during its run are given in the entries. A list of all theatres used by the productions in this volume, broken down into Broadway and Off Broadway, is given in Appendix 10.

20. *Opening Dates*: Following the name of the playhouse is the date on which the production opened, given in numerals with slashes, for example, 9/29/25. Plays that appeared in repertory and were seen in more than one season have their subsequent dates provided in the entries, whenever possible. Dates for repertory productions do not signal the start of a consecutive run but only the first date on which the work was seen during a season. Other dates important to the production, when known, are provided in the entries as well.

21. *Length of Run*: The figure in parentheses that ends most headings signifies the number of performances attained by the work during its run. These figures are not always known, especially for local productions of the ethnic theatre groups. This represents a most puzzling problem for the researcher in the field. It is extraordinary how divergent are the available figures for the runs of plays during the decade. The situation is even more disturbing when one compares the figures given in major secondary reference works based on contemporary materials, since the source of the information pertaining to dates is never given. The principal contemporary sources for determining the length of runs are the annual Burns Mantle *Best Plays of 1920–30* series, the annual New York *Times* summaries, and the summaries found in trade journals such as *Variety* and *Billboard*. The statistics encountered in one source often diverge strikingly from those in another; sometimes the difference is only of one or two performances. For purposes of consistency, the present work has relied mainly on a secondary source, the listings prepared by Maxwell Silverman, a member of the Theatre Collection of the New York Public Library staff, for *Notable Names in the American Theatre*, edited by Raymond McGill (1976). Unfortunately, in double checking these figures, an occasional error of significant proportions turned up. Whenever possible, such errors have been corrected by substituting that figure upon which a majority of

the other available sources agreed. In a number of instances the original newspaper listings were consulted. The best solution would have been personally to make a count of all performances of all productions by studying the daily advertisements; the task, however, was beyond the physical resources of the editor of this work.

The text that follows each heading offers a fairly comprehensive view of the work. It attempts to give the important historical background, a summary of the plot, and an idea of the critical reaction to the play and the performance. Representative quotes of the critics are incorporated verbatim or in paraphrase. Footnotes are not used, and the name of the reviewer is often provided within the sentence by enclosing it in parentheses. When the review being quoted from is unsigned, the newspaper or journal from which it derives is given. The words "New York" have been removed from newspaper names in which they figure; instead, the names are reduced to *Times, Herald Tribune, Sun*, and so on. The name of the publication(s) for which a specific reviewer wrote is provided in Appendix 8. In most cases newspaper reviews appeared the day after a play's opening. Occasionally, however, a play was given a second look in a Sunday column a week or more after the premiere. Most of the critical quotes taken from newspapers are from opening-night reviews; the text does not discriminate, though, between opening night and follow-up notices. Magazine reviews quoted appeared in either weekly or monthly periodicals and can usually be found in the issue closest in time to the opening of a show. In addition to critical quotes, hundreds of anecdotes culled largely from biographical and autobiographical accounts have been incorporated throughout. Since footnotes are not used to document these sources, enough information is given in the entries (author's name or title of the work cited) so that you may find the appropriate work by referring to the Selected Bibliography.

Many plays described in this volume have not been included in earlier accounts of the period. The most complete record of contemporary production available to date has been the annual Burns Mantle volumes; however, Mantle missed a good number of productions that this work contains.

At the end of this book are ten appendices and the Selected Bibliography. The appendices include the list of critics cited in the text, the listing of plays by category, a chronological calendar of all productions of the period, the names of all New York theatres of the decade, a year-by-year statistical breakdown of numbers of productions, a listing of award-winning plays, a list of novels and plays providing source materials for plays and musicals, a list of institutional theatres and their offerings, a list of foreign companies and stars, and a list of the longest running shows of the era.

Holly Hill was responsible for researching and writing almost all of the entries for 1923–1924. Approximately fifty entries for 1920–1921 were written by Mary Ann Messano-Ciesla. The initials of Hill and Messano-Ciesla are given at the end of each of their respective entries. No initials are used to designate the remaining entries, all of which were written by the editor-in-chief, who takes full responsibility for the entire work; he would be happy to hear of any errors or omissions so that corrections may appear in any future editions.

Without the Theatre Collection of the New York City Public Library at Lincoln Center, this book could never have been written. Thanks are hereby tendered to that institution's excellent staff. The newspaper collection of the New York Public Library was likewise of invaluable aid. The staff of the Harry D. Gideonse Library at Brooklyn College went overboard in their willingness to assist; Barbara Scheel was instrumental in obtaining valuable research materials especially for this project, and she has earned a permanent debt of gratitude. I am likewise very grateful to Bill Gargan of the same library. Mark Liwszyc was extremely helpful in providing Russian play titles and George Kait was equally useful in obtaining Yiddish titles. Also very valuable was the Queensborough Public Library, in particular its excellent main branch. I want to thank Marilyn Brownstein of Greenwood Press for her abundant ideas and encouragement. The most irreplaceable component of this project was my indefatigable wife, Marcia, who, as ever, somehow found time amidst her own writing and responsibilities as wife and mother to help me whenever the need arose.

SAMUEL L. LEITER

NOTES

1. Some contemporary sources preferred to count the beginning of the season from June 1 and the end at May 31. This accounts for some of the discrepancies in the statistics cited in Appendix 9.

2. A notable example of an amateur company that received irregular coverage in the press, including the *Times*, was that run by Butler Davenport at his private theatre on East Twenty-eighth Street. Davenport charged no admission for the wicker seats he provided, and did a standard repertory of old and modern classics. His work is not covered here.

Introduction

Undoubtedly the 1920s saw a richer assortment of world drama and theatre technique than has any other decade in our history.
—Glenn Hughes, *A History of the American Theatre, 1700–1950*[1]

The most vivid, fervent, and fruitful years of the American theatre were the 1920s.
—Emory Lewis, *Stages: The Fifty Year Childhood of the American Theatre*[2]

The story of this century's third decade has been too often told to bear extensive repeating here, but an outline of major theatrical developments during the period should prove helpful in putting the entries that follow into a comprehensible perspective.

THE INSTITUTIONAL THEATRES

If the modern American theatre can be said to have been born in the 1920s, its period of gestation may be said to have been that of the 1910s. Likewise, if a single year may be declared to have witnessed the conception, that year would have to be 1915. In 1915 three noncommercial theatre groups were formed, two in New York City and one in Provincetown, Massachusetts. They were the Washington Square Players, the Neighborhood Playhouse, and the Provincetown Players (which had its premiere New York season in 1916). These groups were an outgrowth of the period's Little Theatre movement, designed to challenge the complacency of the commercial stage by introducing the dramas of Europe's most challenging new playwrights, by offering the plays of fledgling American writers, and by staging these works in the imaginative, artistically integrated manner being popularized abroad and at home as the "New Stagecraft." Some authentic examples of the New Stagecraft had been seen in New York, such as when Germany's Max Reinhardt brought his Oriental pantomime *Sumurun* to these shores in 1912 and when France's Jacques Copeau took a two-year residency at Broadway's old Garrick Theatre from 1917 to 1919 with his Théâtre du Vieux Colombier troupe. The inauguration of *Theatre Arts Monthly* in 1917 gave American readers abundant documentation regarding the latest continental developments in staging and design.

The new independent theatre companies, all of which operated under subscription plans, were originally located in what was much later to be known as "Off Broadway," that is, anywhere outside of what the unions were to designate as the geographical and economic parameters setting Broadway apart from its smaller or far-flung competitors. Although most Off Broadway theatres were to find themselves in Greenwich Village, they could just as easily fit the classification if they were located elsewhere in Manhattan, even, if they were small enough, in the midst of the full-size playhouses of the Main Stem itself. To critics of the 1920s, however, the professional theatre in New York was generally referred to as "Broadway," even when a production was nowhere near that street.

The Provincetown Playhouse set up shop at 133 and soon moved to 139 Macdougal Street in the Village, where it had a 220-seat house; the Washington Square Players began at the intimate Bandbox on East 57th Street near Third Avenue and then shifted to Broadway's Comedy Theatre; and the Neighborhood Playhouse took residence at a new theatre built for them by their founders, the wealthy Lewisohn sisters, amidst the melting pot environment of 466 Grand Street on the Lower East Side.

The Provincetown Players were at first a semiprofessional organization that sought primarily to give the new American playwright a platform from which to speak. It was founded by Jig Cook and his wife, Susan Glaspell, playwrights both, and it earned the eternal thankfulness of theatre lovers everywhere for being the company that discovered America's first internationally renowned dramatist, Eugene Gladstone O'Neill. When O'Neill's *Emperor Jones* became a sensation in 1920 and was moved uptown, it precipitated a struggle within the ranks concerning the Provincetown's vaunted "amateur" status versus its going into commercial production. Ultimately, in 1922 Glaspell and Cook departed for Greece; the company closed for a year of rest and then continued until 1929, when economic considerations forced it to close its doors. During this period it was run by several leaders, among them a "triumvirate" composed of O'Neill, Robert Edmond Jones, and Kenneth Macgowan, under the rubric of "The Experimental Theatre, Inc.," which simultaneously managed the Greenwich Village Theatre. During the 1920s the Provincetown achieved lasting fame with plays such as Glaspell's *Inheritors* and *The Verge*; O'Neill's *Hairy Ape, All God's Chillun Got Wings*, and *Desire under the Elms*; and Paul Green's *In Abraham's Bosom*. Contrary to its original aims, it also did some foreign plays and revivals and was responsible for a major production of Anna Cora Mowatt's 1840 *Fashion* and for the American premiere of Strindberg's *Dream Play*. Among the actors it nurtured were Mary Blair, Louis Wolheim, Charles Gilpin, and E. J. Ballantine, and designers Robert Edmond Jones and Cleon Throckmorton had an inestimable effect on the native theatre.

The Neighborhood Playhouse began as an amateur troupe but went professional in 1920. It was founded to serve the cultural needs of the immigrant masses living in the area but soon found itself playing to theatre lovers from all over town. It was more concerned with fostering the art of theatre production in general than with the discovery of important new scripts and concentrated on giving excellent stagings of a largely European repertory of recent plays and revivals; often these plays had a decidedly exotic slant. Their two most renowned presentations were of S. Ansky's *Dybbuk* and the ancient Sanskrit classic *The Little Clay Cart*. They also distinguished themselves with the series of intimate satirical revues *The Grand Street Follies*. Except for one year during which the theatre was closed while the Lewisohn sisters traveled abroad, the Neighborhood offered a half-dozen dramatic programs a year until 1927. Among its most famed discoveries were performers Albert Carroll, Dorothy Sands, and Edith Meiser and designer Aline Bernstein.

The Washington Square Players lasted until 1918 but were reformed under different auspices in 1919 under the name the "Theatre Guild," perhaps the most influential theatre company of its time. Headed by a board of six diverse personalities, it aimed from the start to compete with Broadway on its own turf by doing the best and most farseeing new scripts available in the finest stagings possible. The majority of its early plays were European, for which it was criticized, but it did an enormous service to the theatre in its production of the works of authors such as Franz Werfel, A. A. Milne, Georg Kaiser, Ferenc Molnar, Leonid Andreyev, and others; they specialized in George Bernard Shaw, offering eleven works, new and old, by the aged Irishman during the decade. The Guild did produce one of America's most important works during the early 1920s, Elmer Rice's *Adding Machine*, and in the decade's latter half sponsored a vigorous series of preeminent native plays by writers such as Sidney Howard, S. N. Behrman, Eugene O'Neill, and DuBose and Dorothy Heyward. At one point they attempted a modified repertory system; it grew very confusing all around when they had six plays going on an alternating basis at three theatres; the plan finally deflated when plays such as *Strange Interlude* and *Porgy* proved technically impossible to produce in repertory. The Guild gave America one of its finest designers in Lee Simonson, one of its most distinguished directors in Philip Moeller, and some of its most remarked upon actors in Alfred Lunt and Lynn Fontanne, Edward G. Robinson, Dudley Digges, Helen Westley, Philip Loeb, Henry Travers, Earle Larimore, Margalo Gillmore, and Clare Eames, among many others. The Guild commenced activities at the somewhat out-of-the-way 600-seat Garrick, but had to lease and rent other theatres to allow its plays to run profitably. In 1925 it raised enough money to open the beautiful, but architecturally eccentric, Guild Theatre on West 52nd Street. By the end of the decade the company had 30,000 local subscribers and countless thousands in cities around the nation to which it annually sent its productions.

During the decade a number of other companies attempted with varying degrees of success to stage plays of artistic merit outside the pale of purely commercial considerations. The most outstanding example was the Civic Repertory Theatre, founded in 1926 by actress-director Eva Le Gallienne to do plays in repertory according to the continental plan. She put on three-to-five plays a week at an old theatre on West 14th Street (which would fall into the Off-Broadway category); during the half-dozen years of the Civic Rep's life she offered, at $1.50 top, thirty-four plays in 1,581 performances. She directed most of the plays and acted in most of them as well. Her plays were predominantly European and included classics as well as new works. William Shakespeare, Gregorio Martinez Sierra, Serafin and Joaquin Quintero, Henrik Ibsen, Anton Chekhov, Moliere, and Leo Tolstoy were among the names on her theatre's eclectic list of playwrights.

The respected actor Walter Hampden ran a company along the old-time actor-manager lines, having taken over the Colonial Theatre on Broadway between West 62nd and 63rd streets and renamed it after himself. He offered a respectable series of poetic period dramas, Ibsen's *Enemy of the People* being his sole attempt at anything contemporary in style. Hampden's *pièce de résistance* was Edmond Rostand's *Cyrano de Bergerac*, which he revived on several occasions during the era to continued acclaim. He would have liked to follow a repertory system but was forced by economics to run his offerings as long as the public showed an interest in them.

Of considerable importance was the American Laboratory Theatre, an Off-Broadway troupe and training school set up by Richard Boleslavsky and Maria Ouspenskaya, both formerly of the Moscow Art Theatre. The group experienced varying fortunes from 1925 to 1930; most of its plays were staged by Boleslavsky who, with his staff, was largely responsible for introducing the Stanislavsky system of acting to America. Their plays, staged with a company of novice actors, included the work of Shakespeare, Knut Hamsun, Jules Romains, Eugène Labiche, Victorien Sardou, and moderns such as Clemence Dane and Lynn Riggs.

A principal failure among the institutional theatres that fought for recognition was the National Theatre founded by playwright Augustus Thomas; it succumbed after a disastrously received staging of *As You Like It*. Edward Goodman's Stagers did better with nine productions. A troupe organized under the aegis of Actors' Equity, the Equity Players, gave fourteen plays before being reorganized under Guthrie McClintic for another eighteen productions as the Actors' Theatre. The Garrick Players, led by English player Basil Sydney and his wife, Mary Ellis, shone with only three productions, the New York Theatre Assembly folded after four, and The New Playwrights Theatre, devoted to the scribblings of politically and artistically radical playwrights (Alexander Woollcott called them "the revolting playwrights") gave up the ghost after five, most of them at Greenwich Village's tiny Cherry Lane Playhouse.

THE COMMERCIAL MANAGEMENTS

Broadway's commercial managements clearly benefited from the high-quality work of the institutional theatres, although some enlightened producers, particularly Winthrop Ames, Arthur Hopkins, and John D. Williams, had provided Broadway during the teens with examples of first-rate work on a level with the best that Europe could offer. Hopkins in particular had energized the theatrical scene with a series of plays designed by Robert Edmond Jones and starring John Barrymore, who rose under this tutelage to preeminence as America's leading leading man.

During the 1920s Hopkins actively maintained his esteemed position by noteworthy mountings such as *Anna Christie, Burlesque*, the Barrymore *Hamlet, Machinal, Paris Bound*, and *What Price Glory?* Ames was less busy but presented important works such as *Beggar on Horseback, Escape*, a superbly staged repertory of Gilbert and Sullivan, and the English actor George Arliss in several successful plays. Williams faded out of the picture, but his place was taken by personages such as William A. Brady, Jr., in partnership with Dwight Deere Wiman, Morris Gest in association with F. Ray Comstock, and Jed Harris, Gilbert Miller, and Brock Pemberton.

The more overtly commercial managements, most of which now and then came up with something of more than merely passing value, were headed by the Shuberts, Lee and J. J., acting both in partnership and on their own, and giving Broadway dozens of plays, musicals, revues, operettas, and revivals; David Belasco, master showman since the nineteenth century and nearing the end of a fecund career; and William A. Brady, George M. Cohan, Charles Dillingham, A. L. Erlanger, the firm of Charles Frohman, Inc., Crosby Gaige, John Golden, Arthur Hammerstein, Sam H. Harris, Oliver Morosco, Carl Reed, Edgar Selwyn alone and in partnership with his brother Arch, Laurence Schwab, George C. Tyler, Charles L. Wagner, Lawrence L. Weber, A. H. Woods, and Florenz Ziegfeld, among many others.

There was an unprecedented boom in theatre production in the 1920s, culminating in the record high number of close to 300 offerings during the 1926–1927 season. During the Christmas week of 1927 eighteen new shows opened, eleven on December 26 alone. Every individual with postwar profits to burn seemed to gravitate to Broadway, and the enormous number of failures (more than 70 percent of all productions) is evidence for assuming that most had no idea what they were doing. The harmful effect of hundreds and hundreds of inept productions on the potential theatre audience was incalculable. Nearly 2,500 works were mounted in the decade, an average of 250 a year. This may have been a sign of increasing prosperity; it was no indication at all of artistic quality. Still, with so many productions going forward, it was easier than ever for writers to get produced, and the period did manage to stimulate the creation of the best American playwriting yet to be seen. For most of the decade theatre owners profited from always having their plants in operation, and actors, directors, dramatists, and designers had more opportunities for sharpening their skills than ever before. It was not unusual for an actor to play a half-dozen roles during a single season and not necessarily because he or she belonged to a rep company.

Throughout the 1920s millions of new listeners joined the radio-listening ranks;

radio had begun broadcasting in the very first year of the decade, and soon the phenomenon spread beyond the wildest expectations. There were 20 million radios in use by 1927, and by 1929 radio had become the nation's fourth largest industry. Similarly, theatre had had to compete for years with silent movies. In 1928 Al Jolson's *Jazz Singer* hit the picture palaces, and talkies became the theatre's newest nightmare.

At first sound films had certain economic advantages for theatre people in that they offered talent new and extremely lucrative outlets; they also provided producers with much needed capital for plays with possible movie futures. But in the long run they drained the theatre of its best talent and managed effectively to put an end to the "road," which soon saw its remaining playhouses wired for sound to house the new Hollywood presentations. Sound movies, radio, and the Wall Street crash were too much for the theatre to bear, and the 1930s saw a precipitous drop-off in activity along the Great White Way. In 1930 Burns Mantle complained, "More theatres have gone dark and remained dark in New York than in any other one season that I can recall."[3]

UNIONS AND CENSORSHIP

Further complicating matters for producers of the decade were two increasingly irritating annoyances, the unions and the censors. As early as 1893 when the stagehands were first organized, theatrical labor and management disputes were a bitter pill to swallow for those who were disinclined to view the theatre as an industry. The stagehands, at least, made no claims to being artists, but when musicians, actors, and playwrights organized, the fun of being a producer was considerably decreased. The actors, concerned at first more about general working conditions than about salaries, walked out in a historic strike in 1919; they threatened more than once to repeat that event during the 1920s. In 1924 a dispute arose between Equity and the Producing Managers' Association, representing Broadway's producers, over the issue of a closed shop for Equity. Twenty-seven producers declined to accept Equity's conditions, and another twenty-one formed a subsidiary group, the Manager's Protective Association; the latter agreed to compose their casts of 80 percent Equity members while the remaining 20 percent would be required to pay the equivalent of Equity dues. Before the matter was finished, however, seven shows were forced to ring down their final curtains.[4]

Headaches caused by Equity were coupled with those created by various other theatrical unions. The stagehands, the designers, the hauling companies, the musicians, and others each had restrictive policies and made financial demands— featherbedding was already in full bloom—that cut the profit margin for producers to a bare minimum. Producer Gilbert Miller wrote in a 1928 New York *Times* piece about his union troubles; he claimed that because of the unions, "a play with a well-known star, which played to receipts of $21,000 in Washington, made a profit of only $1,500. Another play, on weekly receipts of $12,000, made a profit for the producer of exactly $10."[5]

A new union roadblock was thrown in front of the producers in 1926 when the playwrights banded together to form the Dramatists' Guild and negotiated the first of the Minimum Basic Agreement contracts by which dramatic authors still are bound. By the late 1920s, then, the theatre's internal costs were escalating so rapidly that it was already beginning to reel when the talkies, the radio, and the crash came down like thunder on its shaky foundations. Even in 1929 a critic like John Anderson could write, in terms that sound depressingly familiar in the 1980s, that the theatre was being forced "to live by the hit—or miss—system in which a play is either an enormous success or an immediate and overwhelming failure."[6]

The unions were a threat at regularly scheduled contract-revision times, but a more persistent sword of Damocles was the ever-present pressure from citizens' groups who shouted jeremiads against the immorality of the stage. The postwar theatre was outspoken, in keeping with its times, and sex and profanity were the spicy ingredients thrown in varying amounts into numerous plays of the era. Usually, the writing managed to stay within the realm of contemporary standards of good taste, but on occasion it caused offense to auditors who consequently clamored for a cleanup. When various self-policing methods among the managers themselves seemed to fail, the law stepped in; the name of District Attorney Joab Banton has come down to us as much because of his involvement in various censorship disputes as for any of his achievements in the world of nontheatrical law enforcement.

The first example of the censor's meddling came with the closing down of *The God of Vengeance*, a powerful foreign drama, during the 1922–1923 season, and the fining of its management. In 1924–1925 the uproar grew more virulent, and a body of 300 citizens was selected as a pool of potential play jurors to sit in judgment on works accused of salaciousness. When claims against *Desire under the Elms, The Firebrand, What Price Glory?* and *Ladies of the Evening* were investigated, the sole action taken was to recommend minor changes in the last three. *A Good Bad Woman* was pressured to close but reopened later in the season and was left alone.

The climactic season for the censor was 1925–1926, when complaints were filed against *The Bunk of 1926, The Captive, The New York Exchange, Sex, An American Tragedy, The Shanghai Gesture, Lulu Belle, The Virgin Man*, and *Night Hawk. The Captive*, a respected hit play from the French dealing with bisexuality, closed voluntarily rather than fight in court, *Sex* shut up shop and its author-star Mae West was hauled off to the pokey, and *The Virgin Man* likewise ended its career, its management suffering court-imposed fines and jail sentences. The naughty revue *Bunk of 1926* obtained an injunction against closing, and by the time the law got around to checking it out it had died of natural causes.

In 1927 the Wales Padlock Law went into effect, giving the legal establishment the power to close a theatre for a year if a play on its boards was found to be immoral. Winthrop Ames tried to forestall the law with a well-reasoned plan for an impartial jury of seven, but despite considerable support, it eventually came to nothing. When *Maya* fell victim to the district attorney's suspicion, it was evicted by its landlord who did not want to risk losing in court and seeing his playhouse padlocked. Two Theatre Guild offerings, *Volpone* and *Strange Interlude*, also caught Banton's eye, but they passed muster without a scratch. A year later *Pleasure Man*, Mae West's rewritten version of her drag queen play *The Drag*, survived only two nights before its cast was carted off in a Black Maria.

THEATRE BUILDING

Perhaps the most visible sign of the decade's mad rush to produce every piece of dramatic flapdoodle that crossed its producers' desks was the incredible activity represented by the construction of Broadway playhouses. Twenty-four legitimate theatres opened their doors during the 1920s, the first being the Times Square in 1920 and the last being the Craig in 1928 (and not the Ethel Barrymore, as is often claimed). The Chanin brothers were alone responsible for the construction of six theatres within a space of five years. The need for theatres led to what Brooks Atkinson called "the most preposterous" playhouse of the era, the intimate Mayfair (within the Broadway area but of Off-Broadway proportions and not included in the total of twenty-four given above). It was built out of a 44th Street restaurant. Atkinson said, "The building was long but it was so narrow that there was no room for side exits for the actors, and there was no backstage space. The dressing rooms were in the basement. The actors had to make awkward entrances through a tiny hutch at the rear and on one side of the stage."[7] The Mayfair's life was very short.

At the turn of the century Times Square was still called "Long Acre Square" and had not yet become a theatrical center. Within thirty years eighty playhouses had been erected within its vicinity. By the 1920s the Shuberts had gained control of the majority of New York's first-class playhouses, which could then be built for about $1 million each. This initial investment could usually be recouped by the owner rather quickly, so theatre building continued apace. As the decade neared its end it became clear that there were more theatres than the traffic could bear, and the process of conversion to movie houses, soon to be followed by demolition of unwanted playhouses, commenced.[8]

PRODUCTION OVERVIEW

New York's theatrical production in the 1920s represented many topics, themes, nationalities, styles, languages, ethnic groups, and backgrounds. Most plays ran for as long as possible, the longest run of the decade being the fabled *Abie's Irish Rose*, which totaled 2,372 performances. Only in the Civic Repertory

Theatre was the long run disdained in favor of alternating several plays a week; even plays that were kept in the repertoire for several seasons failed to establish memorable statistics, since their impact tended to diminish during each season that they were renewed.

Revivals were a major source of production fodder when producers were unable to find appropriate new plays. Dramatic revivals ranged from the Greeks to recent hits; most were unimportant, but some made history. Shakespeare was represented by twenty-one plays in a robust sixty-three productions. (This includes a few revivals in languages other than English, such as Yiddish, French, and German.) *Hamlet* had nine productions, *Macbeth* had six, *The Taming of the Shrew* had seven, and both *Romeo and Juliet* and *Twelfth Night* had five; *The Merchant of Venice* led the pack with twelve, including six in a single season. The most significant Shakespeare revivals included the John Barrymore *Hamlet*; Basil Sydney's modern dress versions of *Hamlet* and *The Taming of the Shrew*; David Belasco's elaborate failure with *The Merchant of Venice*, starring David Warfield; the Jane Cowl *Romeo and Juliet*, which bested Ethel Barrymore's dreary version produced earlier the same season; the Eva Le Gallienne *Romeo and Juliet*; a *Macbeth* with designs inspired by Gordon Craig; the Max Reinhardt *Midsummer Night's Dream*; and several others. Of the 240-odd titles revived (some, as with Shakespeare, more than once), Ibsen's plays were very prominent, *Ghosts* alone receiving seven stagings. The classics were represented by writers such as George Farquhar, Richard Sheridan, Euripides, Moliere, Nikolai Gogol, Aristophanes, Sophocles, William Congreve, Oliver Goldsmith, and Ben Jonson. Of the moderns (other than Ibsen), Chekhov was all the rage, especially after the Moscow Art Theatre showed how he should be done; several of the Russian master's plays that made their local bows in English during the decade were soon restaged with new interpretations. Eva Le Gallienne's *Cherry Orchard* and Jed Harris's *Uncle Vanya* set the standard for other New York productions. George Bernard Shaw's familiar plays were also much in evidence, thanks to the Theatre Guild. Revivals of popular plays of the previous two decades often revealed how quickly dated these works had become.

Musical revivals were largely of well-liked operettas; during one season the Shuberts sponsored a series of such shows, most of them by Victor Herbert, at Jolson's 59th Street Theatre (on West 59th) under the direction of Milton Aborn. Gilbert and Sullivan revivals were a sign of the times, and various Viennese concoctions such as *The Merry Widow* delighted new audiences and old. Thirty-one musical titles were resuscitated from the musical graveyard.

The new American musicals of the decade represented a major step forward in quality as lyricists, composers, and librettists honed their craft, often with the intention of creating a mature form that blended all contributing elements into a harmonious package. Most of the slightly more than 270 new musicals offered were of the catch-as-catch-can variety: a nearly worthless book peppered by unrelated specialty acts and featuring some currently popular performers in the leading roles. Romantic operettas were also much in demand, and the decade saw some highly successful entries in this genre. However, it was not until Jerome Kern and Oscar Hammerstein II's collaboration on *Show Boat* (1927) that the American musical achieved masterpiece status and became the serious art form it has since remained. Other distinguished and popular musicals of the decade included *A Connecticut Yankee, The Desert Song, Funny Face, Good News, Hit the Deck! No, No, Nanette, Oh, Kay!, Rio Rita, Rose-Marie, Sally, Shuffle Along, Strike Up the Band*, and *Whoopee*.

The 1920s were enormously rich in vastly talented composers and lyricists; many of the standards still sung were composed for musicals of the decade. A roster of its Hall of Fame quality songwriters would have to include Irving Berlin, Noble Sissle and Eubie Blake, B. G. De Sylva, Ray Henderson and Lou Brown, J. Fred Coots, Rudolf Friml, Sigmund Romberg, George and Ira Gershwin, Victor Herbert, Raymond Hubbell, Bert Kalmar and Harry Ruby, Jimmy McHugh, Jerome Kern, Cole Porter, Richard Rodgers and Lorenz Hart, Harold Atteridge, Herbert Stothart, Arthur Schwartz, Maurie Rubens, Vincent Youmans, Harry Tierney, Joseph McCarthy, Dorothy Donnelly, Ballard McDonald, Frank Mandel, Harry B. Smith, Oscar Hammerstein II, Otto Harbach, Anne Caldwell, George M. Cohan, Irving Caesar, Noël Coward, and Howard Dietz, almost all of them American.

Most of these tune and wordsmiths also wrote for another phenomenon of the 1920s—the revue. There were all sorts of revues on display: big, intimate, spectacular, plain, home-grown, foreign, black, annual, and one-shot. The big-time annuals were the best known, among them *The Ziegfeld Follies, George White's Scandals, The Passing Show, Earl Carroll's Vanities, The Greenwich Village Follies*, and *The Music Box Revue*. The best of the intimate shows included the multieditioned Russian import, *Le Chauve-Souris*, the British *André Charlot's Revue* and *This Year of Grace, The Garrick Gaieties*, and *The Grand Street Follies*.

The revues were a showcase for outstanding musical, terpsichorean, comic, and design talent. Names like Eddie Cantor, Frank Tinney, Will Rogers, W. C. Fields, Noël Coward, Fannie Brice, Beatrice Lillie, Gertrude Lawrence, Bert Williams, Helen Morgan, and dozens of others of like fame flourished in the revue format. Some of the shows cost fabulous sums to present; often the principal object was to dazzle the audience with fantastic scenic and costume arrangements and effects. Female nudity was commonplace in these popular extravaganzas, yet did not incite the legal powers to action as much as did dramas with scandalous subject matter. Many of the revues prospered because of their topical humor; spoofing current hit shows was one of the most widespread stimulants for laughter.

New plays came to New York not only from native sources but from Austria, Great Britain, Czechoslovakia, France, Germany, Hungary, Italy, Russia, and Spain, to mention only the most prolific sources. America itself gave birth to an array of dramatic talent that quickly rivaled any of these nations' playwrights in critical esteem. Luigi Pirandello, Ferenc Molnar, A. A. Milne, John Galsworthy, George Bernard Shaw, Karel Capek, Nikolai Evreinov, Georg Kaiser,

Sean O'Casey, and Gregorio Martinez Sierra were challenged by rising American stalwarts such as George Abbott (with a host of collaborators), Zoë Akins, Maxwell Anderson, Philip Barry, S. N. Behrman, Marc Connelly (usually with George S. Kaufman), Rachel Crothers, Susan Glaspell, Paul Green, Sidney Howard, George S. Kaufman (with various collaborators), George Kelly, John Howard Lawson, Eugene O'Neill, Elmer Rice, and Robert E. Sherwood, not to mention a gallery of others whose works found outlets not only at home but around the world.

Despite the great number of successful dramatists during the period and the respect they garnered for the native product, it should not be forgotten that they were writing plays for a theatre that operated under auspices that were, above all else, commercial. Several of the notable playwrights just mentioned composed most of their works in collaboration with others. The community approach to playmaking was almost as common during the 1920s as was the conventional solo method. In a business as prone to failure as the theatre, two heads were considered better than one; a surprising number of the era's most successful plays were the product of such cooperative tinkering. Among such efforts were *What Price Glory? Broadway, The Front Page, Dulcy, Berkeley Square, Burlesque, Coquette, Rain, The Bat, Beggar on Horseback, Dracula, The Royal Family*, and *Porgy*.[9]

A significant number of the decade's plays dealt unashamedly with life's most vital concerns; war, politics, religion, sex, alcoholism, Prohibition, drugs, gambling, journalism, the medical profession, psychiatry, prostitution, racial bigotry, divorce, adultery, and homosexuality were among the many subjects given comparatively unvarnished treatment. Contemporary issues were often discussed with a frankness previously unheard on the American stage; as we have seen, dramatists occasionally overstepped the bounds of what many in the theatregoing public considered tasteful, but they persisted nonetheless. Some of their work was clearly written for sensationalistic reasons, but a considerable number of works were intended as meaningful contributions to the issues they confronted. More than ever before, the drama of ideas was making a place for itself in the writing of American playwrights.

Comedy, tragedy, melodrama, and farce were the timeworn forms into which plays of the decade were poured; satire made great strides, as did philosophical and fantastical imaginings; crime plays were rampant, thrillers were abundant, dramas showing domestic tribulations were familiar, small-town life was idolized and refuted, bourgeois values were speared, materialism was both crucified and glorified, and the meaning of existence was agonizingly scrutinized. There was also significant formal experimentation, especially in the mode of expressionism, that attracted native authors such as Eugene O'Neill, Elmer Rice, George S. Kaufman and Marc Connelly, and John Howard Lawson.

One of the most prominent cultural manifestations of the decade was what has been labeled the Harlem Renaissance. Revues, book musicals, and plays featuring black characters and milieus filled the stages of New York season after season. The convention of whites playing blacks in burnt cork makeup continued through the 1920s but came to seem ever more ridiculous as black actors entered the mainstream and demonstrated their abilities. The most noteworthy stimulus to the employment of blacks was the performance of Charles Gilpin in the original production of *The Emperor Jones*; soon actors like Rose McClendon, Frank Wilson, Paul Robeson, and Inez Clough gave proof of a pool of talent that for too long had been neglected. Audiences at musicals and revues clapped enthusiastically to the talents of Miller and Lyles, Bill ''Bojangles'' Robinson, Florence Mills, and Ethel Waters. Most black-related plays of the period were written by white authors; they included *Goat Alley, Porgy, In Abraham's Bosom, All God's Chillun Got Wings*, and *The Green Pastures*. However, black playwrights made their first impact on Broadway now beginning with Willis Richardson's *Chip Woman's Fortune*, and continuing with Garland Anderson's *Appearances*, Frank Wilson's *Meek Mose*, and Wallace Thurman's (with William Jourdan Rapp) *Harlem*. In the musical field the smash hit *Shuffle Along* set a precedent that many others tried to follow.

The Yiddish theatre also made a conspicuous contribution to the ethnic diversity of the New York stage. A corps of active Yiddish theatre companies, mostly situated on the Lower East Side, presented a broad assortment of offerings; most of them were of the heavily sentimental variety called ''shund.'' However, several art theatres of importance existed, among them Maurice Schwartz's Yiddish Art Theatre and Jacob Ben-Ami's Jewish Art Theatre and, later, his New Jewish Art Theatre. The Yiddish companies occasionally produced respected foreign plays before they were seen in English. Important examples include *The God of Vengeance*, Sven Lange's *Samson and Delilah*, and Chekhov's *Uncle Vanya*. Many well-known players of the English stage began their careers in the Yiddish theatre, including Paul Muni, Luther and Stella Adler, Francine Larrimore, Bertha Kalich, and Molly Picon.

New York in the 1920s was a mecca for foreign companies and stars. Three Spanish-speaking companies arrived: Camila Quiroga and the Argentine Players, Madrid's Spanish Art Theatre, and that same city's Maria Guerrero-Fernando Diaz company from the Princess Theatre. Germany sent Max Reinhardt's miraculous productions, seven of them, and France was responsible for the companies of Firmin Gémier (six productions), Maurice de Féraudy (seven productions), Cécile Sorel (seven productions during two visits), Mme. Simone (eight productions), and the Modern French Musical Comedy Company (six productions). From Russia came the highly influential Moscow Art Theatre for two visits during which eleven bills were offered; later came the Moscow Art Theatre Musical Studio, headed by Vladimir Nemirovich-Danchenko, with five programs. Moscow was also responsible for the Habima Players, the renowned Hebrew language group that acted in five plays. Italy proudly shipped the aged Eleanora Duse to America; she presented five plays and then went on to Pittsburgh, where she died. Other Italian stars arrived with far less fanfare, among them Angelo Musco and Giovanni Grasso. Ireland sent the Irish Players of the

Abbey Theatre with two plays. Finally, from England, apart from the many players actively engaged in Broadway productions along with American actors, came the company of Sir John Martin-Harvey with four plays, including *Hamlet* and *Oedipus Rex*. Actress Marie Lohr sponsored two offerings. Ben Greet also arrived, unheralded, with a single performance each of *As You Like It* and *Everyman* played in a school auditorium.

ACTORS, DIRECTORS, AND DESIGNERS

The movies had not yet swallowed whole the best of America's acting talent, and the New York stage remained until the end of the decade a fabulous source of great performances. To list the names of all of those who are still remembered would require too much space; those who are given here are only meant to suggest the wealth of talent available to contemporary playwrights and producers. Of the older school one could mention E. H. Sothern and Julia Marlowe, Otis Skinner, Minnie Maddern Fiske, Charles Coburn, Nance O'Neill, Alla Nazimova, Mrs. Leslie Carter, Ethel Barrymore, Chrystal Herne, Laurette Taylor, Grace George, Billie Burke, John Drew, Lionel Barrymore, Frank Morgan, Fred Stone, Whitford Kane, Holbrook Blinn, Arnold Daly, William Gillette, George Arliss, David Warfield, Richard Bennett, Walter Hampden, Henry Miller, Tyrone Power, and George M. Cohan. This was also a flourishing decade for younger players such as Katharine Cornell, Donald (Donn) Cook, Louis Wolheim, Leo G. Carroll, Roland Young, Alfred Lunt and Lynn Fontanne, Edward G. Robinson, James Gleason, Mary Boland, Margaret Lawrence, Frances Starr, Florence Reed, Constance Collier, Winifred Lenihan, Ralph Morgan, Ian Maclaren, Eric Dressler, Philip Merivale, Rollo Peters, Jacob Ben-Ami, Otto Kruger, Moffat Johnston, John Cromwell, Eric Blore, Roland Young, Dennis King, McKay Morris, Lenore Ulric, Mary Nash, Dorothy Sands, Claiborne Foster, Fay Bainter, Spring Byington, Emily Stevens, Helen Chandler, Lyn Harding, Basil Sydney, Osgood Perkins, Glenn Hunter, Glenn Anders, Jose Ruben, Elliott Nugent, Donald Meek, George Abbott, Henry Hull, Walter Huston, Rosalinde Fuller, June Walker, Helen Menken, Peggy Wood, Ruth Gordon, Tallulah Bankhead, Eva Le Gallienne, Helen Hayes, Elsie Ferguson, Effie Shannon, Clare Eames, Louise Closser Hale, Laura Hope Crews, Anne Harding, Jeanne Eagels, Mae West, Ruth Chatterton, Dudley Digges, John Barrymore, Grant Mitchell, Alice Brady, Morgan Farley, Henry Travers, Tom Powers, Ernest Truex, Claude Rains, Gregory Kelly, Lionel Atwill, Margaret Wycherly, Margalo Gillmore, Blanche Yurka, Alison Skipworth, Pauline Lord, Jane Cowl, Estelle Winwood, Marjorie Rambeau, Ina Claire, Lee Patrick, Fritz Leiber, and Helen MacKellar. Some of these people were at the start of their careers, as were Miriam Hopkins, Judith Anderson, Florence Eldridge, Frederick March, Franchot Tone, Jessica Tandy, Paul Robeson, Paul Muni, Noël Coward, Romney Brent, Leslie Howard, Bela Lugosi, Spencer Tracy, Laurence Olivier, Melvyn Douglas, William Powell, Barbara Stanwyck, Aline McMahon, John Gielgud, Claudette Colbert, Bette

Davis, Sylvia Sidney, Shirley Booth, Cary Grant, Lee Tracy, Humphrey Bogart, James Cagney, Basil Rathbone, Ronald Colman, Sidney Blackmer, Pat O'Brien, Henry Fonda, Lee Strasberg, Walter Abel, Chester Morris, Sam Levene, Sheppard Strudwick, Otto Kruger, Horace Braham, Herbert Marshall, and Charles Bickford. The musical and revue stages claimed brilliant lights such as Fred and Adele Astaire, Zelma O'Neill, the Marx Brothers, Eddie Cantor, Al Jolson, Ruby Keeler, Victor Moore, Bert Lahr, Eddie Buzzell, Helen Ford, James Barton, Guy Robertson, Walter Woolf, Will Rogers, Ed Wynn, W. C. Fields, Irene Dunne, Ginger Rogers, Irene Bordoni, Imogene Coca, Marilyn Miller, Ann Pennington, Helen Morgan, Queenie Smith, Cecilia Loftus, Eleanor Painter, Jack Donahue, Tessa Kosta, Fannie Brice, Florence Mills, Vivienne Segal, Gertrude Lawrence, Beatrice Lillie, and Jeanette MacDonald.

The art of stage direction made enormous strides during the period, and the names of directors were increasingly in evidence in critical reviews. Still, directing credits were erratic, and it is frequently difficult to tell who was responsible for the direction of a show from otherwise detailed credit listings. The idea of a director who specialized in his craft had finally caught on but still was not that widely practiced. One finds dozens of shows directed by their stars, and the notion of a playwright-actor-director-producer was surprisingly common, although it was more usual for two or three of these functions to be combined in the same individual. Almost all important directors of the day also served in another capacity, if not on the show they were staging, in other works of the decade. George Abbott was a director-playwright-actor (later a producer), Winthrop Ames a director-producer, David Belasco a director-playwright-adaptor-producer, Gustav Blum a director-producer, Earl Carroll a director-producer, John Cromwell a director-actor, Rachel Crothers a director-playwright, Dudley Digges a director-actor, Augustin Duncan a director-actor, Walter Hampden a director-actor-producer, Arthur Hopkins a director-producer-playwright (the last on but one major production), Robert Edmond Jones a director-designer-producer, Eva Le Gallienne a director-actor-producer, Howard Lindsay a director-actor-playwright, Lester Lonergan a director-actor, Brock Pemberton a director-producer, Frank Reicher a director-actor, Winchell Smith a director-playwright-producer, and so on. Other conspicuously active or unusually important directors of the 1920s, some of whom had more than one professional theatre talent, included Richard Boleslavsky, Clifford Brooke, R. H. Burnside, David Burton, Allan Dinehart, Basil Dean, Oscar Eagle, Edward Elsner, Harrison Grey Fiske, Sam Forrest, William B. Friedlander, William H. Gilmore, Edward Goodman, Ira Hards, Bertram Harrison, J. C. Huffman, Alexander Leftwich, Fritz Leiber, James Light, Rollo Lloyd, Lawrence W. Marston, Guthrie McClintic, Edgar J. MacGregor, John Meehan, Robert Milton, Philip Moeller, Agnes Morgan, Priestly Morrison, B. Iden Payne, Edward Royce, Maurice Schwartz, Edgar Selwyn, and Hassard Short. Each of these directors offered a minimum of at least ten productions (the listing is selective); of those many directors with at least five presentations the names of George M. Cohan, George Cukor, Myron C. Fagan,

Harry Wagstaff Gribble, George S. Kaufman, George Kelly, Willard Mack, Rouben Mamoulian, George Marion, Gilbert Miller, Clarke Silvernail, Ned Wayburn, and John D. Williams should be mentioned.

Related to the work of the director is that of the choreographer; musical shows obviously made use of his talents, but the term *choreographer* was not yet used in crediting his or her achievements. Choreographers were called dance arranger, dance director, and several other names; they were sometimes not credited at all, and their job was often confused with the director's. Some directors, like Ned Wayburn, were also choreographers, but it is not always clear whether specific directors also staged the dances for their shows. However, the most fertile choreographers of the day were known well enough to be acknowledged for most, if not all, of the shows they worked on. The principal choreographers of the 1920s were David Bennett, Busby Berkeley, Larry Ceballos, Bobby Connolly, Seymour Felix, Bert French, Allan K. Foster, Chester Hale, Jack Haskell, Michio Ito, Sammy Lee, Russell E. Markert, Julian Mitchell, Albertina Rasch, Ralph Reader, Edward Royce, and Ned Wayburn.

Stage designers were coming into their own during the decade, but despite the leaps forward made by these artists, many producers refused to grant them much attention; some producers, like William A. Brady, were notorious for keeping their old scenery in storage and for simply refurbishing it when it could be reused. Thus shows of the decade often failed to credit a set designer. Costume designers were a principal factor in the success of big musicals and revues; however, they were barely acknowledged in straight dramas set in contemporary times, and relatively few of the entries in this book credit their contributions. Program credits for one play after another inform the reader not of the name of a professional costumer, but of some well-known couturiere who provided the stars with their stage clothes. Actresses and actors in modern dramas often were responsible for their own wardrobe selections; the names of their suppliers have not been included in the text. Occasionally, a set designer such as Robert Edmond Jones or Lee Simonson also did the costumes for a show. When it has been possible to determine such contributions, this has been duly noted in the entries. Lighting design, for all of its advances, was not yet the recognized achievement it has come to be, and scene designers working with technicians known as electricians were usually responsible for the lighting the sets and actors received. Some producers, like David Belasco, made a specialty of lighting effects, but they did not take credit on the program for their contributions.

American stage design of the 1920s finally caught up with the best practices then current on European stages. Most of the important designers of the decade were young and continued to have an ongoing influence on stage practices for many years to come. These individuals included Aline Bernstein, Norman Bel Geddes, Claude Bragdon, Robert Edmond Jones, Frederick Jones III, Jo Mielziner, Donald Oenslager, Rollo Peters, Willy Pogany, James Reynolds, Herman Rosse, Lee Simonson, Raymond Sovey, Cleon Throckmorton, Joseph Urban, John Wenger, and Nicholas Yellenti. A number of other designers were less influential but were extremely prolific; they included P. Dodd Ackerman, Watson Barratt, Cirker and Robbins, Gates and Morange, Livingston Platt, Clark Robinson, Woodman Thompson, Sheldon K. Viele, August Vimnera, and Joseph Wickes.

The fame of shows such as the *Ziegfeld Follies, George White's Scandals,* and *Earl Carroll's Vanities* owed an undying debt of gratitude to the imaginations of their costume designers. Some of the most unusual costuming ever created for the stage was seen in these shows; producers squandered many thousands of dollars for the right effects; the artful draping of nude chorus girls with the appropriate bubbles, baubles, and beads was a principal feature of these shows, just as was the creation of astonishing tableaux using yards and yards of material, as when a shining, golden-hued dress was revealed filling the entire stage area. The names of the chief costume designers for these extravaganzas include Gilbert Adrian, Erté, Max Weldy, Kiviette, Charles Le Maire, Cora McGeachey, and James Reynolds.

These times, then, were what Allan Churchill called the "theatrical twenties," when more shows were produced in one city in a ten-year span than ever before or since in the history of the world;[10] when American playwrights first rose to a position of international renown; when two dozen Broadway playhouses were erected in the blink of an eye; and when the New York theatre almost went down for the count on being socked in the box office by the talkies, radio, and the Great Depression. The story of how the theatre groggily picked itself up from the canvas and cleared its head will be told in a succeeding volume of this series for 1930–1940.

NOTES

1. Glenn Hughes, *A History of the American Theatre, 1700–1950* (New York: Samuel French, 1951), 385.

2. Emory Lewis, *Stages: The Fifty Year Childhood of the American Theatre* (Englewood Cliffs, N.J.: Prentice-Hall, 1969), 31.

3. Burns Mantle, ed., *The Best Plays of 1929–1930* (New York: Dodd, Mead, 1930), vi.

4. For an unusually thorough account of the history of Actors Equity and all of its negotiations from its inception through the 1920s, see Alfred Harding, *The Revolt of the Actors* (New York: William R. Morrow, 1929).

5. Quoted in John Anderson, *Box-Office* (New York: Jonathan Cape and Harrison Smith, 1929), 38.

6. Ibid., 43. The most complete and accurate account of contemporary theatre economics is Alfred L. Bernheim (with Sara Harding), *The Business of the Theatre: An Economic History of the American Theatre, 1750–1932* (New York: Benjamin Blom, 1964).

7. Brooks Atkinson, *Broadway*, rev. ed. (New York: Macmillan, 1973), 181.

8. The best source on contemporary theatre building is Mary C. Henderson, *The City and The Theatre; New York Playhouses From Bowling Green to Times Square* (Clifton, N.J.: James T. White, 1973).

9. It should, however, be borne in mind that many of the decade's "collaborations" were barely that; directors, producers, and leading actors often used their leverage to demand coauthorship credit on plays to which they merely had contributed an idea or some revised dialogue.

10. Allan Churchill, *The Theatrical Twenties* (New York: McGraw-Hill, 1975).

THE NEW YORK STAGE, 1920–1930

A

A LA CARTE [Revue] B/D: George Kelly: M/LY: Herman Hupfeld, Louis Alter, Norma Gregg, Paul Lanin, Henry Creamer, and Jimmie Johnson; S: Livingston Platt; C: Maria Willenz; P: Rosalie Stewart; T: Martin Beck Theatre; 8/17/27 (46)

Popular dramatist George Kelly wrote the sketches for this summertime revue; "while far too literary in flavor for the full appreciation of the average Broadway audience, [they] were enthusiastically received by those who caught the spirit of their intent and references," claimed Perriton Maxwell. Yet George Jean Nathan decided that they were "dull." Kelly's contributions concerned golfing manners, backstage vaudeville scandal, and activities on a summer hotel verandah.

The show employed the usual assortment of specialty acts, mainly from vaudeville, and had an assortment of trite new songs and some exciting dance numbers. A mechanical doll number set in a doll shop was highly effective, especially for its use of the talented Harriet Hoctor.

ABIE'S IRISH ROSE [Comedy/Family/Marriage/Religion/Jews] A/P: Anne Nichols; D: Lawrence Marston; T: Fulton Theatre; 5/23/22 (2,327)

When Anne Nichol's play about intermarriage opened, Heywood Broun sneered at it as "a synthetic farce." "There is not so much as a single line of honest writing in" it, he groused, adding, "the play is so cheap and offensive that it might serve to unite all the races of the world in a common hymn of hate." Five-and-a-half years later the play had racked up a long run that would remain unchallenged for fourteen years; its author-producer had become a millionaire. The piece was eventually played worldwide, including a Chinese language version, was revived twice in New York, and made into two films and a radio show.

Inspired by a real-life incident, Nichols wrote the play in less than a week. Despite two very successful West Coast productions she had great difficulty in getting a New York staging, so she invested all of her money and put it on herself. Hurt by mixed reviews, it did poorly at first, but two months of good word-of-mouth turned the tide, and it was soon on its history-making way.

The sentimental farce had a Romeo and Juliet story about Abie Levy (Robert B. Williams) and Rosie Murphy (Marie Carroll), who had met overseas and had been married. Faced at home by their fathers' displeasure at the match, the Jewish Abie palms his wife off as Rosemary Murphyski, and she tells her dad her spouse is Michael Magee. The meeting of Mr. Levy (Alfred Wiseman) and Mr. Murphy (John Cope) sets off the expected detonations, but all is harmonized when the couple undergoes two more marriages, one Jewish and one Catholic, and Rosie has the diplomatic sense to bear twins, thereby uniting old Levy and Murphy in loving grandpahood.

This well-performed work owed much of its success to its appealing cast. Of those who liked it there was the *Evening Journal*, which called it "a lively play...handsomely mounted [with] study and care." The *Times* wrote prophetically, "Personally, we hope to be present at little Rebecca Rachel and Patrick Josephy Levy's second birthday, if not their Hudson-Fulton centennial." Robert Benchley, who despised the play and had to write a weekly note on it for *Life*, came up with barbs such as, "Among the season's worst"; "Where do the people come from who see this thing? You don't see them out in the daytime"; and "Come on now! A joke's a joke."

Abie's Irish Rose was the classic example of a play that began very slowly, drawing its initial audiences by means of cut-rate tickets, and gradually developed into a sensational hit. Only Anne Nichols's faith in it kept it going. From May to October it did not have one profitable week; to keep it alive Nichols had to raise money quickly. She asked gambler Arnold Rothstein for a $30,000 loan; he said yes only when she agreed to let him write all of the insurance on the play for its entire life.

It is also interesting to note that Oliver Morosco later claimed to have made considerable contributions to the script when it was still called *Marriage in Triplicate*, and he produced it on the West Coast before its going East.   ·

ABRAHAM LINCOLN [Dramatic Revival] A: John Drinkwater; D: Gerald Cornell; S: Livingston Platt; P: William Harris, Jr.; T: Forrest Theatre; 10/21/ 29 (8)

In 1919 William Harris, Jr., presented Frank McGlynn in British playwright John Drinkwater's biographical drama about the sixteenth president. The play, which recounts Lincoln's life from his nomination through his assassination in six scenes, ran for 244 performances. Revived by the same producer with the same star in 1929, it eked out only a week's run, despite good notices. As Philo Higley noted, "it showed the same stirring qualities...and the same quiet, moving flow of narrative that are remembered from that earlier production at the Cort." McGlynn's famous portrayal of the Great Emancipator, critics concurred, was still intact. John Hutchens put the revival's failure down to a change in public taste.

ACCUSED (L'Avocat) [Drama/Law/Crime/Romance/French] A: Eugene Brieux; AD: George Middleton; D/P: David Belasco; S: Joseph Wickes; T: Belasco Theatre; 9/29/25 (95)

E. H. Sothern, remarkably youthful looking at the age of sixty-six, portrayed the young laywer Edmund De Verron in what several thought a "talky and dull piece of thesis writing" (John Mason Brown). It was about an attorney who is asked to defend a woman accused of murdering her husband, even though he has long been in love with the woman and discovers that she is guilty of the crime. This lawyer's reputation rests on his never having defended a guilty party, and he is brought on to the case only when another withdraws. He learns as he pieces the facts together that the woman, Louise (Ann Davis), committed the murder to stop her spouse from shooting the man she loved—the attorney himself. De Verron obtains her acquittal, but the relationship is ended.

George Jean Nathan, perturbed by the author's stress on ethical issues, accused Brieux of turning the stage into a lecture hall. Arthur Hornblow, admitting that this was a "ponderous, old-fashioned play," was impressed by its production, and R. Dana Skinner thought it "absorbingly interesting" in its "theme of human will power under terrific stress, and the all too human conflict between emotion, cold reason and idealism."

Sothern was "forceful, sympathetic, convincing" to Hornblow, but Skinner thought he was a florid grandstander. Adaptor Middleton believed the play might have run longer if Sothern had had a more flexible technique. The actor was letter-perfect in his role from the first day of rehearsals and was unable to "unlearn" his speeches where cuts and additions were called for. "Twenty minutes out of the play would have sharpened its intensities and probably made it more than a season's success," claimed Middleton in *These Things are Mine*.

ACROSS THE STREET [Comedy/Small Town/Journalism/Business/Politics/Romance] A: Richard A. Purdy; D/P: Oliver Morosco; S: Joseph Physioc; T: Hudson Theatre; 3/24/24 (32)

In spite of an applauded town meeting scene where two young heros exposed village selectmen who had put a rusty girder into a bridge, *Across the Street* was sent down the tubes by Broadway critics. John Corbin declared that the play illustrated the difference between plain bunk, which it was, and hokum, which still might survive on Broadway. *Across the Street* had won a $3,000 prize and had been a popular attraction on the Chautauqua circuit; James Whittaker stated that the play had been written to please the Chautauqua directors, who gave the prize "a rural jury."

Richard A. Purdy's story certainly extolled small-town life. One young man with business ambitions (Robert Emmett Keane) is sent by his editor-father (Peter Raymond) to revitalize a Vermont newspaper. A local lad (Fred Raymond) who yearns to write inherits his father's dry-goods store. The two change jobs, become great successes, are elected selectmen, and marry village girls.

Both Whittaker and Percy Hammond commented that the comedy bore some resemblance to the "business shows" of George M. Cohan, but, wrote Hammond, the "whole story is much less intelligent than a comic strip in a Sunday newspaper."

H.H.

ADA BEATS THE DRUM [Comedy/Family/Romance/France] A: John Kirkpatrick; D: Geoffrey Kerr; P: John Golden; T: Golden Theatre; 5/8/30 (46)

The boorish behavior of nouveau-riche Americans abroad aspiring to the airs of Continental sophisticates was an old theme rehashed for this comedy made palatable largely through the delicious antics of Mary Boland as Ada Hubbard. This manufacturer's wife has dragged her reluctant spouse (George W. Barbier) and daughter Leila (Nydia Westman) to the South of France in search of distinguished company. Much of the fun develops from her efforts to round up potential guests to visit her rented villa. The eccentric guests she manages to snare lead the play through a maze of comical situations, and the piece ends after Leila has fallen for an American jazz musician whom she will take home to work for daddy's factory.

Conviviality was a keynote of the play, which Brooks Atkinson deemed wanting in funny dialogue but packed with many laugh-provoking situations. Joseph Wood Krutch called it "a more than usually amusing farce" with "both pointed and moderately subtle" thrusts. The play closed early because of Mary Boland's illness.

ADAM SOLITAIRE [Drama/Fantasy] A: Em Jo Basshe; D: Stanley Howlett; S: Cleon Throckmorton; P: Provincetown Players; T: Provincetown Playhouse (OB); 11/6/25 (17)

To most critics this ambitious drama, produced in expressionist style, was a confused and meaningless jumble, notable only for Cleon Throckmorton's exceptionally imaginative setting on the Provincetown's tiny stage. In fifteen scenes, Basshe presented the Job-like tale of John Stafford (Robert Lynn), who suffers one catastrophe after another after his bride's (Clifford Sellers) aunt (Eda Heinemann) reads his fate from a cheap fortune-telling book. In the end, he dies.

Larry Barretto was "completely baffled by the play," and Joseph Wood Krutch called it "desperate nonsense." However, Richard Dana Skinner assailed his critical confreres for their having failed to see this as a "deeply spiritual and moving allegory," told "simply, forthrightly and with great beauty and insight." Stafford's sin, he said, was that of pride in not being willing to "accept the truth of Calvary, that life is a state of suffering, and that suffering is the path to humility and spiritual rebirth."

ADAM'S APPLE [Comedy/Marriage/Crime] A: Test Dalton; D: Charles D. Pitt; P: John J. Kelly; T: Princess Theatre; 6/10/29 (16)

Actors and audience, said *Time*, shared a considerable embarrassment during this "play both flat and flimsy" that the *Times* accused of being "one of the most mystifying of the long series of trivial plays that somehow get produced."

Its vaguely *Importance of Being Earnest*-like action dealt with a married man (Stanley Price) who traipses about town in the evenings by telling his wife (Helen Holmes) of visits to a mythical Uncle John. A burglar (Charles Kennedy), having overheard the truth about this Bunburier, tells the wife, who catches him, that he is Uncle John, and it takes the rest of the play to iron out all of the plot byways to which this revelation leads.

ADDING MACHINE, THE [Comedy-Drama/Marriage/Business/Trial/Labor/ Crime/Death/Fantasy] A: Elmer Rice; D: Philip Moeller; M: Deems Taylor; DS: Lee Simonson; P: Theatre Guild; T: Garrick Theatre; 3/19/23 (72)

Elmer Rice was sitting on his porch one night, thinking about another project, when an entire play on a subject and in a style he had never thought about flashed across his brain. He said in *Minority Report*, "I saw the whole thing complete: characters, plot, incidents, even the title and some of the dialogue. Nothing like it ever happened to me before or since." Obsessed with the play, he scribbled it through the night and continued to do so for days—an experience he likened to "automatic writing." He finished the work in seventeen days and called it *The Adding Machine*. It is still regarded as one of the most important works of the decade.

The Adding Machine was among the first American attempts to use expressionism, a form Rice said he was hardly even aware of at the time. Rice's comedy-drama (which he called "a tragedy") infuriated some critics not only because of his radical dramaturgy but because he used coarse language, sexual innuendo, and themes that blasted holes in the fabric of American judicial and labor practices. However, it drew forth hearty encomiums from others, and the controversy kept houses healthy enough to keep the piece running beyond its scheduled five-week engagement.

Given a production that most commentators agreed was exceptional, *The Adding Machine* began realistically but soon moved into a phantasmagorical telling of how the spineless, inarticulate, conservative clerk Mr. Zero (Dudley Digges), after a quarter century of slaving at a monotonous daily routine of counting figures for the Boss (Irving Dillon), finds out that he is being replaced by an adding machine. Sent berserk by the news, he kills his employer. Following a party at his and his wife's (Helen Westley) apartment, he is arrested, tried, and found guilty. After his execution he is seen in the cemetery, where his soul meets that of a matricide (Edward G. Robinson) and that of Daisy Diana Dorothea Devore (Margaret Wycherly), the woman who used to work with him and killed herself to follow him in death. At the Elysian Fields, the woman's offer of eternal love is spurned by the ever respectable Zero. Finally, his blissful vision of operating a massive adding machine in heaven is presented, only to be interrupted so that he may be sent back to earth for further progress toward regeneration.

The production achieved notable results in several scenes, particularly those of the murder and courtroom. In the former, Zero and Miss Devore, seated on high stools facing one another, declaimed sing-song in alternation an endless stream of figures, culminating in Zero's being discharged. "The desks and the actors whirl about against a wall on which batallions of figures dance," wrote Kenneth Macgowan: "suddenly in a great tumult everything is blotted out with two bloody splashes. Mr. Zero has 'seen red' and committed murder." (These effects were accomplished with the use of a turntable and projections.) The courtroom scene, said the *Times*, showed "the Zero conception of justice, cold, inanimate, relentless, and the contrast between reality and unreality is heightened by the crooked bars and railings and walls."

Among the strongest advocates of the work was Ludwig Lewisohn, who found it superior to *The Hairy Ape* as an example of the form and commented, "Examine [Rice's] play scene by scene, symbol by symbol. The structure stands.... [Here] is an American drama with no loose ends or ragged edges or silly last act compromises, retractions, reconciliations. The work, on its own ground, in its own mood, is honest, finished, sound." Others denied that Rice's play was so capably conceived; they pointed in particular to the heaven scenes following Zero's death when the work "wanders off into a string of episodes that are anecdotal and satiric and without dramatic backbone" (Macgowan). Burns Mantle, in one of his less perspicacious moments, failed to count the work one of the Ten Best Plays of the Year (he chose such now-dated pieces as *Why Not?*, *Mary the Third*, and *The Fool* instead).

The acting was exemplary, with honors going to Digges, Wycherly, Robinson, and Westley.

Rice told several interesting anecdotes about the production. In one he recalled that at the final dress rehearsal a major obstacle arose to progress when a dispute broke out between the carpenters and prop crew about who was responsible for moving the huge adding machine used in the final scene; no one knew whether it was a piece of scenery or a property (Rice didn't remember the decision).

ADMIRAL, THE [Drama/Adventure/Period/Historical-Biographical] A: Charles Rann Kennedy; P: Equity Players; T: Forty-eighth Street Theatre; 4/24/24 (6)

The second of Charles Rann Kennedy's trilogy of dramas written for himself and his wife (Edith Wynne Matthison), *The Admiral* followed the previous season's drama about Christ, *The Chastening*. The *Times* critic found Kennedy's project commendable but the play discursive and lacking in dramatic content. The work featured a discussion between Queen Isabella (Matthison), Columbus (Kennedy), and a girl (Margaret Gage) portrayed as Columbus's friend and partisan.

The Admiral was performed only at special matinees.

H.H.

ADORABLE LIAR, THE [Comedy/Romance/Small Town/Youth] A: Roy Briant and Harry Durant; D/P: Edgar Selwyn; T: Forty-ninth Street Theatre; 8/30/26 (33)

Newcomer Dorothy Burgess made a splash in this play portraying a whimsical seventeen-year-old flapper, Karith, who is the winsome creature of the title. This Florida adolescent with a perverse habit of fibbing dreams of meeting her knight in shining armor; finds him in the person of Alan (Eric Dressler), a young realtor; induces him to climb a ladder to her boudoir so she may be pleasantly compromised; and thereby puts off another girl (Nelly Neil) with hooks out for him. Karith succeeds in winning him for herself.

"It's inconsequential, but entertaining," wrote Ward Morehouse, but Arthur Hornblow found the play to be "anemic." The piece had been called *The Imaginative Girl* before arriving on Broadway.

ADRIENNE [Musical/Romance/Crime/Reincarnation] B/LY: A. Seymour Brown; M: Albert Von Tilzer; SC: a story by Frances Bryant and William Stone; D: Edgar J. MacGregor; CH: David Bennett; P: Louis F. Werba; T: George M. Cohan Theatre; 5/28/23 (235)

Choreographer David Bennett's work with the chorus of this musical was a major factor in accounting for its success. The originality and dynamism of his dance routines, said the *Times*, outshadowed every other part of the show. With humor on the level of lines such as, "Even if he takes a gate, don't you take offense," the talented cast had to work doubly hard to elicit a stir from the summertime auditors.

The star was Vivienne Segal, who played the title role, a believer in reincarnation who nearly loses her valuable jewelry when she wears it to a temple under the impression that she will thereby meet a lover from a past life. Her present boyfriend aids in confounding the plot of several jewel thieves, and the gems remain where they belong.

ADVENTURE [Drama/Romance/Western/Rural/Adventure] A: John Willard; D: Bernard Steele and Rollo Lloyd; S: Nicholas Yellenti; P: Bernard Steele, Inc.; T: Republic Theatre; 9/25/28 (22)

A Wild West romantic melodrama with a dyed-in-the-wool villain, plenty of gunfire, and a true-blue hero who wins the heart of the rancher's daughter. The action begins in New York City, where Dolores Hampton (Roberta Arnold) meets the brave Michael O'Shayne (John B. Litel) when he comes to her rescue in Central Park. He follows her to her father's Wyoming cattle ranch, helps out the old man in his war with the sheep ranchers, shoots the bad guy (Harry D. Southard), and hugs the girl.

"Plot and denouement are as patent as in any movie of the plains and the Western hills," claimed the *Times*.

ADVENTUROUS AGE, THE [Comedy/Marriage/Romance/British/Sex] A: Frederick Witney; D/P: George C. Tyler; T: Mansfield Theatre; 2/7/27 (16)

Mrs. Patrick Campbell, absent from the New York stage for fourteen years, returned in this awful comedy that the *Times* described as worthy only of the amateur stage, and that Percy Hammond termed "an urbane, but half-starved, little comedy with farcical inclinations." Campbell played a forty-five-year-old wife and mother, married for twenty-four years, and longing for rejuvenation in the arms of a young man. Her husband too is itchy, and the pair set their hearts on the young people with whom their own son and daughter are in love. In the end, the middle-agers are overthrown, and youth conquers all.

"It is flat, flaccid, feeble, underfed, futile, foolish and a lot more things which do not all begin with the letter 'F'," wrote the *Times*. Mrs Pat was pitifully overweight and wrinkled, and George Jean Nathan described her as "A Brunhilde creased with the years, an old woman plainly strapped in to the point of discomfort."

ADVERTISING OF KATE, THE [Comedy/Business/Romance] A: Annie Nathan Meyer; P: Lee Kugel; T: Ritz Theatre; 5/8/22 (24)

A tolerable comedy ("ultra-conventional, ingeniously imagined"—Alexander Woollcott) about a very successful advertising woman, Kate Blackwell (Mary Boland), who falls in love with her junior partner (Leslie Austen) and has to put her advertising prowess to work at selling herself in order to draw him away from a rival. Her scheme attracts not only the partner but several other suitors; after various complications she lands the man she is after.

The play's several banalities were balanced by the theme of a perceptive woman using her mental powers to win the man on whom she has set her heart. "Now and then a dull moment [was] offset by many bright and some brilliant ones," wrote Arthur Hornblow. Oldtimer Mrs. Thomas Whiffen, playing an eccentric aunt, stole the show from the younger members of the cast.

AFFAIRES SONT LES AFFAIRES, LES (Business Is Business) [Dramatic Revival/French Language] A: Octave Mirabeau; P: Wendell Phillips Dodge; T: Fulton Theatre; 3/10/24 (4)

Billed by his producer as the Coquelin of his generation, Comédie Française star Maurice de Féraudy brought his own company to perform seven full-length and two one-act plays in New York. For his opening, the star chose a role he had created at the premiere of the play twenty-one years before, and which had been acted in an English version, *Business Is Business*, by William Gillette on Broadway in 1904.

Isador Lechot, nicknamed "the Tiger Cat," is a nouveau-riche entrepreneur who has acquired a nobleman's estate and delights in humiliating its former owner, now the estate manager. Although Lechot's attempts to marry his daughter to an aristocrat fail when she elopes with one of his employees, and his wastrel son is killed in a car accident, the "Tiger Cat" pursues business as usual. Several critics called the play a masterpiece in which Mirabeau took his protagonist apart with a scalpel.

Féraudy was hailed for playing Lechot "with great gusto, and with such

mellowness and spontaneity that he seems to be living in the character rather
than merely acting'' (Robert Gilbert Welsh).

H.H.

AFGAR [Musical/Romance/Sex/French] B: Fred Thompson and Worton David;
M: Charles Cuvillier; LY: Douglas Fuhrer; ADD. M/LY.: Joseph McCarthy and
Harry Tierney; SC: a French work by Michel Carré and André Barde; D: Frank
Collins; C: Paul Poiret; P: F. Ray Comstock and Morris Gest; T: Central Theatre;
11/8/20 (168)

A London hit based on a 1909 French original into which American infusions
were made. It had an Oriental motif, a harem, and a rich Moor clad in grotesque
Oriental draperies. The story involved the absurdity of the life-style of the Moor
(W. H. Rawlins) and his harem as compared to real life. The women in the
harem demand a more conventional marital arrangement, and this leads the
Moor's favorite concubine, Zaydee (Alice Delysia), to strike and almost elope
with the handsome stranger, Don Juan, Jr. (Irving Beebe). Zaydee's strike is a
success, and Don Juan is released to his true love in time for the finale.

The show introduced sexy French singing star Alice Delysia (''a feathered
nobody from France who came to America fresh from a success in the London
music halls''—Heywood Broun). The acrobatic skill of Lupino Lane, who played
the clown Coucourli, heightened the spectacle. The European score was supplemented by James Monaco's ''Caresses'' and several MacCarthy and Tierney
tunes.

M.M.-C.

AFRICANA [Revue/Blacks] B/P: Earl Dancer; M/LY: Donald Heywood; D:
Louis Douglas; T: Daly's Theatre; 7/11/27 (77)

A ''black and tan'' revue starring tall singer-comedienne-dancer Ethel Waters,
new to Broadway. ''It is a frank and uninhibited extravaganza which moves
swiftly and generally contrives to provide an evening's entertainment'' (*Times*).
Fast-paced dance routines mingled with raucous comedy; one of the funniest
sketches was a duologue between a Chinese man and a black sailor. A cakewalk
finale led by Pickaninny Hill was a viewer's delight. *Time* said of Waters, ''Her
70 odd inches are topped by a small closely cropped head. She uses a typical
husky, soft voice to unusual advantage, employs mannerisms frankly and disarmingly Negroid, understands the act of 'living' her songs, so that they take
on dramatic quality. In Harlem, she is queen. In Manhattan, she stopped the
show.''

The show moved to the National Theatre, where it ended its run.

AGE OF INNOCENCE, THE [Drama/Romance/Marriage/Sex/Period] A: Margaret Ayer Barnes; SC: Edith Wharton's novel; D: Guthrie McClintic; S: J. F.
Gallagher; C: Gertrude Newell; P: Gilbert Miller; T: Empire Theatre; 11/27/28
(209)

Some critics shook their heads in befuddlement when, for reasons they could not discern, this verbose dramatization of an Edith Wharton novel became a box-office draw.

Beautifully set and costumed in its 1870s milieu, and excellently performed with Katharine Cornell as its star, the play detailed the plight of Countess Ellen Olenska (Cornell), who flees her marriage to a Polish nobleman and falls in love with Newland Archer (Rollo Peters), who is engaged to her cousin (Eden Gray). The Countess renounces her love so that Newland and her cousin may wed. Forty years afterwards, Newland visits Paris where Ellen lives; although he still adores her, he chooses to keep his memory pure and does not visit her.

Richard Dana Skinner complained that, whereas the play was superior to most, it left him unmoved, because its characters' self-sacrificial motives were not of the highest level. Robert Littell thought it ''a little too literary'' and outmoded. Cornell ''touched the phrases of the dialogue with the flame of her voice,'' said the *Times*. Franchot Tone made his Broadway bow as Newland's son.

This was the first professional writing task undertaken by Margaret Ayer Barnes, who several years later won the Pulitzer Prize for her novel *Years of Grace*. She had been a childhood friend of dramatist Edward Sheldon, who inspired her to undertake the dramatization of Wharton's novel, a project with which he himself had earlier tinkered. Barnes did not take Sheldon's suggestion to write the play seriously, but once she began on it Sheldon continued to follow its progress and to offer important editing and rewrite skills. He refused, however, to take coauthor credit, despite Barnes's entreaties. During its creation, Wharton expressed grave doubts about elements of the adaptation, which sought to alter the nature of the central characters to make them more stageworthy. Wharton's loudest objection was to the idea of giving Newland Archer, a highly conventional character in her book, the qualities of a political crusader modeled after Theodore Roosevelt. However, as Eric Barnes noted in his biography of Sheldon, *The Man Who Lived Twice*, Wharton eventually realized the value of the changes.

AGLAVAINE AND SELYSETTE (Aglavaine et Selysette) [Dramatic Revival] A: Maurice Maeterlinck; AD: Alfred Sutro; P: Afternoon Theatre Company; T: Maxine Elliott Theatre; 1/3/22 (1)

A matinee benefit performance of a Maeterlinck play shown locally in 1916 for a single performance by the Washington Square Players. The mustily romantic drama concerns the friends of the title, rivals for the love of Meleander (William Raymond), and concludes with the suicide leap of Selysette (Eva Le Gallienne) when she realizes that Meleander loves Aglavaine (Clare Eames).

The *Times* wanted to know why Eames and Le Gallienne had bothered with this dreary exercise. ''It is played...in the cataleptic manner which tradition assigns to the Maeterlinck drama and with the non-committed draperies which best suit his plays.''

The idea for this production grew out of an idea of Arthur Row's for a method of allowing actors involved in long run shows to ply their skills at matinee performances of challenging dramas. Lack of financial support killed the scheme.

(1) AIGLON, L' (The Eaglet) [Dramatic Revival/French Language] A: Edmond Rostand; P: Anne Nichols; T: Henry Miller's Theatre; 10/20/24 (8)

Mme. Simone, as part of her seven-play visiting repertory produced by the authoress of *Abie's Irish Rose*, offered this old patriotic Rostand melodrama of 1900, written for Sarah Bernhardt, who was its first "Eaglet," Napolean's weakling son. The role had since been done by various French stars. The declamatory drama struck Ludwig Lewisohn as a work of artificiality and "labored puerilities," and Stark Young said Rostand wrung from the story "every nuance possible, every chance for rhetorical and theatrical device, and every shade of patriotic and tragical emotion."

There was nothing extraordinary about the production, from which two complete acts had been cut, or the acting. Kenneth Macgowan thought it was "well-enough" presented, but Young was shocked by the lack of drama in the costumes and the unfinished makeups.

Mme. Simone was but the palest reflection of Bernhardt in the role, which requires the actress to portray a boy of seventeen. Her acting "was a matter of rather monotonous routine and conventional stage business" (Arthur Hornblow).

(2) TR: Louis N. Parker; D/P: John D. Williams; T: Cosmopolitan Theatre; 12/26/27 (8)

Michael Strange, an actress whose chief claim to fame was her being known as Mrs. John Barrymore, played Rostand's hero in this English-language version. It seemed poorly suited to the new tongue, and its use of an actress to play the Eaglet seemed ever more absurd. Strange was technically ill equipped for the role, physically and emotionally. George Jean Nathan noted that she was "a strapping actress of five feet ten with a chest expansion of at least eight inches and enough vigor to reclaim the whole lost empire of Mongolia." George Marion was Flambeau, William Courtleigh was Metternich, and Effie Shannon undertook Maria Louisa.

AIRWAYS, INC. [Drama/Labor/Business/Aviation/Romance/Crime] A/S: John Dos Passos; D: Edward Massey; P: New Playwrights' Theatre; T: Grove Street Theatre (OB); 2/20/29 (27)

John Dos Passos's experimental offering was desperately in need of the scissors and seemed disunified—effective in spots but not holding together as an entity. The *Times* thought it "a noisy, incoherent but at times . . . extremely interesting and arresting tragedy," but Padraic Colum argued that it was more "a series of disasters" than a tragedy because of the lack of "some heightening of human life, some deepening of human experience."

The two chief characters are an aviator (Winston Lee), who is to be the guiding force behind a new aviation company, and a fiery labor leader (Harry Gordon), who stirs up a strike among oppressed mill workers. The radical loves the spinsterish sister (Edith Meiser) of the flyer, but he goes to jail and is executed on a framed charge when the cops plant a gun on him and arrest him for murder.

The aviator makes his family rich, but he breaks his spine in a crash and will probably die.

"[J]ust what Mr. Dos Passos intends it all to mean is less than lucid," said the *Times*.

ALARM CLOCK, THE (La sonnette d'alarme) [Comedy/Romance/French] A: Maurice Hennequin and Romain Coolus; AD: Avery Hopwood; D: David Burton; S: Paul Allen; C: Evelyn McHortor; P: A. H. Woods; T: Thirty-ninth Street Theatre; 12/24/23 (32)

An Avery Hopwood effort at adapting a Gallic comedy, *The Alarm Clock* failed to go off. Hopwood moved the locale to New York, where a forty-year-old uncle (Bruce McRae) entertains his country nephew (Harold Vermilye) and the youth's fiancée (Marion Coakley). The visitors both cheer and change the uncle's life, for he ends up with the fiancée, and the nephew gets a Follies girl.

Unimpressed with this transposition, George Jean Nathan grumbled, "Entertaining clean sentimental comedy seems to be as far from the talents of the generality of French playwrights as entertaining risque comedy is from the talents of the generality of American." Although the *Times* reviewer called the work wildly amusing and found a collection of one-line "nifties"—such as a girl instructing her maid about flowers from an admirer, "Put them where I won't ever see them. Put them in the kitchen"—Nathan thought the adaptation cluttered with "vaudeville jokes, allusions to Florenz Ziegfeld and Greenwich Village, and wheezes on Prohibition, jazz, and ladies' undergarments."

H.H.

ALEXANDER PUSHKIN [Drama/Period/Marriage/Literary-Biographical/ Romance/Italian/Yiddish Language] A: Valentino Carrera; TR: Abraham Armband; D/P: Maurice Schwartz; S: M. Salzman; T: Yiddish Art Theatre (OB); 1/ 26/28

A Yiddish-language production of an Italian play about the nineteenth-century Russian writer Pushkin, directed by and starring Maurice Schwartz in what was for him an unconventional role. The familiar facts of Pushkin's eventful life were unfolded, including his imprisonment by the Czar for publishing liberal ideas in his poetry, his escape, his romances, his pardon, his marriage, his loss of his idealism as a writer, his elevation to poet laureate, and his death in a duel.

"Although Schwartz was not so appealing...as in some of his earlier roles, he gave, on the whole, a masterful portrayal of Pushkin," commented the *Times*.

ALIAS JIMMY VALENTINE [Dramatic Revival] A: Paul Armstrong; D: Hugh Ford; P: George C. Tyler; T: Gaiety Theatre; 12/8/21 (46)

A new production of a 1909 hit about a master safecracker who escapes from Sing Sing, passes himself off as one Lee Randall (Otto Kruger), but must allow his identity to be revealed when, in a terrific suspense scene, he sandpapers his fingertips until they are bloody and sets to work opening a vault in which a child has been trapped. For some, the play still crackled with old-fashioned melodramatic excitement in this well-staged and well-acted version. Alexander Woollcott called it "a most diverting pastime." But others found the plotting sorely lacking in credibility.

Otto Kruger did a splendid job in the role originated by H. B. Warner, but Margalo Gillmore, in Laurette Taylor's old part as Jimmy's girlfriend, did not fare so well.

ALIAS THE DEACON [Comedy/Small Town/Gambling/Romance] A: John B. Hymer and Le Roy Clemens; D: Winchell Smith and Priestly Morrison; S: P. Dodd Ackerman; P: Samuel Wallach; T: Sam H. Harris Theatre; 11/24/25 (277)

Sometimes referred to as *The Deacon*, this was a successful comedy about a silver-haired card sharp of great charm called by the term used in the title because of his clerical appearance. Berton Churchill's performance as the unctuous gambler was a major delight of the season. The play he was in was really no great shakes given its lack of originality and weak construction, "But it provides a solid evening of entertainment," offered Richard Dana Skinner, "much familiar though never tiresome comedy, and enough intervening pathos to keep the surface emotions pleasantly stirred."

The hokey plot had the Deacon descending from a boxcar to spend some time in a small midwestern town, where he uses his card skills not only to his own pecuniary advantage but to those of the decent local folk, as when he gets the widow Clark (Frances Underwood) off a shylock's hook. He also comes to the assistance of a pair of young lovers (Donald Foster and Mayo Methot), whom he helps bring together.

ALL DRESSED UP [Comedy/Science/Family/Romance] A: Arthur Richman; D: Guthrie McClintic; P: A. H. Woods; T: Eltinge Theatre; 9/9/25 (13)

A "truth serum" called scopolamin was currently gaining some attention in the press as a law-enforcement device. The author of *All Dressed Up* presumed the use of a similar drug as the fulcrum of his potentially interesting play, in which a scientist, Raymond Stevens (Norman Trevor), administers it to his unsuspecting dinner guests, with surprising results. People's social pretenses are stripped away and they behave as their innermost selves dictate. Most notably, the shy young man (James Crane) in love with the scientist's daughter (Kay Johnson) becomes a savage lover, even tearing off his fiancée's gown at the shoulders. The scientist realizes that a degree of hypocrisy in everyday life is necessary for smooth social functioning.

There was much that intrigued the critics about the premise of the play. Joseph Wood Krutch said "It is ingeniously developed and funny throughout in spite of the fact that it never, unfortunately, escapes the somewhat mechanical air which its scheme entails."

ALL GOD'S CHILLUN GOT WINGS [Drama/Race/Blacks/Marriage/Mental Illness] A: Eugene O'Neill; D: James Light; S: Cleon Throckmorton; P: Provincetown Players; T: Provincetown Playhouse (OB) 5/15/24 (43)

A real-life illustration of the racial tension in O'Neill's play won its opening wide publicity. Late in the day of the first performance, New York's Mayor revoked, without explanation, the Gerry Society's permission for children to appear in the play's first scene, which featured an interracial group playing marbles. Director James Light read the first scene for an audience that Percy Hammond described as "composed and tolerant."

The play was variously received, from Hammond's "mildly dull and audacious" to Robert Gilbert Welsh's "Its tragic power is overwhelming." Framed in an expressionistic mode, with a set that moved in on the actors as their problems overwhelmed them, the drama spanned almost two decades. A black boy and a white girl, Jim (Paul Robeson) and Ella (Mary Blair), are friends growing up in the ghetto, are parted in adolescence by her prejudice, and turn to each other when he fails his bar exams and she is abandoned by her lover. Beset by disapproval from all sides, their marriage cannot survive abroad or at home, and Ella drifts into madness and Jim into despair.

Heywood Broun found the play tiresome, because he thought that O'Neill outlined and then sidestepped his problems by turning the black-white into a sane-insane confrontation. Hammond commented that "a bit overdone and breathless, [the play] is a vehement exposition of a marriage between a stupid negro and a stupid white woman."

John Corbin wrote of Paul Robeson that his performance "grips attention and tingles in the nerves. And it is very deeply pathetic, with the pathos one feels for a dumb creature in physical suffering. There are gleams of intelligence also, intelligence of the solider and more intrinsic sort."

The play received another sixty-two performances at the Greenwich Village Theatre (OB) from 8/18/24.

H. H.

ALL THE KING'S MEN [Comedy-Drama/Marriage/Family] A: Fulton Oursler; D: Priestly Morrison; S: Cirker and Robbins; P: Lew Cantor; T: Fulton Theatre; 2/4/29 (33)

Implausible plot developments tripped this promising play up. The author, said Robert Littell, "started off well with an excellent idea...but he...spoiled it with more drama and involution than either we or the reality of the story could endure."

Grant Mitchell played Walter Fairchild, a widower with a young son, who marries Florence Wendell (Mayo Methot) and moves to a new apartment with her when she feels uncomfortable in the one his late wife inhabited. A year later, on the verge of giving birth, she is distraught when Walter leaves her side to rush to his son, reportedly dying of typhoid fever in Switzerland. Mother and stepson survive their crises, but Florence considers running off with another man, abandoning the idea only when he refuses to take along her infant; she realizes the similarity of her maternal feelings to those Walter feels for his boy.

ALL WET [Comedy/Politics/Mental Illness/Marriage] A: Willis Maxwell Goodhue; D: Edward Emery; P: The Players; T: Wallack's Theatre; 7/6/25 (8)

Higgins (Edward Emery), the butler in a wealthy Yonkers home whose married owners (Charles Brown and Mary Duncan) have temporarily departed because of a squabble, takes over control of the household and attempts to institute a Bolshevist program of "nationalizing" the women; his plan runs into unexpected snags, and he eventually is exposed as mentally unbalanced.

The piece was not badly played, and the *Times* enjoyed its humor, but it faded in a week.

ALLEZ-OOP [Revue] B: J. P. McEvoy; M: Philip Charig and Richard Meyers; LY: Leo Robin; D/CH/P: Carl Hemmer; S: Bernard Lohmuller; T: Earl Carroll Theatre; 8/2/27 (119)

J. P. McEvoy's accustomed wit was barely in evidence in the sketches he wrote for this dance-oriented summertime revue. The comedy seemed feeble, despite the efforts of Charles Butterworth of the imbecilic manner and Victor Moore. Skits included a bashful newlywed pair at Niagara Falls, a sanitarium where the patient's nervous condition grows steadily worse, and a burlesque of the Roxy movie theatre's stage show.

Viennese director-choreographer Hemmer created some hard-driving dance routines that shook the stage floor with energy. One number, "Doin' the Gorilla," had the chorus dressed in ape suits. Perriton Maxwell closed his review by saying, "There is nothing to say about the music; it just isn't there."

ALLOY [Drama/Small Town/Marriage/Romance] A: Robert Ritz; P: Lee Kugel; T: Princess Theatre; 10/27/24 (16)

The dreary life of a bickering, poverty-stricken couple in a Pennsylvania mill town was the subject of this exercise in kitchen-sink realism. Real food was cooking on the family stove, but despite the attempt to hold the mirror up to nature, "the moisture of life" (*Times*) was absent.

Pansy Jorgan (Minna Gombell) is unhappily married to an abusive, hard-drinking, frustrated steel worker named Bill (Byron Beasley). After discovering that he has seduced a neighbor, Pansy takes the opportunity to run off with an attractive boarder (Ivan Miller), leaving Bill to fend for himself.

Although well acted, "There was not enough dramatic material in this piece on which to build a play," wrote Arthur Hornblow.

ALL-STAR IDLERS OF 1921 [Revue] D/P: Will Morrissey; T: Shubert Theatre; 7/15/21 (1)

A melange of disconnected and not-well-integrated bits and pieces that lasted at its only performance until 3:30 A.M. A company of approximately thirty well-known entertainers, including Tom Lewis, Ed Wynn, Gitz Rice, Victor Morley, Herbert Corthell, Ned Sparks, and Robert Woolsey, performed in a series of sketches that concentrated on the themes of Prohibition, blue laws, and theatrical unemployment. "It was a combination of burlesque without tights, minstrels without bones and review without a small fortune being spent," noted the *Times*. A brief two-act play by John Emerson offered the only serious note in the proceedings.

An even less effective evening, called simply *Idlers of 1921*, arrived at the Eltinge on 8/8/21 for a single performance; it too was in the hands of Will Morrissey; like the former show, it was composed of members of the Lambs' Club. "The result was [a] haphazard and generally dull affair," reported the *Times*.

ALL-STAR JAMBOREE [Revue] D: William Collier; P: Friars Club; T: Cort Theatre; 7/13/21 (13)

A miscellaneous assortment of entertaining numbers produced by the Friars Club with a company of nearly 100. Working without scenery, the company was nevertheless fun to look at, from its minstrel segment featuring Frank Tinney, William Collier, Eddie Dowling, Lew Brice, and Jack Osterman, among others, to its "Beau Brummels of Broadway" routine, with Bert Kalmar, Harry Ruby, and Eddie Dowling. Lucille Chalfant charmed by her singing, and the evening was rounded out by a George M. Cohan one act, "The Farrell Case." This was one of Cohan's nonsense pieces in the vein of *The Tavern*, being set "yesterday" and "anywhere." A variety of other acts was on the bill, and the result led the *Times* to assert: "It's a good show."

ALOMA OF THE SOUTH SEAS [Drama/Tropics/Romance/Alcoholism] A: John B. Hymer and Le Roy Clemens; D: A. H. Van Buren; P: Carl Reed; T: Lyric Theatre; 4/20/25 (163)

Tropical atmosphere, dark-skinned natives in sexy sarongs, seductive South Seas music, and febrile Caucasians in whites and pith helmets were the ingredients of which plays such as this were composed. John Mason Brown declared, "Inconceivably dull in the writing it has hootchie-kootchied itself into the notoriety belonging to bold and bad plays...set in the South Seas, where few clothes and fewer morals are supposed to be forgiven on the ground of being necessary features of tribal life." Arthur Hornblow said it was "largely hula-hula hokum."

Bob Holden (Frank M. Thomas) is drinking himself to death on the island to which he fled when his fiancée Sylvia (Anne Morrison), thinking him dead in the war, married someone else. He is loved by the island wench Aloma (Vivienne Osborn), herself under the watchful eye of native boyfriend Nuitane (George

Gaul). Redeemed by Aloma's love, Bob is going to marry her when Sylvia and her drunken husband (Richard Gordon) show up. The husband dies in a storm, Bob leaves with Sylvia, and Nuitane ends up with Aloma.

ALT-HEIDELBERG (Old Heidelberg) [Dramatic Revival/German Language] A: Wilhelm Meyer-Forster; D: Ullrich Haupt; P: German Players Association (Deutsche Kuenstled Vereinigung); T: Earl Carroll Theatre; 12/7/24 (4)
   A German-speaking cast led by Ullrich Haupt as Heinrich performed this play, which was the source for the enormously successful Romberg operetta *The Student Prince*, then running in New York. Richard Mansfield had once counted Heinrich among the successful roles of his career. The *Times* thought the production was excellent and noted the presence in the audience of many members of *The Student Prince*'s cast.

AMBUSH [Drama/Family/Marriage/Sex/Prostitution] A: Arthur Richman; D: Frank Reicher; P: Theatre Guild; T: Garrick Theatre; 10/10/21 (98)
   Playwright Arthur Richman's most critically respected work (it was a Best Play of the Year), this peek at the sordid domestic travails of a New Jersey family was a work of often uncomfortable realism that did not please everyone. It served to provide the Theatre Guild with a rare excursion into American drama; in it Florence Eldridge made her first mark with New York's critics.
   Ambush looks at the life of a forty-five-year-old Jersey City clerk (Frank Reicher), who lives by a code of what he deems the highest ideals. This poor, old-fashioned protagonist is confronted by a cynical, selfish wife (Jane Wheatley) and an equally grasping daughter (Eldridge); both women want more material things than their petty existence affords, and the daughter turns to prostituting herself with wealthy men, with her mother's approval, to get what she craves. The drama reveals the father's growing despair as he sees his cherished standards ambushed. At the end, he is reduced to accepting money from one of his daughter's lovers.
   Some critics hailed *Ambush* as one of the best native dramas of its day. Ludwig Lewisohn described this "American tragedy" as true to the principles of Aristotle's commentary in its truthful examination of painful circumstances transmuted through the medium of art. Alexander Woollcott called it "frankly an unpleasant play" but found it was "always interesting, uncommonly well played and...always engrossing."
   To extend its run the play was moved on 11/26/21 to the Belmont Theatre.

AMERICAN BORN [Comedy/Business/Romance] A/D/P: George M. Cohan; S: Joseph Wickes; T: Hudson Theatre; 10/5/25 (88)
   All-around showman George M. Cohan came out of retirement to write, produce, direct, and star in this comedy with a "rather blithering plot" (Alexander Woollcott). "It was of the better type of chewing gum drama, highly

flavored, permanent, perhaps, and lacking in nutrition,'' remarked Percy Hammond.

Cohan played an American youth, Joseph Gilson, who, upon the death of his parents, inherits the family estate in England and goes there to sell it. He meets and falls in love with pretty Jocelyn Pettering (Joan Maclean) and returns to the States with her as his bride. The skimpy plot was basically an excuse for plumping Cohan and his wisecracking ways down amidst the stiff upper lips of the British gentry, where the contrasts between "Are you there?" and "Are you having me on?" could be strikingly demonstrated.

Cohan excelled as the American with a rapid-fire arsenal of quips, and although his play was meager fare, it jolted audiences into not a few laughs.

AMERICAN CHASIDIM (Amerikaner Hassidim) [Comedy/Jews/Religion/ Friendship/Family/Yiddish/Yiddish Language] A: Chune Gotesfeld; D/P: Maurice Schwartz; T: Yiddish Art Theatre (OB); 3/16/28

An uncomfortably barbed satire on the ultra-orthodox sect of Jewry called Chasidism produced by Maurice Schwartz's Yiddish Art Theatre. The *Times* thought he should have had better taste than to enjoy making fun of a religious group. Chasidism was made to seem a ridiculous anachronism in American culture, an archaic fanaticism that did not fit into the New World picture.

The satire was embedded in a plot about two ex-peddlers, now prosperous businessmen, whose friendship is endangered when one of them, a religious man, insists on bringing a Chassidic rabbi to New York. Various complications develop between them and among the members of their respective families, until all is straightened out.

AMERICAN GRAND GUIGNOL [One-Acts] P: Georges Renavent; T: Grove Street Theatre (OB); 1/12/27 (69)

[Program #1] "Cocktail Impromptu" A: Lewis Waller and Dermot Derby; "The Claw" (*La Griffe*) A: Jean Sartene; AD: Dermot Derby; "The Last Torture" A: Jean Bideau; AD: Georges Renavent; "Maid of All Work" (*Petite Bonne serieuse*) A: Gabriel Timmory and Jean Manoussi; AD: Dermot Derby

Georges Renavent, well-known actor of French origin, produced a series of playlets first staged at Paris' theatre of thrills, the Grand Guignol. The first bill consisted of two scare plays, "The Claw" and "The Last Torture," and two farces. "The Claw" was a fairly suspenseful piece about a paralyzed and mute old man's efforts to warn his son of various dangers; "The Last Torture" presented dramatic moments during the Boxer uprising, with gunshots going off throughout the action. Both "The Claw" and "Maid of All Work" had been seen when the Grand Guignol Players visited New York in the fall of 1923.

[Program #2] (2/1/27) "The Morgue" A: Joseph Noel; "A Florentine Tragedy" A: Oscar Wilde; "Butterflies" A: Thomas W. Broadhurst; "Napolean's Barber" A: Arthur Caesar

By the time of the second bill, Renavent's original plan of producing French Grand Guignol plays had been revised to the production of English and American one-acters. The new program began with "The Morgue," set in the title locale, where a man blandly inspects the corpses until he comes across that of his wife; it moved on to an Oscar Wilde piece and then a comic effort called "Napoleon's Barber," ending with "Butterflies," meant to shock, but eliciting laughter instead. *Time* found that "On the whole, there is a great deal of cruelty with a minimum of refinement" in the show.

[Program #3] (2/4/27) "We're All in the Gutter" A: Elfrida and Clarence Derwent; "A Minuet" A: Louis N. Parker; "Casualties" A: Martin Flavin; "The Maker of Images" A: Arthur Caesar

Few pieces on this program had the wherewithal to induce a frisson, and the best piece was deemed to be Flavin's "Casualties," a triangle drama about a drug-addict war veteran (Barton Hepburn) whose wife (Mary Blair) is attracted to his doctor (Owen Cunningham). One of the highlights of the evening was the appearance of singer Helen Morgan in "A Minuet." It was her first appearance in a dramatic role. Otherwise, the program was a dud.

AMERICAN TRAGEDY, AN [Drama/Crime/Trial/Prison/Romance/Sex/Family] A: Patrick Kearney; SC: Theodore Dreiser's novel of the same name; D: Edward Goodman; S: Carolyn Hancock; P: Horace Liveright; T: Longacre Theatre; 10/11/26 (216)

A prologue and four acts totaling a dozen scenes were used to transform Dreiser's voluminous novel into an occasionally stiff, but generally enthralling, episodic drama that gradually built from an uncertain start to a compelling finish in its courtroom scenes. Morgan Farley was Clyde Griffiths, Katherine Wilson was Roberta Alden, and Miriam Hopkins was Sondra Finchley, the chief characters in this tale of a collar-factory employee who seduces one of the women workers and impregnates her; then, having been attracted to a socialite, he allows the girlfriend to drown during a rowing accident, is convicted of murder, and is electrocuted for the crime.

Several critics acclaimed Patrick Kearney's adaptation. "[F]rom the dramatic standpoint little that really matters has been omitted and the result is an absorbing, human, intensely interesting play," commented Arthur Hornblow. But George Jean Nathan thought the adaptor had put only the novel's "bare bones" onto the stage and overlooked Dreiser's "cloak of understanding, meticulous detail and ploughing, earth-turning pity and sympathy." The result was "an obvious murder mystery," he concluded.

Although no official action against it was ever taken, this play was placed on the list of questionable works to be investigated by the District Attorney's office in the wake of complaints by crusaders for censorship.

(1) **AMERICANA** [Revue] B: J. P. McEvoy; M: Con Conrad and Henry Souvaine; ADD. M./LY.: George Gershwin, Philip Charig, Ira Gershwin, and Mor-

rie Ryskind; D: Allan Dinehart; CH: Larry Ceballos; DS: John Held, Jr.; P: Richard Herndon; T: Belmont Theatre; 7/26/26 (224)

An excellently conceived and performed intimate revue that featured Roy Atwell, Charles Butterworth, and Lew Brice (Fannie's brother) to hilarious effect and had fine comedy, good music, and intelligent satire. It was "A witty, ingenious and sophisticated evening of fun-making" (Times). Eschewing lavishness in sets and costumes, it opted for the clever, cartoony style of designer John Held, Jr. A group of six individualistic dancers stood in for the usual array of chorus clones.

Among the best-liked numbers were "Travelogue," in which Roy Atwell played an out-of-towner trying to get directions from New York's melting pot of passersby; a spoof on the Florida real estate boom; and "After-Dinner Speech," in which Charles Butterworth brought the house down as a Rotary Club speaker surrounded on the dais by a half-dozen distinguished citizens represented by wax dummies. George and Ira Gershwin contributed a standout number, "That Lost Barbershop Chord," set in a black barbershop. The show also featured the talented torch singer, Helen Morgan, who, for the first time, performed while sitting on a piano.

(2) M: Roger Wolfe Kahn; LY: J. P. McEvoy and Irving Caesar; D: J. P. McEvoy; CH: Russell Markert, Max Scheck, and George Stamper; S: Herman Rosse; C: Herman Rosse and John Held, Jr.; T: Lew Fields's Theatre; 10/30/ 28 (12)

Edition number two of J. P. McEvoy's satirical revue had little in it to satisfy cravers of original entertainment. Robert Littell limned it as follows: "some mildly amusing ideas done rather badly, and some feeble ideas done no better. Hasty, sour, and lacking in the cheerful gaiety so necessary to skits and music."

Among the show's best features were the dances contributed by a group of black performers and another black number called "Chain Gang." A five-minute condensation of Strange Interlude, done on roller skates, provoked laughs, but much of the remaining material hung heavily with over familiarity.

Following the show's rapid failure, it was revived as New Americana and reopened at the Liberty Theatre with Julius Tannen as M.C., but it too received pans such as that in the Times, which called it a "dull, mediocre entertainment." Opening on 11/29/28 it ran for twelve performances.

AMERICANS IN FRANCE, THE (Les Américains chez nous) [Comedy/ Family/Romance/Marriage/War/French] A: Eugene Brieux; D: Leo Ditrichstein; P: Lee Shubert and Leo Ditrichstein; T: Comedy Theatre; 8/3/20 (23)

A comedy that aimed to comment on the conflict between the American spirit of innovation and that of French traditionalism.

Its central character is Captain Smith (Wayne Arey), who remains in France after the war and turns the rustic estate of M. Charvet (Frank Kingdon) into a center of industrial activity. Nurse Nellie Brown (Harriet Duke) also causes an uproar when Charvet's son (Franklin George) breaks with French tradition and falls in love with her, although his parents had a French girl in mind for him. The customs of the two nations and the criticism of the worship by Americans of utility at the expense of life itself are expressed in terms of emotion rather than in argument.

The play was too intensely French, said Alexander Woollcott, for an American audience to appreciate its many critical points. Also problematic was the need to find a way to make the American characters sound as if they were speaking poor French. The best performance belonged to Blanche Yurka in the role of Henriette Charvet.

M.M.-C.

AMONG THE MARRIED [Comedy/Marriage/Sex] A/D: Vincent Lawrence; S: Gates and Morange; P: Philip Goodman; T: Bijou Theatre; 10/3/29 (44)

Vincent Lawrence's comedy of manners was greeted with polite reservations mixed with cautious approval. Set among the familiar surroundings of affluent Long Islanders, it told of how Ethel Mills (Katherine Wilson), married to the philandering Jack Mills (Frank Morgan), takes revenge on him by sleeping with golf champion William Minot (Edward Leiter). Since she and her husband are still in love, they iron out their conjugal problems by mutually consenting to a double standard for their future conduct.

"On the whole," announced the *Times*, "Mr. Lawrence appears to have made a good deal of his slight material. His characters are feeble, but they speak with some charm." Lawrence's able dialogue sustained the play for most critics, but John Hutchens maintained that the author's "stylistic artistry merely skirted the implications of the central theme."

AMOROUS ANTIC, THE [Comedy/Art/Marriage/Sex] A/D: Ernest Pascal; S: Jo Mielziner; P: Sam H. Harris; T: Theatre Masque; 12/2/29 (8)

A satire on self-consciously sophisticated modern attitudes toward sexual repression such as Susan Glaspell had immortalized in her famous one-act "Suppressed Desires." In *The Amorous Antic* an avant-garde painter (Phoebe Foster) and the avant-garde sculptor (Alan Mowbray) whom she is painting are powerfully drawn toward consummating their passion for one another. The painter's avant-garde playwright spouse (Frank Morgan), not wishing to seem too conventional, struggles to maintain his emotional equilibrium in the face of his wife's desire to have sex with her model once only so as to be rid of her repressions, thus enriching her art.

This was an often-funny piece bordering on farce, with considerable frankness in the lines, but it was too thin for three acts, according to Perriton Maxwell. *Time* thought the dialogue grew "banal and repetitious."

(1) ANATHEMA [Dramatic Revival/Yiddish Language] A: Leonid Andreyev; D/P: Maurice Schwartz; S: Samuel Ostrofsky; T: Yiddish Art Theatre (OB); 2/8/23

An ambiguous, philosophical allegory, originally produced by the Moscow Art Theatre in 1909 but banned after thirty-seven performances for allegedly glorifying the Jews. An earlier New York staging had occurred in 1910, also in Yiddish. In the present version, starring Maurice Schwartz as Anathema and Muni Weisenfreund (later, Paul Muni) as David Leizer, there was "no cohesion, no relation, no bond, visible or invisible, of union among the players"; yet, said the *Times*, the presentation "frequently approached the superb." Schwartz soon after produced the play in an English adaptation, described below.

(2) TR: Herman Bernstein; T: Forty-eighth Street Theatre; 4/10/23 (23)

In this English production Schwartz played David Leizer, and Ernest Glendinning was in the title role. John Corbin was sorely disappointed. He called it "pompous vaporings—a meaningless story enveloped in turgid verbosity."

Andreyev's Faust-like symbolic drama depicts the unsuccessful bid of Anathema, the devil, to enter Heaven and his consequent plot to take revenge by using the pious old Jew David Leizer as a means to his end. David, made enormously wealthy, uses his money to help the poor, but is stoned by them when the flow dries up. Anathema is once more refused admittance to heaven, but the saintly old Jew is allowed to enter.

Andreyev's play baffled the reviewers, although it was given an imaginative production. Ludwig Lewisohn said it offered "too much of turbidness, too much of passionate confusion. . . . [T]here is no controlling and unifying element at the play's core."

"ANCIENT MARINER, THE" and GEORGE DANDIN (Georges Dandin)
P: Provincetown Players; T: Provincetown Playhouse (OB); 4/6/24 (33)
"The Ancient Mariner" [Drama/Sea/Period/One-Act] A: Eugene O'Neill; SC: the poem by Samuel Taylor Coleridge; D: Robert Edmond Jones and James Light; C: Masks by James Light; *George Dandin* [Dramatic Revival] A: Moliere; TR/D: Stark Young; S: Cleon Throckmorton and Robert Edmond Jones; C: Millia Davenport and Robert Edmond Jones

"Mr. O'Neill and his associates have taken art and made it arty," wrote Heywood Broun of Eugene O'Neill's expressionistically conceived setting of Coleridge's poem. O'Neill had only contributed directions for some offstage noises and indicated some pauses, said Broun, but they were enough to botch the ballad. "The swiftness of the tale is gone now, its simplicity." The staging, according to Alexander Woollcott, had masked sailors moving behind the Mariner (E. J. Ballantine) and setting up the semblance of a ship as they swayed to the poem's rhythms, sometimes spoke, and lay dead at the end. Broun described it as "terrifically dreary" and Woollcott as "a nursery entertainment."

These critics had a better opinion of Stark Young's production of Moliere's comedy. Calling it an admirable farce and well played, Broun singled out the "amusing and ingenious" setting. Woollcott found the acting too self-conscious but noted with approval Rosalinde Fuller's chirpy wife as a contrast to her recent Ophelia opposite John Barrymore's Hamlet.

H.H.

AND SO TO BED [Comedy/Period/Sex/Marriage/British] A/D/S: James B. Fagan; P: James B. Fagan under the direction of Lee Shubert; T: Shubert Theatre; 11/9/27 (175)

Restoration-period diarist Samuel Pepys's famous diary made frequent use of the phrase employed as the title of this bedroom comedy, which, appropriately, is concerned with the amatory adventures of the philandering gentleman. Played by the London company, but with American Wallace Eddinger in the lead, it proved diverting, if inconsequential, fare.

Set in 1669, it tells of Pepys's encounter with the lovely singer Mrs. Knight (Mary Grey), whom his servants have rescued from a thief; of his hoped for seduction of the singer, only to have his visit interrupted by that of the king, Charles II (Charles Bryant); of his being hidden by the monarch in a chest when Mrs. Pepys (Yvonne Arnaud) bursts in; of the monarch's deliberate wooing of the diarist's wife as the husband frets in the chest they are sitting on; of the subsequent marital squabble that erupts; and of the ultimate rapprochement that ensues ("and so to bed").

Unequally written, familiar in situation, and unpretentiously played and designed, it nevertheless was a charming exhibition. "You take *And So to Bed* as you would a week-end at a country house," advised Stark Young.

ANDERSH (New Worlds) [Drama/War/Marriage/Business/Mental Illness/Yiddish/Yiddish Language] A: H. Leivick; D/P: Maurice Schwartz; T: Yiddish Art Theatre (OB); 9/25/22

An uneven, but largely engrossing, and extremely well-produced Yiddish drama detailing the inability of a storekeeper named Marcus to relate to the everyday world of business, marriage, and friendship after he returns home from the war. Everything seems to him to be "different" (the English meaning of the title). Finally, he leaves his wife and business, is considered insane, and burns down his store.

The *Times* was impressed by the variety of well-written characters involved, and by the "scenes of exceptional vividness and pathetic-humorous charm." Too much of the action seemed "vague and somewhat bewildering," but the overall effect was "of Sinclair Lewis at his best."

(1) ANDRÉ CHARLOT'S REVUE OF 1924 [Revue/British] B: Noël Coward, Ivor Novello, Ronald Jeans, Douglas Furber, Collie Knox, etc.; M: Noël Coward, Philip Braham, Ivor Novello, etc.; LY: Noël Coward, Ronald Jeans, Dion Titheradge, Douglas Furber, etc.; D: André Charlot; CH: David Bennett; S: Marc

Henri and Laverdet; C: G.K. Benda, Guy de Gerald, Lenief, Louiseboulanger; P: Selwyns; T: Times Square Theatre; 1/9/24 (298)

André Charlot had gained success in London with his unique variety of intimate revues; selecting the best from several of his previous hits, he came to and conquered Broadway with this charming show that introduced New Yorkers to Gertrude Lawrence and Beatrice Lillie. Noël Coward's songs and sketches were a principal contribution, and Alexander Woollcott chose "Parisienne Pierrot" and "There's Life in the Old Girl Yet" as his outstanding contributions.

Percy Hammond found Lawrence, who sang the revue's biggest hit, "Limehouse Blues," beguiling. The song (music by Philip Braham/lyrics by Douglas Furber) had been introduced in London by Teddie Gerard, but Lawrence was so successful with it in New York it soon became one of her trademarks. Heywood Broun described Lillie, whose comic impersonations included an aging soubrette and a march leader (in the greatly liked "March with Me") bungling up her ranks, as "that quite unusual person, an admirable female clown.... Miss Lillie manages to be slim, beautiful and enormously funny all at the same time."

In *A Star Danced*, Gertrude Lawrence claimed that producer Arch Selwyn wanted to cut the "March with Me" number after he saw it in rehearsal. Charlot refused to remove it and it became "the outstanding hit of the Revue." Also commended was sophisticated singer-dancer-light comedian Jack Buchanan. Herbert Mundin was another appreciated performer.

H.H.

(2) [1926 Edition] B/LY: Eric Blore, Dion Titheradge, Philip Braham, Hugh E. Wright, Douglas Furber, Jack Hulburt, Noël Coward, Ronald Jeans, Jack Strachey, Arthur Weigall, Uriell Lillie, Arthur Wimperis, Ivor Novello, Peggy O'Connor, Billy Rose, Al Dubin, Irving Caesar, Eric Fawsett, Hugh Sinclair, George Pughe, and Herbert Mundin; D: André Charlot; P: Selwyns; T: Selwyn Theatre; 11/10/25 (140)

The second of these fabulous *révues intime* was another smash, and the same group of entertainers who headlined the first were still around to put it over. It took several weeks for the show to be pulled into shape with new numbers added and others dropped. Richard Dana Skinner suggested that shows like this, novel when seen in their first editions, were now facing strong competition from a general improvement in Broadway's musical productions and from home-grown small revues. Larry Barretto griped that Lillie and Lawrence were deprived of material as good as they had had in the first version and that there was not enough of them in the show.

Attention-grabbing numbers included Bea Lillie singing a song enticing a mouse to come out of his hole as cards with the lyrics were displayed inviting the audience to sing along; Lillie and Lawrence dressed as hooch-guzzling babes in swaddling clothes engaged in sophisticated badinage in "Fallen Babies," a spoof of Noël Coward's *Fallen Angels*; a Coward ditty "Carrie was a Careful Girl" presented by Lawrence; Lillie's takeoff on an after-dinner musical artiste;

and "Fate," a sketch about a triangular love affair in which the audience was asked to decide the progressive steps in the action.

In *A Star Danced*, Lawrence wrote, "Charlot's revues were characterized by an exquisite economy, a cameraderie between all the players and the audience such as had not been known in America up to this time. . . . His revues did not depend upon spectacular lighting and scenic effects for success. Most of the sketches were played against drapes, which were beautiful in themselves but not breath-taking."

An important part of *Earl Carroll's Vanities* during the 1926-1927 season was the addition of a small-scale version of *Charlot's Revue*. It joined the show on 1/4/27 and remained about a month.

ANDROCLES AND THE LION and "THE MAN OF DESTINY" [Dramatic Revival] A: George Bernard Shaw; D: Philip Moeller; DS: Miguel Covarrubias; P: Theatre Guild; T: Klaw Theatre; 11/23/25 (68)

A Theatre Guild Shaw double-header of *Androcles and the Lion*, the satire on Christian martyrdom in which the tailor (Henry Travers) who removed a thorn from an injured lion's (Romney Brent) paw is rewarded by being served up to the same beast in the Coliseum, and "The Man of Destiny," a one-acter satirizing Napolean (Tom Powers) as seen in a romantic debate with an Austrian female spy (Clare Eames). The responses were mingled.

Richard Dana Skinner found the choice of *Androcles* inexcusable, since the play was, to him, a callous and cynical rejection of historical events deserving of greater reverence. Joseph Wood Krutch, though, noted that its laughter is that "of one who dares to be irreverent because he knows that irreverence can damage only those things which do not deserve to be revered." Miguel Covarrubias's unusual cartoon-like sets had an air of "burlesque" effrontery to them in various critical eyes, but Arthur Hornblow thought they, together with the staging, made the play look "half a Christmas pantomime and half an amazing burlesque."

The most remarked on performance was Edward G. Robinson's Caesar. Said Skinner, "I doubt if an actor has ever caught up in a few inspired moments more of the hollow, pasty, imbecility of the degenerating Roman Empire."

"The Man of Destiny" was a failure as a staging, due largely to the great inadequacies of the casting.

ANGELA [Musical/Romance/Period] A: Fanny Todd Mitchell; M: Alberta Nichols; LY: Mann Holiner; SC: Captain Robert Marshall's play, *A Royal Family*; D: George Marion; CH: Chester Hale; S: Watson Barratt; P: Messrs. Shubert; T: Ambassador Theatre; 12/3/28 (40)

The sexy Annie Russell had starred in the 1900 original from which this operetta-like show was derived. It was a Ruritanian romantic comedy set in the fictional land of Arcacia. *Time* said "the tunes were weak, the jokes wore stays, the trollings were adequate, and Peggy Cornell looked pretty and danced nicely."

"Seldom had a musical piece seemed so dull and archaic," contributed Brooks Atkinson.

Its heroine (Jeannette MacDonald) was a princess in love with a count (Roy Hover) who nevertheless agrees to her parents' demand that she marry a prince. The Prince they select conveniently turns out to be the Count with whom she is in love. The script included a host of old-fashioned gags and devices to complement its hoary plot line.

In the roles of the King and Queen were veterans Eric Blore and Alison Skipworth, but their material was too thin to stand on. "Miss MacDonald brought the only pleasing voice to the comedy," said Atkinson.

ANGELS ON EARTH (M'lochim oif der Erd) [Comedy/Fantasy/Yiddish/ Yiddish Language] A: Chune Gotesfeld; M: George Tueller; D/P: Maurice Schwartz; CH: Charles Adler; S: Boris Aronson; T: Yiddish Art Theatre (OB); 12/10/29

A "Hell and Earth comedy," rollicking in spirit, fantastical in subject, and abundantly humorous in performance, presented by the Yiddish Art Theatre at their new home in the former Fifth Avenue Theatre. Boris Aronson's comically bizarre scenery backed the performances of Maurice Schwartz and Samuel Goldenburg as the Angels Shamsiel and Zafziel who are ordered to leave their delightful home in Hades, where the sinners thoroughly enjoy death, and go to New York and clean up its sin. They get caught up in the wicked fun of New York life and even get married, but their derelictions land them in jail, and they are sent to Hell where they are tried for their misconduct. The outcome is that they are permitted to return to earth.

The *Times* said, this was "the drollest sort of lunacy, emerging in a sort of excited, commedia dell' arte treatment." John Hutchens, who knew no Yiddish, found the production a model "of coordinated clarity." Stella Adler and Lazar Freed were also in the cast.

ANIMAL CRACKERS [Musical/Crime] B: George S. Kaufman and Morrie Ryskind; M/LY: Bert Kalmar and Harry Ruby; D: George S. Kaufman; CH: Russell Markert; S: Raymond Sovey; P: Sam H. Harris; T: Forty-fourth Street Theatre; 10/23/28 (213)

The movie version has preserved much of the wacky horseplay, physical and verbal, engaged in by the zany Marx Brothers in *Animal Crackers*, the 1928 musical designed as a trampoline for their bouncing talents. The plot was a pretext for their craziness. It established them as guests at the posh party of Long Island's Mrs. Rittenhouse (Margaret Dumont), where they engage in the search for the robber of a valuable painting. Groucho portrayed a sun-helmeted African explorer, Captain Spalding; Chico was the Italian immigrant Emanuel Ravelli; and Harpo was the Professor. Zeppo played Groucho's secretary, Jamison.

"George S. Kaufman's book is far from being good and the plot. . .is too foolish to mention," declared *Time*'s critic who could not, however, shake the

memory of Harpo's gags: "when he is through playing the harp, [he] peers like
a prisoner through the strings of his instrument; he pursues a girl quietly wherever
she goes;...on meeting a new person, he offers her his leg to be held and he
whistles strangely, in his own way." Groucho and Chico explored the far-out
reaches of nonsense dialogue and puns, such as Groucho's spoof of the song
"You Took a Bandage Off Me."

The show included several acceptable musical embellishments, among them
"Watching the Clouds Roll By" and "Who's Been Listening to My Heart."
"Hooray for Captain Spalding" remained a theme for Groucho throughout his
career.

ANNA [Drama/Art/Romance/Austrian] A: Rudolph Lothar; AD: Herman Bernstein and Brian Marlow; D: Edgar J. MacGregor; S: Donald Oenslager; P: Samuel
Samach; T: Lyceum Theatre; 5/15/28 (31)

Matinee idol Lou Tellegen appeared opposite the up and coming Judith Anderson in this "verbose and uninspired drama" (*Times*) about a rakish sculptor
and avowed bachelor, Torelli (Tellegen), who, for three acts, is commandeered
into falling in love with and marrying his model (Anderson), who turns out to
be his patron's daughter. It had "as many stupid and inane lines, and as much
sentimental drivel, as" Richard Dana Skinner had "ever heard crowded into a
play." Neither of the players could do much to make the work more bearable.

ANNA ASCENDS [Comedy-Drama/Romance/Literature/Crime/Business] A:
Harry Chapman Ford; P: William A. Brady; T: Playhouse Theatre; 9/22/20 (63)

Well-known actress Alice Brady involved herself in "the worst play that has
been put before the metropolitan audience in many moons," declared Arthur
Hornblow. "[A] grotesquely awkward and preposterous melodrama," was Alexander Woollcott's verdict.

The story's artificial suspense scenes deal with a Syrian immigrant girl, Anna
Ayyobb (Brady), and her rise to the strata of American social life. While working
in a coffee shop, Anna is assaulted by a pimp. She stabs him, and as she runs
from the shop she cries, "Anna ascends." Throughout the play she does just
that—overcoming the return of the pimp and his plan to besmirch her character
and eventually triumphing by writing a novel based on her life and thus earning
$20,000 in royalties. She also satisfactorily concludes a love affair with a decent
young man who has helped her.

M.M.-C.

ANNA CHRISTIE [Drama/Romance/Prostitution/Family/Sea] A: Eugene O'-
Neill; D/P: Arthur Hopkins; S: Robert Edmond Jones; T: Vanderbilt Theatre;
11/2/21 (177)

After going through various revisions, including an out-of-town failure under
the title *Chris Christopherson*, *Anna Christie* opened in New York to great
acclaim and helped Eugene O'Neill ascend another rung on his climb to preem-

inence as America's greatest playwright. In *Anna Christie*, his lifelong preoccupations with the sea, prostitutes, waterfront saloons, and tragic emotion conspired to create what was viewed as a flawed but powerfully affecting play, "the truest, the most searching and the most dramatically consistent study in realism that our playwrights have produced" (Kenneth Macgowan).

O'Neill's fatalistic drama concerns Old Chris (George Marion), a Swedish coal-barge captain who blames the hardships he has suffered on "dat ole davil sea." Chris's daughter Anna (Pauline Lord), reared by relatives on a farm, has become a bedraggled prostitute. She goes East after fifteen years to find her father and soon becomes enmeshed in a torrential love affair with the shipwrecked Irish seaman Mat Burke (Frank Shannon). Spiritually cleansed by contact with the sea, her incipient idealism emerges as typified in the sensational scene when she reveals to Mat and her father the truth about her past. The men overcome their initial shock and disgust, but first they agree to be shipmates on a long voyage of forgetfulness, while Anna is to wait for them to be returned by "dat ole davil sea."

The play's ending stirred some controversy when some critics chose to see it as sentimentally optimistic and others as ironic and cynical.

Anna Christie was one of Burns Mantle's Ten Best of the Year; it also garnered the author his second Pulitzer Prize. The play's critics, however, while acknowledging the playwright's achievement, panned lapses such as the excessive reliance on theatrical trickery and forced developments.

The production was aided immeasurably by Arthur Hopkins's plausible direction, Robert Edmond Jones's atmospheric settings, and Pauline Lord's inspired performance. Arthur Hornblow said, "Pauline Lord is a dynamic creature as the harassed victim of an inexplicable nemesis. Noteworthy was the frugality of her gestures, the gestures of a woman who has lost hope."

ANNIE DEAR [Musical/Marriage] B/M/LY: Clare Kummer; SC: Clare Kummer's comedy *Good Gracious, Annabelle*; D/CH: Edward Royce; P: Florenz Ziegfeld; T: Times Square Theatre; 11/4/24 (103)

A Clare Kummer 1916 comedy hit was converted by the authoress into a Flo Ziegfeld-produced musical comedy, with Kummer contributing her own music and lyrics (with interpolations by Sigmund Romberg and Harry Tierney). Ziegfeld's abundantly talented wife, Billie Burke, played the title role. It was gorgeously produced in the true Ziegfeld manner, with beautiful visuals and a splendid line of chorus girls. Unfortunately, the story seemed buried beneath the production overlay, especially in an extraneous third-act woodland fantasy set to Romberg's music.

Burke's part was that of Annabelle Leigh, who runs away on her wedding day from her husband (Marion Green), and takes a job as housekeeper to a Long Island copper magnate (Ernest Truex); she is located there by her spouse who, because he has shaved off his beard, is not recognized by her, and is thereby wooed back to the married state.

"The first act seems. . . a high tide on the beaches of delight. The second act is well enough. The third, barring a rough and tumble interlude in which Miss Kummer had no hand [presumably the woodland fantasy], is dreadful," reported Heywood Broun.

In her autobiography *With a Feather on My Nose*, Burke noted that she did not have the voice to sustain a big musical comedy. She also claimed that the show might have been more successful if Clare Kummer's contract with Ziegfeld had not prevented the impressario from adding any scenes or numbers she did not create.

ANTONIA [Comedy/Show Business/Marriage/Romance/Hungarian] A: Melchior Lengyel; AD: Arthur Richman; D: Arthur Richman and George Cukor; S: Joseph Urban; P: Charles Frohman, Inc.; T: Empire Theatre; 10/20/25 (55)

Antonia (Marjorie Rambeau), former Budapest opera star, has for ten years been happily ensconsed on her husband's (Lumsden Hare) stock farm, to which she repaired following their wedding. She is enticed back to the city by a flapper niece (Ruth Hammond) who needs her assistance in a love affair with a French officer (Georges Renavent). Antonia is soon attracted to the Captain and he to her, although she manages to resist the temptation of running off with him. Her urge to return to the bright lights and cafes subdued, she returns to her farm and husband.

All this seemed like a musical comedy without the music to both the *Times* and Joseph Wood Krutch, especially as star Marjorie Rambeau sang a couple of songs, and gypsy music figured in several scenes. "[T]he situations and the motivations are nearly all forced and artificial," declared Richard Dana Skinner.

Antonia enjoyed a return engagement of sixteen performances later in the season.

ANTONY AND CLEOPATRA [Dramatic Revival] A: William Shakespeare; D: Frank Reicher; S: Rollo Peters; P: Selwyns i/a/w Adolph Klauber; T: Lyceum Theatre; 2/19/24 (32)

Waggishly declaring that *Antony and Cleopatra* was Shakespeare's "sole attempt to write a play after the Shavian manner," Heywood Broun judged that Shaw had created a better Cleopatra. He thought that Jane Cowl played the role as a present-day flapper, "pert and saucy," and praised the "glorious pace" set by director Frank Reicher. Tragic heights were not reached, however, for Cowl and Rollo Peters as Antony were more like Columbine and Pierrot. Recalling the acting team's Romeo and Juliet from the previous season, Percy Hammond judged Cowl's Cleopatra simply her "adorable Juliet transported to Alexandria." Peters lacked the stature and maturity for Antony and in his beard "looked more like General Grant." Hammond noted that the production used Sir Herbert Tree's cut version in which Antony is onstage more than Cleopatra and found that the production, which featured many physically slight performers "rattling around in stupendous roles," had "something pygmy about it."

Alexander Woollcott, on the other hand, found "as rich, imaginative and generally satisfying a production of the play as this generation is likely to see." To him, Jane Cowl's Cleopatra entered her "into the small company of the Olympians," although he agreed with Broun and John Corbin that Peters was too young and lightweight for Antony.

H.H.

ANYTHING MIGHT HAPPEN [Comedy/Romance] A: Edgar Selwyn; P: Selwyns; T: Comedy Theatre; 2/20/23 (64)

An "inconsequential" (Heywood Broun) farce that "began with a clever first act, carried through to a very amusing second and wound up with a third in which much of the earlier momentum appeared unaccountably dissipated" (Burns Mantle). It was all about a couple of bachelors (Leslie Howard and Roland Young) and their romantic problems. One of them has a chance encounter with the other's fiancée (Estelle Winwood), passes on some information that leads to a rupture between the lovers, and ends up getting drunk with her. Various mishaps develop, but at the end everyone is back with their original mates.

The champagne-drinking scene with Young and Winwood was funny, but the play as a whole never got "away from routine situations and dialogue" (Broun).

APACHE, THE [Drama/Marriage/Music/France] A: Josephine Turck Baker; D: Will H. Gregory; T: Punch and Judy Theatre; 5/7/23 (16)

One of "the worst plays of the season" (*Times*), this forgettable opus was set in a music studio of Paris's Hotel Napolean and examined the fantasies of the jealous husband (Juan de la Cruz) of a gifted Austrian pianist (Thais Margrave), who is as devoted to her art as to her marriage, is sent flowers by a wealthy admirer, and is threatened with murder by her husband in the guise of an Apache. The action turns out to be the husband's dream.

Produced in a hurry with very few rehearsals (no producer was credited) and very little care for sets and props, the work was pretty much of a shambles. "Dramatically," said E. W. Osborn, "the results are at times confusing and occasionally dismaying."

(1) APPEARANCES [Drama/Race/Blacks/Trial] A: Garland Anderson; D: John Hayden; P: Lester W. Sagar; T: Frolic Theatre; 10/13/25 (23)

Appearances was heralded as having been written by Garland Anderson, "The First Negro to Have a Play Produced on Broadway." In fact, Willis Richardson's *Chip-Woman's Fortune*, produced in May 1923, was the premiere black-authored play on the Great White Way. Anderson, a San Francisco bellhop, spent seven years getting the piece produced. He was grateful to Al Jolson, the singer, for reading it and paying for Anderson's trip to New York; Governor Al Smith's presence at a reading of the play helped to attract investors in the production. Anderson claimed that he was inspired to write the play as a service to humankind; it bore traces of being autobiographical and was meant to portray the power of faith. The author's faith was tested when two white actresses, Nedda Harrigan and Myrtle Tannehill, left the show during rehearsals for what some believed to be their bias against appearing with black actors.

The play was considered forceful, but crude, and plagued by "many moments of ponderousness and stiffness. . . . And if the language. . .is not always smooth, if many of the characters are overdrawn, if the plot dips too often into melodrama, the play is none the less moving" (*Times*).

It dealt with the story of a black San Francisco bellhop, Carl (Lionel Monagas), accused by a white woman (Mildred Wall) of attempting to rape her. His friend Rufus (Doe Doe Green) is implicated in the attack as well. The courtroom drama that ensues in the last two acts marshals various witnesses against the black men, who have only truth and no witnesses on their side. Rufus is a stereotyped black character whose comical remarks on the witness stand provide comic relief of the standard variety. Carl has a moment of pathetic valor as he speaks in his own defense; however, he is vindicated not by his innocence but a plot device wherein the plaintiff is revealed as a blackmailer, a deserter from her family, and a light-skinned "Negress."

(**2**) [Dramatic Revival] D: Lee Miller; P: C. Mischell Picard; T: Hudson Theatre; 4/1/29 (64)

A revival of the play with a revised script did better than the original. In this version, the Prosecutor (Rupert La Belle) is revealed as the villain; because the bellhop has convinced Louise Thornton (Martina Martin) that the District Attorney, whom she was planning to marry, is disreputable, the D.A. bribes an adventuress to accuse the black man of attacking her. He thus hopes to discredit him in Louise's eyes.

Only Doe Doe Green of the original cast returned for the revival. The *Times* wrote: "It was recognized at the time of the original production as a sincere but completely naive piece of writing, and a second view gives no reason for altering that opinion."

APPLE CART, THE [Comedy/Politics/British] A: George Bernard Shaw; D: Philip Moeller; DS: Lee Simonson; P: Theatre Guild; T: Martin Beck Theatre; 2/24/30 (88)

Shaw's fortieth play, his first in six years, was written at the age of seventy-three. Described by him as "a political extravaganza," it was a garrulous, three-and-a-half-hour, three-act satire expressed in lengthy monologues and set in England some half-century in the future. The Empire is ruled by the Shaw-like King Magnus (Tom Powers), who confronts a cantankerous labor cabinet intent on depriving him of his veto and upholds against them the principles of enlightened monarchy as opposed to the evils of an irresponsible Democracy. Magnus is later seen passing considerable time with a court lady (Violet Kemble Cooper) desirous of becoming his mistress. Then, the U.S. Ambassador (Frederick Truesdell) arrives and states America's wish to rejoin the British Empire, but Magnus rejects the proposal since it would only make England further subservient to America. Finally, Magnus addresses the Cabinet and threatens to abdicate and become a member of Parliament, rise to prime minister, and with his son on the throne, gain the control he seeks; this leads to the veto issue being abandoned.

The Apple Cart was recommended as intellectual fun, ripe with Shavian rhetoric and ideas, but neither very witty nor dramatically effective. Richard Dana Skinner found it long winded and boringly concerned with matters too exclusively British to matter much to Americans; Joseph Wood Krutch insisted that he remained interested throughout. The acting of Tom Powers and Claude Rains (as the Prime Minister) was highly effective.

APPLESAUCE [Comedy/Romance/Small Town] A: Barry Conners; D: Allan Dinehart; P: Richard Herndon; T: Ambassador Theatre; 9/28/25 (90)

A big hit in Chicago, a relative failure in New York, this comedy was about a small-town fellow who thrives on a theory of spreading around the ''applesauce'' of goodwill, so that one and all may be happy with themselves and life. Allan Dinehart played this cheerful always-do-well character with great ease and honesty (he also directed). The fragile plot had him lose his girl friend (Gladys Lloyd) to Rollo Jenkins (Walter Connolly) and then win her back again.

Arthur Hornblow considered it hokum but agreed that it was ''really excellent of its kind, the comedy comparing well with such . . . successes as *The First Year* and *The Show-Off.* . . . The characters . . . are in a way conventional types, but the author has given them real life.''

APRON STRINGS [Comedy/Marriage/Sex] A: Dorrance Davis; D: Earle Boothe; S: Louis Kennel; P: Forrest C. Haring; T: Bijou Theatre; 2/17/30 (226)

This widely liked farce treated the subject of mother fixation in a vastly amusing manner; it posited a young man, Daniel Curtis (Roger Pryor), whose late mother had had a syndicated advice column in the newspaper. He lives his life in accordance with a sheaf of letters she left him telling him just how to behave in any possible situation. The situation that the play concerns itself with is his marriage to Barbara Olwell (Audray Dale), which he fails to consummate because of various attitudes of punctiliousness imposed on him by his mother's missives. This priggish groom even asks his prospective mother-in-law (Maidel Turner) if the girl has a ''practical working knowledge of the sex relation.'' When his bride runs home to her parents, it takes a few stiff drinks administered by a clever lawyer (Jefferson De Angelis) to get him to submit to nature's urges.

The premise was so amusing, wrote Perriton Maxwell, that it barely mattered that the play was ''weak, ordinary, wordy, silly, and at times positively boring.''

ARABESQUE [Musical/Romance/Period/Africa] B: Cloyd Head and Eunice Tietjens; M: Ruth White Warfield; D/S: Norman Bel Geddes; CH: Michio Ito; P: Norman Bel Geddes and Richard Herndon; T: National Theatre; 10/20/25 (23)

The unique visual talents of Norman Bel Geddes went into making this romance of the Arabian desert a "costly and superbly ornamental production" (Ward Morehouse) in which the designer's innovative decorative sense made mincemeat of an already palsied script. "[I]t is one of the most exciting pictures you will ever see in the legitimate theatre," said *Time*: "As drama it is skinny and undernourished." The critics were overwhelmed by the Bel Geddes genius and were impressed by his use of light to change sets without lowering the curtain.

Set in the picturesque milieu of a Tunisian village, and stocked with colorful types from beggars to sheiks, the work offered "a curious hash of poetry, satire, burlesque, delicacy and gross sensuality" (Richard Dana Skinner) to tell its tale of a sheik (Bela Lugosi) who desires a virgin (Sara Sothern) for his bride but loses her to a virtuous youth (Curtis Cooksey), while himself being seduced by a Bedouine girl (Hortense Alden).

ARABIAN, THE [Drama/Adventure/Africa] A: Gordon Kean; D: Rollo Lloyd; P: Barbour, Conrad, and Bryant; T: Eltinge Theatre; 10/31/27 (32)

Melodrama actor Walker Whiteside returned to New York after a five-year absence, part of which time had been spent touring small cities with this "ten-twent'-thirt' " example set largely in the Arabian desert. George Jean Nathan said he played "the name role made up as an Armenian and comporting himself like a Japanese." Whiteside's vehicle was "a conventional but serviceable piece" (*Times*) about an English-educated Arabian sheik with a grudge against the British for slights suffered at their hands by his English wife. When he has an English regiment trapped in the desert and is prepared to have them annihilated, he relents at the bequest of an English girl (Ellis Baker), who happens to be his long-lost daughter. The playwright was Whiteside himself, writing under a pseudonym.

ARABIAN NIGHTMARE (The Galloping Sheik) [Comedy/Small Town/Adventure/Romance] A: David Tearle and Dominick Colaizzi; P: Clarke Painter; T: Cort Theatre; 1/10/27 (24)

A moderately risible farce that takes its heroine (Marion Coakley) and her spinster aunt (Helen Lowell) from their boring life in Amesbury, Massachusetts, to the Arabian desert after the former inherits a fortune and decides to seek romance and adventure. Her dissatisfaction with her fanciful aspirations becomes manifest after a run-in with an amorous sheik (Charles Millward), but hometown lad Bobbie Mudge (Lorin Raker) arrives to save the day and win the girl.

Partly intended as a satire on the contemporary fad for Arabian romance in books and films, the play was generally amusing but lacked any memorable climaxes. Alexander Samalnam kept waiting for the piece to catch fire, but it never did. The funniest thing in it was Bobbie's rescue of his girlfriend by dressing in drag and outwitting the lustful sheik. *Time* pointed to "a superabundance of stage gags so long standardized" that everyone knew just when to chuckle at them.

AREN'T WE ALL? [Comedy/Marriage/Sex/British] A: Frederick Lonsdale; D: Hugh Ford; P: Charles Dillingham; T: Gaiety Theatre; 5/21/23 (284)

Frederick Lonsdale's British comedy about marital peccadiloes did far better in New York than in London, perhaps, as the *Times* suggested, because its American production focused on the character played by Cyril Maude, whereas abroad the part of the wife as acted by Marie Lohr had been stressed. This wife (Alma Tell) returns from India to discover her husband (Leslie Howard) kissing another woman. Only the clever and charming interference of the philosophically rakish old Lord Grenham (Maude), the husband's father, patches things up when he uncovers an Australian chap who had had an escapade with the wife while she was in India. Lord Grenham marries Lady Frinton (Mabel Terry-Lewis) and all's well that ends well.

John Corbin, like the audience, enjoyed "Mr. Lonsdale's amiable cynicisms, [and] chuckled deeply at his always brilliant and often richly human wit." He said the playwright's intent was to show how we are all philanderers, which makes the world a more pleasant place in which to live.

On 4/13/25 a sixteen-performance return engagement began at the Globe Theatre.

ARIA DEL CONTINENTE, L' (Continental Culture) [Comedy/Family/Italian Language/Italian] A: Nino Martoglio; D: Angelo Musco; P: Italian Art Folklore Theatre; T: Manhattan Opera House (OB); 10/4/27

The English title of this Sicilian comedy played by the visiting company of Italian star Angelo Musco would be *Continental Culture*. Set in a small town in Sicily, it pictured the return of Don Cola Dusciu (Musco) to the embrace of his sister and brother-in-law's family, after his having been away for half a year in Rome recuperating from an appendix operation. But Don Cola is a changed man, a Continental dude, with Milla (Pia Libassi), an attractive female companion who soon is the apple of the local male citizenry's eyes; the female population is resentful. Milla, supposedly sophisticated, is unmasked as a lowly Sicilian girl, and Don Cola drops his posh manner, as town life resumes its ancient course.

The play was rich in realistic Sicilian language, and the acting had a subdued, believable air, according to Walter Littlefield. Luigi Pirandello is said to have worked on it with its author.

ARIADNE [Comedy/Business/Marriage/British] A: A. A. Milne; D: Philip Moeller; S: Carolyn Hancock; P: Theatre Guild; T: Garrick Theatre; 2/23/25 (48)

A whimsical, lighthearted domestic English comedy of marital misunderstanding, played on Broadway before being produced on the London stage. The critics called it "slender," "thin," and "slight." It concerned a young Englishwoman, Ariadne Winter (Laura Hope Crews), whose lawyer husband (Lee Baker) wants her to be friendly to a wealthy client (Harry Mestayer), although the wife complains that the man has romantic designs on her. To bring the matter to a head, the clever Ariadne makes a date for lunch, and possibly more, with the rich old man but returns home when he is detained by business. When the husband realizes how close his wife has come to being *too* friendly, he promises to devote more time to her and less to business.

This was one of the Theatre Guild's less innovative and challenging productions. Compared to some of the author's other works, it was "less entertaining and has infinitely less point," said Stark Young. Well staged and acted, it boasted a luminous performance by Crews.

ARMS AND THE MAN [Dramatic Revival] A: George Bernard Shaw; D: Philip Moeller; DS: Lee Simonson; P: Theatre Guild; T: Guild Theatre; 9/14/25 (181)

War, heroism, and the glorious traditions of soldiery were the targets zeroed in on by Shaw's wonderful 1894 satire (first staged in 1898), here revived by the Theatre Guild in a hit production starring Alfred Lunt as Bluntschli and Lynn Fontanne as Raina. The play's pertinence in the post–World War I years was greater than ever. Its universality was appreciated by Richard Dana Skinner: "His theme is simply the futility and nonsense of self-deception. War, warfare and whereabouts are all accidents." But a few believed, as did John Mason Brown, that *Arms and the Man* had not weathered the storms of time: "It is thin and weak, and its sparkle is somewhat dulled."

To most, Lee Simonson's colorful sets were outstanding and the company's acting of the first water. Most distinguished were the performances of the Lunts. "The romantic Raina of Miss Lynn Fontanne," beamed Skinner, "is crisp and delectable—nothing less—and fittingly matched against the precise common sense of Alfred Lunt."

ARTISTIC TEMPERAMENT [Comedy/Romance/Marriage/Literature] A: Thomas P. Robinson; P/D: Oliver Morosco; T: Wallack's Theatre; 12/9/24 (7)

This "preposterously bad" (Joseph Wood Krutch) product of George Pierce Baker's "47 Workshop" was an outing offering little chance for respected actresses Elisabeth Risdon and Gail Kane to show their stuff. Alexander Woollcott called it a "stale, artless, helpless little comedy."

Its story was about an author, Archie Stanwood (Donald Foster), his wife (Risdon), their thirty-three-year-old spinster guest (Kane), and the spinster's fiancé, a chaste English professor (Austin Fairman). Archie uses the people around him as models for his writing; when the spinster's relationship with the Professor hits some turbulence, Archie woos her, observes her and her fiancé's responses, and, when the woman is prepared to elope with him, announces the completion of his story. He then returns to his wife and the spinster to the Professor.

(1) ARTISTS AND MODELS [Revue] B: Members of the Society of Illustrators, including Rube Goldberg; M: Jean Schwartz; D: Harry Wagstaff Gribble and Francis 'Bunny' Weldon; S: Watson Barratt; P: Messrs. Shubert; T: Shubert Theatre; 8/20/23 (312)

The sensation of showgirls nude to the waist may have partially accounted for this revue's long run, but it was also regarded as tuneful, funny, and visually beautiful. Percy Hammond praised the music as better than that in most revues, and found "there are some fairly successful endeavors to be comic by Mr. Frank Fay." The *Times* reviewer called the semiclad showgirls "the most daring display in years" and singled out the sets for special praise, particularly some Japanese print designs, porcelain statuettes, and a pastoral scene by Watson Barratt.

Originating as their annual production, *Artists and Models* was written and designed by members of the Society of Illustrators. The curtain rose upon a life class in an artist's studio, with the semiclad models appearing one at a time and walking across the stage. Other scenes included a blackface comedian, a ukelele scene, a sketch about critics, a burlesque of professional card tricksters on a vaudeville stage (featuring Frank Fay), and acrobatic dancing by burlesque performer Etta Pillard. A sketch that created a series of pictures from the comic-strip bug house fables was a critical favorite.

H.H.

(2) [1924 Edition] B/D: Harry Wagstaff Gribble; M: Sigmund Romberg and J. Fred Coots; LY: Clifford Grey and Sam Coslow; S: Watson Barratt; P: Messrs. Shubert; T: Astor Theatre; 10/15/24 (258)

The second edition of this pulchritudinous Shubert revue featured "breathtaking spectacles" in many of which "the form divine is displayed bravely and boldly" (Arthur Hornblow). There was not such outrage provoked over the nudity this year as had been the case in 1923, but this may have been because it was "neither as nude nor as ribald" (*Time*) as that edition. Yet the *Times* noted with distaste several moments of comic suggestiveness that it suggested should be eliminated.

Only in an opening scene did the evening purport to have any sort of plot (a New Hampshire girl arrives in Greenwich Village). The rest of the show was devoted to revue and burlesque numbers. Outstanding was Spanish dancer Trini. English comic Barnett Parker was moderately entertaining; ventriloquist Frank Gaby pleased; beautiful Mabel Withee sang well and, in one number, wore a bathing suit and dived into an onstage pool; Valadia Vestoff danced solo; there were sketches and parodies, including one of the Theatre Guild's staging of *Fata Morgana*; and there were new songs, none of them exceptional.

(3) [1925 Edition] B: Harold Atteridge and Harry Wagstaff Gribble; M: Alfred Goodman, J. Fred Coots, and Maurie Rubens; LY: Clifford Grey; D: Alexander Leftwich; CH: Jack Haskell; S: Watson Barratt; P: Messrs. Shubert; T: Winter Garden Theatre; 6/24/25 (416)

The 1925 edition of *Artists and Models* was labeled "the Paris Edition" and sought to bring top Parisian music-hall entertainment to the Broadway revue. Chief of the imports were the eighteen Gertrude Hoffman Girls. "They dance after every conceivable fashion and school,'' wrote Arthur Hornblow; ''they fence with endless litheness and vitality, and clad advantageously in sunflower-hued tights, they perform gracefully upon ropes in the manner of acrobats.''

Scenes the critics liked included ''Mothers of the World,'' in which song-stresses dressed in internationally diverse costumes sang native lullabies; ''Cel-lini's Dream,'' a tableau of feminine beauty in which nary a stitch was worn; ''Pastels,'' another visual delight in which the girls emerged in pastel colors from a giant artist's paintbox; a ''Rotisserie Number,'' displaying various chor-ines dressed as fowls being turned on a spit over a grate; a bubble scene called ''Maid of the Milky Way''; ''Jazz a la Russe,'' in which a *Chauve-Souris*–style bit with American jazz was essayed; and the Hawaiian dance number ''Poi Ball.''

Specialty acts were contributed by the female impersonator and straight-man team of Brennan and Rogers; the vocal talents of Walter Woolf; comic accor-dianist Phil Baker and his stooge Sid Silvers; and many others.

During the run, the Winter Garden celebrated its fifteenth anniversary; to celebrate the occasion, Al Jolson joined the revue on 3/21/26; he had been in the theatre's opening production in 1911. ''For nearly an hour he sang and talked and talked and sang,'' observed the *Times*. Jolson stayed with the show for a month.

(4) [1927 Edition] M: Harry Akst and Maurie Rubens; LY: Benny Davis; ADD. LY: J. Keirn Brennan, Jack Osterman, and Ted Lewis; D: J. C. Huffman; CH: Ralph Reader and Earl Lindsey; S: Watson Barratt; P: Messrs. Shubert; T: Winter Garden Theatre; 11/15/27 (151)

Critics enjoyed this edition's fast-talking comedy lines and sketches, as ex-emplified by talents Jack Pearl, Florence Moore, and Jack Osterman. The humor was conventional but nonetheless amusing. Moore scored with bits such as her playing a nurse who gets a patient to remove his trousers before discovering that the man is there to sell the doctor a subscription. Pearl's German dialect drollery—he said a cynic was where you wash dishes—was likened to the style of Louis Mann, and Osterman held the stage with a paen to Broadway in one of his better numbers. Ted Lewis led the orchestral infusions, and there were specialty standouts such as dancers King and King. Production numbers were appropriately stylish, especially a pantomime on a Chinese junk, ''The Love Boat,'' and scenes set before the Taj Mahal and Rheims Cathedral. One hundred chorus girls provided eye-filling charms, but nudity was not stressed. Burns Mantle called the show ''big, garish, alive with color, not too rough, not too refined, not too messy with clothes nor too revealing of flesh.''

(5) [1930 Edition] M: Harold Stern and Ernie Golden; SC: an English musical comedy, *Dear Love*; D: Frank Smithson and Pal'mere Brandeaux; S: Watson Barratt; C: Ernest Schrapps; P: Messrs. Shubert; T: Majestic Theatre; 6/10/30 (55)

The last in this regularly scheduled series of revues (one more show with the title arrived in 1943) was a dismal letdown, according to the *Times*. It lacked "talent, ideas, taste and a point of view.... [I]t is a dull show which attempts to make up in naughtiness and nudity what it lacks in pace and material." This represented a big change from the previous edition.

The show began life as a musical based on an English work called *Dear Love*, which it was titled during its tryout period. *Dear Love* was gradually transformed into a revue format that assumed the title of the *Artists and Models* series with which it really had little in common. A thread of the plot remained, making the show ambivalent in style.

Phil Baker and his auditorium stooge garnered guffaws with their off-color jokes; Vera Pearce, an English comedienne, was funny in a travesty dance with George Hassell; Aileen Stanley sang several songs, and a variety of other acts were presented to middling effect.

AS YE MOULD [Drama/Marriage] A: Charles Mackay; P: Geoffrey C. Stein, Inc.; T: People's Theatre (OB); 10/19/21 (11)

This first play of Charles Mackay's told of Paul Driscoll (Geoffrey C. Stein), who is set to marry the wealthy widow Mrs. Graham (Helen Lackaye) and thus tries to get the mother (Alice Fleming) of his illegitimate ten-year-old son to assume custody of the child; she fears telling her husband of the boy's existence. Discovering the facts, the husband (Charles Hammond) forgives his wife and accepts legal parentage of her son. Driscoll, though, loses Mrs. Graham.

The general run of critical opinion sided with Louis V. De Foe, who scored the play's radical improbability and said, "It was only an artificial... affair that betrayed the hand of the amateur."

(1) AS YOU LIKE IT [Dramatic Revival] A: William Shakespeare; D: Robert Milton; DS: Lee Simonson; P: American National Theatre; T: Forty-fourth Street Theatre; 4/23/23 (8)

In a season marked by notable Shakespearean productions on Broadway, *As You Like It* proved the least effective; despite an impressive array of talent and the fact that it was the inaugural mounting of the hopeful new American National Theatre company founded by Augustus Thomas, the revival closed in one week.

Robert Milton staged it "with such painstaking reverence, and with such a curious monotony of tone and gesture, that it became not only distinctly tedious, but, at times, actually unintelligible," commented John Farrar. This "mighty good looking bore" (*Herald*) ran until 11:30 P.M., chiefly because of interminable waits occasioned by Lee Simonson's exquisite but clumsy settings. There were some excellent moments early in the play, notably the boisterous wrestling-match scene, but thereafter the pace slackened and grew lugubrious. Chief culprit was star Marjorie Rambeau as Rosalind. "The least of her faults," wrote John Corbin, "is that she sometimes betrays by false emphasis the fact that she did not quite know what she was talking about." A. E. Anson as Jacques "tried to make 'All the world's a stage' seem a light improvisation and broke it up by stirring his drink around, slapping people on the back and walking about. The very effort not to make it seem an elocutionary exercise only heightened the realization that it was'' (Heywood Broun). Margalo Gillmore played Celia and Ian Keith acted Orlando.

(2) D: Fritz Leiber; P: Chicago Civic Shakespeare Society; T: Shubert Theatre; 4/2/30 (2)

Fritz Leiber led a stock company of Chicago actors through a season of nine Shakespearean revivals, including Shakespeare's idyllic comedy. One of their more consistently effective offerings, it prompted Brooks Atkinson to declare, ''Mr. Leiber's company. . . trips through this one daintily. You might be captious about an excess of skipping frolic here and there. But that would not alter the main fact that in a sweet play. . . Mr. Leiber's actors perform sweetly, too, filling an afternoon with pleasantries and beauty.''

The play was cut considerably, and most of Lieber's role of Jacques was gone, making the ''ages of man'' speech his centerpiece. ''As usual, he imposes himself no further on the performance than the circumstances of his part require,'' noted Atkinson. Lawrence Cecil was Orlando, Vera Allen was Rosalind, and Robert Strauss was Touchstone.

Lieber's were nonacademic, straightforward, and conventional productions, stageworthy, if unoriginal, and given competent, but uninspired, mountings.

ASHES [Drama/Theatre/Marriage/British] A: Reginald Goode; P: Lawrence Marston; T: National Theatre; 10/20/24 (24)

A vehicle for emotional actress Florence Reed that offered her strong opportunities but was, at best, a tiresome, sentimental affair. Reed was required to portray Marjorie Lane, a classical American actress, married to a second-rate actor, Rupert Best (Warburton Gamble). Because of her career demands, she entrusts the rearing of her child to an aunt; as she is about to go on one night in *Antony and Cleopatra*, she receives the news of her five-year-old's death; the show, of course, goes on. A couple of years later, her husband is discovered trying to seduce her sister (Gladys Hurlbut), and she leaves him.

Heywood Broun condemned *Ashes* as ''just so much twaddle'' and ''A thing of scraps and stale crusts''; Percy Hammond called it ''rather a tepid entertainment. . . dramatic at times and always literate, but given to dozing now and then.''

ASHES OF LOVE [Drama/Romance/Sex/British] A/P: Vera, Countess of Cathcart; T: National Theatre; 3/22/26 (8)

One of the most meretricious theatre events of the day, this play by Vera, Countess of Cathcart, was an opus self-advertised as based on the actual experiences of its author-star-producer. It was produced before an audience that laughed derisively at all of its attempts at seriousness. ''It is admittedly naive, and recounts with quite an air of discovery a rather childish and undramatic story,'' noted the *Times*. To Ward Morehouse it was ''tedious and mechanical stuff,'' while Wells Root dismissed it as ''dull entertainment and tawdry in tone and purpose.''

Estelle (Countess of Cathcart), married to Lord Rayhaven (Lumsden Hare), meets Lord Anton (Austin Fairman) at a party and elopes with him to South Africa. In that country Anton begins to drink heavily and is unfaithful. Estelle has meanwhile been divorced. She returns to London and is offered remarriage by Rayhaven, but she turns him down.

Shortly after this turkey closed, its authoress-star was deported by the State Department on charges of moral turpitude.

ASSALTO, L' (The Attack) [Dramatic Revival/Italian Language] A: Henri Bernstein; D: Giuseppe Sterni; P: Teatro d'Arte; T: Bijou Theatre; 5/19/29 (1)

The sixth offering of the Teatro d'Arte's busy 1929–30 season was their Italian-language offering of Henri Bernstein's French political drama *L'Assaut* originally seen in New York in English in 1912. The production was not as highly regarded as some earlier works given by the New York-based troupe; Walter Littlefield decided that Bernstein's familiar ingredients seemed ''too obvious, a little worn, a little strained.''

Little remained of interest in the plot about a legislator (Giuseppe Sterni) who is blackmailed by a journalist (Rodolfo Badaloni) for a youthful indiscretion discovered by the latter, and who is exonerated in court and in his sweetheart's eyes. The juicy acting parts gave the company material to play with color, but their effort seemed wasted on an outmoded drama.

ASSUMPTION OF HANNELE, THE (Hanneles Himmelfahrt) [Dramatic Revival] A: Gerhart Hauptmann; TR: Charles Henry Meltzer; M: George D. Copeland; D: John D. Williams with Eva Le Gallienne; S: Mercedes de Costa; P: John D. Williams; T: Cort Theatre; 2/15/24 (3)

The idea for producing special matinees of Hauptmann's Grillparzer Prize play, last seen some dozen years earlier with Mrs. Fiske, was Eva Le Gallienne's. Then appearing in *The Swan*, she persuaded several in that cast, including Basil Rathbone, to join her. Rathbone played Hauptmann's schoolteacher-Christ figure, who carries the young Hannele (Le Gallienne) into the poorhouse of a German mountain village on a stormy night and hovers by her, appearing in her visions, as she lies dying.

The direction was credited to John D. Williams, but it was actually done by Le Gallienne who took over when Williams became ill. It was her first try at direction and so fascinated her that she soon became one of the most active and respected directors of her time. The story of how she undertook the play's direction is found in her memoirs, *At 33*.

Reviews were mixed, from Alexander Woollcott's ''an excellent and a painstaking production, far more elaborate and far better prepared than one expects at these casual special matinees,'' to George Jean Nathan's opinion that Le Gallienne's idea of the play ''seems to be somewhat at variance with the author's.''

The result. . .was the Grand Transformation scene of *Uncle Tom's Cabin* stretched out to two hours and interrupted every now and then by what appeared to be selections from Gorki's *Night Refuge*.''

H.H.

AT MRS. BEAM'S [Comedy/Hotel/Crime/British] A: C. K. Munro; D: Philip Moeller; S: Carolyn Hancock; P: Theatre Guild; T: Guild Theatre; 4/26/26 (222)

Six seasons after its successful London run C. K. Munro's satirical comedy came to New York with Jean Cadell, who had played the part in England, repeating her triumph in the central role of Miss Shoe.

The loosely structured play was produced on the same night that Broadway witnessed another Munro play, the unsuccessful *Beau-Strings*. *At Mrs. Beam's* was about the frustratingly officious old maid Miss Shoe, whose own withered life causes her to pry into everyone's business. She suspects a mysterious couple staying at her boarding house residence of being a notorious criminal (Alfred Lunt) and his next victim (Lynn Fontanne). The scandalmonger is confounded, though, when they turn out to be international thieves who, as the boarders are determining what to do with them, make off with the best items in the resort.

The play displayed an amusing assortment of provincial types and had an excellent battle royal bedroom scene between the Lunts, the first of many they were to make a specialty of. Brooks Atkinson ascribed much of the work's success to the various characterizations, but Richard Dana Skinner assailed Munro for not fully fleshing out his people. To him the play was "dull, sophomoric and fit chiefly for the efforts of amateur theatricals." Yet Stark Young liked it as "a sly comment on English life, on human foibles, a gallery of portraits seen with the eye of a friendly imp."

AT THE GATE OF THE KINGDOM (Ved rikets port) [Drama/University/ Marriage/Norwegian] A: Knut Hamsun; TR: Marta Aresvik Putnam; D: Richard Boleslavsky; P: American Laboratory Theatre; T: American Laboratory Theatre (OB); 12/8/27 (23)

The first play by Nobel Prize-winning Norwegian playwright Hamsun to be done in America, it was an 1895 work laid in the modest home of struggling philosopher Ivar Kareno (Grover Burgess) and his wife (Florence House). Kareno is a man whose ideals prevent him from getting ahead by following the advice of those who tell him to trim his sails and not to make waves by his critical attitudes. His refusal to bend, coupled with his academic preoccupations, leads his wife to leave him for another and to his falling into poverty.

"[I]t proved to be an interesting and provocative drama," claimed the *Times*. Stephen Rathbun, however, could not appreciate the play's finer qualities because of what he deemed a terribly acted, lugubrious staging.

ATLAS AND EVA [Comedy/Family/Marriage] A/P: Harry Delf; D: Ira Hards; T: Mansfield Theatre; 2/6/28 (24)

Originally called *The Nebblepredders*, this innocuous comedy relied for much of its farcical humor on the difficulties of correctly pronouncing that family name. Harry Delf, former musical comedy star turned dramatist and legitimate actor, played Elmer Nebblepredder, a kindly floorwalker, whose family of parasitic relatives lives off his labors and relies on his services in providing boyfriends for its girls and jobs for its unemployed. Finally casting off the shackles of servitude, he decides to enjoy himself with his wife (Leona Hogarth) and not worry about the others.

The *Times* believed Delf had not assembled the familiar materials "with quite sufficient skill to justify the retelling."

AUTUMN FIRE [Drama/Irish/Old Age/Family/Romance/Rural] A: T. C. Murray; D: George Vivian; P: John L. Shine; T: Klaw Theatre; 10/26/26 (71)

Success in London and Dublin preceded this Irish play's New York premiere with an excellent all-Irish cast. Its principal role was that of Owen Keegan (John L. Shine), a robust, athletic, stubborn sixty-year-old farmer who desires a young bride (Julie Hartley-Milburn) and wins her, although his spinster daughter (Una O'Connor) is very upset over the June-December relationship. After a bone-crushing fall from a horse, he realizes the affection existing between his son (Felix Irwin) and his wife and sends the son away in order to hide his debacle from the neighbors. He is a pitiful, lonely being at the end.

E. W. Osborn credited the work for being "full of the simplicity and sincerity that make for the true beauty of art," and the *Times* said that apart from its excessive length, "There is much that is excellent and much that is true in *Autumn Fire*."

AVARE, L' (The Miser) [Dramatic Revival/French Language] A: Moliere; P: Wendell Phillips Dodge; T: Fulton Theatre; 3/11/24 (3)

While on tour during a year's leave from the Comédie Française, where he had acted since 1887, Maurice de Féraudy billed himself as "the greatest living French actor." Alexander Woollcott wondered what Lucien Guitry would think of that, although he found Moliere's play acted "crisply, expertly, entertainingly" by Féraudy and his company. Finding Féraudy's Harpagon—which he had played for thirty years—a joy, the *Times* critic wrote that the actor "is a comedian whose versatility is the best refutation of the theory that prolonged association with the Comédie Française hardens the dramatic arteries." Woollcott remarked that the production's scenery was "of a vintage that would have delighted the penurious Harpagon."

H.H.

AVENTURIERE, L' (The Adventuress) [Dramatic Revival/French Language] A: Émile Augier; P: Messrs. Shubert; T: Thirty-ninth Street Theatre; 11/13/22 (3)

A revival of Augier's swashbuckling romantic melodrama set in fifteenth-century Italy, produced in repertory by the visiting Comédie Française players led by Cécile Sorel.

L'Aventuriere, an 1848 verse play first seen in New York in 1868 and then in several later revivals, comprises a tale of a prodigal son (Albert Lambert), who returns to find his father (Louis Ravet) in the snares of a notorious adventuress (Sorel), his plan to expose the woman's character by seducing her, her growing love for the young man, and her ultimate departure alone.

The leading lady's age was obviously too great for her role, and the dimensions of the Little Theatre only served to accentuate that fact. However, in a part that allowed her "to run pretty well through the gamut of her best moments...Sorel...was in her element.... Her florid style, her flaming jewels, and her incredible gowns completed the picture of La Sorel" (John Corbin).

Cécile Sorel returned with this play in her repertory during the 1927–1928 season and opened it at the Cosmopolitan Theatre for three performances on 12/16/27.

AWFUL TRUTH, THE [Comedy/Romance] A: Arthur Richman; D: Henry Miller; P: Charles Frohman, Inc.; T: Henry Miller's Theatre; 9/18/22 (146)

A piece of romantic comedy ephemera that, despite serious problems of plausibility, pleased most of the critics. It concerned an attractive divorcée (Ina Claire), whose impending marriage to an Oklahoma oil man (Paul Harvey) is threatened by a story he hears about her past. Her first husband (Bruce McRae) bears witness to her character, but he and she fall in love again, and the oil man scurries happily home to the open spaces.

It seemed hard to accept the sophisticated divorcée's innocence, said some. An earlier version of the script had actually established her as guilty, but this had been revised for popular consumption. Heywood Broun noted, "The play depends not upon its plot but upon brisk and amusing dialogue superbly handled." Percy Hammond added that it was "A pretty play..., comprising interesting persons, amusing conversations, [and] smart, romantic situations."

B

BAB [Comedy/Youth/Romance/Family] A: Edward Childs Carpenter; SC: the novel by Mary Roberts Rinehart; D: Ignacio Martinetti; P: George C. Tyler; T: Park Theatre; 10/18/20 (88)

Taken from a Mary Roberts Rinehart book, this play served as a vehicle for Helen Hayes, who depicted impressionable young girlhood with its silly pretensions and pertness. When compared to Booth Tarkington's *Seventeen*, *Bab* was "adolescence rubbed in," wrote the *World*.

Bab is a romantic adolescent weighed down by the incomprehensible problems of life. She comes home from boarding school during a measles epidemic and succeeds in driving her family to near hysteria in a fruitless attempt to make sense out of her lovelorn vagaries. Rather than accept her fictitious lover, the family refuses to sympathize with her innocent deceptions.

Helen Hayes received unanimous praise for her clever portrayal. Ludwig Lewisohn warned, however, that trite plays like this would damage her budding talent.

M.M.-C.

BABBLING BROOKES [Comedy/Legacy/Family] A: E. D. Thomas; D: Edyth Totten; S: Joseph Ticknor; P: Russell Fanning, Inc.; T: Edyth Totten Theatre; 2/25/27 (3)

An inept episodic piece rumored to be the work of actress Edyth Totten and telling in eleven scenes of events in the history of the Brooke family, from 1847 to 1927. The Brookes, in possession of a great portion of Long Island, have been under a curse according to which they shall bear only daughters, and this leads in 1927 to legal difficulties with a will that are finally ironed out by a female lawyer (Totten) belonging to the clan.

"It was all pretty childish stuff—cloudy, dull and crudely put together," wrote the *Times*.

BABES IN TOYLAND [Musical Revival] B/LY: Glen MacDonough; M: Victor Herbert; D: Milton Aborn; P: Jolson Theatre Musical Comedy Company; T: Jolson's Fifty-ninth Street Theatre; 12/23/29 (32)

Victor Herbert's 1903 operetta was seen for the first time since its 1905 revival in this version produced as one of a series of similar resuscitations at the Jolson during the 1929–30 season. There was little to gripe about in the charming show. Calling Herbert "very nearly a great composer," the *Times* critic wrote, "There is magic in the score and melody and wizardry." Leotabel Lane was Contrary Mary, Frank Gallagher was Alan, Betty Byron was Jane, and William Balfour was Uncle Barnaby, the miserly old man who wishes Alan and Jane, his nephew and niece, dead so he may get their inheritance; all were excellent.

BABIES A LA CARTE [Comedy/Legacy/Sex] A: Seaman Lewis; D: Francis Fraunie; P: S. L. Simpson; T: Wallack's Theatre; 8/15/27 (24)

One of three 1927–28 plays with the phrase "a la carte" in their titles, this one was a farce, "as childish, pointless, and unfunny. . .as could possibly be evolved from a central idea which. . .is not without its possibilities" (*Times*). As in *Buy, Buy, Baby* of recent memory, the plot concerned a race to cash in on a legacy by being the first to produce a baby. One sister has hers in Chicago, the other in New York, and there is a debate over which came first, but the news that only a boy baby will be the winner clinches the matter at the end.

The author was the producer, writing under an assumed name. He produced a revision under the title *The Lawyer's Dilemma* on 7/9/28 at the Belmont Theatre, where it ran for twenty-four performances. A new cast and sets did little to improve the play, and the reviews were just as damning as before.

BABY CYCLONE, THE [Comedy/Marriage] A/P: George M. Cohan; D: Sam Forrest; T: Henry Miller's Theatre; 9/12/27 (187)

"Baby Cyclone" is an adorable Pekingese dog belonging to Mr. and Mrs. Hurley (Spencer Tracy and Nan Sunderland) of New York and, in Mr. Hurley's eyes, far too much the preoccupation of his mate. He sells her to a lady in the street for $5, leading to an altercation with the missus and the interference on her part of a stranger, Joseph Meadows (Grant Mitchell), who takes her home with him. Mr. Hurley arrives to straighten matters out, but Mr. Meadow's fiancée (Natalie Moorehead) walks in and turns out to be the Peke's purchaser. Various complications arise over the pup's ownership, until all is peaceably resolved at the climax.

The critics were amazed at how nimbly author Cohan could spin his tenuous idea out to sustain an audience through a full evening's enjoyment. Joseph Wood Krutch asserted that "extraordinarily expert writing keeps it continuously funny," and the *Times* found it "amusing, workmanlike and interesting." Grant Mitchell, the play's star, was admirable, but Spencer Tracy, in his first principal role (specifically written for him), nearly stole his thunder. Richard Dana Skinner said, "Spencer Tracy's masterly delineation. . .is quite the best piece of acting of its kind I have seen in many months. He is not only convincingly at ease at all times, but the variety and sincerity of his facial expressions add sumptuously to the force of every line.''

BABY MINE [Dramatic Revival] A: Margaret Mayo; S: Livingston Platt; P: John Tuerk; T: Forty-sixth Street Theatre; 6/9/27 (12)

A tired 1910 farce revived to give Roscoe "Fatty" Arbuckle a vehicle for his return to the stage (he was said to have done the piece in stock before his scandal-plagued Hollywood career). He played a fellow who, to help out a lady (Lee Patrick) whose husband is upset over her failure to conceive, borrows not one but three babies for her to use in deceiving him.

The *Times* spurned the piece as "pretty dated and mechanical" and found Arbuckle only "fairly satisfactory." First Nighter, however, said that "puffing like an avoirduporpoise, [he] made the [character] live again.''

BACHELOR FATHER, THE [Comedy/Old Age/Family/Romance] A: Edward Childs Carpenter; D/P: David Belasco; S: Joseph Wickes; T: Belasco Theatre; 2/28/28 (264)

Serious critics pooh-poohed the empty sentimentality and improbabilities of this "rather old-fashioned and very ponderously named comedy" (Joseph Wood Krutch), but it was the sort of fare the average playgoer sought. Noting some of the play's hard-to-swallow plot and linguistic features, Krutch commented: "Yet the absurdities are significant only as furnishing examples of the all-pervading unreality which is as conspicuous, though less tangible, in every stroke of the characterization and every element of the atmosphere.''

English character actor C. Aubrey Smith played an egotistical sixtiesh English aristocrat whose libertine youth provided the world with three illegitimate children by separate mothers. Having supported them without ever meeting them, he has them come to his Surrey estate from their homes in Italy, New York, and India. They look dad over, agree to accept him, and the boy from India (Rex O'Malley) falls in love with the girl from Italy (Adriana Dori), happily learning that his father is really someone else. The American girl (June Walker) plans to wed the old codger's solicitor (Geoffrey Kerr).

BACHELOR'S BRIDES [Comedy/Fantasy/Gambling/Romance] A: Charles Horace Malcolm; D: Melville Burke; P: Raye and Co., Inc.; T: Cort Theatre; 5/28/25 (28)

"This is a heavy and commnplace [*sic*] farce," growled Ward Morehouse, and Wells Root snarled that the "idea and construction are generally uneasy.

A young Englishman (Charles Davis) with a past and a fondness for gambling on the horses, is about to be married to an American (Lee Patrick), when a baby is discovered among the wedding gifts. Frightened by the threat of legal suits concerning his imagined paternity, he strives to hide the infant; before the plot is satisfactorily completed the young man has a feverish dream that, as produced, was reminiscent of the expressionist staging used in the *Beggar on Horseback* nightmare. But the resemblance was not a good one. "It seemed an attempt to be expressionistic without a clear conception of the nature of the medium," claimed Root.

BACHELOR'S NIGHT, A [Comedy/Sex] A: Wilson Collison; D: Harry Andrews; P: John Cort; T: Park Theatre; 10/17/21 (8)

A door slamming, girl-chasing farce of no originality or ideas and with very little worth laughing at. Written by a prolific collaborator with authors such as Avery Hopwood, this solo effort was "just as dull as it is innocent," noted the *Times*.

The plot was a mechanical arrangement according to which a bachelor (William Roselle) returns unexpectedly to his flat to find there a number of attractive women. When his mother (Isabel Irving) and a jealous husband turn up, the fur begins to fly. It was overacted like an operetta, griped the *Herald*: "Among the bad plays of the season it is a triumph."

BACK HERE [Drama/Invalidism/Religion/Friendship] A: Olga Printzlau; D: Victor Morley; P: William A. Brady i/a/w I. H. Herk; T: Klaw Theatre; 11/26/28 (8)

Film scenarist Olga Printzlau's second play was, like her first, *Window Panes*, a disaster, closing in only one week's time. Faith healing was its subject, and it had to do with wounded war-veteran Peter Linden (George Meeker), who spreads his ideas among those recuperating at a hospital for shattered soldiers. The cynical Sergeant Terry O'Brien (Melvyn Douglas) does not believe in miracles until the steel plate in his chest saves him during a dance-hall fracas, and the crippled Peter, responding to Terry's challenge, manages to walk.

The *Times* said the dismal effort "could scarcely be described as entertainment," but picked out Melvyn Douglas's performance for its "ease and naturalness" as the evening's best.

BACK PAY [Drama/Romance/War/Sex] A: Fannie Hurst; D: Elwood F. Bostwick; P: A. H. Woods; T; Eltinge Theatre; 8/30/21 (79)

Fannie Hurst was one of America's top fiction writers, especially of emotion-drenched short stories for magazines, when this first play of hers was produced. Based on one of her stories, *Back Pay* reeked of all of the qualities that had made Miss Hurst a popular writer; onstage these qualities bore the stamp of meretriciousness. Hurst's play was not only considered sentimental and tawdry, it also failed to free itself of the fiction writer's reliance on lengthy descriptive dialogue and superfluity of flowery metaphoric expressions.

Hester Bevins (Helen MacKellar) leaves Demopolis, Ohio, and her lover Gerald (Fleming Ward) to run off with a traveling salesman. While being kept by a wealthy New Yorker, she learns of Gerald's war injuries and blindness, takes him home, nurses him until his death, and goes back home, reformed.

This story, wrote Alexander Woollcott, was told "in language that is sometimes incredibly gaudy and with scenes that slosh about in sentiment." It was redeemed, noted Kenneth Macgowan, by Hurst's respect for her central personage: "She gives the woman strength of character all through."

BACK SEAT DRIVERS [Comedy/Business/Crime/Marriage] A: Larry E. Johnson; D: Len D. Hollister; P: Roy Walling; T: Wallack's Theatre; 12/25/28 (16)
Only nondiscriminating audiences found this satirical farce on the current craze in stock-market speculation amusing. It presented the story of two wives (Sylvia Farnese and Tabatha Goodwin) who divert their husbands' (John Litel and Hugh Cameron) finances from potential loss in foolish investments to a phony company they found. The money, however, is seized by their crooked partners, and the husbands have to catch them before it is all gone.
All *Time* could say was that "Spots of this are funny, in a modest way," and the *Times* thought only Hugh Cameron's acting was worth seeing the play for.

BACK TO METHUSELAH [Comedy/Fantasy/Bible/Politics/British] A: George Bernard Shaw; DS: Lee Simonson; P: Theatre Guild; T: Garrick Theatre; 2/27/22; 3/6/22; 3/13/22 (25)
Part I: "In the Beginning" D: Alice Lewisohn and Agnes Morgan; Part II: "The Gospel of the Brothers Barnabas" D: Alice Lewisohn and Agnes Morgan; Part III: "The Thing Happens" D: Frank Reicher; Part IV: "The Tragedy of an Elderly Gentleman" D: Frank Reicher; Part V: "As Far as Thought Can Reach" D: Philip Moeller
When Lawrence Langner and George Bernard Shaw were arranging to have the Theatre Guild produce this longest of modern plays, the Irish playwright told the producer, "Don't bother about a contract.... [I]t isn't likely that any other lunatic will want to produce *Back to Methuselah*!" The play was produced in five parts on three evenings, for all of which the top price for orchestra seats was $9.90, while one could see the three performances for only $3.30 from the rear balcony of the small theatre. The Guild expected to lose money on the play, and it did. Because of the immense amount of work involved, the production was shared with the Neighborhood Playhouse, two of whose directors staged the first evening's presentation. Considerable debate took place concerning the precise method of presentation. Ultimately, the opening night saw Parts I and II, a week later came Parts III and IV, and Part V was staged a week after that. Shaw objected to any cuts in his plays, so the lengthy drama went on *in toto*, but Langner soon convinced Shaw to cut it himself, and these reductions were subsequently introduced, although to no great avail in lengthening the run of nine weeks.
There was little critical adulation dispensed for this garrulous "Metabiological Pentateuch" in which the playwright presents, among a number of topics, his belief that for humankind to perfect itself according to the dictates of Creative Evolution, human beings must develop the ability to live for hundreds, even

thousands, of years. Human life at present, said Shaw, is too brief for men to master those deficiencies of wisdom that contribute to social disharmony. *Back to Methuselah* thus stretches from 4004 B.C., the time of the Garden of Eden, in "In the Beginning," to the year 31920 in "As Far as Thought Can Reach." In that day, 30,000 years hence, people will grow to full maturity in the first few years of life and thereafter devote their lives to thought and some single pragmatic activity, all aimed at one day overcoming entirely their preoccupation with material existence.

Despite a brilliant production, *Back to Methuselah* was largely a tedious, heavy-going experience for critics and spectators. Alexander Woollcott could not help but be "inexpressibly bored by the feeble and repetitious and octogenerian garrulity" of the interminable second part. Arthur Hornblow grumbled at Shaw's "ocean of verbiage," relieved now and then by humor, "with occasional stretches of oppressive dullness, and long-winded to the point of exhaustion to both players and audience." Critics were quick to deride Shaw's dramatic technique and philosophical observations. Chief among the respected performers involved were George Gaul, Margaret Wycherly, Dennis King, Albert Bruning, and Ernita Lascelles.

A first hand account of the Guild's dealings with Shaw in the mounting of this play can be read in Lawrence Langner's *G.B.S. and the Lunatic*. Among the stories he tells is that of the dress rehearsal at which George Gaul, playing Adam, appeared wearing a skimpy loin-cloth; at that moment, Guild member Theresa Helburn was in the auditorium trying to get actress Margaret Wycherly, playing the Serpent, to keep her head out of sight. As Gaul entered, already ill at ease because of his revealing costume and the presence in the theatre of a group of "prim lady social workers," Helburn shouted, "If you think we can't see it, you're very much mistaken." The embarrassed Adam fled the stage as the theatre rocked with unashamed laughter for ten minutes.

BACKSLAPPER, THE [Comedy/Politics/Marriage/Small Town] A: Paul Dickey and Mann Page; P: John Henry Mears and Paul Dickey; T: Hudson Theatre; 4/11/25 (33)

Echoes of George Kelly's *Show-Off* were sounded in this not uninteresting study of a hail-fellow-well-met character, Bob Alden (Harry C. Browne), wed to Beth Lane (Mary Fowler), who left the duller, but ultimately more sincere, John Trainor (Charles Trowbridge) to marry him. Bob, seeking to further his political career so he may be elected, practices his great charm on one and all, is revealed as essentially unprincipled, neglects his wife and alienates her affections, and loses her to the other man.

The majority of the critics were negative. Alan Dale called it a "curious and uncontrolled comedy," and John Ranken Towse penned that "the whole thing is childish and slipshod." The *Times*, though, thought it had "substantial merit," despite its drawbacks.

BAD HABITS OF 1926 [Revue] M: Manning Sherwin; LY: Arthur Herzog; P: Irving S. Strouse; T: Greenwich Village Theatre (OB); 4/30/26 (19)

An amateurish Off-Broadway revue, with unrestrained performances and little subtlety. "The most that one can write of the young people in this show is that they are willing," said Brooks Atkinson. "It was noisy. It was rough in spots and smooth none of the time," added Stephen Rathbun.

Good bits included a takeoff on male choruses, a lecture on the telephone, a dance called "At the Bath," a comic lifeguard song by Willard Tobias, and a burlesque of an all-star cast on an opening night.

BAD MAN, THE [Comedy-Drama/Crime/Adventure/Romance/Western/Rural/ Invalidism] A: Porter Emerson Browne; D: Lester Lonergan; S: Livingston Platt; P: William Harris, Jr.; T: Comedy Theatre; 8/30/20 (320)

"[A] good hair-trigger melodrama through which runs a vein of jovial humor and a thin trickle of social criticism," wrote Alexander Woollcott of this smash hit play. Pancho Lopez (Holbrook Blinn), a Mexican bandit based on the real-life Francisco Villa, captures a ranch in Arizona. The ranch is owned by an invalid American, Gilbert Jones (Frank Conroy), home from the wars and in jeopardy of losing his land to Morgan Pell (Fred L. Tiden), visiting with his wife, Lucia (Frances Carson). Pancho robs a bank to pay off the mortgage and shoots Morgan to save his friend's life. Pancho is a Robin Hood bandit whose philosophy is based on sense not law.

The play was a "clever satire on the familiar Mexican melodrama" (*Independent*), poking fun at the United State's handling of border outlawry; its smooth production was capped by a sensational acting job provided by Holbrook Blinn, who gave the character of Pancho a Shavian aura that made it memorable. The Playgoer said the role fit Blinn's "forceful and commanding personality to perfection."

M.M.-C.

BADGES [Comedy-Drama/Mystery/Crime/Romance] A: Max Marcin and Edward Hammond; D: Edgar J. MacGregor; P: Jules Hurtig; T: Forty-ninth Street Theatre; 12/3/24 (104)

Max Marcin, coauthor of *Badges*, had another popular melodrama, *Silence*, running when this one opened. Unlike the tense, emotional *Silence*, this crook thriller depended for its effect on comedy, especially as embodied in the character of correspondence-school detective Franklyn Green, played with enormous dexterity by Gregory Kelly. This meddlesome oddball was at the heart of a very complex plot about the awkward hotel clerk who wants to be a detective, gets involved in a situation with a young woman (Lotus Robb) whose post-office-employee father has been murdered, and uncovers a gang of bond thieves even the government agents could not locate.

The critics did not consider the story in any way original. John Ranken Towse called it "a pretty childish sort of affair," Stark Young said "it made you think of nothing," and Q. M. claimed the work was based on "one of the most familiar of theatrical devices." Yet all agreed that it was deft entertainment.

BALLYHOO [Drama/Romance/Show Business/Sex] A: Kate Horton; D: Richard Boleslavsky; S: James Reynolds; P: Russell Janney; T: Forty-ninth Street Theatre; 1/4/27 (7)

Carnival life and all of its colorful trappings was the inspiration for this unsuccessful venture directed by Richard Boleslavsky. Its picture of the carny characters did not ring true, despite the presence of types such as barkers, bareback riders, and a strong man. "In the main...it is a somewhat studied picture," noted the *Times*. A couple of weeks later, *The Barker* succeeded where this work did not.

Its chief role was a promiscuous woman bronco rider, Starlight Lil (Minna Gombell), who falls for a society youth (Eric Dressler) but decides to end the romance, believing she is too cheap for him. Her attempts to make him think her unfaithful lead to even worse problems, but the final curtain sees them on the verge of mutual happiness.

BAMBOOLA [Musical/Blacks/Show Business/Romance] B/D: D. Frank Marcus; M/LY: D. Frank Marcus and Bernard Maltin; CH: Sam Rose and Lt. J. Tim Brymn; P: Irving Cooper; T: Royale Theatre; 6/26/29 (27)

Broad comedy, furiously paced dancing, and the talented Isabell Washington gained this ill-fated black musical whatever kudos it attracted. All conventional ingredients of the genre were shoveled on in songs and gags, and a simple story line about a Savannah girl (Washington) who leaves home to venture into northern show biz in a revue with the same title as this musical. Eventually, she becomes a star and marries the show's composer.

With tunes titled "Dixie Vagabond," "Ace of Spades," and "Rub-A-Dub Your Rabbit's Foot," the dance groups called the Bamboola Dusky Damsels and the Bamboola Steppers pounded the Royale's boards with energy.

The *Times* complained that half way through, the show grew tedious, and Richard Dana Skinner reflected a widespread concern that such shows were too imitative of white ones and did not thoroughly exploit "the superb, naive genius of the race."

Some sources give the show's title as *Bomboola*.

BANCO [Comedy/Marriage/Gambling/Sex/French] A: Alfred Savoir; AD: Clare Kummer; D: Robert Milton; S: Livingston Platt; P: William Harris, Jr.; T: Ritz Theatre; 9/20/22 (70)

There was much to enjoy about Clare Kummer's intelligent adaptation of this racy French marital comedy in which Alfred Lunt scored a hit in the title role. Not only was it very well directed and capitally acted, but it remained close in spirit to the original while offering the distinction of Kummer's clever style.

Alexander Woollcott called the play "spirited, original, dauntless and witty," but John Ranken Towse considered it an empty bedroom farce.

Lunt's role was that of a French count nicknamed "Banco" because of his passion for baccarat, which passion leads to his restless wife's (Lola Fisher) divorcing him. She remarries, but Banco intrudes at her new home, distracts the husband (Francis Byrne), keeps the bride occupied throughout a night of card playing, and ultimately wins her back.

Playwright S. N. Behrman was so impressed by Lunt's performance that he reportedly went to see it twenty times in order to study the actor's comic technique.

BANSHEE, THE [Comedy/Crime/Legacy/Mystery/Romance] A: W. D. Hepenstall and Ralph Cullinan; D: Charles J. Mulligan; P: Banshee Inc.; T: Daly's Theatre; 12/5/27 (49)

A melodramatic mystery farce with elements of Irish folklore, Indian mysticism, and hypnotism and packed to the gills with all of the hokum of conventional mystery plays. Banshees are said to have caused Peter Adair's (Joseph Brennan) father's death; when Peter dies after a woman (Lillian Walker) destroys a statue said to be cursed, the banshees are blamed. A fight over a will ensues. The murderer is revealed as an Amazonian native with a blow gun (Richard Whorf). He is captured, the will is settled, and a young couple cement their love affair.

The *Times* thought the production of stock company caliber, and none of the critics did more than shrug at the play's existence.

BARBARA [Drama/Art/Crime/Romance/Italian Language/Italian] A: Gennaro Mario Curci; D/P: Emanuel-Gatti; T: Gallo Theatre; 11/17/29

An Italian prizewinning drama presented in New York following its premiere in Naples; it told of the all-encompassing influence held over a talented Italian painter (Primo Brunetti) working in Paris by his willful model and mistress Barbara (Elvira Curci-Caccia) and of the painter's ultimate release from her spiteful possession by her murder at the hands of a male model (Filippo Caminiti), whom she also has ensnared.

Walter Littlefield found the play very realistically written but verbose and unimaginative in conception. The acting was excellent.

(1) BARE FACTS OF 1926 [Revue] M: Charles M. Schwab; LY: Henry Myers; P: Kathleen Kirkwood i/a/w Murray Phillips; T: Triangle Theatre (OB); 7/18/26 (107)

An intimate Off-Broadway revue that had "to its credit some excellent lyrics, wittily and cleverly wrought...two or three good tunes...and a few ideas," according to the *Times*. Outstanding was an imaginative enactment of Vachel Lindsay's rhythmic poem "The Congo," as chanted by Mary Doerr and performed by silhouetted figures. A "Music Masters" number pictured Mendelssohn, Chopin, and Liszt carping about how Tin Pan Alley stole their best tunes. Various contemporary plays were parodied, among them *Lulu Belle*, *Kongo*, and *The Great God Brown*. The show was not as smoothly professional as critics would have desired, but it was unique enough to garner three months of performances.

(2) [1927 Edition] B: Stuart Hamill; P: Kathleen Kirkwood; T: Triangle Theatre (OB); 6/29/27

A followup to the 1926 original *Bare Facts* revue laughed at Aimee Semple McPherson's evangalism and the Theatre Guild and Provincetown Players' respective offerings of *Ned McCobb's Daughter* and *Rapid Transit*, among other sketches. A "Krazy Kat" and "Missionary Number" also figured on the bill.

(3) [1930 Edition] B: Christopher Morley, Roy McCardell, Steve Claw, Eddie Davis; M: Edwin Cleaves; LY: Edwin Cleaves and Kathleen Kirkwood; P: Kathleen Kirkwood; T: Triangle Theatre (OB); 4/16/30

The final version of this show, produced in the tiny playhouse at Seventh Avenue and Eleventh Street, came nearly three years after its predecessor. It was *Bare Facts of Today*, thus differentiating it from those editions that had been designated by the year of their production. It contained the usual assortment of sketches, songs, and dances and raised absolutely no one's temperature among the professional theatregoers.

BAREFOOT [Comedy/Rural/Southern/Art/France/Romance/Sex] A/D: Richard Barry; P: Native Theatre; T: Princess Theatre; 10/19/25 (37)

The critics balked at this amateurish comedy about a barefoot, red-haired Virginia mountain girl (Evelyn Martin), produced by a theatre group from Mamaroneck, where local audiences enjoyed it greatly. "We doubt if Broadway has seen anything quite so inexplicable, quite so naive, quite so futile as *Barefoot*," sighed Charles Belmont Davis.

Its innocuous tale was of the mountaineer's daughter with artistic talent who succumbs to the tempting talk of a slick northerner (Byron Beasley) with a yen for her flesh who takes her to Paris to study painting; there she learns that he is married, and she rushes back again to her old Virginny home where the lover follows only to be threatened by Pappy's (John M. Kline) shotgun. But the art patron-bachelor (Eugene Weber) who really loves the girl interrupts and makes an honest woman of her.

BARKER, THE [Drama/Romance/Sex/Show Business/Family] A: Kenyon Nicholson; D: Priestly Morrison; S: P. Dodd Ackerman; P: Charles L. Wagner i/a/w Edgar Selwyn; T: Biltmore Theatre; 1/18/27 (225)

Two weeks after the debacle of *Ballyhoo*, a play about life in the carnival midway, came this hit play set in an identical milieu. *The Barker*, in fact, had had to jettison its original title, which was precisely that of the earlier work. The play captured the flashy, sleazy life of the tent shows in an uneven story about a middle-aged barker (Walter Huston), who, when his nineteen-year-old son (Norman Foster) visits, tries to hide the facts of his own debauched life from him but is upended when his hootchie-kootchie dancer mistress (Eleanor Winslow-Williams) inveigles the snake charmer (Claudette Colbert) to seduce the boy. The plan works too well, the lad and the vamp fall in love and depart, the barker is heartbroken and plans to leave the tent show, but the son, happily, sends word that he will resume his law studies while his new wife supports him.

Written by a Columbia University drama professor, the play, said *Time*, "falls short of technical efficiency the while it achieves a glorious fullness of unacademic atmosphere, characterization and emotional conflict." Joseph Wood Krutch liked the original background but censured the author for borrowing familiar melodramatic situations. Colbert and Huston gave fine performances.

BARNUM WAS RIGHT [Comedy/Hotel/Business/Romance] A: Philip Bartholomae and John Meehan; D: John Meehan; P: Louis F. Werba; T: Frazee Theatre; 3/12/23 (88)

Set largely in a weird hotel, this was a *Tavern*-like melange of widely varied ingredients, described by an *Evening Mail* critic as "Ballyhoo farce, ponderously and perspiringly frolicsome, humor with an occasional Cohanesque bon mot brought forth in travail between shootings and bombings" (L.A.F.)

Singer Donald Brian, in his first straight role, was Fred Farell, a young man who sets out to win his true love's (Marion Coakley) hand by convincing her father (Elwood F. Bostwick) of his effectiveness as a businessman. Putting his Barnum-like ideas to work, Farrell creates a booming business by selling the idea of buried treasure at an old manor house, even renting picks and shovels to hopeful fortune hunters. When a long lost set of jewels is uncovered and the reward money of $10,000 made available, Farrell wins the girl without further ado.

BAT, THE [Comedy-Drama/Crime/Mystery/Old Age] A: Mary Roberts Rinehart and Avery Hopwood; SC: a Rinehart novel, *The Circular Staircase*; D: Colin Kemper; P: L. L. Wagenhals and Colin Kemper; T: Morosco Theatre; 8/23/20 (878)

Many consider *The Bat* the best whodunnit of the twenties; it was surely the most profitable. Its plot counted a couple of killings, an arson, a bank theft, and several cases of assault and battery among its violent complications, and the audience was kept guessing throughout concerning the identity of the mastermind villain who gave his soubriquet to the title.

The heroine was Miss Cornelia Van Gorder (Effie Ellsler), a spinster in her sixties, who rents the Long Island country home of a banker reportedly killed out West some few months earlier. It develops that the banker may not be dead at all, that he may have been responsible for a large theft from his firm, and that the money may be hidden in the house where he may be attempting to retrieve it. With a plot ingeniously worked out to include a quartet of others also seeking the cash, the play moves to its exciting conclusion, the revelation that the private detective (Harrison Hunter) hired by Miss Van Gorder is the murdering culprit. During all of this, the antics of the comic maid, played hilariously by May Vokes, provided bursts of comedic relief.

Rinehart's novel had been so well used in creating this drama, said the *Sun* and *Herald*, "that the interest of the audience never flagged for a minute. *The Bat* moves with breathless rapidity, is occasionally somewhat incoherent, but is always engrossing. . . . *The Bat* is . . . the best play of the year."

BATTLING BUTTLER [Musical/Small Town/Sports/Marriage/Friendship/ British] B/LY: Ballard MacDonald, from the original of Stanley Brightman, Austin Melford, and Douglas Furber; M: Walter L. Rosemond; D: Guy Bragdon; CH: David Bennett; S: William E. Castle; C: Kiviette; P: George Choos b/a/w Jack Buchanan and the Selwyns; T: Selwyn Theatre; 10/8/23 (288 +)

Noting that the British production of this hit musical had been running in London for eighteen months B.F. wrote that an American version "applied for naturalization last night" and predicted correctly that it "ought to make a popular and militant citizen."

The book featured Alfred Buttler (Charles Ruggles), a henpecked husband who discovers that he has the same name as a prizefighter (Frank Sinclair). He impersonates the fighter for his wife (Helen Eley) in order to steal away with his best friend (William Kent) on supposed training trips—a 1920s version of Bunburying. The wife and chorus (twelve Tiller-type girls) go to the real Buttler's training camp, and he enjoys the joke so much that he suggests that the husband take his place in the ring with the Alabama Murderer.

The opening-night audience was given pairs of miniature boxing gloves. Ruggles's performance was highly praised, and B.F. called the show "a lively entertainment, well musicked, laden with pretty girls, dashing in its dance features and beaming with the laughable idiocies of Messrs. Kent and Ruggles."

The play was also known as *Mr. Battling Buttler*.

H.H.

BAVU [Drama/Romance/Adventure/Russia] A/D/P: Earl Carroll; T: Earl Carroll Theatre; 2/25/22 (25)

An incident-crammed, old-fashioned melodrama that served to open the new Earl Carroll Theatre. Carroll himself wrote, directed, and produced the "archaic" drama that Alexander Woollcott called an "elaborated and encumbered penny-dreadful." Staged in the manner of "the early Belasco period of trick stagecraft" (Woollcott), it was played mostly "in shadows and some of it in inky blackness," commented Charles Darnton.

The plot deals with Bavu (Henry Herbert), a half-breed Turk who has hidden his spoils gathered during the Russian Revolution in a chimney room in Balta, near the Roumanian border. His maneuverings to get across the border until such time as it is safe to return for his loot fill up the action, which involves an attempt to marry a desperate noblewoman (Helen Freeman) and obtain a passport; his plans are foiled by a commissioner (William H. Powell), who marries the woman himself, kills Bavu, and flees across the border to freedom.

BE YOUR AGE [Comedy/Old Age/Sex/Romance/Medicine] A: Thomas P. Robinson and Esther Willard Bates; D: Ira Hards; P: Richard Herndon; T: Belmont Theatre; 2/4/29 (32)

Spring Byington took the principal role opposite Romney Brent in this fanciful, slightly naughty piece about a wealthy grandmother of close to seventy who submits to a handsome doctor's need for a human guinea pig to further his rejuvenatory experiments. She reverts to a smashing thirty-nine years of age, attracts the physician's attention away from her daughter (Mary Stills), and is on the brink of a sexual escapade with him when a cold undoes the effects of her glandular injections; she returns to her actual age and the old diplomat (John Miltern) who has always adored her.

"The piece is not bad fun and it is aptly acted, though to most people the gland theme would seem to have passed beyond all hope of rejuvenation," declared *Time*. "Often it is dull and more than a bit heavy-footed, but it has moments of gayety and spontaneity," noted the *Times*.

BE YOURSELF [Musical/Southern/Rural/Family/Romance] B: George S. Kaufman and Marc Connelly; M: Lewis Gensler and Milton Schwarzwald; D: William Collier; P: Sidney Wilmer and Walter Vincent; T: Sam H. Harris Theatre; 9/3/24 (93)

Comic-dancers Queenie Smith and Jack Donahue powered this bland musical comedy, the first attempt by Kaufman and Connelly to write a libretto. They had kept it warm since writing it together as *Miss Moonshine* in 1917, when they failed to get it produced. It turned out to be the last of the famous team's collaborations. Most critics thought the book was only sporadically funny. "*Be Yourself* has comedy," claimed Arthur Hornblow, "but only occasionally does it rise above the level of the mediocre."

Basically a spoof of shows about feuding Tennessee moonshining mountaineers, it had a thin Romeo and Juliet plot about the McCleans and the Brennans in which Matt McClean (Donahue), away for a while, returns to his home to find himself caught up in the family feud and in love with the daughter of the rival clan (Dorothy Whitmore). McClean gets so carried away by his family pride at a family banquet that he makes an impassioned speech in favor of more and better murders.

BEATEN TRACK, THE [Drama/Old Age/Family/Death/British] A: J. O. Francis; D/P: Gustav Blum; T: Frolic Theatre; 2/8/26 (19)

A Welsh drama of serious intentions, "not without a certain sincerity, but spoiled by over-literary dialogue and very leisurely action" (Joseph Wood Krutch). This gloomy "dramatization of the relentless tread of death" (Alexander Woollcott) was about a family of Welsh villagers, a young engineer (Gavin Muir) who returns from South America and marries a local girl (Lucille Nikolas) and then refuses to return with his partner to their South American mining operation, and the engineer's grandmother (Eleanor Daniels) who wishes to live long enough to learn of a great-grandson's birth. Through it all stalks the symbolic death figure of the old gravedigger (St. Clair Bayfield), whose grim presence constantly reminds all of the eventuality of the grave.

BEAU-GALLANT [Comedy/Legacy/Romance] A: Stuart Oliver; D: Clarke Silvernail; S: Henry Dreyfuss; P: The Playshop, Inc.; T: Ritz Theatre; 4/5/26 (24)

A dreary character comedy about a New York Beau Brummel (Lionel Atwill) who attempts to live according to the most rigid standards of gentlemanly existence, making of his life a work of aesthetic value and refusing to work to satisfy the needs of his elegant life-style. Indigent and in debt, he accepts the financial aid of his butler's daughter (Marguerite Burrough), refuses a cattle baron uncle's (Dodson Mitchell) legacy of $5 million because it requires that he marry the girl, lets her have the inheritance, and marries a woman equal to his standards of social class.

There was very little drama in this piece, thought the *Times*, merely an excuse for star Lionel Atwill to act a role tailor-made to his urbane specifications. Wells Root was unimpressed by the play's false glamor.

BEAU-STRINGS [Comedy/Hotel/Romance/British] A: C. K. Munro; D: Sigourney Thayer; P: Francis B. Bradley and Sigourney Thayer; T: Mansfield Theatre; 4/26/26 (24)

On the same night that this English comedy (called *Storm* in London) opened, the author's more successful *At Mrs. Beam's* premiered at the Theatre Guild. Like that play, an amusing and meddlesomely eccentric spinster was at the core of the plot. In this case, the lady was Miss Gee (Estelle Winwood), hungry for any man she can sink her claws into, who waits for a likely prospect at the "hydropathic" hotel in the English countryside where the play takes place. She goes after married and unmarried men alike, creates a number of plot complications by her intrusions, and is left without anyone at the end but with a new man under observation.

"[W]hile interesting as an analytical photograph it is a good deal of a drone as a play," reported Percy Hammond; Arthur Hornblow railed at its incessant talkiness.

BEAUX' STRATEGM, THE [Dramatic Revival] A: George Farquhar; D: Howard Lindsay; S: Jules Guerin; P: Players' Club; T: Hampden's Theatre; 6/4/28 (8)

Farquhar's post-Restoration comedy of 1707, written on his deathbed at the age of twenty-nine, was staged as the annual classical revival given by the Players' Club, using one of their top-flight actor lineups. Edgar Lee Masters provided a new prologue for it, David Belasco wrote the epilogue, and the text was bowdlerized to remove those profanities at which 1928 audiences might have blushed. Raymond Hitchcock was Boniface, Wilfred Seagram was Aimwell, Fred Eric was Archer, Dorothy Stickney played Cherry, James T. Powers played Scrub, Helen Menken was Dorinda, Fay Bainter was Mrs. Sullen, Lyn Harding acted Sullen, William Courtleigh acted Gibbet, Henrietta Crosman performed Lady Bountiful, and O. P. Heggie was Sir Charles. The performance was agreeably produced and the work found favor in critical eyes.

Richard Dana Skinner was grateful for reminding "us that a dramatist of two hundred years ago could engage our attention, captivate our interest, and contrive an artificial comedy so neatly as to give it the real sway of illusion."

BECKY SHARP [Dramatic Revival] A: Langdon Mitchell; SC: William Makepeace Thackeray's novel, *Vanity Fair*; D: Dudley Digges; CH: Carola Goya and Lillian Brennard Tonga; DS: Robert Edmond Jones; P: Players' Club; T: Knickerbocker Theatre; 6/3/29 (8)

The annual classic revival of the Players' Club was the force behind this production of the 1899 play, which long had been one of Mrs. Fiske's supremely popular vehicles. Only one week was given over for the staging, despite packed houses. The revival was top-notch in every department. The basically unrevised text still proved viable thirty years after its premiere. Richard Dana Skinner insisted that the story remained contemporaneous and that examples of it could be found in any daily tabloid.

As Becky, Mary Ellis gave what Brooks Atkinson called "the finest performance in her resplendent career" in "a virtuoso role—a hoyden, cruel, mocking, common, yet generous withal, a wretch gallant and base." Basil Sydney played Rawdon Crawley, Moffat Johnstone was Lord Steyne, Cecilia Loftus was Miss Crawley, and Ernest Cossart played Joseph Sedley.

BEDFELLOWS [Comedy/Marriage/Sex] A: Louise Carter; D: Bernard W. Suss; P: Bernard Levey for the Lloyd Productions, Inc.; T: Waldorf Theatre; 7/2/29 (47)

A three-act farce stuffed with tired situations: "if the writing of the piece lacks originality and distinction, its playing is equally uninspired," noted Perriton Maxwell. The effect of the play on the *Times* critic ranged "from complete vacuousness to a sustained yawn."

The innocuous plot dealt with two couples each member of which seeks a marital liason with a member of the other pair, leading to a switcheroo plan as husbands and wives make the appropriate exchanges only to find that no nuptial exchange had been made at all; the remarrier turns out to have been a nut case.

BEFORE YOU'RE 25 [Comedy/Marriage/Politics/Journalism/Family] A: Kenyon Nicholson; P: Lawrence Boyd; T: Maxine Elliott's Theatre; 4/16/29 (23)

A mildly comical farce about a young radical (Eric Dressler) who leaves his family's Chicago home to edit a crusading journal in New York, is hounded from it with his pregnant common-law wife (Mildred McCoy), stays at his parents' comfortable home during her period of childbirth and convalescence, and is persuaded to abandon his radicalism for a secure bourgeois future working in his father's (Fritz Williams) furniture factory.

Much of the comedy derived from the obstacles the couple kept running into whenever they tried to get married. Although he laughed at some of it, Brooks Atkinson concluded, "the excitement seems more forced than genuine, and predicated upon ideas that are not intrinsically comic."

BEGGAR ON HORSEBACK [Comedy/Fantasy/Trial/Music/Business/Romance] A: George S. Kaufman and Marc Connelly; M: Deems Taylor; SC: a German play, *Hans Sonnenstösers Höllenfahrt*, by Paul Apel; D/P: Winthrop Ames; S: Woodman Thompson; T: Broadhurst Theatre; 2/12/24 (224)

Often cited as the only commercially successful expressionist play produced on Broadway, *Beggar on Horseback* was lauded by Percy Hammond as a work that "belittles brass by showing that it isn't gold, and then it goes a whole leap beyond that and shows us gold." Kaufman and Connelly's farce-fantasy satirized American society's preoccupation with big business and moneymaking and extolled artistic integrity.

The job of Neil McRae (Roland Young), a young composer orchestrating cheap tunes, leaves him no time for his symphony. Feeling rejected by the poor girl (Kay Johnson) he loves when she advises him to marry the rich girl pursuing him (Anne Carpenter), he proposes to the heiress and falls asleep. The rest of the play (until the final curtain) consists of dream scenes. First, the composer finds life with his rich wife and in-laws (George W. Barbier, Marion Ballou, and Osgood Perkins) and his job in the family widget factory so intolerable that he kills his spouse and her parents. Then, in a comic-opera style trial, the composer tries to defend himself by presenting a romantic pantomime he had composed with his poor sweetheart, but the court finds this highbrow and sentences him to a factory where great artists produce machine art. There he despairs and tries to get out. He finds that the cage was never locked, walks out, and awakes. He breaks with the rich fiancée and marries the poor girl he loves.

Virtually the only disagreement came over the pantomime sequence, which Alexander Woollcott thought out of sync with the play but which George Jean Nathan applauded and John Farrar thought was so exquisite that it made the rest of the play pale.

Calling attention to the play's "delicate, subtle satire" and "prankful, elfin humor," Woollcott likened it to *Alice in Wonderland* and to a mixture of J. M. Barrie and Sinclair Lewis.

A return engagement opened on 3/23/25 at the Shubert for sixteen performances.

H.H.

(1) BEGGAR'S OPERA, THE [Musical Revival] A: John Gay; D: Nigel Playfair; S: C. Lovatt Fraser; P: Arthur Hopkins; T: Greenwich Village Theatre (OB); 12/29/20 (37)

An importation of the highly respected revival given in England by Nigel Playfair at his Lyric Theatre, Hammersmith. It was produced locally with its London cast and received strong commendation from the critics, some of whom later reviled the public for failing to support it. It was thought a valuable restoration of the long neglected 1728 classic. Gay's ballad opera, which jabbed sharply at old-time politics, Italian opera, and the artificialities of Restoration drama, was judged a virile and uncompromisingly honest look at life. Walter Prichard Eaton said Playfair's staging, "without the meticulous and near-sighted faithfulness of the archaeologist...has still held in high regard the original version...from which prudish minds had hacked away many characteristic portions." Arnold Bennett was credited with helping to restore the text, while Frederick Austin polished up the old score, played on the harpsichord.

(2) P: J. C. Duff i/a/w A. L. Jones and Morris Green; T: Forty-eighth Street Theatre; 3/28/28 (37)
A revival given by a touring English troupe, some of whom had been in the notable production seen here in 1920. Frederick Austin's arrangements were again used, and much of Playfair's staging was retained. However, "It was a sadly staled performance, in which routine and artless slugging had taken the place of spontaneity and delicate charm," according to John Mason Brown.

BEHAVIOR OF MRS. CRANE, THE [Comedy/Marriage/Romance] A: Harry Segall; D: Bertram Harrison; S: Nicholas Yellenti; P: Eugene W. Parsons; T: Erlanger's Theatre; 3/20/28 (31)
Brooks Atkinson said that this intimate drawing-room comedy might have had a chance if it were not so poorly placed in the vast spaces of the Erlanger's stage. Perriton Maxwell blamed the failure on the play's verbosity and forced dialogue. In it, Margaret Lawrence, absent for a few seasons from Broadway, played Mrs. Doris Crane who is confronted by a spouse (Charles Trowbridge) seeking to divorce her so he may wed Myra Spaulding (Isobel Elsom). Surprisingly, Mrs. Crane agrees but only if the adulterous pair can find her a suitable new mate. After several poor choices, they come up with Bruce King (John Marston), a handsome millionaire, and Mrs. Crane is agreeable; however, Myra decides Bruce is an even better selection for herself. Mrs. Crane gets the man, and Mr. Crane gets nothing.
Richard Dana Skinner said, "Its ethics...are simply those of free love.... [T]he play has no value even as an acting vehicle."

BEHOLD THE BRIDEGROOM [Drama/Romance] A/D: George Kelly; S: Livingston Platt; P: Rosalie Stewart; T: Cort Theatre; 12/26/27 (88)
A wide disparity of opinion marked the critical response to George Kelly's serious romantic drama, which Burns Mantle selected as one of the Best of the Year. Its subject was the self-indulgent, jaded sophisticate Tony Lyle (Judith Anderson), whose decadent life-style had not prepared her for the devastation

her heart feels when she falls in love with the handsome, upright Spencer Train (John Marston), who is barely aware of her existence. Realizing that she is incapable of ever capturing his love, she loses all desire to live; her fiancé (Lester Vail), rejected, kills himself. Spencer, at her father's request, speaks to her; she dies of unrequited love.

Percy Hammond said it was one of the year's best, "a good, sane, theatrical study," and Brooks Atkinson called it the author's "finest" work, "sombre, upright, tragic." But a few were dismayed by Kelly's "stilted and forced" dialogue (Richard Dana Skinner) and cardboard characters. Yet, Joseph Wood Krutch thought that "Henry James himself never wrote more subtle or finely tempered dialogue."

Judith Anderson was memorable as Tony Lyle.

BEHOLD THIS DREAMER [Comedy/Art/Marriage/Mental Illness] A: Fulton Oursler and Aubrey Kennedy; SC: the novel by Fulton Oursler; D: Frederick Stanhope; P: George C. Tyler; T: Cort Theatre; 10/31/27 (58)

A "paradox" play, according to the authors, who adapted it from a novel by one of them. *Behold This Dreamer* was a superficial satirical drama that was inspired by a biblical quotation about Joseph and his hateful brethren, who said to one another, "Behold this dreamer cometh. Come now, therefore, let us cast him into some pit. . . . And we shall see what will become of his dreams."

The dreamer here was brush-factory clerk Charley Turner (Glenn Hunter), a misunderstood would-be artist whose henpecking wife (Patricia O'Hearn) and family so fail to appreciate his aspirations for freedom from their fetters that they commit him to a mental home. At the institution he finds the sympathy and happiness he lacked and wins a major art contest, which leads to his release. But once he is back in "normal" society he realizes that the outside world is the crazy one and runs back to the safety of the asylum.

Perriton Maxwell wrote, "At times gently sentimental and satiric, this fable seems weak and hesitant in the telling."

BELLE AVENTURE, LA (The Beautiful Adventure) [Dramatic Revival/ French Language] A: Robert de Flers, Gaston Armand de Caillavet, and Etienne Rey; D/P: Charles Schauten; T: Belmont Theatre; 5/8/22 (8)

The final offering in a three-play repertory offered by a troupe of little-known French actors under Charles Schauten's direction. It had first been seen in New York in an English version staged in 1914.

On the very day that she is to wed Valentin (Gaston Dauriac) Hélène (Mado Ditza) elopes with her real love, André (Schauten). They stay overnight at Hélène's grandmother's home, and André is even berated by the old lady for not fulfilling his husbandly duty when he chooses to sleep on a chair (she thinks the pair are married). Valentin shows up the next day, and Hélène excuses herself for what has happened by blaming the grandmother.

BELLS, THE (Le juif polonais) [Dramatic Revival] A: Leopold Lewis; D: Rollo Lloyd; P: A. E. and R. R. Riskin; T: Bayes Theatre; 4/13/26 (15)

This nineteenth-century melodrama had provided one of the great successes of Sir Henry Irving's career and retained its fame primarily because of his interpretation (Stanislavsky also did an important staging of the work, early in his career, as outlined in detail in *My Life in Art*). But when pulled off the shelf for this first New York revival of the present century, it presented "ancient and insurmountable difficulties" (*Time*), yet had "its moments of melodramatic effectiveness" (Joseph Wood Krutch).

Rollo Lloyd played the role of the Alasatian innkeeper Mathias, whose guilty conscience for the murder, fifteen years before, of a Jew continues to plague him. "We think he did unbelievably well with a part that runs mostly to soliloquy," wrote Larry Barretto.

BELT, THE [Drama/Family/Marriage/Labor/Romance] A: Paul Sifton; M: Heaton Vorse; D: Edward Massey; S: John Dos Passos; P: New Playwrights Theatre; T: New Playwrights Theatre (OB); 10/19/27 (48)

This experimental play's title refers to the automobile assembly line where the workers under the Old Man (George N. Price)—meant to stand for Henry Ford—are exploited by his ruthless demands. Sifton's political play, given an impressively theatricalist mounting, examined the family situation of a disgruntled worker (Ross Matthews), demoted after ten years of robot-like serfdom, whose wife is cheating on him and whose daughter's (Gale De Hart) boyfriend (Lawrence Bolton) is a fiery radical worker who despises the mechanization of men by the industrial process. The action dovetails to a depiction of the boy's leadership of a worker's revolt against the boss's plans to lay them off, a revolt brutally quelled by the militia.

There was a confusion of purposes obvious in the combination of family drama with left-wing polemics. *Time* commented: "Moments of engrossing writing; moments of shrewd staging scarcely salvage the stormy whole." Young unknowns in the cast were Franchot Tone and Eduard Franz.

¡BENDITA SEAS! (Bless You, My Child) [Comedy/Family/Spanish Language/ Argentinian] A: Alberto Novion; D: Hector C. Quiroga; P: Camila Quiroga and the Argentine Players; T: Manhattan Opera House (OB); 12/8/27 (1)

Alberto Novion's most popular play was this high comedy produced by Camila Quiroga's visiting troupe from Argentina. Alison Smith found Quiroga's acting riviting in this piece about a mother who tries to keep her ex-lover Pancho's son Enrique from learning that he is the half-brother of her own boy Javier. But his eventual discovery of the truth leads him to respect her and to beg her not to depart in shame.

BERKELEY SQUARE [Drama/Period/British/Reincarnation/Fantasy/Romance] A: John L. Balderston; SC: Henry James's *A Sense of the Past*; D: Leslie

Howard; S: Sir Edward Luytens; P: Gilbert Miller and Leslie Howard; T: Lyceum Theatre; 11/4/29 (227)

American-born playwright Balderston's drama was a London hit (it was written there) four years before duplicating its success in New York. Suggested by an unfinished James novel, it was, said Perriton Maxwell, "the finest bit of serious drama we have seen thus far this season."

This interesting play was built on a premise related to the theories of the relativity of time posited by Bergson and Einstein. Its hero John Standish (Leslie Howard), a 1928 American who has moved into his ancestral home in London, is completely absorbed in his eighteenth-century antecedents whose diaries and letters he has been assiduously perusing. His enthrallment becomes so complete that he finds himself living as his great-great-grandfather in 1784 where he seems to others to be preturnaturally gifted with clairvoyance. He knows that his ancestor married Kate Pettigrew (Valerie Taylor), but he falls in love instead with her sister Helen (Margalo Gillmore); aware of fate's implacability, he knows he cannot marry Helen, herself gifted with a view of the future. Ultimately dismayed by the conditions of eighteenth-century life, he returns to the present, slowly regains the senses his friends think he has lost, and realizes he can never marry, since his heart remains in the London of Sheridan and Dr. Johnson.

Satire, mystery, whimsy, and tragic poignancy here meshed in a fantastical romance that captured the imagination of thousands. It seemed, however, a despairing play to Richard Dana Skinner, who thought its theme of a man whose life is hopelessly "tied to a dead past" unhealthy, and George Jean Nathan disclaimed it as "obvious theatrical hokum." Most, though, found it a masterfully composed and produced work, with a sensitive, memorable performance by Howard. Burns Mantle chose it as a Best Play of the Year.

BEST PEOPLE, THE [Comedy/Family/Youth/Romance] A: David Gray and Avery Hopwood; P: Charles Frohman, Inc.; T: Lyceum Theatre; 8/19/24 (144)

The generation gap was treated in play after play during the restless twenties, as flapper daughters and cake-eater sons rebelled against the constrictions of parental regulations. *The Best People* offered a typical treatment of the theme.

The action was mainly concerned with the efforts of a father (Charles Richman) to prevent his hootch-guzzling son (Gavin Muir) from marrying a chorus cutie (Hope Drown) and his jazz-loving daughter (Frances Howard) from running off with a Missouri chauffeur (James Rennie). When dad and a brother-in-law (George Graham) get entangled with the chorine and a friend (Florence Johns) after trying to buy the girl off, everything is worked out and the kids get their chosen partners.

The critics treated this comedy of manners as mindless fun of the most conventional sort. Stark Young pointed to the "many stupid, forced and cheap lines and punches," and George Jean Nathan dubbed it "a frank example of box-office pfui, without imagination, without quality, without merit of any kind." It nevertheless had a sizable run.

BETSY [Musical/Romance/Family] B: Irving Caesar and David Freedman; M: Richard Rodgers; LY: Lorenz Hart; D: William Anthony McGuire; CH: Sammy Lee; P: Florenz Ziegfeld; T: New Amsterdam Theatre; 12/28/26 (39)

"[A]n elaborate, loose-jointed but withal fairly routine musical comedy, smacking more than a little of the variety halls," was the *Times*'s assessment of this Rodgers and Hart show, which gave most of its stage duties over to singer and comic actress Belle Baker, a vaudeville favorite. In addition to the songs of Rodgers and Hart, she also interpolated several other tunes, introducing, among them, Irving Berlin's "Blue Skies." However well she did with such melodies, she scored not too highly with the ditties of the show's composers. Still, the show employed to good advantage the talent of entertainers such as Evelyn Law, Bobbie Perkins, Allan Kearns, and, especially, Borah Minnevitch and his Harmonica Orchestra.

The insipid story was about a family the mother of which (Pauline Hoffman) will not allow any of her boys to marry until a suitable mate can be found for sister Betsy (Baker)—which finally transpires.

Rodgers later revealed that he had rushed into the project merely for the chance to work for producer Ziegfeld and had had practically no chance to collaborate with the script writers. He said the experience was painful and that the result was the biggest flop thus far of his career. He was especially dismayed to learn that Berlin's "Blue Skies" had been added to the score and was even more wounded when it became the show's only hit.

BETTER TIMES [Revue] M: Raymond Hubbell; D: R. H. Burnside; P: Charles Dillingham; T: Hippodrome; 9/2/22 (405)

A giant spectacular show, the biggest yet at the mammoth Hippodrome. The "show is by way of being an elephantine Follies," reported Arthur Hornblow. It ran for a full season with its mixture of revue and circus, ballet and pachyderms.

There were extravaganza numbers like "Land of Mystery," an unusual special-effects presentation with dancing skeletons; "Story of a Fan," a lavish routine with dancers dressed as giant fans rising on traps to occupy the entire stage as a gigantic overhead fan glowed in electric lights; "Grand Opera Ball," in which the company emerged from an immense victrola dressed as famous opera characters; and a sensational waterborne finale, "The Harbor of Prosperity," showing Amazons in gold costumes disappearing into the waves and returning on a "ship of dreams." There were animal acts, such as Powers's Elephants, Orlando's Horses, and that inimitable avian star Jacko the crow, who batted barely a feather as he snatched balls and tiny Indian clubs out of the air. Forming a part of one of the acts was a young acrobat, Archie Leach, who later changed his name to Cary Grant. This was the eighteenth and last of the great Hippodrome extravaganzas.

BETTY LEE [Musical/Sports/Romance] B: Otto Harbach; M: Louis Hirsch and Con Conrad; LY: Irving Caesar and Otto Harbach; SC: Rex Beach and Paul

Armstrong's play, *Going Some*; CH: David Bennett; P: Rufus Le Maire; T: Forty-fourth Street Theatre; 12/25/24 (98)

In covering this musical comedy, the last by composer Louis Hirsch who died before it opened, the *Times* drew forth the usual litany of praises and complaints: "Its dancing is of a high order, the personnel is at least satisfactory, the costumes are bright and good-looking, the chorus well-trained. At this point one of the musical comedy stencils must be trotted out: the story is lamentably weak, the humor almost non-existent."

The show was well produced, but it could not effectively turn its 1909 source to account as a libretto. The story dealt with a couple of young men, Wallingford Speed (Hal Skelly) and Lawrence Glass (Joe E. Brown), adrift in California, who get involved in a situation in which the former must pose as a noted runner and race a local youth; he faces lynching if he loses, so Betty Lee (Gloria Foy) and her friends contrive to make him win.

Skelly and Brown, especially the latter, were funnier than their material.

BEWARE OF DOGS [Comedy/Marriage/Romance/Rural] A/D: William Hodge; P: Lee Shubert; T: Broadhurst Theatre; 10/3/21 (88)

Comic-actor William Hodge here provided his own "satirical tale in three wags" in which he was on stage throughout. He played George Oliver, who, seeking a healthy climate for his ailing sister, opens a dog kennel in the country. An assortment of difficulties with the hired help and community complaints about his canine charges lead him to take voluble command of the situation. Everything ends happily, and George plans to marry his sweetheart (Ann Davis).

This was a dog of a play with many off-color references to the doings of hounds that Alexander Woollcott thought were better suited to a smoking car than a stage.

BEWARE OF WIDOWS [Comedy/Romance] A: Owen Davis; D: Guthrie McClintic; P: Crosby Gaige; T: Maxine Elliott's Theatre; 12/1/25 (57)

Owen Davis, one-man play factory, here manufactured an energetic romantic comedy of sorts, "a slightly short-winded piece . . . , a piece that never did quite make up its mind whether to be a sly comedy or a rambunctious farce and ended in a state of faint confusion on the subject" (Alexander Woollcott).

With the beautiful Madge Kennedy as its star, the piece managed to grip the boards for nearly two months. Kennedy was Joyce Bragdon, a widow of three years whose cap is set for Dr. Jack Waller (Alan Edwards), an old flame who resists her advances for three acts until she gets him where she wants him by setting the houseboat they are on adrift.

A purely commercial attempt, the play was too shallowly grounded in character and incident and lacked the necessary clever dialogue to make it interesting.

BEWITCHED [Drama/Fantasy/Aviation/Romance/France] A: Edward Sheldon and Sidney Howard; D/P: John Cromwell; DS: Lee Simonson; M: Arthur Fisher; T: National Theatre; 10/1/24 (29)

A poetic, philosophic, mystical, romantic fantasy—Howard himself called it "a Freudian Fairy Tale"—set in the forest at Auvergne, France, where a young Boston aviator (Glenn Anders), his plane having crashed, is put up for the night at a chateau owned by a marquis (Jose Ruben). As he sleeps beside the fire he dreams himself into the ancient tale of sorcery depicted on the chateau's tapestries wherein the marquis is a sorcerer, his daughter (Florence Eldridge) the source of all sensual temptation (she appears in a half-dozen female guises), and the aviator's conflict that of maintaining his purity through the night. He survives the test, and when he awakens in the morning, he recognizes the maid serving him breakfast as the temptress of his nightmare.

Somewhat uneven and occasionally tedious, it was nevertheless appropriately luscious in language, atmosphere, and feeling. Burns Mantle called it "weird and interesting," Arthur Hornblow said it would "appeal strongly to people in love with love," but Stark Young thought it never fulfilled its intentions. Glenn Anders came in for some hard knocks, but Florence Eldridge was vastly appreciated for her acting.

BEYOND (Jenseits) [Drama/Death/Fantasy/Romance/German] A: Walter Hasenclever; TR: Rita Matthias; M: William Irwin; D: Harold McGee; P: Provincetown Players; T: Provincetown Playhouse (OB); 1/26/25 (14)

An ambitious, experimental attempt to stage a German twenty-two-scene, two-character, expressionist play. This was an uncompromising and difficult piece of subjective reality, with an arbitrary use of time and space. Dialogue was feverish, fragmentary, and often difficult to comprehend. Its two characters were a woman (Helen Gahagan) and her husband's friend (Walter Abel), who arrives at her home drawn by a strange power; during his visit they learn of the husband's death. The husband's spirit inhabits the friend's body, and the wife is soon bound to him by the power of unseen forces. The husband's ghostly presence is felt, there are frequent hallucinatory moments with unusual scenic and lighting effects, and a thin veil of Buddhistic thought appears to provide a foundation for allegorical significance.

The drama, while finding one or two advocates, repelled the majority of critics. George Jean Nathan said *Beyond* "provides about as dull a few hours in the theatre as the human brain can picture."

BEYOND EVIL [Drama/Small Town/Marriage/Blacks/Romance] D: Edward Massey; S: Cleon Throckmorton; P: David Thorne; T: Cort Theatre; 6/7/26 (1)

A raucous, undisciplined audience shouted abuse at the stage when this one-performance flop about miscegenation premiered. "It was the most seditious gathering of first-nighters within the memory of this veteran prothonotary," wrote Percy Hammond.

The lurid drama was about a small-town druggist's (Louis Ancker) bored wife (Mary Blair), who becomes so fed up with her life after being rejected by her lover that she runs off to Harlem, where she lives with a mulatto lawyer (Edouardo Sanchez) and eventually kills herself rather than return to her spouse.

This was deemed "a ludicrous display of scarlet merchandise in the basement of the theatre. It ought not to be allowed and the punishment it got from last night's audience was merciful," Hammond noted. A day after the opening, the play's press agent was notifying critics that the work had been intended as a burlesque on *All God's Chillun Got Wings* and *Lulu Belle*. The show was closed by the police but, according to one source, reopened under some legal device, although the number of performances under these circumstances is unknown.

BEYOND THE HORIZON [Dramatic Revival] A: Eugene O'Neill; S: Cleon Throckmorton; P: Actors' Theatre; T: Mansfield Theatre; 11/30/26 (79)

O'Neill's Pulitzer Prize winner was revived six years after its debut by the Actors' Theatre company. Its tale of the woman Ruth (Aline MacMahon), who, faced by the choice between two brothers, marries the romantic Robert (Robert Keith) rather than the pragmatic Andrew (Thomas Chalmers) and finds unhappiness, was given a fine production.

Joseph Wood Krutch affirmed the play's value as tragedy: "O'Neill turns a play which might have been merely ironic into an indictment not only of chance or fate but of that whole universe which sets itself up against man's desires and conquers them." The *Times* claimed it had "lost none of its power. It remains an inexorable and sometimes majestic tragedy."

BIFF! BING! BANG! [Revue] D/P: Capt. M. W. Plunkett; T: Ambassador Theatre; 5/9/21

The Third Division of the Canadian Army had prepared this soldier revue for presentation in France to Canadian men at war. The company then went on a world tour with it. It was plotless and had an assortment of wartime songs and comic sketches. The outstanding performance was that of a female impersonator, Ross Hamilton, who had "the style and figure of a Ziegfeld beauty" and sang "in an exceptionally fine soprano voice" (*World*). The two comedy sketches each had a wartime background.

The troupe was called "The Dumbells," and each member (men and women) had served an average of eighteen months' duty. A song hit of the evening was "Oh, oh, oh, It's a Lovely War."

BIG BOY [Musical/Sports/Gambling] B: Harold Atteridge; M: James F. Hanley and Joseph Meyer; LY: B. G. DeSylva; D: J. C. Huffman; S: Watson Barratt; P: Messrs. Shubert; T: Winter Garden Theatre; 1/7/25 (48); Forty-fourth Street Theatre; 8/24/25 (120)

No musical comedy star of the decade pleased critics and audiences as much as Al Jolson did. The vehicles he appeared in were secondary to his presence, as in this mediocre piece of hokum in which he blacked up to play his familiar Gus role, here seen as the Negro jockey and stable boy of the Bedfords. He foils the scheme of a gang of connivers to replace him with an English jockey and goes on to triumph as the Derby winner on Big Boy. The horse-race sequence used a treadmill technique such as old-time shows like *Ben Hur* had made theatrically feasible.

The critics paid scant attention to the book or score but gathered their adjectives into posies of praise for the great Jolie. The *Times* declared that "he seems to be an even more vibrant and magnetic figure than ever before. . . . He sings, both seriously and comically; . . . he tells stories, both in character and out of it . . . and, with all of his old skill, he uses his eyes eloquently at the precise moment when the point of a line can be greatly enhanced."

Among the star's best numbers were "California, Here I Come" (introduced during *Bombo*'s 1921 tour), and "Keep Smiling at Trouble" (an interpolation by Jolson, Lewis Gensler, and B. G. DeSylva). "If You Knew Susie" was also heard at one point before Jolson turned it over to Eddie Cantor. Jolson's illness cancelled the show after only 48 performances, but it reopened at the Forty-fourth Street Theatre on 8/24/25 and racked up 120 more performances.

BIG FIGHT, THE [Drama/Sports/Romance/Gambling] A: Max Marcin and Milton Herbert Gropper; D: David Belasco; P: Sam H. Harris and Albert Lewis; T: Majestic Theatre; 9/18/28 (31)

A "meager and hackneyed" (*Times*) melodrama starring ex-world-heavy-weight-champ Jack Dempsey and his movie-star wife Estelle Taylor. "It was a big, costly, restless affair, quite exciting at moments, always lurid and mechanical, and kept moving by the unrestrained hand of David Belasco," declared Robert Littell.

Dempsey played a nice-guy boxer, Jack "Tiger" Dillon, managed by a shady character, Steve Logan (Jack Roseleigh). Both love Shirley (Taylor), the manicurist. Shirley's brother is in the clutches of a gambler crony of Logan's (Arthur R. Vinton), so she has to follow orders and drug Jack to make him lose the big fight on which the gambler will bet a bundle. But the drugs are no match for Dillon's strength, and he KOs his opponent in a vivid onstage fight scene; he gets Shirley for his troubles.

As expected, Dempsey's acting was amateurish, and audiences were surprised to hear his "soft and soprano voice," wrote Perriton Maxwell. His wife and costar revealed little talent for stage acting.

BIG LAKE [Drama/Crime/Rural/Romance] A: Lynn Riggs; D: George Auerbach; P: American Laboratory Theatre; T: American Laboratory Theatre (OB); 4/8/27 (11)

The first produced play by Kansas poet Lynn Riggs was this short, portentous tragedy set in the Oklahoma woods in 1906, before that state had joined the Union. The work was put on by members of Richard Boleslavsky's American

Laboratory Theatre while the master was in Europe. Maria Ouspenskaya aided in its direction. Unfortunately, its attempt to recount a simple tragedy in lyrical, symbolic terms made for ponderous playgoing.

Two sensitive youths, Betty and Lloyd (Helen Coburn and Frank Burk), wander away from a picnic and come across a cabin occupied by a murderous bootlegger and his moll (Grover Burgess and Stella Adler). The boy, out rowing on the lake with Betty, is blamed by the criminal for his own misdeeds, the law enforcers shoot him, and Betty kills herself by leaping into the lake.

Larry Barretto declared, "Pretentious amateurishness can go no further than in *Big Lake*. In it one sees symbolism at its most incoherent, and poetic prose at its dreariest. It is a dead play."

BIG MOGUL, THE [Comedy-Drama/Business/Romance] A: De Witt Newing; D: T. Daniel Frawley; P: Nod Productions, Inc.; T: Daly's Theatre; 5/11/25 (24)

Fiske O'Hara, a corpulent Irish tenor of some popularity, was not gifted enough to carry this melodrama-comedy alone without support from the playwright. It came to New York after a long tour but lasted only three weeks.

It was what was often called a "business play," with the star portraying Peter Quilt, a millionaire Wall Streeter who used to be a plumber. He is in love with his stenographer Marie Lamb (Pat Clary), the daughter of another capitalist (Cameron Mathews), who is out to finagle $7 million away from Quilt. The latter overcomes all difficulties and ends up happily ensconced in his girlfriend's arms.

A folksy entertainment designed for O'Hara's fans, *The Big Mogul* allowed for him to interpolate some of his favorite songs throughout the action. The *Sun* reviled the play as so outlandish that one might almost take it for a burlesque of Wall Street plays.

BIG POND, THE [Comedy/Small Town/Romance/Family/Italy] A: George Middleton and A. E. Thomas; D: Edwin H. Knopf; S: A. J. Lundborg; P: Edwin H. Knopf and William P. Farnsworth; T: Bijou Theatre; 8/21/28 (47)

The authors of this "ingeniously amusing comedy" kept it afloat "by writing amusing lines and keeping the action swift and cleverly eccentric," according to Brooks Atkinson. Excellent performances, especially by Kenneth MacKenna in a dialect role, helped greatly too.

The plot moves from Italy to Vernon, Ohio, to tell the story of how Henry Billings (Harlan Briggs), an American businessman residing with wife and daughter in Europe for a year, returns to America with an impoverished Frenchman (MacKenna) in tow, to see if he will be as attractive to his infatuated daughter (Lucille Nikolas) at home as he was abroad. In Vernon the youth becomes a success in the father's rubber business, but the daughter preferred him as a more sensitive, romantic type and switches her affections to a local boy (Reed Brown, Jr.). (An alternate ending was used on the second night, with the Frenchman getting the girl; this proved more acceptable to audiences.)

This play deserves a small footnote in theatre history for when its tryout was held in Great Neck, New York, the role of the daughter was played by a new actress named Katharine Hepburn. Hepburn has herself admitted that she was released for incompetence.

BILL OF DIVORCEMENT, A [Drama/Family/Marriage/Mental Illness/Romance/War/British] A: Clemence Dane; D: Basil Dean; P: Charles Dillingham; T: George M. Cohan Theatre; 10/10/21 (173)

Selected as a Best Play of the Year, Clemence Dane's Ibsenic drama was one of the author's most successful; it is most well known as the play that helped catapult Katharine Cornell to stardom. To Arthur Hornblow this was "a great play, flawlessly written, superbly acted, a play that you must see at any cost." But the *Independent* was unimpressed by its old-fashioned "tricks of Adelphi melodrama," intellectual counterfeit, and sentimentality.

Dane's drama was set ten years in the future in 1932 when the British government presumably had passed a controversial law permitting a wife whose husband was certifiably insane to divorce him. The play examines the dilemma of a wife (Janet Beecher) who must choose between the man (Charles Waldron) she has been planning to marry and the husband (Allan Pollock) who returns seventeen years after being shell-shocked in the war and whom she has divorced by benefit of the new law. The situation is resolved when Sydney (Cornell), the eugenically minded daughter, aware of the father's streak of insanity, breaks off her planned marriage and promises to devote her life to caring for him.

Burns Mantle noted that Cornell gave "promise of becoming a flashing young genius of the native theatre." Allan Pollock's sensitive performance was deepened by his own experience of shell shock and the slow process of rehabilitation he endured before taking his place on the stage again.

Pollock had seen the play in London shortly after being discharged from the hospital where he had been for nearly three years. He realized that the role of the shell-shocked husband was ideal for him and set about obtaining the American rights to the play. He convinced producer Charles Dillingham, previously associated almost exclusively with musicals and revues, to produce it; it received relatively decent reviews from the second-stringers who reviewed it (the principal reviewers were covering four other shows that night) and far more laudatory notices from the first-stringers who soon got around to examining it. However, the New York public did not seem very interested and the work played to small houses for several weeks; it was on the point of vanishing when there was a sudden upturn in attendance; the attraction was bought by another production firm and the show transferred to the Times Square Theatre, where it had a striking success.

BILLETED [Dramatic Revival] A: F. Tennyson Jesse and H. M. Harwood; P: Grace Griswold; T: Greenwich Village Theatre (OB); 5/9/22 (23)

Margaret Anglin had achieved success as Betty Taradine several years earlier in this English comedy, and now Lois Bolton attempted the role in an Off-Broadway revival. The production was "a thoroughly fine one in all respects" (Arthur Hornblow) and revealed the play as having retained its entertainment values.

The play's somewhat racy story, set during the war, concerns a rural Englishwoman, separated from her husband, who is asked to billet two army officers at her home. To head off any gossip about a married woman billeting two men she sends herself a telegram informing herself of her husband's death. The plot thickens when one of the soldiers turns out to be her spouse (H. Langdon Bruce), using an alias.

BILLIE [Musical/Business/Romance] B/M/LY/P: George M. Cohan; SC: Cohan's farce, *Broadway Jones*; D: Sam Forrest; CH: Edward Royce; T: Erlanger's Theatre; 10/1/28 (112)

George M. Cohan turned one of his popular old farces (of 1912) into this song and dance exhibit in which nearly every character had some terpsichore to perform. A personable, if old-fashioned, presentation, it proved to be the last Cohan musical. It offered little that was new or inventive but gave audiences exactly what they had long expected from a Cohan show. Polly Walker as the title character gained new admirers, there was a hilarious telephone scene in which Val and Ernie Stanton got a wrong number, and plaudits were gained by the vigorous staging.

Its tale was that of the youthful wastrel Jackson Jones (Joseph Wagstaff) who inherits his uncle's chewing-gum factory, which he is talked out of selling by the secretary Billie; he goes on to turn it into a business success and to defeat the malevolent trust and remain an independent.

"Altogether *Billie* is excellent entertainment, clean without being inane," in *Time*'s opinion.

BIRD CAGE, THE [Pantomime/Revival] A: Fernand Beissier; M: P. Mario Costa; DS: James Reynolds; P: Stagers; T: Fifty-second Street Theatre; 6/2/25 (4)

Four special matinees of this piece were given by a Washington, D.C., Little Theatre group, the Ram's Head Players. It was an 1893 French pantomime based on a story by Beissier, supported by P. Mario Costa's melodies. Pierrot (Robert Bell) is the central figure. He is the lover and then husband of Louisette (Josephine Hutchinson), who is expecting an addition to the family. Pierrot, however, is lured by the charms of Fifine (Ruth Harrison) and by card games; he deserts Louisette for these temptations. The child and wife are tended to by an old friend (Richard Elwell). Years later, back comes the tattered and fickle Pierrot to the patient Louisette, who embraces him and takes him in.

The quality of the performance was "only fairly good," as Stark Young pointed out.

BIRD IN HAND [Comedy-Drama/Romance/Family/Hotel/British] A/D: John Drinkwater; P: Lee Shubert; T: Booth Theatre; 4/4/29 (500)

One of the longest running plays of the 1928–1929 season was this Drinkwater comedy, which was unlike the other work of the author, whose fame rested on historical-biographical plays. Drinkwater's sense of humor came as a surprise to the critics, who rejoiced at his expert comic characterizations. Euphemia Van Rensselaer Wyatt observed, "so natural is the dialogue, so cleverly perfect as to detail is the cast—imported direct from London—that the inherent humor in each character becomes entirely patent to the audience who look upon them all as old friends."

The piece deals with the changing attitudes toward English class distinctions as represented by the love affair between Joan (Jill Esmond Moore), the daughter of Thomas (Herbert Lomas), the conservative keeper of the 300-year-old rustic Bird in Hand Inn, and the local squire's (Roddy Hughes) son (Charles Hickman). Thomas is convinced that the son can have only questionable motives in courting Joan, but three wonderfully amusing guests who chance to stop at his inn change his mind. One is a Cockney salesman (Ivor Barnard), another a yeast maker's son (Charles Maunsell), and the third a distinguished barrister (Frank Petley). Finally, the squire himself proposes on the youth's behalf.

The play enjoyed a return engagement on 11/10/30 at the Forty-ninth Street Theatre where it counted sixty-four more performances.

BIT O' LOVE, A [Drama/Marriage/Romance/Religion/British] A: John Galsworthy; D: Robert Milton; S: Donald Oenslager; P: Actors' Theatre; T: Forty-eighth Street Theatre; 5/12/25 (4)

A lesser Galsworthy offering, this one finding the dramatist creating a sentimental tale, with a promising central thesis, yet, as several critics noted, one that is never honestly dealt with but merely made the excuse for theatrical contrivances. Given only at four special matinees, the play was generally frowned on and did not attain a regular run.

It tells of a saintly young rector (O. P. Heggie), who refuses to divorce his adulterous wife (Chrystal Herne) so as not to harm her lover's career and thus displease the wife. When his congregation jeers at him for his decision, he thinks of suicide but decides to go on finding meaning in Christian love.

The play's excessive use of "sentimental platitude" and dramatic trivialities annoyed Stark Young, and George Jean Nathan carped at its obvious plotting and lack of conflict.

BITTER SWEET [Musical/Period/Romance/British] B/M/LY/D: Noël Coward; DS: G. E. Calthrop and Ernest Stern; P: Charles B. Cochran's production presented by Florenz Ziegfeld and Arch Selwyn; T: Ziegfeld Theatre; 11/5/29 (159)

Noël Coward revealed yet another facet of his great versatility when he offered this operetta for which he wrote both score and libretto while also directing it.

Evelyn Laye played the heroine, a role originally created for the London mounting by Peggy Wood.

The plot was a flashback narrated in 1929 by the Marchioness of Shayne (Laye) to her niece (Audrey Pointing), when that young lady is puzzled over whether to marry her fiancée or the jazz musician she loves. The aunt's story of her own romantic life proceeds from 1875 London to 1880 Vienna to 1895 London as she recalls how instead of marrying her own fiancée she ran off with her singing teacher (Gerald Nodin), who later was shot in a duel. She returned to London and married the Marquis of Shayne (John Evelyn).

Euphemia Van Rensselaer Wyatt called *Bitter Sweet* "a well-fashioned and pleasing work, tuneful, and steeped in the kind of romance usually found in revivals from an earlier and quieter day." Coward's tunes included the now standard "Zigeuner" and "I'll See You Again." John Hutchens said the "score, though it is not commanding, touches off the sentimental essence of successive eras, seeking out their wistful charm rather than the easier travesty that might have been accomplished." Only George Jean Nathan growled at the show, finding it juvenile, overly sentimental, derivative, and shopworn.

BLACK BOY [Drama/Sports/Blacks/Race/Sex] A: Jim Tully and Frank Dazey; D: David Burton; P: Horace Liveright; T: Comedy Theatre; 10/6/26 (39)

The title character of this boxing drama was played by Paul Robeson, who cut an impressive figure as the naive young fighter who, without any training, knocks out the white champion (Charles Henderson) and becomes a sports celebrity living in a flashy Harlem apartment with a white mistress (Edith Warren) and a colorful entourage. He loses the big match because of his physical dissipation, sees his hangers on leave him, discovers that Irene is really black, and decides to go to California, where the Japanese are more hated than the blacks.

For some, this was a fairly dynamic, virile play, pungent in speech and atmosphere, with an excellent scene in which the big fight was described on the radio as Black Boy's friends listened in.

Robeson was compelling as the pugilist; when he sang a spiritual it made "all memories of Al Jolson...take the count" for Percy Hammond. George Jean Nathan thought that coauthor Tully's innate honesty had been tampered with and that the decision to have Irene turn out to be Negro was an interpolation aimed at seducing the Broadway audience. John Mason Brown found the work tawdry and shallowly sentimental.

The *Herald Tribune* declared that Paul Robeson "dominates the play by the simpler and surer means of a sheer gianthood of genuineness, native understanding, and deep-voiced likability."

BLACK COCKATOO, THE [Drama/Night Club/Drugs/Orientals/Crime] A: Samuel Ruskin Golding; D: Edgar J. MacGregor; P: Frank Martins; T: Comedy Theatre; 12/30/26 (4)

"[A] leaky, generally preposterous entertainment which plays around the edge of melodrama all evening and never quite succeeds in being one,'' quoth the *Times*. Its shallow plot, which had touches of *Broadway* and *The Shanghai Gesture*, mingled persons such as an assistant district attorney (James Crane); a half-caste New York night-club proprietress, Lily Chang (Anne Forest); and various Oriental and Caucasian dope peddlers and smugglers in a jumble of nefarious schemes during which Lily ensnares the D.A. in a trap and then falls so in love with him that she must become his bride.

BLACK SCANDALS [Revue/Blacks] B/D/P: George Smithfield; T: Edyth Totten Theatre; 10/27/28 (7)

A little-noticed failure of a black revue that the *Times* characterized as ''so naively and disarmingly amateurish that it forestalls any sort of professional criticism.'' Some rapid-fire dance routines and a decent jazz orchestra provided highlights. It had a plot of sorts, about an Alladin's lamp that carries two American blacks, Rastus (Stewart Hampton) and Henry (Clarence Nance), to a mythical kingdom. This was merely the excuse for the interpolation of well-known songs interrupted by ''mirthless stretches of dialogue between the two supposed funmakers.''

BLACK VELVET [Drama/Southern/Race/Labor/Drugs/Blacks] A/D: Willard Robertson; P: M. J. Nicholas; T: Liberty Theatre; 9/27/27 (15)

An incredulous play about an octogenarian southern timber plantation owner (Arthur Byron), whose racial biases are those of the antebellum era, and who cannot face the shifting patterns of black-white relationships; apoplectic at the discovery that his grandson (Nelan Jaap) has been furtively dallying with mulatto Cleo (Nadea Hall) in the canebrake, he dies before he can shoot the youth. Mingled herein are incidents involving black migration to the North for better jobs, a lynching, and cocaine usage among the local blacks.

Critics found the plot and characterizations strained. ''It is a strangely diffuse and unsystematic play,'' cavilled the *Times*, and Alison Smith observed that it was static and ''filled with bombastic and ludicrous dogmatism.''

BLACKBIRDS OF 1926 [Revue/Blacks] D/P: Lew Leslie; T: Alhambra Theatre (OB); 4/12/26

A little-known black revue that ran for six weeks at Harlem's Alhambra, a movie house, and starred dynamo songstress-dancer Florence Mills, around whose talents it was built. The show used none of the usual tableaux seen in contemporary revues, employed a chorus of eight sexy girls, had enormous energy, and was ''a roaring insane asylum of jazz, noise, cacaphony, and tanpandemonium'' (*News*).

BLACKBIRDS OF 1928 [Revue/Blacks] M: Jimmy McHugh; LY: Dorothy Fields; D/P: Lew Leslie; S: Premier Scenic Studios; C: Kiviette; T: Liberty Theatre; 5/9/28 (519)

One of the great revue hits of its day, *Blackbirds of 1928* was the black musical lovechild of the white lyricist-composer team Dorothy Fields and Jimmy McHugh, working together for the first time. It also launched veteran vaudeville tap-dance master Bill "Bojangles" Robinson into the Broadway limelight with his only solo in the show, "Doin' the Low Down," tapped out on a staircase. Adelaide Hall came into prominence as a blues singer; the wonderful songs "I Can't Give You Anything but Love, Baby" (the last word of the title in the original was "Lindy"), "Diga Diga Doo," and "I Must Have That Man" were largely hers. These two made this "the best coon show in town," declared *Time*.

Robinson's terpsichorean talents ensnared most of the plaudits. Richard Dana Skinner said his dancing far surpassed anything like it he had "seen for sheer delicacy, inborn rhythm and perfection of design." Otherwise, he declared the show was "mediocre" and so derivative of white revues as to lack any indigenous Negro spirit. Perriton Maxwell summed it up as a work "not lavishly endowed with wit of a high order or with music above the ordinary [but possessing] the racial trait of abundant speed, clever dancing, and skilled entertainers whose enjoyment in their work crosses the footlights and infuses their audience."

BLANCHETTE [Dramatic Revival/French Language] A: Eugène Brieux; P: Wendell Phillips Dodge; T: Fulton Theatre; 3/18/24 (1)

Brieux's 1892 play was staged by actors of the Comédie Française, led by Maurice de Féraudy, during a visiting season of repertory. John Corbin described the play's theme as "Does education bring happiness when it raises children above, or rather outside of, the mental and social possibilities of their parents?" He declared the problem to be even more pertinent in the postwar years than when the play was first written.

Daughter of peasants who have sacrificed comforts for her education, Blanchette cannot find work after earning her teaching certificate. Her father (de Féraudy) nags her to marry a peasant whose land he covets. Only after being disillusioned by the squire's son she loves does she creep home to wed the faithful peasant.

De Féraudy's portrait of Blanchette's father was called by Corbin "a masterpiece of richly felt nature in finely artistic composition." The play had been done in New York several times since its bow there in 1914.

                                                                                          H.H.

BLESS YOU, SISTER [Drama/Religion/Small Town/Romance/Business] A: John Meehan and Robert Riskin; D: John Meehan and George Abbott; S: Nicholas Yellenti; P: A. E. and R. R. Riskin; T: Forrest Theatre; 12/26/27 (24)

Alice Brady failed to come up with a successful vehicle when she undertook to play the promising role of Mary McDonald, disillusioned daughter of an unappreciated small-town minister (George Alison), who goes into the Bible-thumping business as an evangelist with a Bible salesman (Charles Bickford) as her partner. This theme was subverted, according to the *Times*, when the authors introduced a clumsy love rivalry involving the salesman and another man (Robert Ames).

Here was "a fine idea, imperfectly carried out" (*Times*); it had a rousing tabernacle scene in which Brady, dressed in flowing white robes, held her audience spellbound with her combination of sex appeal and salesmanship. George Jean Nathan characterized the play as "a Broadway attempt to put Elmer Gantry into skirts."

BLIND HEART, THE (El corazón ciego) [Drama/Romance/Spanish/Spanish Language] A/D: Gregorio Martinez-Sierra; P: Spanish Art Theatre; T: Forrest Theatre; 5/7/27 (2)

One of the less-appreciated plays put on by the visiting Spanish Art Theatre, *The Blind Heart* featured prima donna Catalina Barcena in the role of a young lady of Madrid, Maria Luisa, who, after being disillusioned with a boyfriend who left her in the lurch when the road house they had stopped at was raided, elopes with another youth to Africa and eventually realizes that she really loves him.

The *Times* thought Barcena's acting here could have used the restraint she showed in other works but agreed that audiences loved her emotional histrionics.

BLOND BEAST, THE [Drama/Religion] A: Henry Myers; D: Lorenz M. Hart; T: Plymouth Theatre; 3/2/23 (1)

A single matinee performance was given this piece by the author of *The First Fifty Years*. It was about "the conversion of a self-imagined superman and the destruction of his fancied powers of resistance to the wiles of a sentimental world," according to the *Times*. The leading roles were played by Arthur Hohl and Effingham Pinto, and the direction was by the man who was better known as the lyricist partner of composer Richard Rodgers.

The matinee performance was intended to attract a potential producer for a Broadway run. According to *Rodgers and Hart*, by Samuel Marx and Jan Clayton, the author claimed that the producers left en masse before the play began when they received word of a threatened actors' strike. Thus the play never got the hearing it sought.

BLONDE SINNER, THE [Musical/Marriage] B/M/LY: Leon De Costa; D: Edwin Vail; CH: Ralph Riggs; P: Musicomedies, Inc.; T: Cort Theatre; 7/14/26 (179)

A chorus of only four blondes backed this innocuous, but fairly popular, musical in which a Mr. and Mrs. Hemmingworth (Ralph Bunker and Enid Markey) rent a summer home on Long Island and take in boarders to defray the expenses. Aided by detectives, a wife (Marjorie Gateson) seeks to expose the secret co-respondent in her divorce case, and suspicion falls unjustly on Mrs. Hemmingworth before the real sinner, an empty-headed, blonde country girl (Ruth Stevens), is found out.

The show was a labored farce with musical interludes, and its framework was designed to allow for frequent specialty numbers introduced by various boarders. "Any chance of maintaining the pace of farce was lost whenever the action halted completely for a song or dance, with a result that the piece was dull and generally unfunny," observed the *Times*.

BLOOD AND SAND [Drama/Romance/Sports/Marriage/Spain] A: Tom Cushing; SC: Blasco Ibanez's novel, *Blood and Sand*; D: B. Iden Payne; P: Charles Frohman, Inc.; T: Empire Theatre; 9/20/21 (71)

Otis Skinner was in his mid-sixties when he essayed the leading role of the dashing, handsome, young bullfighter Juan Gallardo in Tom Cushing's faithful stage version of Blasco Ibanez's colorful romantic novel of the same name. He proved surprisingly trim and lithe as the daring toreador, "reverting to a bravura style of acting that carries conviction" (Burns Mantle).

The story takes Gallardo from his triumph as Madrid's most popular toreador, to an impassioned affair with the fiery Dona Sol (Catherine Calvert) during which his faithful wife, Rosario (Madeline Delmar), must bide her time, to a three-month period of recuperation from a smashed leg as he waits in vain for a word from his mistress, to his rejection by the faithless woman, to his goring by a bull, and to his last moments as he dies in his wife's arms thinking hers the kiss of Dona Sol.

Burns Mantle called it "a nicely balanced" drama, "a colorful and atmospheric costume play," but Ludwig Lewisohn speared it as "a sentimental tale of illicit passion gaudily tricked out."

The star's young daughter Cornelia Otis Skinner made her Broadway debut in the play, in a tiny role; she describes the experience charmingly in her book *Family Circle*.

BLOOD MONEY [Drama/Mystery/Crime/Romance] A: George Middleton; SC: a story by H. H. Van Loan; D: Ira Hards; P: Mrs. Henry B. Harris; T: Hudson Theatre; 8/22/27 (64)

This "anaemic" thriller (Katherine Zimmermann), comprised of bloodless characters and action, had "an interesting opening, a somewhat scrambled second act and an extremely weak finish," according to Alison Smith. Its heroine (Phyllis Povah) was a blonde stenographer who finds an envelope containing $100,000 in the desk of her late boss Senator Bolton; the cash is soon being sought by a couple of evildoers (Beatrice Nichols and Malcolm Duncan). A chauffeur (Robert Timmins) is slain, and the stenographer accused. She sets sail for Yucatan on the Bolton yacht, where the pursuit of the money continues; it ends with the crooks outsmarted and the money safely bestowed on the heroine, who also wins the late Senator's son (Thomas Mitchell) for her troubles.

BLOSSOM TIME [Musical/Period/Romance/Musical-Biographical/Austrian] B/LY: Dorothy Donnelly; ADD. M.: Sigmund Romberg and Heinrich Berte;

SC: A. M. Willner and H. Reichert's Austrian operetta *Das Dreimädlerhaus*; D: J. C. Huffman; CH: Frank M. Gillespie; S: Watson Barratt; C: Mode Costume Co.; P: Messrs. Shubert; T: Ambassador Theatre; 9/29/21 (516)

A huge hit of its day, this long-running adaptation of a Viennese operetta had been an enormous success in various European capitals under different titles; it had even been done locally in a shabby stock-company version in 1918 in the original German. Its music was all written by the great Austrian composer Franz Schubert, but the orchestrations adapted the melodies for American tastes under the auspices of Dorothy Donnelly and Sigmund Romberg, who made considerable changes in the adaptations done for the original by Heinrich Berte.

The core of the plot was a semifictionalized biographical account of Schubert's (Bertram Cook) life, concentrating on a tragic love affair leading to his early death. The music was largely performed as it was supposed to have been created by the composer, with those moments of inspiration leading to classical pieces such as "Ave Maria" being highlights of the evening.

The critics were depressed by the popularization of the original music and contrasted the Broadway orchestrations unfavorably with the Viennese. On the other hand, they applauded the producers for bringing classical music to Broadway and thereby to the ragtime-jaded ears of American youth, who, it was hoped, would soon be playing this music at their college parties and listening to it on their gramophones.

"Serenade," "Ave Maria," the melody from "The Unfinished Symphony," and "The Military March" were standouts in the lush score, and singers Olga Cook as Mitzi, Howard March as Schober, and Bertram Peacock sang beautifully with feeling and skill.

Blossom Time became a standard work and was revived often, including six additional New York productions, the last in 1943. In the twenties it was seen again on 5/21/23, at the Shubert Theatre (twenty-four performances); 5/19/24, at the Jolson Theatre (twenty-four performances); and 3/8/26 at the Jolson Theatre (sixteen performances).

BLUE BIRD, THE (L'Oiseau bleu) [Dramatic Revival] A: Maurice Maeterlinck; TR: Alexander Teixeria de Mattos; D: Frederick Stanhope; CH: Cleveland Bronner; T: Jolson's Fifty-ninth Street Theatre; 12/25/23 (29)

Maeterlinck's fantastical 1908 play, often revived for young audiences, tells the tale of Tyltyl (Ben Grauer) and Myltyl's (Mary Corday) dream-like journey in search of the Blue Bird in the company of assorted whimsical characters. The present production was mounted as a Christmas entertainment and directed by Frederick Stanhope, who had staged the first New York production some dozen years before. It was warmly greeted by John Corbin, who found that Maeterlinck "has woven into this seemingly naive fantasy far more of wisdom and of humor, of blithe courage and of heroic resignation, of penetrating observation and of deeply quiet thought, than are to be found in many a ponderous tome. And here also the admirably spirited production at Jolson's verifies and re-inforces the inward meaning.''

H.H.

BLUE BONNET [Comedy/Western/Rural/Romance] A: George Scarborough; P: Messrs. Shubert; T: Princess Theatre; 8/28/20 (81)

The author, in satirizing not only cowboys but the whole succession of cowboy plays, succeeded in giving a new twist to a threadbare theme. His story was about Billy Burleson (Ernest Truex), an eighteen-year-old cowboy who has never owned a gun, has no livestock, and doesn't drink or gamble. Near the Mexican border, patrolled by regiments of the National Guard, Terry Mack (Richard Taber) of the ''Fighting Sixty-Ninth'' and Billy fall in love with sixteen-year-old Hope Hillyer. Hope's father, for whom Billy has been working, dies, and Billy makes himself Hope's guardian. In his clumsily heroic way he protects her from those seeking her land and from those who would spread rumors about their relationship; he also wards off the too-persistent attentions of his amorous rival Terry Mack.

Blue Bonnet served to give Ernest Truex a vehicle to display his comic versatility, and he came through with flying colors. The play was described by Alexander Woollcott as ''fairly amusing'' but very crudely produced. Heywood Broun found too much of it ''familiar and dreary stuff.''

M.M.-C.

BLUE EYES [Musical/Romance/Marriage] B: Le Roy Clemens and Leon Gordon; M: I. B. Kornblum; LY: Z. Meyers; D: Clifford Brooke; P: Morris Rose; T: Casino Theatre; 2/21/21 (48)

A musical used as a setting for the main attraction, comedian Lew Fields, who came on again and again, strutted about, waved his arms, and whimpered in ''that vein of aggrieved comedy which is peculiarly his own'' (Alexander Woollcott). The silly show around him, wrote Burns Mantle, was another example of what producers did to ''ruin even such possible stories as their librettists bring them.''

It told the story of down-and-out writer Bobby Brett (Ray Raymond) who is hit by an auto owned by wealthy Dorothy Manners (Mollie King). Dorothy's dad (Carl Eckstrom), thinking Bobby a count, invites him and his two roommates (Andrew Tombes and Fields) to a weekend party in Great Neck. What ensues is a series of comical bits featuring Fields making a fool of himself at the shindig. ''There is little but Lew Fields to recommend *Blue Eyes*,'' moaned Arthur Hornblow, although the critics also singled Andrew Tombes out for praise.

M.C.-C.

BLUE GHOST, THE [Comedy/Mystery/Crime/Romance] A: Bernard J. McOwen and J. P. Riewerts; D: Stephen Clark; P: Jimmie Cooper; T: Forrest Theatre; 3/10/30 (112)

A trite mystery comedy set in a reputedly haunted house by the Pacific Ocean and stuffed with the old standbys of frightened black servants and phosphorescent spooks. The critics hated it, but it strung along for over three months.

A murder has been committed at Dr. De Farmer's (Bernard J. McOwen) castle, a Blue Ghost is suspected, an investigator (Douglas Cosgrove) investigates, a romance gets complicated, and it all turns out to be a whiskey dream of Jasper, the servant (Nate Busby). "[Y]ou could only yawn and agree that it was a very bad dream, indeed," croaked the *Times*.

BLUE KITTEN, THE [Musical/Romance/Family/Night Club/French] B/LY: Otto Harbach and William Cary Duncan; M: Rudolf Friml; SC: Yves Mirande and Gustave Quinson's French comedy *Le Chasseur de chez Maxim's*; D: Edgar Selwyn, Julian Mitchell, and Leon Erroll; CH: Julian Mitchell; P: Arthur Hammerstein; T: Selwyn Theatre; 1/13/22 (140)

Lillian Lorraine, "the Queen of all Showgirldom" (*Evening Sun*), made a flashy return to Broadway as Totoche, a Folies Bergere star, in this musical adaptation of a popular, racy French farce. Lorraine had survived a severe spinal injury, but the revealing backless and nearly frontless gown she wore in Act One had the critics stunned by how little her legendary beauty had been dimmed.

As purified for New York audiences, it told the conventionally far-fetched story of a Parisian *chasseur* (Joseph Cawthorn), a uniformed man of all trades at a fancy night club. His wife and daughter (Lorraine Manville) live at a country home and do not know his true profession. The plot concerns his efforts to keep them from finding out, as well as involving several romantic subplots.

There were bouncy numbers, pretty showgirls, and entertaining performances, but there was little that proved memorable. Arthur Hornblow called the score "dull" and the adaptation "unamusing."

BLUE LAGOON, THE [Drama/Youth/Romance/Tropics/Adventure/British] A: Norman MacOwen and Charlton Mann; SC: H. De Vere Stackpoole's novel, *The Blue Lagoon*; D: Basil Dean; P: Messrs. Shubert i/a/w Basil Dean; T: Astor Theatre; 9/14/21 (21)

Despite its disastrous Broadway showing, *The Blue Lagoon* eventually became popular in several movie versions. The play had been a great hit in London, but when its elaborately produced American production opened, the audience greeted it "with yawns, titters and occasional murmurs of mutiny" (Alexander Woollcott).

The Blue Lagoon is a tropical idyll about two cousins, Dick (as a child, Andrew J. Lawlor, Jr.; as a youth, Harold French) and Emmeline (as a child, Lorna Volare; as a girl, Frances Carson), who are castaways on a South Seas island where they grow up, become lovers, and, eventually, are the parents of a baby. Finally, a search party led by an uncle discovers them.

BLUE PETER, THE [Drama/Marriage/British] A: E. Temple Thurston; D: Edward Goodman; S: Cleon Throckmorton; P: Stagers i/a/w Lumsden Hare; T: Fifty-second Street Theatre; 3/24/25 (39)

The Stagers, a new group with hopes of becoming a permanent ensemble, produced this British work to fairly respectable notices. The general opinion held that the play was an intelligent treatment of a provocative theme but that it was excessively discursive and insufficiently dramatic. Stark Young claimed "it has the quality of a novel rather than a play. . . . As it stands *The Blue Peter* is a kind of psychological sentimental dialogue."

Its hero David Hunter (Warren Williams), formerly a mining engineer in central Africa, has settled in England with his wife (Marjorie Vonnegut) and child, but after six years of office work feels stirring within him the urge to follow the sailing signal, the "Blue Peter," to adventure once more. Tempted by an old mining friend, he strays as far as a Liverpool saloon, where the lure of whiskey and girls are hard to overcome; he manages the feat, though, and returns to the hearth.

BLUEBEARD'S EIGHTH WIFE (La huitieme femme de Barbebleue) [Comedy/Romance/Marriage/Sex/French] A: Alfred Savoir; AD: Charlton Andrews; D: Lester Lonergan and Robert Milton; P: William Harris, Jr.; T: Ritz Theatre; 9/19/21 (155)

A cynical French sex comedy adapted into English with most of the original's bite left out. The result was a suggestive bedroom farce given its principal distinction by the appearance of Ina Claire.

John Brandon (Edmund Breese), a superwealthy American who has worked his way through seven marriages, agrees to marry Monna de Briac (Claire), the daughter of an impecunious nobleman (Ernest Stallard), with the understanding that he will pay her a generous amount if their relationship ends in divorce. Monna contrives to keep John famished for her favors in order to teach him a lesson for the crassly commercial way he bargained for her to be his wife. She also arouses his jealousy to the point where he realizes how much he really loves her.

Ludwig Lewisohn decried the comedy's "flagrant and odious hypocrisy," and Alexander Woollcott observed that the playwright got "a thrill out of seeing how shocking a little comedy he can concoct without having his activities suppressed as a public nuisance."

BLUFFING BLUFFERS [Comedy/Politics/Small Town/Romance] A: Thompson Buchanan and John Meehan; D: John Meehan; P: James P. Beury; T: Ambassador Theatre; 12/22/24 (24)

The *Times* reviewer characterized this poorly received "United States comedy" as "one of those vociferously American plays that have to do with a political boss, a corrupt Senator, a city that needs cleaning up and a hero that undertakes to clean it." The hero in this instance is Dr. Barnes (Edward H.

Robins), a physician who is advised in Washington, D.C., by a crony (Roy Gordon) of a crooked politician, Senator Dawson, that the way to succeed in this country is by bluffing your way along. Barnes sets up practice in an Indiana town where the women have considerable influence; he succeeds here by practicing the bluffing philosophy but remains an honest man. His do-gooder tendencies put him in conflict with the local Irish boss (John T. Doyle). He is saved from difficulties by the townswomen and eventually wins the hand of Senator Dawson's daughter (Enid Markey).

BLUSHING BRIDE, THE [Musical/Romance/Night Club/Show Business] B/LY: Cyrus Wood; M: Sigmund Romberg; SC: a play by Edward Clark; D: Frank Smithson; P: Messrs. Shubert; T: Astor Theatre; 2/6/22 (144)

Sigmund Romberg's next assignment after the great success of *Blossom Time* was this airy concoction for the tired businessman of which the *Tribune*'s B.F. said, "There's a tinge of vaudeville, a shade of revue, a color of burlesque, a hue of musical comedy, a suggestion of concert, and a tincture of the devil himself." The loosely plotted show proved vastly entertaining because of Romberg's songs and the lead performances.

Cleo Mayfield was the popular "theeing and thouing" hat-check girl Lulu Love in Paul Kominski's (Robert O'Connor) cabaret, where her tout boyfriend Coley Collins (Cecil Lean) has taken a job as a sort of chaperone to couples meeting illicitly. The plot displays his efforts to get Lulu to marry him and to keep the well-heeled clientele from getting in his way, but it was all just an excuse for songs, comedy numbers, and cabaret turns. "Plot and story are conspicuous by their absence," said the *Post*.

BOMBO [Revue] B/LY: Harold Atteridge; M: Sigmund Romberg; D: J. C. Huffman; S: Watson Barratt; P: Messrs. Shubert; T: Jolson's Fifty-ninth Street Theatre; 10/6/21 (218)

The new Al Jolson Theatre was opened, appropriately, with the great Jolie himself headlining a spectacular show presented in revue style but loosely linked by a plot about Columbus's discovery of America as aided by his black deck hand Bombo, acted by Jolson in his everpresent blackface guise. *Bombo* was a typical Jolson vehicle, one he was apt to interrupt midway through to ask the audience what they would rather see, him or the show around him, to which the inevitable response was Jolson. He would send the company home and then entertain the crowd nonstop for as long as they were willing.

Bombo had loads of gorgeous scenery and costumes, the money for which Alexander Woollcott thought would have been better spent on adding a comedian or two and some worthwhile singers to the cast, but Jolson's presence made up for any deficiencies the evening might have held. In the show proper he had five songs that he sang from a stage extension that thrust out over the orchestra pit; it replaced the runway so frequently seen in his earlier productions. The great new songs included "April Showers," "Toot Toot Tootsie!" and "California, Here I Come,'' none of them by Romberg who was credited with the score. Only ''April Showers'' (uncredited in the program) was heard on opening night, the others being interpolated later in the run and on tour.

Bombo had a return engagement for thirty-two performances starting on 5/14/23.

BONDS OF INTEREST, THE (Los intereses creados) [Dramatic Revival] A: Jacinto Benavente; TR: John Garrett Underhill; D/P: Walter Hampden; DS: Claude Bragdon; T: Hampden's Theatre; 10/14/29 (24)

Benavente's whimsical, ironic Spanish comedy had introduced the Theatre Guild to New York in 1919; it failed for them and likewise did so for Walter Hampden's company in this revival. Hampden requested that his auditors get into the make-believe spirit of the piece and labored hard to excite their interest; the consensus was that the play was ''a windy, futile and affected bore'' (Percy Hammond).

The commedia plot, about how a clever and rascally servant named Crispin (Hampden) helps his destitute master Leander (Charles Quigley) live high off the hog and marry a rich man's daughter (Ingeborg Torrup), was an excuse for pantomimic drollery that seemed ill suited to the humorless Hampden style, although the actor played with intelligence and craft. John Hutchens said the production was, ''like its acting, diligent where it cries for abandon, and sonorous when it would be brisk.''

BOOK OF CHARM, THE [Comedy/Small Town/Family/Romance/Southern] A: John Kirkpatrick; D/P: Rachel Crothers; T: Comedy Theatre; 9/3/25 (34)

Top writer-director Rachel Crothers here ventured for the first time into the producing field; it also was the first time she staged a play that she did not also write. The piece was an often very funny but unstable satire on contemporary notions of ''charm.'' It took place in a small southern town, where young Joe Pond (Kenneth Dana) seeks to keep his girlfriend (Mildred MacLeod) from going to New York by buying a charm manual and teaching its contents to her unsophisticated family. He finally wins her over when she sees how popular his charm has made him with the local girls.

A simple, artless piece of Americana, *The Book of Charm* sat well with several critics but fared poorly at the box office. ''Its characters were 'sure-fire,' though not too familiar, its lines were honest and amusing, and its movement full of safe and sound absurdities,'' smiled Percy Hammond.

(2) (Charm) [Dramatic Revival] D: Edgar Henning; P: Sam Bacon; T: Wallack's Theatre; 11/28/29 (4)

An ill-fated revival of *The Book of Charm* brought out under the shortened title of *Charm*. Ida May Harper was played by Ann Thomas, Mrs. Wilson by Mabel Montgomery, and Joe Pond by Kenneth Dana (repeating his original role). No revisions were made in the writing, so, according to Alison Smith, it remained "an uneven, faintly amateurish and generally ingratiating little piece with a stereotyped small town plot lighted by surprising flashes of shrewd and authentic humor."

BOOM BOOM [Musical/Sex/Romance/Marriage] B: Fanny Todd Mitchell; M: Werner Janssen; LY: Mann Holiner and J. Keirn Brennan; SC: Louis Verneuil's farce *Oh! Mama!* D: George Marion; CH: John Boyle; S: Watson Barratt; P: Messrs. Shubert; T: Casino Theatre; 1/28/29 (72)

The source for this musical comedy was the French farce *Mlle. ma mere*, known to Broadway as *Oh, Mama!* from its 1925 presentation. The best that could be said of it was that it had plenty of energy. The action was transposed to New York's Park Avenue, the characters were given American names, and the title was a euphemism for making love, as was the same season's *Whoopee*. Perriton Maxwell commented, "Novelty of design is seldom to be found in this musical comedy, but it maintains a rapid pace and a generally exuberant air that prevents the evening from becoming tedious."

The show had a good comic performance by corpulent Frank McIntyre as the philandering husband who writes girls' phone numbers on his shirt cuffs; Cortez and Peggy showed their Spanish dancing skills, Nell Kelly and Jeanette MacDonald came off well in the leading female roles, and a young actor, Archie Leach (later known as Cary Grant), appeared in the small role of Reggie Phipps in which he did some singing.

BOOSTER, THE [Comedy/Family/Friendship/Jews/Romance/Business/Medicine/Austrian] A: Louis Nertz and Armand Friedman; AD: Nat Reid; D: Victor Morley; S: Ward and Harvey; P: Y-DNA, Inc.; T: Nora Bayes Theatre; 10/24/29 (12)

An adaptation of an unlisted Viennese comedy, relocated in a New York apartment, and concerned with the title character, butcher Jacob Stieglitz (Sam Wright), who tries to boost his son's budding career as a doctor by applying to it modern advertising principles; thus kidney ailments, for example, would be treated cheaply on special bargain days. His interference threatens to disrupt the love affair between the son (William McFadden) and the daughter (Jean Newcombe) of his best friend (Lester Bernard), but he is stifled before too much damage is done.

This flop was a "feeble and defenseless" effort (*Times*) that unflatteringly resembled the popular *Potash and Perlmutter* comedies.

BOOTLEGGERS, THE [Comedy-Drama/Prohibition/Romance/Crime] A: William A. Page; D: Frank McCormack; P: Madison Corey and Charles Capehart; T: Thirty-ninth Street Theatre; 11/27/22 (32)

An atmospheric comedy-melodrama peopled by hard-boiled criminals, Broadway types, crooked cops, chorus girls, and shady prohibition agents, the sort of population that served a few years later to turn *Broadway* into a super hit. Here, however, "The best that can be said for the play is that it is not a very good specimen of the ten, twenty and thirty cent drama" (Playgoer).

This pro-hooch, antieighteenth amendment play, jeered at by most of the critics, treats of a bootleggers' war between the kings of New York's illegal liquor traffic, ex-lawyer William T. Rossmore (Robert Conness) of the West Side, and ex-pushcart peddler Vicarelli (Barry Townsley) of the East Side, with a 2,500-case boatload of Scotch the booty. The federal dry agents are deeply involved, hoping to get their share of the action. Murder, revenge, and romance enter the picture before long, and the play ends on a suitably sentimental note.

BORROWED LOVE [Comedy/Theatre/Illness/Marriage] A: Bide Dudley; D: Oscar Eagle; S: Cirker and Robbins; P: John Osborne Clemson; T: Times Square Theatre; 6/17/29 (16)

The first play of the 1929–1930 season was by journalist/critic Bide Dudley and was a four-character comedy that the *Times* described as incoherent and "absurd." It involved the unhappy marriage of John (Richard Gordon) and Grace Carter (Mary Fowler); suffering from a severe case of influenza, John believes that his wife will be better off with another man and introduces her to theatre-manager Tom Bradford (Barry O'Neill). However, Tom refuses to get married, and Grace is determined to stick with John and help him get better.

BOTTLED [Comedy/Prohibition/Romance/Family] A: Anne Collins and Alice Timoney; D/P: Herman Gantvoort; S: Wiard B. Ihnen; T: Booth Theatre; 4/10/28 (63)

The sibling authoresses of this "gentle, folksy little comedy" (*Times*) were Louisville journalists who set the action among a family of Kentucky distillers ruled over by the grand matriarchal figure of wealthy Ellen McMullin (Maud Durand), a lame old Irish widow whose skinflint ways have become the bane of her needy grandchildren. The latter have been left their grandpa's bourbon distillery, which the old crone operates. To make some money, the heirs turn to bootlegging, which leads to some funny business when they hide bottles in every conceivable place. Found out by grandma, who threatens to report them, they muzzle her with their knowledge of her own hooch-making endeavors. There is also a romantic subplot or two involving the grandchildren.

The play's flaws, including excessive length, verbosity, awkward construction, and some poor direction, were observed, but the critics took to its originality, southern flavor, and comic simplicity. *Vogue* reported that the playwrights "devised a play fresh in approach, charmingly gauche, filled with sharp bits of observation and characterization."

BOTTOM OF THE CUP, THE [Drama/Race/Crime/Blacks/Sex/Drugs/Southern] A: John Tucker Battle and William J. Perlman; D: Henry Stillman; P: Mayfair Productions; T: Mayfair Theatre (OB); 1/31/27 (16)

A poorly written drama about Charles Thompson (Daniel L. Haynes), a northern-educated black man who returns to his Mississippi delta cabin to learn that the white girl he loves is pregnant by Robert Kinney (Roderick Maybee), a drug user who is also responsible for a bank robbery. Charles convinces Kinney to marry the girl, reforms him, and then allows himself to be shot by a lynching mob for the crime Kinney committed.

Intended to demonstrate the magnanimity of blacks in the face of white hatred and bigotry, the play's "expression of this thesis was conventional and inept," according to the *Times*. Charles Gilpin was unable to appear in the role of Charles as scheduled, and Haynes had to go on in his stead.

BOTTOMLAND [Musical/Alcoholism/Southern/Blacks] B/M/P: Clarence Williams; D: Aaron Gates and Clarence Williams; T: Princess Theatre; 6/27/27 (21)

A weak black musical produced at the outset of the 1927 summer season; it lacked any distinguished performances and was considered neither fish nor fowl in its tendency to avoid either an out and out exploitation of familiar black entertainment methods or an openly imitative white approach. The *Times* deemed it "an amorphous presentation whose moments, such as they are, are routine and stereotyped."

The show used a great deal of music in proportion to its dialogue, had a too loosely structured book, and an excessively dull pace. It concerned a poor southern black girl (Eva Taylor), who leaves her Bottomland ghetto to travel to Harlem in search of fame and fortune; finding there her best friend Sally (Olivia Otiz) a dispirited and drink-sodden cabaret singer, she returns to the old folks at home.

BOUGHT AND PAID FOR [Dramatic Revival] A: George Broadhurst; D: John Cromwell; P: William A. Brady; T: Playhouse Theatre; 12/7/21 (30)

Bought and Paid For was a 1911 success that had run for more than 400 performances. It depicts a telephone operator (Helen MacKellar) who marries a heavy-drinking self-made man (Charles Richman), who treats his young wife as property and who, in the play's sensational climax, breaks her door down when he insists she honor his conjugal rights. By 1921 it seemed a bit lurid and obvious in its effects, but was "still entertaining" (Alexander Woollcott) and possessed of "plenty of vitality" (Arthur Hornblow).

Three of the original cast members, Charles Richman, Allen Atwell, and Marie Nordstrom, were in the revival.

BOUNDARY LINE, THE [Drama/Marriage/Literature/Romance] A: Dana Burnet; D: Dana Burnet and Morris Green; S: Henry Dreyfuss; P: A. L. Jones and Morris Green; T: Forty-eighth Street Theatre; 2/5/30 (37)

A bumpy play, well developed in spots and depressed in others, about idealistic poet Allan Fenway (Otto Kruger) and the commonplace girl (Katherine Alexander) he marries and for whom he abandons his creative writing to concentrate on their relationship. When they purchase a suburban home, the insecure wife, to his boundary-hating dismay, puts up a fence around it to protect her property; this leads to a confrontation with a farming neighbor (John T. Doyle), whose right of way to a stream is thus cut off. The case goes to court, the wife wins her stand and falls in love with her attorney (Charles Trowbridge), the farmer dies of apoplexy, and Allan leaves for a life on the road.

John Hutchens saw the play as "freighted with the symbolism of Mr. Burnet's favorite thesis—that the creative soul can know no barriers." *Time* reasoned that the author's "dramatic sense is by no means as lucid as his psychology, and his taste is woeful."

BOX SEATS [Drama/Sex/Drugs/Romance/Family/Show Business] A/D: Edward Massey; S: R. N. Robbins; P: Gordon M. Leland; T: Little Theatre; 4/19/28 (28)

A sordid and predictable backstage melodrama that Mori. said was "conceived and executed with childlike innocence of dramatic construction and presented with a complete disregard for human interest possibilities." Gilbert W. Gabriel termed it "all stray episodes and comfortable platitudes and grossly sympathetic chromos of life in the semi-raw."

Hazel Lawrence (Joan Storm), gold digger extraordinaire, has left her husband and family to live life in the fast lane; her husband dies and she takes in her twelve-year-old daughter Dolly (Patricia Barclay), for whose sake she decides to go straight. The pair join a cheap burlesque show, where the mother saves her girl from the lurid intentions of coke-sniffing Monty Slocum (Paul Guilfoyle) by revealing her own affair with him. Mom becomes a *Follies* star in New York, and Dolly weds a wealthy society fellow (Harold Elliott).

BRASS BUTTONS [Drama/Romance/Family/Sex] A: John Hunter Booth; D: Victor Morley; P: Lew Cantor, Inc.; T: Bijou Theatre; 12/5/27 (8)

John Hunter Booth's melodramatic play about a New York Irish cop (Frank Shannon) and the pregnant waif (Muriel Kirkland) he saves from a watery suicide had nothing to recommend it, wrote the *Times*. The cop, failing to get boxer Kid Dickson (Gerald Kent) to admit to being the girl's seducer, marries her himself. A major theme is the close relationship between the officer and his brogueish mother (Beryl Mercer).

BREAKING POINT, THE [Drama/Crime/Mental Illness/Romance/Medicine] A: Mary Roberts Rinehart; SC: the author's novel of the same name; D: Colin Kemper; P: L. L. Wagenhals and Colin Kemper; T: Klaw Theatre; 8/16/23 (68)

"Altogether a rip-snorting third-rater," declared Percy Hammond of Mary Roberts Rinehart's adaptation of her own book. Her plot concerned the dual personality of a young doctor (McKay Morris) who is pursued by a scandal he doesn't remember. Now engaged to the daughter (Regina Wallace) of the doctor (John Doyle) who found him nearly dead and cured him ten years before, the young man is confronted by an actress who was once his lover. In a drunken rage, he had killed her husband, and the shock propelled him into a second personality. Eventually, his personalities integrate, he is cleared of all charges, and he is free to marry his girl and to practice medicine.

Most critics found the plot wildly improbable but engrossing.

H.H.

BREAKS, THE [Comedy-Drama/Rural/Southern/Romance] A: J. C. and Elliott Nugent; D: Augustin Duncan; P: Richard Herndon; T: Klaw Theatre; 4/16/28 (8)

The father and son team of actor-authors, J. C. and Elliott Nugent, appeared opposite each other in this dire flop set in a hamlet of eastern Texas. J. C. played cotton farmer Jed Willis, a tyrannical misogynist who is willing to marry Amy (Sylvia Sidney), his cute housekeeper, to prevent his estate from falling into the hands of his hated relatives, one of whom, the fiery Jim Dolf (Elliott Nugent), is loved by the girl. A gunfight with Jim ends with Jed shot in the groin, and the operation that ensues leaves him sterile. Jim gets Amy, and Jed is snatched up by a blowsy neighbor (Helen Carew); the pre–New York version killed Jed off.

Percy Hammond thought it was "good fruit, ill cooked," and Alexander Woollcott labeled it "an odd jumble of ingenious invention, pawky humor, odd, sporadic charm, and incredibly clumsy craftsmanship."

BRIDAL VEIL, THE (Der Schleier der Pierrette) [Pantomime/Romance/Austrian] A: Arthur Schnitzler; M: Ernst von Dohnanyi; D: Elizabeth Anderson-Ivantzoff; DS: James Reynolds; P: American Laboratory Theatre; T: American Laboratory Theatre (OB); 1/26/28 (38)

The critics were, for the most part, skeptical about this Viennese pantomime dealing with a depressed Sculptor (Harold Hecht), who refuses his friend's entreaties to attend a ball; receives his beloved (Annie Schmidt), who arrives dressed for her wedding (against her will) to another man; takes poison; and is finally joined in death by the Bride.

Richard Lockridge wrote, "Pantomime is a very difficult art. It must have, as its background, sophistication and may only before that background posture at naivety. The present cast provides the naivety in full measure, but its sophistication is, on the whole, that of so many circus acrobats."

BRIDE, THE [Drama/Crime/Romance] A: Stuart Olivier; D: Frederick Stanhope; P: Jewett and Brennan, Inc.; T: Thirty-ninth Street Theatre; 5/5/24 (70)

In an opening-night curtain speech, Peggy Wood noted that her appearance in this crook melodrama was her return to the legitimate stage, and that she planned to alternate between musicals and dramas in the future, although she preferred the latter. To this the critics responded with laments. John Corbin found her ravishing in the title role but thought she was better in musical romances such as *Maytime*. Percy Hammond thought that she was incomplete without music.

The play, by a Baltimore journalist, concerned the adventures of a young woman bolting from a marriage ceremony in her wedding gown, crossing some rooftops, and landing in the Washington Square apartment of two wealthy brothers (Ferdinand Gottschalk and Donald Cameron). There she becomes embroiled in robbery and romance. "Of its kind it is airy and graceful, well-mannered and with a touch of sentimental romance," wrote Corbin, but Heywood Broun found the play below the standard for its type.

Playwright George Middleton revealed in his autobiography *These Things are Mine* that, although he was not credited, he was given a $2,500 advance and half the royalties for rewriting this play the author of which he never met.

H.H.

BRIDE OF THE LAMB, THE [Drama/Family/Religion/Small Town/Marriage/ Sex/Romance/Mental Illness/Crime/Alcoholism] A: William Hurlbut; D: Robert Milton; S: Cleon Throckmorton; P: Alice Brady i/a/w Robert Milton; T: Greenwich Village Theatre (OB); 3/30/26 (103)

This somewhat melodramatic study of the effects on a small-town midwestern family of their confrontation with a handsome, passionate religious evangelist was chosen as one of the Best Plays of 1925–1926. It presented the story of the Bowman family, the alcoholic physician father (Edmund Elton), his neurotic, repressed wife (Alice Brady), their daughter Verna (Arline Blackburn), and what happens when the Reverend Albaugh (Crane Wilbur) sets up his revival tent next to their home and takes up residence with them for a week. By the end of his stay, Mrs. Bowman, having thrown herself at the preacher, has poisoned Dr. Bowman; their daughter has taken to repeatedly confessing her sins; the minister's wife, not seen for eighteen years, returns; and Mrs. Bowman goes raving mad.

William Hurlbut's demonstration of the link between sexual desire and religious frenzy was too heavily laced with Freudian platitudes to please some critics. Others were disturbed by the play's faulty construction, especially the transparent introduction of the preacher's wife near the end.

Although these feelings were widely shared, a good number of the reviewers were shaken by the play's power. Joseph Wood Krutch found "a sturdy competence about the handling of the plot and about the characterization of the principal personages which sustains the interest and keeps alive a vigorous concern for the fate of the people involved."

BRIDE RETIRES, THE (Le Couché de la mariée) [Comedy/French/Marriage/ Romance] A: Felix Gandera; AD/P: Henry Baron; T: National Theatre; 5/16/25 (146)

A contrived French bedroom farce, intended as a marital satire, about a young couple whose impending wedding owes more to parental connivance than romantic leanings. Each has other ties they wish to maintain after the ceremony, but the conjugal situation finds them actually falling in love with each other.

The intent was considered naughty, especially in the boudoir scene when the bride (Lila Lee) gets into bed in her sexy nightgown and insists her new spouse (Stanley Ridges) sleep on the floor. When he objects to her coyness about letting him see her undress, she responds that "the good Lord didn't say you might look at me in my 'undies!' " This led Arthur Hornblow to brand it "an extremely nasty little play" that had lost "All its Gallic sparkle. . .in translation; only its suggestiveness remains."

BRIDGE OF DISTANCES, THE [Drama/Reincarnation/Romance/Orientals/ China/Fantasy] A: John and Elly Scrysmour; M: Frederick Schirmer; D: Ullrich Haupt; S: John Wenger; P: International Playhouse; T: Morosco Theatre; 9/28/ 25 (16)

John Wenger's handsome settings were the most widely admired elements in this lugubrious romantic fantasy set in China present and past. It dealt with the mating between a British aristocrat (Mary Newcomb) and a Chinese diplomat (Ullrich Haupt) in modern Peking and their recognition that they are the reincarnation of Chinese lovers of the past; the play shows in flashback their adventures in a former life when she, as a princess betrothed to him as a prince, was abducted by an English adventurer (Ray Collins). She was saved, the Briton executed, and the lovers ended their lives in double suicide.

The *Times* was impressed by the work's poetic tone and beauty but a more widely held opinion was that of the *Post*, which commented, "The play. . .is exactly as Chinese as chop suey and, as dramatic fare, equally indigestible. It is incredibly naive and pretentiously bad."

British-born actor Clarence Derwent revealed in his autobiography *The Derwent Story* that when a preview audience laughed jeeringly at an actor with a midwestern twang in the role of a British ambassador, the producers decided on the day the play was to open to replace him with Derwent. The latter agreed to take over only on the condition that he not be credited and be allowed to disguise himself with a beard. Derwent learned the role in four hours and was word perfect when the curtain rose.

BRINGING UP FATHER [Musical/Marriage] B: Nat Leroy; M: Seymour Furth; LY/D: Richard F. Carroll; SC: the comic strip by George McManus; T: Lyric Theatre; 3/30/25 (24)

After various versions of this show had successfully toured the nation for a decade, it finally came to Broadway, where, without further ado, it was squashed flat by the critics. Based on the popular Maggie and Jiggs comic strip about a rolling pin-wielding termagant of a wife (Beatrice Harlowe) and her rotund, little, henpecked husband (Danny Simmons), it offered the thinnest of musical-comedy entertainments for an unsophisticated audience and was removed from the boards in three weeks. The *Times* noted, "The production is thoroughly in the mood of the comic strip and may be recommended to those who feel that no day is complete without its portion of the Windjammer Kids [*sic*] and kindred diversions.''

BROADWAY [Comedy-Drama/Show Business/Night Club/Crime/Prohibition/ Romance] A: Philip Dunning and George Abbott; D: George Abbott; P: Jed Harris; T: Broadhurst Theatre; 9/16/26 (603)

George Jean Nathan, reluctant to label the tremendously successful *Broadway* a melodrama, as all his peers were doing, defined it as ''a sharply photographic study of that portion of New York's sewer-life that swirls around the bootlegging night clubs set into a frame of broad but observantly puncturing humor.'' Dunning and Abbott's energetic hit, staged with a remarkable expertise by the authors, gave New York theatregoers two years of exciting, but wholly plausible, entertainment, with some of the best observed characters and slangy dialogue the stage had heard in years. ''The atmosphere all through the evening is tense, thrilling—the real thing,'' wrote Arthur Hornblow. Burns Mantle made it a Best of the Year.

Set in the back rooms of a speakeasy called the Paradise Club, it stewed up a spicy broth of Chicago gangsters, New York bootleggers, cabaret entertainers, cops, jazz, murder, and romance that was to the taste of nearly every critic. Its story was told objectively and matter of factly without special pleading, its situations and tone were as up to the minute as possible, the clash of its characters was consistently interesting, its plot was built with enormous precision and skill, and its performances, especially that of Lee Tracy as the hoofer Roy Lane, were brilliant. ''Each part, no matter how small, has been given an expert and individualized characterization,'' noted Richard Dana Skinner. The character of Roy Lane was based on an actual entertainer, Roy Lloyd, who was hired to understudy Lee Tracy.

The fast-paced, action-filled piece was about Roy Lane's aspirations to move on to the big time, his rivalry for the affection of dancer Billie Moore (Sylvia Field) with bootlegger Steve Crandall (Robert Gleckler), Crandall's murder of competing bootlegger ''Scar'' Edwards (John Wray), the revenge slaying of Crandall by Edwards's girlfriend, and Roy and Billie's success in getting a vaudeville offer.

Before its final title was chosen, Philip Dunning's rough script had been called *The Roaring Forties* and *The Bright Lights*. It had come to producer Jed Harris only after having been rejected by the better established managements. Harris gave the script to George Abbott who found it ''confused. . . , full of wonderful characters and wonderful scenes, but there was no doubt about its possibilities.'' Abbott recalled in his memoirs *''Mister Abbott''* that a major reason for the show's great success was Harris's meeting with Dunning and Abbott following a terrific Atlantic City opening. The producer said, ''This show is going to get by no matter whether we improve it from now on or not. But it will be a much more important production if we eliminate all the cheap jokes. We don't need them. There is enough good comedy so that you can afford to throw out the stuff that downgrades the show.'' Abbott said that this was done and that he successfully used the tactic in later productions. Before the show opened in New York, Harris panicked and sought to have the last act rewritten; he then tried to replace Abbott as director. Both moves were resisted with bitter arguments. When Abbott, who had not signed a formal contract, later learned that he would not get a small royalty as the play's director because of the objections of Harris's partner Crosby Gaige, his relations with Harris grew icy; the pair worked on one more show together, *Coquette*, and the problems encountered during that experience separated the men for good. A good account of the play's backstage traumas can be found in Martin Gottfried's *Jed Harris; the Curse of Genius*.

BROADWAY BREVITIES [Revue] B: Blair Treynor; M/LY: George Le Maire, Archie Gottler, Blair Treynor, Bert Kalmar, Harry Ruby, J. Caesar, and Irving Berlin; P: George Le Maire; T: Winter Garden Theatre; 9/29/20 (105)

A *Follies*-like revue that never achieved its hope of becoming a Broadway annual. Despite a crop of outstanding young tunesmiths, no great hit songs emerged. The show had the usual panoply of lovely girls and settings but was chiefly noteworthy because it starred two great comedians, Eddie Cantor and Bert Williams. Also outstanding was the dancer Ula Sharon, who was paired with Alexis Kosloff in a ballet conceived, surprisingly, by Williams, the famed black entertainer.

Cantor and George Le Maire were amusing in a scene with Cantor the patient of Le Maire's dentist (and then his chiropractor); the chiropractor bit was a steal from the 1919 *Ziegfeld Follies*, in which Cantor had starred, and had to be dropped when Ziegfeld sued. Cantor scored with a mimic virtuoso violin recital (the music being supplied by an offstage fiddler). Williams was less effective than usual in his songs and comedy bits. Edith Hallor was the main female vocalist and was beautiful in various gowns; Hal Van Rensellear was the leading male singer.

The show had mixed reviews. One of the most hateful came from Heywood Broun, who called it ''the worst musical show we ever saw.''

BROADWAY NIGHTS [Revue] B: Edgar Smith; M: Sam Timberg, Lee David, and Maurie Rubens; LY: Moe Jaffe; D: Stanley Logan; CH: Busby Berkeley; S: Watson Barratt; P: Messrs. Shubert; T: Forty-fourth Street Theatre; 7/15/29 (40)

A summertime diversion featuring Dr. Rockwell, the comic quack, Parisienne songstress Odette Myrtil, the Chester Hale Girls, the Allan K. Foster Girls, and various exponents of vaudeville and burlesque. Using blackboard and chalk Rockwell gave a phony lecture on the digestive system (he proved how popcorn causes dandruff) and also played the ''William Tell Overture'' on a flageolet. The chorines pranced about in one routine with beach balls, which they subsequently tossed out to the spectators who were invited to toss them back and ''Hit Your

Baby,'' and appeared before a mammoth rosebush in one number and an orchid background in another. A plot of no apparent logic tied things together.

The show seemed old hat and dull. Francis R. Bellamy said it was ''stupid, vulgar, and full of childish sketches.''

BROADWAY SHADOWS [Comedy/Marriage/Crime] A/D: Willard Earl Simmons; P: Theatres Productions, Inc.; T: Belmont Theatre; 3/31/30 (16)

"Broadway Shadows is a painfully stupid play...completely inundated with the contents of the old hokum bucket,'' announced *Time.* This ''quite terrible'' (*Times*) comedy, which ran only ninety minutes, concerned a social registrite (Howard St. John), whose father (Lawrence C. Phillips) believes he has raised a check (his mother is the guilty party, but he takes the blame). This leads him to move into a tenement apartment, where he gets into all sorts of mishaps with the building's residents. He marries a woman (Lucille Fenton) whose ex-con husband (Leo Dawn), thought dead, returns, gun in hand, but is killed by a friendly blonde neighbor (Majda Torre).

BROADWAY WHIRL, THE [Revue] M: Harry Tierney and George Gershwin; LY: Joseph McCarthy, Richard Carle, B. G. De Sylva, and John Henry Mears; P: Artists' Producers Corporation; T: Times Square Theatre; 6/8/21 (85)

A typical warm-weather revue replete with leggy chorines, pretty costumes, a couple of comics, and lots of tunes. It arrived on Broadway after touring the country for a year. Its stars were Richard Carle, Blanche Ring, and Charles Winninger. Funny moments developed from a grand opera travesty and a scene in a passport office (Richard Carle as a government employee said to a line-waiter: ''I am not here to argue with you; I have been placed here by the government to ignore you'').

''The piece is outwardly fresh, and daintily set and costumed,'' reported the *Times.* The *Telegram* said it had ''plenty of fizz and sparkle.'' A few days later, *The Whirl of New York* opened, and playgoers were justifiably confused by the similar titles.

BROKEN BRANCHES [Comedy-Drama/Family] A: Emil Nyitray and Herbert Hall Winslow; D: Henry B. Stillman; P: Arthur G. Delamater; T: Thirty-ninth Street Theatre; 3/6/22 (16)

An uneven generation-gap drama, its title being a biblical allusion to ungrateful children. It concerned the overindulgent widower Karl Martens (Hyman Adler), who lavishes worldly goods on his children (Raymond Hackett and Beatrice Allen). A close friend (J. M. Kerrigan) tries to convince the man that his spoiling of his children can only lead to heartbreak. When Martens follows the friend's advice, his family life disintegrates; it is only after some fearful imaginings that Martens and his children are happily reconciled.

The happy ending seemed tacked on to several critics, and the only characters worth caring for were the two fathers, one Dutch, the other Irish.

BROKEN CHAIN, THE [Drama/Religion/Jews/Sports/Family] A: William J. Perlman; M: Louis M. Frohman and Abram Elstein; D: Mark Schweid; S: Louis Bromberg; P: Jacob A. Wesler; T: Maxine Elliott's Theatre; 2/19/29 (30)

An unsuccessful, though interesting, study of familial and religious dissension amidst the members of a Lower East Side Chassidic family, the father of which is Rabbi Velvel (Frank McGlynn). The family chain of rabbis is broken when his son turns to prizefighting and his daughter (Mary Fowler) refuses to marry a rabbinical student (Edgar Barrier) chosen by him for her. He pressures her into marriage, she commits adultery, and her sin is later deemed responsible for a series of misfortunes afflicting the congregation. The rabbi's own sin of pride is exposed, however, and he resigns his place to his son-in-law.

"The play . . . has rich overtones of spiritual belief, and succeeds in creating an atmosphere strongly reminiscent of Ansky's *The Dybbuk*," claimed Richard Dana Skinner, who also pointed to its "cumbersome and stilted dialogue." To the *Times* it was "old-fashioned" and "dull."

BROKEN DISHES [Comedy/Family/Small Town/Romance] A: Martin Flavin; D/P: Marion Gering; S: Eddie Eddy; T: Ritz Theatre; 11/5/29 (165)

Martin Flavin was a much-talked-of dramatist when three of his plays were produced on Broadway during the 1929-1930 season. One of the two acclaimed examples was this familiar domestic situation comedy about a midwestern small-town menage ruled over by Jenny (Eda Heinemann), a domineering mother who resents the choice of a husband made by her rebellious daughter Elaine (Bette Davis). Elaine and her milque-toast father (Donald Meek), who strengthens himself with a couple of glasses of hard cider, stand up to her, and Elaine marries her boyfriend (Reed Brown, Jr.) while her mother is at the movies. When Jenny's childhood beau (Duncan Penwarden), whom she keeps saying she should have married, shows up and is revealed as a criminal, Jenny's trap is shut for good.

Donald Meek gave one of his patented henpecked-husband performances to perfection, and Bette Davis continued to make her mark with her budding talents. The play was considered not particularly original, but "as amusing and engaging a farce as Broadway has seen this season," according to Perriton Maxwell. Richard Dana Skinner deemed it a "delicious and generally side-splitting comedy," which had taken time-worn materials and made them "as fresh as the morning dew."

BROKEN WING, THE [Comedy-Drama/Adventure/Rural/Romance/Aviation/ Marriage/Crime/Mexico] A: Paul Dickey and Charles W. Goddard; D/P: Paul Dickey; T: Forty-eighth Street Theatre; 11/29/20 (248)

As a blood relation of *The Bad Man*, *The Broken Wing* presented an entertaining comedy of adventure replete with a panoply of wild Mexican bandits. The story deals with an American aviator, Philip Marvin (Charles Trowbridge), who crashes in Mexican territory and is discovered by Inez Villera (Inez Plummer). Bereft of his money, Philip is held for ransom by a bandit (Joseph Spurin), who is later undone by the American Secret Service. While waiting for the ransom payment, Philip and Inez marry; his amnesia vanishes, and he flies back to the States with his bride.

The high point in the production was when Philip's airplane crashed into the setting, tore away part of a wall, and the audience heard a great whirring sound, moans from the injured airmen, and viewed the plane's wreckage through a cloud of smoke. The play's admixture of "ethnic phraseology, a naive heroine, and mawkish sentiment achieved its burlesque purposes with an ample dose of melodrama," declared Heywood Broun. In the cast were players such as Louis Wolheim and George Abbott.

M.M.-C.

BROKEN WINGS (Con los alas rotas) [Drama/Marriage/Spanish/Spanish Language] A: Emilio Berisso; D: Hector C. Quiroga; P: Camila Quiroga and the Argentine Players; T: Manhattan Opera House (OB); 12/8/27 (1)

This 1917 drama, known in Spanish as *Con los alas rotas*, was in the repertory of visiting Argentine actress Camila Quiroga and was about a married woman whose former lover threatens to reveal to her husband certain old letters of hers unless she becomes his mistress. Despite her efforts, the husband sees the correspondence and promptly kicks her out. Seen after seven years, both the woman and her husband have suffered tragically.

"It was all so stagey and artificial," said L. J., "that Quiroga did not show off to so great advantage" as in some of her other offerings.

BRONX EXPRESS, THE [Dramatic Revival] A: Ossip Dymov; TR: Samuel Golding; AD: Owen Davis; D: Charles Coburn; P: Mr. and Mrs. Charles Coburn; T: Astor Theatre; 4/26/22 (61)

An English-language version of a Yiddish theatre hit, this work met with general disapproval. As adapted, it was "not a good play" and became "an unconvincing *pot pourri* of melodrama, symbolism, musical comedy, burlesque and vaudeville" (Arthur Hornblow).

The Bronx Express is the train taken daily to and from work on Canal Street by immigrant button-maker David Hungerstoltz (Charles Coburn), who has taken the same route for a quarter-century. The play concerns his subway trip in search of his daughter (Hope Sutherland), who ran off when he objected to her poor fiancé. At the core of the drama is his dream in which the subway ads around him come to life and impress him with the madness of his capitalistic beliefs and his arrival at a more accommodating outlook.

Many believed that Charles Coburn was seriously miscast in the role of the button-maker, a role that the great European actor Rudolph Schildkraut had made a great success in when he played it in Yiddish.

BROOK [Drama/Rural/Romance] A: Thomas P. Robinson; P: McKee and Stevens; T: Greenwich Village Theatre (OB); 8/20/23 (16)

The second play of a Boston architect, *Brook* extolled country virtues over city sophistication in the story of a simple backwoods girl (Mary Carroll) who wins back her man (Donald Cameron) from his citybred fiancée (Ellis Baker). Although the *Times* reviewer called it "an uncommonly interesting play, marred but not spoiled, by a good deal of overwriting," more critics agreed with the *Tribune* critic, who wrote that the play's intent was "to show that real love, like running water, will find its own level. And it shouldn't have been such an arduous proposition as the play makes it."

                                                                      H.H.

BROTHER ELKS [Comedy/Business/Romance] A: Larry E. Johnson; P: Walter Campbell; T: Princess Theatre; 9/14/25 (16)

Swift oblivion came to this "dull and witless" (*Commercial*) piece about a young man (Richard Mayfield) who tries to put his abilities to work setting himself up as a corporation and selling stock in himself. The plot complications evolve from the fact that the stockholders own the hero, lock, stock, and barrel. Among the subplots is one in which several women try to gain control of him by cornering the market in his corporation's shares. At the end, the complications are smoothed out, and he gets the girl of his choice.

The *Times* called it "ponderous and slow-witted," and the *Sun* described it as "a vaguely amusing, if strikingly uneventful, comedy of carefully crossed purposes and earnestly involved triangles" for two-thirds of its duration, with the remainder being "much dreary bosh."

BROTHERS [Drama/Drugs/Family/Romance/Law/Crime] A: Herbert Ashton, Jr.; D: Arthur Hurley; S: Nicholas Yellenti; P: John Henry Mears; T: Forty-eighth Street Theatre; 12/25/28 (255)

This successful work was, said Richard Dana Skinner, "a melodrama, frank and unashamed, with many moments of fine theatre and enough tried and true tricks to make it good entertainment for all." Bert Lytell returned triumphantly to Broadway in the double role of twins (he had been in films for a decade). As orphan babies the twins were separated by doctors desirous of testing the effects on them of heredity and environment. One is raised in a wealthy, cultured home, the other in the slums. The rich twin becomes an attorney but also a dope addict and murderer. The poor one, a piano player in a waterfront dive, is an ambitious youth of fine character who is framed for the killing committed by his brother. The attorney defends the innocent brother successfully for his own crime and then dies of an overdose. The acquitted twin is adopted by the rich family in the other's place.

The many improbabilities of the plot were largely made up for by fine acting and direction, although some critics refused to take the play seriously.

(1) BROTHERS KARAMAZOFF, THE (Brat'ya Karamazovy) and "THE LADY FROM THE PROVINCES" (Provintsiyalka) [Russian/Russian Language/Period] P: F. Ray Comstock and Morris Gest; T: Fifty-ninth Street Theatre; 2/26/23 (8)

"The Brothers Karamazoff" [Drama/Family/Invalidism] A/D: Vladimir Nemirovich-Danchenko; SC: Fyodor Dostoievsky's novel; "The Lady from the Provinces" [Dramatic Revival] A: Ivan Turgenev; D: Vladimir Nemirovich-Danchenko and Constantin Stanislavsky

The fifth and final bill presented by the acclaimed Moscow Art Theatre on their initial U.S. visit. This two-part program began with a selection of dramatized scenes from the great Dostoievsky novel and ended with Turgenev's one-act farce.

In opposition to the well-known adaptation of the novel by Jacques Copeau, the Russian version did not attempt to condense the bulky, atmospheric work into a regular play (a fuller adaptation came later). Three revealing scenes only were selected to suggest "the febrile intensity and the minute observation of the most thoroughly Slavic of novelists" (John Corbin). It was assumed that audiences already knew the plot; only four of the many characters were used in this adaptation. Even the central role of Dmitry Karamazoff was excised from the telling, which effectively concentrated on the novel's moods and tone.

The lighter part of the program, Turgenev's 1851 farce, featured Olga Knipper-Chekhova as Daria Ivanovna, a provincial who uses her forceful wiles to overcome all obstacles to reach the big city. Although far older than the character she played, the actress convinced through sheer force of personality and skill. The work was played and written in a style thought to be very much like that of the contemporary Parisian boulevard theatres.

On 11/19/23 the Moscow Art Theatre returned with a more complete adaptation of *The Brothers Karamazoff*. It was played for nine performances without the one-acter on the bill. Although the critics disliked the company's device of an onstage reader bridging gaps between dramatized scenes from Dostoievsky's novel, they considered the actors' ability to make the characters and scenes seem real anyway an artistic feat. Singled out for special praise were Leonid Leonidoff's Dmitry, Vassily Katchaloff's Ivan, and Alla Tarasova's Grushenka. Of the latter, Heywood Broun wrote: "As a general thing, the women of the Moscow Art Theatre have been far less brilliant than the men, but this actress is as good as any except Katchaloff."

Stark Young wrote that the actors "exhibit an understanding, a perfection of ensemble and an inexhaustible study and elaboration of the characters, that must certainly be unequalled in theatres anywhere."

H.H.

(2) (Les Frères Karamazov) [Dramatic Revival] A: Jacques Copeau and Jean Croué; TR: Rosalind Ivan; D: Jacques Copeau; P: Theatre Guild; T: Guild Theatre; 1/3/27 (56)

Jacques Copeau, France's most famous and innovative director, staged this adaptation (spelled "Karamazov") of the great novel with a sparkling cast of Theatre Guild regulars. In 1919 Copeau's own troupe had done the play locally in French. "As a whole," wrote Richard Dana Skinner, "this is probably the most absorbing and authentic drama the New York stage has seen this year."

Alfred Lunt was very good as Dmitri. Lynn Fontanne was Grouchenka, a role she acted "with an amazing outpouring of sheer beauty, disclosing a depth of feeling and emotional power" (Skinner) unsuspected in her recent comic portraits. Dudley Digges was the repulsive Feodor, Edward G. Robinson acted a nearly perfect Smerdiakov, and Morris Carnovsky a touching Aliocha, but George Gaul's Ivan and Clare Eames's Katerina were not on a par with the rest of the company.

Copeau's adaptation was praised for its theatricality and was considered superior to the Moscow Art version. It took well over three hours to perform, though, occasionally dragged, and seemed "nebulous" (Brooks Atkinson) at times about "essential points in the story."

Edward G. Robinson recalled in his autobiography *All My Yesterdays* that one night, after playing a highly dramatic scene, he climbed the set's towering staircase and ripped open the palm of his hand on an exposed nail; although bleeding profusely, he gave no indication of his pain as he stood there during the remaining moments of the act. He later was stitched up and played for several days in a sling but at a matinee performance was in such agony that he had to be replaced, for the first time in his career, by an understudy.

BUBBLE ALONG [Revue/Blacks] T: Garrick Theatre: 6/3/30

A black revue so familiar in construction and execution that the *Times* called it "a shadowy and nondescript entertainment not worth the burnt cork fetched to meet the occasion." The show contained a chorus of a dozen young ladies "enthusiastically out of step," various comic duos, an act in which a spoon was made to dance in a decanter, and a number of songs.

BUCCANEER, THE [Comedy-Drama/Romance/Adventure/Period/Historical-Biographical] A: Maxwell Anderson and Laurence Stallings; D/P: Arthur Hopkins; DS: Robert Edmond Jones; T: Plymouth Theatre; 10/2/25 (20)

The authors of the tremendous hit *What Price Glory?* succeeded it with this tepidly received period romantic-comedy melodrama set in 1671 and picturing the romantic exploits of British naval commander Capt. Henry Morgan (William Farnum), whose conquests and pillaging along the Spanish main bring him into the presence of the beauteous former Lady Elizabeth, now Dona Lisa (Estelle Winwood), the wife of a Spaniard in Panama City. This naval buccaneer, having overreached his commission, is seized and brought back to London, but Charles II (Ferdinand Gottschalk), instead of hanging him, knights him and makes him deputy governor of Jamaica, where he and Lady Elizabeth can be together.

The overall impression was uneven. There was appreciation for much of the quasi-Shavian verbal dexterity, and the characters had a certain liveliness, but faulty construction brought the piece tumbling down. To Richard Dana Skinner, the authors were "not able to achieve that unity of mood and treatment which gives power and . . . sustained interest to a well-constructed play."

BUCKAROO [Comedy/Romance/Sex/Show Business/Crime] A: A. W. and E. L. Barker and Charles Beahan; D/P: Hamilton MacFadden; S: R. N. Robbins; T: Erlanger's Theatre; 3/17/29 (9)

Robert Littell summed up this flop as "sixty-five or more real cowboys, cowgirls, horses, donkeys in a confused, over-populated, badly acted and worse directed melodrama of rodeo life." Yet, Perriton Maxwell, among others, liked it as a "rather faithful picture of a Western rodeo."

It presented the clash between the clean-cut westerners of the rodeo and the Chicago floozies and gangsters they run into while appearing at that city's Soldier Field. Maxine Madison (Ruth Easton), a flashy golddigger, almost succeeds in separating bronco-rider Stray Murfee (James Bell) from his money, but spunky cowgirl Lee Irwin (Nydia Westman) sees to it that this fool and his money are not parted. Stray is shot by a gangster (Clyde Dilson) but still manages to win the championship and Lee's affections.

BULLDOG DRUMMOND [Drama/Crime/Mystery/British] A: "Sapper" (Cyril McNiele); D: Fred G. Latham; P: Charles B. Dillingham; T: Knickerbocker Theatre; 12/26/21 (162)

A rip-roaring melodrama from London, where it was a great hit starring Gerald Du Maurier. This exciting sleuther was the progenitor of a long line of popular detective films, both silent and talkie. Replete "with pistols, poisoned cigarettes, straitjackets, drugs, chloroform, electric doors, knives hurled through the air, and a stage fight so real that blood is drawn" (*Journal*), *Bulldog Drummond* proved that exciting hero-villain epics could still cause lines to form at Broadway box offices.

When Phyliss Benton (Dorothy Tetley) becomes suspicious of the goings on at the hospital next to her home, where her uncle (St. Clair Bayfield) is a patient, she calls in Bulldog Drummond (A. E. Matthews) after seeing his ad in a paper. Drummond, his aide (H. Franklin Bellamy), and Phyliss foil a trio of crooks who are holding a millionaire (George Barraud) prisoner, and Phyliss relaxes in the private detective's arms.

BULLY, THE [Drama/Crime/Romance] A: Julie Helene Percival and Calvin Clark; D: Walter Wilson; P: Mrs. Henry B. Harris; T: Hudson Theatre; 12/25/24 (36)

"[A] somewhat amusingly crude melodrama" (Alan Dale), "gaunt and slovenly drama" (Q. M.), and "a morass of clumsy incompetence" (Percy Hammond) were among the nasty epithets flung at this inflated piece starring Emmett Corrigan.

An overplayed crook drama with Corrigan as master-crook George Moare—
"the bully"—its plot had him contrive a nefarious scheme whereby he, his
bogus wife, Grace (Margaret Cusack), over whom he wields a strange power,
and his assistant crook Billy (James Bradbury, Jr.) take positions in the home
of the Wintons, a wealthy family in Tarrytown, where Moare is to be the secretary
to a young author (Barry Jones). Once inside the house they plan to rob it, but
the plot backfires since they actually have been lured to the home by the family
that knows Moare is the murderer of the late Mr. Winton. Moare and his crony
are caught, and romance flowers for Grace and young Winton.

BUNCH AND JUDY, THE [Musical/Romance/Show Business] B: Anne Caldwell and Hugh Ford; M: Jerome Kern; LY: Anne Caldwell; D: Fred G. Latham;
CH: Edward Royce; P: Charles Dillingham; T: Globe Theatre; 11/28/22 (65)
A poorly plotted, weakly scored, but exceptionally well produced and often
very funny musical comedy that gave Fred and Adele Astaire their biggest roles
yet in a Broadway show. Despite its weak points, the show's positive features
excited many critics; yet it was a dud with audiences and lasted only two months.
It told of Broadway operetta star Judy (Adele Astaire), who gives up her stage
career and moves to Scotland to marry a laird (Philip Tonge), whose Presbyterian
family and acquaintances look down on players. Visited in Scotland by her
former troupe members, Judy rejoins them, leaves her Scotch husband, and gets
married to her ex-leading man (Fred Astaire).
The "singularly dull, old-fashioned book" (Arthur Hornblow) was really an
excuse for comedy and singing and dancing and musical specialty numbers. The
Scotch setting allowed for songs and dances in kilts with bagpipes tooting. A
terrific Highland fling featuring Fred Astaire and Philip Tonge was a standout,
as was a sensational number in which Fred and Adele did a routine on a table
held high in the air by the chorus. During rehearsals of this tricky bit, the Astaires
were often dumped onto the ground since it was very difficult to hold the table
evenly. Astaire wanted the number cut, because he thought it wasn't practical,
but it turned out to be a highlight of the show.
Before the show arrived in New York, character comedian Joseph Cawthorn
fell and broke his leg. This caused an extensive rewrite, so that the brother and
sister team of Johnny and Ray Dooley could be written in in his place.

BUNK OF 1926 [Revue] B/LY: Gene Lockhart and Percy Waxman; M/D: Gene
Lockhart; ADD. M.: Deems Taylor and Robert Armbruster; CH: Adrian Perrin;
P: Talbot Productions, Inc.; T: Heckscher Theatre (OB); 2/16/26 (104)
An intimate satirical revue that began life at the Off-Broadway Heckscher
Theatre at the corner of Fifth Avenue and 104th Street and moved two months
later to Broadway's Broadhurst Theatre, with the addition of several new performers to the cast. The show was largely the brainchild of Gene Lockhart, who
performed in most of its sketches, cowrote its scenes and lyrics, composed its
music, and directed it. Joseph Wood Krutch thought it was "a fairly amusing

revue with little else but its liveliness to recommend it.'' The emphasis was on wit and personality, not on visual beauty and expense.

The sketches and songs were of the usual type, satirizing contemporary culture and manners. There was, for example, a takeoff on Spanish ballroom dancing, a parody of Hollywood, and one, called "A Modest Little Thing," in which Ruth Tester succeeded in "out-Lawrencing Gertrude Lawrence in that actress's own brand of naive-sophisticated ballad" (Helen Walker).

Bunk of 1926 had become the center of a controversy when some of its material proved salacious to the police, who ordered the show shut down. An injunction was granted allowing the revue to stay open, but before further action could be taken, the show closed for lack of ticket sales.

BURGOMASTER OF STILEMONDE, THE (Le Bourgmestre de Stile-monde) [Dramatic Revival] A: Maurice Maeterlinck; TR: Alexander Teixeria de Mattos; D/P: Sir John Martin-Harvey; T: Century Theatre; 11/15/23 (4)

As the third offering of his New York season, Sir John Martin-Harvey introduced Maeterlinck's 1918 antiwar drama. A Belgian Burgomaster (Martin-Harvey) willingly goes to his death before a German firing squad so that his townspeople may be spared reprisals for the murder of a German officer. The Burgomaster's son-in-law by a prewar marriage is a German officer crushed by the Kaiser's military machine when he finds himself head of his beloved father-in-law's execution squad.

The *Times* critic found Maeterlinck's play structurally weak, "with long stretches of inaction and loose thematic threads," and Wells Root called it a "melodrama woven with admirable restraint through a penetrating analysis of the German philosophy." This critic found Martin-Harvey's performance "exceptionally fine throughout, particularly as a display of versatility in contrast with the formal beauty of his *Oedipus*."

This play had been seen in New York in 1919 as *A Burgomaster of Belgium*.

H.H.

BURLESQUE [Comedy-Drama/Show Business/Marriage/Alcoholism] A: George Manker Watters and Arthur Hopkins; D/P: Arthur Hopkins; S: Cleon Throckmorton; T: Plymouth Theatre; 9/1/27 (372)

Barbara Stanwyck went in two years from a job as a cabaret singer, during which she mimicked well-known performers, to an understudy role in *Lily Sue* to a supporting role in *The Noose* to Broadway stardom as Bonny, Hal Skelly's wife in *Burlesque*. Skelly played Skid, an irresponsible, boozing, low comic-dancer who leaves his mate and partner behind on the circuit while he goes on to momentary fame on Broadway, a *Follies* girl on his arm. His deserted wife rejects the temptations of a wealthy cattle baron (Ralph Theodore) to return to her by-now debauched and fallen spouse, and the pair turn up in the last act dancing together in a touring burlesque show, the wife giving the clown the loving support he needs to keep from falling on his face.

A backstage drama in the tradition of *Broadway*, although far less melodramatic and much more sentimental, *Burlesque* was a play of mixed virtues. Brooks Atkinson found it clumsier than *Broadway* and burdened by a story "admittedly commonplace and scattered." Stark Young called it "a lovable, uneven play, often prettily written, sometimes genuinely touching."

Playing a small supporting role was Oscar Levant.

Burlesque had considerable difficulty in getting to Broadway. It originally had been written by George Manker Watters, a man familiar with the lives of burlesque performers; this was his first play. When Arthur Hopkins read it one Saturday evening, he was moved to spend all of the next day rewriting its second act. Watters read the revisions, the author of which was kept secret from him; only when he found the changes worthwhile did Hopkins decide to tell him who was responsible for them.

BUSINESS WIDOW, THE [Comedy/Business/Marriage/Sex/German] A: Alexander Engel and Hans Sassman; AD: Gladys Unger; D: Edward Elsner and Leo Ditrichstein; C: Helen Paul; P: Lee Shubert; T: Ritz Theatre; 12/10/23 (32)

Adapted from an unlisted mid-European original and transposed to a Manhattan setting, this business/marital comedy found few friends. The story of a silly, spendthrift young wife's (Lola Fisher) intrusions upon her older husband's (Leo Ditrichstein) Wall Street business and her flirtations with a Greek adventurer and an interior decorator was deemed of "an artificiality and unreality incredible" by John Corbin. Percy Hammond commented, "It has its graces of speech and motion" and as an entertainment was "well up among the routine second-stringers."

H.H.

BUSYBODY, THE [Comedy/Family/Romance] A: Dorrance Davis; D: Clarke Silvernail; P: George Choos; T: Bijou Theatre; 9/29/24 (65)

A raucous, fast, and furious comedy that made watching the actors "hop around . . . like watching flies trying to extricate themselves from tanglefoot," according to Frank Vreeland. "*The Busybody*," declared the *Times*, "is a farce of incredible crudeness. In trying to tell three or four stories at once it tells no one of them clearly."

It was about a madcap family living in a Riverside Drive apartment, with a busybody of a mother (Ada Lewis), a headstrong daughter (Mildred Florence), chorus girls, private detectives, stolen jewelry, intrusive neighbors, romantic complications, a drunken Swedish servant (Florence Denham), and happy endings.

BUTTER AND EGG MAN, THE [Comedy/Theatre/Business] A: George S. Kaufman; D: James Gleason; P: Crosby Gaige; T: Longacre Theatre; 9/23/25 (241)

"[A] thoroughly amusing farce-comedy dealing with the adventures of a provincial come-on who puts his money into the theatrical business" was George

Jean Nathan's assessment of this hit show in which George S. Kaufman satirized things of which his own experience as a playwright and director had given him firsthand knowledge. The play was chosen as a Best Play of the season. It was Kaufman's sole effort sans collaborator.

Gregory Kelly played Peter Jones, the "butter and egg man" (defined by *Time* as "An individual from out of town with the milk of human kindness in his heart and the root of all evil in his trousers pocket"), a young fellow from Chillicothe, Ohio, with $22,000, who comes to the offices of New York producer Joseph Lehman (Robert Middlemass) and soon has all of his savings tied up in the production of a meretricious piece of hokum called *Her Lesson*. The play flops in Syracuse, but Peter, the naive hick, assumes control over the entire production as sole producer and turns it into a smash hit on Broadway, where its popularity is in danger of growing by leaps and bounds should the police department decide to censor it. Peter also has an obligatory love affair with stenographer Jane Weston (Sylvia Field).

"The patter is bright, abounding in 'wise cracks,' " declared the *Times*, "and the lines are highly charged with sardonic, ill-mannered humor. The structure . . . is quite as full of surprises and entertainment."

BUTTON, BUTTON [Comedy/Mental Illness/Romance/Family] A: Maurice Clark; D: Maurice Clark and H. C. Potter; P: Herman Shumlin i/a/w Mrs. Potter and George Haight; T: Bijou Theatre; 10/22/29 (5)

Button, Button went down the tubes in only five performances despite fine actors in its cast such as Anne Shoemaker, Lynne Overman, and Alison Skipworth. Overman played "Button" Woodhouse, a youth considered to have his family's loosest screws. His aunt (Skipworth), a Freudian faddist, has him released from an institution in order to practice psychoanalysis on him. In a very funny scene she is embarrassed by some of his suggestive revelations. Finally, "Button" elopes with the girl he loves rather than marry the girl his aunt has picked out for him.

Despite its short run, the play did manage to get off some timely satire at the expense of Freudian ideas. However, *Time* called it a one-act stretched to three-act proportions, and the *Times* suggested that it "shares a common failing of being not quite bright," aside from a few glimmers of humor.

BUY, BUY, BABY [Comedy/Sex/Legacy/Family] A: Russell Medcraft and Norma Mitchell; SC: a play by Francis R. Bellamy and Lawton Mackall; P: Bertram Harrison; T: Princess Theatre; 10/7/26 (12)

An inoffensive sex farce that aroused some laughs as well as blushes. Its excellent ensemble was headed by Alison Skipworth as a middle-aged spinster, who, feeling threatened by the population explosion of the Orient, proposes to her childless family that the first of them to have a baby will get $1 million of her money. Various couples rush into action to win the prize, and various amusing situations arise; the money goes at last to a cousin (Maurice Burke), who had been secretly wed to a stenographer (Shirley Booth) and already had produced an infant.

The critics joshed the piece for its racy theme, and some blamed it for indecency. Its humor was blatant, its performance broad, its stage life brief.

BUZZARD, THE [Drama/Mystery/Crime/Politics] A: Courtenay Savage; D: Melville Burke; P: Knox Winslow, Inc.; T: Broadhurst Theatre; 3/14/28 (13)

"*The Buzzard* is a murder mystery, third class, pretty poorly put together," Gilbert W. Gabriel informed his readers. It was intend⌐ ⌐o star tennis champ "Big" Bill Tilden, who had appeared in the author's ⌐ast outing, but the athlete dropped out before the opening.

The mystery involves discovering the killer of a powerful New England district attorney (Eugene Powers), a hated graft taker, who was also the owner of the town newspaper. As in most such exercises, the most suspicious characters turn out to be innocent, and the guilty party emerges as a surprise. The device used to flush the perpetrator was to pretend that the victim had not, indeed, been killed at all, an implausible notion given the fact that the murderer was an intimate member of the household. The killer turns out to be the sympathetic old housekeeper (Clara Blandick) for whom everyone else offers to take the rap.

BUZZIN' AROUND [Musical/Small Town/Theatre/Romance/Family] B: William Morrissey and Edward Madden; M/LY/D/P: William Morrissey; T: Casino Theatre; 7/6/20 (23)

Buzzin' Around was called by contemporaries a "revue" and a "vaudeville," but its semblance of a book allows it to be classed as a musical comedy. It told of a stern father (Walter Wilson) who opposes an actors' colony springing up in his town and of a love affair between his daughter (Elizabeth Bruce) and a singer (Donald Roberts). A benefit performance is arranged, and the show turns into a series of specialty acts. The three Barrymores were burlesqued, as was Theda Bara, but the former was funny enough to lift "the piece out of the class of the ordinary musical revue," according to Arthur Hornblow. Will Morrissey mimicked George M. Cohan, Al Jolson, and Sam Bernard. Magic acts, jugglers, a Chinese wedding spectacle, and a travesty of *The Mikado* also shared the spotlight.

M.M.-C.

BY REQUEST [Comedy/Sex/Marriage] A: J. C. and Elliott Nugent; D: Sam Forrest; P: George M. Cohan; T: Hudson Theatre; 9/27/28 (28)

Three members of the Nugent family performed in this piece written by two of them. The third was Elliott's wife, Norma Lee. Elliott and Norma played a husband and wife from a small town, where he is a journalist. He goes alone to New York City, seeking employment in his profession, and flirts with a blonde literary agent (Veree Teasdale), whom he accompanies in a Pullman to Bar Harbor. His wife accepts the situation but hides in the Pullman and takes her spouse back when he chickens out at the prospect of actually sinning with the other woman.

For all of the ability of its actors, it was "only mildly entertaining and quite harmless," wrote Joseph Wood Krutch. *Time* pointed to its "trite plot and uneven script."

BY THE WAY [Revue/British] B: Ronald Jeans and Harold Simpson; M: Vivian Ellis; LY: Graham John; D: Jack Hulbert; P: A. L. Erlanger; T: Gaiety Theatre; 12/28/25 (177)

A hit intimate revue from the shores of Albion with Jack Hulbert and his wife, Cicely Courtneidge, at its helm. Courtneidge was "An accomplished co-medienne, a clever dancer, [and] a bewitching personality," and Hulbert, "a tall, lean Englishman, is a capital comedian and clever dancer" (Arthur Horn-blow). The show charmed by its clean language and sketches and lack of nudity, novel touches in a decade when flesh and innuendo were staples of the revue form.

The most delightful comedy piece on the varied program was "Greek as She is Taught," in which Courtneidge played a young English lad being kept after school to take a Greek lesson from the master, played by Hulbert, as the sounds of boys outside playing cricket keep interfering with the demeanor of teacher and pupil. This was "one of the most uproariously amusing scenes Broadway has laughed at for some time," opined Hornblow.

On 4/26/26 a spring edition was produced, with about one-fifth new material, in one scene of which, "Passing the Time," Hulbert played a dopey groom who erroneously buys a five shilling clock as an antique. In "Seeing is Believing," he was a blushing near-sighted military officer who is made the butt of ridicule while he is trying to discipline his men.

BYE, BYE, BARBARA [Musical/Romance] B: Sidney Toler and Alonzo Price; M: Monte Carlo and Alma Sanders; P: Adolphe Mayer and Theodore Ham-merstein, Inc.; T: National Theatre; 8/25/24 (16)

A dreadful little musical said to have opened in New York without benefit of an out-of-town tryout because of a Boston stagehands' strike. *Bye, Bye, Barbara* recorded the travails of a circus balloonist, the Great Karloff (Jack Hazzard), fleeing the sheriff for failure to pay his alimony bills, and those of Barbara Palmer (Janet Velie), whose dad (Albert Sackett) won't let her marry movie actor Stanley Howard (Arthur Burckly) until the latter puts up $5,000 to prove his financial security.

Jack Hazzard got a few desperate laughs, and Lillian Fitzgerald interpolated a vaudeville-like routine in which she meowed like a cat, but the show was generally a sorry affair. Percy Hammond wrote, "The music . . . is fairly satisfactory, but the libretto is a subject for despair. A dull anecdote, feebly recited, it limps through two long acts unrelieved by little of anything in the way of jollity."

BYE, BYE, BONNIE [Musical/Politics/Prohibition/Romance/Prison] B: Louis Simon and Bide Dudley; M: Albert Von Tilzer; D: Edgar J. MacGregor; P: L. Lawrence Weber; T: Ritz Theatre; 1/13/27 (125)

Dorothy Burgess furthered her reputation with her fresh and natural charm in this so-so musical that Joseph Wood Krutch thought possessed of ''a genuinely amusing book'' about a soap manufacturer (Louis Simon) who gets arrested during a raid on a speakeasy, spends a month in jail on Welfare Island, changes from a conservative Prohibitionist to a liberal Wet, gets elected to Congress on that platform, and sees both his daughter and his secretary (Burgess) wind up with the fellows of their choice.

This was ''the usual musical comedy unusually well done,'' declared *Time*. The plot showed ''the lamentable results of musical comedy in-breeding, and the music [echoed] the scores of journeyman melody,'' wrote the *Times*. Among the hardworking dancers who danced ''every tune until it is ragged'' (*Times*) was Ruby Keeler.

C

CAESAR AND CLEOPATRA [Dramatic Revival] A: George Bernard Shaw; D: Philip Moeller; S: Frederick Jones III; C: Aline Bernstein; P: Theatre Guild; T: Guild Theatre; 4/13/25 (128)

In 1906 New York first saw this major opus from the pen of George Bernard Shaw. It was seen again in 1913 and then once more in this 1925 Theatre Guild revival done as the premiere staging at the attractive new Guild Theatre. A notable feature of the opening night occurred when President Coolidge in Washington, D.C., pressed a button that turned on the theatre's lights. Shaw's play was greeted as a masterpiece, but the production was a considerable disappointment.

Shaw's witty response to Shakespeare's *Antony and Cleopatra* and *Julius Caesar*, over which the Irish playwright claimed intellectual superiority because of his depiction of the Roman general as a purveyor of his ideas of the Nietzschian superman, was viewed by Stark Young as, "from the standpoint of imagination and theatrical and intellectual contrivance and invention, the greatest of his works."

Mounted with a new prologue and with sumptuous sets, the play ran four hours, and much of it seemed tedious because of inadequacies in the performances. There was a feeling that the simpler virtues of the Forbes-Robertson "ancient front parlor species of production" (George Jean Nathan) had been closer to the playwright's aims.

Lionel Atwill as Caesar found very few who approved of his performance, and Helen Hayes completely lacked the sensual appeal needed for the role. "Miss Hayes is a nice little girl," wrote Nathan, "who suggests sex no more than a rabbit suggests the Archbishop of Canterbury."

Helen Hayes, reportedly, had so wanted the role of the Egyptian temptress that she was willing to do it without salary (she settled for a handsome one, nonetheless). Her drive to succeed in the part was signaled by her attending the first rehearsal with all her lines perfectly memorized. Despite the critics' belief in Miss Hayes's lack of sensuality, her appearance in Aline Bernstein's sensual costumes is said to have so enchanted playwright Charles MacArthur that he began to court her and ultimately made her Mrs. MacArthur.

CAFÉ DE DANSE (La Maison de danses) [Drama/Night Club/ Romance/ Show Business/French] A: Fernand Noziere and Hans Mueller; AD: Clarke Silvernail, Eugenie Leontovich, and Helen Mitchell; SC: Paul Reboux' novel; D: Gregory Ratoff; CH: Anatole Bourman; P: Ben Bernie and Phil Baker; T: Forrest Theatre; 1/15/29 (31)

The Café de Danse, a Barcelona cabaret run by famous ex-dancer Senora Tomasa (Alison Skipworth), was the locale for this adaptation of the popular 1909 French play *La Maison de danses*. One critic called Tomasa a "combined Texas Guinan, Mae West and Helen Morgan of Spain." Business has been suffering since dancer Dolores (Enid Romany), making little money, left for the brighter lights of Paris, where she married banker Solomon Rinkleman (Gregory Ratoff). Working as a drudge at the cabaret is Estrellita (Trini), who is in love with dancer Luisito (Martin Burton), although Tomasa's oily son (Leonard Ceeley) won't leave her be. Dolores returns but refuses to perform, so Estrellita goes on and is a sensation.

The music for this "Frightfully ham" (*Time*) piece was played by Ben Bernie and his famed dance band. "The play never quite comes to life," noted the *Times*. The last eight performances of the piece were under the title *House of Dance*.

CAIN [Dramatic Revival] A: Lord Byron; M: Charles J. McDermott; D: Walter Hartwig; DS: Basset Jones and Alexander Wyckoff; P: Manhattan Little Theatre Club; T: Lenox Little Theatre (OB); 4/8/25 (12)

Although written in 1821 Lord Byron's dramatic poem about the killing of Abel by Cain was never produced professionally in English before this version by an Off-Broadway experimental group was given. It once had been considered a controversial work of unorthodox ideas, but this was of negligible import in 1925. Essentially a closet drama, it received a simple but extremely imaginative embodiment (it was played behind a scrim) on a cramped little stage. For the most part, the critics treated it as an interesting experiment.

The play's first and third acts are set in the Garden of Eden, and the second act shows the airborn Cain (William P. Carleton) and Lucifer (Albert Howson) visiting Hades. The *Evening Post* declared that the play's "poetical points . . . are as true and stirring as the day they were written." Some, though, found it ponderous, nondramatic, and talky.

CALL OF LIFE, THE (Der Ruf des Lebens) [Drama/Period/Crime/Romance/ Military/Sex/Austrian] A: Arthur Schnitzler; AD: Dorothy Donnelly; D: Dudley Digges; S: Jo Mielziner; P: Actors' Theatre; T: Comedy Theatre; 10/9/25 (19)

The critics were unanimous in praising this play's first act as "as devastating a piece of writing as the present season is likely to offer'' (John Mason Brown) and then proceeding to denigrate the latter two acts, especially the third, for having gone to pieces.

The Actors' Theatre staging was extremely capable, although somewhat sentimentalized, but the ponderously depressing play, ''a searching inquiry into whether life is a dream, a tragedy or a farce'' (Arthur Hornblow), found little favor.

''[T]his romantic tragedy of cloying melancholy'' (*Times*), set in Vienna in 1850, presented the story of Marie (Eva Le Gallienne), who murders her ailing, tyrannical old father (Egon Brecher) so that she may have sex with a young officer (Derek Glynne) before he, with his regiment, departs on a suicide mission. She witnesses at her lover's rooms the shooting by a colonel (Hermann Lieb) of his wife for having committed adultery with the same man. The officer kills himself, and another death ensues when Marie's consumptive cousin (Katherine Alexander) passes on.

CALL THE DOCTOR [Comedy/Marriage/Sex] A: Jean Archibald; D/P: David Belasco; T: Empire Theatre; 8/31/20 (129)

A false and unpleasant comedy about ''marriage doctor'' Joan Deering (Janet Beecher), who is called to the home of Howard Mowbray (William Morris). Howard is bored with his wife, Catherine (Charlotte Walker). Deering advises Catherine to ''seem to want to get rid of him.'' She tells her to buy new clothes, go to parties, take long trips away from home, and suggest a divorce to her husband. The instant result is Howard's renewed ardor.

Although the play betrayed a viewpoint on domesticity and masculine nature ''oftener found in rowdy songs at roofgardens,'' balked Alexander Woollcott, director David Belasco managed to salvage the play and, according to Heywood Broun, ''made it seem, for at least an act, better than it actually is.'' As for the theme, the critics questioned whether the Band-Aid approach would heal any marriage. They voted to let Mowbray follow through with the divorce.

M.M.-C.

CAMEL THROUGH THE NEEDLE'S EYE, THE (Velbloud uchem jehly) [Drama/Business/Sex/Romance/Family/Czechoslovakian] A: Frantisek Langer; AD/D: Philip Moeller; S: Lee Simonson; P: Theatre Guild; T: Martin Beck Theatre; 4/15/29 (195)

A commercially successful Theatre Guild offering that most critics refused to take seriously and the success of which they laid at the feet of the Guild's distinguished production personnel. It was a Czech import and was set in Prague, where Susi (Miriam Hopkins) is the illegitimate daughter of a cellar-dwelling family that makes its living by the father's (Henry Travers) feigning fainting spells on the street before rich people and then gaining their money via their sympathy. One such victim is Alik (Elliot Cabot), a wealthy man's tongue-tied son, who finds Susi and begins to live with her; three months pass, and she is no longer ignorant but has gained shrewdness and sophistication, with a high stock-market batting average to boot. Alik's father (Claude Rains) and former fiancée (Mary Kennedy) attempt to break up the pair, but when Susi is instrumental in setting up a model dairy, she and Alik get married and permanently bond their love.

It was an artificial, exaggerated comedy to Richard Dana Skinner, and Robert Littell commented, "There are pleasant and original bits all the way through, but it is a tossed off effort, always empty and quite often dull."

CAMEL'S BACK, THE [Comedy/Family/Sex/Mental Illness/British] A: Somerset Maugham; D: Edgar Selwyn; S: Clifford B. Pember; P: Selwyns; T: Vanderbilt Theatre; 11/13/23 (15)

Somerset Maugham chose his title not from the cliché about the straw that broke the camel's back but from Polonius's answer to Hamlet, " 'tis like a camel indeed." In Maugham's story, an autocratic English barrister (Charles Cherry) and would-be M.P., belittles his wife (Violet Kemble Cooper), tries to bully her sister (Joan Maclean) into marrying a middle-aged crony instead of the young man she loves, and nags his mother (Louise Closser Hale) to move from the hotel whose ambiance she enjoys into the family home. The wife leads the family in a revolt aimed at making the barrister believe he's insane, and after briefly revolting himself by pretending to pursue the family cook, he learns his lesson and gives everyone what they want.

Most critics found the well-acted play an airy trifle; there was general agreement that the first act was very good, the second pallid, and the third fairly strong. John Corbin was disturbed by the production approach, which he argued failed to take advantage of the text's innate possibilities for farce.

H.H.

CAMILA QUIROGA AND THE ARGENTINE PLAYERS T: Manhattan Opera House (OB); 12/8/27

A company of actors led by Argentina's leading actress, Camila Quiroga, appeared in a Spanish-language repertory offering South American, Spanish, and French plays for one performance each. The only plays of theirs reviewed in the English-language press were *Broken Wings* (*Con las alas rotas*), *La fuerza ciega*, *La serpiente*, and *¡Bendita seas!* and even these plays were barely noticed. Entries for these works are found in this volume; other plays presented were *Los mirasoles* (*The Sunflower*), an Argentinian comedy by Julio Sanchez Gardel, 12/12/27; *La virtud sospechosa* (*Suspicious Virtue*), a Spanish comedy by Jacinto Benavente, 12/13/27; *El professor de buenos modales*, a Spanish translation of a French comedy by Paul Armont and Marcel Gerbidon, *L'École des cocottes*, known in New York from its English-language production in 1922 as *The Goldfish*, 12/14/27; another French comedy, *Roberto et Mariana* (*Roberto et Marianne*), this one by Paul Geraldy, 12/15/27; *El zarpazo* (*The Claw*), a respected Colombian comedy-drama by Antonio Alvarez Lleres, 12/16/27; *Los nuevos* *yernos* (*Modern Sons-in-Law*), a Spanish comedy by Jacinto Benavente, 12/17/27; and *La Tendresse*, Henri Bataille's French play, 12/18/27, seen in New York in 1922 in an English version under the original French title.

CANARY DUTCH [Drama/Prison/Crime/Family] A: Willard Mack; SC: a story by John Morosco; D/P: David Belasco; T: Lyceum Theatre; 9/8/25 (39)

A crook drama with gobs of maudlin sentiment heaped on for good measure, written by the actor who played the leading role. Swiss counterfeiter Herman Strauss (nicknamed "Canary Dutch") has served twenty years in the federal penitentiary, where he has long been under the impression that his daughter is dead. He takes up residence upon release at a home for ex-cons, where, after disposing of a man (Albert Gran) who tries to blackmail him into committing another act of counterfeiting, he learns that his daughter (Catherine Dale Owen) runs the very abode at which he is staying.

Mack gave an admirable performance as the aging foreign-accented hero, and his play had considerable vitality in the dialogue, but that was about all it offered. Arthur Hornblow deemed it a "crude, uninteresting old melodrama" unworthy of David Belasco's attention.

(1) CANDIDA [Dramatic Revival] A: George Bernard Shaw; D: Ellen Von Volkenburg; P: Maurice Browne; T: Greenwich Village Theatre (OB); 3/22/22 (43)

Maurice Browne and Ellen Von Volkenburg, coproducers and actors, were proposing to establish a repertory company in New York when they staged this revival of what Alexander Woollcott called "the best play Shaw ever wrote." Ludwig Lewisohn, while admitting that this production of *Candida* was "imperfect," was nevertheless impressed with the company's intelligence, altruism, and clarification of the comedy.

It was generally agreed that Von Volkenburg was seriously inadequate in the title role. She "dwelt heavily, almost lugubriously," noted Arthur Hornblow, "on that wholly delightful heroine's meditative side; her voice aiding in this effect by delivering every line in bible-reading tones." Browne was clearly too old for Marchbanks, and he did nothing particularly noteworthy with the role, but Moroni Olsen was fine as Morrell.

The production was passable for most, but Woollcott thought the play had been "wrenched and distorted."

(2) D: Dudley Digges; S: Woodman Thompson; P: Actors' Theatre; T: Forty-eighth Street Theatre; 12/12/24 (148)

A superlative revival that awed the critics by the depth and polish of each actor's performance. "Both as to ensemble and individual performances it is a production worthy of any theatre in the world," glowed Arthur Hornblow. First put on at three weeks of special matinees, the work was recognized as "one of the few notable productions of the season'' and was mounted commercially for what turned out to be a profitable run.

The play, unlike the updating of recent revivals, was acted in the costumes and settings of the 1890s, when it was written. This was pleasing but not more so than the excellence with which it was enacted. The Morrell of Pedro De Cordoba and the Prossie of Clare Eames were exemplary, but the critics split over Richard Bird's Marchbanks. As Candida, Katharine Cornell, who was still appearing in *Tiger Cats* when *Candida*'s matinees began, achieved one of her most distinguished triumphs. She offered Stark Young ''a deep revelation of the part. Her frail presence had in it something of the light of another world. She was strong, not with womanly aplomb and maternal astuteness, but with an exquisite power to feel and understand.''

After a brief hiatus, the production reopened with Peggy Wood at the Comedy Theatre on 11/9/25. It had twenty-four performances. Wood was, until then, known primarily as a musical comedy actress, and there were those who thought that casting her as Candida was foolish when many serious actresses would have given their eye teeth to play the role. Wood even took it upon herself to convince director Dudley Digges of her suitability. Being a member of the company, she wrote in her autobiography *How Young You Look*, was a revelation. ''Never but once besides have I experienced such orchestral balance of playing . . . led as it was by the invisible conductor of a profound respect for the material to be presented.'' Although her reviews were warm and encouraging, they were not as ecstatic as had been those of Cornell. The *Times* said, ''Miss Wood's performance was adequate, but lacked the perfect Mona Lisa serenty [*sic*] and wisdom which this very difficult part demands.'' Stark Young said that she had made the character ''simpler'' than had Cornell but by that token brought it ''closer to what Bernard Shaw meant by this character in relation to the other characters and to the situation and theme of the play.''

(1) CANDLE LIGHT (Serata d'inverno; Kleine Komödie) [Sex/Italian Language/German] A: Siegfried Geyer; D: Guiseppe Sterni; P: Teatro d'Arte; T: Bijou Theatre; 4/6/29

Candle Light went to New York in September 1929; however, a little noted Italian-language presentation of the German comedy had been seen shortly before under the title *Serata d'inverno (A Winter's Night)*. It was produced by a New York-based company of Italian players led by Giuseppe Sterni. Walter Littlefield wrote that ''Geyer has taken the old paraphrenalia of cross-purpose and impersonation and rendered them superlatively fruitful.'' The troupe was praised for an excellent performance in which director Sterni played the valet, Rodolfo Badaloni acted the master, Daisy T. Raselli was the maid, and Dina Lanzini undertook the mistress. Plot details are given in the following entry.

(2) [Dramatic Revival] AD: P. G. Wodehouse; D/P: Gilbert Miller; T: Empire Theatre; 9/30/29 (129)

The glamorous presences of Gertrude Lawrence, Leslie Howard, and Reginald Owen were almost sufficient in themselves to make this light comedy palatable in its English version; it was deemed a not-altogether-effective romantic "harlequinade" that was founded on a charming, if familiar, premise but that ran out of invention too soon to be wholly satisfying.

Howard (who was replaced by Ernest Glendenning shortly into the run) played a valet, and Owen played his princely master (based on the Austrian Archduke Rudolf). The former impersonates the master to carry off an assignation with the alluring noblewoman (Lawrence) he has invited over, while the master, returning unexpectedly, assumes the valet's livery to help the game along. However, the valet's target ultimately reveals that she too is masquerading, being a parlor maid who has donned her mistress's (Betty Shuster) clothes as part of a prank.

As John Hutchens pointed out, the acting was the major force motivating audience interest; Joseph Wood Krutch maintained that the play "is thin and not tremendously original, but it is easy, skilful, and acted with exceptional suavity." Lawrence was making her New York debut in a nonmusical play; George Jean Nathan found her "a cloying and mannered comedienne," but the *Times* said she was not only beautiful but "lithe and vital and steadily interesting."

The play, seen in England with Yvonne Arnaud before arriving locally, had been titled there *By Candle-Light*. When Wodehouse, the adapter, was asked what relevance the title had to the plot, he responded that it derived from an Austrian proverb, "Choose neither women nor linen by candle-light."

Lawrence, in her autobiography, *A Star Danced*, recalls a performance at which she surprised and delighted Leslie Howard by substituting real sherry for the weak, poor-tasting cold tea provided by the property man. She says the acting of herself and Howard improved noticeably from the substitution and that she and her co-star were actually getting high when the scene drew to an end. Elsewhere, referring to her bow as a straight dramatic actress in this play, she quotes the telegram she received from Noël Coward: "LEGITIMATE AT LAST, DARLING. WON'T MOTHER BE PLEASED?"

CAPE COD FOLLIES [Revue] B/LY/D: Stewart Baird; M: Alexander Fogarty; CH: John Lonergan; P: Cape Playhouse; T: Bijou Theatre; 9/18/29 (29)

An intimate revue originating at the Cape Cod Playhouse and brought to Broadway, where its lack of production expertise made it fair game for the critics, despite a number of excellent ingredients. Cape Cod itself was the subject of much of its humor and song, but it was not funny enough, nor was its music memorable enough, to sustain a run. It did have a freshness and vivacity, however, that made its defects less serious than they might otherwise have been. The most outstanding part of it was a four-vignette scene in which Peter Jorrey impersonated Queen Victoria; also effective were the marionette manipulations of Bobby Fulton and Peggy Ellis's piano playing. A takeoff on Eugene O'Neill's plays contained the line "Go to bed mother and stop gazing beyond the horizon at that there dynamo.'' The *Times* called it "a curious and not highly satisfying mixture of the amateur and professional.'' Lloyd Nolan debuted on Broadway in it.

CAPE SMOKE [Drama/Africa/Tropics/Romance/Sex] A: Walter Archer Frost; D: A. E. Anson; P: Charles K. Gordon; T: Martin Beck Theatre; 2/16/25 (105)

George Jean Nathan may have called this play "a boiler-factory melodrama of the African veldt that substitutes noise for excitement,'' but a number of critics were excited by its chilling episodes, although ultimately faulting it for implausible and contrived plotting, especially in its third and final act. There were witch-doctor curses, venomous snake bites, "pistol shots, and thunder bolts, maniacal convulsions, intrigue and romance'' (Percy Hammond), not to mention sexual titillation in this lurid play.

Cape Smoke was named after the rotgut whiskey that is drunk in the veldt where its febrile story is laid. Four financially troubled Englishmen seeking to flee the nasty place for home embroil an honest Texas millionaire (James Rennie) in a plot to get him so frightened by a trumped up witch-doctor's curse that he will turn over a large sum to them in order to escape with his life. Meanwhile, he falls for the sister of one of them (Ruth Shepley) and eventually uncovers the plot.

CAPONSACCHI [Drama/Period/Italy/Crime/Trial/Romance/Religion] A: Arthur Goodrich and Rose A. Palmer; SC: Robert Browning's poem "The Ring and the Book''; D/P: Walter Hampden; DS: Claude Bragdon; T: Hampden's Theatre; 10/26/26 (271)

Robert Browning's respected poetic treatment of an actual Roman murder case was successfully transformed into this period melodrama set in seventeenth-century Rome. Some of Browning's own blank verse was scattered through the effective play, named after the central character, a noble, spiritually enlightened monk well played by Walter Hampden.

The action begins at a Vatican trial to which Pope Innocent III (Stanley Howlett) is a hidden witness and where the facts behind the murder of Pompilia (Edith Barrett) and her parents are brought out; Caponsacchi begins to explain his role in the events, and a flashback moves the story to Arezzo, where the details of the monk's tragic love for the unhappily wed Pompilia are depicted. When the monk tries to save the woman from a husband (Ernest Rowan) who is slowly killing her, the husband has the man exiled, kills the wife and her parents, and puts the blame on Caponsacchi. The court finds the monk innocent and the husband guilty.

Theatrical, old-fashioned, and obvious it was, but it gripped audiences with its robust story and vivid illusionism. "It proves once more,'' said Gilbert W. Gabriel, "that vitality is not a modern discovery, and that brave deeds and flashing swords have not lost their power strangely to move.''

The play had been a part of Hampden's touring repertory under the title *The*

Ring and the Book, but he changed the name for the New York premiere. Hampden revived it in repertory on 1/24/28, on 11/19/28, and on 11/5/29, bringing its total number of Broadway performances to 384.

CAPRICE (Mit der Lieb Spielen) [Comedy/Sex/Romance/Family/Austrian] A: Sil-Vara; AD/D: Philip Moeller; S: Aline Bernstein; P: Theatre Guild; T: Guild Theatre; 12/31/28 (178)

A frivolous, sophisticated Austrian comedy that benefited enormously from the supersmooth direction of Philip Moeller and the acting genius of the Lunts.

Alfred Lunt played Counselor Albert Von Echardt, who had an illegitimate child with the virtuous Amalia (Lily Cahill) sixteen years earlier; Amalia now brings the boy (Douglass Montgomery) to his father for guidance. Lynn Fontanne was Ilse Von Ilsen, Albert's current romance, a witty, jealous woman, who suspects Amalia of wanting Albert for herself. After trying several ploys to rid Albert of the idealistic youth she succeeds by getting the son to develop a passion for her and then by dashing his hopes by revealing her long-standing intimacy with his father.

British critic St. John Ervine, guesting for the *World*, had never seen the Lunts before. He wrote, "Mr. Lunt's performance was a delightful exhibition of accomplished comedy acting, a fine and accurately observed show of manners. Miss Fontanne startled me with her brilliant artifice. I had not expected to see anything so good. . . . No wonder people are proud of this brilliant pair. They are destined to be prominent in the history of American comedy." Of the play, Robert Littell commented, "It makes much out of very little with sophisticated gaiety, it has a Viennese high polish and wit, and also the Viennese inbreeding and tendency to run in a narrow groove."

CAPTAIN APPLEJACK [Comedy/Romance/Crime/Fantasy/Adventure/British] A/D: Walter Hackett; P: Sam H. Harris; T: Cort Theatre; 12/30/21 (366)

Charles Hawtree starred in this "sure fire hit" (Stephen Rathbun) in London before it came to Broadway with Wallace Eddinger excellent in the title role. A burlesque melodrama produced with an exceptionally fine cast, it was a great success and ran a year. Reminiscent of the fantasy world of *Peter Pan* and the farce adventures of *Seven Keys to Baldpate*, *Captain Applejack* had "enough original humor, surprise and action to make it go. . . . ," according to Arthur Hornblow; it was "good fun as well as good Freud," in Alexander Woollcott's view.

Eddinger portrayed Ambrose Applejohn, a bored English gentleman who longs underneath his dull exterior for a life of dashing excitement. The plot embroils him in an unsought adventure with a gang of thieves; in the midst of events he falls asleep and dreams himself his own swaggering pirate ancestor, Captain Applejack. He cleverly puts down a shipboard mutiny before the always fast-moving action shifts once more to reality and concludes with more adventures among the crooks in Applejohn's home and the ward (Phoebe Foster) with whom he discovers he is in love. Having had thrills to last a lifetime, he plans to live a life of quiet domesticity.

CAPTAIN JINKS [Musical/Romance/Military] B/P: Frank Mandel and Laurence Schwab; M: Lewis E. Gensler and Stephen Jones; LY: B. G. DeSylva; SC: Clyde Fitch's play *Captain Jinks of the Horse Marines*; D: Edgar J. MacGregor; CH: Sammy Lee; S: Frederick Jones III; C: Kiviette; T: Martin Beck Theatre; 9/8/25 (167)

Captain Jinks of the Horse Marines, the 1901 Clyde Fitch comedy hit that made a star of Ethel Barrymore, was seen in a musicalized version in this thinly humorous show produced with beautiful sets and costumes and brought so up to date (the original was set in 1872), including Charleston numbers, that "none who saw the original play would recognize" it (Louis Bromfield). Louise Brown was in the Barrymore role, and her looks and dancing ability were plusses on the show's behalf.

Brown played Madame Trentoni, a Trenton, New Jersey, dancer (she was a singer in the original), who arrives on these shores under the guise of being a French theatrical star and proceeds to engage in a romance with a young man (J. Harold Murray) who is, unlike the horse marine hero of the comedy, merely a member of the Citizens' Marine Corps allowed to don uniforms only on Armistice Day. After various complications, the couple live happily ever after.

Reviews were mixed, but the show caught on. The *Times* liked its music and visuals but deplored its lack of humor. Arthur Hornblow deemed it "commonplace."

CAPTIVE, THE (La Prisonniere) [Drama/Homosexuality/Sex/Marriage/French] A: Eduoard Bourdet; AD: Arthur Hornblow, Jr.; D: Gilbert Miller; S: William E. Castle; P: Charles Frohman, Inc.; T: Empire Theatre; 9/29/26 (160)

A sensationally controversial drama, the first serious treatment of lesbianism seen on Broadway. Bourdet's play, given an accomplished production with a superlative Helen Menken as the doomed victim of a homosexual love, stirred much debate, but the critics were nearly unanimous in their praise for it as a potent work of theatre art. George Jean Nathan termed it "the most finely wrought drama of sex that has come out of France since Porto-Riche's *Amoureuse*." There was commendation for the well-made play's stringent honesty, its lack of sentimentality, its perceptive characterizations, its depth of understanding, and its avoidance of special pleading. A few, like Richard Dana Skinner, voiced their fears that plays like this could "do incalculable harm" to immature minds.

Bourdet's fable examined the tragedy of Irene (Menken), who becomes engaged to Jacques Virieu (Basil Rathbone), of whom she appears to be quite fond. As the first act closes she receives a bouquet of violets, which she kisses passionately. (There was a dropoff in the purchase of violets by women once the play's theme was widely publicized.) Jacques soon has reason to suspect his fiancée of loving another man; he believes it may be his good friend Monsieur d'Aiguines (Arthur Wontner), whose home Irene visits often. In a confrontation with his friend, Jacques learns that Madame d'Aiguines and Irene are lovers. The friend admits that he is too much in love with his wife to leave her but warns Jacques that he can only suffer immeasurably if he marries Irene. Soon, Jacques informs Irene that he knows the truth about her, and she pleads with him to marry her and save her from herself. They wed, but life turns out as d'Aiguines had foretold; Jacques takes up with an old flame, and Irene, aware that she will always be a captive of feelings she is powerless to subdue, leaves her husband.

The Captive was playing to packed houses in its seventeenth week when its producers (Charles Frohman, Inc., was actually backed by the movie firm of Famous Players-Lasky) bowed to the dictates of those who damned it as salacious; without going to trial, it closed down. Gilbert Miller, the firm's representative, wanted to fight the case in court, but his employers overruled him. Basil Rathbone recalled in his autobiography *In and Out of Character* the events surrounding the affair. He had been unaware of any public to-do until one night, as he was putting on his makeup, he was told of a crowd gathering outside. He received a phone call from a Miller employee telling him to be calm and to give his usual performance. He learned that the police might close the play down that night. "As we each walked out onto the stage to await our first entrances we were stopped by a plainclothes policeman who showed his badge and said, 'Please don't let it disturb your performance tonight but consider yourself under arrest!' " The performance was given under these electric conditions, and at its conclusion the cast was carted off to night court by the police. He and Menken were booked and allowed to leave on posting $1,000 bail each. The play was to remain closed pending a trial. The story became headline news in the days that followed and the preliminary hearing a few days later was jammed with witnesses. The entire cast and management were lined up before the judge, but it turned out that the attorney standing there with them was employed only to represent the management. Horace Liveright, the publisher, rose and tried to demand representation for the actors but was silenced. The management lawyer, Max Steuer, declared that Charles Frohman, Inc., was willing to desist from further presentation of *The Captive*. When the actors were asked if they would follow suit, two of them, Ann Trevor and stage manager Percy Shostac, bravely stood up on the play's behalf and expressed their pride to be associated with it. A recess was then granted at Horace Liveright's request. An attorney discussed the issue with the actors at length; they followed his advice to reappear before the bench and accept the judgment *under protest*. Only Percy Shostac refused to do so, for which he received a suspended sentence.

CARAVAN [Drama/France/Crime/Romance] A: Clifford Pember and Ralph Cullinan; M: Jay Gorney; D: Rollo Lloyd; S: P. Dodd Ackerman; P: Richard Herndon; T: Klaw Theatre; 8/29/28 (21)

"Anyone would have thought that this slow vehicle was a bandwagon instead of a gypsy's wain, so pompously did it roll along, so bombastic were the sentiments delivered in it,'' wrote *Time*. Despite a script jammed with melodramatic incident, this play suffered from longeurs and soon gave up the ghost.

Its locale was France, and its plot turned about the dilemma of a nongypsy girl, Alza Gaudet (Virginia Pemberton), raised by gypsies and wanted by two men, Julio (Robert Hyman) and Silvio (Leo Kennedy); the latter wants to sell her into white slavery. Silvio is also the lover of the jealous Chiquita (Elsa Shelley), a married woman. Silvio is killed, suspicion falls on Alza, but, after another murder, Chiquita's husband is disclosed as the perpetrator.

CARMENCITA AND THE SOLDIER [Musical Revival/Russian Language] M: Georges Bizet; D: Vladimir Nemirovich-Danchenko; DS: Isaach Rabinovitch; P: Moscow Art Theatre Musical Studio b/a/w F. Ray Comstock and Morris Gest; T: Jolson's Fifty-ninth Street Theatre; 12/30/25 (58)

A production of Bizet's famed opera *Carmen* as done by the visiting Moscow Art Theatre Musical Studio. It was not an especially adroit presentation, although it offered some novelty in the staging. The libretto was revised for the better, said Richard Dana Skinner, but "The singing is very mediocre, the acting often too heavily underscored, and the tendency toward posed scenes is so great as to impede the flow of dramatic action."

In the telling, Joseph Wood Krutch remarked, "There remains the hard little story as Mérimée conceived it, the story of a love as brief, as fierce, as heartless, and yet as lithesome as the love of two cats or tigers." He believed the production to be "as inhumanly brilliant as the Spanish sun and as cruel as a bull fight." Contrary to Skinner, he loved the acting and believed the cast threw themselves into it "with a glorious abandon."

The work was performed in an atmospheric unit setting using a bridge-like platform in an abstract open-stage arrangement. There was vivid use made of the chorus for visual effect. Much of the score was redistributed to the choral singers, making it "the voice of public opinion intently watching the career of Don Jose," noted Krutch. Olga Baklanova starred as Carmencita.

Carmencita proved to be the most popular of the five works in the company's repertory and was given an extended run of nearly two months.

CARNIVAL (Farsang) [Drama/Romance/Marriage/Hungarian] A: Ferenc Molnar; TR: Melville Baker; D: Frank Reicher; S: Lee Simonson; P: Charles Frohman, Inc.; T: Cort Theatre; 12/29/24 (32)

During the run of Molnar's hit play *The Guardsman*, this 1916 work by the Hungarian dramatist opened, but it met with scorn. The chief interest derived from Elsie Ferguson's performance as the heroine.

Ferguson's role was that of Camilla, a fiery, restless young wife of a domineering country gentleman of middle age (Berton Churchill). Wooed at a fancy ball by young poet Nicholas Kornady (Tom Nesbitt), she is emboldened to suggest elopement with him when she finds a crown jewel lost by the guest of honor. Despite her possession of the means to flight, Kornady's ardor cools at the thought, and Camilla spurns him, gives back the jewel, and returns to her cooped up life with her spouse.

There was a severe critical torrent unleashed on *Carnival*. Heywood Broun called it "one of the dullest plays of the season . . . , heavy-footed and heavy-handed." Ferguson's notices were not much better.

CARNIVAL [Drama/Sex/Show Business/Youth/Romance] A: William R. Doyle; D: Rollo Lloyd; S: Nicholas Yellenti; P: Irving Lande; T: Forrest Theatre; 4/24/29 (20)

A so-so play about backstage life in the garish carnival world, focusing on the doomed love affair of the "cooch" dancer Helen (Anne Forrest) with local seventeen-year-old Bobbie Spenser (Norman Foster). They live together for a while, but she feels he's too good for her; she tries to break up by displaying herself as a cheap performer at an orgiastic men's smoker. He is disgusted and attempts to stop her but only gets wounded by the show's manager (Walter Fenner) for his trouble. To solve the problem Helen substitutes for the show's parachute jumper and leaps to her death.

Brooks Atkinson found the combination of Camille and carnival themes appealing but not as herein presented. Only Anne Forrest, still bearing the marks of a recent car accident, was acceptable, he said. Perriton Maxwell liked the piece and overlooked its episodic structure on behalf of its human story.

CAROLINE [Musical/Period/Southern/Romance] B: Harry B. Smith and E. Kunneke; SC: an Austrian operetta, *Der Vetter Aus Dingsda*, by Herman Haller and Edward Rideamus; M: Edward Rideamus and Alfred Goodman; D: Charles Sinclair; S: Watson Barratt; P: Messrs. Shubert; T: Ambassador Theatre; 1/31/23 (151)

A well-liked operetta with a Viennese score (and several uncredited American interpolations) and a book adapted from an Austrian original to a post–Civil War setting among the belles and the beaux of the late Confederacy. The show, many agreed, "is very pleasant when the orchestra is at work but deadly dull when it isn't" (Arthur Hornblow).

The "factory-made book" (Alexander Woollcott) was particularly deficient in the humor department. Its plot pictured the title figure (Tessa Kosta) forbidden from going to a ball but meeting thereby a handsome stranger (J. Harold Murray), who soon attends to wooing the fair maid. Learning that she pledged her troth ten years before to Roderick Gray (John Adair), whom she has not seen since, he assumes that fellow's name. Eventually, the real Roderick shows up, but by now Caroline and the stranger are in love, so Roderick begins a romance with the second female lead (Helen Shipman).

CAROLINIAN, THE [Drama/Period/Southern/Military/Marriage] A: Rafael Sabatini and J. Harold Terry; SC: the novel by Rafael Sabatini; D: Hamilton MacFadden; P: Charles L. Wagner; T: Sam H. Harris Theatre; 11/2/25 (24)

A history play set in Charles Town, South Carolina, in the 1770s, during the Revolutionary War, and designed as a vehicle for Sidney Blackmer. The tepidly received melodrama was "a workmanlike play on a familiar model—a play filled with redcoats and white wigs, pistols and dueling talk, spies, toasts to his majesty, dusty uniforms and the siege of Charles Town" (*Herald Tribune*). Built like a mystery play, with a fair amount of suspense, the play looked at the activities of the patriotic Harry Latimer (Blackmer), who, after secretly marrying the colonial Governor's daughter (Martha-Bryan Allen), finds himself in various difficulties stemming from his wife's being accused of espionage, followed by himself being suspected of treason. His and his wife's innocence are established, and the play concludes happily.

Arthur Hornblow termed the opus "a very confused and messy bit of Colonial melodrama." Blackmer's histrionics were not admired.

CARRY ON [Drama/Business/Romance/Family] A: Owen Davis; D: Clifford Brooke; S: Livingston Platt; P: Carl Reed; T: Theatre Masque; 1/23/28 (8)

The fecund pen of Owen Davis inked this play as a debut piece for his son Owen, Jr.'s New York acting bow. The juvenile acquitted himself well, but the rickety play stumbled and died within a week.

Junior played the collegiate son of a Yonkers manufacturer (Berton Churchill) whose stanch but blind sense of honor throws his family into poverty when, after his mills go into bankruptcy, he feels himself obligated to pay off all the firm's debts, even though he is not liable. The plot recounts the financial and romantic difficulties of the man's son, daughter (Flora Sheffield), wife (Beatrice Terry), and an old aunt (Elizabeth Patterson) stemming from their enforced poverty.

Percy Hammond rejected it as "a rambling, awkward and at times ridiculous sermonette."

CASANOVA [Drama/Period/Romance/France/Spanish/Historical-Biographical] A: Lorenzo de Azertis; AD: Sidney Howard; M: Deems Taylor; D: Gilbert Miller; CH: Michel Fokine; S: George Barbier; P: A. H. Woods and Gilbert Miller; T: Empire Theatre; 9/26/23 (78)

Katharine Cornell shared kudos with the costumes in this version of the romance between Casanova and Henriette, the mistress who may have been his one true passion. After a pantomime ballet prologue by Michel Fokine, to music by Deems Taylor, Casanova (Lowell Sherman) meets Henriette (Cornell), and they embark upon their affair. Separated by misfortune and mischance after ninety days, the lovers never meet again. Twenty-one years later, Casanova is visited by the daughter (also played by Cornell) born of the liason and dies kissing the floor where her foot had trod.

"Romantic," "spectacular," and "sentimental" were the adjectives most critics applied to the play, which was judged superficial. They split over Sherman's performance, but Cornell was highly lauded. As Arthur Hornblow said, "piquant, vivacious, arch, she was the life of the play."

H.H.

CASTE [Drama/Italy-France/Jews/Family/Romance] A: Cosmo Hamilton; SC: a novel by Cosmo Hamilton; D: Campbell Gullan; S: Herbert Ward; C: Bendel; P: Joe Weber; T: Mansfield Theatre; 12/23/27 (16)

An expensively produced dramatization by the author of one of his own novels. Hamilton's theme was religious intermarriage among the social upper crust. Unfortunately, the play was verbose, slow paced, unclimactic, and poorly put together.

The children of two wealthy and distinguished New York families, the Farquahars and the Lorbensteins, fall in love, face parental interference because of the Gentile-Jewish difference in backgrounds, overcome all obstacles, and live happily ever after. Horace Braham played the Jewish boy, Vivian Martin the Gentile girl.

Percy Hammond called it "a Park Avenue *Abie's Irish Rose*," highfalutin' in tone and appearance but boring to sit through. Some saw the much publicized story of composer Irving Berlin's romance with heiress Ellin MacKay as the source of the plot.

CASTLES IN THE AIR [Musical/Romance] B/LY: Raymond W. Peck; M: Percy Wenrich; D: Frank S. Merlin; CH: Julian Mitchell; P: James W. Elliott; T: Selwyn Theatre; 9/6/26 (162)

Everything about this musical seemed created by formula—its atmosphere, its costumes, its characters, and its music. It was all smoothly enough done, with some talented persons in the leads, but the critics felt they had been there before. A huge hit in Chicago, it did moderately well on Broadway. The *Times* considered it "a large and leisurely entertainment, handsomely produced, and combining the faults and virtues of both musical comedy and operetta." It was short on laughs and bogged down by "A rambling and somewhat burdensome book," revealed the critic. Veteran Julian Mitchell completed the final choreography of his career in it, for he died shortly before the show opened; John Boyle shaped the dances up following his demise.

The plot moved its characters from Westchester County to the European operetta kingdom of Latavia, where the young man John Brown (J. Harold Murray) discloses to the girl he loves (Vivienne Segal) that he is not really just a plain American Joe but the Prince as whom he has been passing himself off.

CAT AND THE CANARY, THE [Drama/Legacy/Mystery/Romance/Mental Illness/Crime] A: John Willard; P: Kilbourn Gordon, Inc.; T: National Theatre; 2/7/22 (349)

One of the great thrillers of its day, *The Cat and the Canary* had a long life in stock and other productions, including several film versions, and is still occasionally produced. Actor-author John Willard, said the *Post*, "wants to make your flesh creep, and uses about every trick known to modern melodrama—secret panels, voodooism, spiritualism, homicidal maniacs, murder, midnight, theft, and all manner of terrifying agencies—to bring about the desired result." These methods kept the audience glued to their seats, only the comic relief segments failing to make their point.

The action takes place in a gloomy manor house, where at midnight on the anniversary of the late owner's death his will is read to the family members. Afraid that one of his heirs might inherit the family's streak of insanity, he has left the estate to young Annabelle West (Florence Eldridge) on the basis of her remaining through the night in the mansion without losing her marbles. Everything possible happens to frighten her, but with the help of the meek fellow (Henry Hull) who loves her, she rides out the storm.

CATSKILL DUTCH [Drama/Period/Small Town/Marriage/Sex/Religion] A: Roscoe W. Brink; D: Robert Milton; S: Livingston Platt; P: Richard Herndon; T: Belmont Theatre; 5/6/24 (7)

Many critics agreed with Stark Young, who declared that this creation from a poet and graduate of George Pierce Baker's "English 47" class at Harvard was long, conscientious, and boring. Set in a Methodist Catskill Mountain village in 1870, the action involved a church Elder (Frederic Burt) who tries to hide his paternity of his servant girl's baby by marrying her off. In a hysteria-packed revival meeting, the girl (Ann Davis) reveals the Elder's sin, and he is disgraced. His wife (Minnie Dupree), previously subjugated in the patriarchal society, makes the Elder pay dearly for his lapse, while the former servant's husband (Kenneth MacKenna) forgives her for the sake of their family.

H.H.

CAUGHT [Drama/Marriage/Crime/Romance] A: Kate McLaurin; D/P: Gustav Blum; S: Jo Mielziner; T: Thirty-Ninth Street Theatre; 10/5/25 (32)

"A morbid, sordid tragedy" (*Herald Tribune*) of lives wasted because of selfishness and greed. Young David Turner (Fairfax Burgher) does not wish to work for his comforts, so he marries a wealthy older woman (Antoinette Perry). Yet when he encounters again the girl (Gladys Hurlbut) he has always loved and learns that she is on the verge of sinning with an older man to make ends meet, he kills his wife and then commits suicide.

"Most of the characters," reported the *Herald Tribune*, were "weak, immoral, wholly uninteresting." The critic found the work "fairly well constructed with fairly good dialogue, but . . . without reason . . . for its being." The *Times* called it "a sturdy melodrama," poorly cast, and unevenly acted.

CAVE GIRL, THE [Comedy/Romance/Rural] A: George Middleton and Guy Bolton; D: George Marion; P: F. Ray Comstock and Morris Gest; T: Longacre Theatre; 8/18/20 (40)

A forest romance about an industrial tycoon, J. T. Bates (John Cope), who organizes a camping trip in the Maine woods to bring together his son Divvy (Saxon Kling) and Elsie Case (Madeline Marshall), the girl he's picked out for him. In the woods, Divvy meets cave-girl Margot Merrill (Grace Valentine). Rather than leave her, Divvy sets fire to the canoes. Margot rescues the stranded campers and rules over them as a benevolent despot. She and Divvy go off to live the free life together.

The production of this "clean and clever comedy" (*Independent*) was in the "hammer-and-anvil school of acting," wrote Alexander Woollcott. "There is something hopelessly 'stock company' about it," argued Arthur Hornblow.

M.M.-C.

CELEBRITY [Comedy/Romance/Sports] A: Willard Keefe; D: Edward Goodman; P: Herman Shumlin and Paul Streger; T: Lyceum Theatre; 12/26/27 (24)

An interesting comic exposé of the world of pugilists and promoters that received decent reviews but could not go the distance. Joseph Wood Krutch saw it as "saltily written, amusingly rowdy, and, except for the presence of a little conventional love interest, refreshingly tough-minded."

Its concern was with a manager, Circus Snyder (Crane Wilbur), who promotes his boxing protegé Barry Regan (Gavin Gordon) into a major celebrity by pushing the angle that the athlete is a polished and highly literate gentleman. Momentarily unhappy in the role, the fighter rejects it but resumes it before the final curtain.

The critics noticed the resemblance of Barry Regan to the well-read contemporary boxing champ Gene Tunney.

CENTURIES, THE [Drama/Jews/Family] A/D: Em Jo Basshe; S: John Dos Passos; P: New Playwrights' Theatre; T: New Playwrights' Theatre (OB); 11/29/27 (33)

A fervid, sprawling, experimental drama employing a huge company of actors, among whom were Franchot Tone and Eduard Franz, to tell in episodic form of the travails of Jewish immigrants in the land of plenty. John Mason Brown believed it was "muddled, inchoate and meagerly acted." Richard Dana Skinner stated, "It is full of telling and sharp character studies [and] it has moments which aspire toward poetic beauty," but its stress on a thesis gave it "all the stilted artificialty of a marionette."

Basshe's "portrait of a tenement house" pictured various rooms in a Lower East Side tenement, where a Russian-Jewish family experiences the jarring transition from life in the old country to life in the new amidst poverty, strikes, brothels, synagogues, and gangsters. In the end they move on to greener pastures in the Bronx.

Well set on three levels and staged expressionistically, it was interesting to observe but too confused to keep interest sustained.

CENTURY REVIEW, THE, and THE MIDNIGHT ROUNDERS [Revue] B: Howard E. Rogers; M: Jean Schwartz; LY: Al Bryan; D: Lew Morton and Jack Mason; P: Messrs. Shubert; T: Century Promenade (Century Theatre Roof); 7/12/20 (150)

The Century Review began at 9:00 P.M. When it concluded, another revue called *The Midnight Rounders* succeeded it, about ll:30 P.M. These plays were "glorified cabaret entertainments," observed the *Times*, which also noted: "most of those who go to the Century Promenade . . . will expect an expensive, expansive entertainment, full of songs and dances, novelties, nonsense, speed and girls—first and last full of girls—and they will get just about what they are looking for."

The shows featured a diverse assortment of entertainers, songs, and spectacle pieces, by persons such as Jane Green, Muriel De Forrest, Jessica Brown, Ted Lorraine, Gladys Walton, Joe Byam, and others, perhaps the best known being singer Walter Woolf. Many of the acts appeared with different material in each show. Charles Darnton selected a black and white ballet in hoop skirts as the most artistic and was also fond of an Apache dance called "Conscience."

Eddie Cantor starred in *The Midnight Rounders* during its pre-Broadway tryout in Philadelphia; he tells some amusing stories of his work on the show in his book *My Life Is in Your Hands*. One of his greatest sketches, "Joe's Blue Front," was born during this show and was repeated in his next show, *Make it Snappy*.

A follow-up edition of the late-night show called *The Midnight Rounders of 1921* arrived on 2/7/21 for forty-nine performances. Principals included Tot Qualters, Olga Cook, Ethel Davis, Harold Murray, Ada Forman, and others. "There are lots of girls who appear and reappear in a series of richly varied costumes in which the quantity of the material is in inverse ratio to the quality; and these girls sing and dance in an aimless . . . fashion in keeping with the drivel of their songs," observed Arthur Hornblow.

CHAINS [Drama/Sex/Family] A: Jules Eckert Goodman; D: William A. Brady, Jr.; P: William A. Brady; T: Playhouse Theatre; 9/19/23 (131)

"Then to hell with respectability!" this play's heroine (Helen Gahagan) shockingly stated when the parents (William Morris and Maude Turner Gordon) of her college lover (Paul Kelly), believing they may have an illegitimate grandchild, urged her to marry their errant son and answered "yes" when she asked if marriage without love was respectable. The drama, which argued a woman's right to sexual freedom if she accepted the consequences and the immorality of marriage for duty, was called by Percy Hammond a variation on *Hindle Wakes* "and does very well by it with the assistance of excellent stage direction and a first-rate cast."

Arthur Hornblow wrote, "The play is well-written and, if one can overlook the false premises, the situations are dramatic enough and of sufficient human interest to compel attention."

H.H.

CHAINS (Kaytn) [Drama/Politics/Prison/Yiddish/Yiddish Language] A: H. Leivick; D/P: Maurice Schwartz; S: Charles Stillwell; T: Yiddish Art Theatre (OB); 2/22/30

A memorable Yiddish Art Theatre production that the *Times* commended for maturity of subject matter, subtlety of direction, and understanding of interpretation.

The play looked at a group of Russian political prisoners incarcerated in a Siberian prison camp in 1905 because of revolutionary activities; they are freed by nearby striking miners whom they seek to proselytize as potential radicals but are again captured and confined to jail.

Written in a poetic tone by one who had himself known life in a Siberian prison camp, the play chronicles the gradual dissolution of the prisoners' fiery idealism as their dreams crumble amidst the agony of their existence.

CHAINS OF DEW [Comedy/Small Town/Marriage] A: Susan Glaspell; D: Ralph Stuart; P: Provincetown Players; T: Provincetown Playhouse (OB); 4/27/22 (16)

Susan Glaspell disappointed with this murky play that critics compared unfavorably to her recent more interesting works *Inheritors* and *The Verge*. Ludwig Lewisohn thought its chief character lacked concreteness and that the author's *bête noir* was her continued preoccupation with "symbolism," a device the critic believed was resorted to when the artist's "energy" had faltered. The play, he stated, "is delicate but its delicacy has no fine edges; it is thoughtful, but its thinking is unclarified."

Midwestern banker-poet Seymour Standish (Edward Reese), feeling himself stifled by his small-town milieu, a dull wife (Louise Treadwell), and an insensitive mother (Agnes McCarthy), takes up with a smart set of New Yorkers. These persons, however, realize that Seymour's bonds are "chains of dew" that he has forged to make himself feel martyred to restrictive forces.

CHALLENGE OF YOUTH, THE [Comedy-Drama/Sex/Youth/Family/University/Small Town] A: Ashley Miller and Hyman Adler; M/LY: Evelyn Adler and Lottie Salisbury; D/P: Hyman Adler; S: P. Dodd Ackerman; T: Forty-ninth Street Theatre; 1/20/30 (24)

There were two new songs interpolated into this "new and nauseating development of the ordeal by sex-problem" (*Time*) play. Like the play, they were forgettable. It was a stereotypical treatment of life among the college-age generation in conflict with their elders; meant as a sermon play, it laid the moralizing on thick in order to point out that the parents are responsible for youth's irresponsible behavior by laying down rules instead of offering wise advice. Stephen Rathbun said, "The play is so poorly written that it is never quite convincing" but, nevertheless, was not "uninteresting."

Hip flasks, jazz, and petting parties were on display in the piece that dealt with a college professor's (Harold De Bray) daughter (Alma Merrick), who has sexual intercourse with a boy (William Lovejoy) during a fete in her own home. Only the young couple's agreement to get married prevents the professor from quitting his job and moving to prevent a scandal.

CHAMPION, THE [Comedy/Sports/Small Town/Politics/Romance] A: Thomas Louden and A. E. Thomas; D: Sam Forrest; P: Sam H. Harris; T: Longacre Theatre; 1/3/21 (176)

To his home in the small English town of Knotley returns William Burroughs (Grant Mitchell), who for fifteen years has been living and flourishing in America; he has become lightweight boxing champion of the world under the name "Gunboat" Williams and has also become a lawyer and a congressman. His father (Arthur Elliott), from whom he long has been estranged, only begins to glow with pride at his pugilistic achievements when he sees how the local aristocrats adore the famous boxer as a native hero. William also wins over the Lady Elizabeth (Ann Andrews) as his bride-to-be.

The Champion was "rather disappointing. . . . Our authors have been too easily satisfied with the old devices of the theatre," in the *Times*'s view. Arthur Hornblow called the piece "perilously flimsy and constructively inept." American slang contrasted with upper-class British locutions provided most of the fun.

CHANGE YOUR LUCK [Musical/Blacks/Prohibition] B: Garland Howard; M/ LY: J. C. Johnson; D: Stanley Bennett; CH: Lawrence Deas and Speedy Smith; S/P: Cleon Throckmorton; T: George M. Cohan Theatre; 6/6/30 (16)

A black musical comedy that faltered because of "a completely enervating and pointless book" (*Times*) that, interfered with, might have been the basis for an enjoyable show. The book was nearly ignored by the succession of specialty acts such as the dance team The Four Flash Devils, dancers Louie Simms and Buster Bowie, comedian Hamtree Harrington, and comic-singer Cora La Redd. Among the cast members was singer Alberta Hunter, who later became a jazz great. What story there was concerned a bootlegging undertaker (Leigh Whipper) who stows his hooch in his large formaldehyde jars.

CHANGELINGS, THE [Comedy/Literature/Family/Marriage/Romance] A: Lee Wilson Dodd; P: Henry Miller; T: Henry Miller's Theatre; 9/17/23 (139)

"Perhaps our first genuine American comedy of manners," Arthur Hornblow wrote about Lee Wilson Dodd's play, which was inspired by Talleyrand's observation *"Plus ça change, plus la même chose."* A middle-aged book publisher and his wife (Henry Miller and Blanche Bates) entertain old friends and contemporaries, a novelist and his wife (Reginald Mason and Laura Hope Crews). The novelist's son, a Yale professor (Geoffrey Kerr), has recently been married to the publisher's daughter (Ruth Chatterton), but all of the characters' relationships are upset when the bride runs away with another man (after finding her mother in her father-in-law's arms). The opposite partners in the parental generation are attracted to each other, but, in the end, all original pairings are confirmed, and the young couple make their parents grandparents.

This was an early example of a dramatist's handling of the Freudian concepts of sexual suppression and frustration. However, Alan Dale thought it was useless: "It was like an old French farce made into a hypocritical debate." Percy Hammond added, "there was an ingenious situation or two and plenty of nimble observations from the pen of Mr. Dodd."

The play enjoyed a week's return engagement from 5/12/24.

H.H.

CHANNEL ROAD, THE [Comedy/Period/Prostitution/France/Sex/Military/War] A: Alexander Woollcott and George S. Kaufman; SC: Guy de Maupassant's story "La Boule de suif"; D/P: Arthur Hopkins; S: Robert Edmond Jones; T: Plymouth Theatre; 10/17/29 (60)

Alexander Woollcott, the drama critic, and George S. Kaufman, major playwriting collaborator and sometime critic, teamed up to pen this comedy based on a de Maupassant story; it was Woollcott's first attempt at dramaturgic construction. The results were not very gratifying, although a few sided with the play. John Hutchens's comments were representative: "Maupassant's lean, hard prose is transformed here to undramatic rhetoric, in the course of which action stops, and literary style struggles, with an audible gasping for breath, to atone for a dearth of dramatic character." Only Sig Rumann and Anne Forrest in the leading roles achieved critical acceptance.

The ironic tale was of a group of French refugees in 1870 fleeing in a diligence from Rouen during the Franco-Prussian War and forced to stop at an inn commandeered by a Prussian lieutenant (Rumann). The officer will allow the party to move on only if the whore submits to him, but she patriotically refuses, leading the other refugees, who had scorned her, to plead with her to agree. She relents, but in a switch from the original, only she and two sisters of mercy are allowed to depart, while the other refugees are left behind in the hands of the Prussians.

CHARLATAN, THE [Drama/Mystery/Crime/Show Business] A: Leonard Praskins and Ernest Pascal; D: Ira Hards; P: Adolph Klauber; T: Times Square Theatre; 4/24/22 (64)

An ingenious idea for a mystery play went awry here because of a lack of technical playwriting skill. This idea was to contrive a whodunnit that involved the illusions conjured up by a magician suspected of murdering his own wife. The magician (Frederick Tiden) is doing his act at Mason Talbot's (William Ingersoll) Florida home when his wife, participating in the disappearing lady routine, really does vanish, only to be found in a trick compartment, poisoned with an Indian drug. The play concerns the complications that ensue as the police attempt to uncover the killer and his or her motives.

Negative reviews sided with Arthur Hornblow's annoyance at the "confusing and irritating" plotting that left him as "hopelessly in the dark" at the end as he was all through; on the positive side was the *Times*, which liked all of the magical hocus-pocus of the action and the suspenseful excitement created.

CHARLEY'S AUNT [Dramatic Revival] A: Brandon Thomas; D/P: Hermann Lieb; T: Daly's Theatre; 6/1/25 (24)

The ever popular 1892 British farce about an Oxford undergraduate who dresses in drag to impersonate another youth's visiting aunt from Brazil, "where the nuts come from," received a decent but short-lived mounting with what the *Times*, without denoting them, called "a number of modernizations." Sam B. Burton was effective as Lord Fancourt Babberly, the masquerading student. A member of the New York cast of 1893, Harry Lillford, made a return in his original role of Brassett.

Joseph Wood Krutch summed up the response: the "revival of *Charley's Aunt* lasts just long enough to demonstrate that this famous farce is still, in spite of the fact that it is neither witty, original, nor credible, genuinely laughable."

CHARM SCHOOL, THE [Comedy/School/Romance/Youth] A: Alice Duerr Miller and Robert Milton; M/LY: Jerome Kern; SC: Miller's novel of the same name; D/P: Robert Milton; T: Bijou Theatre; 8/2/20 (87)

The Charm School offered, according to Alexander Woollcott, "a pleasant, amusing, mildly preoccupying evening" such as summer theatregoers were normally in pursuit of. Its simplistic plot told of a handsome youth, Austin Bevans (Sam Hardy), who inherits a girls' boarding school and thereupon determines to put into practice his educational theory that girls need only to develop their charm to make a success in life. With himself as headmaster and his friends as teachers, he begins his course, only to fall in love with a student (Marie Carroll) while his friends fall for the other girls.

Because the play's manner seemed indeterminate, Woollcott described it as "a curious mixture—a half-heartedly farcical comedy, with one Winter Garden scene effect and one surviving song." The *Sun* and *Herald* censured the show for not maintaining its satirical viewpoint and opting for more commercial effects. The show was musicalized as *June Days* in 1925.

CHASTENING, THE [Drama/Religion/Family] A: Charles Rann Kennedy; P: Equity Players; T: Forty-eighth Street Theatre; 3/12/23 (22)

An unusual three-character play of spiritual faith, produced at a special series of Lenten matinees. This modern miracle play focused on Jesus, Joseph, and Mary, called here the Son (Margaret Gage), the Carpenter (Charles Rann Kennedy), and his Wife (Edith Wynne Matthison). The three are seen at a roadside, where they are briefly resting and discussing the experiences they have just had in the city. The action concerns Jesus's talking his parents into allowing him to follow his nature, regardless of their private wishes for him. During the conversation, the parents come to understand just who their son is.

The work was not universally accepted. Burns Mantle argued that, compared to the prolixity of the Son's parables, "the real Nazarene revealed mystical conceptions by means of simple, homely tales, but he never used mystical tales to explain simple, homely truths." There was sneering at the casting of "a mature and somewhat rogueish woman" (Heywood Broun) as the Son.

(1) CHAUVE-SOURIS, LE (Letuchaya Muish) [Revue/Russian Language/ Russian] D: Nikita Balieff; S: Serge Soudeikine and Nikolai Remisoff; P: F. Ray Comstock and Morris Gest; T: Forty-ninth Street Theatre; 2/1/22 (544)

A Russian vaudeville-type show that became one of the most popular intimate revues on Broadway and fathered several new editions into the forties. It had originated in Moscow over a dozen years earlier when various entertainers would gather at Armenian Nikita Balieff's Bat Restaurant after hours and put on shows for their own amusement, shows that soon became well enough spoken of for them to become regular public entertainments five nights a week. Scattered by the Russian Revolution, many of these artists gravitated to Paris, where Balieff began to organize them once again into shows that soon had France's capital flocking to what was given the silly French name for "bat." Eventually, impressario Morris Gest, partnered by F. Ray Comstock, brought them to New York, where they continued to delight in several manifestations.

The first edition of the *Chauve-Souris* offered thirteen numbers, not all of them of the same high quality, but with several of superlative imagination and professional skill. Presiding informally as M.C. was the rotund, heavily accented Balieff himself, whose manful struggles with the English language contributed greatly to the humor of the program. "Balieff is an extraordinary comedian, Balieff is an uncompromising *regisseur*, and Balieff brings us the ruddy rejuvenating warmth of the peasant where he is most the peasant," wrote Kenneth Macgowan. The program itself remained in Russian and thereby lost none of its native appeal.

The best-appreciated piece on the program was "The Parade of the Wooden Soldiers," a precision dance routine in which various wooden toys came to life. "It is a dream of childhood that these wooden soldiers bring you—a sensation, a memory beyond the reason or the adult imagination, straight from the best remembered of all lands," declared Ludwig Lewisohn. Also delight producing were the Katinka, "a polka, in a good setting and fine make-ups, all from an old style Russian toy, and gay, shrill, droll, and exquisitely sharp and automatic" (Stark Young); and the Chastoushki, a medley of folk work songs. Many of the songs and dances were, though charming, not particularly impressive, and several critics noted that American entertainers could put on an equally well-managed and amusing show.

The original 544-performance run included four editions; the latter three were in the Century Theatre's rooftop playhouse, redesigned in a blaze of Russian colors. Popular numbers such as "The Wooden Soldiers" and "Katinka" remained, but new highlights were introduced in each edition. To the critics, the new editions kept improving over their predecessors.

Edition number two, opening in June, had among its better numbers a Black Hussars drinking song, a peasants' dance of women and soldiers, a mysterious number in which hooded figures sang a strange song, and, above all, "The Clown," a brilliant pantomimic dance impersonation of the circus clown's humor and pathos, performed remarkably well by Kotchetovsky.

Program three, produced in October, saw in "Katinka's Unexpected Romance" the marriage of "Katinka" to one of the wooden soldiers; on opening night, producer Morris Gest gave the bride away, Balieff was the best man, and the wedding guests included John Barrymore, Mary Pickford, Douglas Fairbanks, and other stars. New highlights were a parade of toys to "Malbrough s'en va t'en Guerre;" a serenade of alley cats accompanying a youthful romance, "The Night Idyll;" an exquisitely sung version of Chopin's Etude in G Major; and a samurai dance by Katchetovsky.

With the fourth edition, given in January 1923, and marked by the presence in the audience of the visiting Moscow Art Theatre, there was no "Katinka," but the wooden soldiers were still there, as were new additions such as "Anushka," a Russian novelty song; "Toi Qui Connais les Hussards de la Garde," a French romantic song; and several superb choral arrangements of Russian folksongs.

(2) The *Chauve-Souris* made a return engagement on 9/24/23 for thirty-six performances at Jolson's Theatre and then reappeared with a number of new performers mingled with some of the old in a new version that opened at the Forty-ninth Street Theatre on 1/14/25. This mounting ran for sixty-nine performances. It was an exquisitely polished, and beautifully designed, composed, written, staged, and enacted production that came to New York after first playing in Paris and London. More artistically refined than its forebears, it was strikingly impressive in its variety, visual effects, humor, and general imaginativeness. Nikita Balieff once again headed the company as regisseur and "conferencier" and was now "a trifle more intimate and conversational perhaps" (Stark Young) but with his shrewdly fractured English perfectly intact.

Once more on the program were "The Wooden Soldiers," "Katinka," and "The King Orders the Drums to Be Beaten," but the specialties of the production were its new numbers. Notable were "Stenka Razin," a presentation in song, dance, and scenery of a stirring Volga River legend about a bandit, a beauty, and a barge; "Love in the Ranks," a sketch in which the ascending orders of military rank pay suit to a village grisette, only to have the fat General win the prize; a reverent and moving depiction of the nativity, "The Arrival at Bethlehem" (censored in London); "The Zaporoahtsi," a rousing Dniepper Cossack number based on a painting by Ilya Repin; a hilarious travesty of a Sicilian opera, "A Winter Evening"; a medley of Kreisler songs; "A Country Picnic in a Distant Province," in which were sung songs by Alexei Archangelski (the scene was "an invention that for pure beauty in quality outshone anything the *Chauve-Souris* has done before"—Young); "The Shepherdess Interlude" from the opera *The Queen of Spades*; "The Four Corpses," an opera of tragic gloom and death; and more.

(**3**) [1927 Edition] B/LY: Nikita Balieff; M: Alexei Archangelsky; P: F. Ray Comstock and Morris Gest; T: Cosmopolitan Theatre; 10/10/27 (80)

After an absence of a few years, the *Chauve-Souris* returned with the popular "Katinka" and "Wooden Soldiers" numbers gone forever and with several bits produced in English. Balieff was still in charge and himself constituted, said Richard Dana Skinner, "about three-fourths of the entertainment." Ballet dancer Tamara Geva was introduced in this show; she rapidly rose to fame in America. "Her dancing is shot through with a curious satirical quality which doubtless requires an extraordinary technical equipment. . . . It seems to be an effort to combine two distinct types of dancing in one—the grace of the informal, interpretive dance with the sterner substance of pantomime," wrote Skinner.

Everything seemed new about the revue, except for a revised version of "Love in the Ranks." Comedy dominated more than in past versions, and visual beauty was not as stressed. A "Shooting Gallery" number allowed patrons with air guns handed to them to take pot shots at stage targets; a satirical song, "Where's Our Meyer, Where's Himalaya?" drew laughs; "The Passing of the Regiment" was a highlight with "its teasing music, its foreground of living figures, and its background of passing pasteboard effigies of band, horse, foot dragoons, staff and service of supply"; *La Traviata* was ridiculed; a reverent scene of Calvary was depicted, and so on.

(**4**) [1929 Edition] P: Morris Gest; T: Jolson's Fifty-ninth Street Theatre; 1/22/29 (47)

Nikita Balieff's beloved revue ran into some unwonted critical turbulence during its 1929 incarnation. As Robert Little observed, "The latest program is uneven, containing several dull and tasteless numbers, and there was a certain listlessness and lack of freshness throughout." *Time* commented that it had "gone stale, sterile, incredibly flat."

An entirely new assortment of routines contributed to the show's loss of magic. Also, Balieff's quips, which often had poked good-natured fun at American life, now seemed laced with acid and sat poorly with reviewers and spectators alike. The revue included folksongs and dances, brilliantly colorful sets and costumes, a grisly sketch about Napoleon reviewing the spirits of his dead troops on a battlefield, a kaleidoscopic sketch of Moscow life, a grand-opera burlesque, and an organ-grinder number.

CHEAPER TO MARRY [Drama/Sex/Business/Crime/Romance/Friendship] A: Samuel Shipman; D: John Cromwell; S: Raymond Sovey; C: Maybelle Manning and Alexander; P: Richard Herndon; T: Forty-ninth Street Theatre; 4/15/24 (87)

Arthur Hornblow found *Cheaper to Marry* not representative of Samuel Shipman's best work; he called it racy and full of tricks to please the groundlings but otherwise "crude and dull, wearisome beyond belief," and also badly acted. Percy Hammond wrote, "Mr. Shipman's dramas are like the poetree [*sic*] of Irving Berlin—full of well-meaning but a little ramshackle as to detail."

The story inspiring this debate concerned two close friends and business partners (Robert Warwick and Allan Dinehart). Both fall in love, but while one marries, the other makes his girl his mistress (Florence Eldridge). The latter goes broke and embezzles funds from the business to treat his mistress lavishly and is horrified when her love for him wears out, and she leaves him and refuses to help him return the stolen money. She has fallen in love with another man, but when he learns of her liason, he rejects her. For both, it would have been cheaper to marry.

H.H.

CHECKERBOARD, THE [Comedy/Family/Romance] A: Frederick and Fanny Hatton; D: Clifford Brooke; P: F. Ray Comstock and Morris Gest; T: Thirty-ninth Street Theatre; 8/19/20 (13)

A comedy inspired by Moliere's *Le Bourgeois Gentilhomme* telling of millionaire ash-can manufacturer Joseph Taylor (William Williams), who desires to associate with fashionable and titled persons. He is taken in by a crafty American, Townsend Kellog (Sydney Booth), who enlists the help of Feodor Masimoff (Jose Ruben), a Russian ballet dancer. Masimoff poses as a Russian noble but falls in love with Taylor's daughter Suzanne (Miriam Sears). He refuses to go through with the deception, dulling the edge of the satire with a happy ending.

The queer mixture of melodrama, farce, and Russian dancers encouraged the play's oily sentimentality and turned it into one of those "curious, indigestible melanges of the American stage," wrote Alexander Woollcott.

M.M.-C.

CHEE-CHEE [Musical/China/Orientals/Romance/Sex] B: Herbert Fields; M: Richard Rodgers; LY: Lorenz Hart; SC: Charles Petit's novel *The Son of the Grand Eunuch*; D: Alexander Leftwich; CH: Jack Haskell; P: Lew Fields; T: Mansfield Theatre; 9/25/28 (32)

Fields, Rodgers, and Hart, the twenties' top team of musical-comedy collaborators, fell flat with this Oriental show, which was capsulized by Robert Littell as "Unbelievably dull, more taste than usual as to looks."

The book, based on a comic French novel, was about a Chinese youth (William Williams) whose father (George Hassell) became Grand Eunuch to the Emperor's harem after his birth, and who wishes at all costs to avoid his old man's wishes that he inherit the position. He and his bride Chee-Chee (Helen Ford) escape but are caught, and only a trick devised by Chee-Chee's friend Li Li Wee (Betty Starbuck) fools everyone into thinking him emasculated.

Despite its sumptuous production and unusual Oriental-styled music, the show was vigorously mauled by the critics; its theme was too unpleasant to earn it popular appeal. "It must be admitted," wrote *Time*, "that *Chee-Chee*, though sometimes cute and always dirty, is not consistently amusing." Rodgers, who had collaborated on the show against his better instincts, nevertheless considered it an experiment in unifying book and score. A program note stated, "The musical numbers, some of them very short, are so interwoven with the story that it would be confusing for the audience to peruse a complete list." *Chee-Chee* achieved the shortest run of any Rodgers and Hart work.

CHERRY BLOSSOMS [Musical/Japan/Orientals/Romance/Fantasy] B/LY: Harry B. Smith; M: Sigmund Romberg; SC: Harry Benrimo and Harrison Rhodes's play *The Willow Tree*; D: Lew Morton; CH: Ralph Reader and Michio Ito; S: Watson Barratt; P: Messrs. Shubert; T: Forty-fourth Street Theatre; 3/28/27 (56)

A musical adaptation of a 1917 103-performance fantasy about Westerner Ned Hamilton (Howard Marsh), visiting Japan in the wake of an unhappy love affair, whose purchase of a statue of the willow-tree Princess comes to life when he places a mirror, the soul of a woman, in its bodice. Actually, the Princess is a shopgirl substituted for the statue by the merchant who sold it; this was a change from the original play. The love affair between Ned and Yo-Susa-san (Desiree Ellinger) ends sadly, when she sends Ned back to his English sweetheart and subsequently dies. When Ned returns years later, he finds his daughter by Yo-Susa-san; she is the spitting image of her mother.

Although, for some reason the costumes were "French variations on Japanese motifs," the show, said the *Times*, was a typically lavish Shubert offering, "colorful, tuneful and somewhat trite." The critic was dissatisfied with Romberg's unnecessary blend of Oriental and Western musical modes and detected too clearly the influence of *The Mikado* and *Madame Butterfly*. A nod to Asian theatrical techniques was made through the use of a chorus situated in the orchestra and "chroniclers," who described the action between the acts.

(1) CHERRY ORCHARD, THE (Vishnyovy sad) [Comedy-Drama/Family/Romance/Business/Russian/Russian Language] A: Anton Chekhov; D: Constantin Stanislavsky and Vladimir Nemirovich-Danchenko; P: F. Ray Comstock and Morris Gest; T: Fifty-ninth Street Theatre; 1/22/23 (16)

Chekhov's 1904 masterpiece, never staged professionally in New York, was produced in all of its brilliance by the visiting Moscow Art Theatre as one of several works in repertory. Two decades of playing this revelatory blend of comedy and pathos provided a perfect example of the troupe's standards of ensemble, detailed characterization, intense, yet poetic realism, and human warmth, sincerity, and comprehension.

The Cherry Orchard, in which little seems to happen, pictures the failure of the landed Ranevskaya family to act when they are faced with the sale of their beloved cherry orchard in order to raise the funds needed to maintain their large estate. Held back by their aristocratic values concerning the intelligent manipulation of their finances, they do not heed the warnings constantly placed before them, and the orchard is sold at length to wealthy former serf Lopahin (Ivan Moskvin), who represents the rise of the bourgeoisie. Constantin Stanislavsky played his famous role of Gayeff, and the playwright's widow, Olga Knipper-Chekhova, displayed her art as Madame Ranevskaya.

The critics dwelt on Chekhov's ability to select from life's seemingly secondary moments the essence of his world and its people and to make them seem potent and meaningful. The lack of melodrama, the seeming absence of a plot and conflict, the connection of crises to a symphonically composed milieu of characters and events, the feeling that the drama's concerns were universal, and the emphasis on carefully shaded states of internal turmoil were the gold rings that this work held out to grasping playgoers.

Critic after critic declared that the language barrier dissolved as they viewed the play. Heywood Broun recalled "moments in which we were moved more profoundly than ever before in the theatre"; yet he and others also took great delight in the extensive moments of comedy, played so clearly that no words were needed to convey their meaning. The company, Broun noted, "never had the least temerity about introducing the broadest strokes into this subtle and poignantly tender comedy." Still, John Corbin was one of the minority who claimed that without knowledge of Russian, one could never catch the subtler laugh-inspiring moments.

When the troupe returned in late 1923 the play was given two more performances from 12/15/23.

(2) [Dramatic Revival] TR: George Calderon; D/S/P: James B. Fagan; T: Bijou Theatre; 3/5/28 (6)

This first English-language production of the play in New York was given at a series of matinees in a "scraggly production" that nevertheless could not deny its place "as one of the most thrilling and moving plays of the theatre's literature" (John Mason Brown). Although ill acted and awkwardly translated, enough of an indication of the play's greatness was present to make viewing it worthwhile. George Jean Nathan said the third raters in the troupe obviously thought they were playing something by the author of the tune "When It's Cherry Blossom Time in Tokio." Brooks Atkinson, however, was doubtful that any modern English production could give the piece life, since it was too deeply rooted in a national spirit of time and place. Among the company members were Mary Grey as Madame Ranevskaya and Glen Byam Shaw as Peter.

(3) TR: Constance Garnett; D: Eva Le Gallienne; S: Aline Bernstein; P: Civic Repertory Company; T: Civic Repertory Theatre (OB); 10/15/28 (63)

Eva Le Gallienne's production was the play's first full-scale staging locally.

The exigencies of a repertory schedule, combined with limited financial means, meant a less than perfectly polished mounting, despite Le Gallienne's own good work as Varya and that of guest artist Nazimova as Madame Ranevskaya. Joseph Wood Krutch referred to the "somewhat impromptu air which marks the production" but revelled in the play's magnificence as a work of art. Others, like Robert Littell, thought the troupe had done themselves and Chekhov proud. This critic was prepared to criticize the male performers in the play (except for J. Edward Bromberg as Yasha) and find other defects, but he insisted that "the spirit of that strange marvelous play came through. . . . The company understood what they were trying to do, even if they could not always express it."

As Ranevskaya, Nazimova, said the *Times*, was not as good as Knipper-Chekhova, "But she gave the [role] more beauty, and a deal of fitful charm in her sudden moods." He said that Le Gallienne "gave the truest and most poignant performance of all."

The company kept the play in its repertory and gave it from 9/23/29 for fourteen performances and from 5/4/31 for two performances.

(4) [Yiddish Language] D: Leo Bulgakov; P: Maurice Schwartz; T: Yiddish Art Theatre (OB); 11/7/28

A Yiddish Art Theatre production offered in celebration of the thirtieth anniversary of the founding of the Moscow Art Theatre (MAT). Former MAT actor Leo Bulgakov staged the play in a manner closely resembling that of the great Russian company. "That the Yiddish players should reach the esthetic highlights attained by their Russian prototypes was scarcely to be expected; that they climbed an appreciable distance up the slope is no mean praise" (*Times*). Gaev was played by Maurice Schwartz; he was "finished in the extreme," said the *Times*. Madame Ranevskaya was acted by Helen Zelinskaya, who was not up to the demands of the role.

CHERRY PIE [Revue] M: Eugene L. Barton; LY: Carroll Carroll; D: Harry Wagstaff Gribble; S: Rhea Wells; P: Inter-Theatre Arts, Inc.; T: Cherry Lane Playhouse (OB); 4/14/26 (37)

A modest off-Broadway revue that "proved dull" to *Time* but was enjoyed by the *Times*. It was a compilation of songs and sketches put together by director Harry Wagstaff Gribble and had in its semiprofessional cast a new and promising entertainer, Agnes Lumbard.

Scenes of note (there were twenty-four in all) were "The Fall of an Usher" by Jean Hawthorne and Watson Cady; "The Village Blacksmith," a parody of Longfellow a la O'Neill, Kelly, and Elinor Glyn; and "These Alarming People," a takeoff on the season's most popular plays. The *Times* liked "a somewhat muddled but still rather striking first act finale which shows the Charleston originating from negro spirituals and hymns."

CHICAGO [Comedy/Crime/Prison/Journalism] A: Maurine Watkins; D: George Abbott; P: Sam H. Harris; T: Music Box Theatre; 12/30/26 (173)

Maurine Watkins was a fledgling journalist for the *Chicago Tribune* when she got the idea for this pungent melodrama from one of the court cases she was covering. She quit her reporter job, joined Professor Baker's playwriting course at Yale, wrote *Chicago* there, and before long had a smash hit on her hands. Realistically staged by the man responsible for *Broadway*'s recent success, it made for "swift, vulgar, depressing, and at times excellent theatre," remarked Richard Dana Skinner. Its dialogue was racy, it reeked of the tabloid atmosphere, and it was heavy-handedly satirical in its lampooning of Chicago crook life as depicted in the papers. Audiences were handed Chicago-like newspapers filled with stories of killings and thefts, and tough-looking and acting characters were scattered through the house to add local color to the show.

The beautiful tart Roxie Hart (Francine Larrimore) guns down her lover (Carl Eckstrom); her husband tries to take the rap but not for long. Roxie is turned by a reporter (Charles Bickford) into a national celebrity; the play parodies the process by which tabloid journalism converts killers into heroes. Roxie is tried and acquitted and even invites the jurors to see her new vaudeville act. Roxie is momentarily forgotten at the end when a new murderess kills someone in the courthouse itself.

Burns Mantle selected *Chicago* as a Best Play of the Year.

Dorothy Stickney was then a young ingenue appearing in her first Broadway play, *The Squall*. She was bent on landing the eccentric character role of Old Liz in *Chicago* and made herself up as shabbily as possible to see if she could persuade the producer to give her the part. She was constantly put off, especially because she was so much younger than the character, but she was insistent and got Sam Harris to allow her the concession of watching a rehearsal. During its progress, director Sam Forrest had to stop a scene, because the Old Liz actress had not arrived. Harris and Forrest conferred and then decided to give Stickney a shot. With barely any preparation, she went on and auditioned her heart out. She was cast at once, and told to hand in her notice to *The Squall*. During the rehearsal period, the original star, Jeanne Eagels, threw a tantrum at the director and walked out on the show. She could be found nowhere, so a week before the show opened out of town, Francine Larrimore replaced her. Another out-of-town replacement was director George Abbott, taking over from Forrest.

CHICKEN FEED [Comedy/Marriage] A: Guy Bolton; D: Winchell Smith; S: P. Dodd Ackerman; C: Emma Phillips; P: John Golden; T: Little Theatre; 9/24/23 (146)

Subtitled "Wages for Wives," this Guy Bolton comedy featured a tussle between three women who don't want to beg their husbands for money but to share the family incomes and the men who want to control the purse strings. When one woman asks, "If there weren't any women, who'd mend your clothes?" her man replies, "If there weren't any women, I wouldn't wear any clothes." Things end happily when the characters realize they are all a little wrong. Among the better-known players in the cast were Leila Bennett, Frank McCormack, Arthur Aylsworth, and Roberta Arnold.

Q.M. thought "it all seemed very much lacking in sincerity. Like a man who tries to be funny every time he opens his mouth, it became at times extremely difficult to smile upon," but Arthur Hornblow called it "a good evening's fun." Burns Mantle chose it as a Best Play (bypassing, among other possibilities, Shaw's masterpiece *St. Joan*), because he believed "it best represents its particular type of play, inspiring as much laughter as a farce without losing too completely its hold upon its theme, which is fundamentally both sound and serious."

The play's subtitle was its original title, but this was changed when producer John Golden spied the sign hanging outside of a warehouse owned by his director, Winchell Smith, who had a sideline as a gentleman farmer and merchant; the sign read "WINCHELL SMITH'S CHICKEN FEED."

H.H.

CHIEF THING, THE (Samoe glavnoe) [Dramatic Revival] A: Nikolai Evreinoff; D: Philip Moeller; S: Serge Soudeikine; P: Theatre Guild; T: Guild Theatre; 3/22/26 (40)

An unusual, Pirandellian curio from Russia, described by its author as "a comedy for some—a drama for others," at the end of which the audience was permitted to choose one of two alternate endings or even both. Arthur Hornblow declared that the work dealt with "the idea that the world loves illusions, and to be pleasantly deceived is better than to be wisely but painfully enlightened. Were this philosophy revealed with some measure of clarity or dramatic suspense, one might or might not quarrel with it, provided one were interested."

The symbolical figure of the Paraklete (McKay Morris), a messiah-like figure prophesied by John the Baptist, is seen as a fortune teller listening to the problems of a group of boarding-house residents and then as a theatrical producer who hires a band of actors to play in real life those figures who, if they existed, would bring love and happiness to the people living at the boarding house. Evreinoff never answers the question of the efficacy of the actors' attempts, leaving that for the audience to determine. Instead, he pretends that the whole exercise has been nothing but a harlequinade.

Although this was the play's English-language premiere, it had been given in Yiddish three years earlier by Samuel Goldenberg's Cooperative Irving Place Theatre, with Muni Weisenfreund (Paul Muni).

CHIFFON GIRL, THE [Musical/Prohibition/Music/Romance] B: George Murray; M/LY: Monte Carlo and Alma Sanders; D: Everett Butterfield; CH: Bert French and Francis "Bunny" Weldon; P: Charles Capehart; T: Lyric Theatre; 2/19/24 (103)

Only Eleanor Painter's performance in the title role gave critics much to rave about in describing this humdrum musical. She played a Lower East Side girl of Italian extraction who is sent to study voice in Italy by a patron. She returns a great prima donna and marries not the patron but her old sweetheart (Joseph Lestora). He has—in a twist that added a contemporary tang to what was essentially an operetta—become a bootlegger.

The score was not unmelodious and contained several decent tunes, especially "The Raindrop and the Rose," but the show had a banal book and scarcely any comedy. The *Times* regretted that the distinguished "Miss Painter must perforce make her reappearance in so shoddy and undistinguished a production."

CHILD OF THE WORLD, THE [Drama/Prostitution/Romance/Yiddish/Yiddish Language] A: Peretz Hirschbein; T: Irving Place Theatre (OB); 4/28/22

The emotional actress Bertha Kalich found a colorful role suited to her talents in Hirschbein's *Child of the World*. She played a prostitute whose spiritual awakening derives from her love for a serene toymaker whose withdrawal from worldly relationships convinces her that she can never win his love; she thereupon takes her life in despair.

The play was "more theatrical and pretentious than [Hirschbein's] better-known plays," claimed the *Times*.

CHILDREN OF DARKNESS [Comedy-Drama/Romance/Prison/Sex/Period] A/D: Edwin Justus Mayer; SC: Henry Fielding's *History of the Life of the Late Mr. Jonathan Wilding the Great*; DS: Robert Edmond Jones; P: Kenneth Macgowan and Joseph Verner Reed; T: Biltmore Theatre; 1/7/30 (79)

Mayer's "play in the picaresque manner" enjoyed only a success d'estime in its original presentation and did not meet with commercial popularity until revived for 301 performances by the Circle in the Square in 1958. This costume tragicomedy was set in 1725 in a home adjoining London's Newgate Prison, where Mr. Snap (Walter Kingsford), the corrupt Under-Sheriff, boards paying prisoners. His guests include the debtor Count La Ruse (Basil Sydney), the famous soon-to-be-hanged thief Jonathan Wild (Charles Dalton), the debtor-poet Mr. Cartwright (J. Kirby Hawkes), and old Lord Wainwright (Eugene Powers), poisoner of his wife and her friends. The buxom wench Laetitia (Mary Ellis), Snap's daughter, in love with La Ruse, also cavorts indiscriminately with the other men in a play that is more a series of situations than a sustained story. Wild, thinking he is buying his pardon, is tricked out of his money and then is hanged anyway, while La Ruse, aware that he will never reform, purchases the poet's freedom and kills himself. Laetitia ends up in the sexual clutches of the chilling Wainwright.

Children of Darkness (originally called *The Jailer's* [or *Gaoler's*] *Wench*) was viewed as a somewhat literary, fascinating, artificial comedy filled with an array of cynical, sordid, bawdy, and devilish knaves, barely a one of whom had redeeming features; it smacked of Wycherley and Gay and was "beautifully written with a consistent malice" (Brooks Atkinson). Ornate in language, it needed close attention, but its characters seemed magnetic and truthful and wryly amusing. "The words are an elaborate tapestry which hides the scantiest of plots," concluded Perriton Maxwell. John Hutchens decided Mayer had "caught the fulsome color, malice and wit of eighteenth century England in a scheme that curiously maintains its own detachment."

In his memoir, *The Curtain Falls*, Joseph Verner Reed, the fledgling coproducer of this play, discusses *Children of Darkness* in one of the most detailed descriptions to be found of the production process of any play of the decade. He tells of the difficulties faced by the original director, Lester Lonergan, in handling the talented but tempestuous star Mary Ellis, and of Lonergan's ultimate decision to resign shortly before the opening rather than continue to be humiliated by her. Even the author, who took over the direction, had to face the actress's venom, for he had once been romantically involved with her and now was subject to her "revenge." Reed also provides a fascinating account of the obstacles faced in 1929 by producers when dealing with union regulations; for example, when the stagehands' union was requested to allow its men to take salary cuts to enable the play to continue its run, the union not only refused the request, it required that an extra man be hired to do nothing but ring out the hour of eleven P.M. once each performance on a clock that figured as a prop in the play.

CHILDREN OF THE MOON [Drama/Family/Mental Illness/Aviation] A: Martin A. Flavin; D: B. Iden Payne; S: Cleon Throckmorton; P: Jacob A. Weiser i/a/w A. L. Jones and Morris Green; T: Comedy Theatre; 8/17/23 (109)

Director Louis Calvert died and was replaced by B. Iden Payne during rehearsals of this work, the first play by Martin Flavin. This Freud-influenced play was set on the California coast, where a mother (Beatrice Terry) using the taint of moon madness running through her husband's family to control her children ruins their lives. Fearing his madness, her son had crashed his plane in the war. Now a daughter and the pilot she loves fly off to the moon and are lost over the Pacific.

Critics likened the atmosphere of the play to some of Ibsen's and found merits, variously, in different acts. John Corbin noted that the audience gave a standing ovation after Act Two but thought that the final act was less impressive. Alexander Woollcott concluded that the play never came to life and remained a thing of the theatre, although it was "intense, bold and ambitious."

H.H.

CHILDREN'S TRAGEDY, THE (Kindertragödie), and "THE VAN DYKE"
The Children's Tragedy [Drama/Family/Youth/Sex/German] A: Carl Schönherr; TR: Benjamin F. Glazer; "The Van Dyke" [Dramatic Revival] A: Eugène Fourrier; AD: Cosmo Gordon-Lennox; D/P: Arnold Daly; T: Greenwich Village Theatre (OB); 10/10/21 (8)

Carl Schönherr's German drama dealt with the effect on three children of a forester and his wife of the discovery that their attractive mother is having an affair with a stranger during the father's absence. There are no characters except the sister (Nedda Harrigan) and her two brothers (Phillips Tead and Sidney Carlyle), who are seen spying on the unfaithful parent. As the drama progresses one brother dies of shock after killing the lover, the sister is subjected to an attack when she threatens to reveal the story, and the remaining sibling runs off screaming for assistance.

This was seen by some as a shockingly frank, "deeply, darkly melodramatic" story (*Tribune*), "drab" and "morbid" (*Herald*), "nauseous and repulsive" (Louis V. De Foe). Alison Smith, however, thought it was "a poignant and haunting study," and Alexander Woollcott called the play "simple, moving and genuinely dramatic." What almost all agreed on was the idiocy of the production, which employed three mature actors to play children, thus robbing the work of any veracity or interest it might have held.

In sharp contrast was a short second piece, "The Van Dyke," a one-act French farce starring Arnold Daly, who had toured the vaudeville circuit in it after first introducing it locally in 1907. It told of a man (Daly) who admires everything in another's art collection except a Van Dyck, which he believes to be spurious. After faking a fit of insanity, he manages to steal all of the art works, leaving behind only the Van Dyck.

CHINA ROSE [Musical/China/Orientals/Romance] B: Harry L. Cort and George E. Stoddard; M: A. Baldwin Sloane; D: R. H. Burnside; P: Charles Dillingham, Martin Beck, and John Cort; T: Martin Beck Theatre; 1/19/25 (126)

A month after this "extremely dull" (Joseph Wood Krutch) operetta opened, its fifty-two-year-old composer died. The show itself died two months later. It was an old-fashioned Oriental operetta that Percy Hammond called "Just a sweet old thing, of the kind referred to by this ribald generation as a 'daddy' . . . a florid octogenarian . . . who has left the blessings of retirement for the cruel discomforts of modern, Times Square life."

Using the most conventional of plots, the show concerned itself with virgin Princess Ro See (Olga Steck); the Manchurian Prince Cha Ming (J. Harold Murray), who craves her; the bumbling clowns Hi and Lo (Harry Short and Harry Clarke), who are threatened with beheading if they do not get her for him; the Prince's adoption of a bandit disguise to observe their efforts; and a Chinese young lady who drops phrases such as "Hot stuff!" and "Sure, Mike!" It all added up to "the most astonishingly rubber stamp musical of years and years" (*Times*).

CHINESE O'NEILL [Drama/Adventure/Orientals/China/Romance] A/DS/P: Captain Cushing Donnell; D: Georges Romain; T: Forrest Theatre; 5/22/29 (12)

Machine guns, horse pistols, and other firearms blazed away during the climax of this adventure melodrama about an American soldier of fortune engaged in gun-running along the China coast. Chinese O'Neill (Douglas R. Dumbrille) gets entangled in a dangerous situation when Chang Kai Cheng, "master of the China seas," threatens the destruction of Gerson St. George (Hugh Buckler) for having put a price on the pirate's head. A villain himself, St. George is killed by Chang's associates, but O'Neill wins the heart of St. George's unwilling mistress, the Hon. Nancy Beresford (Audrey Ridgwell), and blows up Chang's gunpowder-laden ship with a well-aimed shot.

"Since the melodrama was rather muddled in the writing, and overtheatricalized in the staging, the enjoyment it provided was often at the expense of the play," smirked Brooks Atkinson.

CHIP WOMAN'S FORTUNE, THE, and SALOMÉ D: Raymond O'Neil; P: Ethiopian Art Theatre; T: Frazee Theatre; 5/7/23 (8)
The Chip Woman's Fortune [Comedy/Family/Blacks/One-Act] A: Willis Richardson; *Salomé* (See separate listing for this play.)

A dual bill given by a visiting black company from Chicago. Willis Richardson's curtain raiser was thought to be the best acted of the troupe's offerings. John Farrar said the piece was "a pointless sketch with neither humor nor tenderness." The play was a domestic comedy about how Aunt Nancy (Laura Bowman) shovels up her savings from the backyard and finds she has not only enough to make the payments on Silas's (Sydney Kirkpatrick) victrola but also to help out her son Jim (Solomon Bruce), just released from jail. With a jazz record playing on the victrola, the company dances as the curtain falls.

This simple comedy is considered the first black-authored work to reach Broadway, although Garland Anderson's *Appearances* attempted to make claim to that distinction a couple of years later. Richardson's play led Robert Littell to write, "It might be described as a mild, sincere comedy of gratitude, surprise, reconciliation, speeding up suddenly at the end into jazz as the phonograph is turned on and all the members of the family dance about the room with that amazingly syncopated motion which seems natural to Negroes but not to us."

CHIPPIES [Comedy-Drama/Small Town/Romance/Family/Sex/Prohibition] A: Luther Yantis; D: George Smithfield; P: F.A.D. Productions, Inc.; T: Belmont Theatre; 5/29/29 (22)

Painsville, Ohio, girl Beth Ramsey (Maud Brooks) flees the boring small-town life for Cleveland's fast lane, where she becomes the mistress of speakeasy operator Tony Perotta (Cullen Landis). News that her mother (Maude Dayton) is dying is brought by her old boyfriend (Warren Colt), and she can only return home with head high if Tony marries her, which he does. She arrives in Painsville only to see her mom stiff in her coffin.

Overly sentimental, stereotyped in all of its characters, and weakly acted, *Chippies* had little chance of success. The *Times* said, "The most significant comment on Mr. Yantis's playwrighting" was the fact that a drunken character who had nothing to do with the action was its sole amusing element.

CHIVALRY [Drama/Trial/Crime/Law] A: William Hurlbut; D: James Durkin; P: Joseph B. Shea; T: Wallack's Theatre; 12/15/25 (23)

A melodrama that failed despite strong expressions of support from several commentators. It begins with a prologue revealing that a sweet young thing (Violet Heming) is about to be tried for the murder of her older lover (Roy Gordon) and then flashes back to describe the events leading up to the killing; during this flashback the girl's nasty, scheming, immoral nature is unveiled. The play then returns to the present, where the male jury pronounces her innocent; it culminates with a sudden reversal on the part of the defense attorney (Edmund Breese), who delivers a stinging rebuke to the jurors for allowing its sentimental notions about women to obstruct the true course of justice. He discloses the truth about his client and then announces his intention of resigning from the bar.

To Arthur Hornblow *Chivalry* was "powerfully written, with a decided punch throughout. . . . Rarely has a native play been more ingeniously contrived or with more powerful interest been produced." However, most went along with Percy Hammond, who called it "a play that ranged from tolerable to terrible, a baffling yes-and-noer."

CHOCOLATE DANDIES, THE [Musical/Sports/Blacks] B: Noble Sissle and Lew Payton; M/LY: Noble Sissle and Eubie Blake; D: Lew Payton; CH: Julian Mitchell; P: R. C. Whitney; T: Colonial Theatre; 9/1/24 (96)

"Undoubtedly one of the best negro musical shows that has been seen in New York," wrote the *Times* of this elaborately produced follow-up to Sissle and Blake's great success with *Shuffle Along*. It was about a race-horse owner (Lew Payton), with two thoroughbreds named Dumb Luck and Jump Steady, who dreams that the former steed has won him a fortune that allows him to set up as president of the Bamville Bank (the show's original title was *In Bamville*). On waking, he learns that a horse named Rarin' to Go has actually won the race, and that the owner (Ivan H. Browning) has landed the pretty Angeline Brown (Lottie Gee) as well. There was critical applause for the revolving platform that allowed the horse race to be shown, and the songs "Bandanaland," "Slave of Love," and "Dixie Moon" were appreciated. One of the funniest scenes was when Payton had a heart-to-heart talk with a real horse, whose head protruded from a stable door. Noticed in the cast was young Josephine Baker, billed as "That Comedy Chorus Girl."

Sissle later asserted that this show represented his best score.

(1) CHOCOLATE SOLDIER, THE (Der Tapfere Soldat) [Musical Revival] B: Rudolph Bernauer and Leopold Jacobson; TR: Stanislaus Stange; M: Oscar Straus; S: Rollo Wayne; P: Messrs. Shubert; T: Century Theatre; 12/12/21 (83)

A worthwhile resuscitation of the popular 1909 opera bouffe parody of George Bernard Shaw's *Arms and the Man*, with a Viennese score by Oscar Straus. Kenneth Andrews said the show "has not aged in the least . . . and will probably never age appreciably." New Straus music was added to the score, but the awkward book remained unrevised. Alexander Woollcott claimed that the music was superior to anything then playing in town, called the production "generally able'' and ''well-sung—barring an occasional tendency toward shrillness,'' and, when ''My Hero'' was sung, thrilled to it as when he first heard it performed. Tessa Kosta and Donald Brian were members of the cast.

(2) D: Milton Aborn; S: Rollo Wayne; P: Jolson Theatre Musical Comedy Company; T: Jolson's Fifty-ninth Street Theatre; 1/27/30 (25)
One of the series of old light operas revived by Milton Aborn at Jolson's Theatre during the 1929–1930 season. Charles Purcell sang Captain Bumerli, Alice MacKenzie was Nadina, Vera Ross was Aurelia, Vivian Hart was Mascha, Roy Cropper was Spiridoff, and John Dunsmore was Colonel Popoff; all were in admirable voice. M.G. noted, ''The music is as delightful and the book of course as clever as ever.''

CINDERELLA ON BROADWAY [Revue] B/LY: Harold Atteridge; M: Bert Grant and Al Goodman; D: J. C. Huffman; P: Messrs. Shubert; T: Winter Garden Theatre; 6/24/20 (126)
Due to open as *Rip Van Winkle, Jr.*, this Shubert revue suddenly changed its title to *Cinderella on Broadway*. Although plotless, it did have a loose frame in which Cinderella searched for Prince Charming. Two acts and twenty-two scenes were employed to fill the frame. The *Times* observed that ''there is not even a thread to hang the many scenes together.'' The best thing about the premise was its basis for a spectacular ball scene with a staircase transmogrified out of a gigantic silk slipper. Also lavishly depicted were ''The Jewelled Castle'' and ''The Top of the World'' scenes. In the latter the chorus was envisioned as a human roulette wheel.
Things the critics liked included Swedish comic El Brendel; dancer Jessica Brown; a slack wire act, Mijares; soprano Llora Hoffman; mimic Georgie Price; and an ape impersonator, Tarzan. A sour voice came from the *Evening Sun*: ''The scenery . . . is unattractive and the book is insipid and unimaginative.''

CINDERS [Musical/Crime/Romance] B/LY: Edward Clark; M: Rudolf Friml; D/CH/P: Edward Royce; T: Dresden Theatre; 4/3/23 (31)
One of the more blatant examples of the Cinderella theme, so prevalent in early twenties musicals, was here embodied in a fairly attractive, fast-paced entertainment. Despite being ''a familiar show with stock characters and situations'' (Percy Hammond), its ''Pretty girls, attractive costumes, well-staged ensembles, and, above all, its leading player and singer, Miss Nancy Welford'' (*Sun*) led several critics to recommend it.
Its threadbare plot concerns Cinders (Welford), a modiste's shopgirl with Cinderella aspirations, who, failing to deliver a gown on time, decides to wear it to the ball herself, becomes the belle of the party, and is the object of the wealthy hostess's son's (W. Douglas Stevenson) attentions. During the fete she foils a jewel theft but is herself left open to suspicion; she is forced to hit the

streets, cold and forlorn. As things turn out, she is cleared of the theft and returns to her admirer's arms.

The libretto set few hearts on fire, but Friml's score was valued for its tunefulness.

CIRCLE, THE [Comedy/Marriage/Romance/British] A: W. Somerset Maugham; D: Clifford Brooke; P: Selwyns; T: Selwyn Theatre; 9/12/21 (175)

A hit play of the 1921–1922 season and a Burns Mantle Best Play of the Year. W. Somerset Maugham's lithe drawing-room comedy was "a searching, malicious and richly entertaining" (Alexander Woollcott) work in which Time, ever repeating itself in circular fashion, plays the principal role.

Maugham's ironic comedy brought back to Broadway the seasoned star Mrs. Leslie Carter, who had not been seen on a New York stage in years, and paired her with one of Broadway's grand old men, John Drew. This veteran duo played the roles of Lady Catherine Champion-Cheney and her lover of more than thirty years, Lord Porteus, a couple who eloped in their youth, leaving only a note on a pincushion for the lady's unhappy husband (Ernest Lawford). No longer avid lovers, the pair yap at each other like the aging spouses they indeed are. When they pay a surprise visit to the lady's son (Robert Rendel), whom she has not seen in all these years, they learn that his young wife, Elizabeth (Estelle Winwood), is planning just as they did to run off with someone else (John Halliday). Lady Champion-Cheney and Lord Porteus do their best to dissuade Elizabeth and her lover Edward from their planned elopement, but even the tale of their own woes can do nothing to cool the pair's ardor, and they depart, much to the scandalous pleasure of the 1921 audience.

Arthur Hornblow, as did many others, said the play contained "sparkling lines, keen satire, distinguished acting, added to an absorbing and very human story."

The play moved to the Fulton Theatre after five months at the Selwyn Theatre.

CIRCUS PRINCESS, THE (Die Zirkusprinzessen) [Musical/Circus/Romance/Russia/Austrian] AD: Harry B. Smith; B/LY: Julius Brammer and Alfred Grunwald; M: Emmerich Kalman; D: J. C. Huffman; CH: Allan K. Foster; S: Watson Barratt; P: Messrs. Shubert; T: Winter Garden Theatre; 4/25/27 (192)

An operetta abounding in entertaining features, from its romantic plot to its spectacularly realized circus background to its lavish decor to its Emmerich Kalman Viennese score. The legitimate performers were joined by an assortment of real circus acts, including daredevil rider Poodles Hanneford, tightrope acrobat Bee Starr, and a passel of clowns.

The libretto; adapted from a Viennese work, was set in 1912 Russia and concerned Prince Orloff (Guy Robertson), whose family problems lead him to join the circus, where he falls in love with Princess Fedora (Desiree Tabor), becomes involved with her in an intrigue, and finally reaches a happy conclusion in a fancy hotel in Vienna.

"The costumes and staging were particularly effective," reported First Nighter, "but the dialogue was exceedingly weak and the music just fair."

CITTA MORTA, LA (The Dead City) [Dramatic Revival/Italian Language] A: Gabriel D'Annunzio; P: F. Ray Comstock and Morris Gest; T: Century Theatre; 11/27/23 (2)

"A thwarted line of playgoers was coiled round the building like an angry snake," noted the *Herald* critic of the thousand people turned away from the performance he attended of *The Dead City*. This reviewer found visiting star Eleanora Duse's role most suited to her of all in her current repertoire: "The spell woven by her moving hands and by the moonlit magic of her voice wrought an ancient and mystic princess."

Duse's role in the Symbolist drama about archaeologists beset by an ancient curse while excavating a Homeric tomb in Mycenae was that of the Cassandra-like blind wife of one explorer. At the end, groping her way to a pool where the corpses of the other characters lie, she cried out: "I can see! I can see!" John Corbin commented, "As Duse renders that cry, it is as if the ancient curse were lifted from one and all of them."

H.H.

CITY CHAP, THE [Musical/Romance/Small Town] B: James Montgomery; M: Jerome Kern; LY: Anne Caldwell; SC: Winchell Smith's play *The Fortune Hunter*; D: R. H. Burnside; CH: David Bennett; DS: James Reynolds; P: Charles Dillingham; T: Liberty Theatre; 10/26/25 (72)

A likable, but average, musical comedy based on a hit 1909 comedy that had starred juvenile lead John Barrymore in his first legitimate theatre role. Richard "Skeets" Gallagher now essayed the part, that of the "city chap" down on his luck who travels from New York to a small town to woo and wed the banker's daughter (Ina Williams) whom he finds not nearly as appealing as the blonde, blue-eyed girl (Phyllis Cleveland) of the country druggist. He succeeds as an entrepreneur with his notion of opening a jazz-tearoom at the drugstore and marries the pharmacist's daughter.

"Two or three excellent songs, some frenzied dancing and a small supply of jokes are here and there included," was *Time*'s assessment, and the *Sun* deemed it "a highly efficient, zestful and polished musical comedy." In a small role, George Raft danced "gorgeously," declared Ward Morehouse. Also in the cast was the delightful Irene Dunne.

CITY HAUL [Comedy/Politics/Crime/Romance] A: Elizabeth Miele; D: Harry Wagstaff Gribble; P: Gil Boag; T: Hudson Theatre; 12/30/29 (77)

"[A] clever, fast-moving bit of satire on one of our most substantial American jokes—municipal politics" (Perriton Maxwell). Numerous facets of city corruption were revealed in this diverting piece that honed in on the abuses of Timothy MacHugh (Herbert Rawlinson), mayor of an Illinois city, a charming and debonair scoundrel, his finger in every pie; the mayor finds himself on the brink of disaster when a tax scam he operates is about to be uncovered; he is saved by the shrewd thinking of his ex-con male secretary (J. Anthony Hughes), whose love affair with the mayor's daughter (Dorothy Lebaire) his Honor has been frowning on until now.

Essentially a character study of the rapscallion civic leader, *City Haul*'s plot was a triviality worth little except as a springboard for the introduction of numerous amusing character types. Actor Rawlinson made up as New York's Mayor Jimmy Walker, and this may have been why the show ran into booking trouble and was forced to leave the Hudson for the Eltinge Theatre.

CLAIR DE LUNE [Drama/France/Period/Romance] A/M: Michael Strange; SC: Victor Hugo's novel *The Man Who Laughed*; D: E. Lyall Swete; P: Charles Frohman, Inc.; T: Empire Theatre; 4/18/21 (64)

Michael Strange, better known as Mrs. John Barrymore, authored this adaptation of a Hugo work in which her husband played Gwymplane, the grotesque mountebank, and his sister Ethel played Queen Anne. So potent was the draw of this team that crowd-control police had to be called in on opening night to handle the mobs.

Set in a late eighteenth-century environment suggestive of Versailles and the fashions of Marie Antoinette, *Clair de Lune* recounted the fable of Gwymplane who, with Dea (Jane Cooper), the blind girl, entertains at the Queen's palace and is drawn into the Queen's scheme to prevent the marriage of the Duchess of Beaumont (Violet Kemble Cooper) to Prince Charles (Henry Daniell). The highlight comes when the strange Duchess, fatally attracted to the distorted Gwymplane, toys erotically with him, and he kisses her feet. Finally, the girl dies, and Gwymplane kills himself.

This was judged a melancholy, decadent play of a poetic and literary manner. Most reviews were pejorative in tone, as in Alexander Woollcott's comments that it was ''feeble much of the time and incorrigibly pretentious always.'' John Barrymore helped design the production, and Ludwig Lewisohn thought his conception placed him ''in the front rank of our scenic artists.''

CLAIRE ADAMS [Drama/Marriage/Sex/Crime/Journalism] A: Daniel N. Rubin; D: Priestly Morrison; S: Redington Sharpe; P: Tom Weatherly; T: Biltmore Theatre; 11/19/29 (7)

Critical disgruntlement scuttled this absurd melodrama in one week's time. It was, said *Time*, ''a sordid, ordinary tragedy conceived and acted without much imagination.'' Its theme was the perils of New York life for those who move there from their small home towns. The title character (Mildred MacLeod) leaves Waco, Texas, with her new husband (Charles Starrett), a reporter and would-be novelist, for Greenwich Village, where their marriage goes flat; she takes a lover, wealthy Clyde Price (Buford Armitage), she had known back home and then takes up with his cousin (Charles Ritchie), whom she gets to murder Clyde. Jail beckons for Claire as her husband phones in his account of the events to his paper.

This play was on the verge of opening with the title *Undertow* when its name was revised.

CLAW, THE (La griffe) [Dramatic Revival] A: Henri Bernstein; TR: Edward Delaney Dunn and Louis Wolheim; D/P: Arthur Hopkins; S: Robert Edmond Jones; T: Broadhurst Theatre; 10/17/21 (115)

The first-night audience at this 1906 Bernstein drama coughed their way through a turgid work about a Paris newspaper publisher, Achille Cortelon, chewed up, digested, and eliminated by a worthless wife (Irene Fenwick); yet their appreciation of Cortelon's portrayer, Lionel Barrymore, was genuine. Barrymore's genius was the only important thing about this "fairly old-fashioned" (Arthur Hornblow) exercise. It roamed over many years in following the career of Cortelon from his peak of power as a respected radical-socialist political leader to his fatal infatuation with the scheming vamp Antoinette, who ruins his career and elopes with a lover, while he is saved from the wrath of an angry mob only by the intrusion of death.

The play was found wanting in "sincerity and dramatic intensity" by Hornblow and reviled by Alexander Woollcott for its formlessness and repetitious plotting. The work succeeded commercially though; Barrymore, disgruntled by his recent failure in *Macbeth*, later revealed in his autobiography *We Barrymores*, "I would have departed the theatre [for films] four years sooner if this one had not worked out."

Bernstein's drama had been produced locally in 1909, in German, with the title *Die Kralle*.

CLIMAX, THE [Dramatic Revival] A/D: Edward Locke; S: P. Dodd Ackerman; P: Samuel Wallach; T: Forty-eighth Street Theatre; 5/17/26 (8)

Revived seventeen years after its 1909 success, this old four-character melodrama with a Svengali theme seemed laughably out-of-date with its heroine who grows enraged by the expletive "damn" in the mouth of a lover. Its story of a promising singer (Dorothy Francis), the ardor of her two suitors, the use by one of them of autosuggestion to make her believe she has lost her voice so he may marry her, her realization that she can still sing, and the happy ending that ensues were all redolent of old-fashioned theatrics, but there was nonetheless a residue of entertainment to be derived from its performance.

To A.T. it was "rather inconsequential drama," and Percy Hammond thought the actors, for all of their earnestness, "were retarded by the limping gait of their ancient vehicle." Two members of the 1908 company, Albert Bruning and Effingham Pinto, played their original roles. *The Climax* had been revived once before, in 1918.

CLINGING VINE, THE [Musical/Business/Romance] B: Zelda Sears; M: Harold Levey; D: Ira Hards; P: Henry W. Savage; T: Knickerbocker Theatre; 12/25/22 (188)

Famous comic actress Zelda Sears turned musical-comedy librettist to provide star Peggy Wood with this very well-appreciated show that the critics hailed for its depth and skill. Since musicals with thematic values were so rare, *The Clinging Vine* scored heavily for its "novel plot and . . . most eye-appealing character" (*Times*). "Here is a piece with an intelligent book, some charming music and a capital cast," noted Arthur Hornblow. The relative paucity of the score made the show more a "comedy with music" than a conventional musical comedy.

Peggy Wood played a pragmatic and hardheaded businesswoman who kowtows to no man. While East on business, she visits her sophisticated grandmother (Louise Galloway), who teaches her to land a man by playing the demure clinging vine. She wins the heart of a poor young inventor (Charles Derickson) and also manages to turn a neat profit in a deal she puts over on the local businessmen.

In a minor role in her Broadway debut was Irene Dunne.

CLOISTER, THE (Le cloître) [Drama/Verse/Religion/Belgian] A: Émile Verhaeren; TR: Osman Edwards; S: Sheldon K. Viele; P: Theatre Guild; T: Garrick Theatre; 6/5/21 (2)

Only Theatre Guild subscribers got to see Symbolist poet Verhaeren's blank verse and prose play of 1900, given at two special end-of-season performances. It presents the conflict between the patrician monks at a cloister and the plebian monks who aggressively seek to take over the cloister's leadership. Central to the drama is the plight of Dom Balthazar (Georges Renavent), suffering the pangs of guilt for a parricide committed ten years earlier; he confessed his crime to the prior but now feels he must confess to his brother monks. When this fails to cleanse him, he confesses publicly before the worshiping congregation and is thereupon cast out of the cloister to undergo the punishment of the outside world.

Nicely designed and well played by one or two, the remainder of "the performance . . . was not conspicuous for its excellence," noted the *Times*. The play was deemed not sufficiently dramatic to sustain interest.

CLOSE HARMONY [Comedy/Alcoholism/Marriage/Romance] A: Dorothy Parker and Elmer Rice; D/P: Arthur Hopkins; S: Woodman Thompson; T: Gaiety Theatre; 12/1/24 (24)

The Main Street temperament and environment embodied in Sinclair Lewis's novels was seen as an influence on this unevenly received Parker-Rice collaboration. It was a comedic study of suburban married life in which a henpecked husband, Ed Graham (James Spottswood), whose wife of thirteen years (Georgie Drew Mendum) will not even permit him to play the mandolin at home, warms to Belle Sheridan (Wanda Lyon), a former Follies girl who, with her alcoholic husband (Robert Hudson), has recently moved next door.

Generally, the critics censured the play for its uninteresting characters and milieu. Noting the accuracy of its dialogue, Joseph Wood Krutch nevertheless questioned why an audience would be interested in "a hero weak to the point of insignificance." Heywood Broun, however, was interested, and called *Close Harmony* "the bitterest of the current comedies and one of the brightest," a play with truthful humor and emotional validity.

CLOUDS [Drama/War/Romance/Invalidism/Mental Illness/Small Town] A: Helen Broun; D: Edward Elsner; P: Woodhouse Productions, Inc. i/a/w Walter O. Lindsey; T: Cort Theatre; 9/2/25 (22)

A mawkish drama that Percy Hammond called "a messy little canard" that presented young veteran Richard Adams (Ramsey Wallace), whose shell shock has caused him to go blind and whose disability threatens to alienate the girl he loves (Marian Swayne). The youth's saccharine-sweet mother (Louise Carter) learns that Richard's blindness may be cured by another shock; she thereupon both simulates madness and tells the son that he will lose his girl. The ploy works, and Richard gets to say, "I can see. I can see," and to embrace his girl and mother before the curtain falls.

"Through the dampness of the sentimentalities which moisten this play . . . it was difficult to distinguish the author's purpose," announced Brooks Atkinson. "*Clouds* is not entertainment for the hard-boiled," exclaimed Percy Hammond.

Actress Louise Carter was rumored to be the author, writing under a pseudonym. The play was revived for sixteen performances on 1/25/26, having been trimmed considerably.

CLOUDS OF THE SUN [Drama/Verse/Period/Religion/Art/Romance] A: Isabel Fiske-Conant; T: Cloisters (OB); 5/6/22 (1)

A benefit performance for orphans of the French Army and Navy was given of this play at the Cloisters, a reproduction of a medieval French cloister located in Manhattan's Washington Heights. It was acted in the inner and outer courtyards in beautifully designed costumes, with musical settings suggestive of the medieval period and with a cast made up of professionals and amateurs. Best known of the players was Clare Eames, who figured as a reader of the Prologue. The unusual presentation had a plot about an artist named Gaston Le Fevre (Barry Irvine), who vows to wed only she who is identical to the girl he painted in a moment of inspiration; when he meets Alysoun (Sydney Thompson) and falls in love with her, he remembers his vow and leaves to fight in the Crusades. When he returns, he discovers that Alysoun, by constant pondering on the girl's portrait, has become her very image, so he now can marry her.

CLUBS ARE TRUMPS [Comedy/Sports/Business/Romance] A: Leslie Hickson and W. Lee Dickson; P: Walter Hast; T: Bijou Theatre; 10/14/24 (7)

"In *Clubs Are Trumps*," groaned Stark Young, "the theatrical season may boast that it hit bottom." The play was a cheerless farce about a George M.

Cohan-like young man (Harry Green), an ad writer for a soup company, who believes he can find success in his field by becoming a better golfer. He practices in his bedroom, and then goes out to play his first game as if a veteran of the links. The experience ends in embarrassment, but he stays with his theory, reappears at the club tournament a half-year later, ends in a tie with his rival for the soup magnate's daughter (May Collins), makes the connections he sought, and gets the girl.

Much of the comedy came from golfing quips, but they were insufficient to warrant many guffaws.

CLUTCHING CLAW, THE [Drama/Mystery/Spiritualism/Crime/Drugs] A: Ralph Thomas Kettering; D: Rollo Lloyd; P: Barbour and Bryant; T: Forrest Theatre; 2/14/28 (23)

A stereotypical murder mystery set in a manor house. During the prologue, a murder is committed and the subsequent action concerns the attempts of an exceptionally clever young newspaper man (Ralph Morgan) to use his amateur detective abilities to unearth the culprit. His sleuthing makes asses of the police force. A seance in which a ghost materializes figures as part of the plot, as does a gang of dope sellers.

Richard Dana Skinner recommended *The Clutching Claw* only to the most avid mystery fan who would "not likely leave the theatre until the final curtain shall leave him fumbling for his hat and coat in the dark."

COBRA [Drama/Sex/Marriage/Friendship] A: Martin Brown; D: Henry Stillman and William B. Friedlander; P: L. Lawrence Weber; T: Hudson Theatre; 4/22/24 (240)

Noting that the cobra-serpent character was not new, John Corbin wrote, "but as written and as Judith Anderson plays it, it is of such vitality and authenticity in evil as to hold one breathless upon every word and gasping for what is to follow." Loving a college athlete (Louis Calhern), a woman (Anderson) marries his friend (Ralph Morgan), because he is rich and generous. Four years later she lures her love to a hotel, but he leaves after they have dinner together. She is killed when the hotel burns down, and her almost-lover ponders whether to go on letting the grief-stricken husband idolize her memory or to tell him the truth. The husband learns of his wife's character from another source, and his friend marries a pure stenographer and settles down.

Martin Brown's drama was generally praised as good entertainment and the actors as excellent.

H.H.

COCK O' THE ROOST [Comedy/Romance/Family/Literature] A: Rida Johnson Young; D: James Forbes; S: Livingston Platt; P: Dramatists' Theatre, Inc.; T: Liberty Theatre; 10/13/24 (24)

George Kelly's *Show-Off* spawned a number of imitators, *Cock o' the Roost* being one of them. The loudmouth in this comedy was Jerry Hayward (Donald Foster), a dynamic but poor go-getter of the most self-confident sort, who, in love with the daughter (Katherine Wilson) of a writer of cheap detective fiction (Harry Davenport) whose labors on behalf of his wife (Elizabeth Risdon) and daughter's comforts are threatening to give him a nervous breakdown, manages to reorganize the family's life, set them up in a model tenement, and arrange so the father can have a year off to write his masterpiece. Jerry foils a wealthy rival for the daughter's hand, and the curtain falls when they are clearly headed for a happy future.

A work of unabashed optimism and good cheer, the comedy caused H.S. to consider it "good entertainment" of the fast moving, smart dialogue variety. But *Time* said, "Only the most blandly vacuous and the veriest tyros of the theatre can regard *Cock o' the Roost* favorably."

COCK ROBIN [Comedy-Drama/Mystery/Theatre) A: Philip Barry and Elmer Rice; D/P: Guthrie McClintic; S: Jo Mielziner; T: Forty-eighth Street Theatre; 1/12/28 (100)

A reasonably effective mystery of the whodunit variety that dealt with a murder committed during a charity performance of an amateur suburban theatre group. The dead man is Hancock Robinson (Henry Southard), a nasty fellow, who meets his end by a knife in the back and a real bullet substituted for a blank in the play-within-the-play's duel scene. A dozen or so suspects are brought into the limelight until the guilty party, a drama coach (Edward Ellis) with noble intentions, is detected.

The piece was dismissed by George Jean Nathan as a mere throwaway by its distinguished authors, but Joseph Wood Krutch liked it enough to say that "the authors have managed both to keep within the bounds of the remotely possible and to create characters solid enough to produce an illusion of life." John Mason Brown dubbed it a cross between *The Trial of Mary Dugan* and *The Torch Bearers*; it was neither consistent melodrama, he said, nor an acute enough satire on amateur theatre.

COCOANUTS, THE [Musical/Hotel/Southern/Business] B: George S. Kaufman; M/LY: Irving Berlin; D: Oscar Eagle; CH: Sammy Lee; S: Woodman Thompson; C: Charles Le Maire; P: Sam H. Harris; T: Lyric Theatre; 12/8/25 (375)

After years of vaudeville popularity and a Broadway success in the revue-like antics of *I'll Say She Is* a year earlier, the four Marx Brothers, Zeppo, Chico, Groucho, and Harpo, careened rowdily onto the Great White Way in this lavishly designed hit musical with a plot by George S. Kaufman and a score by Irving Berlin. The skimpy story was merely an excuse for their riotous clowning; it plunked the risible siblings down at a luxurious Florida hotel, where Henry W. Schlemmer (Groucho) is a hotel manager and real estate wheeler-dealer taking advantage of the local real estate boom. Groucho touted his property as "the

biggest development since Sophie Tucker.'' There were perfunctory plot stratagems such as a jewel theft, with suspicion thrown on the innocent shoulders
of the matronly victim's (Margaret Dumont, in her first appearance as a Marx
Brothers' straight man) niece's (Mabel Withee) fiancé (Jack Barker); these details, though, were only the framework for the crazy Marx Brothers shenanigans,
in the course of which so many ad-libs were created by the comics that Kaufman
is reported to have said once in surprise, ''Say, I really think Groucho just spoke
one of my lines as I wrote it.''

Harpo was Silent Sam, Chico was the Italian dialect-speaking, piano-playing
Willie the Wop, and Zeppo was Jamison, a straight character participating as a
romantic plot element. Groucho delivered a nonstop stream of quips and puns,
such as his reference to a ''poultry'' amount of cash, his comparison of a girl's
eyes to a blue serge suit, and his suggestion that the lovers repair to the mushroom.

Even more popular was the gifted Harpo, whose pantomimic and musical
genius had the critics singing his praises as a clown of Chaplinesque stature.
Much of Harpo's humor was improvised, too, as when he established a running
gag by chasing a blonde across the stage in the middle of someone else's scene.
At such a time Groucho was likely to wise-crack something like, ''First time I
ever saw a taxi hail a passenger.''

Although the critics did not all admire Berlin's music, the songs were nothing
to scoff at. ''A Little Bungalow,'' ''We Should Care,'' ''Lucky Boy,'' and
''The Monkey Doodle-doo'' were among the more popular selections. Four new
songs joined the show for its revised summer edition in 1926, when the singing
Brox sisters entered the cast. A return engagement opened on 5/16/27 for sixteen
performances at the Century.

COLD FEET [Comedy/Medicine/Marriage] A: Fred Jackson and Pierre Gendron; D: Edgar J. MacGregor; P: Biltmore Producing Co., Inc.; T: Fulton Theatre;
5/21/23 (24)

A sodden farce that no quantity of energetic acting by the shallow company
could redeem from the refuse heap of triviality to which the critics abandoned
it.

Its implausible premise placed the wedding of Coralie (Annette Bade) to Count
De La Tour (Louis D'Arclay) in the home of best man Dr. Nolles (Glenn Anders),
the man Coralie jilted, so that she, feeling dizzy while changing from her bridal
gown, could come into his office in her underwear to ask for a restorative. The
confused physician mistakenly gives her chloral, a knockout potion, instead and
soon has his hands full hiding her unconscious person in his bedroom as he is
forced to drug one after another of the inquisitive folk who come around looking
for her.

''All of the actors worked vigorously and loudly and were obviously determined to let the audience share even the stagiest of whispers,'' wrote the *Times*.

COME SEVEN [Comedy/Blacks/Marriage] A: Octavius Roy Cohen; SC: a story in the *Saturday Evening Post*; D: Mrs. Lillian Trimble Bradley; P: George Broadhurst; T: Broadhurst Theatre; 7/19/20 (72)

A one-dimensional comedy of stereotyped black characters, all of whom were played, and very obviously so, by white actors in burnt-cork makeup. "The effect was that of a vaudeville dialogue vastly extended," carped Heywood Broun. A few good jokes were not sufficient compensation for paper-thin characters and a total lack of illusion.

The plot dealt with a crapshooting husband (Arthur Aylesworth) who "borrows" his wife's (Lucille LaVerne) diamond ring and hocks it to raise cash for a Ford flivver. The complications arrive in fast order when the pawnbroker lends it to a young woman (Gail Kane) on whose finger it is spotted by the wife, and the husband has to buy a new ring as a substitute.

Walter Prichard Eaton was offended that his colleagues on the daily papers had not condemned the piece as outright trash.

(1) COMEDIAN, THE (Le comédien) [Comedy-Drama/Theatre/Marriage/French] A: Sacha Guitry; AD/D/P: David Belasco; T: Lyceum Theatre; 3/13/23 (87)

Only one night after his biographical drama *Pasteur* opened on Broadway, Sacha Guitry saw his *Comedian* come to town, but the former, thought by the critics to be superior, closed quickly, while the present work had a modest run. It starred Lionel Atwill, for the third time playing a Guitry role originally intended for Lucien, the actor-dramatist's famous father. David Belasco adapted the French play, bowdlerizing it in the process, much to the dismay of Arthur Hornblow, himself a distinguished translator.

The Comedian's eponymous hero is a middle-aged actor (Atwill), consumed by vanity, who charms an eighteen-year-old visitor (Elsie Mackaye) to his dressing room into going on tour with him and, within ten days, marrying him (she remained his mistress in the original). When the untalented girl demands the right to act with him, he is forced to choose between her and his art; he opts for the latter, loses her, and declares to his dressing-room mirror that tomorrow night, he has "a rendezvous with 1,200 people."

Heywood Broun supported this work in which "comedy, farce, tragedy and the broadest sort of burlesque" were included. But Kenneth Macgowan called it "hokum," John Farrar judged it to be "a heavy monotonous piece," and the *Times* thought it "disappointing."

(2) (L'Attore) [Dramatic Revival/Italian Language] D: Giuseppe Sterni; P: Teatro d'Arte; T: Bijou Theatre; 3/10/29

An Italian adaptation of Guitry's play given by a New York-based company of Italian players; it was close to the original text, which had been severely tampered with in Belasco's version. Giuseppe Sterni played the Lionel Atwill role. "Giuseppe Sterni is an actor of great repose and of an immense fund of reserve, which is felt rather than demonstrated. He plays with consummate skill, tact and finish,'' wrote the *Times*, and his company was entirely adequate to its tasks.

COMEDIENNE (La comédienne) [Comedy/Theatre/Romance/Family/French] A: Paul Armont and Jacques Bousquet; AD/P: Henry Baron; D: Gustave Rolland; T: Bijou Theatre; 10/21/24 (16)

A tepid French comedy, the locale of which was transferred from Paris to New York, about an aging and vain theatrical star, Helen Blakemore (Charlotte Walker), who, sensing that her glamor is fading when her lover leaves her for a younger woman, retires from the stage to a farm in Virginia, taking there her married son (Alexander Clark, Jr.) and his family. In the third act a new Barrie script comes her way, and she not only decides upon a comeback but also regains the man she loves.

George Jean Nathan observed, ''*Comedienne* is the modern French boulevard theatre in a sentimental mood, and when the modern French boulevard theatre gets into a sentimental mood, it is...pretty awful.''

COMEDY OF ERRORS, THE [Dramatic Revival] A: William Shakespeare; D: Raymond O'Neil; P: Ethiopian Art Theatre; T: Frazee Theatre; 5/15/23 (7)

A Chicago-based company of black actors, the Ethiopian Art Theatre, directed by Raymond O'Neil, a white man, produced this play as part of a brief stand that also included *Salomé* and *The Chip Woman's Fortune*. Shakespeare's comedy of twins and mistaken identities was given a jazz interpretation, with offstage music accompanying most of the action and the play set in a circus-tent environment, the scenes being changed in view of the audience by four clowns under the guidance of a top-hatted ringmaster.

The overdone staging could not elevate the play, and Ludwig Lewisohn complained that this farce was ''inconceivably trivial as well as inconceivably faded.'' The show tried to be a high-energy-level romp, but ''there seemed to be very little of the true inspiration of extravaganza anywhere on the premises.... [T]he attempted grotesquerie creaked at the hinges,'' reported the *Times*.

COMEDY OF WOMEN, THE [Comedy/Sex/Romance] A: Leo de Valery; D: Edward Elsner; S: Eddie Eddy; P: Leo de Valery i/a/w Edward Elsner; T: Craig Theatre; 9/13/29 (5)

''The less said about the embarrassing proceeding the better,'' was Joseph Wood Krutch's way of disposing of this egregious disaster written by and starring Leo de Valery in the role of an irresistible Park Avenue Don Juan who goes through one woman after another until he ends up marrying one of them. The *Times* said it was ''as ingenuous and dispiriting an evening in the lesser theatre as has been provided in many months.''

COME-ON MAN, THE [Comedy/Crime/Romance/Family] A: Herbert Ashton, Jr.; D: Herbert Ashton; S: Eddie Eddy; P: Roy Walling; T: Forty-ninth Street Theatre; 4/22/29 (24)

Herbert Ashton, Sr., and Jr. starred in this modest melodramatic crook comedy authored by the latter and directed by the former. In it the Strange family, father William (George McQuarrie), wife Marguerite (Jane Marbury), and daughter Betty (Mary Wall) are Park Avenue sophisticates who use their polished manners to filch baubles and such from their invited guests. Handsome young Jimmie McGuire (Ashton, Jr.) is hired to attract moneyed widows to this fashionable thieves' den. He and Betty become romantic partners. When a theft is in progress later, a detective (Harold Webster) tries to foil it, but Jimmie and a buddy (Ashton, Sr.) turn the tables and reveal the detective as a crook and themselves as undercover cops.

"Despite its more than familiar material and uninspired acting," reported Perriton Maxwell, "*The Come-on Man* proves fairly interesting at all times and offers moderate, inoffensive entertainment."

COMIC, THE [Comedy/Theatre/Marriage/Hungarian] A: Lajos Luria; AD: James L. A. Burrell and Lawrence R. Brown; D: J. C. Nugent; P: John Jay Scholl and William J. Perlman; T: Masque Theatre; 4/19/27 (15)

This ho-hum Budapestian comedy by a pseudonymous author was repudiated by most critics. "It is not very deftly written and in places borders dangerously on burlesque, but it was always amusing," said First Nighter. Conceived as a play within a play, it dealt with marital infidelity as seen in a theatre troupe peopled by figures such as the Comedian (J. C. Nugent), his Actress-wife (Patricia Collinge), the Author (Cyril Keightly), the Pupil (Rex O'Malley), and the Manager (Malcolm Williams). To test his belief that the Author and the Actress are having an affair the Comedian tries to trick them into compromising themselves, but they are too quick for him; however, the Actress eventually goes off with the Manager.

COMMAND PERFORMANCE, THE [Comedy/Theatre/Romance] A: C. Stafford Dickens; D: Clifford Brooke; S: Raymond Sovey; P: Herman Shumlin; T: Klaw Theatre; 10/3/28 (29)

In Robert Littell's mind, this was a "wooden farce-romance about Balkan kings and queenlets; stale variations on an old theme, very badly performed." The setting was somewhere called Moldavia; the debauched prince is among a group of roughnecks who try to attack an actress. The actor (Ian Keith) who saves her is hauled before the prince's mother (Beatrice Terry) and told that the only way for Moldavia to conclude a treaty with Wallachia is for him to woo and win their princess (Jessie Royce Landis) by proxy for the dissipated prince. He accepts the mission, falls in love for real and, when the prince abdicates, marries the girl himself.

Instead of the usual Ruritanian trappings of such romances, this one was done in sophisticated modern dress, with many familiar 1928 touches. That was its sole claim to novelty.

COMMAND TO LOVE, THE [Comedy/Romance/Politics/Austrian/Sex] A: Rudolph Lothar and Fritz Gottwald; AD: Herman Bernstein and Brian Marlow; D: Lester Lonergan; S: Ovida Bergere; P: William A. Brady, Jr., and Dwight Deere Wiman i/a/w John Tuerk; T: Longacre Theatre; 9/20/27 (236)

A "highly entertaining and scabrous comedy" (Joseph Wood Krutch) about a French attaché at the Spanish court whose chief function is to romance the ladies of the court in the interests of international relations. Gaston (Basil Rathbone), in love with the French Ambassador's (Henry Stephenson) wife (Violet Kemble Cooper), is commanded to love Manuela (Mary Nash), wife of Spain's War Minister (Ferdinand Gottschalk). Carrying out his orders with aplomb, Gaston's actions are responsible for the successful signing of a treaty between France and Spain; he is given an ambassadorship to Peru.

The naughtiness of the plot and double entendres titillated the reviewers who thought the Austrian play was a good example of French farce. Perriton Maxwell called it "A sophisticated Continental comedy, exposing everything but the bedding; clever, splendidly acted, but not without jolts to one's sensitiveness." When the police demanded some cleaning up of the action, the producers, according to George Jean Nathan, obliged "by making the leading woman put on skirts instead of pajamas and explaining the change with a line that was twice as dirty as anything that had been in the script before."

COMMODORE MARRIES, THE [Comedy-Drama/Marriage/Sea/Period] A: Kate Parsons; SC: Tobias Smollet's novel *The Adventures of Peregrine Pickle*; D/P: Arthur Hopkins; S: Robert Edmond Jones; T: Plymouth Theatre; 9/4/29 (37)

A dramatization of an eighteenth-century novel of which the *Times* admitted, "You can hardly shut your eyes to its dramatic shortcomings, its lack of structure and its impulsive changes in mood," but such drawbacks were abundantly rectified by "its moments of broad comedy and hard-headed dignity" and by a magnificent portrait of the commodore by Walter Huston. John Hutchens was impressed by the writer's imagination and resourcefulness and counted the staging important.

The eccentric, slightly mad Commodore Trunnion lives in a house fitted up like a seagoing vessel and commanded by him as if it were one. To get her hands on his fortune Miss Pickle (Eda Heinemann) weds him and soon converts his nautical surroundings to more conventional ones. Eventually, amid evidences of her insincerity, he makes her walk the plank back into single life and resumes his course with hearty cheer.

COMMON SIN, THE [Drama/Marriage/Sex/Crime] A/D/P: Willard Mack; S: Rollo Wayne; T: Forrest Theatre; 10/15/28 (24)

"[A] sprawling, artificial melodrama whose very lack of tautness makes for a corresponding lack of interest on the part of the spectator," opined the *Times*.

Jim Steele (Thurston Hall), unhappily married and in dire financial straits, would have killed himself had not an old flame, Bobo Aster (Lee Patrick), come to his aid with a promise of $300,000. She plans to get the money by sleeping with a certain wealthy man, but she discovers Steele's wife, Helen (Millicent Hanley), in the man's apartment. Helen, threatened by Bobo with blackmail, murders Steele, and Bobo is placed under suspicion, but Bobo finally tricks the wife into a confession.

The play had been variously called *Bobo's Bargain*, *Bad Debts*, and *Paid Off* before opening in New York.

COMPLEX, THE [Drama/Mental Illness/Sex/Marriage] A: Louis E. Bisch; D: Miss Percy Haswell; P: The Reed Producers, Inc.; T: Booth Theatre; 3/3/25 (47)

The first example of the Freudian psychoanalytic genre in which the action consists largely of the probing by an analyst into a patient's mind to discover the root of a serious mental problem. The author was himself a psychiatrist. The play began promisingly as a matinee production and then eked out a regular run that lasted a month.

The central problem was that of a young newlywed (Dorothy Hall) who, unable to consummate her marriage on her wedding night, enters analysis, and learns that she has a father complex stemming from her belief in a paternal ideal for a father she has never seen and believes dead. She uncovers the fact that her father is alive and no one to be proud of, overcomes her complex, and returns to her husband's arms.

John Ranken Towse noted, "the calculated artifice of the whole structure is so transparent that the pretense of its having a scientific foundation to rest upon becomes a trifle ridiculous."

COMTE OBLIGADO (Count Obligado) [Musical/French/French Language] B/LY: André Barde; M: Raoul Moretti; P: Modern French Musical Comedy Company i/a/w J. A. Gauvin; T: Jolson's Fifty-ninth Street Theatre; 3/11/29 (4)

One of several French comic operas given in repertory by a visiting French troupe. It was a harmless and pleasant musical diversion that charmed by its spirited and catchy tunes. The company's rotund and hilarious star was Hans Servatius, who played the title role, an elevator operator at a fashionable couturiere's who comes into a fortune and amuses himself by impersonating an aristocrat, Count Obligado, so that he can mingle with those he formerly had to cater to in his elevator. "M. Servatius appears in a succession of ridiculous get-ups, sings, dances, minces, sighs and collapses through a long perspiring performance,'' reported the *Times*. He had the spectators in stitches in a number called "The Caravan,'' in which, dressed as a Bedouin with a camel tied to his ample waist, he led a march that went from the stage through the aisles.

CONFLICT [Drama/War/Marriage/Aviation] A: Warren F. Lawrence; D: Edward Clarke Lilley; S: P. Dodd Ackerman; P: Spad Producing Co., Inc.; T: Fulton Theatre; 3/6/29 (52)

Robert Littell commented of this play's hero, "attractive, baffled, conceited, self-mistrusting, unhappy and completely maladjusted, [he] comes to life more than the play warrants through the natural, capable acting of Spencer Tracy, a young man with a sure touch and an ability to concentrate on the character he is trying to create. With good opportunity, Mr. Tracy ought to be heard from more emphatically in the future.'' Of his vehicle, *Time* remarked, "It is an exceedingly interesting study of the blind arrogance of one of War's own children in conflict with the equally blind forgetfulness of the world to which he returned. It just misses being a fine play.'' Most, however, found the writing spotty and inconsistent.

Richard Banks (Tracy), a drab, ineffectual clerk, is drafted and becomes a heroic flight commander, much decorated. The war over, his fame inflates his ego, he weds the upper-class girl (Peggy Allenby) who once scorned him, and he seeks success beyond his abilities. Finally, his marriage crumbles, and he finds his proper station as a commercial aviator.

The play's fine cast included players such as Edward Arnold and Albert Dekker.

CONGAI [Drama/Tropics/Romance/Sex/Military] A: Harry Hervey and Carleton Hildreth; SC: Harry Hervey's novel of the same name; D: Rouben Mamoulian; S: Cleon Throckmorton; P: Sam H. Harris; T: Sam H. Harris Theatre; 11/27/28 (137)

Congai is the Vietnamese word for the unwed wife of a white colonial. The play treats in vivid melodramatic fashion the relations between the indigenous population of what was then French Indo-China and the French colonials. Its heroine, a daughter of a native woman and a Frenchman, is Thi-Linh (Helen Menken), prevented from marrying the village boy she loves, Kim Khouan (Theodore Hecht), because of her heritage and forced to become a *congai* herself. While Kim is off fighting for France, she works herself up to a position of influence as a general's *congai*, meanwhile seeing to the raising of her son by Kim in the old village. When Kim returns after many years, she is prevented from running away with him by the appearance of her boy, who kills the General for insulting his mother. The Governor (H. Dudley Hawley) keeps her as his *congai* as the price for hushing up the crime.

Lavishly produced and well acted, *Congai* was, nonetheless, "pure drivel, and as consecutive drama...merely does not exist,'' as Richard Dana Skinner put it. Nothing, said the *Times*, "could save the piece from the deadly effect of a constant striving after something that it could never reach.''

CONGRATULATIONS [Comedy/Theatre/Politics/Small Town] A: Morgan Wallace; D: Edward Clarke Lilley; S: Rollo Wayne; P: Lawrence Shubert Lawrence; T: National Theatre; 4/30/29 (39)

The author of this often-amusing satire on hick politics gave his name, oddly enough, to the hero, played by Henry Hull. This fictional Morgan Wallace is a Missouri stock-company actor and manager who is asked to run for mayor as a dummy candidate and turns out to be more popular than the machine politicos thought, since he garners all of the idolizing women's votes.

The play was meant as a spoof and had many broad touches, such as labeling its locale Hokum City. "The idea of the comedy," assessed the *Times*, "is a good one and remains in the end considerably superior to the writing, which never aims higher than the box-office grating." Preston Foster made his New York debut in the play.

CONNECTICUT YANKEE, A [Musical/Fantasy/Period/Romance] B: Herbert Fields; M: Richard Rodgers; LY: Lorenz Hart; SC: Mark Twain's novel *A Connecticut Yankee in King Arthur's Court*; D: Alexander Leftwich; CH: Busby Berkeley; DS: John T. Hawkins, Jr.; P: Lew Fields and Lyle D. Andrews; T: Vanderbilt Theatre; 11/3/27 (421)

Rodgers, Hart, and Fields teamed up again to produce another top hit with this satirical musical based on Mark Twain's classic about a contemporary Hartford fellow (William Gaxton) who, hit on the skull by a champagne bottle during a bachelor party, returns to the days of King Arthur, where he introduces the benefits of modern industrial organization. Soon sandwich boards read "I would fain walk a furlong for a Camel" and the like. The dialogue's anachronistic mixture of 1920s slang with Arthurian English ("methinks yon damsel is a lovely broad") provided much of the humor, although this palled. An excellent score, choreography, and designs helped ride this winner to success.

Fields's book did not slavishly copy the Twain original but tackled it from an altogether fresh viewpoint. The major contribution, though, was the score, of which Perriton Maxwell noted, "Ingratiating melodies that make you ache to remember them.... And lyrics abounding in satire, sentiment and the most provoking rhymes that a nimble brain ever conceived." "My Heart Stood Still," originally heard in a 1927 London revue, was interpolated after it caught on abroad. "Thou Swell" nearly was cut in the pre-New York tryout. "On a Desert Island with Thee" and "I Feel at Home with You" were other top numbers.

CONNIE GOES HOME [Comedy/Theatre/Romance] A: Edward Childs Carpenter; SC: a story by Fannie Kilbourne; D: Frederick Stanhope; P: Kilbourn Gordon, Inc.; T: Forty-ninth Street Theatre; 9/6/23 (19)

Sylvia Field delighted critics as the title character in what Percy Hammond called an "ambrosial" entertainment in its writing, staging, and acting. Not many agreed, judging from the short run it enjoyed. A stranded nineteen-year-old actress, Connie, refuses to compromise her virtue for success on Broadway and heads back to the Illinois orphan's refuge she calls home. To get there at half-fare, she dresses in her last theatrical costume, as a child of eleven. On the train she meets a young man and is subsequently adopted by his millionaire uncle. The youth is engaged to a vamp but turns his affection to Connie when he sees her dressed in an evening gown.

John Corbin enjoyed this "idyllic yet homely romance," but Heywood Broun's opinion was more widespread: "People of average sophistication in the ways of life, or the theatre, will enjoy some of *Connie Goes Home* and hate the rest. Very simple folk ought to have the time of their lives."

H.H.

CONSCIENCE [Drama/Marriage/Prostitution/Crime/Mental Illness] A: Don Mullally; D: Roy Walling; P: A. H. Woods; T: Belmont Theatre; 9/11/24 (132)

There was sharp dissension regarding the merits of this pretentious melodrama (which made its bow at an Off-Broadway matinee but moved uptown for a good run); all agreed that in the person of young Lillian Foster, an unknown from a western stock company, the theatre had made a definite find. Foster's career did not develop as her advocates would have imagined, although she did act in nearly a dozen more Broadway plays through 1948, but in *Conscience* she appeared a veritable "Western Duse," as Alan Dale expressed it.

The vehicle for this auspicious debut was an uneven piece in four acts, the first and last of which are set in a snowbound Yukon cabin during a storm. Here Jeff Stewart (Ray B. Collins), former radical laborer of idealistic notions, is on the verge of a mental breakdown as he relives his earlier domestic entanglements. The intervening two acts display the sequence of events that led him to lose his job, leave home to find another, return to discover his illiterate waitress wife (Foster) a prostitute, and end up killing her. In the last act, haunted by his conscience as represented by his wife's ghost, he wanders off into the snow to die.

George Jean Nathan sniffed at the play as a "cheap melodrama," and Stark Young thought the conception imaginative but unfulfilled.

CONSTANT NYMPH, THE [Drama/Romance/Music/Marriage/British] A: Margaret Kennedy and Basil Dean; M: Eugene Goosens; SC: Kennedy's novel of the same name; D: Basil Dean; S: George W. Harris; P: George C. Tyler and Basil Dean; T: Selwyn Theatre; 12/9/26 (148)

A London triumph that successfully adapted to the stage a widely read and respected novel; the "particular virtue" of the work was the depth of its characterization, wrote George Jean Nathan. The play mingled pathos and comedy in its telling of a romantic story about a precocious child-woman, the creature of the title, young Teresa Sanger (Beatrix Thomson), who loves from afar the brilliant young musician Lewis Dodd (Glenn Anders), who lives in her bohemian household (called "Sanger's Circus") in the Tyrol. Lewis impulsively marries the dilettante Florence Churchill (Lotus Robb), however, but the marriage is soon on the rocks. Lewis runs off to Brussels with the "nymph" he has come to love, but she dies of a heart lesion not long afterwards.

The death of Teresa struck a false note for Richard Dana Skinner, for it made her loss "neither a tragedy of renunciation. . .nor a tragedy of atonement [but] a tragedy of accident" and, thus, "not really a tragedy at all." But it was "powerful on its own planes," averred *Time*, and Brooks Atkinson insisted that the play had caught exactly the spirit of the original, "the hilarity shot through with pathos, the struggle, the passion, romance, wisdom, nostalgia and. . .the luminous beauty that lightens every scene."

CONSTANT WIFE, THE [Comedy/Marriage/Sex/British] A: W. Somerset Maugham; D: Gilbert Miller; P: Charles Frohman, Inc.; T: Maxine Elliott's Theatre; 11/29/26 (295)

Maugham's mildly naughty drawing-room comedy about the double standard in marital relations scored a smart success both because of its stylistic felicities and the graceful comic charm of its star, Ethel Barrymore. "It is a deft and sparkling comedy of no overwhelming importance," judged the *Times*. Some, like the moralistic Richard Dana Skinner, inveighed against the play's suggestion that the way to handle infidelity "is to abolish all standards whatsoever," but most accepted the thesis as an example of sophisticated modern thinking.

Maugham's heroine, Constance Middleton, discovering that her husband of fifteen years (C. Aubrey Smith) has been having an affair with her best friend (Veree Teasdale), indulgently extricates him from disaster when the friend's husband finds him out; however, she gets even, to her mate's consternation, by opening a profitable business and running off to vacation abroad for six weeks with an old flame (Frank Conroy).

The play's problems were noted, some finding the theme trivial, others the epigrammatic dialogue "machine-turned and. . .heavy-handed" (Gilbert Seldes). "But it is well written," countered Arthur Hornblow, and "it sparkles with the usual Maugham wit." Barrymore seemed younger and more attractive than in years. The play was chosen as one of the year's Ten Best by Burns Mantle.

COQUETTE [Comedy-Drama/Southern/Romance/Sex/Small Town/Crime/Family/Trial] A: George Abbott and Ann Preston Bridgers; D: George Abbott; S: Raymond Sovey; P: Jed Harris i/a/w Crosby Gaige; T: Maxine Elliott's Theatre; 11/8/27 (366)

A collaborative effort between George Abbott and an actress upon whose recollections of life in the South the story was based. It was originally called *Norma's First Affair*. (George Jean Nathan maintained that the plot was derived from a North Carolina murder case, and that verbatim use was made of transcripts and news stories pertaining to it.)

Helen Hayes, in a role that was a career milestone, played Norma Besant, a southern small-town belle, whose father, Dr. Besant (Charles Waldron), still lives by the old codes. The flirtatious and white-lieing Norma is besieged by many suitors, but her affections are reserved for the roughneck scamp Michael Jeffery (Elliot Cabot), much to Dr. Besant's discomfort. When Michael is driven to reveal his intimacy with Norma, Dr. Besant shoots him dead. He stands trial, and the pregnant Norma, unable to claim for the jury a virtue she does not possess, commits suicide, thinking thus to save her father's life.

Considerable respect was achieved for the excellent dialogue, truthful situations, and perceptive character drawing; only the final act seemed prefabricated.

Of Hayes's astonishing acting, John Mason Brown wrote, "It is by far the best performance of her career, lacking in all [her familiar] mannerisms. . . and possessing a burnished authenticity. In the course of a single evening, and with a sincerity that almost hurts, Miss Hayes changes from the silly, light-headed. . . little heroine. . . into a woman whose whole being has been subdued and broken by tragedy.''

The casting of Hayes was extremely controversial, since she was known as the quintessential player of virginal flapper roles. There were few who would have trusted her with a role demanding emotional power. Her success in the role made producer Jed Harris look like a genius.

George Cukor was hired to direct, but he and Miss Hayes, old friends, could not rehearse effectively together since they kept laughing at the old-fashioned southern mannerisms of the characters. Hayes then demanded that coauthor Abbott take over the reins, but he agreed only on the condition that Harris, whom he hated, not attend the rehearsals. The latter did, however, seek to make major changes in the script. There are conflicting stories of who made what revisions. Abbott said in his book "*Mister Abbott*," "Once again I resisted him and we had harsh words, but we opened. . . without the changes." According to Catherine Hayes Brown, Hayes's mother, in her book *Letters to Mary*, when Harris turned up at the Atlantic City tryout, he tore the show to pieces and so riddled the actress that she threw down her script and shouted, "I didn't know this was Euripides. I thought it was a simple play about plain people. I won't go on until you get out of here!" Nevertheless, Hayes continued to be bothered about the weak second-act curtain and her complaints got Harris to work with Abbott and Bridgers to fix the scene before the Philadelphia opening: "Jed had worked a miracle on that second act curtain," said Mrs. Brown. Harris, however, has a different story; according to his *Dance on the High Wire*, he was instrumental in rewriting the script from the start, even to the point of giving it its title. (Abbott has said Harris loved to take undue credit for revising others' scripts). Harris stated that he was unhappy with Abbott's slambang directorial style on *Coquette* and actually finished the job himself. He further claimed to have made the needed second-act changes by himself. When the authors heard the dialogue with which Harris had replaced theirs, they confronted him in anger, but he answered them with biting sarcasm. This meant the end of the relationship between Harris and Abbott, which at one point had promised to be one of the most exciting of the period.

CORNERED [Comedy-Drama/Crime/Family] A: Dodson Mitchell; D: John McKee; P: Henry W. Savage; T: Astor Theatre; 12/8/20 (141)

"[A]n intricate and implausible melodrama" (Alexander Woollcott) marking the return to the stage from films of Madge Kennedy, who played a dual role in it, resorting when need be to quick changes.

She began the play as Mary Brennan, a virtuous girl raised among crooks, who tries to go straight but returns to the criminal life for a final caper. This involves her impersonating a society belle of whom she is a double. She does her job well, and the crooks are able to burgle the home of Mary Waring with impunity, but when Mary returns unexpectedly, the plot is forced to reveal, after various complications, that the women are really twins, separated as infants following a sea disaster.

CORTEZ [Comedy/Films/Mexico/Romance] A: Le Roy Clemens and Ralph Murphy; D: Ira Hards; P: Jack Linder; T: Mansfield Theatre; 11/4/29 (8)

Handsome Lou Tellegen, one-time leading man to Eleanora Duse and Sarah Bernhardt, had several Broadway flops in the 1920s, the last being this tiresome comedy in which he played a Castillian bandit, a descendent of the explorer Cortez, who kidnaps a Hollywood film company on location in Mexico and drags them to his castle hideaway. His exploits in routing a group of Mexican troublemakers, however, have been preserved on celluloid. He woos the leading lady (Helen Baxter), who plays along in hopes of saving her troupe. When she confesses her deception, he relents and the company leaves for Hollywood. He goes there later and learns that he has become a motion-picture sensation. This helps him win the actress on her own turf.

"Mr. Tellegen is emotionally expert but. . . he is working with material which is hardly adult," scolded the *Times*.

COSI SIA (Thy Will Be Done) [Drama/Family/Religion/Italian/Italian Language] A: Tommaso Gallarti-Scotti; P: F. Ray Comstock and Morris Gest; T: Century Theatre; 11/14/23 (2)

No critic was impressed by this Eleanora Duse vehicle in which a mother (Duse) bargains with the Virgin to give up her adored lover and make an annual pilgrimage to the Virgin's mountain shrine if only her dying child may live. Her prayer is answered, and twenty-three years later, as the mother is making her yearly pilgrimage, her son returns from America with boisterous friends and rejects her in shame. The mother prays at the shrine for her son's soul and dies saying the words of the title, which translate as "Thy will be done."

John Corbin commented that Duse's art abundantly compensated for that lacking in the play: "Under her touch the Mother becomes an incarnation of divine tenderness and sorrow.... Her face is as profoundly expressive as a Rembrandt portrait." Stark Young described the actress as not being one whose performance could be enjoyed as supreme craft or analyzed in pieces: "It will not allow that separation of the craft from the meaning.... It is only slowly that you see what labor and skill has gone to make up that creation in Duse's soul in the outer forms of an art."

H.H.

COUNT OF LUXEMBOURG, THE (Der Graf von Luxemburg) [Musical Revival] AD: Glen MacDonough; B: A. M. Willner and Robert Bodanzky; M: Franz Lehar; LY: Basil Hood and Adrian Ross; D: Milton Aborn; S: Rollo Wayne; P: Jolson Theatre Musical Comedy Company; T: Jolson's Fifty-ninth Street Theatre; 2/17/30 (16)

The season of 1929–1930 saw a series of operetta revivals produced at Jolson's Theatre under the direction of Milton Aborn. *The Count of Luxembourg*, a 1912 Viennese piece with a Franz Lehar score, had a book that now seemed silly, but its music was still impressive. It told of a grand duke (Florenz Ames) who arranges to have a beautiful commoner (Manila Powers) he wishes to marry gain noble rank by wedding her temporarily to an impecunious count (Roy Cropper). His plans go awry when she and the Count fall in love. "Love Breaks Every Bond," "Are You Going to Dance," and "I'm in Love" were the crowd-pleasing numbers.

The show was well performed and staged. The *Times* noted that it remained "fresh and vigorous; that the Lehar tunes still float out gently and with zest."

COUNTESS MARITZA, THE (Gräfin Maritza) [Musical/Romance/Austrian] AD: Harry B. Smith; B/LY: Julius Brammer and Alfred Grunwald; M: Emmerich Kalman; D: J. C. Huffman; CH: Carl Randall and Jack Mason; S: Watson Barratt; P: Messrs. Shubert; T: Shubert Theatre; 9/18/26 (321)

A hit operetta, based on a Viennese original. Profusely mounted, lushly melodic, and, for the most part, effectively performed by a company of sixty-four, it nevertheless lacked an intelligent book. "Was anything more artificial, hopelessly old-fashioned, ponderous and heavy ever put together?" queried Arthur Hornblow.

Former Metropolitan Opera House prima donna Yvonne D'Arle was a mediocre leading lady in this saga of a nobleman (Walter Woolf) who chooses to gain the trust of the Countess he adores by taking employment as her overseer, revealing his true identity only when the plot's exigencies finally require it.

Time said that "romantically inclined" audiences would like the show, if they could overlook its "turbulent succession of flat puns and desperate buffoonery."

A return engagement played from 4/9/28 for sixteen performances at the Century Theatre.

COURAGE [Drama/Marriage/Fantasy/British] A: Isabel Kemp; D: Reginald Pole; P: Threshold Matinee Theatre; T: Princess Theatre; 1/19/27 (10)

A matinees-only production of a play about a marital triangle. The husband (Reginald Pole) returns to his deserted wife (Lillian Foster) after three years in Africa with a mistress who has just died. The spirit of the dead mistress comes between wife and husband, and the wife, who had planned on remarrying, finds herself stuck with a man whose inner needs are cared for by a ghost.

The piece made some negative commentary on the unpopular British divorce law but had little pertinence to a New York audience. The *Times* declared that "the author's hand is not an expert one and the play emerges as something less than so-so."

COURAGE [Comedy/Family/Sex] A: Tom Barry; D: Priestly Morrison; S: R. N. Robbins; P: Lew Cantor; T: Ritz Theatre; 10/8/28 (283)

The second Broadway play with this title in less than two years was a very popular Pollyanna comedy starring Janet Beecher. The *Times* maintained that its shopworn theme was treated with freshness, and that its leading actress was deserving of the ten curtain calls she took; however, child-actor Junior Durkin almost stole the show.

Beecher's role was that of Mary Colebrook, a midwestern widow with seven kids, the youngest of which, Bill (Durkin), is the illegitimate offspring of a long-standing love affair. She goes to Boston with her brood in search of sustenance from her wealthy family, but Bill's illegitimacy is the cause of her being rejected. When someone who has grown fond of Bill dies and leaves him a $500,000 legacy, Mary and the kids can return home and she can marry Bill's pop.

The *Times* was struck by how "extraordinarily well written" the comedy was, and Richard Dana Skinner termed it "one of those curious outcroppings of excess sentimentality mixed with a lot of tough truth which fall somewhere between good drama and hokum."

COURTESAN [Drama/Sex/Crime] A: Irving Kaye Davis; D: Leo Bulgakov; S: P. Dodd Ackerman; P: Joseph F. Leone; T: President Theatre; 4/29/30 (7)

One-person plays are no longer unusual, but they were in 1930 when this early example was produced. Elsa Shelley (formerly known as Bertha Broad), making much use of the telephone, played a three-act drama about a kept woman named Alice Trevor and her relations with nine other (unseen) characters. Hurt by her paramour's friends, she keeps an assignation with a musician in her apartment building, but she murders him when he treats her like a prostitute. She then leaps from her balcony to the street, eighteen stories below.

The play seemed banal and melodramatic, and Shelley's performance, while adequate, was not the type to sustain such writing. Joseph Wood Krutch found that the imagined offstage voices and the phone business was so overused that the novelty wore off. Brooks Atkinson characterized the play as "sordidly un-imaginative and intrinsically dull."

COURTING [Comedy/Romance/Family/Scottish] A: A. Kenward Matthews; D: Archibald Forbes; P: Lee Shubert; T: Forty-ninth Street Theatre; 9/12/25 (41)

A quaint Scottish Cinderella comedy brought to New York with its London company; it was an "amusing, simple, clean little play [that came] like a breath of Spring bearing the fragrance of a field of heather" (Arthur Hornblow). John Anderson said, "It is charming, wistful at times, but much too slight."

It told a familiar tale of a Scotch farm family ruled by a stiff-necked, Bible-fearing father (J. Nelson Ramsey) who heeds the preachments of the minister (John Duncan) and attempts to stifle the amorous yearnings of his son (Kenneth Grant) and daughter (Jean Clyde). The daughter disobeys her father and goes to the Laird's ball, where the young English boarder (Vernon Sylvaine) has taken someone else, but she and the Briton are eventually united in romantic bliss.

COUSIN SONIA (Ma Cousine de Varsovie) [Comedy/Romance/French] A: Louis Verneuil; TR: Herbert Williams; D: Edward Elsner; DS: Joseph Physioc; P: Sonia Productions, Inc.; T: Central Park Theatre (OB); 12/7/25 (24)

A "somewhat sedulously risque French farce" (*Times*) performed in a tiny, new Off-Broadway playhouse at Fifty-ninth Street and Fifth Avenue ("the stage was almost in the spectators' laps"). It had formerly served as the chapel of La Salle College. Alison Smith reported that "there were moments when the mechanics of the play sagged a bit from old age."

The acting of this work was clumsy, except for Marguerita Sylva, who played the lead and also sang several songs in French and Italian. She portrayed a beautiful young homewrecker who has romantic ties with a young artist (Douglas MacPherson) and a married banker (Hugh O'Connell), whose doctor has told him to give up business and write off-color stories to shore up his health. The banker's wife (Katharine Hayden) is a flirt involved with the physician. Sylva's character entered the scene to distract the men and help work out a satisfactory denouement for the married couple.

There were only polite comments on the play and production.

COUTURIÈRE DE LUNEVILLE, LA (The Dressmaker of Luneville) [Comedy/Romance/Sex/French/French Language] A: Alfred Savoir; P: George C. Tyler and Hugh Ford; T: Gaiety Theatre; 3/25/24 (2)

During her 1924 visit to New York, the famous French actress Mme. Simone ventured forth in this French farce, played at two matinees, in which she acted Irene, a one-time village dressmaker, now a renowned film star, who returns to her town to take revenge on the lover (Jose Ruben) who was responsible for her illegitimate child. She appears in several disguises to carry out her plan.

"There is only the slightest of plausibility to the plot, which is kept adroitly alive by the regular injection of sprightly comedy scenes and even opportunities for protean efforts,'' declared the *Times*. Mme. Simone's ''gift for light comedy . . . served to carry her audience beyond the improbability of her scenes into a state of constant merriment,'' said the critic.

H.H.

CRADLE SNATCHERS [Comedy/Marriage/Sex/Youth] A: Russell Medcraft and Norma Mitchell; D: Sam Forrest; P: Sam H. Harris b/a/w Hassard Short; T: Music Box Theatre; 9/7/25 (485)

A sure-fire hit farce that ran well over a year and became an international success. ''It is a boisterous piece,'' declared *Time*, ''offensive to those of temperate taste, and probably very funny to the rest.'' ''Here is a genuinely entertaining play, full of laughs, witticism, and smart dialogue,'' reported Arthur Hornblow.

Three wealthy wives of early middle age (Mary Boland, Edna May Oliver, and Margaret Dale), determined to get even with their philandering husbands (Cecil Owen, Stanley Jessup, and Willard Barton), contract with three shiny-haired college youths (Humphrey Bogart, Raymond Guion, and Gerald Philips) to spend the weekend together with them at a Glen Cove, Long Island, house. The unpolished young suitors, seeking to earn the $2,000 they are being paid, go a bit too far in their advances to please the ladies and meet resistance, leading to a second act in which the latter trio appear ''with their hair down, badly dissheveled, slippers off, hair awry.'' At the end, the husbands appear at the house with a trio of flappers and are startled to discover their wives in its occupancy and even more so to witness the ladies' departure.

As one of the comically gauche young men, Humphrey Bogart was singled out for applause.

A return engagement opened on 5/2/27 at the same theatre for sixteen showings.

(1) CRADLE SONG (Cancion de cuna) [Drama/Spanish/Religion/Youth] A: Gregorio Martinez-Sierra; AD: John Garrett Underhill; D: Augustin Duncan; T: Times Square Theatre; 2/28/21 (4)

The first New York showing of *Cradle Song* came at a brief series of special matinees, six years before the 1911 play became an annual feature of the Civic Repertory Theatre's program. Its sentimental story is simply that of the discovery by the members of a convent of a foundling, of her being raised there for eighteen years by the loving nuns, and of her eventual departure into the world when she reaches the age of eighteen. Very little happens in the play other than various events that expose the maternal qualities of the cloistered nuns. The chief roles are those of Sister Joanna of the Cross (Angela McCahill), who is in charge of bringing the girl up; the girl Teresa (Florence Flinn) herself; and the prioress (Louise Randolph).

The *Times* summed the piece up as ''a delicate story of thwarted mother love, rather deliberately undramatic . . . , and leaving unmistakably the impression that it approaches its subject too gingerly for the purposes of the theatre.'' Ludwig

Lewisohn was greatly impressed by the staging: "Nothing...could be better than the groupings and movements and gestures of the nuns through which their unexpressed pathos is symbolized."

(2) [Dramatic Revival] D: Eva Le Gallienne; S: G. E. Calthrop; P: Civic Repertory Company; T: Civic Repertory Theatre (OB); 1/24/27 (52)

Eva Le Gallienne's company made this quiet work into one of their most cherished possessions; they produced it in repertory five more times through 1932, giving it a total of 180 performances. Despite its having been seen locally before, Burns Mantle chose it as one of Ten Best Plays of the Year.

George Jean Nathan found it "a distinctly refreshing adventure," and Richard Dana Skinner claimed it was "really a very profound study of the strongest human emotions, wrought with all the skill and tempered suspense of the most stirring drama."

Notable was the achievement of Le Gallienne as both Sister Joanna of the Cross and as director. "The whole movement and flow of the piece is faultless, replete with humor and tenderness" (Skinner).

(3) and "FRAGELINA ROSINA" [Spanish Language] D: Gregorio Martinez-Sierra; P: Spanish Art Theatre and Crosby Gaige; T: Forrest Theatre; 5/9/27 (1)

Madrid's visiting Spanish Art Theatre, of which *Cradle Song*'s author was the artistic director, staged the play during the same season as the version described above. It proved "the most distinguished of" the troupe's five presentations, thought the *Times*. "The delicately expressive playing of these Spaniards brings out all the tenderness, gentle humor and soft pathos of the play."

Staged by the playwright with Catalina Barcena as Sister Joanna, the play was given the smooth ensemble performance it deserved. The author appeared between the acts to read the narrative bridging the eighteen-year lapse that occurs before Act Two begins. A one-act comedy of his, "Fragilina Rosina," was given as an afterpiece. Barcena played a girl whose romantic inclinations get her into trouble with a trio of boyfriends.

CRAIG'S WIFE [Drama/Marriage] A/D: George Kelly; S: Sheldon K. Viclc; P: Rosalie Stewart; T: Morosco Theatre; 10/12/25 (360)

George Kelly's trenchant character study of a selfish woman who puts her own security over the happiness of a normal married life gave, by its title, a new phrase to the language to describe someone with a pathological interest in the care of her home. His Harriet Craig (Chrystal Herne) was a microscopically precise cross-section of a creature whose "harshness, pathos, egotism, intelligence" were held up to inspection in a play that led Stark Young to state, "You sit through much of *Craig's Wife* quite spellbound, gripped by the reality of the characters and at the same moment delighted by the manifest craft of their presentation."

Mrs. Craig does not love Mr. Craig (Charles Trowbridge). She seeks only total control of her home, so that she may be its autocratic mistress and reign in it supreme and alone. Her home is a temple of cleanliness and order. Her accommodating spouse only becomes fully enlightened concerning her cold, obsessive nature after a murder and suicide at a friend's house he has visited that very night lead her to disclose that her fear regarding his involvement in the case stems from her insecurity about how she will be affected and not from her concern for him. He walks out on her after destroying an *objet d'art* she cherishes. Mrs. Craig is a pathetic person alone in her house at the end.

The critics, though not unanimous, generally agreed that *Craig's Wife* was one of the finest serious dramas of American life yet written. It won the Pulitzer Prize and was named a Best Play of the Year. Most critics tempered their enthusiasm with reservations, however. Several shared George Jean Nathan's belief that "The leading defect. . . lies in its author's effort to broaden the aspect and importance of his theme by departing from the specific to the general." Others were displeased by the play's verbosity.

Kelly's great directorial skill helped immeasurably in the production, and a fine cast was led by Chrystal Herne's magnificent portrayal; she captured "the suave manner, the icy loftiness, the metallic obstinacy, the fluttering meticulousness, the piercing sarcasm" of Mrs. Craig, according to Richard Dana Skinner.

CRASHING THROUGH [Comedy-Drama/Sex/Romance/Family] A: Saxon Kling; D/P: Oliver D. Bailley; S: P. Dodd Ackerman; T: Republic Theatre; 10/29/28 (40)

Consuelo Poole (Rose Hobart), uppity daughter of divorced upper-class parents, is gazing through her luxurious New York home's skylight at a handsome young riveter working on a neighboring project when she decides to revolt against her galavanting family's shallow code and break off her engagement to socialite Richard Jefferson (Robert Harrigan). Just then the riveter crashes through into her sun room. Romance buds, Consuelo breaks free of her class strictures, and the youth (Gavin Gordon) moves into her life. They proudly take up living together, she becomes pregnant, and they finally give in to parental pressure to get married.

The material was skillfully handled, "although not without a good many rather awkward jumps from one tone to another and at the very last with some quite unnecessary and exceedingly jarring rough language," thought Arthur Ruhl. The *Times* also derided the play for its shifts in mood and declared it to be "pretentiously overwritten."

CREAKING CHAIR, THE [Drama/Mystery/Crime] A: Allene Tupper Wilkes; REV: Roland Pertwee; D: E. E. Clive; S: Livingston Platt; P: Carl Reed i/a/w E. E. Clive; T: Lyceum Theatre; 2/22/26 (80)

A conventional mystery drama with an "inept plot" (Arthur Hornblow), it was by an American but was about British characters and had already run in London to approving audiences. In New York it stumbled in critical esteem. It "creaked sometimes as much in its construction as in its wheel-chair" (Frank Vreeland).

Taking place in an English country house, it had its stock quota of hands emerging from curtains to shut off lights, thunderstorms, spectral visitors flitting through French doors, shots in the dark, and foolish detectives. It was about the desperate efforts made to retrieve a bejewelled headdress taken from a Nile tomb by Egyptologist Edwin Latter (Reginald Mason), confined to a wheelchair. A murder occurs, and the cast tries to find its perpetrator, who turns out to be an Egyptian (Brandon Peters) seeking to return the booty to its original resting place.

CREDITORS (Fordringsägare) and "THE CONSTANT LOVER" D: Maurice Browne; P: Maurice Browne and Ellen Von Volkenburg; T: Greenwich Village Theatre (OB); 5/2/22 (8)
Creditors [Dramatic Revival] A: August Strindberg; "The Constant Lover" [One-Act/British] A: St. John Hankin

Strindberg's 1880 autobiographical marital drama set in a Swedish hotel room was produced for a one-week Off-Broadway engagement. It followed the curtain raiser of St. John Hankin's 1908 "Constant Lover," on which the critics failed to comment.

Creditors deals with a case of a man's hatred for and revenge upon his ex-wife. Thekla (Ellen Von Volkenburg) has married Adolph (Maurice Browne), who has helped her write a novel in which she mocked and libeled her former spouse Gustav (Reginald Pole). Seeking revenge, Gustav gains a strange power over Adolph and convinces him that Thekla is unfaithful, thus causing him to die of an epileptic fit.

The few critics who turned out came away with mixed impressions. M.B. said, "Its very conception is a symptom of disease.... It is quietly dramatic until its morbid falsity wearies the auditor."

CREOLES [Comedy-Drama/Southern/Romance/Period] A: Samuel Shipman and Kenneth Perkins; D: Harry Benrimo; S: Norman Bel Geddes; P: Richard Herndon; T: Klaw Theatre; 9/22/27 (28)

A costume drama set in New Orleans in 1850 and dealing with the convent-bred girl Jacinta (Helen Chandler), who refuses to marry the debauched family creditor Monsieur Merluche (George Nash) to forestall her mother's (Princess Matchabelli) having to mortgage the family household. Instead, Jacinta tries to convince the Mexican sea-dog of a pirate El Gato (Allan Dinehart) to make her his mistress; he doesn't—he makes her his bride.

"[O]ne may certainly put it down as a bit of painted card-board in which the actors are called upon to utter profoundly unbelievable lines," remarked Richard Dana Skinner.

CRICKET ON THE HEARTH, THE [Comedy/Family/Period/Russian/Russian Language] A: Boris Suskevitch; SC: Charles Dickens's story *The Cricket on the Hearth*; D: Ivan Lazareff; P: Russian Chamber Theatre; T: Cherry Lane Playhouse (OB); 5/24/25

A well-done staging in Russian of the same adaptation of Dickens's 1846 story that had been in the repertoire of the Moscow Art Theatre for a number of years. It was not the version used at one time by Joseph Jefferson III as a curtain raiser. The cast of expatriate Russian players included several former Moscow Art Theatre members, including Leo Bulgakov, who played Caleb Plummer, and Barbara Bulgakov, who was Mrs. Peerybingle.

The adaptation centered on the plight of Caleb and his blind daughter Bertha. Stark Young said "the achievement was unequal but always sympathetic and sincere. The same purity of intention, the same exact and flowing exchange between the various players" was seen as when the Moscow Art company came to New York two seasons before.

CRIME [Drama/Crime/Romance] A: Samuel Shipman and John B. Hymer; D: Guthrie McClintic; S: P. Dodd Ackerman; P: A. H. Woods; T: Eltinge Theatre; 2/22/27 (186)

A tough, unshaven underworld melodrama that was inferior literature but explosive theatre. "Its values are quite false and artificial throughout," sermonized Richard Dana Skinner. "But there is no denying the sheer entertainment value of its hokum."

Eugene Fenmore (James Rennie), smooth gentleman crook with a code of ethics concerning bloodshed, masterminds numerous robberies committed by his gang; he forces a young engaged couple (Sylvia Sidney and Douglas Montgomery) into fronting a daring jewelry heist in which a rival gang member (Chester Morris) kills someone. The youngsters are headed for the electric chair, but Fenmore turns himself in and saves their lives.

There was vivid humor as well as suspense here; a brutal scene of police third-degree tactics drew comment, as did the tense and elaborately staged jewelry theft. To heighten the atmosphere, radio reports of New York robberies were blared during the scene waits.

CRIME IN THE WHISTLER ROOM, THE [Drama/Family/Romance] A: Edmund Wilson; D: Stanley Howlett; S: Cleon Throckmorton; P: Provincetown Players; T: Provincetown Playhouse (OB); 10/12/24 (23)

Confused responses were the outcome of Edmund Wilson's attempt to use expressionist devices to tell a story of a waif named "Bill" (Mary Blair), introduced into the decorous home of wealthy Long Islanders by their social-worker daughter (Mary Morris), of the nightmare she experiences in which she is confronted by the resounding clash between her own nature and those of the prim and stifling folk she has encountered in the family's Whistler Room, and of her morning flight from the house with the poet Simon (E. J. Ballantine) when she learns of her pregnancy.

Although excellently performed by most of the company, especially Blair, the play itself was vague and incoherent to various commentators. Frank Vreeland called it "inchoate, phantasmagoric, transcendental—everything that is not drama in any sense of the word." Stark Young, however, thought it was "engaging, sometimes bitingly drawn, and often suggestive of a fresh quality in the theatre."

CRIMINAL CODE, THE [Drama/Crime/Prison/Law/Romance] A: Martin Flavin; D/P: William Harris, Jr.; S: Albert R. Johnson; T: National Theatre; 10/2/29 (174)

The most respected and widely discussed of the three Martin Flavin dramas that hit Broadway during the 1929–1930 season was this interesting prison drama, which Burns Mantle selected as a Best Play of the Year. Flavin's cynical play was about "the inexorability of the criminal code" (*Times*) and was considered one of the most authentic pictures of penal life and the harm it can inflict ever to have been put on the stage. The only element that spoiled the critics full appreciation was a gratuitous love interest. Perriton Maxwell thought "there is about it that fine consciousness of reaching beyond the lives of the men who are its players to strike out for a generalization which makes the play meaningful beyond its own episodes. And that, in the end, *is* playwriting."

A prologue and twelve swiftly moving scenes were deployed to present the tale of one Robert Graham (Russell Hardie), a young man convicted of manslaughter and sent to prison for a ten year stretch. The D.A. (Arthur Byron) who convicts him later becomes the prison warden. Seven years pass until a parole is in sight; Graham witnesses a murder, but since he has now accepted the criminal code, he refuses to name the killer. Relentlessly goaded by a prison official, he kills the man and sacrifices his chance for release. To deepen the pathos, Flavin suggested a love relationship with the warden's daughter (Anita Kerry). Because of negative critical responses to this device, Flavin revised the play by removing the romantic ending. "The effect was to strengthen the play greatly as a social document," claimed Burns Mantle.

CRISS CROSS [Musical/Romance/Aviation/Adventure/France] B/LY: Otto Harbach and Anne Caldwell; M: Jerome Kern; D: R. H. Burnside; CH: David Bennett; S: James Reynolds; P: Charles Dillingham; T: Globe Theatre; 10/12/26 (210)

Fifty-three-year-old acrobatic comedian Fred Stone continued to surprise by his feats of agility, as when he came swooping over the stage hanging by his heels from an airplane and flipped a girl off the ground into the air machine. The girl was played by his daughter Dorothy, and another role was filled by Allene Stone, his wife. Dorothy's virtues were most evident in the dance numbers, but the versatile Tiller Sunshine Girls were the evening's main terpsichorean delight.

The show itself was a sumptuous affair, set in far-flung places such as Fable-Land, southern France, and Algiers. It included a cast of fantastical characters woven through a thin plot about a French schoolgirl (Dorothy Stone), her threatened claim to an Algerian fortune, her romantic travails, and her rescue from worry by the clever flier Christopher Cross (Stone).

A tuneful Jerome Kern score supported an expensively mounted production, abundant with opulent sets and costumes. The *Times* recommended it as entirely entertaining, save for Stone's old jokes, and *Time* acknowledged that this "big-dress parade is possessed of every grace except humor."

CRITIC, THE [Dramatic Revival] A: Richard Brinsley Sheridan; D: Agnes Morgan and Ian Maclaren; DS: Aline Bernstein; P: Neighborhood Playhouse; T: Neighborhood Playhouse (OB); 5/8/25 (38)

A high-spirited romp of a revival of Sheridan's 1778 spoof on the theatre world of his day, smacking of burlesque and often hysterically funny. John Ranken Towse called it "an exceedingly credible achievement" and observed that the old play, infrequently produced, was "replete with wit, satire and exuberant humor, and still so 'up to date' in spite of its age."

Although designed with period costumes, there was a free-wheeling approach taken; thus an old justice was dressed "in a Salvation Army Santa Claus robe, a pair of wire spectacles, a tangle of whiskers and an aviator's helmet," wrote Wells Root. There were also some contemporary references to the theatre world of 1925.

The best performance was that of Dorothy Sands as both Mrs. Dangle and the confidant. Ian Maclaren's Puff was likewise commended but not as widely.

CROOKED FRIDAY, THE [Drama/Romance/Crime/British] A: Monckton Hoffe; D: Dennis Neilson-Terry; S: Rollo Wayne; P: Messrs. Shubert i/a/w B. A. Meyer; T: Bijou Theatre; 10/8/25 (21)

A crook play "of ineffable banality" (Arthur Hornblow) that strained credulity. It starred the British husband and wife team of Dennis Neilson-Terry and Mary Glynne. Neither came off particularly well, despite their attractiveness, in this preposterous piece. It was about the wealthy Michael Tristan (Neilson-Terry) who, having as a boy of ten discovered a foundling with the tatoo "Friday" on her arm only to subsequently lose her, locates her many years later after she has become a world-traveled crook residing as Felicity Erewhon (Glynne) in the United States. He anonymously arranges for a $2,000 monthly allowance to be paid her but gets her to believe she is keeping him, in order to arouse her affections. Various complications follow, including the presence of another boyfriend, a theft, and Michael's arrest, until all is satisfactorily resolved.

"A surprised audience gasped at the primitiveness of it all," remarked Alan Dale.

CROOKED GAMBLERS [Comedy-Drama/Business] A: Samuel Shipman and Percival Wilde; D: Robert Milton; P: A. H. Woods; T: Hudson Theatre; 7/31/ 20 (81)

Taylor Holmes left Hollywood to be featured in this production about John Stetson (Holmes), a manufacturer of automobile tires. Content to get rich slowly, he shuns Wall Street. His partner Bob Dryden (Purnell Pratt), urged by a stock manipulator, Turner (Felix Krembs), to turn the business into a stock company, convinces Stetson to do so. The stock rises, and Stetson's friends invest heavily. Then comes the crash. Turner wants to sell the stock short and buy in at a lower price and start another boom. Stetson fights him and, just when he seems to be losing, comes through victoriously.

The play scored points for originality from some critics. Its plot differed from the usual run of Wall Street plays in that Stetson was made to loathe the Street, but "the moral framework is purely conventional and the economic prattle childish," noted Ludwig Lewisohn.

M.M.-C.

CROOKED SQUARE, THE [Comedy/Prison/Romance] A: Samuel Shipman and Alfred C. Kennedy; D: Frederick G. Stanhope; P: Mrs. Henry B. Harris; T: Hudson Theatre; 9/10/23 (88)

"Mr. Shipman's latest effort has all the naivete of popular melodrama and may conceivably be popular," wrote the *Times* critic, but added that its appeal was to morons. In the story, a young southern woman (Edna Hibbard), stranded in Manhattan, asks help from a man on the street and is arrested as a street walker. Sent to a reformatory, she is released and smuggled into a wealthy family's home to aid a fake detective agency by ferreting out a scandal. She falls in love with the son (Kenneth MacKenna) and, aided by a Russian prince, a questionable English nobleman, a Japanese chauffeur (T. Tamamoto), a loquacious butler, and two maids, double-crosses her employers, saves the family, and wins the son.

The *Tribune*'s reviewer commented: "In language, motion, theme and development it surpassed uncommon faith, transgressed all earthly laws and was, in short, 100 per cent Martian."

H.H.

CROOKS' CONVENTION, THE [Comedy/Crime/Religion] A: Arthur Somers Roche; D: Leo Donnelly; S: Ward and Harvey Studios; P: Irving Lande; T: Forrest Theatre; 9/18/29 (13)

Arthur Somers Roche asked in this comedy what would happen to the nation if all of the crooks reformed and thereby put an end to crime. He took "three tedious acts of satire" (*Time*) to give the answer that the police would be put out of business, newspapers would have nothing to report, industries would topple, and there would be no sinners for the churches to redeem. "His answer," said *Time*, "is not remarkably trenchant, nor is his playwriting adept."

Roche's plot contrived a convention of a dozen crook union representatives who become converted by evangelist "Revival" Hunt (Leo Donnelly) and vow to give up the rackets for a virtuous life. When this leads to social disorder, the criminals resume their wonted shootouts, robberies, and other such activities. "[A]s satire," said Francis R. Bellamy, "it is so heavy footed that it practically sticks to the floor."

CROSS MY HEART [Musical/Romance] B: Daniel Kusell; M: Harry Tierney; LY: Joseph McCarthy; D/CH/P: Sammy Lee; S: P. Dodd Ackerman; T: Knickerbocker Theatre; 9/17/28 (64)

Harry Tierney and Joseph McCarthy came up empty handed with their score for this last collaboration of theirs on Broadway. The most appreciative word *Time* could muster to describe it was "cunning." Ernest Boyd called it "Standardized merchandise."

Its plot, reminiscent of *The Would-Be Gentleman*, treated of a corpulent social-climbing mother, Mrs. Gobble (Lulu McConnell), who seeks to marry her reluctant daughter Elsie (Doris Eaton) to the Maharaja of Maha (Eddie Conrad), who is really in the employ of Elsie's boyfriend Charles (Bobby Watson). After a silly Mamamouchi-like ceremony, Mrs. Gobble realizes what a fool she is and lets Charles wed Elsie. Meanwhile, a romantic subplot concerning a society youth (Clarence Nordstrom) masquerading as a band leader is brought to a fruitful conclusion.

CROSS ROADS [Drama/Youth/University/Romance/Sex] A: Martin Flavin; D: Guthrie McClintic; S: Robert Edmond Jones; P: Lewis E. Gensler; T: Morosco Theatre; 11/11/29 (28)

The least successful of the three Martin Flavin plays that followed one another in quick succession on Broadway during the season of 1929–1930. The play's problems stemmed largely from mechanical and implausible plotting. It dealt with the love affair of a pair of college youths, Michael (Eric Dressler) and Patricia (Sylvia Sidney). Sexually frustrated, he wishes to give up med school to get married; she opposes his wish. He meets a willing flapper (Irene Purcell) and takes her to a roadhouse. A raid follows and then the threat of scandal and the girl's blackmailing father. Patricia tries to revenge her wounded feelings by a fling with the college rake (Franchot Tone), who gets killed when their car crashes. Michael and Patricia reconcile their differences, and he decides to concentrate on his career.

The play offered insights into the personal problems of college youth and had sensitive dialogue. Richard Dana Skinner reported, "It has too many good moments to be discarded as sheer rubbish, and yet, . . . it is [often] so inept and bungling that you wonder how it ever came to actual production."

CROWN PRINCE, THE (A trónörökös) [Drama/Romance/Crime/Period/Hungarian] A: Ernest Vajda; AD: Zoë Akins; D: Lawrence Marston; S: Watson Barratt; P: L. Lawrence Weber; T: Forrest Theatre; 3/23/27 (45)

A romantic tragedy based on well-known events in the Austrian royal family in 1889 (the "Meyerling affair"). The play purports to answer what remained an unsolved mystery. Vajda combined "color, intrigue, regal ceremonies, romance and death" (Brooks Atkinson) in an expertly crafted piece that kept spectators firmly in place during its fanciful, sentimental progress.

The Crown Prince (Basil Sydney) is married, but he really loves the Baroness (Mary Ellis), which angers both his wife (Kay Strozzi) and his father, the Emperor (Henry Stephenson). The latter uses various means to persuade the Baroness to poison the Prince, and then he tries to betray the woman by telling the Prince the condition of his wine. But the Prince, dismayed, chooses to quaff the potion, and his mistress follows suit.

CROWNS [Drama/Religion/Romance/War/Verse] A: John Luther Long; S: Cleon Throckmorton; P: Players Co., Inc.; T: Provincetown Playhouse (OB); 11/9/22 (8)

A pretentious attempt by a fledgling Off-Broadway group, the Players Company (an offshoot of the Provincetown Players), to do a new blank-verse play as a tryout for possible Broadway production. The attempt crashed instantly, for the play was notably deficient.

Its plot was of the Romeo and Juliet variety, with the Prince (Benjamin Kauser) and Princess (Margaret Mower) of rival houses in love with one another and each of them imbued with the teachings of Jesus but forced to wage war against each other by political leaders. Misunderstandings prepared by their underlings eventuate in the Princess's suicide as the Prince gets to her side too late to prevent it.

"It is all maniacal piffle, hopelessly lacking in beauty, sonorousness, in charm and in fancy," opined Laurence Stallings.

CUP, THE [Drama/Crime/Religion/Romance] A: William Hurlbut; D: Edgar J. MacGregor; P: Joseph E. Shea; T: Fulton Theatre; 11/12/23 (16)

"*The Cup* is a play glorifying American filth. It is the foulest-mouthed, cruelest, least ingenious piece of 'realism' which has come to Broadway in this highly profane and richly vulgar season," wrote Q.M. John Corbin was milder, holding that there was considerable crude force in the melodrama, weakened by straying into religious paths. The combination of religion—the story concerns a cheap crook and his girlfriend (Tom Moore and Josephine Victor) whose souls may be saved when he accidentally steals the Holy Grail and she almost dies returning it to a priest—and of crude language disturbed some critics. One word, apparently said for the first time on a Broadway stage (no critic indicated what word), shocked audiences.

H.H.

CYCLONE LOVER, THE [Comedy/Romance] A: Fred Ballard and Charles A. Bickford; D: Al Roberts and Roy Walling; P: W. Herbert Adams and Roy Walling; T: Frolic Theatre; 6/5/28 (31)

Many critics left this piece in midperformance, agreeing with Percy Hammond that "its values as an entertainment are meager." The cyclone lover is a timid insurance agent (Harold Elliott) who loves a wealthy girl (Emily Graham), herself infatuated with a swinish portrait artist (Theodore Hecht) of Greenwich Village. He insures the girl, at her father's behest, against her marriage to the painter; then, to protect her from the painter's wiles, he snatches her away just as she is about to be secretly wed and gradually overcomes her objections in time for her to agree to be his bride.

CYMBELINE [Dramatic Revival] A: William Shakespeare; D: Julia Marlowe and E. H. Sothern; P: Marlowe and Sothern i/a/w the Messrs. Shubert; T: Jolson's Fifty-ninth Street Theatre; 10/2/23 (15)

Cymbeline, rarely produced in America, was given its second twentieth-century New York mounting in this production. It marked the first time in at least a dozen years that Julia Marlowe essayed a new Shakespearean character.

Cymbeline proved an inauspicious opening of E. H. Sothern and Julia Marlowe's New York season of Shakespeare, with productions of *Romeo and Juliet*, *Twelfth Night*, *Taming of the Shrew*, *Merchant of Venice*, and *Hamlet* to follow. Although Sothern's Posthumous "was finely spirited and impassioned" according to John Corbin, Julia Marlowe's Imogen was a disaster: "Of late years Miss Marlowe's mannerisms have steadily grown on her—overwrought and fallacious pathos alternating with outbursts of fake passion. Worst of all is an extreme deliberation in utterance, further retarded by fake pauses that destroy poetic rhythm and even rob her scenes of their prime quality of spontaneity and passion." Alan Dale, however, liked both Sothern and Marlowe, commenting that she played "with her old charm, and with new force. She gave a tragic vehemence to many of the scenes. It was almost like a new Julia Marlowe."

Of particular interest to John Corbin was the visual approach taken. Corbin, who before becoming a critic for the *Times* had designed productions of *The Winter's Tale* and *The Tempest*, displayed scholarly knowledge of the Elizabethan stage in a review that recounted in detail Sothern's masterly use of Elizabethan practices that made his *Cymbeline* "by far the most scholarly, artistic and richly colored of the recent Shakespearean revivals." Sothern had come up with a setting closely approximating the layout of the Shakespearean theatre, using the then-popular notion of an "inner stage" or "alcove" decorated with draperies, with doorways set into the walls on either side of the alcove. This allowed for speedy playing and a minimum of time wasted for scene shifts; however, Sothern elected in the cave and battle scenes to go for "heavy Victorian scenery that involves delay in proportion as it is magnificent."

H.H.

CYRANO DE BERGERAC [Dramatic Revival] A: Edmond Rostand; TR: Brian Hooker; D/P: Walter Hampden; DS: Claude Bragdon; T: National Theatre; 11/1/23 (250)

The great significance of this *Cyrano* revival was its introduction of Brian Hooker's version of the play, which has remained the most popular translation to date. John Corbin called Hooker's work "more redolent of the original than any other." Stark Young quibbled that it was smooth and actable but too simplified in spots and too prudent in conversation.

Launching Walter Hampden's season of classical repertory with his own company, the production as well as the star's project won wide acclaim. Comparing the performances of Cyrano by Richard Mansfield and Coquelin to Hampden's, the *Evening Telegraph*'s critic noted that Mansfield had excelled in the death scene, Coquelin in the play's lighter scenes, and "It remained for Mr. Hampden to be equally expressive in both the lighter and the more serious aspects of this great comedy."

Young thought Hampden's a slight talent lacking in style, "not a great actor but a fine centre of theatrical belief and labor," but Corbin commented, "Mr. Hampden's Cyrano is an interpretation of great physical vigor, deep truth and intensity of passion," who really fenced yet seemed to improvise verses during the first-act duel, made one believe he could rout one hundred attackers, radiated bravura in the moonman scene, and, at the end, "soared high in the region of tragic pathos."

Hampden's Cyrano returned to New York at the actor's own theatre on 2/18/26 and ran for 96 performances. An even longer run was produced beginning 12/25/28, again at the Hampden, when it totaled 143 performances. Many considered Cyrano the role of the actor's career. "There is something in that false and grotesque nose which releases the real Hampden," surmised Richard Dana Skinner. "Perhaps he identifies his own idealistic nature more closely with this hero than with any other. At all events, he puts into Cyrano a volume of feeling and warmth which many find lacking in his portrayals of other noble parts."

Designer Claude Bragdon, in his book *More Lives than One*, gives a precise account of his production scheme for this drama. He describes the need for a "heavy" production with numerous locales and architectural features and tells how he devised a unit set to simplify the staging. Two wagon-stages were used, one being eighteen inches above the stage floor, the other seven feet higher than the first. Each was a "house on wheels" with their four sides covered by flats bearing all the needed architectural elements. "By rolling the wagons into different positions and exposing different faces at different times. . . it was possible to meet all of the acting requirements and at the same time differentiate the various scenes sufficiently to deceive all but the most expert and analytical eye.''

H.H.

CZARINA, THE (A cárnö) [Comedy/Period/Romance/Russia/Historical-Bio-graphical/Hungarian] A: Melchior Lengyel and Lajos Biro; AD: Edward Sheldon; D: Gilbert Miller; P: Charles Frohman, Inc.; T: Empire Theatre; 1/31/22 (136)

Doris Keane, after touring in the United States and abroad for nine years in the sensational Edward Sheldon romantic melodrama *Romance*, opened on Broadway in a hopeful follow-up to her previous success. Alexander Woollcott announced that ''she has done it again.'' Several other daily reviewers agreed; the consensus, however, was that *The Czarina*, a romantic comedy based on Russia's Queen Catherine the Great, was ''the sheerest theatrical clap-trap, made High Hokum by dint of a thoroughly beautiful setting, radiant costuming and the still magic name of Charles Frohman'' (Arthur Hornblow), the late producer whose name continued to head an active production company.

Edward Sheldon's adaptation of a popular Hungarian play concentrated on the glamorous Czarina's (Keane) tempestuous love life, beginning with her introduction to Count Alexei Czerny (Basil Rathbone), a lieutenant in her army, who arrives to warn her of a conspiracy against the throne and her life and is rewarded by being made her lover. Later, unhappy in his subservient role as the Czarina's stud, he joins the conspirators and is defeated and condemned to death. Catherine, meanwhile, has no trouble in kindling a new amour with the handsome new French Ambassador (Ian Keith). Her former lover is pardoned and even granted an estate.

D

DADDY DUMPLINS [Comedy-Drama/Legacy/Family/Youth] A: George Barr McCutcheon and Earl Carroll; SC: "Mr. Bingle," a story by George Barr McCutcheon; D/P: Earl Carroll; T: Republic Theatre; 11/25/20 (64)

A Daddy Longlegs–Pollyanna sort of play about Henry Dumplins (Maclyn Arbuckle), a hearty old bachelor who adopts seven orphans. He brings them up amidst luxury until his inheritance is claimed by his cruel cousin (Percy Moore). The children are sent to a home, while Daddy goes to live in a tenement house. Later the cousin relents, and the whole family is reunited on Christmas Eve.

The piece was tailor-made for lovers of sentimentality and engendered "a new note of wholesomeness, charity, love of home and parentless children of the streets," declared Charles Darnton. The *Times* described it as "a simple and human story, told with a number of artful touches, and possessed of an undeniable appeal."

M.M.-C.

DADDY'S GONE A-HUNTING [Drama/Marriage/Art] A: Zoë Akins; D/P: Arthur Hopkins; S: Robert Edmond Jones; T: Plymouth Theatre; 8/31/21 (129)

An intensely promising, but incompletely fulfilled, marital drama about a poor young couple. The husband (Frank Conroy) tries to shed his family obligations so he may pursue his artistic goals. The wife (Marjorie Rambeau) turns to another man (Lee Baker). Five years later, the husband returns to be near his dying child, but he remains true to his vision and will not rekindle his relationship with his wife.

Some of the reviews of *Daddy's Gone a-Hunting* reveal how powerfully and directly Akins's writing had broken new ground in its truthfulness and integrity to the people it portrayed. Alexander Woollcott thought this "finely wrought and distinguished play," so similar in outline to many conventional dramas, was unique to itself, "so distinctive is the thought and expression" of the dramatist.

But Ludwig Lewisohn was sorely irked by the sentimental deathbed contrivances of the final act. He did, however, admire the author's "peculiar grace" in avoiding a happy ending.

DAFFY DILL [Musical/Romance] B: Guy Bolton and Oscar Hammerstein II; M: Herbert Stothart; LY: Oscar Hammerstein II; D/CH: Julian Mitchell; P: Arthur Hammerstein; T: Apollo Theatre; 8/22/22 (69)

A piece of summer fluff, designed to show off the talents of vaudevillian Frank Tinney and his supporting star Georgia O'Ramey in a nearly plotless series of twelve episodes consisting of various vaudeville turns. Tinney was in all of the episodes, and when neither he nor O'Ramey were present, the more than twenty scantily clad chorus girls ("The girl who wore stockings and shoes was an object to attract attention"—Q.M.) "gyrate and chirrup" (Alan Dale).

The specialty numbers were conducted in the interstices of a sketchy and meaningless plot concerned with a Cinderella story about the love of an old-fashioned girl (Irene Olsen) for a millionaire (Guy Robertson) who feels burdened by his riches.

DAGGER, THE [Drama/Crime/Legacy/France/Romance] A: Marian Wightman; D: William B. Friedlander; P: L. Lawrence Weber; T: Longacre Theatre; 9/9/25 (5)

Another lurid melodrama of the Paris underworld with an Apache hero and a hooker with a heart of gold. The Apache (Ralph Morgan) is a Montmartre criminal called the "Dagger"; a former member of high society, he has turned to crime because he has been tricked out of the legacy to which he was entitled. This brave young crook engages in a romance with a local girl (Sara Sothern) with whom, after various adventures, he is finally united at the curtain's descent, by which time he also has been cleared of all criminal charges.

The critics were incredulous that such a play could still get a Broadway production. This "childish rubbish" was recommended by Alexander Woollcott "to that not inconsiderable minority of the theatregoing public which is not quite bright."

DAGMAR (Tilla) [Drama/Sex/Romance/Hungarian] A: Ferencz Herczeg; AD: Louis Anspacher; D: B. Iden Payne; S: Frederick Jones III; P: Charles Bryant; T: Selwyn Theatre; 1/22/23 (65)

A torrid "sex extravaganza" (Arthur Hornblow) about the nymphomaniacal Countess Dagmar (Alla Nazimova), who flits from lover to lover until she begins a liason with Andre Belisar (Charles Bryant). Belisar accepts her offer to kill her if she is ever unfaithful, and when she returns to the arms of another romance (Gilbert Emery), Belisar thrusts a knife into her throat.

There was little respect for this "worthless, meretricious play," which the Playgoer regretted did not kill off the heroine earlier, "thus making more promptly a good riddance to bad rubbish." A strong feeling existed that the Russian star actress who was the chief excuse for this "incredible piece of maudlin stuff" (Laurence Stallings) had erred egregiously in choosing so lamentable a script, and that her recent stardom in films had cheapened her tastes.

DAISY MAYME [Comedy/Romance/Family] A/D: George Kelly; S: Livingston Platt; P: Rosalie Stewart; T: Playhouse Theatre; 10/25/26 (113)

An acidulous domestic comedy, directed to perfection by its author. Kelly's gift for detailed, photographically observed characterization was apparent, but the piece seemed too determinedly bitter in outlook to Brooks Atkinson, and Arthur Hornblow was dissatisfied with his "commonplace" lines and thin story. George Jean Nathan thought it was too artful a depiction of reality.

Daisy Mayme was named for the character of the loud, but good-natured, spinster (Jessie Busley) whom realtor Cliff Mettinger (Carlton Brickert) meets in Atlantic City and brings home to his suburban household of dependent and jealous female relatives. The latter raise their hackles at the idea that she may steal their breadwinner from under their noses—which she does.

Burns Mantle made it a Best Play of the Year, but Richard Dana Skinner asserted, "There is not much sparkle to *Daisy Mayme*, little adventure, and what humor there is becomes in time monotonously ironic." However, Joseph Wood Krutch declared it to be "not merely funny, [but,] like *Craig's Wife*, exciting as well."

DAME AUX CAMÉLIAS, LA (Camille) [Dramatic Revival/French Language] A: Alexander Dumas *fils*; P: Messrs. Shubert; T: Thirty-ninth Street Theatre; 11/19/22 (4)

Dumas *fils'* nineteenth-century classic of the pathetic love affair of consumptive courtesan Marguerite Gautier (Cécile Sorel) and Armand Duval (Albert Lambert) was revived in the original language by a troupe of actors from the Comédie Française and the Odéon, led by Sorel. Her production was an attempt to update the work to the 1920s; it was performed to a jazz background, but the effect seemed odd, especially in the shoddy mounting using "queer, flat, old scenery" and "misfit wigs." Further marred by a late curtain and excessive scene waits, the "utterly unillusive" (*Times*) production faltered badly and half of the opening-night crowd departed in midperformance.

In terms of physical type and appropriate age, Sorel and Lambert were wrong as the lovers; Camille, for example, "had the bounding physique of a well-preserved matron who has just escaped stoutness" (*Times*). Nevertheless, she was "full of life, vigor and emotion," said the *Tribune*. Sorel's Camille followed the broad outlines of her predecessors in the role, but she introduced a novel touch at the end when she "only faintly indicated the dread disease" instead of being medically accurate. "There was nothing repulsive in her death," said Charles Pike Sawyer, just "a sudden collapse in the arms of Armand almost immediately following their reconciliation."

Sorel returned with *Camille* in her 1926 month-long repertory at the Cosmopolitan, where, beginning on 12/6/26, she gave it twelve performances. Rolla Norman was her Armand for the occasion. The production was an improvement over that of 1922.

DAMN THE TEARS [Drama/Sports/University/Mental Illness] A: William Gaston; M: Ruth Warfield; D: Sigourney Thayer; S: Norman Bel Geddes; P: Alexander McKaig; T: Garrick Theatre; 1/21/27 (11)

"[W]ild eyed trash of an uncommon order," was Gilbert W. Gabriel's assessment of this noisy, pretentious, obscure expressionistic effort at an "ironic play in seven scenes." It told the dismal story of a star college baseball player (Ralph Morgan), who, failing to hit in the clutch, grows depressed, breaks training, and is kicked off the team. He gradually sees his life slip into the haze of insanity as he becomes a Chaplinesque tramp and is finally picked up by the cops as a mindless vagrant when he wanders onto the ball field of his former glory.

Produced in an unusual manner with several well-staged scenes suggesting the disintegration of the central character's mind, it nevertheless quickly grew tiresome. Puppets designed by Remo Bufano were used in one scene to suggest the eccentric movement of cheerleaders, and manikin spectators responded on cue. The play also employed film sequences to explore the hero's confused state of mind.

DAMN YOUR HONOR [Comedy-Drama/Period/Crime/Romance/Sex] A/D: Bayard Veiller and Becky Gardiner; DS: Lee Simonson; P: Vincent Youmans; T: Cosmopolitan Theatre; 12/30/29 (8)

A swashbuckling costume melodrama that seemed to Perriton Maxwell like a "thumping movie in flesh and blood"; however, he conceded that as a play it was "the merest piffle." The colorfully produced saga, set on the isle of Barataria and in New Orleans, presented the dashing pirate hero La Tour (John Halliday), who steals the jewels of the Governor's (Frederick Worlock) wife Cydalese (Jessie Royce Landis) and, when she boldly comes to his camp to ask for them back, steals her heart; finally, after numerous action-packed situations, he makes off with her for good on his ship.

Audiences weren't sure whether the piece was meant to be taken seriously or as a burlesque. At one point a pirate girl (Peggy Shannon) sacrifices her life for the pirate captain. Seeing a touch of blood on her blouse he declares, "But—you're wounded!" Dropping to the floor, she cries out, "Damn it! I'm dead!"

DANCE OF DEATH, THE (Dödsdansen) [Dramatic Revival/German Language] A: August Strindberg; T: Princess Theatre; 12/16/23 (3)

Strindberg's brutal exploration of the dark side of marriage, first produced in 1905, was given a German-language staging that introduced actress Irene Triesch to Broadway in the role of Alice. The *Times* critic lamented that Strindberg's play "utterly fails to repay a sustained attendance upon it, and it breaks down completely as the vehicle for the display of her emotional abilities by any actress whatsoever.'' He judged that Triesch probably accomplished as much with her role as possible: ''Despite her obvious possession of the ability to portray emotion amounting almost to hysteria, she played with a calculated restraint that very few other actresses would have imposed upon themselves,'' and he expressed a hope to see the German star in another play. Her only other performance here came in a single performance of *Rosmersholm*, given in German, in February 1924.

H.H.

DANCERS, THE [Drama/Show Business/British] A: Gerald Du Maurier; D: William Devereux; P: Messrs. Shubert; T: Broadhurst Theatre; 10/17/23 (133)

''A more unabashed, barefaced specimen of cheap dramatic hokum has not been seen in these parts for many a moon,'' Arthur Hornblow wrote, while the *Tribune*'s critic declared that Du Maurier's play, a huge success in London, was ''a first-class, oldtime British melodrama, done in a smart, new-fashioned way.'' Richard Bennett took the Du Maurier role of Tony, a poor young man loved but rejected by a flapper (Florence Eldridge). Tony goes to Canada, where he runs a dance saloon and is loved by Maxine (Kathlene MacDonell, in the role in which Tallulah Bankhead had made her London debut). He inherits a fortune and returns to the flapper. But she, having become pregnant, kills herself. Six years later, Tony and Maxine, who is now a star, meet and rekindle their romance.

Richard Bennett gave a ''sensitive, manly and indeed very elevated performance,'' claimed Hornblow, but he concluded that it was not enough to knit a disjointed play.

H.H.

DANCING GIRL, THE [Musical/Marriage/Sea/Romance] D: J. C. Huffman; S: Watson Barratt; P: Messrs. Shubert; T: Winter Garden; 1/24/23 (142)

No authors or composers were credited with creating this show, which, despite a whisper of a plot, was really a revue designed to open the newly refurbished Winter Garden with a confectionary entertainment. According to the *Times*, the show was pieced together of materials originally used in the popular Raymond Hitchcock revues called *Hitchy-Koo* (there were four editions), with contributions from Cole Porter, Harold Atteridge, and Harry Wagstaff Gribble.

Set mostly aboard an ocean liner, with its story about a romance between a first-class passenger and a Spanish dancing girl (Trini) in the steerage section, the show offered abundant excuses for vaudeville turns. Among them was boxer Benny Leonard, who staged a comic bout with Jack Pearl and an exhibition with a pro fighter, and Marie Dressler in a burlesque rendition of the Jeanne Eagels hit *Rain*.

This was ''a shimmering and generally well-dressed revue,'' lacking, however, in ''any real wit'' (*Times*).

DANCING MOTHERS [Comedy-Drama/Family/Romance/Sex/Marriage] A: Edgar Selwyn and Edmund Goulding; D/P: Edgar Selwyn; T: Booth Theatre; 8/11/24 (311)

Flappers were the subject of many twenties plays and Helen Hayes got to play a heavy share of them. Her flapper role in *Dancing Mothers* was another in the pattern. With its strong cast, excellent mounting, and surprise ending, the play became one of its season's strongest hits and was named a Best Play of the Year.

Generally, the play was viewed as old hat and, aside from its conclusion, predictable. George Jean Nathan wrote that the authors "have viewed life with all the shades down and the electric lights up. Their characters are not out of homes, but out of stage dressing rooms; they achieve reality only in an occasional line of dialogue."

Dancing Mothers concerns a bored mother (Mary Young), bored father (Henry Stephenson), and hot-blooded, hooch-swilling daughter (Hayes). When the wife becomes aware of the father's philandering and the daughter's meandering, she decides to go them one better; she drops her domestic airs, has an affair with her girl's flashy beau (John Halliday), and, in a conclusion that made the play unique for its genre, leaves her family for a happier future with him.

Arthur Hornblow's belief that the "unexpected twist at the end saved it from being utterly commonplace and is likely to carry it to success" was widely shared.

Helen Hayes's mother, Catherine Hayes Brown, in *Letters to Mary*, recounted how she and Hayes sought to turn down Edgar Selwyn's offer of the role of the flapper daughter. They chose to ask for the exorbitant sum of $750 a week and were shocked when Selwyn agreed without hesitation. Brown went on to say, "She was never happy in the part, and I always felt it was just retribution for Mommy [Hayes] and me for being such worms.... Mommy did work harder in that part than she ever did in any other to put as much in it as she could to justify that salary."

DANGER [Drama/Marriage/Romance/Sex/British] A: Cosmo Hamilton; D/P: Carle Carlton; T: Thirty-ninth Street Theatre; 12/22/21 (79)

An unsuccessful, sensationalistic example of "the clinical drama," which "pretended to probe deep into the soul of a sexless and over-ambitious woman" (Arthur Hornblow) but was really a stage version of the kind of garish story found in cheap magazines. Alexander Woollcott called it "a highly varnished bit of artificiality" written in "pretentious language."

Stage and film star H. B. Warner met with "disaster" (Charles Darnton) in this shallow exposé of a British marriage in which barrister John Fitzroy Scorrier (Warner) weds a self-described "modernist" (Marie Goff), the social-climbing daughter of a horse trainer, who refuses to have sex with him from their wedding night on and plans to reap the financial benefits of her marriage in a nation where the husband has no recourse to divorce. Scorrier turns for succor to his secretary

(Kathlene MacDonell), whom he impregnates and plans to marry after having his first marriage annulled.

Warner acted well, but Leslie Howard, playing his bungling friend Percy Sturgess, was greeted as the play's best performer.

DANTON'S DEATH (Danton's Tod) [Dramatic Revival/German Language] A: George Büchner; D: Max Reinhardt; P: Gilbert Miller; T: Century Theatre; 12/20/27 (16)

New York's first view of George Büchner's 1835 play, a standard tragedy in Germany, came with Max Reinhardt's remarkable production seen during his Berlin company's 1927–1928 visiting season. Büchner had died at twenty-four, and his play did not see a production until sixty years later. Startlingly ahead of its time, it used an epic style to project the story of the French Revolution leader of the title, exceptionally well played by Paul Hartmann, whose conflict with the ruthless Robespierre, equally well portrayed by Vladimir Sokoloff, is the seed of the action. The weary rationalist procrastinator is paired against the icily dogmatic pragmatist in a battle that leads to the former's confrontation with the guillotine. Swirling about the multiscened, fragmented action are a host of other historical personages, such as poet Camille Desmoulins (Hans Thimig), Danton's wife Lucile (Lili Darvas), and the cruel St. Just (Arnold Korff).

Forty-seven characters combined with a multitude of extras (Americans trained in only a week to give a striking impression of a squalling mob) to turn the mounting into a sensational staging with crowd scenes and atmospheric effects unusual to even hardened theatregoers. Reinhardt's genius for stagecraft overwhelmed most critics, as he molded a total theatre picture of the frenzied Revolutionary period. Most memorable was the scene before the tribunal in which, unsuccessfully, Danton defended himself. Through the use of actors planted in the house, the audience was swept up into the events of the plot. The company's acting was loudly commended, Brooks Atkinson mentioning their "freedom in gesture, compass and timbre of vocal tones, bodily posture, suppleness of fingers and wrists, all confident and sure of touch." Stark Young, who had reservations about the overall quality of the troupe, found that "the chief interest. . . was the production itself with regard to the light, the transition from one setting to another, the immense mechanics of the physical stage, and the management of the mass scenes."

DARK, THE [Drama/Marriage] A: Martin Brown; D: George Cukor; S: Livingston Platt; P: William A. Brady, Jr., and Dwight Deere Wiman; T: Lyceum Theatre; 2/1/27 (13)

A short-lived, but not ineffective, and often gripping piece about a handsome, would-be inventor (Louis Calhern), whose tinkering with a device to help his wife (Ann Andrews) overcome her fear of the dark misfires, blinding him and scarring his face so horribly that he must wear a mask. His vain, beauty-worshipping mate suffers terribly from the strain; he confronts her about a suspected love affair and rips his mask off, but the sight so shocks her that she finds her love for him returning in a rush.

Alexander Woollcott deemed the work "chock full of finely wrought, cunningly whipped-up agonies." *Time* said the plot was "forced" and psychologically unsound but had "moments of theatrical power." The *Times*, though, said it was "fashioned. . . out of shoddy."

DARK ANGEL, THE [Drama/War/Romance/British] A: H. B. Trevelyan; D/P: Robert Milton; S: Livingston Platt; T: Longacre Theatre; 2/10/25 (64)

Another variation of the shopworn sentimental Enoch Arden story by an author rumored to be popular British writer Michael Arlen writing pseudonymously. Arlen himself denied the rumor.

The Dark Angel had moments of sparkling verbal high comedy, but it was viewed by many as essentially lachrymose and banal, as well as overly familiar in subject matter. Joseph Wood Krutch, for one, could not see why he had "to sympathize with the sham sorrows of sham people created by some technician rubbing his hands behind the scenes."

This drama of honor and self-sacrifice dealt with Kitty (Patricia Collinge) and Hilary (Reginald Mason); the latter is reported killed in action, and Kitty eventually falls in love with another chap (Barry O'Neill). Hilary turns out to be alive but blind; Kitty, with Hilary's support, chooses to marry the other man.

DARK MIRROR, THE [Drama/Family/Business/Marriage] A: Irving Stone; D: Adele Gutman Nathan; P: Lenox Hill Players; T: Cherry Lane Playhouse (OB); 11/9/28 (32)

A five-act tragedy of urban American life; it moves from 1910 to 1950, each act marking a passage of ten years. Three generations of a family are depicted. The father (Jerome Seplow) dies when he loses the job he has had for many years, and his wife (Adeline Ruby) becomes a successful realtor. Her son (Mitchell Marcus), however, ruins the business, fights with his wife (Mary Hallett), and sees his daughter (Syd Brenner) go bad; the family dies in poverty.

"It contains many flashes of true characterization, but lacks in smoothness and continuity," noted L.E.J.

DAUGHTER OF MME. ANGOT, THE (La Fille de Mme. Angot) [Musical Revival/Russian Language] AD: Vladimir Nemirovich-Danchenko and Mikhail Galperin; B: "Clairville," (Louis François Nikolaie), Paul Siraudin, and Victor Koning; M: Charles Lecocq; D: Vladimir Nemirovich-Danchenko; DS: Maria Gortinskaya; P: F. Ray Comstock and Morris Gest; T: Jolson's Fifty-ninth Street Theatre; 12/28/25 (8)

La Fille de Mme. Angot was a popular and often revived opera bouffe, first produced in Paris in 1872 and seen in New York a year later. The present production of this piece, set during the French Directory period, was given by the visiting Moscow Art Theatre Musical Studio as part of a repertory season exploring their "Synthetic Theatre" ideals. The leading role was sung by Na-diezhada Kenarskaya, but Olga Baklanova as Lange was best liked by the critics. Otherwise, the troupe displayed little genius at singing. The faithful adaptation of the original was not good enough to prevent the critics from being bored. The *World* said it was "a so-so operetta" that "dragged into dulness." Joseph Wood Krutch called it a "rather trifling and faded French operetta with an undistinguished score." Olin Downes, observing that it was a triumph of setting and costume design, thought that the Russian qualities of the production over-powered the material and swamped the necessary Gallic sparkle.

DAWN [Drama/Youth/Sex/Family/Romance] A: Tom Barry; P: Sidney Wilmer and Walter Vincent; T: Sam H. Harris Theatre; 11/24/24 (48)

To most critics Emma Dunn's performance was the only notable element in what *Time* called a "dull and arrantly absurd" play about a Rhode Island family of understanding mother (Dunn), rebellious flapper daughter (Zita Johann), and rigidly puritanical father (Howard Lang).

The father represses the daughter's instincts, but the mother goes so far as to allow her to have her friends over for a party. Another repressed girl at the party commits suicide. When the father learns that his daughter has had sex with a boyfriend, he insists on her getting married to the fellow, but the mother in-tercedes, claiming "I came to you as she is going to her sweetheart" (the sweetheart being another lad, not the one she slept with).

Joseph Wood Krutch said the play was "hopelessly unreal," but Arthur Horn-blow warmed to it as having "distinct merit and really tragic force."

DAWN OF IRELAND, THE [Drama/Politics] A: Hugh Stanislaus Stange; P: Will Morrissey; T: Lexington Theatre (OB); 10/1/20

A little-known Off-Broadway play based on the Irish political troubles and virulently anti-English in sentiment. "[S]ave for a few moments when it becomes unconsciously funny, it is a singularly wordy, dreary and uninspired work," noted the *Times*.

DEAR ME [Comedy/Theatre/Friendship/Romance] A: Luther Reed and Hale Hamilton; D: Winchell Smith; P: John Golden; T: Republic Theatre; 1/17/21 (144)

"[A] fairly effective retelling of the perennial Cinderella legend" (*Times*) involving April Blair (Grace LaRue), a drab kitchen maid with a voice. She works in a Home for Artistic and Literary Failures and has a penchant for writing herself letters addressed "Dear Me." Her success-oriented philosophy turns the home's residents into achievers. A new inmate (Hale Hamilton) writes a play and builds a theatre for April, bringing her fame but leading her to neglect her roots. In the end she acknowledges her old friends.

The play's Pollyanna platitudes were designed for the matinee trade. The trouble with Pollyannas, argued Alan Dale, "is that they are selfish at heart and think of the effect on their own soul if they can make others swallow optimism."

M.M.-C.

DEAR OLD ENGLAND [Comedy/Romance/British] A: H. F. Maltby; D/P: Elwood F. Bostwick; S: P. Dodd Ackerman; T: Ritz Theatre; 3/25/30 (23)

Following its London success, this English "satirical farce" bored the New York critics with its story of a group of English aristocrats, made paupers by the effects of World War I and forced to live in abandoned tram cars on the Sussex Downs wasteland, where they keep up the pretences of good breeding. The daughter (Mary Vance) of Lady Shoreham (Gladys Hanson) takes a menial job at her former manorial residence; she and the bourgeois youth (Reginald Sheffield) who has purchased the place fall in love and live happily ever after.

The play's laughter owed much to the considerable degree of low-comedy horseplay engaged in, including lots of crashing into broken-down furniture. There was also a paper-eating goat and satire based on down-and-outers practicing dignified customs amidst abject squalor. Joseph Wood Krutch said, "The general impression...is that of a superior college play, but there is both good humor and entertainment."

DEAR SIR [Musical/Romance] B: Edgar Selwyn; M: Jerome Kern; LY: Howard Dietz; D: David Burton; CH: David Bennett; S: Raymond Sovey; P: Philip Goodman; T: Times Square Theatre; 9/23/24 (15)

A musical comedy noteworthy for Jerome Kern's contributions but otherwise irreparably mediocre. It starred Oscar Shaw and Genevieve Tobin as the romantic leads, he an eligible society bachelor, she a southern debutante in the big city who repulses his proposal because of his rakish reputation. She enters a popularity contest at a Park Avenue street fair where the young millionaire bids for her services at an auction and wins them for a week. She goes to work for him as his temporary maid, is tamed by his affections, and falls in love with him.

The show proved a disappointing box-office failure despite some strong reviews. It was expensively produced with a forty-member chorus and had a funny performance by bumbling comic actor Walter Catlett, but its book was leaden. Frank Vreeland said Kern's music was "not always his best," although Stephen Rathbun thought it "gay, blithe and melodious." Newcomer Howard Dietz's lyrics were very well appreciated; the *Times* acknowledged him a worthy successor to P. G. Wodehouse. Dancer Clare Luce gained some attention in a small part when she exhibited her skill at kicking the back of her head with her toes.

DEAREST ENEMY [Musical/Period/Military/War/Romance/Historical-Bio-graphical] B: Herbert Fields; M: Richard Rodgers; LY: Lorenz Hart; D: John Murray Anderson; CH: Carl Hemmer; S: Clark Robinson; C: Mark Mooring,

Hubert Davis, and James Reynolds; P: George Ford; T: Knickerbocker Theatre; 9/18/25 (286)

The first Broadway collaboration of Rodgers and Hart was this hit show described by the *Times* as an "operetta with more than a chance flavor of Gilbert and Sullivan." The critics were greatly charmed by the show's elegant period settings, the novel background of the book, and the excellent melodies and lyrics of the songs. Helen Ford, in the ingenue role, outdid herself by the charm of her performance.

The show was based on an actual historical incident, the occasion when Mrs. Robert Murray (Flavia Arcaro) entertained with food and wine the chiefs of staff of the British forces one night during the Revolutionary War, thereby giving General Putnam (Percy Woodley) and his 3,000 Continentals the opportunity to move unhindered from the Battery to Harlem Heights, where they joined General Washington (H. E. Eldridge). The idea for the show came to Rodgers and Hart when they chanced upon a plaque on a Thirty-seventh Street building commemorating the event. Attendant upon the historical incidents were the usual romantic and comic interludes conventional to shows of the genre.

Herbert Fields's book was superior to most of the day, but there was some carping over his recourse to sexual innuendo. Hart's witty lyrics were also a bit risque. Arthur Hornblow remarked, "The score is really delightful, combining as it does refinement and genuinely sustained melody throughout. Richard Rodgers. . .is one of the coming lights of his particular field." Numbers appreciated by the reviewers included two that became standards, "Here in My Arms" and "Bye and Bye."

DEATH OF PAZUKHIN, THE (Smert' Pazukhina) [Dramatic Revival/Russian Language] A: Mikhail Saltykov-Schedrin; D: Ivan Moskvin and Vassily Luzhsky; S: Ivan Gremislavsky; P: F. Ray Comstock and Morris Gest; T: Jolson's Fifty-ninth Street Theatre; 2/11/24 (10)

Saltykov-Schedrin's 1857 *Volpone*-like comedy, in which he satirized religious superstition, official corruption, and private greed under the Imperial regime of the midnineteenth century, was given by the visiting Moscow Art Theatre during their third New York repertory season in a year.

An aged miser, Pazukhin (Vassily Luzhsky), lies dying, a box of negotiable securities hidden under his bed. As they vie for the inheritance, his relations are revealed as hypocritical religionists, discharged bureaucrats, and degraded officers.

John Corbin found the play's story and situations negligible but its characters "as boldly limned and as various as in a cartoon by Hogarth" and wonderfully acted: "Once more we have the Stanislavsky miracle of a comedy vitalized and spiritualized in every moment of every part." The great Ivan Moskvin triumphed in the role of Pazukhin's son. Alexander Woollcott observed, "Surely there never were eyes in the theatre that said so much as his—hurt, bewildered, stricken eyes that looked out over such a set of whiskers as seldom graces even the stage of the Moscow Art Theatre.''

H.H.

DEATH TAKES A HOLIDAY (La morte in Vacanze) [Comedy-Drama/Death/ Romance/Italian/Fantasy] A: Alberto Casella; AD: Walter Ferris; D: Lawrence Marston; S: Rollo Wayne; P: Lee Shubert; T: Ethel Barrymore Theatre; 12/26/ 29 (181)

It took several years of adaptive work on what originally was what Burns Mantle called ''a fairly rollicking comedy'' to turn this Italian play of the supernatural into a viable Broadway commodity. Politely received, it took time to develop an audience but soon became a hit. What Stark Young viewed as a ''fantastic, philosophical, grotesque and finally poetic play,'' beautifully enacted by Philip Merivale and Rose Hobart, was about the visit paid to earth by Death (Merivale) in the person of Prince Sirki, guest at a nobleman's castle, where for three days he plans to discover why mortals so fear him. His presence, he warns his ducal host (James Dale), is to be a secret; during his stay nothing dies; life blooms as never before, and his personality wins over all of the houseguests, while he himself falls deeply in love with the pure young Princess Grazia (Hobart), who carries no fear of him. Finally, he departs, taking Grazia with him, but she goes as one who knows nothing of the boundary between death and life, for she has the vision to see beyond illusion.

''The nostalgia of the infinite is in it, and a rare loveliness like the twilights of da Vinci,'' wrote Euphemia Van Rensselaer Wyatt. Perriton Maxwell was unhappy with the too tragic conclusion but was awed by the play's originality and touching beauty. Yet the *Times* found much of it a pedestrian treatment of a vastly promising theme. Burns Mantle chose it as a Best Play of the Year.

(1) DEBURAU [Comedy-Drama/Period/Romance/Verse/Family/French/Theatre] A: Sacha Guitry; AD: Harley Granville-Barker; D/P: David Belasco; S: Ernest Gros; T: Belasco Theatre; 12/23/20 (189)

Counting cast, crew, and musicians, this French adaptation required 128 salaried employees to produce it. The mounting was highly adept and represented one of David Belasco's finest directorial achievements. He captured with sensitivity and imagination Guitry's highly thought of play about the nearly forgotten early nineteenth-century pantomime star of the Théâtre des Funambules, Jean Gaspard Deburau (Lionel Atwill), player of Pierrot and one time lover of Marie Duplessis (Elsie Mackay), the Lady of the Camellias. The plot tells of his eventual handing on of the tradition to his actor-son Charles (Morgan Farley) once he has come to realize the painful evanescence of fame.

Alexander Woollcott called the work ''a bitter sweet comedy which is itself the comedian's credo and apology, a study of the illusions and the ironies, the hurts and the compensations, the truths and the pretenses which make up the pageant of the theatre.'' Harley Granville-Barker's rhymed verse translation was not entirely successful, but Atwill's performance of the demanding title role was a major contribution, as were those of a highly distinguished cast supporting him.

Arthur Hornblow shared the opinion of many in judging *Deburau* ''old material skillfully handled. . . [,] an impressive, appealing play.'' Burns Mantle chose it as a Best Play of the Year.

(2) One act of the play was staged as a curtain raiser to *Mozart* when Sacha Guitry himself played in New York in December 1926.

DECISION [Comedy/Family/Romance/Legacy/Small Town] A: Carl Henkle; D: Alan Alyn; S: Anthony Continer; P: Robert Sterling; T: Forty-ninth Street Theatre; 5/27/29 (56)

A trivial example of hokum and sentimentality, set in Worcester, Massachusetts and dealing with a local miss, Nancy Lane (Margaret Barnstead), who for a decade takes care of her late sister's two children, inherits a fortune from a wealthy relative (the kids get even more), and has to fight for its possession against greedy relations who try to cheat her out of it. A law court decides in her favor, and she also marries the simple fellow by whom she long has been loved.

Brooks Atkinson had to ''withhold his support'' from this offering for the following reasons: ''the plot, the dialogue, the characters and the performance.''

DEEP CHANNELS [Comedy/Sex/Romance] A: J. W. Von Barre and Paul Krafft; D: Joseph Edmond Soraghan and Herschel Mayall; P: J. W. Von Barre; T: Waldorf Theatre; 10/18/29 (4)

The critics scratched their benumbed scalps at this doleful epigrammatic comedy about an upper-class woman (Frances Johnson) sexually drawn to her manly groom (Jesse W. LeRoy); he also is the love object of the maid servant (Angie Allen), who kills herself when she spies the mistress and groom making love. The mistress turns from the groom, unsatisfied, and weds a doctor (Stephen Clark).

Robert Littell's words summed up the response: ''After a few feeble efforts to convince ourselves that a play if bad enough can also be funny, we all relapsed into numbness and asphyxiation.''

DEEP HARLEM [Revue/Blacks] B: Salem Whitney and Homer Tutt; M: Joe Jordan; LY: Homer Tutt and Henry Creamer; D: Henry Creamer; P: Samuel Grisman; T: Biltmore Theatre; 1/7/29 (8)

An attempt to put in musical form the epic history of black people beginning in ancient Africa, progressing through American nineteenth-century tribulations in the antebellum and postbellum South, and ending in the locale indicated by the title. It was produced in typical Broadway revue fashion (the *Times* criticized it for aping the methods of the Shuberts and Ziegfeld), with the stress on extravagant production numbers. *"Deep Harlem,"* said the *Times,* "represents...the negro musical entertainment in a juvenile and undisciplined form."

DEEP RIVER [Musical/Race/Southern/Period/Romance] B/LY: Laurence Stallings; M: Frank Harling; S: Woodman Thompson; D/P: Arthur Hopkins; T: Imperial Theatre; 10/4/26 (32)

A colorful, controversial attempt at "native opera," the music of which was characterized by Arthur Hornblow as "Italian jazz, with much Puccini, and little jazz." George Jean Nathan averred, "If *Deep River* is an opera, native or otherwise, *Die Gotterdammerung* is a drawing room comedy." Most critics said it fell short of its aims; few agreed that the music was accurately described as jazz. Some thought it impossible for jazz to be used as opera music. Nathan, for one, insisted that "Jazz is a too cheap and shallow musical medium to evoke, convey and further any save cheap and shallow emotions."

Laurence Stallings's libretto, which John Mason Brown considered "undramatized, submerged in dreary talk," was about a tragic love rivalry over a beautiful quadroom girl (Lottice Howell) between a white Kentuckian (Frederick Burton) and a dark-skinned Creole (Luis Alberni) in the voodoo immersed world of 1835 New Orleans. Both men die in a duel.

Gilbert Seldes thought the work's sorest oversight was the complete lack of dancing, for this would have given it "its real character," since ballet, he believed, not opera, was the natural outlet for jazz.

DEEP TANGLED WILDWOOD, THE [Comedy/Theatre/Small Town/Romance] A: George S. Kaufman and Marc Connelly; D: Hugh Ford; S: W. H. Mathews; T: Frazee Theatre; 11/5/23 (16)

Percy Hammond described Kaufman and Connelly's approach in this play as taking the formula of Winchell Smith, who wrote about people turning small towns into metropolises and making a pet of it after tying a can to its tail. In the comedy, a successful young playwright (James Gleason) has a flop, decides he has become jaded in New York, and returns to his home town of Millersville for fresh inspiration. There he finds that the town has boomed, and its citizens have discovered smoking, drinking, jazz, and fashion. He falls in love with the only old-fashioned person he meets (Mildred Booth), a fellow adopted New Yorker who is visiting Millersville. They go back to Broadway for their honeymoon.

Hammond commended Kaufman and Connelly for a "giddy satire," but *Time*'s critic thought that the writing team had "finally missed fire," for the play was "unsubstantial though studded with smart lines." This was the most serious flop of the team's collaborations.

H.H.

(1) DELUGE, THE (Syndafloden) [Dramatic Revival] A: Henning Berger; AD: Frank Allen; D/P: Arthur Hopkins; S: Robert Edmond Jones; T: Plymouth Theatre; 1/27/22 (45)

Swedish playwright Henning Berger had traveled about through the American heartland in the 1890s and later put into this play much of what he had observed of American life. It had been unsuccessfully produced by Arthur Hopkins during sultry summer weather in 1917, but Hopkins did not abandon it; he restaged it in this tightened and somewhat more effective version in 1922. Its new cast included the young, not yet well-known, Edward G. Robinson as a Scandinavian immigrant.

Meant as a satire on human nature, the ironic play imagines the plight of a group of people trapped in a saloon by flood waters during a storm. Their innate nobility shines through under duress, but their selfishness returns when the threat has passed.

Alexander Woollcott termed the piece "a searching and sardonic comedy" that should bring its producer "a mild glow of pride." However, Louis V. De Foe thought it had a "lack of substance."

(2) [Hebrew Language] P: Habima Players of Moscow; T: Cosmopolitan Theatre; 1/11/27 (6)

The Habima Players, in New York with their repertory of plays, gave this revival of the play in Hebrew. Its excellent staging, with very interesting scenes of pantomime, was impressive, as were the Hebraic chants sung by the characters in their moment of gloom. The *Times* said the work "moved with a vitality which pleased" all who were present.

The Deluge was something of an anomaly among the Habima's productions, being their first effort at a contemporary piece in modern dress on a non-Jewish subject. After unsuccessfully attempting to adapt it to a Jewish milieu, it was produced with its original background but with the retention of a Chassidic musical accompaniment.

DEMI-MONDE, LE [Dramatic Revival/French Language] A: Alexander Dumas *fils*; P: Messrs. Shubert; T: Little Theatre; 11/14/22 (3)

Dumas *fils'* 1855 drama about Suzanne (Cécile Sorel), a courtesan who attempts through marriage to the soldier de Nanjac (Albert Lambert) to get into high society, was a staple of the French repertoire brought to New York during a short French season led by Cécile Sorel and a company of Comédie Française and Odéon actors. There were no such extravagant responses to the company as were soon to be accorded the Moscow Art Theatre, but the critics were impressed by the actors' respect for the traditions. Sorel's gifts and training were of great service to her as well.

The once daring play, originally rejected by the Comédie Française, only to be done there twenty years later, was beautifully gowned and capably performed but lasted far too long because of irksome scenery changes. "The denouement is dramatic in the extreme, but the action drags from a present day viewpoint," decided the *Sun*.

Sorel returned to New York with this play in her repertory and gave it three performances from 11/30/26 at the Cosmopolitan Theatre.

DEMI-VIRGIN, THE [Comedy/Marriage/Sex/Films/French] AD: Avery Hopwood; SC: a French original (uncredited); D: Bertram Harrison and Charles Mather; P: A. H. Woods; T: Times Square Theatre; 10/18/21 (268)

This sex farce, based on an uncredited French original, came to New York with a scandalous reputation attendant upon its having been closed by the Pittsburgh police. Despite its attempted naughtiness, however, the worst the critics could say was that "Its name is the most provocative detail" (Louis V. De Foe). Percy Hammond thought it was "as roguish as a nude cadaver."

Produced by A. H. Woods, whose career was largely devoted to just such bedroom romps, *The Demi-Virgin* was a weak attempt to expose the immorality of the Hollywood film colony with its reputed absorption in fleshly concerns. Its plot revolves around the interrupted marriage of film stars Gloria Graham (Hazel Dawn) and Wally Dean (Glenn Anders), a relationship that crumbles when an old flame of Wally's calls him in the wee hours on his wedding night, thus arousing Gloria's jealous ire. Thereafter Hollywood knows Gloria as "the demi-virgin." Wally's efforts to win back his estranged bride succeed when the studio forces them to finish the film they were making before the separation.

The most risque element in the play was a strip-poker scene. Its presence led the *Times* to refuse to advertise the show by its title. Producer A. H. Woods thereupon advertised by telling in his ad how many people had attended the farce running at the Eltinge (to which it had moved). His device helped create a long run.

DEPTHS, THE (Flamme) [Drama/Music/Prostitution/Romance/Sex/Austrian] A: Hans Mueller; P: Arch Selwyn i/a/w Adolph Klauber; T: Broadhurst Theatre; 1/27/25 (31)

Jane Cowl made a big mistake in choosing the role of Anna, the prostitute with a soul as pure as driven snow, in this translation from the German. Carlton Miles characterized it as a "turgid mess" in which the star "abandoned all the nuances of her talent for a florid fling at the broader spaces. *The Depths* is decidedly pump-and-tub stuff."

It dealt with a Viennese whore who falls in love with a young composer (Rollo Peters), who, when he realizes her profession, takes her to his home and tries to raise her to a level of respectability. She makes progress, but when she seeks to attend her lover's first symphony performance, her way is barred. She descends once again into the depths and ends up killing herself.

This piece was known in its original as *Flamme* (*The Flame*) and had a wide success in Europe following its 1920 premiere. When Cowl staged it in a Chicago tryout, she titled it *Who Knows*, and it was treated as salacious goods by the critics.

DESERT FLOWER, THE [Drama/Western/Romance/Crime] A: Don Mullally; P: A. H. Woods i/a/w Messrs. Shubert; T: Longacre Theatre; 11/18/24 (31)

The acting of Helen MacKellar glowed amidst the murkiness of this unoriginal melodrama in which she played the stepdaughter of a brutal alcoholic (Robert Cummings), living in a Nevada boxcar where she nurses her infant stepsister. She runs away, taking the child with her, when she meets a young tramp prospector (Robert Ames) and takes up dancing in the Bullfrog Saloon. The stepfather catches up with her, but she kills him, and only at the last moment is the prospector saved from being hung for the crime. The picturesque ingredients of wisecracking dance-hall girls, gold prospectors, a whiskey-toting villain, and a frank and honest heroine were not enough to relieve the play of its awkward construction and lack of inventiveness.

Percy Hammond thought it "a drowsy old timer, pursuing its uneventful way among the homicides and romances of the Nevada gold fields," and others found it padded with unnecessary incidents and people.

DESERT SANDS [Drama/Romance/Sex/Africa/Adventure] A: Wilson Collison; D: Harry Andrews; P: Shelton Wheeler; T: Princess Theatre; 2/13/22 (16)

Wilson Collison's four-character romantic melodrama, set in the sands of the Sahara, had all of the exotic, but conventional, appurtenances of desert plays— an oasis, a beautiful tent, a star-filled sky, and even a belly dancer. The clumsy dramaturgy and merely competent acting, however, led to its early demise.

Arthur Landron (Edmund Lowe) and Hugh Berndon (Norman Trevor), former lovers of Lady Marchbanks (Virginia Hammond), have fled their scandalous involvement with her to take up life on the Sahara. Berndon lives with Kadra (Anzonetta Lloyd), a native dancer. Lady Marchbanks pursues the men but is unhappy about Berndon's mistress. Kadra slays Landron, and Lady Marchbanks departs with Berndon, leaving the disconsolate girl behind.

The promising "contents were assembled and arranged so improbably and with such a halting awkwardness that they left many of us cold and skeptical," growled Percy Hammond.

DESERT SONG, THE [Musical/Romance/Adventure/Africa] B/LY: Otto Harbach, Oscar Hammerstein II, and Frank Mandel; M: Sigmund Romberg; D: Arthur Hurley; CH: Bobby Connolly; S: Woodman Thompson; C: Vyvyan Donner and Mark Mooring; P: Laurence Schwab and Frank Mandel; T: Casino Theatre; 11/30/26 (465)

A recent spate of Riff uprisings in Northern Africa clearly inspired this famous operetta, which had a long run and gave rise to many revivals. The show was also indebted to contemporary interest in Arabian adventures as exemplified by the career of T. E. Lawrence and the Rudolph Valentino film *The Sheik*, which had a similar plot. First called *Lady Fair*, it was the initial collaboration of Sigmund Romberg and librettists Hammerstein and Harbach. It starred Vivienne Segal (who took over the female lead at the last moment), Eddie Buzzell as the comic lead, Pearl Regay as the native girl interest, and Robert Halliday as the dual-role principal character. The show did not receive unanimous approval, especially as its somewhat heavy book tended to bog things down. "The question of how simple-minded the book of a musical comedy can be was debated last night,'' carped Richard Watts, Jr., ''and the verdict arrived at was 'no end.' '' But ''the excellent and sometimes rather imposing score...and the stirring and resonant male chorus...provoked considerable enthusiasm,'' noted the *Times*. The *Sun* extolled its ''pageantry, romance, ringing music, vitality and humor.''

The melodramatic plot was set in French Morocco, where the leader of the insurgents, ''The Red Shadow'' (Halliday), loves Margot Bonvalet (Segal), who, in turn, yearns for the Governor's son Pierre (also Halliday), a seeming wimp. Abducted by the Red Shadow, Margot resists him at first but soon falls for his manly ways; the Red Shadow puts up no defenses when attacked by the Governor and, consequently, sees his men desert him. The Red Shadow then identifies himself as the Governor's son, and Margot embraces the same man she has always loved.

The Desert Song contributed melodies such as the title song, generally called ''Blue Heaven,'' ''One Alone,'' ''Romance,'' ''Sabre Song,'' ''It,'' and ''Riff Song.''

DESIRE UNDER THE ELMS [Drama/Rural/Family/Romance/Period/Crime/ Sex] A: Eugene O'Neill; DS: Robert Edmond Jones; P: Provincetown Players; T: Greenwich Village Theatre (OB); 11/11/24 (208)

Eugene O'Neill's starkly realistic, somber study of passion and greed on a nineteenth-century New England farm, later acknowledged as one of his greatest plays, was not unanimously approved of at its debut. Several critics were disturbed by its unrelenting seriousness and were happy to get back into the fresh air when it was over. The work, which was chosen as a Best Play of the Year, elicited sharply varying responses. In fact, Joseph Wood Krutch remarked, ''To me it is the most admirable play of the year, to others it is doubtless the most hateful.'' After premiering at the Greenwich Village Theatre, the drama was successfully transferred to Broadway's Earl Carroll Theatre under the producership of A. L. Jones and Morris Green.

Desire Under the Elms is about a rock-hard, 1850s, God-fearing, Bible spouting, seventy-six-year-old Maine farmer, Ephraim Cabot (Walter Huston), who has two sons by his first wife and a third, Eben (Charles Ellis), by a second; he marries a third wife, four decades younger than himself. The older sons leave for California; the younger remains, because he believes the land to be his own, stolen by his hated father from his sainted mother. Eben and the new wife, Abby (Mary Morris), are passionately attracted; they have an affair, and Abby has a baby, which the old man thinks his own. Eben believes Abby will, through the new heir, seize the farm, so she, to prove her love, kills the infant. At the end, the sheriff marches the pair off to prison, leaving Ephraim alone on his farm.

One of the most memorable features of *Desire Under the Elms* was the unusual setting devised by Robert Edmond Jones according to the detailed description and sketch of the author. One side of the farmhouse occupied the stage, with wall sections removed as needed to reveal the action inside. This device allowed some scenes to be played in one area, while characters in another area were exposed to view, although they were not the principal focus of attention. A scene with Abby in her bedroom and Eben in his, separated by a wall, was particularly evocative.

Richard Dana Skinner could find no true tragedy in the play, "because there is no real struggle indicated, no resistance to the onslaught of evil, no vision on the part of the victims of the higher things they have lost." In Heywood Broun's view, the work was overly melodramatic and predictable. Louis Bromfield, however, was stirred by the presence of "all the fine elevation of Greek tragedy and ten times the sense of reality. Indeed, it is so real and tragical that one leaves the theatre in a state bordering on exhaustion.... The play...is the best analysis of the witch burning brand of Puritanism that has yet been done in America."

Mary Morris and Walter Huston gave vividly etched performances of their roles.

Produced at a time of increasing virulence against salacious plays, *Desire Under the Elms* was confronted by considerable outrage against its subject and treatment. The District Attorney even ordered its closing, but the protests that arose against this decision forced him to reconsider. A jury was appointed to investigate, and they recommended that the play be allowed to continue its run, unrevised. Still, audiences seeking cheap thrills attended the work *en masse* and laughed at every innuendo. It got so bad during one performance that actor Charles Ellis was forced to step out of his role and warn the spectators that if their foolish behavior did not stop the play would not go on.

DETOUR, THE [Drama/Rural/Romance/Family/Marriage/Art] A: Owen Davis; D: Augustin Duncan; P: Messrs. Shubert; T: Astor Theatre; 8/23/21 (48)

The critics were nonplussed to realize that Owen Davis, whose reputation rested on the most obvious sort of melodramaturgics, had written in *The Detour* "a sober, sincere and very frequently successful attempt to tell the truth about character and to let us look at some of the irony that makes life" (Kenneth Andrews).

The play is set on a farm where Helen (Effie Shannon) has scrimped and saved for years so that her daughter Kate (Angela McCahill) can study for an art career. Tom (Willard Robertson), a neighboring young farmer who loves Kate and wishes to open a garage on his property, is forced to raise money by selling his land to Helen's dour, land-hungry spouse (Augustin Duncan). Helen and Kate's plans are detoured as well when they are told by an expert of Helen's lack of talent; the play ends with dreams deferred and Kate planning to marry Tom.

The Detour showed a tendency toward monotony and sentimentality and had climax speeches that seemed "too carefully arranged and rhetorical," but it was still "a straightforward and moving study of the conflict of false ambitions with the hard realities of farm life," according to Kenneth Macgowan.

DEVIL IN THE CHEESE, THE [Comedy/Fantasy/Romance/Family] A: Tom
Cushing; D/P: Charles Hopkins; S: Norman Bel Geddes; T: Charles Hopkins
Theatre; 12/29/26 (165)

A dazzlingly illusionistic mountaintop setting contributed by Norman Bel
Geddes was the preeminent virtue of this "inept and awkward" (Brooks Atkinson) comedy about a would-be American archaeologist (Robert McWade) who
digs up a magical piece of cheese in Meteora and, upon eating it, is empowered
by a genie to see into his seventeen-year-old daughter's (Linda Watkins) mind.
There he reads that she is deeply in love with the bothersome young steamship
steward Jimmie Chard (Frederic March). A fantasy within this fantasy occurs
as the daughter envisions herself nursing Jimmie back to health on a desert
island, followed by Jimmie's becoming president. The device also allowed for
two actors to play the role of the father, one as he viewed himself, and one as
the girl saw him, that is, as a misanthropic crab. When Jimmie later rescues the
archaeologist and his family from Greek bandits, the way is cleared for the
eventual nuptials.

The fantasy sequence was well conceived, there were some effective comic
and melodramatic moments, and the cast, in which Bela Lugosi and Dwight
Frye also had parts, was nothing to be shy of. However, the play was not of a
whole. Richard Dana Skinner, while regarding it as "quite good theatre," nevertheless said it was "utter nonsense."

DEVIL TO PAY, THE (Eva Bonheur) [Comedy-Drama/Family/Romance/
Dutch] A: Herman Heijermans; TR: Caroline Heijermans-Houwing and Lillian
Saunders; D: Edward Goodman; S: Cleon Throckmorton; P: Stagers; T: Fifty-
second Street Theatre; 12/3/25 (12)

Dutch playwright Herman Heijerman's 1917 play was a loudly acclaimed
work in its native Holland; staged in New York it seemed hackneyed, its morality
dated, and its dramaturgy plodding. Percy Hammond claimed it was "a dreary
two hours with some voluble Dutch persons and their wordy troubles."

The play's set revealed the upstairs and down of Mynheer Jasper's (Whitford
Kane) home wherein he resides with his daughter Marie (Mary Ricard), his wife
(Ethel Strickland), and others, including the hateful widow Eva Bonheur (Margaret Wycherly), who holds a lien on the house. The central plot concerns the
seduction of Marie by a young musician (Alexander Kirkland), her subsequent
pregnancy, and the dismissal of the unworthy youth by the girl and her family
despite his offer of marriage; their decision is based on the father's philosophy
that to inflict a "crippled soul" upon his daughter as a marriage partner would
be tragic and that she is better off having an illegitimate child. Even the nasty
Eva Bonheur is touched by this decision.

DEVIL WITHIN, THE [Drama/Mystery/Crime] A: Charles Horan; P: Rock
and Horan, Inc.; T: Hudson Theatre; 3/16/25 (24)

A formula play that was recognized as pure hack work and could not sustain more than three weeks of performances. Filled to the borders as it was with all of the conventional tricks and devices of mystery plays, it seemed to Alexander Woollcott almost like a travesty of the genre. "It is an unevenly written and somewhat reminiscent reproduction from the school of *The Bat*," observed Q.M.

It told about wealthy John Blackwood (Henry W. Pemberton), a man recently returned to Westchester County, who, after giving a number of persons ample reason to hate him unto death, is done in on his wedding eve by one of them with a paper knife. Everyone falls under suspicion, except for the actual killer, which personage is uncovered at the conclusion.

DEVILS [Drama/Religion/Southern/Rural/Sex] A: Daniel N. Rubin; D: John Cromwell; S: Livingston Platt; P: William A. Brady, Jr., and Dwight Deere Wiman; T: Maxine Elliott's Theatre; 3/17/26 (29)

Time called *Devils* "brutal and unpleasant, but a sound and at times swiftly exciting piece of dramaturgy." A similar tone of mingled distaste and appreciation was expressed by a number of reviewers. The play, like *Rain* and several other works of the decade, strove to show the tragic effects of the relation between fervid religiosity and sexual passion. It was set in the southern backwoods farming community where the ignorant inhabitants practice a fundamentalist religion based on fear of a wrathful God as preached by a fanatically demonic minister (John Cromwell). An innocent teenage orphan, Jennie (Ruth Mero), recently come to live with her sexually frustrated uncle (David Landau) and his chore-burdened wife (Jennet Adair), is blamed by the fiery pastor as the reason for the destruction of the cotton crops by the boll-weevil; this leads to his exorcism of the devils infesting her, her admission that her uncle raped her, and her eventual madness and suicide.

DEVIL'S DISCIPLE, THE [Dramatic Revival] A: George Bernard Shaw; D: Philip Moeller; DS: Lee Simonson; P: Theatre Guild; T: Garrick Theatre; 4/23/23 (192)

Bernard Shaw's 1897 blend of philosophical comedy and melodrama, set in New England during the Revolutionary War, had not been revived in New York since Richard Mansfield introduced the piece twenty-six years previously. Mansfield's performance of Dick Dudgeon, the radical Puritan who aligns himself with the Devil to spite his hypocritical relations, was renowned to the point that theatregoers who never saw it were aware of its accomplishments. Basil Sydney's portrayal of the role was considered less effective, but it did have its advocates, notably John Corbin, who said it "seemed wholly satisfactory, a really distinguished accomplishment." Roland Young's General Burgoyne, however, was the most lauded performance in the revival.

The Guild's mounting received mixed notices. Kenneth Macgowan said it "suffers heavily from bad direction," but the *Times* allowed that the play "scored one of the few great comedy hits of the season."

DEW DROP INN [Musical/Hotel/Business] B: Walter De Leon and Edward Delaney Dunn; M: Alfred Goodman; LY: Cyrus Wood; P: Messrs. Shubert; T: Astor Theatre; 5/17/23 (52)

Billed as lightweight fare for the hot summer months, this dreary musical had only one thing going for it, the inimitable terpsichorean art of former vaudevillian James Barton. Barton played a hotel porter who manages to pump up the selling price of his hotel by pushing a rumor that there is buried treasure on the property. The book and music were completely forgettable, but Barton's flying feet remained indelibly imaged in the minds of those who saw him. "When he begins to dance even a cautious reviewer should begin to consider using the word 'genius,' " raved Heywood Broun: "In his medium Barton creates a superb and final beauty and so 'genius' will have to be the word."

DIAMOND LIL [Comedy/Period/Sex/Romance/Crime/Prostitution] A/D: Mae West; SC: a suggestion of Mark Linder's; D: Ira Hards; P: Jack Linder; T: Royale Theatre; 4/9/28 (323)

A vehicle by and for the inimitable Mae West, sex comedienne par extraordinaire. "Propped up under the arm-pits by a dress that might have been designed by the stage carpenter" (*Time*), she acted the title role of a late 1890s Bowery grande dame living with saloon and brothel keeper Gus Jordan (J. Merrill Holmes). The play was a lusty melodrama about Lil's attraction for a Salvation Army officer (Curtis Cooksey), who turns out to be a police captain and who snares the white-slave-trafficking Gus, thus getting Lil for himself. "Boy, I knew you could be had," she says to her new lover at the end.

West's first show since the scandalous *Sex*, which cost her ten days in the pokey, was not as lubricious but managed to convey enough of the star's penchant for leering epigrams, torso-wriggling innuendo, and eye-rolling nuance to capture attention. All of the good lines were hers, and her grandiose gay nineties costuming made her the undoubted center of attention. The play included lots of New York slang, plenty of action, singing waiters, and a good deal of lurid atmosphere, but its plotting was banal. John Mason Brown described it as "sorry and wooden," but the star's outrageous campiness covered all defects. During the play, she sang a novel rendition of "Frankie and Johnny" that the *Times* labeled "a profanation."

Although West took full credit for the writing, what she really had done was to appropriate material created by Mark Linder in a Bowery sketch called "The Frame Up" which he had later expanded into the full-length play *Chatham Square*. She came up with the new title and adapted the script to her special brand of rowdy humor. Among the actors she cast for it were young Jack LaRue as the Spanish lover and Harold Gary, in his Broadway debut, as the Bowery Terror. The show established West as a major star.

DIANA [Drama/France-Russia/Sex/Show Business] A: Irving Kaye Davis; D: Hugh Ford; S: Cirker and Robbins; P: L. Lawrence Weber i/a/w Hugh Ford; T: Longacre Theatre; 12/9/29 (8)

A seriously muddled attempt to do a biographical play based on the life of renowned modern dancer Isadora Duncan, with episodes in Paris, Moscow, and Nice detailing her tragic love affairs, the death of her children in an accident, and her own bizarre demise when her lengthy scarf caught in an auto's wheels and strangled her to death. The play was a meretricious one stressing Isadora's far-flung sex life and failed to give more than the cheapest surface picture of her character. The names of the actual figures in the dancer's life were altered for stage purposes. Mary Nash was completely unsuited for the leading role, and the result, said the *Times*, was "sound and fury, signifying nothing."

DICE OF THE GODS, THE [Drama/Drugs/Family/Italy/Romance] A: Lillian Barrett; S: Gates and Morange; D: Harrison Grey Fiske; P: H. H. Frazee; T: National Theatre; 4/5/23 (20)

The critics fired shattering salvos aimed at quickly annihilating this "sleazy, disorderly and generally negligible piece" (Alexander Woollcott) in which America's foremost stage star, Mrs. Fiske, returned to Broadway. Commentators called her taste into question for having chosen this "indifferent and rather improbable play" (*Evening Telegram*), in which there was neither life nor skill.

The central role was that of Virginia socialite Patricia Baird (Fiske), who becomes a morphine addict, leaves her husband, loses her home and standing, takes a lover, and descends into the snake pit. She becomes a liar and thief, ends up in a shabby flat in Florence, and tries to get her daughter (Ernita Lascelles) to marry a wealthy older man. Ultimately, she kills herself with a drug overdose.

Before arriving in New York the play bore first the title *Paddy* and then *The Last Card*.

(1) DIFF'RENT [Drama/Sex/Small Town/Romance] A: Eugene O'Neill; D: James Light; P: Provincetown Players; T: Provincetown Playhouse (OB); 12/27/20 (74)

A month after *Diff'rent* opened Off Broadway, it moved to Broadway's intimate Princess Theatre (on 2/4/21) to complete its run. It was a grim tragedy of sexual repression in a New England seaport village, telling of Emma Crosby (Mary Blair), who breaks off her pending wedding to Capt. Caleb Williams (James Light) when she learns of his previous South Seas dalliances; she no longer considers him "diff'rent" from the ordinary run of men. After three decades have passed, the middle-aged and heavily made up Emma loses her head over young wastrel Benny Rogers (Charles Ellis), who is really only interested in her money. The shock of this relationship leads the still-devoted Caleb to kill himself, and Emma, hearing of his death and realizing Benny's disdain of her, prepares to do as Caleb did.

Alexander Woollcott was moved by O'Neill's dialogue but thought the author had lost interest midway through the play and allowed it to "stumble on to a dull and conventional conclusion." Kenneth Macgowan said that "The effects that O'Neill secures are powerful and they seem in the last analysis truthful."

Yet he judged it inferior as a play probing spiritual values to *The Emperor Jones* and thought it "a step backward for its author."

(2) [Dramatic Revival] **and "THE TRIUMPH OF THE EGG"** D: Helen Freeman; S: Cleon Throckmorton; 2/10/25 (23)
"The Triumph of the Egg" A: Sherwood Anderson and Raymond O'Neil
  An Off-Broadway double bill consisting of a revival of O'Neill's 1920 study of a sexually frustrated spinster combined with a one-act curtain raiser by Sherwood Anderson and Raymond O'Neil that encountered mixed reviews. *Diff'rent* was still not a critic's favorite. Despite a superlatively acted mounting, Bernard Simon wrote that the work bordered on the "obscene" and that the author had grown sufficiently since it was first produced "not to be forced to confront his past." But Joseph Wood Krutch insisted that it remained "the best American play to date," and he found it "difficult to understand how anyone, even though he found the theme distasteful, could fail to appreciate the extraordinary conciseness and force of the dialogue."
  The other piece, based on an Anderson short story, was practically a monologue in which the proprietor (John Huston) of a Pickleville, Ohio, hash house rambles garrulously on to two of his customers. "This he does for a straight half hour that is a tax on the patience of anyone to listen to," commented C.L.E.

DINNER IS SERVED [Comedy/Marriage/Sex] A/D: Alan Mowbray; P: George L. Miller and Elmer Powell; T: Cort Theatre; 8/15/29 (4)
  British-born actor Alan Mowbray wrote and performed in this doomed marital comedy. The *Times* said he had given himself "a dull part in a dull comedy." This "well bred, though uninspired" comedy of manners concerned a wife's (Beatrice Hendricks) attempt to stimulate her husband's (Mowbray) waning sexual passions by interesting him in the maid (Gaby Fay), only to have him suddenly fill with desire for her while the maid becomes caught up with the wife's father (Edward Emery).

DIPLOMACY (Dora) [Dramatic Revival] A: Victorien Sardou; TR: Gerald du Maurier; D: Campbell Gullan; P: George C. Tyler; T: Erlanger's Theatre; 5/28/28 (32)
  Sardou's popular, well-made play of 1877 received its fourth revival of the century in this "famous actor" mounting that played it in modern dress and thereby robbed it of its 1870s period allure. *Time* thought the old drama—in which a foreign spy and thief, the Countess Zicka (Helen Gahagan), is found out by the smooth ambassador Henri Beauclerc (William Faversham) who recognizes her telltale perfume—so well performed that it "seemed nearly as neat and sparkling" as a half-century earlier, but O.G.V. thought it was dated. Stark Young found the actors, despite their fame, inept, suggesting "none of Sardou's world of form and but little of the *soigné* world that we are asked to believe is theirs."

The distinguished cast included Rollo Peters as Julian, Jacob Ben-Ami as Michael Orloff, Margaret Anglin as Lady Fairfax, Georgette Cohan as Mion, Tyrone Power as Markham, Cecilia Loftus as Mme. La Marquise De Rio-Zares, Frances Starr as Dora, and Charles Coburn as Baron Stein.

DISHONORED LADY [Drama/Sex/Crime] A: Margaret Ayer Barnes and Edward Sheldon; D: Guthrie McClintic; P: Gilbert Miller i/a/w Guthrie McClintic; T: Empire Theatre; 2/4/30 (127)

Guthrie McClintic directed his wife, Katharine Cornell, in this sensational study of the neurotic, oversexed Madeleine Cary. Cornell's dynamic, realistic, multifaceted acting drew plaudits, but the play was seen as "simple and not very pure melodrama, heavy handed, [and] furnished with scenes of passion which not infrequently suggest the adjective 'cheap' " according to Perriton Maxwell.

Based on a real person and events of 1857 that transpired in Glasgow, *Dishonored Lady* dealt with a New York woman of means who, planning to marry a wealthy Englishman (Francis Lister) she loves, rids herself of her Argentinian lover (Fortunio Bonanova) by first sleeping with him one last time and then poisoning him. She is tried and acquitted, because of a faked alibi, but in the end sees all of her male relatives and friends wash their hands of her forever.

The critics bewailed Cornell's presence in rubbish like this, which, no matter how brilliantly she played, dimmed her lustre. The role originally was intended for Ethel Barrymore.

Several years after it closed, *Dishonored Lady* became the subject of a noted plagiarism suit. Its authors sued Metro-Goldwyn-Mayer for using material from their rejected screenplay in Metro's film based on the story as it was also told in the novel *Letty Lyndon* by Mrs. Belloc Lowndes. The judge ruled in favor of the defendant because the play and the novel were based on the same source; the decision was eventually reversed because the film actually had been based on the *Dishonored Lady* treatment; final judgment, which took seven years to arrive, awarded Sheldon and Barnes more than a half million dollars, at the time considered enormous damages in such a suit.

DISTANT DRUM, A [Comedy-Drama/Romance/Sex/Marriage] A: Vincent Lawrence; D/P: William Harris, Jr.; S: Livingston Platt; T: Hudson Theatre; 1/20/28 (11)

Excellent dialogue could not overcome clumsy plotting in this ironical Vincent Lawrence drama about an attractive gigolo (Louis Calhern) who lives off the money with which adoring women ply him. While attempting to break off an affair with a Mrs. Wilson (Mary Newcomb) so he may run off with the wealthy bachelorette Edith Reed (Katherine Wilson) he is shot dead by Mr. Wilson, who has learned of his spouse's illicit liason.

"*A Distant Drum*," wrote Percy Hammond, "is a well acted and ambitious mediocrity, full of promises unfulfilled." Joseph Wood Krutch was very favorable to the play because of the honest depiction of the interesting central character, cad though he was. George Jean Nathan even defended the work as a "brilliant. . .American comedy" that the critics failed to understand.

DIVERSION [Drama/Romance/Crime/Family/British] A: John Van Druten; D: Jane Cowl; S: Rollo Peters; P: Adolph Klauber; T: Forty-ninth Street Theatre; 1/11/28 (61)

A melodrama of love, betrayal, murder, and suicide made palatable by the author's gift for sympathetic and convincing characterizations. As in Van Druten's *Young Woodley*, a young man is led astray by his feelings for an older woman. Here, law student Wyn Hayward (Richard Bird), after a fling in Italy with alluring actress Rayetta Muir (Cathleen Nesbit), is dumped by her in London and proceeds in his rage to strangle her. He confesses his deed to his physician father (Guy Standing) and persuades him to give him the poison that will end his life.

Brooks Atkinson declared that "Two or three fervently truthful bits of acting and two or three forceful situations more than balance the rough edgings of" the piece. Joseph Wood Krutch thought the only excuse for the author's use of "one of the cheapest and most hackneyed stories" was the chance to present the father and son scenes; otherwise, he said the play alternated "between the lurid and the maudlin." When the box office faltered, Van Druten rewrote the play so that the actress was only made unconscious, and the young man escaped the charge of murder.

DIVIDED HONORS [Drama/Crime/Marriage/Romance] A: Winnie Baldwin; D: William B. Friedlander; S: Willy Pogany; P: K.A.L.; T: Forrest Theatre; 9/30/29 (40)

Kenneth Stewart (Guido Nadzo) is an author with a penchant for women and alcohol; during a binge with Vina Chase (Glenda Farrell) he marries her, although he loves Angela Bannerman (Jane Kim), who gets shot by Mary Lane (Doris Freeman), herself in love with him. Vina takes the rap, is acquitted, and departs so that Kenneth can have Mary.

"Conceived by a vaudeville actress,. . .this pastiche of variety show emotions and humors succeeds in being very elaborate balderdash" (*Time*). The *Times* panned the unskillful writing, the "rather ordinary plot," and the lack of "theatrically credible" characters.

DIVORCE A LA CARTE [Comedy/Marriage] A/D: Samuel Ruskin Golding; P: Drama Associates, Inc.; T: Biltmore Theatre; 3/26/28 (8)

A mere eight performance run resulted from reviews such as that of Richard Watts, Jr., who noted his surprise at "such an incredibly amateurish and thoroughly stupid striving after comedy." Golding's "satirical farce" aimed at the evils of divorce depicted a squabbling upper-class married couple (Hale Hamilton and Regina Wallace) who allow a friend (Geoffrey Harwood) to arrange their

Mexican divorce for them. They marry their respective corespondents, and finally, after discovering that they still love each other, learn that their divorce is not legal, and that they still are husband and wife.

DIXIE TO BROADWAY [Revue/Blacks] B: Walter De Leon, Tom Howard, Lew Leslie, and Sidney Lazarus; M: George W. Meyer and Arthur Johnston; LY: Grant Clarke and Roy Turke; D/P: Lew Leslie; T: Broadhurst Theatre; 10/29/24 (77)

A very enthusiastic response greeted this black revue produced in the manner of the successful white ones of the era, such as the *Follies* and *Vanities*, but with less stress on feminine pulchritude. The show had some good comics, such as Shelton Brooks and Hamtree Harrington, but no single comedian of exceptional ability. There were familiar tableaux, such as "The Evolution of the Colored Race," a series of black impressions of famous white performers, black takeoffs on *Chauve-Souris* specialties such as the wooden soldiers, various outstanding dance numbers, a smartly costumed and light-complexioned chorus of beauties ("the high-yellers are positively pink and cream"—Gilbert Seldes), an excellent jazz orchestra, and, above all, the sensational and diverse talents of the inimitable Florence Mills, making her final Broadway appearance before her untimely death.

DR. DAVID'S DAD (Dr. Stieglitz) [Comedy/Family/Medicine/German] A: Armand Friedman and Louis Nertz; AD: Carrington North and Joseph J. Garren; P: Feldon Productions, Inc.; T: Vanderbilt Theatre; 8/13/24 (5)

As *Dr. Stieglitz*, this comedy was an enormous German-language hit in Berlin and Vienna, but New York had its fill of it after less than a week of performances. The *Times* reported that it was "hokum throughout, hokum of line, of character, of incident, of theme." The reviewers had expected it to be a German *Abie's Irish Rose* but found it nothing of the kind.

It begins on the eve of Old Stieglitz's (Egon Brecher) son David's (Bruce Elmore) graduation from medical school. The deliriously happy father is soon upset when he learns that the high-toned family of his son's fiancée refuses their permission to let her marry the young physician. Then the father gets so meddlesome in helping out around the son's office that the doctor has to kick him out.

DOCTOR KNOCK (Knock) [Comedy/Medicine/Business/French] A: Jules Romains; AD: Harley Granville-Barker; D: Richard Boleslavsky; DS: Clement Wilenchick; P: American Laboratory Theatre; T: American Laboratory Theatre (OB); 2/23/28 (23)

French star Louis Jouvet had made the hit of his career in this satire on medicine and hypochondria seen in New York in an English version directed by Richard Boleslavsky with Robert H. Gordon in the title role.

Jules Romains's delightful comedy concerns a rapscallion of a physician who turns the country practice he purchases into a source of enormous profit by playing on the credulity of his patients and getting them to think they are suffering from a host of ailments that they proceed to nurse with hilarious avidity. By the end, all of the town's residents are in bed, and the place has become a mecca for those seeking a diagnosis of their ills.

There was serious dissatisfaction with the director's excessively broad interpretation, which employed cartoon-like sets and characters and labored buffoonery. "Lampoon scenery with murderous knives and saws decorating the doctor's consulting room wages constant battle with the lines; and putty noses, clown pants and furious moustachios turn the actors into mountebanks," complained Brooks Atkinson. John Anderson said the play had been "virtually ruined by arty clap-trap." Still, the *Sun* praised it as "rollicking good fun," and Barclay V. McCarty believed Boleslavsky had succeeded excellently in "interpreting a piece prone toward heaviness in a light, bizarre manner."

DOCTOR'S DILEMMA, THE [Dramatic Revival] A: George Bernard Shaw; D: Dudley Digges; S: Jo Mielziner; C: Aline Bernstein; P: Theatre Guild; 11/21/27 (115)

A stirringly well-played revival of Shaw's satire on the medical profession, not seen in New York since its 1915 premiere there. Baliol Holloway played the role of the famous doctor Sir Colenso Ridgeon, who is faced with the dilemma of using his TB cure to save the life of a mediocre physician (Henry Travers) or a disreputable but gifted painter (Alfred Lunt) whose wife (Lynn Fontanne) he loves. A beautifully blended ensemble, in which Helen Westley, Dudley Digges, Earle Larimore, and Ernest Cossart also figured, helped make the showing a success.

Time said, "For those who still...revere as magic an agile comedy immaculately acted, it will be a blessing." John Mason Brown cautioned about the play's prolixity but said that its theme "In the hands of Shaw...becomes a fascinating conflict of viewpoints, a discussion that, because of Shaw's uncanny skill both as an expositor and a dramatist holds the interest throughout, and somehow involves the heart as well as the mind." But Joseph Wood Krutch argued that its satire was familiar and its thesis not arousing. Brooks Atkinson thought it was "long, garrulous, inconclusive and overreaching."

DOLLY JORDAN [Comedy-Drama/Romance/Period/Theatre] A/D: B. Iden Payne; S: Rollo Peters; P: John Cort; T: Daly's Theatre; 10/3/22 (7)

How he managed the feat is not now known, but B. Iden Payne, author and director of this play, also staged another play, *That Day*, which opened the same night. Both were catastrophes. *Dolly Jordan*, at the newly christened Daly's (formerly the Sixty-third Street Theatre) was Payne's first attempt at playwriting. Ludwig Lewisohn said "he should know better."

The play was a biographical treatment of Dorothy Bland, better known as Dolly Jordan (Josephine Victor), a stage favorite in London and Dublin during the Georgian era. Thirty-eight years are traversed in episodic fashion, presenting the actress's professional as well as romantic conquests.

A work of "sentiment and third-rate historical gossip" (Lewisohn), *Dolly Jordan* was "a poor play" with "passages of lofty rhetoric and sonorous banality" (Lawrence Stallings).

DON JUAN (L'Homme à la rose) [Drama/Romance/Period/French] A: Henri Bataille; AD: Lawrence Langner; S: Lee Simonson; P/D: Frank Reicher; T: Garrick Theatre; 9/5/21 (14)

The oft-dramatized legend of Spain's great lover furnished yet another play in this respectable 1920 example from the pen of France's Henri Bataille. According to this telling Don Juan (Lou Tellegen), presumed dead, is really alive; he has chosen to retire while his legend is undimmed. The play has him scorned by the woman he loves and then makes him suffer the indignity of paying a kitchen wench for sexual services rendered. His vaunted prowess, he learns with anguish, survived only as long as he could claim ownership of his name and reputation.

Don Juan seemed tedious to some, but this seems mainly because of the ineffectiveness of matinee idol Lou Tellegen as the great romancer. He looked the part, but "Somehow his role seems to strike no responsive chord in" him, said Arthur Hornblow.

DON Q., JR. [Comedy/Crime/Youth] A: Bernard S. Schubert; D: Arthur Hurley; T: Forty-ninth Street Theatre; 1/27/26 (14)

The only reason any fuss was made over this silly play was the presence in it, in his professional stage debut, of tennis hero William T. Tilden, in a supporting role. The play, reported the *Times*, had "nothing to do with tennis—and not a great deal with anything else, for that matter."

The true star of the event was child-actor Billy Quinn, who played the title role, that of a twelve-year-old boy who holds up a store for $150 so he may send a friend and his wife (John McGrath and Maxine Flood) to Arizona for health reasons. He is caught and sent to a reform school, where he overcomes a villain and is befriended by the shy reform-school clerk played by Tilden.

On 2/19/26 the play reopened as *That Smith Boy* as the first offering at the new 300-seat Mayfair Theatre on East Forty-fourth Street next to the Claridge Hotel. It rang up thirty-four performances.

DONA MARIA LA BRAVA (Dona Maria the Brave) [Drama/Verse/Period/Crime/Spanish/Spanish Language] A: Eduardo Marquina; P: Maria Guerrero-Fernando Diaz Company of Madrid; T: Manhattan Opera House (OB); 5/17/26 (1)

The stars of Spain's Teatro de la Princesa, Maria Guerrero and Fernando Diaz, visited New York during their tour of the Western Hemisphere with a varied repertoire; their first offering locally was this emotional period play, first done in 1909, written for the stars, and dominated by Guerrero's fiery histrionics. A tragic drama of maternal passion, it allowed the actress to let the stops out on her theatrical technique.

According to the *Times*, "She more than dominated the scene. She devastated it. Her first rush upon it was a perfect whirlwind of screams, groans, sobbings and quivering flesh." The spectacular play, considerably cut for touring, filled the vast stage space with effective crowd scenes, but the *Times* would have preferred something by Calderon or Echegaray.

The plot was about a murder at the Spanish court committed by the King's son (Diaz Mendoza y Guerrero) and of his death at the hands of the victim's wife.

DONOVAN AFFAIR, THE [Drama/Mystery/Crime] A: Owen Davis; D: Albert Lewis; S: Nicholas Yellenti; P: Albert Lewis i/a/w Donald Davis; T: Fulton Theatre; 8/30/26 (128)

A formula mystery play by potboiler-specialist Owen Davis, in which a dinner host is murdered early on and the remainder of the action is taken up with a comic detective's (Paul Harvey) attempts to solve the crime, with suspicion touching one and all, until the supposedly least likely suspect turns out to be the guilty party.

John Mason Brown believed it to be "thorough and skilled in the horrific, if familiar, means it commands for twisting and untwisting the spectator's spin." The awkward and unnecessary intrusions of humor were the only distractions for Arthur Hornblow. To the *Times* critic the central motive of the pursuit of a magical turquoise ring that gave its wearer an unnatural power over women provided an aura that led to "an evening of steadily mounting interest."

DON'T BOTHER MOTHER [Comedy/Family/Romance/Theatre] A: E. B. Dewing and Courtenay Savage; D: Albert Bruning; P: Bender and Storm; T: Little Theatre; 2/3/25 (3)

E. B. Dewing, coauthor of this three-performance failure, was an actress in its ineffective cast. It was put on only at special matinees. The story concerned an attractive actress of early middle age (Mary Hall), still youthful looking enough to be cast as a younger woman, who resents her actual age and keeps it as much a secret as possible, not even allowing her husband of twenty years or her growing children to get involved in her public life. She has often, as now, been in love with her leading men, but a young dressmaker (Margaret Mower) is also after the same fellow (Joseph Macauley); the dressmaker wins the actor, and the actress turns back to the bosom of her family.

John Ranken Towse described it as "an exceedingly feeble affair, at once extravagant and tame, and altogether pointless."

DON'T TELL [Comedy/Romance/Family/Gambling/Scottish] A: Graham Moffat; P: William Morris; T: Nora Bayes Theatre; 9/27/20 (16)

A Scottish play about which the only things clearly Scottish, according to the *Times*, were its Glasgow setting and the fine Scottish burr with which its speeches were shouted. Its principal interest lay in its depiction of various Scottish characters.

Graham Moffat, whose successful Scottish comedy *Bunty Pulls the Strings* had been seen here in 1911, played the leading role in *Don't Tell* to little avail. It dealt with the household of John Cameron (Moffat), a well-to-do plumber. His young son John Willie (George Tawde) has a passion for the horses and other vices. He steals and pawns his mother's (Margaret Noble) jewelry and filches money from other family members. An outbreak of family unrest arises involving militant Suffragism, a suspicion of kleptomania, and suits of love, which seem bound to go wrong.

The piece seemed confused and aimless to Heywood Broun, among others.

M.M.-C.

DOORMAT, THE [Comedy/Literature/Sex/Romance] A: H. S. Sheldon; D: David G. Fischer; P: Edward Whiteside; T: Punch and Judy Theatre; 12/7/22 (5)

A disastrously received comedy about young Lucy Cavender (Lois Bolton), fed up to here with being her family's "doormat," who takes a job as secretary to a millionaire writer (Harry Benham), whose publishers have told him that if he wants to write more truthfully about women, he should get to know them better. While helping him to write one of his books, Lucy discusses with him the sex and name of a child to be introduced into the story; a scandal ensues when the butler reports what he overheard and misinterpreted. The writer ends up divorcing his present wife after the scandal is cleared up and marrying his secretary.

"It was stupid, amateurish and badly acted," scolded Percy Hammond, and Alexander Woollcott added that it was a "hopelessly forlorn and incompetent little play. . . abetted by a strikingly inferior performance."

DOPE [Drama/Drugs/Crime] A: Hermann Lieb ("second episode" by Joseph Medill Patterson); T: Forty-eighth Street Theatre; 1/4/26 (2)

A clumsily structured melodrama expanded to full-length proportions from actor Hermann Lieb's very successful vaudeville one-act of the same title. The result, reported Percy Hammond, was "of no account." "The original sketch was stuck in the middle of a lot of ill-written and shiftless anecdotes having nothing whatever to do with its story, its manner or its purpose. . . . [I]t was a botch."

The eventful action concerned illicit drug dealing in cocaine and morphine, the drug-related death of the daughter of a society matron (Jennie A. Eustace), the investigation of the circumstances by the District Attorney (Robert T. Haines), the involvement of the matron as landlady of a drug dealer's place of business and a brothel, the deferential attitude of the police to folks from high society, and so forth.

DORA MOBRIDGE [Drama/Small Town/Legacy/Sex/Family] A: Adeline Leitzbach; D: J. Kent Thurber; S: Charles Teichner; P: Louis Isquith; T: Little Theatre; 4/19/30 (9)

Originally called *Dollars and Sex*, this misadventure was about a Glendale, New Jersey, woman, Dora Mobridge (Louise Carter), a respected and loved friend, neighbor, mother, and human being who inherits a fortune. This leads to the news that she was raised in a Milwaukee bawdy house, although retaining her purity. Immediately, townsfolk and family shun her as one unclean, but the tide soon turns in her favor, and her family, at least, apologizes.

It was "very depressing," said the *Times*, to contemplate this "most pathetic venture of the season."

DORIAN GRAY [Drama/Crime/Drugs/Fantasy] A: David Thorne; SC: Oscar Wilde's novel *The Picture of Dorian Gray*; D: Augustus Thorne; P: Oscaria Theatre Corporation; T: Biltmore Theatre; 5/21/28 (16)

Lait. of *Variety* correctly predicted a brief existence for this appalling muckup of Wilde's famed story. He said, "With profane and uninspired hands they modernize and adapt him, and with clodding feet they personate him."

The inexperienced young actor, Howard Cull, who played Dorian, had good looks but lacked anything like the talent needed for the difficult role. Dorian is an ideally beautiful young man who is prompted by his evil genius to revere his own attractiveness. A painting of him by a friend has captured both Dorian's looks and soul. Dorian becomes enmeshed in many scandals, sexual and drug-related; although he maintains his beauty, his portrait reveals his growing degeneracy. Finally, he is murdered by the brother of an abandoned girlfriend.

DOVE, THE [Drama/Crime/Mexico/Gambling/Romance/Night Club/Sex] A: Willard Mack; SC: a story by Gerald Beaumont; D/P: David Belasco; S: Joseph Wickes; T: Empire Theatre; 2/11/25 (159)

The Dove was an object lesson in the genius for realistic and atmospheric staging for which producer-director David Belasco was renowned. "This Mack play is a pretty poor play," wrote George Jean Nathan, "and always obvious melodrama which Belasco contrives to turn into a pretty good theatrical exhibit by painstaking attention to details that are not worth painstaking attention." With stars Holbrook Blinn and Judith Anderson turning in sensational performances, this "rattling, bright colored, old-style" work (Arthur Hornblow) made a considerable impression on audiences.

A Mexican border town was the locale of the action, which depicted the rapacious behavior of the nation's wealthiest citizen, Don Jose Maria Lopez y Tostado (Blinn), a slick oil merchant, who desires the sultry, yet virginal, cabaret singer Dolores (Anderson), who, in turn, loves the American gambler Johnny Powell (William Harrigan). Don Jose interferes in the relationship of Johnny and Dolores, using his power to convince the latter to succumb to his lust, but he eventually gives up his quest and grants the lovers their freedom.

The romantic south-of-the-border ambiance of this guns, gambling, and girls melodrama was etched with enormous skill by all of the production elements.

A return engagement arrived at the Empire Theatre on 8/24/25 for forty-eight performances.

DOVER ROAD, THE [Comedy/Romance/Marriage/British] A: A. A. Milne; D/P: Guthrie McClintic; T: Bijou Theatre; 12/23/21 (324)

One of the major successes of the season, *The Dover Road* added another feather to the cap of British author Milne. It was produced in New York (after being rejected by the Theatre Guild) even before it reached London and introduced Guthrie McClintic at the auspicious start of what became an outstanding directorial career.

Milne's fanciful, light drawing-room comedy supposes that a wealthy bachelor, Latimer (Charles Cherry), decides that many conjugal mishaps can be avoided if the parties get better acquainted before saying their vows. Taking advantage of his house's location on the road from Dover, whence eloping couples were wont to travel on route to France, he contrives to force a pair of couples to stop at his home, as if at an inn. His plan works wonders, and he even winds up with one of the women (Molly Pearson).

The Dover Road was "delightful entertainment from start to finish," wrote Arthur Hornblow, and Burns Mantle selected it as one of his Ten Best of the Year. Louis De Foe found its plot "fragile" but its "dialogue...bright with intelligent humor." Of McClintic's staging, Alexander Woollcott noted that "his advent takes on the nature of an occasion."

The amusing story of how McClintic managed to get this play produced, despite various tribulations, is told in his book *Me and Kit*.

DOWN STREAM [Comedy-Drama/Sex/Rural] A: Alexander C. Herman and Leslie P. Eichel; S: Dickson Morgan; P: Thomas Wilkes; T: Forty-eighth Street Theatre; 1/11/26 (16)

A short-lived drama of a young man's coming of age aboard a riverboat plying the Ohio River. The youth, well played by Rex Cherryman, is a spineless lad at first, one with little experience of women when he signs on to work the towboat Speedwell. On board he meets the sexy harridan and cook's wife, Mazie (Roberta Arnold), a rough-natured dame who likes her men hard-boiled. But Mazie takes an interest in the naive boy, teaches him a thing or two about her gender, and then, when he has reached a man's estate, but before he can get too serious about her, dismisses him so he may return the wiser to his family and sweetheart back in his Kentucky hometown.

"The trouble" with the play, claimed Percy Hammond, "seemed to be that it loitered too often in footless conversation." Robert Coleman rejected it as "a sluggish and top-heavy" work, and the *Times* thought it was "as rough in technique as its deck hands are in conversation."

DRACULA [Drama/Mystery/Medicine/Fantasy/Romance/Crime/British] A: Hamilton Deane and John Balderston; SC: Bram Stoker's novel of the same name; D: Ira Hards; S: Joseph Physioc; P: Horace Liveright; T: Fulton Theatre; 10/5/27 (265)

In its day, *Dracula*, the quintessential vampire chiller, was a truly frightening experience, even though 1927 audiences were far more sophisticated than those who, twenty-five years earlier, had fainted while reading the novel on which it was founded. *Time* declared of the drama, "It is a chamber of horrors to raise the most jaded hair." Alexander Woollcott warned, "Ye who have fits prepare to throw them now." The play's unevenness was noted by some, but few denied its power to make the flesh crawl.

The Transylvanian Count Dracula (Bela Lugosi), "undead" for five centuries, revives nightly from his coffin to seek out the blood of fresh victims but must return before sunrise. Those into whom the vampire sinks his fangs gradually succumb to his state of being, becoming the slaves of his will until they too turn into the "undead." Various victims are bitten by the fiend, including Lucy (Dorothy Peterson), the niece of Dr. Seward (Herbert Bunston). Diagnostician Professor van Helsing (Edward Van Sloan) arrives to search out and destroy Dracula. Crosses serve as protective talismans as van Helsing and others discover the Count's resting place and drive a stake through his heart.

Dracula has since become widely familiar through its many stage and screen versions. Hungarian actor Bela Lugosi's interpretation of the vampire led to a career of playing this and other horror roles in films, and he is indelibly linked with the part. Still, 1927 critics were reserved about his performance. Brooks Atkinson, for one, thought he was "a little too deliberate and confident" and could have played more frantically and mysteriously.

The production scored high grades for its atmospheric staging with its wolf howls, eerie lighting, flying bats, and billowing gauze curtains.

(1) DRAGON, THE [Comedy-Drama/Fantasy/Irish] A: Lady Gregory; P/D: Dudley Digges; T: Earl Carroll Theatre; 12/26/22 (6)

Lady Gregory's Irish folk play was originally written as *The Awakening of a Soul* in 1917 and was later changed to *The Change of Heart* and finally to *The Dragon*. It was produced in New York for a series of special holiday matinees aimed at a youthful audience.

In this "mildly amusing and, in one or two of its moments,... thrilling little fairy story" (Q.M.) a gigantic dragon (John Waller) swimming across the Irish Sea with his heart set on eating the pretty Princess Nuala (Gladys Hurlbut) before she can get married—which would make him disinterested in her—is overcome by the maiden's groom-to-be (Albert Carroll), a cook who is really a Prince in disguise.

"The dialogue is rather long-drawn, but the action is full of folk humor and of facile inventions inspired by the amiable faculty of wonder," claimed John Corbin.

(2) [Dramatic Revival] D: David Elliott; S: Frances Keating; P: Jitney Players; T: Cherry Lane Theatre (OB); 3/25/29 (5)

The play's second showing of the decade was by a group of traveling troupers who were in town for a brief presentation of their two-play repertory (the other work was Sheridan's *Trip to Scarborough*). Their work was energetic but amateurish. The *Times* claimed that the play "demands no highly specialized type of acting and puts few restraints upon those who undertake it."

DREAM GIRL, THE [Musical/Reincarnation/Fantasy/Romance/Period] B: Rida Johnson Young and Harold Atteridge; M: Victor Herbert; SC: *The Road to Yesterday*, a play by Beulah Dix and E. G. Sutherland; D: J. C. Huffman; CH: David Bennett; S: Watson Barratt; C: Eleanor Abbott; P: Messrs. Shubert; T: Ambassador Theatre; 8/20/24 (118)

The score for this moderately successful musical was composed shortly before Victor Herbert's death; produced posthumously, it represented his last effort for the theatre. The *Times* said the music would "surely be found to rank high in the total product of his work." Of the songs, the most popular proved to be the title number.

Just as much delight was taken in the appearance of Fay Bainter in the lead, after several seasons of playing in straight plays. Her costar, Walter Woolf, was considered the stage's finest baritone. The plot was based on a hit comedy of 1906; it had to do with Elspeth (Bainter), a young woman who dreams herself to be Lady Elizabeth Tyrell, a creature of three centuries earlier. All of her friends appear in period costumes but retain their twentieth-century characters, and even the radio pops up in some scenes. Her boyfriend Jack (Woolf) is seen as cowardly at first but eventually rises to heroic stature to rescue her from the villain.

"Combining the fantasy of *Peter Pan* with the delicate satire of *Alice-Sit-By-The-Fire*, the piece is a charming product of the poet's fancy," beamed Arthur Hornblow.

DREAM MAKER, THE [Drama/Adventure/Crime] A: William Gillette; SC: a story by Howard E. Morton; D: David Burton; P: Charles Frohman, Inc.; T: Empire Theatre; 11/21/21 (82)

Author-actor William Gillette was deeply into his maturity when he brought this "unashamed and entertaining melodrama" into New York with himself in the stellar role. "The play itself is shallow and full of fissures, but Mr. Gillette manages through his gentle charm and his guileful methods to make it a show, if nothing else," commented Alexander Woollcott.

The far-fetched play pictured the star as Dr. Paul Clement, an aging physician who learns that the daughter (Miriam Sears) of an old flame has fallen into the clutches of the Red Mike gang of blackmailers; they are contriving to make her believe that, under the influence of a glass of champagne, her honor has been compromised, thereby forcing her to pay a heavy sum for their silence. Dr.

Clement devises a skillful series of stratagems to deceive the three villains into giving him their fingerprints and also manages to calm the distraught girl by convincing her that everything was but a nightmare. Finally, by slipping the gang some drugged whiskey and getting them completely nauseated, the doctor obtains their confessions and saves the day.

DREAM PLAY, THE (Et drömspel) [Drama/Fantasy/Swedish] A: August Strindberg; TR: Edwin Bjorkman; D: James Light; S: Cleon Throckmorton; P: Provincetown Players; T: Provincetown Playhouse (OB); 1/20/26 (26)

Off Broadway's seedbed of experimentation, the Provincetown Playhouse, was the ideal place for staging this work that prefigured so much of the modernist movement of the 1920s and that, like all of Strindberg's playwriting, had so influenced the Provincetown's own great product, Eugene O'Neill. This premiere American production of the Scandinavian author's 1907 multiscened, multi-character fantasy was daring in attempting to mount so technically and intellectually challenging a piece on a stage as cramped as the Provincetown's. But the production approach, effective as it was in certain scenes, was heavy footed in its use of different backgrounds for each locale, thereby necessitating tedious shifting that slowed the action. The fatal effect was of disconnectedness rather than fluidity.

The critics were pleased to note the artistry with which Strindberg employed expressionist techniques that had lately become sham and labored devices as managed by a number of contemporary writers. Joseph Wood Krutch was deeply moved by the sincerity with which the play recreated the nightmare vision Strindberg had of life, with its passions, perversions, and pains. The expressionistic form, with its characters who transmogrify into other characters, its places that become new ones without apparent reason, its strange events and personages, all seemed truthful and poignant evocations of lived experiences seen through the feverish brain of the playwright-dreamer.

The plot of this influential work is designed to elucidate the dramatist's belief that "Men are to be pitied," a refrain heard in it frequently. Strindberg's elusive work pictures the descent to earth of Indra's daughter (Mary Fowler) to determine why men are so unhappy. She views and participates in numerous symbolic scenes in which she seeks enlightenment about man's condition, until at the end, she reascends to heaven feeling "the whole of life's pain" as a castle flares into flames and a flower bud on its roof blossoms into a huge chrysanthemum.

DREAMS FOR SALE [Comedy-Drama/Business/Small Town/Romance/Family] A: Owen Davis; D/P: William A. Brady; T: Playhouse Theatre; 9/13/22 (13)

There was a light in the gloom cast by the critics over this "well meaning little fiasco" (Lawrence Reamer), and it emanated from the glowing reviews given newcomer Helen Gahagan at the start of the exceptional career that led her from stage to political stardom.

This is a New England play involving a pair of feuding families, with rival forests and pulp mills a motivating force in the action. There is also a romantic plot involving Ann Baldwin (Gahagan), Arthur Nash's (John Bohn) girlfriend, who is in love with Jim Griswold (Donald Cameron). Anne only realizes how much Jim means to her after she shoots him; after some explosive situations the plot ends happily for all.

Romance, melodrama, comedy, and farce banged noisily against each other in this "rickety" (Alexander Woollcott) construction. The *Telegram* laughed at this "most disastrous production of this and many another season."

DRIFT [Drama/Romance] A: Maurice V. Samuels, with Hyman Adler; D: William S. Rainey; S: Joseph Mullen; T: Cherry Lane Playhouse (OB); 11/24/ 25 (13)

An unimportant Off-Broadway work, *Drift* was a verbose melodrama about a down-and-out elderly musician Rigo Karolyi (Hyman Adler), who becomes involved in a mistaken identity plot wherein a pair of lovers are identified as siblings but, when their blood relationship turns out not to exist after all, are told that they may return to their romantic interests in one another. The play was well stocked with villains, villainesses, gypsy violinists, millionaires, a girl threatened with a fate worse than death, a betrayed mother, and the like.

"Sense and sensibility went by the beaverboards in this preposterous thing," snapped A.T., and the *Times* claimed that the work "uses every device known to hokum in order to intrigue the audience and explain the action."

DRIFTING [Drama/Period/China/Romance/Orientals/Adventure] A: John Colton and D. H. Andrews; D: John Cromwell; P: William A. Brady; T: Playhouse Theatre; 1/2/22 (63)

A large-cast costume melodrama, the most distinctive feature of which was that a young player named Humphrey Bogart made his Broadway debut in it in a pair of minor roles (his billing for one was as H. D. Bogart).

Set in China, the "lavish and colorful" (Arthur Hornblow) production featured Alice Brady as Cassie Cook of the Yellow Seas, a Massachusetts deacon's daughter who has been cast out by her stern father for an innocent prank and becomes a femme fatale in the cabarets and byways of Asia. Caught up in a Tartar uprising, she is rescued by tough American ex-soldier Badlands McKinney (Robert Warwick); the pair, outcasts both, recognize in each other what they need to fulfill themselves. They undergo various exciting adventures and live happily ever after.

Alexander Woollcott noted of Bogart's premiere that he was "inadequate," a judgment he later admitted was premature.

DRUMS OF JEOPARDY, THE [Drama/Crime/Romance] A: Howard Herrick and Harold MacGrath; D: Ira Hards; P: Alfred E. Aarons; T: Gaiety Theatre; 5/ 29/22 (8)

A panned dime-novel crook melodrama with neither effective acting nor a decent script. It had to do with a refugee Russian prince named, of all things, John Hawksley (C. Henry Gordon), who escapes from the Bolshevists to New York with two priceless emeralds called the "Drums of Jeopardy" that are reputed to bring bad luck to their possessor. A huge Bolshy, Boris (Paul Everton), pursues him with the aim of snatching the gems and killing the Prince. Finally, he is stopped by the heroine's (Marion Coakley) godfather "Cutty" (William Courtleigh), a Secret Service agent, and the big fellow is deported to his homeland. The gem set is broken up to break their spell, and John and Kitty become engaged.

Heywood Broun argued that "The exposition was often muddled as well as tedious," and John Ranken Towse claimed that "the ingredients are imperfectly mixed and badly cooked."

DRUNKARD (OR THE FALLEN SAVED), THE [Dramatic Revival] A: Anonymous; D: William Dorsey Blake and Norvell Thompson; S: Norvell Thompson; C: Ena Hourwich; P: Macdougal Street Players; T: Macdougal Street Playhouse (OB); 12/30/29

The Provincetown Playhouse was renamed for this revival of the 1840s melodrama about the dangers of demon rum. The best thing about the weakly done production, said the *Times*, was its incidental music.

DUEL, LE (The Duel) [Dramatic Revival/French Language] A: Henri Lavedan; P: Messrs. Shubert; T: Thirty-ninth Street Theatre; 11/16/22 (2)

Seen locally in 1906 in an English version, Lavedan's well-made problem play was given in French by the troupe led by Cécile Sorel that came to New York in 1922. Sorel herself did not appear in this piece about the duel between a doctor (Georges Sellier) and his priest brother (Albert Lambert) for the soul of a married woman (Rachel Berendt) with whom the physician is in love. Albert Lambert played Abbé Daniel with "all the declamation that a French actor could ask for," noted the *Times*.

DULCY [Comedy/Business/Marriage/Films/Romance] A: George S. Kaufman and Marc Connelly; D: Howard Lindsay; P: George C. Tyler and H. H. Frazee; T: Frazee Theatre; 8/13/21 (246)

With the title role in *Dulcy* Lynn Fontanne came into her own as one of the luminaries of the American stage. *Dulcy*, Kaufman and Connelly's first hit, was a worthy vehicle for her gifts as a light comedienne, being a successful depiction of the bromide-spouting Dulcinea, a character featured in the popular New York *Tribune* column of Franklin Pierce Adams. This well-meaning but meddlesome young wife, forever pronouncing platitudes such as "let sleeping dogs lie," "a time and a place for everything," and "live and let live," is happily married to Gordon Smith (John Westley), who hopes to cement a big deal with a certain businessman (Wallis Clark). To further her husband's ambitions, the eager Dulcy invites a small group over for the weekend, with the businessman and his wife

(Constance Pelissier) the guests of honor. During the party Dulcy keeps trying to help her spouse out but never opens her trap without putting her foot in it and nearly kills the deal. There are some vastly amusing scenes, including a lengthy narration by an effeminate screenwriter guest (Howard Lindsay) of his new epic scenario *Sin*, a suspected jewel theft, the discovery that a sophisticated guest (Gilbert Douglas) is a harmless imposter, and the elopement of a young couple (Norma Lee and Gregory Kelly). At the end, Dulcy triumphs, and as she utters some final bromides, Gordon closes her jabbering lips with a kiss.

The critics ignored the plot and relished the situations, the characters, the sparkling dialogue, and most of the performances. There was also effective satire on the movies and on advertising mingled in the action. "[T]he plot, as in a musical comedy, is secondary and. . .distinctly second rate," wrote Alexander Woollcott, but the play has so much wit that "it is amusing all the time," and some of its scenes "reach a level of sheer satiric comedy not often achieved by American playwrights."

Of Miss Fontanne, Kenneth Macgowan raved, "From the coif of her hair to the teetering of her feet, she is a complete and penetrating picture of busy and obvious silliness."

According to Scott Meredith's *George S. Kaufman and His Friends*, the Dulcy character was originally introduced for Fontanne by Kaufman in his rewritten version of the 1918 comedy *Someone in the House* by Larry Evans and Walter Percival.

DUMB-BELL [Comedy/Business/Romance/Small Town] A: J. C. and Elliott Nugent; D: Howard Lindsay; P: Richard Herndon; T: Belmont Theatre; 11/26/23 (2)

The Nugent family, vaudeville successes before turning to playwriting and directing, won more plaudits as performers than dramatists with *Dumb-Bell*. J. C. Nugent was cited by the *Times* critic for his "humor and pathetic charm" as a village nit-wit who stumbles on the invention of a new toy. Developing the toy into a money maker enables a young man (Kenneth MacKenna) to foil the plan of his snobbish mother to prevent his marriage to a poor girl (Ruth Nugent).

The *Times* critic viewed the heroine as a *Peg 'o My Heart* type and the nitwit as freshly imagined, although he found that the plot and at least two of its main characters "were old, bad stuff when the Victorian theatre was still at its stagiest." Wells Root called the play "a rather tepid solution of fantasy and fact."

The play was seen only at a pair of matinees.

                                                                              H.H.

DUNCE-BOY, THE [Drama/Southern/Mental Illness/Crime/Sex/Family] A: Lula Vollmer; D: Henry Stillman; P: Art Theatre; T: Daly's Theatre; 4/1/25 (43)

Lula Vollmer's folk plays of the mountain people of North Carolina, *Sun Up* and *The Shame Woman*, were big successes of 1923. She followed them up with another folk play in *The Dunce-Boy*, but this one came a cropper despite some fine writing and performances. As Arthur Hornblow observed, "It is not that the author has not written with surety of appeal and a proper stage command, but her fable is unpleasant." Stark Young considered it "one of the most nobly and sincerely aimed" plays of the season but one that had not quite achieved its goals.

The title character, Tude Huckle (Gareth Hughes), is a nineteen-year-old suffering from mental retardation. His sexual instincts are aroused by a young schoolteacher (Mary Carroll) boarding in his house; his sympathetic mother (Antoinette Perry) tries to avert a problem by telling him that the girl will die if he should touch her. When Tude sees the teacher become the unwilling object of an insistent lover's attentions, he kills the man and eventually throws himself under a buzzsaw and dies.

DUST HEAP, THE [Drama/Adventure/Romance/Jews/Sex] A: Paul Dickey and Bernard J. McOwen; D: Paul Dickey; P: Lyle D. Andrews i/a/w James Shesgreen; T: Vanderbilt Theatre; 4/24/24 (20)

Several critics commented on *The Dust Heap*'s likeness to *Abie's Irish Rose*, and the *Times* concluded: "So at the end we have Rebecca's Irish Patrick." Little good was found in this melodrama about a wandering Jew (George Farren) searching the Yukon for his long-lost daughter (Inez Plummer). She is kidnapped by a French Canadian (Louis Bennison) and destined for white slavery. Just as she is about to be ravished, God strikes her kidnapper dead with lightning, and a birthmark exposed in the struggle reveals her as the Jew's daughter. Since she is not, as supposed, a half-Indian foundling, she is free to marry the Mountie (Robert Strange) who loves her.

The miscegenation issue reminded Heywood Broun of *All God's Chillun Got Wings*. There were so many influences on the work, he wrote, that "no fewer than 12 standard types of drama here have been combined. . . . The authors have managed to retain the worst features of each."

H.H.

(1) DYBBUK, THE (Der Dibuk) [Drama/Romance/Jews/Family/Fantasy/Death/ Religion/Yiddish/Yiddish Language] A: S. Ansky; D/P: Maurice Schwartz; T: Yiddish Art Theatre (OB); 9/1/21

New York's introduction to what has since become a classic drama of Judaic mysticism came in a Yiddish Theatre presentation; the play originally had been written in Russian, was translated into Yiddish by the author when the censor banned it, and saw its first publication in Hebrew. This Hebrew version was then retranslated and revised for the play's premiere in Warsaw in 1920, shortly after Ansky's death. It came to New York in a staging at the Irving Place Theatre, occupied at the time by the Yiddish Art Theatre. The title was spelled "Dibbuk." The *Times* said, "It is a strange, stark and gloomy play, that hovers on such a perilous broderland [*sic*] of consciousness as Faustus evokes." The company gave a sensitive rendition of the haunting drama, with a triumphant performance of the doomed maiden by Celia Adler and with Maurice Schwartz playing the main rabbi. Two "special matinees" were given at Broadway's Apollo Theatre on 12/8 and 12/9/21. The plot is given below, in entry 3.

(2) [Dramatic Revival/Yiddish Language] D: David Herman; P: Boris and Harry Thomashefsky and William Rolland; T: Thomashefsky's Broadway Yiddish Theatre; 1/29/24

A revival by the Vilna Troupe from Vilna, Poland, which came to New York after a Berlin engagement. This was the famous company that gave the play its world premiere in 1920. The *Evening Post*'s J.P.L. reported unpleasant scenes in the lobby when there weren't enough seats. Praising a cast of "general excellence" in this tale of a dead lover's soul reaching out to draw his beloved to him, J.P.L. wrote that, "Dim lighting and sombre settings were provided to accentuate the mysticism which permeated the play and many of the most moving scenes were enacted in the shadows, with telling effect." The production was renowned for the vivid expressionistic techniques it employed.

H.H.

(3) AD: Henry G. Alsberg; M: Joel Engel; D: David Vardi i/a/w Alice Lewisohn; DS: Aline Bernstein; P: Neighborhood Playhouse; T: Neighborhood Playhouse (OB); 12/15/25 (120)

Ansky's controversial and influential "mystic melodrama" of possession and exorcism in an East European Chassidic community received its first showing in English in this staging. It was something of a sensation in its exotic setting, theatricalized manner, and fantastical story and has remained one of the more unusual products of the modern theatre, being given numerous worldwide mountings.

The story concerns the death of the student-mystic Channon (Albert Carroll) when he learns that the father (Marc Loebell) of Leah (Mary Ellis) wants a more prosperous groom for his daughter. Leah is possessed by Channon's soul, and this *dybbuk* must be exorcised from her. The spirit departs, but Leah dies and joins her lover in the afterworld.

To nearly every critic the play and production were "a memorable triumph," offering a folk play of surpassing beauty, philosophy, humanity, and poetry. "The production, in its authentic representation of Jewish religious custom, its incorporation of Jewish sacred and folk music, and its superb artistry in the arrangement of groups—especially remarkable in the scene where the poor are gathered in the courtyard on the wedding day and weave their uncanny weird and terrifying dance about the bride—is beyond criticism, and one that will long be memorable," expounded Helen Walker. *The Dybbuk* was chosen as one of the Best Plays of the Year. The company revived the work on 12/16/26, three days after the opening of the Habima version. It lasted for forty-one showings.

(4) [Hebrew Language] M: Joel Engel; D: Eugene Vakhtangov; S: Nathan Altman; P: Habima Players of Moscow; T: Mansfield Theatre; 12/13/26 (24)

A revival by the visiting Habima Players of Moscow who presented their legendary version in the Hebrew language. The piece was given a highly theatricalist interpretation by Eugene Vakhtangov, the famed protegé of Constantin Stanislavsky. Vakhtangov's staging incorporated his notions of the play as a revolutionary work, a struggle by its protagonists Leah and Channon against the established religious and cultural order of Chassidism. Furthermore, according to Emanual Levy's *Habima; Israel's National Theatre*, the director emphasized the class struggle between the wealthy Reb Sender and the lower classes who attend the wedding ceremony. The production's overtly stylized and grotesque makeups, eccentric pantomime and expressionistic scenery and props, bizarre vocalizations, choral effects, and strange music did not prevent the actors from breathing "unmistakable intensity into their roles," commented *Time*. Interested viewers got to compare the presentation with the more realistic version at the Neighborhood Playhouse, revived several days later. The Neighborhood mounting did not greatly pale by comparison, since it had been staged by a former Habima player who knew the work thoroughly but who chose a less bold way of expressing it. Atkinson liked the lights and settings of the local mounting better than he did those of the Hebrew actors. However, he was stunned enough by the Habima's phantasmagorical staging to declare, "the effect is astonishing— as unreal as the mystic legend of the play, as profound in its searching of the emotions, supple, resilient and varied. . . . It is a method extraordinarily beautiful when it is perfectly welded and polished," as it was here.

DYNAMO [Drama/Religion/Sex/Small Town/Crime/Science/Family] A: Eugene O'Neill; D: Philip Moeller; S: Lee Simonson; P: Theatre Guild; T: Martin Beck Theatre; 2/11/29 (66)

O'Neill described *Dynamo* as part one of a trilogy (never completed) that would deal with what he saw as the great malaise afflicting the world, "the death of an old god and the failure of science and materialism to give any satisfying new one for the surviving primitive religious instinct to find a meaning for life in." This experimental play used a number of striking devices to convey its message. In Act One, two houses were seen side by side on stage with all of their rooms exposed (as in *Desire Under the Elms*); *Strange Interlude*-like asides and soliloquies revealed inner thoughts; and the characters were more abstractions than rounded individuals.

The story was that of Reuben Light (Glenn Anders), disillusioned son of a Connecticut fundamentalist minister (George Gaul), who seeks religious meaning not in the divinity worshipped by his father but in the force of electrical power represented by a dynamo. He loves Ada Fife (Claudette Colbert), cynical daughter of his atheist neighbor (Dudley Digges), a mortal enemy of his father's. He eventually kills Ada, repenting of her lure for him. He is himself killed when he casts himself upon the dynamo that has given him little succor and proven an unsatisfying deity.

Critical antipathy doomed the play. George Jean Nathan compared it to cheap melodrama, and Ernest Boyd called it a work of shallow and "adolescent pre-tentiousness." O'Neill himself later admitted that *Dynamo* was in too ragged a state for production. It was also the first O'Neill play to be produced without the author in attendance (he was engaged in foreign travels).

O'Neill prepared detailed drawings of what he wanted the set to look like (based on his visit to the Stevenson, Connecticut, generator plant). The entire cast visited the plant to soak up the proper atmosphere. Lee Simonson's final set designs, employing O'Neill's sketches and his own study of the Stevenson plant, provided a striking image combining realism and constructivism in a novel pattern.

E

EARL CARROLL'S SKETCHBOOK [Revue] B: Eddie Cantor; M/LY: E. Y. Harburg and Jay Gorney; D: Edgar J. MacGregor; CH: Le Roy Prinz; C: Florence Weber; P: Earl Carroll; T: Earl Carroll Theatre; 7/1/29 (392)

Earl Carroll, famed producer of the *Vanities* series, presented this colorfully caparisoned summertime revue with a book by comedian Eddie Cantor; the only follow-up was a 1935 edition. A variety of beautiful staging effects were designed to display nubile female forms; there were the usual comic sketches and the standard musical interpolations. Cantor, then appearing in *Whoopee*, was seen in a talking film clip "which catches his rolling eye and muffles his treble speech in hot-potato tones" (Brooks Atkinson). Carroll appeared in the clip as well and was shown bargaining with the star over the latter's salary. The show's comedy was not very successful; it relied on ribaldry about sex and bathroom matters. One laughworthy skit had a cop enter a speakeasy and ignore the illegal drinking while reprimanding the patrons about their unlawful parking outside. Also good was a bit with Patsy Kelly playing a woman calmly taking a bath as her bathroom fills with a plumber and policemen. Will Mahoney's special brand of slipping, sliding comic dancing was a hit; the Three Sailors succeeded with their acrobatic zaniness; William Demarest scored in a slapstick stint with Kelly, who sang "Fascinating You" to him; and the chorus danced effectively.

(1) EARL CARROLL'S VANITIES [First Edition] [Revue] B: William Collier; M/LY/P/D: Earl Carroll; CH: Sammy Lee and F. Renoff; S: R. Reid MacQuire; C: Paul Arlington; T: Earl Carroll Theatre; 7/5/23 (204)

Earl Carroll was a master showman whose taste for spectacular revues packed with sensationally displayed, breathtakingly beautiful showgirls placed him amongst that pantheon of producers of which Flo Ziegfeld was king. Over the stage door to his theatre hung a sign announcing, "Through These Portals Pass the Most Beautiful Girls in the World." His annual revues were based on a standard formula of exquisite tableaux and front-line comic and musical talents;

the only major artists discovered in his shows, however, were Patsy Kelly and Lillian Roth.

The first of his *Vanities* revues opened with a parade of beauties representing other top revues; from amongst them was born the new revue, represented by Alice Weaver. Beauties such as Peggy Hopkins Joyce, Dorothy Knapp, and Carlena Diamond figured in the act's finale called "Furs," in which each stood for another fabulous fur as "When the Snowflakes Fall" was played. The second act featured sketches such as "Jazzmania" and "Insanities of 1923." Vaudeville comedian Joe Cook was a big hit with his various bits, among them "One Man Vaudeville." Arthur Hornblow wrote that Cook "frolics his way through the whole program doing his various stunts, and there is unrestrained joy and not a dull moment while this kind of fun-maker is on the stage."

H.H.

(2) [Second Edition] B: William Collier; M/LY/D/P: Earl Carroll; CH: Sammy Lee; DS: Max Ree; T: Earl Carroll Theatre; 9/10/24 (134)

This was actually the first edition to which the producer's name was prefixed; it proclaimed its purpose to be that of "exalting the human form." Expensive and well produced, it had an army of 108 chorus beauties; in one scene a nearly naked girl swung back and forth on a pendulum. The first-act finale employed a spangled revolving staircase on which stood dancer Charles Fredericks with all of the chorines arranged in revealing garments. Another spectacular number, "Twenty-Four Lovely Hours," showed each hour represented by a *Vanities* girl.

The major problem was the weakness of the comedy segments, a common sore spot. Despite the presence once more of Joe Cook, the jokes and routines were stale. The *Times* asserted that Cook's verbal humor was slighted so that he could concentrate on acrobatic comedy. His funniest scene, "The Electrical Laboratory," had in it a young comic named Dave Chasen who nearly stole the show. The headline singer was Sophie Tucker, who, as the "High Priestess of Pep," seemed out of place in her numbers, although Alan Dale referred to her as "sinuous and alluring."

(3) [Third Edition] B: William Grew, Jimmy Duffy, Arthur "Bugs" Baer, Blanche Merrill, Julius Tannen, Lester Allen, Owen Murphy, Jay Gorney, and Bozeman Bulger; M: Clarence Gaskill; LY: Ray Klages, Louis Alter, Fred Phillips, Irving Bibo, Owen Murphy, and Jay Gorney; D/P: Earl Carroll; CH: David Bennett, Sonia Gluck; S: Willy Pogany; C: Charles Le Maire; T: Earl Carroll Theatre; 7/6/25 (197)

Edition number three was marred by an accident to a chorus girl who was hit by a moving stage prop and had to be carried off, but the show proceeded to capture plaudits for its combination of taste, beauty, and good entertainment. Julius Tannen was the main comic and garnered many laughs, and the headline acts that backed him included Bobby Folsom, Oscar Lorraine, Marjorie Peterson, Vivian Hart, Jessica Dragonette, and the Three Whirlwinds.

Novelty was introduced via an eight-foot forestage leading to a pit that swallowed up exiting performers; several tables with guests around the perimeter suggested a cabaret environment.

(4) [Fourth Edition] B: William A. Grew; M: Clarence Gaskill; S: Willy Pogany; C: Charles Le Maire; D/P: Earl Carroll; T: Earl Carroll Theatre; 12/28/25 (243)

The cabaret environment only hinted at in the previous edition became the principal feature of the fourth. A forestage was added to the stage proper, with the orchestra placed at the theatre's side. The audience was invited to dance on the forestage before the show began and during the intermission, and ginger ale was served to the thirsty. Scantily clad girls marched down the aisles as usherettes. The audience was too self-conscious to make much of the invitation to dance, and the plan did not catch fire.

Like others in the series, this was an edition filled with gorgeous nudes, good tunes, and lovely decor. Louis Bromfield wrote of the opulence: "It is the kind of performance popularly associated with the idea of Babylon."

Julius Tannen was the arch M.C., but laughter was a scarce commodity. Only comic Ted Healy and a burlesque sign-painter's "ballet" were sure-fire chuckle getters. Dorothy Knapp was introduced as "the most beautiful girl in the world," and Joe Cook and Frank Tinney did what they could to draw laughter.

It was during the run of this edition that Earl Carroll was arrested for violating the Prohibition law by giving a backstage party on 2/22/26 during which a showgirl took a bath in a tub reported to have been filled with champagne (it was really highly diluted sherry). Carroll spent four months in jail for the offense.

(5) [Fifth Edition] B: Stanley Rauh and William Grew; M/LY: Grace Henry and Morris Hamilton; D/P: Earl Carroll; CH: David Bennett; T: Earl Carroll Theatre; 8/24/26 (154)

The fifth edition brought back many popular players of earlier versions, including M.C. Julius Tannen, blackface clowns Moran and Mack, Harry Delf, and Dorothy Knapp; Smith and Dale, Yvette Rugel, Wells and Brady, and Magda de Bries were also on hand. Carroll made extensive revisions to his playhouse, decking it out in full Spanish garb to make the event a "Night in Spain," as if the show were a Spanish garden party. It was as sumptuous an offering as ever but proved generally dull, with not much doing in the laugh department.

(6) [International Edition] B: Ronald Jeans; M/LY: Grace Henry and Morris Hamilton; ADD. M.: Noel Gay and Dick Addinsell; ADD. LY.: Ronald Jeans, Donovan Parsons, Howland Leigh; D/P: Earl Carroll; CH: Anton Dolin, David Bennett; DS: Bernard Lohmuller, August Vimnera; T: Earl Carroll Theatre; 1/4/27 (151)

This was an interpolation into the framework of the regular revue of the British intimate revue created by André Charlot, which had recently been so popular in New York. Tannen, Moran and Mack, the chorines, and the spectacle numbers were still around, but the show now took its cue from Herbert Mundin and Jessie Matthews as the chief song and comedy performers. Sketches and satirical songs made up the ballast of this revue within a revue; the most enjoyable bit was a spoof of the Grand Guignol, which had the players lurch into a musical comedy number whenever the action reached a gory climax. The *Times* noted that this production was "one of the most fully clothed of all the town's eye-appeasing saturnalias."

(7) [Seventh Edition] B: W. C. Fields and Paul Gerard Smith; M/LY: Grace Henry, Morris Hamilton, Ned Washington and Michael Cleary, Jean Herbert and Bernard Maltin, Paul Jones, George Whiting and Joseph Burke, Ray Klages and Jesse Greer, Louis Alter, Herbert Magidson, Jo Trent and Peter De Rose, Ernie Golden, Jack Le Soir, Ray Doll, and Abner Silver; D: Edgar J. MacGregor; CH: Busby Berkeley; S: Hugh Willoughby; C: Mabel Johnston and William Matthews; P: Earl Carroll; T: Earl Carroll Theatre; 8/6/28 (200)

The chief reason for attending the seventh edition of the *Vanities* was the return to Broadway of W. C. Fields, who cowrote the book, and the new-to-Broadway antics of stuttering comedian Joe Frisco. An array of gorgeous corybantes included many beauty-contest winners, from Miss Universe to Miss Brooklyn, and Carroll boasted that the girls earned the highest salary of any similar entertainers in the history of the theatre. Much flesh was shown, and Dorothy Knapp and Beryl Halley were the two most prominent exhibitors of it.

The show had the usual run of allegorical tableaux, such as the "Temple of Mythology" and "The Spider and the Butterfly," and an unusual mechanical ballet based on a visit to a Ford motor plant, with the dancers dressed in futuristic rubber costumes.

Field's best sketches had him in one called "At the Dentist's," with Ray Dooley, Gordon Dooley, and Martha Morton joining in the fun, and another called "Stolen Bonds" during which he kept receiving shovelfuls of snow in his face. Frisco's funniest moments included a parody of Helen Morgan crooning "The Man I Love" and one in which he spoofed the dance-marathon craze. Gilbert Seldes summed up his impression of the show: "The music I found terrible, the setting uninteresting, the mass display of bodies not particularly well done. Nevertheless, with two stars and a terrific go, the *Vanities* manage to please vast audiences."

The final editions of the *Vanities* were in July 1930, August 1931, September 1932, and January 1940.

EARTH [Drama/Religion/Blacks/Southern/Rural] A: Em Joe Basshe; M: Hall Johnson; D: Earle Browne; S: Cleon Throckmorton; C: Evelyn T. Clifton; P: New Playwrights' Theatre; T: Fifty-second Street Theatre; 3/9/27 (26)

A drama of southern Negro spiritual emotionalism produced in alternating repertory with Lawson's *Loud Speaker*. An all-black company presented it. The play seemed earnest but incoherent in its attempt to depict the emotional conflict in a village of rural blacks between their perceptions of the Christian and Voodoo faiths.

Set in the 1880s, the play focused on the Job-like plight of a self-righteous woman Deborah (Inez Clough), who, despite her devotion, has undergone various tragedies. Because of her apostasy she is blamed by the blind preacher (Daniel L. Haynes) for a great forest fire actually ignited by a Voodoo leader (William Townsend). The villagers revert in fear to the pagan faith, but Deborah kills the Voodoo leader; she is ultimately slain by the villagers who blame their continuing woes on her; as they leave they sing "Free at Last."

Brooks Atkinson dubbed this a "pedestrian drama," relieved only by its ceremonial aspects, but Richard Dana Skinner approved of it as "a play of deep feeling."

EARTH BETWEEN, THE, and "BEFORE BREAKFAST" D: James Light; P: Provincetown Players; T: Provincetown Playhouse (OB); 3/5/29 (30)
The Earth Between [Drama/Rural/Family] A: Virgil Geddes; "Before Breakfast" [Dramatic Revival] A: Eugene O'Neill

A double bill presenting a revival of O'Neill's bitter 1916 one-act monologue about a nagging wife (Mary Blair) battering away verbally at her offstage husband's nerves until he slits his throat with a razor, followed by a rural drama skirting the theme of incest. It tells of a selfishly possessive Nebraska farmer (Carl Ashburn) who bars all of the area men from courting his pretty daughter Floy (Bette Davis). He is even responsible for the death of a boy (William Challee) in whom she has shown an interest. He succeeds in keeping Floy a spinster who will care for him as he ages.

The new play, an "inarticulate, halting yet at times inexplicably effective farm tragedy" (Robert Littell) introduced New York to the talents of Bette Davis, who received widespread commendation. The *Times* critic said of her, "Miss Davis, who is now making her first professional appearance [this is not accurate; she had acted professionally outside of New York], is an entrancing creature who plays in a soft, unassertive style." In her autobiography *The Lonely Life*, Davis recalled that when she first read the play it did not appear "that the father's compensative demands on the child were excessive; but it never occurred to me for one moment just how fully he wanted her to replace her mother.... [Director] Jimmie Light, treasuring my naïveté, never enlightened me as to what the play was about.... What I didn't know wouldn't hurt me—it helped me. I was as innocent as the girl in the play." As for O'Neill's one-acter, it was rejected as too gloomy and depressing.

EASIEST WAY, THE [Dramatic Revival] A: Eugene Walter; D/P: David Belasco; T: Lyceum Theatre; 9/6/21 (63)

One of several revivals of popular realistic dramas from the not-too-distant past that producers fell back on when Broadway's business seemed depressed. *The Easiest Way* still served to grip its audiences with its theatrically vivid and, for its day, honest depiction of a kept woman's dilemma. A shocking naturalistic work in 1909, because of its situations and language (its heroine's last-act line,

234   EAST LYNNE

"I'm going to Rector's to make a hit, and to hell with the rest," became famous), in 1921 it remained "an uncommonly forceful and satisfying play" (Alexander Woollcott). Minor changes only had been made to update the text, the director was once again David Belasco, and leads Frances Starr and Joseph Kilgour returned to their original roles of Laura Murdock and Willard Brockton.

EAST LYNNE [Dramatic Revival] A: Mrs. Henry Wood; D: James Light and Stanley Howlett; S: Cleon Throckmorton; P: Provincetown Players; T: Provincetown Playhouse (OB); 3/10/26 (38)

A satirical revival of the nineteenth-century melodrama, played by the Provincetown Players for laughs in hopes of turning it into a success like that they had recently enjoyed with a similarly burlesqued treatment of *Fashion*. The company gave the play a carefully costumed, set, and acted production, but the results failed to garner the sought for chuckles. Several critics suggested that the play would have been better off played straight, and that it probably still had a capacity to wring tears from its auditors. There were also those who believed the aims of the spoof to have been misdirected, since contemporary drama by no means had moved so far away from the old conventions as the players seemed to think: "first nighters have beheld several equally maudlin dramas this season." frowned Brooks Atkinson.

EAST OF SUEZ [Drama/China/Marriage/Romance/Orientals/British] A: W. Somerset Maugham; D: Lester Lonergan; P: A. H. Woods; T: Eltinge Theatre; 9/21/22 (102)

"A sultry Oriental melodrama" (Alexander Woollcott), set in China, that Heywood Broun called "archaic and conventional" but that the *Evening Journal* claimed was "an extremely smooth, well-rounded and plausible drama, intense in its interest throughout."

Written by Maugham after his travels in Asia, it deals with Daisy (Florence Reed), a sexy Eurasian vamp, engaged to Henry Anderson (Leonard Mudie), who revenges herself on his friend George (John Halliday) for having jilted her by putting him in a compromising position. He kills himself, however, and this leads to Daisy becoming the property of Lee Tai Ching (Howard Lang) to whom her Chinese mother sold her long ago.

This was mechanical and predictable stuff, argued Broun. Still, several critics enjoyed the play greatly, because its exciting theatrical currents overcame intellectual hesitations. Florence Reed, in the type of role she made a specialty of, "was alluring, ferocious and dominant by turn" (Charles Darnton).

The play might have had a longer run if star Florence Reed had not quit the show after a brouhaha with producer Al Woods.

EASTER (Påsk) and "ONE DAY MORE" [Dramas] D: Edward Goodman; S: Albert Bliss; C: Fania Mindell; P: Stagers; T: Princess Theatre; 3/18/26 (28)
Easter [Religion/Mental Illness/Family/Romance/Swedish] A: August Strind-

berg; TR: Velma Swanston Howard; REV: Michael Strange; "One Day More" [Sea/Romance/Old Age/British/One-Act] A: Joseph Conrad; SC: Conrad's short story "Tomorrow"

A double bill consisting of a one-act by Joseph Conrad and a 1901 three-act play by Strindberg. The former was a sketch reminiscent of the short sea plays of O'Neill. It depicted the patient waiting of a senile old man (Whitford Kane) for a son who had run off to sea sixteen years earlier. Also waiting is a young girl (Josephine Hutchinson) who has idealized his character. The son (Warrren William) returns but is unrecognized by his father, and the girl realizes that her image of him was false. The *Times* called the play clumsy in its exposition, uncertainly developed in its action, and trivial in theme.

The main piece found the critics in differing states of mind. Many were baffled and bored by it, others were inspired and touched. The uncharacteristic drama found Strindberg dealing with mystical themes within a realistic framework. It is set at Easter time, its first act being on Maundy Thursday, its second on Good Friday, and the third on Easter Eve. Music from the appropriate movements of Haydn's "The Seven Last Words of Christ" introduces each act.

Easter is a somber parable drama about the Heyst family. Among the characters is a son Elis (Warren William), a teacher; a daughter Eleonora (Michael Strange), a sixteen year old just escaped from an insane asylum, who bears powers of extrasensory perception; the son's fiancée (Rita Romilly), whom Elis believes has betrayed him with a friend; Frau Heyst (Judith Lowry), who, with her son, bemoans her shame about the imprisonment of her husband for embezzlement; and Lindquist (Arthur Hughes), the threatening family creditor. The family undergoes feelings of guilt, shame, and jealousy but, through the presence of the scorned Eleonora and her Christ-like love, discovers peace and surcease from suffering.

Among *Easter*'s severest critics was John Mason Brown, who esteemed it "a messy, often ludicrous version of the Crucifixion in Modern Dress."

EASY COME, EASY GO [Comedy/Rural/Crime/Illness] A: Owen Davis; D: Priestly Morrison; S: Nicholas Yellenti; P: Albert Lewis and Max Gordon i/a/ w Sam H. Harris; T: George M. Cohan Theatre; 10/26/25 (180)

A successful play said to be the one hundredth from the copious pen of Owen Davis. *Time* disputed the figure, claiming Davis actually had produced about 130 pieces, making him the most financially successful living playwright.

Easy Come, Easy Go was an often very funny farce plagued by an inability to keep the comic inventiveness going throughout. Otto Kruger and Victor Moore played Dick Train and Jim Bailey, two slick crooks who flee from a bank robbery aboard a Pullman and hide out at a secluded health farm until the heat cools off. They get embroiled there in various plots and subplots, including the bamboozling of a vacationing millionaire (Edward Arnold) and the love affair of Dick with a girl (Mary Halliday) at the resort.

The *Times* roared at this "hilarious farce," but the more general opinion was, as Richard Dana Skinner observed, that it dragged "heavily toward the end." The 1929 musical *Lady Fingers* was based on this script.

EASY MARK, THE [Comedy/Small Town/Business] A: Jack Larrie; D: Edward Goodman; S: Sheldon K. Viele; P: Independent Theatre; T: Thirty-ninth Street Theatre; 8/26/24 (104)

Walter Huston, recently very successful in *Mister Pitt*, was far less effective in this simpleminded comedy in which he played Sam Crane, a small-town optimist with dreams of making a fortune out of a clever business deal. Sam invests his family's $6,000 in a piece of real estate deceitfully presented to him by sharpers as valuable oil property. He loses his money only for oil to be discovered and the sharpers to attempt to buy back the land cheaply before he learns of the gusher. Some suspense is generated by Sam's readiness to sell. When he learns that the gusher was merely salt water, the otherwise slow-witted and guileless hero puts one over on the villains by selling them back the land for $190,000.

Huston's natural talent and personality got him through his unconvincing role. Several critics said that only those who believed in Santa Claus could have accepted the events of this plot. "It is, in a word, stupid and amateurish material, and utterly dull," said George Jean Nathan.

EASY STREET [Drama/Marriage] A: A/D/P: Ralph Thomas Kettering; T: Thirty-ninth Street Theatre; 8/14/24 (12)

This drama, which was critically and financially successful during an eighteen-week run in Chicago, met only with horse laughs and raspberries from the New York theatre community. An uneven work that veered radically from melodrama to domestic comedy, *Easy Street* was about a narrow-minded suburban husband (Ralph Kellard) who suspects his wife's (Mary Newcomb) motives in going frequently into town. Although he thinks she is having an affair, she has actually been working to supplement the family income but has not told him because of fear of wounding his pride. He tells her to leave; she packs; he looks inside her bag and finds a baby's garment. "Darling, can this be true?" he asks. The curtain falls as reconciliation dawns.

"*Easy Street*" is amateurish, dull and absurd throughout," cavilled the *Times*.

EASY TERMS [Comedy/Family] A: Crane Wilbur; D: Frank McCormack; T: National Theatre; 9/22/25 (15)

Crane Wilbur, film actor and author of the fairly successful horror play *The Monster*, wrote and acted in this flop comedy that boasted little more than a sterling performance by character man Donald Meek. A satire on life in a commuter's family, it dealt with a New York City office worker (Meek) whose wife (Mabel Montgomery), sister, and chiropractor (Wilbur) talk him into buying a suburban home, despite his wish to remain in the comfortable city apartment he has lived in for seventeen years. The chiropractor turns out to be a villain after the wife's savings and the virtue of a young lady (Suzanne Caubet) residing with the family. All ends well, however, and the chiropractor is revealed for the dastard he is.

"Mr. Meek...plays suavely, entertainingly," wrote the *Times*, in a play that is "only occasionally amusing and even less frequently authentic."

EASY VIRTUE [Comedy-Drama/Marriage/Romance/British] A: Noël Coward; D: Basil Dean; S: George W. Harris; P: Charles Frohman, Inc., i/a/w J. P. Bickerton, Jr., and Basil Dean; T: Empire Theatre; 12/7/25 (146)

Noël Coward's third play seen on Broadway in the early part of the 1925–1926 season led some critics to think of him as facile. The present opus recounts the conflict between John Whittaker's (Robert Harris) bride Larita (Jane Cowl), a free thinker with a past, and his snooty upper-class family. Tensions become exacerbated, and Larita smashes an expensive statuette, shouting "I always hated that damn thing!" and leaves her callow husband for good.

There were many for whom the drama was a modern-day retelling of the familiar plot epitomized by Sir Arthur Wing Pinero's *The Second Mrs. Tanqueray*. Coward did not deny the resemblance; he said in his book *Present Indicative*, "My object in writing it had been primarily to adapt a story, intrinsically Pinero in theme and structure, to present-day behaviour; to compare the déclassée woman of today with the more flamboyant demi-mondaine of the nineties." He was convinced that the old-fashioned Pinero quality was intensified by what he believed Jane Cowl's tendency to overdramatize her big scene with the statuette. At any rate, he realized that her histrionics were largely responsible for the play's healthy showing at the box office.

Critics who enjoyed the piece pointed to its brittle wit, its chic characters and milieu, the snappy flourishes with which it was developed, and Coward's overall theatricalism of effect. These strengths, though, elicited distrust in George Jean Nathan, who compared the "nervous and terse" dialogue to silent film subtitles, called the climaxes arbitrary and unoriginal, and criticized the name-dropping proclivity of the characters.

EDGAR ALLAN POE [Drama/Marriage/Alcoholism/Literary-Biographical/Period] A: Catherine Chisholm Cushing; D: Arthur Hurley; T: Liberty Theatre; 10/5/25 (8)

Some found this biographical drama about the great American writer hard to take seriously. Poe lovers, wrote Alison Smith, would find the "net result...sacrilege" and "a burlesque of his life."

The piece was staged with a long list of characters, and the action shifted from Richmond, Virginia, to Baltimore to Fordham, New York, and back to Baltimore. The story followed Poe's (James Kirkwood) disinheritance by his father, his engagement to Virginia Clem (Lila Lee), his rise in literary esteem, the death of Virginia, and Poe's own demise as a drunkard in which estate he was reduced to reciting "The Raven" for a drink.

This was a pretentious, pompously written elegy inflated in its language, melodramatic in its handling, and with its hero portrayed as "a megalomaniac" (*Times*). It "seemed unreal throughout" to Ward Morehouse.

EGOTIST, THE [Comedy/Marriage/Sex/Theatre] A: Ben Hecht; P: Lee Shubert; T: Thirty-ninth Street Theatre; 12/25/22 (49)

Ben Hecht's first play—he was already a respected journalist—showed great promise; Arthur Hornblow went so far as to call *The Egotist* "one of the gayest and best comedies of the season."

Viennese actor Leo Ditrichstein acted Felix Tarbell, the egotistic middle-aged playwright whose words and phrases win over woman after woman but whose various insecurities prevent him from consummating the situations in which his ardent personality embroils him. When his infatuated leading lady (Mary Duncan) lures the happily married man to her apartment and proceeds to seduce him in a scene climaxed by her appearance in a "Salome dance costume consisting mainly of two brass ashtrays and the absence of seven veils" (Alexander Woollcott), the hapless poseur hero hurries home before his vows are broken. Unhappily, his wife (Maude Hanaford), assuming his reputation to be true, decides to mate with a stock broker, and Felix is left alone and disconsolate at the curtain.

ELECTRA [Dramatic Revival] A: Sophocles; TR: Edward Hayes Plumptre; D/ P: Margaret Anglin; S: Livingston Platt; T: Metropolitan Opera House; 5/3/27 (2)

Margaret Anglin was fifty-one when she revived Sophocles's Greek tragedy for two performances at the cavernous Metropolitan Opera House. She had given it in 1918 for a single presentation at Carnegie Hall, its sole previous mounting in New York. She was indifferently supported by a modest company, but her own performance was appropriately regal and compelling. The piece suffered from insufficient rehearsal and a lack of classical training for the principals. The chorus of fifteen was effectively drilled and did their work efficiently. "Simple in their infrequent gestures, clad in loose, colored garments, gathered in symmetrical groups on each end of the stage, they serve their purposes commendably," observed Brooks Atkinson.

The staging and mood were severe, austere, reverent, and majestic; little dabbling in realistic detail was discernible. Of the starkly sable-garbed Anglin Richard Dana Skinner averred, "something greater than the actress herself was astir, something ageless in the human soul," but Joseph Wood Krutch noted a lack of "variety of tone" and a greater degree of "sincerity" than "genius." "Yet," he added, "there is probably no other American actress who could do it as well."

Anglin's Aegisthos was Charles Dalton, her Clytemnestra was Ruth Holt Boucicault, and her Orestes Ralph Roeder. When she revived the play on 12/1/

27 for thirteen performances at the Gallo Theatre, Ian Maclaren took Aegisthos and Antoinette Perry Clytemnestra, with Roeder resuming Orestes. The production was much improved, especially in the choral passages.

ELMER GANTRY [Drama/Sex/Religion/Small Town] A: Patrick Kearney; SC: Sinclair Lewis's novel of the same name; D: Joseph H. Graham; P: Joseph Shea; T: Playhouse Theatre; 8/9/28 (44)

Sinclair Lewis's widely read muckraking novel about the hollow cant of professional evangelists was not very well translated into dramatic form in this middling effort, which concentrated on the amorous misadventures of its hero as its method of unifying the book's diverse strands. It had several good scenes but did not mesh its melodramatic and comedic qualities into a satisfying blend. In one part it sought to make the audience part of a revival meeting, with sinners rushing from their seats to the stage.

The play was credited to Patrick Kearney, but Thompson Buchanan actually wrote the third act. Its title character (Edward Pawley) is a philandering evangelist who becomes a success in the "salvation racket" while simultaneously fulfilling his lustful urges toward the women he encounters, including a deacon's daughter (Gwendolyn Hathaway) and a female revivalist, Sharon Falconer (Adele Klaer), who eventually goes up in flames when the Atlantic City Tabernacle burns down.

"[F]lat and disorderly" was Brooks Atkinson's assessment, and Alison Smith considered it a "cheap and chaotic attempt. . . to make salvation pay."

ELMER THE GREAT [Comedy/Sports/Small Town/Romance/Gambling] A: Ring Lardner; SC: Lardner's stories *You Know Me, Al*; D: Sam Forrest; P: George M. Cohan; T: Lyceum Theatre; 9/24/28 (40)

Sardonic humorist Ring Lardner was responsible for this baseball comedy about a talented, thickwitted, and boastful small-town minor-league pitcher, Elmer Kane (Walter Huston), who prefers to remain in Gentryville, Indiana, where he can be near the girl he adores (Nan Sunderland), who is also his employer, rather than go off to play in the majors for the New York Giants. Only when she fires him does he join the team. He has an up and down life, making good as a player but going broke from gambling. Manipulated by crafty sharpers, he nearly throws a crucial game to gain back some cash. A way out is found, and all ends happily.

As wonderfully played by Walter Huston, Elmer was one of the season's brightest characters, but the play did not stand up to scrutiny. The *Times* maintained that Lardner had "stirred bits of farce, drama and melodrama into a strange medley of unrelated entertainment; as a playwright he is neither supercilious nor subtle." Lardner claimed the play as produced was not a fair representation of the one he had written. Joseph Wood Krutch asserted that producer Cohan had turned the "ivory-headed pitcher into a hero and replaced most of the original satire with homely sentiment."

ELSIE [Musical/Marriage/Family/Show Business] B: Charles W. Bell; M/LY: Eubie Blake and Noble Sissle; Monte Carlo and Alma Sanders; SC: A. L. Erlanger's comedy *The Dislocated Honeymoon*; D: Edgar J. MacGregor; CH: Walter Brooks and Bert French; P: John Jay Scholl; T: Vanderbilt Theatre; 4/2/23 (40)

Comedienne Luella Gear, in her second Broadway role, was propelled into the limelight in this otherwise pedestrian show that the *Times* called "on the whole, so-so." The *Times* critic thought the material better than its performers, Gear excluded, and recommended it only for "musical comedy addicts." But the *World* found it "A delightful little musical show," well cast in all departments, and John Farrar considered it "so well played and danced by everyone . . . that we have many thanks for an entertaining afternoon."

Once again Cinderella had her hand in influencing the trite plotting, this time in a tale about a musical-comedy performer named Elsie (Marguerite Zender), who has to overcome all of her rich husband's family's objections to her entering their ranks by charming the pants off everyone.

ELSIE JANIS AND HER GANG [Revue] CN/D/P: Elsie Janis; T: Gaiety Theatre; 1/16/22 (56)

After touring abroad with her "home-made revue" (Alexander Woollcott), Elsie Janis brought it back to Broadway, where it surprised by its scenic tattiness at a time when lavish productions were all the rage. As the featured performer, Janis was her usual entertaining self as a travesty comedienne, her solo segment being the highlight of the evening. Other top-notch moments were "The Bonus Blues," sung in an employment office by a chorus of nine ex-soldiers, a sketch set in Montmartre, where Janis sang the French version of Fannie Brice's Ziegfeld Follies hit "My Man," called here "Mon Homme," Janis's "gorgeous" (Woollcott) dance numbers, and the stuttering comedy of Charlie Lawrence.

ELTON CASE, THE [Drama/Gambling/Sex/Crime] A: William Devereux; D: Mrs. Lillian Trimble Bradley; P: George Broadhurst; T: Playhouse Theatre; 9/10/21 (17)

A dramatized attempt to offer a solution to a much-publicized unsolved murder case of a year earlier involving a party named Elwell. The author's approach titillated by its ingenuity, but it was not meant as a serious answer to the crime.

The play pretended that Marjorie Ramsey (Chrystal Herne) slew whist expert Robert Elton (Byron Beasley) rather than pay him off sexually for a gambling debt he had covered for her. It also suggested that the District Attorney and the police hushed up the case to protect a certain prominent woman who had been present at the scene. "Thus," scoffed Alexander Woollcott, "you are sent away from the theatre grinning at the author's notion of an invisible empire—and an invisible empress."

EMBERS (Aprés l'amour) [Comedy-Drama/Romance/Sex/Marriage/French] A: Pierre Wolff and Henri Duvernois; AD: A. E. Thomas; D/P: Henry Miller; T: Henry Miller Theatre; 2/1/26 (33)

A fine company of actors toiled earnestly but without reward in this adaptation about the typically French concerns of marriage and infidelity. The effect, wrote K.A.L., was "like playing Yankee Doodle on a Stradivarius."

The mathematically precise plot ("as orderly and as lifeless as a syllogism"— Joseph Wood Krutch) disclosed a husband, Francois (Henry Miller), and his young mistress Germaine (Florence Shirley), the man's estranged wife, Gabrielle (Laura Hope Crews), and her lover Fournier (Nicholas Joy). Both women become pregnant and give birth to boys. Fournier leaves Gabrielle when her impending motherhood is made known. Germaine dies in childbirth. Francois and Gabrielle are reconciled. Francois secretly switches the infants in their cribs so that he may raise his own son. Gabrielle's son is then adopted as a playfellow for the child, but his mother is not told of his true identity.

K.A.L. said the piece should have been called *Embryos* instead of *Embers*, and Richard Dana Skinner accused it of sentimentality, dragginess, and insincerity.

(1) EMPEROR JONES, THE [Drama/Blacks/Race/Tropics/Politics] A: Eugene O'Neill; D: George Cram Cook; S: Cleon Throckmorton; P: Provincetown Players; T: Provincetown Playhouse (OB); 11/1/20 (192)

O'Neill's explosive drama began its successful life in a tiny Macdougal Street theatre and, after two months, beginning with several matinees at the Selwyn Theatre, where it shared the bill with "Tickless Time," a 1918 one-act by Susan Glaspell and George Cram Cook, moved into Broadway's small Princess Theatre. It was continually revived at its Off-Broadway home theatre through the 1920s: 5/6/24 for twenty-one performances; 12/15/24 for fourteen performances; 1/11/25 (at Broadway's Punch and Judy Theatre) for twenty performances; 2/16/26 for thirty-five performances; 11/10/26 at the Mayfair Theatre for eighty-one performances; and 2/11/25 with *The Dreamy Kid* sharing the bill at the Fifty-second Street Theatre for twenty-four performances. Aside from the eventual replacement of Charles Gilpin in the lead by Paul Robeson, the production remained essentially the same in each mounting; its overall quality gradually improved over what was at first a rough-edged mounting.

Composed in one act with eight scenes, *The Emperor Jones* recounts the story of ex-Pullman porter and ex-con Brutus Jones, who has escaped from a U.S. prison to a West Indian isle, where he has wangled his way through unscrupulous means to being the island's ruthless emperor. Extorting the natives by virtue of a self-created legend that only a silver bullet can kill him, he realizes he must flee; the drama concentrates on his pursuit through the jungle, which is largely depicted through atmospheric effects as the pursuers close in, with tom-toms pounding an ever more insistent beat as the tension mounts. Jones's imagination stirs up personal and racial memories that close in on him until at last he is felled—by a silver bullet.

Kenneth Macgowan took great pleasure in noting that "Here, as in no other American play except that 'sport,' *The Yellow Jacket*, there is genuine imagination both in the material and in the structure of the drama. These eight short scenes shake free from the traditional forms of our drama; they carry forward easily and honestly upon the track of discovery."

Jones's transformation from self-confident ruler to half-insane fugitive required exceptional acting, which Charles Gilpin gave it, leading Alexander Woollcott to observe, "His is an uncommonly powerful and imaginative performance, in several respects unsurpassed this season in New York." It was considered a radical experiment to have a black actor play a black role in a major drama by a white writer, and the choice of Gilpin stirred some debate in theatre circles of the day. When Gilpin was invited by the Drama League to a dinner for those who had made distinguished contributions to the season, a number of league members protested about the presence of this black actor among the white guests. The situation was inflated to the status of a public scandal through the extensive newspaper reports on it but was amicably resolved when what would have been a dinner for 300 guests attracted 1,000 who insisted on dining with the talented new actor.

The Emperor Jones was notable on other accounts as well. It gave New York its first view of a new theatrical device, a plaster sky dome or *kuppelhorizonte*, based on German models. It nearly wiped out the Provincetown's nest egg of something over $500 and was installed over vigorous objections when George Cram Cook, the company's founder and the play's director, insisted on its use. It resulted in exceptionally effective lighting effects that could be reflected off its curving, rough-textured, plaster surface.

(2) [Dramatic Revival] 5/6/24 (21)

This revival is listed because it is the one in which Paul Robeson drew attention as Brutus Jones.

Woollcott called O'Neill's drama "a singularly stirring play woven out of unshopworn materials with a leaping imagination" and the production better than the original. Robeson, he wrote, had "a voice unmatched in the American theatre. This dusky giant unleashed in a great play provides the kind of evening that you remember all your life." When Robeson appeared for curtain calls in a checkered bathrobe, P.V. wrote that he made such a figure "that one might have been pardoned for wondering just what he'd do to Harry Willis."

H.H.

(3) [Dramatic Revival] 11/10/26 (81)

Gilpin returned to the leading role several times; by the time of this revival, he had lost whatever magic he had shown in 1920. Tragedy stalked his life, and he was unable to cope with the pressures of fame. *Time* said of his acting in this mounting, "his present work rings hollow, artificial." The role of Smithers was enacted by future playwright-director Moss Hart.

ENCHANTED APRIL, THE [Comedy/Romance/Marriage/Italy] A: Kane Campbell; SC: the novel by "Elizabeth"; D: John Hayden; S: Sheldon K. Viele; P: Rosalie Stewart; T: Morosco Theatre; 8/24/25 (32)

A very popular recent novel dramatized to modest effect. It had a number of warm admirers, but a crew of disappointed viewers as well. Among the former were Arthur Hornblow, who called it "a satisfying and entertaining comedy." Yet George Jean Nathan claimed it possessed only "a measure of witty dialogue that struggles to sustain a feeble play."

The source of this contention was a comedy about four disparate London women—two unhappy wives (Elizabeth Risdon and Merle Maddern), a queenly dowager (Alison Skipworth), and a pretty, bored, young thing (Helen Gahagan)—who answer an ad to rent a picturesque Italian villa and spend a month there sans mates, smoothing out their psyches and getting their nerves in shape. Their misadventures make up most of the action, during which some droll events transpire.

ENCHANTED COTTAGE, THE [Drama/Fantasy/War/Romance/Marriage/British] A: Sir Arthur Wing Pinero; D: Jessie Bonstelle and William A. Brady, Jr.; P: William A. Brady, Ltd.; T: Ritz Theatre; 3/31/23 (64)

A sentimental fantasy, written late in the distinguished career of Sir Arthur Wing Pinero and construed by numerous critics to be an unworthy imitation of his successful younger rival, James Barrie. The play had its avid defenders, like John Corbin and John Farrar, but it met with reluctant appreciation from some and downright opposition from others.

Oliver Bashforth (Noel Tearle), a maimed veteran, falls in love with and marries the homely Laura Pennington (Katharine Cornell). Soon the couple shed their unattractive selves to become golden lovers. Laura dreams that she is the loveliest of honeymooners ever to have shared her cottage. The "miracle" of her and Oliver's transformation is not apparent to their relatives, and the couple realize that love has made them beautiful in each other's eyes.

The Playgoer typified the objections to this play when he wrote, "The play attempts to soar, but falls to earth." Everything was too obvious, he noted, without mystery or shadows. John Corbin, however, insisted that Pinero was writing about social conditions in an attempt to inspire war ravaged Britons so that "their lives might be beautified and ennobled, their strength and virtue preserved for Britain's future."

Katharine Cornell was luminous as Laura, Farrar calling her "little short of miraculous."

ENCHANTED ISLE [Musical/Romance] B/M/LY: Ida Hoyt Chamberlain; D: Oscar Eagle; P: American Allied Arts, Inc.; T: Lyric Theatre; 9/19/27 (32)

Concert singer Ida Hoyt Chamberlain wrote the book, lyrics, and music for this "naive and harmless" (*Times*) musical about eastern debutante Maria Whozis (Marga Waldron), who is pursued by an effete Italian nobleman (George E.

Mack) but who really loves a handsome forest ranger (Greek Evans); after a plot circumstance separates the lovers, the obstacle is removed, and the pair are united. The action transpired in southern California and aboard a yacht.

ENCHANTMENT [Comedy/British] A: Joseph Jefferson Farjeon; D: Robert Rendel; S: Clark Robinson; P: Enchantment, Inc., i/a/w the American Theatre Association; T: Edyth Totten Theatre; 4/27/27 (9)

A bland English comedy with an English cast; its dialogue "was heavy with infant chit-chat, dull though clean" (Perriton Maxwell). This remark was meant ironically, since the play was offered by a group pledged to nonsalacious presentations.

Enchantment was a class-conscious satire about a foursome who take refuge in a country cottage from a blizzard and proceed to pass themselves off as lords and ladies, while the real lord and lady who soon arrive join the masquerade and role play as a maid and butler.

Brooks Atkinson asked, "why should contentiously clean drama materialize in thin entertainment, as it always does? Is sin the only stirring force?"

ENDLESS CHAIN, THE [Comedy-Drama/Marriage] A/D: James Forbes; P: A. L. Erlanger; T: George M. Cohan Theatre; 9/4/22 (40)

Margaret Lawrence and Kenneth MacKenna gave sparkle to this fair-to-middling piece about keeping up with the Joneses and what happens when one lives beyond one's means.

Amy and Kenneth Reeves are a young couple; she lavishes upon herself all of the material goods in which she enviously sees her friends abounding. Her idea is to give the impression that her spouse is doing quite well, thank you, and when a move to the city from the suburbs promises to advance Kenneth's chances, they decide to chance it. The bills accumulate, however, and Amy even curries favor with an influential businessman (Harry Minturn) on her husband's behalf, only to have the man misconstrue her intentions. "The threads of this plot are gathered together at last in a somewhat too artful knot, with scraps of paper and delayed telegrams and elaborate misunderstandings a trifle mechanically maintained" (Alexander Woollcott).

To Percy Hammond this was "rather a bright, serious comedy," but the *Telegraph* noted too many obvious plot devices.

ENEMY, THE [Drama/War/Family] A: Channing Pollock; M: Reynell Wreford; D: Robert Milton; P: Crosby Gaige; T: Times Square Theatre; 10/20/25 (202)

Channing Pollock, after a career of hack playwriting, began in the 1920s to compose serious, if platitudinous and melodramatic, dramas with ethically or spiritually relevant themes. Such was this jeremiad against the cruelty and folly of militarism, inspired by the quote, "Oh wad some power the giftie gie us to see oursels as others see us." Burns Mantle summed up the drama's theme: "That hate is the real enemy of humanity; that wars are inspired by hate; that there is no real difference between peoples and that if hatred and greed are banished from the earth there will be no more war.'' Mantle chose the work as a Best Play of 1925–1926.

Pollock's preachment was set in a Vienna flat as seen in June 1914, shortly before the outbreak of the war; scenes set in August 1914, March 1917, and June 1919 followed, showing the effects of the holocaust on the ''enemy'' side so as to point up how, apart from hatred itself, there are no ''enemies'' in war.

The critics viewed a shrewdly affecting play in *The Enemy*, one that demonstrated the author's talent at manipulating his audience's feelings by resorting to the most obvious tricks of his trade. The main objections raised to the work was that it was more a propaganda philippic than a work of dramatic art. Richard Dana Skinner was especially vociferous in his indictment, referring to the play's ''muddled thinking'' and its ''well-meant fallacies.''

In his autobiography *Harvest of My Years*, Pollock reported that a principal role was filled by Fay Bainter only at the very last moment and that the opening was going to be postponed had the actress not been signed up. Bainter accepted the part at two in the morning and, to Pollock's amazement, at ten the same morning had learned all the many lines for her first act.

(1) ENEMY OF THE PEOPLE, AN (En folkfiende) [Dramatic Revival] A: Henrik Ibsen; P/D: Robert Whittier; T: Manhattan Opera House (OB); 9/6/20

A two weeks' engagement of Ibsen's satiric 1883 play about the rights of the minority was given a mediocre production in this mounting. The *Times* said it ''was far from smooth'' and seemed to have needed more rehearsal. Robert Whittier played Dr. Stockmann and ''came perilously close to burlesque'' in his portrayal.

(2) [Russian Language] D: Constantin Stanislavsky; S: Ivan Gremislavsky; P: F. Ray Comstock and Morris Gest; T: Jolson's Fifty-ninth Street Theatre; 12/3/23 (5)

John Corbin mistakenly noted that this Moscow Art Theatre production of the play was its first in New York since that of Beerbohm-Tree twenty-five years earlier; he judged the Russian ensemble acting great, particularly in the town-meeting scene, where he recognized Olga Knipper-Chekhova and Ivan Moskvin in small parts. He could not identify but commended the actor playing a drunken intruder continually ejected from the meeting—an interesting staging detail, particularly since this was one of the few Moscow Art presentations whose direction was credited solely to Stanislavsky. Corbin found Vassily Katchaloff's Dr. Stockmann a noble creation, the making of the martyr ''of the finest spiritual insight.''

H.H.

(3) D/P: Walter Hampden; DS: Claude Bragdon; T: Hampden's Theatre; 10/3/27 (127)

A successful restaging by Walter Hampden. The play was seen as argumentative and polemical but soundly dramatic and true. The mass-meeting scene was especially well staged, and Hampden's performance as Stockmann was one of his finer efforts. "Hampden finds abundant opportunity to show how human is the unworldly, scientific altruist Ibsen has created, and how closely his problems and perplexities coincide with those of many a man to-day when idealism and cheap self-interest are in sharp conflict," wrote Perriton Maxwell.

Hampden brought the play back for twenty-four more performances beginning on 11/5/28.

ENGAGED [Musical Revival] B: W. S. Gilbert; M/LY: Brian Hooker; D: Edward T. Goodman; S: Robert E. Locher and Cleon Throckmorton; C: Robert E. Locher; P: Stagers; T: Fifty-second Street Theatre; 6/18/25 (44)

W. S. Gilbert's 1877 burlesque of Victorian plays, written sans Arthur Sullivan's musical collaboration but revived in this production with music and lyrics by Brian Hooker, proved "boisterous, merry and hilarious" (*Times*). It compared favorably with the three recent Gilbert and Sullivan revivals seen in New York. The music, although credited to Hooker, was actually "found" by him, the composers being Arthur Sullivan and several others of the nineteenth century, supplemented by a few new melodies by Porter Steele written in the Victorian mode. Although the original work was a straight farce, the revival's fifteen songs require that it be classed as a musical.

The straightforward plot was about Cheviot Hill (J. M. Kerrigan), an ardent and smug youth who is always falling in love with and proposing to women and who becomes embroiled in complications when a Svengali-like friend (Jay Fassett) tries to prevent him from marrying, because that would mean an end to the friend's income.

ENOUGH STUPIDITY IN EVERY WISE MAN (Na vsyakogo mudretsa dovolno prostoty) [Dramatic Revival/Russian Language] A: Alexander Ostrovsky; D: Vladimir Nemirovich-Danchenko; S: Ivan Gremislavsky; P: F. Ray Comstock and Morris Gest; T: Jolson's Fifty-ninth Street Theatre; 12/5/23 (5)

Ostrovsky poked fun at Russian aristocrats and bureaucrats of the midnineteenth century in this 1868 tale of a clever and handsome young man who taunts the rich with his wit. Realizing he'd be wiser to court them, he pours his satire into a diary. Just as success and marriage to an heiress are about to be his, an older beauty whom he has used steals the diary and reads it aloud before his victims. When they all enjoy what is said about the others but not themselves, the young man declares that they are so stupid that they need him more as a friend than an enemy. After he leaves, the victims decide that the young man is right, and the older beauty volunteers to take charge of the rascal.

Percy Hammond speculated that the play was probably enjoyed more by the Moscow Art Theatre's devotees than by outsiders, but John Corbin found Ostrovsky's story and characters so effective "that the final impression is of intense modernity." Corbin gave the honors of the performance to Constantin Stanislavsky, "who played a slow-witted and pompous old General of the old school. There was no undue repression here. Stanislavsky strutted and attutidinized, rumbled and hemmed, spouted heroic verse.... [I]n the inner humor of facial play, the watery eye, the glassy stare and the mincing lips—he was unrivalled."

H.H.

ENTER MADAME [Comedy/Marriage/Music] A: Gilda Varesi and Dolly Byrne; D/P: Brock Pemberton; S: Robert Edmond Jones; T: Garrick Theatre; 8/16/20 (366)

Actress Gilda Varesi coauthored this vastly popular drama under the name Guilia Conti, but when Brock Pemberton produced it, she acted its lead under her own name. It marked Pemberton's entry into the ranks of Broadway's top director-producers and led Varesi to inform the public that the central role was based on her own mother, Mme. Elena Varesi, who had died only two months before the work was staged.

The central role was that of Mme. Della Robbia, a capricious and temperamental prima donna married to an American (Norman Trevor) who has tired of her constant traveling and of her irresponsible and theatrical way of life. He seeks the companionship of one who will be a domestic helpmeet. To retain her spouse, the opera star invites him and his new love for a final dinner and this proves his undoing when a nostalgic conversation sweeps away all thoughts of departure.

The play seemed extremely adroit in its depiction of the opera singer's milieu, and much comedy derived from the dialogue in which music was a constant reference point. The critics found *Enter Madame* "a delightful play excellently acted" (Heywood Broun), with truthful people, a well-worked-out plot, and an exceptional performance by Varesi in her first Broadway starring role.

Varesi had been appearing in *The Jest* when she told Pemberton of her play; when Arthur Hopkins, for whom Pemberton had been working, fired him, Pemberton covered up his new status by telling friends he was going to become a producer. With money borrowed from a cousin, he put on *Enter Madame* and became a major force on Broadway.

EPISODE [Comedy-Drama/Marriage] A: Gilbert Emery; D: Melville Burke; P: Lee Shubert; T: Bijou Theatre; 2/4/25 (21)

An uneven triangle-drama placed among the well-bred, fashionable, and clever New York sophisticates of the day. Reviews ranged from warm to tepid, and the play, which featured its author in a leading role, ran only three weeks.

The episode in question is one that occurred years earlier between Evelyn Rysedale (Kathlene Macdonell) and Herbert Ballinger (Gilbert Emery), an old friend of the long-married Rysedales. Their brief affair, now but a faded memory, comes to light, and the trio of husband (William Courtleigh), wife, and ex-lover sit in stately furnishings as, with total aplomb and politesse, they attempt as decent people to discuss and iron out their feelings. At the end, Evelyn prepares to pursue a divorce.

The play was praised for its intelligent, civilized dialogue, its expert handling of the central thesis without recourse to excessive theatricality, and its Ibsenic methods of bringing the past to bear on present situations. However, George Jean Nathan disassembled the piece to reveal its numerous "amateurish" contrivances.

ERMINIE [Musical Revival] B/LY: Harry Paulton; REV: Marc Connelly; M: E. Jakobowski; D: Charles C. Fais; S: Norman Bel Geddes; P: George C. Tyler and William Farnum; T: Park Theatre; 1/3/21 (108)

An 1886 comic opera that brought veteran Francis Wilson back to recreate his role of Cadeaux and teamed him with another top old-timer, De Wolf Hopper, as Ravennes, thus giving nostalgia lovers plenty to crow about. It was splendidly produced, its music still was listenable, and the stars made even its dated comedy enjoyable. Especially interesting were the exceptional designs of Norman Bel Geddes: "these are of a beauty that is comparatively new in the theatre," advised Alexander Woollcott.

Erminie is the show that contributed "Lullabye and Good Night" to posterity.

ESCAPE [Drama/Crime/British/Prostitution] A: John Galsworthy; D/P: Winthrop Ames; T: Booth Theatre; 10/26/27 (176)

A high-principled and morally perplexing drama that gave Leslie Howard his first fully starring role on Broadway and was roundly supported by glowing reviews. Howard played Matt Denant, a gentleman who—coming to the aid of a prostitute in Hyde Park—accidentally kills a plainclothes detective, is found guilty of manslaughter, escapes from prison after serving two years of a five-year sentence, and is depicted in the main action of the play as a fugitive over a forty-hour span. He meets various persons in his bid for freedom and finally surrenders rather than compromise a kindly parson (Austin Trevor). "It's one's decent *self* one can't escape," he declares.

The play dramatizes the moral dilemma of those toward whom the fugitive turns for help. The wavering of many of these people is objectively examined, as are their motives for hindering or succoring the unjustly convicted Denant. Stark Young found it "a delightful evening's entertainment" but not a profound one. John Mason Brown stated that Winthrop Ames's production was a masterpiece of understatement. But Gilbert Seldes panned the episodic structure, Richard Dana Skinner the overtly black and white characterizations, and George Jean Nathan the excessive sentimentality.

Of Howard's brilliant acting, *Time* reported: "For almost any U.S. actor, the part would have been impossible; for Mr. Howard it is a goal unerringly achieved."

Howard could be somewhat absentminded as an actor. One night during the run of *Escape* he found himself in his dressing room instead of onstage, where he was supposed to be hiding under a bed when the curtain rose. The stage carpenter had to cut a hole in the scenery wall so that Howard could crawl into place unseen by the audience while actress Frieda Inescourt tried to cover for him. He may have been distracted, since his days at the time were occupied in rehearsing and directing his own play, *Murray Hill*, which was soon to open.

ETERNAL JEW, THE (Der Eybiker Yid: Der Fremder) [Drama/Jews/Religion/Period/Yiddish/Hebrew Language] A: David Pinski; D: Vsevold Mchedelov; S: N. E. Yakulow; M: Alexander Krein; P: Habima Players of Moscow; T: Mansfield Theatre; 12/20/26 (9)

Moscow's Habima Theatre made a vivid impression during their visiting 1926–1927 season. Led by founder and principal actor Nahum L. Zemach, it offered the present work among others in its repertory. Stylized in its staging and decor, and perfectly crafted in its ensemble, the play swept audiences "away from all minor points of criticism to silent admiration for the atmosphere created, for the integrity of spirit it conveys and for the sense of being transported back 2,000 years to a living reality," wrote Richard Dana Skinner.

The drama was a 1906 one-act lengthened by the inclusion of musical passages. It told of the destruction of the Temple and the fall of Jerusalem at the hands of the Romans. The legend of the Wandering Jew is explained as originating in the temple's downfall and not, as others would have it, in the Crucifixion. The action develops in the town of Birath Arba, several days ride from Jerusalem. Here a child destined to be the Messiah is said to be present. The man seeking the child is scorned, however, until the mother of a child born the hour of the temple's destruction arrives. But the child vanishes, and the man takes up his eternal search for him.

The play is also known in English as *The Stranger*.

EVA THE FIFTH [Comedy/Theatre/Small Town/Romance] A: Kenyon Nicholson and John Golden; D: John Golden; P: John Golden and Edgar Selwyn; T: Little Theatre; 8/28/28 (63)

An innocuous, but diverting, backstage comedy starring the charming Claiborne Foster as Hattie Hartley, member of a barnstorming *Uncle Tom's Cabin* troupe stranded in Hiawatha, Kansas. Hattie is the company's fourth-generation player of Little Eva and may have to wed the wealthy undertaker (Philip Barrison) to get the company out of the red. Her bratty younger sister Oriole (Lois Shore) goes on in her stead at a benefit for flood sufferers; however, having stuffed herself with chocolates, she doubles up with stomach pains and plays the famous death scene as a hilarious combination of burlesque and tragedy. Hattie eventually resumes the role and marries the Simon Legree of the show (Buford Armitage), and the company moves on.

Most critics were extremely pleased by the play's mix of sentiment and comedy and by its clean language. Richard Dana Skinner said the highbrows would sniff at it, but he thought it was "one of the pleasantest and best sustained comedies of a simple order that have appeared for many months."

EVER GREEN LADY, THE [Comedy/Family/Prohibition/Romance] A: Abby Merchant; D: J. M. Kerrigan; P: David Wallace; T: Punch and Judy Theatre; 10/11/22 (14)

"A fair to middling, intermittently amusing little comedy" (Alexander Woollcott) about an Irish grandmother (Beryl Mercer) who, when her son becomes wealthy, is unable to shake her fondness for life in the Greenwich Village tenement where she has lived so long, ministering to the residents by taking in washing and preparing moonshine for them. When her son's family betake themselves to Palm Beach and send her to Lakewood, New Jersey, she hies herself back to the tenement and resumes her old life-style, using a washroom boiler transformed into a still to produce a whiskey that cures the locals of the flu epidemic raging among them. A subplot deals with her granddaughter's (Beatrice Miles) love for a journalist (Charles Ellis).

EVERYDAY [Comedy-Drama/Family/Small Town/Politics/Business/Romance] A/D: Rachel Crothers; P: Mary Kirkpatrick; T: Bijou Theatre; 11/16/21 (30)

Rachel Crothers could not duplicate with this play the success she had had with her previous effort, and the critics found many faults with it, despite its excellent company and performances. It bore an interesting premise but fell apart in the telling. The premise was that a young woman, Phyllis Nolan (Tallulah Bankhead), returning home to her small midwestern town after traveling about Europe for five years, would come back with high and worthy ideals and be confronted by meanness, narrowness, and venality, especially that of her tyrannical father (Frank Shannon). The drama is played out against a background of political cynicism and unscrupulous financial dealings. Phyllis rebels against parental dictates concerning her choice of a mate and runs off with a disillusioned war vet (Henry Hull).

Among the fissures uncovered were the play's loquacity, its lack of credible characters, and its inconsistency. S. Jay Kaufman noted of Bankhead, whose reviews were generally good, that "Her work isn't as sustained as it should be. A moment or two of fire and then charm and then she stands back as if to say, 'Well, that's that,' until her next cue arrives."

(1) EVERYMAN (Via Crucis) [Dramatic Revival] A: Anonymous; AD: Hugo von Hofmannsthal; TR: Sybil Amherst and Dr. C. E. Wheeler; P: Sir John Martin-Harvey; T: Century Theatre; 11/12/23 (4)

An English version of von Hofmannsthal's modern adaptation in German of the anonymous medieval morality play called in German *Jedermann* and here titled *Via Crucis*. It was offered as one of Sir John Martin-Harvey's plays during his 1923 season. Laurence Stallings found it a "morality hodge-podge," not as impressive as the troupe's *Oedipus*, and the English star's Everyman "a foppish fellow, a wastrel of too mincing and graceful a mien.... All of the pretty graces and furbelows of actory tradition were persisted in assiduously.'' The rhyming translation was stilted, the settings shabby, the music and choreography ''clownish,'' and only the costumes good, he said. The *Times* saw it differently, as ''rather a delightful anachronism, seasoned with a fresh naivete.''

H.H.

(2) (Jedermann) [German Language] D: Max Reinhardt; M: Einar Nilson; P: Gilbert Miller; T: Century Theatre; 12/7/27 (14)

Max Reinhardt brought his world-famed production of von Hofmannsthal's modern treatment of the old morality play *Everyman* to New York in repertory with several other Reinhardt-directed masterpieces. Conceived for outdoor presentation on the steps of a cathedral during Salzburg's summer festivals, it seemed somewhat hemmed in at the Century; reactions varied. A feeling prevailed that Reinhardt's showmanship had denuded the tale of its primitive simplicity and naivete and replaced it with a twentieth-century show-business knowhow that seemed at odds with the text. ''Everyman crept into a grave that was nearer to Hollywood than Heaven,'' remarked John Mason Brown. Still, the regisseur's genius at spectacle was widely praised. The centerpiece of the staging, a banquet scene at which the title figure (Alexander Moissi) feels the call of Death (Vladimir Sokoloff) was described by Stark Young as ''being without eloquence or power of any kind, and without taste,'' but Brown, like most others, found it ''a banquet in which very little happened but much seemed to happen, in which the whole tempo of the speeches and the shifts in grouping gave variety and even expectancy to threadbare theatrical cliches.'' Brooks Atkinson acclaimed such features as the summoning of Everyman by voices placed all around the theatre during this scene.

A nearly bare, three-leveled setting backed by stark Gothic arches allowed for swift and efficient movement and tableaux. Light, color, dance patterns, music, rich costumes, and props benumbed the senses; only Moissi and Sokoloff, among the cast, seemed able to overcome the theatrical trappings to give performances of memorable sweep, power, and imagination, ''the former in tragic eloquence; the latter in comic extravagance'' (Perriton Maxwell).

One other production of *Everyman* was seen during the decade; it was produced by a troupe under Sir Ben Greet for a single off-Broadway performance in November 1929, but reviews are not available.

EVERYTHING'S JAKE [Comedy/Prohibition/France/Family/Business/Alcoholism] A: Don Marquis; D: Walter Greenough; S: Edgar Bohlman; P: New York Theatre Assembly; T: Assembly Theatre; 1/16/30 (76)

Don Marquis's popular character Clem Hawley (Charles Kennedy), the Old Soak, once the subject of a successful comedy, played a supporting role in this new work about his friend, Jake Smith (Thurston Hall), the bootlegger. These fellows and two of their cronies comprised a risible quartet that provided considerable laughter in a threadbare, sprawling, predictable plot. ''It is old fashioned humor, to be sure. But somehow or other, it manages to be freshly amusing,'' was Perriton Maxwell's comment.

Long Island bootlegger and barkeep Jake Smith is talked by his wife (Jean Adair) and daughter (Eleanore Bedford) into taking them to Paris, and he brings his boozy buddies along for the fun. There they get into various encounters; in the best liked of them Jake takes tea with an earthy countess (Ethel Morrison), who recognizes in him a kindred spirit and consummates a profitable business deal with him on the spot.

EVE'S LEAVES [Comedy/Sex/Marriage] A: Harry Chapman Ford; P: Ray Collins; T: Wallack's Theatre; 3/26/25 (12)

A pompously overwritten play that sounded more like a nineteenth-century melodrama than a 1925 marital comedy. *Eve's Leaves* prompted bursts of unsought laughter and fluttered away in short order. Played by ''a queer troupe of artless unknowns'' (Percy Hammond), this ''utterly preposterous play'' concerned a wife, Eve Corbin (Elwyn Harvey), whose husband cannot afford to pay for the expensive clothes she desires. To indulge her desires, she purchases the clothes, wears them a single time, and returns them. When a dressmaker (Benedict MacQuarrie) discovers her ploy, he makes an arrangement with her by which she can wear the clothes by serving as his agent with her friends. This plan evolves into one whereby the couturier requests Eve's body in return for his garments. The poor woman is tempted, but she eventually decides against it and announces that bassinets and maternity clothes will now be her preoccupation.

EXCEEDING SMALL [Drama/Marriage/Illness] A: Caroline Francke; D: Rachel Crothers; S: Rollo Wayne; P: The Actors' Theatre; T: Comedy Theatre; 10/22/28 (72)

A tragic ''slice-of-life'' treatment of a poor young married couple, very much in love, who, faced by the husband's (Eric Dressler) imminent death of a heart ailment, choose to commit double suicide rather than for the wife (Ruth Easton) to go on alone.

Despite its depressing premise, a number of critics found the play a worthy, if unsatisfying, contribution. Richard Dana Skinner declared, ''The dialogue runs crisp and true and human. The characterization is excellent, until the last scene, and many of the scenes, as brought to life by Rachel Crother's intelligent direction, achieve a rare poignancy.'' Still, Skinner could not accept the conclusion as faithful to the earlier development of the characters. But Robert Littell was one of those won over ''in spite of clumsiness and sentimentality, by the tragedy of its subject and the honesty of its writing.''

EXCESS BAGGAGE [Comedy/Show Business/Marriage] A: John McGowan; D: Paul Dickey; S: P. Dodd Ackerman; CH: John Boyle; P: Barbour, Crimmins, and Bryant; T: Ritz Theatre; 12/26/27 (216)

A hit backstage comedy-melodrama in the manner of *Broadway* and *Burlesque* starring Eric Dressler and Miriam Hopkins as Eddie Kane, tightrope actor, and pretty Elsa McCoy, his "excess baggage" wife. Comedy, pathos, and suspense were fairly well mixed in a plot about the five-a-day vaudeville performers whose relationship is turned topsy-turvy when the "excess baggage" gets a movie contract, prompting Eddie to quit the show when he realizes how empty the act is without her. Depressed by the life of a film star's spouse, he returns to vaudeville, has an accident, but rejoices when his wife rushes to his side.

Part of the play required Eric Dressler to do a daring tightrope stunt on a wire stretched between the stage and the theatre's gallery. In Perriton Maxwell's opinion, the play's effect derived from "the banter and badinage of vaudeville stars and lesser luminaries." Richard Dana Skinner appreciated the truthful atmosphere but found it difficult to become "concerned about the fate of any individual."

EXCITERS, THE [Comedy/Romance/Legacy/Crime/Youth] A: Martin Brown; D: Edgar Selwyn; P: Selwyns; T: Times Square Theatre; 9/22/22 (35)

Tallulah Bankhead's vivid personality and physical appeal were among the few draws to this implausible and mixed bag of a play, in which farce, satire, crook melodrama, and vaudeville elements clashed uncomfortably. It had to do with a band of restless flappers who call themselves the "Exciters" and who go around looking for thrills. Among them is eighteen-year-old "Rufus" Raud (Bankhead), who is involved in a car accident from which she may not survive; to satisfy a clause in a will guaranteeing her family a large sum of money if she marries, she is wed to a burglar (Allan Dinehart) caught in the house that very night. As such plays would have it, she recovers, falls in love with her husband, and learns that he is a detective, not a crook.

"This is a very childish story and Martin Brown has not animated it with any very free flow of wit and humor," barked Heywood Broun.

Burns Mantle offered this unusual view of Bankhead: "Her bored air she has acquired through two seasons of successful playing, her beauty is an excuse for any hero's playing, and she springs lightly to the call of the melodramatic scenes. A gifted young woman upon whose shoulders we fear success is weighing a little heavy. She looks tired and a bit fed up with her work."

EXILE, THE [Comedy-Drama/Period/Theatre/Politics/France] A: Sidney Toler; D: Jose Ruben; P: Joseph Sidney, Inc.; T: George M. Cohan Theatre; 4/9/23 (32)

The actor-author of this far-fetched costume melodrama could not attend its opening night since he was currently appearing in the hit play *Kiki*. But those who were there saw an old-fashioned work, "of the stage stagey, and only rarely convincing" (*Times*).

It takes place in 1792 in France, where young nobleman Jacques Cortot (Jose Ruben), having been exiled because of a slight to the Queen, slips back into the country and pulls the strings that will enable his beloved, singer Berenice Millet

(Eleanor Painter), to join the Comédie Française and produce a play of his. Cortot and Millet, meanwhile, are privy to the creation by Rouget de L'Isle (Sidney Riggs) of the "Marseillase." When the Revolution erupts and the mob bursts into Cortot's home, Berenice saves herself from harm by launching full voiced into de L'Isle's stirring theme.

Laurence Stallings said singer-actress Eleanor Painter was being wasted "in a rather musty, quasi-historical drama."

EXILES [Drama/Literature/Marriage/Sex/Romance/Irish] A: James Joyce; D: Agnes Morgan; S: Russel Wright; P: Neighborhood Playhouse; T: Neighborhood Playhouse (OB); 2/19/25 (29)

James Joyce's only play, first produced in Germany, was finished in 1915, before he wrote his great novel *Ulysses*. It lacks the innovative spirit characteristic of the author's books and is clearly under the spell of Ibsenic techniques. Produced Off Broadway in a dully respectable mounting, it interested but failed to make a vital place for itself in critical estimation.

Set in 1912 Dublin, it focuses on a respected and self-consciously unconventional writer, Richard Rowan (Ian Maclaren), and his common-law wife, Bertha (Phyllis Joyce), who return from a self-imposed exile to become enmeshed in a quadrangular relationship with Robert Hand (Malcolm Fassett) and Beatrice (Dorothy Sands), Robert's cousin. Bertha and Robert are on the brink of an affair in which Richard refuses to meddle on the idealistic grounds that Bertha should be free to do as she pleases. As Joseph Wood Krutch pointed out, "the play ends in complete despair. Alienated from his wife and from his friend, doubtful of his own motives, the hero stands sure of only two things: the intensity of his own suffering and the fact that he has never bowed to any convention or accepted any compromise."

The drama was charged with being too literary, cerebral, and undramatic, as well as somewhat dated in its characters' concern with a morality that no longer seemed daring.

EXPRESSING WILLIE [Comedy/Business/Art/Romance] A/D: Rachel Crothers; M: Rachel Crothers and John Eagan; S: Woodman Thompson; P: Equity Players, Inc.; T: Forty-eighth Street Theatre; 4/16/24 (293)

The distinguished first-night audience could hardly have anticipated, wrote John Corbin, "the perfect conjunction of play-writing, acting and stage management that unfolded itself as if by miracle" in *Expressing Willie*. He could only compare the opening with *The Swan*'s but noted with satisfaction that Rachel Crothers's was an American play and one that showed the perfection of her powers. Her wit provoked hilarity, and the variety and subtlety of characterization made the actors "seem lifted to genius."

Crothers had been unable to sell commercial managements her story of Willie (Richard Sterling), a millionaire toothpaste manufacturer in awe of the phony artistes and cafe-society parasites who surround him in his Long Island mansion, prating about self-expression. Trying to help, Willie's mother (Louise Closser Hale) imports from their old midwest home town Minnie, a mousey music teacher (Chrystal Herne) who had loved him. At first Minnie takes the phonies to be real but eventually proves herself their superior both artistically and personally. She also succeeds in winning Willie from a predatory actress, saving him and his money from the shallow poseurs who gabble about self-expression but have nothing to express.

H.H.

EXTRA [Comedy-Drama/Journalism/Romance/Business/Politics] A: Jack Alicoate; D: Walter Wilson; P: Jack Alicoate and William Collier, Jr.; T: Longacre Theatre; 1/23/23 (23)

Newspaper plays were common in the twenties, and this was a fair example of the type. Its story was about how John H. King (Howard Truesdell), wishing for certain business reasons to have his newspaper business go bankrupt, left for Europe after putting the paper in the hands of his devil-may-care son Wallace (Chester Morris) and his bibulous buddy (Charles Lawrence). A drinking binge of theirs leads the friend to write a front-page editorial reversing the paper's former political stance. With its new reformist policies, the paper's circulation increases, ad rates go up, and advertisers clamor for space. The paper becomes a great success, the son is a crony of the progressive new mayor, and indictments against the shady dealings of the father are set aside by the son's influence at City Hall.

"There is no excuse whatsoever for the appearance of *Extra* in a Broadway theatre," was the *Sun*'s nasty response. But the *Evening Telegram* thought that, apart from "a number of clumsy and ineffective comedy scenes," the events were "breezy."

EYVIND OF THE HILLS (Bjoerg-Ejvind og hans hustru) [Drama/Period/ Rural/Sex/Crime/Romance/Icelandic] A: Johann Sigurjonsson; TR: Henninge Krohn Schanche; D: Frank Conroy; S: Livingston Platt; P: Frank Conroy and Charles Henry Meltzer; T: Greenwich Village Theatre (OB); 2/1/21 (22)

An interesting 1911 tragedy from Iceland, originally written in Danish and set in a rural environment in the eighteenth century. The story involves the passionate love of a farm widow, Halla (Margaret Wycherly), and her overseer Eyvind (Arthur Hohl), who is revealed as an outlaw who stole a sheep; the pair run off to live as outcasts in the hills for many years, and the play depicts the gradual dissolution, under extreme pressure, of their love, of Halla's two infanticides, and of the starving couple's eventual suicide.

"It is about as gloomy, and morbid, and depressing as any play could be," claimed Arthur Hornblow. Kenneth Macgowan was among those who thought it was "a finely imagined and poetically written tragedy." The chief problem lay with the uninspired mounting. Most agreed that Edward G. Robinson in the supporting role of Arnes gave the best acting in the production.

F

FACE VALUE [Comedy/Romance/Sex/Italian] A: Sabatino Lopez; AD: Solita Solano; P: Lee Shubert; T: Forty-ninth Street Theatre; 12/26/21 (41)

An "empty and somewhat pointless farce" (Alexander Woollcott) starring foreign-born matinee idol Leo Ditrichstein in an eccentric comic role that required him to wear a makeup of brick red hair and thick hornrimmed spectacles. The role was that of Cuban Jose Henriquez, an exceedingly homely man who sets out to prove that women may first notice good looks but that under the right circumstances he can win a woman by sheer force of his personality. Various women fall prey to his charms, but chiefly Alma Curtis (Frances Underwood), whom he is near to seducing, despite her affection for a handsome lover, when her husband (Orlando Daly) arrives. Jose convinces him that nothing immodest was going on, and his funny looks lend credence to his claims of innocence. The play ends following Henriquez' successful wooing of his ward Arabella (Clara Mackin).

Played in an "ugly, cheap and garish" setting, *Face Value* was "intolerably dull" (Arthur Hornblow).

FAILURES, THE (Les Ratés) [Drama/Prostitution/Marriage/Theatre/French] A: H. R. Lenormand; TR: Winifred Katzin; D: Stark Young; S: Lee Simonson; P: Theatre Guild; T: Garrick Theatre; 11/19/23 (40)

George Jean Nathan insisted that this play's author, for all of his vaunted prowess as an experimentalist, owed his success to his understanding of the commercial values that made for effective theatricality. Nevertheless, *The Failures* was a commercial flop.

In Lenormand's story, He (Jacob Ben-Ami), a young playwright, and She (Winifred Lenihan), an actress, are happily married but impoverished. Lacking the character to sustain their high ideals through a run of bad luck, She turns to prostitution to support them as they tour on one-night stands with a broken-down provincial troupe. He accepts her sacrifice until He can bear their lives no longer and kills her and then himself.

John Corbin declared that a three-volume novel would not tell more about the characters, and Joseph Wood Krutch commented that such "people are to be found everywhere, whose aspiration outruns talent and character." "Simply and swiftly staged, artfully mounted and superbly acted," wrote Alexander Woollcott of the production. The distinguished cast included Sterling Holloway, Helen Westley, Henry Travers, Morris Carnovsky, Jo Mielziner, and Dudley Digges.

H.H.

FAIR CIRCASSIAN, THE [Comedy/Romance/Period] A: Gladys Unger; D: Clifford Brooke; P: Miss Newell; T: Republic Theatre; 12/6/21 (7)

A "hopelessly feeble" (Ludwig Lewisohn) romantic comedy set in 1819 when the Persian Ambassador (Claude King) to the British court brings as a gift to the Prince Regent (Louis Wolheim) a beautiful Circassian maiden, Zora (Margaret Mower). Zora soon learns that she is no longer a slave, for Britain has made that status illegal, and she begins to act her newfound role of a free woman with gusto. During the lengthy drama she becomes engaged to an English gentleman but eventually winds up as the wife of the Ambassador, formerly her master, who has loved her all along.

Colorfully set and costumed, with some lovely period touches, this play had certain resemblances to Shaw's *Pygmalion*, but in spite of "much that is quaint and engaging and unshopworn" (Alexander Woollcott), it lacked an actress of sufficient versatility and appeal to rouge its rough complexion.

FAITHFUL HEART, THE [Comedy-Drama/Family/Hotel/British] A: Monckton Hoffe; D: Frederick Stanhope; P: Max Marcin and Frederick Stanhope; T: Broadhurst Theatre; 10/10/22 (31)

This London hit did not do very well on Broadway, despite a number of strongly approving reviews. Its "old fashioned and somewhat excessively mellow and sentimental" strains were embodied in an "adroitly written and beautifully played" (Heywood Broun) work featuring performances by Tom Nesbitt and Flora Sheffield of great restraint, honesty, and economy.

Nesbitt portrayed Waverly Ango, a sailor who once had a passing affair with a Southhampton seaside wench (Sheffield) resulting, unbeknownst to him, in her pregnancy and consequent death in childbirth. Two decades pass, and Waverly, after a notable war career, is ready to take a respectable landlubber's job and marry an upstanding Southhampton woman (Daisy Markham) when he is confronted, without malice, by the daughter he never knew he had. He does the right thing and gives up his dreams of retirement to captain a tramp steamer with his child by his side.

FAKE, THE [Drama/Marriage/Crime/Drugs/Alcoholism/Politics/British] A: Frederick Lonsdale; D: Frank Reicher; P: A. H. Woods; T: Hudson Theatre; 10/6/24 (89)

A melodramatic problem play with a fairly sensational denouement, a generally excellent all-British cast, and an outstanding performance by Godfrey Tearle.

Lonsdale's drama examines the six-year marriage of an upper-class politician's (Orlando Daly) daughter to an earl's son (Frank Conroy), who is an alcoholic, drug abuser, and wife mistreater. The wife (Frieda Inescort) is forced to endure the relationship because of her father's fear of scandal in his ascending career. A family friend, the adventurous older man Geoffrey Sands (Tearle), befriends the husband and solves the wife's problem by conspiring to murder the man and make his death look like a drug-related suicide. He then confronts the pompous father and strips bare his soul to reveal him for the fake he is.

Stark Young compared the play to a second-rate novel, and Robert Littell believed it to be a well-constructed "simplification of life into heroes and villains."

FAKIR RAHMAN BEY [Miscellaneous/Solo] D: Prof. Victor Bertelloni; P: A. H. Woods and Arch Selwyn; T: Selwyn Theatre; 5/25/26 (24)

Three weeks of demonstrations of the "Science of Fakirism" by a supreme exponent, the Italo-Egyptian fakir Rahman Bey. The fakir's program was devoted to feats showing the power of the human will over the material obstacle of the human body. Among his feats were his lapsing into a cataleptic state so that a heavy stone placed on his chest could be demolished with a sledgehammer; the piercing of his cheeks by long needles; the puncturing of his breast by similar needles to at least a quarter of an inch's depth; the insertion through his flesh at his adam's apple of a sharp dagger; his burial alive in a coffin covered with sand for a lengthy period, sans oxygen; exhibitions of his powers of mind reading and thought transference; and his hypnotic influence on small fowl and animals, as well as human beings.

FALL GUY, THE [Comedy/Romance/Drugs/Crime/Prohibition/Family] A: James Gleason and George Abbott; P: Messrs. Shubert i/a/w George B. Mc-Lellan; T: Eltinge Theatre; 3/10/25 (177)

Actor-playwright James Gleason accomplished the difficult task of creating two hit plays in one season without ever having written a play before. Both were collaborations, and the present one was chosen by Burns Mantle for his Best Plays of 1924–1925, although its run was nowhere near as long as Gleason's other work.

The Fall Guy takes place in a cheap upper–West Side flat where unemployed druggist's clerk Johnnie Quinlan (Ernest Truex) resides with his nagging wife (Beatrice Noyes). Johnnie gets mixed up with bootleggers who agree to pay him for carrying their goods; he is caught and, when the satchel with the hooch is opened, a false bottom containing heroin is revealed. Johnnie escapes jail by his cleverness, and, at the end, after the real villain (Hartley Power) is nabbed, Johnnie is preparing for a career as a federal detective.

Melodrama and comedy were present in equal proportions in this popular work that several hailed as an example of true American genre playwriting, especially because of its racily authentic dialogue. Percy Hammond stated that it was "completely acted, completely staged, and...entitled to a place among the top notchers of American shows."

FALL OF EVE, THE [Comedy/Marriage] A: John Emerson and Anita Loos; P: John Emerson; T: Booth Theatre; 8/31/25 (48)

There was little dissension from Joseph Wood Krutch's assessment that "the irresistably amusing Ruth Gordon takes complete charge of a poor play called *The Fall of Eve* and makes it very funny in spite of itself." Gordon portrayed Eva Hutton, the wife of young lawyer Ted Hutton (Arthur Albertson), whose business relationship with a beautiful actress for whom he has been working as a tax consultant leads, via the agency of a rumor-mongering spinster (Cora Witherspoon), to Eva's great jealousy. However, when she gets drunk and finds herself having spent the night at the home of two bachelor friends of Ted's, she believes she has betrayed him. Of course, her fears are unfounded, the bachelors never touched her, and her spouse is completely innocent.

Objections to the comedy were typified by Richard Dana Skinner who censured its unoriginal story, lack of subtlety, "artificial thesis,...cumbersome exposition and situations that are far from exalted."

FALLEN ANGELS [Comedy/Marriage/Sex/British] A: Noël Coward; D: Guthrie McClintic; S: Jo Mielziner; P: Actors' Theatre; T: Forty-ninth Street Theatre; 12/1/27 (36)

A fragile Noël Coward comedy involving two married women, Julia Steroll (Fay Bainter) and Jane Banbury (Estelle Winwood), who as younger spirits had both loved the same Frenchman (Luis Alberni); five years into their respective marriages they are on the verge of meeting him again. They spend an entire act drinking champagne and liquors, growing progressively more inebriated and squabbling; the play concludes when their former lover finally arrives in Act Three.

The comedy was seen as a one-scene effort, everything being built around the boozing of the two women and the rest displaying a lack of invention. Brooks Atkinson said he grew bored by the last act, and John Mason Brown called it "a fairly hilarious vaudeville sketch, sandwiched between two lamentably thin acts."

In England, where Edna Best and Tallulah Bankhead were the play's first stars, *Fallen Angels* kicked up a ruckus because of its revelation that both Julia and Jane had had premarital sexual relations with the same lover. The play was branded as salacious and led Coward to write, in a preface to the printed version, "I...deny very firmly the imputation...that I wrote *Fallen Angels* in order to be 'daring' and 'shocking.' Neither of these exceedingly second-rate ambitions has ever occurred to me." The play created little controversy on Broadway.

FALSTAFF [Comedy/Period/Romance] A: James Plaisted Webber; M: Porter Steele; LY: Brian Hooker; SC: Shakespeare's character, Sir John Falstaff; D: Richard Boleslavsky and Henry Stillman; CH: Richard Boleslavsky and Ted Shawn; P: Charles Coburn; T: Coburn Theatre; 12/25/28 (15)

Although billed as a comedy, the inclusion of much original music and lyrics could conceivably have classed *Falstaff* as a musical. It was an entertaining concoction based on Shakespeare's beloved fat knight, played by Charles Coburn and pieced together from *Henry IV, Henry V,* and *The Merry Wives of Windsor.* The possibilities inherent in the subject matter, though, were not well realized by the awkward production, in which several actors were miscast, and the staging seemed disunified. Still, a number of encomiums came forth, such as Richard Dana Skinner's that this was a "rollicking comedy interspersed with some delicious music, catching thoroughly the old English feeling."

In addition to the familiar Shakespeare scenes, the play added a love affair between Prince Hal (John D. Seymour) and Anne Page (Kathryn Reece). St. John Ervine was one critic dissatisfied with the interpolation.

Shepperd Strudwick, at the start of his career, played the small part of a Herald.

FAMILY AFFAIRS [Comedy/Marriage/Family/Sex] A: Earle Crooker and Lowell Brentano; D: Arthur Hopkins; S: Cirker and Robbins; P: Arthur Hopkins and Lawrence Weber; T: Maxine Elliott's Theatre; 12/10/29 (7)

The affairs intimated in this scrawny comedy's title were of the extra and premarital type; however, the play was so poor that not even Billie Burke's bedazzlements could get audiences to sustain it. It was a contrived bit of hackwork about a well-to-do East Sixties matron (Burke) who tries to handle her spouse's (Frank Elliott) philandering and her son's (Joseph McCallion) derelictions with a show girl (Leona Beutelle) by throwing a weekend bash for all concerned, including her daughter (Elaine Temple) and her fiancé (Edmund George) and a young man who stands in as her gigolo (Bruce Evans). Things work out well; the husband's mistress (Audrey Ridgewell) flees, the gigolo gets the daughter, and the son will wed his chorine.

"Largely through lack of movement, the situation descends to the flat and even plane of talkiness from which it is never lifted," barked Perriton Maxwell.

FAMILY FAILING, THE [Comedy/Family/Romance/British] A: Elfrida and Clarence Derwent; D: Clarence Derwent; T: Princess Theatre; 6/9/25 (1)

A play produced for only a single matinee tryout performance. It was billed as being cowritten, but the actual author was Elfrida Derwent, Clarence Derwent's sister. It had to do with two families that, out of stubborn pride, pose before one another as more well off than they are. The husbands are a grocer and a bacteriologist. The deceptions stem from the snobbishness of their wives, who are half-sisters. Eventually, their children grow up and fall in love with one another, and the family pretensions are revealed for what they are.

The *Herald Tribune* reported that "the audience is always a jump ahead of the action and . . . scenes suffer in consequence."

The Family Failing had originally been staged by Annie Horniman at her theatre in Manchester, England.

FAMILY UPSTAIRS, THE [Comedy/Family/Romance] A: Harry Delf; D: Sam Forrest; P: Sam H. Harris i/a/w Albert Lewis and Max Gordon; T: Gaiety Theatre; 8/17/25 (72)

A respectable kitchen-sink comedy of domestic affairs in the squabbling lives of the Heller family, streetcar inspector father (Walter Wilson), loquacious, housewifely mother (Clara Woodbury), pretty older daughter (Ruth Nugent), cocky son (Theodore Westman), and younger daughter (Lilian Garrick). The *Times* considered it a detailed and truthful cross-section of an example of New York middle-class life and values, filled with humorous and closely observed banalities of the domestic routine, but Gilbert W. Gabriel was annoyed by the play's sentimentality and structural problems.

Mrs. Heller is preoccupied with obtaining a suitable mate for her daughter, but when an eligible male (Harold Elliott) does visit the homely Heller parlor, she puts on such airs in her effort to sell her child's desirability that the poor fellow is scared off, to the utter disgust of the girl. Ultimately, he is brought back and a happy conclusion is achieved.

FAN, THE (L'Eventail) [Comedy/Romance/French] A: Robert de Flers and Robert de Caillavet; AD: Pitts Duffield; D: Edgar J. MacGregor; P: Wallace Munro; T: Punch and Judy Theatre; 10/3/21 (32)

A conventional French comedy of wit and "flirtatious" situations, well constructed, replete with "bright chatter" (Charles Darnton), and not particularly offensive to pure-minded theatregoers.

Well played by a company led by Hilda Spong, the play told the tale of Giselle (Spong), a young widow who has a way with men and who uses her feminine wiles to lure a friend's (Eva Leonard-Boyne) philandering husband (Harold Heaton) away from another woman and also finds time to rescue the married ingenue Blanche (Beatrice Miller) from her predisposition to melt at the approach of any likely male. She herself meets her lost lover (Ian Maclaren) of a decade earlier and successfully reattaches herself to him.

Although confined to "pretty well beaten paths," *The Fan* was produced "without the loss of the spice, the lightness of touch or the swiftness of movement upon which a French comedy depends," noted Alexander Woollcott.

FANATICS, THE [Comedy/Marriage/Family/Romance/Sex/British] A: Miles Malleson; D: Leon M. Lion; P: A. H. Woods; T: Forty-ninth Street Theatre; 11/7/27 (16)

A thesis drama in favor of trial marriage, this British import was not especially well written but came "to the point with sincerity and blunt, artless honesty," noted Brooks Atkinson. *Time* thought it was "hampered by fitful mediocrity."

Those brave young people whose determination to live their lives as they see fit are the "fanatics" of the title. The leading character is John Freeman (Richard Bird), a disillusioned product of World War I, who attributes the problems of the day to the outmoded marital institution and proclaims that marriage should be entered into only when, after living together, couples determine the depth of their compatability. When his fiancée (Rose Hobart) refuses this arrangement, he tries it with someone else (Anita Kerry), leading to the disruption of the engagement. After a lengthy discussion of the issues, sister Gwen (Joan Maclean) determines to be a mistress before she will be a wife.

FANNY [Comedy/Western/Rural/Crime/Romance] A: Willard Mack and David Belasco; D/P: David Belasco; S: Joseph Wickes; T: Lyceum Theatre; 9/21/26 (63)

Fannie Brice stepped out of her revue and vaudeville career to essay a straight acting role in this melodramatic comedy, but her choice of material was not especially savvy. She took the title role in what was a threadbare, dime-novel fable of Fanny Fiebaum, a brash Jewish girl from New York, who serves as a wealthy old woman's (Jane Ellison) companion. While staying at an Arizona ranch owned by the woman's late brother, she helps foil a gang of desperadoes seeking a hidden cache of money and falls in love with a law-enforcement agent (Warren William) disguised as a crook, who turns out to be Jewish.

"[E]ven its best moments showed signs of inferiority," claimed Percy Hammond. Brice delivered many of her quips in Yiddish, making the play amusing only to those conversant with the language, but her comical nuttiness was appreciated. She had some moments of pathos, but her best scenes showed her as the slangy, cross-eyed, grinning, crooning eccentric she had made famous.

According to Norman Katkov in *The Fabulous Fanny* [*sic*], Fannie Brice's decision to do a straight play caused considerable head shaking on the Main Stem, since it was difficult to think of her as a legitimate actress. She so wanted to do it, though, that she was very accessible to David Belasco's repeated wooing of her with what was clearly a lousy script. Not being used to regular stage direction—she preferred to employ a good deal of improvisation in her performances—she was nonplussed by the overwhelming demands Belasco, a notorious perfectionist, made upon her. At one key rehearsal, Belasco had her repeat and repeat a scene with which he was dissatisfied, but she could not please him at all. She said to her coactor John Cromwell, "I probably could have done what he wanted...but I can't understand a goddam word he's saying." Her problem, it seems, is that she had no idea of what Belasco meant by telling her to stop "declaiming." Once Cromwell told her what the word meant, she played the scene to everyone's delight.

FANNY HAWTHORN (Hindle Wakes) [Dramatic Revival] A: Stanley Houghton; P: Vanderbilt Producing Company; T: Vanderbilt Theatre; 5/11/22 (36)

Hindle Wakes was a greatly respected British play of 1912 that failed to attract an audience in New York. Revived to acclaim in 1921 under the title *Fanny Hawthorn*, with Whitford Kane repeating his original role of the father, it once again demonstrated its author's integrity, gift for characterization, structural deftness, and humor, leading Arthur Hornblow to describe it as "one of the best plays of modern times." However, New York again cold shouldered it, and it survived only a month.

The once controversial story told of a poor Lancashire lass (Eileen Huban) who becomes pregnant but refuses to marry her wealthy seducer, regardless of conventional dictates.

With its old story propped up by a modern feminist viewpoint, *Fanny Hawthorn* was seen as "a salutary and corrective comedy" (Alexander Woollcott).

FANSHASTICS; OR, THE MERRY WIVES OF GOTHAM [Comedy/Period/Marriage/Family/Romance] A: Laurence Eyre; M: song "Heart 'o Mine" composed by Victor Herbert; S: William E. Castle; P: Henry Miller; T: Henry Miller's Theatre; 1/16/24 (96)

Two woman who share a "fanshastic" bond of sympathy and goodwill are, ever unbeknownst to them but revealed to the audience in a prologue set in Ireland in 1830, twin sisters separately adopted at birth. Forty-three years later, one (Grace George) is the wife of a millionaire (Berton Churchill) and the other (Laura Hope Crews) is wed to a squatter (Arthur Sinclair) on the rich man's property. In spite of their husbands' feud, augmented by the millionaire's son (William Hanley) wanting to marry the poor man's daughter (Mary Ellis), the women remain friendly.

Alexander Woollcott found that the play fell "somewhat short of being a sheer delight," and John Corbin thought the scenes between the sisters wonderful but the main plot contrived and silly. The acting was greatly lauded.

H.H.

FANTASTIC FRICASEE, A [Revue] D: Andre Chotin; P: Marguerite Abbott Barker; T: Greenwich Village Theatre; (OB); 9/11/22 (111)

A patchwork revue consisting of dramatic sketches, ballets, a ukelele-playing singer, satirical bits, and a marionette show, the overall effect being uneven and "incredibly dull" (Laurence Stallings). Ben Hecht and Maxwell Bodenheim's one-act play "The Master Poisoner," written in blank verse and done in Grand Guignol style, was mocked, as was Arthur Caesar's satirical piece "When the Dead Get Gay," set in a New York mausoleum and involving two cadavers chatting about such topical concerns as Prohibition. "[A]s dull as an obituary," was Percy Hammond's verdict.

Jeannette MacDonald was one of the as yet unsung singers in the revue.

FAR CRY, THE [Drama/Family/France-Italy/Romance/Art] A: Arthur Richman; D/P: Robert Milton; S: Livingston Platt; T: Cort Theatre; 9/30/24 (31)

One of the theatre's most respected directors, Robert Milton, launched into independent production with this "somewhat unpalatable play" (*Time*). As in the author's more widely admired *Ambush*, an upright father tries to control the waywardness of his errant daughter, who has lost her faith in marriage. The locales here are Paris and Florence; the chief characters, a sophisticated but morally lax mother (Winifred Harris) and daughter (Margalo Gillmore), the mother's estranged husband (Claude King), the divorcée daughter's American art student boyfriend (Kenneth MacKenna), his mother (Lucile Watson), and the Italian Count (Frederick Worlock) for whom she leaves the artist. Ultimately, she follows her father's advice and returns to America to marry the artist.

"Its story is conventional and uninteresting. . . . Nor does the writing compensate for the lack of originality and virility of idea. The dialogue is banal, rarely amusing, never brilliant," observed Arthur Hornblow.

FARMER'S WIFE, THE [Comedy/Romance/Rural/British] A: Eden Phillpotts; D: Charles Coburn and Walter Edwin; S: Watson Barratt; P: Lee Shubert; T: Comedy Theatre; 10/9/24 (100)

A London success transplanted to good effect on Broadway, with Mr. and Mrs. Charles Coburn effective in the leads. A play of character and incident rather than one of plot, this English folk comedy was set among the farm society of Devonshire, where farmer Samuel Sweetland (Coburn), missing his late beloved wife, decides to take a new bride. Aided by his charming housekeeper Araminta (Mrs. Coburn), he draws up a list of the neighborhood's five most eligible women and pursues each in turn, with some highly comic proposal scenes presenting his adventures. Turned down by all, he suddenly realizes the wonders of Araminta herself; by the time he makes his choice, the others, too late, are having second thoughts about him.

Arthur Hornblow thought this "unusually good entertainment of a novel, refreshing kind. . . . The piece is genuinely funny." To the *Times* it was "a flavorsome, though somewhat caricaturish comedy."

FASHION [Dramatic Revival] A: Anna Cora Mowatt; AD: Brian Hooker; M: songs of the 1840s, arranged by Deems Taylor and Brian Hooker; D: Robert Edmond Jones and James Light; S: Robert Edmond Jones, Cleon Throckmorton, and Reginald Marsh; C: Kira Markham and Robert Edmond Jones; P: Provincetown Players; T: Provincetown Playhouse (OB); 2/3/24 (240)

The Provincetown Players chose to spoof Anna Cora Mowatt's comedy about Americans aping European fashions and manners and ignoring homegrown virtues. Brian Hooker's new version shortened Mowatt's 1845 original, added a dozen period songs, and accented its "archaic absurdities." The actors trumpeted asides to the audience through hollowed palms and accented old techniques of performing. The production featured footlights, an enlarged sentimental Valentine for a curtain, and a two-piece orchestra. Ludwig Lewisohn found all "exquisitely done, of an adorable innocence." Audiences showed their approval by hissing the villain, cheering the virtuous, and leaving the theatre singing. Several critics, though, believed the piece might have been better served if played straight.

Notable players involved included Mary Blair, Clare Eames, Helen Freeman, Stanley Howlett, Mary Morris, and Walter Abel.

H.H.

FASHIONS FOR MEN (Úri divat) [Drama/Romance/Business/Hungarian] A: Ferenc Molnar; TR/D: Benjamin Glazer; P: Maurice S. Revnes; T: National Theatre; 12/5/22 (89)

Broadway's favorite Hungarian playwright scored a mild success with this light 1914 comic romance, summed up by Kenneth Macgowan as "A novel combination of continental sophistication and sentimental comedy, deft and amusing."

Peter Juhasz (O. P. Heggie) is a saintly haberdashery store proprietor who raises no protest when his chief salesman (Clarke Silvernail) runs off with his wife (Beth Merrill) and the store's receipts, leading him to bankruptcy. Peter and his cashier (Helen Gahagan) take up employment on the estate of a count (Edwin Nicander), who desires the cashier as his mistress while the cashier eyes the Count as a wealthy potential spouse. Peter is set up in his store again by the Count who seeks to get him out of the way, and Peter and the cashier eventually realize that life would be rosy if they were to get married.

A few critics treated the play with derision, among them Ludwig Lewisohn who berated "its brittleness and inner factitiousness." John Corbin was one, however, who argued that "never has character been more freshly sensed in the theatre or more keenly observed." He said, "It is a comedy of indescribable freshness, and authenticity of character."

FASHIONS OF 1924 [Revue] M: Ted Snyder; LY: Harry B. Smith; D: Alexander Leftwich; CH: John V. Lowe; P: Fashion Productions, Inc.; T: Lyceum Theatre; 7/18/23 (13)

Billed as the first of an annual series of revue-fashion shows exhibiting ensembles by the foremost American designers and forecasting trends of the coming season, *Fashions of 1924* opened with a sketch featuring characters such as Needle, Thread, Headdress, and Silk. The twenty-six scenes included Forecasts of Sportswear, Beach Wear, Afternoon Wear, Furs and Footwear, plus "The Great Lover-Chapters of Women's Dresses 1450–1924" and "Dans Le Jardin de Fashion." Among them were interspersed numbers such as "Sweethearts," "When the Cat's Away," "The Triangle," and "The Real Thing." The performers included Eugene O'Neill's future wife Carlotta Monterey.

The *Times* noted, "As a matter of fact, it contains more good material than any of the other revues in town, but a good deal of its value has been dissipated by failure to shape it to the best advantage. . . . [T]he finishing hand of a [Florenz]

Ziegfeld or a [George] White is missing.'' Among the show's best performers were Jewish dialect comic Jimmy Hussey and legitimate actor Arnold Daly, making his first appearance in a revue.

H.H.

FAST LIFE, THE [Drama/Romance/Sex/Marriage/Crime/Prison] A: Samuel Shipman and John B. Hymer; D: A. H. Van Buren; P: A. H. Woods; T: Ambassador Theatre; 9/26/28 (20)

"[H]ideous and nauseating claptrap with a real electric chair. Not badly acted. Claudette Colbert very natural and lively. Yards of bogus sob-stuff,'' ran Robert Littell's nutshell description of this lurid melodrama. ''Better had this piece been called Slow Death,'' added *Time*.

Its large cast was embroiled in a plot about a pretty lady (Colbert) loved by three men, secretly married to one of them (Donald Dillaway), and discovered in bed with him by a misunderstanding suitor (Donald McClelland). This leads to the man's being shot and the blame landing on the husband; just as he is about to be executed in the chair, the Governor, whose own son (Chester Morris) has confessed, has the juice turned off.

FATA MORGANA (A délibáb) [Comedy/Rural/Marriage/Youth/Sex/Hungarian] A: Ernest Vajda; TR: James L. A. Burrell; D: Philip Moeller; DS: Lee Simonson; P: Theatre Guild; T: Garrick Theatre; 3/3/24 (254)

The Theatre Guild achieved a noteworthy success with this Hungarian comedy. According to a program note, the title means ''mirage.'' Vajda's heroine was called Mrs. Fay and represented a kind of mirage frequent on the plains of his country.

Set in a farmhouse on just such a plain, on a sweltering midsummer night, the play featured the seduction of George (Morgan Farley), an eighteen-year-old student, by a sophisticated visitor (Emily Stevens) from Budapest. The next morning her husband (Orlando Daly) and George's family return from an all-night fair, and George proposes to Mrs. Fay before all. She struggles to deceive her prosaic but rich husband and to convince the idealistic George that love is a mirage. His illusions shattered, George lies to the husband to save her honor and goes back to his books.

John Corbin found that ''Life in this remote Hungarian household is illumined with a thousand touches of genial observation and humor which make it as living and familiar as one of our own folk plays.'' George Jean Nathan called *Fata Morgana* the ''most adroit comedy on the duet of sex in modern drama'' and praised Vajda for using implication rather than milking situations, leaving much to the audience's imagination and handling his theme with ''wit and irony and a deep psychological sense and fulness of reflection.'' In addition to the actors mentioned, Helen Westley and Josephine Hull gave fine performances.

H.H.

FATAL WEDDING, THE [Dramatic Revival] A: Theodore Kremens; D: Harry McRae Webster; P: Mary H. Kirkpatrick; T: Ritz Theatre; 6/2/24 (16)

A revival of a 1901 melodrama presented in a faithful rendering of its original, now laughable, style; the sets, costumes, lighting devices, and even the old-time lantern slides warning the audience not to stamp its feet were reproduced. To the *Times* the result was an evening of "excellent fun."

The plot of the dated piece was about a jealous woman (Ann Crawford) who seeks to damage a friend's (Mildred Southwick) marriage. She succeeds in her mean-spirited attempt but is herself the victim of the friend's revenge at her own nuptials.

FATHER, THE (Fadren) [Dramatic Revival] A: August Strindberg; AD: Robert Whittier; D: Allan Dinehart; P: Robert Whittier b/a/w Richard Herndon; T: Belmont Theatre; 5/11/28 (11)

Strindberg's famous 1887 naturalistic drama about a wife who battles her husband over control of their daughter's destiny and succeeds by having the man declared insane was given an unevenly acted revival with Robert Whittier as the Captain, Florence Johns as Laura, Peggy Keenan as Bertha, and Kate Mayhew as Margaret. Whittier also produced and adapted the play. "This probably accounts for the fact that the only incompetent actor in the cast is Robert Whittier, and that what is obviously a strong, though a biting, morose and scalding play appears as a paroxysm of unintelligent ranting," declared Richard Dana Skinner.

(1) FAUST [Dramatic Revival] A: Johann Wolfgang von Goethe; AD: Henry Irving; T: Edyth Totten Theatre; 1/3/27 (24)

Sir Henry Irving's acting edition of Goethe's classic was given at this intimate theatre after not having been seen in New York since 1901. The production was barely noticed, being rather slapdash, especially as concerned the lighting, which was so dark during the "apotheosis" of Marguerite (Eleanor Laning) that the audience had to be informed of the play's having concluded. Gene Lockhart played Mephisto and Parker Fennelly was Faust. According to the *Times*, "Irving's edition subdues philosophy to the drama and turns a poem into a melodramatic costume tragedy, but there is something living in the play which histrionics cannot thwart."

(2) AD: Graham and Tristran Rawson; M: Wolgang Zeller; D: Friedrich Holl; S: Lee Simonson; CH: Bernard Day; P: Theatre Guild; T: Guild Theatre; 10/8/28 (48)

A far more ambitious revival was that of the Theatre Guild, which mounted an English translation first done in London in 1924 (this was the Guild's earliest staging of a classic drama). The director was imported for the occasion from the Berlin Volksbühne; however, the reviews were among the sharpest pans the Guild ever had received. It all seemed "surprisingly meager and wooden" to Brooks Atkinson, who was particularly offput by the lack of "compelling romance" projected by Faust (George Gaul) and Marguerite (Helen Chandler). As Mephistopheles, Dudley Digges gave what some thought one of his finest performances. There were many criticisms made of the unpoetic, plodding adaptation and the necessarily abbreviated text (seventeen scenes crammed into a two-and-a-half-hour production). Some even took Goethe to task for poor dramaturgy and ideation. Joseph Wood Krutch reported: "*Faust* moves through its many scenes with a meandering listlessness and reaches, with the death of Marguerite, a pathetic conclusion which, so far as the play is concerned, is no conclusion at all. . . .*Faust* is not a supremely great drama."

(1) FEDORA [Dramatic Revival] A: Victorien Sardou; D/P: Marie Lohr; T: Hudson Theatre; 2/10/22 (12)

Sardou's turgid nineteenth-century romantic melodrama was revived by British star Marie Lohr and her visiting company for that actress's debut in New York. The play only rattled the more loudly for Lohr's extravagant performance, of which Charles Darnton said she established herself "as an emotional actress of uncommon power."

New York had last seen *Fedora* in 1905, when Sarah Bernhardt played it on tour, and many theatregoers could also remember the performances of Fanny Davenport and Bertha Kalich in the title role. As Russian Princess Fedora Romazova, who turns over Count Louis Ipanoff (Herbert Marshall) to the police for a murder she later learns was justified and then poisons herself when she realizes she loves him, Lohr had a personal triumph, but the play itself was dated and hokey.

This was thirty-one-year-old Herbert Marshall's first Broadway show. Having lost his right leg in the war, he nevertheless had an active stage and screen career.

(2) [German Language] D: Alexander Leftwich; P: Lee Shubert and A. H. Woods; T: Frazee Theatre; 1/23/24 (5)

Tillia Durieux's performance in German of Sardou's heroine inspired Alexander Woollcott to comment: "So, to the strange experiences of a polyglot season which has already included a Russian performance of an Italian comedy and an Italian performance of a Norwegian tragedy, one must now add this German performance of a trashy French melodrama which the theatre was learning to forget." He wrote that Durieux "gave such an exhibition of the disordered countenance, the writhing limb and the heaving bosom of a discarded school of acting as had not been seen in these regions for many a long day."

H.H.

FIELD GOD, THE [Drama/Southern/Rural/Marriage/Death/Religion/Small Town] A: Paul Green; D/P: Edwin R. Wolfe; S: Louis Bromberg; T: Greenwich Village Theatre (OB); 4/21/27 (45)

Shakespearean actor Fritz Leiber tackled the southern dialect role of Hardy Gilchrist, a powerful, religion-defying North Carolina farmer, whose success the fanatical neighbors look upon as the devil's work. Hardy and his neurotic wife's (Adelaide Fitz-Allen) niece Rhoda (Ruth Mason) fall in love. Before any sin has transpired, Hardy's wife, believing them lovers, is fatally shocked by the supposition and curses them as she dies. Rhoda and Hardy marry and suffer a series of Job-like misfortunes as if Mrs. Gilchrist's spirit were haunting them. Gilchrist succumbs to "the God who is in us" only when he loses his infant to illness.

The play, compared by some to *Desire Under the Elms*, was bogged down by superfluities, lacked a sense of proportion, was long winded and sometimes muddled, but had an uncommon power, vivid characters, and hearty humor. Joseph Wood Krutch wrote that "The image of a primitive society which [Paul Green] projects. . . with an apparently effortless ease has an extraordinary depth and solidity." He deemed it "a genuine folk-tragedy," better even than the more highly acclaimed *In Abraham's Bosom*.

FIESTA [Drama/Politics/Sex/Family/Mexico] A: Michael Gold; D: James Light; S: Cleon Throckmorton; CH: Tamiris; P: Provincetown Players; T: Garrick Theatre; 9/17/29 (39)

New Masses editor Michael Gold authored this disappointing play. Perriton Maxwell observed, "*Fiesta* is deadly serious without being impressive. Mr. Gold has attempted an allegory of modern Mexico struggling to free itself from the dominion of capitalistic aristocracy, but he has made the grievous error of burying whatever reality his theme might have possessed in a great deal of high-sounding oratory with Tolstoian philosophy as its background." Various critics thought the play's intellectual idea was valid and interesting but weakened by faulty creative writing.

Fiesta tells of rancher Don Enrique (Carl Benton Reid), who returned from the wars with Tolstoy's principles in his heart and who desires to educate his peons to where they can take control of his land. The symbol of his goals is in the young orphan girl Guadalupe (Virginia Venable). He soon realizes the enormity of his task when the peons refuse to abandon their more irresponsible behavior. Guadalupe is seduced by Don Enrique's brother (Jack La Rue), and the angered landowner dismisses his philosophy and ends up shooting an old peon.

FIFTY MILLION FRENCHMEN [Musical/Romance/France] B: Herbert Fields; M/LY: Cole Porter; S: Norman Bel Geddes; D: Edgar "Monty" Woolley; CH: Larry Ceballos; C: James Reynolds; P: E. Ray Goetz; T: Lyric Theatre; 11/27/29 (254)

Cole Porter's first smash hit musical was set in his favorite city and used a Herbert Fields satirical libretto to follow the caperings of American summer tourists through Paris's favorite haunts—the Ritz Bar, the American Express Company, the Café de la Paix, Longchamps racetrack, the Claridge Hotel, Chateau Madrid, and Zelli's—designed with flair by Norman Bel Geddes. The slim story concerned wealthy American Peter Forbes's (William Gaxton) $25,000 wager to friend Michael Cummins (Jack Thompson) that he can, within a month, without relying on his cash, win the heart of Terre Haute tourist Looloo Carroll (Genevieve Tobin). He takes on various jobs to do so, from gigolo to magician to tour guide, thus motivating the constant shift of locales.

With Thompson's elegant dancing, Gaxton's boyish charm, and the talents of Tobin and supporting players Helen Broderick, Evelyn Hoey, and Betty Compton, this was a splendid show, which the *Times* described as "brisk, crack-brained, smartly accoutred and modishly salacious." Francis R. Bellamy exclaimed that it "contains the most amusing lyrics and some of the funniest scenes Broadway has witnessed this winter." Gilbert Seldes said of Porter, "His musical gift is almost entirely that of a wit, but his talent is so great that he can take any style of popular music and write in it, reserving for his finest pieces the abundant flow of his satire." The great song hits from the show included "You've Got That Thing," "You Do Something to Me," "You Don't Know Paree," and "Find Me a Primitive Man." Director Edgar "Monty" Woolley, once Porter's Yale instructor, was in charge of his first Broadway show.

FIFTY-SEVEN BOWERY [Comedy-Drama/Jews/Crime/Family/Romance] A: Edward Locke; D: Edward Elsner; S: Eddie Eddy; P: C. W. Morganstern; T: Wallack's Theatre; 1/26/28 (28)

Edward Locke's comedy-melodrama, chock full of lines that came straight out of the gaslight days, was a laughably awkward attempt to create interest in a story about an honest Jewish pawnbroker of the Bowery who gets mixed up with the criminal element. Jake Rosenberg (Hyman Adler) is induced by his college son Manny (John D. Seymour) to hock jewels that turn out to be goods stolen from the hoi polloi by Edward Van Clive (Robert Brister). When Jake's involvement is detected and he is going to be arrested, an Irish detective (Howard Healy) comes to the rescue, gets Van Clive to confess during an offstage torture scene, and all works out acceptably.

"The plot is as transparent as a night-club hostess' good-fellowship," snapped *Variety*'s Abel. The *Times* classed it as "a curiously archaic and mushy hodge-podge."

FINAL BALANCE, THE [Comedy-Drama/Romance/Fantasy/Mental Illness/Business/Yiddish] A: David Pinski; D: Theodore Viehman and James Light; S: Mordecai Gorelik; C: Evelyn Clifton; P: Provincetown Players; T: Provincetown Playhouse (OB); 10/30/28 (28)

A symbolical drama translated from the Yiddish and featuring a baker (E. J. Ballantine) who becomes rich by acting on a dream suggestion that the town's old flour will cure townspeople of insanity induced by eating this year's bread. He corners the old flour and prevents only three from partaking of the new bread, his nagging wife (Mary Michael), his partner (William Franklin), and a married roomer (Emily Graham) he loves. A fortune is earned selling the antidote flour, but he cannot win the roomer's affections. He causes his wife and her lover to go mad and also the roomer's spouse (Berne Lenrow). But he still cannot conquer the roomer, so he gives her his last piece of antidote bread for her husband and then hangs himself.

The directors of the play suggested that it was about money not having the power to buy true love, but Perriton Maxwell thought it was all "much ado about nothing." "The only question is," asked the *Times*, "was the play worth doing at all?"

FIND DADDY [Comedy/Marriage] A: Tadema Bussiere; D: Rollo Lloyd; S: Nicholas Yellenti; P: W. I. Percival; T: Ritz Theatre; 3/8/26 (8)

A Hollywood, California, bungalow living room was the setting for this inexpert nonstop farce whose "absurd characters were so busy doing nothing that they hadn't time to do anything" (Robert Coleman). Its idea was that a husband (Horace Braham), separated for a time from his wife (Dorothy Peterson), and unaware of her pregnancy, is not told by her of the child's birth, because she wants to surprise him with the news on his birthday a day later. A cousin (Enid Markey) agrees to assume the guise of a maid and act the part of the baby's mother until the proper moment arrives to make the announcement. A number of complications develop, and various people claim the child's paternity or maternity until all is suitably resolved.

"It was a labored, unfunny and thoroughly stenciled farce," judged the *Times*, and nothing the able cast of actors did could dislodge this opinion.

FINTA GIARDINIERA, LA (The False Lady Gardener) [Musical Revival] AD: Harrison Dowd; M: Wolfgang Amadeus Mozart; D: Helen Freeman; T: Mayfair Theatre (OB); 1/18/27

A production of a long-lost Mozart operetta discovered in the New York Public Library's Music Room by Macklin Morrow, who conducted; it may have been the piece's first staging since it was performed at the Munich court of the Elector of Bavaria on January 13, 1775, and subsequently in revised form in Leipzig. A libretto sparkling with risque dialogue concerned the amorous intrigues of three pairs of lovers. Excellently sung and smartly produced, it featured performers such as Weyland Echols, Dorothy Chamberlin, Helen Sheridan, Norma Millay, and John Campbell. Agnes DeMille was a delightful Columbine in her dance solo.

The *Times* said that "Mozart's gossamer music, [was] like a butterfly for lightness and iridescent flashing color." The composer was twenty-one when he wrote it.

FIORETTA [Musical/Romance/Period/Italy] B/P: Earl Carroll; AD: Charlton Andrews; M/LY: George Bagby and G. Romilli; ADD. LY.: Grace Henry, Jo Trent, and Billy Rose; D: Clifford Brooke; CH: Le Roy Prinz; S: Clark Robinson; C: William H. Mathews and Charles Le Maire; T: Earl Carroll Theatre; 2/5/29 (111)

A romantic musical set in eighteenth-century Venice and peopled by an array of outstandingly beautiful young women (*"Fioretta* as a beauty show must outshine everything that has been or can be put on"—Padraic Colum).

The story was a compilation of scenes plagiarized from such romantic predecessors as *The Three Musketeers*, *La Tosca*, and *Don Cesar de Bazin*. According to Robert Littell, only "Fannie Brice's humorous and strangely attractive leers and antics helped to redeem the show from utter boredom."

Carroll's famed *Vanities* showgirl Dorothy Knapp played the peasant Fioretta, who loves a count (George Houston) but is hindered in her romance by the lecherous Duke of Venice (Theo Karle). He sentences the Count to death for duelling, marries her to the condemned man so she may be elevated to the rank of countess for his own interests, but is foiled by the schemes of Julio (Leon Erroll), who helps the Count to escape and the lovers evade the Duke's ruthless desires.

Brice stopped the show when she warbled "What Did Cleopatra Have That I Haven't Got?" and "Wicked Old Willage of Wenice." Otherwise the music was without distinction. Top names in the cast included Leon Erroll and Lionel Atwill.

FIREBRAND, THE [Comedy/Romance/Period/Italy/Sex/Art] A: Edwin Justus Mayer; M: Maurice Nitke, Robert Russell Bennett; D: Arthur Hurley; S: Woodman Thompson; P: Laurence Schwab, Horace Liveright, and Frank Mandel; T: Morosco Theatre; 10/15/24 (287)

Edwin Justus Mayer's first play, a successful costume-drama spoof on the romantic milieu of Florence in the age of the Medicis, was based more on inspiration than documentation; it purported to be an account of several adventures involving the temperamental, dashing Renaissance sculptor Benvenuto Cellini (Joseph Schildkraut). The play paid little heed to the accuracy of its characters' behavior or language; it was a bedroom farce in which the people "concerned refuse to be frightened by their historical significance. They talk like human beings—if often like the human beings that [farce writer] Avery Hopwood knows," wrote Stephen Vincent Benet.

The complex plot pictured the fiery Cellini after his having slain an enemy. He is sought for hanging by the slow-witted, henpecked Duke (Frank Morgan). The Duke soon is diverted by his passion for the beauteous model Angela (Eden Gray) with whom Cellini is in love. Soon various complications arise, including the Duke's connivances to bed Angela and the Duchess's (Nana Bryant) maneuvers to do likewise with the sculptor. More murders, bedroom mixups, and counterplots ensue; at the end the Duke gets his heart's desire, and the artist is once more ensconced in the ducal favor.

The Firebrand (made into an unsuccessful musical, *The Firebrand of Florence*, in 1945) was selected as a Best Play of the Year. The play contained some questionable material and led the city's "play jury" to investigate it. Backed by the power of the District Attorney, the jurors requested certain changes in the business and script; the producers, not wishing to have their show padlocked, acceded, and the show continued its run.

FIRST FIFTY YEARS, THE [Drama/Marriage] A: Henry Myers; P: Lorenz Hart and Irving Strouse; T: Princess Theatre; 3/13/22 (48)

A work of exceptional interest, this was the first play by Henry Myers, whose subsequent career did not fulfill the promise shown here. The at-the-time unusual drama was written for just two characters, Ann and Martin Wells (Tom Powers and Clare Eames), whose married lives during a period of fifty years, beginning in 1872, are observed in seven intensely dramatic scenes. The characters are viewed on the occasion of their paper, wooden, tin, crystal, silver, and golden wedding anniversaries. With cynical and unromantic intent, Myers shows them beginning life together as rosy-cheeked lovers, descending into quarrelsome spouses, becoming silent partners for a ten-year stretch, shifting to a "strangers but not enemies" (Stark Young) status, growing ever more resigned to their fate, and ending in a sort of emotionless twilight zone of the soul.

The episodic structure of brief, swift scenes moved the play along effectively, and the author was praised for his constructive skill and character insight. His choice of concentrating on the undramatic lives of his people without recourse to major crises outside of those organic to their natures was considered exceptional. Alexander Woollcott called the work "a *tour de force*" that kept his interest sustained throughout.

FIRST FLIGHT [Drama/Period/Romance/Adventure/Historical-Biographical] A: Maxwell Anderson and Laurence Stallings; D/P: Arthur Hopkins; S: Jo Mielziner; T: Plymouth Theatre; 9/17/25 (11)

The first produced play by the collaborative team of Anderson and Stallings since their immense success with *What Price Glory?* Like their *Buccaneer*, which came next, it was a period drama of romance and adventure, but it was a critical disaster.

It dealt with the young Andrew Jackson (Rudolph Cameron) as he was in 1788 while stopping over in the Free State of Franklin on route to Nashville, where he hoped to prevent the separation of Franklin from North Carolina. Here he encounters the rowdy, hot-headed, swift-drinking, self-consciously honorable local frontier gentry, gets mixed up in their affairs, engages in a pair of pistol duels, and experiences love in the person of seventeen-year-old Charity Clarkson (Helen Chandler).

Mentioning both its good and bad points, George Jean Nathan said, "The play is... ; heavily conversational, it moves with disturbing slowness...; it shows...disregard for compact form.... Yet there is in it...a fine ring of brave beauty and the soft melody of an understanding tenderness."

FIRST LAW, THE (Pervy Zakor) [Drama/Rural/Romance/Politics/Russian] A: Dmitry Scheglov; AD: Herman Bernstein and Leonid Snegoff; D: Leonid Snegoff; S: Rollo Wayne; P: N.S.R. Productions, Inc.; T: Theatre Masque; 5/6/29 (8)

The first Soviet Russian play to be produced in America. Brooks Atkinson denigrated it as "an intolerably amateur piece of playmaking," although he conceded that it may have lost something in translation.

To an abandoned hut in a Siberian forest during a blizzard come Ollan Stevens (Frances Carson) and Henry Woodhouse (Reginald Goode). She is the upper-class daughter of a mining engineer; he is her fiancé. Flight from the revolutionary forces has brought them here. A triangle plot ensues when the Bolshevist Vladimir arrives for shelter. Vladimir wins Ollan and kills the effete Woodehouse. Her capitalistic instincts reassert themselves when she is rescued, and she abandons Vladimir to return to the comforts of her own kind.

FIRST LOVE (Pile ou face) [Comedy/Family/Romance/French/Sex] A: Louis Verneuil; AD: Zoë Akins; D: George Marion; S: Watson Barratt; P: Messrs. Shubert; T: Booth Theatre; 11/8/26 (50)

A mediocre adaptation from the 1924 French play *Pile ou face* about an impoverished, unmarried bohemian young couple in Paris—he (Geoffrey Kerr) a cabaret singer of noble blood, she (Fay Bainter) a Rumanian medical student—his wealthy father's (Bruce McRae) attempt to get him to marry a business associate's daughter, and the medical student's essay at getting much needed cash from a man whose interest is more than platonic. The man turns out to be the youth's dad, so all eventuates satisfactorily.

Known as *Parakeets* in its original American version, the work "distinctly has its moments," said Brooks Atkinson, "but it is spread pretty thin over three acts." Katharine Zimmermann wrote, "The piece sags sadly in between whiles, burdened with an excess of sentimentality."

FIRST MAN, THE [Drama/Marriage] A: Eugene O'Neill; D/P: Augustin Duncan; T: Neighborhood Playhouse (OB); 3/4/22 (27)

Produced during the same year that saw productions of Eugene O'Neill's *Anna Christie*, *The Hairy Ape*, and *The Straw*, *The First Man* (originally called *The Oldest Man*) was typically concerned with human suffering and possessed of bursts of raw emotion; however, as Alexander Woollcott pointed out, it was "prolix, circuitously repetitive and clumsy of gait."

The First Man is a domestic drama about the Jaysons of Bridgetown, Connecticut. He (Augustin Duncan) is an anthropologist selfishly devoted to his work. When he learns that his plans to travel on an expedition to Tibet to find the remains of "the first man" will have to be shelved because his wife (Margaret Mower) is pregnant, he grows jealously enraged, refuses to accept the news, and even wishes the baby born dead. Following a scene in which the wife delivers a son offstage, with her labor cries audible to the audience, and then dies, the husband comes to terms with his new fatherhood. He goes off on his trip, promising to take up his duties as a parent when he returns.

The scene of the offstage birth was considered "extremely frank," if somewhat "indelicate," to Arthur Hornblow and others.

FIRST MRS. FRASER, THE [Comedy/Marriage/British] A: St. John Ervine; D: Grace George; S: Livingston Platt; P: William A. Brady; T: Playhouse Theatre; 12/28/29 (352)

One of the Best Plays of 1929–1930 was this London success that met with equal popularity in New York, where Grace George starred in the role created by Marie Tempest.

It was a polite comedy about a wealthy gentleman, James Fraser (A. E. Matthews), who, having divorced his decent wife, Janet (George), after many years of marriage so that he might wed nineteen-year-old Elsie (Carol Goodner), now wishes to dispose of his incompatible young bride. Janet's advice is sought; she thinks up a plan to shed Elsie by getting the younger woman embroiled with another man. At the end, Fraser is intent on wooing back the first Mrs. Fraser.

Because Elsie was depicted as an amalgam of all of the less attractive traits often attributed to contemporary youth, Ervine's play was thought to have a touch of unbecoming peevishness. Perriton Maxwell said it was "a pleasant, often vivacious little comedy, marred only by the spleen which he insists on venting against the younger generation." "The dialog is sedately witty rather than wisecracking," noted *Time*.

FIRST MORTGAGE [Drama/Family/Sex/Small Town] A: Louis Weitzenkorn; D: Jose Ruben; S: Jo Mielziner; P: W. P. Farnsworth and H. M. Hayman; T: Royale Theatre; 10/10/29 (4)

Half a week was all this suburban family play could muster. Its hero was Elmer Gray (Walter Abel), who, having purchased a bungalow in High Falls, New Jersey, begins to crumble under the pressures of the monthly mortgage payments and the installments on his furniture. While his wife (Beatrice Hendricks) is off having a baby, he has an affair with neighbor Gracie Turner (Leona Maricle). He burns his house down to get rid of its burdens, but his father advances the money for a new one. He will continue to live out his gray days in High Falls.

The *Times* concluded, "It was a pinchpenny play without fervor, and, accordingly, it took on the color of its environment."

FIRST STONE, THE [Drama/Marriage/Sex/Small Town/Family] A: Walter Ferris; SC: a story by Mary Heaton Vorse; D: Eva Le Gallienne; P: Civic Repertory Company; T: Civic Repertory Theatre (OB); 1/13/28 (19)

This play, constructed about the double-standard theme, was set in Cape Cod, where a Portuguese trucker (Egon Brecher), gone from his wife and family for long stretches at a time, learns that in his absence his spouse (Eva Le Gallienne) has been keeping occupied with a local fellow. He tosses her out, but she, with the support of her children (Josephine Hutchinson and Charles McCarthy), returns and brazens the situation out; unable to cast the first stone, the husband lets her stay.

"Both play and performance make rather bare use of the bare material at their disposal," commented the *Times*. This critic found the play essentially truthful but "inelastic, uneventful and abrupt" and lacking the proper shading. Richard Dana Skinner said it was uneven yet convincing and perceptive.

FIRST YEAR, THE [Comedy/Marriage/Small Town/Family] A: Frank Craven; D: Winchell Smith; P: John Golden; T: Little Theatre; 10/20/20 (725)

An unpretentious comedy of young married life that became the biggest hit of its playwright-star's career and one to which reviewers would subsequently always refer as a standard of his achievement. "Simple, human and joyous is *The First Year*," began the *Times* review, which went on to detail the many homely but honest touches the author had assembled to spread a sense of warmth and familiarity over the audience.

The excellently produced work starred Craven as Thomas Tucker, an unromantic midwestern youth who woos and wins Grace Livingston (Roberta Arnold). After they are wed, a climactic dinner party for a business connection turns into a shambles; Grace grows disconsolate with her penny-pinching lifestyle and returns home to her mother. Thomas girds his loins, accomplishes a highly profitable real estate deal with the railroad company, which seeks a parcel of land he owns, and earns enough money to win back his wife's affections.

Walter Prichard Eaton decided that this was a play of significance because of the depth of its satiric realism and the accuracy with which all of the characters were limned. Joseph Wood Krutch, in his book *American Drama since 1918*, noted how perfectly the play captured the materialistic spirit of 1920: "To make a lot of money, to make it quick, and to make it by some method which rendered the magnitude of the result delightfully disproportionate to the effort involved was regarded as the most inspiring possible example."

FIVE O'CLOCK GIRL, THE [Musical/Romance] B: Guy Bolton and Fred Thompson; M/LY: Bert Kalmar and Harry Ruby; D: John Harwood; CH: Jack Haskell; S: Norman Bel Geddes; P: Philip Goodman; T: Forty-fourth Street Theatre; 10/10/27 (278)

Time capsulized this hit musical in these terms: "The jokes were moldy, the dancing deft, and the vast chorus uncommonly bewitching." Richard Dana Skinner jotted that it had "a barely adequate book, no voices worth mentioning, and all the mechanical routine of chorus and spotlighted principals." "Thinking of You" was the show's best song.

Mary Eaton starred as Patricia Brown, an assistant in a cleaning establishment who everyday at five o'clock talks on the phone with the good-looking Gerald Brooks (Oscar Shaw), whom she has never met. When she does meet him, she poses as a debutante and wears clothes borrowed from her firm. Gerald finds out the truth, but since this is a Cinderella story, it doesn't matter in the end.

Comedienne Pert Kelton was a standout in the show, especially during a show-stopping number in which she mimicked Spanish diseuse Raquel Meller.

FLAME OF LOVE [Drama/Period/China/Orientals/Romance/Fantasy] A: Maurice V. Samuels and Malcolm LaPrade; M: Ernest LaPrade; D: Frank Reicher; S: Eric Pape; C: Ami Mali Hicks; P: G. W. McGregor; T: Morosco Theatre; 4/21/24 (32)

Billed as a romantic drama of ancient China, *Flame of Love* was set in fourteenth-century Canfu. In a competition, a young weaver (Brandon Peters) seeks to reproduce the flaming pattern that wafted the weavers' goddess to heaven. He must, according to legend, remain pure to accomplish his task, but he falls to the temptation of a beautiful Circassian (Lenita Lane). The goddess takes pity on him, however, and enables him to win both the competition and the girl.

The Playgoer declared that the wrong medium had been chosen, for the story would make a charming book for an opera. The *Times* critic praised the care with which the production was mounted but found the play dull: "the continued stately procession of the play's formal language...cannot but tire."

H.H.

FLAMME, LA (The Flame) [Drama/Family/Sex/Marriage/French] A: Charles Méré; P: William A. Brady; T: Playhouse Theatre; 2/11/23 (1)

A single matinee performance was offered of this French work about Cleo (Jane Grey), who regains her son Hugh (Kenneth MacKenna) from her estranged spouse only when the latter is on his deathbed. She ends her affair with Boussat (John Cromwell) but returns to him when Hugh proves incapable of elevating her life.

Reviews are not available.

FLESH [Comedy-Drama/Prostitution/Sex/Romance] A: A. J. Lamb; D: Charles Hanna; P: United Arcades, Inc.; T: Princess Theatre; 5/7/25 (4)

A. J. Lamb, author of the popular old song "The Bird in the Gilded Cage," was responsible for this "absolutely incredible play" (*Times*), which was so dumbly conceived that the audience roared with laughter at the most inappropriate moments.

The terribly produced, written, acted, and staged play was about a girl (Madeline Davidson) who learns that her fiancé (William Balfour) frequents a certain fast woman of the town (Grayce Connell) and decides to arrange with the latter to surprise the fellow by waiting for him in the other's bed. When she does, she is witness to the visit of both the fiancé and the other woman's boyfriend (Edwin Guhl) and the fight that then breaks out. The young woman then decides to wed a certain doctor (George Patton) instead.

Following the opening-night debacle, a prologue was added informing the audience that the work was meant as a travesty on sex plays and was not intended to be taken seriously.

FLIGHT [Comedy/Sex/Romance] A: Susan Meriwether and Victor Victor; D: Lemist Esler; S: Livingston Platt; P: Laura D. Wilck; T: Longacre Theatre; 2/18/29 (41)

Because this frank and suggestive play about an unmarried flapper's sexual adventuring was not consistently sincere, Richard Dana Skinner declared, "its passages of would-be daring become merely cheap and inexcusable—when they are not likewise, one is compelled to add, childish and absurd."

Cynthia Larrimore (Miriam Hopkins), influenced by the marital dissatisfaction of her parents, which has led them to be promiscuous, follows a similar path with Terry Hamilton (John D. Seymour), but when she falls for John Hill (Donald Dillaway), her past with Terry returns to haunt her. Unsure whether Terry or John is the father of her soon-to-be-born infant, she contemplates abortion, but John salvages the situation by agreeing to remain with her and be the child's parent.

The Pollyanna ending was cloying, and the play leaned too heavily on sentimentality to be accepted as veracious.

FLORIANI'S WIFE (Come prima, meglio diprima) [Drama/Marriage/Family/Italian] A: Luigi Pirandello; TR: Ann Sprague MacDonald; D: Margaret Wycherly (with Henry Stillman); S: Livingston Platt; P: Greenwich Village Theatre b/s/a/w Cornelia Penfield Lathrop; T: Greenwich Village Theatre (OB); 10/1/23 (16)

"Far more surely than *Six Characters in Search of An Author*, the play at the Greenwich Village Theatre stamps Luigi Pirandello as an original dramatist of note" wrote John Corbin of *Floriani's Wife*. An ironic tale of a woman (Margaret Wycherly) driven by her husband into a lover's arms and induced to return home thirteen years later as the husband's second wife, the play focuses on the relationship of the mother-stepmother to her sixteen-year-old daughter (Mary Hone). The girl has made a cult of her "dead" mother's virtues and ultimately drives her "stepmother" away.

Corbin found Pirandello's ability to extract comedy from the painful situations in the play "a feat beyond any but a master of human reality." The *Tribune*'s critic thought that the play possessed "gloomy possibilities, though it was acted so vaguely that they were sometimes in the shadows."

H.H.

FLORIDA GIRL [Musical/Crime/Romance] B/LY: Paul Porter, Benjamin Hapgood Burt, and William A. Grew; M: Milton Suskind; D: Frederick Stanhope; CH: David Bennett; P: Earl Carroll; T: Lyric Theatre; 11/2/25 (40)

A musical comedy produced by revue master Earl Carroll; its lavish costuming and nimble dancing were its standout creative achievements, but it contained excellent performances by leads Lester Allen, Vivienne Segal, and the zany acrobatic comedy trio the Ritz Brothers.

As was often the case, the book was a mediocrity, possessing a few good gags meagerly distributed through its action. Its plot was about a detective, Sandy (Allen), with a dog named Satan (Anally Pupp), and his efforts to recover by midnight a slipper containing $100,000 in smuggled diamonds stolen from the dainty foot of the heroine Daphne (Segal) upon her arrival at Coral Gables, Florida. Using many disguises, Sandy accomplishes his task, and Daphne's romance with Henry Elkins (Irving Beebe) prospers.

Ward Morehouse reported that the show was "expensively staged, stunningly costumed, and...a rollicking and jubilant entertainment when it is dancing."

FLOSSIE [Musical/Romance] B/M: Armand Robi; LY: Ralph Murphy; P: Charles Mulligan; T: Lyric Theatre; 6/3/24 (16+)

Arthur Hornblow said this musical's "dubious distinction" was to have "the most banal book of any play of the season. The dialogue was crude beyond belief." A good jazz chorus was not enough to save this poor example of musical comedy from drifting away after a few weeks.

Its story was about a girl, Flossie (Doris Duncan), who tries to fool a clever uncle into believing that she is married to Archie (Sydney Grant), who really loves Bessie (Alice Cavanaugh). The uncle forces the issue by putting the couple into embarrassing situations until the truth emerges, and Flossie gets to marry the boy she really loves.

FLYING HIGH [Musical/Aviation/Romance] B/LY: B. G. De Sylva, Lew Brown, and Jack McGowan; M: B. G. De Sylva, Lew Brown, and Ray Henderson; D: Edward Clark Lilley; CH: Bobby Connolly; S: Joseph Urban; C: Charles Le Maire; P: George White; T: Apollo Theatre; 3/3/30 (355)

This was to be the last Broadway show on which the outstanding team of De Sylva, Henderson, and Brown collaborated, since De Sylva decided to go his own way thenceforth. Actually, the success of this blockbuster was not tied so much to their own contributions as it was to the hilarity induced by the ribald, low-down comedy of "Bert Lahr whose eyes are close together and easily crossed, who emits ape-like noises and resorts to other equally obvious antics. His most successful gag is a vulgar parody of a procedure common to all medical examinations" (*Time*). This gag caused the audience to howl for sixty-two seconds by B. G. De Sylva's clock. After being whirled about in a spinning machine, Lahr's character was handed a glass by the doctor, who said, "You know what to do with that." At first the dizzy clown did not understand. Then his face lit up in comprehension; he chuckled as he took a hip flask out of his pocket and poured the liquor into the glass. He handed it to the physician, saying "Here you are boy, that's all I can spare." Coauthor McGowan had bet $5 that the audience would be offended; John Lahr, in *Notes on a Cowardly Lion*, his biography of his father, Bert, said "The scene he thought would be offensive...became the biggest single laugh in the history of the American stage."

During the out-of-town tryouts the show was in serious trouble; the original sets were completely replaced, and producer George White redid all of the choreography and direction. When it opened in New York, the show came through "as one of those perfectly effortless entertainments which charm the beholder from the beginning and make him forget his surroundings and himself" (Francis R. Bellamy).

The plot involved the rivalry of two pilots in a transcontinental air-mail race. Lahr was "Rusty" Krause, a mechanic who breaks a record by keeping a plane in the air longer than anyone else, simply because he doesn't know how to land. The hero, Tod Addison (Oscar Shaw), wins his race and wins his girl (Grace Brinkley), whom he first met when he landed a plane on her New York apartment-house roof.

Lahr's side-splitting bits included his being pursued by the obese singer Kate Smith, playing his would-be girlfriend Pansy. Lahr and Smith had a running feud during the show; he disliked her for her relative lack of experience and poor sense of comedy; she was mad at him for his ad-libs at her expense (he once called her "Etna" onstage). Lahr scored singing "Mrs. Krause's Blue-Eyed Baby Boy." Smith did likewise with "Red Hot Chicago."

FOG [Drama/Mystery/Crime/Sea] A: John Willard; D: Arthur Hurley; S: Nicholas Yellenti; P: Lorton Production, Inc.; T: National Theatre; 2/7/27 (97)

A scenically interesting, but dramaturgically insipid, mystery melodrama set on a Long Island wharf and then in the rolling, rocking cabin of an old schooner cut loose in foggy Great South Bay. Bernard Simon considered "the evening...a great deal more sedative than thrilling," and First Nighter averred,"It's great child's play, but no play for an adult with more than the allowed thirteen-year-old intelligence."

The piece had to do with evil deeds upon the yacht during a formal party; several guests were thrown overboard, the host never appeared, and a black servant with the appearance of an African savage wandered through the action. At the end, a time bomb was set to go off in five minutes, and some suspense was whipped up by the search for it. Audiences were caught up sufficiently by the tension to scream out instructions to the threatened characters. Robert Keith and Vivienne Osborn were the principal players.

FOG-BOUND [Drama/Romance/Marriage/Small Town/Religion] A: Hugh Stanislaus Stange; D: Alfred Hickman; S: Nicholas Yellenti; P: Richard Herndon; T: Belmont Theatre; 4/1/27 (27)

A "worthy but faltering" (Brooks Atkinson) vehicle for Nance O'Neil. She portrayed a woman from a small Long Island fishing village who marries a fanatical fisherman-preacher (Alfred Hickman) at the insistence of her parents; when her true love, the sailor Lem (Curtis Cooksey), returns eighteen years later to claim her from her loveless marriage, she turns him down for fear that her daughter, who would be left behind, would suffer at the hands of the narrow-minded citizenry.

Nicholas Yellenti's atmospheric surfside setting was a highly effective backing for this well-produced staging, abundantly provided with numerous sound and lighting effects. Several noted the play's affinity to those of O'Neill, but the resemblance was like the way "morning cigar butts recall a comfortable evening of adventurous talk," declared Richard Dana Skinner.

FOLLOW THRU [Musical/Sports/Romance] B: Laurence Schwab and B. G. De Sylva; M/LY: B. G. De Sylva, Lew Brown, and Ray Henderson; D: Edgar J. MacGregor; CH: Bobby Connolly; S: Donald Oenslager; C: Kiviette; P: Laurence Schwab and Frank Mandel; T: Chanin's Forty-sixth Street Theatre; 1/9/29 (401)

Ernest Boyd enthused about this "musical slice of country club life": "It is undoubtedly one of the most amusing, tuneful, and attractively staged plays of its kind in the entire annals of musical comedy." With Irene Delroy and Zelma O'Neal as rival leading ladies fighting for the attention of handsome John Barker, and with John Sheehan and Jack Haley arousing bursts of bawdy laughter, the show's performance was in highly capable hands.

There was a lot of locker-room-level comedy in the romantic plot about a young professional golfer (Barker) who gets involved with a pretty miss (Delroy) to whom he gives lessons, following which she cops a country-club championship from her lover rival (Madeline Cameron) and also nabs the pro.

The *Times* glowed over this "fast, impudent and generally insane frolic." It had "Gymnastic dancing, agreeable songs, funny lines and the pace that kills." Song favorites introduced that are still heard included "You Are My Lucky Star," "Button Up Your Overcoat," and "I Want to Be Bad." Eleanor Powell, in the small role of Molly, attained her first Broadway success, and O'Neal, playing the role of Angie, a girl seeking to land wealthy Jack Martin (Haley), scored the show's biggest hit.

FOOL, THE [Drama/Religion/Labor] A: Channing Pollock; D: Frank Reicher; P: Selwyns; T: Times Square Theatre; 10/23/22 (272+)

A much talked-of problem play that Burns Mantle chose as one of the Ten Best of the Year. Critics took clear-cut sides in their reviews, and the controversy thus generated helped *The Fool* to snowball into a substantial run.

Daniel Gilchrist (James Kirkwood), a young minister returned from the horrors or war, strives to instill in his wealthy parishioners his compassionate brand of Christian socialism but is rebuffed and driven from his post. He meets with cold shoulders from the miners he seeks to aid and then from the people at a settlement house. Here a miracle occurs as a crippled girl (Sara Sothern) throws away her crutches and awes the crowd by the fool's mystical power. Finally, he is visited in his garret by a representative (Henry Stephenson) of the mining firm, who offers him a lucrative position, which he turns down to continue his selfless work for the underprivileged.

Pollock was trying to demonstrate what would happen if a contemporary man tried to live his life like Christ. His story actually was inspired by the life of St. Francis of Assisi. What many reviewers could not accept in this "routine melodrama of the spirit" (Arthur Hornblow) was its "deplorably mawkish" (Laurence Stallings) attitude, the way in which "dignity is sacrificed for melodrama" (Charles Darnton). Many, however, were deeply moved by this message play, but they too often were distracted by the work's shallow devices. Among *The Fool*'s advocates was Alexander Woollcott, who judged it a "vigorous, hard-hitting, intensely dramatic play."

Channing Pollock devoted a chapter of his autobiography *Harvest of My Years* to *The Fool*. He said that he had worked intermittently on it for over a dozen years, and finally decided to write it in earnest when he had grown weary of his usual work as a hack dramatist. He drew its title from an Alfred Lord Tennyson quote, "They called me in the public squares/The Fool that wears a crown of thorns." Upon completion of the script it was promptly shown to and turned down by twenty-eight producers, none of whom wanted to put on a serious play with a religious theme. The producer who did agree to do it, Arch Selwyn, did so without even hearing the entire work, the reading of which was interrupted by Selwyn's aching tooth. After producer Sam H. Harris took a twenty-five percent interest in the play, it was tried out in a Los Angeles stock company with Richard Bennett in the lead as Gilchrist. Bennett left the show, but Sara Sothern, an unknown, went on with the show to New York and London where she gained kudos. She retired early but her daughter became the famous film star, Elizabeth Taylor. When Sam Harris bowed out of the production, fearing a debacle, author Pollock took over his share of the show. Before the show could be produced on Broadway, all the sets were destroyed in a warehouse fire. They were rebuilt on the cheap, since the originals had not been insured. One flat continued to flap in the wind throughout the run. The show opened to very weak business, with only $500 in the house on the second night. Pollock, formerly a press agent for top producers, set to work to promote the piece, especially after receiving numerous letters of support from prominent persons who had attended the first performances. He took a quarter-page newspaper ad citing their letters, and headlined it "ARE ALL THESE MEN FOOLS?" A letter-writing and speech-making campaign followed, and the show was further aided by sermons in its favor from local pulpits. By the fourth week, the show, once in danger of early death, began to sell out, and soon extra matinees were added to increase the weekly total of performances to twelve. Seven companies toured with the play that season, five million playgoers got to see it, and over $1 million in profit was earned. According to Ward Morehouse in *Matinee Tomorrow*, Pollock asserted, "The critics didn't like it because I didn't lie down and play dead. . . . I've had thirty-two productions and out of all that I've only received eight good notices. But I've made a million and a half and I can tell anybody to go to hell, including the critics.''

FOOL'S BELLS [Comedy/Fantasy/Romance/War] A: A. E. Thomas; M: Percy Wenrich; SC: a story by Leona Dalrymple; D: Walter F. Scott; P: Donald Gallaher and James W. Elliott; T: Criterion Theatre; 12/23/25 (5)

The Criterion Theatre, for years devoted to the cinema, returned to the legitimate with this five-performance turkey of a "comedy fantasy" by the well-known A. E. Thomas. It began with a prologue set in the present, revealing David Hewitt (Donald Gallaher), a self-conscious hunchback who has written a play about a fantasy hunchback; this play-within-the-play is then enacted, occupying most of the drama, before returning to the present in an epilogue. In the play-within-the-play the hunchback is shown as a man who, through the positive power of good deeds, attains happiness and a straightened spine. He is aided by the fair tenement lass Lucy Grey (Sara Sothern) whom he loves. In the epilogue, the playwright, convinced of his viewpoint, leaves his sweetheart behind as he departs to take part in World War I.

Time wrote the play off as "something terrible"; Percy Hammond said it "lost its mind and went to pieces in several unstrung and unnecessary episodes." The best things on view were the character portrayals of Donald Meek and Beryl Mercer in supporting roles.

FOOLS ERRANT [Drama/Marriage/Labor/Romance] A: Louis Evan Shipman; D: B. Iden Payne; P: Messrs. Shubert; T: Maxine Elliott's Theatre; 8/21/22 (64)

An improbable drama about a hardy idealist, Eric Brierly (Cyril Keightley), who, having given up the good life to live and work among the depressed miners of Minnesota, returns East to visit Fanny, his former heart's affection (Lucile Watson), who married in his stead John Pritchard (Vincent Serrano). When he learns that John is having an affair with Greta (Alexandra Carlisle), he attempts to help Fanny out by convincing Greta to come back with him to Minnesota as his wife. Eric and Greta's life among the miners brings them truly close to one another, but John and Fanny fail to be reconciled; when John dies and Fanny seeks out Eric, she learns that she has become an unwanted third wheel.

The hero, intended as "a quixotic ass," seemed more "a foolish ass," "much too priggish to be endured" (Heywood Broun). The dialogue sounded inflated: "The people. . .talk like the better sort of English essayists. . . . But they seldom, if ever, say dramatic things" (Kenneth Macgowan).

FOOTLIGHTS [Musical/Show Business/Romance] B/LY: Roland Oliver; M: Harry Denny; D: Francis "Bunny" Weldon; S: August Vimnera; P: The Tom Cat, Inc.; T: Lyric Theatre; 8/19/27 (43)

An egregiously poor spoof of musical comedies in the making, *Footlights* combined the specialty acts of conventional vaudeville, a lot of running about in the audience, and a boy meets girl theme within a loose plot about small towner George Weston (J. Kent Thurber), who is induced by producer Jacob Perlstein (Louis Sorin) and burlesque queen Violet Wilding (Ruth Wheeler) to invest $20,000 in their show. He loses the money but finds true love with Hazel Deane (Ellalee Ruby) and goes back home with her in his arms.

"It is. . . one of those plays," declared the *Times*, "which cause little sidewalk groups to debate. . . whether or not it is the worst they have ever seen."

FOR ALL OF US [Comedy/Religion/Invalidism/Alcoholism/Business/Family/ Romance] A/D: William Hodge; S: Watson Barratt; P: Lee Shubert; T: Forty-ninth Street Theatre; 10/15/23 (216)

Called "the apostle of wholesomeness in the theatre" in the *Times*, playwright and longtime star William Hodge portrayed Tom Griswell, a ditch digger converted to a Bible-based philosophy of clean mind and body during a thirty-day jail hitch for drunkenness. The laborer's happy whistling outside his home attracts the attention of a wealthy, partially paralyzed banker (Frank Losee), who invites Tom inside. Tom converts the banker, whose paralysis disappears, and discovers his long-lost daughter in the person of the banker's stenographer. The banker gives his blessing for the stenographer and his son to marry.

Although he found the play given to moralizing, the *Times* critic praised Hodge for gaining his effects quietly and gave him a left-handed compliment for so underplaying stock situations that the play did not seem the kind "characteristically written by an actor."

H.H.

FOR BETTER OR WORSE [Comedy-Drama/Sex/Marriage] A: Allen de Lano; D: Tom Powers; T: Mansfield Theatre; 1/31/27 (16)

A befuddled piece about a spoiled, pompous, educated young man (Tom Powers), who marries the illiterate orphan girl (Gladys Hurlbut) working as a servant in his mother's home when the evidence of his seduction swells her womb, only to discover that the disparity in their interests is driving him to distraction. When the wife declares their child is not his, the husband is finally able to calm down and begin to smooth out the kinks in their relationship.

"As a play it is all for the worse," ventured *Time*, while the *Times* judged it "Lopsided, overwritten and overplayed.

FOR GOODNESS SAKE [Musical/Marriage] B: Fred Jackson; M: William Daly and Paul Lanin; LY: Arthur Jackson; ADD. M.: George Gershwin; ADD. LY.: Arthur Francis (Ira Gershwin); D: Priestly Morrison; CH: Allan K. Foster; P: Alex A. Aarons; T: Lyric Theatre; 2/20/22 (103)

"An agreeable if not brilliant musical" (Alexander Woollcott) that came alive mainly because of the unique dance and comedy talents of the youthful siblings Fred and Adele Astaire. Not much could be done to salvage the weak plot and shallow dialogue. There were some good tunes (including the Gershwin interpolations "Someone" and "Tra-la-la"), some pretty girls, and a couple of comic moments. The piece was about how Perry Reynolds (John E. Hazzard) incurs his wife's (Marjorie Gateson) unwarranted jealousy when seen removing a speck from a pretty woman's eye; he is made miserable by his wife's vengeful flirtations and plans to make her think he has committed suicide but fails when she overhears the plot. He ends up an unwelcome visitor under his own piano and dining table, a situation that Hazzard exploited for all of its humorous value. Also funny in the piece was comic actor Charles Judels.

The Astaires played the supporting roles of the young lovers Lawrence and Suzanne; Woollcott noted how skillful they were becoming as comedians, "particularly the feminine member of the team." Robert Benchley wrote, "When they dance everything seems brighter and their comedy alone would be good enough to carry them through even if they were to stop dancing (which God forbid!)." The show was the first association of the Astaires with George Gershwin (whose brother Ira, under another name, provided some lyrics) in what was to be an important professional relationship in coming years.

FOR VALUE RECEIVED [Drama/Romance/Literature] A: Ethel Clifton; D: Augustin Duncan; T: Longacre Theatre; 5/7/23 (48)

A bromidic melodrama of ultimately requited love in which contrivances of plotting ran side by side with strong dramatic values. It was "good average entertainment," opined Burns Mantle. "A little stiffly written in certain passages, it frequently erupts with the type of emotional scene that was more popular a decade ago than it is today."

The plot concerns the relationship between successful writer Almeric Thomson (Augustin Duncan) and his attractive secretary Beverly Mason (Maude Hanaford), who travel together as husband and wife so that Beverly can better minister to the writer, who is losing his vision. Almeric's coolness toward her leads Beverly to the arms of Lawrence Banning (Louis Kimball). A charge of embezzlement against her by the writer's lawyer eventuates in her disclosure that she took the money because she had actually written Almeric's best-selling works and that the money was spent on her crippled sister's (Eleanor Griffith) music schooling. She had thus paid fully for value received. After a year's separation, Almeric and Beverly are reconciled.

FORBIDDEN; OR, VIRGINIA RUNS AWAY [Comedy/Youth/Sex/Romance/Family] A: Sydney Rosenfelt; P: John Cort; T: Daly's Sixty-third Street Theatre; 10/1/23 (8)

"An Ibsen theme Mack Sennetized" proclaimed L.W. of this comedy about a rebellious seventeen-year-old girl (Josephine Stevens) who tries to elope with a callow youth. A sympathetic aunt sends her to a Freudian analyst (Harry

Minturn), who, in thirty-six hours, understands her soul and wins her love and her hand. B.F. found the work "a bright and sophisticated comedy with pleasant banter and cheerful plot."

H.H.

(1) FORBIDDEN ROADS (El Caudal de los hijos) [Drama/Marriage/Spanish/ Spanish Language] A: Jose Lopez Pinillos; P: Maria Guerrero-Fernando Diaz Company of Madrid i/a/w Walter O. Lindsey; T: Manhattan Opera House (OB); 5/22/26 (1)

The visiting company of Guerrero and Diaz from Madrid's Princess Theatre offered *El Caudal de los hijos* as part of their eight-play repertoire, but reviews are not available.

(2) [Dramatic Revival] AD: Roland Oliver; D: Henry Stillman; P: Walter O. Lindsey and James E. Kenney; T: Liberty Theatre; 4/16/28 (16)

An English-language version of *El Caudal de los hijos*, titled *Forbidden Roads* but more accurately called *The Heritage of the Children*. It was "a play with a moderately interesting story, but which is both written and acted in a hammer-and-tongs fashion" (*Times*).

The theme of the play was Honor, presented in a story about a husband (Robert Bentley) who, to save the honor of his young son, forbears from killing the man who is about to have an affair with his wife (Judith Voselli). When the son (Alan Birmingham) reaches manhood, he finds himself in the same marital entanglement and, for the same reason, at his parent's urging, lets the would-be seducer go. When the wife (Maxine Calvert) attempts to run off with her lover, the mother shoots her.

Perriton Maxwell considered this "a dull and rarely interesting preachment upon the honor of a family name."

FORTUNE TELLER, THE [Musical Revival] B/LY: Harry B. Smith; M: Victor Herbert; D: Milton Aborn; P: Jolson Theatre Musical Comedy Company; T: Jolson's Fifty-ninth Street Theatre; 11/4/29 (16)

A new production of the Victor Herbert comic opera first seen in New York in the 1898–1899 season and with Tessa Kosta in the triple role of Musette, Irma, and Lieutenant Feodor. It was produced as one of a series of Milton Aborn operetta revivals put on at Jolson's Theatre.

In her tripartite performance of the ballerina, gypsy maid, and manly soldier, Tessa Kosta "had sweetness and charm, and carried all the romantic illusions intended by the composer," jotted the *Times*. Aside from her performance, the show seemed ill prepared, but the score, especially "Gypsy Love Song," still impressed.

49ERS, THE [Revue] CN: George S. Kaufman and Marc Connelly; B: George S. Kaufman, Morrie Ryskind and Howard Dietz, Franklin Pierce Adams and

Arthur Samuels, Robert Benchley and Dorothy Parker, Heywood Broun, Montague Glass, Ring Lardner, Marc Connelly, and so on; D: Howard Lindsay; P: George C. Tyler; T: Punch and Judy Theatre; 11/7/22 (15)

A comedy revue inspired by a one-night amateur revue written by members of the literary clique known as the members of the Round Table at the Algonquin Hotel. That show had been called *No, Siree!* and many of its participants took part in the creation and performance of this show. The new work's title came from its being given at a theatre on Forty-ninth Street. Sketches were contributed by more than a dozen famous and not-so-famous humorists. The work was dependent for its success on the quality of its satire, and in this sphere it was uneven. Critical response was disappointing, and it folded early.

A principal weakness was the use of vaudevillian May Irwin as mistress of ceremonies. Marc Connelly stated in his memoirs *Voices Offstage* that he took over on the second night and did far better in the role than she.

On the program were bits such as Kaufman's "Life in the Back Pages," which depicted American life as lived in the magazine ads; "Power of Light," Morrie Ryskind and Howard Dietz's Russian burlesque; a parody of musical comedies with business themes by Franklin Pierce Adams and Arthur Samuels; Robert Benchley and Dorothy Parker's historical pastiche, "Nero"; Heywood Broun's "A Robe for the King"; Montague Glass's satire on the funeral business, "Omit Flowers"; a now-famous nonsense skit by Ring Lardner, "The Tridget of Greva"; and a Connelly created midwestern folk dance, "The Dance of the Small Town Mayors."

FOUNTAIN, THE [Drama/Period/Romance/Fantasy/Historical-Biographical] A: Eugene O'Neill; M: Macklin Morrow; D/DS: Robert Edmond Jones; P: Kenneth Macgowan, Robert Edmond Jones, and Eugene O'Neill; T: Greenwich Village Theatre (OB); 12/10/25 (24)

It took Eugene O'Neill four years to get this play, written in 1921, produced, and even then he had to participate in its mounting as a coproducer. Its Off-Broadway staging gained much atttention, but the artistic triumphs were the sets and staging of Robert Edmond Jones. O'Neill's play was a vast disappointment, especially since it marked a turning from what he half-ironically called in a program note themes of "morbid realism" to those of historical romance. O'Neill noted that he was interested in writing not a historically accurate play but an invention based on the historical characters of Columbus (Henry O'Neill) and Ponce de Leon (Walter Huston); the latter was drawn more as fiction than fact. But the playwright failed to embody his drama in terms as theatrically satisfying as those he had achieved in his best earlier plays, and *The Fountain* emerged as "an evening of pageantry, badly proportioned, diffuse and wearisome, despite the poetic beauty of its conception" (Brooks Atkinson).

This long and often tedious eleven-scene play chronicled Ponce de Leon's quest for the fountain of youth. He was seen as a young adventurer in Granada, as a passenger on Columbus's new world-bound flagship, in Puerto Rico, falling unhappily in love with the daughter (Rosalinde Fuller) of a former mistress, discovering Florida, being betrayed by the Indians as he drank from what he presumed the source of eternal youthfulness, and dying in a scene replete with the visions of various symbolic figures from his past after he has learned, as John Mason Brown expressed it, that the fountain of youth "did not exist except in youth renewing itself afresh from generation to generation and perpetuating its own ideas."

FOUR IN HAND [Comedy/Marriage/Austrian] A: Paul Frank and Siegfried Geyer; AD: Roy Briant and E. L. Gerstein; T: Greenwich Village Theatre (OB); 9/6/23 (4)

An adaptation from the German that proved to be seriously flawed and amateurish in conception and execution. "The acting was in thorough keeping with the dramaturgy," advised the *Times*. Galina Kopernak, a Russian actress, appeared as the Wife, a temperamental person who acquires a divorce because her husband (Robert Rendel) does not provide adequate proof of his jealousy but who remarries him once his jealous nature is apparent.

H.H.

FOUR ONE-ACT PLAYS [One-Acts] A: Clare Kummer; D: W. H. Gilmore; T: Punch and Judy Theatre; 2/28/21 (12)
"Bridges" [Comedy]; "The Choir Rehearsal" [Musical]; "The Robbery" [Comedy]; "Chinese Love" [Musical/China]

A program of four one-acts that received mostly approving notices. Two of the offerings were musicals, and the material ranged from sophisticated farce to small-town farce. "The Robbery," in which a New York couple return to their apartment unexpectedly to find their daughter (Ruth Gillmore) sleeping in the arms of a stranger (Sidney Blackmer) who turns out to be an innocent youth from across the street, was the best liked. Kummer's skill was praised highly, and "her dialogue in each case has the charm characteristic of her comedy satire and the naive way in which she works up to her climaxes is delicious," declared *Variety*.

FOUR ONE-ACTS [One-Acts] P: Inter-Theatre Arts; T: Little Theatre; 1/28/23 (1)

A bill of four one-acts employing the distinguished services of players such as Tom Powers, Moffat Johnston, Elliot Cabot, Gladys Hurlbut, Margaret Wycherly, and Henry O'Neill. The plays were Claude Habberstad's "Cat Comes Back," Lascelles Abercrombie's "Staircase," Constance Wilcox's "Heart of Frances," and Harry Wagstaff Gribble's "All Gummed Up." Not much is known about their contents. The *Times* observed that "The plays successfully realized the illusions of comedy, tragedy and fantasy variously intended by their authors."

FOUR WALLS [Drama/Crime/Romance/Jews] A: Dana Burnet and George Abbott; D: George Abbott; S: Cirker and Robbins; P: John Golden; T: John Golden Theatre; 9/19/27 (144)

Thirty-two-year-old Paul Muni, then known as Muni Wisenfrend, was a sensation in this, his second English-speaking role after years of work in the Yiddish theatre. *Four Walls* (originally titled *The Prisoner*) offered him a superb part in a rousing melodrama in which his character, Benny Horowitz, was a Lower East Side hoodlum just released from Sing Sing after a five-year stay and determined to go straight. His home-brewed philosophy is to steer clear of all social and romantic encumbrances and remain completely his own man. But circumstances go against him; when a ruckus over his former girlfriend (Jeanne Green) leads to his accidental killing of another gangster, he chooses to surrender to the cops rather than to the lying wiles of the lady in question.

A large cast of Lower East Side types (some of them acted by familiar Yiddish theatre players, such as Clara Langsner and Muni's wife, Bella Finkel) gave a flavorful background to this theatrical but engrossing play. "*Four Walls* is a play to see, a vivid dramatic photograph of a phase of New York life," wrote Perriton Maxwell. The leading actor, wrote Richard Dana Skinner, gave to his role "a richness and understanding rarely seen on the English-speaking stage." Lee Strasberg and Sanford Meisner had minor roles in the drama.

The role of Benny was a departure for Muni, who had specialized in old-man roles.

FOUR-FLUSHER, THE [Comedy/Small Town/Legacy/Romance/Business] A: Caesar Dunn; D: Edgar J. MacGregor; P: Mack Hilliard; T: Apollo Theatre; 4/13/25 (65)

A rags to riches story about a hapless small-town shoe-store clerk, Andy Whittaker (Russell Mack), who would like to wed a certain dowager's (Margaret Dumont) daughter (Sue MacManamy) and become store manager; he learns that a millionaire uncle (Spencer Charters) may die of a weak heart and leave him about a million dollars. The comedy involves mainly Andy's high living, when, with word of the prospective legacy bruited about, he is extended credit by all of the businesses in sight, only for him to crash when the inheritance seems not to be forthcoming; he rises again, however, on the strength of a shoe arch he invents and sells for a fortune. He marries a pretty cashier instead of the dowager's girl.

Broadly humorous, this comedy, a first play, was deemed "a simple and unpretending" work by Ward Morehouse, who described it as "a play that is artificial of line, plot and characterization." Joseph Wood Krutch was disturbed by the overt acquisitive materialism of this and similar works and noted how closely the author had struck a spark of kinship with those who attended its run.

FRANK FAY'S FABLES [Revue] CN/B/LY/D: Frank Fay; P: Harry L. Cort; T: Park Theatre; 2/6/22 (32)

Musical numbers, both sung and danced, and acted sketches, both comic and melodramatic, served up by genial host, writer, and director Frank Fay comprised this pleasant diversion at the Park Theatre (called the Park Music Hall during the run). Some amusing, tuneful, and well-staged selections were done by a quartet comprised of Fay, Bernard Granville, Eddie Carr, and Herbert Corthell. The foursome was delightful as the "Three Musical McGluckens," playing their grand finale on metal radiators. Among the other good performers was Fania Marinoff, who did an old-time Western melodrama skit with Fay and Granville.

FREDDY [Comedy/Marriage/Romance/Sex/British] A/D: C. Stafford Dickens; S: P. Dodd Ackerman; P: Murray Phillips; T: Lyceum Theatre; 7/16/29 (63)

A quadrangular comedy about the romantic interrelationships of a husband (C. Stafford Dickens), wife (Beatrice Terry), bachelor (Raymond Walburn), and bachelorette (Vera Neilson) in which the first aims for the fourth and the second goes for the third, but which ends with numbers three and four seeking each other out. "It was familiar material in the less pretentious theatre, and put together with obvious effort, but it was acted with more style than you might have expected," reported Brooks Atkinson.

FREE SOUL, A [Drama/Mystery/Crime/Gambling/Trial/Romance/Law/Alcoholism] A: Willard Mack; SC: the novel of the same name by Adela Rogers St. John; D: George Cukor; P: William A. Brady; T: Playhouse Theatre; 1/12/28 (100)

Stephen Ashe (Lester Lonergan), alcoholic society attorney, has brought up his daughter Jan (Kay Johnson) to be a totally free and unconventional soul and has not denied her the acquaintance of the gamblers and sporting men with whom he himself is friendly. When her dad fails to stay on the wagon, despite his promise, she weds a gambler (Melvyn Douglas) who shortly afterwards shoots Jan's former society boyfriend (Henry Whittemore) for paying undue attention to his wife. The gambler is acquitted at his trial, thanks to the attorney's help; the latter dies at the end.

"All this made an acceptable melodrama for the inexacting," said *Time*. The *Times* critic was entertained throughout, but called the play "florid and more than a little implausible. . . . It is a play of unashamed theatricalism, of . . . hokum adroitly employed."

An interesting sidelight on this production is the fact that during its run, veteran producer William A. Brady took over Lester Lonergan's role and performed it with remarkable vigor and panache, even though he did not trouble to learn his lines.

FRENCH DOLL, THE (Jeunes filles de palaces) [Comedy/Romance/Family/French] A: Paul Armont and Marcel Gerbidon; AD: A. E. Thomas; D: W. H. Gilmore; P: E. Ray Goetz; T: Lyceum Theatre; 2/20/22 (120)

A. E. Thomas's Americanized version of this French fluff was "A Boulevard salad with very little dressing,'' according to Arthur Hornblow. The plot of this ''heavy-footed comedy'' (Kenneth Andrews) was a well-worn one about a poor Gallic family that hopes to strike it rich by having their pretty daughter Georgina (Irene Bordoni) marry into money. The wheels of their rapacious plan are turning smoothly and the millionaire they are aiming for (Thurston Hall) is nearly theirs, but Georgina finds herself in love with the equally impoverished young Philip (Don Burroughs) and cannot bring herself to wed the wealthy man. Finally, after various obstacles are overcome, the play ends happily, if with excessive sentimentality.

Throughout, its ''bright and never too dull'' dialogue made it ''good fun'' for Alexander Woollcott, but Hornblow thought that without the fine acting of the company the piece would have been ''of the sleeping variety.'' Irene Bordoni's ''immaculate and radiant'' (Andrews) performance was enlivened by a few interpolated songs, one of which, the naughty George Gershwin/B. G. De Sylva ''Do It Again,'' was encored.

FRENCH LEAVE [Comedy/War/France/Sex/Marriage/Military/British] A: Reginald Berkeley; P: Marc Klaw, Inc.; T: Belmont Theatre; 11/8/20 (56)

Used to kick off the Coburns's season, this was a belated war play about the British army at the front. Capt. Harry Glenister's (Alexander Onslow) pretty wife, Dolly (Mrs. Coburn), defies regulations and comes to headquarters disguised as Mlle. Juliette, a Paris singer. Brig.-Gen. Archibald Root (Charles Coburn) suspects her of being a spy; her husband not only is liable to a court-martial, he must also observe Root's amorous interest in Dolly. But the truth emerges, Dolly's charm pacifies the general, and all is forgiven.

Kenneth Macgowan declared that the only success achieved by the piece was in the performance of comic character-actor Dallas Welford as a discipline-loving corporal. Referring to its old-fashioned nature, Alexander Woollcott said it could ''be roughly described as one of those plays in which two men, each looking for the same woman, crawl around in the dark until they bump into each other.''

M.M.-C.

FRIEND INDEED, A [Comedy/Small Town/Journalism/Business/Romance] A: Bernhard Voight and Clayton Hamilton; P: Mary Forrest; T: Central Park Theatre (OB); 4/26/26 (16)

''An artless little racket'' of a play produced Off Broadway with a ''generally amateurish'' company (*Herald Tribune*), it was set in the town of Tarkington, Indiana, and offered insights into the local newspaper business. The *Times* said it was ''a little truer to the theatre than it was to newspapers.''

Its plot concerned a journal whose lagging circulation is boosted by the scheme of a sharp young fellow (Roland Hogue) to print a phony story about a burglary and thus scoop the rival paper. This clever gentleman saves the day and marries the heiress (Ruth Easton).

FROM MORN TO MIDNIGHT (Von Morgens bis Mitternacht) [Drama/ Crime/Family/Sex/German] A: Georg Kaiser; TR: Ashley Dukes; D: Frank Reicher; DS: Lee Simonson; P: Theatre Guild; T: Garrick Theatre; 5/14/22 (2); Frazee Theatre; 6/5/22 (56)

Considered one of the finest examples of the German expressionist style of playwriting (then experiencing a European vogue), *From Morn to Midnight* was the first major play in this much-discussed style to reach New York. It had premiered under Max Reinhardt in Germany in 1917, a year after its publication and five years after it was written. Only the adventurous Theatre Guild had the courage to show this unique work to Broadway, first in a subscriber-only pair of performances and then to audiences at large when the play was shifted to the Frazee Theatre. The play's influence on Americans who attempted to borrow its techniques was seen in works such as John Howard Lawson's *Processional* and Elmer Rice's *The Adding Machine*.

From Morn to Midnight concentrated on evoking in two parts and seven "stations" the inner world of an automaton-like Everyman, the Cashier (Frank Reicher), whose fantasies of escape are spurred by the presence in his bank of the beautiful Lady (Helen Westley); he seizes a 60,000 marks deposit and flees. The play follows his eventful day "from morn to midnight" as a fugitive; ultimately, he is turned in to the police for the reward by a Salvation Army girl (Ernita Lascelles), and kills himself, dying as all of the lights go out from a short circuit.

This gripping modern allegory on a person's useless martyrdom to money was written and produced in a manner designed to evoke a vivid fantasy world of people without names or individual identities, all of them seen from the viewpoint of the central character's feverish brain. The Theatre Guild staging was an "extraordinary" (Alison Smith) one with a brilliant company and imaginatively suggestive settings by Lee Simonson.

FRONT PAGE, THE [Comedy/Journalism/Politics/Crime/Romance/Prostitution] A: Ben Hecht and Charles MacArthur; D: George S. Kaufman; S: Raymond Sovey; P: Jed Harris; T: Times Square Theatre; 8/14/28 (281)

It was commonly believed among critics that stories about newspaper life did not make good plays until this ground-breaking comedy-melodrama appeared and became the exception that proved the rule. It opened only thirteen days before another heralded play about journalists, Ward Morehouse's *Gentlemen of the Press*, appeared, the latter being only a modest 128-performance hit but supporting the former's evidence that no matter what the background, an effective treatment could make it palatable.

The Front Page, a Best Play of the Year, and frequently revived since its inaugural mounting, was a side-splitting comedy about Chicago crime reporters written by two former Chicago newspaper men. Its juicy dialogue was considered pungent and honestly expressive of the salty speech native to its milieu, and the tag line "The son-of-a-bitch stole my watch" has become famous. The play's inside look at the profane behavior and dedicated professionalism of its subjects gained it a reputation for honesty, while offering audiences a group of characters and a number of situations that kept them continually involved. "Most admirably directed by George S. Kaufmann [*sic*], *The Front Page* simply swept along and swept its audience off their feet with its speed, boisterousness, veracity and that quintessential hokum which is 'good theatre.' " Lee Tracy, Osgood Perkins, and Dorothy Stickney gave what were among the finest portrayals of their careers in it.

Set in the press room of the Chicago Criminal Courts Building, it gathered together a motley crew of vulgar card-playing, unkempt, wise-cracking reporters and placed them in the midst of a plot in which (1) reporter Hildy Johnson (Tracy) is desirous of leaving the *Herald-Examiner* to marry Peggy Grant (Frances Fuller), much to the chagrin of his hard-boiled editor Walter Burns (Osgood Perkins), who schemes to stop him, while (2) Earl Williams (George Leach), condemned murderer, escapes his captors and, wounded, hides out in the press room's rolltop desk. To Burns's delight, Hildy is drawn into covering the case while the bride waits at the station. Once all is resolved, in a swirl of cops, politicos, and the gunman's prostitute girlfriend (Stickney), Hildy leaves, but Burns manages to put one last obstacle in the path to his departure.

Richard Dana Skinner and a few others argued that the play's success was owing strictly to its brilliant staging and acting. As writing he said it was "a hodgepodge of plot mechanics, vast improbabilities, deliberate hokum and faked sentimentalities." But Robert Littell maintained that, "*The Front Page*, farcical and improbable as it may seem when you take a second look at its framework, at the time of seeing it first has the sharp taste of novelty and the tumultuous unexpected surprises of real life."

It should, perhaps, be added that producer Jed Harris claimed in his memoirs *A Dance on the High Wire* that he was responsible for much of the plotting used in the play. He also noted that director Kaufman oversaw much of the writing and came up with the play's title. Harris declared that the play was based on real Chicago journalists: "It was one of the marvels of *The Front Page* that although all the characters were actual people, nobody ever thought of suing us for invasion of privacy. Indeed they all turned up for the opening night in Chicago and simply wallowed in delight. When the curtain fell at the end of the first act, the roar that rose from the auditorium sounded like the bellowing of a herd of wild animals. . . . Above this din one great monster of a voice could be heard yelling: 'MAKE IT MORE PERSONAL!' "

Dorothy Stickney, who played the tart Molly Malloy had a scene where she had to jump out of a window to her death. To accomplish this, a hole was dug in the stage floor outside the setting window, and the actress dove onto a mattress set up in the basement. On the dress rehearsal night, she banged her elbow in the process and did not realize until three days later that she had chipped the bone. She had to play for three weeks in a cast with her arm in a sling matching her black lace dress.

The Front Page was the first play for which George S. Kaufman received sole credit as director; he went on to become one of Broadway's greatest comedy directors as well as one of its most successful playwrights. A major problem he had in *The Front Page* concerned Dorothy Stickney's reluctance to speak her entrance line, "I've been looking for you bastards." According to Howard Teichman's *George S. Kaufman*, the director got the prim actress to speak the line by taking her aside and telling her that the words were "inserted solely for the purpose of arousing sympathy from the audience for the character she was playing."

FUERZA CIEGA, LA (The Blind Destiny) [Drama/Marriage/Sex/Spanish Language/Uruguayan] A: Vincente Martinez Cuitino; P: Camila Quiroga and the Argentine Players; T: Manhattan Opera House (OB); 12/6/27 (1)

A Uruguayan drama presented by a visiting troupe from Buenos Aires; their outstanding performer was the actress Camila Quiroga. This work was "a strange mixture of vaudeville and melodrama," noted the *Times*. It was awkwardly directed and given to outmoded tactics such as allowing actors to stop the action as they acknowledged applause.

The tempestuous drama concerned a marriage in which the husband discovers that his wife was formerly seduced by his own father and is consequently urged by the wife to commit patricide. As the wife, Quiroga justified all of the advance publicity bestowed on her, but the role was deemed unworthy of her talents.

FUNNY FACE [Musical/Romance/Crime] B: Fred Thompson and Paul Gerard Smith; M: George Gershwin; LY: Ira Gershwin; D: Edgar J. MacGregor; CH: Bobby Connolly; S: John Wenger; C: Kiviette; P: Alex A. Aarons and Vinton Freedley; T: Alvin Theatre; 11/22/27 (250)

Fred and Adele Astaire soared across the boards in this, their third Gershwin musical, and were joined by elaborately comedic performances given by Victor Moore and William Kent, who made golden humor of cracks such as the one about turning in one's "chivalry for a Cadillac." Fred and Adele, reported Brooks Atkinson, "have not only humor but intelligence; not only spirit but good taste; not only poise but modesty; and they are not only expert eccentric dancers but they never make an ungraceful movement." With these players and a score counting among its riches "High Hat" (performed by Fred in tails with a similarly dressed chorus), "S'Wonderful," the verbally felicitous "Babbitt and the Bromide," "Funny Face," "He Loves and She Loves," and "My One and Only," the banal plot was a mere bagatelle offering an excuse for first-rate singing, acting, and dancing.

Adele Astaire was Frankie, and Fred was her protective guardian Jimmie Reeve. Desiring her pearls, which Jimmie has locked in a safe, Frankie conspires with boyfriend Peter (Allan Kearns) to snatch them. Complications crop up when burlesque burglars Herbert (Moore) and Dugsie (Kent) turn up in search of the gems, but Frankie gets what she wants at the end.

The show's success was not predictable, since its creative period had been shaken by the defection of book writer Robert Benchley, who was replaced by Paul Gerard Smith. The title was also changed, from *Smarty*. Victor Moore's role was incorporated at nearly the last moment. The production opened the new Alvin Theatre (its name was a combination formed from those of producers Alex A. Aarons and Vinton Freedley) on Fifty-second Street.

FURIES, THE [Drama/Crime/Mental Illness/Romance] A: Zoë Akins; D: George Cukor; S: James Reynolds; P: John Tuerk; T: Shubert Theatre; 3/7/28 (41)

All this overblown play offered, said Robert Littell, was "some remarkably fine acting by Miss Laurette Taylor, some stunningly original sets by Mr. James Reynolds, and a brand new variety of strained and luxurious meaninglessness." It was about the murder of the wealthy husband of Fifi Sands (Taylor) shortly after he accedes to her request for a divorce. The District Attorney (Alfred Kappeler) arrives to investigate. The murderer seems to be Owen MacDonald (Frederick Worlock), in love with Fifi, who, like Claudius in *Hamlet*, conspired with her to rob Fifi's son (Alan Campbell) of his legacy. The killer turns out to be Oliver Bedloe (A. E. Anson), an insane lawyer, also in love with Fifi; he solves everything by diving out of an apartment window forty-two stories up.

The play was not in typical mystery play form but was adorned "with dinner table conversation, with quotations from poetry, with roulades from an orchestra back-stage, and with all the pomp and ceremony of high circumstance," according to Brooks Atkinson.

The Furies was also notable for its use of *Strange Interlude*-like asides (the O'Neill classic had opened a month earlier) and for its deployment of expressionistic scenic devices that, by their use of odd angles and various distortions, clearly suggested the insanity of the killer.

G

GALA NIGHT [Comedy/Show Business/Romance] A: Laurence Eyre; M: Mortimer Browning; D: Edith Ellis; S: Joseph Mullen; P: Hunter Williams; T: Erlanger's Theatre; 2/25/30 (15)

James Rennie played romantic opera-star Paval Zala in this long-winded, pretentious, unfunny comedy about the backstage carryings on and intrigues in a Budapest opera troupe. Paval, actually an American, is the object of one lustful prima donna after another, and the play chronicles his efforts to elude the love-hungry female hordes and settle down with his secret bride, Luti Bender (Desiree Tabor), the company understudy.

In Perriton Maxwell's view, *Gala Night* was "an attempt at satire, lost in a maze of words and ineffectual complications. An occasional well-turned line does not compensate for an evening of pretty clumsy claptrap."

GAMBLING [Comedy-Drama/Gambling/Crime/Mystery] A/P: George M. Cohan; D: Sam Forrest; T: Fulton Theatre; 8/26/29 (155)

Conventional in story and development, this lively drama by and starring George M. Cohan proved to be a competent piece of theatre. More of the interest lay in the detailed underworld characterizations allowed most members of the supporting company than in the detection of the motivating crime.

Cohan portrayed Al Draper, a professional gambler, keen-witted and honest, who puts his cleverness to the task of tracking down the murderer of his adopted daughter. He gets involved with various dubious personages along his quest, which seems to be leading to his discovery of the killer when he turns out to have been following a false scent. Finally, the murderer (Douglas MacPherson), a youth who had eloped with the girl, confesses and commits suicide.

"*Gambling*, while it is full of the most expert kind of theatrical effects taken one by one, in the sum total is a hoax on the audience and not—like *The Tavern* of humorous memory—an intended one," opined Francis R. Bellamy.

An interesting sidelight on the play's history is that the leading role in the out-of-town tryouts was played by the still-unknown Clark Gable; Cohan chose to fire Gable and rewrite the play to star himself.

GAME OF LOVE AND DEATH, THE (Le Jeu de l'amour et de la morte) [Drama/French/Period/Politics/Marriage/Romance] A: Romain Rolland; TR: Eleanor Stimson Brooks; D: Rouben Mamoulian; DS: Aline Bernstein; P: Theatre Guild; T: Guild Theatre; 11/25/29 (48)

A windy literary play, bordering on closet drama, which Romain Rolland wrote as one segment of a twelve-play epic interpreting in his own terms the French Revolution and on which he had been working for a quarter of a century. The work was crushed by a lack of dramatic interest and a preponderance of rhetoric. "Some of this language sounds consciously flowery, some of it bombastic, and a little of it like the fine writing it probably is," noted the *Times*.

The melodramatic content of this history play set in 1794 Paris concerned a Girondist, Courvoisier (Frank Conroy), who gives aid to a political fugitive, Vallée (Otto Kruger), when he learns that his own wife (Alice Brady) is in love with him and then calmly remains behind with her to die at the guillotine after Vallée has fled.

The play, wrote John Hutchens, had the "sentiment of '. . . a far, far better thing that I do now. . .' always effective, always a little too eager to rescue blankness with pathos." The most lustrous performance was that of Claude Rains as Carnot. Appearing in the crowd scenes was Henry Fonda, making his Broadway debut.

GANG WAR [Drama/Crime/Prohibition] A/D/P: Willard Mack; S: Rollo Wayne; T: Morosco Theatre; 8/20/28 (77)

An action-packed melodrama about rival Chicago gangs and gunfighting. The rivals in question are the Castoldi gang and the Kelton gang; the subject of their enmity is bootlegging territory. Al Castoldi (Anthony Spirella) is bumped off on the church steps; his girlfriend (Beatrice Nichols) also meets her maker; Duke Kelton (Louis Kimball) is snatched by Castoldi's men, led by Joe Magelli (Donald Kirke); and Kelton's men fly over and drop bombs on the place in retaliation (the theatre was suffused with smoke from the special effects).

Robert Littell's capsule review: "several hundred revolver shots, and a fine example of the tameness of too much excitement." Perriton Maxwell added, "*Gang War* is the transcription of a dime novel from an earlier day, furbished up with current news and rank language and hung upon a prohibition peg."

GARDEN OF EDEN, THE [Comedy/Romance/Austrian/Sex] A: Rudolph Bernauer and Rudolph Oesterreicher; AD: Avery Hopwood; D: Edwin H. Knopf; S: Joseph Mullen; P: Arch Selwyn; T: Selwyn Theatre; 9/27/27 (23)

A shopworn comedy adapted from the German and, aside from the acting of Alison Skipworth, proving "singularly unrewarding" to Brooks Atkinson. It had a Cinderella story about a young woman (Miriam Hopkins) who, on the verge of marriage to an upper cruster (Douglass Montgomery) she met at Monte Carlo's Eden Hotel, is revealed as a lower-class pretender with a scandalous past as a cabaret singer; this cools her groom's ardor. She tears off her wedding gown before the shocked assembly and walks off in her undies. Fortunately, a dashing Spanish prince (Russ Whytal) offers her his affection, and she willingly accepts it.

Miriam Hopkins played the role taken in the earlier London version by Tallulah Bankhead.

GARDEN OF WEEDS [Drama/Show Business/Crime/Sex/Marriage] A/D: Leon Gordon; S: George W. Howe; P: Leon Gordon i/a/w W. Herbert Adams; T: Gaiety Theatre; 4/28/24 (16)

An unidentified critic declared that Leon Gordon's being an actor showed in his writing, for his "characters behave less like human beings than Samuel French catalogues," and called the show "an attempt to inveigle the box office with the old dodge of palming off smut in terms of moral indignation."

Alexander Woollcott wrote that the audience, anticipating another Gordon hit like *White Cargo*, was disappointed by his tale of a wealthy man (Lee Baker) with an Asbury Park mansion with a garden by the sea. There he tests his theory that the most beautiful human flowers are weeds at root by mixing decent and degenerate Broadway showgirls. When one (Phoebe Foster) saves herself by marrying a good man (Warburton Gamble), the human weed-gardener haunts her until the husband kills him.

H.H.

GARDENER'S DOG, THE (El perro del hortelano) [Dramatic Revival/Yiddish Language] A: Lope de Vega; AD/D: Boris Glagolin; TR: Harry Bransky; S: A. Soudelkin; P: Maurice Schwartz; T: Yiddish Art Theatre (OB); 9/5/27

A revival of Lope de Vega's sixteenth-century comedy under the direction of Boris Glagolin of Moscow's Revolution Theatre, here making his American directorial debut. Maurice Schwartz's Yiddish Art Theatre was put through boisterously energetic paces at his command, and the *Times* discovered that where there is shouting and horseplay, there is not necessarily humor.

De Vega's complex comedy concerns the efforts made by a Neapolitan countess to woo her secretary away from a maid in her household; she acts like the "gardener's dog" in her ambivalent treatment of him, and only when a deception convinces her that he is of high birth does she marry him. The play, known in Spanish as *El perro del hortelano* (sometimes translated as *The Dog in the Manger*) belongs to Lope's cape-and-sword play genre.

Glagolin's production was filled with stage tricks and gimmicks. The lack of a curtain, the visible shifting of scenes, the use of the aisles, the release of doves into the audience were some of them. The show seemed too frantic and breathless in its effort to be amusing, but it nevertheless proved an interesting experiment.

(1) GARRICK GAIETIES, THE [Revue] B: Morrie Ryskind, Benjamin Kaye, Newman Levy, and Sam Jaffe; M: Richard Rodgers; LY: Lorenz Hart; D: Philip Loeb with Herbert Fields; DS: Carolyn Hancock and Miguel Covarrubias; P: Theatre Guild; T: Garrick Theatre; 6/8/25 (231)

The first of several editions of a revue produced by the Junior Group of the Theatre Guild, the *Garrick Gaieties* started life as a two-performance show, was extended to some additional matinees, and before long began a regular Broadway run, thereby putting the composer-lyricist team of Rodgers and Hart permanently on the twentieth-century theatrical map. Their first fully professional engagement was a big hit from which, of their contributions, two standards emerged, "Sentimental Me" and "Manhattan," both introduced by Sterling Holloway and June Cochrane, with help from James Norris and Edith Meiser on the former.

The Garrick Gaieties was conceived in the vein of the intimate revues then becoming popular. It was mounted under Guild auspices to raise money for the new Guild Theatre's tapestries; inexpensively produced, it cost only $5,000 and made much more than that.

Like the *Grand Street Follies*, most of the show's fun proceeded from its parodies of recent productions; among the targets of this mockery were the plays the Guild itself had staged, including *They Knew What They Wanted* (here travestied as "They Didn't Know What They Were Getting"), *Fata Morgana*, and *The Guardsman*. Diseuse Ruth Draper was delightfully spoofed by Hildegarde Halliday, and Peggy Conway did a devastating takeoff on Pauline Lord. Among the other stars mimicked in good fun were the Lunts and Richard Bennett.

In all, twenty-three numbers were presented by a cast containing many future stalwarts of stage and screen. In addition to play parodies, Guild put-ons, and song and dance numbers, there was a political sketch joshing the conventional domesticity of President Calvin Coolidge, another poking fun at William Jennings Bryant's involvement in the *Scopes* "monkey" trial, a beautifully designed (by Miguel Covarrubias) Mexican cafe scene featuring dancer Rose Rolanda (the designer's wife), and a "jazz-opera" by Rodgers and Hart, "The Joy Spreader," about a salesgirl (Betty Starbuck) and a clerk (Romney Brent) locked by mistake in a department store for the night. This last was soon dropped in favor of "Sentimental Me."

(2) [Second Edition] M: Richard Rodgers; LY: Lorenz Hart; D: Philip Loeb; CH: Herbert Fields; P: Theatre Guild; T: Garrick Theatre; 5/10/26 (174)

Edition number two in this series of informal revues was another success, especially with its hilarious travesties on the season's serious and not-so-serious theatrical offerings. The work was not up to the level of the previous effort, however, being too self-conscious about doing as well.

For the most part, this was a "bright, lively, and refreshing" (Joseph Wood Krutch) show, and although the critics were not as taken by the Rodgers and Hart score as they were a year earlier, "Mountain Greenery" was a major contribution. Among the shows parodied were *The Glass Slipper*, *Androcles and the Lion*, *Goat Song*, *The Chief Thing*, and *The Dybbuk*. A memorable inclusion was a takeoff on musical comedies called ''Rose of Arizona,'' set in a hotel on the Arizona-Mexican border. ''Tennis Champs'' satirized sports stars Bill Tilden Bill Tilden and Helen Wills, a Blue Danube routine was well danced, the skit called ''Home Sweet Home'' mocked American optimism, ''The Psychopathic Ward'' poked fun at the effects of magazine ads on impressionable minds, and ''Burglary a la Mode'' ridiculed a family that hires a crook to steal their goods so they may get into the papers.

(3) [Third Edition] B: H. Alexander, Carroll Carroll, Ruth Chorpenning, Leopoldine Damrosch, Gretchen Damrosch Finletter, Landon Herrick, Sterling Holloway, Benjamin M. Kaye, Newman Levy, Dorian Otvos, and Louis M. Simon; M: Marc Blitzstein, Aaron Copland, Vernon Duke, Basil Fomeen, Harold Goldiman, William Irwin, Ned Lehak, Everett Miller, Peter Nolan, Willard Robeson, Charles M. Schwab, and Kay Swift; LY: Allen Boretz, Ruth Chorpenning, Ira Gershwin, E. Y. Harburg, Sterling Holloway, Paul James, Ronald Jeans, Malcolm McComb, John Mercer, Henry Myers, Louis Simon, and Josiah Titzell; D: Philip Loeb; CH: Olin Howland and Stella Block; S: Kate Drain Lawson; C: Kate Drain Lawson and Louis Simon; P: Theatre Guild; T: Guild Theatre; 6/4/ 30 (155)

After a hiatus of four years, this intimate revue made a successful return with a cast led by Albert Carroll, Philip Loeb, Edith Meiser, and Sterling Holloway. Also present was fresh young comedienne Imogene Coca, making her local bow. Twenty-seven scenes and songs, by an army of creative talents, including many great names in American theatre history, took off on contemporary persons and on show business with the usual lack of reverence. It offered ''the wittiest topical satire of the season,'' commented Francis R. Bellamy. Hilarity emerged from the show's highlight, the skit ''They Always Come Back,'' in which Loeb impersonated former Police Commissioner Grover Whalen who had taken a job with Wanamaker's Department Store. Wearing a gardenia and top hat, Loeb sang ''I'm back among the drapers/Because the daily papers/Hadn't room enough for Jimmy [Walker] and me.'' Wanamaker's was seen as an example of how police methods could be used in department-store management. The skit infuriated Whalen. The familiar play burlesques included Carroll mimicking Mei Lan-Fang as he might have acted in *Strictly Dishonorable*. Despite a plethora of top songwriting talent, none of the music compared with the earlier *Garrick Gaieties* contributions of Rodgers and Hart.

A fall 1930 edition benefited from new material contributed by Rodgers and Hart and Herbert Fields; a dazzling young comedienne named Rosalind Russell made her local bow in this revised version.

(1) **GAY PAREE** [Revue] B: Harold Atteridge; M: Alfred Goodman, Maurie Rubens, and J. Fred Coots; LY: Clifford Grey; D: J. J. Shubert; S: Watson

Barratt; P: Messrs. Shubert i/a/w Rufus Le Maire; T: Shubert Theatre; 8/18/25 (181)

The title locale had little to do with the contents of this expensive revue, which had scenes set in Venice, Florida, Times Square, Sheba, and elsewhere. *Time* characterized it as "a fair spectacle, noisy, rowdy in spots, and intermittently entertaining," but it was clear the critics were growing bored with shows of this ilk.

The revue included among its thirty-four numbers one called "Wide Pants Willie," a collegiate dance routine led by Margie Finley; various tableaux called "Vision of Hassan," "Wedgewood Curtain," and "Venetian Nights," using brilliantly colored sets and costumes; "The Opera in 1860"; the sketches of Billy B. Van and George Le Maire; the rustic comedy of Chic Sales, including his "The Country Church Choir"; a burlesque singing and piano recital featuring Winnie Lightner and Eddie Conrad; and the Negro songs of duo Salt and Pepper.

(**2**) [1926 Edition] M/LY: Alberta Nichols and Mann Holiner; D: J. C. Huffman and Charles Judels; CH: Seymour Felix; S: Watson Barratt; P: Messrs. Shubert; T: Winter Garden Theatre; 11/9/26 (175)

A second and last edition following the familiar pattern: girls, comics, spectacle, nudity, dances, songs, and sketches. One superlative routine was on the theme of fans, from Spain to Japan, and it concluded with a tableau of an immense fan made of feathers and girls. Among the most applauded acts were homespun comedian Chic Sales, whose Yankee character spoofs were offbeat and rib tickling—a piece called "He Knew Lincoln" mingled comedy and pathos to good effect; Winnie Lightner; Parisian entertainer Jane Aubert; acrobatic dancer Chester Fredericks; and a host of others. The *Times* called the show "good and serviceable."

GENERAL JOHN REGAN [Dramatic Revival] A: George A. Birmingham; D: Joseph Augustus Keogh; S: William G. Gaskin; C: Jenny Covan; P: Irish Players; T: Irish Theatre (OB); 1/29/30 (28)

The Irish Theatre, formerly the Greenwich Village Theatre, produced this 1913 satirical farce set in the Irish town of Ballymoy, but although the play seemed worthy of new life, the production suffered on a number of accounts. Too few of the actors seemed Irish, and the acting was generally dismal.

The plot dealt with an American millionaire's son (John F. Clearman), stranded in the sleepy town, who pulls off a hoax to wake up the indolent citizens by convincing them to erect a statue in honor of a native son, Gen. John Regan, a hero in Bolivia, who never existed.

Wilella Waldorf found the production "crude and often positively distressing."

GENIUS AND THE CROWD [Comedy/Sex/Music/Romance] A: John T. McIntyre and Francis Hill; D/P: George M. Cohan; T: Casino Theatre; 9/6/20 (24)

This play marked George M. Cohan's debut as an independent producer and the severance of his long association with Sam H. Harris. The play he chose for the occasion was a trivial affair revolving around Philippe Trava (Georges Renavent), a young violinist with great appeal for women. This female attention disgusts rather than flatters him, and he refuses to continue his career. Later, he is tricked into returning to the concert stage when told that his secretary, whom he loves, is about to marry someone else. Off to Carnegie Hall he goes to get her and play as he has never played before.

The production ran off the track into the crudest of burlesque and "revealed in half a dozen spots that Cohan is a little out of his league," wrote Alexander Woollcott. Heywood Broun said the play was languid and obvious, while Ludwig Lewisohn observed that it depended upon "a wilted picturesqueness flavored by speeches in the best style of the...*Family Herald.*"

M.M.-C.

GENTLE GRAFTERS [Drama/Romance/Sex] A: Owen Davis; D: Sam Forrest; P: Sam H. Harris; T: Music Box Theatre; 10/27/26 (13)

A spindly piece of Owen Davis hackwork about a pretty young woman named Sally (Katharine Alexander), who decides to use men for all they are worth because of a slight a man had paid to her late mother. Together with a greedy middle-aged acquaintance, Cora (Charlotte Granville), she moves up in the world and acquires a fancy apartment, gifts, and clothes, much of it by faking her credit rating. Finally, the stores begin to get wise to her. The impecunious Dick Cameron (Robert Cameron) plans to marry her, but when Cora sees her meal ticket about to vanish, she lies that Dick is going to wed someone else, and the heartbroken Sally runs off for an auto jaunt with several other fellows.

Percy Hammond loved Alexander's acting but called the play "heavy-handed," and Brooks Atkinson said it "seemed commonplace in its expression and defective in its construction."

GENTLEMEN OF THE PRESS [Comedy/Journalism/Romance] A: Ward Morehouse; D: George Abbott; S: R. N. Robbins; P: Thomas E. Jackson and H. S. Kraft; T: Henry Miller's Theatre; 8/27/28 (128)

This newspaper play was vastly overshadowed by the enormously successful *Front Page*, which opened only two weeks earlier; still, it had a good run and earned some approbatory comments. The plot was considered trivial; the characters true to life. Taking up the latter theme was Gilbert Seldes: "The newspaper men were newspaper men as every cub reporter and every experienced city editor knows them." The author was himself a drama critic for the *Sun* and knew whereof he wrote. But Robert Littell noted, "A stab at real character and the suggestion of a real story are ruined by sentimentality, irrelevance, clap-trap, cheap humor, a mediocre performance and an inability to keep going in any one direction."

Its central character was Wick Snell (John Cromwell), a newshound who leaves his paper to become a press agent, a career he finds disillusioning and which he rejects to go back to his paper's city room desk. A romantic involvement figures as a subplot.

Russell Crouse, *Evening Post* columnist and future successful playwright, debuted as an actor in a small role. His *World* critic-wife Alison Smith wrote of him: "In the group of minor reporters one figure emerged as dimly familiar. The name, it seems, is Crouse. He was greeted by a kindly burst of applause...and he received at least one telegram from a former editor stating (we hope not ambiguously), 'Your work was unbelievable.' To this we may add that he gave the best back view of a city newsman ever presented in a ten-line part and in a five-minute big emotional scene with a ham sandwich."

GENTLEMEN PREFER BLONDES [Comedy/Sex/France/Romance] A: Anita Loos and John Emerson; SC: Anita Loos's novel of the same name; D/P: Edgar Selwyn; T: Times Square Theatre; 9/28/26 (201)

Anita Loos coadapted her sensationally popular diary-style novel about Lorelei Lee (June Walker), the blonde golddigger from Little Rock, into this successful comedy that led to an even more successful 1949 musical and then to a major movie hit. Edna Hibbard played the malapropistic Lorelei's hard-boiled, wise-cracking brunette buddy Dorothy Shaw. George Jean Nathan believed the popularity of Loos's work could be found in her care at creating rounded characters for whom funny lines could be written rather than by writing gags and then trying to fit a character to them: "[H]er characters are completely alive, reported with an ear of absolute pitch and caught brilliantly in detail."

Walker and Hibbard had trouble looking exactly like the wonderful Ralph Barton illustrations that accompanied the book, but their excellent talents soon got them over this hurdle. Their vehicle concerned Lorelei's "education" at the hand of wealthy button-maker Gus Eisman (Arthur S. Ross), her Paris-bound shipboard escapades, her romance with Philadelphia playboy Henry Spoffard (Frank Morgan), her efforts to improve her mind, and her penchant for diamonds, among other things.

Brooks Atkinson realized that the play was not great literature, but he appreciated its effective opportunism in making the most of its materials. But John Mason Brown thought otherwise: "It is a talky and rather lame collision of most...of the enchanting episodes of the book, that is sadly in need of editing."

(1) GEORGE WHITE'S SCANDALS OF 1921 [Revue] B: "Bugs" Baer and George White; M: George Gershwin; LY: Arthur Jackson; S: Herbert Ward; C: Albertina Randall Wheelan, Alice O'Neill, Ada Fields, and Gilbert Adrian; D/CH/P: George White; T: Liberty Theatre; 7/11/21 (97)

The third edition of this annual summer revue was considered superior to its predecessors; it was congratulated on the color and realism of its spectacle, the novelty and style of its costumes, and the performing talents of several of its contributors. The show consisted of two acts and twenty scenes set mostly in

New York, but with locales as far flung as the South Seas, the Winter Palace in Moscow, the Panama Canal, the North Pole, the Flying Dutchman, and biblical times with Samson (Lester Allen) and Delilah (Ann Pennington) as well. The material was a variety of Gershwin songs, dances, and comic sketches, the intent being to satirize events of the past annum; "the satire does not go very far or very deep," commented the *Times*. Although it often was funny, the humor too often seemed forced and heavy, lacked subtlety, or fell flat, despite the efforts of comics such as George Bickel, Lester Allen, and George Le Maire. Other important talents were the black mammy entertainer Teresa Gardela with her "Aunt Jemima" act (the *Times* thought her the evening's biggest hit with her rendition of plantation songs); dancer Ann Pennington, whom the *Herald* said was getting "chubby"; and black-face singer-comedian Lou Holtz.

(2) [1922 Edition] B: George White, W. C. Fields, and Andy Rice; M: George Gershwin; LY: B. G. De Sylva and E. Ray Goetz; D/CH/P: George White; S: John Wenger and Herbert Ward; C: Ada Fields, Erté, Max Weldy, Alice O'Neill, and Charles Le Maire; T: Globe Theatre; 8/28/22 (89)

The fourth edition of the *Scandals* featured favorites such as W. C. Fields, Winnie Lightner, and dancer-producer George White, but the act that made the audiences go wild (they were "set to swaying like a wheat field touched by the wind"—Alexander Woollcott) was the first act finale provided by jazz band-leader Paul Whiteman and his Palais Royale Orchestra. With the set representing "The Patent Leather Forest"—actually a white staircase adorned with chorus girls in black patent leather gowns—the band launched into Gershwin's "I'll Build a Stairway to Paradise" and then encored it as the girls dropped their skirts so suddenly that the audience gasped. Winnie Lightner participated by singing the lyric and Pearl Regay by dancing to it.

To shorten the show after opening night Gershwin and De Sylva's twenty-minute jazz opera about blacks (played by whites in burnt cork), "Blue Monday," a foretaste of *Porgy and Bess*, was excised. Few critics warmed to it, but it survived in a revised form known as "135th Street."

W. C. Fields, abandoning Florenz Ziegfeld for the occasion, was mildly effective with his "The Radio Bug" bit that Sime. called "the first radio comedy around," but he went flat in his numbers about baseball and auto traffic. Other than "A Stairway to Paradise," the show's score was average, although "I Found a Four Leaf Clover" found favor.

(3) [1923 Edition] B: George White and William K. Wells; M: George Gershwin; LY: B. G. De Sylva and E. Ray Goetz; ADD. LY.: Ballard MacDonald; D/CH/P: George White; C: Cora McGeachey, Max Weldy, and Erté; T: Globe Theatre; 6/18/23 (168)

The fifth edition of *George White's Scandals*, featuring twenty-five scenes, prompted Laurence Stallings to comment that the Queen of Sheba might have felt inferior after seeing the show. He found "little distinction in the music, and only a fair amount in the settings, but in the costumes the new *Scandals* have combined an unequalled lavishness with the most astounding loveliness.'' One of the most startling visual effects, according to the *Times*, was a curtain into which nude girls were stitched. A rare jewel number, ''one of the most exquisite scenes that has yet been revealed in revue,'' was rated outstanding.

Other scenes included dancing by the Tiller Girls, comic and clog dancer Tom Patricola, comedy team Johnny Dooley and Leslie Allen, and a rose number danced by Marga Waldron.

H.H.

(4) [1924 Edition] B: George White and William K. Wells; M: George Gershwin; LY: B. G. De Sylva; D/CH/P: George White; C: Erté and Max Weldy; T: Apollo Theatre; 6/30/24 (196)

Another standardized product from the George White factory of lavishly done revues. ''The new *Scandals*,'' noted Arthur Hornblow, ''is not sensationally better than its predecessors and not less good. Both the costumes and the lack of them are brilliant features, and the gorgeous scenes melt into each other with bewildering effect.''

Costumes and seminude girls were the main attractions, but there were some talented performers on hand and a few excellent songs. Among the latter was Gershwin's brilliant ''Somebody Loves Me,'' sung by winsome Winnie Lightner in an overproduced spectacle number in which famous romantic heroes of the past and present paid her suit. This was the composer's last *Scandals*, since White refused his bid for a raise in his $125 a week salary.

In addition to Lightner, headline numbers included the comedy-dancing of Tom Patricola, the mandolin-playing comedy of Will Mahoney, the antics of Lester Allen, the dancing of Alice Weaver, and the singing of Helen Hudson and Richard Bold. A sketch called ''Ah'' was a ''social melodrama'' composed entirely of dialogue using that word; Brooke Johns and Ann Pennington's dancing was travestied by Allen and Patricola; a fur-shop sketch showed the chorines garbed in beautiful furs and gowns; a ''Charleston'' number led by the McCarthy Sisters had toes tapping; and a special lighting technique changed the bathing suited chorus into marble statues—one of them even lost her arms to resemble the Venus de Milo.

(5) [1925 Edition] B: George White and William K. Wells; M: Ray Henderson; LY: B. G. De Sylva and Lew Brown; D/CH/P: George White; C: Erté and Max Weldy; T: Apollo Theatre; 6/22/25 (169)

Edition number seven was the musical product of De Sylva, Henderson, and Brown, but the talented trio could not come up with any hits; there were some fine talents in the company, but their efforts did not make this edition distinguished. Helen Morgan, soon to burst forth in stardom in *Show Boat*, contributed little of note.

Comic dancer Tom Patricola and songstress Helen Hudson were back in the show again, and they were abetted by performers such as Harry Fox, the comedian, the broad comedy duet of Dooley and Morton, the singing McCarthy

Sisters, the Albertina Rasch dancers, and the comics Miller and Lyles, who worked in blackface. Dooley scored with an impersonation of Irving Berlin singing "All Alone" as sixty chorus girls stepped over and around him; and there was a funny sketch of a melodrama done in Charleston dance style by a supposed stock company from the city that gave the dance its name.

The show was a hit despite carping such as Arthur Hornblow's to the effect that its lyrics, music, and humor were banal, that its girls' figures looked "the worse for wear," and that the costumes resembled "the machinations of the president of the 'Happy Girls' Glee Club' when they give a 'play' in the social community hall."

(6) [1926 Edition] B: George White and William K. Wells; M: Ray Henderson; LY: B. G. De Sylva and Lew Brown; S: Gustave Weidhaas; D/CH/P: George White; C: Erté, Max Weldy, Gustave Weidhaas, W. Oden-Waller; T: Apollo Theatre; 6/14/26 (432)

There was a lot of bickering over the $55 a seat charged to the opening of this eighth edition, but it was, as *Time* reported, "the sovereign of the series." It is regarded by many as one of the best revues ever unveiled. Arthur Hornblow, who insisted that the show was "dull and lacking in pep," admitted that some of the numbers "as regards color, novelty and splendor in design and execution" were as lovely "as anything of the kind ever attempted."

The show began with the entire chorus singing "Talent Is What the Public Wants" as they coyly undressed on each stanza. Ann Pennington introduced "The Black Bottom," a De Sylva, Henderson, and Brown dance hit that became the successor to the Charleston; and the song-writing trio came up with another all-time standard, "Birth of the Blues," as well. "This Is My Lucky Day" marked another top hit emerging from their fertile pens. "Birth of the Blues" was given a spectacular staircase routine, with Willie Howard dressed as Beethoven and Eugene as Liszt. Harry Richman's job was to convince them that the blues was real music; he won them over with a rendition of Gershwin's "Rhapsody in Blue." Richman also introduced "This Is My Lucky Day" and sang "The Girl Is You" with Frances Williams.

The Howards had a very amusing love-triangle bit using two telephones, with Willie speaking to his girlfriend as his wife hovered nearby, and with the girlfriend's husband getting in her way at her end of the line.

This edition netted the longest run in *Scandals* history.

(7) [1928 Edition] B: George White and William K. Wells; M: Ray Henderson; LY: B. G. De Sylva and Lew Brown; D/P: George White; CH: Russell Markert; S: W. Oden-Waller and Gustave Weidhaas; C: Erté, Max Weldy, and Charles Le Maire; T: Apollo Theatre; 7/2/28 (240)

Edition number nine featured Ann Pennington, the Howard brothers, Harry Richman, Frances Williams, Tom Patricola, and the Russell Markert Dancers. It had been two years since the most successful show in the series opened, and the present version, although nothing to sneeze at, could not surpass it. "[I]t is too sedulously imitative and too content to follow along the paths of its predecessor,'' opined the *Times*. The comedy bits too frequently resembled the old ones, and there were not many top flight songs from the De Sylva, Brown, and Henderson tune factory, which herein offered their last *Scandals* score. An effective routine parodied the talkies; the first Broadway spoof on *Strange Interlude* had funny moments; a tribute to Victor Herbert gained notice; and the spectacle numbers were lovely, specifically one using a trick curtain that could open into differing patterns. The best of the songs included ''I'm on the Crest of a Wave'' and ''An Old-Fashioned Girl.''

(**8**) [1929 Edition] B: George White, William K. Wells, and Irving Caesar; M/ LY: Cliff Friend and George White; D/CH/P: George White; S: Ted Weidhaas, Gustave Weidhaas, and W. Oden-Waller; C: Erté, Max Weldy, Orry-Kelly, Charles Le Maire, and Cora McGeachey; T: Apollo Theatre; 9/23/29 (159)

In this edition White opened with a number celebrating the show's tenth birthday. Its theme song was ''Bigger and Better Than Ever'' (*Time* said the tune was ''piffle, the sentiment. . .mere braggadocio''). An array of resplendent girls, in various states of dishabille, filled the eye in the many tableaux numbers, and headliners Frances Williams and Willie and Eugene Howard worked hard to support the proceedings (''The show. . .suffers a little from lack of variety among its principals''—Perriton Maxwell). A new number called ''Bottoms Up'' tried without avail to rival White's past successes with dance crazes such as the Charleston and the Black Bottom, and there were spectacle scenes incorporating giant effigies inspired by European carnivals. A team of female dancers who tapped on their toes drew kudos. A finale in which White himself and various performers adorned in rubber costumes took a dip in an onstage pool closed the exhibition.

GERTIE [Comedy-Drama/Romance/Sex] A: Tadema Bussiere; D/P: Gustav Blum; S: Nicholas Yellenti; T: Nora Bayes Theatre; 11/15/26 (248)

Pat O'Brien's acting was the most genuine in this comedy-drama about a poor working girl (Constance Mackay) who wants to bag a society millionaire (Edward Reese) for his bank account but learns that he wants her for one thing only, and it isn't marriage. However, the nice, steady Irish garage worker (O'Brien) who really loved her all along is agreeable to becoming her permanent mate.

According to J.H., ''The opus appeared on the level with those melodramas wherein the heroine hisses, 'You cad,' and the villain hisses back with, 'Now you're in me power, me gal.' '' ''It provided. . .an inoffensive evening in the minor theatre,'' noted Richard Watts, Jr., even though it was ''pretty much of a bore.'' Still, the show fooled all of the critics and climbed to an impressive number of performances.

GET ME IN THE MOVIES [Comedy/Films/Romance/Sex] A: Charlton Andrews and Philip Dunning; D: Ralph Murphy; S: Nicholas Yellenti; P: Laura D. Wilck; T: Earl Carroll Theatre; 5/21/28 (32)

An implausible farce about a Sheboygan, Michigan, lad, Johnny Loring (Sterling Holloway), who wins a film-writing prize for his clean-minded scenario, goes to Hollywood, is besieged by the mothers of actresses and the actresses themselves who will go to any lengths for a part, and yet remains chaste for his small-town sweetheart.

Variety ridiculed the play's premise by declaring that even "the most obscure extra in the deaf and dumb racket knows that an eastern author has about as much drag in L.A. as a Knight of Columbus in Birmingham." Wilfred J. Riley knocked it as "a cheap, tawdry and vulgar bedroom farce, poorly written, acted and directed." Sterling Holloway, in his first leading role, was thought grievously miscast.

GET TOGETHER [Revue] D: R. H. Burnside; P: Charles Dillingham; T: Hippodrome; 9/3/21 (397)

New York's largest theatre, the financially plagued 6,000-seat Hippodrome, home of mammoth spectacles, was host to this extravagant revue that held its audience entranced by the humor and skill of its performers. The show had a variety of contrasting acts, much like a vaudeville show, but had no singers. Clive Cook appeared on the screen in a comedy film short, "The Toreador," and there was great fun provided by Powers's Performing Elephants who amused with the help of the Marceline and Moron clown act. Acrobatic clowns the Three Bobs performed with a sensational juggling bulldog and a show-stealing crow named Jocko that caught balls thrown to it from the audience. A spectacular ballet by premier dancer Michel Fokine and his wife, Vera Fokina, "The Thunder Bird," was a pretentious Aztec legend-based work, but Fokina charmed with her "Dying Swan" ballet. Musician Ferry Conway played music on everyday objects, and a full-scale ice show imported from Germany told a Russian tale, "The Red Shoes," starring the whizzing skates of Charlotte.

GETTING EVEN [Comedy-Drama/Sex] A/D/P: Nathaniel Wilson; S: Cleon Throckmorton; T: Biltmore Theatre; 8/19/29 (4)

A tedious, episodic, thirty-four scene pseudosymbolistic calamity that offered merely "a profusion of clipped words, stiff postures and cloying attitudes," in Brooks Atkinson's opinion. By the third act, the theatre was rocking with unintended peals of laughter.

The play covered eleven years, from ages eleven to twenty-two, in the life of Irish maidservant Veronica Mathilda McConnell (Georgia Clarke), from her Pollyanna childhood to her tragic death. Her days with an ethereal married couple, during which she plows through man after man as she gets even with what for some reason was left vague, are covered, until, following the wife's death, the husband proposes to her. She dies, though, of an abortion.

Percy Hammond called it memorable as "the world's worst play."

GETTING GERTIE'S GARTER [Comedy/Sex/Marriage] A: Wilson Collison and Avery Hopwood; D: Bertram Harrison; P: A. H. Woods; T: Republic Theatre; 8/1/21 (120)

A frivolous three-act sex farce that mildly scandalized several reviewers. Its authors used a plot line very similar to that of their recently popular *Up in Mabel's Room* (which also featured Hazel Dawn). Here young Ken Walrick (Donald MacDonald) struggles to recover from his former girlfriend Gertrude (Dawn) a gem-studded garter with a small photo of himself in it that he gave to her. He wants neither her new husband (Louis Kimball) nor his new wife (Dorothy Mackaye) to discover it in her possession. The complications that ensue take one and all to a second-act barn setting, where one female character finds herself minus her clothes and appears in a straw-covered horse blanket, rubber boots, and a bridal veil.

Even the title was meant to be taken two ways in this double-entendre-larded farce, but wit and subtlety were largely absent from the otherwise "gorgeously active" (Alan Dale) farce, which offered "considerable amusement by virtue of tremendous pace and a certain naive hilarity," according to Heywood Broun.

GHOST BETWEEN, THE [Comedy/Marriage] A: Vincent Lawrence; D: W. H. Gilmore; T: Thirty-ninth Street Theatre; 3/22/21 (128)

The "ghost between" is the memory of Ethel Brookes's (Laura Walker) idolized husband, who dies in the prologue. Ethel agrees to marry the kindly surgeon Dr. John Dillard (Arthur Byron) but only as a matter of convenience. When Richard Hunt (Glenn Anders) tries to elope with her, Ethel and John realize that they have buried the ghost and that theirs can now be a marriage in more than name only.

Vincent Lawrence's play, which he claimed took fourteen years to get produced, was considered "a strikingly original and amusing romance" by the *American*'s critic. Alexander Woollcott found the dialogue captivating, and the plethora of laughter in the piece was duly noted. But the *Evening Post* thought much of the laughter was out of place and that the piece was "an extraordinary hodge-podge of styles."

GHOST PARADE, THE [Drama/Mystery/Crime] A: Hadley Waters; D: Charles K. Gordon; S: Clark Robinson; P: Charles K. Gordon i/a/w H. T. Curley; T: Lyric Theatre; 10/30/29 (13)

The locale of this flop mystery melodrama was in the headquarters of Major Ainslee (Oswald Marshall), in an old temple in the mountains of northern India. The temple seems haunted with ghosts. The ghosts are merely the contrivances of the major who is engaged in smuggling arms to rebellious relatives; his scheme is uncovered by the apparently evil Hindu Suma Singhi, who, in reality, is British detective Cyril Teetam (Clarence Derwent).

"It is a venture in more than one way distressing," groaned *Time*.

GHOST TRAIN, THE [Drama/Mystery/Drugs/Crime/British] A: Arnold Ridley; D: Norman Houston; P: A. H. Woods and Arch Selwyn; T: Eltinge Theatre; 8/25/26 (62)

This British hit flopped on Broadway but later became one of the most popular and often revived mysteries among amateur groups worldwide. Several film versions of it also were produced.

The American mounting, although played by a mixed British and American cast, was set at a Maine railway station that has a reputation for being haunted by a ghost train that passes by nightly; to look upon it is said to bring certain death. When a party of six travelers is held up here because of a wreck down the line, the proceedings lead to the revelation that the train, which actually does appear (mechanical effects by Langdon McCormick), is no spook at all but a transport vehicle for drugs and other contraband. A supposedly foolish member of the party turns out to be a clever detective (Eric Blore).

Brooks Atkinson noted that "this unevenly written melodrama...abounds in silent, moving, mysterious lights, death thuds, shrieks, uncanny signal bells, sudden darkness-while dirty work's afoot." Among the derailed actors were Claudette Colbert and John Williams.

(1) GHOSTS (Gengàngere) [Dramatic Revival] A: Henrik Ibsen; D/P: Mary Shaw; T: Punch and Judy Theatre; 2/6/22 (21)

Very little attention was paid to this revival of Ibsen's classic, which was produced by actress Mary Shaw in tandem with her revival of *Mrs. Warren's Profession*. Shaw was the original American Mrs. Alving, having first played the role in the 1890s. She reappeared in the part on several occasions, including a 1917 version sponsored by the Washington Square Players.

Of this revival the *Times* said, "It is a fairly competent and reasonably well acted presentation....Miss Shaw's characterization has deepened with constant performance, and, if it has also taken on certain mannerisms with the passing of time, these are perhaps excusable." Also noteworthy was Everett Butterfield's Oswald. The *Times* critic jibed at the play's generally awkward staging and production values.

(2) (Spettri) [Italian Language] P: F. Ray Comstock and Morris Gest; T: Century Theatre; 11/6/23 (2)

A performance by Eleanora Duse in Italian; the play was called *Spettri* in this version. Several critics complained about distracting prompting, which Alexander Woollcott declared was a tradition of Italian theatre. Laurence Stallings judged that Memo Benassi, who played Oswald, outacted the great star both in this play and *The Lady from the Sea*. Woollcott speculated that Duse varied more than most according to the tide of her health and spirits: "It was an astounding being who swayed with the woe of Mrs. Alving.... But it was a frailer and an older being, less ringing of voice and more fumbling of touch.'' Stark Young declared that she put distinction into the role, despite her low opinion of the character.

H.H.

(3) D: Hilda Englund; T: Princess Theatre; 12/1/25 (2)

There were two revivals of *Ghosts* in the 1925–1926 season. The first, starring and directed by Danish actress Hilda Englund, was an unimportant one given only at two matinees. Englund headed an ''ill-assorted'' cast. The play was described in a program note as having been staged in accordance with the business used at its first Scandinavian presentation.

''Miss Englund's Mrs. Alving was patient and noble and long suffering, with, unfortunately, too much emphasis placed upon the length and the quality of the suffering and too little upon the iron rectitude of a character born into an unrighteous world,'' wrote the *Times*. Alison Smith noted, ''Regina [Mabel Vanet] emerged inexplicably as a buxom soubrette with everything but a backward kick to her exits, and... Pastor Manders [Franklin Ramsay] had the engaging youthfulness of Barrie's Little Minister.''

(4) D: Dudley Digges; P: Actors' Theatre; T: Comedy Theatre; 3/16/26 (29)

The second revival of this play in the 1925–1926 season was far better than the first, although *Time* claimed that it was ''patchy'' and that Lucile Watson's Mrs. Alving was ''disappointing.'' Most other critics were more positive, but John Mason Brown agreed that the production was not very effective. ''Its first act was whispered in sombre notes as if *Ghosts* were a mystery play of sex. Even after that it counted on brow-clasping and foot-tapping to serve as thermometers to the passing emotions.''

The production by the Actors' Theatre, recently responsible for a revival of *Hedda Gabler*, which moved to matinees so that *Ghosts* could hold the boards at night, was generally considered a fine one with a noteworthy performance of Oswald by Jose Ruben, who had played the role in a 1917 mounting.

As Mrs. Alving, Watson seemed to the *Times* reviewer ''to lack tragic depth,'' but Hammond thought that she acted ''with beauty, charm, and a patient, cynical smile, making that troubled widow quite the most recognizable lady you have ever seen in the part.''

(5) TR: William Archer; REV/D: Harrison Grey Fiske; S: David Gaither; P: Charles D. Coburn and Patterson McNutt; T: Mansfield Theatre; 1/10/27 (24)

An insipidly cast revival partly salvaged by the excellence of the sixty-one-year-old Minnie Maddern (Mrs.) Fiske's technique in the role of Mrs. Alving. Mrs. Fiske's novel approach lit up the usually gloomy play with touches of satirical wit and humor; *Time* thought this inappropriate to the sombre tragic tone, and Richard Dana Skinner declared that it mismatched with the attack of the star's less-than-satisfactory company. Gilbert Seldes took Mrs. Fiske to task for her numerous comedic interpolations, which made her seem intent on "the destruction of every other actor": "If Mrs. Fiske had not babbled and shouted through the rest of the play, her violent hysterics at the end. . .would have been extraordinarily affecting." Yet Brooks Atkinson found the star's Helen Alving "intelligible, subtle and uncommonly wise."

The most admired of the supporting actors was Theodore St. John as Oswald.

(6) (Die Gespenster) [German Language] D: Max Reinhardt; P: Deutsches Theatre; T: Yorkville Theatre (OB); 2/7/28 (3)

Max Reinhardt's troupe of actors had recently made a conquest of New York with their repertory of plays staged by the great regisseur. Several of the actors in the company offered a presentation of *Ghosts* at a small theatre on East Eighty-sixth Street before returning to Germany. It was sponsored by a local group of amateurs called the Deutsches Theatre. Produced under the German title *Die Gespenster*, it starred Reinhardt's most sensational actor, Alexander Moissi, as Oswald; Hedwig Pauley played Mrs. Alving, Eduard von Winterstein was Manders, Vladimir Sokoloff was Engstrand, and Maria Solveg played Regina.

In this version, Oswald became the focal point, and, according to the *Times*, this made more sense than when Mrs. Alving's role was stressed, and it seemed nearer to Ibsen's intentions. Moissi in the part justified the interpretation with brilliancy. "Not the least effective of his. . .scenes was the one in which, without uttering a sound, but solely in his manner of pacing the stage, he revealed to the audience how rapidly the insanity had come upon him" (*Times*).

The other actors were up to Moissi's ability and offered a display of the fine things that good training can do for a talented ensemble. The *Times* noted, "There was a Continental thoroughness one seldom sees in this country."

(7) [German Language] S: Eduard Munch; P: Morris Gest and Edgar Selwyn; T: Forrest Theatre; 2/5/29 (5)

Alexander Moissi once more led a band of first-rate German players through this play, but none of the players from his 1928 production was involved in this staging. It was given during a tour of the troupe with a production of Tolstoy's *Redemption*. Johanna Terwin was the new Mrs. Alving, and the decor was created by famed Scandinavian artist Eduard Munch. The *Times* found the mounting "superb": "Against the meagerest background—frowzy furniture, shabby hangings, ugly doors—these actors show themselves alert to every impulse lurking in the story." Terwin was "infinitely compassionate in a fertile, womanly performance with no false strokes. . . .Her acting reminds you of the immortal Chekhova," applauded the *Times*. The critic went on, "As Oswald, Moissi is physically too solid and. . .rather too mature. By virtue of sheer, magnetic talent. . ., however, he not only overcomes these handicaps, but actually makes them count in his favor. This is a powerful, tempestuous Oswald—no weakling, no snivelling voluptuary."

GIFT, THE [Drama/Art/France/Romance/Illness] A: Julia Chandler and Alethea Luce; M: tone poem by Anna Lambert Steward; D: Clifford Brooke; S: Joseph

Physioc; P: Anna Lambert Steward; T: Greenwich Village Theatre (OB); 1/22/ 24 (7)

"Lighting the candle of understanding in the heart" was a line seized upon by critics as an example of the "flowery verbiage" in this drama. In Paris, a rich, young American painter (Pedro de Cordoba) is more successful as a spendthrift and Don Juan than as an artist. Although he dallies with others, his idealistic model (Doris Kenyon) tries to arouse his love through her devotion and her practice of the belief that the compelling force behind every worthy purpose is understanding. When she dies of tuberculosis, her spirit finally draws the painter away from dissipation toward greatness.

Burns Mantle called the work "one of those honest attempts to express a helpful philosophy that is never quite able to kick itself free from the restraining hands of the theatre" and thought that it seemed artificial in spite of earnest staging.

H.H.

GINGER [Musical/Romance] B: Harold Orlob and H. I. Phillips; M/P: Harold Orlob; D: Walter Brooks; S: P. Dodd Ackerman; T: Daly's Sixty-third Street Theatre; 10/16/23 (30)

"Amateur night" and "indescribably poor" were a couple of phrases used by the *Times* to characterize this musical about an engaged couple on a trial honeymoon chaperoned by the title character's aunt. Sibylla Bowhan was applauded as a personable soubrette and a good dancer, and Joe Mack and Olive May also won approval. Before arriving on Broadway, the show had been called *Take a Chance* and *Money and the Girl*.

GINGER SNAPS [Revue/Blacks] B/LY/D: Homer Tutt, Donald Heywood, and George Morris; M: Donald Heywood; CH: George Stamper; S: Ben Glick; C: Hilda Farnum; T: Belmont Theatre; 12/31/29 (7)

To the *World* critic, this was a "completely unbearable" black revue, and the *Times* exclaimed, "Less than nothing was added to the midtown New Year's Eve gayety" by the show. A few good dance numbers were the only high spots, but on the whole the terpsichorean contributions were not as good as in other such works.

GINGHAM GIRL, THE [Musical/Romance/Business] B: Daniel Kusell; M: Albert Von Tilzer; LY: Neville Fleeson; D: Daniel Kusell and Edgar J. MacGregor; CH: Sammy Lee; P: Laurence Schwab and Daniel Kusell; T: Earl Carroll Theatre; 8/28/22 (322)

From tiny acorns, mighty oaks do grow could have been the motto of the *Gingham Girl* for the show evolved from an Eddie Buzzell vaudeville sketch called "A Man of Affairs" into one of the biggest hits of the season. Its petite stars, Buzzell being 5'2" and Helen Ford 4'11", were major reasons for its popularity, although Buzzell, a vaudeville performer, was here making his Broadway debut.

Only a week before coming to Broadway this folksy little show was being played out of town as *Love and Kisses*. When the name was changed to suggest the kind of frocks worn by its heroine, a gingham proscenium arch was added to the set design.

Unlike many of its contemporaries, *The Gingham Girl* was a legitimate musical comedy, not a revue disguised as one by virtue of a skeletal plot. The *Herald* called it "a jiggling, jingling, joshing show, the kind that Broadway likes, all the way."

Buzzell played John Cousins, a wise-cracking hick, and Ford was his rural flapper girlfriend Mary. The plot had John leave the countryside to come to New York. With $100 given her as a parting present by John, Mary follows him and soon sets up in the city a terrifically successful cookie business. Eventually, the pair are reunited making fast-selling Blue Bird cookies together.

The show's song hit that endured was "As Long as I Have You."

GIRL AND THE CAT, THE (La niña y el gato) [Comedy/Crime/Romance/Spanish/Spanish Language] A: Carlos Arniches; D: Gregorio Martinez-Sierra; P: Spanish Art Theatre and Crosby Gaige; T: Forrest Theatre; 5/5/27 (3)

The versatile prima donna of the visiting Spanish Art Theatre, Catalina Barcena, displayed her range by playing the broadly comic lead in this boisterous slapstick piece by the popular and fertile Arniches that captured many laughs by its funny lines and movement. "It goes with the vim of a Tiller chorus and the humor of a movie comedian," observed the *Times*.

Barcena enacted a virtuous drudge working in a thieving family's household. A snowstorm awaits her and her pet cat, bird, and dog when she refuses to engage in a robbery. While huddled for warmth in a park, the cat eats the bird. She takes shelter in a kindly home but decides to turn crook; when, after stealing a picture, she chooses to reform by replacing it, she is caught but forgiven. Romance with another servant soon develops.

GIRL FRIEND, THE [Musical/Sports/Gambling/Romance] B: Herbert Fields; M: Richard Rodgers; LY: Lorenz Hart; D: John Harwood; CH: Jack Haskell; S: P. Dodd Ackerman; P: Lew Fields; T: Vanderbilt Theatre; 3/17/26 (306)

Sam White and Eva Puck had appeared in an earlier flop show by Rodgers, Hart, and Fields, *The Melody Man*, and they reappeared in the present hit, the second in a row for its creators, following *Dearest Enemy*. Eccentric dancer and comic White played chicken-rancher and six-day bicycle racer Leonard Silver, and Puck, a popular vaudeville entertainer, played his girlfriend and trainer, Mollie Farrell. Silver's training includes pedalling with a wheel attached to a churn on a Long Island farm. He gets involved with a promoter (Frank Doane) who puts him into a fixed race, and he also gets mixed up with the promoter's sister (Evelyn Cavanaugh), but all turns out well and he wins the race and is happy with Mollie at the end.

The big Rodgers and Hart hits were the romantic "Blue Room" and the Charleston number "The Girl Friend." Arthur Hornblow called the show "tuneful and breezy," and the *Times* found it "generally captivating," with "adroit and well-fashioned rhymes" and "very agreeable tunes." Field's book was nowhere as successful as the score, Hornblow declaring it not funny, and Richard Dana Skinner dismissing it as "doleful."

GIRL IN THE SPOTLIGHT, THE [Musical/Show Business/Romance] B/LY: Richard Bruce; M: Victor Herbert; D/P: George W. Lederer; T: Knickerbocker Theatre; 7/12/20 (54)

Veteran musical producer-director George Lederer staged his last Broadway show with this Victor Herbert operetta about a poor Irish drudge (Mary Milburn) who learns by heart the songs of a composer (Ben Forbes) staying at the boarding house where she works; when the prima donna of his new show refuses to go on, she does so in her place to acclaim as well as to wedding bells with the songwriter.

Critics found the plot worthwhile and well developed but saved their accolades for Herbert's score. The work was ably performed and presented, but no hit songs emerged from it, and it lasted only as long as the summer. "Taken all in all," reported the *Evening Post*, "it was a most delightful entertainment for those who love real music, wholesome fun, pretty girls, and clever dancing." Popular eccentric dancers Hal Skelly and Johnny Dooley were responsible for much of the enjoyment.

GIRL TROUBLE [Comedy/Youth/Sex/Family] A: Barry Conners; D: Allan Dinehart; P: Richard Herndon; T: Belmont Theatre; 10/25/28 (22)

Girl Trouble, snapped Robert Littell, was "feeble rubbish," and *Time* discovered in it "a disturbing lack of comic inspiration." Director-star Allan Dinehart frittered his talents away on the role of Jimmy Lockhart, a shy adolescent with an overprotective mother (Lucia Moore) who annuls his precocious marriage to a carnival girl (Dorothy Hall) only to see him thereafter ensconced in constant girl trouble. Finally, his affair with another femme leads his mom to permit the boy and his former bride to retie the knot.

GIRL WITH THE CARMINE LIPS, THE [Comedy/Marriage/Sex/Law] A/ P: Wilson Collison; D: Priestly Morrison; T: Punch and Judy Theatre; 8/9/20 (16)

Early in the century an anonymous actress had toured in a vaudeville piece called "The Girl with Auburn Hair." Wilson Collison tried to stimulate curiosity in his new farce by employing a similar device, which also served to protect his amateurish leading lady who was apparently making her professional debut. The play was "a mirthless and vulgar farce" (Alexander Woollcott) that no amount of publicity mongering could infuse with life.

A female lawyer of doubtful ethics (anonymous) seeks to apply the old Band-Aid cure to save the marriage of Peter (Wilfred Clark) and Jane (Grace Menken). A couple of chippies are sent to the husband's apartment, where they get drunk and put on sexy undies. Peter's alcoholic fog keeps him from being aware of their behavior. His wife and her mother show up, and a raucous chase scene follows. All is straightened out when the lawyer confesses her plan to arouse Jane's jealousy.

"[N]o redeeming virtues whatever," said the *World*.

M.M.-C.

GIVE AND TAKE [Comedy/Labor/Business/Romance] A: Aaron Hoffman; D: W. H. Gilmore; P: Max Marcin, Inc.; T: Forty-ninth Street Theatre; 1/15/23 (188)

"[A] mixture of humor, hokum and sentiment" (Playgoer) that, despite generally tepid reviews, had enough laugh-motivating steam to turn it into a considerable success.

It featured top character actors George Sidney and Louis Mann as, respectively, foreman and owner of Bauer's Canning Factory, and close friends for years. Just when the firm seems to be tottering financially, the employees rise in protest demanding numerous benefits. Kruger, the foreman, sides with the workers, who are further supported by the owner's socialist-minded son (Robert W. Craig), whose suggestion it is to turn the place over to the workers to run. The revolutionary plan fizzles, but things work out when the workers dip into their pockets to save the company from failure, and the son devises a clever sales scheme. There is also a romance fulfilled between the son and the foreman's daughter (Vivian Tobin).

No serious intent was behind the radical politics of the comedy, merely a desire to provide a fun-filled farce. In one breath the play extols the slogan of "Industrial Democracy" and in the next frowns upon the Bolshevists of Russia.

GLASS OF WATER, A (Le verre d'eau) [Dramatic Revival] A: Eugéne Scribe; D: Maria Germanova; DS: Jean Bilibine; P: American Laboratory Theatre; T: American Laboratory Theatre (OB); 3/5/30 (9)

Scribe's French five-act comedy of 1840 set at the court of England's Queen Anne (Maria Germanova) and in which, amidst political embroilments, Captain of the Guards Arthur Masham (Britton Diller) attracts the monarch's attentions, as well as those of the Duchess of Marlborough (Emily Floyd) and commoner Abigail Churchill (Angela Mulinos). It provided a chance for this Off-Broadway company to "give an incredibly bad account of themselves," wrote Brooks Atkinson: "Except as a classroom exercise, *A Glass of Water* is pretty worthless and may now be permitted to rest in peace."

GLASS SLIPPER, THE (Az üvegcipö) [Comedy/Hungarian/Prostitution/Romance/Sex] A: Ferenc Molnar; D: Philip Moeller; DS: Lee Simonson P: Theatre Guild, under the management of Charles Frohman, Inc.; T: Guild Theatre; 10/19/25 (65)

A disunified comedy-drama that pleased some but displeased many others. It followed the tribulations of a fantasizing, sex-starved nineteen-year-old kitchen drudge, Irma Szabo (June Walker), who is in the employ of a Budapest boarding house, where she is deeply in love with her Prince Charming, a surly forty-eight-year-old carpenter, Lajos Sipos (Lee Baker), himself the lover for ten years of the slatternly landlady (Helen Westley). Although the landlady also lusts after a younger boarder (George Baxter), who in turn feels similarly toward Irma, she marries the older man, to the chagrin of the wench who thereupon gets drunk and applies to a whorehouse for work. The play concludes in a police station, where the bordello madame defends her practice, and others appear as witnesses on Irma's behalf. The carpenter finally decides that Irma is really for him.

Those who enjoyed the play did so primarily because of the depiction of the young waif's "whimsical, half-sad, half-gay character" (*Times*), which was likened to a Barrie portrait, especially as played by June Walker, whose personal reviews were raves. But the piece failed to hold up structurally, was patently artificial and manipulative, offended several reviewers by its situational and linguistic frankness ("I found nothing but dirt"—Arthur Hornblow), confused reality with fantasy, and seemed overlong.

GLORY [Musical/Romance/Small Town/Business] B: James Montgomery; M: Maurice de Packh and Harry Tierney; LY: James Dyrenforth and Joseph McCarthy; D: Bert French; P: Vanderbilt Producing Company; T: Vanderbilt Theatre; 12/25/22 (74)

Another countrified show glorifying rural virtues, *Glory* was by the author of the great hit *Irene*, which it echoed in style but could not match musically. It was "good, light, lyrical entertainment," Heywood Broun assured his readers. What the *Times* especially liked about the music was how "the songs spring naturally from the score and from the plot."

The heavily plotted show was about the people in a small New England town, where Hiram Dexter (Jack Clifford), the richest but most tight-fisted man, owns a local factory as well as the home of Abner Moore (Peter Lang), the town soak and father of the prettiest girl, Glory (Patti Harrold). A young man (Walter Regan) arrives, sets up a booming business, saves Glory from a forced (but phony) marriage to Lem King (Raymond Hackett), sees Glory defeat Hiram's daughter in a popularity contest, and, amidst setting other matters right, wins Glory for himself.

GLORY HALLELUJAH [Drama/Hotel/Death/Religion] A: Thomas Mitchell and Bertram Bloch; D/P: Guthrie McClintic; T: Broadhurst Theatre; 4/6/26 (15)

Henning Berger's *Deluge*, seen in a revival several seasons earlier, may have inspired this drama, for both plays were basically about the same subject, that is, how people react when the end of their lives is near. Berger had his characters trapped in a saloon during a flood; the present work pictured its personages as lowly residents of a seedy Lower East Side hotel who have heard it reported that the world will die in seven days when a comet shooting across the sky will absorb the sun's heat, causing the earth to freeze. Each of the characters finds a way of dealing with the situation; one of them, a scrubwoman (June Walker), afraid to die because of her sins, is so inspired by a tramp's (Charles Bickford) tale of God's benificence that when the scare is over and the sun shines again, she shoots herself to seek a less cruel existence.

June Walker was wonderful, but the play, despite moments of promise, was "mere sound and fury, signifying nothing" (George Jean Nathan). "It is cleverly managed, well acted and ingenious," declared Joseph Wood Krutch, "but clever manipulation and ingenuity do no more than produce a sort of semi-conviction and a mild desire to see how it will turn out."

GO EASY, MABEL [Musical/Sex/Marriage] B/M/LY: Charles George; D: Bertram Harrison and Julian Alfred; P: Hudson Productions Company, Inc.; T: Longacre Theatre; 5/8/22 (16)

A talent-wasting piece of "unutterable piffle" (Arthur Hornblow) that bore notice only because of the presence of the versatile Estelle Winwood and the delightful ex-Mrs. George M. Cohan, Ethel Levey, who had not been seen locally in several years. With these and several other talented performers (including Margaret Dumont of later Marx Brothers fame), and a decently mounted production to boot, author-composer Charles George (rumored to be a pseudonym for several collaborators) could do nothing interesting script or music-wise. "It is the kind of musical play," declared Alexander Woollcott, "in which the chorus is brought on when a character goes to the telephone and says: 'What? Girls for my new musical play? Send them up.' "

The inane plot concerns the faded marriage of Ted and Mable Sparks (Will J. Deming and Estelle Winwood), who are advised by friends to dally with others so as to rekindle the sparks in their own marriage; much of the humor depended on the excessively flirtatious behavior of the pretty stenographer (Levey) Ted lures to fulfill his side of the arrangement.

GO WEST, YOUNG MAN [Comedy/Show Business/Romance] A/M: Fay Pulsifer; D: Hal Briggs; S: Charles Auburn; P: Westminster Productions; T: Punch and Judy Theatre; 11/12/23 (48)

A tale about a lad (Percy Helton) studying barefoot dancing in New York, the Texas girl (Kay Johnson) he meets there and follows home, and his efforts to win the girl by foiling an oil swindler; this comedy was seen by the *Times* critic as satirizing esthetic dancing, boarding houses, and oil stock promoters "in a blood curdling fashion." The *World*'s critic wrote, "It is not only the worst play in New York, it is the worst play that was ever produced in New York and the acting was below the playwriting." The *Herald*'s reviewer, however, found that "The play had originality and a good deal of real fun in it."

H.H.

(1) GOAT ALLEY [Drama/Blacks/Romance/Sex] A: Ernest Howard Culbertson; D: Cecil Owen; P: Alice Wade Mulhern; T: Bijou Theatre; 6/20/21 (8)

The producers of this play were intent on demonstrating its sociological accuracy as a picture of contemporary black life. Not only did a piece about it appear in the *Medical Review of Reviews*, but a doctor addressed the audience about the play's truthfulness before the rising of the curtain. This did not avail the play greatly, since it was exceptional in neither scientific nor artistic terms.

A black cast, presumably amateur, performed the "crude and inexpert play" (*Times*) that only now and then showed sparks of vitality. The *Times* opined that whatever realism it had could as easily have been projected "by professional actors in blackface."

Because it had a racy plot not unlike Eugene Walter's *Easiest Way*, audience members under twenty were not allowed in by the management. This plot was set in a Washington, D.C., ghetto and focused on Lucy Belle (Lillian McKee), an ignorant, indigent young woman totally in love with Sam Reed (Barrington Carter); while he is in jail, however, she is driven to a series of unwilling affairs. Upon his release, the angry Reed, refusing to accept her and her illegitimate child, kills her.

Ludwig Lewisohn decried the sanitizing the play had undergone at the hands of the "sociologists and propagandists" in prettifying the ending, which originally had the mother, Medea-like, kill both her child and herself.

(2) [Dramatic Revival] D: Egon Brecher; P: Toussaint Players; T: Princess Theatre; 4/20/27 (13)

New York's second staging of this play lasted only a bit longer than the original did. Only its all-black cast was of interest to *Time*, which termed the play "an undistinguished dish of canned melodrama." Others scorned its "sociological value." The *Times* called it "a crude and uneven work." This production, the reviewer noted, "serves to dispel what seems to be a prevalent illusion—namely that all negroes are good actors. Although there are some first rate performances, there are also others which are pretty bad."

GOAT SONG (Bocksgesang) [Drama/Period/Romance/Politics/German] A: Franz Werfel; TR: Ruth Langner; D: Jacob Ben-Ami; DS: Lee Simonson; P: Theatre Guild; T: Guild Theatre; 1/25/26 (58)

After a season that disappointed many because of the flabbiness of its selections, the Theatre Guild sprang this bombshell of realism, expressionism, and symbolism on New York, with controversial effect. Reviews ranged from the confused to the ecstatic, but the event was recognized as a milestone for the Guild.

Werfel's play occurs in the 1790s in a Slavic country region. It draws its title from the Greek word for tragedy and also implies the ancient idea of the ritual scapegoat. *Goat Song* depicts the dilemmas that arise when a landed family's son, half-beast/half-man, consigned since birth to a prison, escapes and is used by rebellious farmers as a symbol of their revolt. Juvan (Alfred Lunt), the student who leads the peasants, frees the monster (said to represent the Dionysiac force in humans) when Stanja (Lynn Fontanne) enters its cage to cut its bonds. The beast is killed, the rebellion quelled, and Juvan, after he and Stanja declare their mutual love, executed. Stanja reveals to the monster's mother that she is bearing its child.

Viewers debated the symbolical meanings of the work, which is rich in allusions, folklore, poetry, and superstitions. Whatever its significance, one critic asserted that the dutiful search for meanings led many to lose "sight of a really bully play" (Larry Barretto). However, Brooks Atkinson found it chaotic, "ponderous and unwieldy." In the brilliant cast were Blanche Yurka, George Gaul, Helen Westley, Edward G. Robinson, Frank Reicher, and, in a small role, Harold Clurman.

GOD LOVES US [Comedy-Drama/Business/Labor] A: J. P. McEvoy; D: Guthrie McClintic; S: Woodman Thompson; P: Actors' Theatre; T: Maxine Elliott's Theatre; 10/18/26 (32)

A satirical play with an undertone of tragedy about the enslavement of modern humans to the American religion of commerce. Set within an admirably suggestive constructivist setting that resembled the hidden girders and beams of a skyscraper, the piece made a definite impression but lasted a mere month. It was an episodic play, backed by jazz music and staged so that its multiple locales could be represented cinematically within the set's various levels through selective lighting. Somewhat expressionist in form, and not unlike *The Adding Machine* in theme, its central character was Hector Midge (J. C. Nugent), a greeting-card writer and assistant sales manager whose quarter century of devoted service is ignored and who loses his chance at becoming sales manager when the job goes to the boss's snooty son (Cebra Graves). Defeated in his search for other employment, he resumes his former dead-end job.

Time thought that "nothing on the current stage satirizes so incisively, originally, the cruel banalaties of 'big business go-getters.' " One who thought otherwise was Brooks Atkinson, who found it "verbose and desultory."

GOD, MAN, AND THE DEVIL (Got, Mentsh, und Taivel) [Drama/Yiddish/Family/Fantasy/Jews/Yiddish Language] A: Jacob Gordin; D/P: Maurice Schwartz; S: Mordecai Gorelik; T: Yiddish Art Theatre (OB); 12/21/28

Maurice Schwartz and Lazar Freed of the Yiddish Art Theatre offered a memorable acting duel in Jacob Gordin's Faust-like drama in which Schwartz played Masik, the Satanic figure, and Freed Dubrovner, the poor scribe. Masik makes it possible for the scribe to win a great sum of money, which eventuates in the latter's bringing pain, unhappiness, and poverty to his family and neighbors, ending with his suicide.

Robert Littell said this "half-allegorical, half-realistic play" was "extraordinarily interesting," more because of the production's quality than the writing itself: "The acting is more florid, richer, more expressive than ours, but it always stays within the limits of its own style....More interesting even than the acting are the strange and imaginative settings of Mordecai Gorelik."

(1) GOD OF VENGEANCE, THE [Dramatic Revival/Yiddish Language] A: Sholem Asch; D: Rudolph Schildkraut; T: Irving Place Theatre (OB); 11/3/21

A violently powerful Polish 1907 play written in Yiddish that raised storms of protest in some quarters because of its torrid subject matter. This emotional drama was produced in Berlin by Max Reinhardt and was seen not long afterwards in its original Yiddish in New York. Rudolph Schildkraut, who had played it for Reinhardt, acted it in New York in German, Yiddish, and, finally, in English. His 1921 Yiddish production was ragged except for his own brilliant acting. He played brothel-keeper Yekel Shepshovitch, a sinner whose aspirations for salvation are tied up in the soul of his daughter Rifkele, whose purity he wishes to preserve as moral vindication of his own degradation. But the god of vengeance leads her to become a prostitute and a lesbian, destroying Yekel's hopes for her and for himself. He consigns his wife and child to his own brothel at the end.

The *Times* said the play "remains still one of the finest plays of the Yiddish theatre, the most powerfully realistic, the most moving and human, the most sincere and compassionate in its comprehension of human striving."

(2) T: Provincetown Playhouse (OB); 12/20/22 (137)

Schildkraut's English staging opened Off Broadway but soon proved popular enough to transfer to Broadway's Apollo Theatre on 2/19/22, where it completed its run. The controversial work now stirred the ire of the Society for the Suppression of Vice, and the star had to spend a night in jail when the play was temporarily closed down.

The fiery work was, said Kenneth Macgowan, "so badly presented that it seemed only some grotesquely comic horror." Heywood Broun, approving the play as "honest and highly skillful," was shocked by the more blatant of its features, especially a kissing scene between two women. There was strong approval of Schildkraut's work in his English-language debut: "his piety, his confusion, his aspiration and despair, his humility and ugliness and paternal devotion and violence, all are rendered with absolute truth," claimed Stark Young.

According to Schildkraut's actor son, Joseph (in *My Father and I*), a protracted court battle over the play's alleged salaciousness ensued with leading figures in American culture and law, such as Oswald Garrison Villard, H. A. Overstreet, and Dr. Henry Neumann coming to Asch's defense. Still, the outcome was a negative decision against the production; Schildkraut and his producers were fined $200 each.

GODS OF THE LIGHTNING [Drama/Labor/Politics/Crime/Trial] A: Maxwell Anderson and Harold Hickerson; D: Hamilton MacFadden; P: Hamilton MacFadden and Kellogg Gary; T: Little Theatre; 10/24/28 (29)

A fictionalized, propagandistic account of the notorious seven-year *Sacco-Vanzetti* case in which two anarchists were executed for a murder of which many believed them to be guiltless. The result, to Joseph Wood Krutch, was "one of the most effective dramas of social protest which it has ever been my privilege to see." The coauthors, he claimed, set up their proposition "with a passionate eloquence which never falters." The play did infuriate many by its ideology, which insisted that America was a land in which only the wealthy capitalists had complete freedom, and that an insidious tyranny lurked behind such symbols as the stars and stripes.

The plot follows the tragic tribulations of International Workers of the World labor-agitator Macready (Charles Bickford) and Italian anarchist Capraro (Horace Braham) when they are framed for a murder committed by their rebellious friend Suvorin (Leo Bulgakov). The powerful trial scene, manipulated by a calculating D.A. (Robert Brister) and a biased judge (Douglas Wood), finds them guilty and they are sentenced to die by electrocution.

The play used numerous details of the actual case, even some of the judge's recorded statements, but greatly simplified the action to melodramatic proportions. In spite of generally positive notices, the play was removed in less than a month. Among the capable cast members was Sylvia Sidney as Macready's sweetheart.

GO-GO [Musical/Night Club/Romance/Show Business] B: Harry L. Cort and George E. Stoddard; M: C. Luckyeth Roberts; LY: Alex Rogers; D: Walter Brooks; P: John Cort; T: Daly's Theatre; 3/12/23 (138)

Noise, speed, and energy were the ingredients that stood out in this otherwise barely memorable show about a romantic mixup stemming from the hoary device of twins. Jack Locksmith (Bernard Granville) falls in love with nurse Isabel Parker (Josephine Stevens) in France and then looks her up in the States only to come across her cabaret singer twin Florabel (played by the same actress) instead. By the end of Act Two his error is corrected, and he and Isabel find each other again.

The comedy elements here were conspicuous by their nonpresence, despite feeble tries at puns, burlesque-like costumes, and eccentric characters. The ballads were unexceptional, but the rhythm numbers were fast and furious, and several critics likened them to the best of the black revues. The *Evening Mail* called *Go-Go* ''the fastest white show Broadway has ever seen. . . . It is greased-lightning jazz, super-syncopation even to the supers. The chorus seemed inexhaustible.''

GOIN' HOME [Drama/Blacks/Marriage/Sex/War/Military/Race/Friendship/France] A: Ransom Rideout; D/P: Brock Pemberton; S: Raymond Sovey; T: Hudson Theatre; 8/23/28 (77)

An earnestly written prizewinning drama (known as *Deep River* in little theatre circles) about white-black race relations shortly after World War I in a French seaport town, where New Orleans black man Israel du Bois (Richard Hale, a white actor), released from the Foreign Legion, marries cafe proprietress Lise (Barbara Bulgakov), she believing him a prosperous man back home. To the cafe comes the white Major (Russell Hicks) for whose family Israel formerly worked as a servant and with whom he was raised. When the horrified Major discovers that Lise's only interest in Israel is his presumed wealth, he convinces the black man to return to the United States with him. But the officer gets drunk, and Lise seduces him. When a primitive Senegalese friend (Clarence Redd) realizes the Major's betrayal, he tries to kill him, but Israel shoots the African and goes home with his white friend.

Euphemia Van Rensellaer Wyatt summed up the themes: ''the contrast between the domesticated and the primitive Negro and the division of loyalty in a black soul between the white master and its own flesh and blood.'' The play seemed too filled with coincidences and sentimentality; yet it retained a great interest and power that overcame strong reservations. Richard Dana Skinner remarked, ''there is no doubt of the strength with which the theme is handled in the main, nor of the diverting and frequently gripping theatrical character of many of the scenes.''

GOLD [Drama/Mental Illness/Crime/Sea/Family] A: Eugene O'Neill; D: Homer Saint-Gaudens; P: John D. Williams; T: Frazee Theatre; 6/1/21 (13)

A lesser O'Neill effort, its fourth act being a reworking of an earlier one-act of his, ''Where the Cross is Made.'' The new play was a clear failure. Arthur Hornblow wrote: ''Its gloom is so utterly unrelieved as to defeat its dramatic purpose. It is tediously reiterative and scenes of keen psychologic verity are followed by those of conventional banality. It is feebly constructed, so palpably episodic, that it doesn't hang together.''

Its story follows Captain Bartlett (Willard Mack), who, his whaling ship wrecked in the Malay Archipelago, finds, with his crew, a treasure chest. He stands by and lets two of the men be killed when they declare it worthless. He is rescued and plans to go back to retrieve the buried treasure, but remorse for the men's deaths gnaws at him until he loses his mind; his wife (Katherine Grey) dies, his son (E. J. Ballantine) goes mad, and after the Captain dies, the treasure is revealed as junk.

GOLD BRAID [Drama/Military/Marriage/Romance/Tropics] A: Ann Shelby; D: Gene Gowing; S: David S. Gaither; P: Louis A. Safien; T: Theatre Masque; 5/13/30 (7)

Married unhappily to the unpleasant Major Rodney (Edward Reese), an American Intelligence officer stationed in the Philippines, Linda Rodney is commanded by her promotion-seeking husband to spy on Julio Cortez (Alen Devitt), a suspected Moro rebel. But she has fallen in love with Julio and will not reveal his secrets. She decries her husband's methods and promises Julio to wait for him in America.

Atmospheric tropical effects, gunfire, flashing knives, tom-toms, and the like could not vivify this dank melodrama of tired clichés and stereotypes. Noting that things were then going poorly in Washington, D.C., Brooks Atkinson wrote in his review, "No one expects the drama to be better than the government."

GOLD DIGGERS, THE (Die Gold Greber) [Comedy/Jews/Romance/Yiddish/ Yiddish Language] A: Sholem Aleichem; AD: D. Berkowitz; M: Herman Zaetzky; D/P: Maurice Schwartz; T: Yiddish Art Theatre (OB); 12/2/27

A noisy, raucous staging of a Sholem Aleichem (the "Jewish Mark Twain") story about a town whose residents believe superstitiously that Napoleon buried gold in their Jewish cemetery when he was retreating from Moscow. A visiting American Jew, aware that the legend is apocryphal, plays a trick on the town by impersonating a ghost and informing the town's leading citizen that the American knows about the buried treasure. The town digs up the graves in their search for the gold, while the American elopes with the leading citizen's daughter.

"Notwithstanding the continuous racket, aided and abetted by the uproar of the audience's laughter, the play is amusing and again reveals Sholem Aleichem's insight into Jewish life," remarked the *Times*.

GOLDEN AGE, THE [Drama/Rural/Romance/Family] A: Lester Lonergan and Charlton Andrews; D: Lester Lonergan; S: Nicholas Yellenti; P: John Tuerk; T: Longacre Theatre; 4/24/28 (6)

The critics did so thorough a hatchet job on *The Golden Age* that it could not find breath enough to live one week. Gilbert W. Gabriel declared it "an unholy bore in those moments when it did not topple over into burlesque."

It was placed in the peaceful, idyllic setting of Enchanted Land, Utah, and was about a family living in primitive contentment among the Indians; they take in a "Stranger Man" (Warren William), betroth him to their youngest (Leila Frost), but watch him leave when he is revealed by a pair of air mail carriers whose plane has crashed as an impotent war fugitive.

GOLDEN DAWN [Musical/Africa/Blacks/Romance/Tropics/Religion] B: Otto Harbach and Oscar Hammerstein II; M: Emmerich Kalman and Herbert Stothart; D: Reginald Hammerstein; CH: David Bennett; S: Joseph Urban; C: Mark Mooring; P: Arthur Hammerstein; T: Hammersteins's Theatre; 11/30/27 (200)

The opening of the elaborate new Hammerstein Theatre at Broadway and Fifty-third Street, built in memory of nineteenth-century opera impressario Oscar Hammerstein by his son Arthur, was marked by this successful, lavishly presented operetta's debut. Metropolitan Opera singer Louise Hunter was assigned the leading role of Dawn, blonde African high priestess, whose tribe resides near a German prison camp. She is desired by the black overseer Shep Keyes (Robert Chisholm) and an English prisoner of war, Steve Allen (Paul Gregory); she manages to end up with Steve, whom she loves, after learning that she is really white.

Gorgeous sets and native masks and costumes, ritual dances, and African superstitions gave the show an aura of the exotic; Richard Dana Skinner said that only its excessive comic relief and conventional chorus numbers stood in the way of its being an opera. Stark Young berated the "dreadful book" of this "dull and trashy entertainment." In the small role of Anzac was the unnoticed new actor Archie Leach (later Cary Grant), making his Broadway bow.

GOLDEN DAYS [Comedy/Small Town/Youth/Romance/War] A: Sidney Toler and Marion Short; D: Sidney Toler; P: George C. Tyler and A. L. Erlanger; T: Gaiety Theatre; 11/1/21 (40)

A pleasant romantic comedy with a new twist on the familiar Cinderella story. Emphasizing a milieu of youthful charm as well as inanity, it employed a large cast of juveniles and ingenues, all of them appropriately cast for age.

Helen Hayes starred as the sweet but poor little country maid Mary Anne, whose local yokel boyfriend William (Robert Fiske) deserts her for a sophisticated city cutie (Selena Royle). She regains his attention by faking a liason with another fellow (Donald Gallaher), but by the time William realizes his mistake, Mary Anne and the new boy are in love.

Alexander Woollcott found the comedy "surprisingly spontaneous and true" at many points, and he especially savored the "delicious" chatter of the youthful characters. However, he confided, "the play is uninspired in too many of its scenes to be continuously beguiling."

(1) GOLDFISH, THE (L'École des cocottes) [Comedy/Marriage/Romance/French] A: Paul Armont and Marcel Gerbidon; AD: Gladys Unger; D: Stuart Walker; P: Messrs. Shubert; T: Maxine Elliott's Theatre; 4/17/22 (169)

Known in its mother tongue as *L'École des cocottes* Armont and Gerbidon's "excellent French play [was] done into hash for the American boulevards," snarled Arthur Hornblow, "under the latest contribution to the zoological series of play titles." According to this critic, Gladys Unger's adaptation Americanized the Gallic delicacy in its shift of the locale from Paris to New York, its transformation of "the piquant mistress of a young, struggling artist" to "the hardshelled, chorus-brained wife of a jazz song writer," and its plot of a woman using various lovers on her ascent up the ladder of society made into a similar ascent with new husbands filling in for new lovers.

In its new trappings the comedy told of social-climbing Jenny Jones (Marjorie Rambeau), who works her way through two divorces and one husband's death to the point where she is about to become wife to the Duke of Middlesex (Dennis Cleughs); however, sentimental memories of her humble past rush in, and since by chance her first love (Wilfred Lytell) shows up just then, she melts with him into the night wearing the same poor frock she wore when they were lovers six years before.

Ten weeks into its run the show transferred to the Astor Theatre.

(2) [Dramatic Revival/Spanish Language] P: Camila Quiroga and the Argentine Players; T: Manhattan Opera House; 12/14/27 (1)

An unreviewed revival, under the title *El professor de buenos modales*, given in Spanish during a week-long stay by Argentina's famed actress Camila Quiroga.

GOLEM, THE [Drama/Jews/Fantasy/Period/Religion/Yiddish/Hebrew Language] A: H. Leivick; D: Boris I. Vershilov; S: Yignat Nivinsky; M: Moshe Milnar; P: Habima Players of Moscow; T: Irving Place Theatre (OB); 2/4/27

One of the most famous works of the Yiddish drama was this powerful religious work based on Jewish legend, written by the great Yiddish poet Leivick after he had emigrated from Russia to America, but offered to New York in a Hebrew version by the Habima company of Moscow, which had premiered the work in 1925.

A work of deep profundity and religious symbolism, it is set in Prague in the sixteenth century and depicts the creation by the Rabbi of Prague, the "Maharal" (B. Tchemerinsky), of a monstrous figure, the Golem (A. Meskin), out of clay, to be used by the Jews as a defensive weapon against the enemies of their religion. The creature is a mindless destructive force, controlled only by the Rabbi's powers. The Messiah (A. Rovina) and Elijah (G. Tchechik-Efrati) are sent away so that the Golem can pulverize the Jews' persecutors. Struggling with internal demons of hate and fear, the Golem turns against the Jews; the people continue to suffer from their new oppressor. Finally, the Rabbi finds the potent words that allow him to subdue the monster and transform him back to clay.

In the Habima staging, noted the *Times*, "Action, word and gesture are welded into a unity which combines the vividness of accomplished pantomime to the sonority of dramatic speech." After the *Dybbuk*, *The Golem* was the Habima's greatest success and remained in the repertoire for three decades.

GOOD BAD WOMAN, A [Drama/Sex/Romance/Crime] A: William J. McNally; P: William A. Brady and A. H. Woods; T: Comedy Theatre; 2/9/25 (17)

A lurid, sordid play that brought on an antivice crusade headed by District Attorney Joab Banton. Helen MacKellar played a low-class, gauche woman of shady character, a wicked femme who turns her nature to good uses in the working out of the plot. So rough was it by contemporary standards that the D.A. managed to close it after seventeen performances. He claimed, "In my opinion no deletion or alteration, either in the dialogue or the action, can make it morally fit." However, the producers went ahead and made some minor changes and reopened the play on 6/22/25 to a packed house. There was, according to the reviews, very little change from the first staging. It ran for sixty-four performances with Josephine Evans in the MacKellar role.

The plot concerned the morally loose Eileen Donovan (MacKellar) who seduces Archie Capper (Donald Cameron) on her first night back in town and later arranges with her blacksmith father (Walter Law) to kill the husband of the woman (Edith King) Archie loves so the pair can be happy together.

Joseph Wood Krutch said the play "outdoes all current plays in three directions: none is so violent, so coarse, or so absurd."

GOOD BOY [Musical/Theatre/Romance] B: Otto Harbach, Oscar Hammerstein II and Henry Myers; M/LY: Herbert Stothart, Bert Kalmar, and Harry Ruby; D: Reginald Hammerstein; CH: Busby Berkeley; S: John Wenger; P: Arthur Hammerstein; T: Hammerstein's Theatre; 9/5/28 (253)

A multiscened backstage musical using so many sets that the stage was equipped with treadmills to make the scenery changes as swift as possible. The idea came to Oscar Hammerstein after seeing Piscator's Berlin staging of *The Good Soldier Schweik*. *Good Boy* is the show that introduced Helen Kane's inimitable little-girl-voiced rendition of "I Wanna Be Loved by You," which led her to be labeled the "Boop-de-Boop Girl." John Wenger's sets depicted various New York locales; one scene was unusual as "one side of a hotel room swung around to become a balcony from which the lovers were vouchsafed a glimpse of Central Park and the panorama of the city," wrote the *Times*. Busby Berkeley made cunning use of the treadmills in a mechanical doll number with a bevy of chorines kept moving in interesting formations.

Eddie Buzzell was Walter Meakin, the country bumpkin from Arkansas who venture forth to conquer Broadway with his brother Cicero (Charles Butterworth); he meets and loves pretty chorus-girl Betty Summers (Barbara Newberry). She gets him a chorus boy's job, and they separate, but a doll he creates gives a show's producer a great idea for a number, he earns much money, and he gets Betty back.

Charles Butterworth was the best-liked performer as the loutish farm boy forever putting his hands above his head and saying, "Oh, the pity of it all." Also scoring well was Borrah Minevitch of harmonica-playing fame.

GOOD FELLOW, THE [Comedy/Family] A: George S. Kaufman and Herman J. Mankiewicz; D: Howard Lindsay and George S. Kaufman; P: Crosby Gaige; T: Playhouse Theatre; 10/5/26 (8)

George S. Kaufman took a heavy beating with this one-week flop cowritten with Herman J. Manckiewicz, his coworker on the drama desk of the New York

Times. Arthur Hornblow called it "a nondescript play in three acts, utilizing much old material rather clumsily and developing little that is new." It had to do with a *Show-Off*-like hail-fellow-well-met character, Jim Helton (John E. Hazzard), who is so enamored of his Wilkes-Barre, Pennsylvania, lodge, the Ancient Order of Corsicans, of which he is the Grand Napoleon, that he gets himself tied up in a scheme to raise $10,000 so that their convention can take place in Wilkes-Barre; he fouls up the works, ends up in a domestic mess, and finally resigns from his beloved brotherhood.

Taking a cue from *The Would-Be Gentleman* of Moliere, the authors interpolated a sidesplitting, though out-of-place, spoof on secret-society initiation rites. A considerable number of fraternal-order members took umbrage at the play's mockery of their ritual methods. The play gave Kaufman his first directorial credit, which he shared with Howard Lindsay.

GOOD HOPE, THE (Op Hoop van Zegen) [Dramatic Revival] A: Herman Heijermans; TR: Lilian Saunders and Caroline Heijermans-Houwink; D: Eva Le Gallienne; S: Cleon Throckmorton; P: Civic Repertory Company; T: Civic Repertory Theatre (OB); 10/18/27 (49)

In 1908 Ellen Terry had played this 1900 Dutch tragedy in New York during one of her tours. It now was restaged by the Civic Repertory Company with Eva Le Gallienne directing and playing Jo. Although not thoroughly well performed, the production was respectable, and the play was appreciated as a worthwhile contribution. Alexander Woollcott said, "The play, though it has in it compassion and truth, has a rambling gait," and Brooks Atkinson summarized it as "a rugged, noble drama, seething with humor, hatred and the black fate of the seaman."

Heijerman's realistic thesis drama, reputed to have influenced Dutch maritime laws, was about the unscrupulous shipowners who, secure in the knowledge that their losses are insured, send their fishing boats out to sea despite serious weaknesses in them, as well as about the North Sea fishing-village families who suffer the dread of seeing their men folk go off to watery deaths.

GOOD MORNING, DEARIE [Musical/Romance/Crime] B/LY: Anne Caldwell; M: Jerome Kern; D/CH: Edward Royce; P: Charles Dillingham; T: Globe Theatre; 11/1/21 (347)

Good Morning, Dearie had an innocuous title and an overly conventional rags to riches Cinderella book, but its musical excellences were so conspicuous that Kenneth Andrews called it "the best musical comedy of the year." In Arthur Hornblow's words, "It is amusing, the personnel is admirably picked and pulchritudinous. Jerome Kern's music is melodious and mellifluous, albeit a trifle monotonous—while the staging and costuming are marked by variety and ingenuity of movement and capital taste."

The story line on which the music and dancing were hung followed pretty, young shopgirl Rose-Marie (Louise Groody), who is loved by millionaire Billy

Van Cortlandt (Oscar Shaw), and who also has a bothersome ex-con boyfriend, Chesty (Harland Dixon). The plotting involves the two rivals in a Chinatown dance-hall brawl and later has Chesty attempting to steal the family jewels from Billy's wealthy sister (Roberta Beatty) during a fete being thrown at her fancy home; fortunately, Rose-Marie appears there in disguise to foil the crook and end up in Billy's arms.

The tuneful show, from which the Hawaiian melody "Ka-lu-a" became a standard, also included "Blue Danube Blues" and "Every Girl" among its finer numbers; "Look for the Silver Lining," a Kern hit from *Sally*, was put in for good measure. During the show's run Kern was sued by Fred Fisher, a songwriter who claimed that "Ka-lu-a" had plagiarized Fisher's "Dardanella." Kern had to pay damages of $250.

GOOD NEWS [Musical/University/Romance/Sports] B: Laurence Schwab and B. G. De Sylva; M: Ray Henderson; LY: Lew Brown and B. G. De Sylva; D: Edgar J. MacGregor; CH: Bobby Connolly; S: Donald Oenslager; C: Kiviette; P: Laurence Schwab and Frank Mandel; T: Chanin's Forty-sixth Street Theatre; 9/6/27 (551)

From the moment the audience entered the playhouse, they were absorbed in the rah-rah atmosphere of this collegiate musical about the upcoming big football game between Tait College and Colton. The ushers wore old-fashioned college jerseys, and George Olsen's jazz orchestra contributed cheers to the atmosphere. At the show's conclusion, wrote Brooks Atkinson, the spectators had been witness to "a constantly fast entertainment with furious dancing, catchy tunes played to the last trombone squeal, . . . excellent singing and genuine excitement in the last few scenes during the football game."

Good News became the quintessential college musical, with its dormitory dizziness, sorority silliness, pajama parties, locker-room laughter, school spirit, and romantic rhubarbs. Its story deals with Tom Marlow (John Price Jones), the Tait football captain, who will be prevented from playing in the big game if he can't pass Astronomy. Tutored by his supposed fiancée's (Shirley Vernon) girl-friend (Mary Lawlor), he falls in love with the girl, passes the course, and plays in the game; the winning play, however, goes to Bobby Randall (Gus Shy), who transforms Tom's fumble into a lateral pass and runs for a touchdown. A treadmill was used to make the game's staging more exciting.

Costuming, setting, and choreography were valued assets, but so were such players as Zelma O'Neal, who became a star on the basis of her performance of the hit tunes "Varsity Drag" and the title song. "The Best Things in Life Are Free," "Lucky in Love," "The Girls of Pi Beta Phi," and "Just Imagine" were other rousing numbers in this multihit-song show.

GOOD OLD DAYS, THE [Comedy/Prohibition/Religion/Crime/Romance] A: Aaron Hoffman; D: Howard Lindsay and Aaron Hoffman; P: A. H. Woods; T: Broadhurst Theatre; 8/14/23 (71)

Kidding the Volstead Act, this comedy (originally called *Light Wine and Beer*) featured two saloon keepers whose friendship is tested by Prohibition. Nick (George Bickel) becomes a bootlegger, but Rudolph (Charles Winninger) is converted at Madison Square Garden by Billy Sunday and becomes an enforcement officer. After several skirmishes, Rudolph decides he was wrong and frees his daughter to marry Nick's nephew with his blessing.

"A good deal the sort of farce at which you are likely to laugh in haste and repent at leisure," wrote Burns Mantle. Percy Hammond thought: "This is a good example of the hot-dog drama, providing, as it does, much mental nutrition for those whose deepest thoughts are of ice cream cones and all-day suckers."

H.H.

GOOD TIMES [Revue] B/D: R. H. Burnside; M: Raymond Hubbell; P: Charles Dillingham; T: Hippodrome; 8/9/20 (455)

A mammoth revue seen at the gigantic Hippodrome. A huge company of vaudeville artists was combined with elaborate scenic arrangements to provide an evening of spectacle, music, comedy, dancing, and a potpourri of other entertainments. Among numbers scoring heavily were English music-hall clown Ferry Conway, the Hanneford family of equestrians, bicycle-performer Joe Jackson, a bevy of diving girls who performed in the theatre's immense water tank, singer Belle Story, an elephant act, an English pantomime act, and various others, fifteen in all. Among the extravagant and spectacular scenes was "Shadowland," in which shadow effects of dancing ladies dressed in Greek costumes were created, and "The Valley of Dreams," showing a poetic landscape of hills and mountains. A grand finale had an international theme and was climaxed by a giant American flag constructed of streamers held by the many chorus girls. Of the six annual extravaganzas thus far held at the Hippodrome, critics rated this the best.

A young acrobat appearing in one of the acts was then known as Archie Leach, now, Cary Grant.

GOOSE HANGS HIGH, THE [Comedy/Family/Marriage/Youth/Small Town] A: Lewis Beach; S: Livingston Platt; P: Dramatists' Theatre, Inc.; T: Bijou Theatre; 1/29/24 (186)

The Dramatists' Theatre was founded by a group of American playwrights, including Pulitzer Prize-winner Owen Davis, to produce their own plays without the intervention of middlemen. This first venture was not one of their own works, however. Lewis Beach's comedy was about two hardworking parents, the Ingals (Norman Trevor and Katherine Grey), who have sacrificed to put their three children through college. When the three (John Marston, Eric Dressler, and Miriam Doyle) arrive home for Christmas talking about socialism, Freud, and study abroad and behave in a manner described by their grandmother as "rotten spoiled," their parents realize that discipline is needed as much as self-sacrifice. The father's loss of his job brings out all of the good qualities in his brood, who decide to chuck school and marriage and support the household. Dad decides not to take back his job, when it is offered to him, and to continue with his more satisfying pursuit of horticulture.

"A spirited and sentimental panorama of life in an American home," wrote Percy Hammond, "shrewdly and observantly written, its stage direction is finished, its acting excellent and its audience appreciative."

                                                                                H.H.

GORILLA, THE [Comedy/Mystery/Theatre/Crime] A: Ralph Spence; D: Walter F. Scott; P: Donald Gallaher; T: Selwyn Theatre; 4/28/25 (257)

A mystery-play parody that the public loved, which reappeared in at least three film versions. "It is a tumble of all the things that have ever gone into mystery plays—shootings, secret panels, prowling gorillas, lights that go out, dangling skeletons, hidden stairways, trap doors, shadows, screams, comic detectives, and what not" (*Times*).

The show was a rip-roaring laugh getter, and the opening-night audience continued cheering for five minutes after the final curtain fell. "About ninety-nine per cent of the piece is monkey business," quipped Arthur Hornblow, who compared it to George M. Cohan's *Tavern* in effect. The comic highlight came when the actor dressed in a gorilla suit jumped into the auditorium and ran around amidst the spectators.

The extremely complex plot concerned a young playwright of thrillers (Robert Strange), his girlfriend (Betty Weston), her father (Frederick Truesdell) to whom the dramatist reads his play in hopes of getting the old man to produce it, and the confusing events that transpire involving a zoo's escaped gorilla (Harrry A. Ward), a crook named the Gorilla, and a couple of funny cops (Frank McCormack and Clifford Dempsey).

The show had an eight-performance return engagement during the 1925–1926 season.

GOSSIPY SEX, THE [Comedy/Marriage/Romance] A: Lawrence Grattan; SC: a vaudeville sketch; D: Sam Forrest; P: John Golden; T: Mansfield Theatre; 4/19/27 (23)

The gender referred to by this title was man, not woman, and the play's proponent of gossip was Danny Grundy, a character, beautifully acted by English player Lynne Overman, whose well-meaning efforts at being friendly take expression in his incessant babble of unfounded chatter. A trio of marriages are disrupted by his rumor-mongering, and one person is nearly slain, but even after this, and when he has won the girl he loves, Danny's mouth keeps working.

It was "An ambling, unimportant, but sometimes amusing comedy" to the *Times*, and Alison Smith declared it to be "a preposterous, creaky and genuinely hilarious farce." The play had been developed from an eighteen-minute vaudeville sketch.

GRAB BAG, THE [Revue] B/M/LY/P: Ed Wynn; D/CH: Julian Mitchell and Ed Wynn; T: Globe Theatre; 10/6/24 (184)

A successful Ed Wynn revue that the great comedian wrote by himself to set off his oddball talents. It boasted "graceful dancing, good singing, tasteful costumes and colorful settings, nimble, pretty girls and comedy—ceaseless comedy" (Charles Belmont Davis). Audiences were thrown into convulsions of merriment by the Wynn sense of humor. He was on almost all evening long, even in other performers' numbers, but never became a hindrance. The others included vaudeville comics Albert Shaw and Samuel Lee, singers Jay and Janet Velie, and dancers Katherine Witchie and Madeline Fairbanks. A group of eight men billed as the Volga Boys did Russian songs, and a trio of contortionists called the Le Grohs were diverting.

Wynn's music and lyrics were only passable, but his comedy was one of a kind. Robert Benchley cited one moment as illustrative of his antics. Wynn had come on with a large bass-viol as if to play a number. "As he stands absorbed in preliminary explanation, the instrument, which is made of rubber and inflated, slowly collapses until, by the time the artist is ready to play, he discovers nothing in his hand but a deflated wreck."

GRAND DUCHESS AND THE WAITER, THE (La Grande Duchesse et la garçon d'étage) [Comedy/Hotel/French/Romance] A: Alfred Savoir; AD: Arthur Richman; D: Frank Reicher; P: Charles Frohman, Inc.; T: Lyceum Theatre; 10/13/25 (31)

Elsie Ferguson's career as a leading lady was thrown into serious jeopardy by her vehicles during this period; she followed the disaster of Ferenc Molnar's *Carnival* with this unfortunate outing in a Savoir play, which cast her as a Russian expatriate noblewoman, the Grand Duchess Xenia, staying at a Swiss hotel with her coexiled relatives. There a passion for her flowers in the lowly waiter Albert (Basil Rathbone), who turns out to be the son of the president of the Swiss Republic. She, however, likes him better as a waiter. He follows her to Deauville, where she opens a cabaret with members of the Russian nobility as its staff and with Albert back in waiter's garb to suit the Duchess's tastes.

There were some lighthearted moments in the piece, and some found it periodically charming, but it provoked little interest and "was of indefinite consequence," declared *Time*. According to the *Times*, it mingled "brisk, Gallic farce with sentimental comedy, without enhancing the unity of its effect."

GRAND DUKE, THE (Le gran-duc) [Comedy/Romance/French] A: Sacha Guitry; TR: Achmed Abdullah; D/P: David Belasco; T: Lyceum Theatre; 11/1/21 (131)

Lionel Atwill played the title role in this lightweight Parisian concoction written by Sacha Guitry for his famous actor-playwright father, Lucien. The clumsy translation was staged with consummate ease by "the deft and sensitive hands of David Belasco" (Alexander Woollcott). Robert Allerton Parker rapped the producer-director for neglecting Guitry's best works and importing "trivial and unimportant works" such as this, especially one from which all of the piquancy of the original had been excised.

The Romanoff nobleman Grand Duke Feodor Michaelovitch (Lionel Atwill), exiled by the Russian Revolution to Paris, passes the time giving lessons in English (which he barely understands) to a millionaire plumber's (John L. Shine) daughter, Marie (Vivian Tobin). Marie falls in love with the handsome son (Morgan Farley) of her singing teacher (Lina Abarbanell), the Grand Duke recognizes the singing teacher as an old flame, the son is revealed to be the Grand Duke's illegitimate child, the young people are betrothed, and the plumber proposes to the singing teacher and plans to be a third, but secret, wheel in their relationship. "[T]he moral of the comedy... is not good," advised Hornblow.

(1) **GRAND GUIGNOL PLAYERS, THE** [One-Acts/French/French Language] P: Selwyns; T: Frolic Theatre; 10/15/23 (9)
"Sur le banc" A: Henry Hirsch; "Au rat mort, cabinet no. 6" A: André de Lorde and Pierre Chaine; "Une Nuit au bourge" A: Charles Méré; "Le Court Circuit" A: Benjamin Rabier and Eugène Joullot

During its seven-week season, the famous French horror theatre presented twenty-six one-act plays. Of their opening bill, Q.M. complained that the advance publicity stressing the company's ability to overcome the language barrier by the clarity of their acting was misguided; he found only one of their four plays comprehensible. This was "Au rat mort, cabinet no. 6," a 1908 piece seen in New York in 1913 under the title "A Pair of White Gloves." It was a tale of revenge in which a Russian woman (Jane Méryem), impersonating a courtesan, entices a Russian general (Paul Bernier) who was responsible for her sister's death and strangles him with a pair of white gloves after revealing her identity. The *Times* thought "Une Nuit au bourge" ("A Night in a Den") was the best play. It involved a sadistic Italian prince (Leo Brizard), a duchess (Marcelle Gylda) whom he frightens by pretending to be an Apache, her killing of the Prince, and the entry of a gang of real Apaches who assume that she is one of them. In "Sur le banc" ("On the Bench"), cited by the *Times* as the most original piece, an old man (Maurice Henriet) forestalls a seduction by telling the story of an affair in his life to a young couple on a park bench. "Le Court Circuit" ("The Short Circuit") was a 1915 comedy about a jealous nobleman (Marcel des Mazes) disguising himself as an electrician so that he can observe his mistress making love to a real electrician (Robert Seller), who is disguised as a prince; he eventually gets fed up and walks out on his mistress.

Corbin found the bill gentle for the Guignol's reputation. The sets and lighting were thought sorely lacking in atmosphere.   H.H.

(2) 10/22/23 (9)
"Nounouche" A: Henri Duvernois; "Au coin joli" A: Frederic Boutet; "L'Horrible Experience" A: André de Lorde and Alfred Binet

The Guignol's second program included at least one real shocker, "L'Horrible Experience" ("A Horrible Experience"), with its story of a surgeon (Paul Bernier) who tries to revive his slain daughter by means of an electric battery but dies himself when the muscles of her hands close on his throat. In "Nounouche" the servant girl Nounouche (Jeanne Bay) takes over the henpecking role of a man's (Marcel des Mazes) recently deceased wife. "Au coin joli" recounted what happens when a criminal returns to the scene of his crime.

(3) 10/29/23 (9)
"Alcide Pepie" A: Armant Massart and Alfred Vercourt; "Les Crucifés" A: André-Paul Antoine and Charles Poidlous; "Sur la dalle" A: André de Lorde and Georges Montignac
Three more one-acts; "Sur la dalle" ("On the Slab") presented a killing in a morgue; "Alcide Pepie" was named for its central character; and "Les Crucifés" ("The Crucified") was about the supernatural means of revenge taken by the spirit of a crucified man on those responsible for his death.

(4) 11/5/23 (9)
"Catherine Goulden" A: E. M. Laumann; "Un Peu de musique" A: Gaston Cronier; SC: a novelette by Eugène Fourrier; "Les Trois Masques" A: Charles Méré; "The Unknown Lady" A: George Middleton
When Russian actress Alla Nazimova's sketch "The Unknown Lady" was deemed too bold for the Keith Vaudeville Circuit with its propagandistic anti–New York State divorce-law theme, it was allowed to join the Grand Guignol for a week of performances. The play, banned in England several years earlier when it was called "Collusion," had been a vaudeville smash until closed because of protests lodged by an unnamed person. Its author provides some interesting background on it in *These Things Are Mine*. On the same bill was "Catherine Goulden," about a servant (Marcelle Gylda) who slays her master with an axe after she has been turned out of the house; "Les Trois Masques" ("The Three Masks"), a tragedy set in Corsica, is concerned with a theme of Corsican familial vengeance; and "Un Peu de musique" ("A Little Music"), is based on a Eugène Fourrier novelette, and is a farce that was notable for a lengthy monologue delivered by Leo Brizard.

(5) 11/12/23 (9)
"Gardiens de phare" A: Paul Cloquemin and Paul Autier; "Seul" A: Henri Duvernois; "Le Système du docteur Goudron et du professeur Plume" A: André de Lorde: SC: Edgar Allen Poe's story "The System of Dr. Tarr and Professor Feather"; "Le Kama Soutra" A: Régis Gignoux
Program number five mingled comedy and chills in its selections. "Gardiens de phare" ("Keepers of the Lighthouse") was a grisly piece about a father (Léo Brizard) and son (Paul Bernier) manning a lighthouse and the father's being forced to strangle his son when he goes insane and attacks him; in "Seul"

("Alone"), the plot concerned the disillusionment of a woman (Marcelle Gylda) upon visiting the studio of a charming poet (Marcel des Mazes) she had admired; the piece based on a Poe story dealt with the discovery of a pair of journalists that the inmates of an insane asylum have taken over its management; and "Le Kama Soutra" recounted the amusing developments incumbent upon the discovery by a middle-class family of India's ancient book of sexual love, the *Kama Sutra*.

(6) 11/19/23 (9)
"Le Bonheur" A: Serge Veber; "Le laboratoire des hallucinations" A: André de Lorde and Henri Bauche; "La Fiole" A: Max Maurey
  The audience had a tough time taking seriously the central shocker on this bill, "La Laboratoire des hallucinations" ("The Laboratory of Hallucinations"), when it depicted an insane man's attempt to operate on the skull of the surgeon (Paul Bernier) who had rendered him mad in revenge for having an affair with his wife; there was more appreciation of "Le Bonheur" ("Happiness"), a gently allegorical fable about a man (Louis Defresne), disappointed when he learns that his cousin (Maurice Henriet) has not returned from America with anything to bring him happiness, who is told by his relative that he should consider himself happy to have a home, a family, and food in the larder. "La Fiole" ("The Vial") was an inconsequential farce about a woman (Simone Hermann) who downs an elixir of youth before her bedraggled lover (Marcel de Mazes), who sent for it, can drink it himself.

(7) 11/26/23 (9)
"Prenez madame" A: Maxime Girard; "Sol Hyams, brocanteur" A: Jean Bernac; SC: a novel by W. W. Jacobs; "La Griffe" A: Jean Sartene; "Petite Bonne serieuse" A: Jean Manoussi and Gabriel Timmory
  The final bill of the Grand Guignol consisted of the thriller "La Griffe" ("The Claw") about an old peasant (Maurice Henriet) whose speech has been paralyzed but whose strong hands strangle his daughter-in-law (Jane Méryem) when he sees her lead her husband to a certain death; another thriller, "Sol Hyams, brocanteur" ("Sol Hyams, Pawnbroker"), based on a well-known novel; "Prenez madame" ("Take Madame"), a comedy in which a husband (Marcel des Mazes), learning of his wife's (Jane Méryem) rendezvous, gets there first and moralizes over checkers with the lover (Maurice Henriet); and a farce, "Petite Bonne serieuse" ("Maid of All Work"), with the usual Gallic sexual innuendoes. This piece was later done in English by the American Grand Guignol (see that entry).

(1) GRAND STREET FOLLIES, THE [Revue] B/LY/D: Helen Arthur and Agnes Morgan; M: Great composers, arranged mostly by Lily May Hyland; ADD. M./LY.: Albert Carroll; C: Alice Beer and Polaire Weissmann; P: Neighborhood Playhouse; T: Neighborhood Playhouse (OB); 6/13/22 (12)

This soon-to-become legendary Off-Broadway revue began as a giveaway to the Neighborhood Playhouse's 1921–1922 season subscribers. The Playhouse had been giving informal burlesques of its own work annually since 1912, but they had remained private for the theatre's "family." Alice Lewisohn conceived the notion of showing the sketches to the public when nothing suitable could be found to end the subscription season. The show that was developed was labeled "A low brow show for high grade morons" and soon became so popular that the two subscribers' performances had to be supplemented by ten more for the public at large, most of whom had never been to 466 Grand Street before. The revue had to close for various reasons but could have drawn audiences all summer if it had wished to remain open.

This first edition established the format for subsequent programs, that is, songs, impersonations, and sketches all designed to ridicule both the Playhouse's productions and those of the uptown theatres. Edition number one opened with "In the Beginning," a bit depicting the world's first drama critics, Adam Stale and Eve, moved into takeoffs on leading personalities and plays of the day and, in the second half, used a *Chauve-Souris*-like framework as a means of introducing the acts. Albert Carroll was in this first *Follies*, and he became a stalwart of later editions. A year's hiatus was taken before the *Follies* resumed on a regular basis in May 1924.

(2) [Second Edition] B/LY: Agnes Morgan; M: Lily May Hyland; D: Helen Arthur; CH: Albert Carroll; DS: Aline Bernstein; P: Neighborhood Playhouse; T: Neighborhood Playhouse (OB); 5/20/24 (172)

After viewing the second showing of the *Follies*, the *Times* critic wrote, "All cover themselves with glory." He found here "more inherent ingenuity than any of the revues of Broadway." The show opened with a group of characters— Heywood, Alec, Kenneth, John, Percy, and Bob—outward bound on the SS *Algonquin*, accompanied by stowaways Ludwig and Stark. Alison Smith commented that the actors made this spoof of critics "horribly realistic," aided by life-like masks designed by sculptor Jo Davidson.

There were burlesques of *This Fine-Pretty World* and *Blanco Posnet*, two flops of the season, a Russian art sketch, a medieval tragedy about the old Irish legend of Teapot Dome, and a Shakespeare spoof that kidded the new scenic school by revealing a stage filled with only eleven flights of steps. The epilogue sent up *The Miracle* and several shows by having Saint Joan, Queen Victoria, Beatrice Lillie, and Tondeleyo meeting in a Bel Geddes cathedral.

In the show were actors Aline McMahon, Agnes Morgan, Joanna Roos, and Albert Carroll, among others.

H.H.

(3) [Third Edition] B/LY: Agnes Morgan; M: Lily May Hyland; D: Helen Arthur; CH: Albert Carroll; S: Russel Wright; C: Aline Bernstein; P: Neighborhood Playhouse; T: Neighborhood Playhouse (OB); 6/18/25 (166)

This annual intimate burlesque and satire revue opened the 1925–1926 theatrical season; the past season's theatrical and film productions again offered fodder that, as digested by these sprightly talents, emerged as good-natured, rib-tickling entertainment.

Among the varied assortment of funny sketches was "They Knew What They Wanted under the Elms," in which O'Neill's respected "tragedy was turned into farce with the aid of a Ray Dooley baby, a gorilla, and a few simultaneous love-bouts in the three-walled farmhouse" (Arthur Hornblow); "What Price Morning Glories?" in which Albert Carroll played Sergeant Quirt as a satin pajamaed pansy; an Italian Grand Opera version of *Abie's Irish Rose*, "L'Irlandesa Rosa Dell'Abie," in honor "of the consolidation of the Irish Free State and Palestine"; and *The Wild Duck* travestied as a Sheridan comedy with such characters as Mr. Ekdal Scandal and Mr. Gregers Tattle.

The show, claimed Larry Barretto, "possesses a flavor, an originality, which survives even a lack of the splendor offered by the uptown revues."

(4) [Fourth Edition] B/LY/D: Agnes Morgan; M: Lily May Hyland, Arthur Schwartz, and Randall Thompson; DS: Aline Bernstein; P: Neighborhood Playhouse; T: Neighborhood Playhouse (OB); 6/15/26 (55)

Edition number three closed the 1925–1926 season, as its predecessor had opened it. The intent of the show, to satirize the year's plays, was the same, but it was encased in a very loose plot about a North Pole real estate boom, and this tended to dampen and constrict the fun, making it somewhat less effective than earlier versions. Its run was the shortest of the series.

The plot outline, used only in the first half, disclosed a Florida real-estate promoter parachuting into an Eskimo settlement and thereupon attempting to establish a North Pole Florida resort region. The promoter goes to New York to get the notables there to invest in his scheme, and these celebrities are impersonated by the company. Among them are Mother Goshdarn [Mother Goddam, from *The Shanghai Gesture*], Craig's Wife, the Great God Brown, Irving Berlin, and Texas Guyem [Guinan], among others. The second half of the program incorporated a staging of *Uncle Tom's Cabin* by the Northern Lights Art Theatre in the vein of Russian constructivism and taking off on the recent New York productions of the Moscow Art Theatre Musical Studio. A freight elevator transported the dead souls to heaven. In another sketch, a possible Theatre Guild staging of "Jack and Jill" was spoofed.

(5) [Fifth Edition] B/LY/D: Agnes Morgan and others; M: Max Ewing and others; DS: Aline Bernstein; P: Neighborhood Playhouse; T: Neighborhood Playhouse (OB); 5/19/27 (148)

The majority of the familiar Grand Street regulars returned for this fourth edition, the last to be staged at the Neighborhood Playhouse. The production marked the disbandment of the experiment at that noble center; it played there for two weeks before trekking uptown to reopen, somewhat revised, at the Little Theatre.

Much of the revue spoofed the shows of the season that had run into censorship trouble with D.A. Banton who had found them "awfully rude, for they acted in the nude." The satire was itself blue by contemporary standards. As in the past shows much delight was taken in the impersonations of famed performers. Albert Carroll, Dorothy Sands, Paula Trueman, Otto Hulicius, and George Heller did their risible versions of Ethel and John Barrymore, Mrs. Fiske, Jane Cowl, Henrietta Crosman, Laura Hope Crews, Alexander Woollcott, and Moran and Mack. The latter pair of blackface clowns was imagined in a Richard Brinsley Sheridan parody called "The School for Rivals." A clever bit burlesqued in a Gilbert and Sullivan manner President Calvin Coolidge as a chorus of reporters tried in vain to stir the complacent chief executive to give evidence of thought.

"Their satire," penciled Joseph Wood Krutch, "is as irreverently salty and their spirit is as impudent as it ever was."

(6) [Sixth Edition] B/LY/D: Agnes Morgan; M: Max Ewing, Lily May Hyland, and Serge Walter; CH: James Cagney; P: The Actor-Managers; T: Booth Theatre; 5/28/28 (144)

The next to last edition of this annual revue was created for a Broadway playhouse, the first of the line to bear that distinction. Its most memorable contribution was the presence of James Cagney as both choreographer and company dancer.

The show's specialty of burlesqueing the season's past productions led to a musical comedy version of *Coquette*; a farce combination of *Porgy* and *The Doctor's Dilemma*; a political spoof on Calvin Coolidge, Al Smith, and Herbert Lehman called "Strange Inner Feud"; a Reinhardt parody set on the steps of the Forty-second Street Library and with Albert Carroll doing Romeo as Alexander Moissi would have done him and Dorothy Sands doing a Mae West Juliet; a takeoff on *Marco Millions* called "Marked Millions" and pointing at the Teapot Dome scandal; and many other bits and musical numbers. The framework was the wandering about town of old Trader Horn, who encounters the various shows being ribbed.

(7) [Seventh Edition] B/LY/D: Agnes Morgan; M: Max Ewing and Arthur Schwartz; ADD. M./LY.: William Irwin and Serge Walter; CH: Dave Gold; P: The Actor-Managers; T: Booth Theatre; 5/1/29 (85)

The 1929 edition was the last. Once more it produced its zany parodies of the theatre season, but this time out its feet were dragging more apparently than ever before. With its new veneer of Broadway glitter it seemed to lack its old inner vitality and was too much like its neighborhood competition. A chorus line was added in the process but its dancing was commonplace. "As a total production," lamented Richard Dana Skinner, "the current show is...'neither maid, wife nor widow.' "

The impersonations of Paula Trueman, Albert Carroll, and Dorothy Sands were the highlights. Carroll was his usual brilliant self in spoofs of Beatrice Lillie in *This Year of Grace*, Constance Collier in *Serena Blandish*, Fannie Brice in *Fioretta*, and Gertrude Lawrence in *Treasure Girl*, but fell flat with his Harpo

Marx in *Animal Crackers*. Trueman hit the mark as Katharine Cornell in *The Age of Innocence* but came a cropper as Ruth Gordon in *Serena Blandish*. As Irene Bordoni and Lenore Ulric in *Paris* and *Mima* Dorothy Sands excelled herself. Eddie Cantor and Bert Lahr were imitated by others, among them James Cagney.

The show's premise was a succession of scenes looking at famed historical events through modern eyes. The siege of Troy seen as a Belasco staging and Paul Revere's ride reported via a *Front Page* telephone sketch were examples. A revised version was produced on 6/18/29 with some new material substituted for weaker sketches. Talking pictures, Morris Gest, and modern musical groups were among the targets of the additions.

GRANITE [Drama/Marriage/Crime/Rural/British] A: Clemence Dane; D: Richard Boleslavsky; P: American Laboratory Theatre; T: American Laboratory Theatre (OB); 2/11/27 (70)

Richard Boleslavsky's staging gained kudos, but Clemence Dane's play remained unsatisfactory. The director's approach to the strange drama was to do it in a frankly and consistently theatricalist manner, which succeeded in gripping the spectator, said Joseph Wood Krutch, despite disbelief in the dramatic substance. The play had been a last-minute substitution for *Danton's Death*, which the company never did get to put on. It was rehearsed hurriedly, and Francis Ferguson, then a company member, declared that Boleslavsky produced it for purely commercial reasons, since the American Lab was low in funds. "He didn't like it. He knew exactly how to stage it....He did it beautifully: the atmosphere was so thick you could cut it with a knife." The piece was so successful with audiences that the company accepted offers to move it to the intimate Mayfair Theatre on West Forty-fourth Street, where it ran for seven weeks beginning on 2/28/27; a final week was played back at the Lab's own theatre.

Dane's offbeat play took place on bleak Lundy Island, where farmer Jordan Morris (Herbert V. Gellendre) is so granite-like that his despairing wife (Blanche Tancock), in love with his half-brother, calls upon the devil's aid to rid her of her dilemma. A Nameless Man (Robert H. Gordon) appears, having been shipwrecked; he kills the farmer, freeing the wife to marry the half-brother (George Macready), but the stranger kills him too and takes over the wife and her property.

The author's ambivalency about whether the Nameless One was indeed the devil irked some critics, but they approved the sense of dread it provoked. The play was revived by the troupe on 11/29/27 for twenty-six more showings.

(1) GREAT ADVENTURE, THE [Dramatic Revival] A: Arnold Bennett; S: Frederick Bentley; P: Neighborhood Playhouse; T: Neighborhood Playhouse (OB); 2/25/21

A revival of British author Arnold Bennett's comedy, first seen locally in 1913. Alexander Woollcott called it "an original and diverting comedy of temperament." Ian Maclaren took on the part of frail artist Ilam Carve, who, when his valet dies of pneumonia, arranges for him to be buried in Westminster Abbey as if it were Carve himself who had died. The artist looks on interestedly at the circumstances surrounding his own funeral, but when he begins anew his career with a different painting technique, he is eventually found out. Deirdre Doyle was Janet Cannot, the cockney wife who provides a warm home for the painter. "The scenes in her living room are played with a beautiful sincerity," remarked Ludwig Lewisohn; he found that "the Neighborhood Playhouse has set itself a new standard of significant and harmonious execution."

(2) D/P: Reginald Pole; T: Princess Theatre; 12/22/26 (30)

The revival Reginald Pole directed, produced, and starred in was a dreary, unimpressive business. Pole's acting was "amateurish," thought Brooks Atkinson, and the play's structure seemed faltering, its dialogue lacking in "distinction." Spring Byington as Janet gave the production what merit it possessed.

The show squeezed out an additional sixteen performances in a return engagement that opened on 1/24/27 at the Edyth Totten Theatre.

GREAT BROXOPP, THE [Comedy/Marriage/Family/Business/Romance/British] A: A. A. Milne; D: B. Iden Payne; P: B. Iden Payne and Lavarack, Inc.; T: Punch and Judy Theatre; 11/15/21 (66)

A mildly received comedy of English life, the chief feature of which was its satire on advertising. It looked at the career of James Broxopp (B. Iden Payne), whose advertising genius turns "Broxopp's Beans for Babies" into a nationally known item. On the ads is one of his sons, pictured at the age of three as the Broxopp baby. The plot follows the plight of this son (Fred Shirley), now grown and in love, who is unhappy with the jests aimed at him because of his name. He gets his dad to change his name and live like a country squire but sees him grow uneasy in this guise and return to the world of business using a new name and selling a "cheese for chickens."

Alan Dale appreciated some of the humor and subtlety but adjudged the whole "a patchwork affair" that often dragged tediously. To Alexander Woollcott it was "a slightly uneven but generally gorgeous comedy."

GREAT DAY [Musical/Southern/Romance/Period] B: William Cary Duncan and John Wells; M/P: Vincent Youmans; LY: William Rose and Edward Eliscu; D: Frank M. Gillespie; CH: Le Roy Prinz; S: Gates and Morange; T: Cosmopolitan Theatre; 10/17/29 (37)

This disappointing musical contributed two classic Youmans songs to appreciative music lovers, "More Than You Know" and "Without a Song," which far outlived its life of one month. Moreover, star Marilyn Miller's objections had removed another great number, "Time on My Hands," before the show opened. Other good songs in the score were the title number and "Happy Because I'm in Love." *Great Day* came to town after a miserable four months' preopening period in which many creative heads rolled, among them that of future song-writing great Harold Arlen (who was to play a casino piano player).

The old-fashioned show itself was a "bromidic and tedious musicomedy" (*Time*) about a nineteenth-century Louisiana belle (Mayo Methot), forced to sell her plantation to a villain (John Haynes), who converts it to a Spanish casino but who is eventually given his comeuppance by the stalwart hero (Allan Prior), who makes it possible for the girl to marry him.

GREAT FORTUNE, THE (Der Groise Gevins) [Comedy/Family/Romance/Jews/Yiddish/Yiddish Language] A: Sholem Aleichem; D/P: Maurice Schwartz; T: Yiddish Art Theatre (OB); 12/8/22

An adaptation of Sholem Aleichem stories sometimes called *The Big Lottery*, *The Big Win*, and *The Two Hundred Thousand*. It tells of what happens when a poor Russian family wins a 200,000-ruble lottery; the news turns out to be a mistake, but by the time the family learns the truth, they realize that they are better off being poor. The *Times* thought that the adaptation was too long and clumsy and that if the minor role of Kopel, the poor suitor of the daughter of the house, had been enlarged, it would have guaranteed the success of the piece. Perhaps that is because the part was played by Muni Weisenfreund, later known as Paul Muni.

GREAT GATSBY, THE [Drama/Romance/Prohibition/Crime] A: Owen Davis; SC: the novel by F. Scott Fitzgerald; D: George Cukor; P: William A. Brady; T: Ambassador Theatre; 2/2/26 (113)

A year after the publication of F. Scott Fitzgerald's quintessential 1920s novel, its dramatization appeared on Broadway. Various commentators were surprised at how well the prolific Owen Davis had done in transferring the story to the stage. The tale—intact in a prologue and three acts—was about how handsome Jay Gatsby (James Rennie), née Gatz, of no social background, falls in love with Daisy Fay (Florence Eldridge), comes home from the war to find her wed to the wealthy Long Islander Tom Buchanan (Elliot Cabot), amasses a fortune as a master bootlegger, pursues his obsession with Daisy who will not divorce the philandering Tom to marry him, and is killed by a chauffeur (a garage owner in the book) who believes him to be having an affair with his wife (mistress in the novel). "[T]he characters realized in the flesh are uncannily close to the prose portraits of the book," reported Richard Dana Skinner.

In the opinion of Larry Barretto, "The lines have been left intact, the spirit of the book has been preserved, and the result is a play whose comedy shades into tragedy, whose sordidness is lifted sometimes into nobility—the most delicate satire we have yet seen on the world of form and manners where the best bred are sometimes the most shabby, and the worst bred shine with innate decency." Others could not forgive the play its sentimentality and egomaniacal hero.

GREAT GOD BROWN, THE [Drama/Marriage/Sex/Romance/Friendship/ Prostitution/Fantasy] A: Eugene O'Neill; D/DS: Robert Edmond Jones; P: Kenneth Macgowan, Robert Edmond Jones, and Eugene O'Neill; T: Greenwich Village Theatre (OB); 1/23/26 (271)

O'Neill's symbolic mask-drama began Off Broadway and then moved first to Broadway's Garrick and next to the Klaw; it was a hotbed of controversy during the 1925–1926 season and has remained one of the dramatist's most perplexing but fascinating creations. It was named a Best Play of the season by Burns Mantle.

O'Neill's play focused on four characters, their names chosen to suggest their allegorical significance: Dion Anthony (Robert Keith), who represents the joyous, creative Dionysian spirit in conflict with what the author called the "life-denying spirit of Christianity as represented by St. Anthony"; Margaret (Leona Hogarth), the Faustian Marguerite or "eternal girl-woman" of simple virtue, devoted to "maintaining the race"; Cybele (Anne Shoemaker), the Earth Mother, a "pariah in a world of unnatural laws," and William A. Brown (William Harrigan), the Babbit-like symbol of materialistic success, prosperous without, hollow within.

These characters all wear masks to cover their true natures (Brown goes maskless during the first part) and remove them when outward pretence is dropped. Their story, covering eight years, is of the love of Dion and Brown, childhood friends, for Margaret; of the artist Dion's deep sensitivity masked by the face of Pan to express his outward cynicism in a world that cannot fathom his inner self; of Margaret's love for the masked aspect of Dion and her marriage to it; of Dion's evolution into a Mephistophelian mask of dissolution; of his swallowing his scruples and going to work for the successful businessman Brown; of his discovery of spiritual solace in the arms of the prostitute Cybele, with whom he need wear no mask; of the death of Dion from the anguish of a martyred life; of the assumption of his mask by Brown who passes for Dion in Margaret's eyes; of Brown's need to assume the mask of a successful businessman to alternate with that of Dion; of Brown's announcement as Dion that Brown is dead; of his flight from the police who seek Dion's murderer; of his death; and of his discovery of faith in Cybele's final words to him.

The actor's deft performances with and without their masks placed this work on a constantly intriguing but often baffling level; the play grew increasingly complex and hard to follow in the later portions, from the point where Brown assumes Dion's mask and is accepted by Margaret in that guise. Nearly every critic mentioned his or her difficulty in grasping all of the symbolism, but only a few, like Arthur Hornblow, condemned the play outright. More common were opinions like John Anderson's who termed this "a superb failure. . . . It is a conflict of humanity, masked and unmasked, of shifting values, hidden identities, of shy, frightened souls lurking behind the frozen faces of desperate pretense."

GREAT MUSIC [Drama/Music/Romance/Drugs/Crime/Illness/Tropics/Italy-France] A: Martin Brown; M: C. Linn Seiler; S: John Wenger; P: George Backer; T: Earl Carroll Theatre; 10/4/24 (44)

An ambitious but overstuffed and unsatisfying drama, called by its author "the dramatic interpretation of Eric Fane's Symphony in D Minor." Using a cast that, with supernumeraries, came to seventy-five members, and with a full-sized symphony orchestra providing musical accompaniment, the productions's scope was impressive, but its dramatic substance turned out to be, as Percy Hammond remarked, "a gloomy gymkhana, all excited and hysterical over nothing at all."

Martin Brown's melodramatic epic purported to tell the story of anguished American composer Eric Fane's (Tom Powers) struggle to write the symphony he hears raging in his head. The plot takes him from Paris to Rome to Port Said to the South Seas, where he encounters various women, drugs, and finally leprosy and his wife's suicide before he finally can compose his masterpiece. Music accompanied most of the action. The score provided by C. Linn Seiler was, like the play, "utterly commonplace" (Fred MacIsaac).

GREAT NECKER, THE [Comedy/Films/Romance/Sex] A: Elmer Harris; D: J. Fred Butler; S: Rollo Wayne; P: Chamberlain Brown; T: Ambassador Theatre; 3/6/28 (39)

A raucous and silly farce that a few critics thought would have served better as a musical comedy. Robert Littell said it had "lots of gags—the kind you use once and throw away—about short skirts and long kisses and cocktails and 'experience' and bridal chambers and twin beds and deceiving husbands and petting and necking and the sex life of the pond lily."

The wealthy, middle-aged bachelor hero (Taylor Holmes) is both a ladies man and a resident of Great Neck, Long Island—thus the title. He wants to wed the sixteen-year-old daughter (Irene Purcell) of a sexually frustrated movie censor (Blanche Ring) whose positive opinion he desires on a movie he is coproducing. He is shocked to discover that the girl is more knowledgeable about the naughty facts of life than he and switches his attentions to a more mature lady (Marjorie Gateson).

GREAT POWER, THE [Drama/Family/Fantasy/Politics] A/D/P: Myron C. Fagan; S: Livingston Platt; T: Ritz Theatre; 9/11/28 (22)

Time's comment: "This dreadful piece contains all ordinary and extraordinary horrors of uninspired writing for the stage." Its central figure was Power (John T. Doyle), a powerful millionaire whose machinations on Wall Street and in politics strike fear in all lesser beings. He nearly meets his match in young Joan Wray (Minna Gombell), whose senator brother he wishes to defame, only to learn that Joan is his own daughter by an abandoned wife. After dying of a heart attack, Power must face the Judgement Seat in Heaven, where his misdeeds are enumerated. The scene is really a dream, Power revives to make amends for past cruelties, and Joan becomes affianced to Power's stepson (Alan Birmingham).

GREAT SCOTT [Comedy/Family/Labor/Romance/Small Town] A: Howard E. Koch; D: Albert Bannister; S: Anthony Continer; P: L. A. Safian; T: Forty-ninth Street Theatre; 9/2/29 (16)

After two weeks of performances, this flimsy play disappeared, primarily because of "a plot which revealed little of novelty or interest and characters cut from the too familiar patterns of small town comedy," Perriton Maxwell said.

Delancey Scott (Ray Harper) graduates from college with a headful of learning, takes employment in the factory where his dad (Walter Horton) and brother (Millard F. Mitchell) work, incites the laborers to strike successfully, and gains the love of the boss's daughter, but he doesn't get the promotion he seeks; he then takes a job as a schoolteacher.

GREAT TEMPTATIONS, THE [Revue] B: Harold Atteridge; M: Maurie Rubens; LY: Clifford Grey; D: J. J. Shubert; S: Watson Barratt; P: Messrs. Shubert; T: Winter Garden; 5/18/26 (197)

An ostentatiously elaborate summertime revue described by Joseph Wood Krutch in these terms: "There is nothing in it that is new, but they have taken bigger and better for their motto. I never. . . saw in any revue so many girls, dressed and undressed, so bewildering a variety of decor, or so much and such vertiginous dancing as this one presents." The humor of the show was hard to find, even with the presence of some good comedians and with M.C. Jack Benny ("an unusually reserved comic for the Winter Garden"—Wells Root) introducing the acts.

There was a spoof of *The Shanghai Gesture*, with Hazel Dawn effectively mimicking Florence Reed, but a soon-to-be seen *Grand Street Follies* version did an even funnier takeoff. Parisian dance team Roseray and Capella were agile and sensuous, singers Charlotte Woodruff and Halfred Young were good, an 1896-style showgirl routine in the fashion of those formerly done at Koster and Bial's Music Hall was memorable, and a display of female beauty dressed as flowers in "A Garden of Memories" was artistically conceived.

GREAT WAY, THE [Drama/Romance/Spain/Prostitution/Music] A: Horace Fish and Helen Freeman; D: Helen Freeman and Reginald Pole; P: Helen Freeman; T: Park Theatre; 11/7/21 (8)

An attempt to create an elaborate, picturesque atmospheric drama of Spanish life as a vehicle for Helen Freeman who codirected, cowrote, produced, and starred in it. The effect, however, was a "pallid melodrama" that "paints in pale pastel shades Spanish pictures that should be in the boldest of contrasting colors," according to the *Herald*.

The Great Way involved Dulce (Freeman), a Spanish streetwalker rejected by Jose Luis (Moroni Olsen), who chooses an Englishwoman (Duval Dalzell) instead. Dulce becomes a famous opera star, meets Jose, now married, once again and vows to remain worthy of him.

The critics scoffed at the piece and its performance as bathetic claptrap; the *Sun* said it was not worthy of a high school drama society.

GREEN BEETLE, THE [Drama/Mystery/Orientals/Crime] A: John A. Willard; P: Kilbourn Gordon; T: Klaw Theatre; 9/2/24 (63)

John Willard's *Cat and the Canary* was one of the greatest mystery play hits of the early twenties. *The Green Beetle*, another thriller, was not nearly as good. It was a drama of vengeance set among the cunning denizens of San Francisco's Chinatown.

The villain is the crafty, sinister, philosophical, flowery-speeched Chang Hong (Ian Maclaren), proprietor of a curio shop, who seeks revenge on the American that, years earlier, raped his beloved Suey-Yen in Shanghai. He lures the man (Percy Moore) and his wife (Florence Fair) to his establishment, causes the former to suffer a heart attack, drugs the latter into servility, and then sets out to destroy the couple's daughter (Lee Patrick), who is in possession of a jade ring called the Green Beetle. Chang's attempt falters, and he falls victim to his own blood lust in Act Three.

Arthur Hornblow accused the play of being an overstuffed sketch, dragged out to three unnecessary acts, and Percy Hammond damned it as "naive, incoherent, babbling, irksome, and generally incredible."

GREEN GODDESS, THE [Drama/Adventure/Orientals/British] A: William Archer; D/P: Winthrop Ames; T: Booth Theatre; 1/18/21 (440)

William Archer's first play, after a brilliant career as a critic and translator of Ibsen, disproved his own claim that he could not himself write a play. It was a greatly successful work that gave George Arliss one of the crowning triumphs of his career in the role of the Raja of Rukh. Despite Archer's own battle against meretriciousness in drama, his play had no literary value and was "commercial melodrama of the most conventional kind," according to Arthur Hornblow.

Into an inaccessible area of India ruled over by the anti-British Raja of Rukh crashlands a plane bearing Major Crespin (Herbert Waring) of the Indian Army, his wife (Olive Wyndham), and Dr. Traherne (Cyril Keightley). The Oxford-educated ruler treats the survivors graciously but plans to kill them in return for the planned execution of three of his own politically subversive brothers by the Indian government. When Mrs. Crespin refuses the Prince's one condition for saving her party, their fates are sealed. However, they manage to send out a message via the wireless and are rescued in the nick of time by the British Flying Corps.

Alexander Woollcott informed his readers that Archer had "attempted nothing more—nor less—than a suave and mannerly hair-raiser, and while his play will not touch your heart nor quicken your mind, it is practically certain to have a most agitating effect upon your scalp." "Mr. George Arliss," wrote Ludwig

Lewisohn, "gave a performance of such pliancy and precision that he seemed to flash and darken like a polished blade in alternate sunshine and shadow."

An anecdote connected with this play concerns Olive Wyndham, who, before she even read the script, dreamed about being held a prisoner in a palace by a fantastic-looking jailer; playwright Archer later told the actress that a precisely similar dream had inspired him to write the play.

According to the star, George Arliss, the play had suffered from an exceedingly weak third act, and the only thing that saved it was the weird lighting devised by Winthrop Ames to suggest a mood of "impending catastrophe." On the day that the lights were being changed the author phoned Ames's office but was told by his secretary that the director was at the theatre "relighting the third act." Archer rushed over to the theatre in great anger, only to find out that the secretary had said "relighting" and not "rewriting."

Director Guthrie McClintic reported in *Me and Kit* that the dry, meticulous Arliss was far from William Archer's own conception of the role. Arliss turned out to be very effective at tactfully convincing the author to revise his dialogue to fit the actor's unique style. On opening night, the angular actor delivered a pun-filled speech that began, "This success does not surprise me for when you have a good Archer with good Ames you can't miss."

GREEN HAT, THE [Drama/Romance/Sex/France/British] A: Michael Arlen; SC: Michael Arlen's novel of the same title; D: Guthrie McClintic; S: P. Dodd Ackerman; P: A. H. Woods; T: Broadhurst Theatre; 9/15/25 (237)

Michael Arlen's disappointing adaptation of his own best-seller was one of the most ballyhooed events of the 1925–1926 season. It came to New York after rousing acclaim in other cities. The international Arlen vogue created an avid audience interest that led to speculators selling opening-night seats for more than $100 each, but the critical response to the play was a frown, although the performance of Katharine Cornell as the heroine Iris March was one of the triumphs of the day. It placed the actress's name above the lights for the first time in her career.

The play tells a tale of sex and love and family honor among a group of wealthy British sophisticates; the scenes are set at Deauville, Mayfair, Paris, and in an English country house; about ten years transpires between the first and last scenes. The plot concerns the thwarted love affair of Iris, a beauty known all over for her green hat and yellow Hispano Suiza, and Napier Harpenden (Leslie Howard); as a result of the objections of Napier's father (Eugene Powers), Iris marries Boy Fenwick, but Boy kills himself on their wedding night after revealing that he has contracted venereal disease. Iris lies to protect Boy's name and says he died "for purity" upon discovering her own past transgressions. She proceeds to sleep with many men to satiate her love needs, and only Napier learns from her the truth about Boy. He marries Venice (Margalo Gillmore). Iris suffers various forms of emotional and physical retribution; disillusioned with Napier she drives her car into a tree, killing herself.

Richard Dana Skinner had not read the book. He found the play "a rather loosely and at times very poorly constructed play wound about a theme which might have been poignantly beautiful, but which missed both beauty and song" by a wide margin. Others found it dull and shallow, but Brooks Atkinson thought it was a work of great atmospheric beauty.

GREEN PASTURES, THE [Comedy/Religion/Bible/Blacks/Southern/Rural] A/D: Marc Connelly; SC: Roark Bradford's stories *Ol' Man Adam and His Chillun*; S: Robert Edmond Jones; P: Laurence Rivers; T: Mansfield Theatre; 2/ 26/30 (640)

One of the most notable efforts of the decade, a Best Play choice for 1929–1930 and the year's Pulitzer Prize Winner was Marc Connelly's warm and reverent retelling of the Old Testament as explained by a rural black Louisiana Sunday-school teacher to his naive youthful brethren. Unusual in many ways, the all-black play became a colossal hit and has since been performed numerous times all over the world. Its leading player, sixty-six-year-old Richard B. Harrison, who acted De Lawd, had never performed professionally before but instantly became famous for his profoundly gentle, dignified, and moving portrayal.

Connelly announced that his purpose was to present his material according to the language and folklore of "untutored black Christians." "Unburdened by the differences of more educated theologians they accept the Old Testament as a chronicle of wonders which happened to people like themselves in vague but actual places and of rules of conduct, true acceptance of which will lead them to a tangible, three-dimensional Heaven."

Many scoffed at the play's commercial possibilities, and only novice producer Rowland Stebbins (using the *nom de théâtre* of Laurence Rivers) came forth with the needed funds. The play caught on at once and ran for a solid year and a half, followed by five years of touring and two New York revivals, in 1935 and 1951.

Produced with splendid folk-style sets and with a background of spirituals resoundingly sung by the Hall Johnson Choir, *The Green Pastures* recounted in the child-like terms of black folk fantasy eighteen scenes of the Bible, from the Garden of Eden to the story of Noah to Moses and the Pharoah to the Battle of Jericho to the debauchery of Babylon to God's envisioning of the Crucifixion. De Lawd was seen as a kindly white-haired country preacher in frock coat working at a rolltop desk, Heaven was a place for grand fish frys, Babylon was a Harlem night club, and so on. Marc Connelly's superb direction was a tour de force of movement, lighting, pacing, and rhythm. *Time* noted that "The all-Negro cast perform with a combination of spontaneity, vigor, and accomplished artistry which exemplifies the race at its dramatic best."

Most critics were beside themselves with admiration in trying to eulogize the play. Brooks Atkinson was representative: "From almost any point of view, *The Green Pastures* is a play of surpassing beauty. As comedy, fantasy, folklore, religion, poetry, theatre—it hardly matters which.... And Marc Connelly has lifted his fable of the Lord walking on the earth to those exalted heights where utter simplicity in religious conception produces a play of great emotional depth and spiritual exaltation—in fact the divine comedy of the modern theatre.''

A bit of commotion was raised when the play became a hit, because it was claimed that Roark Bradford had not been given sufficient credit for the original work on which the play was based; the Pulitzer Prize committee completely failed to mention his contribution. Public acknowledgement of Bradford's work was duly made. A detailed history of the play's creation may be found in Connelly's memoir, *Voices Offstage*.

GREEN RING, THE (Zelyunue Kul'tso) [Comedy/Youth/Family/Russian] A: Zinaida Hippius; S: Warren Dahler; C: Aline Bernstein; P: Neighborhood Play-house; T: Neighborhood Playhouse (OB); 4/4/22 (30)

Zinaida Hippius was a respected Russian poetess whose *Green Ring* had been successfully staged in Moscow in 1914. Several reviewers considered her comedy deep, perhaps even more insightful into the minds of young people than the better-known *Spring's Awakening* of Wedekind.

Set in 1912, it concerns a secret society of Petrograd youth called the Green Ring, which gets together to discuss various weighty subjects, including sex, religion, politics, and suicide, and to pass resolutions condemning the insensi-tivity and ineffectuality of their elders. The main plot action concerns the group's earnest attempts to help solve the problems faced by new member Sonia (Joanna Roos) with her estranged parents (Eugene Powers and Pamela Gaythorne). Their solution involves the girl's finding happiness with a philosophical older man (Ian Maclaren) who attends the Green Ring's meetings.

Arthur Hornblow described the play as ''a lifeless story garnished with a quantity of insincere talk,'' with a ''general effect. . . of dreariness,'' but Kenneth Macgowan said it was a ''rare, understanding and Olympian. . . study of youth.''

(1) GREENWICH VILLAGE FOLLIES OF 1920, THE [Revue] B: Thomas J. Gray; M: A. Baldwin Sloane; LY: John Murray Anderson and Arthur Swan-strom; D: John Murray Anderson; DS: Robert Locher and James Reynolds; P: The Bohemians, Inc.; T: Greenwich Village Theatre (OB); 8/30/20 (217)

The second edition of this annual revue, begun in 1919 by John Murray Anderson, was memorable on several accounts, but the critics dwelt principally on its exquisite visual delights. ''It is a shimmering thing of silks and satins, of gold cloths and silver cloths, of soft drapes and splashing color effects, of costumes surely as stunning as any which ever have graced the revue stage,'' noted the *Times*. The *Evening Telegram* said the sets were reminiscent of those created by Gordon Craig and Leon Bakst. Many of the production routines went over well, among these a samovar number that employed a procession dressed in medieval Russian costumes and that climaxed in a sensational dance by Ivan Bankhoff and Mlle. Phebe. The masks of Benda made a startling impression as worn by dancer Margaret Severn in ''The Golden Carnival.'' Comedy was entrusted to the teams of Meyers and Hanford, Collins and Hart, and, most successfully, Bert Savoy and Jay Brennan (Savoy was a top female impersonator of the day). Frank Crummit, singer-comedian, traipsed through the exhibition as M.C.

The show employed a lot of nudity, especially in its "The Naked Truth" opening number. Other popular numbers were "Just Sweet Sixteen," with chorines dressed as cake and candles; "Come to Bohemia," a ribbing of a Greenwich Village dive; "The Krazy Kat's Ball," based on the comic strip; and a perfume allegory, "Tsin," in which the beauties masqueraded as various fragrances in bottles while Rimsky-Korsakoff's "Scheherazade" was played.

(2) [Third Edition] B: Thomas J. Gray; M: Carey Morgan; LY: John Murray Anderson and Arthur Swanstrom; D: John Murray Anderson; DS: Robert Locher and James Reynolds; P: Bohemians, Inc.; T: Shubert Theatre; 8/31/21 (167)

The *Greenwich Village Follies* made their first incursion onto Broadway after their two previous Greenwich Village presentations and thereby lost, according to Arthur Hornblow, "whatever advantage the village *cachet* and their isolation downtown gave them," for now they had to compete with the big-time revues of the Great White Way.

Essentially a glorified vaudeville show, this *Follies* was a succession of specialty acts, mixed with a parade of gorgeously dressed beautiful girls in various tableaux; John Murray Anderson's tasteful stage arrangements, the masks of Benda, and the use of outstandingly lovely lighting effects were combined with memorable results. "Nothing more beautiful than the color effects has been seen on the New York stage in years," clapped Charles Pike Sawyer. Production numbers "When Dreams Come True," "Snowflakes," and "In Silver and Black" were highly praised, particularly "Silver and Black" in its Art Nouveau Aubrey Beardsley styling. One number revealed beauty Florence Normand wearing form-fitting black tights, the same she wore in the previous year's show as "the black cat," and another presented her "entirely nude except for some gilded leaves discreetly arranged" (Hornblow). Irene Franklin and Rosalinde Fuller were singers who lent grace to the evening.

(3) [Fourth Edition] B: George V. Hobart; M: Louis M. Hirsch; LY: John Murray Anderson and Irving Caesar; D: John Murray Anderson; CH: Carl Randall; DS: Reginald Marsh, Cleon Throckmorton, Howard Greer, James Reynolds, Erté, Ingeborg Hansell, Earl Payne Frank, Blanding Sloane, Alice O'Neill, Georgianna Brown, Dorothy Armstrong, Pieter Myer; P: The Bohemians, Inc.; T: Shubert Theatre; 9/12/22 (209)

With exquisite curtain, scene, and costume designs, the 1922 edition was extremely handsome. From the moment the audience entered the Shubert to witness the Reginald Marsh show curtain depicting famous Villagers of the day, including Donald Ogden Stewart, John Dos Passos, and F. Scott Fitzgerald, they knew they were in for a visual feast of "pictures brilliant, flashing and bizarre" (Alexander Woollcott).

Dancing was a vital element in the show's success, with Ula Sharon, Marjorie Peterson, and Alexander Yakoleff competing for terpsichorean honors. The dance highlight and the gorgeous centerpiece of the program was the Ballet Ballad, the first example of an item found regularly in later editions of the show, this one being the adaptation of Oscar Wilde's poem "The Nightingale and the Rose," danced by Sharon and Yakoleff.

The comic partnership of Bert Savoy and Jay Brennan struck gold with their naughty antics in which Savoy, a blatantly swishy female impersonator, told risque limp-wristed anecdotes about his friend Margie. Nothing else in the show provoked as many hearty yocks.

Tableaux and spectacles were represented by one picturing a famous mezzotint, accompanied by Beethoven's "Moonlight Sonata"; another featuring dolls in movement; "Sweetheart Lane," set in Washington Square Park; and "You Are My Rainbow," a lush Hirsch ballad performed to a colorful ballet. The best-known song from the show was an interpolation, "Georgette," by Lew Brown and Ray Henderson.

(4) [Fifth Edition] B: Lew Fields; M: Louis A. Hirsch and Con Conrad; LY: Irving Caesar and John Murray Anderson; D: Lew Fields and John Murray Anderson; CH: Larry Ceballos and Michio Ito; D: John Murray Anderson; DS: Howard Greer, Ingeborg Hansell, and James Reynolds; P: The Bohemians, Inc.; T: Winter Garden; 9/20/23 (131)

For its fifth edition, this *Follies* moved from the Shubert to the Winter Garden. James Craig found the revue's distinguishing feature its costuming, and the *Times* critic commented that John Murray Anderson had contributed "a number of hauntingly beautiful scenes." He found dull "The Gardens of Kama," a fantasy on Laurence Hope's love lyrics of India set to the music of Amy Woodforde-Finden, but Craig thought the costuming here and in a Spanish dancing fiesta was outstanding.

Craig complained that there was not enough comedy, although "diminutive Daphne Pollard, the English comedienne, did some first-rate clowning," and Tom Howard, a former comedian for Minsky's burlesque shows, had some amusing sketches. The *Times* critic found a starving-on-a-raft sequence to be hilarious. Craig praised the dancing of Martha Graham, Ula Sharon, the Spanish Casinos, the show-stopping Buster West and the acrobatic Mandells. The *Times* noted that the chorus was large, beautiful, and generally underdressed. In the show were such performers as Joe E. Brown, Marion Green, Eva Puck, and Sammy White.

H.H.

(5) [Sixth Edition] B: Lew Fields and Irving Caesar; M: Cole Porter, Owen Murphy, and Jay Gorney; LY: Cole Porter, Irving Caesar, and John Murray Anderson; D: John Murray Anderson; CH: Larry Ceballos; DS: James Reynolds, Ingeborg Hansell, and Herman Rosse; P: The Bohemians, Inc.; T: Shubert Theatre; 9/16/24 (131)

Another spectacularly produced, excessively long, formless edition of this series, from which critics departed with a feeling as if of being bloated from overeating. "It contains so much," complained Arthur Hornblow, "girls, costumes, tableaux, drolleries—that half the time you can't see the forest for the trees."

Jennie and Rosie Dolly, better known as the Dolly Sisters, were first in the hearts of the critics, with blackface comics Mack and Moran a close second. The Dollys did a pathos-ridden morality sketch called "Destiny," a Parisian Apache production number about a streetwalker in which Jennie's acting talents were displayed; and their dance numbers were outstanding, including one done with four trained collies who joined precisely in their steps. Oscar Wilde's "Happy Prince" was transmogrified into an exquisitely designed Ballet Ballad featuring dancer Anna Ludmilla as the Swallow, and future top choreographer Robert Alton was the Prince; Parisian comic Manuel Vega did an uproarious wrestling match with a dummy; and various other conventional but expertly produced numbers were exhibited. The music for these numbers was at first provided by Cole Porter, but his songs were eventually replaced by Owen Murphy and Jay Gorney numbers. Porter's contributions had included "I'm in Love Again."

Spectacle numbers included "Liebestraum," based on Liszt's composition; "Wait for the Moon," a white and green fantasy; and "The Hall of Mirrors," in which the chorus girls created mirror images of one another.

(6) [Seventh Edition] M/LY: Harold Levey and Owen Murphy; D: Hassard Short; CH: Larry Ceballos and Alexander Gabrilov; S: Clark Robinson; C: Mark Mooring, Charles Le Maire, and Gilbert Adrian; P: The Bohemians, Inc.; T: Chanin's Forty-Sixth Street Theatre; 12/24/25 (180)

The large-scale revue format was beginning to grind itself into dust when this edition appeared; it did little to retard the onrush of the inevitable. The bloom was off the rose, novelty was as scarce as snow in July, and the creative impulses behind the shows had, for the most part, withered. As Arthur Hornblow bemoaned, "these sublimated vaudeville shows are nothing like as good as they used to be. They are dull as to wit, impoverished as to invention."

The Greenwich Village Follies sought new life in the work of master revue director Hassard Short, who took over John Murray Anderson's chores. Short's genius was not alight for the occasion, however, and the production was merely acceptable in the familiar vein, being extremely meager in the laugh department. Short's specialty, beautiful production numbers using mechanized elevator platforms, were in abundance, and the stage pictures were attractive but only conventionally so.

Comediennes Florence Moore and Renie Riano, songstress Irene Delroy, and comics Tom Howard and Frank McIntyre fought a losing battle to stir empathy with dreary material. Numbers cited by the critics included a "Lady of the Snow," featuring melting figures of Jack Frost and human snowballs, and travesties of hit plays such as *The Vortex* and *Cradle Snatchers*. A "Spring Edition" with a batch of new players and numbers appeared on 3/15/26.

This show ended the regular editions of the series; a final stab at keeping the *Follies* alive came two years later.

(7) [Eighth Edition] B: Harold Atteridge; M: Ray Perkins and Maurie Rubens; LY: Max and Nathaniel Lief; S: Watson Barratt; C: Ernest Schrapps; D: J. C. Huffman; CH: Ralph Reader; P: The Bohemians, Inc.; T: Winter Garden Theatre; 4/9/28 (128)

The final edition of the series was no better or worse than its worthy predecessors; it offered "a brazen fast-moving, shiny extravaganza, containing the usual quota of good dancing and...not an overabundance of humor" (*Times*). Doctor Rockwell was its comic highlight, he being a clown "who bounces his rubber teeth on the floor and gives little talks through his nose," according to *Time*. Vaudeville headliners Blossom Seeley, Benny Fields, and Bobby Watson were in the show, as was songstress Grace LaRue. Comic duo Jans and Whalen provided fun; Carlos and Valeria danced acrobatically; the Chester Hale Girls did a calypso dance with two other groups, one of them taught by Martha Graham; Evelyn Law, former Ziegfeldian, danced solo; and there were weak travesties of plays such as *The Command to Love*, *The Trial of Mary Dugan*, and *Silent House*.

GREENWICH VILLAGERS, THE [Revue] B: Menlo Mayfield and Ballard MacDonald; M/LY: John Milton Hagen, Marion Gillespie, and Menlo Mayfield; T: Grove Street Theatre (OB); 8/18/27 (5)

An intimate Off-Broadway revue focusing on the eccentricities of Greenwich Village but lacking "wit, cleverness [and] originality," not to mention talent, declared the *Times*. Another revue, *Bare Facts*, part of a short-lived series, had disbanded after a quarrel between its creators and its management, and the former refashioned their contributions into this new offering. Sketches, off-color humor, a couple of tunes, and the like were thrown together to be quickly forgotten as soon as the curtain fell.

GREY FOX, THE [Drama/Historical-Biographical/Period/Politics/Romance/ Crime/Italy] A: Lemist Esler; D: William A. Brady, Jr., and Lemist Esler; S: Jo Mielziner; P: William A. Brady, Jr., and Dwight Deere Wiman; T: Playhouse Theatre; 10/22/28 (88)

This elaborately staged product of George Pierce Baker's playwriting course at Yale was an ambitious biographical account of the cunning Italian Renaissance thinker and Florentine political adviser Niccolo Machiavelli (Henry Hull). Machiavelli is first shown as an idealist sent by the Republic of Florence on a diplomatic mission to Caterina Sforza, Duchess of Imola (Chrystal Herne), for whom he has a passionate regard. Her ultimate duplicity leads him to adopt a cynical philosophy of opportunism. He is next seen as instrumental in carrying out a mass murder of Cesare Borgia's (Edward Arnold) enemies and finally is shown as an old man writing *The Prince* in exile.

Many agreed with Richard Dana Skinner who found that the play failed to clarify the Italian political background but nevertheless often caught fire and projected "much of the turbulent passion of the renaissance." Some sided with *Time*, which observed, "An overwritten text and an overdressed cast somehow made it seem improbable, uninteresting."

GRINGA, LA [Drama/Period/Romance/Mexico] A: Tom Cushing; D/P: Hamilton MacFadden; S: P. Dodd Ackerman; T: Little Theatre; 2/1/28 (21)

Brooks Atkinson said that "Most of the staples of the untutored native-girl drama" were decked out in *La Gringa*, about a roving 1885 New England sea dog, Captain Bowditch (George Nash), who finds a torrid half-breed schoolgirl Carlota (Claudette Colbert), in a Mexican convent and takes her back with him as his wife to his New Bedford, Massachusetts, sister (Clara Blandick) (the marriage, however, was phony). He discovers that the Spanish legacy Carlota was entitled to is gone, and he loses her to the schoolteacher Caleb Sprague (Paul Wright). She leaves Caleb to keep his reputation clean, and she then poisons Bowditch before fleeing on a schooner bound for south of the border.

Claudette Colbert's beauty and appeal were the only glowing flames in this "silly, tiresome rumpus," said Gordon M. Leland.

GRINGO [Comedy-Drama/Romance/Crime/Mexico] A: Sophie Treadwell; D/P: Guthrie McClintic; T: Comedy Theatre; 12/14/22 (29)

Sophie Treadwell's first produced play was based on her considerable travels in Mexico as a journalist. Essentially a melodrama, it failed to capitalize on innate entertainment values by developing the characters or action in a way bound to elicit the proper proportions of sympathy and revulsion.

Set in the mountains of Mexico's back country, *Gringo* presents a story of a group of "poor white trash" Americans whose ideals and behavior are meant to be contrasted with those of the natives. The principal action concerns the kidnapping of the group by a bandit-revolutionary (Jose Ruben), his demand for money, and his eventually successful wooing of the half-breed Bessie (Edna Hibbard), daughter of two of his victims.

Heywood Broun judged *Gringo* a work "of great promise and some extraordinarily interesting achievement which does not quite come off," and Alexander Woollcott voted it "a lively, colorful and continuously interesting play." Arthur Hornblow, however, insisted that "Its dialogue and the general behavior of its characters are as unreal as Santa Claus in Armenia."

GROUNDS FOR DIVORCE (Válóperes hölgy) [Comedy/Marriage/Hungarian] A: Ernest Vajda; AD: Guy Bolton; D/P: Henry Miller; S: Clara Fargo Thomas; T: Empire Theatre; 9/23/24 (130)

Hungarian playwright Ernest Vajda's high comedy, for all of its forced charm, was not very amusing, and it was as much Ina Claire's scintillating acting as any of the author's devices that kept the chatty piece around for its profitable run.

Claire's talents were expended on the role of Denise Sorbier, elegant wife of the dashing Paris divorce lawyer Maurice (Philip Merivale), who so neglects her in the interest of his lovely clients that he even forgets their anniversary, thus prompting his irate wife to pitch an ink bottle at him to good effect. She takes the route her husband specializes in and goes off to Rome for a year but returns when he is on the brink of marriage. Her strategy is to incur Maurice's jealousy through the advertisement of a liason with an Italian lover (Georges Renavent). This time the fiancée is ignored, precipitating a bottle of red ink flying through the air. By Act Three, husband and wife have worked out their difficulties and have been happily reunited.

Like so many foreign plays adapted for Broadway, this one underwent meddlesome tampering. Arthur Hornblow grumbled, *"Grounds for Divorce* is a mirthless comedy, with the merest skeleton of a plot, obvious lines and a total lack of the effervescent qualities one expects in a first class comedy."

GUARDSMAN, THE (A testör) [Dramatic Revival] A: Ferenc Molnar; S: Jo Mielziner; P: Theatre Guild; T: Garrick Theatre; 10/13/24 (274)

The critical opinion was generally in agreement on this high comedy of Molnar's—the play was fluff but the production and the acting were of absolutely top quality. "The cast make it seem far better than it really is," said Robert Littell. The Guild was scolded for dallying with such piffle, but there was little doubt that Alfred Lunt and Lynn Fontanne (in their first starring roles in the same play since becoming "The Lunts") were giving among the finest demonstrations of acting technique available on the Main Stem. An earlier version of the play, *Where Ignorance Is Bliss*, had failed in 1913 after eight performances.

The situations in *The Guardsman* develop from the jealousy of an actor (Lunt) of his young actress wife (Fontanne) whom he suspects of having a romance with a certain Russian Imperial guardsman; to test his suspicions he courts the wife by flowers and notes, presumably sent by the Guardsman, sets up a rendezvous with her, and ultimately gets familiar enough to kiss her, following which he removes his disguise. Seeing him in this light, she laughs and says she was not fooled one whit by his ploy and knew all along who he was. Both the audience and the actor are left deliberately puzzled by her statement—is she or is she not telling the truth?

Joining the Lunts in this escapade were Dudley Digges, Helen Westley, Philip Loeb, and Edith Meiser.

The Guardsman moved after a month to the Booth, where it finished out its excellent run.

GUEST OF HONOR, THE [Comedy/Literature/Family/Romance] A/D: William Hodge; P: Lee Shubert; T: Broadhurst Theatre; 9/20/20 (75)

John Weatherbee (William Hodge), an unrecognized writer, has been caring for Jack (Graham Lucas), an orphaned boy. As John is about to be evicted from his studio, he receives a $500 check for advance royalties on some verse he sent to a women's literary club. He is invited to be the guest of honor at the club by a young woman (Alice Bricker) who turns out to be the boy's aunt. A battle for Jack's custody ensues, but all is solved when John and Helen marry.

The play afforded William Hodge only a moderate vehicle for his talents. The points made by the dialogue were ''obvious and a little too deliberate,'' observed Alan Dale; they could have served as ''the sidewalk conversations of vaudeville,'' added Alexander Woollcott. This critic called the play ''an old-fashioned, home-made, deep-dish comedy which was never meant for New York.''

GUIBOUR: UN MIRACLE DE NOTRE DAME, COMMENT ELLE GARDA UNE FEMME D'ESTRE ARSE [Dramatic Revival/French Language] AD: Anna Sprague MacDonald; P: Yvette Guilbert; T: Thirty-ninth Street Theatre; 3/1/22 (5)

A French work from the Middle Ages that had been introduced locally in 1919 at the Neighborhood Playhouse, starring French actress Yvette Guilbert, who was responsible for the present five-performance revival. This miracle play (not reviewed by the press in this incarnation) was about a woman named Guibor (Elizabeth Moffatt) who slays her son-in-law Aubin to halt the dismaying rumors of which she has been the victim. She is saved from death at the stake by the intervention of the Virgin Mary.

GUILTY ONE, THE [Drama/Marriage/Crime/British] A: Michael Morton and Peter Traill; D: Edward Elsner; P: A. H. Woods; T: Selwyn Theatre; 3/20/23 (31)

After nearly nine years of film acting, Pauline Frederick returned to the stage, but her vehicle turned out to be a flop that Heywood Broun unceremoniously labeled ''a bad play, so terrible and fearsome that its ineptitudes are far beyond the realm of opinion.''

The plot, really one enormous red herring, concerns Ronald Short's (Charles Waldron) demand that his wife (Frederick) stop seeing her lover Dick Raston (Noel Leslie) if she does not wish to see the husband kill him. Shortly after she declares that she intends to leave Ronald for Dick, she is informed that the latter has been murdered by the former. The rest of the play involves the tormenting experiences she is subjected to as a result of the crime, but it is revealed toward the end that no murder has taken place, all of the proceedings having been arranged by Ronald as a means of teaching his wife a lesson.

GUINEA PIG, THE [Comedy/Theatre/Sex/Romance] A/P: Preston Sturges; D: Walter Greenough; S: William Bradley Studio; T: President Theatre; 1/7/29 (64)

Preston Sturges, soon to become one of Hollywood's most respected screenwriters and directors, offered *The Guinea Pig* as his first play. Its premise was not new, but it garnered many mildly complimentary comments. The play was based on a personal experience, recounted in James Curtis's biography of Sturges, *Between Flops*. Sturges was seeing a successful actress (unnamed) who constantly fought with and ridiculed him. After one particularly ferocious argument, she told him that to her, he was nothing but a guinea pig for the main character in a play she was writing. This crack inspired him to get even by writing a play that would be better than hers. He set to work at once, obsessed with the project, and came up with *The Guinea Pig*. When he couldn't find a New York producer, he convinced the Wharf Players of Provincetown, Massachusetts, to do it in the summer of 1928. Still unable to get the play produced in New York, Sturges learned that for an absolute minimum of $2,500 he might be able to produce it himself. He raised the money, which proved to be insufficient, and worked out several deals that allowed him finally to get the work on the boards. One such deal was an arrangement with the Leoni Brothers, Forty-eighth Street restaurateurs, to do the play in the intimate Edythe Totten Theatre that they owned and to rename it the ''President,'' after the hotel it faced. The well-known dialect actor Alexander Carr was hired, not for his usual $2,500 a week salary but for a more affordable sum plus 10 percent of the gross and the payment of his $750 worth of hotel bills. The production money was gone before the show could open; to get an audience for tryout purposes, Sturges convinced the wealthy suburban community of Scarborough to let him preview the play for them for two nights. These performances cost him only $60.

Carr played Sam Small, a Jewish furrier *cum* producer, who tells a young female playwright (Mary Carroll) that she must get more life experience before her work can be truthful. She thereupon selects a young male dramatist (John Ferguson) as the guinea pig on whom she will practice the art of seduction to learn just what he would say when cornered. After momentary emotional obstacles are overcome when the heroine's motives are exposed, the two authors discover that they love one another.

Stark Young detected ''plenty of humor and sentiment,'' the *Times* claimed that, despite its apparent aimlessness, the play was ''so completely unpretentious that time and again you are drawn to it,'' and Ernest Boyd termed it ''An amusing comedy.''

GUNS [Drama/Prohibition/Crime/Romance] A: James Hagan; D/P: Jack Kingsberry; T: Wallack's Theatre; 8/6/28 (48)

A ''completely unoriginal'' (Richard Watts, Jr.) gangland melodrama with echoes of numerous other plays in the genre; it was implausible, used outdated slang expressions, and had a foggy plot about beer runners and smuggling aliens across the Mexican border. The action ranged from speakeasies in New York and Chicago to the Mexican border and included a misguided miss (Suzanne Bennett) embroiled in underworld operations, an undercover federal detective (Hugh Thompson) operating amidst the crooks, and assorted gunslinging murderers and bootleggers. Action afficionadoes got a full share of bullets and blood, and romantic spectators were happy to see the good girl win the federal officer's heart.

GYPSY [Drama/Sex/Marriage/Family] A: Maxwell Anderson; D: George Cukor; P: Richard Herndon; T: Klaw Theatre; 1/14/29 (64)

Burns Mantle chose this play for his Best Play collection, despite its commercial failure, because it represented "an honestly written drama inspired by changing social standards and values, a play of purpose, the artistic integrity of which cannot be questioned whatever the reaction to its characters and story."

Maxwell Anderson's title character (Claiborne Foster) is a sexually promiscuous young wife, married to a handsome, decent musician (Lester Vail), and unable, because of traits apparently both learned and inherited from her fickle thrice-married mother (Mary Young), to keep from having affairs. Finally, she sees that her only escape from herself is suicide. The opening-night version, rejected by the critics, had a telephone call interrupt her self-inflicted death by gas; another man's request for her favors led her to continue living. By night two, the suicide was carried out.

Richard Dana Skinner reasoned against the idea of inherited infidelity as destructive of Gypsy's sense of free will; Ernest Boyd thought she was an "unconvincing" character and said the subject was better suited to comedy than drama; and Robert Littell said the play "is overwritten, it contains much smart, semi-epigrammatic dialogue..., and in many spots it is soft or perfunctory."

GYPSY FIRES [Drama/Romance/Crime] A: Allan Davis; D: A. H. Van Buren; S: Clark Robinson; P: William Caryl for Golden Love, Inc.; T: George M. Cohan Theatre; 12/7/25 (16)

A colorful saga of a gypsy girl's love for a nongypsy lad that Wells Root said was "a gutteral melodrama, intermittently convincing and always interesting," but that the *Evening Sun* rejected for its "stale dialogue, incongruous and unoriginal humor and...superficial and bungling character development."

The unlikely heroine was a gypsy, Morella O'Neil (Lillian Foster), who spoke with a brogue. With her drunken Irish dad (J. M. Kerrigan) she lives among a gypsy band encamped in a New England forest. The Romeo and Juliet-type romance has her in love with upper-class artist Carroll Lankford (Arthur Albertson), whose snobbish parents are repelled by the match; the gypsy queen (Alice Fischer) also objects to the affair. The drama includes the knife killing of the girl's father and the mauling to death by a trained bear of the murderer before true love conquers all impediments.

GYPSY JIM [Comedy/Family] A: Oscar Hammerstein II and Milton Herbert Gropper; D: Clifford Brooke; S: Clifford Pember; C: Charles Le Maire; P: Arthur Hammerstein; T: Forty-ninth Street Theatre; 1/14/24 (48)

Just when the Blake family—parents, son, and daughter—is about to fall apart due to personal and professional problems, Gypsy Jim (Leo Carrillo) knocks at their door, convinces them of his almost supernatural powers, restores their faith in themselves, and sets all on roads to success. Later, Jim is revealed as an eccentric millionaire who applies practical charity when he sees it is needed.

Although he rated the play at nursery level, Percy Hammond deemed it "one of those helpful extravaganzas that stimulate the innocent of heart to noble emotions and kindly deeds." Alexander Woollcott mused that the comedy seemed "to have been written without an atom of thought or skill, and yet. . . somehow does not bore you at all."

H.H.

H

H.M.S. PINAFORE [Musical Revival] B/LY: W. S. Gilbert; M: Arthur Sullivan; D: Milton Aborn; S: Rollo Wayne; P: Messrs. Shubert; T: Century Theatre; 4/6/26 (56)

A lavish, spectacular revival of the Gilbert and Sullivan classic with an enormous representation of the ship of the title occupying all of the Theatre's immense revolving stage. It was only slightly less pictorially stupendous than the revival offered in 1916 at the gigantic Hippodrome, also produced by the Shuberts. A chorus of 100 plus, a few hundred gowns and uniforms, and an all-star cast went far toward making this a well-liked staging. Fay Templeton, who had gained considerable weight during her recent retirement, made a plump Buttercup, Marion Green was an excellent Captain Corcoran, William Danforth a droll Dick Deadeye, and John E. Hazzard a comic delight as Sir Joseph Porter.

The scale of the show, wrote John Mason Brown, hampered the clarity of Gilbert's lyrics, and the music was not as effective as intended when played as accompaniment to revue-like production numbers. But Arthur Hornblow claimed that the lyrics and tunes sounded better than ever, especially when sung by "a chorus that lifted the roof."

HABITUAL HUSBAND, THE [Comedy/Sex/Marriage] A: Dana Burnet; D: Dudley Digges and Josephine Hull; S: Woodman Thompson; P: Actors' Theatre; T: Forty-eighth Street Theatre; 12/24/24 (11)

The "habitual husband" is Rodney Kingsley (Grant Mitchell), who has been married to Anne (Margalo Gillmore) for a couple of years, with the "modern" understanding between them that as soon as one tires of the other, they are to seek a separation. When Anne's ex-roommate Hilda (Diantha Pattison) visits, Rodney is distracted by her, and the pair are soon planning to run away together; Anne encourages the decision but then demands to be taken along. She manages to win back her mate through various devices, including a family recipe for angel-food cake.

"[T]oo slow for farce and too implausible for comedy," was Heywood Broun's assessment. "It begins briskly and amusingly and holds that pace for a single act. After that the dawdling sets in."

HAIL AND FAREWELL [Drama/Romance/Period/France] A: William Hurlbut; D: B. Iden Payne; P: Joseph B. Shea; T: Morosco Theatre; 2/19/23 (41)

A *Camille*-like romantic drama set in 1871 France, on the Riviera and in Paris, and starring Florence Reed as Isabella Echevaria, a crafty, pipe-smoking, high-class Spanish courtesan whose lovers have included nobles and wealthy commoners but who now, for the first time, falls dangerously in love with the handsome young Philippe, Comte de Villeneuve (Paul Gordon), a prospective diplomat. When Isabella learns that the relationship, which has been blissful, threatens Philippe's career, she takes the only way out, suicide, dying in her lover's arms. "She dies by slow poison to slow music," noted the *Herald*. "The young man sings a ballad, 'Hail and Farewell,' as she takes the potion behind his back."

"The drama is loosely strung together by much flatulent dialogue," observed the *Times*.

HAIRY APE, THE [Drama/Sea/Labor/Politics] A. Eugene O'Neill; D: Eugene O'Neill and James Light; DS: Robert Edmond Jones and Cleon Throckmorton; P: Provincetown Players; T: Provincetown Playhouse (OB); 3/9/22 (120)

Clearly the most controversial drama of the 1921–1922 season and one of the major works of the decade. Given a mesmerizingly effective production, *The Hairy Ape* received notices ranging from ecstatically positive to nastily negative. Kenneth Andrews acknowledged the fineness of its conception but said "The dialogue is clumsy, redundant, and painfully rhetorical" and couched in "the most primitive, the most ineffective kind of play writing." Others dismissed it as a piece of blatant International Workers of the World (IWW) propaganda. A favorite critical theme was the play's extensive use of strong language. Patterson James was so shocked by it that he branded O'Neill "Archpriest of the Unwashed Drama and pet divinity of its Unsoaped Patrons." The New York City Police Department even threatened at one point to close the show on the grounds of obscene language.

Such negative attitudes served only to stoke the coals of curiosity, and it was not long before the Off-Broadway presentation leaped from the pan of Macdougal Street to the fire of Broadway's Plymouth Theatre, where it opened on April 17.

Written in the pounding rhythms of expressionistic technique, with a potent substructure of symbolist and realistic methods, *The Hairy Ape* concentrates on the plight of Robert Smith (Louis Wolheim), a human behemoth known as "Yank," who swells with pride at the strength and endurance he displays stoking the furnace of a transatlantic liner. Only when the slumming daughter (Mary Blair) of a steel magnate recoils in horror on seeing him in his dark, fiery stokehole, does this "hairy ape" lose confidence in his sense of belonging and begin his rapid and tragic descent into ruin. In eight swiftly moving scenes, O'Neill takes the audience from the liner's stokehole and hurricane deck to Fifth Avenue in New York, where Yank collides with unfeeling passerby mannikins, to prison on Rikers Island, to an IWW meeting, where he is ejected as a spy, and to the Central Park Zoo, where he enters the gorilla cage and is crushed to death and left there by the ape who occupies it; Yank, at last, has found where he "belongs."

Hornblow thought the play deserving of the Pulitzer Prize (another O'Neill drama, *Anna Christie*, won it) for being "a study profound and moving in its picture of the futility of brute power in its sole opposition to the conventions of society and the overwhelming authority of capitalistic control...*The Hairy Ape* is apocalyptic in its message."

The acting, except for a weak spot represented by Mary Blair (she was replaced on Broadway by Carlotta Monterey, who thereby met O'Neill and not long after married him), was exceptional but none more so than that provided by Louis Wolheim, the brutish looking intellectual who played Yank. He "played expertly and with every indication of the role's characteristics," wrote Percy Hammond.

HALF A WIDOW [Musical/War/Military/Romance/France] B/LY: Harry B. Smith and Frank Dupree; M: Shep Camp; D: Lawrence Marston and Edwin T. Emery; S: P. Dodd Ackerman; P: Wally Gluck; T: Waldorf Theatre; 9/12/27 (16)

It took ten years to bring this musical about a World War I romance between an American and a French girl from page to stage; interest in it after its production was as minimal as that preceding it. George Jean Nathan decided it was "a deadly stupid hoof and yodel show."

The story, which had faint resemblances to *What Price Glory?* concerned an American captain (Halfred Young) in love with Babette (Gertrude Lang), whom he marries before leaving for the front, where he expects to be killed. His money will go to her, and she can then marry the French lad she loves. But the officer lives, and Babette decides to stay wed to him when he returns.

HALF MOON, THE [Musical/Romance/Family] B/LY: William Le Baron; M: Victor Jacobi; D: Fred G. Latham; P: Charles Dillingham; T: Liberty Theatre; 11/1/20 (48)

The Half Moon was a half-baked composition with a top-heavily talented cast featuring Joseph Cawthorn in the lead as Henry Hudson Hobson. The feeble libretto of this "rather thin, too sugary" (*Times*) show had Mr. Cawthorn's character oppose the marriage of his son (Joseph Santley) to a Boston socialite (May Thompson), because he suspects her of being a snob; she proves that she isn't, so the wedding proceeds. Cawthorn did what he could to pull laughs from the material, but it proved a nearly impossible task. Musically, the show was a step better, but none of its songs endured. Cast members of note who sank with the schooner included Maude Eburne, Edna May Oliver, Ivy Sawyer, and Oscar Shaw.

HALF-CASTE, THE [Drama/Tropics/Alcoholism/Romance] A: Jack Mc-Clellan; D: Edgar J. MacGregor; T: National Theatre; 3/29/26 (63)

Tropic paradises with their brown-skinned beauties were seductive locales for 1920s playwrights, as witness exotic wares such as *The Bird of Paradise*, *Aloma of the South Seas*, and the present melodrama, set in Samoa. In this "story of love and sacrifice in a Land of Forgotten Men" a handsome, young, alcoholic playboy (Frederick March) is yachting in the South Seas, where, years earlier, his father also had sailed and had had a romance with a native maiden, leaving a half-caste daughter behind. The young man, fiancée (Helenka Adamowska) in tow, arrives at the island and soon falls for Tuana (Veronica), a girl who is revealed as his half-sister before he marries her. The father, thought dead, turns up as a beachcomber (Frederick Perry) and makes the revelation. The girl ends up stabbing herself to death.

The play, meant as a diatribe against the evils of whiskey, "was all a brazen and half-conscious caricature, depending on its sensational outbreaks to sell itself," thought Percy Hammond.

HALF-GODS [Drama/Marriage] A: Sidney Howard; D/P: Arthur Hopkins; S: Albert R. Johnson; T: Plymouth Theatre; 12/21/29 (17)

The critics were suprised to see how poorly Sidney Howard's inspiration had served him in this play that the *Times* said seemed to have been written by a rank novice instead of a distinguished dramatist. The play sought to be an excoriating although satirical examination of the hell of a married life experienced by lawyer Stephen Ferrier (Donn Cook) and his selfish, ineffectual, dissatisfied wife of eight years, Hope (Mayo Methot). She listens to the psychiatric diagnosis of two professors, one a Freudian and the other a German, who tells her that her only function is to bear children. She and Stephen battle vigorously through nine scenes to the brink of divorce proceedings, only to be reconciled to starting over after a brutal physical confrontation with one another.

"There is a great deal of implied social criticism in the lines and text," Perriton Maxwell pointed out, "but...nothing which is very effective or important seems to emerge."

HALF-NAKED TRUTH, THE [Comedy/Art/Romance] A: N. Brewster Morse; D: Douglas Wood; P: Mabel Ryan; T: Mayfair Theatre (OB); 6/7/26 (41)

This "pleasant but undistinguished little comedy" (*Sun*) had to vie for audience attention on opening night with a theatre cat that paraded on stage in the midst of a scene and settled down for the duration. The critics spent more words on him than on the play.

The plot dealt with a misunderstanding between New York tenement types

Charlie Smith (Ray Collins) and his girlfriend Mamie (Marguerite Mosier) over his attraction for the vampiress-sculptor Clarice Van Doren (Eva Balfour) for whom he has been secretly posing as a model. After a night spent pondering the issue in Central Park, he reveals the truth, and soon the statue is itself unveiled to critical appreciation of its masculine perfection. Noble young Charlie becomes the center of media attention, is even offered a film contract, and moves West with Mamie to a ranch.

The play was, to Brooks Atkinson, "amateurish in every respect" and, to Charles Belmont Davis, "one of the most naive dramas ever" produced on Broadway.

(1) HAMLET [Dramatic Revival] A: William Shakespeare; D/P: John E. Kellard; T: Manhattan Opera House (OB); 12/6/20 (4)

John E. Kellard, who had produced a record-breaking 102-performance run of *Hamlet* in 1912 at the Garden Theatre, brought a company including Ian Keith, Edward Forbes, Fredda Brindley, and Dora Fellows to New York with a five-play Shakespeare series, none of which seems to have gained the slightest attention from the critics. Kellard played all of the leading roles.

(2) D/P: Fritz Leiber; T: Lexington Theatre (OB); 12/27/20 (3) (and others; see entry)

Fritz Leiber, a dedicated though not brilliant Shakespearean actor, appeared in New York in various roles drawn by the Bard; only a year before this revival he had essayed Hamlet and would return with it several more times during the decade. The *Times* wrote of him in 1920: "He knows his Hamlet and physically and in characterization fits the popular Hamlet. His figure, lean and trim, and his poetic masque are well suited to the part, and while he fails to carry one to the heights of tenseness contained in the action, he still keeps one's attention concentrated on the wistful, melancholy brooding which dominates the Prince of Denmark." Virginia Bronson played Ophelia, and John C. Hickey was Polonius; they outclassed a mediocre troupe.

Leiber's Hamlet was back on 12/27/21 at the same theatre for two performances, on 1/23/22 at the Forty-eighth Street Theatre for one performance, and on 3/24/30 at the Shubert for five performances. At the Shubert he headed the Chicago Civic Shakespeare Society's production and played in eight other Shakespeare plays as well. William Courtleigh was Claudius, Philip Quin was Polonius, Virginia Bronson—once Leiber's Ophelia—was Gertrude, and Marie Carroll was Ophelia.

Of his repertory, Hamlet was among Leiber's most successful roles. Perriton Maxwell thought he both "caught and held the mood of the play in his interpretation." "Mr. Leiber's performances," noted John Hutchens, "which point the direction and establish the tone of the plays, are controlled and coherent, though they have nothing to do with the other and inspired Shakespeare who is to be acted for his great poetry and not explained in his narrative." But Brooks

Atkinson thought the actor's stress on ensemble and the telling of a pithy story made the play so clear that this was "the most coherent Hamlet this courier has ever seen.... His is a straightforward Hamlet—no muddy-mettled spouter of lines, but a character alert to all the relationships of the drama, clarifying the dialogue with simple gestures, waiting his time without slackening pace, keeping his diction clean and his mind on edge."

Sets for this last named revival were by Herman Rosse and costumes by William Henry Matthews.

(3) D/P: Walter Hampden; DS: Claude Bragdon; T: Broadhurst Theatre; 5/4/21 (8) (and others; see entry)

Walter Hampden had introduced his Hamlet to New York several years earlier and showed it there often on later occasions, such as the present revival. Other twenties stagings of Hampden's version came at Hampden's Theatre on 10/10/ 25 for sixty-eight performances and at the same playhouse on 1/4/28 for thirteen showings. The most memorable of these came in 1925, a month before Basil Sydney upset all preconceptions with his modern-dress production; Ethel Barrymore was Hampden's Ophelia for the exhibition, which played in repertory with *The Merchant of Venice*, in which Barrymore was Portia.

The Hampden *Hamlet* was three and three-quarters hours long and felt it. A little cut text allowed the *Times* to appreciate "the sheer dramatic greatness of this play," and Hampden's meticulous, clearly worked-out production left nothing vague or overlooked. The note struck by his acting was of the heroic. Many were bored, but Richard Dana Skinner described his noble Dane as a straightforward, triumphant being who never wavered from his course of avenging his father's death, and who, once he was convinced of the truthfulness of the ghost's tale, moved without any indecision toward the inexorable conclusion.

Barrymore was more effective as Ophelia. She had "an unexpected youthfulness and an expected radiance," wrote John Mason Brown of the forty-six-year-old star.

Claude Bragdon designed a clever, carefully selective setting that used a curtain as a background for down-front scenes while upstage ones were being changed. A detailed account of his conception is provided in his *More Lives Than One*.

(4) E. H. Sothern and Julia Marlowe; T: Century Theatre; 11/7/21 (11)

E. H. Sothern and Julia Marlowe, he as Hamlet and she as Ophelia, had been seen in their touring production of the play so many times over the years that their arrival did not stir up much critical attention, and there is barely any coverage of note to draw on in describing their production. When they returned to New York for their last local mounting of the play, on 10/29/23 at Jolson's Fifty-ninth Street Theatre for seven performances, the *Times* noted: "Mr. Sothern's Hamlet...was in every way equal to his past appearances in the part—in the clarity and consistency of its conception and execution it has not been excelled. Miss Marlowe's Ophelia was a delicate and graceful characterization. In the mad scene, particularly, she played with an admirable restraint and a full recognition of the scene's essential connection with the entire play.''

(5) D/P: Arthur Hopkins; M: Robert Russell Bennett; L: George Scheff; DS: Robert Edmond Jones; T: Sam H. Harris Theatre; 11/16/22 (101)

When John Barrymore's performance as Hamlet came to an end after 101 performances, a record that he boasted exceeded the acclaimed 100 performance-run of Edwin Booth (but was actually one short of John E. Kellard's 1912 record of 102 at the Garden Theatre), the production was going strong with houses sold out for several weeks more, requiring that producer Hopkins refund a sizable sum to ticket holders. Broadway's Shakespearean event of the decade, it had brought to the American stage a controversial staging headed by an epochal performance of the title role.

Barrymore's Hamlet, although not perfect and subject to erratic changes at different performances, has never been equaled in general esteem by any other American actor. The qualities it purveyed were ''illusion, a sense of reality'' (*Tribune*), and a low-keyed believability unmarred by artificiality of tone; thoughtfulness, as Hamlet ''seemed to be searching, searching, for some explanation of the curious eventfulness of his life'' (Alan Dale); physical beauty and gracefulness, wit, perception, economy, psychological depth, precision, a conversational tone that nevertheless respected the verse and its rhythms, sympathy, intelligence, virility, unity, subtlety, irony, a lack of trickery, intensity, sophistication, ''clarity of outline and a beauty of the spirit that heightens to radiant humanity and deepens to soul tragedy'' (John Corbin).

The critics saw a Hamlet who seemed flawlessly true and honestly concerned with the problems of the drama. ''We give you our word that this sweet prince is a distraught, though mysterious, human being; not a prolonged and loquacious query,'' declared the *Tribune*.

Barrymore played not madness but feigned madness. Freud entered the picture in Hamlet's seemingly incestuous relationship with Blanche Yurka's attractive Gertrude.

Those who found fault with the performance cited a general lack of deep feeling in the playing, the emotional scenes never quite arousing significant pity for the character. Stark Young wanted to see not so cerebral an interpretation but one with ''the sense of a larger inner tumult'' suggestive of greater suffering.

This *Hamlet* made a number of important textual cuts; still, it ran over four hours and was considered complete. The beautiful set did not slow things down, since it consisted of a unit scheme that allowed the action to move swiftly without the need for shifts. Jones's design was very controversial, since it set the play within an architectural plan dominated by a central arch and a set of stairs that occupied the middle-stage area, thereby cramping the actors' movements. The set's flexibility seemed awkward when it came to the burial of Ophelia, for, as Broun stated, the funeral seemed to be taking place ''in the front parlor.''

Another hotly questioned idea was the use not of a visible ghost but of a wavering spot of light to suggest its presence. When the offstage voice of the ghost (Reginald Pole) did not seem to come from the light, the effect seemed laughable.

The company supporting Barrymore was a decent one; no one was unusually effective, and the Ophelia (Rosalinde Fuller), Claudius (Tyrone Power), and Gertrude (Blanche Yurka) were thought to be good.

The production made a return visit on 11/26/23 and played at the Manhattan Opera House for twenty-four performances. Among the changes was the substitution of an actor dressed in ghostly garments to portray Hamlet's father instead of using a beam of light.

(6) D/P/DS: Sir John Martin-Harvey; T: Century Theatre; 11/19/23 (8)

John Corbin found the *Hamlet* brought here by Sir John Martin-Harvey "always interesting and frequently of high distinction . . . the most novel feature is the vividness with which the play stands forth as a story and as a drama." Also notable was the ensemble, as opposed to the star performance.

Corbin described the British actor's Prince as fundamentally poetic. He read the lines with an "unfailing sense of the meaning," but displayed a limited voice range and missed the subtler overtones of Hamlet's mental play, his sly wit, melancholy, and whirling tempers. These qualities were denoted rather than fully expressed, but Hamlet as a "sweet, gentle Prince stands out as not since Forbes-Robertson." The *Tribune* critic thought that Barrymore proved the modernity and universality of Shakespeare, and that Martin-Harvey was "a more singing player."

H.H.

(7) D: James Light; S: Frederick Jones III; C: Aline Bernstein; P: Horace Liveright; T: Booth Theatre; 11/9/25 (88)

Basil Sydney's interpretation brought to New York its first modern-dress staging of Shakespeare's tragedy; viewers seemed to find the experiment eminently worthwhile, if not triumphant. The production came hard upon the heels of a revival of Walter Hampden's version, which was still on the boards, so there was ample scope for comparison with a traditional mounting.

George Jean Nathan revealed all of the prejudices he held against the modern-dress approach before seeing it; he marshaled every argument he could to ridicule the concept, but he discovered on watching it in the theatre that he felt "like an ass," for the production was "actually more interesting, more exciting, more moving and more vivid than any *Hamlet* of other days" he had witnessed. What he and others saw onstage was a *Hamlet* that was not as electric as it was merely because its garments were modish and its accoutrements familiar, but because it was a superbly staged and acted work of theatre art.

The new approach brought great lucidity to the play. *Hamlet*, deprived of all of the fustian of period vestments, stood forth, said *Time*, as "a credible, relatively simple and most amazingly shrewd commentary on human weaknesses." In the present staging, social rank and character type were so clearly delineated by costuming that the play's humor as well as its pathos seemed far more natural than before.

James Light's direction introduced a court at which the King (Charles Waldron) wore a cutaway or flannels as the need arose; Polonius (Ernest Lawford) was a well-groomed gentleman with a monocle; Hamlet appeared at various times in a double-breasted suit, dinner jacket, plus fours, sporting cap, and smoking either a pipe or cigarette (of great use in the soliloquys); Gertrude (Adrienne Morrison) had her hair bobbed and wore the latest Paris fashions and also smoked; the soldiers wore contemporary military garb, Ophelia (Helen Chandler) dressed in the frocks of 1925s flappers; the first gravedigger (Walter Kingsford) had on a bowler, smoked a pipe, and worked in shirtsleeves; and so on. The telephone was much in evidence, and Polonius was killed by a pistol shot, not a sword. The lines were spoken colloquially with little attempt at the rhythms of the verse and thereby made the words carry a freight of meaning often lost to modern audiences. Strangely, as the *Times* pointed out, the dialogue was "purged of the more bawdy licences of Elizabethan speech."

The principals all gave highly respected performances, but the stellar contribution was that of Lawford as Polonius; he made the role "fatuous, supercilious, plausible to the extreme" and not at all the usual "doddering old fool" (*Times*). Sydney's Prince was "as honestly thought out and as rationally projected a Hamlet as" George Jean Nathan ever saw. But to Richard Dana Skinner he was too continually "neurotic and emotional" and should have been more heroic in the Hampden vein.

Frederick Jones's sets were spare and simple and allowed a smooth flow to the staging but may have been too black to allow Hamlet the necessary contrast for his character.

[HAMMERSTEIN'S] NINE O'CLOCK REVUE [Revue/British] B: Harold Simpson and Morris Harvey; M: Uriel Lillie, Max Carewski, M. D. Lyon, Harry Coleman, Jack Strachey, and Kenneth Duffield; LY: Harold Simpson, Arthur Weigall, Dion Titheradge, and Graham John; D: Geoffrey Wilmer; CH: Raymond Midgley; G: Charles Le Maire; P: Arthur Hammerstein; T: Century Roof; 10/4/23 (12)

This series of English sketches and specialties was imported from London's Little Theatre. Among the American critics the favorite was a love-quadrangle sketch done first in an English and then in French style, using not dialogue but only sounds. The *Evening Mail*'s critic found that "Nothing could be more delicious than this contrast between the staid bored English and the lively temperamental French manner of telling the same story." Also praised was designer Charles Le Maire, who "has had a happy inspiration in draping his stage with gray velvet. These neutral curtains, with the aid of the new lighting systems, change their tones constantly, and the simple props that are added make singularly satisfying stage pictures." Although he found the singing and dancing wan, Heywood Broun thought the revue was "among the most ingenious of current musical shows."

H.H.

HAND OF THE POTTER, THE [Drama/Sex/Family/Mental Illness/Crime/ Jews] A: Theodore Dreiser; D: George Cram Cook; P: Provincetown Players; T: Provincetown Playhouse (OB); 12/5/21 (21)

Famed novelist Theodore Dreiser's somber drama, which he had had great difficulty in selling to commercial managements and had to have staged Off Broadway, met with little approbation. Kenneth Macgowan wrote that it was "a study in degeneracy with no more illumination in it than you can find in *Psychopathia Sexualis*," and the *Post* dubbed it "a morbid and unsavory piece."

Dreiser's play is a detailed exploration of the progressive stages of insanity in poor Russian-Jewish immigrant Isadore Berchansky (J. Paul Jones). The twenty-one-year-old Isadore is an "epileptic degenerate" who roams freely and rapes and murders eleven-year-old Kitty Neafy (Millie Bolend); he is captured, is tried, and commits suicide. Dreiser attempts to demonstrate that Isadore is as much to be pitied as a victim of society as condemned as a perpetrator of evil.

Ludwig Lewisohn, loudest of the play's defenders, declared that it was "remarkable" how closely the author "had penetrated by the sheer closeness of his relation to life to the last necessities of a tragic action in such a world as we perceive. He substitutes the concept of tragic guilt for sin," a concept most were not prepared to accept. Various commentators have since come to consider this a work of importance. W. David Sievers, in *Freud on Broadway*, noted that it was "the most trenchant piece of naturalism until *Dead End* some fourteen years later" and that it was an outstanding example of Freud's ideas applied to drama.

HANDY MAN, THE [Comedy-Drama/Crime/Small Town/Romance/Religion] A: Fred Wall and Ralph Murphy; D: Edgar J. MacGregor and Lawrence Grattan; P: Sam Comly, Inc.; T: Thirty-ninth Street Theatre; 3/9/25 (48)

A play of faith, in the vein of *The Servant in the House* and *The Passing of the Third Floor Back*, but with neither the literary significance of those works nor the acting talent that was needed for the Christ-like title role. The *Evening Post*'s critic described the play as "a story which holds the attention and a set of characters who, if they are not entirely free of melodramatic touches, are on the whole a group of very interesting people."

"The handyman" (Tim Murphy) is Chris, a genial small-town carpenter, who, while working on a house, comes in contact with Nellie Nelson (Margaret Cusack), a young female pickpocket, who has become romantically involved with the son (Glenn Burdette) of the family that owns the place. Her aim is to get the youth started on a life of crime, but old Chris applies the balm of his folksy wisdom to the problem and sets matters on their rightful course.

HANGMAN'S HOUSE [Drama/Romance/Rural/Sports] A: Willard Mack; SC: Donn Byrne's novel of the same name; D: William A Brady, Jr.; S: Louis Kennell; P: William A. Brady, Jr., and Dwight Deere Wiman; T: Forrest Theatre; 12/16/26 (4)

Time said that this play, when compared with the author's two other then-current Broadway melodramas, was "a theatrically diseased mess." The action was set in Ireland's countryside and followed the love affair of young gentleman Dermot McDermot (Walter Abel) and Connaught O'Brien (Katherine Alexander), an affair that is impeded by her father (Joseph Kilgour), a judge called "the hangman," who forces her to wed the mean-spirited John D'Arcy (Jack Shannon). This villain even kills her race horse after Dermot rides it to victory. Finally, the villain kills himself, and his wife, who has remained pure despite a year of marriage, is free to return to the hero.

A major fault was the ineptly staged horse race, using treadmills, which allowed a clearly loping horse to beat one with flying feet.

HAPPY [Musical/University/Romance] B: Vincent Lawrence and McElbert Moore; M: Frank Gray; LY: Earle Crocker and McElbert Moore; D: Walter Brooks; P: Murray Phillips; T: Earl Carroll Theatre; 12/5/27 (82)

A frail book, routine but pleasant score, and hardworking cast had enough pep to squeeze this ordinary musical for almost three months of performances. It was the season's second campus musical, but *Good News* had nothing to fear from its divagations.

Its action had to do with Hadley College student Siggy Sigler's (Percy Helton) attempt to earn $100,000 of his own to entitle him to his family's fortune and his involvement in several campus love affairs, especially that in which he helps out Jack Gaynor (Fred Santley), the poet who wants to be a Broadway lyricist, in his romance with Lorelei Lynn (Madeleine Fairbanks).

There were some acceptable performances, and the dance routines were snappy; still, the *Times* predicted that the show would "find it difficult going."

HAPPY HUSBAND, THE [Comedy/Marriage/Sex/British] A: Harrison Owen; D: A. E. Matthews; S: Nicholas Yellenti; P: Gilbert Miller; T: Empire Theatre; 5/7/28 (72)

An insouciant British marital farce about a woman, Dot Rendell (Billie Burke), who, surprised at a sophisticated weekend party by an educated burglar (John Williams) during an interlude with a man (A. E. Matthews) other than her husband (Lawrence Grossmith), admits her guilt only to have the other guests pooh-pooh her confession as a coverup for a more likely suspect (Ilka Chase); piqued by her spouse's inability to conceive her guilty of dereliction, she goes to great lengths to convince him of her scandalous potential, making him somewhat less happy than he was.

"The play," said *Time*, "is full of easy-going wit which requires no pregnant pauses to speed it on its way. The people are lazy and likable." Several critics censured Burke for a mannered performance. "She is the essense of squirm and if her twistings and slinking are her idea of simulated youth someone should whisper in her pretty ear that it is painfully wrong," snapped Perriton Maxwell.

HAPPY-GO-LUCKY [Comedy/Romance/British/Family] A: Ian Hay (John Hay Beith); SC: Ian Hay's novel of the same name; D: W. H. Gilmore; P: A. H. Woods; T: Booth Theatre; 8/4/20 (79)

A Broadway showing of a London hit called there *Tilly of Bloomsbury* and based by the author on his own novel. Tilly Welwyn (Muriel Martin-Harvey) is a dress designer who fears her aristocratic boyfriend's (Barry Baxter) parents will look down on her because of her parents' humble occupations. The boyfriend's parents (George Giddens and Mrs. Edmund Gurney) come to visit, and Tilly makes her folks put on airs, even inducing the bailiff's man (O. P. Heggie) to play the family butler. Comic mishaps bubble up, and Richard's family squirms, but he refuses to take their class snobbishness seriously and remains with Tilly.

A threadbare theme was made delectable through witty speech and charming characters. Several critics likened the characterizations to those of Dickens. Alexander Woollcott, for one, called the tale "stale and silly," but applauded "a stageful of people done with quite Victorian heartiness and imagination."

HAPPY-GO-LUCKY [Musical/Family] B/LY: Helena Phillips Evans; M: Lucien Denni; D: Fred G. Latham; P: A. L. Erlanger; T: Liberty Theatre; 9/30/26 (52)

"The book is stupid, comedy entirely lacking, and there is a marked artificiality in the settings and the acting of the principals," opined Arthur Hornblow; Richard Dana Skinner asserted, "it is cut from the most ordinary of goods, with music that is fair to middling, dancing that . . . is uninspired, and comedy that . . . would never give support to the theory that we are a humorous people."

The leading character was Chester Chapin (Taylor Holmes), a curmudgeon who drives his family batty by his touchy ways until they soften him up by overdoses of flattery; he sheds his beard and brashness and soon is eating out of his children's hands.

HAREM, THE (A hárem) [Comedy/Marriage/Sex/Hungarian] A: Ernest Vajda; AD: Avery Hopwood; D/P: David Belasco; S: Joseph Wickes; T: Belasco Theatre; 12/2/24 (183)

Ferenc Molnar's *Guardsman*, running on Broadway when this play opened, was about a man who disguises himself to see if he can seduce his wife. Vajda's *Harem*, a "fifth-rate paraphrase of Molnar's" play (George Jean Nathan), reversed the situation and had a veiled wife trying to tempt her suspected husband. This was the author's fourth production of the 1924–1925 season.

Vajda's comedy was considered far more racy than *The Guardsman*, and some accused it loudly of being obscene. Meretricious as it was, however, it contained an abundance of laughs, and George Jean Nathan admitted that its bluer jokes had in him an appreciative auditor. Nevertheless, he went on, "Aside from its periodic honkatonk jocosities, *The Harem* is not worth criticism."

Belasco star Lenore Ulric played Carla, who meets the attractive Manon (Virginia Hammond) by chance and is told by her that all husbands are unfaithful. Carla defends her husband, Roland (William Courtleigh), from the charge. To test Roland's fidelity a ruse is carried out in which the wife, in disguise, seduces her spouse; when she confronts him with the truth, he cheerfully replies that he knew it was she all along.

Belasco was once again picked on for peddling rubbishy wares, but the play caught on and had a good run. A large part of its success stemmed from Ulric's sensual and appealingly varied acting.

HARLEM [Drama/Crime/Blacks/Sex/Family/Gambling] A: Wallace Thurman and William Jourdan Rapp; SC: the short story "Cordelia the Crude," by Wallace Thurman; D: Chester Erskin; P: Edward A. Blatt; T: Apollo Theatre; 2/20/29 (94)

There were sixty black actors and one white actor (a detective played by Arthur Hughes) employed for this "Episode of Life in New York's Black Belt," a rambunctious melodrama set among the poor but flashy populace of the title neighborhood. Coauthor Wallace Thurman, who was black, was recognized as an important member of the Negro Renaissance movement of the day; he had written the original version of this play, then called *Black Belt*, and was aided in its revision by white author Rapp. One of only two serious full-length dramas by blacks to reach Broadway in the twenties, *Harlem* was the first black-authored attempt at a realistic picture of life in the black community. A "Glossary of Harlemisms" was distributed to spectators to aid them in following the authentic dialogue.

The drama involved the South Carolina Williams family, which has moved to Harlem where its financial problems are pressing. To meet their rent payments, the family throws paid admission orgiastic Saturday-night rent parties, where the local population behaves in unbridled fashion. Gambling, lust, dancing, drinking, and cussing occupy their time. Daughter Cordelia (Isabell Washington) is a promiscuous creature, whose dalliance brings about the death of one of her boyfriends (Billy Andrews), a racketeer. The killer (Ernest R. Whitman) is himself shot by the white cop. Another lover (Richard Landers) is unjustly accused of the first killing, but he is cleared in Act Three. Cordelia departs alone intending to make "de whole world look up at me."

George Jean Nathan declared of the play that "with all its holes, it gets under the skin of the characters and their lives and it has all the actuality of an untouched up photograph, . . . a dozen and one vivid hints of niggerdom at its realest."

A second engagement of the play was at the Eltinge from 10/21/29 for sixteen performances.

"HARLEQUINADE, THE" and "INNOCENT AND ANNABEL" D: Agnes Morgan; P: Neighborhood Playhouse; T: Neighborhood Playhouse (OB); 5/10/ 21 (25)
"The Harlequinade" [Comedy/Period/Theatre/Fantasy/British] A: Harley Granville-Barker and Dion Calthrop; CH: Albert Carroll; DS: Esther Peck; "Innocent and Annabel" [Comedy/One-Act] A: Harold Chapin

"The Harlequinade" is a brief piece originally written to serve as a curtain raiser for George Bernard Shaw's *Androcles and the Lion*. Its charming premise allows a quartet of gods to descend to earth and journey through history, watching the progress of Harlequin in various theatrical periods. Each episode is commented on by Uncle Edward (Whitford Kane) and his niece Alice (Joanna Roos), seated at the side of the proscenium. Theatre styles seen are the Italian Commedia dell'Arte, eighteenth-century British, and, in a switch from the published script that ends with a satire on Henrik Ibsen, that of the "Bronx Art Theatre" of the future. The last proved the most amusing in its spoof of fashionable modernistic tendencies in lighting and design.

The *Times* enjoyed it, but Ludwig Lewisohn thought it was a waste of the Neighborhood's talented performers.

Sharing the program was the one-acter "Innocent and Annabel," an extremely light but somewhat entertaining episode, given a "shaky and heavy-handed performance" (*Times*).

"The Harlequinade" was transferred to Broadway's small Punch and Judy Theatre with a revival of Lord Dunsany's "Night at the Inn," first done by the Playhouse in 1916; opening on 6/14/21, the program lasted only for fifteen performances and contributed to the decision of the Neighborhood's benefactresses, the Lewisohn sisters, not to move any more plays to Broadway.

HARRY DELMAR'S REVELS [Revue] B: William K. Wells; M: Jimmy Monaco, Jesse Greer, and Lester Lee; LY: Billy Rose and Ballard MacDonald; CH: Harry Delmar, Sam Rose, and Chester Hale; S: Clark Robinson; C: Jeanne Hackett; P: Samuel Baerwitz and Harry Delmar; T: Shubert Theatre; 11/28/27 (114)

A very pleasing revue in the *Follies-Scandals* vein, with a cast headed by names such as Winnie Lightner, Frank Fay, Patsy Kelly, and Bert Lahr in his Broadway debut after a career in burlesque and vaudeville. Milton MacKaye said, "Delmar turned out a glittering and fairly ponderous affair, filled with mirror cloth and rhinestones, girls and ga-ga." There were comedy sketches, including a spoof of foreign-language art theatres; Lahr and his partner-wife, Mercedes, did their old bit, "What's the Idea," about a dopey cop and a sexy Spanish dancer; Lahr performed in a skit called "The Four Horsemen—Don Quixote, Paul Revere, Ben Hur, and Jesse James," playing the latter; and songs that were noticed included "Say It with Solitaire," "My Rainbow," "The Jigaboo Jig," and "Nagasaki Butterfly." John Lahr, in his biography of his father, *Notes on a Cowardly Lion*, pointed out that the show also had an inter-

polation by Jimmy McHugh and Dorothy Fields that was largely ignored but
became a great hit when reintroduced in *Blackbirds of 1928*; its title was "I
Can't Give You Anything but Love, Baby."

The show did poorly at the box office and was sustained by investments in it
made by its stars, including Lahr. Since this made Lahr a part owner of the
show, songwriter Billy Rose sued him for $40 of unpaid salary. Lahr thought
this was so ridiculous that he withdrew the money from the bank in pennies and
lugged it down Broadway to Rose's office. When he dumped it on the desk of
Rose's manager, he was told it wasn't legal tender, and he had to carry the
4,000 pennies all the way back to the bank.

HARVEST [Drama/Rural/Family/Romance/Sex] A: Kate Horton; D: John
Cromwell; P: Messrs. Shubert i/a/w John Cromwell; T: Belmont Theatre; 9/19/
25 (17)

A dreary drama of Michigan farm life in which a half-dozen or so dull characters sat around "boring themselves and all within earshot" (*News*) about what
failures they all were. The imminent failure of the corn crops is also a chief
concern, as is the need for rain. The Swiss farmer (Augustin Duncan) and his
wife (Louise Closser Hale) bemoan the fact that their daughter (Ethel Taylor)
has transgressed with the young man (Frederic March) visiting the neighborhood
for the summer. However, when the clouds open up, their dismay is lifted, and
they make no fuss when the daughter decides not to marry the boy.

This was an "unimpressive" (*Herald Tribune*) work that had commendable
performances of its middle-aged rustics by the reliable Louise Closser Hale and
Augustin Duncan.

HASSAN [Drama/Verse/Adventure/Period/Romance/British] A: James Elroy
Flecker; M: Frederick Delius; D: Basil Dean; CH: Michel Fokine; S: George
W. Harris; P: A. L. Erlanger; T: Knickerbocker Theatre; 9/22/24 (16)

A great hit in London, this spectacular poetical romance by a poet who died
in 1915 was elaborately, but dully, produced. Despite its extensive scenery and
richly decorative costumes, it failed to ignite. George Jean Nathan commented,
"Flecker wrote a play rich in the music of romance and poesy, as beautiful a
thing of its kind as has appeared in recent dramatic literature; [Basil] Dean staged
it with all the imagination and rhythm of a sailor's stoker."

The story dealt with an Arabian nights' adventure set in ancient Baghdad and
focusing on the middle-aged confectioner Hassan (Randal Ayrton), who loves
the courtesan Yasmin (Mary Nash), is rejected by her, falls into the company
of the Caliph (James Dale), saves him from assassination, observes his cruelty,
and deserts him for a journey to Samarkand with Ishak the poet (Murray Kinnell).

HASSARD SHORT'S RITZ REVUE [Revue] CN/D: Hassard Short; T: Ritz
Theatre; 9/17/24 (109)

Hassard Short, who had created some of Broadway's most successfully lavish productions in the *Music Box Revues*, rose to the top of the heap with this highly acclaimed show that Arthur Hornblow called "the liveliest, snappiest, most pulchritudinous spectacle" he had seen in years. Packed to the gills with gorgeous tableaux, scantily clad beauties, button-bursting comics, and matchless sets and costumes, the revue was, apart from some off-color material purveyed by the team of Jay Brennan and Stanley Rogers (Rogers was the look-alike replacement for female impersonator Bert Savoy, who had died recently when struck by lightning), a masterpiece of good taste.

The audience was enthralled by an exquisite drop curtain of gold and black silk and gauzy silken semitransparent draperies that allowed for fabulous lighting effects; the hilarities of comedienne Charlotte Greenwood in a sketch called "Her Morning Bath"; the blue humor of Brennan and Rogers; the drolleries of m.c. Raymond Hitchcock; the singing of Tom Burke; the terpsichorean accomplishments of Alberta Vitak; and the allure of barely draped female forms, especially in a number that displayed the famed courtesans of history.

HAUNTED HOUSE, THE [Comedy/Mystery/Crime/Literature] A: Owen Davis; D: Howard Lindsay; P: Albert Lewis and Max Gordon; T: George M. Cohan Theatre; 9/2/24 (103)

All of the characters in this burlesque of mystery plays had names like "The Tramp," "The Bride," "The Wife," and so on. Called "a farce crook mystery play" by Stark Young, it took place in a haunted country house and brought together a large and varied assortment of eccentric characters such as The Novelist (Wallace Eddinger), striving to write a thriller, who attempts to solve a murder by using Freudian techniques to analyze the suspects' minds; he is searching for the complex that will explain the killing. The Novelist soon discovers that the methods he is using could as easily prove himself as guilty as anyone else.

The show was somewhat vague and uneven in comedy and quality, but enough laughs were involved to keep it on the boards for a respectable run. It began strongly but could not sustain its momentum. "The stride of the playwright grows choppy, and the whole affair ends with a tame and inane solution," nagged Heywood Broun.

HAVOC [Drama/Romance/War/British] A: Harry Wall; D: Leo G. Carroll; P: Messrs. Shubert; T: Maxine Elliott's Theatre; 9/1/24 (48)

One of three war plays that opened in the same week early in the 1924–1925 season. Following a half year's run in London, it could draw in New York for only a month and a half, even with its original English cast.

Reviews were generally favorable. Arthur Hornblow termed it "A frankly theatrical though none the less gripping melodrama [with] a cluster of gripping performances that rank with the very best." The play revealed how a woman could wreak more havoc on the men who loved her than the enemy they were battling at the front. Its two officer heroes, Dick Chappell (Ralph Forbes) and Roddy Dunton (Leo G. Carroll), both love Violet Derring (Joyce Barbour); she leads Dunton to believe she loves him but becomes engaged to his friend and comrade while Dunton is at the front. Dunton's jealousy causes him to put Chappell's life in danger during battle, but the officer, blinded, escapes with his life. The guilt-racked Dunton kills himself, Chappell returns to find that Violet has forgotten him, and he discovers his love for Dunton's sister (Molly Johnson).

HAWK ISLAND [Drama/Crime] A/D: Howard Irving Young; S: Willy Pogany; P: Thomas Kilpatrick; T: Longacre Theatre; 9/16/29 (24)

Clark Gable's second Broadway appearance came in this three-week flop described by Euphemia Van Rensselaer Wyatt as "a very badly constructed piece of work which seemed only to give a set of extremely uninteresting people the chance to be rude to each other, and to theorize about a murder in which neither players nor audience seemed to have the slightest real interest." However, Perriton Maxwell described it as a gripping and clever melodrama, which he allowed the grade of C+.

Hawk Island, the locale, is a lonely place off the New England coast, where bachelor host Gregory Sloane (Gable) is giving a weekend party for several young couples. Sloane and a murder writer (Charles Halton) decide to enliven things by faking the latter's murder and making Sloane seem guilty. The hoax goes over well until Halton really is killed by a jealous husband and the evidence points to Sloane. An ingenious plot solution gets him off the hook, however, before it is too late.

HAY FEVER [Comedy/Family/Romance/Theatre/Literature/British] A: Noël Coward; D: Noël Coward and Laura Hope Crews; P: Messrs. Shubert; T: Maxine Elliott's Theatre; 10/5/25 (49)

Noël Coward's comedy (written in three days) has become a perennial of the modern stage, appearing in numerous revivals, including two in New York, but its first Broadway production ran for only a month and a half. In London it had been a hit. It arrived during Coward's first big Broadway season, when his succession of new plays made him the theatre's fair-haired boy.

The general opinion was that *Hay Fever* was a clever piece of machinery, made palatable largely because of the excellence of its actors, especially Laura Hope Crews. Richard Dana Skinner described it as "a meticulous little comedy of English character written, one might imagine, as an amusing stunt and dependent upon rapid dialogue and the invincible humor of human nature laid bare."

The slender plot depicts an eccentric English family in their suburban home. There is the retired actress-mother Judith Bliss (Laura Hope Crews), forever dramatizing her life by slipping into snatches of dialogue from her old plays and being abetted by her children and spouse; her absent-minded novelist husband, David (Harry Davenport), who likes to keep his spectacles dangling from his right ear; and her contentious son Simon (Gavin Muir) and daughter Sorel (Frieda Inescourt). Each has invited a private guest to the house for the weekend but has not told the others; the guests arrive and are made the victims of the rude, bizarre, and risible behavior of their hosts, until they can bear it no longer and take their leave, unheeded by the querulous household members.

In his autobiography, *Present Indicative*, Coward claims he wrote the play "in about three days." The eccentric actress upon whom he based the character of Judith Bliss was the American star, Laurette Taylor. Coward laid the blame for the work's New York failure on a very poorly acted opening night performance, which Laura Hope Crews made seem even more hopeless by a valiant attempt to make the most of her opportunities.

HE LOVED THE LADIES [Comedy/Romance/Legacy/Small Town] A: Herbert Hall Winslow; D: Jack Roseleigh; P: Lepane Amusement Company; T: Frolic Theatre; 5/10/27 (7)

A flop comedy produced in the intimate rooftop playhouse above the New Amsterdam Theatre, from whence the musical sounds of *Lucky* came crashing through reminding auditors of the more fortunate spectators below.

The late Hamilton Wayne had loved many ladies in his day, but when he died, his estate was willed to a hitherto unknown illegitimate daughter, Audrey Le Salle (Lillian Ross). The matrons of Waynesburg raise hell about the upstart, until she reveals the contents of a box of letters to Wayne now belonging to her in which all of their reputations are besmirched. The housekeeper (Louise Carter) is revealed as her mother, Wayne's nephew (Lyons Wickland) becomes her fiancé, and she burns the missives in a gesture of goodwill.

"It is a badly written, poorly acted play," ran Arthur Hornblow's assessment. This show was such a box-office fiasco that at one performance the curtain rose to a completely empty house.

HE UNDERSTOOD WOMEN [Comedy/Sex/France/Marriage] A: Frances Lynch and Michael Kalleser; D: Frank G. Bond; P: Michael Kalleser; T: Belmont Theatre; 8/15/28 (37)

Ernest Boyd thought that this "continental comedy" was an "incredible" attempt to emulate French sex comedy; *Time* reported that "Nothing in the play, its characters, its situations or its continental idiom is fresh or interesting."

The hero was Julien Roman (Joseph Granby), a rakish *boulevardier* with a long string of feminine conquests, who is trapped by the Baron Le Long (William Augustin) in the arms of the Baroness (Hilda Spong); he shoots the husband in a duel and marries the Baroness's maid Aline (Peggy Allenby) in order to produce a son to whom he can hand on his masterly ways with women; when he learns that all of his amours were shallow victories and that his own wife has deceived him, he turns her out, and undergoes various tribulations before being reunited with her.

HE WALKED IN HER SLEEP [Comedy/Marriage/Sex] A: Norman Cannon; P: Superb Plays Corporation; T: Princess Theatre; 4/4/29 (20)

A six-character "amateurish" (*Times*) farce about a husband (Ralph Roberts) who believes his wife (Beatrice Nichols) is cheating on him, sneaks out of bed one night hoping to make his wife jealous, does so, and then discovers that she has been faithful all along. Brooks Atkinson reported, "a farce with less true farcical substance I have seldom seen."

HE WHO GETS SLAPPED (Tot, kto poluchaet poshchochiny) [Drama/ Romance/Circus/Russian] A: Leonid Andreyev; TR: Gregory Zilboorg; D: Robert Milton; DS: Lee Simonson; P: Theatre Guild; T: Garrick Theatre; 1/9/22 (308)

Leonid Andreyev's cynical, philosophical, and symbolical drama set in the world of a French circus was welcomed as one of the most unusual and worthwhile seen in years. Given a lauded, but much debated, interpretation by the Theatre Guild, the play had a long run, even though most audiences were baffled by its elusive ideas.

The play takes place in the circus green room, outside of a city like Lyon or Marseille, and tells the story of a mysterious stranger, an intellectual of repute who has become disillusioned with his inability to make real contact with the world through his ideas—another man has popularized them and also run off with his wife—and who decides to become a clown named He (Richard Bennett); his ultimately successful act involves his being slapped consistently to which he responds as if the slaps were signs of acclamation rather than of ridicule. In the circus he becomes enmeshed in the unhappy love affair of the circus owner's (Ernest Cossart) lion-tamer wife, Zinida (Helen Westley), with Bezano (John Rutherford), the equestrian, and is himself drawn into a heart-breaking passion for the naive, artless, young bareback rider Consuelo (Margalo Gillmore). The girl's alleged father, Mancini (Frank Reicher), arranges for Consuelo to marry a wealthy baron (Louis Calvert), and when the clown cannot prevent the union, he poisons her and himself, after which the Baron ends his own life with a pistol.

Andreyev's play was a fascinating intellectual enigma for contemporary Broadwayites. Eschewing the central role's bitterness for its qualities of Christ-like sacrifice, Richard Bennett scored strongly with audiences but found little favor with reviewers like Stark Young, who believed the play to be "a tragic fantasy around the ironical career that truth and distinction meet at the hands of the common mass of men." Guild producer Lawrence Langner, in his autobiography, *The Magic Curtain*, recalled that Bennett "gave a brilliantly romantic performance but seemingly hadn't the least idea of the character he was playing." On another critical front, many believed the production stressed the play's picturesque aspects at the expense of its profundity.

Ludwig Lewisohn was representative of those who thought the play and production were masterful. "The Theatre Guild production is sensitive to an almost morbid point, consummate in its emphasis, modulation, rhythm of tone, color, movement."

During its successful run, *He Who Gets Slapped* was moved from the Garrick (on 2/13/22) to the Fulton; on 5/20/22 it returned to the Garrick.

HEAD FIRST [Comedy-Drama/Business/Marriage] A: Willis Maxwell Good-hue; P: Oliver Morosco; T: Greenwich Village Theatre (OB); 1/6/26 (5)

Broadway producer Oliver Morosco produced this Off-Broadway fiasco as a vehicle for his wife, Selma Paley, whose talents met with scarce approbation.

The play was about a filing clerk (Louis Kimball) whose lack of ingenuity gets him fired, only for his dutiful wife (Paley), upon inquiring of the boss (Byron Beasley) the reason for the dismissal, to land his job instead. Her success is terrific, and she is soon earning enough to put her husband on a $2,000 a month allowance while she goes to Paris to run the firm's branch there. Her spouse goes into the garbage-hauling business and makes out well, but when his wife returns, their essential incompatibility leads to a separation.

Percy Hammond trashed the play as "an inept, disjointed and overblown muddle."

HEAD OR TAIL (Fej vagy irás) [Comedy/Marriage/Hungarian/Fantasy/Prostitution] A: Laszlo Lakatos; AD: Garrick Truman; D: Clarke Silvernail; P: Henry Baron; T: Waldorf Theatre; 11/9/26 (7)

An unconvincing, strangely constructed Hungarian triangle comedy about a husband's (Philip Merivale) attempts to determine the fidelity of his wife (Estelle Winwood). The play shifted gears without warning from a conventional first act to a second act set in a brothel, with the same actors now playing different characters. It was meant to suggest the husband's imagined conception of how his own life was reflected by the behavior of those who frequent such a place. Arthur Hornblow suggested "the author's vagaries are a novel way of saying that 'we' are only 'we' but also a good many other people." In Act Three, the play returned to its original personages to satisfactorily resolve the man's dilemma.

Crudely staged, the piece led *Time* to exclaim, "it is doubtful whether the play . . . can ever succeed in expressing with even moderate success, the cleverly conceived theme."

HEADQUARTERS [Drama/Family/Drugs/Crime] A: Hugh Stanislaus Stange; D: Joseph Graham; S: P. Dodd Ackerman; P: Sidney Wilmer, Walter Vincent, and Alfred E. Aarons; T: Forrest Theatre; 12/4/29 (13)

Onetime ladies' idol William Farnum, heavier than in his salad days, but still heroic looking, played police detective Bill Regan whose job is to investigate the double slaying of his film-star wife, Mimi Sharon (Lea Penman), and her lover, actor Richard Condon (George Baxter). A daughter (Mildred Mitchell) by his previous marriage is the most likely suspect, but her innocence eventually is established and the actor's dope addict wife (Florence Johns) arrested.

The piece seemed to the *Times* derivative, predictable, and unlife-like.

HEADS UP! [Musical/Prohibition/Romance/Crime/Sea] B: John McGowan and Paul Gerard Smith; M: Richard Rodgers; LY: Lorenz Hart; CH: George Hale;

S: Donald Oenslager; C: Kiviette; P: Alex A. Aarons and Vinton Freedley; T: Alvin Theatre; 11/11/29 (144)

This Rodgers and Hart musical began life as a show called *Me For You*, with an Owen Davis book, which flopped in Detroit after two weeks. The original stars were retained, many of the sets and costumes salvaged, the score (except for two excised songs) kept intact, and a whole new book added to produce what became a modest hit. The show managed to open in New York despite the Wall Street crash. Victor Moore was its established star, and relative newcomer Ray Bolger was the player whose career was greatly boosted by it.

The mildly beguiling show had a good deal of its action set aboard a yacht, the Silver Lady, and provided a book about how a lowly cook with a three-times prison record (Moore) is working on the yacht, which is being used, without its owner's knowledge, for rum smuggling by a Captain Denny (Robert Gleckler). Coast Guard officer Mason (Jack Whiting) pursues the smugglers and wins the heart of its owner's daughter (Barbara Newberry).

The show was judged routine; only "A Ship without a Sail" and "Why Do You Suppose" gained many bravos. The *Times* labeled it "a fairly lively diversion." An example of its tired humor was Moore's definition of a *mutiny* as an afternoon performance.

HEARTBREAK HOUSE [Comedy-Drama/Family/War/British] A: George Bernard Shaw; D: Dudley Digges; S: Lee Simonson; P: Theatre Guild; T: Garrick Theatre; 11/10/20 (128)

Heartbreak House, Shaw's "Chekhovian" tragi-comedy, published in 1919, premiered in New York before reaching London. This first new Shaw play to be done locally since 1914 was very respectably greeted, even by those who found it variously flawed. Kenneth Macgowan, for example, argued that it played far better than it read: "It is still a largely incohesive mass of interesting speeches coming from interesting character studies. But instead of proving somewhat dull and rather nauseous in places, *Heartbreak House* becomes in actual performance a lively, highly amusing and finely thoughtful play." Alexander Woollcott added that "*Heartbreak House*, despite the doldrums of tedium into which its second act flounders toward the end, is quite the larkiest and most amusing one that Shaw has written in many a year."

As Macgowan noted, "The total effect of the play is a disillusioned and bitter picture of the moral slackness of liberal England in the face of the war's challenge." Some saw not merely England, but Europe itself, as the target of the attack. Shaw's "Fantasia in the Russian Manner on English Themes" was set in 1914 Sussex in a shiplike mansion, "Heartbreak House," owned by Captain Shotover (Albert Perry), an octogenarian creator of destructive inventions, in which he lives with his daughter Hesione Hushabye (Effie Shannon) and her husband, Hector (Fred Eric). A weekend house party draws there a representative cross-section of English society; not much action occurs as the discursive and provocative play moves along: young Ellie Dunne (Elizabeth Risdon) is dismayed to learn that the man she is really in love with is Hesione's philandering husband, who presently flirts with Shotover's daughter Lady Ariadne (Lucile Watson); Ellie proclaims that she wants to wed the Captain; capitalism—represented by tycoon "Boss" Mangan (Dudley Digges)—is seen as of little avail in saving Europe; Shotover foresees shipwreck for Britain; a burglar (Henry Travers) is caught; and an air raid (sounding like a Beethoven symphony) is launched, killing Mangan and the burglar, but thrilling all of the rest.

The work has many themes and was considered slippery, although a brilliantly stimulating evocation of Shaw's despair in the face of war's effect on the world and the need for an answer to the challenge facing humankind: "Either out of that darkness some new creation will come to supplant us, as we have supplanted the animals, or the heavens will fall in thunder and destroy us."

Heartbreak House was the first Shaw play to be done by the Guild, which became the chief sponsor of his work on the American stage. Lawrence Langner has told the story of how the Guild dealt with an apparent difficulty encountered after they realized that their Hesione Hushabye, Effie Shannon, was blonde while Shaw calls for someone with "magnificent black hair." Shannon refused to wear a wig or dye her hair. To cover a reference to her hair in the dialogue by Ellie, the Guild decided to have the line slurred. When Shaw saw photos of the show he noticed that Shannon was fair haired and wanted to know if any lines had been cut without his permission. Langner, fearful of upsetting the Irish author, told him the truth and asked what he would have done. Shaw gave him a smile, said "That's all right," and Langner relaxed. The story of the Theatre Guild's experiences with Shaw in their production of this play can be found in Langner's *The Magic Curtain* and *G.B.S. and the Lunatic*.

HEARTS ARE TRUMPS (Atout . . . coeur) [Comedy/Marriage/Romance/French] A: Felix Gandera; D: Clifford Brooke; S: August Vimnera; P: Henry Baron; T: Morosco Theatre; 4/7/27 (20)

A saucy French comedy whose sauce was excessively watered. The implausible story was about a young woman (Vivian Martin) who marries a man claiming to be a certain count and discovers that he is not whom he claims to be but that she is legally wed to the nobleman whose name she now bears; she seeks a divorce so that she may marry her cousin, meets the real Count (Frank Morgan)—her legal spouse—and falls in love with him (and he with her).

The critics passed on this old-fashioned and mostly uninteresting attempt. Brooks Atkinson said it "degenerates into pointless persiflage and general unrest among the characters," and Katharine Zimmermann referred to its "Neolithic jokes."

HEAVEN-TAPPERS, THE [Drama/Prison/Religion/Prohibition/Southern/Rural/Romance] A: George Scarborough and Annette Westbay; D: Edwin Carewe; P: Lee Shubert i/a/w Edwin Carewe; T: Forrest Theatre; 3/8/27 (9)

An "incredible" (Brooks Atkinson) melodrama about phony religionists, Kentucky moonshiners, mountaineer love, poisoned hooch, and repentent sinners. Its action is set in a federal prison cell, a Blue Ridge mountain camp, and a moonshiner's hut. A trio of crooks, one female and two male, masquerade as religious prophets in a scam designed to cheat the moonshiners of their money. They outfox the cunning Kentuckians with their assumed devotional fervor, but when the chief moonshiner (Louis Bennison) gets religion, so does the girl-crook (Margaret Lawrence) who has been preying on him.

"*The Heaven-Tappers* had neither the force of a big idea, the grip of an interesting plot nor the delineation of a single human character. It was a blatant demonstration of bad taste and offensive dialogue," declared Arthur Hornblow.

HEAVY TRAFFIC [Comedy/Marriage/Sex] A: Arthur Richman; D: Bertram Harrison; P: Charles Frohman, Inc.; T: Empire Theatre; 9/5/28 (61)

The "heavy traffic" of the title was the stream of men who moved relentlessly through the love life of the flirtatious middle-aged wife, Rosalie West (Mary Boland). Her complacent spouse (Reginald Mason) changes his tune and offers her a handsome divorce settlement when he falls for Isabel Mancini (Kay Strozzi), sister of his wife's present lover (Edward Crandall). But Rosalie refuses the divorce and Isabel refuses to have her brother named as corespondent. All is saved when an English private eye (A. E. Matthews), hired to follow Mrs. West's peccadiloes, promises further evidence forthwith.

The *Times* said that the author, using an epigrammatic comedy of manners style, "assumes a cleverness of wit and situation that is not always borne out by his play." Richard Dana Skinner turned his back on it as "unspeakably boring as well as deliberately perverse."

(1) HEDDA GABLER [Dramatic Revival] A: Henrik Ibsen; T: Little Theatre; 10/4/20 (4)

The first of several twenties revivals of Ibsen's classic study of feminine psychology came in this shoddy mounting at the Little Theatre where it expired after a brief series of matinees. The star of the occasion was one Borgny Hammer, reputedly a Norwegian actress who had played at the National Theatre of Christiana. "Mme. Hammer plays Hedda in a majestic and formidable manner," reported the *Times*: "Even the catlike darts and thrusts of the restless lady she must needs render with a kind of operatic dignity and deliberation, so imperfect is her present mastery of our alien tongue."

(2) TR: William Archer; D: Robert Edmond Jones; S: Woodman Thompson; P: Equity Players; T: Forty-eighth Street Theatre; 5/16/24 (6)

Praising with a faint damn, John Corbin found that in this revival of *Hedda Gabler* "The cast throughout, in fact, is quite perfect—except in those qualities of imaginative intensity which are needed to make the play viable." As Hedda, Clare Eames's problem was "a certain self-consciousness. Doubtless she never really listens to her own voice or inwardly admires her archaic and angular attitudes; but there are times when she gives one the impression of so doing." This was a pity, Corbin thought, because at times Eames's performance was the best since Mrs. Fiske's, but it missed "Hedda's underlying white heat of rage."

Corbin found Dudley Digges's Tesman perfect and Margalo Gillmore's Thea admirable. Roland Young played Judge Brack "honestly, loyally, skillfully," but the audience—used to him as a comedian—laughed at almost everything he said and did. Corbin sympathized: "Seldom has so well poised and forthright a performance miscarried so jovially." Fritz Leiber was the competent Eilert Lovborg.

H.H.

(3) D: Dudley Digges; P: Actors' Theatre; T: Comedy Theatre; 1/26/26 (59)

The production seen briefly in May 1924 was restaged by Dudley Digges with several cast changes, notably Emily Stevens in the role of Hedda. This revival brought to four the number of Ibsen plays running on Broadway during the 1925–1926 season. Joseph Wood Krutch said that of them all it was "both the finest play and the finest performance."

The production was not up to the Actors' Theatre's even more commendable recent revival of *The Wild Duck*, but it had various excellencies of which to boast. Chief among them was the Tesman of Dudley Digges. Digges's performance so perfectly suited his actions to his dialogue that Brooks Atkinson had to return to the text to determine if the actor was not adding gags of his own. Emily Stevens also gave a rich portrayal, but it was not consistent. "Emily Stevens," said John Mason Brown, "is mannered and occasionally over-emphatic, . . . but her Hedda is continuously arresting and often brilliant in its quick shifts of mood." Louis Calhern was her lover Eilert.

(4) TR: Julie Le Gallienne and Paul Leyssac; D: Eva Le Gallienne; DS: Aline Bernstein; P: Civic Repertory Company; T: Civic Repertory Theatre (OB); 3/26/28 (15)

Eva Le Gallienne's production of *Hedda Gabler* starred the director-producer in the title role; Paul Leysacc's acting as Tesman was "amazingly perfect," said Brooks Atkinson, but Le Gallienne was a disappointing Hedda. Playing against a simple setting of artfully arranged gray draperies, wearing modern dress clothing (short skirts and bobbed hair), and smoking numerous cigarettes, she was the most obvious culprit in what John Mason Brown called "a badly paced and tepidly acted" revival: "Miss Le Gallienne's Hedda is curiously literal and immature. She plays her almost entirely for what the lines say rather than for what they do not say, which is only a fairly definite way of implying that she does not play Hedda at all." In Richard Dana Skinner's minority view, this was a superior production to that of Emily Stevens in 1926: "It is less spectacular, less tortured, yet not a whit less dramatic." Le Gallienne's portrayal he deemed to be "a masterpiece" of realism.

The Civic Repertory revived the piece on 10/3/28 for eleven performances, on 2/6/30 for three performances, and on 12/6/30 for six performances. Le Gallienne played it in later Broadway revivals as late as 1948.

(5) D: Blanche Yurka; P: Actors' Theatre; T: Forty-ninth Street Theatre; 2/2/29 (25)

Blanche Yurka was the Hedda in this version, which allowed audiences to compare her with Le Gallienne, who was then reviving the work with her company. Yurka's reviews were mixed. Robert Littell described her: "Miss Yurka's Hedda was a thoroughly good job—a little too bored at times, at others not quite biting or terrifying enough—and Miss Yurka has a rich and well modulated voice." *Time* printed a split-column comparison of the two Heddas. Le Gallienne was found to have the lissomness of figure, the angularity of form to create the image of a cruel woman. Her crisp speech was thought appropriate to the hypertense character. Yurka's height and burliness were noted as too ample for the role, and her languorous effects were "not of a bitter neurotic, but of a temporarily awkward marble slowly reverting to stone." "Her voice," said *Time*, was of "a drifting sadness" that was not Hedda-like. Yet Richard Dana Skinner thought she was as true to the character's satanic motives as possible. "Miss Yurka's Hedda is not static. She grows in evil before your eyes, so that the play achieves a definite sense of moment." Brooks Atkinson thought that she overcame her native drawbacks by sheer skill, and that her manuscript burning scene was "more cruel and cataclysmic" than he had ever seen it. Of the supporting cast, only Ralph Roeder's Eilert gained approval.

HELEN OF TROY, NEW YORK [Musical/Business/Romance] B: George S. Kaufman and Marc Connelly; M/LY: Bert Kalmar and Harry Ruby; D: Bertram Harrison and Bert French; S: Sheldon K. Viele and Jimnolds; C: Kiviette, Gilbert Clark, Inc., and Millia Davenport; P: Rufus Le Maire and George Jessel i/a/w/ Sidney Wilmer and Walter Vincent; T: Selwyn Theatre; 6/19/23 (193)

This modestly successful musical boasted two "firsts." Although the *Tribune*'s critic found their music "only so-so, if it is that," the score was the first by the team of Kalmar and Ruby. The book was Kaufman and Connelly's first produced collaboration on a book musical. In their tale of a stenographer (Helen Ford) who loses her job because her boss objects to his son's romantic interest in her, and who then invents a product for a rival company that leads to both a business and a marital merger, Kaufman and Connelly introduced to musical comedy the business satire of their *To the Ladies*.

The *Tribune*'s man thought the result was above the intelligence of the average musical comedy audience but that it was "a bright travesty, poulticed a little with ballads and a love story." The *Herald* commended "the perfect musical comedy . . . [and] unceasingly delightful book."

The whole cast was admired, but superlatives belonged to dancer-comedienne Queenie Smith, who played the stenographer's little sister.

The story of the devious methods used by producer Rufus Le Maire to finagle backing from bootleggers and Nick the Greek, a notorious gambler, is detailed in Scott Meredith's *George Ŝ. Kaufman and His Friends*. He practically tricked song-and-dance man George Jessel into investing $10,000, his life's savings, in the show, and Jessel in turn fast-talked producers Wilmer and Vincent into putting up $100,000. None of the producers earned a penny from the show's run, however, as its expenses ate up all the profits.

H.H.

HELENA'S BOYS [Comedy/Family] A: Ida Lublenski Erlich; SC: a story by Mary Brecht Pulver; D: Harrison Grey Fiske; P: Charles L. Wagner; T: Henry Miller Theatre; 4/7/24 (40)

Most critics agreed that *Helena's Boys*, a vehicle for Mrs. Fiske, was twaddle, although Percy Hammond found it to be "an intelligent satire, acted and directed well and much better than a 'good show.' "

Mrs. Fiske played Helena, the mother of two young sons (Guy Pendleton and Reggie Sheffield) newly converted to radical ideas. She tames their radicalism by pretending conversion to extreme views, feigning drunkenness, and threatening to live with her suitor.

Several critics saw this comedy of generational conflict in which the older character wins as a poor relation to *The Goose Hangs High* and *We Moderns*.

H.H.

HELL-BENT FER HEAVEN [Drama/Rural/Religion/Family/Romance] A: Hatcher Hughes; D: Augustin Duncan; S: Alonzo Klaw; P: Marc Klaw, Inc.; T: Klaw Theatre; 1/4/24 (matinees, 16); 2/5/24 (112)

Beating George Kelly's *Show-Off* in a bitter contest that resulted in two jurors publicly denouncing the verdict and one resigning from the jury, *Hell-Bent fer Heaven* won the Pulitzer Prize for Drama in 1923. The award appears to have been granted because Columbia University professor Brander Matthews intervened on behalf of his colleague, Hughes, with the president of Columbia, which handled the award. The play was also chosen as the Best Play of the Year.

Hughes's play is set in Kentucky's Blue Ridge Mountains, where the religious fanatic Rufe Pryor (John F. Hamilton) aims to eradicate Sid Hunt (George Abbott) from the picture, because Sid's presence means not only that Rufe will no longer be needed around the Hunt household but that Rufe will have to cease his pursuit of Sid's girlfriend Jude Lowry (Margaret Borough). Rufe incites old clan hatreds between the Hunts and Lowrys, nearly causes Sid to be shot, and blows up a dam before he is found out and the two families are reconciled. The play's ending underwent a revision from having Rufe trapped and about to die in his self-created flood to allowing his escape, despite the other characters' desire for vengeance.

The story is "trivial, unimportant," wrote L.W., but "the humanity of these primitive Americans, their religiosity, their long and irritable memories, the tang of their speech . . . grow together. . . . It is the most moving American drama we have seen on Broadway since...*Beyond the Horizon*." On the other hand, there were a few opinions like Alan Dale's: "This melodrama...has some strength, all of which does not materialize, owing to faulty construction."

The show was first seen at a series of matinees as the theatre for which it was intended was occupied with a new hit. It met with such approval from the public that the special matinees went on for a month before it was transferred to a regular run, where it added another 112 performances.

H.H.

HELLO, DADDY! [Musical/Sex/Romance] B: Herbert Fields; M: Jimmy McHugh; LY: Dorothy Fields; D: Alexander Leftwich and John Murray Anderson; SC: a German farce, *The High Cost of Loving*; CH: Busby Berkeley; S: Herman Rosse; C: Charles Le Maire; P: Lew Fields: T: Mansfield Theatre; 12/26/28 (196)

The Fields family, father Lew and children Dorothy and Herbert, were the brains behind this hit based on a German farce in which Lew Fields had starred in 1914. Fields once again was the respectable Henry Block, a gentleman who, with friends Anthony Bennett (Wilfred Clark) and Edward Hauser (George Hassell), is active in the Purity League but who for years has been supporting the child of a dancer he knew in his youth, believing it to be his. Ditto his friends. When the silly, pimple-faced, alleged son (Billy Taylor) turns up with "Hello, Daddy" forever spouting from his lips, embarrassment ensues until it is discovered that he is not the child of any of those who have been paying for his upbringing. A romantic subplot between two others offered a touch of sentiment.

The plot was patently "preposterous," grumbled *Time*, but the show was very well done, with comedienne Betty Starbuck gaining accolades, especially in a show-stopping comic number with Billy Taylor when they sang "In a Big Way."

HELLO, LOLA! [Musical/Small Town/Romance/Youth] B/LY: Dorothy Donnelly; M: William B. Kernell; SC: Booth Tarkington's novel and play *Seventeen*; D: Seymour Felix; T: Eltinge Theatre; 1/12/26 (47)

Tarkington's novel *Seventeen*, successfully dramatized in 1918 with a cast led by Ruth Gordon and Gregory Kelly, did not come to life again in this unhappy musicalization that "made rather a hash of it," as Percy Hammond observed. It offered "little more than a noisy jumble of song and dance, with none of the delightful quality that made the original so winning an entertainment." Richard Dana Skinner thought the material was inappropriate for musical comedy, others thought it was a vulgarization of the original and one with not a touch of true laughter. The casting of adult actors as adolescents also rankled the critics.

The plot line was retained. It told of the boyish affection of young Willie Baxter (Richard Keene) for the affected, "baby-talking" Lola Pratt (Edythe Baker) visiting the Parcher family and of the comic lengths he goes to, including the theft of his father's (Ben Hendricks) best suit, to impress her.

HELLO YOURSELF [Musical/University/Theatre/Gambling] B: Walter De Leon; M: Richard Myers; LY: Leo Robin; D: Clarke Silvernail; CH: Dave Gould; S: P. Dodd Ackerman; C: Charles Le Maire; P: George Choos; T: Casino Theatre; 10/30/28 (87)

A sophomoric "Rah! Rah!" musical comedy set on a college campus and featuring Fred Waring and his Pennsylvanians, the choral singing group. "Say That You Love Me" and "He-Man" were two of the show's better melodies. All in all, the piece was "not half bad," in Perriton Maxwell's opinion.

The silly book dealt with a student (Al Sexton) who is about to be expelled from Westley University on suspicion of gambling but whose girlfriend, niece of the school president and daughter of a Broadway producer, gets her dad to finance a play the youth has written and thereby saves the day. The *Times* suggested that the show had hit potential if its humor could be improved.

HELL'S BELLS [Comedy/Small Town/Romance] A: Barry Conners; D: John Hayden; P: Herman Gantvoort; T: Wallack's Theatre; 1/26/25 (139)

A complexly plotted farce that met with both stinging rebukes and gladsome laughter. Its central characters were two Arizona prospectors, "Jap" Stilson (Tom H. Walsh) and D. O. O'Donnell (Eddie Garvie), who come back to the former's Connecticut home town, where rumor has it that they are millionaires. A conspiracy evolves among Stilson's relatives to get him declared insane so that they can get their hands on his money, leading him to reveal that he is actually flat broke. Romantic subplots were included for each partner. The play's title derived from Stilson's frequent use of it as an expletive.

Alan Dale claimed "[I]t handed me some of the fattest laughs I have had lately.... [I]t has two characters that are tremendously droll." To Q.M. it was "a hard working and artless concoction, farce and comedy and burlesque in turns."

In small roles Humphrey Bogart and Shirley Booth carried themselves with relative distinction.

HENRY—BEHAVE! [Comedy/Mental Illness/Family/Business] A: Lawrence Langner; D/P: Gustav Blum; S: Nicholas Yellenti; T: Nora Bayes Theatre; 8/23/26 (96)

Theatre Guild bigwig Lawrence Langner was the author of this flimsy third-rater of which Arthur Hornblow declared, "A more callow and vapid attempt at playmaking rarely has been foisted on a sorely tried public." It concerned an excessively strict Long Island community pillar, Henry Wilton (John Cumberland), whose rigid puritanical ideas are tossed away when he loses his memory in an accident and proceeds to behave in precisely the drink-guzzling, girl-chasing, rug-cutting ways he has condemned. He loses a major business opportunity, but his new personality leads him to be made a candidate for Congress;

when he gets back his wits later that same night he decides to continue acting the part of the good-timer.

Elisha Cook, Jr., and Edward G. Robinson were among the supporting players trapped in this lead balloon. Pat O'Brien made his Broadway debut in the play.

HENRY'S HAREM [Comedy/Family/Romance] A: Fred Ballard and Arthur Stern; P: The Playshop; T: Greenwich Village Theatre (OB); 9/13/26 (8)

A "slim, faltering, obvious, but always raucous affair" (*Times*) about a young bachelor, Henry (Al Roberts), whose vow not to marry until his three sisters are first provided with mates leads to complications when he falls in love. The plot concerns his clever and successful maneuvers at finding husbands for the sisters.

Loudly acted, it sounded to the *Times* reviewer as if the cast had rehearsed in Yankee Stadium.

HER CARDBOARD LOVER (Dans sa candour naïve) [Comedy/Romance/ French] A: Jacques Deval; AD: Valerie Wyngate and P. G. Wodehouse; P: Gilbert Miller and A. H. Woods; T: Empire Theatre; 3/21/27 (152)

Jeanne Eagels, busy for four years in New York and elsewhere with her remarkable success in *Rain*, ventured forth in a new and much-awaited role in this thin, conventional French triangle farce, only to have the spotlight stolen from her by the lustrous acting of her as-yet nonstar leading man, Leslie Howard. Eagels played Simone, a young divorcée still crazy about her ex- (Stanley Logan), who, to help her keep him at bay, hires André (Howard), a young man who really loves her, to play her lover. Eventually, she falls in love with André for real.

The play was indeed comic, and coadapter Wodehouse was given much of the credit for the laughter. First Nighter reported, "The crackle of Wodehouse's wit enriches the lines of every speech and punctuates every situation." Stark Young thought it was "more pleasantly expert than average," but Brooks Atkinson claimed it was "uneven...with dull and amusing scenes by turns; and no more substance than thistle down." Eagels was too boisterous for French farce, and her costar, according to Atkinson, played "buoyantly with droll flourishes and a sustaining sardonic intelligence." At the curtain, the audience shouted for "Howard, Howard, Howard," when Eagels stepped forth for her bows.

Eagels had replaced Laurette Taylor, who had tried acting the piece in an out-of-town production a year earlier. Eagels revised the first word of the original title from "the" to "her" and soon began to demand that various actors be dismissed. After the show opened, she improved her performance but put on a "star" act that had others in the play annoyed. She demanded a red carpet from her dressing room to the street and pulled some irresponsible bits while onstage. At one performance she ad-libbed to Howard that she wanted a glass of water; when she repeated her request, the actor walked off the stage and into his dressing room, forcing an end to that night's show. On another night she appeared to pass out in her stage bed, and the show was again cancelled in midperformance. Through it all, she suffered from various ailments (she was to die tragically young in 1929) and heavy drinking. On the road with the show in Chicago, she became hysterical over a tiff with a lover, and the evening's performance was cancelled. Equity forbade her from acting again for eighteen months, and although she appeared in vaudeville, she never performed on a legitimate stage again.

The story of Laurette Taylor's unfortunate experiences with this play is told in Marguerite Courtenay's *Laurette*.

HER FAMILY TREE [Musical/Reincarnation/Spiritualism] B: Al Weeks and Arthur "Bugs" Baer; M/LY: Seymour Simons; D: Hassard Short; P: Nora Bayes; T: Lyric Theatre; 12/27/20 (90)

An elaborately staged show designed as a vehicle for Nora Bayes. Her character was seen entertaining some friends when the conversation turned to reincarnation. Through the ministrations of a "Ouija" board and a seeress with a crystal ball, it is revealed that Bayes is really one Dora Goldberg, and she and her friends travel back through the ages to experience her former lives. This gave the book writers the chance to burlesque various historical periods and for Bayes, wearing a succession of blonde wigs, to play a girl of the old West, a Chinese maiden, a girl of the minuet period, a damsel of the crusade period, and Japhet's wife in a Noah's Ark scene.

Arthur Hornblow thought it was "too lavish an entertainment," but Alexander Woollcott decided it was "an ambitious, generally entertaining and overlong musical comedy." Julius Tannen and Frank Morgan offered ample support.

HER FIRST AFFAIRE [Comedy/Sex/Literature/Romance] A: Merrill Rogers; D/P: Gustav Blum; S: Nicholas Yellenti; T: Nora Bayes Theatre; 8/22/27 (138)

"It is pleasant, light fare," said *Time* of this fairly successful piece in which a self-consciously advanced young flapper (Grace Voss), determined to have a fling before settling down to marriage, selects her favorite novelist (Stanley Logan), whose writings depict the joys of free love, as the object of her first "affaire." After getting the writer's wisely complacent wife (Aline MacMahon) to agree to the arrangement, the flapper tries in vain to seduce the rather uptight author; finally, she returns to her conventional fiancée's (Anderson Lawler) arms a chastened woman.

Perriton Maxwell termed the play "rather refreshing," and the *Times* called it "a moderately passable sex comedy" that ran out of gas and survived "the evening only with difficulty."

HER FRIEND, THE KING [Comedy/Romance] A: A. E. Thomas and Harrison Rhodes; D: F. Gatenby Bell; P: L. Lawrence Weber; T: Longacre Theatre; 10/7/29 (24)

A "polite, romantic and occasionally humorous comedy" (Perriton Maxwell) that served to bring one time matinee idol William Faversham back to Broadway. He played a dethroned monarch of a Ruritanian nation, Constantia-Felix, living in Swiss exile, where he meets a rich American widow, Mrs. Hastings (Ara Gerald), with whom he was once in love; she helps restore him to his throne and herself to his heart. The romance of Princess Lydia (Katherine Kohler) and Prince Otto (Hugh Sinclair) forms a subplot.

To the *Times* it was a charmless play, "by no means unpleasant in its vague ramblings and never causing even the slightest acceleration of the heart-beats."

HER SALARY MAN [Comedy/Marriage/Romance] A: Forrest Rutherford; D: Harry Andrews; P: John Cort; T: Cort Theatre; 11/28/21 (32)

The author of this first play was a Western businessman who succeeded in devising a mildly comic piece that, despite weak construction and a lack of polish, had "here and there a fresh idea," was "clean, and. . .often quite amusing" (Arthur Hornblow).

Its premise was that Emily Sladen (Ruth Shepley), a young heiress, in order to escape a life of chaperonage by her silly, old-maid aunt (Edna May Oliver), seeks for a man to marry. The terms are that the marriage will be strictly a business arrangement, with the husband being paid a salary provided he leaves town once the ceremony is completed. After the expected complications, the husband (A. H. Van Buren) returns to her demanding to be a husband in fact as well as name. Several more obstacles are overcome, the pair do become a true bride and groom, and all ends for the best.

HER TEMPORARY HUSBAND [Comedy/Legacy/Marriage] A: Edward A. Paulton; P: H. H. Frazee; T: Frazee Theatre; 8/31/22 (95)

This was "the kind of reckless and infrequently credible piece we used to see oftener in the early nineties than in these later seasons," wrote Alexander Woollcott. It was activated with a conventional plot device of the time, a will, in this case one that cautions a young heiress (Ann Andrews) that she will forfeit her inheritance if she weds one Clarence Topping (Henry Mortimer). Hoping to outfox the will maker, she decides to marry some decrepit senior citizen, get the money, and then, when he kicks the bucket, move in with old Clarence as she had wanted to do in the first place. However, handsome young Tom Burton (William Courtleigh) learns of her scheme, makes himself up as a senile old fogey, and weds the girl, only to then reveal himself to her and attempt to win her on his own—which he does.

HER UNBORN CHILD [Drama/Sex/Romance/France] A: Howard McKent Barnes and Grace Hayward; REV/D: Melville Burke; P: Majestic Productions, Inc.; T: Eltinge Theatre; 3/5/28 (52)

This tearjerker had a sensational title and theme; it had been available in vastly popular touring versions for a decade but had never before been shown in New York. Revised and updated, it failed to excite the critics but seems to have stirred its audiences. Its thematic bombshell was the subject of birth control (that is, abortion), which was brought up by a high-fashion, aristocratic woman during a long discussion; the author's attitude was decidedly reactionary, and the applause that greeted the more moralistic epithets demonstrated the agreement of the auditors.

The play itself was a schmaltzy saga of a pregnant single woman (Ivy Mertons) who is refused an abortion and, after turning down the repentant father's (Theodore Hecht) initial plea for marriage, gains her gray-haired mother's (Effie Shannon) support and changes her mind. The moral was, "motherhood is God's greatest gift to humanity."

"Few plays ever came to Broadway that have provoked such a concerted use of hankies," noted Ibee., who said the play "belongs out where it came from." Wilella Waldorf observed that "A young man named Elisha Cook, Jr. indicated that he might be unusually competent in kid-brother roles in another play some time."

A second run at the Forty-eighth Street Theatre began on 6/11/28 for twenty-four performances.

HER WAY OUT [Drama/Politics/Romance/Prostitution/Sex] A: Edwin Milton Royle; D: Walter Wilson; P: Associated Players; T: Gaiety Theatre; 6/23/24 (24)

An adequate melodrama about a Washington, D.C., woman (Beatrice Terry) with a past, who is asked to restrain a fiery young senator (Edward Arnold), just arrived in town, but who falls in love with him and admits to once having been a brothel madam (a flashback shows her in her former role). Unexpectedly, he wants her, warts and all, and the play ends happily, although the original conclusion, suggested by the title, had her committing suicide. The *Times*, which found much of the play absorbing, thought the author should have retained the first ending.

Arnold and Terry were very good, especially the latter; also in the cast was Josephine Royle, the author's daughter.

HERE'S HOWE! [Musical/Romance/Business] B: Fred Thompson and Paul Gerard Smith; M: Roger Wolfe Kahn and Joseph Meyer: LY: Irving Caesar; CH: Sammy Lee; S: John Wenger; C: Kiviette; P: Alex A. Aarons and Vinton Freedley; T: Broadhurst Theatre; 5/1/28 (71)

Passable fare for a summer evening in 1928, this musical boasted the enthusiastic presence of Ben Bernie's orchestra, with Bernie's virtuoso conductorship and violin playing contributing to much of the fun. The conventional book, which allowed for the insertion of the usual specialty numbers, was about young love—Billy (Allan Kearns), an auto factory mechanic, and Joyce Baxter (Irene Delroy), a secretary. Billy sacrifices Joyce's love when his boss (Arthur Hartley) wants to make her his traveling companion. Ups and downs occur in their fates until they are reunited, and they go into the combined filling station-tea room business on the Boston Post Road.

Richard Dana Skinner judged the show "a general melange of familiar materials, plot and characters, popular fallacies, routine dances, etc., etc."

HERO, THE [Comedy-Drama/War/Crime/Sex/Marriage/Family] A: Gilbert Emery; D: Sam Forrest; P: Sam H. Harris; T: Longacre Theatre; 3/14/21 (matinees, 4); 9/5/21 (80)

The Hero was first produced as a matinee-only production but several months later returned in a regular mounting at the Belmont Theatre and became a *success d'éstime*, its original leading player being replaced by Richard Bennett. Alexander Woollcott was only one of many who urged his readers to see this ironic work that explored the question of what true heroism is.

During the war n'er-do-well brother Oswald (Robert Ames) apparently redeemed himself by a career of valiant heroics in the Foreign Legion. Brother Andrew (Bennett) stayed home, struggling to care for his family, despite a small income. Welcomed home as the conquering hero, Oswald soon seduces Marthe (Fania Marinoff), the refugee Belgian maid, and attempts the same with his doting sister-in-law Hester (Alma Belwin). Finally, he dies before he can run off with the church funds he has stolen, having performed a final courageous act in saving a child from a kindergarten fire. Yet no one, no matter what he has done, condemns his previous acts of dishonesty or immorality. Which brother, the play asks, is the true hero—the morally or the physically brave one?

This plot, said Heywood Broun, was superficially old-fashioned but was raised to artistic heights by Emery's dramatic insights. Burns Mantle chose it as one of his Ten Best of the Year.

HIDDEN [Drama/Sex/Marriage] A: William Hurlbut; D/P: David Belasco; S: Joseph Wickes; T: Lyceum Theatre; 10/4/27 (80)

A typically realistic Belasco production supported this somber piece described by Gilbert W. Gabriel as "A play with every grim intention to be medical, honest and profound. . . . But uneven, [and] badly caked, blundering into the stale and silly."

The verbose drama dealt with Violet (Beth Merrill), a virginal young woman living with her sister Ellen (Mary Morris) and handsome brother-in-law Nick (Philip Merivale). Her monomaniacal sexual desire for Nick causes her to tell lies that break up his marriage; she seduces him and then kills herself to avoid the guilt.

The critics treated the work as an example of Freud's influence on dramaturgy. Brooks Atkinson deemed it "the kind of forced drama that breeds active dislike. . . .*Hidden* never seems quite true . . . because every episode is dictated from the casebook."

HIGH GEAR [Comedy/Marriage/Family] A: Larry E. Johnson; D: Roy Walling; T: Wallack's Theatre; 10/6/27 (20)

"[A] decidedly inoffensive and decidedly machine-made entertainment" (*Times*) starring Shirley Booth in a predictable but complex assortment of farcical adventures about a young wife whose written descriptions to her wealthy California uncle of her fancy way of life are put to the test when Uncle (Erman Seavey) comes to visit. Borrowed furnishings, silver, servants, and the like are introduced to impress the relative; Harvey (William Skelley), her spouse, must play the butler when the hired one turns out to be a crook, and the complications thicken when someone must be found to play the husband.

HIGH ROAD, THE [Comedy/Romance/Theatre/British] A/D: Frederick Lonsdale; S: Clara Fargo Thomas; P: Charles Dillingham; T: Fulton Theatre; 9/10/28 (144)

Lonsdale's British drawing-room comedy about class prejudices, while not up to his best earlier efforts in George Jean Nathan's mind, made a strong showing with a cast of first-rate English actors, including Herbert Marshall and Edna Best. The play's smart veneer covered a routine plot about a titled young man (John Williams) whose family disapproves of his actress fiancée (Best). The actress melts the family and wins them over, meanwhile shifting her affections to another aristocrat (Marshall), whose duty is to another woman. Unable to marry him, the actress goes back to the theatre.

Richard Dana Skinner was happy to discern "a sense of proportion and values in this simple story . . . a shrewd, clean-thinking and very human comedy, with an undertone of high-spirited renunciation." *Time* said the piece might have been even better had it been written as "a true and biting comedy instead of an exceptionally witty tragedy."

HIGH STAKES [Drama/Marriage/Crime/Sex/Romance] A: Willard Mack; P: A. H. Woods; T: Hudson Theatre; 9/9/24 (120)

A "cheap melodrama" (George Jean Nathan) about a sixtyish millionaire (Wilton Lackaye) whose twenty-three-year-old wife (Phoebe Foster) has married him to get her hands on his money and is scheming to do so with her houseguest lover (Fleming Ward) until the plot is foiled by the husband's clever younger brother (Lowell Sherman), a would-be dramatist.

Heywood Broun disposed of the work as "cheap, tawdry, vulgar and pretty generally disgusting" because of its sexual innuendoes. Arthur Hornblow noted that "it's many a moon since I have sat through a piece so amateurishly put together, so barren in ideas and interest, so tedious in action, crude and dull in dialogue."

HIGH-HATTERS, THE [Comedy/Crime/Mental Illness] A: Louis Sobol; D: Ralph Murphy; P: Louis Isquith, Inc.; T: Klaw Theatre; 5/10/28 (10)

An unoriginal wise-cracking farce using a premise very much like that of the

1925 *Easy Come, Easy Go*. In the present venture, the two crooks, Bim (Gilbert Douglas) and Cookie (Thomas H. Manning), are failed vaudeville performers, and their scam is to get admitted to a sanitorium from whence they can fleece wealthy neighborhood residents of their belongings while being considered innocent nut jobs undergoing treatment.

E. W. Osborn advised playgoers to laugh this one off, which its brief life suggests they did. Perriton Maxwell derided the affair as "one of the most inane, inept and stupid dramas of this or any other season." Among what Maxwell called "the group of incompetents who formed the cast" was the youthful Robert Montgomery.

HIM [Comedy/Romance/Homosexuality/Theatre/Fantasy] A: E. E. Cummings; D: James Light; P: Provincetown Players; T: Provincetown Playhouse (OB); 4/18/28 (21)

One of the most unusual and abstract plays of its time, *Him* (also spelled *him*) was an ambitious failure that some have since come to view as an important contribution to America's experimental theatre. Few could make sense of this expressionist-surrealist farrago of psychology and burlesque. "Others," wrote *Time*, "undeceived by the play's pretenses, by its dreary smut, by its fairly frequent lapses into complete and trite absurdity, by long stretches in which the author...had obviously fallen into the immature fallacy of trying to tell all about life in a single paragraph, found partially concealed in its three spasmodic acts many specimens of acute and mordant understanding as well as a fair quantity of mordant wit."

Involving the relationship of Him (William S. Johnstone) and his girlfriend Me (Erin O'Brien Moore), as fantasized under ether administered to her during childbirth by a doctor (Lawrence Bolton) who appears in different guises during the delirium, *Him* was a kaleidoscopic succession of unusual scenes presided over by three masked old Weirds. They sit knitting in rocking chairs while a play Him has written for popular consumption is spasmodically enacted. Its diverse sequences have a ribald vaudeville quality and include things such as a black rendition in song and dance of "Frankie and Johnnie," a portrait of Mussolini speechifying to a band of homosexuals, and a sideshow with a barker announcing an exotic dancer who turns out to be Me.

Cummings tried to forewarn spectators of the play's special nature by a program note in which, among other things, he told them to sit back, relax, and enjoy the piece, not for its likeness to other plays but on its own terms. "DON'T TRY TO UNDERSTAND IT, LET IT TRY TO UNDERSTAND YOU." Gilbert Seldes found the directions hard to follow, but explained the work as "a tragic fantasy....The conflict is announced at the very beginning, when the girl says, 'Why should we pretend to love each other?' and the man says that his life is based on three things—that he is a man, an artist, and a failure." The play's ultimate purpose, Seldes averred, was to show how "the unconscious burlesques our conscious life."

The play marked the local debut of Lionel Stander, who played the effeminate First Fairy.

HINDU, THE [Drama/Adventure/Crime] A: Gordon Kean and Carl Mason; D: John Harwood; T: Comedy Theatre; 3/21/22 (71)

A creaking mystery melodrama set in Scotland Yard and at a palace in Somnouth, India. It served as a vehicle for Walker Whiteside, who was rumored to be the actual author. *The Hindu* showed the influence of William Archer's very popular *Green Goddess*, which recently had served George Arliss very well. It purported to be filled with unique twists and a surprise ending, but, as Arthur Hornblow noted, "Only the brain of an infant could possibly be mystified by anything that transpires." Its chief interest lay in its use of trick furniture and stage effects.

A British diplomat, Morgan (Ian Maclaren), has been fomenting rebellion among Prince Tamar's people in hopes of gaining control of the country's foodstuffs. Scotland Yard sends a female operative (Sydney Shields) to uncover the plot, but she barely escapes Morgan's clutches. The Prince saves the woman and then seems to have her in mind for his own uses, but he turns out to be not only a disguised Scotland Yard detective but the woman's husband.

HIS QUEEN [Comedy-Drama/Romance/Politics/British] A: John Hastings Turner; D/P: Oliver Morosco; T: Hudson Theatre; 5/11/25 (11)

Romantic melodrama sat uncomfortably next to comedy in this costumed farrago of old-fashioned appearance and little appeal.

The example of what Wells Root called the "Graustark school" of theatre concerned itself with a young Yonkers model (Francine Larrimore) who marries the assistant floorwalker (Charles Brown) at the shop she works in and then discovers that she has been made queen of some far-off kingdom. She takes up her regal duties but is unhappy to become the object of a revolutionary band's political enmity. Her love for their leader (Robert Warwick) is unavailing as a palace skirmish with the rebels leads to her stopping a bullet intended for his breast.

"Most of the characters spoke too much and too unnecessarily," groused Alan Dale. Some were upset by the heroine's untimely and stylistically jarring death.

HIS WIFE'S LOVER [Musical/Marriage/Jews/Yiddish/Yiddish Language] B: Sheine Rochel Semkoff; M: Abe Ellstein; LY: Boris Rosenthal; D/P: Ludwig Satz; CH: Chaim Adler; S: Alex Chertoff; T: Satz Yiddish Folks Theatre (OB); 10/20/29

The conflict at the core of this Yiddish musical comedy concerned the efforts of a handsome young actor (Leon Gold) to win a $10,000 wager by convincing his mysogynist uncle (Joseph Schoengold) that a true woman exists. The actor disguises himself as an old man, marries a needy tenement girl (Fanny Lubritzky), but does not possess her love. He comes to her as his good-looking self to test her fidelity, but she refuses his temptations, and the uncle loses his $10,000.

Some able burlesque clowning and lively music salvaged this show, which the *Times* said was "Hackneyed in plot [and] limited in the apparatus of production so essential to this type of entertainment."

HIT THE DECK! [Musical/Sea/China/Romance] B: Herbert Fields; M: Vincent Youmans; LY: Leo Robin and Clifford Grey; SC: Hubert Osborne's play *Shore Leave*; D: Alexander Leftwich; CH: Seymour Felix; S: John Wenger; C: Mark Mooring; P: Lew Fields and Vincent Youmans; T: Belasco Theatre; 4/25/27 (352)

The first musical ever staged at the Belasco Theatre was this big hit based on a 1922 comedy that had been produced by David Belasco. *Hit the Deck*'s chief musical gift to posterity was the rousing "Hallelujah," sung by Stella Mayhew made up as a black mammy. Louise Groody, the original Nanette of *No, No, Nanette*, played Loulou, the Newport coffee-house owner who follows her boy-friend "Bilge" Smith (Charles King) around the world to China before he will consent to marry her—but only after she agrees to give up her inheritance to her first child so it need not seem that Bilge is marrying her for her money.

"Hallelujah's" popularity was matched by another Youmans perennial, "Sometimes I'm Happy," but both songs actually had been written in earlier years for other occasions. Richard Dana Skinner called *Hit the Deck!* "a bright and quick stepping musical play" with a story "as Cinderella-like and harmless as an April zephyr." Brooks Atkinson was pleased to notice the unwonted masculinity of the male chorus members and applauded the show's music, spirit, and choreography, much of which involved the free-wheeling movements of the white-duck garbed sailors. Designer John Wenger contributed a "spectacular scene depicting the forward deck of the U.S.S. Nebraska from web mast to rolling gun turret," reported Atkinson.

HITCHY-KOO OF 1920 [Revue] B/LY: Glen MacDonough and Anne Caldwell; M: Jerome Kern; D: Ned Wayburn; P: Charles Dillingham; T: New Amsterdam Theatre; 10/19/20 (71)

The fourth and last in this series of annual revues possessed "a great deal of gay nonsense, about twice the usual ration of novelty, some brilliant costuming and a fine lot of talent," stated Alexander Woollcott. It began with a comic routine in which G. P. Huntley, Julia Sanderson, and Raymond Hitchcock debated the question of which of them was the show's star. The point was moot, since there were others who nearly stole the show away from them. They included Billy Holbrook as the hilarious forelegs of a racing horse, the acrobatic dancers known as the Mosconi Brothers, and Florence O'Denishawn with an expert Egyptian *pas seul*. The show's comedy seemed dated, and an old-time vaudeville melodrama burlesque, "For Pity's Sake," occupied too much stage time. A Little Old New York segment took spectators back to the presidential campaigns of Blaine and Cleveland. Although there was not much to remember Jerome Kern's score by, there was the beautiful young soprano Grace Moore, who came into her own, even after the tune Kern wrote for her, "The Wedding Cake," was appropriated by Julia Sanderson. Moore became known as "The Girl Who Lost Her Pants" after a contretemps in one scene when her panties fell off during a dance in which she wore a hooped gown.

HOBOKEN BLUES [Drama/Blacks/Fantasy] A: Michael Gold; M: Edward A. Ziman; D: Edward Massey; S: William Gaskin; P: New Playwrights' Theatre; T: New Playwrights' Theatre (OB); 2/17/28 (16)

Michael Gold's "white fantasy on a black theme" met with ruthless critical opposition. It was a free-form, semiexpressionistic play, acted in blackface and supported by a considerable amount of song and dance, about Sam Pickens (George Bratt), a shiftless black man who returns to Harlem after a twenty-five-year absence to find it tragically given over to the evil values represented by the white man's capitalism.

It was staged with various experimental devices to realize its kaleidoscopic, fragmentary script. Brooks Atkinson called it "less a story than a potpourri of revival meetings, horse cars, cake-walk gallipolades, saloon palaver, cabaret and circus scenes and processionals up and down the aisle." He also termed it "simply boring."

HOLD EVERYTHING [Musical/Sports/Romance] B: B. G. De Sylva and John McGowan; M: Ray Henderson; LY: B. G. De Sylva, Lew Brown; D: Bertram Harrison; CH: Jack Haskell and Sam Rose; S: Henry Dreyfuss; P: Alex A. Aarons and Vinton Freedley; T: Broadhurst Theatre; 10/10/28 (413)

The trio of De Sylva, Henderson, and Brown conspired to create another in their list of musical hits in *Hold Everything*, a show also blessed by a wondrous crew of comedy merchants, including Victor Moore, Bert Lahr ("a clown capacious in the mouth but enjoyably constricted above the eyebrows"—*Times*), and Nina Olivette, a Fannie Brice-like clown and dancer. The show was Lahr's debut in a Broadway book musical. He played Gink Shiner, a punchdrunk pug who is so dumb that when his girlfriend shouts "For two cents I'd knock you out myself," he rejoinders, "You're mercenary, you're mercenary!" He had better material to work with than the hapless Moore, who, as a fighter's manager, had to struggle to overcome banal dialogue. The handsome romantic leads were played by Jack Whiting and Ona Munson. In the score were tunes such as "Too Good to Be True" and "You're the Cream in my Coffee." During its tryout period, the show seemed destined for failure, but it became a big Broadway hit.

The modest book was burdened by a tale about Sonny Jim Brooks (Whiting), a welterweight championship contender, and his romantic problems with Sue Burke (Munson) and Norma Lloyd (Betty Compton), the society girls who want him. He is scheduled to fight the champ in an upcoming bout, but through various contrivances of the plot, Gink, his sparring partner, fights him instead and wins; he also captures the heart of the girl he loves.

Bert Lahr's reviews were raves. St. John Ervine wrote of him in admiration: "This man is funny. He can make old, tired stuff seem new and original. . . . Mr. Lahr can obtain laughter by merely distorting his features. . . . His resourcefulness is astonishing."

Since Victor Moore was a very quiet, restrained player, Lahr used to try to make him laugh, even breaking wind on stage to do so. After Moore retaliated by smearing Limberger cheese on a prop-reducing cabinet in which Lahr had to sit with his head sticking out, Lahr got even by sending the quavery-voiced actor a note supposedly coming from a fraternal group seeing the show; he was asked to mention the names of some of the club's members during the show and was promised a big reaction. Moore worked the names into the script, but not one of them drew the hoped for response. Finally, Moore walked offstage muttering, "I'm a son-of-a-bitch, if I'm going to mention another name." Lahr never revealed the actual source of the note.

HOLIDAY [Comedy/Family/Romance/Alcoholism] A: Philip Barry; D/P: Arthur Hopkins; S: Robert Edmond Jones; T: Plymouth Theatre; 11/26/28 (230)

Hope Williams had proved so successful in the role of Fanny, the heroine's friend, in Barry's *Paris Bound* that he wrote *Holiday* to use both the character (now called Linda Seton) and the actress's talents. This comedy of manners among New York's superrich was even more respected than its predecessor. Linda Seton was seen as the unconventional socialite sister of Julia (Dorothy Tree), the latter engaged to the unconventional lawyer Johnny Case (Ben Smith), a young man who wishes to retire early with the money he's made on the stock market and to enjoy life as a holiday while he can. This view runs into opposition from Julia and her capitalistic father (Walter Walker), but, backed by the alcoholic Seton brother Nick (Donald Ogden Stewart) and the snappy Linda, Johnny sticks to his guns. At the end, the two unconventional souls, Linda and Johnny, come together, and Julia is left behind.

Brilliantly cast, designed, and staged, *Holiday* was a treat in all departments. Richard Dana Skinner congratulated Barry on his "masterpiece." The best thing about the writing was not the plot but the dialogue, a Barry forte. Joseph Wood Krutch said it was "both delightfully witty and thoroughly humane as well, . . . [H]is dialogue is not of the sort which can be quoted in fragments and it is almost too unsubstantial to be subject to analysis, but it ripples in one gay and continuous stream throughout the piece."

Williams's reviews were noteworthy, but many wondered whether her success was not owing more to her skill at playing herself than at impersonating a character. Her understudy, Katharine Hepburn, did not get to show her gifts in the role until she played it in the 1938 screen version. The casting of Donald Ogden Stewart, the noted humorist, in the role of Nick, was considered another stroke of genius.

HOLKA-POLKA [Musical/Family/Romance/Czechoslovakian] B: W. Walzer; TR: Derick Wulff; AD: Bert Kalmar and Harry Ruby; M: Will Ortman; LY: Gus Kahn and Raymond B. Eagan; D: Oscar Eagle; CH: Busby Berkeley; S: Livingston Platt; P: Carl Reed; T: Lyric Theatre; 10/14/25 (21)

An operetta adapted from an European original as a showcase for the singing and dancing talents of Orville Harrold and his daughter Patti. Busby Berkeley contributed the excellent dance ensembles, there were many fine voices in the troupe, the Harrolds were in fine fettle, and the "conservative," that is, nonjazz, music was pleasant; however, as the *Sun* pointed out, "The humor of the piece is palpably forced and far from satisfying," although character comedienne May Vokes contributed some glimmers of amusement wherever possible.

The unsubstantial book cast Patti Harrold as a Czech art student who does not know that the man who raised her is her father, who has romantic experiences with two men in Prague, and whose position is threatened, but for whom all works out satisfactorily in the end.

HOLY TERROR [Drama/Romance/Family/Crime/Labor/Small Town/Trial] A: Winchell Smith and George Abbott; D: Winchell Smith; P: John Golden; T: George M. Cohan Theatre; 9/28/25 (32)

An uneven large-cast melodrama coauthored by two of Broadway's leading lights, starring one of them and directed by the other. Its subject was the character of Dirk Yancey (George Abbott), a straight-shooting West Virginia mountaineer raised in the intense climate of a family feud with the Chapmans; this rough and tough, rotgut-drinking gent is made chief of police when a mining strike occurs. He has long loved the Mayor's (Bennet Musson) wife (Leona Hogarth), so when the Mayor is killed, the hired coal company detectives sent there to stem the strike have him arrested for the murder. But the Holy Terror escapes hanging, becomes a hero, is tried and cleared of the slaying, and marries the widow.

Alexander Woollcott termed it a "somewhat sedulously virile but none the less stirring and engrossing play" during the first act but dead thereafter, and the *Times* detected two plays present in the guise of one. Abbott was approved for his heroic, manly characterization.

In his memoirs, "*Mister Abbott*," Abbott revealed that he actually ended up directing the play when Winchell Smith became ill. He noted also that this play had begun as a collaboration between himself and Maxwell Anderson, but that producer Golden arranged for Anderson to forgo the project in favor of Smith. Abbott recalled: "it seems to me that neither Winchell nor I was the right author for this [play]. We made it into a show, a melodrama, whereas its only hope was to be treated in a more important way—to delve deeply into the causes of feuds and hatreds."

HOME FIRES [Comedy/Marriage/Family] A: Owen Davis; D: Hugh Ford; P: Messrs. Shubert; T: Thirty-ninth Street Theatre; 8/20/23 (48)

Preceded by *The Detour* and the 1922 Pulitzer Prize drama *Icebound*, *Home*

Fires was the third of Owen Davis's serious studies of American life. Whereas *Icebound* had been a gloomy drama, the new work was a comedy about a suburban family. An ever-understanding and resourceful wife (Frances Underwood), whose husband (Charles Richman) loses his job and flirts with a neighbor's wife, and whose restless teenage daughters run temporarily wild, manages to straighten out everyone's messes and to keep the home fires burning.

John Corbin greeted the play as "fresh and funny," noting that the harsh realism of *Icebound* had become more genial and, he would like to think, more truly American. Some critics accused Davis of idealizing the mother too much. Heywood Broun declared: "We remember no character we have ever detested so thoroughly as the incessantly obliging Mary."

HOME TOWNERS, THE [Comedy/Romance/Friendship] A/P: George M. Cohan; D: John Meehan; S: Joseph Wickes; T: Hudson Theatre; 8/23/26 (64)

A sporadically funny, weakly constructed Cohan farce that satirized the narrow-mindedness of Main Street America through the boisterous character of P. H. Bancroft, ably played by Robert McWade. This South Bend, Indiana, yokel arrives in New York for the wedding of his childhood pal Vic Arnold (William Elliott) to Beth Calhoon (Peg Entwistle), twenty years the junior of her millionaire groom. Bancroft immediately casts aspersions on the motives of Beth and her family in desiring this marriage. His suspicions prove to be unfounded, and after he nearly wrecks his friend's plans, everything is righted at the end.

Richard Dana Skinner thought it "a meandering, and occasionally highly amusing," work that fell apart in the denouement; lagging tempo was also annoying. "It's entertaining noisiness makes up for its lack of substance," ventured Brooks Atkinson, who noted the usual Cohan "Americanisms,...retorts, threats, vain boasts, [and] sundry and diverse 'cracks' " filling the dialogue.

HOMME ET SES FANTÔMES, L' (Man and His Phantoms) [Drama/Spiritualism/Romance/French/French Language] A: H. R. Lenormand; D: Firmin Gémier; T: Jolson's Fifty-ninth Street Theatre; 11/13/24 (3)

The third production to open in the repertory brought to New York by Firmin Gémier's company from Paris's Odéon Theatre. Written by a contemporary writer whose third New York production of the year this was, it displayed the work of "an adept craftsman...,with variety and daring in the construction of his scenes," but with a lack of "power," according to Stark Young.

An unconventional tragedy, it dealt with the Man (Gémier), a Don Juan whose callous treatment of the women he loves and abandons is depicted; he soon meets suffering inflicted on him for his deeds, grows past the physical need for women as his health fades, and becomes enmeshed in spiritualist experiences. Gradually, he becomes unduly subject to the pressure of his ex-mistresses and dies as he struggles with their phantoms.

Most thought the play was pretentious, but Edmund Wilson took it seriously as an interpretation of "Don Juan in the light of modern psychology...[as a] cold-blooded immoralist who deliberately defies Heaven and abandons the women he has seduced with unnecessary harshness." In Wilson's view, Lenormand sees Don Juan as a homosexual whose life might have been different had he recognized the meaning of his behavior.

HOMME QUI ASSASSINA, L' (The Man Who Murders) [Drama/Romance/ Crime/Marriage/French/French Language] A: Pierre Frondaie; SC: a novel by Claude Farrère; D: Firmin Gémier; T: Jolson's Fifty-ninth Street Theatre; 11/ 10/24 (3)

French "*homme du théâtre*," Firmin Gémier and his company of Odéon actors performed this play in repertory during their visiting season in New York. It was a pentagonal affair played with such ensemble unity that A.G.H. Spiers remarked, "Not even Stanislavsky's admirable veterans surpassed in this respect the young company trained and led by Firmin Gémier."

Unfortunately, despite the blaring campaign on the troupe's behalf, this first play staged by them turned out to be "a melodramatic potboiler" (George Jean Nathan) performed with nothing of unusual note by the star. It concerned the efforts of Sir Archibald Falkland (Charles Vanel) and his mistress to get Lady Falkland (Germaine Rouer) out of the picture by arranging with the rakish Prince Cernuwitz (Marcel Chabrier) to betray her. Another gentleman (Gémier) interrupts the scheme by slaying Falkland; his own love for Lady Falkland is dashed when he learns that she loves the Prince.

HONEST LIARS [Comedy/Sex/Romance] A: Robert Weenolsen and Sherrill Webb; D: Frank Smithson; P: George MacFarlane; T: Sam H. Harris Theatre; 7/19/26 (97)

"It is but poor stuff, tawdry and vulgar," declared Arthur Hornblow, an opinion seconded by Richard Dana Skinner, who snapped that this piece was "as stupid and inept an evening as one could well devise."

The farce was a mad assortment of crazy incidents taking place among assorted loonies at a sanitarium. Among them are a drunk (Neil Pratt), a comic maid (Margaret Walker), a detective (Jay Wilson), and a pair of lovers. One of the latter (Robert Woolsey) is being sought for having been involved in a roadhouse raid from which he escaped with one of the doctor's wives by stealing a taxi in the rear of which a set of twins had been deposited.

HONEYDEW [Musical/Music/Business] B/LY: Joseph Herbert; M: Efrem Zimbalist; D: Hassard Short; P: Joe Weber; T: Casino Theatre; 9/6/20 (200)

Internationally renowned violinist Efrem Zimbalist composed the score for this humdrum operetta and succeeded in producing several appreciated tunes, among them "Oh, How I Long for Someone," "The Morals of a Sailor Man," and "Drop Me a Line." The *Times* asserted that Zimbalist had not "written down'' for Broadway but had ''merely marshaled his skill as a musician of parts and rung the bell with ease and confidence.''

The ''quite barren'' libretto told of eccentric composer Henry Honeydew (Hal Forde), whose father-in-law promotes his exterminating business by using one of Henry's songs, ''The June Bug,'' as a giveaway to customers buying one of his products. This plugging makes the song a hit and Henry a success.

A return engagement opened on 5/16/21 for forty-nine showings.

HONEYMOON LANE [Musical/Small Town/Romance/Fantasy/Show Business] B/M/LY: Eddie Dowling and James Hanley; D: Edgar J. MacGregor; CH: Bobby Connolly; P: A. L. Erlanger; T: Knickerbocker Theatre; 9/20/26 (353)

''[A] palatable bit of candy for romantic sweethearts,'' said Arthur Hornblow of this musical confection. Richard Dana Skinner was annoyed by the frequent jokes at the expense of ''male perverts,'' a type of gag he said was ''almost standard in the musical shows,'' but he loved the music and the dancing, if not the banal book and lyrics. All of it was the responsibility of Eddie Dowling, who also played the lead. The ''sticky sentimentality'' of the show was made bearable, wrote *Time*, by the dancing of Florence O'Denishawn, who moved ''through it all like a fairy on a moonbeam.''

The opulently produced show was about a couple of small-town young lovers (Dowling and Pauline Mason); she leaves him behind at the pickle factory to pursue a Broadway career, falls in love with the pickle maker's son, and is headed for stardom, before it all turns out to be a dream; she and her boyfriend remain ever after on Honeymoon Lane in Cannington, Pennsylvania.

The show's greatest contribution was the young singer Kate Smith who came on late in the evening playing Tiny Little, reported by the *Times* to weigh in at 200-250 pounds. ''As a dancer and coon-shouting 'blues' singer she proved unusually adept, and stop the show she did.''

HONEYMOONING [Comedy/Marriage/Sex/Spiritualism/Southern] A: Hatcher Hughes; D: Marion Kerby; S: Livingston Platt; P: the company; T: Bijou Theatre; 3/17/27 (20)

A vastly disappointing follow-up to the author's Pulitzer Prize *Hell-Bent fer Heaven*, this play elicited numerous expressions of derision. E. W. Osborn claimed it ''achieves a unique standing in unbelievableness.'' ''Partly through clumsiness in the acting, partly through the puerility of the dialogue and invention, the story emerges as scattered, pointless confusion, somewhat frantic in its expression,'' exclaimed Brooks Atkinson.

The company itself produced this ridiculous farce about a young couple who discover on their honeymoon at a southern roadhouse that their marriage is not legal, followed by various complications; they include the groom's (Lorin Raker) faked suicide to win back his bride (Marie Louise Dana), their involvement with a spiritualist (LeRoi Operti) who performs seances, and a scene in which the husband plays dead while filling the inside of a coffin as his loved ones try to reach him in the spirit world.

HONOR BE DAMNED! [Drama/Law/Crime/Sex/Romance] A/D: Willard Mack; P: Willard Mack b/a/w David Belasco; T: Morosco Theatre; 1/26/27 (45)

All-around theatre man Willard Mack starred in this melodrama of his own devising about a rising young Irish lawyer, John Connell, in with New York's shady politicos, who agrees to defend Lou Buckley (Carl Gerard), guilty of murder, and concocts an ingenious case based on a self-defense plea. When Connell learns that Buckley seduced his sister (Ruth King) and got her pregnant, he walks out on the case, to the consternation of the backroom boys who are not told the reason. A suitor for the sister turns up willing to marry her, so Connell breathes easier, and he honors his earlier pledges and agrees to take on the case.

Supposedly based on an actual incident, the play failed to have the right stuff; it was "a compact, fairly effective play, with at least one decidedly effective scene," but it was "sufficiently archaic" in its view of life to make it seem drearily outmoded, said the *Times*.

HONOR OF THE FAMILY, THE (La Rabouilleuse) [Dramatic Revival] A: Émile Fabre; AD: Paul Potter; SC: Honoré de Balzac's story "Un Ménage de Garçon"; P: Charles Frohman, Inc.; T: Booth Theatre; 12/25/26 (33)

Otis Skinner's third New York production of this 1908 adaptation from the 1903 French play *La Rabouilleuse* betrayed "a script that is decidedly frayed and a supporting company that is decidedly shoddy," in John Mason Brown's opinion. "All the motives of the drama are false; the piece is heavily weighted down with fustian," agreed Brooks Atkinson. The exercise was effective chiefly for giving Skinner another chance to display his marvelously rich characterization as Colonel Bridau, the nephew of an old miser, who turns up at his uncle's home to clean it out of those with designs on his coffers.

HONORS ARE EVEN [Comedy/Romance/Crime/Theatre] A/D: Roi Cooper Megrue; P: Selwyns; T: Times Theatre; 8/10/21 (70)

A talky romantic comedy about pretty, well-to-do, clever Belinde (Lola Fisher), who is indifferent to the many suitors who ask for her hand but runs into emotional difficulties when she meets sophisticated playwright John Leighton (William Courtenay), who thinks the way to win her is to play hard to get. She realizes that her problem can be solved by fighting fire with fire. When Leighton sees that he may lose her to the villain of the piece (Henry Mowray), a jewel thief, he makes the proper moves and gets the girl.

This "uneven but generally amusing" play, "a curious mixture of comedy of manners and crook melodrama'' (Heywood Broun), was mildly received, its best features being some smart dialogue and a winsome heroine, played engagingly by Lola Fisher.

HOSPITALITY [Comedy-Drama/Family/Marriage] A: Leon Cunningham; D: Augustin Duncan; P: Equity Players; T: Forty-eighth Street Theatre; 11/13/22 (46)

The Equity Players produced this interesting drama as part of a season of noncommercial works; although marred by structural and character problems, there was enough here of dramatic and theatrical values, in the writing and the playing, to gain the work modest effusions of respect.

Treating material not dissimilar from that soon to be powerfully recorded in Sidney Howard's *Silver Cord*, *Hospitality* presented a portrait of Jennie Wells (Louise Closser Hale), a self-sacrificing but smothering mother and a domineering, proud, gritty woman, ''overworked, illiterate, hard, shrewd, inexpressive'' (Walter Prichard Eaton), who has never stinted on her maternal duties toward her son Peter (Tom Powers), but who also has never shown outwardly the tenderness of a mother's love and affection. Dissatisfied with the wealthy girl of loose morals Peter has married, Jennie contrives to break up the marriage and then proceeds to suffer a heart attack and die in her son's arms.

The *World* argued that the first two acts were ''incredibly, monstrously dull, talky, unreal'' but that the play came to vivid life in the third.

HOT CHOCOLATES [Revue/Blacks] B: Eddie Green; M: Thomas ''Fats'' Waller and Harry Brooks; LY: Andy Razaf; D: Leonard Harper, Danny Dare, and Harry Ruskin; P: Connie and George Immerman; T: Hudson Theatre; 6/20/29 (228)

One of the few late-twenties black revues to make a dent on Broadway, this one made it through the dog days well into the meat of the following season. It sported a chorus of lovelies whom Francis R. Bellamy was at pains to describe as light enough in complexion to adorn a white chorus line, had a first-rate score by ''Fats'' Waller and Harry Brooks, and had a host of stageworthy talent. The show (billed as ''A New Tanskin Revel'') originated at Harlem's popular night spot, Connie's Inn, and its opening scene was set there as the ''customers'' started to arrive. There followed a succession of sketches and musical numbers, with some memorable dancing, solo and chorus.

The show introduced Waller's classic ''Ain't Misbehavin','' which was one day to have a Broadway revue named after it. ''Jazzlips'' Richardson was the evening's mirth provoker and Margaret Simms its principal female singer; Louis Armstrong, a member of the orchestra, gave a solo on the trumpet at one point.

HOT PAN [Comedy/Period/Western] A: Michael Swift; D: James Light; S: Cleon Throckmorton; P: Provincetown Players; T: Provincetown Playhouse (OB); 2/15/28 (28)

Although parts of this "rough-and-ready comedy" greatly delighted Brooks Atkinson, he had to confess that it was "shapeless, crude and sophomoric" and acted by a bunch of amateurs. The satire lashed out at numerous targets on its disorderly journey, including business ethics, political chicanery, and feminine wiles; it missed more bull's-eyes than it hit.

Inspired by Anatole France's satire *Penguin Island*, *Hot Pan*'s crude japes were embedded in a plot taking place in a Hot Pan, California, saloon during the gold rush days of 1849. A lode of gold is discovered under the planking, leading to a maelstrom of fervid activity, most of it concerned with gaining possession of the precious ore.

Time's verdict was that "Flashes of vivid satire, bits of brutal delight gleamed in the dialog like gold nuggets. The rest was sand and water." Eduard Franz and Barbara Bulgakov were members of the cast.

HOT WATER [Comedy/Theatre/Business/Romance] A: Helena Dayton and Louise Bascom Baratt; D: Jose Ruben; T: Lucille La Verne Theatre; 1/21/29 (32)

Lucille La Verne, a character actress long known for her old hag in Lula Vollmer's *Sun Up*, produced and starred in this flop about an elderly janitress and former footlights favorite who dishes out good deeds and money on behalf of the ungrateful wretches who require her help. She invents a special umbrella called a "showersol" but goes broke trying to market it, fails in a comeback attempt at acting, and is finally rescued from destitution by a lodger who succeeds in selling the showersol and also in winning her as his wife.

A poor performance only further damaged this "pitifully weak play" (*Times*). The Lucille La Verne Theatre was the old Princess, renamed for the occasion.

HOTBED [Comedy-Drama/ University/Sex/Family] A: Paul Osborn; D: Brock Pemberton and Antoinette Perry; S: Raymond Sovey; P: Brock Pemberton; T: Klaw Theatre; 11/8/28 (19)

Paul Osborn, student of Yale playwriting professor George Pierce Baker, was the author of this first play. It had a sound premise but was dramaturgically feeble, according to George Jean Nathan. "*Hotbed*, though crude," offered Robert Littell, "was well enough made to give us the primitive satisfaction of seeing an enemy pounded into the dirt, and some of it was quite entertaining as well."

An attack on puritanism, *Hotbed* centered on the bigoted Rev. David Rushbrook (William Ingersoll), who zealously fulminates against the laxity of youth who attend the nearby university. He strikes out at a young instructor (Richard Spencer) for having a girl student in his rooms and has him dismissed, only to learn that the girl in question is his own daughter (Alison Bradshaw), who is only too happy to be cast out of the house.

Preston Sturges, future film genius, played a small role in the play.

HOTEL MOUSE, THE [Musical/Crime/Romance/Hotel/French] B: Guy Bolton; M: Armand Vecsey and Ivan Caryll; LY: Clifford Grey; SC: a French work, *La souris d'hôtel*, by Paul Armont and Marcel Gerbidon; D: John Harwood; P: Messrs. Shubert; T: Shubert Theatre; 3/13/21 (88)

The Gallic plot of this frothy little show was supplied by prolific Boulevardiers Gerbidon and Armont, but its Americanization was the work of the ubiquitous Guy Bolton. Its chief *raison d'être* was the presence in the title role of tiny, versatile Frances White.

Its fragile plot concerned the clever Mauricette's thieving ability, which baffles the Riviera police who are on the alert for her following her successful hotel burglaries. One night she finds herself trapped in a room with baritone Wally Shields (Taylor Holmes), who protects her from the detectives lurking outside and ends up marrying her.

Composer Ivan Caryll died in the midst of writing the score, and the task was completed by Armand Vecsey. The most Alexander Woollcott could say of the music was that it was "pleasantly tinkling," but the *Women's Wear* critic claimed the show had "catchy and sparkling light music, witty lines, lyrics which arise naturally out of the situation, and comedy with a touch of romance and true love."

HOTEL UNIVERSE [Drama/France/Mental Illness/Hotel/Fantasy/Friendship/Romance] A: Philip Barry; D: Philip Moeller; S: Lee Simonson; P: Theatre Guild; T: Martin Beck Theatre; 4/14/30 (81)

Philip Barry's ambitious psychological drama, a surprising shift from his recent drawing-room comedy successes, was greeted with responses ranging from reverent appreciation to outright scorn. The play, performed without an intermission, is set on a July eve in Toulon, France, to which Ann Field (Katherine Alexander) has brought her father, Stephen (Morris Carnovsky), a brilliant physicist whose mind appears to have become unhinged, for recuperation. Their residence is an old hotel filled with mystical associations. To them on a visit come a group of Ann's wealthy, soul-sore, and disillusioned friends, several of them suicidal. Under the spell of the place, and through Stephen's subtle manipulation, each relives without a change of scene early painful experiences from which they emerge as if healed with a healthier outlook on life. Stephen enacts for each the figure(s) in their lives whose influence was most crucial in souring their perspectives. His daughter and Pat Farley (Glenn Anders) are enabled to further their affair, but old Stephen dies in his wheelchair as a symbolic white cock crows optimistically of the future.

Criticisms of the play found it opaque and verbose. Joseph Wood Krutch referred to its "pompous platitudes of a sentimental and second-hand mysticism." But Perriton Maxwell, while aware of certain drawbacks, was gripped by its "consistently effective material." A fine cast, including Ruth Gordon, Franchot Tone, Phyllis Povah, and Earle Larimore, played in one of Lee Simonson's finest settings.

HOUSE AFIRE [Comedy/Marriage] A: Mann Page; D: Clifford Brooke; P: Arthur Fisher; T: Little Theatre; 3/31/30 (16)

Perriton Maxwell gave this undeveloped comedy "a fairly low C," because its generally acceptable premise had been inadequately employed. The play concerned a wife (May Collins), unhappy in her New Jersey suburban environment, who wishes to live in the city. When her home burns down and she lives it up on the insurance proceeds, she is suspected of having torched the place herself. By the end, the actual incendiary is caught.

The play's characters were "wholly theatrical," noted *Time*, "limned without originality or wit." In the role of the suspected arsonist's spouse was noted comic actor John E. Hazzard.

HOUSE DIVIDED, THE [Drama/Family/Prostitution/Greek] A: Spyros Melas; T: Punch and Judy Theatre; 11/11/23 (1)

An uncredited adaptation of a glum family drama by one of Greece's respected modern dramatists. It depicted a shallow and mercenary mother, smugly respectable elder and irresponsible younger son, and self-sacrificial elder daughter (whose prostitution provides the family's chief source of income) and naive younger daughter betrayed by a lover. According to John Corbin it had "the air of uncompromising realism." He found that the European milieu and lack of any humor rendered the play too "far removed from our knowledge and sympathy."

HOUSE OF FEAR, THE [Comedy/Mystery/Spiritualism/Crime] A: Wall Spence; D: Elmer H. Brown; P: Ray Productions, Inc.; T: Republic Theatre; 10/7/29 (48)

A "mystery farce" with a central character, Mme. Zita (Effie Shannon), whose occupation as a spiritualist led to an evening of laughs and thrills as bodies and parts of bodies floated about and things such as "sliding doors, secret panels, blood stains and the odor of lotus blossoms" (Perriton Maxwell) played their appointed roles. The *Times* said it combined "the worst features" of burlesque and mystery in "a childish hodge-podge" about how Mme. Zita creates a scary seance to drive a confession from a murderer guilty of the crime for which her son has been imprisoned in Sing Sing.

HOUSE OF SHADOWS, THE [Drama/Mystery/Spiritualism/Fantasy/Romance] A: Leigh Hutty; S: Livingston Platt; P: William A. Brady, Jr., and Dwight Deere Wiman i/a/w J. H. Del Bondio; T: Longacre Theatre; 4/21/27 (29)

A meager mystery melodrama designed to scare theatregoers by the venerable device of strange goings on in a haunted mansion. It lacked surprises, bored the audience, and failed to convince. "The illusion of reality was about 99 percent absent," advised Stark Young. What little comedy relief it offered came from a servant called Darkey (Tom Mosely) played in blackface.

The usual haunting paraphernalia were unwrapped from mothballs to support a plot about a reputedly haunted house being investigated by a Harvard professor (Tom Powers) interested in spiritualism, when a pretty female (Marguerite Churchill) intrudes on a stormy night seeking shelter from an evil pursuer. The action sees the latter (James S. Barrett) killed off, a romance sprout between the professor and the damsel, and the discovery that the evidences of ghosts is owing to the tricks of an old miser (Frank Peters) hiding in the walls and protecting a pirate treasure.

HOUSE OF USSHER, THE [Drama/Jews/Crime/Romance/Business/Gambling/Family/British] A: H. V. Esmond; D: Edward Elsner; P: Wainwright and Brennan i/a/w Playhouse owners; T: Fifth Avenue Playhouse (OB); 1/13/26 (20)

Known in its original English version as *Birds of a Feather*, this "journeyman drama" (Brooks Atkinson) was about Constance Ussher (Rosalined Fuller), the willful daughter of a wealthy Jewish financier (Clarence Derwent), whose money has been made by means both fair and foul; she rebels against her overbearing father's wishes. To attract her father's non-Jewish secretary (Fairfax Burgher) she forges a check for 1,000 pounds, gambles with it on the stock market, and makes a bundle, shocking the young man by her criminality. However, she sees him return with 1,000 pounds he has won at the races to wipe out her theft. When the father learns of her sinful alliance with the secretary, he gives in to her demands.

John Mason Brown described it as "an elaborately built but generally dull comedy of manners"; Henry Longan Stuart wrote, "The languid action was punctuated by epigrams of the blear-eyed, knock kneed, and stammering kind popularized by the late Oscar Wilde."

Early in the run the Fifth Avenue Playhouse, a small theatre near Twelfth Street, was seriously damaged by a fire that broke out in the middle of a performance. Clarence Derwent, the star, suspected producer George Brennan of setting it to get him out of paying that week's salaries. When it turned out that Brennan had no title to the play, Derwent arranged to get it himself. He reopened the play uptown on 6/7/26 at the intimate Mayfair, where it ran through the summer; it then moved to the Forty-ninth Street Theatre and finally back to the Mayfair. By the time it closed it had accrued 205 performances, not counting the original 20. Still, it failed to earn a profit. The tale of Derwent's trials with the piece is set down in his *Derwent Story*.

HOUSE OF WOMEN, THE [Drama/Family/Labor/Sex/Religion/Romance] A: Louis Bromfield; SC: Louis Bromfield's novel *The Green Bay Tree*; D/P: Arthur Hopkins; S: Robert Edmond Jones; T: Maxine Elliott's Theatre; 10/3/27 (40)

An adaptation of his own first novel by Pulitzer Prize-winning Louis Bromfield; the novel's title was the same as that of a sensational 1933 drama of homosexuality by Mordaunt Shairp. Brilliantly played by its leading actresses, *The House of Women* failed to register because of faulty playwriting. Brooks Atkinson claimed for the characters a depth and meaningfulness he said was sorely lacking in the play's dialogue and construction and in the author's weakness as a dramatic story teller.

Two sisters are contrasted; their wise, widowed mother (Nance O'Neil) is the axis around which they revolve. These women are the Shanes; the hot-blooded beauty (Elsie Ferguson) turns down Governor Bascom (Walter Abel) as a husband, despite their illegitimate offspring; frustrated sister Irene (Helen Freeman), in love with the politician, turns for solace to Catholicism. Later, a dynamic labor leader–preacher (Curtis Cooksey) attracts the siblings' eyes. He loves Lily, thus terribly hurting the abusive Irene. The old lady dies, telling Lily to marry the man.

HOUSE UNGUARDED [Drama/Journalism/Crime/Marriage/Sex] A: Len D. Hollister and Lester Lonergan; D/P: Bernard Steele; S: Nicholas Yellenti; T: Little Theatre; 1/15/29 (39)

The unusual plot method of this melodrama foreshadowed that which later was so much more effectively used in the Japanese drama *Rashomon*. The premise in both plays is, briefly, what is truth? In *House Unguarded* a tragedy has transpired. Each of the three acts gives a different version of it. Unlike *Rashomon*, the first two versions are not those of the participants but of outsiders, two newsmen (Jerome Daley and Frank Knight) piecing the story together. Act Three presents the tale as it actually occurred, according to the words of a character central to its action. The story itself concerns the murder of a Panama Canal Zone man (Lester Lonergan) whose wife (Shirley Warde) has been having an affair with a naval officer (John Marston); the killer is revealed as an Asian orderly in the household. The twist is that the most improbable of the three explanations turns out to be the truthful one.

Despite its intriguing device, the play failed to exploit its potentialities. "Clumsy, mildly entertaining," was Robert Littell's concise view.

HOUSEBOAT ON THE STYX, THE [Musical/Fantasy/Death/Period] B: Kenneth Webb and John E. Hazzard; M/LY: Monte Carlo and Alma Sanders; SC: stories by John Kendrick Bangs; D: Oscar Eagle; CH: Ray Perez and Chester Hale; S: Willy Pogany; C: John Booth; P: Ned Jakobs; T: Liberty Theatre; 12/25/28 (103)

A well-known group of turn-of-the-century satirical stories was turned into an operetta in which many famed historical personages, including Queen Elizabeth (Blanche Ring), Salome (Virginia Watts), Sappho (Millicent Bancroft), Ponce de Leon (Sam Ash), Shakespeare (John Osborne Clemson), and others are gathered together in Hades. When the men set up an exclusive, no-women permitted houseboat stag party, the women decide to see what's cooking there for themselves; after an adventurous conflict between Captain Kidd (John E. Hazzard) and his cohorts versus the Male Shades, the ladies are only too glad to leave the men in peace.

Time thought it "mounted to hilarity" and said, "Its songs, while not entirely novel, are cheering." But Richard Dana Skinner found it long and dull.

HOUSEPARTY [Drama/University/Youth/Sex/Crime] A: Kenneth Phillips Britton and Roy Hargrave; D: Harry Wagstaff Gribble; P: A. L. Erlanger and George C. Tyler; T: Knickerbocker Theatre; 9/9/29 (178)

A frat-house library at Williams College, Williamstown, Massachusetts, formed the background to this "streaky play, one containing some crudely effective and gripping scenes and blessed with a capacity to hold the interest until the ultimate curtain" (*Times*).

Out of the closely observed milieu emerged a tale of an easy town girl (Harriett MacGibbon), who, attempting to blackmail Alan Bradford (Roy Hargrave) for making her pregnant, is accidentally killed by him. He hides her corpse in a closet and behaves nonchalantly until his nerves begin to go. The deed is disclosed, and he is acquitted; a nervous breakdown ensues, but he is saved from suicide and prompted to seek professional help.

HOUSES OF SAND [Drama/Orientals/Race/Romance] A: G. Marion Burton; D: Daniel V. Arthur and Clifford Brooke; P: Michael Mindlin; T: Hudson Theatre; 2/17/25 (31)

The critics shelled this "unrelievedly dull" (*Times*) drama of potential miscegenation with devastating invectives. George Jean Nathan called it "awful gaga of the *East is West* variety."

With an accompaniment of offstage Puccini music to heighten its *Madame Butterfly* pathos, *Houses of Sand* studied the effects of an East-West romance between Arthur Demarest (Paul Kelly), strangely drawn toward things Oriental, and Miss Kane (Vivienne Osborne), a pidgin-English speaking maiden of Japan. Following the hindrance of the lovers' plans by their respective fathers, the youth discovers that he is the half-Nipponese offspring of a sinful liason his father, Pinkerton-like, had had with a Japanese girl, and this enables the couple to marry without fear of upsetting too many racial apple carts.

Charles Bickford made his New York debut in this play.

HOW COME? [Musical/Blacks/Prohibition] B/M/LY: Eddie Hunter; D: Sam H. Grisman; P: Criterion Productions, Inc.; T: Apollo Theatre; 4/16/23 (40)

Comedian Eddie Hunter provided the only bright spot in this seriously disapproved black musical, of which Hunter was the writer and composer. He was "an authentic funny man and far more amusing than anyone put forward in" such hit black shows as *Shuffle Along* and *Liza*, according to Heywood Broun.

What story there was concerned the attempt by one Rastus Skunkton Lime (Hunter) to cheat the Mobile Chicken Trust Corporation out of its hard-earned funds. The company's former treasurer, seeking to recoup the money thus lost, establishes a bootleg liquor setup, fronted by a shoeshine parlor. Hunter had a hilarious jail-break scene in which he went to noisy and violent lengths to carry out what he believed a clever escape plan only to learn that his jailer was deaf and blind.

HOWDY, KING [Comedy/Western/Politics/Romance] A: Mark Swan; D: Clifford Brooke; P: Anne Nichols; T: Morosco Theatre; 12/13/26 (48)

A far-fetched, although sometimes comical, farce that was notable more because *Abie's Irish Rose* author Anne Nichols produced it than for its intrinsic merit. It told the story of an American cowboy rancher Johnny North (Minor Watson), who visits Europe to sell horses, falls in love with an American tourist (Harriett MacGibbon), and becomes king of the Graustarkian kingdom of Eldorado when his relationship to the late leader there is revealed. He becomes embroiled in palace politics, including being made chief of the revolutionists, and helps establish a republic to supercede the outmoded monarchy.

George Jean Nathan called it "a trashy comedy...aimed at the boob box-office with a cannon," but Richard Dana Skinner thought "it all comes off with a sure touch and some excellent satire."

HOW'S YOUR HEALTH? [Comedy/Illness/Romance/Friendship] A: Booth Tarkington and Harry Leon Wilson; D: R. H. Burnside; S: Cirker and Robbins; P: Lyle D. Andrews and R. H. Burnside; T: Vanderbilt Theatre; 11/26/29 (46)

A pleasant although slight farce about a hypochondriac, Lawrence Satterleigh (Roy Atwell), whose friends Sam Catterson (Herbert Corthell) and Dr. Pepper (Donald Brian) inveigle him into going to a party to take his mind off his worries but where he proceeds to frighten all of the guests into numerous fears for their health and very lives; especially scared are the two scoffers who originally got him to attend the party. Meanwhile, the love of a young lady he meets (Virginia O'Brien) restores the original imaginary invalid to booming health.

"The plot...is of the slightest, the play itself lacks body, and the humor, though side-splitting at times, wanes too often," wrote Euphemia Van Rensselaer Wyatt.

HUMAN NATURE [Drama/Marriage/Literature/Sex/Romance] A: J. C. and Elliott Nugent; D: J. C. Nugent and Frederick Stanhope; S: Joseph Urban; P: Gene Buck; T: Liberty Theatre; 9/24/25 (4)

The father-son team of playwrights, J. C. and Elliott Nugent, came a cropper with this major disaster to which the opening night audience "objected...sharply, and laughed at the most poignant passages" (*Time*). "The acting, the direction, the settings were superb," declared Alan Dale, but the play was poor fish, "herring on a golden platter."

Bess Flanders (Mary Duncan), would-be novelist, marries aging novelist Mr. Hale (Brandon Tynan) for his intellectual stimulation, when she learns that the young and handsome Jim Trayne (John Marston) is already wed. Upon meeting

Jim again several years later, when his wife (Sue MacManamy) has become an invalid, her passion erupts and they have an affair, leading to her pregnancy. They separate, though, each to bear their burdens, and old Hale agrees to raise the baby as his own.

The play, originally called *Gunpowder*, failed to explode.

HUMBLE, THE [Dramatic Revival] A: Laurence Irving; SC: Dostoievsky's novel *Crime and Punishment*; D: Bertram Forsyth; S: Livingston Platt; P: Carl Reed; T: Greenwich Village Theatre (OB); 10/13/26 (21)

First produced in New York in 1908 as *Crime and Punishment*, this was an adaptation of the great Russian novel of that name. E. H. Sothern had then played Raskolnikoff. An even earlier version, *Rodion the Student*, by C. H. Meltzer had been a Richard Mansfield vehicle. Basil Sydney now essayed the difficult role of the atheistic philosophical student who kills an evil man (David Landau), believing in the justice of ridding society of oppressive persons, but is tracked down and imprisoned. The play retained some of its power and interest and offered various players fine opportunities for their talents. Brooks Atkinson commented, "In spite of much theatricalism and oratory in the construction of the play, [it] still sputters occasionally with creepy emotion." The gruelling inquisition scene in which the student is given the third degree by the magistrate Bezak, brilliantly played by Sidney Greenstreet, was the production's highlight. Mary Ellis was spiritually noble as Sonia.

HUMBUG, THE [Drama/Sex/Science] A/D: Max Marcin; S: P. Dodd Ackerman; P: Flintmar Productions, Inc.; T: Ambassador Theatre; 11/27/29 (13)

Hypnotism was the subject of this play, which *Time* said "quavers between melodrama and advanced psychology with notable contributions to neither." Hypnotist Dr. Alexis Collender (John Halliday) uses his technique to gain the favors of his women subjects. The plot reveals him wielding his power over two such victims (Kay Strozzi and Eleanor Griffith) in his attempt to win a place in the Academy for the Advancement of Science and Art. His application is opposed by the husband (Paul Harvey) and fiancé (King Calder) of these women, and one of them manages to turn the quack's devices against him and to shoot him fatally.

HUMMING BIRD, THE [Comedy/War] A: Maude Fulton; D: Robert Ober; P: Frank Egan; T: Ritz Theatre; 1/15/23 (40)

Former vaudevillian Maude Fulton had starred in one Broadway play before 1923, *The Brat*, a 1917 hit that was the product of her own pen. She could not duplicate the feat in her fatuous comedy *The Humming Bird*.

In the role of Toinette, "The Humming Bird," Fulton impersonated a young Parisian Apache (she seemed, at thirty-seven, too old for the role) who, to escape her past, has gone to New York, where for three years she has kept house for a starving artist (Robert Ober) and a cub reporter (Andrew Mack). Another

Apache, the brutal Charlot (Walter Wills), has trailed her here; although he presents a fierce demeanor, he turns out to be after her not for foul purposes but because she is to be decorated by the French government for getting fifty Apaches to join the fray at Chateau Thierry when Paris was threatened by the Boche.

The show's glowing moment was a second-act Apache dance, but for the rest, it "lagged boringly," "lacked coherence . . . and failed to interest," declared the *Sun*.

HUMORESQUE [Comedy-Drama/Music/War/Family/Jews] A: Fannie Hurst; D: J. Hartley Manners; T: Vanderbilt Theatre; 2/27/23 (31)

One of the most unusual roles ever played by Laurette Taylor was that of Sarah Kantor, the poverty-ridden Lower East Side Jewish mother, who, in Fannie Hurst's maudlin play, sacrifices the best years of her life so that her son Leon (Luther Adler) can achieve fame as a violinist. This Leon does, but when the war arrives, he packs his musical instrument away and leaves his mother to enter the fray.

Of the "inconclusive" (Alexander Woollcott) drama, based on a Hurst story and already seen as a film, the critics had not much worthwhile to say. Heywood Broun denoted it as "certainly not a good play. The detail throughout is rich, the dialogue often superb both in its humor and its tang." But Leon's character seemed implausible, and the play was repetitious, said Broun.

Commentary concentrated on the enormous skill of the star's interpretation. Taylor had prepared by spending days sitting in a Bronx tailorshop run by Russian Jews, observing their mannerisms and dialect. Despite the presence of a largely Jewish cast, she seemed to Woollcott, "more Jewish than any of them."

HUNDRED YEARS OLD, A (Papa Juan) [Comedy/Romance/Old Age/Family/Spanish] A: Serafín and Joaquín Álvarez Quintero; AD: Helen and Harley Granville-Barker; D/S: James Whale; P: Gilbert Miller; T: Lyceum Theatre; 10/1/29 (39)

Veteran star Otis Skinner, seventy-one, enacted beautifully the principal role of the beloved 100-year-old Papa Juan in this sentimental, leisurely, and well-liked Spanish comedy. Papa Juan, preparing to celebrate his centennial, insists that the entire large family, warts and all, be invited to his birthday party. This allows various interestingly observed characters to appear; the play takes more time detailing their idiosyncracies than in constructing a developed story. A romance arises between two of his great-grandchildren when Papa Juan expresses his wish for great-great descendents.

This simple play was "a series of genre pictures, memorable for their truth and beauty rather than for their intensity of emotion or tenseness of situation," said Euphemia Van Rensselaer Wyatt, who observed an almost total lack of conflict in the play.

HUNKY DORY [Comedy/Romance/Scottish] A/D: Macdonald Watson; P: Marc Klaw, Inc.; T: Klaw Theatre; 9/4/22 (49)

A Scottish comedy, seen previously in London and Montreal, that charmed several critics, despite having "what is probably the worst plot of the last ten years" (*Times*).

Set in a Scottish lowland town, the whimsical piece was named after its wastrel hero, an admirer of John Barleycorn, whose ingenuity is expended in avoiding any sort of labor. The plot deals with romantic complications concerning the widow Macfayden (Frances Ross Campbell); the bootmaker Specky Todd (Robert Drysdale); the plumber who wants to be an artist, Peter Maguffie (Macdonald Watson); Specky's adopted and Hunky's actual daughter Jenny (Nell Barker); and the wealthy, young David Low (F. Manning Sproston). Numerous contrivances and coincidences are used to carry out and conclude the story, and all ends satisfactorily.

Farce, pathos, and melodramatics were spicily mixed together in this modest import. The *Telegraph* said it was "Fresh, clean and wholesome as a brisk heather scented breeze."

HURRICANE [Drama/Family/Prostitution/Business/Romance] A: Olga Petrova; S: Olga Petrova and Clifford Pember; P: Richard Herndon; T: Frolic Theatre; 12/25/23 (125)

"Glum and interesting play made eventful by the fact that Olga Petrova acts away for dear life in it," wrote Alexander Woollcott of the actress-playwright's vehicle. Petrova's character stabs her tyrannical Russian immigrant father to protect her invalid mother and to escape a forced marriage. Fleeing with a white slaver, she becomes a prostitute in Kansas City and moves East to win success as an interior decorator. Although courted by two men who know her history, she kills herself when a disease from her past manifests itself.

George Jean Nathan thought the play was a compendium of Broadway hokum: "The exhibit is a post-graduate study in the star actress play of commerce." Alexander Woollcott commented, "It is a shrewd, blunt, aggressively feministic tragedy, and yet the author of it, instead of stamping on in square toed shoes, takes her minor curtain calls drooping all over the less expensive members of the troupe like a specially draped lambriquin. . . . Nay, the same perversities run through the whole performance like shoddy in silk."

H.H.

HUSH MONEY [Drama/Crime/Romance] A: Alfred G. Jackson and Mann Page; D: William B. Friedlander; P. Charles K. Gordon; T: Forty-ninth Street Theatre; 3/15/26 (56)

Justine Johnstone was a former Ziegfeld girl attempting to make a career as a legitimate actress with her role in this play. *Time* wrote of her: "Miss Johnstone is the most beautiful blond leading woman in the land. She is not the best actress, but she is easily good enough for this inconspicuous little crook play."

The piece was based on an actual jewel theft of which coauthor Jackson learned in his capacity as a journalist. It dealt with the struggle of reformed crook Harry Bentley (Kenneth Thomson) to overcome the negative feelings of others about his past and to marry an upper-class girl (Johnstone). He is framed for the robbery of a pearl necklace but manages to clear himself and to foil the crooks responsible, one of whom is the investigating detective. He marries the girl at the end.

I

I WANT MY WIFE [Comedy/Romance/Legacy/Family] A: B. M. Kaye; D: Ralph Murphy; S: P. Dodd Ackerman; P: Murray Phillips; T: Liberty Theatre; 3/20/30 (12)

An egregiously outmoded farce having to do with bachelor Alfred Towder (Herbert Yost), who stands to earn a million-dollar legacy if he marries, and whose sister Cecilia (Spring Byington) tries to operate on his susceptible mind by drugging him, so that when he awakes he will think he is wed to Janet Macauley (Patricia Barclay). The plan backfires, however, when Alfred's actual bride, whom he married during an amnesiac spell in Philadelphia, turns up.

"The various states of unconsciousness and semi-consciousness experienced by the hero of the entertainment are shared, unfortunately, by the audience," wrote *Time*.

I WILL IF YOU WILL [Comedy/Mystery/Crime] A: Crane Wilbur; D: Mrs. Lillian Trimble Bradley; P: George Broadhurst; T: Comedy Theatre; 8/29/22 (15)

This play was a combination bedroom farce and mystery comedy set on New Year's Eve in a fashionable three-room hotel suite with seven doors promptly set to swinging open and slamming shut. It embodies "just about all of the conventional mechanics of this type of play," jeered Q.M.

The "incredibly dull" piece (*Times*) was about the theft from the suite of a $30,000 necklace belonging to the young wife (Leila Frost) of a soused husband (William Roselle) during a New Year's Eve party, the wife's culpability in the crime, the wild search by all concerned for the missing gems, the revelation that the thief is a female detective (Lilyan Tashman), and the involvement in the action of a handsome young fellow (Edmund Lowe), presumed to be the thief, but actually a rich gent in search of some thrills.

ICEBOUND [Drama/Legacy/Romance/Rural/Family] A: Owen Davis; D: Sam Forrest; P: Sam H. Harris; T: Sam H. Harris Theatre; 2/10/23 (170)

One of several notable dramas by the productive Owen Davis that demonstrated his skill at quality playwriting after a feverish career of writing cheap melodramas. Its virtues were recognized by its being chosen by Burns Mantle as a Best Play of the Year, and by its being the 1922–1923 Pulitzer Prize winner. Considered slightly inferior to his recent *Detour*, it nevertheless appealed more effectively to Broadway audiences and finished with a handsome total of 170 performances.

Reviews were mixed for this "vivid and biting study of a New England family" (Playgoer), the Jordans, a clan with their emotions encased in blocks of ice. John Craig said the play "ought to be called a bit of grim genre painting, rather than drama, drawn with a bold hand and sharply etched with the acids of biting satire," but Heywood Broun considered it frequently false, contrived, and implausible, "a mixture of things fine and things shoddy." Disagreeing, Charles Darnton wrote that "It is bleak realism warmed by romance, narrow as the life it depicts, yet human and interesting with genuinely affecting moments."

Davis disclosed the waiting of a family of greedy, selfish Jordan survivors for the offstage death of tightfisted old Grandma Jordan, so that they may learn what she has left them in her will. The good, old lady has expected their greedy response and has left her estate to a ward, Jane (Phyllis Povah), who nursed her for six years, the girl being requested in the will to use the money to regenerate the wastrel grandson Ben (Robert Ames), an arsonist under indictment. Ben goes to work for Jane on the farm in return for her signing his bail bond, but when she discovers another girl (Boots Wooster) in his arms, she is ready to grant him the property and leave. Ben eventually learns how much Jane really loves him and decides to marry her. Meanwhile, the action shows how the mean-spirited Jordans have been trying to cheat Jane of her legacy.

In his book *I'd Like to Do It Again*, Owen Davis wrote that famed producer David Belasco had wanted to do this play. When Belasco couldn't promise the impatient author an immediate production, the latter gave copies of the manuscript to three other producers the same Friday morning, insisting that they could have it only if they agreed by Monday noon to buy it. That same day he ran into vaudeville producer Max Gordon, partner of Al Lewis, a pair seeking to branch out into legitimate theatre production. Gordon persuaded Davis to let him read the last copy of *Icebound*, which he spied in Davis's pocket. On Sunday morning, Gordon informed the playwright that he and Al Lewis were going to produce the drama as silent partners in association with Sam Harris. When, on Monday, every producer to whom Davis had offered the script called to accept it, Davis had to tell them it was already spoken for. He confessed, "[I]t took me about five years to square myself."

IDLE INN, THE [Dramatic Revival] A: Peretz Hirshbein; AD: Isaac Goldberg and Louis Wolheim; D/P: Arthur Hopkins; S: Robert Edmond Jones; T: Plymouth Theatre; 12/20/21 (25)

Jacob Ben-Ami was being hailed as one of the great actors of his time when he appeared in this misbegotten adaptation of Hirshbein's Yiddish folk play in the original of which he had distinguished himself when it was played two years earlier by the Yiddish Art Theatre. A promising company was crushed under the weight of a poorly staged and ineptly translated play that was almost completely deficient in just those powerful, haunting, tragicomic peasant qualities possessed by its previous production. Large amounts were cut, including all of the fourth act, and the peasant idiom was pruned. As Stark Young noted, "The rich flavor is sponged down, the violence and racy abandon halved....The emotional rhythm of the scenes is slowed up and often sterilized."

The Idle Inn is a Romeo and Juliet-type story of misguided parental influence in a daughter's choice of husbands. Set in a Russian village, it recounts the love story of the womanizing, swaggering, and passionate horse thief Eisik (Ben-Ami) and his docile cousin Maite (Eva MacDonald), who is betrothed against her will to the mealy-mouthed Mendel (Edward G. Robinson). At the wedding feast Eisik shows up and steals the bride away by arranging to occupy the superstitious minds of the others with strange effects. Eisik and Maite are sought for in the woods, but when they are found at last, a mystical power prevents them from being separated.

IF [Comedy/Adventure/Fantasy/British] A: Lord Dunsany; M: Edmond Rickett; D: Agnes Morgan; S: Aline Bernstein; P: Actor-Managers i/a/w Sidney Ross; T: Little Theatre; 10/25/27 (23)

A new troupe made up of many former Neighborhood Playhouse actors and directed by a former *doyenne* of the Grand Street theatre produced Lord Dunsany's dream-comedy half a dozen years after its London staging. The play was a "pleasantly whimsical theme while it remains in the realm of fantasy," decided Perriton Maxwell, "but when it deals with the more Shavian bits of philosophy the little comedy becomes a bit top-heavy and assumes the form of a leaden object balancing itself on a balloon in mid-air."

Its fable was that of stuffily proper Englishman John Beal (Walter Kingsford), who, offered a magic crystal with which he can relive the past, travels back ten years in time and takes a train he had missed only to have it lead him into adventures in far-flung Persia, where he becomes a mighty but pompous potentate whose rule is eventually overthrown. Threatened with murder by his enemies, he awakes and finds himself secure in his dull, conventional British world.

IF I WAS RICH [Comedy/Marriage] A/D: William Anthony McGuire; SC: a short story by Clyde North and J. B. Rethy; T: Mansfield Theatre; 9/2/26 (92)

A shakily built, derivative, yet generally amusing, slangy comedy about a poor shipping clerk, Jimmy Sterling (Joe Laurie, Jr.), married to a spendthrift (Mildred MacLeod), who persuades her mate to pass himself off as a Brazilian rubber-plantation owner's heir as a way of ingratiating himself with supposedly wealthy folk who can advance his status. The ploy backfires, the wife nearly succumbs to the advances of her boss, the rich man to whom Jimmy lied turns out to be broke, and only a reversion to an honesty-is-the-best-policy standard gets the characters out of hot water.

The author "neither devised telling situations nor deftly exploited them," believed Arthur Hornblow, and Brooks Atkinson took issue with its "false sentimentalities and hackneyed conceptions."

IF THE RABBI WANTS (Vos der Rebe Vil) [Musical/Religion/Spiritualism/ Jews/Romance/Yiddish/Yiddish Language] B/LY: N. Stuchkoff; M: A. Ellstein; D/P: Ludwig Satz; CH: Francis "Bunny" Weldon; S: Alex Chertoff; T: Yiddish Folks Theatre (OB); 12/22/29

A "Chassidic operetta" that was in effect a burlesque on Chassidic practices and on the ritual of exorcising dybbuks. Ludwig Satz played a doctor who was forced out of town when he fell in love with the daughter of a devout man and who turned to doing exorcisms for a living. When (his true identity being unknown) he is called on to exorcise a dybbuk from his own former sweetheart the day she is to wed a rabbi's son, he pretends that the spirit possessing her is that of the departed doctor and thereby arranges to marry her himself. They elope before the father can stop them.

The audience enjoyed this "farcical caricature of Chassidism, mildly seasoned with bawdiness, in no uncertain terms," reported the *Times*.

IF WINTER COMES [Drama/Marriage/War/Trial/British/Romance] A: A.S.M. Hutchinson and B. Macdonald Hastings; SC: A.S.M. Hutchinson's novel of the same name; P: Charles Dillingham; T: Gaiety Theatre; 4/2/23 (40)

Over half a million copies had been sold of A.S.M. Hutchinson's novel *If Winter Comes* before it found its way to the stage. The title had become a popular catchword in England, where the play was first produced. Its New York reception, like that in London, was cool.

Dramatizing a lengthy novel is a problem that has defeated many playwrights. This was one of those occasions. Too much of the book had to be omitted for it to become a cohesive, consistently compelling play. Heywood Broun reported that the adaptation was drawn "largely out of the melodramatic material which came at the fag end of the book."

Cyril Maude played the noble, patriotic, Quixotic leading role of Mark Sabre, a man of the lower middle classes, who leaves his disgruntled wife (Mabel Terry-Lewis) to go to war to fight for civilization and returns from combat wounded. He takes in young Effie Bright (Peggy Rush), mother of an illegitimate child, but loses Mrs. Sabre as a result. While he is away Effie swallows poison and Mark must undergo third-degree questioning in a courtroom scene to determine his complicity in the affair. Various melodramatic developments occur, Mark's position in the community is salvaged, and he and Lady Tybar (Lydia Bilbrooke) are united.

I'LL SAY SHE IS [Revue] B/LY: Will B. Johnstone; M: Tom Johnstone; D: Eugene Sanger; CH: Vaughn Godfrey; P: James P. Beury; T: Casino Theatre; 5/19/24 (313)

Famous as vaudevillians, the four Marx Brothers left the Keith Circuit, which tried to hold them, to appear in this Broadway revue. Of the first night audience, the *Times* critic noted that both those familiar and unfamiliar with the Brothers' antics "joined equally in the boisterous laughter. Such shouts of merriment have not been heard in the Casino these many years." Percy Hammond found the show funny but not special except for the Brothers, who made up "a comic carnival." In addition to the Marx quartet, Q.M. mentioned a half-nude Apache dance and lovelier chorus girls than were even necessary considering the "hilarious nonsense all evening." Lotta Miles was cited as a good singer and great beauty.

The twenty-four scene revue had a slight story line in which Beauty (Lotta Miles) seeks thrills. Her trip to a Chinatown opium den (where the Apache dance takes place) leads to a charge of murder, on which Groucho defends her. Dabbling in hypnosis lands Beauty in a dream sequence in which she is Josephine, Groucho is Napoleon, and his three brothers are Josephine's lovers. In one sequence, Groucho was Napoleon, in another he was Cinderella.

Groucho and Harpo received the most praise, Q.M. commenting that there must have been a time when Ed Wynn and Leon Errol gave such promise to the comic stage.

                                                                        H.H.

ILLUSIONISTE, L' (The Illusionist) [Comedy/Romance/Show Business/ French/French Language] A/D: Sacha Guitry; P: A. H. Woods; T: Chanin's Forty-sixth Street Theatre; 1/10/27 (16)

The visiting French company led by the Guitrys put on this fresh satirical romantic comedy of 1917 to general approval. Sacha played the vaudeville magician Teddy Brooks to the Miss Hopkins, a presumably English entertainer, of his wife, Yvonne Printemps. Actually, Miss Hopkins knows only two words of English, although her songs are sung in that tongue. A failure to communicate marks the pair's first encounter, he thinking her English, she thinking the same of him. He pays court to another woman (J. Leclerc), but his promises are mere illusions; a quarrel develops, and he happily returns to Miss Hopkins, their language barriers soon crumbling to dust.

The Guitrys were accomplished players of such frothy material. First Nighter wrote, "[H]ere is a piece which is pure [French] comedy...but handled as the Guitrys do it, there is nothing to offend the most prudish."

IMAGINARY INVALID, THE (Le malade imaginaire) [Dramatic Revival] A: Moliere; D: Mr. and Mrs. Charles Coburn; P: Mr. and Mrs. Coburn in cooperation with the Departments of English and Comparative Literature and

Romance Languages and the Institute of Arts and Sciences of Columbia University; T: University Gymnasium (OB); 7/25/22 (4)

A mixed company of amateurs and professionals essayed Moliere's comedy with Charles Coburn and his wife playing Argan and Toinette and directing the effort. The staging was in honor of the Moliere tercentenary; it proved a surprisingly amusing production, and the play, said the *Times*, was "still a vigorous piece." "Mr. Coburn made a blowzy, blundering invalid, playing true to his part, apparently, and certainly giving the spectators a broad comedy treat," noted the *Times*.

IMMODEST VIOLET [Comedy/Southern/Romance/Sex/Youth/Politics] A: David Carb; D: John Cromwell; P: William A. Brady; T: Forty-eighth Street Theatre; 8/24/20 (1)

A single matinee performance doomed this not-especially horrendous first play to quick oblivion. Reminiscent of both *Hindle Wakes* and *Lightnin'*, it told of an audacious heroine, Violet Rose (Marie Goff), who desires to attend a woman's suffrage convention in Texas. This leads her to being discovered in a compromising situation with the shy bookkeeper Arthur Bodkin (Kenneth MacKenna) to whose room she goes in search of a loan for carfare. They run off, and Arthur gets into trouble for violation of the Mann Act, as he has crossed the state border with Violet in tow. He is acquitted when Violet convinces the jury that "to the pure all things are pure."

Immodest Violet is the earliest play of the decade to deal, if only parenthetically, with the subject of woman's suffrage, which had only recently been enacted as the Nineteenth Amendment to the Constitution. The play, wrote Kenneth Macgowan, may have been "better suited for some local theatre, than for the competition of Broadway." However, Alexander Woollcott thought it was superior to a lot of the plays then running.

IMMORAL ISABELLA [Comedy/Period/Spain/Romance/Marriage] A: Lawton Campbell; D: Mabel Brownell; S: Watson Barratt; P: Chamberlain Brown; T: Bijou Theatre; 10/27/27 (60)

A historical satire compared in tone to the more successful *Road to Rome* of Sherwood. Modern slang came forth from famous characters of the past, namely, Queen Isabella of Spain (Frances Starr); King Ferdinand (Reginald Mason), who wore a nightshirt through most of the proceedings; and Christopher Columbus (Julius McVicker), among others. Columbus and Isabella are lovers, and Columbus has been sent on his voyage to the New World by Ferdinand to get rid of him. Returned in triumph, and still hot for the Queen, he is once more dispatched by her royal spouse. References to "the Knights of Columbus" and "Columbus Circle" were the sort of anachronisms on which the piece thrived.

Brooks Atkinson insisted that the piece was "fairly transparent and the wit exploded with the dull boom of the 'wise-crack.' " Frances Starr, said Perriton Maxwell, was wasted in "a dreary evening of banalities."

IMMORTAL THIEF, THE [Drama/Period/Prostitution/Crime/Religion] A: Tom Barry; M: Elliot Schenck; D/P: Walter Hampden; S: Claude Bragdon; C: Ami Mali Hicks; T: Hampden's Theatre; 10/2/26 (25)

A humorless, dignified, episodic, religious spectacle drama set in Jerusalem and cast with Walter Hampden in the role of one of the two thieves who died at Calvary with Christ. The pageantry elements were present in full scale, with a large, colorfully dressed cast of biblical characters; the seriousness of the undertaking could not be faulted. However, Tom Barry's too-literary play was not very stageworthy and "seemed to be merely a rather stagey melodrama, ill-becoming its incidental chronicle of the Crucifixion," wrote the *Times*.

Hampden played Marius Rufinus, cruel gang leader, whose love for a prostitute (Edith Barrett) leads him to sacrifice himself for her sake when she kills, in self-defense, a wicked brothel keeper (Robert Paton Gibbs); having been redeemed by this act, he achieves eternal salvation and dies on the cross.

"[T]o many the play seemed more of pulpit than theatre," announced *Time*.

IMPORTANCE OF BEING EARNEST, THE [Dramatic Revival] A: Oscar Wilde; D: Dudley Digges; P: Actors' Theatre; T: Comedy Theatre; 5/3/26 (64)

A not-particularly distinguished revival that served its purpose well enough. The play itself "revealed once more its brittle and unsubstantial, yet often corruscating qualities" (Arthur Hornblow). The critical reaction to the mounting varied, but no one was excited. John Mason Brown believed the playing was too realistic. He thought only the Cecily (Patricia Collinge) and Gwendolyn (Haroldine Humphreys) scenes had the proper quality of "frank unreality and...persuasive make-believe." Brooks Atkinson thought Dudley Digges's staging had moments of extraneous comic business and that the playing was externally self-conscious. Digges was an effective Chasuble, Lucile Watson a competent Lady Bracknell, Vernon Steele an intelligent John Worthing, and Reginald Owen a polished Algernon.

IMPROVISATIONS IN JUNE (Improvisationem im Juni) [Comedy/Romance/Family/German] A: Max Mohr; AD: Susan Behn and Cecil Lewis; D: Eva Le Gallienne; DS: Aline Bernstein; P: Civic Repertory Company; T: Civic Repertory Theatre (OB); 2/26/28 (14)

This play had been enormously popular in Germany but failed to snare attention in New York. The Civic Rep company gave it "a rather ratty performance," sneered Alexander Woollcott.

Meant as a satire on the excesses of American plutocracy in postwar Europe, the offbeat allegorical comedy concerned a pompous American Croesus (Walter Beck), who thinks money is the answer to all problems. His misunderstood son (John Eldridge) finds sympathizers among the Old World folk he meets at a Salzburg castle purchased by his father; they despise the materialism of the machine-crazed world. The son triumphs over his depression when an improvisational comedian's (Egon Brecher) daughter (Josephine Hutchinson) leads him to realize that he must not get trapped by the degenerate values of those like his father but must find salvation through personal integrity.

The play's mixture of expressionism and realism was unusual, but it was doomed by an inept production. Still, Richard Dana Skinner admired it as "an allegory of the modern world, where faith rests only in humanity, and evil only in the passions of men."

A single additional performance was given on 11/10/28.

IN A GARDEN [Comedy/Theatre/Romance/Marriage] A: Philip Barry; D/P: Arthur Hopkins; S: Robert Edmond Jones; T: Plymouth Theatre; 11/16/25 (73)

This wordy high comedy was too tenuously hung upon a metaphysical substructure to satisfy the critics; apart from Laurette Taylor's beautiful acting as the wife, it attracted few compliments.

The play envisioned a successful dramatist Adrian Terry (Frank Conroy), whose modeling of his female characters upon his wife has made her neurotically concerned with the meaning of all of her actions. Adrian is stimulated by a friend's remark that "every wife is the mistress of another man in her heart" to test it as the premise for a new work. He establishes the external conditions that prevailed when his wife and a certain ex-lover (Louis Calhern) first met but is shocked at his wife's apparently revived romantic feelings. Apprised of the deception, the wife departs to seek the life of spontaneity her marriage has denied her.

Barry was accused of verbosity and mechanical plotting. Gilbert W. Gabriel dubbed the play "a labored exploitation of meager and dispirited material." However, Alexander Woollcott supported the piece, finding it "searching, subtle, and brushed with a kind of gentle graciousness of its own."

On the play's opening night, Laurette Taylor embarrassed and angered her author and producer by making a curtain speech, saying, "Perhaps our playwright isn't ready yet. Perhaps we did a disservice to his brilliant talent by producing him too soon."

IN ABRAHAM'S BOSOM [Drama/Blacks/Southern/Race/Rural/Marriage/Family] A: Paul Green; D: Jasper Deeter; S: Cleon Throckmorton; P: Provincetown Players; T: Provincetown Playhouse (OB); 12/30/26 (200)

Paul Green's look at the lives of rural North Carolina blacks, his first play staged in New York, won the Pulitzer Prize (and was also a Best Play selection). When first produced, Off Broadway, it was not much thought of by most reviewers; when it later developed that it was under consideration for the Pulitzer, instead of closing because of small houses, it was moved (in February 1927) to Broadway's Garrick Theatre, where it received better notices but did not live long. Following its garnering the prize in May, it reopened Off Broadway for six weeks and was revived there on 9/6/27 for seventy-seven extra performances. Its February opening had been marked by the assumption of the leading role by understudy Frank Wilson when Jule Bledsoe was fired for failing to appear. Wilson's notices were outstanding.

The award itself was controversial, and there were many who thought it a poor selection, given the competition. An unusual choice because of its racial content and regional origins, Green's "folk tragedy" proved to have a potent force, riddled with effective comedy and elevated by poetic beauty but to be marred by its polemics, its length, and its faulty construction. It tells of Abraham McCranie (Bledsoe), the illegitimate son of a white plantation owner (L. Rufus Hill) and a black woman, who fights all opposition, including that of his white half-brother Lonnie (H. Ben Smith), in his burning desire to educate the illiterate black workers. He loses his job after beating one of his students in a fit of frustration and moves with his wife, Goldie (Rose McClendon), to the city where his son (R. J. Huey) becomes a petty criminal. Moving back to the country to resume his teaching career, he is forced to confront the angry local whites, is sorely taunted by Lonnie, kills him, and is gunned down by a vengeful mob.

Representative of those supporting the work was Brooks Atkinson, who wrote, "*In Abraham's Bosom* glows with the purging white flame of authentic, tragic character study." Richard Dana Skinner remarked, "Few plays of recent times have stripped the tortured soul of a man so bare, few have shown the same exaltation of humble heroism." But Joseph Wood Krutch found it not much more than "highly interesting prentice work," and Stark Young, agreeing that it was "moving and profound," faulted its dialogue as "flat and...hastily written."

In Abraham's Bosom was inspired by an incident in Paul Green's boyhood (told in detail in Ward Morehouse's *Matinee Tomorrow*), when he saw a dignified black schoolteacher who had alighted from a train struck across the cheek, viciously and without cause, by a cane in the hands of an engineer.

IN HIS ARMS [Comedy/Family/Romance] A: Lynn Starling; D: Guthrie McClintic; P: Sam H. Harris; T: Fulton Theatre; 10/13/24 (40)

A antiquated play with pretentions to being a drawing-room comedy that was headed by a cast of top-drawer performers, with comedienne Margaret Lawrence in the leading role. George Jean Nathan termed the opus "a vulgar sentimental farce," and Robert Littell turned it down as "A mediocre and wooden piece."

Elise (Lawrence), very shortly to wed the lumpish artist Ernest (Geoffrey Kerr), meets a sentimental Dutchman, Tom van Ruysen (Vernon Steele), and falls in love with him. The action of the play charts her gradual separation from the prudish Ernest and attachment to Tom in the day or two before the wedding, culminating in her decision before the final curtain falls to marry the Hollander. The title comes from her answer to the question she is asked at the end, regarding where she intends to spend her honeymoon.

(1) IN LOVE WITH LOVE [Comedy/Romance] A: Vincent Lawrence; D: Robert Milton; S: Livingston Platt; C: Gilbert Clark; P: William Harris, Jr.; T: Ritz Theatre; 8/6/23 (122)

Lynn Fontanne gained raves for her role as a girl who finally admits that she was "in love with love" when she accepted an engagement ring from an older suitor (Robert Strange) while also toying with a shy pursuer (Henry Hull), whose friend (Ralph Morgan) encouraged his suit. The girl realizes that she truly loves the friend and chases him in Act Three.

Heywood Broun commended the girl's initiation of a love scene as daring to flaunt the theory that audiences don't like the female to pursue and to propose and found this play better than Lawrence's previous *Two Fellows and a Girl*. John Corbin thought Lawrence's character drawing skillful and his sense of what was theatrically effective unfailing.

H.H.

(2) [Dramatic Revival] D/P: Joseph Shea; T: Cosmopolitan Theatre; 5/14/28 (8)

An unheralded revival featuring Miriam Meehan in the Lynne Fontanne role, Percy Helton in the Henry Hull role, Philip Tonge in the Robert Strange role, and Brandon Tynan in the Ralph Morgan role.

IN THE CLAWS OF LIFE (Livet ivold) [Comedy/Theatre/Sex/Marriage/Russian Language/Norwegian] A: Knut Hamsun; M: Ilya Sats; D: Vladimir Nemirovich-Danchenko; S: Ivan Gremislavsky; P: F. Ray Comstock and Morris Gest; T: Jolson's Fifty-ninth Street Theatre; 11/29/23 (3)

Critics praised Chekhov's widow, Olga Knipper-Chekhova, for her portrayal of an actress with a checkered past and an elderly doting husband. Concerned with the actress's love affairs with a South American playboy and a temperamental lieutenant, the 1910 play was by Norwegian novelist Knut Hamsun, who won the Nobel Prize for literature in 1920. Noting that, for the first time in the Moscow Art Theatre's New York appearances, the producers had not provided critics with a translation of the play, John Corbin thought it was difficult to understand. The *Telegram's* reviewer, however, thought the piece was the most readily adaptable to the American stage among those presented by the Russians. The play was staged during the company's second visit to New York.

H.H.

IN THE NEAR FUTURE [Comedy-Drama/Medicine/Romance/Marriage] A: Abraham Goldknopf; P: Mutual Theatre Society, Inc.; T: Wallack's Theatre; 3/10/25 (3)

Produced at only three matinees, this work by a physician seemed to have been created to propound certain medical ideas of the author's. Richard Watts, Jr., on viewing this work filled with preposterous chatter about medicine, the soul, the subconscious, and the future, said, "It is perhaps the most incredibly bad play which has been seen on Broadway this past season."

Its plot dealt with a doctor's wife (Harriet Harbaugh) who tries to prevent a younger woman (Jean Madison) from marrying a man who might neglect her. To find out what the younger woman's fiancé is like, the doctor's wife gets romantically involved with him; later, under ether on her husband's operating table, she talks freely of her feelings, and the husband must decide whether to let her live or die.

IN THE NEXT ROOM [Drama/Mystery/Romance/Crime] A: Eleanor Robson and Harriet Ford; SC: *The Mystery of the Boule Cabinet*, a novel by Burton E. Stevenson; D: Guthrie McClintic; P: Winthrop Ames and Guthrie McClintic; T: Vanderbilt Theatre; 11/27/23 (164)

One coauthoress and the first-night audience of this spine-tingling melodrama excited almost as much interest as the play. Eleanor Robson had been a highly regarded actress in the previous decade, best known as the title character in Paul Armstrong's drama *Salomy Jane*. She gave up her career to marry millionaire socialite August Belmont, and on the opening night of her play the house was crowded with social celebrities.

The play opened with two murders in the home of a Washington Square art collector (Wright Kramer). Conflicts involved an American-born French duchess (Merle Maddern) fearing a divorce scandal and seeking love letters and a famous diamond necklace concealed in a Boule cabinet, a famous French cook (Claude King) who stole the Mona Lisa, a British sleuth (also Claude King), a gabby butler (George Riddell), and a terse reporter (Arthur Albertson) who pursues the mysteries and an heiress (Mary Kennedy). Most thought the play was unoriginal but highly effective and often chilling and the production excellent. James Sinnott concluded: "one of the best-played melodramas that Broadway has known in all its history. . . . Guthrie McClintic has staged *In the Next Room* with exceptional care." Percy Hammond declared, "thrill follows thrill until . . . you are . . . quite limp from quivering."

H.H.

IN THE NIGHT WATCH (La veille d'armes) [Drama/Sea/Trial/Military/War/French] A: Claude Farrère and Lucien Nepoty; AD: Michael Morton; D: Frederick Stanhope; P: Messrs. Shubert; T: Century Theatre; 1/29/21 (113)

An import from Paris via London and reminiscent, to the *Times*, of Drury Lane melodrama. The naval engagement in Act Three "with guns booming, the signal lights winking and the seamen charging up and down the companion ways through the smoke" was exciting stuff. The remainder of the offering was shoddy.

Middle-aged Commander de Corlaix (Robert Warwick), married to the young Eugenie (Jeanne Eagels), is ordered to take his cruiser into battle but has not had time to clear the ship of his wife and her lover, on board for a birthday party. He is unaware of their continued presence on the ship. The lover dies when the ship is sunk, and de Corlaix faces a court martial, but his wife comes to the rescue by confessing her marital malfeasance in order to reveal what she overheard concerning the real reason for the ship's loss.

The show was in a ragged state on opening night, and some scenes had to be left out to get the play on in time. Although most of the well-known players in the cast were wasted, Eagels was able to give "an uncommonly good performance," according to the *Times*.

INDISCRETION [Drama/Sex/Theatre/Politics/Romance/Italy] A/D/P: Myron C. Fagan; S: Eddie Eddy; T: Mansfield Theatre; 3/4/29 (40)

Margaret (Minna Gombell) and Bob (Harland Tucker), although unwed, are sharing a home together in Venice. His railroad magnate father in America is stricken ill, and Bob rushes to his bedside, promising to return. He never does. Margaret becomes a major actress over the next eighteen years. Bob, married, becomes a senator. He has believed a scandalous story about her and doesn't learn its falsity until fate once more brings them together. She learns that he did not mean to betray her and that a villain (Arthur R. Vinton), at whom the audience hissed, has done all of the dirty work. The young man Margaret desires turns out to be Bob's daughter's fiancé, and the daughter (Betty Lancaster) is revealed as her own long-lost child.

Robert Garland censured the play for a confusing, incident-strewn plot, the *Times* saw too much purple writing and obvious melodramatics, and *Time* thought it more a joke than a play.

INFINITE SHOEBLACK, THE [Drama/University/Youth/Romance/Africa/British] A: Norman MacOwan; D: Leslie Banks and Norman MacOwan; S: Leslie Banks and Rollo Wayne; P: Lee Shubert; T: Maxine Elliott's Theatre; 2/17/30 (80)

A dourly tragic drama "steeped in Carlyle mysticism and moral principle" (Brooks Atkinson), with settings in Edinburgh and Cairo, and treating of the love between the impecunious Scotch student Andrew Berwick (Leslie Banks), preparing for his actuarial exams, and the promiscuous professor's daughter Mary (Helen Menken), whom he finds on his doorstep after she has run away from home. She needs to regain her health in Spain so Andrew finances her trip by taking a bribe from someone who wishes to substitute his exam papers. He later runs into her in Cairo, where she is a general's mistress and living well on money left by an aunt. He struggles for her soul, and she renounces her legacy and way of life to marry him and live frugally, but death comes in childbirth.

This was seen as a philosophical drama, based on a Carlyle passage, contrasting the characters of two vastly opposite persons. It was "a very pretty play, a very thoughtful play, and not always an effective one," summed up Perriton Maxwell.

(1) INHERITORS [Drama/University/Politics] A: Susan Glaspell; D: James Light; S: Cleon Throckmorton; T: Greenwich Village Theatre (OB); 3/21/21 (26)

Although negatively reviewed by most of the daily critics, *Inheritors* was eventually recognized as one of the more significant American plays of the early twenties. One of the few who acknowledged its value was Ludwig Lewisohn, who said it was "the first play of the American theatre in which a strong intellect and a ripe artistic nature have grasped and set forth in human terms the central tradition and most burning problem of our national life quite justly...without acrimony or compromise.''

The play moves from 1879 to 1920 to recount the story of two midwestern farmers, Silas Morton of pioneer stock and Felix Fejevary, a Hungarian immigrant. The latter's liberal beliefs strongly influence his friend. Silas founds a college to perpetuate the liberal ideal, and this college is then seen in 1920 when the immigrant's son not only has become a conservative member of the Board of Trustees but has a son who is even more reactionary. A college professor (James Light) upholds the liberal principles but is stifled. Morton's granddaughter (Ann Harding) has similar, if even more radical, beliefs and goes to her martyrdom refusing to be gagged.

A return engagement played on 5/21/21 for seventeen showings.

(2) [Dramatic Revival] D: Eva Le Gallienne; P: Civic Repertory Theatre; T: Civic Repertory Theatre (OB); 3/7/27 (21)

Eva Le Gallienne played the supporting role of Aunt Isabel and the granddaughter's role fell to Josephine Hutchinson in this revival. Richard Dana Skinner observed that ''The weakness of the play lies in its too obvious effort to teach a lesson by the milestone method. There are too many parallels and coincidences of speech and action. And at times, too, the dialogue becomes a trifle rhetorical. But to balance this, there is a great deal of sheer poetry and an abundance of authentic feeling woven into the play, not to mention its sharp and often scathing social analysis.''

Le Gallienne's company returned to the play on 2/11/28 for seven repertory performances and on 10/26/29 for six more. There was another Civic Repertory resuscitation of *Inheritors* in 1931.

INK [Comedy-Drama/Journalism/Sex/Prohibition/Romance] A: ''Dana Watterson Greeley''; D: T. Daniel Frawley; S: Albert Bliss; P: Charles L. Wagner; T: Biltmore Theatre; 11/1/27 (15)

A familiar subject, set within the world of newspaper publishing, propelled this lame ''satiric melodrama'' of which Brooks Atkinson remarked, ''It is rambling, ill-digested entertainment.''

This ''unusually stupid, tepid and unconvincing effort'' (Lait.) was about the sanctimonious publisher (Charles Richman) of his wife's (Eleanor Woodruff) newspaper, who is having an affair with an actress (Kay Strozzi), a fast liver also carrying on with his drama critic (Robert Hyman) and a bootlegger (Brandon Evans). Scandal emerges when the actress and the other two men kill two others in a car crash shortly after she has left the publisher asleep in her bed. Inspired by the managing editor, the paper cries out for justice, and the publisher, exonerated when the bootlegger jumps from a window, loses his wife to the managing editor (William Harrigan).

''Dana Watterson Greeley'' was a pseudonym for a pair of midwestern journalists who wrote the play.

INNOCENT EYES [Revue] B: Harold Atteridge; M: Sigmund Romberg and Jean Schwartz; LY: Harold Atteridge and Tot Seymour; D: Frank Smithson; CH: Jack Mason and Seymour Felix; S: Watson Barratt; P: Messrs. Shubert; T: Winter Garden; 5/20/24 (119)

With legs valued in Paris at $50,000 each, Mistinguett was a famous French music-hall dancer when she made her Broadway debut in this revue designed for her. John Corbin described her as "an artist of stature and power. A blond of the type that led Julius Caesar to prefer the women of Gaul to the men, she has the presence of a grenadier and the commanding glance of a field marshal." Arthur Hornblow was less impressed, noting that the French star was no longer young or thrilling as a performer, but most critics agreed that she was compelling in her most famous sketch, an athletic Apache dance in which she killed the brute mistreating her after he threw her into the Seine, and she emerged soaked and enraged.

Corbin complained that the rest of the show was negligible and the humor awful, an example being Mistinguett's remark that her pearls were given her by a king and another character's reply of "Tut."

H.H.

(1) INSPECTOR GENERAL, THE (Revizor) [Dramatic Revival/Yiddish Language] A: Nikolai Gogol; D: Vladimir Viskovksy; P: Maurice Schwartz; T: Yiddish Art Theatre (OB); 10/8/22

A resoundingly successful staging in Yiddish of Gogol's satirical Russian classic of 1836 in which he ridicules the corruption of a provincial city's government. As Khlestakov, the opportunist who takes advantage of the local politicians' erroneous belief that he is the visiting inspector general come to check up on them, Maurice Schwartz found one of his most congenial roles, which he "played gracefully, humorously and with an underlying strain of gravity" (*Times*), while his "huge, hunch-backed, fumbling, red-faced" servant was brilliantly handled by Muni Weisenfreund, later known as Paul Muni. The staging was in the hands of a visiting Soviet director from the Theatre Korsch, Moscow. The *Times* thought the casting was perfect, the acting excellent, and the staging memorable.

(2) D: Maurice Schwartz; P: Classic Theatre, Inc.; T: Forty-eighth Street Theatre; 4/30/23 (8)

Maurice Schwartz restaged the play for an English-speaking company and again took the role of Khlestakov in this production, but the result was an egregious flop. The Broadway company, in which the servant Osip was played by William A. Norton, had not one actor of note other than Schwartz. Critics who had not seen it during its sixteen-week run in Yiddish wondered why its reputation was so outstanding. Heywood Broun said that, viewed against the tradition of American comedy, the play seemed "a feeble farce," and Ludwig Lewisohn thought Gogol was too dependent on mechanical comic contrivances.

John Corbin said of the acting that it was "abundantly unreal but not abundantly amusing."

INSPECTOR KENNEDY [Drama/Crime/Mystery/Romance] A: Milton Herbert Gropper and Edna Sherry; S: Cleon Throckmorton; P: William Hodge; T: Bijou Theatre; 12/20/29 (43)

An unmysterious mystery play produced as a vehicle for William Hodge, who usually wrote his own plays. He acted the title character, a police detective, brought in to solve a murder case. Perriton Maxwell observed, "when Mr. Hodge is absent from the action the play becomes a pretty dull piece of business indeed." The irascible Inspector Kennedy's job is to investigate the demise of a hated narcotics smuggler (Walter Watson), who arranged his own death so that the guilt would fall on the fiancé (Maurice Burke) of the girl (Margaret Mullen) who refused his advances. Finally, the fiancé is cleared and the culprit adduced.

INTERFERENCE [Drama/Mystery/Crime/Romance/Death/British] A: Roland Pertwee and Harold Dearden; D: Campbell Gullan; P: Gilbert Miller; T: Empire Theatre; 10/18/27 (226)

Spit and polish acting helped sustain this suave British melodrama of blackmail and murder through a seven-month run. Arthur Wontner and A. E. Matthews played the roles handled in the London hit version by Gerald Du Maurier and Herbert Marshall. Wontner was Sir John Marley, distinguished physician, whose wife (Phoebe Foster) is being blackmailed by Deborah Kane (Kathlene MacDonnell), in whose hands are the love letters she once wrote to her now supposedly dead first husband, Philip Voaze (Matthews). But Voaze is alive, although threatened by an ailment with imminent death; he poisons his former mistress Deborah and, when Sir John is about to be arrested on suspicion of the murder, turns himself over to the law with the line, "For delivery to Bow Street Station, marked 'fragile.' "

This was a sophisticated drawing-room melodrama "which prides itself on taking even its climaxes with a certain well-bred calm," smiled the *Times*. A return engagement opened for eight cut-rate performances on 5/7/28 at the Cosmopolitan Theatre with a new cast and a top price of $1.00.

INTERNATIONAL, THE [Comedy-Drama/Politics/Labor] A/D: John Howard Lawson; M: Edward A. Ziman; S: John Dos Passos; P: New Playwrights Theatre; T: New Playwrights Theatre (OB); 1/14/28 (27)

Despite the potential of this free-wheeling "play with music's" theme, Alexander Woollcott found it "almost excruciatingly uninteresting." Cast in the form of a musical comedy, Lawson's work crammed numerous contemporary topics into a compressed and episodic twenty-one scene presentation in order to satirically ridicule capitalism, imperialism, and international relations. The *Times* described the approach as "literal realism": "There is a vague background of expressionism, a constructivist stage setting, and jazz interludes in which the theme of the moment is reduced to lyric and sung by eight stenographers, or communists, or whatever they happen to be at the time.''

The controversial subject underlying the experimental work was the stirring up of an unsuccessful Communist revolution on a global scale, an uprising stemming from the economic manipulations of Wall Street financiers. Joseph Wood Krutch said it was ''sometimes painfully heavyfooted, but sometimes illuminated with...moments of uncanny power.'' Franchot Tone and Eduard Franz were in the cast.

INTERNATIONAL REVIEW, THE [Revue] B: Nat Dorfman and Lew Leslie; M: Jimmy McHugh; LY: Dorothy Fields; D: Edward Clarke Lilley; CH: Busby Berkeley and Harry Crosley; S: Anthony W. Street; P: Lew Leslie; T: Majestic Theatre; 2/25/30 (95)

A lot of effort and cash (more than $200,000) was expended on this colorful revue, but *Time* exclaimed that it was ''in general gaudy, vulgar and provides little opportunity for the best efforts of its talent.'' Standing out was a dramatic dance number set in Montmartre and featuring Anton Dolin, formerly of the Ballets Russe, as a murderous Apache; Dorothy Fields and Jimmy McHugh's great songs ''Sunny Side of the Street'' and ''Exactly Like You,'' both sung by Gertrude Lawrence; a moving rendition of ''Pagliacci'' by Italian opera singer Radaelli; and a waltz by dancers Moss and Fontana.

The show revealed gobs of flesh on its nubile chorus girls, one of whose routines had them spell out the word ''International'' on a flight of stairs. Lawrence had little of worth to do in her banal sketches and left the show during the run. Florence Moore and Jack Pearl had similar bad luck with their comedy bits. Harry Richman was another name performer starring in the revue.

INTIMATE REVUE, AN [Revue] B: Marita Resler, James Reynolds, and others; M: Herman Hupfeld; D/CH/DS: Joseph Mullen; T: Cherry Lane Theatre (OB); 11/17/25

A little-known Off-Broadway revue that played only on Sunday nights at the Cherry Lane and used a cast recruited from the *Garrick Gaieties*, supplemented by other young talents. It was very simply but imaginatively done, and Robert Coleman called it ''unpretentious, intimate and brief.'' Using only a piano accompaniment, it offered divertissements such as a Charleston by Stella Block, a satire on *The Vortex* called ''More Sex'' by Marita Resler, and ''A Sunday Evening in the Gay 90's'' by famed designer James Reynolds, dealing very humorously with a daughter's (Edith Meiser) inflicting of various tortures on her family after she returns from an European tour.

INTIMATE STRANGERS [Comedy/Romance] A: Booth Tarkington; D: Ira Hards (or Booth Tarkington); P: Florenz Ziegfeld, A. L. Erlanger, and Charles Dillingham; T: Henry Miller's Theatre; 11/7/21 (91)

This lighthearted romantic comedy could not sustain the charm and originality of its opening act but nevertheless pleased by its superb acting and disingenuousness. Constructed on a fragile plot, it revealed its author "never in a hurry, never in the least self-conscious, and never dull," according to Kenneth Andrews. Alexander Woollcott said the work ranged "from utterly charming to rather stupid" and was ultimately disappointing. It had been written by Tarkington specifically for Alfred Lunt, who had scored so sensationally in *Clarence*. Although Ira Hards was credited with the direction, Billie Burke, in her autobiography, *With a Feather on My Nose*, said that the playwright himself staged the work.

Two strangers, Ames (Lunt) and Isabel (Billie Burke), meet at a country railroad station when they are stranded there for the night. They fall in love, although Ames is momentarily bedazzled by Isabel's flapper niece (Frances Howard), who arrives in the morning. Isabel, a sure-footed matron, manages to recapture Ames's interest, and at the end marriage is definitely in the offing.

Lunt and Burke made a marvelous romantic duo and gave to the play an enormous share of its appeal.

INTRUDER, THE [Drama/Sex/Marriage] A: Paul Eldridge; D/P: Edward Sargent Brown; S: August Vimnera; T: Biltmore Theatre; 7/25/28 (5)

A forgettable event marked only by the appearance of a good new actress, Viola Frayne. She played a doctor's assistant who is seduced by the physician (Richard Gordon), who is lonely during a two-week absence of his wife; she has his child and six years later returns to demand that he divorce his wife (Anne Sutherland) and confess his paternity. She ultimately drops her claims, when she sees how deep his relationship is with his wife.

The play was "amateurish" but promising to the *Times* and "reasonably interesting" to Richard Dana Skinner, who saw it as a *Hamlet*-like study of the doctor.

INVITATION AU VOYAGE, L' [Drama/Marriage/Romance/French] A: Jean-Jacques Bernard; AD: Ernest Boyd; D: Eva Le Gallienne; DS: Aline Bernstein; P: Civic Repertory Company; T: Civic Repertory Theatre (OB); 10/4/28 (19)

This delicate, cerebral 1924 French play about a woman's romantic illusions was given a sensitive Civic Repertory production. Its simple story concerns Marie-Louise (Eva Le Gallienne), the bored wife of a businessman (Donald Cameron), who believes she is in love with her husband's partner, abroad in Argentina for years (he never appears); when she learns that he has returned, she goes to see him but returns disillusioned, aware that her love was just a dream.

The author's gentle manner pleased some critics, among them the *Times* reviewer, who wrote, "something about the quietude of his writing, the bold simplicity of his design, makes for a loveliness of emotion." But Robert Littell considered it "a grey, flat stretch of unsalted poetry, curiously combining sign-post obviousness and delicate implications that misfire."

A single additional performance was given by the company on 1/31/30.

IOLANTHE [Musical Revival] B/LY: W. S. Gilbert; M: Arthur Sullivan; D/P: Winthrop Ames; S: Woodman Thompson; T: Plymouth Theatre; 4/19/26 (255)

This extremely popular Gilbert and Sullivan comic opera, seen numerous times on the New York stage, had its longest run there in this production, put on under the tasteful and creative guidance of Winthrop Ames. The show was a high watermark of Gilbert and Sullivan staging during the decade. The critics were overjoyed by the piece itself, then one of the less-often-seen works in the canon.

This joyous ribbing of the British House of Lords received what John Mason Brown called "one of the most perfect Gilbert and Sullivan revivals this generation has been permitted to see. It is sung so that its lyrics do not interfere with the music, and the music does not drown out the lyrics. . . .Its principles and choruses alike bubble over with the jubilancy of their work."

The uniformly excellent company was much remarked on, although special praise went to Ernest Lawford's Lord Chancellor, Vera Ross's Fairy Queen, John Barclay's Earl of Mountararat, and Adele Sanderson's Iolanthe.

A return engagement was effected on 11/14/27 at the Royale Theatre for twelve performances. It ran in repertory with *The Mikado* and *The Pirates of Penzance*.

IPHEGENIA IN AULIS [Dramatic Revival] A: Euripides; M: Walter Damrosch; D: Margaret Anglin and Maurice Browne; S: Raymond Sovey; P: Oratorio Society of New York; T: Manhattan Opera House (OB); 4/17/21 (2)

A rare revival of this Greek tragedy directed by and starring Margaret Anglin, who played Clytemnestra. The most memorable part of the event was the star's acting, described by Alexander Woollcott, who thrilled to "the splendor of Miss Anglin, the lovely music of her voice and the prodigious, the amazing energy that is her's and her's alone among the actresses of the American stage." Ludwig Lewisohn, however, wrote that she "plays. . .with passion but with less iron forcefulness than one had, perhaps, a right to expect."

The adaptation was pieced together from several translations; it concluded by having Iphegenia saved by Artemis, leading to a scene of jubilant belicosity as the Greek soldiers whooped off to make war on Troy, and Clytemnestra was left sad and solitary by the departing Agamemnon (Eugene Powers). The choruses were directed by Maurice Browne in a manner derided by Woollcott as "an abomination" but defended by Lewisohn for their "wild and natural grace."

Maurice Browne, the codirector, wrote in amusing detail about this production in *Too Late to Lament*. He said it was an enormous undertaking with more than 400 people employed on the crews and with several hundred extras. The difficulty of dealing with these people was exacerbated when Anglin and Walter Damrosch, the conductor, developed a heated enmity for one another. Finally, the star stamped out, threatening to return simply to "walk through" her role on opening night. The last ten minutes of the play had not been rehearsed, and there had been no dress rehearsal. Browne restaged the play to throw emphasis onto Iphegenia (Mary Fowler). On the night, just as Anglin was preparing to make her entrance in a horse-drawn chariot, the animal bolted and threw her to the ground, bruising her. This so charged her up that, neglectful of her pain, she remounted the chariot and drove on stage in a furious dash; she proceeded to act "Mary Fowler, Damrosch, her own Company and the entire New York Symphony Orchestra clean off the stage." The final ten minutes were brilliantly improvised. After eighteen curtain calls, during which Anglin and Damrosch bowed together and kissed one another, she followed the curtain's final descent by turning to the respected conductor and slapping him in the face.

IS ZAT SO? [Comedy/Sports/Romance/Crime] A: James Gleason and Richard Taber; P: Earle Boothe; T: Thirty-ninth Street Theatre; 1/5/25 (634)

A vastly successful farce starring James Gleason, one of its coauthors, and concentrating on the activities of two characters, simple-minded boxer "Chick" Cowan (Robert Armstrong) and his feisty, bullying, but fatherly manager "Hap" Hurley (Gleason). The latter's favorite retort provides the title of the play. When it was not focusing on "Chick" and "Hap," the piece was "pretty bad" (*Times*), but such moments were rare.

The laughs were produced by the incongruity of the comic duo's being set down in the midst of a swank Fifth Avenue home as butler and second man, when the scion of the family (Sidney Riggs), seeing their destitute condition, takes them in. This dissipated young man wants the pair to put him back into sound physical condition so he can take on a villainous brother-in-law (John C. King). Both Chick and Hap develop romances with young women in the household, there is an onstage boxing match between Chick and a chauffeur, and the villain is foiled.

ISABEL and "SHALL WE JOIN THE LADIES" D: Frank Reicher; P: Charles Frohman, Inc.; T: Empire Theatre; 1/13/25 (31)

Isabel [Comedy/Science/Marriage/Romance/German] A: Curt Goetz; AD: Arthur Richman; "Shall We Join the Ladies" [Drama/One-Act/Mystery/Crime/British] A: James M. Barrie

A double bill consisting of Curt Goetz's lightweight German comedy *Isabel* and a one-act by James M. Barrie. The one-act, contrary to normal practice, closed the program.

Isabel was based on "the dog-tired triangle," as George Jean Nathan put it. Its heroine (Margaret Lawrence) was the lovely wife of an absent-minded biology professor (Lyonel Watts); she had married him thinking him to be the one who saved her from an embarrassing predicament many years earlier. The man who was actually responsible, a handsome young playwright (Leslie Howard), turns up as a house guest and soon a potential affair is in the air. The wife must choose between her husband and the new man, and when the curtain falls, she is on her way to a garden encounter with the latter.

Expertly played by a superb group of five actors, this frail piece was an enjoyable time passer. The effect was of "a merry, sparkling bit of triviality," wrote Arthur Hornblow.

The Barrie play, the first act of an unfinished four-act play that has nevertheless gained popularity, is a murder mystery in which a dozen guests are finishing their weekend at a wealthy host's home by having a final dinner, when he announces that he has invited them because all were present on the eve of his brother's death in Monte Carlo. The revelation elicits guilty responses from all, and even the host seems a possible murderer, but no solution is forthcoming when the play reaches its conclusion.

The play's reviews were mixed. Heywood Broun claimed it was not "up to the best which our own authors have done." Stark Young, though, said it was "a fresh quality from Barrie's inexhaustible talent."

IT ALL DEPENDS [Comedy/Sex/Romance] A: Kate McLaurin; D: John Cromwell; S: Livingston Platt; P: John Cromwell and William A. Brady, Jr.; T: Vanderbilt Theatre; 8/10/25 (16)

An unsuccessful comedy that may have been "a little too preachy to please frivolous Broadway" (Arthur Hornblow) but that garnered a few appreciative reviews and considerable flack. The whims and wiles of "a couple of cigarette-smoking flask-sucking, yellowback-reading flappers" (George Jean Nathan) were presented in a tale that had them deciding that sexual attraction counts more heavily than love, and that an affair with a married man is the cat's pajamas. Shirley Lane (Katherine Alexander) strikes up a relationship with her neighbor's spouse, and she dismisses her mother's warnings about the effect on the man's wife. She comes around, however, when she learns that her roommate Maida (Lee Patrick) is carrying on with her (Shirley's) own father (Norman Trevor) and sees how her mother is hurt. She realizes now that "it all depends...."

IT IS THE LAW [Drama/Mystery/Crime/Law] A: Elmer Rice, D: Lester Lonergan; P: Samuel Wallach; T: Ritz Theatre; 11/29/22 (121)

Elmer Rice had brought the film technique of the flashback to a Broadway play in his popular 1914 courtroom drama *On Trial*. Now the former lawyer turned playwright used the device again and in another stirring melodrama involving the workings of the legal system. *It Is the Law* had coincidence and improbability in good measure, as many critics pointed out, but its hair-raising action and suspenseful development gave audiences little chance to contemplate until later the inadequacies of the story.

Told in seven scenes, the play begins with a shooting and then moves back eight years to explain why the killer cannot be prosecuted. The action reveals that the murderer has already done time for killing the same man, but that the first murder was a fake and that the presumed victim had planned the whole thing to steal his rival's girl. The killer was played by Ralph Kellard, the mastermind by Arthur Hohl, and the girlfriend by Alma Tell.

Heywood Broun complained of inconsistencies and obvious foreshadowing but agreed that it did "possess suspense and several striking situations." "Mr. Rice...is...a complete master of artful ingenuity," noted the *Evening Telegram.*

IT IS TO LAUGH [Comedy-Drama/Jews/Family/Romance] A: Fannie Hurst; SC: a story by Fannie Hurst; D: Rollo Lloyd; S: P. Dodd Ackerman; P: Barbour, Crimmins, and Bryant; T: Eltinge Theatre; 12/26/27 (37)

Fannie Hurst produced "A maudlin, over-sentimental" play (Perriton Maxwell) in this stage version of one of her own stories. It was a Jewish family saga about the immigrant Goldfish household, moved from their humble but comfortable Division Street flat on the Lower East Side to a fancy Upper West Side apartment at the instigation of their financially successful son Morris (John Davidson). Father (Irving Honigman) and mother (Bella Gudinsky) are unhappy, and their daughter (Edna Hibbard) rebels by marrying a counterfeiter (Frank Beaston), who eventually goes straight after coming out of prison. Papa dies at the conclusion.

IT NEVER RAINS [Comedy/Romance/Family/Business] A: Aurania Rouverol; D: Paul Martin; P: Hyman Productions; T: Republic Theatre; 11/19/29 (178)

A successful comedy that did not exceed the author's previous hit, *Skidding*, but did well enough to be given a revival on 12/24/31 for twenty-three showings.

It took place in Los Angeles, where the Rogers family of husband (Jack Bennett), wife (Ann Dere), and son (Carl J. Julius) are visited by the eastern Donovan family of husband (Phil Kelly), wife (Fay Courtenay), and daughter (Sidney Fox). The plot concerns the sale of a piece of real estate by Mr. Rogers to Mr. Donovan, the difficulties encountered between the two families when the sale is considered criminal, the ultimate proof that it was legal, and the simultaneous love affair between the Rogers son and the Donovan daughter.

A play deemed a good example of "the stock farce tradition" (*Times*), it had a decent apportionment of pleasantries and entertaining chit-chat. "[T]he fabric of this play is mere burlap," declared *Time*.

IT'S A BOY! [Comedy/Small Town/Marriage] A: William Anthony McGuire; D: Sam Forrest; P: Sam H. Harris; T: Sam H. Harris Theatre; 9/19/22 (64)

Small-town drama continued to appeal to playwrights of the period, as seen in this typical example in which a young married couple, after testing the heady waters of the big city, return disillusioned to their simpler rural environment. William Anthony McGuire, author of a hit example of the genre, *Six-Cylinder Love*, here penned "a sufficiently interesting comedy, although lacking the freshness that marked the earlier piece," noted the *Times*.

In the prologue, the couple Chester and Phyllis Blake (Robert Ames and Dorothy Mackaye) become parents of a bouncing baby boy. Chester is a contented local businessman whose wife forces him to take a lucrative job in New York when an offer comes along. The sparkle in their champagne soon goes flat, though, and they leave life in the fast lane for a new life back in Pennsylvania.

IT'S A GRAND LIFE [Comedy/Family/Marriage/Sex] A: Hatcher Hughes and Alan Williams; D: Harrison Grey Fiske; P: A. L. Erlanger and George M. Cohan; T: Cort Theatre; 2/10/30 (25)

An "odoriferous" (*Time*) farce designed for the indubitable talents of Mrs. Fiske. As usual, the critics bewailed the fact that this leading actress had chosen to appear in such a rank contrivance as this "unconvincing rubbish" (Richard Dana Skinner) about a New York matron of extraordinary self-sacrificial tendencies. Mrs. Tyler, matriarch of an obstreperous family—the husband (Cyril Scott) philanders (one of his former mistresses has his baby in the Tyler apartment), the daughter (Leona Beutelle) carries on with married men, the son (Andrew Lawlor, Jr.) marries a chorine who formerly was a chippie of the old man's—handles her domestic peccadilloes with wit and understanding. Mrs. Fiske gave a notably effective comic performance, but her material was considered distasteful and crude.

The play's original title was *The Family Blues*. Mrs. Fiske was reportedly dismayed by its critical reception and thereupon launched a revival of *The Rivals* to clear her name of besmirchment.

IT'S A WISE CHILD [Comedy/Romance/Family/Sex/Small Town] A: Laurence E. Johnson; D/P: David Belasco; S: Joseph Wickes; T: Belasco Theatre; 8/6/29 (378)

This long-run play, which was seen in New York again in 1933, was produced and directed by seventy-five-year-old David Belasco and proved to Brooks Atkinson to be "a resourceful comedy written in dialogue that at times is tremendously funny."

Joyce Stanton (Mildred McCoy), looking for an out from her engagement to dyspeptic banker G. A. Appleby (Harlan Briggs), lets him think she is pregnant by a rival, bank clerk Roger Baldwin (Humphrey Bogart), whom she thinks she loves. The family is in a turmoil, especially as a maid (Leila Bennett) has the identical maternal dilemma (as a result of a liason with the iceman [Sidney Toler]). Roger decides that Joyce is not the girl for him, but that's all right, since attorney James Stevens (Minor Watson) fits the bill for Joyce dandily.

Style more than content was the going concept here, said Atkinson, and Perriton Maxwell observed, "Mr. Johnson has supplied plenty of laugh-provoking lines—lines which are not so funny in themselves but which, in connection with the characters and the situations and by their very unexpectedness, develop a surprising amount of irresistible humor."

During this play's tryout in Atlantic City the author and the aged producer got into a heated dispute on the boardwalk when Belasco ridiculed one of Johnson's scenes. Johnson spat back that Belasco's ideas were antiquated to which the Bishop of Broadway responded by commanding the playwright to revise the script. In a moment the pair were going for each other, and only the intercession of some actors kept them from each other's throats.

IT'S UP TO YOU [Musical/Romance/Business/Family] B/LY: Douglas Leavitt, Edward Paulton, and Harry Clarke; M: Manuel Klein, John L. McManus, and Ray Perkins; D: Frank Stammers; CH: David Bennett; P: William Moore Patch; T: Casino Theatre; 3/28/21 (24)

The number of worthwhiles was not large in this mediocre work "made of standardized materials," according to Alexander Woollcott. The hero was not so much a person in difficulties "as a business in difficulties," he said.

It was all about Ned Spencer (Charles King), who is in love with Harriet Hollistar (Betty Pierce). Her mother (Florence Earle) prefers that she marry the rich Freddy Oliver (Ray George). Ned wins Mrs. Hollistar's approval when, with two friends, he forms a realty company and sells a parcel of cheap swamp land for a bundle.

The most negligible factor in this "ordinary example of the stereotyped musical show of the day" (Arthur Hornblow) was its music. Most of the entertainment's pleasure rested with the dancers.

M.M.-C

IVANOFF [Dramatic Revival/Russian Language] A: Anton Chekhov; D: Vladimir Nemirovich-Danchenko; P: F. Ray Comstock and Morris Gest; T: Jolson's Fifty-ninth Street Theatre; 11/26/23 (7)

Their Chekhov productions were unquestionably the critics' favorites among the Moscow Art Theatre's presentations. Their production of *Ivanoff* impressed the *Times* critic as being one of their most brilliant. Vassily Katchaloff's Ivanoff was to Lawrence Stallings "a Hamlet without the music of Shakespeare." There were also sterling jobs done by Constantin Stanislavsky as the senile count and Leonidoff as the overseer.

Chekhov's melancholy play, first produced in 1887, and subsequently rewritten several times, tells the tale of the unfortunate marriage of the debt-ridden Nikolai Ivanoff to the Jewess Anna, who despite her sacrifices on his behalf loses his love to Sasha, the daughter of a friend; reviled by Anna when she discovers him with Sasha, Ivanoff strikes back at her cruelly and tells her she is dying. A year or so later she has passed away, and he is set to marry Sasha, but his guilt so overwhelms him that he cancels the wedding and commits suicide.

Stark Young expostulated on the play's qualities: "I saw more than ever the likeness between Chekhov's method and Shakespeare's.... Without using any means that might not be perfectly possible and actual, Chekhov contrives to give us the utmost shock and centre of the life he portrays.... And out of this modern and realistic art I got something of the same thing that comes off from Shakespeare: the tragic excitement, the vivacity and pathetic beauty,... the thrill that comes from a sense of truth."

Ivanoff received another two performances from 2/24/24 when the company returned for a final visit.

H.H.

IVORY DOOR, THE [Comedy-Drama/Fantasy/Romance/Period/British] A: A. A. Milne; D/P: Charles Hopkins; S: Cleon Throckmorton; T: Charles Hopkins Theatre; 10/18/27 (312)

A typically whimsical A. A. Milne fantasy, somewhat too cloyingly precious for all tastes, and on the whole respected far more in script form than as realized in what many thought a muddled production. Generally understood as a parable about how people cherish their traditions rather than progress, even when stared at by truth in the face, it took its audience back in time to a mythical kingdom, where the bachelor monarch King Perivale (Henry Hull) decides on his wedding day to venture through the fabled Ivory Door, from whence no traveler has returned. His fate is to be denied his throne by his people who now claim he is a fake. Princess Lelia (Linda Watkins), who recognizes him, goes through the door and is met with the same treatment; the pair is declared dead, so they return in the guise of ordinary lovers and sacrifice their rights to the throne for the sake of freedom and truth.

"The undertones of the play are powerful, startling, exquisite," commented *Time*: "As overwritten by Mr. Milne, overacted by Henry Hull, and overproduced, it becomes a despair to the intelligent." Richard Dana Skinner, though, found it "an evening of unencumbered delight."

IZZY [Comedy/Romance/Films/Business/Jews] A: Mrs. Lillian Trimble Bradley and George Broadhurst; SC: the "Izzy Iskovitch" short stories of George Randolph Chester and Lillian Chester; D: Mrs. Lillian Trimble Bradley; P: George Broadhurst; T: Broadhurst Theatre; 9/16/24 (71)

There were several who compared this comedy to the more successful *Merton of the Movies*. Its Horatio Alger plot followed young Izzy Izkovitch (Jimmy Hussey) on the rags to riches trail as he blazed a career in the film business. Izzy, desiring to become a mogul, convinces a gaggle of wealthy uncles to back his ventures as a producer in Hollywood. He works his way up from office boy to partner and general manager of a film company, meeting on the way a lovely actress named Prudence Joy (Isabelle Lowe), whom he turns into a star; when he discovers that her real name is Rosenblum, he marries her.

Q.M. called *Izzy* "a picture of the commercial chaos inside the film industry which was both faithful and of extreme satirical smartness." Frank Vreeland thought its plot was too lacking in obstacles for Izzy to tackle and too hungry for cheap laughs.

J

JACK AND JILL [Musical/Romance] B: Frederic Isham and Otto Harbach; M: Augustus Barratt and Alfred Newman; LY: Otto Harbach, John Murray Anderson, and Augustus Barratt; D: John Murray Anderson; S: Frederick Jones III; P: Chelsea Producing Corporation; T: Globe Theatre; 3/22/23 (92)

More a revue than a musical comedy, this show did nonetheless possess a story line, "utterly threadbare" (Heywood Broun) though it may have been. Aside from the delicious delights of Ann Pennington's dances, seconded by the charms of Clifton Webb's nimble feet, *Jack and Jill* fell down the hill with its "heavy and spiritless" dialogue (Broun), "wishy washy songs," and "painful attempts" (*Post*) at humor.

The plot was about the nouveau riche Mrs. Malone (Georgia O'Ramey), an antique lover who buys an old chair said to have been made of the cherry tree chopped down by George Washington. Whenever someone sits on it they begin to spout their truthful feelings about others. This premise was used to resolve a love story about a girl (Virginia O'Brien) who wants a certain fellow (Donald MacDonald) while her mother prefers someone else (Clifton Webb) for her.

JACK IN THE PULPIT [Comedy/Legacy/Religion/Small Town/Crime/Romance] A: Gordon Morris; D: Elwood F. Bostwick; P: Robert Ames and Elwood F. Bostwick, Inc.; T: Princess Theatre; 1/6/25 (7)

"[A]s foolish and hollow a piece of theatrical balderdash as one is likely to see in a month of Mondays" was Alexander Woollcott's opinion of this embarrassment.

Robert Ames played a crook named Jack who is informed that if he completes his theological studies and becomes the rector of a church in Rosedale Junction he will inherit a million dollars. He and his three cronies agree to follow through; they move to the town, Jack becomes the rector, and he weds his childhood sweetheart. The trio, having discovered God, reform and find local love interests, and at the end Jack moves dramatically toward his pulpit as the choir sings "Onward Christian Soldiers."

JACOB SLOVAK [Drama/Small Town/Jews/Sex/Romance] A: Mercedes de Acosta; D: James Light; S: Cleon Throckmorton; P: Joseph P. Bickerton, Jr.; T: Greenwich Village Theatre (OB); 10/5/27 (21)

A play about religious bigotry in a small New England town; Jacob Slovak (Jose Ruben) is a Polish Jew working as a clerk in an alien milieu. Seductively attractive because of his sensitive, foreign ways to a local belle, Myra Flint (Miriam Doyle), he has an affair with her; although pregnant with his child, she rejects him in favor of local boy Hezekiah Brent (Richard Abbott), and Jacob is run out of town by her father and others.

Stark Young thought that Jacob's character was not fully fleshed out, but that the others were three-dimensional and the action steadily more engrossing. The *Times* judged the play as "honest and interesting," with "several fine and touching emotional scenes," but harmed by an overliteral portrayal of the conflict between Jacob and the locals.

JACOB'S DREAM (Jaaćob's Traum) [Drama/Verse/Bible/Family/Religion/Austrian/Hebrew Language] A: Richard Beer-Hoffman; M: M. Milner; D: B. M. Suskevitch; S: R. R. Falk; P: Habima Players of Moscow; T: Mansfield Theatre; 1/3/27 (16)

One of the Hebrew-language offerings staged by the Habima Theatre during its 1926–1927 stay in New York. It was a 1918 literary tragedy by a distinguished Austrian author; it was conceived as the prelude to his major opus, *The History of King David*, an uncompleted trilogy intended as an interpretation of Jewish belief and legend. *Jacob's Dream*, set in the biblical period of the Patriarchs, was given a highly formalized expressionistic mounting by the Habima and had a strong, nearly operatic score written to accompany its action. In the opinion of the *Times*, however, the production suffered the drawback of failing to sufficiently evoke the superhuman figures of the angels and archangels who figure in the tale; they were simply too concrete for convincing stage portrayal.

The story is that of the devout and far-seeing Jacob (L. Warshawer) and his conflict with his passionate, earth-bound brother Esau (Nahum Zemach), who is enraged that his younger sibling has contrived to steal the paternal blessing belonging to him—Esau. Jacob pacifies Esau and then dreams of a debate with the archangels and Satan or Semael (Benjamin Zamach) and learns that his blessing also bears a curse that will bring suffering to the Jews in their great religious mission. He sings out at the end that he has changed his name to one who strove with God—Yisro-El.

During its New York stay the company split up; one faction under Nahum Zemach tried to start a second Habima and revived *Jacob's Dream* on 11/12/27 at the Neighborhood Playhouse, but audiences did not care to attend and it soon vanished.

JADE GOD, THE [Drama/Mystery/Crime/Romance/British] A: William E. Barry; SC: the novel by Alan Sullivan; D: Walter Greenough; P: Ben Stein; T: Cort Theatre; 5/13/29 (105)

It wasn't the butler who did it in this English murder mystery; it was the housemaid (Margaret Wycherly). What she did was to fall under the influence of a jade idol in the possession of John Millicent (Ronald Dexter) and to kill its owner with a Malay creese. The object of the play is for novelist Jack Derrick (Richard Nicholls), who loves Millicent's sister (Lyle Stackpole), to ply his amateur sleuthing skills cleverly enough to weed out all suspicious persons who might have killed the man, until he arrives at the perpetrator herself. A bumbling Scotland Yard detective (Stanley Harrison) abets him in the search.

The piece was traditional in every way and only moderately interesting. It had a "sophomoric quality" to the *Times* critic, who described Wycherly as being forced "to speak enigmatic lines in a sepulchral tone of voice and to walk about in a prescient daze that resembles the somnambulism of Lady Macbeth."

JANE, OUR STRANGER [Drama/Marriage/France] A: Mary Borden; SC: the novel of the same name; D: William Perry Adams; S: Sheldon K. Viele; P: Herman Gantvoort; T: Cort Theatre; 10/8/25 (4)

Ward Morehouse said of this mediocrity that it was "a shoddy, hollow play, a stagey artificiality that does not appear to have been worth producing."

Its plot was set in France, where wealthy American heiress Jane Carpenter (Selena Royle), married to the insincere Marquis Joigny (Clarke Silvernail), loses him to a princess (Kay Strozzi) with whom he elopes. Alone, Jane realizes how much better off she is without him. When they meet two years later, she is the superior one, and she refuses to have anything to do with him or his paramour.

JARNEGAN [Drama/Films/Sex] A: Charles Beahan and Garrett Fort; SC: Jim Tully's novel; D: Ira Hards; S: Clark Robinson; P: Charles K. Gordon and Paul Streger; T: Longacre Theatre; 9/24/28 (138)

This unexceptional dramatization of a Jim Tully novel about the evils of Hollywood is remembered chiefly because it marked the debut of the beautiful Joan Bennett. She acted opposite her father, Richard Bennett, who played the title role, that of a rebellious, blaspheming, and womanizing tramp turned major film director, which he portrayed "with gutteral roars, hobnails, stubble-beard and a chest expansion," according to *Time*, which found it all "profane and exciting." Jarnegan sees future star material in the person of sixteen-year-old Daisy Carol (Joan Bennett) and grows insanely angry at the sinful film world when, seduced by another director (Robert Cain), and fatally affected by an abortion, Daisy dies. He drunkenly breaks into a lavish party and denounces the principals in the starkest terms.

Melodramatic toughness and soppy sentimentality were bedpartners in this uneven play of which Richard Dana Skinner said, "I have seldom sat through so many long stretches of antiquated wisecracks and painfully obvious off-color lines." Sam Levene and Lionel Stander were among the extras in the third-act party.

JAY WALKER, THE [Comedy-Drama/Family/Romance/Crime] A: Olga Printzlau; D: A. H. Van Buren; P: Benjamin F. Witbeck; T: Klaw Theatre; 2/8/26 (17)

A play of "kitchen sink" realism, written with all the usual commonplaces in character in dialogue and characterized by Alan Dale as "one of the futile, the ridiculous, the inexplicable events of the season."

Laid bare was the life of a poor family on West 112th Street, the mechanic son (Reed Brown), the slaving, self-sacrificing, gray-haired dressmaker mother (Jennet Adair), the arrogant daughter (Mary Daniel), and a handsome traffic cop boarder (Curtis Cooksey). The quarrelsome daughter has run off and married a wealthy upper-class man; she returns home when he beats her, steals $100 from her mother, flees to California, is indicted for manslaughter, jumps bail, comes home with the mother's stolen cash preparing to escape to Europe, and is turned over by her grieving parent to the law.

JAZZ SINGER, THE [Comedy-Drama/Family/Show Business/Jews/Religion] A: Samson Raphaelson; SC: Samson Raphaelson's short story "The Day of Atonement"; D: Albert Lewis; P: Albert Lewis and Max Gordon i/a/w Sam H. Harris; T: Fulton Theatre; 9/14/25 (315)

The show that was adapted into the first feature-length sound film (actually a silent film movie with segments of song and speech) was a sentimental comedy of New York Jewish family life starring George Jessel in the role made famous on screen by Al Jolson, whose life suggested some of the material in the drama. The show was an instantaneous success. The *Times* reported that it was "a shrewd and well-planned excursion into the theatre, concerned with a theme of obvious appeal, and assuredly so written that even the slowest of wits can understand it." Many of the critics were negative, but the public didn't mind, and the play was soon "standing room only."

The script was at first called *The Day of Atonement*, after the original story author Raphaelson had published in *Everybody*'s magazine. The rough script was short, but Jessel, director-coproducer Albert Lewis, and the playwright worked together to expand it to full-length stature.

A Lower East Side milieu was the setting for the simple tale of Cantor Rabinowitz's (Howard Lang) anguish when told by his son Jack (Jessel) that he wishes to make a career not in the synagogue like his father and grandfathers before him, but clowning and singing in blackface on the stage. When his father lies dying at the end, the "jazz singer" returns to his bedside and then takes his place in the temple on Yom Kippur, prepared to follow his family tradition.

Jessel, whose career had been primarily in vaudeville, emerged a fine actor in this dramatic role. He noted the play's universal appeal in his autobiography *The World I Lived In*: "I played one performance for a thousand priests; I acted scenes from the play in churches and temples across the United States. It became a subject for sermons in every city we played." Jessel was very hopeful of doing the movie version of the play and even starred in the first talkie monologue, a two-reel short called *Talking to Mother*. He was practically set to do *The Jazz Singer* film when he found that the script had the character return to Broadway at the end and even had his mother encouraging him from a box seat. Jessel refused to do this revised version and suspected that Jolson was behind the rewriting; he also was experiencing contract difficulties with the film's producers, the Warner brothers. Soon, he learned that Jolson had signed to play the role; Jolson had agreed to help finance the film, and the company needed every penny it could grab.

Broadway's *The Jazz Singer* was reprised for sixteen performances on 4/18/27 at the Century Theatre.

JEALOUS MOON, THE [Drama/Show Business/Fantasy/Romance] A: Theodore Charles and Jane Cowl; M: Hugo Felix; D: Priestly Morrison; S: Jo Mielziner; P: William A. Brady, Jr., and Dwight Deere Wiman; T: Majestic Theatre; 11/20/28 (72)

Jane Cowl, the great star actress, cowrote this Pierrot fantasy and played its leading female role, that of Judy, a marionette operator of Columbine loved but ignored by Pierrot operator Peter Parrot (Philip Merivale). After a prologue introducing the human characters, the play explores Peter's Commedia Dell'Arte dream in which he becomes Pierrot and undergoes various romantic difficulties with Columbine (Cowl) and a flame-tressed temptress (Joyce Carey) culminating in Columbine's tragic death in his arms. He awakens for the epilogue and happiness with Judy ever after.

The tenuous material was given an opulently designed staging but quickly deteriorated in its second act into "an unconscionable series of attitudes and empty gestures," stated the *Times*. "*The Jealous Moon* is so sweet that it excites a mental toothache," cracked *Time*.

JEALOUSY (Monsieur Lambertier) [Drama/Marriage/Crime/French/Sex] A: Louis Verneuil; AD: Eugene Walter; D: Guthrie McClintic; P: A. H. Woods; T: Maxine Elliott's Theatre; 10/22/28 (136)

Known in French both as *Monsieur Lambertier* and *Satan*, this "extraordinarily ingenious" (*Times*) drama employed only two actors, John Halliday and Fay Bainter. George Jean Nathan attacked the play for its "detheatricalization" of its material by depending more on inference than action, but Ernest Boyd exclaimed that the actors "contrived to hold an audience for three acts which were as full of incident as if the stage were crowded with action."

The two characters are Maurice and Valerie who, after a period of living together, get married, only for their wedding night to turn into a jealous conflagration when Maurice begins to suspect Lambertier, the wealthy old sensualist who has been Valerie's "guardian," of having seduced her. He ultimately goes to prison for strangling the man, who indeed did have an intimate relationship with Valerie.

John Halliday only took on his role after Glenn Hunter dropped it during the tryout period, director Guthrie McClintic had experimented with it, and English actor Richard Bird had not worked out in it.

JENNY [Comedy/Marriage/Family/Romance/Sex] A: Margaret Ayer Barnes and Edward Sheldon; D: Frederick Stanhope; S: Jo Mielziner; P: William A. Brady, Jr., and Dwight Deere Wiman; T: Booth Theatre; 10/8/29 (111)

Attorney John R. Weatherby (Guy Standing) is barely tolerated by his rakehell family, from his frivolous wife (Katherine Emmett) to his dissolute and promiscuous grown children. Enter like a breath of spring famed actress Jenny Valentine (Jane Cowl), who devises a plan to get John into her clutches at a Canadian campsite, where she has him to herself for over a month. John goes home determined to be lord of his castle, meets with the usual rebuffs, watches as Jenny nails the incorrigible family with a diatribe on their behavior, and goes off with her, leaving the rest to their own devices.

"[I]t is a relapse into shop-worn romance," barked the *Times*; Perriton Maxwell believed that Cowl's superb acting almost single handedly saved "this rather incredible tale"; *Time* wondered why she even bothered "to appear in such a stale, superficial play."

JERRY-FOR-SHORT [Comedy/Romance/Family] A/D: William A. Grew; P: Eugene Productions, Inc.; T: Waldorf Theatre; 8/12/29 (64)

A satirical vehicle for Irish favorite Fiske O'Hara who played John Hartwell, a boorish Westchester nouveau riche attempting to gain the approval of high society so that the snobbish Mrs. Manners (Marie Louise Dana) will allow her son Robert (Joseph Fay) to marry his niece Betty (Lorna Carroll). When the hired butler (Cameron Mathews) is reported to have inherited a title, the lady's snobbishness softens, but the title turns out to be a mistake. At length, Mrs. Manners relents and gives her blessing to the young couple.

Perriton Maxwell could not stomach the unsophisticated play, and Richard Dana Skinner said, "The situations are too trite and the working out of the plot is too artificial to provoke serious comment."

JEST, THE (La cena delle beffe) [Dramatic Revival] A: Sem Benneli; D/P: Arthur Hopkins; S: Robert Edmond Jones; T: Plymouth Theatre; 2/4/26 (78)

In 1919 Arthur Hopkins had produced this 1909 romantic Italian period melodrama of Renaissance Florence with the brothers Barrymore to great acclaim. Unable to reclaim these actors for a revival, Hopkins mounted it with Basil Sydney and Alphonz Ethier in the roles originally embodied, respectively, by John and Lionel. To *Time* it was a quality revival that nearly equalled, and in some ways surpassed, the original staging, but Richard Dana Skinner told his readers not to waste time on it, because, apart from the Duse-like acting of Maria Ouspenskaya in a small role, the performances were "without serious worth." Joseph Wood Krutch declared that Basil Sydney, Violet Heming, and Alphonz

Ethier were good, and that Ethier (who had taken over from Lionel seven years earlier) overtopped them all. Many thought he was an improvement, but Sydney's blond-wigged Gianetto was generally considered inferior to that of John Barrymore.

(1) JEW SUSS [Drama/Period/Family/Sex/German/Politics/Jews/Yiddish Language] A: Lion Feuchtwanger; AD/D: Maurice Schwartz; SC: Feuchtwanger's novel *Power*; S: Boris Aronson; P: Maurice Schwartz; T: Yiddish Art Theatre (OB); 10/18/29

The famed old Proctor's Fifth Avenue Theatre at Twenty-eighth Street and Fifth Avenue was now the home of Maurice Schwartz's Yiddish Art Theatre, which opened their 1929–1930 season with this adaptation of German author Lion Feuchtwanger's novel *Jud Süss*, known in English as *Power*. The *Times* dismissed it as a "dull and prolix" treatment of a costume history set in eighteenth-century Germany at the court of Wurtemburg. The same material was eventually distorted into a virulent anti-Semitic tract for a movie made in Hitler's Germany.

Jew Suss is a study of the eponymous hero's (Samuel Goldenburg) voracious lust for power, which leads to his becoming financial minister to the kingdom of the lascivious Duke Karl Alexander (Schwartz). Benign only to his daughter Tamar (Judith Abarbanell), Suss keeps her safe from the Duke's seductions in a forest castle, but the Duke manages to outwit him, only to see the daughter leap to her death before submitting to him. The crushed Suss is prevented from taking sweet revenge when the Duke dies.

Although the *Times* found *Jew Suss* unpleasant and vague of purpose, it lauded the expert production, with special plaudits for Schwartz's acting and direction. Stella Adler was among the lesser players in the cast.

(2) (Josef Suss) [Dramatic Revival] AD: Ashley Dukes; D: Reginald Denham; P: Charles Dillingham i/a/w J. C. Williamson, Ltd.; T: Erlanger's Theatre; 1/20/30 (40)

Shortly after the Yiddish production of this work, a British adaptation titled *Josef Suss*, successful in London, arrived on Broadway with Maurice Moscovitch in the title role. Malcolm Keen was the Duke, and the daughter, here called Naemi, was Janet Morrison. The play seemed to falter in its surge for grandeur, because in Perriton Maxwell's opinion, Ashley Dukes's treatment failed to sustain the drama's sweep. John Hutchens blamed the problem on a flawed and careless production. The work seemed "like mechanical puppetry" to *Time*. According to Peter Bauland in *The Hooded Eagle*, the show's producers had altered its title from *Jew Suss* to *Josef Suss* for fear of offending theatregoers.

JEWELLED TREE, THE [Drama/Africa/Period/Fantasy/Romance] A: Garrett Chatfield Pier; M: Sandor Harmati; D: Lawrence Marston; S: Willy Pogany; P: Pierce-Tollman Corporation; T: Forty-eighth Street Theatre; 10/7/26 (36)

Critics scratched their pates over this "Egyptian fantasy," adorned with colorful settings but ineffectively acted by a giant cast and clunkishly written. Placed in 1350 B.C., or the Eighteenth Egyptian Dynasty, a bit after King Tut-ank-hamen's demise, it offered a novel scenic milieu but standard dramatic fare. Its author was better known as an Egyptologist than as a playwright. To the *Times* his work was "a somewhat hollow and pretentious fable" that for all of its probable authenticity seemed "synthetic." Joseph Wood Krutch labeled it "a ponderous and unimaginative spectacle."

It dealt with a quest made by Rames (Walter Petrie) on behalf of Tutankha-men's widow Ankheson (Olive Valerie) for a jewelled tree whose fruit possesses the virtue of making its eater forever young and lovely. Rames finds the tree but falls in love with its spirit Ata (Reva Greenwood). Ankheson turns old and ugly from the fruit, and Rames weds Ata, who is made human by the gods.

JIM JAM JEMS [Musical/Journalism] B/LY: Harry L. Cort and George E. Stoddard; M: James Hanley; D: Edward J. MacGregor; P: John Cort; T: Cort Theatre; 10/4/20 (105)

A quartet of comic virtuosos, Joe E. Brown, Frank Fay, Ned Sparks, and Joe E. Miller, were the principal reasons for attending this otherwise standard offering that the *Times* described as "very long and sometimes dreary." More a melange of vaudeville and cabaret than an integrated musical comedy, the show provided a shallow plot about an innocent New York girl (Ada Mae Weeks) whose uncle (Stanley Forde), fearing scandal, refuses to let her mix in society, but who escapes his surveillance by doing the town on the arm of an inquisitive reporter (Fay) writing a story. Weeks demonstrated abundant musical and comedic talents in her soubrette role.

During its run the show changed its name to *Hello Lester*, but reverted to *Jim Jam Jems* when business failed to increase.

JIMMIE [Musical/Night Club/Legacy/Family] B/LY: Otto Harbach, Oscar Hammerstein II, and Frank Mandel; M: Herbert Stothart; P: Arthur Hammerstein; T: Apollo Theatre; 11/17/20 (69)

Plots about inheritances peppered the shows of the decade, and *Jimmie* was just one more example, here applied in a musical-comedy setting. It served to inaugurate Forty-second Street's new Apollo Theatre and gave Frances White a shot at stardom in the title role. The *Times* declared the work "a lavishly gowned and splashy piece with a nearly humorless book,...brought up to the standard of good entertainment by the presence of Miss White."

She played a waitress and cabaret singer raised by Vincenzo Carlotti (Paul Porcasi), who, aware that she is due to inherit a fortune, tries to substitute his own girl as the heiress; the plot is uncovered, and Jimmie gets not only her money but is reunited with the father (Ben Welch) who had thought she was lost forever.

A few good songs such as "Jimmie," "Cute Little Two by Four," and "Baby Dreams" emerged from the show.

JIMMIE'S WOMEN [Comedy/Legacy/Marriage/Romance/Family] A/D: Myron C. Fagan; S: Gates and Morange; P: B. F. Witbeck; T: Biltmore Theatre; 9/26/27 (217)

Another in the endless series of plays involving the ridiculous dictates of some late person's will. Jimmie Turner (Robert Williams), heir to a fortune, can't get a penny unless he marries the girl of his trustee's choice. The trustee (Charles Abbe) wants the girl to be his flapper daughter Teddie (Lucia Laska), but she loves Algernon Simpson (Junior Cook), while Jimmie's eyes are for actress Gypsy Adair (Minna Gombell). The inciting incidents are ignited when a beautiful stranger is introduced by Teddie's parents to woo Algernon away, leaving Teddie free for Jimmie. The fact that the stranger is Gypsy, who has secretly wed Jimmie, is the source of all the mayhem that ensues.

"Thoroughly artificial, repetitious, and often painfully tiresome, the piece is redeemed...by some bright lines and amusing situations," thought the *Times*. Regardless of such pans, the play was a hit.

JITTA'S ATONEMENT (Frau Gitta's Sühne) [Comedy-Drama/Marriage/Austrian] A: Siegfried Trebitsch; AD: George Bernard Shaw; D: Lester Lonergan; P: Lee Shubert; T: Comedy Theatre; 1/17/23 (38)

The Austrian author of this unsuccessful work was the man who had translated Shaw's plays into German. Shaw returned the compliment by doing this play into English, but the result, said Heywood Broun, was "the most unworthy piece with which his name has ever been connected." Evidence of Shaw's contribution peeped forth only sporadically; for the rest, the work was an uneven effort smacking a bit too strongly of the theatre and not enough of life. Whatever there was of wit and cleverness in the dialogue and spirit, the critics tended to attribute to the Irish playwright who, indeed, had altered Trebitsch's serious drama into "a near comedy."

Jitta Lenkheim (Bertha Kalich) flees the site when the man (John Craig) with whom she has been having an affair—her husband's (Francis Byrne) literary collaborator—dies of a heart attack. When the truth comes out about their relationship, it delights the dead man's daughter (Beth Eliott), who is happy to know the woman of her father's pleasure, and his wife (Thais Lawton), who is pleased that the mistress was of a suitable class. Jitta's spouse, however, disavows his late collaborator's theories, but the play intimates that he and Jitta will once again be partners, for this is to be her "atonement," performed to save from scandal the reputations of the dead man's relations.

The play had been offered by Shaw to the Theatre Guild, which produced most of his plays during the decade, but when Yiddish Theatre star Bertha Kalich requested the rights, the Guild acquiesced. Shaw was not entirely happy to have her do the play, fearing she would ignore his comedy and "revert to the unrelieved gloom of the original," according to a letter published in Lawrence Langner's *G.B.S. and the Lunatic*.

JOAN OF ARC [Drama/Period/Historical-Biographical/Religion] A: Donal Haines; SC: Mark Twain's book *The Recollection of Joan of Arc*; D: Le Roi Operti; T: Hampden's Theatre; 4/23/26 (1)

An adaptation of Mark Twain's account of the life of the Maid of Orleans, produced for a single showing with a cast consisting of actors in Walter Hampden's repertory company. The title role was played by Twain's daughter, Clara Clemens, a singer here making her acting debut. The play was structured to alternate staged vignettes with the reading of long passages of narration. It lacked action, was irritatingly read by the director Le Roi Operti, and had little of dramatic interest. Clara Clemens proved to be a one-note actress.

Clemens brought the piece back on 4/14/27 for nine "special performances" at the Edyth Totten Theatre.

JOHANNES KREISLER (Die Wunderlichen Geshichten des Kappelmeisters Kreisler) [Drama/Fantasy/Romance/Music/Period/German] A: Carl Meinhard and Rudolph Bernauer; AD: Louis N. Parker; M: E. H. Von Reznicek; D: Frank Reicher; S: Sven Gade; P: Selwyns; T: Apollo Theatre; 12/20/22 (65)

This "fantastic melodrama" in forty-one scenes, imported from Germany, was so expensively and elaborately produced, with a giant company of actors and advanced technical effects, that even good houses could not sustain it for more than a two-month run. The critics were split. Robert Allerton Parker therefore called this "a triumph of mechanics over drama." But Ludwig Lewisohn declared it a significant work of German legend and fairy-tale inspiration that simply could not reach an audience that did not share its internal references.

Johannes Kreisler was technically expressionistic, but thematically romantic, with a touch of symbolism. It was inspired by the life and work of E. T. Hoffman, the composer who is really the Kreisler of the story. Johannes Kreisler (Jacob Ben-Ami) is a melancholy composer who, on the last night of his life, narrates to a friend (Erskine Sanford) the story of his past, with the focus on the three women he loved, each of whom represents another manifestation of his feminine ideal, Undine, about whom he has attempted to write an opera. The story shifts to the past in dream-like flashbacks and is enacted all over the stage via the use of surprising, scenic and lighting devices. Finally he meets his early love, Julia (Lotus Robb), again, but only in a vision, and flies to her (wires were used), only to learn the next day that she died at the moment of their "reunion." He too then passes away.

JOHN [Drama/Bible/Religion/Period] A: Philip Barry; D: Guthrie McClintic; S: Norman Bel Geddes; P: Actors' Theatre; 11/4/27 (11)

Philip Barry's disappointing biblical drama about the life of John the Baptist (Jacob Ben-Ami) was a noble flop; Constance Collier was Herodias, and Norman Bel Geddes created potent stage designs, but Barry's interpretation of scripture lacked "progressive movement" for all of its beauty and high-mindedness, said Brooks Atkinson.

Set in A.D. 30, it depicted the evangelical Baptist as ''a surly Elias, addicted to sudden fits of anger'' (Percy Hammond). Although his Old Testament evangelism is rivaled by that of Christ, he refuses the political seductions of the incestuous Herodias, who will make him a general if he agrees to quell the growing power of Jesus, whose gentle ways he fails to comprehend. He is beheaded but dies not unwillingly; he believes that Jesus, of whose identity as the Messiah he has become convinced, will wield the sword against the sinful Herodias and raise the Jews to their wonted might. (Christ does not appear in the play.)

Joseph Wood Krutch discerned ''the stuff of great tragedy'' in *John*, and he, as well as others, blamed its failure on Barry's inability ''to manage his narrative.'' Ben-Ami's accent was a hindrance, as was Guthrie McClintic's tediously unimaginative staging.

(1) JOHN FERGUSON [Dramatic Revival] A: St. John Ervine; P: Theatre Guild; T: Garrick Theatre; 5/23/21 (24)

After the Theatre Guild's first production, *The Bonds of Interest*, had failed, the company came back to life with its first success, *John Ferguson*, staged on 5/12/19. A year later the now-prospering Guild briefly revived the play in the present production, with Augustin Duncan and Dudley Digges repeating their roles, respectively, of John Ferguson and James Caesar. The 1915 play, set in County Down, Ireland, recounts the tragic travails of John, a crippled farmer, as he awaits the money from his wealthy brother in America that will prevent foreclosure of the farm's mortgage. The play was ''as absorbing now, as gripping, as it was during its first presentation,'' said the *Times*.

(2) P: The Repertory Theatre; T: Belmont Theatre; 6/20/21 (10)

No sooner had the Theatre Guild revival of the play closed than virtually the same group of players produced it at another playhouse, calling themselves the Repertory Theatre. In Dudley Digge's role now was J. M. Kerrigan, a popular Irish actor who had played the part in the original Dublin production and who was very effective in it.

(3) D: Augustin Duncan; P: Charles Mulligan; T: Theatre Masque; 1/17/28 (9)

A third revival was given for matinees only with a cast including only one of the original Guild cast, Augustin Duncan, who also directed. Barry McCollum, who played Clutie John McGrath in the above revivals, repeated that role, while Richard Whorf and Miriam Hopkins were among the newcomers. The *Times* found the chief interest of the revival in watching the up and coming Hopkins: ''After a little early compromise with the accents and manners of County Devon, Miss Hopkins found her artistic feet and gave a good account of herself in the scene of hysteria.'' Duncan, now blind, was as expert as ever.

JOHN GABRIEL BORKMAN [Dramatic Revival] A: Henrik Ibsen; D/P: Eva Le Gallienne; S: G. E. Calthrop; T: Booth Theatre; 1/29/26 (7)

Eva Le Gallienne was the moving force behind the performance at a series of matinees of this late (produced 1887) Ibsen work. She played Ella, Egon Brecher was Borkman, and English actress Helen Haye was Mrs. Borkman. This was one of four Ibsen revivals running concurrently on Broadway at the time. The play seemed dry and stuffy, its somber, reflective mood not very appealing. Burns Mantle called it "macabre," and John Mason Brown said it seemed "more aged" than the other Ibsen works on view. The performances were admirable. Brooks Atkinson wrote of the perfection of the ensemble: "the dominant impression is of a well-joined group exposition, instinct with understanding."

Le Gallienne and Egon Brecher were at the time appearing in her production of Ibsen's *Master Builder*. The presentation of these two works gave her the impetus to found her renowned Civic Repertory Company in 1926. In her autobiography, *At 33*, Le Gallienne described the combination of farce and tragedy she faced at *Borkman*'s dress rehearsal. The rehearsal was scheduled at midnight after she and Brecher had appeared in *The Master Builder* at the Princess Theatre. Things first got underway at two in the morning; one mishap after another kept the company working until the last act finally began about dawn, with the show scheduled to open several hours later. During this last act, after the scene had changed from the front of Borkman's house to an icy path in the mountains, Le Gallienne and Brecher, unfamiliar with the set and moving about on the darkened stage, got fouled up in some black velour curtains and couldn't find their way to their proper places. Although nearly hysterical they kept their control and spoke their solemn lines with straight faces. Soon after, when the property snow began to fall on them, it turned out not to have been prepared properly and came down in a deluge, entering the actors' noses and mouths. They struggled to maintain their composure as they looked at each other, but when "amidst a final flurry of tremendous violence, a coat-hanger descended. . . and fastened itself in Brecher's beard," the players "burst into roars and screams of uncontrollable laughter." The rehearsal was ended at that point, and everyone left with nothing but disaster seeming to loom on the horizon. However, as so often happens after a catastrophic dress rehearsal, the opening went beautifully without a hitch.

This revival was produced in repertory by Le Gallienne's noble Civic Repertory Company as their fourth production, starting on 11/9/26 for fifteen performances. It was revived periodically by them through 1930, arriving for seven performances on 1/28/28, two performances on 1/28/29, and a single performance on 3/28/30. In the 1926 mounting Beatrice Terry was outstanding as Mrs. Borkman, Egon Brecher was "a theatrical Borkman, earnest enough, but with only rare moments of effectiveness," in Richard Dana Skinner's view, and Le Gallienne was a competent Ella. "She never quite extracts the full emotional power from a scene and is afflicted with a large number of mannerisms," wrote Skinner.

JOHN HAWTHORNE [Drama/Rural/Religion/Sex/Crime/Marriage] A: David Liebovits; D: Philip Moeller; P: Theatre Guild; T: Garrick Theatre; 1/24/21 (4)

The first American play to be produced by the Theatre Guild was this much-derided work given only at a series of matinees. It was a tragedy dealing with Kentucky farmhand John Hawthorne (Warren Kreck), who is discovered in his affair with the farmer's (Eugene Ordway) wife (Muriel Starr), kills him, and runs off to hide from the law. When the young atheist refuses the woman's attempt to lead him to God, she tells the authorities where to find him, but he kills himself first.

Among those who jeered at the play was Alexander Woollcott, who called it "continuously dull and uninteresting." Ludwig Lewisohn, while assailing its numerous defects, discerned in it an ambitious and authentic strain of tragic dimension and even berated Woollcott for his fatuous criticism of this and other works.

JOKER, THE [Drama/Crime/Marriage/Mystery] A: Arthur Goodrich and W. F. Payson; D: Colin Kemper; P: L. L. Wagenhals and Colin Kemper; T: Maxine Elliott's Theatre; 11/16/25 (16)

A mystery melodrama about how easygoing, none-too-reliable, but likable Dick Hamill (Ralph Morgan) is accused of stealing $70,000 in bonds from his office, is loaned the amount by a pal, and is trusted by his wife, Virginia (Leona Hogarth), while he takes a year to solve the crime and clear his name. The villain he discovers to be his friend Grant Nugent (Walter Gilbert), who has been seducing his wife and is also the killer of Dick's father.

No mystery was sustained, since it was soon clear who the bad guy was, and the play descended, said Charles Belmont Davis, into irksomeness. Alison Smith rejected the piece as "a long-winded and leaden melodrama."

JOLLY ORPHAN, THE (Dos Frohliche Yosehmele) [Musical/Jews/Legacy/Yiddish Language/Yiddish] B: William Siegel; M: Joseph Rumshinsky; LY: L. Gilrod and Molly Picon; D: Jacob Kalich; CH: Charles Adler; P: Joseph Rumshinsky and Jacob Kalich; T: Kessler's Second Avenue Theatre (OB); 12/22/29

Molly Picon cavorted enchantingly in this operetta vehicle produced in Yiddish; she was herself partly responsible for the lyrics. "In a kitchenmaid's costumes or in her home-made pink flannel one-piece pajamas she is her unfettered self, exacting all the humor and pathos out of her role as a wistful orphan waif," commented the *Times*.

The threadbare sentimental plot followed her fortunes as she rose from poverty to a million-dollar legacy. Two songs that stood out were the title tune (in Yiddish, "Dos Frohliche Yosehmele") and "Delightful to Be a Poor Man" ("A Mechayeh zu sein a Captsen").

JOLLY ROGER, THE [Comedy/Fantasy/Romance/Adventure/Sea] A: A. E. Thomas; D/P: Walter Hampden; S: John Wolcott Adams and Raymond Sovey; C: Charles Chrisdie; T: National Theatre; 8/30/23 (52)

With incidental music including the overture from *The Pirates of Penzance* and old sailor chanties, this fantasy launched by Walter Hampden as a preliminary to his repertory season took place Sometime off the coast of Somewhere. The hero (Pedro De Cordoba) takes over a pirate ship with a dead captain and mutinous crew. He discovers and falls in love with a beautiful girl (Carroll McComas) disguised as a cabin boy. After they are marooned on a desert island for a month, she decides she loves him too, and a mysterious way of escape is found for them.

John Corbin praised the very beautiful sets of the ship's deck and cabin and the island but found the play to be an operetta without music: "The only thing that is lacking is plausibility, not to say reality." Heywood Broun thought the comedy was "the dreariest play of the season," "romance reduced to slow motion."

H.H.

JONESY [Comedy/Family/Gambling/Theatre/Romance/Youth] A: Anne Morrison and John Peter Toohey; SC: a series of stories by John Peter Toohey; D/P: Earle Boothe; S: Rollo Wayne; T: Bijou Theatre; 4/9/29 (96)

A diverting hokey family farce, the gist of whose complex plot was about college freshman Wilbur Jones (Raymond Guion), who loves Diana (Helen Brooks), an actress (her play has been raided), who is the niece of Mr. Jackson (Percy Moore), a powerful local businessman. Wilbur, bound by a gambling debt, sells his dad's car to raise cash. Mr. and Mrs. Jones (Donald Meek and Spring Byington) try to break up the romance, but Mr. Jones begins to relent when he learns that Diana's uncle is the man from whom he seeks a job. Other complications come from Mr. Jones's accusing the man who has bought his car of stealing it. The cheeky son Jonesy cuts his parental apron strings, saves the day, gets his dad the job, and wins the girl.

"Wit and humor do not obtrude seriously upon this skit," informed the *Times*, "But here is the illusion of humor." "*Jonesy* is too forced for straight comedy and lacks the stamina for farce," stated Euphemia Van Rensselaer Wyatt.

JONICA [Musical/Romance] B: Dorothy Heywood and Moss Hart; M: Joseph Meyer; LY: William Moll; D/P: William B. Friedlander; CH: Pal'mere Brandeaux; T: Craig Theatre; 4/7/30 (40)

This musical, which marked Moss Hart's writing debut in New York, was about a cute, naive girl (Nell Roy), who leaves the convent to attend a New York wedding, and gets involved on the train with a fat man (Bert Matthews) and an actress (Joyce Barbour). She mistakenly winds up at the groom's bachelor party instead of at the bride's home, gets mixed up in several complications in which the fat man and the actress also get embroiled, meets her old boyfriend (Jerry Marquis), and decides with him to tie the knot.

Jonica bombed with the critics, the *Times*, for example, deciding that "At its best...*Jonica* is a moderately pleasing but undistinguished pastime. Unfortunately, it isn't always at its best." Hart ultimately denied having been responsible for much of what was seen, claiming an anonymous play doctor rewrote his share of the libretto.

JOSEPH [Comedy/Bible/Sex/Period] A: Bertram Bloch; M: Joseph Rumshinsky; D: George S. Kaufman; S: Redington Sharpe; P: John Golden; T: Liberty Theatre; 2/12/30 (13)

An iconoclastic retelling in satirical terms of the biblical story of Joseph, played by George Jessel "as glib, crafty and loquacious as a Jewish press agent (timest)." The familiar plot events of Joseph's being sold into slavery, where he becomes leader of Potiphar's (Ferdinand Gottschalk) slaves; of his rejection of Potiphar's wife Neris's (Ara Gerald) advances; and of his subsequent incarceration and evolution into an interpreter of Pharoah's (Douglas Dumbrille) dreams were intact but viewed from a 1930 perspective. Thus Joseph rejects Neris more from fear of being thrown to the crocodiles than for moral reasons. Joseph applies his native common sense and salesmanship to every problem and makes a success in the face of constant adversity.

George Jessel could not have been bettered, and most critics enjoyed the comedy, with *Time*, for one, calling it "one of the season's more amusing pieces." Still, it died very young.

Jessel was John Golden's partner in producing the venture and was given permission to close it if he liked. On closing night, the dejected Jessel, for the only time in his career, kept the curtain up at the end to address the audience, dressed in full biblical makeup and costume. Choosing not to go through all of the usual tearful farewells with his cast, he made a sentimental little speech to the audience, saying farewell to and for the company and then signaled the curtain to drop. He then stepped off the stage, walked up the aisle, "makeup, robes, and all, hailed a cab. . .and went home" (Jessel, *The World I Lived In*).

JOURNEY'S END [Drama/War/Military/Alcoholism/British] A: R. C Sherriff; D/S: James Whale; P: Gilbert Miller b/a/w/ Maurice Browne; T: Henry Miller's Theatre; 3/22/29 (485)

To many contemporaries, *Journey's End* was the best play of the 1928–1929 season. As a war play, it seemed to various commentators an even more powerful and realistic work than the acclaimed *What Price Glory?* It was a first play, written by a thirty-two-year-old insurance agent for an Englishmen's amateur group consisting of rowing-club members and based on the author's own experiences at the front. It failed to interest the commercial London managements but caught important eyes when given a Sunday-night performance by the Stage Society. This led to its enormous worldwide success in the years to come. Its lack of women, its completely British atmosphere, and its depressing conclusion convinced *Variety* that it could never succeed commercially in New York; its almost 500 showings made bosh of this prediction.

The play's reception was remarkably positive. It was lauded as a masterpiece, as one of the greatest works of the modern drama. Several critics admitted to being so overwhelmed that they had difficulty writing about it. Beyond its immediate poignancy as a reminder of recent anguish, said Richard Dana Skinner, "it remains somehow a thing of worth and tragic beauty and poetic valor in its own right—the portrait of men who are universal and therefore of all times, the story of a valiant fight between fear and relentless duty such as men must wage so long as hate breaks forth between nations."

It is March 1918 in the foul dugout at St. Quentin, thirty-six hours before the German attack. Half a dozen officers are gathered here, a cross-section of sharply drawn British types: the athletic Captain Stanhope (Colin Keith-Johnston), soothing his cracking nerves with alcohol; the sensitive schoolmaster Osborne (Leon Quartermaine); the hysterically frightened Hibbert (Jack Hawkins); the dull cockney Trotter (Henry Wenman); the idealistic newcomer Raleigh (Derek Williams); and the comic cook Mason (Victor Stanley). Four others, including a German prisoner (Sol Dowday), are also introduced. The central incidents concern a raid carried out by Osborne and Raleigh, Osborne's death, and, later, Raleigh's. Finally, a shell explodes, and the dugout's doom is realized.

Journey's End's few negative responses were buried in a mountain of adulation. George Jean Nathan enumerated what he saw as the drama's virtues (the organic relation of emotion to character, the lack of overdramatization, and the sense of ever-felt external forces), but his list of criticisms suggested an excessive deployment of "cheap theatrical fetches" at crucial moments, an implausible stress on all of the characters' "stupendous heroism," and the surprising lack of profanity. Burns Mantle chose it as a Best Play of the Year.

Several critics asserted that it was difficult to single out individual actors for praise in a company which gave a brilliant ensemble performance.

JOY OF SERPENTS, THE [Comedy/War/Romance] A: Frederick Schlick and J. Barry McCarthy; D: A. Montague Ash; S: Martin Sloane; T: Playshop Theatre (OB); 4/4/30

The tiny Playshop Theatre at 133 Macdougal Street was the old Provincetown Playhouse with a new name. The play, reminiscent of, but inferior to, O'Casey's *Silver Tassie*, was set in an English war hospital, introduced a cross-section of the wounded patients and presented a romance between a maimed flyer and a nurse. The *Times* termed it "self-consciously literal and cheaply humorous."

JUAREZ AND MAXIMILIAN (Juarez und Maximilian) [Drama/Period/Historical-Biographical/Mexico/German/Politics] A: Franz Werfel; TR: Ruth Langner; D: Philip Moeller; DS: Lee Simonson; P: Theatre Guild; 10/11/26 (42)

An episodic, large-cast, philosophical history drama in thirteen scenes about the ill-fated 1865–1867 reign of the Austrian ruler Maximilian as emperor of Mexico. It was very warmly received by various critics, but it was, according to Norman Nadel's *Pictorial History of the Theatre Guild*, "the only one of fifteen consecutive plays produced by the Guild's Acting Company which was not financially successful.'' Werfel's pessimism, according to which he saw life "not as a struggle between good and evil... but between two principles inscrutably complex; even, perhaps, between two evils'' (Joseph Wood Krutch), informed this epic work of the idealistic monarch, encouraged by Napolean III to form a Mexican empire, only to desert him to the guns of Benito Juarez, leader of the insurgent Mexican forces. Juarez himself is never seen in the play, which focuses on the Hamlet-like character of Maximilian (Alfred Lunt), a man tragically out of joint with the circumstances swirling about him.

Despite a lavish production, this was one of the Guild's less-polished presentations. Lunt looked the emperor to a "T", but his garbled diction hindered his performance. The play was too disconnected, and it seemed sluggish and uninvolving. John Mason Brown said the play "rarely substitutes theatre for the facts it has to tell.'' Good performances were turned in by Edward G. Robinson, Dudley Digges, Arnold Daly, and Clare Eames.

JUDAS [Drama/Bible/Period/Religion/British] A: Walter Ferris and Basil Rathbone; D/C: Richard Boleslavsky; S: Jo Mielziner; P: William A. Brady, Jr., and Dwight Deere Wiman; T: Longacre Theatre; 1/24/29 (12)

Since his adolescence, actor Basil Rathbone had been intrigued by questions concerning the relationship of Christ and Judas such as why Christ chose Judas as one of his disciples when he knew that he would betray him. After intensive study of the problem he was startled to read about a German author who had written a book on this issue. He shared his ideas with Walter Ferris, a would-be writer who worked as a teacher, and the pair decided to collaborate on a play. In his autobiography, which discusses the experience in great detail, Rathbone describes his involvement in the project as an obsession.

Rathbone played the eponymous hero in this biblical drama, but it turned out to be only "soft and dismal rubbish upon a sincerely conceived Biblical footnote'' (Robert Littell). It sought to interpret the betrayer of Christ as an intellectual agitator, who, misunderstanding Christ's purpose, believes his mission can best be accomplished by military conquest of the Romans. His betrayal is conceived as a ruse to spur the Savior to violent action.

The *Times*'s chief criticism was that, no matter how honorable the theme, the subject matter demanded a treatment at least on a par with its own grandeur. Under such circumstances, said the critic, "mediocre plays seem more egregious than usual, and the roar and rant of the acting sound particularly hollow.'' The play marked director Boleslavsky's last production for the New York theatre before he turned westward toward a Hollywood career.

JUDGE'S HUSBAND, THE [Comedy/Marriage/Law/Politics/Family/Prohibition/Trial] A: William Hodge; D: Thomas Coffin Cook; P: Lee Shubert; T: Forty-ninth Street Theatre; 9/27/26 (112)

William Hodge wrote this vehicle for his own comic talents and played it successfully on the road before its New York opening. He acted Joe Kirby, a guy whose judge-wife (Gladys Hanson) is so preoccupied with a bid for the governorship that he must assume the role of homemaker in her absence. He does not prosper in this capacity nor does his daughter (Ruth Lyons), whose social activities demand the presence of a strong maternal assist. When Joe disappears for a couple of days Mrs. Judge Kirby's ire is aroused, and she sues for divorce on grounds of adultery; she acts as both plaintiff and judge in the case, while Joe, a former barrister, is defendant and attorney. The funny court-room scene is the climax, as Joe proves his innocence (he was away protecting his daughter) of his wife's charges and also manages to discommode a lawyer with designs on his spouse. Mingled with this tale is some business relating to Prohibition; a man's arrest for having liquor in his car leads to the revelation that the judge placed it there after being gifted with it by a group of leading citizens.

Arthur Hornblow noted "There is some good satire in *The Judge's Husband*—but a little too much play to the gallery of anti-feminists."

JUDY [Musical/Romance] B: Mark Swan; M: Charles Rosoff; LY: Leo Robin; SC: Mark Swan's farce *Judy Drops In*; D: John Hayden; CH: Bobby Connolly; P: John Henry Mears; T: Royale Theatre; 2/7/27 (104)

Mark Swan turned his 1924 farce *Judy Drops In* into this mildly received musical starring a too-plump Queenie Smith as the girl who takes up with a group of Greenwich Village fellows as their housekeeper and ends up marrying one of them (Charles Purcell). The *Times* called it "another thoroughly routine musical show." It put its emphasis on energetic dancing, while its book, lyrics, music, and humor barely scraped by. The only thing of note, according to First Nighter, was that the show "opened...with a bluntly posed nude who exits rapidly, taking with her the last of the bare facts to be exposed and leaving darkness and disappointment to a dastardly discouraged audience."

JUDY DROPS IN [Comedy/Romance] A: Mark Swan; P: John Henry Mears; T: Punch and Judy Theatre; 10/4/24 (43)

A contrived and stereotypical little comedy of the *La Boheme* mold that at times effected "an air of charm and whimsy" (*Times*) and that was characterized by *Time* as "one of those clean, wholesome entertainments to which you can take your great aunt. Almost anyone else would be bored to death."

In a Greenwich Village studio apartment called the "Rookery" live several rambunctious young men, including a sculptor, a medical student, and a painter; their names are Tom (George Meeker), Dick (Edward H. Wever), and Harry (Frank Beaston). Also residing there is a lawyer named Jack (Donald Gallaher). Locked out of her home by her strict stepfather because of her late hours, a girl named Judy (Marian Mears) turns up at the Rookery past midnight, dressed in a pierrette costume worn to a ball. The fellows take her in and she proceeds to reform them, with she and Jack becoming romantically involved.

JULIE [Drama/Rural/Alcoholism/Family/Romance] A: Arthur Corning White; D: Arthur Hurley; P: Homeric Productions, Inc.; T: Lyceum Theatre; 5/9/27 (8)

A northern New Hampshire farm was the setting for this "deadly dull" (First Nighter) flop about a whiskey-drenched Canuck mother (Alison Skipworth) who seeks to palm her virgin daughter Julie (Betty Pierce) off on Pierre (Edward Arnold), a fat Canuck bootlegger, in return for a supply of hooch. Julie suffers the anguish of a love for Lee Stone (Alexander Clark, Jr.), which is hindered by his mother's (Blanche Frederici) opposition to this girl she believes to be the parent of a bastard child. Only when it is finally revealed that the child is that of Phoebe (Mildred Southwick), whom Mrs. Stone had wanted as a daughter-in-law, is everything happily resolved.

Richard Dana Skinner walked out in the middle, and the *Times* maintained that "The main story and the main characters never bring conviction for a moment."

(1) JULIUS CAESAR [Dramatic Revival] A: William Shakespeare; D/P: John E. Kellard; T: Manhattan Opera House (OB); 12/16/20 (4)

John E. Kellard led a troupe of mostly third-rate players in a repertory of five Shakespearean plays at the Manhattan Opera House, but reviews are not available. One of the better actors in the company was Ian Keith.

(2) D/P: Fritz Leiber; T: Lexington Theatre (OB); 12/3/20 (1)

Fritz Leiber led several troupes of earnest actors through Shakespeare's paces during the twenties and received generally respectable reviews for his sincere but not especially significant interpretations. His *Julius Caesar* productions were seen in the revival cited in the heading on 12/30/21 at the same theatre for one performance, on 1/19/22 at the Forty-eighth Street Theatre for three performances, and on 4/30/30 at the Shubert Theatre for two performances; the Shubert run was the actor's most attended to of the decade, since it was with a new company he led, the Chicago Civic Shakespeare Society, as part of a visiting nine-play repertory of the Bard's works.

Leiber played Marc Antony in the 1930 revival, Hart Jenks was Caesar, William Courtleigh was Brutus, Lawrence H. Cecil was Cassius, Kathryn Collier was Calphurnia, and Virginia Bronson was Portia. "The production was fairly concise, well paced and, in respect to Mr. Leiber's personal contribution, interesting," reported the *Times*. Somewhat tired vocally, Leiber "offered a vivid, resourceful and adequately incendiary portrayal." He played the funeral scene "with a showmanlike ardor and craftiness that would have swayed rabble even less prepared to be swayed than" the extras in the production. William Courtleigh's Brutus had dignity but lacked passion, although his scene with Cassius was effective.

(3) M: Charles L. Safford; D: John Craig; S: Norman Bel Geddes; P: Players' Club; T: New Amsterdam Theatre; 6/6/27 (8)

Staged as the annual Players' Club classic revival, *Julius Caesar* suffered from a short rehearsal period, lack of careful casting, and inadequate direction. Only Norman Bel Geddes's distinctive settings gained universal acclamation. "With his usual flare for telling simplicity, Mr. Geddes has built nearly all of his effects around a few columns so lighted and arranged as to give an unmistakably authentic mood without the least effort at popular realism," wrote Richard Dana Skinner.

Basil Rathbone was Cassius ("It was most unflattering to his histrionic ability"—First Nighter), Tyrone Power was a dull and funereal Brutus, William Courtleigh was a dignified, authoritative Caesar, and James Rennie was a suprisingly good Mark Antony, bringing to the role "a truly thrilling energy and reserve force" (Skinner).

Well-known players, among them James T. Powers, Pedro de Cordoba, and Joseph Kilgour, embodied the minor roles. Mary Young was an excellent Portia. Among the rabble were famous names in the literary and visual arts, such as Don Marquis, Edgar Lee Masters, and Clayton Hamilton.

JUNE DAYS [Musical/Romance/School] B: Cyrus Wood; M: J. Fred Coots; LY: Clifford Grey; SC: the play *The Charm School*, by Alice Duer Miller and Robert Milton; D: J. J. Shubert; P: Messrs. Shubert; T: Astor Theatre; 8/6/25 (85)

Another dismally unexciting musical based on the same old noncreative instincts that had brought so many of its ilk crashing to the ground. Inspired by a mildly appreciated comedy of 1920, it had none of the appeal of the original and offered only the talents of Elizabeth Hines, "she of the handsome, athletic figure and graceful dancing" (Arthur Hornblow), as an incentive to keep spectators interested. The book "lacked sprightliness among other things, and . . . may fairly be estimated as insufficient," nagged Percy Hammond.

June Days had for its plot the romantic things that happen at a suburban school run by a young man (Roy Royston) who believes the curriculum should specialize in charm.

JUNE LOVE [Musical/Sports/Romance] B: Otto Harbach and W. H. Post; M: Rudolph Friml; LY: Brian Hooker; SC: Charlotte Thompson's book *In Search of Summer*; D: George Vivian; P: Sherman Brown; T: Knickerbocker Theatre; 4/25/21 (48)

June Love garnered few compliments other than those accorded its performers such as singer Else Alder, comic Johnny Dooley, and dancer Bertee Beaumont. The book and music were of the insipid and soon-forgotten sort, despite the reptutations of the originators.

Dooley played a golf expert who tries to keep his friend Jack Garrison (W. B. Davidson) from falling for Mrs. June Love (Alder), not realizing that she's a widow. The amateur-golf-champ Garrison weds her when he finds out the truth.

The critics thought such a lightweight show was being produced a little early in the season; the *Sun*, for instance, said, *June Love* might be all right in June, but it is a little too summery for April.

JUNE MOON [Comedy/Show Business/Romance] B: Ring Lardner and George S. Kaufman; M/LY: Ring Lardner; SC: a Ring Lardner short story; D: George S. Kaufman; S: W. Oden-Waller; P: Sam H. Harris; T: Broadhurst Theatre; 10/9/29 (272)

The laugh riot hit of 1929–1930, selected by Burns Mantle as a Best Play and considered an earthy and unconvincing satire on the money-grubbing milieu of Broadway music publishing known as Tin Pan Alley. Based loosely on a well-known Lardner short story "Some Like Them Cold," the play pictured the meeting and falling in love on a New York-bound train of Schenectady's Fred Stevens (Norman Foster) and Edna Baker (Linda Watkins); his arrival among the sharp-witted tunesmiths in Manhattan, where, despite his colossal naiveté, he becomes a success as a lyricist with a silly number called "June Moon"; the attempt of a composer's gold-digging sister-in-law (Lee Patrick) to win him; and his eventual entrapment by the girl he gave his heart to on the Pullman.

Superlatively cast and staged, with thoroughly individualized characters, the comedy was a sure-fire smash. "While it is continuously and uproariously funny, often for its local allusions, the satire deepens to an irony evolved from character as faithfully here as in any of a score of the terse and revealing Lardner tales. His ear for the American vernacular, his talent for setting it down in all its slurred and slangy economy, have come over to the stage in biting dialogue, fresh and cruel," expounded John Hutchens.

The details on how this play came to be written and rewritten in the process of turning it into a hit are revealed in Scott Meredith's *George S. Kaufman and His Friends*. Meredith also tells of the depression Ring Lardner suffered during the run, despite his success, and of his decline into alcoholism and contemplation of suicide.

JUNK [Comedy/Romance/Crime] A: Edwin B. Self; D: Charles Coburn; S: Joseph Techner; P: James Shesgreen and Edward Vroom; T: Garrick Theatre; 1/5/27 (9)

It took great restraint by some critics not to describe this play by the one word of its title. The play, a first by its author, was a "sprawling, ramshackle" affair (*Times*) starring veteran Sydney Greenstreet as a rotund junkman, Ernest John, whose good Samaritanism led him in his youth to take part in a bank robbery to help pay for an old lady's (Alice May Tuck) operation. A killing occurred during the crime. A quarter of a century later, one of the robbers has become governor (Calvin Thomas), but he is in hot water because a dying convict has mentioned his name in connection with the theft. The fat man, formerly in love with the Governor's wife (Marguerite Mosier), intercedes to take the blame on his own shoulders, which he succeeds in doing, but a bullet ends his life prematurely.

(1) JUNO AND THE PAYCOCK [Comedy-Drama/Legacy/Marriage/Politics/ Family/Irish] A: Sean O'Casey; D: Augustin Duncan; P: H. W. Romberg i/a/w John Jay Scholl; T: Mayfair Theatre (OB); 3/15/26 (72)

Dublin and London were ecstatic over this work, since recognized as a modern masterpiece, but in New York its reception was somewhat cooler. *Time* offered a couple of reasons for this: "One is unfamiliarity with Irish politics and the other the not particularly capable production."

In O'Casey's play, laughter and horror coexist, and scenes of tragedy are often contrapuntal to scenes of farce. The effect of the sudden introduction of a tragic note into the predominantly comedic mode created, said Arthur Hornblow, "a poignancy that is overwhelming." This serio-comic tone runs through the story of the Boyles, a Dublin family of 1922, when Irish political clashes between the Free Staters and the Irregulars had cast the nation into a bloody civil war. Captain Boyle (Augustin Duncan) is a lazy, unemployed, shiftless, drunken, strutting "paycock," as his wife calls him. She, Juno (Louise Randolph), is a noble, hardworking, heroic figure of maternal strength. Her salary supports the household. Their son Johnny (Barry McCollum) has been crippled by his actions in the political fighting. The daughter Mary (Isabel Stuart Hill) is out of work because of a strike. There is also the paycock's equally n'er-do-well parasitic wastrel buddy Joxer Daly (Claude Cooper). The action follows this group through the discovery that the Boyles have inherited a fortune, their consequent expenditure of money on ostentatious furnishings, the revelation that the legacy is an error, and the repossession of the goods. There is also the subplot of the daughter's romance with the English teacher (Charles Webster), who departs, leaving her pregnant, after he learns that there will be no inheritance, and the execution of Johnny by the Irregulars for his having betrayed a neighbor's son.

Responses to the play were sharply varied. Speaking for the negatively minded, Joseph Wood Krutch argued that the work was one of merely local interest and that in New York it was "only a rather bungling affair which though frequently amusing reveals the inexperienced hand of its author in its halting action and its frequent lapses into conventional theatre.... [O'Casey] lacks the art to give his perceptions any really forceful expression." On the other side stood Hornblow, for whom this was "a really great play, rich in laughter and rollicking humor, astonishingly true in its types, tender and sincere in its humanity and pathos."

The play was given at the new 300-seat Off-Broadway Mayfair on Forty-fourth Street east of Broadway.

(2) [Dramatic Revival] P: The Irish Players i/a/w George C. Tyler; T: Gallo Theatre; 12/19/27 (25)

As played by the visiting Irish players from Dublin, O'Casey's play came to life as few who had seen its earlier New York staging could have envisioned. However, poor direction and lighting marred the work for many.

O'Casey's writing was thunderously applauded for its incisive drawing of Irish character, its imaginative grasp of authentic atmosphere, and its comic honesty; his plot was deemed of only secondary value.

John Mason Brown, describing the similarity in "lack of restraint" that marked the acting, wrote: "In moments of fisticuffs (and there are many), their own exuberance makes them overstep the bounds of comedy and leap into farce. In the lulls in action and the preparatory stretches their methods demand a readjustment from playgoers accustomed to the insistent drive of American productions. . . . Both their slowness and their expansiveness prove, . . . however, to be the proper—almost inevitable—manner of giving the plays their final authenticity."

The most significant contributions were those of Arthur Sinclair as the Paycock, Sara Allgood as Juno, Maire O'Neill as Maisie Madigan, and Sydney Morgan as Joxer.

JUST A MINUTE [Musical/Romance/Show Business] B/D: H. C. Greene; M: Harry Archer; LY: Walter O'Keefe; CH: Russell Markert; S: P. Dodd Ackerman; P: Phil Morris and H. C. Greene; T: Ambassador Theatre; 10/8/28 (80)

This show offered little to advance the art of musical comedy; in fact, it threatened to hinder that advance. The *Times* asserted, "It is not a good show; in spite of certain lamentable features, particularly an appallingly weak book, it is not quite a bad one."

A thread of a plot held this jerrybuilt show together; it was about a girl persuaded by her songwriter boyfriend to get friendly with a Broadway producer on behalf of the songwriter and his partner; however, the girl and the producer start a serious affair. In the main, the show was really a series of vaudeville acts, with Arthur and Morton Havel the chief comic interests.

JUST BECAUSE [Musical/Romance] B/LY: Anne Wynne O'Ryan and Helen S. Woodruff; M: Madelyn Sheppard; D: Oscar Eagle; P: Just Because, Inc.; T: Earl Carroll Theatre; 3/22/22 (46)

Although female dramatists were not uncommon in the twenties, few musicals were written entirely by the distaff side. *Just Because* was an exception, but it did not help make the show a success. A "feeble" (*Times*) book and lyrics and unexceptional tunes supported a story about a man (Frank Moulan) with nine daughters living in the country next door to a millionaire (Charles Trowbridge), who, contrary to his claims of being a woman hater, is raising a group of girl orphans to become model young ladies. A romance ensues between the yougest of the daughters (Jane Richardson) and the millionaire when the girl figures she can land him if she dresses and behaves like one of his young charges.

Top dance honors went to Queenie Smith as one of the daughters.

JUST BEYOND [Drama/Family/Rural/Marriage/British] A: Reginald Goode; D: A. E. Anson; S: Clark Robinson; P: Charles K. Gordon; T: National Theatre; 12/1/25 (7)

This play's setting, Gundra-mundra (Just Beyond), in New South Wales, Australia, was its most unusual feature. It was a talky but fairly interesting melodrama of life on an Aussie sheep ranch to which a shell-shocked officer (Cyril Keightly) returns from the war with his American bride (Wanda Lyon) so that they may settle down to a life of sheep raising with his family. A long drought so unnerves him that he suspects his brother (Leslie Barrie) of planning adultery with his wife. He comes to his senses when stunned by a bolt of lightning, precursor to the sought-for heavenly downpour.

"The materials woven into this febrile fancy were for the most part coarse," stated Wells Root. The work (formerly titled *Drought*) was filled with sentimental touches and treacly characters; at one point a live kangaroo bounded about the stage.

JUST FANCY [Musical/Romance/Southern] B: Joseph Santley and Gertrude Purcell; M: Joseph Meyer and Philip Charig; LY: Leo Robin; SC: A. E. Thomas's farce *Just Suppose*; D/P: Joseph Santley; CH: Chester Hale; T: Casino Theatre; 10/11/27 (79)

A musical version of the 1920 play that saw Leslie Howard make his New York debut. Joseph Santley, who cowrote the book and directed and produced it, played the Prince of Wales and Ivy Sawyer played Linda Lee Stafford, the American belle the Prince falls in love with during his visit to this country. Possibly to avoid embarrassing the heir to the British throne, the musical's action was set back to the Victorian era, and the Prince in question was made Edward VII; a prologue set in the present revealed an aged Aunt Linda Lee (Mrs. Thomas Whiffen) recalling her youthful escapade before the lights dimmed and action flashed back to the crinolined past.

The husband and wife team of Santley and Sawyer were "charming with just the right touch of sentiment to make their scenes affecting," said the *Times*. Otherwise, the show was overproduced, with too many heavy, slow-shifting sets. Comic actors Raymond Hitchcock and Eric Blore were subdued by the inanity of their material, but the dance routines, largely in the hands of the Chester Hale girls, were skillfully done.

JUST LIFE [Comedy/Marriage/Family/Show Business/Sex/Romance] A: John Bowie; D: Oscar Eagle; S: Nicholas Yellenti; P: Jacob Oppenheimer; T: Henry Miller's Theatre; 9/14/26 (80)

The clash between the staid conservatism of the Victorian mode and the loose liberalism of the modern underpinned this crudely written piece starring Marjorie Rambeau as a famous opera singer. Larry Barretto opined that she "struggled gallantly through this morass of platitudes, but...could not save the play"; Brooks Atkinson added that, despite the title, it had no relation to life.

Madame Bernice Chase (Rambeau) gives up her retirement to go back on the operatic stage to help her husband (Clyde Fillmore) out of monetary and legal problems (he has passed bad checks). She goes abroad for the better part of a year but returns to find her spouse in love with another woman; her daughter (Vivian Tobin), a profligate in the truest flapper style, runs off with the young man she loves. Madame Chase thereupon finds a lover (Boyd Marshall) among her chosen friends and plans to meet the fellow in Rome.

JUST MARRIED [Comedy/Sex/Sea/Romance] A: Adelaide Matthews and Anne Nichols; D: J. C. Huffman and Clifford Stork; P: Jules Hurtig i/a/w Messrs. Shubert; T: Comedy Theatre; 4/26/21 (307)

"*Just Married* is another ordinary, cut-to-pattern bedroom farce, the bedroom this time being a stateroom de-luxe on an Atlantic liner," wrote Arthur Hornblow. Lynne Overman as the farcical hero received superlative notices and was largely responsible for the hit proportions achieved by the piece.

Overman portrayed Robert Adams, a gentleman who, while inebriated, boards a liner docked at Bordeaux and takes up occupancy in a stateroom that is shared by single Roberta Adams (Vivian Martin), who believed her roommate would be another female. It requires several acts before she can straighten the mixup out with the Witters, the couple chaperoning her, but by then Roberta and Robert are in love.

"Barring the fact that it has no single element of novelty it may be ranked as fair to middling," was Heywood Broun's decision.

JUST SUPPOSE [Comedy/Romance/Southern] A: A. E. Thomas; T: Henry Miller's Theatre; 11/1/20 (88)

A prophetic little comedy that just supposed that the Prince of Wales (Geoffrey Kerr), visiting in Washington, D.C., encounters at a Virginia home replete with southern moonlight and fragrant breezes pretty American Linda Lee (Patricia Collinge) and falls instantly in love with her but must in the end give her up when she refuses to force him to abdicate on her behalf. Of course, when the real Prince of Wales fell for Mrs. Wallis Simpson some years later, no such denouement eventuated.

"There is much that is interesting and a good deal that is exceedingly charming in the somewhat awkwardly built but prettily decorated comedy," wrote Alexander Woollcott. Among the better performances was that of English actor Leslie Howard, making his New York debut as the Prince's clownish chum.

Just Suppose became *Just Fancy* when it was made into a musical comedy in 1927.

K

K GUY, THE [Comedy/Films/Crime] A: Walter De Leon and Alethea Luce; D: Melville Burke; S: Theodore Kahn; P: Irving and Charles Yates; T: Biltmore Theatre; 10/15/28 (8)

Infrequent humor and flimsy construction were responsible for this play's youthful demise. One of many twenties comedies about Hollywood, it was set in the lunchroom of the Idol Film Company and combined one story about a hunt for a forger who always adds a "k" to his phony check signatures with another about a new movie actor who may or may not be the forger.

The stories were not well fused, but the evening was salvaged to a degree "by the brightness of its dialogue" (*Times*). *Time* said it was "somewhat amusing."

KANSAS CITY KITTY [Comedy/Romance/Illness] A: Roland Oliver; S: Joseph A. Physioc; T: Gansevoort Theatre (OB); 9/26/29 (2)

A Greenwich Village offering about Kitty (Evelyn Platt), a pretty girl who uses her looks to get ahead with her tubercular boss whom she eventually weds and vows to help cure. The *Times* found some of the characters "natural and entertaining," others less so, and had little of a concrete nature to offer concerning other aspects of the piece.

KARL AND ANNA (Karl und Anna) [Drama/German/Prison/Marriage] A: Leonhard Frank; TR: Ruth Langner; SC: Leonhard Frank's novel of the same name; D: Philip Moeller; S: Jo Mielziner; P: Theatre Guild; T: Guild Theatre; 10/7/29 (49)

Karl and Anna had been very successful in its native Germany, but it bombed in its Theatre Guild showing. This Enoch Arden variation had certain ripe moments, but the play as a whole bore only bitter fruit. It supposed that a German soldier, Karl (Otto Kruger), having escaped from a Russian prison camp where he learned from his friend Richard (Frank Conroy) all about the latter's wife, Anna (Alice Brady), goes to her in Berlin, passes himself off as her much-changed spouse, wins her love—even though she is aware of the ruse—and retains it even when Richard himself eventually returns.

It was a promising play until its third act, claimed the *Times*. Perriton Maxwell believed "that its theme is dependent on the fusion of such subtle, subjective forces that it could never have been effectively worked out in the objective medium of the theatre." Joseph Wood Krutch's disappointment arose because "It is flat, it is spiritless, and it leaves the spectator not so much unconvinced as unconcerned." The choice of this play proved seriously disturbing to various critics who saw in it a symptom of the Guild's growing weakness as a result of its having expanded its New York and road-show operations enormously in recent years.

KATERINA (Vekaterina Ivanovna) [Drama/Marriage/Sex/Russian] A: Leonid Andreyev; TR: Herman Bernstein; D: Eva Le Gallienne; DS: Aline Bernstein; P: Civic Repertory Company; T: Civic Repertory Theatre (OB); 2/25/29 (19)

A melancholy 1912 Russian drama concerning "the fact that the infliction of an injustice on a person may have the effect of dehumanizing that person" (Padraic Colum). Alla Nazimova played the title role, that of a woman whose jealous husband (Walter Beck) has not only unjustly accused her of adultery but has shot three times at her. She packs her bags and leaves with her children and soon descends into a life of casual degeneracy in revenge against her husband's accusations. Realizing what he has wrought, the husband tries to make up, but her spiritual murder has been accomplished, and it is too late; she has become what she was censured for being.

Nazimova gave what was considered by some a Duse-like enactment of her role in this tragic, relentless, but uneven drama. Colum thought its tone was too masochistic and the heroine too romanticized. Richard Dana Skinner wished to see more of a spiritual struggle on her behalf but commended the play's power.

KATJA [Musical/Romance/British] B: Frederick Lonsdale; M: Jean Gilbert; LY: Harry Graham; D: Lewis Morton; CH: Guy Kendall; P: Messrs. Shubert; T: Forty-fourth Street Theatre; 10/18/26 (113)

One of two Lonsdale works that opened simultaneously, *Katja* was an operetta that Arthur Hornblow said offered "Good music, plenty of humor, interesting story, effective scenery and entertaining cast—a much too rare combination in musical productions." Lonsdale's dialogue had been Americanized, but four of the London cast's leading players came to these shores to perform it. The titular role was played by Lillian Davies, whom George Jean Nathan thought was far too old for it.

Katja depicted the many events transpiring in a single night at Monte Carlo, all of them involving the story of Princess Katja and Prince Ivo (Dennis Hoey), whose estates were snatched by Prince Carl (Allan Prior) and who have taken to performing as dancers to earn their keep. Carl encounters them when he visits

the home of Count Orpitch (Bruce Winston), and he falls for Katja; only after
various developments, including several murder attempts (Ivo is a villain who
desires Katja), do things conclude satisfactorily.

KATY DID [Comedy/Prohibition/Romance] A: Willis Maxwell Goodhue; D:
Oscar Eagle; P: Edward Whiteside and J. J. Levinson; T: Daly's Sixty-third
Street Theatre; 5/9/27 (8)

This "domestic comedy with foreign relations" was "a play generally afflicted
with acute infantilism," commented the *Times*. It was concerned with Katie
Donovan (Juliette Day), a Childs Restaurant waitress who meets a hungry dish-
washer, Carlo Emarri (Romney Brent), who happens to be the King of Suavia;
she marries him, and they become enmeshed in various adventures involving
his activities as a bootlegger.

KEEP IT CLEAN [Revue] B: Jimmy Duffy and Will Morrissey; M/LY: Jimmy
Duffy, Will Morrissey, Lester Lee, Harry Archer, Benny Ryan, James Hanley,
Clarence Gaskill, Violinsky, Charles Tobias, and Harry Converse; CH: Russell
Markert; T: Selwyn Theatre; 6/24/29 (16)

This turkey came and went very early in the season. It was an intimate revue
for which Will Morrissey and Jimmy Duffy were largely responsible, as writers
and performers, and was judged by the *Times* "a hodge-podge of vaudeville,
revue and night club specialties." It lacked originality in all areas. Morrissey
tried to amuse with a comic monologue filled with too many theatrical in-jokes,
Douglas Stanbury's singing of "Marching Home" seemed out of place, there
was a tasteless comedy song about the Lindbergh-Morrow nuptials sung by
Duffy, and Morrissey's wife, Midgie Miller, stood out as the show's freshest
talent, especially in a Bea Lillie impersonation set in a sketch called "English
Actors at Home."

KEEP KOOL [Revue] B/LY: Paul Gerard Smith; M/ADD. LY.: Jack Frost;
D: Earl Lindsay; S: H. Robert Law; C: Kiviette; P: E. K. Nadel; T: Morosco
Theatre; 5/22/24 (148)

Heywood Broun noted that *Keep Kool*'s advertising slogan had been "Positively and absolutely no dramatic critics in this cast," but that "their show is
excellent despite this omission," because it had a revue's prime requisite, "pace,
a pace precise, cumulative and contagious." Broun thought this was an ensemble
show, although he singled out contralto Ann Butler, comedian Johnny Dooley,
song and dance man Charles King, and veteran Hazel Dawn.

The *Times* critic praised these performers as well as Ina Williams's clowning,
and found the show to be "a workmanlike revue of the better order." He noted
that lyricist–book writer Paul Gerard Smith's name had been appearing on revue
programs for several seasons as a writer of sketches used to separate musical
numbers. Several critics found amusing Smith's scene in which Eugene O'Neill,

Avery Hopwood, and George M. Cohan treated the same subject in their distinctive styles.

H.H.

KEEP SHUFFLIN' [Musical/Blacks/Crime] B: Flournoy Miller and Aubrey Lyles; M: Jimmy Johnson, Thomas "Fats" Waller, and Clarence Todd; LY: Henry Creamer and Andy Razaf; P: Con Conrad; T: Daly's Sixty-third Street Theatre; 2/27/28 (104)

A black musical that hoped to become a follow-up to *Shuffle Along*, the major black show of the decade, which had played at the same theatre with the same colibrettists and stars, Miller and Lyles. They had not much in the way of good comedy to fool with, and the show's tunes, although zesty, were unexceptional. Although described as a book show, it employed a large number of specialty numbers; there were twenty-two songs in the score. Top dancing talents Billy Yarbough and Maude Russell made a strong mark, as did pit pianist and co-composer "Fats" Waller, whose enthusiastic keyboard pounding drew considerable attention.

The onionskin plot had Miller and Lyles once more playing Steve Jenkins and Sam Peck, a pair of shiftless types who head a utopian group called the Equal Got Club for which they plan to dynamite the Jimtown bank and hand out equal proportions of the loot, keeping a mite more for themselves. When they obtain the cash, they can't spend it, since everyone has closed up shop so as not to have to work anymore.

(1) KEMPY [Comedy/Small Town/Romance] A: J. C. Nugent and Elliott Nugent; D: Augustin Duncan; P: Richard G. Herndon; T: Belmont Theatre; 5/15/ 22 (212)

J. C. Nugent had been a headliner in vaudeville for many years; although he had written many plays, none had been accepted for New York production until *Kempy*. He wrote the piece while on the vaudeville circuit, using some material he already had employed in his popular vaudeville sketch, "The Rounders." Later, he read the material to his fledgling actor son, Elliott, then appearing in the pre-New York tour of *Dulcy*. Elliott's comments were so perceptive he was commissioned to rewrite the play and receive coauthor credit. When the play finally was produced, it also had the benefit of uncredited additions by Howard Lindsay. Various producers turned the play down, however, most agreeing, as J. C. Nugent said in his autobiography, *It's a Great Life*, "that it was too simple and too unpretentious for sophisticated Broadway." The play was tried out in Pennsylvania by a pair of producers, but dropped before going on to New York. Finally, Nugent convinced Richard G. Herndon to put it on by offering to bring it in for $6,000 (Herndon thought it needed $10,000), half of which he would put up himself, thereby becoming the uncredited coproducer. Nugent cast the show with his daughter Ruth in a supporting role and Elliott in the title part. Nugent himself wanted to play the role of the fortyish Duke Merrill, but was persuaded that he would do much better in the character role of Old Man Bence. The show went on to become a major hit of the season and established the father and son team as a major writing and acting force on Broadway during the decade.

The play was a nonsensical romantic trifle about a poor small-town New Jersey youth, "Kempy" James, who practices plumbing while studying to be an architect; he goes to a home to do a job, and meets there a girl, Kate (Lotus Robb), who has just quarreled with her lawyer fiancé, Duke Merrill (Grant Mitchell). Within a half-hour the young man and the girl are on their way to a Justice of the Peace to get married; however, on their wedding night Kate's father kicks Kempy out of the house and sends his daughter to bed. In the morning, the matter is placed in the clever lawyer boyfriend's hands, and he comes up with a solution that works things out amicably for everyone.

Arthur Hornblow said "the play contains all the ingredients a veteran of the theatre knows so well how to employ—surprise, humor, clever lines, gaiety, human interest," to which was added enough "fantasy and whimsical imagination [to make] the entire evening delightful entertainment."

(2) [Dramatic Revival] D: J. C. Nugent; P: Murray Phillips; T: Hudson Theatre; 5/11/27 (48)

An appreciated restaging of the 1922 hit with the Nugent family redoing their original roles. Richard Dana Skinner noted of J. C. Nugent: "His range is somewhat limited by physical appearance and vocal equipment, but within that range he can be as moving an actor as we have on the stage. His work is notable for its great simplicity and the perfection of its detail."

Elliott Nugent appeared only in the early showings of the revival, and then left for another engagement, his role being taken by Anderson Lawlor. Lotus Robb was once again in the role of Kate Bence.

KEPT [Comedy/Old Age/Alcoholism/Romance] A: Pierre Gendron; D: Ira Hards; S: Albert Bliss; P: Chamberlain Brown; T: Comedy Theatre; 9/17/26 (11)

An inept, and quickly vanished, piece about a disillusioned young architect, Norman Henderson (Robert Williams), who is involved in a drunken-driving accident, thereby bringing him into contact with a lonely old lady (Minnie Dupree), at a nursing home, whose maternal instinct he arouses. She moves in with him to his New York apartment but is eventually rejected when Norman slips back into despondency and goes on a binge at the instigation of his mistress Vera (Zola Talma). He then repents and takes the old lady back into his heart.

Minnie Dupree's performance was all that could be recommended of this clumsy effort, which Brooks Atkinson deemed an old-fashioned package of "theatrical sentimentalism" during which much of the audience departed.

KIBITZER, THE [Comedy/Jews/Family/Business/Romance/Gambling] A: Jo Swerling and Edward G. Robinson; D/P: Patterson McNutt; T: Royale Theatre; 2/18/29 (127)

Leo Rosten's *Joys of Yiddish* defines a *kibitzer* as "someone who kibitzes—that is, gives unasked for advice, especially a bystander-observer at a game." Such is I. Lazarus (Edward G. Robinson), this play's central character, a cigarstore merchant of Amsterdam Avenue, who offers his unsought opinions on everyone's contemplated wagers. When he visits the office of the Wall Street millionaire father (Eugene Powers) of the boy his daughter (Jeanne Greene) loves, he saves the financier from a crazed secretary and cannot come up with a decision when told to name his own reward. He is given power over a sizable chunk of steel stock, installs a ticker tape in his shop, sells his cronies shares in the potential profits, and watches the stock climb in price. Before he can make up his mind when to sell, the stock plummets. He is saved because a weakminded relative gave the order to sell when the price was at the top.

The Kibitzer, coauthored by star Edward G. Robinson, was a favorite; he gave one of his most admired impersonations in it. Richard Dana Skinner, who lauded the play's universality, irony, sentiment, and hilarity, said Robinson gave "a wholly creative character study" as Lazarus.

According to Robinson's autobiography *All My Yesterdays*, the play had been a failure in Atlantic City. Some time later, after Robinson had been in two other plays, he got together with Swerling to discuss *The Kibitzer*. Swerling took Robinson's ideas down on the typewriter. The actor was surprised to see that the rewritten play gave him coauthorship credit.

KID BOOTS [Musical/Sports/Prohibition/Romance] B: William Anthony McGuire and Otto Harbach; M: Harry Tierney; LY: Joseph McCarthy; D/CH: Edward Royce; P: Florenz Ziegfeld; T: Earl Carroll Theatre; 12/31/23 (479)

Eddie Cantor and ex-Follies solo dancer Mary Eaton headed the cast of this hit musical, but it was the former who was credited with most of its success. The *Herald*'s critic wrote that "To hear him explain a sex complex during a little putting contest . . . is to throw back one's head and drop ten years off one's life." Charles Belmont Davis noted that neither Cantor nor Eaton were peerless as singers, dancers, actors, or comics, but both had a rare appeal: "Personality, supposedly; the ability to establish a friendly relationship with not an audience, but all the separate individuals in an audience."

Capitalizing on current interest in golf and bootlegging, the book had Cantor as Boots, a caddy master at an exclusive Palm Beach club. Boots deals in crooked balls and bootleg booze, accidentally giving his best friend a bad ball, which loses him the club championship, but managing to arrange a love match between the friend and an heiress (Eaton). In one scene, Boots bumbles into the ladies locker room, the better to provide an opportunity to display the chorus girls. Some critics commented that the show was reminiscent of *Sally*, with its popular comedian and golden-haired dancer as central figures, although *Kid Boots* suffered by comparison. The critics found the score lively, but it was an interpolated song by Harry Akst, "Dinah," that became the popular hit.

According to Charles Higham's *Ziegfeld*, the idea for this show came when the librettist, composer, and lyricist had gathered together for purposes of devising a new Eddie Cantor show. Cantor arrived wearing such an outlandish golfing outfit that they decided at once to write a show around his getup. After a great deal of work had been done on the show, the initially enthusiastic Ziegfeld suddenly decided against doing it; he changed his mind only after the dismayed Cantor improvised the entire show for him, taking all of the roles.

Cantor's story is somewhat different as found in his book *My Life Is in Your Hands*. He says that the composer and lyricist devised the idea of a show about golf. Cantor gives a very detailed account of the entire production, shedding light on how musicals of the decade were often shaped specifically to highlight a star performer. Many of the notions incorporated into the show were actually conceived by Cantor. When the show finally ended its New York run, said the comedian, it had grossed $1,750,000.

H.H.

KIDDISH HASHEM [Drama/Period/Jews/Yiddish/Yiddish Language] A: Maurice Schwartz; SC: a novel by Sholem Asch; D/P: Maurice Schwartz; T: Yiddish Art Theatre (OB); 9/14/28

Kiddish Hashem's title, meaning the sanctification of the Holy Name, was here used to imply martyrdom for Judaism, especially as signified by the oppression of the Tartars and Cossacks. The play was a three-act, seventeen-scene episodic saga based on the 1648 Cossack uprising and massacre of Ukranian Jewry. "Although unwieldy and soft in the current production," wrote Brooks Atkinson, "it is shot through with the hopes and disasters of a far-scattered race; it is imaginative, emotional, devout, grim." Atkinson may have derided the production, but Robert Littell wrote that it displayed "great life and energy, some very remarkable acting (in particular by Maurice Schwartz), and some magnificent tableaux."

KIKI [Comedy/Romance/Show Business/French] A: André Picard; AD/D/P: David Belasco; T: Belasco Theatre; 11/29/21 (580)

David Belasco directed and adapted this sentimental Parisian Boulevard comedy, but his version put the material through an "American deodorizing process" (Arthur Hornblow) that removed all taint of the risque from what was in its French original a more realistic view of the mores of its milieu. Belasco also produced "an abominable" (Alexander Woollcott) translation in which the language of the Parisian lower classes became a strange collaboration between French phrases and the argot of Broadway showgirls. "*T'en fais-pas*, I'll hand him a dirty wallop," went one line. The play itself was decidedly second-rate stuff, but its title role allowed Lenore Ulric to perform so brilliantly that the critics tossed their adjectives into the air for joy.

Kiki is a Paris *gamine*, a chorus girl with a crush on her theatre's manager (Sam B. Hardy), who is married to but estranged from the star performer (Arline Fredericks); the latter is seeking to get him back. In the best-liked comedy scene,

Kiki, faced with a choice between becoming the mistress of Baron Rapp (Max Figman) or returning to the streets, pretends to be the victim of a cataleptic trance. The play ends with Kiki and the manager happily in love with each other.

Writing of Ulric's acting, Ludwig Lewisohn noted: "Miss Ulric's playing is perfect. She has made over her body. Every gesture, every step, her very nerves and sinews are drenched with Kiki." Before it closed, *Kiki* had become the longest running Broadway play derived from a French original.

KILLERS [Drama/Marriage/Mystery/Trial/Crime] A: Louis E. Bisch and Howard Merling; D: Howard Merling; P: Contemporary Theatre, Inc.; T: Forty-ninth Street Theatre; 3/13/28 (23)

A lumpishly constructed, but occasionally involving, melodrama; the *Times* said it was "wabbly" and suffered from "strangely scattered quality." Its story told of a woman (Cynthia Blake) who hires several gangsters to kill her philandering husband (George Clarkson); he is shot in a speakeasy but not, apparently, by the gunmen, who, as it turns out, are arrested and found guilty. They are incarcerated and then escape from prison; one of them (Harold Vermilyea) is about to go to the electric chair, which is shown in the last scene, when the wife confesses that she is the killer.

"With too much plot and thirty-four characters, *Killers* misses fire," noted *Time*: "Its message: 'We are all killers at heart.' "

KILPATRICK'S OLD-TIME MINSTRELS [Revue] AD: Henry Myers; D: Walter F. Scott and J. A. Shipp; P: Thomas Kilpatrick; T: Royale Theatre; 4/19/30 (8)

The last time a minstrel show came to New York was in 1908, according to *Time*, so this example was welcomed with some interest. However, despite the authenticity of the material, the public was unconcerned. The all-black show employed burnt cork for its lighter members and used colorful costumes, a sartorially resplendent Mr. Interlocutor (Henry Troy), and songs such as "When the Bell in the Lighthouse Rings" and "Trans-mag-ni-fi-can-bam-dam-u-ality."

The weakest part was the variety act or Olio section, in which a ventriloquist, female impersonator, and singers were presented before an old-time advertisement-cluttered show curtain. This material, said Brooks Atkinson, was "labored and spasmodic."

KING CAN DO NO WRONG, THE [Drama/Romance/Politics/Crime] A/D: Frank S. Merlin; P: James W. Elliott; T: Theatre Masque; 11/16/27 (13)

An unnamed South American kingdom was the setting for this middling melodrama about the efforts of the gold-braided Baron Reus (Lionel Atwill), chief of the Secret Police, to track down, despite many dangers, the assassin of the Crown Prince (Guy Phillips), to whom he was devoted; actually, the Prince was a devilish fellow who tried to seduce the Baron's niece and did deflower the fiancée of the American envoy (Larry Fletcher). Reus is swept up into a revolution, becomes a hero, wins the widow (Leona Hogarth) of his late traitorous rival (Felix Krembs), reveals the envoy—who shoots himself—as the assassin, and is elected president of the new republic.

It was merely "pretentious claptrap," maintained Percy Hammond who also ridiculed the gaudy costumes and demeanor affected by Atwill as the stately hero.

KING HENRY IV (PART I) [Dramatic Revival] A: William Shakespeare; D: Henry Herbert; S: Charles B. Falls; P: Players' Club; T: Knickerbocker Theatre; 5/31/26 (8)

Not since 1896 had New York seen Shakespeare's great historical drama focusing on the relationship of Prince Hal and Sir John Falstaff and on the rebellion of Hotspur against King Henry IV. The production, given as the annual classical revival of the Players' Club, employed the distinguished services of a long list of well-known actors, and their script was one edited by Brian Hooker, to which a prologue especially written for the old star John Drew was prefixed.

There ensued a memorable presentation, marked by several distinguished performances but marred by the roughness to which such ill-rehearsed "all-star" mountings were susceptible. Otis Skinner was Falstaff; Philip Merivale, Hotspur; Peggy Wood, Lady Percy; Basil Sydney, Prince Hal; William Courtleigh, Henry IV; and Blanche Ring, Mistress Quickly.

The play itself received only tepid appreciation. Richard Dana Skinner, for instance, thought it was more two plays than one, "a comedy and a romantic tragedy," and Brooks Atkinson wrote, "most of this history moves ponderously across the stage." The mounting itself, stated Burns Mantle, had "dignity and form, if not much lift," and Wells Root declared that it "fell between the flamboyant and the casual. . . . There is little daring . . . but much satisfaction." The principal textual innovation was the interpolation of the Shallow (Guy Nichols)-Silence (J. M. Kerrigan) scene from Part II, to add comic relief.

KING HENRY V [Dramatic Revival] A: William Shakespeare; D/P: Walter Hampden; DS: Claude Bragdon; T: Hampden's Theatre; 3/15/28 (51)

The present century had seen only two revivals of this chronicle play, one in 1900 with Richard Mansfield and one in 1912 with Lewis Waller, before Walter Hampden's respectful 1928 interpretation. It was designed with artful simplicity using draperies, a few selected pieces of furniture, and ingenious lighting. Richard Dana Skinner thought the sets "not only facilitate rapid changes of scene, but have a rare beauty not at all in the line of conventional realism." But Hampden's staging and performance were less widely admired. The dignity and seriousness of purpose everywhere apparent tended to dampen whatever life was in the piece and make it largely uninteresting.

Joseph Wood Krutch described the event as "somewhat uneven, but on the whole satisfactory enough in a generally conventional fashion. . . . Mr. Hampden is rather too gravely mature to give an ideal representation of the fiery young monarch.''

(1) KING LEAR [Dramatic Revival) A: William Shakespeare; D/P: Reginald Pole: T: Earl Carroll Theatre; 3/9/23 (2)

Shakespeare's solemn tragedy of the British King ill served by two of his three daughters had last been seen in New York in 1918 in one of Robert Mantell's recurring productions. The present ineffective mounting, shown at two matinees under the direction of and starring British actor Reginald Pole, was given in Elizabethan costumes that hampered the otherwise uninventive production. Pole further alienated the critics by casting a woman (Beata Karm) in the role of the Fool. ''To make matters worse,'' wrote Stephen Rathbun, ''the actress spoke her lines rapidly and what she said was often unintelligible.''

Pole, only in his early thirties, was too young for the role, aside from being ''an actor of little emotional power'' (Rathbun). He and his cast spoke in the studied declamatory tones of elocutionists, while behind them stood a dull and dreary looking set of black drapery, pulled aside by pages whenever necessary to suggest a change of scene. Some platforming also was used. There were few people left in the house when the final curtain fell.

(2) D: Fritz Leiber; P: Chicago Civic Shakespeare Society; S: Herman Rosse; T: Shubert Theatre; 3/31/30 (3)

A revival included among nine Shakespearean productions brought to Broadway by Fritz Leiber at the head of the Chicago Civic Shakespeare Society. Joseph Wood Krutch proclaimed it ''the most unsatisfactory of'' Leiber's revivals: ''[N]o matter how vigorously Mr. Leiber vociferated he never once succeeded in convincing the audience that his passion rose to a height which would justify the wildness of the words he was called upon to utter.'' Yet Krutch had to admit that the production revealed new depths in the play for him, especially in its revelation both of a profound nihilism and of advanced methods of expressing it. The scene on the heath seemed as good an example of modern expressionism as any.

In Brooks Atkinson's estimation the play was excessively cut, the characters pared to the bone, and certain scenes seemed unmotivated. He noted that the version used was Edwin Booth's as edited by William Winter, one that no longer was tenable. He deemed the mounting unexciting and too noisy with offstage effects (Tchaikovsky's music was heard thundering during Cordelia [Marie Carroll] and Lear's reunion). He described Leiber's Lear as ''hoary-headed, gnarled with weary age. . . . It is a Lear of petulance, grimness and wrath,'' but one that declined into ''tired declamation.'' The supporting cast was competent, nothing more.

KING SAUL (Saul Hamelich) [Drama/Bible/Old Age/Period/Yiddish/Yiddish Language] A: Paul Heyse; D/P: Maurice Schwartz; T: Yiddish Art Theatre (Nora Bayes Theatre); 9/17/25

The Yiddish Art Theatre took up a brief residency at Broadway's Bayes Theatre for this biblical drama based on the first Book of Samuel and starring Maurice Schwartz in the title role. The *Times* found his acting poignantly expressive as the aged patriarch and recommended the performance for its dramatic strength.

KINGDOM OF GOD, THE (El reino de Dios) [Drama/Religion/Spanish] A: Gregorio Martinez-Sierra; TR: Helen and Harley Granville-Barker; D: E. M. Blythe (Ethel Barrymore); S: Watson Barratt; C: Orry Kelly; P: Lee Shubert; T: Ethel Barrymore Theatre; 12/20/28 (93)

Ethel Barrymore was the distinguished star of this sensitive, although tenuous, Spanish drama produced for the opening of the new theatre erected in her name. It turned out to be the next-to-last theatre built on the Great White Way for nearly fifty years. Barrymore's portrayal of Sister Gracia did not overcome whatever restlessness "the frailty and shapelessness" (Brooks Atkinson) of the play induced, however. Despite a mixed reception, it was chosen as a Best Play of the Year.

The work covers the life of Sister Gracia in three acts, taking her from ages nineteen to seventy, and studies the growth of her wisdom and benevolence as a nun in the Order of St. Vincent de Paul, devoted to ministering to the ill and to teaching children. She is seen at three stages of her career, as a young woman caring for the residents of an old men's home, as a woman of nearly thirty in a home for unwed mothers, and as an aged and lame Mother Superior at the head of a poverty-stricken orphanage.

The large cast provided a detailed background for a character study of the central role, but there was little of gripping action or emotionality until the last act when Sister Gracia had the opportunity to disclose her inmost feelings in a speech to her starving orphans. Barrymore's work was admired, but not universally; her supporting cast was considered inferior.

KISS IN A TAXI, THE (Le Monsieur de cinq heures) [Comedy/Marriage/Romance/Sex/French] A: Maurice Hennequin and Pierre Veber; AD: Clifford Grey; D: Bertram Harrison; P: A. H. Woods; T: Ritz Theatre; 8/25/25 (103)

For her next Broadway outing after the debacle of *The Wild Wescotts*, in which she debuted, Claudette Colbert chose this mildly diverting French farce in which she played the Montmartre-cabaret entertainer-mistress of banker Leon Lambert (Arthur Byron), who passes himself off to those concerned as a certain bookkeeper in his own employ. Lucien (John Williams), the youth who loves the girl, is told she is the older man's daughter, which goads him into persuading Lambert to acknowledge her as his illegitimate child, "this blossom of inadvertance." Lambert is on the verge of giving up the girl, but when his wife (Janet Beecher) learns of her existence, she insists on adopting her, thus making the sugar daddy a real daddy after all.

"Simplicity in construction and invention in the dialogue would greatly enhance this bit of nonsense,'' suggested the *Times*, which thought the play must have suffered in its move from Paris to Broadway. Arthur Hornblow deemed it ''suave and hilarious,'' though.

KISS ME [Musical/Art/Sex/Marriage/French] B: Richard Kessler; AD: Derick Wulff and Max Simon; M: Winthrop Cortelyou; LY: Derick Wulff; SC: a French farce; D: Edward Elsner; S: August Vimnera; P: J. J. Levinson; T: Lyric Theatre; 7/21/27 (28)

Based on an unspecified French farce as adapted by a German playwright, *Kiss Me* was simply ''a decidedly routine musical entertainment'' (*Times*), old-fashioned in tone and detail. Its would-be naughtiness stemmed from a naive plot about an American painter (Ralph Whitehead) in Paris whose commission to paint a Persian shah's (Joseph Macauley) favorite wife requires him to marry his secretary (Desiree Ellinger) so that he may enter the Shah's harem. Irked by her wife-in-name-only status, the secretary occupies most of the show's time by seducing the painter and fending off other aspirants to her charms.

KISSING TIME [Musical/Romance/France] B: George V. Hobart; M: Ivan Caryll; LY: Philander Johnson; SC: a French play by Adolf Philipp and Edward Paulton; D/CH: Edward Royce; P: Empire Producing Corporation; T: Lyric Theatre; 10/11/20 (65)

A background located amongst the millinary establishments of Paris permitted an array of gorgeous clothes in this modest musical based on an uncredited French comedy. A score of little distinction was not abetted by a libretto of first-rate quality. There were some good dances, especially a chicken dance, ''Kik-erikee,'' performed by Edith Taliaferro, Dorothy Maynard, Paul Frawley, and Frank Doane, but not much more.

It told of a young lady (Taliaferro) who poses as the bride of a young man (Frawley), whose employer insists that all of his workers be married. Complications arise when the boss falls for the fake wife, and the piece concludes when the girl discovers that her pretend spouse is the very man her folks have chosen for her to wed.

To the *Times* the show had ''An ingratiating score, a cohesive but none too amusing story, and a general sprightliness of movement.''

KITTY'S KISSES [Musical/Romance/Hotel] B: Philip Bartholomae and Otto Harbach; M: Con Conrad; LY: Gus Kahn; SC: Philip Bartholomae's farce *Little Miss Brown*; D: John Cromwell; CH: Bobby Connolly; P: William A. Brady; T: Playhouse Theatre; 5/6/26 (170)

''*Kitty's Kisses* is an unimportant musical comedy with a shattering succession of excellent dance numbers,'' went *Time*'s report on this show. It served well its purpose of providing light fare for summer theatregoers.

Its scrawny, but complex, book demonstrated the contretemps emerging from a situation in which Kitty Brown (Dorothy Dilley), having lost her purse and cash, is erroneously taken by the management of the Wendel Hotel for the wife of a Mr. Dennison (Mark Smith) and is ushered into his rooms, which are the bridal suite. The next morning she learns the compromising fact that she has spent the night with a married man, but since the man has a wife (Frances Burke) who wants a divorce, since her lawyer is a young man (John Boles) Kitty met on the train, and since Kitty and the lawyer have fallen in love, everything is straightened out in time for a happy ending.

KONGO [Drama/Africa/Sex/Tropics/Prostitution/Drugs] A/D: Chester De Vonde and Kilbourn Gordon; S: Nicholas Yellenti; P: Kilbourn Gordon; T: Biltmore Theatre; 3/30/26 (135)

A feverish, colorful, exciting melodrama of life in the torrid zone, where the tropical soil nourishes those whose lives are circumscribed by sex, vengeance, dope, disease, whiskey, and sadism.

In the heart of the Congo lives the half-paralyzed trader Flint (Walter Huston). This masterful but cruel man dreams of revenge on the hateful trader Kregg (Frederic Burt). Flint drives Kregg's daughter into prostitution but then learns that she is really his own child. After the girl, Annie (Florence Mason), falls in love with a dope-crazed doctor (Richard Stevenson) she helps to cure, she and the doctor are aided by Flint to escape the frenzied blacks seeking to make a sacrifice of her. Kregg dies by a native spear, and Flint remains alone in the jungle.

The piece was "gripping theatre," said Arthur Hornblow, but "The acting was superior to the play."

KOSHER KITTY KELLY [Musical/Romance/Family/Jews] B/M/LY: Leon De Costa; D: A. H. Van Buren; P: Arch Productions, Inc.; T: Times Square Theatre; 6/15/25 (105)

A not-entirely unsuccessful attempt to write a dialect musical in the vein of *Abie's Irish Rose*, this Jewish-Irish romantic farce played through the summer of 1925, closed briefly, and was given a return engagement that ran for two more months. It told of the romance of Morris Rosen (Basil Loughrane) with Kitty Kelly (Helen Shipman). In the working out of their love relationship it develops that Kitty's mother (Dorothy Walters) was married to a man who had previously been the husband of a Mrs. Feinbaum (Jennie Moscowitz). In the end, Mrs. Feinbaum's daughter Rosie (Beatrice Allen) winds up with Morris, and one Patrick O'Reilly (Fred Santley) pairs off with Kitty.

Percy Hammond reported of the show that "it proved to be a merciless and incompetent bore." Much of the humor came from words like *schlemiel* and phrases like "Bad cess to yez."

(1) KREUTZER SONATA, THE [Dramatic Revival/Yiddish Language] A: M. Katz; T: Jewish Art Theatre (OB); 10/2/20

The Kreutzer Sonata, based on a story by Leo Tolstoy, had been an important part of the Yiddish theatre repertory since its introduction in 1906 in a Jacob Gordin version starring Bertha Kalich, who revived it on a number of occasions. The present production was of a new adaptation by M. Katz for Jacob Ben-Ami's Jewish Art Theatre; its star was the great Rudolph Schildkraut. The story was of Miriam, a Russian Jewess, deserted by her Christian lover and hastily married to another man (Schildkraut) to escape the scandal of her pregnancy. Years later, after they have settled in America, her husband abuses her child and loves her younger sister. Discovering them together, Miriam kills both and goes mad.

Ralph Block found the piece "distorted, exaggerated, [and] melodramatic" but admired greatly Schildkraut's acting: "we have no native actor who can hint at so many resources and reserves as Shildkraut [*sic*] implies in his present role."

(2) A: Jacob Gordin; AD: Langdon Mitchell; D: Harrison Grey Fiske; P: Lee Shubert; T: Frazee Theatre; 5/14/24 (61)

Yiddish theatre star Bertha Kalich, who divided her time between the Yiddish and English-language stages, revived her favorite vehicle in this 1924 staging. The critics thought the piece was old-fashioned but her acting still effective.

H.H.

L

LACE PETTICOAT [Musical/Southern/Race/Romance] B: Stewart St. Clair; M: Emil Gerstenberger and Carle Carlton; LY: Howard Johnson; D/P: Carle Carlton; CH: J. J. Hughes; T: Forrest Theatre; 1/4/27 (15)

The second musical of the 1926–1927 season (after *Deep River*) to use the background of New Orleans and characters of mixed blood to tell a "tenuous" (*Times*) romantic story. This tale concerns the love affair of young naval Lieutenant Paul Joscelyn (Tom Burke) and Renita (Vivian Hart) and the attempt by another suitor Raymond De La Lange (Luis Alberni) to separate the pair by falsely claiming that Renita is a quadroon. The truth comes out at last, and the Mardi Gras can be enjoyed by the lovers with peace of mind.

The show was strictly conventional, including its familiar musical comedy staples of a drunk scene and blackface humor. Popular dance numbers were the "Creole Crawl" and "Skeleton Ghost," the latter being a spooky bit using phosphorescent paint to suggest dancing bones.

LADDER, THE [Drama/Fantasy/Reincarnation/Period/Romance] A: J. Frank Davis; D/P: Brock Pemberton; S: Raymond Sovey; C: Robert Edmond Jones; T: Mansfield Theatre; 10/22/26 (794)

A beautifully and expensively designed play on the subject of reincarnation, which came in for hard critical knocks, but which was kept going for two seasons, despite very thin houses, by the money provided by a Texas millionaire, Edgar B. Davis, who let interested spectators in for free. His object was to spread the doctrine of reincarnation far and wide. Gilbert Seldes said, "The play seemed . . . entirely without significance and the acting almost uniformly bad. The principals alone avoided the monotony of badness by being a little worse."

The action moved from the present (1926) in New York to an English castle in 1300 to London in 1670 to New York in 1844 and back to the present. The same actors appeared in each scene as different characters. Antoinette Perry portrayed Margaret Newell, who, while conversing about reincarnation to two of her suitors, drifts off to dream of her earlier lives and wakes up to choose the man she really loves (Vernon Steele) and had never wed in previous centuries. The piece derived its title from the following lines of Josiah Gilbert Holland, published in the program: "Heaven is not reached at a single bound, / But we build the ladder by which we rise / From the lowly earth to the vaulted skies; / And we mount to its summit round by round."

LADIES DON'T LIE [Comedy/Aviation/German/Romance] A: Paul Frank; AD: Herman Bernstein; D: Edward Sargent Brown; S: Nicholas Yellenti; P: Radiant Productions, Inc., i/a/w Edward Sargent Brown; T: Gallo Theatre; 10/10/29 (12)

This flop German comedy from an unlisted original inaugurated a series of low-price productions at the Gallo (seats ranged from 50¢ to $2). The play itself proved to be "a mild little comedy which suffers so badly from malnutrition that it barely finishes out the evening" (*Times*).

The loquacious play concerned three gentlemen (Charles Richman, Dodd Mehan, and Richard Sterling), all of them intimates of Thea (Spring Byington), who have run off to a deserted island for temporary sanctuary from the fair sex. Thea arrives by plane to ruffle their complacency; the men become embroiled in a tug of war over her, but she elects to take off with the charming flyer (Stanley De Wolf) who brought her there.

LADIES LEAVE [Comedy/Sex/Marriage] A: Sophie Treadwell; D/P: Charles Hopkins; S: Robert Edmond Jones; T: Charles Hopkins Theatre; 10/1/29 (15)

Sophie Treadwell, talented author of *Machinal*, provided here a drawing-room comedy of cuckoldry, "which, lacking the sprightliness to carry off this theme, became eventually boring," according to Perriton Maxwell.

Zizi Powers (Blyth Daly), a preoccupied editor's (Walter Connolly) dissatisfied wife, seeks psychiatric help from the Viennese practitioner Dr. Jeffer (Charles Trowbridge), who advises her to take a lover (Henry Hull). The lover fails to satisfy her needs, and her husband is displeased with the arrangement, so Zizi runs off to Vienna with the doctor himself as her goal.

LADIES' NIGHT (IN A TURKISH BATH) [Comedy/Sex] A: Avery Hopwood and Charlton Andrews; D: Bertram Harrison; P: A. H. Woods; T: Eltinge Theatre; 8/9/20 (375)

This play was a substantial hit and later became a summer-stock stalwart. The story was that of the overly shy husband Jimmy Walters (John Cumberland), whose friends take him to a bohemian ball to cure him of his shyness regarding female flesh. When the place is raided by the cops he escapes, dressed in drag, into an adjoining ladies' turkish bath and is joined there by his similarly disguised pals (Charles Ruggles and Edward Douglas). Acres of visual stimulation are hereby afforded to male voyeurs. Among the beauties displayed in the original staging were Evelyn Gosnell, Eleanor Dawn, Allyn King, and Judith Voselli. Lots of fun evolves as the trio tries to avoid detection.

Alexander Woollcott scored *Ladies' Night* as "a somewhat laborious farce" of the most meretricious sort, and Arthur Hornblow censured it because "The complication is hackneyed, the humor forced, the dialogue incredibly dull." He went on, "The insistence on fleshy backs and bare legs begins to sicken one, and we wonder how . . . there are to be found actresses willing to make such a show of themselves."

LADIES OF THE EVENING [Drama/Prostitution/Sex/Art/Romance] A: Milton Herbert Gropper; D/P: David Belasco; T: Lyceum Theatre; 12/23/24 (159)

Broadway's prudes were irate over this meretricious opus that Arthur Hornblow labeled "a coarse, lurid play of New York underworld life. . . . The play is not only disgusting in the intimate details it reveals of the life of a prostitute, but certain of its scenes are actually nauseating in their unveiled coarseness and salaciousness." In his review, Hornblow described the most "revolting" scenes as those in which a streetwalker urged her "John" to get on with his business so she could get back to her beat and one in which two harlots in desperate need of cash phone men in other hotel rooms soliciting their attentions.

The play's theme was that of "Pygmalion and Galatea." A well-to-do young sculptor, Jerry Strong (James Kirkwood), wagers with his cronies that he can reform the sleaziest of prostitutes by providing her with the proper moral environment. He takes the streetwalker Kate (Beth Merrill) into his studio, where, for three months, she works as his model; the two, without realizing it, fall in love. When Dot, Kate's old associate, arrives and tells her that she is the pawn in a bet, Kate departs and goes back to her sordid profession. Jerry, distraught, searches for her, finds her waiting on tables, and marries her.

Most of the discussion about the play centered on its tawdry appeal. George Jean Nathan termed it "a large platter of dollar-grabbing smut. . . . The thing is sewerage, cheap, vulgar and contemptible."

A return engagement played at the same theatre for twenty-four performances from 8/17/25.

LADIES OF THE JURY [Comedy/Trial/Law/Crime] A: Fred Ballard; D: Harrison Grey Fiske; S: Gates and Morange; P: A. L. Erlanger and George C. Tyler; T: Erlanger's Theatre; 10/21/29 (80)

Mrs. Fiske sailed forth at age sixty-four as the lorgnette bearing Mrs. Livingston Baldwin Crane, a flustery New Jersey socialite, in this satirical courtroom farce about her experience while serving on a jury trying a Mrs. Gordon (Germaine Giroux) for the murder of her millionaire spouse. Although her eleven peers vote for a verdict of guilty, the indomitable Mrs. Crane uses a bagful of con man's devices to wheedle the others into changing their minds. Mrs. Gordon gains her acquittal at last.

The piece seemed "hilariously funny" to the *Times*, and Perriton Maxwell labeled it "a pleasantly inconsequential farce [to which] Mrs. Fiske brings life, movement and charm." The sharply sketched cross-section of types and the lively situations kept the juices flowing and provided a worthwhile evening of pleasure. Mrs. Fiske gave a "sweeping performance, rich in suggestion, continuity, and, always, surety," noted John Hutchens.

An important feature of the production was the presence of Wilton Lackaye, one-time star, in the role of the judge. In Archie Binn's *Mrs. Fiske and the American Theatre* it is reported that Lackaye's failing memory forced him to read his part from papers scattered about on his character's desk.

LADY, THE [Drama/Marriage/France/Romance/Family] A: Martin Brown; D: Lester Lonergan; S: Clifford B. Pember; P: A. H. Woods; T: Empire Theatre; 12/4/23 (85)

Spanning twenty years, with locales in England and France, *The Lady* told the story of a popular soubrette (Mary Nash) who marries a feckless gentleman (Austin Fairman). After the marriage shatters and the heroine sends her son away rather than surrender him to her snobbish father-in-law, she struggles until she becomes owner of a bar in Havre. There she meets her grown son and tries to save him from a murder charge without revealing her identity to him.

The *Times* critic declared that the play was a "frank, unblushing and glorious melodrama, filled to the hilt with maudlin, beer-gardenish sentiment." Percy Hammond called it a "large masterpiece of frank and honest bad playwriting."

H.H.

LADY ALONE [Drama/Romance/Sex/Marriage] A: Laetitia McDonald; D: Lionel Atwill; P: L. Lawrence Weber i/a/w David Wallace; T: Forrest Theatre; 1/20/27 (45)

A drawing-room play of polite society that had the veneer of comedy but was fundamentally tragic in its working out. Its heroine Nina Hopkins (Alice Brady) is an impoverished socialite who seeks to find security through a marriage of convenience with Stephen Brett (Joseph Kilgour), an older man. However, the chance for a renewed relationship with Craig Neilson (Austin Fairman), the man she really loves, arises, and she dismisses Stephen to await Craig's divorce, living with him until it is finalized. When he decides against remarriage, Nina overdoses on sleeping powders.

"Here are no tumultuous passions or great actions," reported Joseph Wood Krutch, "but a story which, as worked out with great delicacy and verisimilitude, affords an absorbing study of the conflict between natural impulse and the fixed traditions of a society." But Brooks Atkinson found it "thin and repetitious." Alice Brady's performance was deeply moving.

LADY, BE GOOD! [Musical/Family/Show Business/Legacy/Romance] B: Guy Bolton and Fred Thompson; M: George Gershwin; LY: Ira Gershwin; D: Felix Edwardes; CH: Sammy Lee; S: Norman Bel Geddes; C: Jenkins, Kiviette, Iverson, and Henneage; P: Alex A. Aarons and Vinton Freedley; T: Liberty Theatre; 12/1/24 (330)

After an extended engagement on the London stage, where they became the toasts of the town, Fred and Adele Astaire returned to a Broadway hungry for their great talents in this wonderfully successful George and Ira Gershwin show (originally called *Black-Eyed Susan*) that put the young composer and lyricist team firmly at the head of their profession. In addition to the Astaires, there was excellent comic acting by Walter Catlett, a sparkling chorus put through their paces by Sammy Lee, spirited ukelele playing by Cliff Edwards, outstanding sets by Norman Bel Geddes, and a first-rate score with nary an exceptional voice to sing it.

The Astaires played Dick and Susie Trevor, a brother and sister dance team down on their luck and forced to play at private parties. They are kicked out of their apartment, leading to an amusing scene in which Susie tries to arrange their furniture in a cosy setting around a lamp post. Dick can solve their financial problems if he weds a certain rich girl who loves him but for whom he does not care. To avoid having her sibling make the sacrifice, Susie conspires with a shyster attorney (Catlett) to impersonate a Mexican widow and gain a $4 million inheritance. The scheme does not succeed, but Dick and Susie do find true love, the latter with a millionaire (Alan Edwards), the former with a girl named Shirley (Kathlene Martyn).

The *Sun* referred to "The brilliant Gershwin score—brisk, inventive, gay, nervous, delightful." Included among the numbers were "Fascinating Rhythm," "Little Jazz Bird," "Oh, Lady, Be Good!," and "So am I." The great "The Man I Love" was dropped from the show before its New York opening, because a producer found it static.

The Astaires, especially Adele, dominated attention. Adele seemed to have blossomed into a comic actress reminiscent of Beatrice Lillie's manner and astonished critics by her all-around scope. Stark Young tried to describe the Astaire team's dancing style but admitted its impossibility: "[O]f the Astaires what wins all hearts is a certain pure dance quality. . . . It is abstract as music is, scarcely imitative at all, quite free and complete in itself. It is agile, clever, tricky, whatever you like to say about it."

LADY BILLY [Musical/Romance] B/LY: Zelda Sears; M: Harold A. Levey; D: John McKee; P: Henry W. Savage; T: Liberty Theatre; 12/14/20 (188)

Yet one more variation on the *Twelfth Night* premise of a man attracted to a boy who turns out to be a woman in disguise. The woman here is an eccentric Rumanian Countess (Mitzi) known as "Lady Billy" who makes ends meet by charging tourists to view her reputedly haunted castle, and who enjoys passing herself off as the gardener's son. An American engineer (Boyd Marshall) likes the "boy's" company and tells him to go to America as a boy soprano, which "he" does; finally, the Countess feels able to doff her masquerade and marry the man.

"The distinction of *Lady Billy*," advised Ludwig Lewisohn, "centers wholly in the diminutive actress who calls herself Mitzi. She has a silvery, bell-like little singing voice that mocks delicately at the perfection of its own production and use; she has incredible lightness of movement which she also treats with a touch of self-mockery; she is aware of the slight ache of morbidity in her impersonation of a boy.'' The show was otherwise modestly adorned with ''some pleasantly sentimental numbers,'' wrote the *Times*.

LADY BUG [Comedy/Crime] A: Frances Nordstrom; D: Priestly Morrison; P: Philip Klein; T: Apollo Theatre; 4/17/22 (5)

A middling satirical farce about a superliberal but scatterbrained do-gooder who gets caught up in all of the latest social fads only to have them recoil on her when least expected. The playwright's sister Marie Nordstrom played Marion Thornton, whose current preoccupation is to help out ex-cons upon their release from prison. She puts up at her home an alleged murderer (Edward Poland) for whom she gives a fancy party. Her husband (John Cumberland) and the butler (Denman Maley) scheme to show the ex-con up as a means of curing her obsession, but the butler gets drunk, the ploy goes awry, and the ''killer'' turns out to be nothing more than an alimony cheat.

''*Lady Bug* crawls along in a slow and monotonous fashion,'' yawned Arthur Hornblow, with its poor dialogue and clumsy handling.

LADY BUTTERFLY [Musical/Romance] B: Clifford Grey; M: Werner Janssen; SC: *Somebody's Luggage*, a farce by Mark Swan and James T. Powers; D/CH: Ned Wayburn; P: Oliver Morosco; T: Globe Theatre; 1/22/23 (128)

Pretty girls and lots of dancing forced the book, lyrics, and comedy of this revue-like musical comedy to take a back seat. Very little of the humor remained from the 1916 farce that inspired the show, and only Maude Eburne, the comic dancer, was consistently amusing.

Beginning with a realistic first-act ship-boarding scene in which the gangplank was lowered to the third row of the orchestra, so that the passengers could march down the aisles to embark and followed by the use of moving sets to suggest the ship's departure into the wings, the show offered a number of impressive visual treats.

The typically implausible plot had to do with the impersonation by Alfred Hopper (Florenz Ames) of an Australian heir en route to marry Enid Crawford (Marjorie Gateson), whom the Australian has never met. All of this transpires because of a luggage and ticket mixup on the channel boat to England; the ensuing complications were sufficient to keep the numbers coming and the audience entertained.

The music was unexceptionable, but pleasant, ''not too new to be startling and not too old to waken sacred memories'' (*Times*). The general effect was of ''beautiful stage pictures, clever scenic effects, prettily conceived dance patterns, tuneful music, an agreeable cast, good comedians and a chorus worthy of the Globe stage,'' declared the *Tribune*.

LADY CLARA [Comedy/Romance/British] A: Aimee and Philip Stuart; D: Stanley Logan; S: Rollo Wayne; P: Lee Shubert; T: Booth Theatre; 4/17/30 (28)

The hackneyed story (as in *Pygmalion, Peg o' My Heart,* and so on) of the rough-edged but golden-hearted lower-class miss who wins her way into the affections of the upper classes by her shining virtues was trotted out again for this play, which served as an unworthy vehicle for the talented Florence Nash. A success in London with the title *Clara Gibbings,* it recounted the saga of a cockney barmaid who learns that she is the illegitimate child of the Earl of Drumoor (T. Wigney Percival), and schemes to reveal her secret if she is not allowed to marry the Earl's nephew (Terence Neill). She charms his snobbish family, but, seeing their dissolute ways, decides her own class is where she belongs.

"Audiences detected a trite and true strain in its structure," commented *Time,* and Brooks Atkinson put it down as "undistinguished stock drama."

LADY CRISTILINDA, THE [Comedy-Drama/Romance/Circus/Art/Religion/Invalidism/British] A: Monckton Hoffe; D: Robert Milton; S: Livingston Platt; P: William Harris, Jr.; T: Broadhurst Theatre; 12/25/22 (24)

Fay Bainter and Leslie Howard had the romantic leads in this sentimental work about a bareback rider and a circus sketch artist. The play was less a romance than a work of inspirational religiosity in its tale of equestrienne Lady Cristilinda, star of a shabby English circus and the artist Martini whom she relinquishes at his upper-class father's request. His portrait of her is doctored to resemble a masterpiece and ends up in the possession of the chapel of St. Etheldreda, whose likeness it is claimed to be. The circus girl, now crippled, travels to the church and begs those who know the truth not to disclose it, since the painting has taken on a holy meaning for the faithful. Her wish is granted, and the play closes with the picture viewed in the light of flickering candle flames.

The inconsistency of this well-acted play was its greatest flaw, for it took the audience "into the sheerest realms of dramatic illusion and straightway [cast] it down into the ruts of bathos," said Laurence Stallings. But most critics respected it, Arthur Hornblow calling it "a reverential and unusual piece of work, marked above all by a sensitive humor."

LADY DEDLOCK, THE [Drama/Period/Crime/Mystery/Family] A: Paul Kester; SC: Charles Dickens's novel *Bleak House*; D: Margaret Anglin; S: Carol Sax and Livingston Platt; C: Lucien Labaudt; P: Murray Phillips and J. J. Leventhal; T: Ambassador Theatre; 12/31/28 (50)

One more in a string of failed attempts to dramatize the novels of Dickens; it starred Margaret Anglin in the double role of Lady Dedlock and her French maid. The tradition of doubling these roles began with a late nineteenth-century adaptation called *Chesney Wold*, starring Fanny Janauschek. Anglin seemed uncomfortable in the maid's part. The work "remained a conscientious but uninspiring effort'' (*Herald Tribune*). The complexities of the material with its expository requirements were overwhelming and far from satisfactorily mastered.

Lady Dedlock believes her illicit daughter (Margaret Shackelford) to have died in childhood; the girl is still alive and set to marry the son (Robert Harrigan) of Lady Dedlock's spouse (St. Clair Bayfield). Her husband's evil solicitor Tulkingham (John Ivancowich) discovers the truth about her shady past and her relationship to the bride, but before her child's happiness can be imperiled her maid kills the solicitor. The lady wanders without food for days and dies on her lover's grave, but her daughter marries happily.

LADY DO [Musical/Romance] B: Jack McClellan and Albert Cowles; M: Abel Baer; LY: Sam M. Lewis and Joe Young; D: Edgar J. MacGregor; CH: Busby Berkeley; P: Frank L. Teiler; T: Liberty Theatre; 4/18/27 (56)

A poorly conceived libretto, excessive length, and forgettable music were among the most prominent of this show's flaws. It starred vaudeville female impersonator Karyl Norman as a man who pursues his dream girl Dorothy (Nancy Welford) by pretending to be a woman, so that his love rival may fall for him, thus leaving Dorothy for himself. The humor came from the expected devices of double entendre, hidden cigars, sudden voice shifts, and so on. Only an excellent chorus made the critics smile. The *Times* did not care for the star, who, more often than not, seemed like a Mask and Wig Club player than a convincing drag performer.

LADY FINGERS [Musical/Crime/Rural/Romance] B: Eddie Buzzell; M: Joseph Meyer; LY: Edward Eliscu; SC: Owen Davis's comedy *Easy Come, Easy Go*; D: Edward J. MacGregor; CH: Sammy Lee; S: Ward and Harvey Studios; C: Kiviette; P: Lyle D. Andrews; T: Vanderbilt Theatre; 1/31/29 (132)

A modestly successful musical for the tired businessman "who wants his imagination lulled to sleep instead of pricked into startled wonderment" (Francis R. Bellamy). It followed the plot of its 1925 source and managed to stir up a good deal of amusement through its balanced mix of spirited dance and extravagant burlesque-flavored comedy. "Played with the infectious freshness of a college frolic, set to good tunes and decked out with pleasing costumes, *Lady Fingers* relieves the midwinter tedium a good deal," stated Brooks Atkinson.

Eddie Buzzell held the old Otto Kruger role, and John Price Jones essayed that of Victor Moore. Both were excellent.

LADY FOR A NIGHT, A [Comedy/Mystery/Fantasy/Marriage] A: Hutcheson Boyd; D: John Meehan; P: Chamberlain Brown; T: Forty-ninth Street Theatre; 4/16/28 (8)

The old device of creating a series of unusual situations and then explaining that everything was a dream supported this "silly and somewhat incoherent play" that was "pretty much a mess," according to the *Times*. It was "just a bad musical comedy libretto with the tunes unfortunately omitted,'' opined the *Herald Tribune*.

A family on Staten Island, in need of a servant, gets one in the shape of a kookie department store salesgirl (Esther Howard), who behaves in an outrageously independent way; soon various things meant to burlesque mystery plays intrude, including a murderous preacher, a shooting, the police, bootleggers, and so on, until the mad tangle is dismissed as the wife's (Dorothy Hall) bedtime hallucinations.

LADY FROM ALFÁQUEQUE, THE (La consulesa) and "ON THE HIGH ROAD" (Na bolshoi doroge) D: Eva Le Gallienne; S: Aline Bernstein; P: Civic Repertory Company; T: Civic Repertory Theatre (OB); 1/14/29 (17)
The Lady From Alfáqueque [Comedy/Spanish/Small Town] A: Serafín and Joaquín Álvarez Quintero; TR: Helen and Harley Granville-Barker; "On the High Road" [Comedy/One-Act/Marriage/Russian/Alcoholism] A: Anton Chekhov; TR: Constance Garnett; SC: Chekhov's story "In the Autumn"

Eva Le Gallienne kept the Quintero brothers' 1914 play in her company's repertory for three seasons, reviving it on 9/30/29 for eight performances, and on 10/9/30 for nine more. A Spanish comedy of manners, it was thought to be "as successful a piece of sheer theatre as the" troupe had yet presented, noted Robert Littell. Critics welcomed it as a masterpiece of dramatic simplicity.

Its fragile plot, very well performed, was intended as "a skit upon provincial pride," declared Euphemia Van Rensselaer Wyatt. The lady of the title is Fernandita (Alma Kruger), a Madrid businessman's wife who bears such a deep affection for her Andalusian small home town of Alfáqueque that when she is visited at her home by natives of the town she becomes the softest of touches. Even when a poet who is not from Alfáqueque inveigles his way into her heart by lying that he is, and goes on to seduce her daughters and those of a neighbor, she allows him to remain after hearing his poem in honor of Alfáqueque.

On the same bill was an early Chekhov one-act, censored during his life and discovered after his death. It was set in a dingy inn during a storm and concerned a drunken tramp (Egon Brecher), once wealthy, who encounters his beautiful ex-wife (Alla Nazimova); she is untouched by his degradation and sweeps out. The tramp, however, has retained his decency and throws his coat across a freezing derelict.

(1) LADY FROM THE SEA, THE (La Donna del mare; Fruen fra havet) [Dramatic Revival/Italian Language] A: Henrik Ibsen; P: F. Ray Comstock and Morris Gest; T: Metropolitan Opera House; 10/29/23 (1)

Opening the New York segment of a London-America tour ended by her death in Pittsburgh the following spring, the sixty-four-year-old Eleanora Duse received a twenty-minute ovation from a sold-out house. The *Tribune* reported that 161 extra seats were added to the theatre for Duse's scheduled performances—and that one man paid $500 for a pair of seats cajoled from the line of ticket holders.

Coproducer Gest, quoted in the *Times*, declared that the box office took in $30,000, at the time the largest receipts in Broadway history of a regular dramatic performance.

Critics agreed that the play was inferior Ibsen and a poor choice for the opening and that the supporting company of Italian players was mediocre, but most were enraptured by Duse. Percy Hammond thought that she seemed tired and fragile, but that "If she was not Ellida she was Duse." John Corbin commented that Duse's voice was "of a silver twilight." In the thirty years since she had first appeared in America, he reflected, "no voice has been heard even faintly resembling hers—nor is such a voice ever likely to be heard again."

H.H.

(2) D: Cecil Clovelly; P: Actors' Theatre; T: Bijou Theatre; 3/18/29 (24)

Blanche Yurka starred in this Ibsen revival during a season in which she also played the title role in *Hedda Gabler* and Gina in *The Wild Duck*. Her interpretation and the production as a whole were thought to have fallen short of Ibsen's play. Brooks Atkinson lamented, "Miss Yurka is none too happily cast." The play itself, largely because of its murky symbolism and its implausible conclusion, also failed to please. Richard Dana Skinner argued that the play's ending, in which Ellida's obsession with the memory of a youthful lover is cured by her husband's (Edward Fielding) granting her permission to do as she pleases, was "a last-minute trick," an excuse to present a thesis "on the importance of feminine freedom." The suddenness of the psychological maneuver was too much for him to gulp down. In her autobiography *Bohemian Girl* Yurka herself saw the play as "pure psychoanalysis" but found that the abrupt transition of the final act was impossible to play convincingly.

LADY IN ERMINE, THE [Musical/Romance/Fantasy/Military/Period/Sex/British] B: Frederick Lonsdale and Cyrus Wood; M: Jean Gilbert and Alfred Goodman; LY: Harry Graham and Cyrus Wood; SC: *Die Frau im Hermelin*, a Viennese operetta by Rudolph Schanzer and Ernest Welisch; D: Charles Sinclair; CH: Allan K. Foster; S: Watson Barratt; P: Messrs. Shubert; T: Ambassador Theatre; 10/2/22 (238)

Ruritanian romance, the background fodder fed into so many European operettas, was made easily digestible in this successful costume show presumably set in the time of Napoleon's invasion of Italy. Known in its London run as *The Lady of the Rose*, the show introduced the full-voiced Walter Woolf to Broadway. The evening's major song contribution, warbled by Wilda Bennett, was the Sigmund Romberg interpolation "When Hearts Are Young." The critics revelled in this "thoroughly delightful" (*Tribune*) work, and the *Times* called it "genuinely musical and dramatic."

The Lady in Ermine told a dashing tale of Colonel Belovar (Woolf), quartered with his troops at the castle of Mariana (Bennett), a beauty he seeks to seduce.

In a drunk scene enacted as he awaits a rendezvous with Mariana, a portrait of the "lady in ermine," the castle's erstwhile mistress, comes alive and dances with him; he thereby realizes his true love for Mariana.

LADY IN LOVE, A [Comedy/Period/Romance/Marriage/Sex] A: Dorrance Davis; D: Rollo Lloyd; P: A. E. and R. R. Riskin; T: Lyceum Theatre; 2/21/27 (17)

An ersatz Restoration comedy replete with the stock characters, adulterous situations, and risque language of the genre but weakened by the author's inability to prevent himself "from betraying the modernity of his sensibilities by introducing motives and sentiments . . . alien to the pattern of the Restoration mind," wrote Joseph Wood Krutch.

Peggy Wood ("charming to no purpose"—First Nighter) was the 1680 Mayfair heroine Clarissa, in love with Captain Bragdon (Gavin Gordon) but married to old Sir Barnaby (Rollo Lloyd), whom she wed to save her father from debtor's prison. The plot arranges for Barnaby to think himself Bragdon's murderer, so that the Captain's corpse may be left alone with Clarissa for her to minister to it. The desired cuckoldry takes place, of course, for Bragdon is very much alive.

LADY KILLER, THE [Comedy/Films/Crime/Romance] A: Alice and Frank Mandel; D: Franklyn Underwood; S: P. Dodd Ackerman; P: Morosco Holding Company, Inc.; T: Morosco Theatre; 3/12/24 (13)

"Immature as a tadpole and almost as intelligent," wrote Percy Hammond of this tale about a Hollywood screenwriter's (George Alison) secretary (Claiborne Foster), whose imagination is overstimulated by filmdom fantasies. When the boy (Paul Kelly) she loves is charged with murder, she confesses to the crime, because she believes no jury will convict a pretty girl. The crime turns out to be a hoax, and the secretary is released to be married. Hammond grumbled: "It was not farce, melodrama, burlesque or entertainment . . . just a hysterical nursery tale, feebly related." He found Claiborne Foster to be "of the supercutie type, simpering, pigeon-toed and fond of grimacing" and the rest of the cast awful. Most of his colleagues agreed on all points.

James Gleason, in a fairly brief role as a derby-hatted detective, gained most of the acting honors.

H.H.

LADY LIES, THE [Comedy/Sex/Romance/Family] A: John Meehan; D: David Burton; S: Jo Mielziner; P: Joseph Santley, Theodore Barter, and John McGowan; T: Little Theatre; 11/26/28 (24)

One critic thought this was an "amusing, intelligent and generally convincing comedy" (M.G.), but most sided with Robert Littell, who called it "a good idea made incredible. . . . [A]fter the first act one ceases to believe."

Forty-year-old widower Robert Rossiter (William Boyd), with three fond children ranging from age eighteen to fifteen, has been living with Joyce Roamer

(Shirley Warde) for seven years and is pressured by his New England puritan relatives to throw her over for a more respectable and permanent relationship with a certain socialite to whom he becomes engaged; however, with his kids' pleas in his ears and his own newly awakened awareness of his real feelings, he rejects the fiancée and hitches up with Joyce.

LADY OF THE LAMP, THE [Comedy-Drama/Fantasy/China/Drugs/Romance/Orientals/Adventure] A: Earl Carroll; D/S: Earl Carroll; P: A. H. Woods and Earl Carroll; T: Republic Theatre; 8/17/20 (111)

A red-blooded melodrama, telling of celestial love while unfolding a romantic fantasy of ancient China. Arthur White (George Gaul), an artist, is invited to dinner at the home of his friend Li Fu Yang (Brandon Hurst), a Chinese philosopher. While inspecting Yang's art collection he smokes opium to widen his emotional experiences. He thinks he is a Chinese emperor and the protector of Princess T'ien Tao (Eileen Wilson), becomes a great hero, but sees the girl die only to live again as he wakes up to encounter a young American lady in whom T'ien's spirit is reincarnated.

This was the fourth Chinese-oriented play within two years and "by far the best," wrote Ludwig Lewisohn. Henry Herbert as a Manchu emperor was deemed the finest actor in the piece. The play was exquisitely produced and took "high rank as spectacle," in Alexander Woollcott's view. But the frequent injections of humor at dramatic moments almost killed the play, Arthur Hornblow noted.

M.M.-C.

LADY OF THE ORCHIDS, THE (La Greluchon délicat) [Comedy-Drama/Sex/French] A: Jacques Natanson; AD/P: E. Ray Goetz; D: William H. Gilmore; T: Henry Miller's Theatre; 12/13/28 (20)

A continental comedy starring Peggy Hopkins Joyce, former Ziegfeld beauty and best known for her frequent marriages. "It is an old-fashioned piece in the Sardou-Dumas *fils* tradition," penned Ernest Boyd, "with all the roses and raptures and despairs of the unvirtuous when true love conflicts with financial interest."

Joyce was the seductive Parisienne Simone, kept by a wealthy middle-aged lover (Kenneth Hunter) and dallying with various younger admirers; one of them, Henri (Edward Crandall), she falls in love with; the older man endows her with sufficient largess for her to keep the youth, while he assumes the other corner of the triangle.

LADY OF THE ROSE [Drama/Marriage/Theatre] A: Martin Flavin; D: Henry Herbert and Jacob Weiser; P: Jacob A. Weiser; T: Forty-ninth Street Theatre; 5/19/25 (8)

A Pirandellian drama that was only momentarily effective and was marred by faulty playing.

It told of a playwright (Henry Herbert) whose wife (Margaret Mower) turns out to be less than the ideal woman he has always cherished and about whom he wrote a play, never staged, in his youth. One day, the play is discovered and produced, without his being told. When he views the production, with his wife in the lead, he decries the desecration of his masterpiece, rejects his wife for crushing his dream, and dies.

The heavy and pretentious drama was not intriguing enough to hold the attention or to fire the imagination, revealed Stark Young. He said it was "wandering and sentimental and unconvincing."

LADY SCREAMS, THE [Comedy-Drama/Romance/Crime] A: Everett Chantler; D: Edward Broadley; P: Charles J. Mulligan; T: Selwyn Theatre; 5/2/27 (8)

Lucy West (Betty Weston) receives a seven-year suspended sentence with a year's parole for shooting Walten Hensen (Anthony Hughes). Ruth Harrison (Dana Desboro) takes her into her home for the year of her parole. Lucy is tempted by Ruth's $50,000 pearls, and when they are snatched, she is suspected. The crook she shot is the perpetrator; he is caught, while Lucy relaxes in the arms of the fellow (Allan Tower) she loves.

"All in all, *The Lady Screams* is but a plaintive moan," commented W.O.T. Stephen Rathbun recommended it for a Pulitzer Prize as the year's worst play.

LADY'S VIRTUE, A [Drama/Marriage/Sex] A/D: Rachel Crothers; S: Watson Barratt; P: Messrs. Shubert; T: Bijou Theatre; 11/23/25 (147)

Rachel Crothers's "trite and true" plot devices were enlivened by her considerable theatrical talents to provide an entertaining play, "cleverly and adeptly assembled," said the *Times*. To Arthur Hornblow it was "melodramatic in spots and occasionally a little mawkish" but was nevertheless enjoyable.

Its threadbare situation had a bored husband (Robert Warwick) and wife (Florence Nash) visited by a famed opera singer (Mary Nash) and her retinue, with the husband and the diva having a fling and the wife engaging in her own philandering with a city bachelor, but with the spouses returning in the end to each other's arms.

Despite its "shrewd observation of American life," Joseph Wood Krutch thought its discussion of morality was muddled.

LAFF THAT OFF [Comedy/Romance] A: Don Mullally; D: Roy Walling; P: Earl Carroll; T: Wallack's Theatre; 11/2/25 (390)

Quadrangular comedies about three young men and a girl set in New York boarding houses or Greenwich Village flats were not uncommon in the twenties, and Don Mullally's was only the latest arrival in this vein. Stock characters, including a couple of stage Irishmen, were other conventional accoutrements of this diverting, if somewhat shopworn, piece.

Its story was that of Leo the bachelor (Alan Bunce), who picks up a pretty waif (Shirley Booth), brings her to the apartment he keeps with two other single lads, gives her the job of doing their housework, neglects her when the other two fall for her, sees her run off with the trio's $600 savings only to return two years later as a budding film star, and finally falls in love with her.

Most critics looked down their noses at this "sloppy tale for five-year olds with scarcely a probable moment in it" (*Herald Tribune*), but the *Times* thought it was an excellent example of commercially viable comedy, one of those "that mean nothing, get nowhere and keep the audience in chuckles from beginning to end." Shirley Booth "played with discretion and charm," noted Alan Dale, and Alan Bunce came into his own as a light comedian "of charm and ability" (Louis Bromfield).

LALLY [Comedy/Music/Romance/Family] A: Henry Stillman; D: John D. Williams; S: Livingston Platt; P: Carl Reed i/a/w Norman C. Stoneham; T: Greenwich Village Theatre (OB); 2/8/27 (60)

Lally reminded various viewers of the then-current English success *The Constant Nymph*, although it allegedly had been written earlier. Its eponymous hero (Claude Rains) is a free-loving composer living in chaos with his four children in a huge Hudson River home. Each child is by a different mother. The mothers each also have provided Lally with themes in his operatic writing, but his latest work awaits a major new inspiration, which comes to him in the shape of Judith Montfiori (Anne Morrison). A noble type, she leaves him, despite his pleas, so that he may through his suffering create the great music still dormant in him. The climax arrives when the strains of his masterpiece are heard from offstage.

The piece seemed monotonous, windy, and disconnected; one trite scene singled out represented a discussion of the great composers "as though they were being checked off on an inventory list," wrote First Nighter.

LASS O' LAUGHTER [Comedy/Legacy/Romance/Scottish] A: Edith Carter and Nan Marriott Watson; D: Ira Hards; P: Henry W. Savage; T: Comedy Theatre; 1/8/25 (28)

The "English Mary Pickford," Flora Le Breton, made her Broadway debut in this short-lived Scottish Cinderella comedy that Q.M. branded "a weak-kneed and unimaginative little thing."

The beautiful blonde actress portrayed Lass, a Scottish drudge who learns that she is an heiress descended from Lord Maxwell. The young Earl (Leslie Austen), previously thought to be the heir, is rejected by his fiancée now that the money is going to someone else. Disturbed, he wanders about the family mansion until he encounters the charming Lass, who is unfazed by the compromising situation (she is wearing her silk pajamas). They fall in love, and their engagement is announced. It is then learned that Lass is not legally the heiress, but since the Earl will marry her, it does not matter.

LAST MILE, THE [Drama/Prison/Crime] A: John Wexley; SC: Robert Blake's playlet "The Law Takes Its Toll"; D: Chester Erskin; S: Henry Dreyfuss; P: Herman Shumlin; T: Sam H. Harris Theatre; 2/13/30 (285)

The Last Mile was considered a brutally authentic and powerfully relentless view of prison life (*Time* termed it "the most repulsive play now to be seen"); it was inspired by a short play published in the *American Mercury* by a man condemned to die in a Texas penitentiary. An actual prison uprising also influenced the writing. Wexley's work caused a considerable commotion among theatregoers and had a tremendous effect on the careers of both Spencer Tracy, who acted the role of "Killer" Mears in New York, and Clark Gable, who played it on the West Coast.

An anticapital punishment melodrama, *The Last Mile* was set in the death house of Oklahoma's Keystone State Penitentiary. In Act One the inmates awaiting execution in the electric chair converse in dialogue based largely on Blake's verbatim account. In Act Two Chicago murderer "Killer" Mears contrives to spark a mutiny among the half-dozen doomed prisoners. The rebellion flares, two officials are slain, and the uprising is brutally crushed.

"The author has not created a drama. Rather he has turned loose a fine camera and a red-hot pen upon a bit of life that we usually keep hidden.... It is all real, close to the ground, stripped of every shred of illusion," explained Perriton Maxwell. Faults included excessive sentimentality, too obvious a use of comic relief, and the sometimes too pointed stressing of the thesis. "Spencer Tracy," noted Richard Dana Skinner, "puts the final seal on his qualifications as one of our best and most versatile young actors."

LAST NIGHT OF DON JUAN, THE (La Dernière nuit de Don Juan) and "THE PILGRIMAGE" ("Le Pèlerin") [French] D: Robert Milton; M: Macklin Morrow; S: James Reynolds; C: Millia Davenport; P: Kenneth Macgowan, Robert Edmond Jones, and Eugene O'Neill; T: Greenwich Village Theatre (OB); 11/9/25 (16)
The Last Night of Don Juan [Drama/Fantasy/Period] A: Edmond Rostand; TR: Sidney Howard; "The Pilgrimage" [Comedy/One-Act/Old Age] A: Charles Vildrac; TR: Sigourney Thayer

Rostand's Don Juan play gained keen critical approval, although there was dissatisfaction with its acting and directing. George Jean Nathan found in it "all those elements of ironic beauty and sardonic tenderness and lively imagery and wide knowledge of the heart of man which go into the being of lasting drama."

The story treats of Don Juan's (Stanley Logan) winning from the Devil (Augustin Duncan) a reprieve of ten years in which to do even more wicked things, only to have the masked ghosts of the 1,003 betrayed women in the great libertine's life appear when the decade is up to damn him to perdition. If he only can find love for one of them his soul will be saved; but he cannot, and so he goes to hell, as a character in the Devil's puppet play, crying out madly, "I'll make them laugh!" of the little girls he will forever be playing to.

"The Pilgrimage" was played as a curtain raiser; the few who commented on it believed its presentation was far superior to the main piece and that Augustin Duncan, who was not liked as the Devil, was quite acceptable in it. A comedy, it was about an old man (Duncan) revisiting for nostalgic reasons the small home town of his childhood after being away for forty years. The black sheep of his family, he is derided by a relative and leaves, turning down an invitation to dinner.

LAST OF MRS. CHEYNEY, THE [Comedy-Drama/Romance/Crime/Sex/ British] A: Frederick Lonsdale; D: Winchell Smith; S: James Reynolds; P: Charles Dillingham; T: Fulton Theatre; 11/9/25 (283)

''[A] crook hickpicker'' was the term George Jean Nathan used demeaningly to write off this very successful British drawing-room comedy that was chosen one of the Best Plays of 1925–1926. Ina Claire and Roland Young were heaped with accolades for the lighthearted esprit with which they displayed their comedic skills as the romantic leads.

The stereotypical premise of the play allowed Claire to portray Mrs. Cheyney, who turns up in London society after a supposed widowhood spent in Australia; she is sought after by two eligible bachelors, one of them Lord Arthur Dilling (Young). Mrs. Cheyney turns out to be a jewel thief with her eye on a certain string of pearls. When Lord Arthur discovers her profession, he offers her a choice of evils: the police or a romp in bed. When she chooses the former, he comes to respect her, and the plot culminates in their romantic union.

The critics cited Lonsdale's wit and charm as reasons for his appeal, despite his nonsensical plot. Arthur Hornblow maintained that it was ''one of the thinnest and at the same time most beguiling comedies in several seasons.''

LAST WALTZ, THE (Der Letzte Waltzer) [Musical/Romance/Military/Adventure/Austrian] AD: Harold Atteridge and Edward Delaney Dunn; B: Julius Brammer and Alfred Grunwald; M: Oscar Straus; D: J. C. Huffman and Frank Smithson; S: Watson Barratt; P: Messrs. Shubert; T: Century Theatre; 5/10/21 (185)

A version of an Oscar Straus operetta in which the Viennese hero was turned into an American naval officer (Walter Woolf) and which was set in one of those Balkan countries so dear to the cliché-ridden hearts of contemporary librettists. The critics adored its score, which included several non-Straus interpolations for the dance numbers.

The innocuous plot placed the officer and his sailor friend (James Barton) in the midst of political troubles, which featured a local damsel in distress (Eleanor Painter). The officer rescues her from a prince's lustful grasp, a slew of adventures arise, the officer and the sailor come through bravely, and they return home each with a bride of his choice.

Walter Woolf and Eleanor Painter were among the best operetta talents of the day, but comic dancer James Barton stole the show. ''He is a fine clown and the best and most ingenious of our comic opera dancers,'' noted Heywood Broun.

LAST WARNING, THE [Drama/Mystery/Crime/Theatre] A: Thomas F. Fallon; SC: Wadsworth Camp's novel *The House of Fear*; D: Clifford Brooke; P: Michael Mindlin and Michael Goldreyer; T: Klaw Theatre; 10/24/22 (236)

Two young, unknown producers, never having put on a play before, were responsible for this sensational hit mystery play that several critics ranked well above earlier smashes in the genre such as *The Bat* and *The Cat and the Canary*. Percy Hammond said it had "enough shivers to satisfy" mystery lovers for a full season.

Thomas F. Fallon's story tells of the leasing by theatre-manager-turned-detective Arthur McHugh (William Courtleigh) of a haunted Broadway playhouse that has been closed for five years since the star of its hit play *The Snare*, a Mr. Woodford, vanished, presumably having been slain. McHugh, desiring to revive the play, reassembles the entire cast and brings back the director, his aim being to solve the puzzle and rid the place of the reputed curse hanging over it. Strange phenomena occur during the rehearsals, leading all to suspect the actor's ghost, said to be jealous of anyone attempting his old role, as the culprit. One weird occurrence succeeds another, including an invasion of giant tarantulas and the murder of the leading man. Soon there are police stationed in the theatre to protect the audience, and a play-within-the-play is performed, with ushers handing out programs to the spectators; as the climax approaches, the cops even begin to shoot at spirits in the boxes. Finally, the perpetrator is disclosed as the one least likely to have been responsible.

LAUGH, CLOWN, LAUGH (Ridi, Pagliacco!) [Drama/Romance/Show Business/Mental Illness/Italian] A: Fausto Martini; AD: David Belasco and Tom Cushing; SC: a tale by Grimaldi; D/P: David Belasco; S: Stroppa of Milan; C: George Hadden; T: Belasco Theatre; 11/28/23 (136)

A beautifully produced and directed tragi-comedy that met with mixed reviews; most critics found parts stunning but the whole a bit dull and strained. Heywood Broun called it an excellent one-act done in three.

Lionel Barrymore learned to do a spectacular front flip as Tito, an Italian vaudeville clown, in this adaptation of Martini's *Ridi, Pagliaccio!* itself a version of a familiar tale by Grimaldi which was the basis for Ruggiero Leon Cavallo's opera. In a Rome psychiatrist's office, Tito meets Luigi (Ian Keith), an aristocrat turned player. Tito is given to uncontrollable fits of sobbing, because he hopelessly loves his young ward and partner (Irene Fenwick); Luigi to fits of laughter, because he has had too much of wine and women. The prescription for both is a normal, happy love, but Tito's partner falls in love with Luigi while feeling obligated to Tito. The clown sends her to marry Luigi and kills himself.

Barrymore was considered somewhat uneven, and Stark Young referred to him as "sincere and wistful" but not a convincing clown.

H.H.

LAUGHING LADY, THE [Comedy/Marriage/Romance/British] A: Alfred Sutro; D/P: Arthur Hopkins; S: Robert Edmond Jones; T: Longacre Theatre; 2/12/23 (96)

Ethel Barrymore drew only mixed notices for her acting in Alfred Sutro's drawing-room comedy, which echoed Oscar Wilde and Henry Arthur Jones.

The old-fashioned play, "an effective second-rater," as the *Tribune* expressed it, was deftly written with many sparkling epigrams but had an ending that upset several critics by its implausibility. The lady of the title is Mrs. Marjorie Colladine (Barrymore), whose dull husband, Hector (McKay Morris), divorced her on the basis of purely circumstantial evidence. Hector's interest in her is revived when she develops an attachment for his lawyer (Cyril Keightly), but the lawyer's wife feels it would be best for Marjorie to become his mistress until the affair fades of its own volition. In the conclusion jumped on by the critics, Marjorie returns to her spouse, consigning the barrister to a similar condition with his wife. "Thus," wrote Arthur Hornblow, "there are four miserable people in the world instead of two."

(1) LAUNCELOT AND ELAINE [Drama/Romance/Verse/Period] A: Edwin Milton Royle; SC: Alfred Lord Tennyson's "Idylls of the King"; D: Edward Elsner; S: Livingston Platt; P: Playwright and Players' Company; T: Greenwich Village Theatre (OB); 9/12/21 (32)

A respectable dramatization of the Launcelot and Elaine romance. Edwin Milton Royle did his work "in a manner which is at once scholarly, faithful to the original poetic conception and finally impressive," Arthur Hornblow said. The poetic play was staged Off-Broadway in a widely admired mounting that offered Royle's two actress daughters, Selena and Josephine, an exceptional opportunity for their professional debuts.

Royle borrowed liberal portions of Tennyson's blank-verse dialogue and produced a long, literary, but often touching drama of the unrequited love of Elaine (Josephine Royle) for the sad knight who suffers inwardly for his illicit love affair with King Arthur's queen, the beauteous Guinivere (Selena Royle); the most beautiful and moving part of the presentation was the arrival near the end of a funeral barge bearing the white body of Elaine to Camelot.

(2) [Dramatic Revival] D: Calvin Thomas; S: P. Dodd Ackerman; C: Livingston Platt; P: Round Table Productions, Inc.; T: President Theatre; 3/8/30 (25)

The Royle sisters reappeared in their father's play in its 1930 Broadway revival. "[E]nunciated . . . with true stock company grandiloquence" (*Time*), the piece appeared a leaden literary exercise lightened only momentarily by shafts of beauty. Two hours of inflated blank verse proved trying, and the acting was too pompously oritund to maintain interest. Only the Royles rose above the mundane acting company.

LAUNZI (Egi és földi szerelem) [Drama/Family/Romance/Mental Illness/Sex/Hungarian] A: Ferenc Molnar; AD: Edna St. Vincent Millay; D/P: Arthur Hopkins; S: Robert Edmond Jones; T: Plymouth Theatre; 10/10/23 (13)

Several critics complained about being unable to hear chunks of this Molnar play because of mumbling by the players, among whom were several respected talents, including Pauline Lord, Edward G. Robinson, and Adrienne Morrison.

Madness befell Molnar's innocent young heroine Launzi (Lord), when she found the boy she loved (Saxon Kling) infatuated with her alluring mother (Morrison). Unsuccessful in a suicide attempt, she lives as if dead, wearing angel's wings on which she eventually tries to fly from a tower window; she falls to her death.

Heywood Broun observed that "There is something inevitably undramatic about madness. The insane are on the other side of a gulf which even sympathy cannot bridge." Arthur Hornblow observed: "It is all very morbid and painful, not to say gruesome and sacreligious."

H.H.

LAW BREAKER, THE [Drama/Crime/Romance] A: Jules Eckart Goodman; P: William A. Brady; T: Booth Theatre; 2/1/22 (90)

A familiar cops and crooks melodrama in which a reformist thesis mingles conventionally with a story of romance. Blanche Yurka played Joan Fowler, daughter of a banker (Clifford Dempsey) whose institution has been robbed of $60,000. Joan is convinced that crooks are really just as decent as honest folks, but that a streak of irresponsibility turns them from the straight and narrow. When Jim Thorne (William Courtenay) is caught, Joan undertakes to reform the burglar on her own. Thorne, feeling guilty, returns the stolen loot and then is tempted by Joan's valuable necklace, which he wants for Kit (Marguerite Maxwell), a girlfriend. He changes his mind at the last minute and tries to flee, but Kit, trying to protect him, is wounded by a cop's bullet. True love dawns, and Jim decides she is the girl for him.

The Law Breaker was a talky, overlong drama weighted with sociological discussions and suffering from "excessive slowness and its tendency to obscure its own point by prolixity" (Alan Dale). Yet Percy Hammond thought it was "bountiful," if burdened by a "minimum of credibility."

LAWFUL LARCENY [Comedy-Drama/Law/Crime/Marriage/Romance] A: Samuel Shipman; D: Bertram Harrison; P: A. H. Woods; T: Republic Theatre; 1/2/22 (225)

A popular comedy melodrama with a surfeit of improbabilities but one that was nevertheless "rather entertaining," said Alexander Woollcott. It labored under stilted language and clumsy plotting but posed the interesting question of why a woman stealing another's jewels is acting illegally, while a woman who steals another's husband is committing "lawful larceny."

Happily married couple Andrew (Allan Dinehart) and Marion Dorsey (Margaret Lawrence) run into difficulties when Andrew becomes enthralled by "vampire" Vivian Hepburn (Gail Kane), an adventuress who strips men bare of all they are worth. Marion learns of her mate's undoing and takes revenge by getting a job with Vivian and stealing all of the treasures in the vamp's safe. In the ensuing shouting match between the rival women, held in the presence of a judge (Felix Krembs), the theme is sounded: all a woman whose husband has been stolen from her can do is to institute a civil law suit, but the offender will not go to jail.

Arthur Hornblow said "the pace is rapid and there is never a dull moment," although "one's credulity is strained."

LAZYBONES [Comedy-Drama/Small Town/Romance/Sex] A: Owen Davis; D: Guthrie McClintic; P: Sam H. Harris; T: Vanderbilt Theatre; 9/22/24 (72)

An excellent example of the stereotypical rural drama, replete with all of the stock village types and typified by the great hit play *Lightnin'* to which the critics agreed it bore a strong resemblance. Although it ran fewer than eighty performances, it was warmly received, and some even predicted long-run status for it.

George Abbott gave a solidly believable performance as Steve Tuttle, the shiftless but sincere local yokel who comes home one day with a baby, brings it up with his mother's (Amelia Gardner) help, allows the village folk to think he is its father, refuses to divulge who its mother is, loses his suspicious girlfriend as a result, and falls in love with the girl when she grows into a pretty teenager (Martha–Bryan Allen). Finally, it is revealed that the actual mother is the sister of Steve's former fiancée, who had been deserted by her worthless lover. Steve's reputation is restored.

Arthur Hornblow termed the opus "well conceived, the characters exceptionally and accurately drawn and the play excellently acted."

LEAH KLESCHNA [Dramatic Revival] A: C.M.S. McLellan; D: Jessie Bonstelle; S: Louis Kennel and Entwisle; P: William A. Brady; T: Lyric Theatre; 4/21/24 (32)

"Such purity and dullness is incomprehensible in ye theatrical year of 1924," commented Arthur Hornblow about this revival of the forerunner of American "crook plays," a melodrama about a girl thief (Helen Gahagan) who goes straight after a saintly would-be victim (William Faversham) preaches to her. John Corbin found that the thief's central conflict, between the saintly man and her rascally father (Arnold Daly), had truth and that the play was "still the most honestly motivated and emotionally convincing" of its type.

Mrs. Fiske had played the thief Leah Kleschna in 1904 and had added an epilogue showing the reformed thief living in the country. Corbin praised the deletion of the epilogue but found everything else about the revival inferior.

H.H.

LEAP, THE [Comedy/Family/Romance] A: Jessy Trimble and Eugenie Woodward; D: Whitford Kane; P: Town and Country Players, Inc.; T: Cherry Lane Playhouse (OB); 5/22/24 (12)

Because the Cherry Lane Theatre had recently opened with an experimental work (*The Man Who Ate the Popomack*), Alison Smith was surprised to see the playhouse offer this play, which seemed to have "wandered up a bit timidly straight from the gentle, innocuous days of the eighteen-nineties." She thought that the comedy, about a shy spinster who captures her attractive mother's young suitor on his honeymoon eve, should be laid in lavender, although she commended the acting. The *Times* found the play "a very light but eminently sophisticated little comedy."

H.H.

LEDGE, A [Drama/Romance/Crime/Business] A: Paul Osborn; SC: a short story by Henry Holt; D: Walter Greenough; S: Edgar Bohlman; C: Jean Blackburne; P: New York Theatre Assembly; T: Assembly Theatre; 11/18/29 (16)

The second production of the socialite-oriented New York Theatre Assembly was, like its first offering, a dud. Paul Osborn's title derived from his central incident when Richard Legrange (Leonard Mudie), believed by his firm's partners to have stolen its bonds, is punished by being forced to walk along the four-inch ledge from one window to another of their office, 200 feet above the ground. The partners think he will fall and be declared a suicide, but he manages the feat and is forgiven; he even wins the hand of the boss's (Augustin Duncan) wife (Marguerite Burrough), who gave him the bonds to hold after they had been stolen by the man (Gage Clarke) with whom she thought she was in love.

"The harrowing quality of the ledge scene," averred *Time*, "fails to mitigate . . . Osborn's long, tedious stretches."

LEGATAIRE UNIVERSEL, LE (The Residuary Legatee) [Dramatic Revival/French Language] A: Jean-Francois Regnard; P: Wendell Phillips Dodge; T: Fulton Theatre; 3/19/24 (1)

A classic French comedy of 1708, produced in repertory by the visiting company led by Comédie Française actor Maurice de Féraudy. In this verse comedy, de Féraudy played Crispin, the clever servant. His poor young master is rejected by the mother of a rich girl as her daughter's suitor. Crispin tricks his master's old, ill uncle into signing a will in the young man's favor, so that he becomes an heir suitable to the rich girl. Crispin also looks out for himself. The will dictates that the nephew gets the estate, Crispin an annuity, and a comely female servant a cash gift on condition that she marry Crispin.

H.H.

LEGEND OF LEONORA, THE [Dramatic Revival] A: Sir James M. Barrie; D: Edward Elsner; S: Livingston Platt; P: William A. Brady; T: Ritz Theatre; 3/29/27 (16)

A replication of Barrie's 1914 play that had run for 136 performances with Maude Adams as Leonora. This slender bit of whimsy—about a charming, solicitous, young, widowed mother (Grace George) who is acquitted of the crime of pushing a fellow traveler off a train when he refused to close a window to make her sniffy-nosed daughter more comfortable—seemed cloyingly sentimental in 1927. Brooks Atkinson found it "faintly tedious," and Richard Dana Skinner accused it of being "dated." Grace George was, said Atkinson, "delightful. Slender, erect, alert and pleasantly sweet, she carries Leonora through her various dilemmas without a misstep."

LESSON IN LOVE, A [Comedy/Sex/British] A: Rudolf Besier and May Edginton; D: William Faversham; P: Lee Shubert; T: Thirty-ninth Street Theatre; 9/24/23 (75)

This combination comedy of manners and thesis play was titled *The Prude's Downfall* when presented in London. A widow (Emily Stevens) cuts dead a friend who has had an affair, and the French Captain (William Faversham) wooing her sets out to teach the prude a lesson. He leads her to the brink of an affair himself, and when she sees that she too is capable of passion, produces a marriage license.

The critics agreed that the genres did not combine well, and the characters were not very sympathetic, but they admired the acting of Stevens and Faversham. "Even though the dialogue be human and bright, conversation which takes until ten o'clock to posit a dramatic situation does not make for an entirely satisfying play," summed up Arthur Hornblow.

H.H.

LET AND SUB-LET [Comedy/Romance] A: Martha Stanley; D: Paul Edouard Martin; P: Lionel A. and Jack Hyman; T: Biltmore Theatre; 5/19/30 (40)

A hot-weather time passer lacking "the originality and freshness so necessary to effectiveness with the always brittle qualities of farce," asserted Perriton Maxwell. Its implausible plot dealt with a young lady of Larchmont (Dorothea Chard) whose parents leave for Europe thinking she has already sailed and will meet them there, while their home is sublet to a couple of bachelors. The girl has actually been hiding and emerges after her folks' departure; she passes herself off to one of the bachelors (George Dill) as the niece he has been expecting, manages to send the real niece (Betty Lancaster) off when she arrives, and falls in love with the bachelor uncle before the family returns.

"The first act is amusing, the second finds the machine gasping stertorously for new material, and the third is given over . . . to explaining what you have known for an hour," informed the *Times*.

LET US BE GAY [Comedy/Marriage/Romance] A/D: Rachel Crothers; P: John Golden; T: Little Theatre; 2/21/29 (132)

Rachel Crothers's sophisticated light comedy (which had a plot noticeably similar to that of *Meet the Prince*, which opened less than a week later), a hit that Burns Mantle chose as one of his Ten Best, was considered by some her best work yet.

Francine Larrimore turned in a fine job as Kitty Brown, who leaves her mate

Bob (William Williams) when he is unfaithful and three years later meets him again at a Westchester house party. She has been invited by Mrs. Boucicault (Charlotte Granville), the shrewd, cantankerous old lady of the house for the express purpose of luring Bob away from a young flapper (Rita Vale) he is after. The old lady doesn't want him to break up the engagement of this niece to a nice young fellow, nor does she know Kitty once was wed to Bob. Kitty is surprised that Bob is drawn to her when he sees all of the other men present attending upon her; a happy ending is effected.

"The almost Parisian frankness of modern New York society is excellently presented," praised Francis R. Bellamy, "yet the truths about love and hope and the ideal of fidelity which seem to inhabit the human heart . . . are never lost sight of."

LETTER, THE [Drama/Crime/Orientals/Romance/Tropics/Sex/Marriage/British] A: W. Somerset Maugham; SC: a story by Maugham; D: Guthrie McClintic; P: Messmore Kendall; T: Morosco Theatre; 9/26/27 (105)

Somerset Maugham's melodrama of passion in the tropics, still being produced in the 1980s, was met with mingled feelings. It was considered meretricious by many, Stark Young, for one, calling it "mostly trash," but its colorful story and brilliant Katharine Cornell performance gave it considerable interest for playgoers.

It unfolded a plot in which Mrs. Leslie Crosbie (Cornell), wife of an English planter in Singapore, pumps five bullets into the body of Geoffrey Hammond (Burton McEveilly), her secret lover, and then covers up her motives by claiming she acted in self-defense when Hammond tried to rape her. Her real reason is the discovery of his affair with a Chinese woman. The English community rallies to her cause, and she is cleared, but not before she has purchased for $10,000 a revealing letter written by her to Hammond and possessed by his Oriental mistress. She must inform her husband of the facts, and this will color their lives ever after. At the end she reveals that she still loves the man she slew.

Young maintained that Maugham had in no way developed the promising elements of his story, and that the talk was "bald and empty, . . . trite and futile." Brooks Atkinson, however, agreed that it was thin stuff but stuff in which, because of the sordid, exotic atmosphere, he was completely absorbed.

LETTY PEPPER [Musical/Romance/Business] B: Oliver Morosco and George V. Hobart; M: Werner Janssen; SC: Charles Klein's play *Maggie Pepper*; D: George V. Hobart; P: Oliver Morosco; T: Vanderbilt Theatre; 4/10/22 (32)

A dreary and unfunny musical based on a Charles Klein comedy of 1911, which only the eccentric cavortings of gawky star comedienne Charlotte Greenwood saved from complete ignominy. Greenwood played an ambitious department-store cashier fired by her envious supervisor but hired back and made a buyer when she meets and tells her troubles to young Mr. Colby (Ray Raymond), who, to her surprise, turns out to be the store's owner. Although threatened by the nasty supervisor, she makes the business a success, overcomes the wiles of the proprietor's haughty fiancée, and wins the affections of Colby himself.

Faced with forgettable music and a "dire libretto" (Alexander Woollcott), Greenwood had her spindly arms full trying to animate the moribund show.

LIANE, LE (Ties That Bind) and "IL CANTICO DEI CANTICI" ("The Song of Songs") [Drama/Italian/Italian Language] D: Giuseppe Sterni; P: Teatro d'Arte; T: Bijou Theatre; 4/21/29
Le Liane (Africa/Tropics/Race/Blacks] A: Gino Rocca; "Il Cantico dei cantici" [Religion/Romance] A: Felice Cavalloti

Le Liane was named for a tropical clinging vine with lotus-like properties; the name was meant to symbolize "the ties that bind." The play was staged in its original Italian by a local troupe that gave a typically polished, incisive performance of it. It concerned Riccardo (Rodolfo Badaloni), a man living in self-imposed exile on a Congo rubber plantation. The place is managed by the mulatto Oto (Giuseppe Sterni), who tries to prevent Riccardo from returning to Italy, fearing that without him there he, Oto, will fall a victim to the blacks he has mistreated. When he fails to stop Riccardo's departure, Oto strangles himself with the liane "which is thus transformed from a symbol into a force," according to Walter Littlefield.

The play was compact and suspenseful, thought Littlefield.

Also on the bill was "Il Cantico dei cantici," a one-act in which Sterni played "a bashful theological student who is won from his holy calling by reciting the Song of Solomon with his cousin Pia [Nera Badaloni]" (Littlefield).

LIDO GIRL, THE [Drama/Sex/Romance] A/D: Edward Elsner; P: Hyman Productions, Inc.; T: Edyth Totten Theatre; 8/23/28 (60)

A play that the *Times* placed among those annual offerings "that are literally so bad as to defy description." *Time* called it "a monstrosity." The critics mercilessly ripped apart the acting and the writing. Its heroine was a promiscuous Greenwich Village belle (Ethel Fisher), whose appeal inspires poets and sculptors; the play is principally concerned with her various amours and with one lover in particular, a bridge builder (Frank R. London), but she leaves him when an ex-boyfriend, freed from prison, offers to take her with him to Australia.

LIGHT OF ASIA [Drama/Orientals/Religion/Period] A: Georgina Jones Walton; M: Elliott Schenck; SC: Edwin Arnold's poem; D/P: Walter Hampden; CH: Ruth St. Denis; DS: Claude Bragdon; T: Hampden's Theatre; 10/9/28 (23)

A sincerely intended, reverently produced, but dull retelling of the life of Siddartha, Prince of the Sakkyas, and founder of Buddhism, as based upon a story in the nineteenth-century version of Sir Edwin Arnold. It had been written by theosophist Georgina Jones Walton about ten years earlier but had not been staged until now. Walter Hampden played the Buddha in this ornately uninventive effort denoted by the *Times* as "a commonplace pageant that contains none of

Buddha's serene wisdom save an interpolated maxim or two. . . . [N]either play nor acting catches the selfless dignity and nobility of a great fount of universal wisdom.'' Richard Dana Skinner saw the main defect being the inertia of the subject matter and its lack of conflict and suspense in the outcome.

LIGHTS OUT [Comedy-Drama/Films/Crime/Romance] A: Paul Dickey and Mann Page; D: Walter Wilson; P: Mrs. Henry B. Harris; T: Vanderbilt Theatre; 8/16/22 (12)

The producer of this comedy-melodrama chose the hottest night of the summer to open her ''moderately amusing'' (*Times*) play. The critic for *Variety* was right when he guessed that ''The high-brows won't like it,'' but he was dead wrong when he assumed the piece would go over with the masses who would savor its ''neat love story, . . . mystery, . . . corking crook angle and . . . touch of the motion picture stuff.''

When a band of thieves learn that the satchel they wish to steal from Egbert Winslow (Robert Ames) contains film scenarios, they hatch a scheme whereby the would-be writer will create scenarios based on their real-life adventures. One of them, designed to expose another crook (C. Henry Gordon), is produced, leading to the crook's capture and Egbert's landing of the daughter (Marcia Byron) of the bank president, who is cleared of the crook's crime.

LIKE A KING [Comedy/Business/Small Town] A: John Hunter Booth; P: Adolph Klauber; T: Thirty-ninth Street Theatre; 10/3/21 (16)

A completely predictable comedy of small-town life about Nat Alden (James Gleason), a young man who returns to his home town in a borrowed Rolls-Royce determined to convince the folks there that he is a success. Soon his whirlwind ways inspire the local citizenry to invest in a hydroelectric project; he even manages to bamboozle the Rolls's owner out of his car. The play ends with a shining future (financially and romantically) in store for the big fibber.

The characters were each a bucolic stereotype. The ''naive and unpretentious'' (Alexander Woollcott) comedy had its share of humor and charm, but it was extremely thin stuff. The show was remade as a musical, *Talk about Girls*, in 1927.

LILIES OF THE FIELD [Comedy-Drama/Prostitution/Sex/Romance] A: William Hurlbut; D: Harry McRae Webster; P: Garrick Productions; T: Klaw Theatre; 10/4/21 (169)

A strikingly mixed bag of virtues and vices, William Hurlbut's play about kept women was racy enough to make it a modest hit.

Mildred Harker (Marie Doro) is divorced from her unfaithful husband (Roy Walling) and loses custody of her young daughter. Influenced by a friend (Josephine Drake) and believing her child to have died, she moves in with a millionaire (Norman Trevor) who agrees to keep her. After a year she falls in love with the man and then learns that her girl is alive. The Croesus offers to marry her, and her husband agrees to give her custody of the child.

Woollcott thought the plot was "as uningenious, ungainly and generally incredible as any" seen on Broadway in years but found "immensely entertaining" those portions that had "an assortment of gaudy courtesans sitting around loose and chatting over their lives in a humorous and philosophical manner."

(1) **LILIOM** [Comedy-Drama/Sex/Romance/Marriage/Fantasy/Hungarian] A: Ferenc Molnar; TR: Benjamin F. Glazer; D: Frank Reicher; S: Lee Simonson; P: Theatre Guild; T: Garrick Theatre; 4/20/21 (300)

Liliom, which Burns Mantle chose as a Best Play of the Year, was first produced unsuccessfully in Budapest in 1909 and went to New York in a renowned Theatre Guild staging in 1921. Originally a failure, it was revived in its home city after the war, and this led to its New York production. After its generally enthusiastic welcome locally, it transferred to the Fulton Theatre.

The episodic play, in "seven scenes and a prologue," employed poignancy and satire to tell its simple tale of the crude carnival barker (his name in Hungarian means "roughneck") with a penchant for flirtation who wins the total love of the housemaid Julie (Eva Le Gallienne), whom he beats, despite his affection for her. She gives up her job to live as the bride of this Liliom (Joseph Schildkraut); when she conceives, the overjoyed roustabout tries with his pal the Sparrow (Dudley Digges) to stage a robbery to get needed cash. The attempt fails miserably, and Liliom kills himself rather than go to prison. The play then shifts styles to become a fantasy set in heaven, where Liliom appears before a police court judge (Albert Perry) who tells him he must remain there for fifteen years and then will be granted a day's reprieve on earth to redeem his soul. The basically unregenerate thief returns on the fated day, stealing a star for his young daughter (Evelyn Chard) as a gift. She does not recognize him, and her behavior leads him to slap her, but after he has gone, Julie, told of the incident, knows that it was Liliom.

Liliom's blend of fantasy and reality was judged experimental and indicative of new directions being taken by the drama. The writing, translation, direction, decor, and acting gained most critics' admiration; the play has remained popular in its dramatic form as well as in its tremendously successful musicalization by Richard Rodgers and Oscar Hammerstein II, *Carousel*. Edmund Wilson's remarks may be taken as representative: "*Liliom* . . . is such a very good play that one hardly knows what to say about it. The theme is slight and rather sentimental, but it is handled so deftly and lightly and redeemed with such sharpness and wit that the result is a drama of dignity." Although Schildkraut and Le Gallienne were long remembered for their portrayals, several reviewers, Wilson among them, thought they were not fully acceptable. But much approval was accorded Hortense Alden as Marie, Digges as the Sparrow, and Helen Westley as Mrs. Muskat. As a total production, many considered it the Guild's best to date: "A scrupulous respect for reality is combined in it with a strong and sober imaginative sense," commented Ludwig Lewisohn.

Joseph Schildkraut jotted in his autobiography *My Father and I* that, aside from a Viennese production, *Liliom* had been tepidly received in several European stagings before its New York success. A Broadway mounting starring John Barrymore was abandoned when Arthur Hopkins decided it would never sell to the general public. Schildkraut persuaded the Guild to do the play on the basis of a German version he read to several of its directors. He was also responsible for getting Le Gallienne cast as Julie. She herself had longed to do this play for years, having known it in a version called *Daisy*. In her autobiography *At 33*, Le Gallienne recalled how brilliantly Schildkraut played on opening night, while she, she thought, "was playing badly." "I was so nervous that my mouth was parched and dry. I was tied up in a thousand knots. . . . It was a nightmare." The next day she was amazed at the success she had made in the part.

(2) [Dramatic Revival/Yiddish Language] S: Willy Pogany; T: Irving Place Theatre (OB); 9/9/21

This Yiddish-language production ran simultaneously with the Guild's staging; it was notable for its use of settings by Willy Pogany that were comparable in excellence to those of Lee Simonson's. The *Times* noted a rude and unruly audience but found the production exceedingly worthwhile and lauded the appearance of a new Hungarian actor, Martin Ratkay, in the title role.

LILY SUE [Drama/Rural/Western/Romance] A: Willard Mack; D/P: David Belasco; S: Joseph Wickes; T: Lyceum Theatre; 11/16/26 (47)

A long-winded cowboy melodrama through which David Belasco presumably sought to make Beth Merrill a star. Merrill's costar was the author, who enacted an 1890s Montana sheriff, one of many men in love with Lily Sue (Merrill), a homesteader's pretty daughter, but whose chief rivals are cowhand Duke Adams (Curtis Cooksey) and n'er-do-well Louis Lindgard (Joseph Sweeney). When the latter is killed while peeping at Lily Sue's disrobing, the sheriff jails Duke as the culprit, and he is near to being hanged when the murderer is revealed as Lily Sue's brother (Leslie M. Hunt), who turns out to have justifiable reasons for shooting Lindgard.

The play's torrent of words was "heaped together with a singular disregard of dramatic values," complained Arthur Hornblow. For two acts barely any visible plot obtained; the third act packed in more action than the drama could contain.

LION TAMER, THE (Le Dompteur, ou l'anglais tel qu'on le mange) [Comedy/Circus/French/Marriage] A: Alfred Savoir; TR: Winifred Katzin; SC: a short story by Jacques Théry; D: Agnes Morgan; DS: Aline Bernstein; P: Neighborhood Playhouse; T: Neighborhood Playhouse (OB); 10/7/26 (33)

A symbolic French "satirical fable" that was considered by many sporadically intriguing and aesthetically inconsistent. Its allegorical intent was to pit a man of high ideals of justice and a believer in revolution against a brutish but practical oppressor of the masses. The tale concerns the English Lord Lonsdale's (Ian Maclaren) attempt to overcome the cruel circus lion-tamer Angelo (Otto Hulicius) by seeing one of his lions bite his head off. The lions, however, accept their subjugation, so the lord seeks to win the circus man's equestrienne wife, Arabella (Dorothy Sands), as a way of weakening the husband. He then turns to being a lion tamer himself, fighting fire with fire, but the lions eat him up, only for his place to be assumed by his son, a replica of himself, suggesting that the conflict will be eternal.

Richard Dana Skinner's feelings were shared by several reviewers. He was "delighted with the swift satire of the first act and dismally disappointed by the commonplace bedroom farce material of the second—a disappointment which the resumption of satire in the third act could not dispel."

LISTENING IN [Comedy/Mystery/Spiritualism] A: Carlyle Moore; D: Ira Hards; P: Milton Productions; T: Bijou Theatre; 12/4/22 (91)

Dubbed an "emotional comedy" by its author, *Listening In* was really a chiller with comic overtones, a "spook play" such as was then highly popular. Taking place in a big haunted house, with a sufficiently scary apparition from the beyond as one of its ghostly highlights, the play's various faults were overlooked in the wake of its shiver-inducing effects.

A major problem was the stylistic confusion between macabre melodrama and frisson farce. John Coomber (Ernest Glendinning), for reasons vaguely explained ("The worst expository dialogue I've ever heard . . . explains the obscurity"— Arthur Hornblow) agrees to reside in a haunted house for as long as it takes to establish or disestablish the presence there of a communicative spectre. The greenish glowing wraith that does appear turns out to be, through the automatic writing it inspires, a very helpful aide in matters financial and otherwise but is ultimately revealed as a mesmeric apparition conjured up by a clever illusionist and hypnotist.

LITTLE ACCIDENT [Comedy/Sex/Romance] A: Floyd Dell and Thomas Mitchell; SC: Floyd Dell's novel *An Unmarried Father*; D: Joseph Graham and Thomas Mitchell; S: Raymond Sovey; P: Crosby Gaige; T: Morosco Theatre; 10/9/28 (304)

The critics delighted in this jolly comedy about a bridegroom (Thomas Mitchell) who is rehearsing for his wedding when he learns that another girl (Katherine Alexander) has had his baby. He rushes off to the hospital (where a hilarious scene amongst expectant papas transpires) to kidnap the infant rather than see it put up for adoption by its career-minded mother. He fights off the attentions of his boarding-housekeeper's daughter (Patricia Barclay) and his fiancée (Elvia Enders), only to reconcile with his baby's mom and begin plans for their nuptials.

"It is easily one of the best-written and most amusing current entertainments."

smiled Robert Littell, "a little wobbly perhaps in the last act, when the comedy begins to turn into farce." "Ingenuous and yet very smart, *Little Accident* is full of laughter that keeps its place," wrote *Time*. Thomas Mitchell was described by Littell as "an extraordinarily good comedian. His gestures, his pantomime, his way of letting us know what is going on inside his head . . . are admirable." Burns Mantle selected the play as one of the Best of the Year.

LITTLE ANGEL, THE (Rozmarin Néni) [Comedy/Romance/Sex/Period/Hungarian] A: Ernest Vajda; TR: John S. Vajda; AD: J. Jacobus (Jeannette J. Druce); D: Herbert Druce; S: Willy Pogany; P: Brock Pemberton; T: Frazee Theatre; 9/27/24 (49)

One of two plays by Hungarian Ernest Vajda opening the same week on Broadway, this was a satire on the familiar tale of an innocent young pretty who gets pregnant but has no idea of how it happened.

The play is set in 1840. Anita (Mildred Macleod) is made love to by a young count (Robert Strange) while she is in a faint, which he presumes to be a ruse of modesty. The girl gets pregnant, and her family puts pressure on the Count to do the honorable thing. The girl protests that she has no idea of what occurred. The marriage is effected, and the girl's powerful aunt (Clare Eames) intends to have the Count sued for a divorce, but the couple fall in love, and the divorce plans are shelved.

Some were displeased at what Alan Dale called a "foolish, inept and ponderously piffling" play. In George Jean Nathan's view, "To get the full aroma of Hungarian light comedy, a half-French, half-Viennese touch is essential; and the play in its local revealment has all the bouquet of a bottle of Poland water."

LITTLE CLAY CART, THE (Mrcchakatika) [Dramatic Revival] A: Attr. to King Shudraka; TR: Arthur William Ryder; D: Agnes Morgan and Irene Lewisohn; DS: Aline Bernstein; P: Neighborhood Playhouse; T: Neighborhood Playhouse (OB); 12/5/24 (69)

A unique theatrical event, the reverent staging of an ancient Sanskrit play by the Neighborhood Playhouse, in a remarkably sustained and imaginative production that combined acting, direction, and design into a work of great enchantment. Eschewing the merely "exotic and the quaint" (Joseph Wood Krutch), the staging was faithful to the spirit of the play. Krutch expostulated: "Here . . . the spectator will be able to see a genuine example of that 'pure theatre' of which theorists talk. . . . Here he will see acting which has abandoned all pretense of literal imitation but which is yet strikingly beautiful and impressive; staging which belongs frankly to the make-believe of children at play but which is nevertheless artistically satisfying; and, in addition, a play wholly artificial yet profoundly moving because it is not realistic but real."

This classic Sanskrit work, written sometime in the middle of the first millenium A.D., and produced in a Rajput-influenced setting, tells of the love of the poor merchant Charudatta (Ian Maclaren) and the courtesan Vasantasena

(Kyra Alanova) and of the various obstacles that arise to keep them apart. Among these are her being strangled by a vicious prince (Harold Minjer) and Charudatta's being tried for the crime, only to be freed when she shows up alive at the last moment.

The play was produced again with minor cast changes on 11/8/26 for thirty-nine performances.

LITTLE CLOWN, THE (Der Kleiner Payets) [Musical/Romance/Jews/Family/Theatre/Yiddish/Yiddish Language] B: Joseph Lateiner; AD: William Siegel; M: Joseph Rumshinsky; D: Jacob Kalich; CH: Rose Gordon; P: Joseph Rumshinsky and Jacob Kalich; T: Kessler's Second Avenue Theatre (OB); 3/14/30

Molly Picon was the star of this Yiddish operetta based on an episode in the comedienne's own life. She played Stella, an actress, whose romance with a young rabbi (Muni Serebrov) betrothed by his parents to marry an important man's daughter leads his mother to dismiss her. The familyless Stella concocts an aunt (played by Picon) of sufficient respectability to induce her boyfriend's parents to see Stella perform. This eventuates in their acceptance of her as their daughter-in-law.

Picon's vehicle was a tuneful, ingratiating one, and the *Times* reviewer liked it considerably.

LITTLE EYOLF (Lille Eyolf) [Dramatic Revival] A: Henrik Ibsen; DS: Jo Mielziner; P: William A. Brady, Jr., and Dwight Deere Wiman; T: Guild Theatre; 2/2/26 (7)

A revival of Ibsen's play, first staged in 1895 and last seen in New York in 1910 starring Nazimova. It was given only at special matinees, and its cast was comprised of some of the most respected of New York's actors. Coming as it did amidst a rash of Ibsen revivals, the play did not fare well, either as drama or as production. ''Reginald Owen played Allmers so that his endless self-deception, his cant, and his fine phrases . . . were not clearly defined. Although Clare Eames always understood and illumined the burning jealousy and the frank unmorality of Rita, she often indicated rather than suggested the passion of the real Rita. Margalo Gillmore's Asta had a moving and direct quality completely lacking in Helen Menken's tricked and artful Rat Wife,'' wrote John Mason Brown.

The chief faults of the play itself seemed to lie in its lack of external action, and its reliance on the discussion of past events. Its strength was seen in the fine discernment of Ibsen's characterizations.

LITTLE JESSIE JAMES [Musical/Sex/Romance] B/LY: Harlan Thompson; M: Harry Archer; D: Walter Brooks; S: P. Dodd Ackerman; C: Mabel E. Johnston; P: L. Lawrence Weber; T: Longacre Theatre; 8/15/23 (385)

A bed that appeared and vanished as needed was so important to this musical that one critic included it in his cast list. Some critics likened the book by New

York newspaperman Harlan Thompson to French bedroom farce, most liked its racy jokes, and one song, "I Love You," survived long after the show, itself the biggest musical hit of the 1923–1924 season.

In this early example of the economical one-set show with a small chorus (of only eight), the title character (so called because she gets what she wants by fair means or foul) pursues a young man in his New York apartment. Paul (Jay Velie) and his roommate are poor, lazy, and involved with various women until Jessie (Nan Halperin) lands him after saving him from another man's wife (Miriam Hopkins, making her Broadway debut).

Paul Whiteman's Band was called "the James Boys" in the program and the musicians were introduced individually, a touch the *Times* critic thought a bit much. He thought that "the most refreshing member of the cast is a young woman named Miriam Hopkins, possessed of a Francine Larrimore manner, a tremendous head of yellow hair and two nimble legs."

H.H.

LITTLE MINISTER, THE [Dramatic Revival] A: James M. Barrie; D: Basil Dean; P: Charles Dillingham; T: Globe Theatre; 3/23/25 (16)

A revival of Barrie's popular 1897 play, frequently staged since the turn of the century, but not after this production, in which Ruth Chatterton starred as the little Scottish gypsy girl who turns out in the end to be Lord Rintoul's daughter, Lady Babbie. In 1925 *The Little Minister*, wrote Joseph Wood Krutch, seemed "pretty trifling and convincing neither as romance nor as realism."

It was generally agreed that, as Gilbert W. Gabriel phrased it, this was a "stilted laborious revival" and that Chatterton was not up to the demands of the role that Maude Adams had been so exquisite in years before.

LITTLE MISS BLUEBEARD (Kisaszony férje) [Comedy/Music/Sex/Marriage/Hungarian] A: Gabor Dregely; AD: Avery Hopwood; D: William H. Gilmore; S: Hermann Rosse; P: Charles Frohman i/a/w E. Ray Goetz; T: Lyceum Theatre; 8/28/23 (175)

Irene Bordoni's nine costumes, which James Craig called "each a stage masterpiece in itself," caused more excitement than any other feature of this production. John Corbin wrote that the play "affords Irene Bordoni an admirable vehicle for the brilliant and varied gowns she wears so well, for three or four delightful little songs, and for her very considerable charms of personality and of the art of amative comedy."

In Hopwood's adaptation, Collette, a comely French woman in love with Larry (Bruce McRae), a composer, is introduced to him as the wife of his best friend (Stanley Logan), who claims to have committed bigamy by marrying her under Larry's name. To solve the problem, Larry agrees to cover for his friend by letting the woman stay in his apartment. Soon, he falls in love with her and marries her for real. It is revealed that the friend had concocted the events as a scheme designed to win a wager that Larry would not always be a bachelor. The plot allowed for Bordoni to sing songs by E. Ray Goetz, Paul A. Rubens, B. G. De Sylva, and others; the show was even billed as a "song-play."

H.H.

LITTLE MISS CHARITY [Musical/Romance] B: Edward Clark; M: S. R. Henry and M. Savin; SC: a farce, *Not with My Money*; CH: Sammy Lee; P: Richard G. Herndon; T: Belmont Theatre; 9/2/20 (76)

A 1918 farce that had run for only eleven performances was resurrected in the shape of this musical comedy, its plot line "agreeably interrupted with dances and generally enlivened with some vaguely familiar but extremely danceable music," according to Alexander Woollcott. Its fable was about philanthropic young heiress Angel Butterfield (Juanita Fletcher), whom three crooks try to fleece of her fortune when they learn of her search for someone to manage its charitable dispersion. Angel's plan to build a model town for starving rent strikers hits a responsive chord in them, and they forgo their dishonest schemes so as to fulfill her dream. One of them (Frederick Raymond, Jr.) even marries her. Veterans Marjorie Gateson and Frank Moulan were the other two would-be swindlers.

LITTLE NELLIE KELLY [Musical/Crime/Romance] B/M/LY/P: George M. Cohan; D: George M. Cohan; CH: Julian Mitchell; T: Liberty Theatre; 11/13/22 (276)

George M. Cohan still had plenty of talent to provide when he wrote, composed, and codirected this hit musical comedy, which joshed the mystery play genre as often as it joshed itself. "The charm of Mr. Cohan's play is that he never takes the book seriously. He lets no opportunity slip by without spoofing his own efforts and taking the playgoers into his confidence," wrote the *Tribune*.

Dedicated to his parents (the romantic leads had the same first names as they, Jerry and Nellie), this powder keg of a musical was in the much-loved Cohan vein of dynamite dancing, supercharged sentimentality, and explosive humor. The author borrowed "all the standard props of the successful musical comedies of the last two or three years" (*Tribune*) to tell the story of Police Captain Kelly's daughter, Nellie (Elizabeth Hines), adept salesgirl, loved by the wealthy Jack Lloyd (Barrett Greenwood) as well as her jealous childhood sweetheart Jerry Conroy (Charles King); Jerry's suspicions of Jack are tied into a plot about a stolen string of pearls of which Jerry, until near the end, is thought to be the thief.

LITTLE OLD NEW YORK [Comedy/Period/Family/Legacy/Romance] A: Rida Johnson Young; D: Sam Forrest; P: Sam H. Harris; T: Plymouth Theatre; 9/8/20 (311)

New York City in 1810 formed the milieu for this hit comedy that Ludwig Lewisohn disparaged as sketching the old town "with the depth and imaginative grasp of a newspaper headline.'' Among the characters were the German-accented John Jacob Astor (Albert Andrews), Cornelius Vanderbilt (Douglas J. Wood), and Washington Irving (Frank Charlton). Genevieve Tobin acted the leading role, that of Patricia O'Day, an Irish lass who, at her father Michael's (Alf T. Helton) urging, comes over from Eire dressed as a boy so as to inherit a fortune meant for Michael's son, if he had one. When she learns that her ruse will cheat Larry Delevan (Ernest Glendinning), a cousin with whom she is in love, out of the money, she confesses the truth.

Alexander Woollcott considered the production enchantingly acted and compared Tobin to Maude Adams; he said the play was fascinatingly depictive of the persons and history of New York's early citizens and called it ''A lace-valentine play, a thing of twin hearts cut in the bark of an old play, a comedy of obvious banter, all prettily tricked out in the costumes and phrases of a hundred years ago.''

LITTLE ORCHID ANNIE [Comedy/Marriage/Homosexuality/Sex] A: Hadley Waters and Charles Beahan; D: Frederick Stanhope; P: Myra Furst; T: Eltinge Theatre; 4/21/30 (16)

Annie Westlake (Betty Lawrence) is the most ingenuous little sweetheart of a model, who harbors no suspicion that the men who lavish money, steel stocks, and Rolls Royces on her might have something salacious on their minds. With the money she has been sending young Danny Flynn (James Norris) through Yale. One Christmas eve, two of her wealthy admirers arrive to collect their due, and a brouhaha ensues, with Danny filling out the quadrangle and proving he's Annie's spouse. The men are hauled off to the police station.

The play contained many cracks upon homosexuality at the expense of a gay designer (Franz Bendtson) as delivered by a hard-boiled femme (Kitty Kelly); they became ''very tiresome indeed'' (Perriton Maxwell). The play itself was a ''rather determinedly smutty comedy,'' thought *Time*.

LITTLE POOR MAN, THE [Drama/Period/Verse/Religion] A: Harry Lee; D: Charles Warburton; CH: George Miles; S: Albert Bliss and Howard Claney; C: Marion De Pew; P: Clare Tree Major; T: Princess Theatre; 8/5/25 (35)

A verse play claiming the distinction of having won the $500 William Lindsey Prize of the Poetry Society of America for the best American poetic drama, but that, like many other prize plays, was sadly deficient on the stage. Pomposity marred the writing and the acting, the latter delivered ''by a band of ardent elocutionists,'' according to Percy Hammond, who found the play ''a saintly bore.''

The work was an incident-crammed biography of the life of St. Francis of Assisi (Jerome Lawler), into which all the principal facts of that holy person's life appear to have been inserted. There was sympathy expressed, said the *Times*, but ''little interpretation.''

LITTLE SHOW, THE [Revue] B: Howard Dietz, Newman Levy, George S. Kaufman, Fred Allen, and Marya Mannes; M: Arthur Schwartz (and others); LY: Howard Dietz; D: Dwight Deere Wiman; CH: Danny Dare; S: Jo Mielziner; C: Ruth Brenner; P: William A. Brady, Jr., and Dwight Deere Wiman i/a/w Tom Weatherly; T: Music Box Theatre; 4/20/29 (321)

Fledgling lyricist Howard Dietz, then working as a publicist for MGM pictures, was sitting in a speakeasy when he overheard Tom Weatherly and Dwight Wiman discussing their ideas for a new, intimate Broadway revue. Based on his own lack of good fortune on Broadway, he advised them against the venture and recited for them his poem "Lament for the Failures." They were immediately interested in his talent and signed him on as lyricist for their planned production *The Little Show*. They put him in touch with a young composer, Arthur Schwartz, who had once before refused a collaboration with him, and the team of Dietz and Schwartz was thereby launched on one of the most successful partnerships in American popular music.

The Little Show was a hugely popular production featuring a cast of extraordinarily gifted persons; Richard Dana Skinner said of it, "The music is engaging, some of the sketches are excellent in their brevity, and the effect of lavish entertainment is provided by an astoundingly small cast and remarkably little scenic extravagance." Its theme was New York life, and it came across "like an animated issue of such smart charts as *Vanity Fair* and *The New Yorker*," said *Time*. Fred Allen, whose "voice sounds as though it ran over a ratchet," came into prominence as the leading comic; Clifton Webb displayed his versatile dancing skills and introduced the song classic "I Guess I'll Have to Change My Plans" (originally composed for a boy's camp lyric written by Lorenz Hart); Libby Holman became a star when she sang songs such as "Moanin' Low" (with Ralph Rainger's music and accompanied by Webb's dancing) and "Can't We Be Friends?" (by James Warburg and Kay Swift) in her sultry tones; Romney Brent caused loud laughter to erupt; the theme song was "Hammacher Schlemmer—I Love You"; the tunes "I've Made a Habit of You" and "Little Old New York" were introduced; George S. Kaufman's famous sketch "The Still Alarm" was premiered; and so on. Brooks Atkinson rejoiced in the show as "gay, sardonic, trifling and remarkably good fun." Since the sequels to *The Little Show* were called *The Second Little Show* and *The Third Little Show*, this one is sometimes referred to as *The First Little Show*.

LITTLE SPITFIRE, THE [Comedy/Marriage/Crime/Family] A: Myron C. Fagan; D: A. H. Van Buren; P: B. F. Witbeck; T: Cort Theatre; 8/16/26 (201)

A hit comedy that the critics considered a lame affair because of a machine-made plot, relieved only by some snappy wisecracks. Arthur Hornblow branded it "dull and uninteresting," and the *Times* claimed it was like a "naive" cross between a Eugene Walter and George Kelly piece. It retold the familiar fable of the Bronx chorus girl, here named Gypsy (Sylvia Field), who weds a Southampton socialite (Louis Kimball) and is looked on by his family as an interloper.

The complications involve money stolen from the family firm by Gypsy's brother (Andrew Lawlor, Jr.), her attempt to save his neck only to be discovered by her mate in a certain man's (Dudley Hawley) rooms, and the ultimate working out of the details to the mutual satisfaction of the married couple and their families.

Sylvia Field walked off with the acting honors in a work suffering from "some incredibly bad casting and costuming," commented Richard Dana Skinner.

LIVE AND LEARN [Drama/Marriage/Sex] A: Lincoln Kalworth; D: Richard Irving; P: Michael Kallesser; T: Wallack's Theatre; 4/9/30 (5)

Very near the bottom of the 1929–1930 season's totem pole was this "thin little wisp of domestic dramaturgy" (*Time*). The curtain line of Act One, "The whole thing has been a mistake, a failure," gave the press a sharp hook on which to hang the play, which contained, said Brooks Atkinson, "some of the worst dramatic writing of modern times." The author was reported to be the producer hiding behind a pseudonym.

The essence of this triviality concerned the intrusion of blonde good-looker Annette Roberts (Beatrice Nichols) into the already bumpy home life of Harold (Allen Chase) and Mabel Fuller (Lois Jesson); Harold's disillusion with Annette and Harold's devising a stratagem to dump Annette and get Mabel back filled out the dramatic action.

(1) LIVING CORPSE, THE (Zhivoi trup; Der Lebende Leichnam) [Dramatic Revival/German Language] A: Leo N. Tolstoy; AD: August Scholz; D: Max Reinhardt; P: Gilbert Miller; T: Cosmopolitan Theatre; 1/23/28 (8)

In 1918 John Barrymore starred in this 1911 Russian play under the title *Redemption* (in England it was called *Reparation*). The present version was presented as part of the repertory season given by Max Reinhardt's visiting company in 1927–1928. Alexander Moissi, the great German star, played the leading role of Fedja. The *Times* believed the production to be the company's finest. "Using only a few indicative backgrounds and cutting the darkness of his stage with spotlights, [Reinhardt] frankly turned his theatre over to his actors," wrote John Mason Brown. The Slavic atmosphere was only partly attained, the emphasis going to the minutely detailed characterizations of each player.

Tolstoy's somber play concentrates on the plight of the worthless drunk Fedja who, to allow his wife the chance to marry a decent man, lets it be thought that he has killed himself. When the truth one day emerges, Fedja's only solution for absolving his wife (Helene Thimig) and her new husband (Eduard Winterstein) from legal complications is to commit suicide for real.

Both Thimig and Moissi were unusually luminous, wrote the critics, and Richard Dana Skinner expostulated on Reinhardt's directorial precision in capturing the rhythmic and ensemble values required.

Moissi returned to New York in this play with a non-Reinhardt company on 11/19/28 for a limited run of twenty performances at the Ambassador Theatre. This time it was titled *Redemption*.

(2) TR/D: Jacob Ben-Ami; DS: Aline Bernstein; P: Civic Repertory Company; T: Civic Repertory Theatre (OB); 12/6/29 (33)

This revival reverted to the title *The Living Corpse*. It was one of the most respected of the Civic Repertory Theatre's productions and employed Jacob Ben-Ami (who also translated and directed the play) as Fedja; Josephine Hutchinson as Lisa, the wife; and Donald Cameron as Victor, the second husband. Arnold Moss and Robert Lewis were in small roles. It was the heavily accented Ben-Ami's performance that drew most attention. His performance compared favorably with the interpretations of Barrymore and Moissi, although, as John Hutchens pointed out, the production, unlike theirs, stressed the play as a whole more than the central role.

Richard Dana Skinner found the mounting too consciously trying to avoid comparisons with Reinhardt's but believed the staging was "a competent, well-ordered piece of work, lacking brilliancy, but shot through with sincere power." Eva Le Gallienne was very good in her brief comedy role as Anna Karenina.

LIVING MASK, THE (Enrico IV) [Drama/Mental Illness/Italian] A: Luigi Pirandello; TR: Arthur Livingston; D/P: Brock Pemberton; DS: Robert Edmond Jones; T: Forty-fourth Street Theatre; 1/21/24 (36)

Noting that the title of Pirandello's *Henry IV* had been changed for its Broadway premiere lest audiences confuse it with Shakespeare's play, Alexander Woollcott found the feigned pretense of Pirandello's madman at being Henry IV of the Holy Roman Empire "is an old game. Hamlet played it, and indeed this *Living Mask* is a *Hamlet* with the poetry and the beauty and the divine spark left out."

Pirandello's play, which has since become appreciated as one of his finest works, concerns the case of a man who suffered an accident during a festival and has for years lived under the delusion that he is Emperor Henry IV (Arnold Korff). When, abetted by several others, Marchioness Mathilde (Ernita Lascelles) devises a plan to snap him back to reality by introducing to him her own daughter (Kay Strozzi), who resembles her as she was in youth, the situation goes askew, the "madman" kills someone, and he is thereafter condemned to living the rest of his life as his fantasy character, even though he has thrown off the chains of madness.

J. Ranken Towse complained that most of the actors could not be heard because of slovenly diction and that the play "impresses more by its oddity than its depth." The *Sun* critic, however, lauded the "highly successful production of grippingly impressive drama."

H.H.

LIZA [Musical/Romance/Crime/Blacks] B: Irvin C. Miller; M/LY: Maceo Pinkard; ADD./LY.: Nat Vincent; D: Walter Brooks; P: Al Davis; T: Daly's Theatre; 11/27/22 (172)

Liza did not run as long, but the critical response to it was nearly as favorable as that meted out to the decade's first smash black musical, *Shuffle Along*. There was scant attention paid to the "rather weak" book (*World*), and the comedy pickings (the comics, though black, wore blackface) were decidedly sparse; the format and look of the show were uninspired and savored more of vaudeville than of musical comedy. But *Liza* did have drive and pace and rhythm and spirit enough to energize the Great White Way for several months.

What plot there was concerned the collection of money for a monument to the late mayor of Jimtown, giving the local dandies and other smooth denizens a chance to line their pockets with the donations. When the populace notices that Dandy (Thaddeus Drayton), the beau of Squire Norris's daughter Liza (Margaret Simms), seems to be prospering, suspicions of graft begin to emerge (the Squire is behind the monument plan), but these suspicions are allayed; Dandy and Liza announce their coming nuptials. One funny scene took place in a cemetery where a couple of graverobbers were scared silly by a ghost.

The show's outstanding feature was its dynamic chorus routines, including the "Charleston Dancy," leading the *World* to call it "the fastest dancing show ever seen on Broadway. . . . These agile colored youngsters," the critic exclaimed, "dance with their hands, legs and bodies and no steps seem too difficult for them to do in unison."

The show's first title was *Bon Bon Buddy, Jr.*

(1) LOCANDIERA, LA [Dramatic Revival/Russian Language] A: Carlo Goldoni; D: Constantin Stanislavsky; P: F. Ray Goetz and Morris Gest; T: Jolson's Fifty-ninth Street Theatre; 11/21/23 (7)

Opinions were divided over the merits of Carlo Goldoni's play, also known as *Mirandolina* and *The Mistress of the Inn*, and Stanislavsky's staging of it for the Moscow Art Theatre. John Corbin recognized that the director had, contrary to recent practice, mounted all five acts of the original play and included two female characters—actresses masquerading as grande dames—usually cut out. Corbin commented that the production seemed very much in the festive spirit of the *Chauve-Souris* revues. Percy Hammond found the play a bore but was regaled by the frolicsome fun of the acting: "They abound in color and vivid moments, and they fascinate." Stark Young, however, found no joy here: "They took a play that comes out of an old civilization, a gracious and cynical tradition of social culture, and made it lively, empty, laborious, and a little boorish." There were equally mixed responses to the acting of Olga Knipper-Chekhova as one of the actresses and Stanislavsky as Ripafratta.

H.H.

(2) TR: Helen Lehmann; D: Eva Le Gallienne; P: Civic Repertory Company; T: Civic Repertory Theatre (OB); 12/6/26 (32)

Enthusiasm, devotion, and high ideals were the decisive virtues behind the Civic Repertory's revival of this eighteenth-century comedy. Le Gallienne's company was unpolished, with many foreign and local accents, and weakened by the director's choice of acting in plays she also staged, but it was nevertheless a worthwhile resuscitation of the classic. The respectful mounting featured Le Gallienne as Mirandolina, the innkeeper who circumvents the attentions of three nobles staying there to marry her servant Fabrizio (Alan Birmingham).

The *Times* critic said the work "floated lightly into an audience which was already prepared to enjoy and applaud this commendable repertoire experiment. It is an enjoyable little play, compact of asides, soliloquies, petty artifices and 'straight' characters, fitted to an elaborately unsophisticated treatment of a pleasant little theme." Richard Dana Skinner thought Le Gallienne's work had "sparkle and a great deal of refreshing spontaneity." Egon Brecher played Ripafratta.

The troupe returned to the play on 10/21/27, 10/12/28, 1/4/30, and 4/25/31, thereby establishing it as a mainstay of their repertory.

LOCKED DOOR, THE [Comedy/Marriage/Sex] A: Martin Lawton; D: Priestly Morrison; P: Jacob A. Weiser and Bela Blau; T: Cort Theatre; 6/19/24 (20)

An unoriginal marital comedy that vanished in less than three weeks. Its plot was like that of many French farces, but it was insufficiently developed and, aside from some decent laughs here and there, failed to tickle many spectators into giggling.

The story was that of young newlyweds Richard (Charles Trowbridge) and Muriel (Eleanor Woodruff); the groom wants to go on having a romantic affair with his bride, as if there never was a wedding. He is convinced that marriage will stale his affections. The disgruntled Muriel, advised by friends, locks him out on their wedding night. After being forced to spend the night picking her lock, Richard admits defeat and settles into conjugal bliss.

The author, commented the *Times*, "in no way attempts to elaborate the theme or express his opinions." With its "labored first act and . . . decidedly conventional third act," the play lumbered along to certain failure.

LOCURA DE AMOR (Lovesickness) [Drama/Marriage/Mental Illness/Spanish/Spanish Language] A: Manuel Tamayo y Baus; P: Maria Guerrero-Fernando Diaz Company of Madrid; T: Manhattan Opera House (OB); 5/19/26 (1)

The Princess Theatre Company of Madrid paid a visit to New York with a repertory including this play, starring its leading lady Maria Guerrero. She played the role of an insanely jealous queen, whose fears of her husband's philandering drive her over the brink. The crucial scene saw her madly interrogating her ladies-in-waiting about the handwriting on a letter sent to the King. Ultimately, her spouse lies dying, and she stands near his bed, whispering that he will live "under her heart" forever.

LOGGERHEADS [Comedy/Religion/Romance/Irish] A: Ralph Cullinan; P: Whitford Kane and Barry Macollum; T: Cherry Lane Theatre (OB); 2/9/25 (70)

An Irish melodrama that John Mason Brown considered "violent and perplexing" and an "outlandish mixture of every Irish dramatic brew from Boucicault to St. John Ervine." Joseph Wood Krutch called it "old-fashioned but effective up to the last act."

Ellen Halpin (Gail Kane), lives with Corny Halpin (Whitford Kane), brother of her late husband. He loves her but has kept the fact to himself. She is on the outs with the Barrett family, one of whose members slew her husband, but she loves Christie Barrett (Earle House), who has been long gone overseas. On his return, Ellen's daughter (Joanna Roos) contrives to end the family feud so that her mother may marry Christie, while she will become a nun.

The acting of Joanna Roos and Whitford Kane kept this weak play going far longer than might otherwise have been the case. The piece began Off-Broadway but then moved to Broadway's Gaiety Theatre, where it lived out its days.

LOLLIPOP [Musical/Family/Romance] B: Zelda Sears; M: Vincent Youmans; LY: Zelda Sears and Walter De Leon; D: Ira Hards; CH: Bert French; S: Sheldon K. Viele and William Castle; P: Henry W. Savage, Inc.; T: Knickerbocker Theatre; 1/21/24 (145)

Termed "weakly Cinderella-ish" but fresh and breezy, this musical's book featured an orphan nicknamed "Lollipop" (Ada-May) who is adopted by a rich but crotchety woman (Zelda Sears). In her new home she clears herself of a charge of stealing her benefactor's purse and meets an attractive plumber and marries him after they have danced in and out of trouble. Two hit songs emerged from Vincent Youmans's first full score—"Tie a Little String around Your Finger" and "Take a Little One Step" (reused in *No, No, Nanette*). Book-writer and lyricist Zelda Sears played the rich adoptive mother, the *Times* critic noted, "with great unction, and remaining modestly in the background throughout the evening." The greatest success of the cast was the British Tiller Girls dancers, about whom the *Evening Post*'s Charles Pike Sawyer commented: "each new lot sent over by that remarkable teacher [John Tiller] seems better than ever, for each lot has something new to show."

This was one of seven shows forced to close following a producers' dispute with Actors' Equity.

H.H.

LOLLY [Comedy/Romance/Family] A: Fanny Heaslip Lea; D: Walter Greenough; P: New York Theatre Assembly; T: Assembly Theatre; 10/16/29 (29)

A stale romantic comedy about lost and found love involving the case of lovesick Lolly Carroll (Mary Young), a frivolous dowager with a nineteen-year-old daughter (Eleanore Bedford). Lolly manages to escape the attentions of a Latin gigolo (Alberto Carrillo) for the worthier embraces of a lover (Hugh Miller) gone two decades in South America, who also turns out to be her flapper daughter's father. The epigrammatic dialogue contained remarks such as, "Children should be the result of love, not love the result of children."

"*Lolly* is . . . a talkative and tedious play, whose chief freshness is to be found in its occasional patches of shrewd and telling dialogue," observed the

Times. The work was the premiere offering of a new subscription group aimed at society audiences and playing in the renamed Princess Theatre on Thirty-ninth Street.

LOMBARDI, LTD. [Dramatic Revival] A: Frederick and Fanny Hatton; D: Cecil Owen; P: Murray Phillips; T: George M. Cohan Theatre; 6/6/27 (24)

Leo Carrillo, who starred in the original 1917 hit production of this comedy, returned to do it ten years later in a low-priced revival produced as the third in a series of such works being offered by Murray Phillips. Carrillo played one of his specialty Italian dialect parts as the kindhearted-to-a-fault dressmaker who, when he is unable to win the love of the model he desires (Rita Vale), settles for his assistant (Helen Deddens).

The *Times* thought the piece was a bit worse for wear, but to Richard Dana Skinner it was "full of good comedy and quite a little pathos."

LOOSE ANKLES [Comedy/Sex/Romance] A: Sam Janney; D/P: Brock Pemberton; T: Biltmore Theatre; 8/16/26 (161)

Sam Janney's comedy suffered from a split personality; it succeeded admirably in its argot-strewn, cynically humorous depiction of young New York gigolos who prey on older women by acting as dancing partners at public dance halls, but it disintegrated into "insipidity" and "vapid farce" (John Mason Brown) when it ventured to tell the story of an heiress (Kathleen Comegys) who can cash in on a will only by getting married, which she does not want to do. To make a point of her refusal, she decides to create a scandal by being compromised by a lounge lizard. The one she chooses, however, is Gil (Harold Vermilyea), really a good lad at heart who refuses to hurt the girl's reputation. They fall in love and marry.

The scenes among the gold-digging men provided material for laughter-producing characterizations and dialogue "of considerable briskness and satiric point," declared Richard Dana Skinner. Much of the remainder of the play was "crudely written and crudely conceived" (John Mason Brown). The best performance was that of Osgood Perkins as one of the professional lovers.

LOOSE ENDS [Drama/Marriage/British] A/D: Dion Titheradge; P: Sam H. Harris; T: Ritz Theatre; 11/1/26 (40)

Dion Titheradge wrote, directed, and played the leading role in this well-acted, somewhat sentimental British drama of married life among the contemporary smart set. A largely English company was enlisted to perform it. Actress Nina Grant (Violet Heming) falls in love with and marries Malcolm Forres (Titheradge) after nearly running him over and subsequently recognizing in him finer qualities than those of the men in her dissolute circle. Some time later she is scandalized to learn that her model consort is an ex-convict who spent fifteen years in prison for murder (albeit a justifiable homicide). He agrees to her request for a divorce, which can be granted only if he is guilty of adultery; Nina changes her mind when another woman (Molly Kerr) gladly agrees to help Malcolm satisfy the legal requirements.

The play depicted a Noël Coward-like world of sophisticated poseurs, but not cynically. "The story it tells," noted Arthur Hornblow, "is human enough, if not altogether plausible, and the characters are well and amusingly drawn."

LOS ANGELES [Comedy/Films/Sex/Romance] A: Max Marcin and Donald Ogden Stewart; D: Sam Forrest; P: George M. Cohan b/a/w Max Marcin; T: Hudson Theatre; 12/19/27 (16)

A formula comedy with melodramatic underpinnings about scandalous goings on in Hollywood. Originally known as *A Hollywood Party*, its title was changed at the suggestion of producer George M. Cohan. It "emerged as desultory and only fair-to-middling entertainment," wrote the *Times*.

Ethel Grierson (Frances Dale), a New York blonde, travels with a phony "aunt" (Alison Skipworth) to filmland, where, passing herself off as a virtuous convent-bred girl, she is employed by a film magnate to involve a certain actor (Alan Brooks) in a scandal as a ploy to prevent him from shifting to another firm. Her mercenary involvement turns to a romantic one, and the play follows her struggles to prevent a real scandal and at the same time land the guy.

LOST [Drama/Romance/Marriage] A: A. E. Thomas and George Agnew Chamberlain; SC: a novel by George Agnew Chamberlain; D: Rollo Lloyd; S: P. Dodd Ackerman; P: Ramsey Wallace; T: Mansfield Theatre; 3/28/27 (8)

"A rather faltering and underwritten tale" (*Times*), based on a novel by one of the codramatists, about a Connecticut couple, the Lansings, and their marital bugaboos. Gerald Lansing (Ramsey Wallace) goes to Brazil to have it out with Alan Wayne (James Crane), the man with whom he believes his wife (Mona Kingsley) ran off (she actually had second thoughts and didn't go). While in Brazil Gerald takes up with a native beauty (Rosalinde Fuller); when Alice arrives to straighten things out, the girl conveniently kills herself.

LOST SHEEP [Comedy/Family/Prostitution/Romance/Sex/British] A: Belford Forrest; D: Marion Gering; S: Watson Barratt; P: George Choos and Jack Donahue; T: Selwyn Theatre; 5/5/30 (96)

The titillating premise of this British comedy disturbed some critics, but others found it harmless enough. Parson William Wampus (Ferdinand Gottschalk), his wife (Cecelia Loftus), and three daughters take temporary residence while their new home is being prepared at a house formerly famed as a bordello. A host of complications is thus unleashed when the brothel's customers come around, unaware of a changeover in the occupants, and try to engage the services of Mrs. Wampus and her girls. One innocent youth (Rex Cherryman) falls for one of the girls (Sidney Fox) and tries to lead her from her shameful path. He succeeds in winning her as his bride-to-be.

The play could not sustain interest indefinitely on the thin thread of its central misunderstanding and eventually began to pall. Too many obvious contrivances had to be called on to milk the situation. Perriton Maxwell declared, "it is but a passable bit of farce and one which remains credible only if you are not in too critical a mood."

A return engagement played for sixteen performances from 8/18/30.

LOUD SPEAKER [Comedy/Politics/Family/Journalism] A: John Howard Lawson; M: Eugene L. Berton; LY: Edward Ellison; D: Harry Wagstaff Gribble; S: Mordecai Gorelik; P: New Playwrights Theatre; T: Fifty-second Street Theatre; 3/2/27 (29)

The most unusual aspect of *Loud Speaker* was its constructivist set and acrobatic acting style, suggestive of the Russian director Meyerhold's innovations. "Stairways run up and down with good-natured abandon; chutes lead on and off on either side; doors, windows, desks, divans, a fireplace, a safe, a trusty musket and a screen complete the whirligig stage fittings," wrote Brooks Atkinson. A jazz band accompanied the action. Actors slid down chutes and catapulted over furniture before delivering innocuous lines. Joseph Wood Krutch loved this "all but plotless fantasia," because it was "the nearest approximation yet seen in New York of the spirit of the Commedia dell'Arte."

Lawson's poorly received expressionistic farce satirized numerous American customs from occult religions to Freudian psychology to tabloid journalism to the hypocrisy of politics. These elements jostled one another without mercy, claimed Atkinson, who nevertheless found it "tiresome" because of a story lacking "distinction" and "commonplace" acting. This story dealt with the election campaign of a dull millionaire gubernatorial candidate (Seth Kendall), who, upon experiencing the disintegration of his family's life, takes out his frustration on the public in a condemnatory radio speech, only to have the public take it as a speech of blazing integrity for which he is elected to run New York State.

LOUIE THE 14TH [Musical/German] B: F. and J. Wilhelm; AD: Arthur Wimperis; M: Sigmund Romberg; D/CH: Edward Royce; P: Florenz Ziegfeld; T: Cosmopolitan Theatre; 3/3/25 (319)

Opening-night seats to this work were obtainable from scalpers for $100 each. Those who paid the price got relatively fair value in return, for the show proceeded to become a solid hit that ran for nearly a year. With its expected Ziegfeld-produced extravagances, it was "*hors concours*," wrote Arthur Hornblow: "Its huge choruses, male and female, its gorgeous costumes, striking pageants, lovely stage settings—to say nothing of the magnificent service of gold plate by the Gorham Company, displayed in the banquet scene—are worth all of the $300,000 the production is said to have cost."

Based by an English writer on an unlisted German show, it was set in the French Alps and starred the comic actor Leon Errol as an army cook *cum* mountain guide *cum* phony aristocrat named Louie Ketchup who gets invited by wealthy American Paul Trapman (J. W. Doyle) to be the fourteenth guest at his lavish dinner party, where Louie promptly proceeds to make a comical ass of himself.

Sigmund Romberg's score was not first-rate, but there was much popular and critical acclaim for one number, "Homeland," sung by Harry Fender. The show's chief attraction was Leon Errol, but the star was hampered by an inept book that had barely any genuine humor in it.

LOVE [Drama/Family/Marriage] A: Evelyn Scott; D: George Cram Cook; P: Provincetown Players; T: Provincetown Playhouse (OB); 2/19/21 (14)

A play examining with Freudian intent the subject of mother-love as expressed in a woman's jealousy of her daughter-in-law. Ludwig Lewisohn said the play was "notably better than its title. Its action . . . is straight and true; its dialogue is veracious and well-molded." Only an offstage suicide at the end marred the full realization of the writer's treatment, he thought.

Carroll Lamont (Ida Rauch) has married Claude Mayfield (William Rainey) as his second wife and has also thus become stepmother to his son from a previous marriage. As in that earlier relationship, Claude's mother's (Virginia Chauvenet) insane jealousy goes to work at destroying the marriage until Claude resolves the dilemma by killing himself.

LOVE AND DEATH [Musical/One-Acts/Russian/Russian Language] SC: the writings of Alexander Pushkin; D: Xenia Kotlubai; DS: Ivan Gremislavsky and Nikolai Iznar; P: F. Ray Comstock and Morris Gest; T: Jolson's Fifty-ninth Street Theatre; 1/11/26 (7)

"Aleko" [Marriage/Sex] B: Vladimir Nemirovich-Danchenko; M: Sergei Rachmaninoff; SC: Pushkin's "The Gypsies"; "The Fountain of Bakhchi-Sarai" [Marriage/Sex] M: Anton Arensky; "Cleopatra" [Period/Sex] B/M: Reinhold Gliere; SC: Pushkin's *Egyptian Nights*

A triple bill of musical one-acts produced in repertory by the Moscow Art Theatre Musical Studio, led by Vladimir Nemirovich-Danchenko, during their 1925 stay in New York. This was the first program they produced based on Russian, not foreign, materials. "Aleko" was an 1891 Rachmaninoff opera created when the composer was only eighteen; Samuel Chotzinoff said it was not much to be proud of: "The score is insipid and undistinguished." It concerned Aleko (Pyotr Saratovsky), a wanderer, who weds a gypsy (Veronica La Touche), discovers her affair with a young gypsy (Nikolai Permyakoff), kills them, and is cast out by the tribe. "The Fountain" revealed the Khan (Vladimir Lossky) reminiscing at the Fountain of Tears about a love affair of five years earlier, when his wife (Olga Baklanova) threatened his new mistress (Nadizhda Kemarskaya) with death. This opera and "mimo-drama" was not especially noteworthy. Finally, there was the ballet of "Cleopatra," about how the Roman Flavius (Misael Speremsky) agrees to one night of love with Cleopatra in exchange for his own life on the morrow.

LOVE AND INTRIGUE (Kabale und Liebe) [Dramatic Revival/German Language] A: Friedrich Schiller; D: Max Reinhardt; P: Gilbert Miller; T: Cosmopolitan Theatre; 1/16/28 (8)

Schiller's eighteenth-century romantic tragedy was presented in the original German by Max Reinhardt's impressive company during their 1927–1928 repertory season in New York. As with the great regisseur's handling of Shakespeare, this play saw the sharp edge of the editorial scissor so as "to speed the action or to point the high accents," noted the *Times*. Reinhardt's version compacted the five-acter into two and drove the action relentlessly forward in a swiftly moving, excitingly dramatic mounting. "Reinhardt and his actors played this overwrought drama with all the perfervid exaggeration that alone can make it bearable today, as if they believed in every phrase they uttered and attitude they struck," said John Mason Brown.

The production, unlike Reinhardt's others, seemed classically austere and not self-consciously modernized. A sort of Teutonic Romeo and Juliet, it tells of the great love between a couple of widely varying social classes and of their fateful end by poisoning. Helene Thimig made her first major New York appearance in it as Luise and awed various critics, Lili Darvas made an impact as Lady Milford, Vladimir Sokoloff was the serpentine Wurm, and Alexander Moissi was memorable in the tiny role of the president's valet.

LOVE AND POLITICS (Liebe und Politik) [Drama/Jews/Politics/Yiddish/Yiddish Language] A/D/P: Max Gabel; T: Gabel's Public Theatre (OB); 10/20/29

A half-English, half-Yiddish melodrama produced at a theatre on Second Avenue known for its prolific author-producer's output of moralistic melodramas inspired by Broadway hits. One of Gabel's few plays to be noticed in the English-language press, it was considered by the *Times* reviewer "the best balanced and best performed" work he had witnessed at this playhouse. The plot was a Romeo and Juliet story told in terms of a struggle between a crooked political group in power and a reform party trying to overcome them. Only the deaths of their children bring the heads of the rival parties to a reconciliation.

LOVE BIRDS [Musical/Romance] B/LY: Edgar Allen Woolf and Ballard MacDonald; M: Sigmund Romberg; D: Edgar J. MacGregor and Julian Alfred; P: Wilner and Romberg; T: Apollo Theatre; 3/15/21 (103)

"Musical comedy production has reached the zero mark in this offering," grumbled Arthur Hornblow: "It is like all the others, only worse. There is not a single new thing in it excepting the scenery and the clothes, and there is a sinful waste of money. . . . It is a lamentably weak attempt to transplant a lot of vaudevillians . . . into musical comedy." The show that provoked these acidulous remarks was a formula arrangement that employed veterans such as Pat Rooney and his wife, Marion Bent (who stole the show), Elizabeth Murray, Eva Davenport, Tom Dingle, and Emilie Lea in the service of a story about a girl (Elizabeth Hines) who joins a Persian sultan's harem to avoid marrying the man her mother has chosen for her, and who is finally rescued by the fellow (Barrett Greenwood) she really adores.

LOVE CALL, THE [Musical/Western/Period/Romance/Military] B: Edward Locke and Harry B. Smith; M: Sigmund Romberg; LY: Harry B. Smith; SC: Augustus Thomas's play *Arizona*; D: J. C. Huffman; CH: Earl Lindsay; P: Messrs. Shubert i/a/w L. Lawrence Weber; T: Majestic Theatre; 10/24/27 (81)

A routine retelling in musical comedy form of Augustus Thomas's once respected melodrama of the Golden West, *Arizona*. The action was moved back from 1894 to 1869, but the story of how the whites at Henry Canby's (W. L. Thorne) ranch are threatened by Black Hawk Indians on the warpath and are rescued at the climactic moment by the cavalry—all of it tied in with elements of romance, honor, and seduction—gave the producers ample matter for a colorful, if formula, presentation. It seemed to Brooks Atkinson "as dated as a Frederick Remington print," and *Time* announced, "Fair music, fairer chorus girls scarcely compensate for a deadly lack of laughter."

LOVE CHILD, THE (L'Enfant de l'amour) [Drama/Romance/Sex/French] A: Henri Bataille; AD: Martin Brown; D: Bertram Harrison; P: A. H. Woods and Charles L. Wagner; T: Cohan Theatre; 11/14/22 (169)

A serious drama that, like the lighter products of A. H. Woods's sponsorship, had certain off-color and sensational qualities. The *Herald* called it "the frankest play of the season." It served "principally as an excuse for a remarkably well chosen cast to let loose the best serious acting of the season on a wholesale scale," claimed the *Herald*. The reactions of the critics to Martin Brown's adaptation were unenthusiastic.

Janet Beecher acted Laura Thorne, a role established in Paris by the great Réjane. Laura, for seventeen years the mistress of Paul Brander (Lee Baker), whose wife has been insane for years, believes her chance to marry Paul has arrived following Mrs. Brander's death. Paul, however, faced by a promising public career, decides to move on without Laura, ignoring his previous promises to her. Laura's son Eugene (Sidney Blackmer), of a previous union, neglected by his mother because of her attentions toward Brander, fights for his mother's cause by threatening to compromise Brander's daughter (Juliette Crosby), but when Brander gives in, Laura rejects him and prepares to nourish her relationship with her son.

LOVE CITY, THE (Yoshiwara) [Drama/Fantasy/Drugs/Orientals/Sex/Prostitution/German] A: Hans Bachwitz; D: Stuart Walker; P: Sessue Hayakawa; T: Little Theatre; 1/25/26 (24)

A house filled with motion-picture celebrities turned out on opening night to view this Oriental melodrama from Germany (originally called *Yoshiwara*), starring and produced by Japanese screen idol Sessue Hayakawa. The play was but "a dawdling affair" (*Herald Tribune*), and Hayakawa was not particularly noteworthy in his Broadway debut as Chang Lo, the villainous Chinese brothel keeper and opium dealer who runs the House on the Hill of Delight for the pleasures of interested Europeans.

This purveyor of forbidden ecstacies keeps prisoner the English-speaking Tze-Shi (Catherine Dale Owen), a beauty who lures men to his establishment. Here, an Englishman (Earle Larimore), in a drug-induced stupor, dreams that his wife is Tze-Shi and that she is having an affair with Chang Lo. When he wakes, he kills the Chinese in a duel and is himself slain by a bullet.

LOVE DREAMS [Musical/Romance/Invalidism] B: Anne Nichols; M: Werner Janssen; LY: Oliver Morosco; D: Oliver Morosco and John McKee; P: Oliver Morosco; T: Times Square Theatre; 10/10/21 (40)

This so-called melody drama was "a rather ingenious combination of musical comedy and sentimental drama" (*Times*) with a book by the soon-to-be-famous authoress of *Abie's Irish Rose*. Nichols's schmaltzy story tells of how a sexy pseudo-European Broadway star, Renee D'Albret (Vera Michelena), allows her press agent (Harry K. Morton) to promote her image as a torrid vamp, since all she really wants is to make enough money to care for her crippled sister Cherry (Marie Carroll). The love interest involves Renee's attachment to Larry Pell (Tom Powers), whom she gives up when Larry and Cherry fall in love. Cherry's illness is cured by Larry's doctor brother (Orrin Johnson), and a romance begins between the M.D. and the actress.

Drama and music did not mix in this bungled effort, noted Arthur Hornblow. The critics were surprised that the chorus had no singing to do ("thank heavens," sighed Hornblow).

LOVE DUEL, THE [Comedy-Drama/Romance/Sex/Hungarian] A: Lili Hatvany; AD: Zoë Akins; D: E. M. Blythe (Ethel Barrymore); S: Watson Barratt; P: Lee Shubert i/a/w Gilbert Miller; T: Ethel Barrymore Theatre; 4/15/29 (88)

A vehicle for Ethel Barrymore in which the star's excellent performance served to demonstrate the inadequacy of the material for her talent. It was a sophisticated romantic allegory, set in Switzerland, with its leading characters called He (Louis Calhern) and She (Barrymore). During the play they are referred to as Carlo and Lydia. Each is a figure with far-flung Continental love conquests. Worthy opponents, they meet and engage in a duel of romance; whoever first brings the other to his or her knees is the victor. During the action, She gives birth to an illegitimate child. This leads to the decision being a draw.

Excessive sentiment and puppet-like characters were negative aspects that damaged the work's credibility. Richard Dana Skinner extolled Barrymore's "charm and beauty" while damning the piece for "the most preposterous situations and the most absurd artificialities of plot, situation and character."

LOVE 'EM AND LEAVE 'EM [Comedy/Romance/Gambling] A: George Abbott and John V. A. Weaver; D: George Abbott; P: Jed Harris; T: Sam H. Harris Theatre; 2/3/26 (152)

John V. A. Weaver, popular versifier of American slang, teamed up with experienced Broadway-hand George Abbott, to compose this likable melange of colloquialisms in which the tartness of the speech patterns, as suggested by the title, was the main ingredient. Joseph Wood Krutch put it succinctly: "The plot is thin and conventional, but it is made into a genuinely amusing comedy by the raciness of the dialogue." Arthur Hornblow found it "an extremely interesting comedy, idiomatically correct, very well cast and well played."

The action takes place in a boarding house and in Ginsberg's Department Store. Much of the activity concerns preparations for a pageant being put on under the auspices of the store's Welfare Association. The major portion of the plot deals with sisters Janie (Katherine Wilson) and Mame Walsh (Florence Johns), their rivalry over the affections of store-clerk Billingsley (Donald Macdonald), Janie's underhanded methods of capturing him, her gambling away of the association's money, her noble sister's crap-shooting luck at winning it back, the switch of Billingsley's attentions to her, and the consequent pursuit of other bachelors by the chastened Janie.

LOVE EXPERT, THE [Comedy/Small Town/Journalism/Romance] A: John Kirkpatrick; D: Gustav Blum; P: Gustav Blum i/a/w Arthur Tupper Jones; T: Wallack's Theatre; 9/23/29 (16)

"The Love Expert" is Miss Alice (Helen Holmes), the advice to the lovelorn columnist for a local paper who answers a Mary Jackson's (Natalie Wykes) query about whether she should marry Chester (Owen Cunningham) or Tony (William Lovejoy) by visiting Mary with her own fiancé, reporter Tom Jones (Earl McDonald). Tom solves the dilemma by leaving Miss Alice and getting Mary to select him.

The *Times* called this "absurd affair" childish and puerile, and *Time* quoted the one line it liked: "Women don't really change their minds. Their minds simply get tired resting on one side, and turn over."

LOVE FOR LOVE [Dramatic Revival] A: William Congreve; D: Robert Edmond Jones and Stanley Howlett; S: Robert Edmond Jones; C: Milia Davenport; T: Greenwich Village Theatre (OB); 3/31/25 (47)

A ripping good revival of Congreve's Restoration classic that allowed highly favorable comparisons to be made with it and the author's more renowned *Way of the World*, staged somewhat less delightfully earlier the same season. Gilbert W. Gabriel said, "the town has known no lark this season more delightful" and found the production "brimming with grace, wit and beauty." Most critics claimed, as did Joseph Wood Krutch, that the unexpurgated bawdy jokes had an "indecency . . . as robust and boisterous as [they are] intellectually accomplished."

What truly put the work over was the fineness of the acting. The best performances were Edgar Stehli as Tattle, Rosalinde Fuller as Miss Prue, Adrienne Morrison as Miss Frail, Helen Freeman as Angelica, and E. J. Ballantine as Foresight.

The show returned on 9/14/25 for sixteen performances at Daly's Theatre before going on tour.

LOVE HABIT, THE (Pour avoir Adrienne) [Comedy/Marriage/Romance/Sex/ French] A: Louis Verneuil; AD: Gladys Unger; D/P: Brock Pemberton; T: Bijou Theatre; 3/14/23 (69)

Unlike the conventional Broadway adaptations of French farces, which were so bowdlerized and Americanized that they bore scant relation to their originals, *The Love Habit* was refreshingly true to its source, causing Heywood Broun to claim the play as being ''almost historic'' and worthy of being designated ''educational drama.''

Louis Verneuil's naughty bedroom romp, delightfully enacted by a highly gifted troupe, tickled many critics pink with its witty telling of a story in which an attractive young man (James Rennie) insists on pursuing a married woman (Florence Eldridge) for purposes of adultery; he goes so far in his quest as to blackmail the woman's husband (Ernest Cossart) not to interfere for fear of his revealing to the wife his extramarital dalliance with a certain cabaret danseuse (Fania Marinoff).

It was ''an amusing farce that at times attains downright hilarity,'' laughed Arthur Hornblow, who thought it ''quite the best comedy importation of the present season.''

LOVE, HONOR, AND BETRAY (L'Ennemie) [Comedy/Fantasy/Death/Sex/ Romance/French] A: André-Paul Antoine; TR: Frederick and Fanny Hatton; D: Lester Lonergan; S: Nicholas Yellenti; P: A. H. Woods; T: Eltinge Theatre; 3/ 12/30 (45)

Clark Gable made his last Broadway appearance in this play in a cast that counted Alice Brady, Wilton Lackaye, George Brent, and Glenda Farrell among its talented players. The ''satire,'' which Brooks Atkinson decided was not particularly satiric, took place in a graveyard, where the shades of three men who had been involved with a certain temptress (Brady) in life appear to discuss her and their attitudes toward women. Gable was the Lover whom her sex needs wore out, Mark Smith the corpulent Husband who died of frustration at being stuck with her, and Robert Williams the Young Man who killed himself for her. Episodes from their lives with her are enacted in flashback, and they laugh as they watch her unsuccessfully trying to woo her handsome Chauffeur (Brent) away from her own daughter (Farrell).

Perriton Maxwell found nothing here to convince him ''that it was anything but a tedious, heavy, somewhat bewildered and entirely obvious concoction which hovered between satire and comedy and occasionally slipped over the border into farce.''

LOVE IN A MIST [Comedy/Romance/Southern] A: Amelie Rives (Princess Troubetskoy) and Gilbert Emery; D: Gilbert Emery; P: Charles L. Wagner; T: Gaiety Theatre; 4/12/26 (120)

A drawing-room comedy about a mendacious Virginia woman, Diana Wynne (Madge Kennedy), who finds good reasons for failing to divulge the simple truth. Her prevarications lead her into a predicament in which she has promised herself to the Italian Count Varrelli (Tom Powers), with whose war injuries she sympathizes, and with Gregory Farnham (Sidney Blackmer), the young man to whom she becomes betrothed. When the Count arrives on the evening of the betrothal and shoots himself (but not fatally) on learning of it, Diana's falsehoods come back to haunt her, and she nearly loses Gregory as a result.

Diana's constant pretexts for avoiding the truth were greatly enjoyable, and the scene of the near-suicide had a potent effect, although it jarred with the play around it. But the work's potential was "smothered by amateurish playwriting," according to Brooks Atkinson: "[C]lumsiness in the handling of the dramatic material joins with a scarcity of invention in keeping the piece dull and heavy-footed," but to Joseph Wood Krutch it was "a thoroughly amusing farce written with brightness and speed." Two years later it emerged as a musical called *Say When*.

LOVE IN THE TROPICS [Comedy-Drama/Marriage/Tropics/Crime] A: Arthur Corning White; D: Cyril Raymond; P: Clark Ross; T: Daly's Theatre; 10/18/27 (15)

An obvious tropical melodrama set in the Philippines on a plantation that middle-aged Hugh Blanton (E. J. Blunkall) has purchased. His young, blonde wife (Isabel Baring) is respectably eyed by plantation-manager Dick Gray (Walter N. Greaza) but not so respectably pursued by the Spaniard Mendoza (Benedict MacQuarrie). Mendoza kills Blanton, the blame is placed on Gray, but Mendoza is found out before Gray's execution.

The poorly acted play "moved with a jerkiness that suggested an author not intimately familiar with his material," said the *Times*. *Time* called it "trite torment.''

LOVE IS LIKE THAT [Comedy/Romance] A: S. N. Behrman and Kenyon Nicholson; D: Dudley Digges; P: A. L. Jones and Morris Green b/a/w Stuart Walker; T: Cort Theatre; 4/18/27 (24)

Basil Rathbone gave a smooth performance as an exiled, penniless Russian prince in this second-rate romantic comedy. He meets and falls for Cassandra Hooper (Ann Davis), a rich New Yorker from Oklahoma, aboard an ocean liner; becomes a hit in her snobbish circle of parvenus; is sought after by title-hungry Kay Gurlitz (Catharine Willard); and seeks to rid himself of her by pretending to be a fake. His efforts to woo Cassandra get him nowhere, since she loves someone else, so he walks off with dignity into the night.

"Although many of the lines are delightfully bright, *Love Is Like That* seems dreary entertainment," reported Brooks Atkinson, and Alexander Woollcott advised that the "play seems to be heavy-footed, awkward, implausible and only fitfully interesting."

LOVE LETTER, THE [Musical/Romance/Fantasy/Hungarian] B/LY: William Le Baron; M: Victor Jacobi; SC: Ferenc Molnar's play *The Phantom Rival*; D/CH: Edward Royce; S: Joseph Urban; P: Charles Dillingham; T: Globe Theatre; 10/4/21 (31)

A highly praised show that seemed to have all of the earmarks of a hit but that lasted only a month and may have led to the fatal heart attack suffered several weeks after its closing by the show's despondent thirty-seven-year-old composer. Producer Dillingham provided gorgeous costuming and sets, the latter brilliantly designed by Joseph Urban, to decorate an operetta based on a Molnar play produced in 1914 by David Belasco (it was revived as *A Tale of the Wolf* in 1925).

Miriam Charlot (Carolyn Thompson), unhappy with the unattractive choice of a husband made for her by her mother (Katharine Stewart), fantasizes about Philip (John Charles Thomas), her true love, who wrote a love letter to her when he went off several years before and promised to come back—in what guise he could only guess. Miriam dreams of him arriving in various romantic roles, but when he does appear for real, it is as a successful businessman (Molnar's original had him arrive as a dullish hick). The lovers are happily united.

"[S]heer melody, beautiful voices and romantic plot," combined with "many gifted players" (Arthur Hornblow), raised this work well above the ordinary musical of the day. In supporting roles were Fred and Adele Astaire, who, as usual, stole the show by their dancing and comic skills, especially in their "Upside Down" song choreography.

In Fred Astaire's autobiography *Steps in Time*, he told the story of how choreographer Edward Royce developed the "Upside Down" number. Royce first had Adele circle the stage as if she were riding a bicycle as the band kept going "um-pah, um-pah." He then had Fred join her, shoulder to shoulder. He took a five-minute break and, when he returned, said, "What we need here . . . is a 'nut' number. It should make no sense at all in lyrics and then the dance should be silly and tricky until you both drop into this run-around thing and then eventually you just run offstage. I think it'll bring down the house." He then instructed the composer and lyricist to write a song to fit the number, which they did to critical acclaim. Astaire went on to say, "That run-around finish became a trademark of ours and we used it in five different shows over a period of about ten years."

LOVE NEST, THE [Comedy/Marriage/Films/Alcoholism] A: Robert E. Sherwood; SC: a Ring Lardner short story; D: Agnes Morgan; S: Aline Bernstein; P: Actor-Managers i/a/w Sidney Ross; T: Comedy Theatre; 12/22/27 (25)

Ring Lardner's bitter satirical tale of Hollywood was transformed into this theatrical dud by Robert E. Sherwood for the new troupe composed of ex-Neighborhood Playhouse actors. The best material in the play was that attributable to Lardner's story; around it, said the *Times*, Sherwood created "mechanical" material, unsubtle in structure and dialogue.

Its subject was the phony glamor attached by the fan magazines to the supposedly happy married life of a famous director (Clyde Fillmore) and his pretty wife (June Walker). The wife's solace actually comes from the bourbon she consumes, and she is in an alcoholic haze when she reveals the truth to an avidly listening reporter (Paula Trueman) who has come to interview her. At the end, she runs off with the butler (G. G. Thorpe) and her three kids.

LOVE SCANDAL, A [Comedy/Romance/Marriage/British] A: Carlo de Navarro and Sydney Stone; D: Armand Robi; S: William Castle; C: Madama Soffi Stein; P: Calvert, Inc.; T: Ambassador Theatre, 11/5/23 (32)

"There is nothing more harrowing than a group of intelligent people standing around repeating epigrams that don't ep," wrote *Time*'s critic about the dialogue in *A Love Scandal*. Set in Scotland, the comedy concerned the vain efforts of a wealthy man's wife (Mona Kingsley) to keep an American flapper (Edith Taliaferro) from winning a successful young playwright (Percy Waram) the wife had once loved but rejected when he was poor and unknown.

Although a few critics found the play diverting, most held the language to be its chief failing. The *Herald*'s critic wrote that all of the characters "spoke in stilted phrases and elaborately devised figures of speech even in the most heated moments, so that occasionally a declaration of love sounded like a little eloquent bit of psychoanalysis."

H.H.

LOVE SET, THE [Comedy/Family/Crime/Romance] A: Thomas Louden; D/P: Gavin Muir; T: Punch and Judy Theatre; 3/19/23 (8)

An excessively mechanical, thickly plotted, and altogether boring romantic comedy that the critics all loudly sniffed at. It concerned a girl, Gertrude (Catherine Dale Owen), who is prepared to ignore the warnings of her socialite foster father (George Alison) and marry a farmhand who rescued her from a runaway horse. In the melange of plot events that follow, Gertrude's actual father (Russell Morrison) is cleared of a robbery charge, the farmhand is revealed as an underhanded lout, and tennis-champ Tom Sheridan (Gavin Muir) wins Gertrude's hand.

The critical thunder included comments such as the *Tribune*'s: "The score at 11:15 p.m. was 'love all' and apparently nothing doing for Mr. Louden's play."

LOVE SONG, THE [Musical/Period/Musical-Biographical/Romance/Hungarian-German] B: an unlisted text by Ferago, Nador, Klein, and Bredenschneider; AD: Harry B. Smith; M: Jacques Offenbach, arr. by Edward Kunneke; D: Fred G. Latham; CH: Kosloff; S: Watson Barratt; P: Messrs. Shubert; T: Century Theatre; 1/13/25 (167)

A spectacularly produced, dazzlingly effective operetta with a company of 250, with gorgeous costuming and scenery worth a king's ransom in gold. Based on an imagined love affair of nineteenth-century composer Jacques Offenbach (Allan Prior) with the woman who became Napolean IV's wife, the Empress Eugenie (Dorothy Francis), it had a score abundant with the composer's great melodies, as well as several additions by Edward Kunneke, who did a masterful job of selecting and arranging all of the music.

Q.M. wrote that the theatre "blazed . . . with a magnificence in melody and movement and color," and Stark Young called this "The most stupendous of the musical plays." A marvelous chorus, outstanding voices among the principals, grand-scale staging, a romantic plot lightened by amusing comedy (Odette Myrtil scored strongly in the comic role of actress Hortense Schneider), excellent tunes, a unified conceptualization, and a lovely ballet in scenes representing *La Belle Hélène* were among the operetta's visual and aural joys.

LOVELY LADY [Comedy/Romance/Family] A: Jesse Lynch Williams; D: Colin Kemper; S: Cleon Throckmorton; P: L. L. Wagenhals and Colin Kemper; T: Belmont Theatre; 10/14/25 (21)

Successful dramatist Jesse Lynch Williams ran afoul of the critics with this piece about a fortyish widow, Mrs. Julia Deshiels (Elisabeth Risdon), who sets out her snares for two men, hoping to get one. They are her attorney Linton (Bruce McRae) and his nineteen-year-old son (William Hanley). The father and son only gradually learn of the other's involvement, and when they do, they both decide, for the sake of their wife and mother (Lily Cahill), to do without Mrs. Deshiels.

Seeking a laugh-provoking comedy, Williams arrived instead at an excessively artful and mechanical work, said the *Times*, despite the presence of workable moments. This critic found the characters basically plausible, but Burns Mantle insisted that they were "impossibly exaggerated and quite unbelievable." Audiences were a little uncomfortable with a scene in which young Linton and his flapper girlfriend (Miriam Hopkins) chatted about birth control.

LOVELY LADY [Musical/Romance/Hotel/French] B: André Birabeau; AD: Gladys Unger and Harold Levey; SC: the French farce *Déjeuner de soleil*; D: J. C. Huffman; CH: David Bennett and Chester Hale; S: Watson Barratt; P: Messrs. Shubert; T: Sam H. Harris Theatre; 12/29/27 (164)

Brooks Atkinson spent at least half of his review of this musical comedy based on a French bedroom farce discussing the Chester Hale Girls, which made up the dancing chorus, and lamenting their repetitious platoon choreography. Of the innocuous show, he claimed that "the music seems commonplace, the jokes and the 'gags' serve their purpose perfunctorily." Edna Leedom, the leading lady, got fine notices but seemed all there was to praise. Her comic acting was delightful, her singing average. Her role was that of a young woman at a fancy Paris Hotel who gets the good-looking Paul de Morlaix (Guy Robertson) to pass himself off as her husband and winds up actually marrying him. Perriton Maxwell observed that the show was "least successful when time is devoted to the unfolding of the inconsequential plot."

LOVERS AND ENEMIES (Vragi) [Comedy-Drama/Marriage/Russian] A: Michael Artzybasheff; TR: Mme. Strindberg; D: Agnes Morgan; P: Grand Street Follies Company; T: Little Theatre; 9/20/27 (2)

A Russian tragi-comedy staged at a pair of matinees using no scenery but with costumes and makeup. The performance was mediocre, except for the contributions of Eva Condon and former Moscow Art Theatre actor Leo Bulgakov. According to the *Times*, the play had a veneer of Chekhovianism but was completely devoid of the master's philosophical foundation and his love for human beings. Richard Dana Skinner said it had "a relentless candor" in its study of "love in all its aspects" but fell down in its failure to touch on "the creative force of suffering."

The play, which in Russian means merely *Enemies*, is part of a 1913 trilogy that was very successful in its native land. It was meant as an examination of the marriage bond and true love as represented in the cases of three married couples, young and old, and well or ill matched according to the temperaments of the respective partners. The author's viewpoint condemned the institution of marriage as almost inevitably leading to misery.

LOVE'S CALL [Drama/Mexico/Romance/Adventure] A/D: Joe Byron Totten; M: Arthur Bergh; P: Joe Byron Totten and L. M. Simmons; T: Thirty-ninth Street Theatre; 9/10/25 (20)

This "play of primitive passion" set in Mexico was a laughably inflated melodrama produced with a very attractive atmospheric setting and with lots of local color in the staging. It depicted the handsome gringo hero Clyde Wilson Harrison (Mitchell Harris)—referred to in the dialogue by his tripartite name—falling in love with the spicy Guadalharra half-breed Piquita (Galina Kopernak). Later, captured and held for ransom with his fiancée Sue Gertrude Madison (Norma Phillips) in Devil's Pass by the bandit Don Pedro de Scarillo (Robert Gleckler), he is saved from his captor's bullet by Piquita, Scarillo's mistress, who places herself in its way, with fatal results.

Tempestuous Mexican spitting, flashing knives, hot kisses, pistol fire, ringing curses, and purple rhetoric embroidered this foolish play to no avail. Frank Vreeland called it a "bit of theatrical doldrums."

LOVES OF LULU, THE (Erdgeist) [Drama/Sex/Homosexuality/German] A: Frank Wedekind; TR: Samuel A. Eliot, Jr.; D: Ullrich Haupt; P: Forty-ninth Street Theatre; 5/11/25 (16)

"[A]n unpardonably bad production of" Wedekind's *Erdgeist* or *Earth Spirit*, here called *The Loves of Lulu* as if to make it seem a frothy comedy, rankled John Mason Brown and other critics. There was outrage over the inept translation ("so bad as to make it partially unintelligible"—Edmund Wilson) but even more over the draggy, uncreative direction and incompetent acting. The audience laughed frequently at what Gilbert Seldes said should have been a "somber and terrifying" work.

Wedekind's drama, first staged in 1898, highly controversial for its frank treatment of sex, as well as for its protoexpressionist techniques, was a work vastly respected by critics with their pulse on the currents of the modern theatre; this disastrous staging damaged the play's reputation in America, however.

The play examined the "earth spirit" or sexual urge; in it the temptress Lulu (Margot Kelly) wends her way through numerous erotic affairs, destroying her lovers in the process. Among her acquaintances, Lulu counts at least one lesbian friend as well.

Arthur Hornblow saw the work as a depiction "of the evil, destructive earth-spirit which breaks all that is winged in man and soils his clearest vision."

(1)LOWER DEPTHS, THE (Nad ne) [Dramatic Revival/Russian Language] A: Maxim Gorky; D: Vladimir Nemirovich-Danchenko and Konstantin Stanislavsky; P: F. Ray Comstock and Morris Gest; T: Fifty-ninth Street Theatre; 1/15/23 (16)

The Moscow Art Theatre produced Gorky's famous view of derelicts living in a doss house as the second of its five programs during its first season visiting America. Under the title *Night Lodging* it had a brief run (directed by Arthur Hopkins) in English in 1919. Two foreign-language presentations had also been seen locally.

The play is an intimately detailed presentation of underworld life, the misery, degradation, and spiritual longing that come to the lowly creatures gathered around the huge warmth-giving stove in the shabby slum environment. The characters, all based on people Gorky actually knew, were given startlingly believable characterizations by the gifted company.

Every player was artistically accomplished in interpretation and execution, making it difficult to single out individuals for special praise. As the pilgrim Luka, Moskvin's performance was "amazing in its simple kindness, its shrewd wisdom and its spiritual intensity," said John Corbin. Nikolai Alexandroff as the down and out alcoholic Actor provided "the most moving acting" the Playgoer had seen in ages, and Stanislavsky played Satine "with great force and distinction" (Corbin); Katcheloff as the Baron and Olga Knipper-Chekhova as the prostitute Nastaya likewise distinguished themselves.

Three more performances were offered from 12/8/23 during the troupe's second New York visit.

H.H.

(2) (At the Bottom) TR: William L. Laurence; D: Leo Bulgakov; DS: Walter Walden (after original Moscow Art Theatre designs); P: Leo Bulgakov Theatre Associates, Inc.; T: Waldorf Theatre; 1/9/30 (71)

The third major production of this play gave it a third title, *At the Bottom*; its distinguishing feature was the very contemporary colloquial American dialogue into which William L. Laurence had translated it. For most, the slangy wise-cracking lines seemed bizarrely out of place in what would otherwise have been a well-done presentation. Former Moscow Art Theatre member Leo Bulgakov's production attempted to capture the Moscow style in acting and design. There was much appreciation of the ensemble quality of the performance and the sharply individualized characterizations achieved. "The total effect," wrote John Hutchens, "which is of an exalted realism, is swift and inevitable. It is theatre that belongs to each of its actors; and acting—as a pattern of significant character—is the first thing in it." The majority agreed; yet Brooks Atkinson maintained that the performance was "strident and rough-edged in tone" and not well orchestrated. Walter Abel as Vaska, Richard Hale as Satin, Edgar Stehli as Luka, Barbara Bulgakova as Nastya, Anne Seymour as Natasha, and Mary Morris as Visilisa were among the most warmly commended players.

LOYALTIES [Drama/Jews/Crime/Law/British] A: John Galsworthy; D: Basil Dean; P: Charles Dillingham; T: Gaiety Theatre; 9/27/22 (222)

An outstanding work of its time, John Galsworthy's *Loyalties* was an easy choice for Burns Mantle's Ten Best Plays of the Year. Performed beautifully by an all-English cast while its original production was still running in England, this play impressed New York's critics by its incorporation of socially relevant themes within an almost perfectly constructed three-act format with well-rounded characters, excellent dialogue, an intriguing and compellingly interesting story, and the aura of lifelikeness in all of its aspects.

Called by Alexander Woollcott a modern retelling of *The Merchant of Venice*, the play deals with the demand of a wealthy Jew, Ferdinand De Levis (James Dale), that the popular young aristocrat Dancy (Charles Quartermaine) be prosecuted for stealing 1,000 pounds from his room at a home where he is staying as a guest. De Levis claims loyalty to his faith in his pursuit, and Dancy's friends and wife obstruct the law out of loyalty to the man. When Dancy's guilt is proved, his lawyer abandons him so as not to be disloyal to his profession, and Dancy kills himself out of loyalty to his position when the police come battering at his door.

The play's treatment of anti-Semitism seemed to some to guarantee its topicality, but there were those who claimed that De Levis's being Jewish was not so much the point as his being an outsider in a society of those who banded together on grounds of class loyalty. The author scrupulously avoided taking sides, setting up his situations and letting them play themselves out, but it was hard for many not to feel the weight of sympathy to be on the Jew's side, despite his not being depicted in fully admirable terms. Some, like Heywood Broun, preferred having a clearer picture of where Galsworthy stood on the issues.

The author's general theme was clearer. In Walter Prichard Eaton's words, it was "that however fine a thing loyalty may be, each separate loyalty must be correlated to a larger view of life, a larger sympathy, than the individual race or code before it can avail much in the modern world."

Director Basil Dean declared in his autobiography *Seven Ages* that A. L. Erlanger, who was actually coproducing the play with Charles Dillingham, was so worried that the New York Jewish populace might be offended by the portrait of De Levis that he asked Dean to get Galsworthy to change the character from a Jew to a Scotsman. As it was, no one who saw the play thought of it as in any way anti-Semitic.

(1) LUCKEE GIRL (Un Bon Garçon) [Musical/Romance/French] B: André Barde and Maurice Yvain; AD: Gertrude Purcell; M: Maurice Yvain and Maurie Rubens; LY: Max and Nathaniel Lief; D: Lew Morton; CH: Harry Puck; S: Watson Barratt; P: Messrs. Shubert; T: Casino Theatre; 9/15/28 (81)

An adaptation from the French musical *Un Bon Garçon*, with a score by "the Irving Berlin of Paris," the composer of "Mon Homme." Robert Littell said it had "Joyous, galloping music, and one of the most sordidly nasty collections of humor on record." *Time* declared that its components were borrowed "from a thousand previous productions of the same kind."

The main reason for recalling the piece is that it gave Irene Dunne her first starring role on Broadway. She played Arlette, a Montmartre midinette in love with Lucien (Irving Fisher), who is betrothed to a girl in his home town. She sets out after him in the company of the roly-poly waiter Hercules (Billy House) and convinces him to marry her rather than the country wench.

The rotund vaudevillian Billy House drew many chuckles, and the score was both plentiful and melodic (although much of it consisted of interpolations, with only four of the original tunes remaining). One of the songs, "Come on, Let's Make Whoopee," predated that season's Eddie Cantor success, *Whoopee*. Of the new star, the *Times* observed, "Irene Dunne is far from being the least attractive participant in the exhibit."

(2) (Un Bon Garçon) [Musical Revival/French Language] D: J. A. Gauvin; P: Modern French Musical Comedy Company; 3/18/29 (4)

When the Modern French Musical Comedy Company visited the city in 1929, they brought this show over as part of their repertory. The droll M. Servatius, their leading performer, played the obese waiter (here called Achille), Arlette was taken by Sonia Alny, and Lucien was played by Gaston Garchery.

"There is an abundance of lively lilting songs and a considerable sprinkling of dancing,'' reported the *Times*, which selected as the show's high spot Achilles's instruction of a group of country folk in the intricacies of the Charleston, a dance that to local eyes looked different from the version to which they were accustomed.

LUCKY [Musical/Crime/Romance] B/LY: Otto Harbach, Bert Kalmar, and Harry Ruby; M: Jerome Kern; D: Hassard Short; CH: David Bennett and Albertina Rasch; S: James Reynolds; P: Charles Dillingham; T: New Amsterdam Theatre; 3/22/27 (71)

Few musicals could have had a more promising list of names associated with them; apart from the first-rate creative team listed above, it sported a cast including Joseph Santley, Richard "Skeets" Gallagher, Ivy Sawyer, Ruby Keeler, Walter Catlett, and Mary Eaton. Even Paul Whiteman's band appeared in the second act for a lengthy exhibition of their gifts (they offered treats such as a full version of Gershwin's "Rhapsody in Blue"). Several critics were overjoyed by it all, but Brooks Atkinson represented the majority when he sneered at the show's dismal humor and the dependence of the "rambling book" on dance numbers to see the evening through.

The story moved from the novel setting of Ceylon to New York in telling its fable of a romance between American tourist Jack Mansfield (Santley) and Ceylonese pearl diver Lucky (Eaton) and their involvement with pearl smuggling and buried treasure.

LUCKY BREAK, A [Comedy/Romance/Small Town] A: Zelda Sears; M: Harold Levey; P: American Producing Co.; T: Cort Theatre; 8/11/25 (23)

Zelda Sears, a librettist for several musicals, turned to the legitimate with this comedy, but the *Times* said she had "remained at heart a librettist. *A Lucky Break* is at best naive entertainment.''

The plot was reminiscent of Shakespeare's *Timon of Athens* but with a Pollyanna ending; it was only incidental to the author's preoccupation with amusing rural types. The play dealt with a Wall Street millionaire (Walter Macfarlane) of middle years who decides to test human nature by returning to his home town pretending to be broke. His worst fears are conquered when the citizens greet him with generosity. He even ends up marrying a local belle.

˙ Percy Hammond regarded it as "a cunning mixture of wise saws, marmalade, three barrytone roles [there were three songs interpolated into the script] and characters from the stock-pot of rural comedy.'' A half-year later, the play was musicalized as *Rainbow Rose*; like its legitimate version, it flopped.

LUCKY ONE, THE [Comedy-Drama/Romance/Family/Crime/British] A: A. A. Milne; D: Theodore Komisarjevsky; S: Lee Simonson; P: Theatre Guild; T: Garrick Theatre; 11/20/22 (32)

A. A. Milne's productivity at this period began to invite skepticism about the quality of his output, and *The Lucky One* was one work that could not abide close scrutiny—thus Arthur Hornblow's comment: ''The piece is a job-lot of scenes wrenched out of a Milne note-book and fastened together without much thought to the general picture."

This is a play about two brothers, Gerald (Dennis King), "the lucky one," and Bob (Percy Waram). Everything comes easy to the former; the other leads a dull, plodding life, always second best. However, events lead Gerald's fiancée (Violet Heming) to shift her affections to Bob, who emerges as the victorious brother.

The consensus was that the play was middling and damaged further by a miscast production. However, despite the casting errors (attributable to the Guild), Russian director Komisarjevsky, making his American bow, was impressive. "There was a warmth of treatment and a generosity of feeling that betokened something very real to come" from future stagings, thought Arthur Hornblow.

LUCKY SAM McCARVER [Drama/Marriage/Night Club/Prohibition] A: Sidney Howard; D: John Cromwell; S: Jo Mielziner; P: William A. Brady, Jr., and Dwight Deere Wiman i/a/w John Cromwell; T: Playhouse Theatre; 10/21/25 (30)

A flawed, but highly interesting play, unconventional, offbeat, and considered worth seeing. The *Times* said it was "worthy of the most recent Pulitzer Prize winner." Audiences, however, were sparse. Howard later claimed that the play was not accepted by the public because it failed to give them the melodramatic trappings it sought, such as a happy ending.

Howard's "four episodes in the rise of a New Yorker" followed the travails of self-made speakeasy-owner Sam McCarver (John Cromwell), an ambitious, rough-hewn man who saves a dissolute society beauty (Clare Eames) from implication in a murder committed in his establishment. Brooks Atkinson noted in *The Lively Years* that the first act, set in the Club Tuileries on New Year's Eve, was "an excellent portrait of the depraved mood of the Twenties—graphic, extravagant, reckless, dissipated; also corrupt on a colossal scale from top to bottom. Prohibition had made a lawbreaker of everyone who had any self-respect." McCarver marries the flighty upper-class woman, becomes a ruthless Wall Street manipulator, and leaves his wife when her decadent tastes revolt him. She refuses his offer of financial support and then dies of heart disease in his presence; he recovers from his initial shock and departs as soon as he recalls a business engagement.

Joseph Wood Krutch labeled the work "an honest and honorable" failure, muddled by plot complexities. None of the critics denied the excellence of the acting by Eames and Cromwell.

LUCKY SAMBO [Musical/Business/Blacks] B/M/LY: Porter Grainger and Freddie Johnson; D: Leigh Whipper and Freddie Johnson; CH: Freddie Johnson; P: Harlem Productions, Inc.; T: Colonial Theatre; 6/6/25 (9)

A not-very-novel, but enjoyable, black musical comedy that, like others of its time, made do with a smidgen of a plot and stereotypical characters in order to overcome with a storehouse of dancing and singing talent. The microscopic story was about how a couple of fellows, Rufus Johnson (Joe Byrd) and Sambo Jenkins (Tim Moore), get snared in a phony oil-stock-selling scam manipulated by Jim Nightengale (Clarence Robinson) and after several setbacks find themselves in the money when the oil starts gushing.

What the troupe had to offer was a "reckless profusion" of "fast and furious dancing" and "robust and plaintive comedy," said the *Times*. The latter element was largely provided by actors Byrd and Moore in cracks such as Byrd's to a girlfriend, "What did you do with the $4 I promised you last night?"

LULLABY, THE [Drama/Sex/Family/Crime/Prostitution] A: Edward Knoblock; D: Fred G. Latham and Edward Knoblock; S: William Cameron Menzies; P: Charles Dillingham; T: Knickerbocker Theatre; 9/17/23 (148)

Although Alan Dale thought that the Camille-like heroine of this play set in France felt so sorry for herself that no one else could pity her, Arthur Hornblow felt compassion and sympathy for the old tart Madelon (Florence Reed). Trying to keep a young girl from meeting her lover, Madelon tells her life story (in flashbacks)—a teenage unwed mother, mistress of men who let her down, giving up her child to foster care, drifting into street-walking. Her one point of honor became avoiding going with sailors after she learned that her son had joined the navy; because of a tussle with one sailor who was killed, she spent twenty years in prison. In the epilogue, Madelon finishes her cautionary tale to the young girl.

Hornblow found that playwright Edward Knoblock had "succeeded in dishing up old material in a new and picturesque way. What he gives us is a rapid action, very human story," and he thought Florence Reed was superlative as Madelon.

H.H.

LULU BELLE [Drama/Blacks/Prostitution/Crime/Sex/Romance] A: Edward Sheldon and Charles MacArthur; D/P: David Belasco; S: Joseph Wickes; T: Belasco Theatre; 2/9/26 (461)

A meretricious drama of black life given one of the most spectacular and photographically detailed productions of its time. A huge company of about 115 (75 of them black) was kept on the boards for a year and a half in what purported to be a play about a mulatto prostitute from the pavements of Harlem who uses her appeal to move up the ladder to become a nobleman's mistress in Paris. The leading roles were played in blackface by respected players such as Lenore Ulric and Henry Hull, while lesser black characters were acted by members of that race.

The play's meager plot was smothered under the tons of realistic scenery and army of characters. Brooks Atkinson observed "tenement houses represented exactly from door to fire-escape, and the square is set with lampposts, fire signal boxes, electric signs and all the requisite paraphernalia to the last detail." In one scene a Ford rumbled across the Belasco stage, packed with actors. Jazz was heard through much of the action, and Ulric, who used a Harlem dialect, got to sing a few popular ditties as well as do a rousing Charleston. The piece had obvious interest for a white public then very much intrigued by the manifestations of life among the black citizenry, but the production remained, withal, "a complete vulgarization of the material with which it deals" (Joseph Wood Krutch).

LYRIC DRAMA [One-Acts] P: Neighborhood Playhouse; T: Neighborhood Playhouse (OB); 4/5/27 (31)
"Tone Pictures" and "The White Peacock" [Musical] CH: Irene Lewisohn; DS: Aline Bernstein; "Commedia dell'Arte" [Comedy] TR: Amelia Defries; AD: Ann MacDonald; M: Howard Barlow; "Ritornell" [Musical/Romance] M: Bela Bartok; CH: Irene Lewisohn and Francis Edwards Faragoh; DS: Esther Peck
The closing production of the Neighborhood Playhouse (apart from the last edition of the *Grand Street Follies*) after twelve years of unusual and provocative presentations with a core of talented players was this evening of fragile one-acts and dance pieces.
Irene Lewisohn conceived the dance patterns for several "Tone Pictures," and there was a slapstick based on a commedia dell'arte piece from the seventeenth century. The latter centered on Arlecchino (Albert Carroll) and Columbina (Paula Trueman) and was an interesting museum piece but not particularly vital as a theatre work in 1927. Then came a Hungarian dance selection, "Ritornell," the evening's most effective selection.
The evening drew mixed reviews, Richard Dana Skinner noting a sense of creative fatigue, and Brooks Atkinson, a "supremely enjoyable" presentation.

(1) LYSISTRATA [Dramatic Revival/Russian Language] A: Aristophanes; AD: Dmitry Smolin; M: Reinhold Gliere; D: Vladimir Nemirovich-Danchenko; P: Moscow Art Theatre Musical Studio i/a/w F. Ray Comstock and Morris Gest; T: Jolson's Fifty-ninth Street Theatre; 12/14/25 (9)
Included in the repertoire brought to New York by Nemirovich-Danchenko's Musical Studio was this musical version of *Lysistrata*, Aristophanes's great comedy about a women's sex strike designed to prevent their men from warring. Actually, according to the *Times*, there were only about fifteen minutes given over to the performance of music in the production; yet the piece seemed, as produced, more musical than dramatic. The director's scheme had been to create a "Synthetic Theatre" blending all of the contributory theatrical arts into a conceptual unity; *Lysistrata*, more than any other work shown, succeeded in reaching this goal. Using a daringly ribald, relatively unbowdlerized text (a spicy English version by Gilbert Seldes was given to spectators), the Russian actors demonstrated a surprising versatility of technique; Nemirovich-Danchenko's staging was "done in a spacious design of rowdy humors, clowneries, buffonnade, even burlesque, yet disciplined and ordered and planned," noted the *Times*.
The production employed a striking setting suggestive of the Greek atmosphere

and employing a central platform with several flights of stairs that could be swung around to create different vistas and provide variety. With a classically blue sky behind the white columns, the exceptionally well-designed groupings and movements of the actors made an unforgettable impression. Of especially noteworthy quality was the chorus, excellently employed to carry the play's emotional currents; much of the action involved having them act in the aisles. The overall acting of the company was praised as being exemplary of ensemble standards; three actresses alternated as Lysistrata, Olga Baklanova, Lydia Belyakova, and Yelizaveta Gundobina.

(2) AD: Gilbert Seldes; M: Leo Ornstein; D/DS: Norman Bel Geddes; CH: Doris Humphrey and Charles Weidman; P: Philadelphia Theatre Association, Inc.; T: Forty-fourth Street Theatre; 6/5/30 (252)

This production remains the only commercially successful one of *Lysistrata* ever to be staged in New York, even though at least a half-dozen attempts were to follow. It began as an offering in Philadelphia, where it was a smash, before it trekked to Broadway. With Norman Bel Geddes's acclaimed "rich-hued, towering Acropolis" (*Time*) as its setting; Violet Kemble Cooper as Lysistrata; the alluringly garbed Miriam Hopkins as Kalonika; Hortense Alden as the lustful Myrrhina; Ernest Truex as the fidgety, sex-starved Kinesias; and a bawdy new translation, it proved a delectable dessert for Broadway palates.

Some viewed the piece as an example of vulgar, if not particularly objectionable, wit. "It handles the facts of life with about as much reserve as your pet comedian handles a custard pie," sniffed Richard Dana Skinner. Several others sided with him in believing that it "has too long and boring passages to be inherently good entertainment."

The brilliant company, which also included Sidney Greenstreet, Hope Emerson, Eric Dressler, and Albert Von Dekker, made the most of Bel Geddes's spirited direction, but it was Bel Geddes's designs that garnered most of the critical kudos.

M

MABEL ROWLAND [Miscellaneous/Solo] T: National Theatre; 11/18/23

Mabel Rowland, like Beatrice Herford and Ruth Draper, was an accomplished actress who appeared in programs during which she offered solo performances of sketches she had written to display her virtuosity at characterization. In her first full evening of sketches she proved capable of presenting "a thoroughly delightful and amusing evening's entertainment," said the *Times*. This critic, comparing her to Herford and Draper, said "Her individual offerings are much shorter and her material a good deal more blunt and simple than theirs." Her comic touch was a major ingredient. Sketches seen on opening night were called "Selling Seeds in the Basement," "What Every Husband Knows," "In the Mountains," "Say It with Flowers," "Mother and Son on a Pullman," and so on. She was accompanied by harpist Beatrice Weller and a chorus of nine girls.

(1) MACBETH [Dramatic Revival] A: William Shakespeare

John E. Kellard produced, directed, and starred in the play as part of a brief Shakespearean repertory at the Manhattan Opera House from 12/9/20 for four showings. Fritz Leiber, also heading a Shakespearian repertory troupe, did it at the Lexington Theatre on 12/28/20 for four showings and on 12/26/21 for one showing. He also did it at the Forty-eighth Street Theatre on 1/16/22 for three showings. Reviews for these presentations are not available.

(2) D/P: Arthur Hopkins; M: Robert Russell Bennett; DS: Robert Edmond Jones; T: Apollo Theatre; 2/17/21 (28)

This production, despite its failure, has continued to be among the play's most famous, chiefly because of the fantastical designs of Robert Edmond Jones. The star was Lionel Barrymore, who, in his only Shakespearean role, proved unable to pass muster. "I do not mind telling you that I was no good in *Macbeth*," he bluntly stated in his autobiography *We Barrymores*. Referring to the McBride ticket agency, Heywood Broun, in his review of the play, offered this now-famous quip about the work: "Lay on MacDuff, Lay off McBride."

The sets of Jones were productive of much controversy. Discussing the Inverness setting, Alexander Woollcott said they resembled "a giant molar tooth pitched rakishly in space." Writing of the heath scene, he said, "The curtain rises on a black curtained stage of infinite depth and height. Glaring down on the centre are three five foot masks of dull silver. The eyes of these masks focus on a ring around which stand three interminable figures in crimson crepe. These hags . . . wear masks of bronze. . . . Startling?. . . . Yes. But of the scene's own atmosphere . . . not an atom." Of those few who claimed the sets to be significant there was, for example, Kenneth Macgowan, who gave an extensive analysis of them in *Theatre Arts*, in which he called them "epoch making" and printed reproductions of them.

No critic, however, found Lionel Barrymore's work as the Thane of even the slightest worth. Typical was Ludwig Lewisohn, who said he acted the part "as a creature of no tragic austerity, no vision of fatality, no splendor, and no gloom. He is rough, sordid, unintelligent, ignoble." Walter Prichard Eaton said the production offered "the worst acting in a so-called first-class Shakespeare production" he had seen in thirty years.

Julia Arthur, modest as was her performance, towered over Barrymore in the role of Lady Macbeth, and only one or two minor players seemed capable of filling their roles.

(3) D/P: Walter Hampden; DS: Claude Bragdon; T: Broadhurst Theatre; 4/19/21 (6)

Walter Hampden brought his touring Shakespeare troupe to Broadway with a repertory of works including *Macbeth*, which opened his stay. It was a disappointment. Alexander Woollcott said it had not "a single scene played with real tragic power or beauty or distinction." Hampden, as so often during his career, failed to move or thrill his auditors and was classed as a thorough and conscientious player of intelligence but little inspiration. His mediocre company included Mary Hall as Lady Macbeth; hers seemed vastly inferior to Julia Arthur's recent performance. The play offered several touches of originality in the staging, such as having Lady Macbeth faint following the banquet scene rather than trudge wearily off to bed. The final battle with MacDuff was energetically and convincingly executed.

(4) D: James K. Hackett; S: Woodman Thompson; P: Equity Players; T: Forty-eighth Street Theatre; 3/15/24 (33)

James K. Hackett's second Broadway appearance, after a successful tour abroad as Shakespeare's tormentedly ambitious Scotsman, won comments ranging from James Whittaker's "the greatest of contemporary Macbeths" to the *Times* critic's "most nearly adequate since Henry Irving." The latter noted that between his 1920–1921 season Macbeth and his performances abroad, Hackett had studied the role with the late Louis Calvert, "who was in most ways the ablest Shakespearean director of his time," and his characterization had improved. The *Times* critic found that Hackett showed Macbeth the warrior, ambitious nobleman, and bloody tyrant but also "the underlying goodness which turns to weakness, the morbid mysticism which has more than a touch of psychic degeneracy. His Macbeth is true kinsman to Hamlet and to Marc Antony."

Some debate was sparked by Clare Eames's Lady Macbeth. Whittaker liked her "relentless anguish," but Lawrence Stallings criticized her acting "in the pace of a Mack Sennett thriller." The ensemble was not of an especially noteworthy distinction.

H.H.

(5) D: Douglas Ross; DS: Gordon Craig; P: George C. Tyler; T: Knickerbocker Theatre; 11/19/28 (64)

Although respected actor Lyn Harding played the title role opposite Florence Reed in this version, its chief interest lay in the fact that its sets were inspired by ideas contributed by the major living theorist of stage design, Gordon Craig, few of whose designs were ever actually realized during his career. Craig contributed only some sketches and ideas on coloring and remained 4,000 miles away during the production, but his input was sufficient for George Jean Nathan to expound that "These few flashes of Craig" revealed him as "the one and only authentic scenic artist of the modern theatre." Euphemia Van Rensselaer Wyatt observed of the multileveled set, "Unlike the deep reds and blues of Mr. Jones's *Hamlet* and *Richard III* which gave against the massive stonework the feeling of medieval stained glass, Mr. Craig has a certain luminous quality which suggests highly glazed enamel. The colors of his costumes are also clear and fresh. Each scene is eminently suggestive of the text." However, Richard Dana Skinner found much of the scenery an unsuccessful compromise between the old illusionism and the newer symbolism. Many condemned in particular the old-fashioned methods of the banquet scene, with its too obviously corporeal ghost.

Douglas Ross's staging took expert advantage of the scenic layout, but not all of the acting was on a par with it. Harding's notices were mixed. Skinner said "he was a big, soft, overgrown weakling, afraid of his own shadow," a not-uninteresting interpretation marred by elocutionary speech methods. Reed, subbing for Margaret Anglin, who had had an accident in rehearsal, was far weaker, this being her first role in Shakespeare. Joseph Wood Krutch likened her work to that of a melodrama heroine rather than a classic tragedienne. Basil Gill's Macduff was excellent, as was Percival Vivian's Porter.

(6) D: Fritz Leiber; S: Herman Rosse; C: William Henry Matthews; P: Chicago Civic Shakespeare Society; T: Shubert Theatre; 3/25/30 (4)

The Macbeth on this occasion was once more Fritz Leiber, at the head of his new Chicago Civic Shakespeare Society troupe, visiting with a nine-play repertoire of the Bard. These stagings were nonacademic, uncluttered interpretations, swiftly paced, with performances of adequate, but not outstanding, calibre. *Macbeth* was even more rapidly played than the other works, too much so for Perriton Maxwell, and the cuts made the motivations less clear than they should have been. One such excision was that brief one in which the English forces agree to hide themselves behind branches as they attack. When the messenger subsequently reported that Birnam Wood was coming to Dunsinane, the moment had not been prepared for.

Leiber's production stressed the action as a murder melodrama, and detailed characterizations were not permitted to impede the rush of events. This approach robbed the work of poetic heights but made it theatrically vivid. The *Times* critic wrote of Leiber's work: "He has a certain authority and he knows at all times what he is about, but he is fairly inflexible and he lacks the physical impressiveness that Lyn Harding brought to the part.... He speaks rapidly, in a strong voice that last night was without shading, but every word is clear." Virginia Bronson was his Lady Macbeth, as she was a decade earlier, and fared not too well; Hart Jenks handled Banquo (his ghost was seen as a green light), and William Courtleigh acted Macduff.

MACHINAL [Drama/Sex/Crime/Prison/Trial] A: Sophie Treadwell; M: Frank Harling; D/P: Arthur Hopkins; S: Robert Edmond Jones; T: Plymouth Theatre; 9/7/28 (93)

The Ruth Snyder-Judd Gray murder case was one of the most notorious of the day; it had an influence on Sophie Treadwell, the journalist-dramatist responsible for this work. Her play was a highly impressionistic, at times expressionistic, episodic account of the debilitating effects of the modern mechanistic routine on the soul of its central figure, the Young Woman (Zita Johann). It created a brief sensation but failed to sustain a long run. Clark Gable made his mark in it as the character labeled "A Man."

Treadwell's grim Freudian melodrama, strikingly directed, used skeletized characters; repetitious, stacatto dialogue; and sudden dramatic developments to tell of how the Young Woman, a repressed stenographer passionately attracted to the Man she meets in a speakeasy, thereupon murders her hated spouse (George Stilwell) and is found out, convicted, and executed for the crime.

The banal facts of the tale were given the air of something novel by the dynamic staging, sets, and lighting. Many saw the work as a tragedy of devastating potency and depth; Perriton Maxwell called it a "forceful, beautiful, thrilling play." Joseph Wood Krutch admired the playwright's failure to provide artificial rationalizations for the heroine's crime and her insistence on simply reporting the tragic outcome stemming from trivial impulses. Gilbert Seldes observed many faults but said they were "swept away by the tempest of feeling which Miss Treadwell has written into the lines." But some condemned the work as unwholesome, hollow, incomplete, and unconvincing. Richard Dana Skinner accused the Young Woman of being "a psychologically deranged moron."

MAD DOG, THE [Drama/Sex/Crime/Western/Romance] A: George Scarborough; P: Messrs. Shubert; T: Comedy Theatre; 11/8/21 (15)

"[A] hot, violent and smoky melodrama" (Alexander Woollcott) of the American Southwest that gave Conway Tearle an excuse to return to the stage after some time spent in films. Tearle's choice of a play was a poor one, and he did little to elevate its interest in his role of Rab Mobley, grimy convicted killer on the lam from a Colorado penitentiary. On his way to the Mexican border, Mobley wanders into the San Pablo Mission, sees Maria (Helen Menken), the beautiful ward of the padre (Forrest Robinson), and rapes her; he flees, returns with a guilty conscience, begs Maria to kill him, and is shot but does not die. After being nursed back to health he wins Maria's heart, reforms, and, with the blessing of padre and sheriff (William Harcourt), takes off with her for south of the border.

MAD HONEYMOON, THE [Comedy/Romance/Crime] A: Barry Conners; D: Hal Briggs; S: Gates and Morange; P: William A. Brady i/a/w Sidney Wilmer and Walter Vincent; T: Playhouse Theatre; 8/7/23 (14)

This innocuous-sounding tale of an elopement secretly aided by the bride's (Boots Wooster) formally disapproving father (George Pauncefort), and interrupted by crooks who are after government bonds they had hidden in her fur coat, was covered with gore. John Corbin declared that the audience laughed at rather than with the play, Percy Hammond dismissed it as terrible, and Heywood Broun noted that it had all of the theatrical clichés of bad plays from the last decade.

H.H.

MADAME PIERRE (Les Hannetons) [Dramatic Revival] A: Eugène Brieux; AD: Arthur Hornblow, Jr.; D: Robert Milton; P: William Harris, Jr.; T: Ritz Theatre; 2/15/22 (37)

Eugene Brieux's "bitter, murderously mysogynistic comedy" (Alexander Woollcott) had been seen in New York under the title *The Incubus* in 1909 and as *The Affinity* in 1910. Both versions starred Laurence Irving and Mabel Hackney. Now Roland Young and Estelle Winwood appeared in an "uncommonly adroit and sensitive" adaptation that revealed the author's subjugation of his thesis tendencies to tell the tale of "the bitter enchainment that can ensue from a man's taking a mistress," according to Arthur Hornblow.

The roles for which the leads seemed so suited were those of Parisian wench Charlotte and fortyish scientist Pierre. The action presents their strained relationship and the emotional ties that keep them together despite their mutual bitterness. When Charlotte leaves Pierre in a fit of temperament, he is happy to see her go but agrees to take her back when urged by friends to do so.

MME. POMPADOUR [Musical/Period/Romance/Historical-Biographical/Austrian] AD: Clare Kummer; B/LY: Rudolph Schanzer and Ernest Welisch; M: Leo Fall; D: R. H. Burnside; P: Charles Dillingham and Martin Beck; T: Martin Beck Theatre; 11/11/24 (79)

This Viennese operetta had been a popular European hit for two and a half years. It made New York headlines because film star Hope Hampton was to play its leading role—her first as a Broadway actress—but she was replaced just before the opening by Wilda Bennett. The play was the first to be done at the beautiful, new, Byzantine-inspired Martin Beck Theatre on West Forty-fifth Street.

The production was exceptionally handsome, with sumptuous costumes and sets, but Clare Kummer's adaptation of the libretto was weak and contained "hardly a shred of humor" (*Times*).

Set in the eighteenth century at the court of Louis XV, the operetta displayed the king's beautiful mistress, Mme. Pompadour (Bennett), engaged in a fling with Rene, the Count d'Estrades (John Quinlan), whom, just in time, she learns is her brother-in-law, thus sending her back to the arms of the King.

Leo Fall's Viennese score contained "moments of infinite beauty . . . which are designed to make the very stars twinkle more brightly," wrote Q.M.

MADAME SANS-GÊNE [Dramatic Revival/French Language] A: Victorien Sardou; D: Mme. Simone; P: Anne Nichols; T: Henry Miller's Theatre; 11/3/24 (24)

One of the plays in the repertory of the French star Mme. Simone during her 1924 season in New York. The old Sardou piece, once one of the stock items of the late nineteenth century, was "as buoyant and full of crisp humor" as when first acted, according to Arthur Hornblow, and showed the star off to good advantage, because it offered her opportunities to display her comic skills. Stark Young also enjoyed the creaking old vehicle, in which the star played Catherine Hubscher, a laundress whose husband is made Marshal of France, leading her to become Duchess of Dantzig or Madame Sans-Gêne. As Young viewed the production, "The playing was lively and intelligent, the ensembles the best in town. . . . Mme. Simone played with . . . dash and bravura. . . . She played, too, with an evident love for the character and its joyous tradition."

MADAME X (La Femme X) [Dramatic Revival] A: Alexandre Bisson; AD: John Raphael; D: Cecil Owen; P: Murray Phillips; T: Earl Carroll Theatre; 7/6/27 (23)

Murray Phillip's project of reviving not-too-long-dead plays at popular prices was behind this resuscitation of a 1908 French drama first seen locally in 1910 and in which Sarah Bernhardt had appeared in Paris. Carroll McComas played Jacqueline, and Rex Cherryman was her son Raymond Floriot. The old tearjerker was about a youth raised by his father after Jacqueline, his mother, has left her spouse; the son finds himself one day acting as the defense attorney, in his first case, for a murderer he does not know to be his mother.

The play appeared dated to the *Times*, but there were many sodden hankies by the end of the performance. Rex Cherryman gave the standout acting demonstration, and *Time* said McComas "seemed real in spite of her struggle with late Victorian anguish."

MADCAP, THE (Fruit vert) [Musical/Romance/Family/French] B: Régis Gignoux and Jacques Théry; AD: Gertrude Purcell and Gladys Unger; M: Maurie Rubens; LY: Clifford Grey; D: Duane Nelson; CH: Harry Puck; P: Messrs. Shubert; T: Royale Theatre; 1/31/28 (103)

A French farce turned into a Broadway musical starring Mitzi; out of town it had been called *Green Fruit*. The *Times* found the libretto "tenuous and fairly routine." It gave the Hungarian-born star a chance to play an eccentric role, that of twenty-year-old Chibi, who passes herself off as twelve so that her mother may justifiably tell Lord Clarence (Sydney Greenstreet) that she is twenty-nine. The predictable situations arise, but Chibi's mother gets her man, and Chibi also gets hers.

Mitzi was moderately amusing in the inane piece, but little that was original was on view. Arthur Treacher made his New York bow in a small role.

MADE FOR EACH OTHER [Comedy/Mystery] A: John Clements and L. Westervelt; P: Upson Rose; T: Fifty-second Street Theatre; 9/29/24 (16)

A humdrum comedy, postponed frequently before its opening, that "proved to be a mechanically complicated mystery somewhat hindered in its development by the dogged playing of the majority" (Wells Root). Alan Dale left after an hour, "appalled" at the "amateurish" effort.

This "extremely dull and badly written play" (*Times*) made extensive use of the flashback technique as it presented a young man's account of why he was late to his wedding. The events that had delayed him (he was whisked away by his love rival) were enacted three times—once to show the villain's side of the story, another to show the young man's fabrications, and the third to show what really happened. A similar idea was to inform the much more successful *Rashomon* many years later.

MADE IN AMERICA [Drama/Business/Romance] A: Mr. and Mrs. H. Gulesian; D: John Ravold; T: Cort Theatre; 10/14/25 (71)

A crude but sincere opus by an Armenian couple who wrote it as a paean to the country they revered for having given them a life of prosperity and freedom. The autobiographical work followed the experiences of a young Armenian (Horace Braham), who, with his sister (Rosalie Herrup), flees the oppression of his native land to become an immigrant in America. They are seen first going through the immigration procedures at Ellis Island and then setting up a new life for themselves, with the lad falling in love with the daughter (Jane Chapin) of the Immigration Commissioner (Brandon Evans) and then becoming a Park Avenue art shop owner.

"Amateurish" was Stephen Rathbun's verdict on the clumsy melodrama, while G.L.E. stated, "It is full of hokum and well-frayed claptrap, and yet it strives to tell a good story and succeeds in doing so." Future star Earle Larimore made his Broadway debut in the supporting role of Bill Pickering, a journalist.

MADELEINE AND THE MOVIES [Comedy/Films/Fantasy] A/D/P: George M. Cohan; T: Gaiety Theatre; 3/6/22 (80)

George M. Cohan and his daughter Georgette appeared in this skimpy little "melodramatic farce" concocted by the former "out of some things he happened to find in the icebox when he was in a hurry" (Alexander Woollcott) in order to provide a vehicle for the latter. Cohan was not in the cast at the opening but decided shortly thereafter to take the role of movie-star Garrison Paige from James Rennie and play it himself, hoping thereby to boost the box-office take.

The inconsequential piece, in which critics saw traces of Cohan's hits *The Tavern* and *Seven Keys to Baldpate*, was a dream play that toyed with conventions of reality and fantasy. It begins with movie-star Paige coming home late one night to find young Madeleine (Georgette Cohan) asleep on a sofa. She explains that he is being sought by her father and brother who think her worship of him on the screen goes further than that in real life; various incidents intrude; in the end all of the confusion, the frequent midnight visitors, and the incessant phone calls turn out to be the feverish dreams of Paige's sleeping valet (Frank Hollins), who nodded off while reading a thick scenario.

MADEMOISELLE BOURRAT [Drama/Sex/Family/French] A: Claude Anet; TR: the author; D: Eva Le Gallienne; DS: Aline Bernstein; P: Civic Repertory Company; T: Civic Repertory Theatre (OB); 10/7/29 (26)

"*Mademoiselle Bourrat*," wrote John Hutchens, "is not an important play. It is only a kindly one of dim, shifting moods, compassionate, severe and droll. But if occasionally it is self-conscious and evasively literary, it is also quietly actable." "It is ... a study of conflicting maternal instincts, with many exceedingly tender scenes. It is unsparingly frank ... but not in the salacious manner," thought Richard Dana Skinner.

Josephine Hutchinson gave a touching performance as the title character, a convent-bred girl of supreme innocence whose small-town life is strictly regulated by her narrow and protective mother (Alma Kruger). Moved by the handsome gardener's (Robert Ross) appeal, Mademoiselle Bourrat allows him to make love to her, becomes pregnant, and drives her mother into a frenzy trying to protect the secret from turning into a scandal. The baby dies soon after birth, but the piano teacher (Harold Moulton) noticed all and uses his perception to win the maid as his bride.

MLLE. MODISTE [Musical Revival] B/LY: Henry Blossom; M: Victor Herbert; D: Milton Aborn; P: Jolson Theatre Musical Comedy Company; T: Jolson's Fifty-ninth Street Theatre; 10/7/29 (48)

The sixth New York presentation of this operetta since its hit inauguration in 1905 proved to be the last; it was given as one in a series of Herbert revivals occupying the Jolson Theatre during the 1929–1930 season. Twenty-four years after making its local bow, the original star, Fritzi Scheff, returned to sing its leading role of Fifi. "The star is in good voice, sings with spirit, and has lost surprisingly little of her sparkle, her *abandon*, and her ease among the higher notes,'' noted Euphemia Van Rensselaer Wyatt.

Mlle. Modiste's production was expert in every way, and the book and score had served the test of time quite well, although the humor frequently seemed dated. As usual, favorite numbers were ''Kiss Me Again,'' ''The Nightingale and the Star,'' ''The Mascot of the Troupe,'' and ''I Want What I Want When I Want It.''

MADRAS HOUSE, THE [Drama/Sex/Business/British] A: Harley Granville-Barker; D: Agnes Morgan and Alice Lewisohn; P: Neighborhood Playhouse; T: Neighborhood Playhouse (OB); 10/29/21 (80)

Granville-Barker's 1910 provocative comedy of Edwardian mores opened the Neighborhood Playhouse's eighth season. Kenneth Andrews was one who condemned it as a ''four-act talk'' because of its reliance on carefully crafted dialogue and ideas and lack of plotting. But Robert Allerton Parker praised it ''as the most significant play in New York,'' one that all American dramatists should be forced to attend. The Neighborhood mounting proved to many that the play was stageworthy and not simply a closet drama, as some had said.

The play was a discursive satire on the confusing sexual attitudes of modern man toward women, a subject of even more piquancy in 1921 than 1910. Ludwig Lewisohn asserted that no other play had ''called attention to the pervasive and voluntary sexuality of the whole of Western civilization.'' The author's ideas were brought out in a variety of cases, from the six sexually frustrated spinster daughters of semiretired drapery-dealer Henry Huxtable (Whitford Kane) to Constantine Madras (Montague Rutherford), the Madras House textile emporium's director who has left his wife and converted to Mohammedism to satisfy his polygamous desires, to the shopgirl (Ernita Lascelles) who has thrown herself into an affair with Madras and becomes pregnant, to the alluring models whose clothing is meant to arouse the opposite gender, and so on.

The play proved so popular with local audiences that it was allowed to finish its run at Broadway's National Theatre, where, however, indifference cut short its life.

MADRE [Drama/Family/Sex/Spanish] A: Rafael Marti Obera; TR: Alfred Hickman; D: Henry Stillman; P: The Players; T: Lenox Hill Theatre (OB); 12/30/23 (14)

A stilted translation was partly blamed for the failure of this Spanish play about a mother's (Nance O'Neil) efforts to keep peace between her son and stepson, rivals for the stepson's bride, after her husband's death. Although the *Times* critic thought that O'Neil ''made the most of an ungrateful role that was in no way adequate to her talents,'' he commented about the play: ''Into the prominent chinks of inaction between his bits of drama, the author has inserted sophomoric and wandering bits of philosophy about the disintegration of the human soul and what he obviously considers related subjects.''

H.H.

MAGDA (Heimat) [Dramatic Revival] A: Hermann Sudermann; TR: Charles Edward Amory Winslow; D: Edgar J. MacGregor; P: Lawrence J. Anhalt; T: Forty-ninth Street Theatre; 1/26/26 (24)

Sudermann's 1893 German drama remained a vigorous, if thematically dated, work in this resuscitation, with Bertha Kalich in the star role formerly played by such greats as Eleanora Duse, Sarah Bernhardt, and Mrs. Pat Campbell. Kalich had played the role previously in Yiddish. The play was respected as an excellent example of dramaturgic craftsmanship of the well-made school.

In the title role of the daughter who flies in the face of paternal authority in a home hidebound by conventional morality, Kalich received mixed notices. Richard Watts, Jr., praised her quiet restraint in "an admirable performance of the slightly more rhetorical school of acting," and Joseph Wood Krutch said she gave "a vigorous and effective if not particularly subtle performance."

MAGGIE THE MAGNIFICENT [Comedy/Family/Romance] A/D: George Kelly; S: Livingston Platt; P: Laurence Rivers, Inc.; T: Cort Theatre; 10/21/29 (32)

A bitterly realistic domestic comedy about the dissension between a daughter, who aspires to better things, and her mother, whose outlook is distressingly humdrum. It was one of George Kelly's few failures.

The daughter is Margaret "Maggie" Reed (Shirley Warde), whose sensitive artist father died during her childhood, and who has been raised by her slatternly mother (Marion S. Barney) with whom she has little in common. Slapped by Mrs. Reed after she insults a gin-guzzling aunt, Maggie leaves home to take residence at a glamorous country estate temporarily occupied by her boss and serves there as his social secretary. This action touches off an eventual reconciliation of sorts between Maggie and Mrs. Reed, and the former accepts a proposal of marriage from the young man (Frank Rowan) she admires.

John Hutchens noted a confusing ambivalence regarding Maggie's goals in contrast with a surer sense of her mother's character; *Time* opined that Kelly's "species of talking photography [had] taken a formless, tedious picture." Playing Maggie's brother and sister-in-law in sharply etched portrayals were James Cagney, who acted "with clarity and grace," and Joan Blondell, a "gum-chewing, posing, brazen jade" (*Times*).

MAGIC [Dramatic Revival] A: G. K. Chesterton; D/P: Randolph Somerville; T: Gansevoort Theatre (OB); 12/16/29 (7)

A revival of Chesterton's British drawing-room comedy, one of the rare plays by the essayist, poet, and novelist. It proved a chatty, intellectual piece, touching on numerous subjects in a not-very-theatrical way. Most of the action is in the Duke's (Parker Wilson) parlor where the Chesterton-like Duke converses with his guests, a conjuror, a doctor (Richard Ceough), and a preacher (John Keehan), chiefly about the topic of faith. Despite a merely passable performance, the play, said the *Times*, "endures competently and well." It had been introduced to New York in 1917.

MAGIC RING, THE [Musical/Fantasy/Romance/Adventure] B/LY: Zelda Sears; M: Harold Levey; D: Ira Hards; CH: David Bennett; P: Henry W. Savage; T: Liberty Theatre; 10/1/23 (96)

Several critics saw Zelda Sears and Harold Levey's new musical as an attempt to recreate, but not as successfully, the Cinderella story of their previous season's *Clinging Vine*. A vehicle for the Hungarian singing-comedienne Mitzi, the book featured her as a poor organ grinder, who comes upon a magic ring in an antique store and sets off on adventures that culminate in her marrying a Chicago meat-packing heir. "A graceful, amusing and characteristic book that gives the diminutive star every gracious opportunity for the display of her indubitable talents and her quaint tabloid personality," wrote Arthur Hornblow, who also praised Boyd Marshall as the romantic lead and Sydney Greenstreet as the antique store owner: "a character actor with a fine sense of individuality and values ... generously amusing." The *Times* and *Tribune* critics cited the beauty and singing of Jeanette MacDonald in a supporting role.

H.H.

MAGNOLIA [Comedy/Southern/Family/Period/Adventure/Romance/Gambling] A: Booth Tarkington; D: Ira Hards; S: P. Dodd Ackerman; C: Charles Chrisdie and Co.; P: Alfred E. Aarons, Inc.; T: Liberty Theatre; 8/27/23 (40)

Percy Hammond wrote that Booth Tarkington's new play "is a luscious semi-burlesque, making delectable fun of certain gaudy habits of the South before the war. Among these are its specious chivalry, its florid romance, its murderous feuds and its melodramatic Mississippi steamboat gambling." In a Mississippi small town in the 1830s, Tom (Leo Carrillo) is reviled for the gentle Quaker ways he learned in the North. His refusal to duel or even to fight so infuriates his father (J. K. Hutchinson) that he sends Tom to live in the woodshed. The young man runs away and drifts into a Natchez gambling house, where he sheds his gentle manners and learns to fight and shoot. Seven years later Tom returns home as a famous gunfighter, is revenged upon his detractors, and wins his cousin's love.

John Corbin observed, "there are many arid wastes in the dialogue and the total result is disappointing. The truth is that our author's satire steps on the toes of his romance, and both play football with probability."

H.H.

MAGNOLIA LADY, THE [Musical/Family/Romance/Southern] B/LY: Anne Caldwell; M: Harold Levey; SC: Alice Duer Miller and A. E. Thomas's play

Come into the Kitchen; D: Hassard Short; CH: Chester Hale; S: William E. Castle; P: Henry Miller; T: Shubert Theatre; 11/25/24 (49)

A musical comedy in which Ruth Chatterton decided to try her legs at dancing and singing; she had played the lead in the straight comedy of 1916 on which the book was based. The experiment did not pan out. *Time* bluntly stated, "Ruth Chatterton is not a good musical comedienne. She sings only mildly and dances doubtfully. Her charm is forced a trifle out of focus by the unfamiliar medium and her emotional accomplishments are not required."

Chatterton's role was that of a southern belle, Lily-Lou Ravenal, whose once-proud family is now indigent. To get a wealthy Englishman (Ralph Forbes) who only wants white employees—he was a Yankee in the source play—to rent their mansion, they pass themselves off as the house's servants. At the close, Lily-Lou and the Englishman are very much in love.

There were some fine performances, especially the comic one by Richard "Skeets" Gallagher as a Ravenal family member, but the show garnered no more than polite reviews.

MAIN LINE, THE [Comedy/Family] A: Grace Griswold and Thomas McKean; D: Horace Sinclair; S: Arthur Ebberts; P: Comedy Producing Company, Inc.; T: Klaw Theatre; 3/25/24 (27)

"Something which only the mother of the author could love" was one critic's estimate of this play, in which coauthor Grace Griswold was featured as a Philadelphia society matron who hires a social reformer (Jo Walker) to democratize her household. The servant-reformer soon has the place completely reorganized and accomplishes numerous good deeds, among them the inspiring of a young man of the house (Murray Bennett) with ambition.

The *World*'s critic concluded, "so much preaching and other drool as was let loose in this show. It's all very democratic, but it's pretty tough on democracy to make it such a terrible bore."

                                                                                            H.H.

MAIN STREET [Drama/Marriage/Small Town] A: Harvey O'Higgins and Harriet Ford; SC: Sinclair Lewis's novel of the same name; P: Messrs. Shubert; T: National Theatre; 10/5/21 (86)

A well-done dramatization of Sinclair Lewis's sprawling novel of small-town America, this play had the virtue of condensing into succinct theatrical terms material that took the novelist hundreds of pages to describe. Lewis's satire on Gopher Prairie, Minnesota's provincial milieu, was here seen largely through the eyes of the characters Doc Kennicott (McKay Morris) and his wife, Carol (Alma Tell), who respectively represent the fundamental clash of pro and con vis-à-vis the town. Carol's foolish haughtiness in looking down on the life around her and the simple humanity of Will Kennicott came through with great clarity in the adaptation. Played with sincere realism, the drama, said Arthur Hornblow, evoked sympathy for both its central characters, despite the fact that their attitudes contrasted so vividly. Although structurally "ramshackle and ungainly" (Alexander Woollcott), the play had substance and was strong enough to stick around for several months.

MAÎTRESSE DE ROI (Mistress of the King) [Drama/Period/Romance/French/ French Language/Historical-Biographical] A: Adolph Aderer and Armand Ephraim; M: Arthur Honneger; D: Theodore Komisarjevsky; S: A. Allegri; P: Messrs. Shubert; T: Cosmopolitan Theatre; 11/30/26 (17)

One of the plays produced to highlight the art of aging but still lovely Comédie Française star Cecile Sorel during her 1926 visit. The play was a new, though old-fashioned, telling of the story of Madame Du Barry (Sorel), mistress of Louis XV (Louis Ravet), but it was not considered as interesting as Richepin's *Du Barry* of years earlier. "[T]here is little that rises above the obvious and the commonplace," ventured Arthur Hornblow. As a vehicle for Sorel, it served its purpose, though. She looked ravishing in the period costumes and was completely convincing in her role. She moved through the drama "vivaciously with the excitability of temperament. Graceful and imposing, she describes this glamorous royal mistress in high colors and unsubdued vocal tones," commended Brooks Atkinson.

The work was produced with totally authentic props and furniture valued at $600,000. It marked the first example seen in New York of the direction of Russian emigré Theodore Komisarjevsky.

MAJOR BARBARA [Dramatic Revival] A: George Bernard Shaw; D: Philip Moeller; S: Redington Sharpe; P: Theatre Guild; T: Guild Theatre; 11/19/28 (73)

New York's favorite Shaw producers once more revived to good effect a play by the witty Irishman, this time his 1905 tale of the Salvation Army girl (Winifred Lenihan) whose father is Sir Andrew Undershaft (Dudley Digges), the munitions maker *cum* social reformer. Its last act, given over to lengthy rhetoric, was not as stimulating as Shaw had intended, but the critics greatly appreciated the remainder of the work. The *Times* man thought that it seemed a wittier and more satirical piece than when first seen locally in 1915. Joseph Wood Krutch claimed that Shaw's viewpoints appeared so diverse that it was impossible to pin any one of them on him, thereby making the play "positively obscure." Richard Dana Skinner, however, had no trouble discerning Shaw's notion that a full stomach has more virtue "than all the religions, the priests, the scholarship, the poetry and the heroism of all time rolled together."

The superb acting company included Elliot Cabot as Cusins, Helen Westley as Lady Britomart, and Percy Waram as Bill. Lenihan disappointed as Barbara, lacking the requisite spark and vivacity of the role.

MAJOR NOAH [Drama/Period/Historical-Biographical/Jews/Religion/Yiddish/ Yiddish Language] A: Harry Sackler; D/P: Maurice Schwartz; S: Alex Chertoff; T: Yiddish Art Theatre (OB); 2/15/29

A biographical drama based on the life of one of America's first nationally prominent Jews, Mordecai Manuel Noah (1785–1851), a man of enormous versatility as writer, politician, and diplomat, who first spoke the phrase, "Millions for defense, but not one cent for tribute."

The piece was founded on an historical incident according to which the members of New York's Bachelor's Club played a prank on Noah (Maurice Schwartz) by getting him to believe he had been chosen to free the Jews from bondage. Inspired by the notion, Noah swings into alarmingly energetic action to realize a visionary haven for his people on an island near Buffalo and is only dissuaded from his zealotry when the woman he loves (Celia Adler) convinces him to forgo it for her sake.

"Mr. Sackler's play," opined the *Times*, "is probably more interesting as wordy biography than drama."

MAKE IT SNAPPY [Revue] B/LY: Harold Atteridge; M: Jean Schwartz; D: J. C. Huffman; CH: Allan K. Foster; S: Watson Barratt; P: Messrs. Shubert; T: Winter Garden; 4/13/22 (96)

The Winter Garden, home to a series of popular Al Jolson revues, gave way for one headlining singer-comedian Eddie Cantor; the verdict was that Cantor was surely one of the most risible men on any stage. "Cantor is almost alone," said Gilbert Seldes: "He has managed to outdistance Leon Errol and James Barton by his versatility and by his vitality." "He works like a Trojan," observed Alexander Woollcott, "playing and singing each song as though under the impression that an angry uncle lies in wait in the wings to choke him to death if he does not score an instantaneous . . . success." Cantor's sketches included one as a hapless lover in huge galoshes; another as a character he had introduced in *The Midnight Rounders*, Max the tailor in the "Joe's Blue Front" scene, handling a customer who wants a coat with a belt in the back—he figures out the costs by writing in chalk on the coat's black fabric; one that showed him as a cab driver; one in which he mimicked Rudolph Valentino in a harem sketch; and one in which he played a meek applicant for the job of a cop. He also sang and danced and toward the evening's end appeared in blackface with his trademark white-rimmed glasses and white gloves.

The other acts on the overlong program included dance teams, acrobats, and singers, as well as lavish chorus-girl numbers. In his autobiography *My Life Is in Your Hands*, Cantor recalled that the title for this revue was born when J. J. Shubert heard an elevator boy urge the crowd into his car using the same words. Cantor's book gives some background on his comic scenes; it also mentions the role he played in "discovering" new talent among the cast, especially the acrobatic Kelo Brothers and the singing McCarthy Sisters.

MAKE ME KNOW IT [Comedy/Blacks/Politics/Sex] A: D. Frank Marcus; D: D. Frank Marcus and Sam Rose; P: Wallace Davis; T: Wallack's Theatre; 11/4/29 (4)

A black cast played this critically pulverized political melodrama; *Time* reported that their "vigor and skill [were] purposeless in a banal, disorganized play which depends for impetus on such lines as these: 'But I am too old to marry you.' 'Daddy, you have pep and life enough for me—make me know it.' "

A Harlem-like background was used to depict a play of political corruption concerning the machinations of Bulge Bannon (A. B. Comathiere), a party boss who seeks to clean up his ward by getting a black candidate elected. The play used a variety of violent episodes as well as a subplot in which the boss falls for his sultry adopted daughter (Vivienne Baber).

MAKERS OF LIGHT [Drama/Romance/Sex/School/Small Town] A: Frederick Lansing Day; S: Warren Dahler; P: Neighborhood Playhouse; T: Neighborhood Playhouse (OB); 5/3/22 (21)

This stark modern tragedy was first done in Harvard's 47 Workshop. At New York's Neighborhood Playhouse it generated admiration but was not thought suited to commercial presentation.

Set in a small New England town among the members of the local school system, the piece focused on the increasing attachment of a misunderstood seventeen-year-old boy (Albert Carroll) and his lonely twenty-nine-year-old Latin teacher (Adrienne Morrison) for one another. They fall in love, and the teacher gets pregnant; this frightens the youth so much he commits suicide.

The frank situation was presented against a background that depicted the malicious gossip brought on by the affair, as well as the financial and emotional privations undergone by teachers at the school board's hands. It impressed by its "entire lack of self-consciousness" (Kenneth Andrews), penetrating characterizations, and avoidance of easy answers.

MAKROPOULOS SECRET, THE (Věc Makropulos) [Comedy/Fantasy/Czechoslovakian] A: Karel Capek; AD: Randal C. Burrell; D: Charles Hopkins; S: Cleon Throckmorton; P: Charles Hopkins i/a/w Herman Gantvoort; T: Charles Hopkins Theatre; 1/21/26 (108)

An intriguing philosophical melodrama that John Mason Brown declared was "a breathless mystery play around the question of longevity, which is more surely written and much better-characterized than either . . . *R.U.R.* or *The Insect Comedy*" by the same author. Not everyone agreed, but the theme was of sufficient fascination to warrant a decent run.

The central character is Emilia Marty (Helen Menken), an opera star 350 years old, born on Crete in 1587, and able to have survived so long because of a formula discovered by her alchemist father. She finally realizes that prolonged life has not brought her happiness. A legal complication forces her to give up the "Makropoulos Secret," and a debate rages among those who might wish to acquire it, but when no taker has the courage to try it, a girl (Joanna Roos) destroys it.

Some, like John Mason Brown, were enthralled by the adroitness of the writing, especially during the fifteen-minute debate on the merits of eternal life. Much of the remainder of the play seemed tedious to various critics. A few later considered the piece a response to Shaw's *Back to Methuselah*, but this is untenable since Shaw's play is of a later date. An opera version by Leoš Janáček is well known.

MALIA [Dramatic Revival/Italian Language] A: Luigi Capuana; T: Royal Theatre (OB); 9/9/21

Sicilian star Giovanni Grassi opened a twelve-week repertory season with this Italian play, first seen in New York in 1908, when Grassi and a troupe of visiting players introduced it. It was set on Mount Aetna among a barbaric people and concerned Iana's (Signora Carolina Bragglia) passion for her sister's husband, Cola, although she is betrothed to Ninu (Grassi). Her family seeks to exorcise by witchcraft her evil yearnings; alone with Cola, she cannot help herself and suffers a fit during which he rapes her. Ninu then kills Cola with a razor.

Grassi, said the *Times*, "invests [his role] with an ominous importance and reveals in his brief scenes an extraordinarily varied and distinguished art. His comedy is as sly and deft and plaintive as Joe Jackson's but it is in his hours of grief and fear and anger that he wins his countrymen."

MALINDA [Musical/Blacks/Southern/Night Club/Romance] B: Dennis Donoghue; M/LY: Roland V. Irving and Earl B. Westfield; D/P: Kathleen Kirkwood; CH: Leonard Ruffin; T: Triangle Theatre (OB); 12/3/29

A little-known black "musical drama of the South and Harlem" produced at a tiny theatre at 128 Seventh Avenue. The *Times* found it coarse edged but "heavily freighted both with native talent and that peculiar property of the negro race—spontaneity." It had a banal book about a Miami schoolteacher (Ida Bennet) who falls into the clutches of a city smoothie (Albert Chester) and becomes a cabaret singer in Harlem, where she is saved by her boyfriend, Detective Jim Johnson (Webb Richardson).

MALQUERIDA, THE (The Passion Flower) [Dramatic Revival/Spanish Language] A: Jacinto Benavente; P: Maria Guerrero-Fernando Diaz Company of Madrid i/a/w Walter O. Lindsey; T: Manhattan Opera House (OB); 5/18/26 (1)

A Spanish repertory company from Madrid's Princess Theatre, led by Maria Guerrero and her husband, Fernando Diaz, offered a week of selections including Benavente's 1913 play, seen in New York at the Greenwich Village Theatre in 1920. Set in a small Castilian town, it explores in tragic terms the incestuous passions of a peasant and his stepdaughter and the response to the relationship of the emotionally distraught mother, played here with fiery histrionics by Maria Guerrero. Victor Lemaitre, writing in the *Columbia Spectator*, was quoted by Burns Mantle: "It was grim, quiet tragedy prepared unbendingly by the author. . . . There was a conviction to [Senora Guerrero's] lines, a portrayal of weariness and the little false momentary happiness before despair, that was nothing short of really great art.''

MALVALOCA [Drama/Romance/Spanish] A: Serafín and Joaquín Álvarez Quintero; TR: Jacob S. Fassett, Jr.; D: Augustin Duncan; S: Woodman Thompson; P: Equity Players; T: Forty-eighth Street Theatre; 10/2/22 (48)

The new company called the Equity Players provided this 1912 Spanish drama of romance as their first offering; it was generally panned, getting them off to a shaky start from which they eventually recovered.

This product of the Quintero brothers was a "picturesque, romantic and symbolical transaction" (Percy Hammond), restrained and poetic in mood and verbose and nondramatic in effect. It deals with Malvaloca (Jane Cowl), the ex-mistress of Salvador (Frederic Burt), who, upon visiting him in a hospital where he is being treated for a foundry accident, meets his handsome partner Leonardo (Rollo Peters). Leonardo's goals include recasting the local convent bell, which has been cracked. Malvaloca and Leon fall in love, but the shadow of her doubtful past troubles him. Following his recasting of the bell, her prayers that her past could also be recast are answered, and Leon overcomes his hesitation and agrees to marry her.

Walter Prichard Eaton argued that the play's authentic values had evaporated in translation, that whatever had made the work important in Spain meant "astonishingly little in America." Stark Young blamed the failure on the actors.

MAMA LOVES PAPA [Comedy/Marriage] A: Jack McGowan and Mann Page; D: John Hayden; P: Oxford Producing Co.; T: Forrest Theatre; 2/22/26 (25)

"[A]n exceedingly thin and conventional farce" (Joseph Wood Krutch) about newlyweds Joe (Lorin Raker) and Nan Turner (Sara Sothern) of Great Neck, Long Island. Nan suspects her insurance salesman mate of unfaithful dalliance following her discovery that he has insured the beauteous legs of French dancer Mlle. Desiree (Zola Talma). She takes revenge by doing some philandering of her own, during which she attends a party also visited by Joe and the dancer, and runs into the expected complications before the expected conclusions can be reached.

This workmanlike endeavor was well performed, with a good comic portrayal of a jovial drunk by John E. Hazzard. The piece was compared to a comic strip but on a very slightly higher level of artistry.

MAN AND THE MASSES (Masse-Mensch) [Drama/Politics/Prison/Marriage/German] A: Ernst Toller; TR: Louis Untermeyer; D/S: Lee Simonson; P: Theatre Guild; T: Garrick Theatre; 4/14/24 (32)

Ernst Toller's work, set in 1918–1919, is also known as *Masses and Men*. It is a famous example of expressionism and alternates visionary abstractions of reality with dream sequences. It was written while the author, a political activist, was in prison. Its seven "pictures" present the saga of a political revolution of workers led by a Woman from the upper classes (Blanche Yurka) who leaves her Husband (Ullrich Haupt), a conservative, for the fight. Despite her pleas for no killing, the revolution turns bloody under the direction of the Spirit of the Masses (Jacob Ben-Ami); the revolt is stifled ruthlessly by the state, and the Woman goes to prison. She refuses the offers of aid from her Husband and from the Spirit of the Masses, for she recognizes her guilt and must expiate it. She is shot by the firing squad.

Alexander Woollcott thought that Toller's expressionistic drama about social revolution in Germany had been used to show off the new stagecraft: "Here was a lure for the Guild directors to do a dull play just because they could do it beautifully. And when they had done it as beautifully as anyone could ask, it remained a dull, heavy-footed, essentially uneventful play." Several critics praised Blanche Yurka and Jacob Ben-Ami, but the real star proved to be director-designer Lee Simonson. Some found the play largely incomprehensible, and Heywood Broun noted, "the essential thrill of drama is lacking."

H.H.

MAN FROM TORONTO, THE [Dramatic Revival] A: Douglas Murray; D: Albert Bannister; P: Albert Bannister and Elmer Powell i/a/w Miller and Gold-reyer; T: Selwyn Theatre; 6/17/26 (28)

In 1918 Henry Miller and Ruth Chatterton had starred in this British play under the title *Perkins*. It failed then and was now revived only to flop again. The original was first staged in London in 1916, and a successful 1926 revival there sparked the New York attempt. Wells Root said of the play that it was "often old-fashioned to the point of imbecility, and always obvious."

A rich old man has died and required in his will that for the Evonshire widow Mrs. Calthorpe (Beatrice Hendricks) to share in his $3,750,000 legacy, she must marry his nephew, the Canadian rancher Fergis Wimbush (Curtis Cooksey). Determined to see if she likes this rough-mannered provincial boor, she impersonates a parlor maid when he arrives. It is in this guise that she wins his clumsy but honest heart before agreeing to the wedding.

MAN IN EVENING CLOTHES, THE (Un Homme en habit) [Comedy/ Marriage/French] A: André Picard and Yves Mirande; TR: Ruth Chatterton; D/ P: Henry Miller; T: Henry Miller's Theatre; 12/5/24 (11)

Known in France as *Un Homme en habit*, this weak French comedy, blandly translated by Broadway star Ruth Chatterton, proved an embarrassment to distinguished actor-director-producer Henry Miller, who intimated in a curtain speech that this might be his farewell production (it was not—he appeared in *Embers* in 1926). The play was ridiculed by George Jean Nathan as "utter dullness" and by the *Sun* as "a foolish, singularly archaic farce."

Miller played a wealthy Parisian who goes broke but is allowed by the bankruptcy laws to keep one suit of clothes. He chooses evening wear, and his adventures thus garbed are recounted. On the outs with his much younger and cold wife (Carlotta Monterey), he has spent his funds on other ladies. In his new-found life as a pauper he meets his wife again, and a reconciliation ensues.

MAN IN THE MAKING, THE [Drama/Business/University/Family] A: James W. Elliott; D/P: John Meehan; T: Hudson Theatre; 9/20/21 (22)

Produced and directed by a former George M. Cohan stage manager and actor, this play revealed various Cohan-like qualities. But it lacked Cohan's vitality; was overlong, inflated, and didactic; and had only a few notes of sincerity and truth sprinkled through it.

The author's point was that only a self-made man was worthwhile, that sending one's sons to college was tantamount to sending them to Sing Sing, and that no matter what advantages a parent provides, life itself is the greatest teacher and molder of character. His play showed the results of a self-made businessman's (Paul Everton) shipping his son (Donald Gallaher) off to school; the boy encounters there little more than booze and parties. Only when he picks up some lessons in the school of hard knocks do things pay off for him and does his father come around to seeing things differently.

"A somewhat scattered and unconvincing play," judged Alexander Woollcott.

MAN OF THE PEOPLE, A [Drama/Period/Politics/Southern/Historical-Bio-graphical/War] A/P: Thomas Dixon; SC: Thomas Dixon's novel *The Southerner*; D: Augustin Duncan; T: Bijou Theatre; 9/7/20 (15)

A Lincoln biography by the author of the book on which the film *Birth of a Nation* was based. Called "the drama of the supreme crisis in Lincoln's life," it moved from a glimpse of the future president as a boy to his days in the White House. The central action has to do with Lincoln's (Howard Hall) being asked to withdraw as the Republican nominee in the upcoming election; when confidence is restored to his administration following Sherman's capture of Atlanta, he decides to run.

Closely following the authentic facts of Lincoln's life, the play seemed a worthy dramatic effort, Robert Allerton Parker even claiming for it "a more sympathetic presentation of Civil War times" than John Drinkwater's famous Lincoln drama. Howard Hall was a respectable Lincoln, despite his dissimilarity in appearance to the Great Emancipator.

MAN OR DEVIL [Drama/Fantasy/Period/Romance] A: Jerome K. Jerome; D: Lawrence Marston; P: Messrs. Shubert; T: Broadhurst Theatre; 5/21/25 (20)

An outmoded fantasy play set in a seventeenth-century Dutch town that proved the third failure in a row for star Lionel Barrymore, who nevertheless gave a fine performance. He played Nicholas Snyders, the town's wealthy but iron-hearted seller of pawned goods, who exchanges his soul with that of the handsome young sea captain Jan (McKay Morris) through the intermediation of a mysterious

Peddler (Thurlow Bergen), who provides a magic wine for the transaction. The Captain becomes a miserly money grubber, the junk dealer a glad-handed friend to one and all. Even the junk dealer's pretty drudge Christine (Ruth Findlay) rejects Jan, although she long had loved him. Only in the last act are things set aright again over another glass of the potent potion.

The play's characters and virtues were of cardboard, and there was little discernible subtlety or sophistication, claimed Charles Belmont Davis, who also found the work repetitious, draggy, and inconsistent. Wells Root termed it "an injudicious mixture of fact and fantasy."

This was Barrymore's last play before his departure for Hollywood.

MAN WHO ATE THE POPOMACK, THE [Drama/Fantasy/British] A: W. J. Turner; D: Reginald Travers; S: Frederick Jones III; C: Joseph Mullen; P: Cherry Lane Players, Inc.; T: Cherry Lane Theatre (OB); 3/24/24 (52)

Off Broadway's Cherry Lane Theatre opened its doors with a fanciful tragicomedy about a young British lord (William S. Rainey) who decides to test people's hypocrisy. He eats of the popomack, a delectable Eastern fruit with the unfortunate side effect of causing extreme body odor. Deserted by all of the people who had fawned on him and disgusted by their trivial standards, he kills himself.

Burns Mantle thought the play was intelligently written and cast and acted competently. The *Times* critic praised the performances and situations in this "bitter and sometimes deep-biting commentary on the world—not quite built for the practical theatre, and obscured now and then by a somewhat diffused treatment."

H.H.

MAN WHO NEVER DIED, THE [Drama/Crime/Mystery/Trial/Law/Fantasy] A: Charles Webster; D: Ralph Stuart; S: Cleon Throckmorton; P: Provincetown Players; T: Provincetown Playhouse (OB); 12/12/25 (23)

Off Broadway's Provincetown Playhouse had begun to irk the critics by its production of abstruse experimental plays, one of which was this exercise in "adolescent mysticism" (Joseph Wood Krutch). The *Evening Graphic* declared it a vague, baffling folderol that, despite momentary cogency, descended into "an incohate [*sic*], mystical meandering."

The strange drama began much like a conventional murder mystery with the depiction of parallel murders committed by two men of their wives' lovers. One man, Holt (Harold Vosburgh), slew to preserve the sanctity of his home. The other man, Uwyng (Bennett Southard), accepted his wife's right to a lover and killed the man by accident. Holt's jury acquits him, but Uwyng's jury fails to understand his compassionate ways, and he is condemned to a lengthy sentence. Uwyng believes himself immortal and more than human, a man not subject to human codes. The epilogue shows him twenty years later, unaged.

MAN WITH A LOAD OF MISCHIEF, THE [Comedy/Period/Romance/British] A: Ashley Dukes; D: Ruth Chatterton; S: Rollo Wayne; P: Lee Shubert; T: Ritz Theatre; 10/26/25 (16)

A wordy, but witty and disarming, literary conceit that starred distinguished players Robert Loraine and Ruth Chatterton. This British comedy is set in the early nineteenth century at an English wayside inn to which come a Lady (Chatterton) and her Maid (Bertha Mann) after having been rescued on the road in a coaching accident by a Nobleman (Loraine) and his Man (Ralph Forbes). The Lady has been escaping from her neglectful lover. The pompous Nobleman fails to seduce her, but his Man succeeds and finally flees with her. His master, meantime, has contented himself well enough with the Maid.

This imaginative period satire, ornamental in language, philosophical in thought, and sprightly in style, was base metal given the sheen of gold by its polished manner. The *Times* said, "Mr. Dukes's play is drivel, gibberish and claptrap. It is also thoroughly delightful." "[I]t manages to achieve a very distinct flavor by the artful blending of romance and irony," explained Joseph Wood Krutch.

MAN WITH RED HAIR, A [Drama/Crime/Mental Illness/British] A: Benn W. Levy; SC: Hugh Walpole's story; D: John D. Williams; P: Charles L. Wagner; T: Garrick Theatre; 11/8/28 (19)

A powerful performance by Edward G. Robinson stood many hairs on end in this gruesome Grand Guignol shocker; Euphemia van Rensselaer Wyatt was too scared to remove her coat throughout and ran from the theatre forgetting to take her purse when it concluded. Too strong for most tastes, it soon disappeared.

The play was a melodramatic study of a brutal red-haired sadist, Mr. Crispin, who believes that by inflicting pain he is uplifting human nature. He lives in a Cornwall cottage with three Japanese servants whose tongues he has removed. Two men (Barry O'Neill and Harold Vermilyea) and a woman (Mary Kennedy) come under the maniac's influence. His attempts at slowly torturing the men, who try to save the woman from being forced to wed Crispin's son (Kirby Hawkes), are overturned by the rebellious servants, who intend to give him everything he's given others.

To Richard Dana Skinner the major trouble was that the play "touches very few universal qualities, or, at least, only in so exaggerated a form as to make them seem quite apart from human experience."

MANDARIN, THE (Die Mandarine) [Drama/Mental Illness/Fantasy/Austrian/Sex] A: Paul Frank; AD: Herman Bernstein; D: W. H. Gilmore; P: Mandarin Play Producing Co., Inc.; T: Princess Theatre; 11/9/20 (16)

Paul Frank's *Faust*-like play, in German, had included material based on Sigmund Freud and Richard Kraft-Ebbing. But the New York version was bowdlerized into an "unidiomatic and . . . hundred percent Broadway production," according to Ludwig Lewisohn. It dealt with a neurasthenic Baron (Brandon Tynan), who meets a stranger (Mario Majeroni) claiming to be a doctor. A deal is struck whereby by accepting a Chinese doll, the Baron becomes totally successful with women, taking one after the other. But happiness does not come from these easy conquests, and when the Baron tries to rid himself of the Mandarin doll, now grown to life size, he cannot. All turns out to be a madman's delusion suffered in a mental institution.

Billed as "a play of another world," the piece was as interesting as "watching bacteria strike poses under the microscope" to Alan Dale.

MANHATTAN [Comedy/Romance/Literature] A: Leighton Osmun and Henry Hull; D/P: John Cromwell; T: Playhouse Theatre; 8/15/22 (89)

Plots about poor girls who strike it rich were among the most prominent of the decade, as in this rags-to-riches saga of Lory (Marguerite Maxwell), the working girl, who finds herself both a fortune and a wealthy husband to boot. No one took it seriously, and only its good cast and occasionally clever dialogue made it bearable summer entertainment.

Forty-year-old Duncan Van Norman (Norman Trevor), member of high society, hires a female secretary, Lory, falls in love with her, rejects her when she inherits a fortune, because he does not want the world to think he married for money, and is snared only when she locks him in her apartment and throws away the key.

A not-particularly original story was enlivened by smart talk with many epigrams. Alexander Woollcott jeered at it as "an artificial and desperately epigrammatic comedy . . . [that] rings about as true as a bad quarter," but Charles Pike Sawyer thought the play succeeded at its goal of being "a trifle light as air, intended solely for entertainment."

Helen Gahagan made her local debut in the small role of Sybil Herrington.

MANHATTAN MARY [Musical/Show Business/Romance] B/M/LY: B. G. De Sylva, Lew Brown, Ray Henderson, William K. Wells, and George White; D/P: George White; C: Erté; T: Apollo Theatre; 9/26/27 (264)

Ed Wynn laid 'em in the aisles as Crickets in this extravagant show that the *Times* denoted as "a sumptuous and rather ingenious blending of musical comedy and the revue form." Wynn's familiar humor had him talking about his odd inventions and his relatives, and he also displayed his dancing skill. In one bit he led the orchestra and scratched his back with the baton. Nor was he above going over to a spectator and asking him, "Wasn't I good?"

The device that moved the action along was a rags-to-riches fable about a showgirl (Ona Munson) who builds a successful career for herself as a star of *George White's Scandals*. White appeared as himself in a memorable dance routine, "The Five Step," that threatened to become a popular dance sensation. Other dancers who added class to the show were Harland Dixon and Doree Leslie; Lou Holtz's Yiddish comedy bolstered the laughs of Ed Wynn.

MANHATTERS, THE [Revue] B: Aline Erlanger and George S. Oppenheimer; M: Alfred Nathan; LY: George S. Oppenheimer; D/CH: David Bennett; P: Manhatters Company; T: Selwyn Theatre; 8/3/27 (77)

A summertime comedy and music revue; youth predominated amongst its creators and performers, and they tried their hardest, but the show had little of novelty to offer. Thematically concerned with Manhattan life, it revealed two dozen scenes set in places such as Chinatown, Gramercy Square, the Metropolitan Museum, and the "Roxymount" Theatre. Sally Bates was noticed for her singing of tunes such as "Kleptomaniac" and "Orphans of the Brainstorm," Eleanor Shaler was a songstress standout with her renditions of sentimental Gay Nineties melodies and with a comedy turn at a tombstone, and dancer Jacques Cartier gained approval with his Chinese sword-dance number and a Congo voodoo routine.

The show had begun as an amateur performance by the Cellar Players of the Hudson Guild and then was produced professionally Off Broadway; two weeks after its Greenwich Village inauguration, it ventured onto the Great White Way. Brooks Atkinson said that it "lacks the firm touch and the professional competence that make for satisfactory evenings in the theatre," but Abel. thought it "ever-lively and alert."

The twelve-year-old "St. Louis Blues" was heard in the show, but a well-liked song, "Nigger Heaven Blues," was removed when blacks complained that it was offensive.

MAN'S ESTATE [Drama/Romance/Family/Marriage/Sex/Small Town] A: Bruce Gould and Beatrice Blackmar; D: Dudley Digges; S: Cleon Throckmorton; P: Theatre Guild; T: Biltmore Theatre; 4/1/29 (48)

What the *Times* characterized as one of the Guild's "less enterprising moments" was this unoriginal piece about Jerry and Sesaly (Earle Larimore and Margalo Gillmore), a couple of youthful midwesterners who find that a moonlight dalliance has left her pregnant. The liberal-minded pair agree that she will marry him and live abroad with the baby until he has finished architecture school (a decision that shakes the moral foundations of the family). They wed, but Jim finally realizes that he must assume a "man's estate," and the couple settle down in town, where he will work in an uncle's hardware store.

"Despite a sly and purring humor in some of the scenes, it is a little clipped and thin," decided the *Times*. George Jean Nathan declared that its only saving grace was a few lines on couples living together before marriage and on the justice and relative safety of abortions. Producer Jed Harris had given up on the play during a pre-Broadway tryout production, and the Guild was censured for trying to salvage it.

MAN'S MAN, A [Comedy-Drama/Marriage/Sex] A: Patrick Kearney; D: Edward Goodman; P: Stagers; T: Fifty-second Street Theatre; 10/13/25 (120)

One of the season's most commendably written and performed new American plays, *A Man's Man* was by no means an altogether happy comedy. It told a painful story about a poor, self-deluding young couple, the Tuttles (Dwight Frye and Josephine Hutchinson), both of whom seek to make a success of their lives. He wants to be an Elk, she a movie star. Each is bamboozled by a hustler, Charlie Groff (Robert Gleckler), the husband losing money, the wife her marital fidelity. Learning that they have been duped, the couple squabble fiercely but reconcile in time for the final curtain.

The play's uncompromising honesty, sincerity, and pathos were much valued by the critics. Richard Dana Skinner thought it presented its tale "with caustic realism and fine sympathy" and that its last act had great beauty and understanding. Joseph Wood Krutch viewed it as an example of "the bedraggled muse of modern tragedy" in its emotional strength coupled with an inability to exalt.

MAN'S NAME, THE [Drama/Illness/Marriage/Rural/Sex] A: Marjorie Chase and Eugene Walter; D: Bertram Harrison; P: A. H. Woods; T: Republic Theatre; 11/15/21 (24)

Marjorie Chase was rumored to have written and Eugene Walter rewritten this triangle melodrama that most of the critics found gripping and well done and for which a long run was mistakenly forecast. Suspense, sharp dialogue, and intense situations marked this work taking place in a cabin in the Rockies, where writer Hal Marvin (Lowell Sherman) has gone with his wife (Dorothy Shoemaker) to recuperate from tuberculosis. The action concerns the husband's discovery that the wife had spent a night in a hotel with another man (Felix Krembs) to obtain the money needed for his recovery. The conclusion has the husband wounding the visiting other man in the hand with a gun so that he will never forget the incident.

"Here was an interesting and virile play," wrote Charles Darnton, who regretted, however, the play's essential predictability.

MANY A SLIP [Comedy/Romance/Sex] A: Edith Fitzgerald and Robert Riskin; D: Robert Riskin; S: Cirker and Robbins; P: Lew Cantor; T: Little Theatre; 2/3/30 (56)

A small cast of bright talents toiled dutifully on behalf of this cliched comedy in which the issue of a phony pregnancy again reared its tiny head. The very same season the device had been used in *It's a Wise Child*. Still, there were occasionally worthwhile comic moments in what was described by the *Times* as "labored and obviously manufactured to snare easy laughs."

Jerry (Douglass Montgomery) and Patsy (Sylvia Sidney) are living together in a Greenwich Village apartment, and she so wants him to marry her that she takes her mother's (Dorothy Sands) advice and tells Jerry that she's expecting. He weds her and fills the house with baby toys, only to uncover the ruse and leave. Finally, she gets him back when she learns that she really is *enciente*.

MANY WATERS [Drama/Theatre/Fantasy/Marriage/British] A: Monckton Hoffe; D: Leon M. Lion; P: Arch Selwyn and Charles B. Cochran i/a/w Leon M. Lion; T: Maxine Elliott's Theatre; 9/25/29 (119)

Monckton Hoffe's "extraordinarily good sentimental play" was, said Brooks Atkinson, "a poignant, graceful little caprice, which is acted with fervent simplicity by an excellent company." Others also found vibrant words of praise for it.

Hoffe's purpose was to demonstrate that no one's life, no matter what one might judge from superficial externals, is commonplace; his episodic plot presented a playwright (Ronald Simpson) and a producer (Aubrey Dexter) arguing in the latter's office over whether audiences want plays to be realistic mirrors of actuality or escapist fantasy. The producer illustrates his reason for presenting the former by pointing to the dramaless lives of a dull couple, the Barcaldines (Ernest Truex and Marda Vanne), who arrive on the matter of a house rental; a chronicle drama ensues following the Barcaldines through their many faithful years together, during which all of the dramatic elements of which the producer mistakenly believes their lives empty are enacted. Numerous scenes and characters pass by until the dramatist realizes that his preconceptions regarding such supposedly humdrum people are erroneous; he agrees henceforth to write light-weight works for their enjoyment having learned that "many waters cannot quench love, neither can the floods drown it."

(1) MARCH HARES [Comedy/Sex/Romance] A: Harry Wagstaff Gribble; D: W. H. Gilmore; P: Messrs. Shubert; T: Bijou Theatre; 8/11/21 (60)

An interesting, but confusing, Freudian satire concerning an unpleasant, egomaniacal hero, Geoffrey Wareham (Alexander Onslow), a teacher of elocution, engaged to Janet Rodney (Adrienne Morrison), who teaches the same subject. The apparently less-than-virile young man (there is a touch of latent homosexuality in his behavior) frustrates his demonstrative fiancée by his seeming indifference. She introduces him to the sensual Claudia (Norma Mitchell); when that vamp's allure seems to be developing a response, Janet flirts with Geoffrey's friend Edgar (Brandon Peters). Mutual jealousy brings Janet and Geoffrey together again for a happy ending.

Several critics complained of the comedy's static and fuzzily worked-out action ("as an example of premeditated incoherency, [it] is a masterpiece"—Louis V. De Foe), its difficult-to-like, eccentric characters ("a lot of disturbed, unbalanced, even unhinged erotomaniacs"—P.F.R.), its decadent Oscar Wildeish manner, and its self-conscious air of artificiality.

(2) [Dramatic Revival] P: Inter-Theatre Arts; T: Little Theatre; 3/11/23 (4)

A limited-engagement revival produced at three matinees and one evening performance. It was apparently an improvement over the original presentation of a season earlier, although some of the same actors were involved in both. The *Globe* applauded "a cast which is even better than its first group of players" and noted that the comedy's "quality was obscured when . . . first produced by a performance that was unfortunate in several particulars." "[I]t is one of the most delightful things we have ever seen," asserted Robert Benchley. The standout contribution was made by Moffatt Johnston as Geoff.

(3) D: Daniel Frawley; P: Charles L. Wagner; T: Little Theatre; 4/2/28 (20)

Once again this respected satire sprang up in a twenties' revival; despite "uneven playing," it was still "full of deliciously nonsensical fun," thought the *Times*. The critic did admit, though, that the play was not "expertly written or fully sustained," and Richard Dana Skinner believed it to be "a reasonably amusing and witty play without sufficient passion or fire or human feeling underneath it to carry it beyond the limits of those who like cleverness for its own sake."

Richard Bird failed as Geoff, and Vivian Tobin was adequate as Janet, but Dorothy Stickney as Claudia and Josephine Hull as Mrs. Rodney were exceptionally good.

MARCO MILLIONS [Comedy/China/Italy/Romance/Orientals/Period/Business] A: Eugene O'Neill; D: Rouben Mamoulian; DS: Lee Simonson; P: Theatre Guild; T: Guild Theatre; 1/9/28 (102)

Eugene O'Neill's globe-trotting epic satire on American babbitry—a satire that not a few believed would have had more sting four or five years earlier before the point became overly familiar through other treatments—was given a remarkably munificent staging by the Theatre Guild. Direction and design were significant contributions, but the play met with varying reactions.

Marco Millions is a romantic, philosophical, comic, and often poetic work about the Venetian traveler Marco Polo (Alfred Lunt), depicted as the counterpart of an insensitive modern American go-getter businessman, who journeys with his uncle (Ernest Cossart) and father (Henry Travers) to the court of the sagacious Kublai Kaan (Baliol Holloway); he loses whatever poetic sensibilities he once possessed, evolves into a paragon of crass materialism, is given free rein in Cathay, and wins the love of Princess Kukachin (Margalo Gillmore), who is betrothed to the Kaan of Persia (Morris Carnovsky). He accompanies her on her voyage to be married but blindly fails to recognize the depth of her feelings for him (which ultimately causes her death of a broken heart). Finally, he returns in profitable triumph to Venice and his fat fiancée as the soul-stricken Kaan grieves over the Princess's demise.

Joseph Wood Krutch, comparing it to other O'Neill plays, said "it has a purity of outline and a delicacy of execution equalled by none of the others." John Mason Brown thought it was "written with a haunting and savage beauty that lifts the play far above the mockery which is ordinarily aimed at Kiwanians." In Richard Dana Skinner's view, "It has much beautiful writing and much that is distinctly commonplace. It offers gorgeous opportunities in stage settings, but very few moments of authentic drama."

The Guild revived the play on 3/3/30 at the Liberty Theatre for eight performances with Earle Larimore as Marco, Sylvia Field as Kukachin, and Henry Travers as Chu-Yin (first played by Dudley Digges). *Time* said it seemed "more ponderous in its satire" than before.

MARIA GUERRERO AND FERNANDO DIAZ DE MENDOZA AND THE PRINCESS THEATRE COMPANY OF MADRID; P: Walter O. Lindsey; T: Manhattan Opera House (OB); week of 5/17/26

Spain's famed Princess Theatre Company, led by Maria Guerrero and Fernando Diaz de Mendoza, received only sporadic attention in New York's English-language press. Works of theirs reviewed and/or given entries in this volume were *Locura de amor*, *Dona Maria la brava*, *La malquerida* (*The Passion Flower*), and *El caudal de los hijos* (also seen in New York in English as *Forbidden Roads*, and described under that entry). Other plays in the repertoire were *Don Juan Tenorio*, Jose Zorilla's famous 1844 retelling of the Don Juan legend, seen in Spain every year early in November, 5/20/26; *La condesa Maria* (author not listed), 5/21/26; and *Cancionera* by the Quinteros, 5/21/26.

MARIE ANTOINETTE [Drama/Period/Romance/France] A: "Edymar"; D: Grace George and John Cromwell; S: Joseph Wickes; C: Miss Fields; T: Playhouse Theatre; 11/22/21 (16)

Alexander Woollcott thought this production premature and the play not ready to face the public in so "halting and ragged a performance." What he called "a turgid and majestical romance" and "not either deeply moving or overwhelmingly dramatic" was by the pseudonymous Edymar. The critics approved the handsome mounting but, like Woollcott, abhorred the overly sentimental, historically inaccurate play.

Grace George starred as Marie of Austria, better known as Marie Antoinette, the extravagant, romantic queen of France, whose affair with Swedish nobleman Count Axel Ferson (Pedro de Cordoba) led to his leaving her to go to America with Lafayette. She pays for her peccadiloes by being beheaded, but the scene of the execution suggested that she gave her life to the revolutionists in order to save those of King Louis and their children.

MARINERS [Drama/Marriage/Romance/British] A: Clemence Dane; D: Guthrie McClintic; S: Jo Mielziner; P: Actors' Theatre; T: Plymouth Theatre; 3/28/27 (16)

Pauline Lord, looking for a suitable role following her great success in *They Knew What They Wanted*, did not find it in this lumpy import about an ill-fated marriage. The analysts concluded that the piece was structurally unsound and unfocused. The unsuitable couple here were a noble, brilliant clergyman (Arthur Wontner) and a vulgar, temperamental former barmaid (Lord); her behavior destroys his promising career, but he maintains his affection for her through two decades of hell; when he dies of the flu, for which she is partly responsible, she shows her own deep love by dying on his grave. A romantic subplot shows a young woman taking heart from the older couple's marital relationship.

Stark Young said, *"Mariners* is deadly with talked motives, flat and arbitrary analyses, and an exhausting determination to lay out a theme."

MARJOLAINE [Musical/Period/Family/Romance] B: Catherine Chisholm Cushing; M: Hugo Felix; LY: Brian Hooker; SC: Louis N. Parker's play *Pomander Walk*; D: Russell Janney and W. H. Post; CH: Bert French; P: Russell Janney; T: Broadhurst Theatre; 1/24/22 (136)

Louis N. Parker's *Pomander Walk* had been a hit romantic comedy in 1910 and pleased many critics in its being turned now into "a charming operetta," which offered the sentimental story in a "winsome" new guise (Arthur Hornblow). The adapters were faithful to the period play, which tells of a budding romance in 1805 between sweet Marjolaine Lachesnais (Peggy Wood) of Pomander Walk, London, and handsome, young, naval officer Jack Sayle (Irving Beebe); the romance is interfered with by the girl's mother (Nellie Strong) and the boy's father (Worthe Faulkner), who had themselves once been lovers. After the usual obstacles are overcome, Marjolaine and Jack are united, and the lovers' parents decide to follow their hearts to a new romance of their own.

There was nothing especially noteworthy about the music, lyrics, comedy, or plot, but Peggy Wood was beguilingly lovely and coquettish.

MARJORIE [Musical/Romance/Theatre] B/LY: Fred Thompson, Clifford Grey, and Harold Atteridge; M: Sigmund Romberg, Herbert Stothart, Philip Kulkin, and Stephen Jones; CH: David Bennett; P: Embassy Productions, Inc.; T: Shubert Theatre; 8/11/24 (144)

Composed and written by a conglomerate of seven men, this show was simply a deft and likable one with barely a smidgin of creative inspiration or novelty. "*Marjorie*, like most song and dance shows," exclaimed Arthur Hornblow, "is bewilderingly hazy and thin. . . . But as these sorts of attractions go nowadays, it is snappy, good entertainment, superior to many in its class."

One of its brightest spots was the comedy element supplied by the delightful farceur of the *Follies*, Andrew Tombes. Tombes played a press agent in a thin plot about how Marjorie Daw (Elizabeth Hines) sells her brother's (Richard "Skeets" Gallagher) play to a producer (Roy Royston) who is in love with her and whom she allows to believe that she is the playwright. Using the same title, the press agent rewrites the play, the producer puts it on, and Marjorie and the producer get engaged.

MARQUISE, THE [Comedy/France/Period/Romance/Family/British] A: Noël Coward; D: David Burton; S: Jo Mielziner; P: Kenneth Macgowan and Sidney Ross; T: Biltmore Theatre; 11/14/27 (82)

Billie Burke returned to straight comedy in this play's title role, played successfully in London by Marie Tempest. She was "loveliness itself in . . . powdered wig and ... frills and ruffles'' (*Times*). Her part was of the forty-two-year-old, eighteenth-century French Marquise who, having had a son (Rex O'-Malley) by one man (Reg Owen) and a daughter (Madge Evans) by another, returns to the latter (Arthur Byron) after eighteen years in time to prevent the convenience marriage of her two half-siblings to one another. The two former lovers still want her, but she chooses the girl's father as her spouse.

The *Times* claimed that this Coward play was compounded of high comedy and farce, with an unusual amount of situation, considering the author's other plays: "It is a play written with all of Mr. Coward's impudence and about half of his accustomed skill at dialogue.'' Burke displeased some, like Joseph Wood Krutch, by being "so coyly arch as to be frankly embarrassing.''

MARRIAGE BED, THE [Comedy-Drama/Marriage/Sex] A: Ernest Pascal; SC: the author's novel of the same name; D: Robert Milton; P: Sam H. Harris i/a/ w Felix Young; T: Booth Theatre; 1/7/29 (72)

"[A] very creditable piece of dramatic work'' (Richard Dana Skinner), pro-marriage in theme, about a married man, George (Allan Dinehart), who falls for and philanders with a young woman (Helen Flint), and whose wife (Ann Davis) refuses him a divorce for what she takes as a passing fancy. When she discovers that her own sister (Helen Chandler) is in the sad position of the other woman in her own life, she relents, but by now George no longer wants the divorce and is happy to be taken back.

Francis R. Bellamy argued that the author's ideas on marriage were confused and that the play was "a curious combination of Victorian emotionalism, and what is called ultra-modern, hard-boiled intellectualism.''

MARRIED—AND HOW! [Comedy/Marriage] A: Ray Hodgdon; D: Priestly Morrison; P: Phil Bush; T: Little Theatre; 6/14/28 (36)

Flo and Phil Ballinger (Dulcie Cooper and Robert Bentley), newly married, are faced by the cutoff in Phil's funds from his millionaire dad (Walter Jones), because the latter doesn't approve of Phil's chorus-girl bride. Dissension grows between the couple over their alternatives, until Phil is struck by a car driven by his brother-in-law (George Le Guere). Flo gives up her threats of divorce to care for Phil, and Papa comes through with lots of mazuma to make the union flourish.

"Piecing together the old lumber of the theatrical workshop the author was ingenious enough to keep his play moving toward a foregone conclusion,'' observed Brooks Atkinson. The evening was, he said, "neither ... original nor ... tedious; it was commonplace.''

MARRIED WOMAN, THE [Dramatic Revival] A: C. B. Fernald; D: C. A. De Lima; P: Norman Trevor; T: Princess Theatre; 11/24/21 (51)

American author C. B. Fernald, long resident in England, had had this play produced in London a decade earlier; it was also seen briefly in 1916 at New

York's Neighborhood Playhouse. The play was dated and, though technically adroit, was "as stale in every way as a twenty-year-old newspaper is stale," quipped Alexander Woollcott. Kenneth Macgowan stated that it was excessively literary and not sufficiently stageworthy, for all of its well-meant treatment of the marriage relationship.

Fernald's thesis drama about marriage was described by some as a coda to Ibsen's *A Doll's House*. Sylvia (Margaret Dale), the disillusioned heroine, having married for love, soon finds that the conjugal institution is not what she expected and that her individualism is being sapped by her wifely duties. She married in the face of all of the evidence she needed to prove how fleeting is romantic love but still cannot accept it when her own marriage founders on the same well-worn rocks. She handles her dilemma by leaving her spouse (Percy Waram) and turning to the cynical bachelor Hugh Dellamy (Norman Trevor) with whom she agrees to live without benefit of clergy, regardless of the scandal she knows will follow.

MARRY THE MAN [Comedy/Sex/Family/Marriage/Romance] A: Jean Archibald; D: Priestly Morrison; P: Clyde Elliott; T: Fulton Theatre; 4/22/29 (8)

What was then conveniently called "companionate marriage" was the subject of many plays. This one came down hard against the notion, but it seemed "like a girls' high school debate badly given," exclaimed Robert Littell.

It had to do with a fellow (Lester Vail) living with his companionate bride (Vivian Martin) but afraid of the instability of such arrangements who tricks the lady into marrying him by announcing his imminent nuptials to a fictitious woman. Amazed, she weakens, and they dash off to their own marriage ceremony.

The play was called *Companionate Marriage* before arriving locally.

MARRY THE POOR GIRL [Comedy/Romance] A: Owen Davis; D: Priestly Morrison; P: Oliver Morosco; T: Little Theatre; 9/23/20 (18)

Owen Davis, one-man play factory, offered this formula bedroom farce, but it had little appeal for theatregoers. Alexander Woollcott discerned in it nothing but "an ordinary and somewhat rowdy farce" subjected to a "helter-skelter production and hammer-and-tongs performance."

The familiar forced-marriage plot was about a drunken bachelor (William Roselle) who sleeps by mistake in the room of a demure bachelorette (Isabelle Lowe) during a Long Island weekend party and is forced to marry the girl to keep the tongues from wagging. To protect him, his friends make out that he is a bigamist, but, as everyone could have foretold, he and the girl decide to stay man and wife before the curtain falls.

MARTINE [Drama/Romance/Rural/French] A: Jean-Jacques Bernard; TR: Helen Grayson; D: Richard Boleslavsky; DS: Robert Edmond Jones; P: American Laboratory Theatre; T: American Laboratory Theatre (OB); 4/4/28 (16)

A delicate 1922 French play, "somewhat elusive but progressively interesting'' (*Times*), about a pretty country girl (Ruth Nelson) who falls in love with a Paris newspaperman (George Macready) visiting his grandmother (Frances Williams); when he inevitably goes off to marry his chic Paris fiancée (Mary Steichen Martin), she weds a dull local farmer (Herbert V. Gellendre).

The young company struggled with this modest piece. They were not a ''cast . . . to glow about; they remind more of elocution students experimenting with difficult gestures in a mass recital,'' said Mark Barron. Nevertheless, various commentators discerned acting of great sensitivity and insight in the work of Ruth Nelson.

MARY [Musical/Romance/Business] B/LY: Otto Harbach and Frank Mandel; M: Louis Hirsch; D: Sam Forrest; CH: Julian Mitchell; P: George M. Cohan; T: Knickerbocker Theatre; 10/18/20 (220)

George M. Cohan received no writing or directing credit for this show, but it was common knowledge that he had so rewritten the book (even changing its name from *The House That Jack Built*) and had added so much to the fast-paced staging that it was a perfect example of what was deemed ''Cohanization.'' Compared to other musicals, Burns Mantle said, ''it is the pepperiest and the most tastefully staged, it has the most lucid story and the best cast. Its chorus is a herd of bounding antelope with chiffon flying from their antlers.'' Even more responsible than these flavorsome components for the show's hit status was its best-selling song ''The Love Nest.'' With several other melodic offerings, it made for a memorable musical entertainment. Commenting on the many well-worked-out dance routines, Arthur Hornblow noted, ''It seems impossible that so much vigorous gymnastic work was ever crowded into one musical comedy before.''

The shallow libretto was about a Kansas girl, Mary (Janet Velie), who loves Jack Keene (Jack McGowan) and who plans to marry someone else for money so Jack's impecunious family may share in the profits. Jack, however, who is involved in trying to establish a business selling ''portable houses,'' makes a fortune when he strikes oil; Mary can now give herself to him, and he can forget the widow (Florrie Millership) who has been pursuing him.

MARY JANE McKANE [Musical/Business/Romance] B/LY: William Cary Duncan and Oscar Hammerstein II; M: Herbert Stothart and Vincent Youmans; D: Alonzo Price; CH: Sammy Lee; S: Gates and Morange; C: Charles Le Maire; P: Arthur Hammerstein; T: Imperial Theatre; 12/25/23 (151)

The critics were respectful to enthusiastic about the book and music surrounding this story of a pretty country girl (Mary Hay) who is fired as a stenographer when she catches the eye of her employer's son (Stanley Ridges), starts her own business with her swain, and gets him and his father's blessing in the end.

Mary Hay, recalled Arthur Hornblow, was more plump and older than in her *Follies* appearances, but ''as cute and unaffected as ever.'' Perhaps of most importance in this production's record is that it opened the new Imperial Theatre.

The *Herald*'s critic commented: "It is one of the most tasteful of the latter day theatres of the Shuberts and achieves the feat of concentrating 1,650 into an orchestra and single balcony without the faintest suggestion of crowding the mourners."

                                                                                    H.H.

MARY, MARY, QUITE CONTRARY [Comedy/Theatre/Romance/British] A: St. John Ervine; D: David Belasco; S: Ernest Gros; P: David Belasco b/a/w Harrison Grey Fiske; T: Belasco Theatre; 9/11/23 (86)

Minnie Maddern Fiske's association with David Belasco began with this comedy about a London actress who goes to a country village to hear a young poet (Francis Lister) read his Joan of Arc play for her. She fascinates both the poet, who is engaged to his cousin (Nora Swinburne), and his uncle, a confirmed bachelor, until she rearranges all of their lives and exits laughing.

The play was pronounced fair, Mrs. Fiske the fairest. The *Times* critic called her a dream, "gay, inconsequent, abounding in inspired insolences. . . . It is brittle comedy, artificial at times as the character is, yet a feat of extraordinary artistry of which only this one woman in the world is capable."

An innovation was a new lighting scheme, which Belasco dedicated to his star. The *Tribune*'s critic commented: "Spots, foots and border lights are abandoned, with the result that such glows as illuminate *Mary, Mary, Quite Contrary* are less human than novel and much more natural." According to Mrs. Fiske's biographer Archie Binns, in *Mrs. Fiske and the American Theatre*, the credit given Belasco for the lighting should have gone to Mrs. Fiske's husband, Harrison Grey Fiske.

                                                                                    H.H.

MARY ROSE [Drama/Fantasy/Marriage/Family/Death/British] A: James M. Barrie; D: B. Iden Payne; M: Norman O'Neill; P: Charles Frohman, Inc.; T: Empire Theatre; 12/22/20 (128)

A not-especially-bodacious performance of this fantasy was partly responsible for its not having run longer. Barrie's whimsical drama, a Burns Mantle Best Play, and which some saw as an allegory of death, toyed with ideas of time and the afterlife in a way that was often poignantly affecting; some, though, found it confused and bathetic.

It began with the return of an Australian soldier (Tom Nesbitt) to the manor house in which he had spent his childhood before running off to sea at twelve. During his visit the play flashes back to the house as it was years before, when occupied by Mary Rose (Ruth Chatterton) and her parents. Mary once had disappeared for a month while staying at "The Island That Likes to Be Visited" in the Hebrides. After marriage and motherhood arrive, she again disappears on the island but does not return for twenty-five years; when she does, she is still young and child-like, but her parents and spouse have aged greatly and her child, whom she seeks with great longing, has been gone for years and is nearly forgotten. This apparently so shocks her that she dies. Finally, her spirit goes to the Aussie, whom she does not recognize as her son; her spirit is released, and she returns to her empyrean.

"It is a curiously austere and deeply moving play," wrote Alexander Woollcott, but the Playgoer found its quaint dialogue "a bit thin and its fancifulness ... a trifle stale." Ludwig Lewisohn discerned a "Spiritual triviality" and cloying sentimentality in Barrie's outlook. Ruth Chatterton proved a serious disappointment in the role intended to bring Maude Adams back to the stage.

MARY STUART and "A MAN ABOUT TOWN" P: William Harris, Jr.; T: Ritz Theatre; 3/21/21 (40)
Mary Stuart [Drama/Period/Marriage/Romance/Historical-Biographical/British] A: John Drinkwater; D: Lester Lonergan; "A Man about Town" [Pantomime]
Mary Stuart was a historical drama about Mary Queen of Scots (Clare Eames) produced on Broadway before being seen in its author's native England. It was marred by a prolix and repetitious modern-day prologue that could have been cut, but Drinkwater's play proper drew commendable notices for its excellent lines, its psychologically acute portrait of Mary, and the exceptional performance of Eames. The production also marked the opening of the Ritz Theatre.

The brief work, which did not purport to be historically accurate, presented Mary as a woman who can love two men, her husband, Darnley (Charles Waldron), and the Italian David Riccio (Frank Reicher), a fact that leads Darnley to have his rival executed; at the end the amorous Mary is preparing for a rendezvous with Bothwell (Thurston Hall).

The play suggested that Mary never had someone worthy of her ability to love, a man whose love would have inspired her to be as great as she was capable of being. Kenneth Macgowan noted that Drinkwater had written "almost the ideal dialog for the future play of high emotion and romantic color." Ludwig Lewisohn, though, thought that verse, not prose, would have better suited it.

To round out the evening, a comic pantomime was performed by esteemed nonprofessional members of the Comedy Club such as Henry Clapp Smith, Austin Strong, and Deems Taylor.

MARY THE THIRD [Comedy/Marriage/Sex/Family] A/D: Rachel Crothers; P: Lee Shubert; T: Thirty-ninth Street Theatre; 2/5/23 (163)
Rachel Crothers's satire on the marriage state was selected as a Best Play of 1922–1923 by Burns Mantle. As usual, said the *Times*, Crothers "devoted herself to tilting at modern manners, institutions and tendencies," with her picture of a contemporary flapper and her feeling about free love and marriage.

To tell her story, the playwright chose to present three generations of women, all named Mary and all played by Louise Huff, beginning with a prologue set in 1870, moving to a scene in 1897, and concluding with most of the action set in 1923. The purpose is to show the nature of the courtships experienced by the first two Marys as background to the family situations exposed in the modern portion of the play.

Considered the author's finest play to date by some, *Mary the Third* aroused Ludwig Lewisohn to praise it, apart from "its falsely happy ending," as "as thoughtful, delightful, and crisp a comedy as any American has written." Arthur Hornblow, however, wrote that Crothers had contributed neither "to modern thought" nor "to current drama. Her play is for the most part cumbersome, creaky with the machinery of propaganda and 'ideas,' and dramatically ineffective as a result of being fundamentally unreal."

MASK AND THE FACE, THE (La maschera il volto) [Comedy/Marriage/ Italian] A: Luigi Chiarelli; AD: Chester Baily Fernald; D/P: Brock Pemberton; S: Raymond Sovey; T: Bijou Theatre; 9/10/24 (13)

A highly reputed example of the Italian theatrical mode called the "theatre of the grotesque," a form that established the foundation for the plays of Pirandello. Originally produced in 1916, the play came to Broadway following a big London success. Another version, translated by Somerset Maugham, was scheduled for production by Gilbert Miller the same season but did not get put on until 1933. The present version was egregiously inept, both as a translation and production, and remained for less than two weeks. George Jean Nathan accused the adaptor of converting "amusing ironic comedy into a dull London drawing room comedy."

Count Grazia (William Faversham) boasts that if he ever finds his wife unfaithful he will murder her. When the wife (Catherine Willard) is discovered in a compromising situation with a friend (Austin Fairman), the Count ignores the wife's pleas of innocence, sends her away, and bruits it about that he has killed her. This makes him a local hero. At the wife's public funeral, she shows up wearing a veil and, after a funny scene, is reunited with the Count.

MASK OF HAMLET, THE [Drama/Politics/Crime/Romance/Italian] A: Ario Flamma; D: Cecil Owen; P: Excelsior Drama Corporation; T: Princess Theatre; 8/22/21 (8)

A "lurid melodrama" (Alexander Woollcott) translated into "stilted and almost always absurd" English (*Evening Post*) from the Italian. It depicted a man, Marvin (Harmon MacGregor), who has changed his name to Marx and abandoned his wealthy family for a Greenwich Village flat with his Russian Communist comrades. He is used by them to plant a bomb in Wall Street and kill many people. Afraid that he may squeal, a comrade (Laura Walker) stabs him to death.

Flamma's play sought to explain the background to an actual unsolved Wall Street explosion that had rocked the financial district on 9/22/20.

MASKED WOMAN, THE (La Femme masquée) [Drama/Marriage/Sex/Legacy/Medicine/French] A: Charles Méré; AD: Kate Jordan; D: Bertram Harrison; P: A. H. Woods; T: Eltinge Theatre; 12/22/22 (117)

Few critics took this melodramatic farrago seriously, agreeing in the main that its *raison d'être* was to offer Lowell Sherman another meaty villain role and Helen MacKellar another chance to act one of her familiar virtuous young women roles.

Sherman was the wealthy Baron Tolento, given three months to live by Dr. René Delatour (John Halliday). Hoping to be named the beneficiary in the Baron's will so that she can give her spouse the money for his laboratory, the doctor's wife, Diane (MacKellar), attends the Baron's farewell party, masked. After an unsuccessful attempt to seduce her, the Baron dies, and his will reveals a legacy for Diane. His idea had been to make the doctor jealous, but a witness to the foiled seduction clears the doctor's mind of doubt.

The result, said Heywood Broun, was "cheap melodrama played with a good deal of spirit."

MASQUE OF VENICE, THE [Comedy/Literature/Romance/British] A: George Dunning Gribble; D: Brock Pemberton; S: Jo Mielziner; P: Brock Pemberton, William A. Brady, Jr., and Dwight Deere Wiman; T: Mansfield Theatre; 3/2/26 (15)

Despite its dismally brief run this English comedy was not an all-round critical disaster. Larry Barretto did call it a "fiasco," and Richard Dana Skinner did use it as a laboratory specimen for demonstrating "Why Plays Leave Broadway," but Joseph Wood Krutch maintained that it was "quite entertaining . . . and its witty lines have the advantage of a genuinely literary polish." The reasons for its demise seem to have lain largely in the areas of casting and direction.

Arnold Daly played Jonathan Mumford, the Byronesque hero-novelist staying in Venice with his live-in girlfriend Egeria (Selena Royle) and coming into contact there with various literary friends. Among them are Jack Cazaneuve (Kenneth MacKenna), a descendent of Jacques Casanova, and Sophia Weir (Antoinette Perry), whose relationship is fostered by Mumford. It comes to naught, as does that of Mumford and Egeria, and Sophia and Mumford are left planning a play together.

MASTER BUILDER, THE (Bygmester Solness) [Dramatic Revival] A: Henrik Ibsen; D/P: Eva Le Gallienne; S: G. E. Calthrop; T: Maxine Elliott's Theatre; 11/10/25 (78)

A season in which Ibsen revivals were a marked characteristic saw Eva Le Gallienne's involvement in two of them, *John Gabriel Borkman* and the present play, both produced under her own management as an experiment which culminated in her decision to found the Civic Repertory Company in 1926. *The Master Builder* was given at special matinees at first but soon was produced for an open run at the Princess Theatre.

Le Gallienne played Hilda Wangel, in addition to directing and producing. Little enthusiasm for the 1892 play was expressed. The *Times* critic was panegyric, but John Mason Brown thought it "puzzling and repetitious, clouded in the emphasis of its theme, and unsparing in its stress of false leads." Alexander Woollcott considered it "overstrained, arduous," and too blatantly symbolic, and Richard Watts, Jr., censured its cold intellectualism. There were warmer feelings for the production, staged in modern dress against simple backgrounds. "It was a completely acted version, if hardly a brilliant one," offered Watts. Woollcott found Le Gallienne's work "as good . . . as she has ever done. Its last moments are alive with a finely communicated exaltation."

The production soon after produced by the Civic Rep was basically the same. That company put on the play on 11/1/26 for twenty-nine performances, on 11/1/27 for fourteen performances, on 10/31/28 for six performances, on 9/19/29 for five performances, and on 2/18/31 for three performances, all of them in alternating repertory with other works.

MASTER OF THE INN, THE [Drama/Hotel/Romance/Alcoholism/Mental Illness/Medicine] A: Catherine Chisholm Cushing; SC: Robert Herrick's novel of the same title; D: Hubert Druce; S: John Wenger; P: Hubert Druce and William Streett; T: Little Theatre; 12/22/25 (41)

An uncomfortably old-fashioned romantic play, in appropriately decorative language, about a Virginia surgeon and innkeeper (Robert Loraine) whose inn is devoted to healing without charge the spirit and the flesh of those who visit. He explains to his guests that his mission began when his beloved (Virginia Pemberton) betrayed him to elope with a young doctor, Toney Norton (Ian Keith). This couple are now his guests, he a defeated drunkard, she a mental case as the result of a crack on the head with a decanter. He heals the pair, his only reward being the knowledge of doing good.

Time called the piece a complicated and generally unconvincing contraption "that wasted the talents of British star Robert Loraine." A setter brought on in the first act amused both actors and spectators by bounding off the stage and up the aisle before he could be stopped.

MATINEE GIRL, THE [Musical/Romance] B/LY: McElbert Moore and Bide Dudley; M: Frank Gray; D: Oscar Eagle; CH: Sam Rose; P: Ed Rosenbaum, Jr., for Edmund Enterprises, Inc.; T: Forrest Theatre; 2/1/26 (25)

A stereotypical musical comedy that fluttered few pulses and was neither very good nor very bad. Richard Watts, Jr., called it "reasonably agreeable entertainment," despite its awful libretto, and the *World* enjoyed it as "clean, breezy, [and] full of catchy music." An example of its not-appreciated humor was the line, "When we cross the Gulf Stream, I'll wear my golf suit."

Set mostly on a yacht and patio, it followed the ploys of "Bubbles" Peters (Olga Steck) to land matinee-idol Jack Sterling (James Hamilton) by disguising herself as a cabin boy aboard his Cuba-bound yacht. Once there she dresses normally and wins his affections.

MATING SEASON, THE [Comedy/Sex/Romance] A/D: William A. Grew; P: David Chasen; T: Selwyn Theatre; 7/18/27 (24)

William A. Grew wrote, directed, and starred in this trivial bedroom farce, which gave him so many of the lines that it seemed, said the *Times*, more like a monologue than a play. It was also, said the critic, "just about as laboriously unfunny as a farce can be." Its substance was the complications attendant upon the pursuit by playwright Jack Stratford (Grew) of his sister-in-law (Lillian Walker) and the pursuit of Stratford by his wife's aunt. Bedroom complications occupied all of Act Three.

MATRIARCH, THE [Drama/Family/Business/Jews/British] A: G[ladys] B[ronwyn] Stern and Frank Vernon; SC: Stern's novel *The Tents of Israel*; D: Frank Vernon; P: Messrs. Shubert; T: Longacre Theatre; 3/18/30 (15)

A sorry dramatization of a Gladys Bronwyn Stern novel, which gave critics fuel for their belief that novels rarely make good source material for plays.

Constance Collier acted the title role, Anastasia Rakonitz, iron-fisted matriarch of a long-established family of Jewish jewellers. She lives entirely for her family and its honor. The plot concerns the handing on of the Rakonitz torch to her granddaughter Toni (Jessica Tandy), who will become the new matriarch.

Typical of the critical reactions was John Hutchens's comment that the play's "Indecisiveness lay in the conflict that so often affects dramatized novels, that conflict between true and interesting characterization and the slothful form containing it." The play marked the local debut of twenty-year-old Jessica Tandy of whom Brooks Atkinson wrote, "Jessica Tandy has a part deeper than most and she plays with pride and fresh sincerity."

MATRIMONIAL BED, THE (Au premier de ces messieurs) [Comedy/Marriage/Sex/French] A: Yves Mirande and André Mouézy-Eon; AD: Seymour Hicks; D: Bertram Harrison; P: A. H. Woods; T: Ambassador Theatre; 10/12/27 (15)

A speedily paced French bedroom farce, the title of which referred to a large piece of furniture that occupied much of the action. The play had been a London hit under the name *Mr. What's His Name*. It laid an egg on Broadway.

M. Noblet (John T. Murray), thought dead, has been suffering from amnesia. His wife (Lee Patrick) has remarried. He turns up at her home as a rakish hair dresser. A hypnotist has enabled him to recall everything before the accident, so when he sees his ex-wife he thinks he merely has been asleep. The tangles that follow stem from his rivalry with the new spouse (Kenneth Hill) to occupy the title prop with the wife that night. An undressing scene involving the two men, during which they both leaped onto the bed to be its first occupant, was the comic highpoint.

Katharine Zimmermann declared the farce "about as provocative of amusement as a dentist's chair."

MAURICE CHEVALIER [Revue] P: Charles Dillingham; T: Fulton Theatre; 3/30/30 (18)

Beginning with this appearance, French singer and actor Maurice Chevalier made it a regular occasion to headline a major New York recital; there were six more Broadway shows titled by his name through 1965. His 1930 show wove a spell of magic that even the raised houselights at the end failed to diminish. The audience demanded more, and the star was happily forced to comply. He emerged to offer "Valentine" and then sent his auditors joyously on their way.

Chevalier had appeared previously in a *Midnight Frolic* produced by Florenz Ziegfeld. He came back to Broadway after working in Hollywood films and was "burdened with the lush romance of a theme song or two, but with enough of his shimmering French ballads to make an hour pass with disheartening rapidity. . . . For Mr. Chevalier has the volatile personality and the expertness of touch that translate ballads into high comedy" (*Times*).

Sharing the program was Duke Ellington ("the djinn of din"—*Times*) and his Cotton Club Orchestra, supplemented by agile black dancers Aninias Berry and Henry Wetzel. Ellington played "Awfully Sad," "Mississippi Dry," "St. Louis Blues," "When You're Smiling," and "Liza." A third segment was devoted to the dancing talents of young Eleanor Powell.

MAYA [Drama/Prostitution/Sex/French] A: Simon Gantillon; TR: Ernest Boyd; D: Agnes Morgan; DS: Aline Bernstein; P: Actor-Managers i/a/w Gertrude Newell; T: Comedy Theatre; 2/21/28 (15)

This unusual French drama of a Marseilles prostitute, seen in Paris in 1924 and subsequently in Berlin and London, gave Aline MacMahon her first major Broadway role. She was outstanding in the role of Bella, the streetwalker whose life is traced by the episodic action in nine scenes showing her being visited by a succession of clients. The depiction of her character is essentially an exploration of her symbolic status as an illusory creature who is all things to all men. As an East Indian mystic explains her, she is Maya, a combination of Mary, the Mother of Desire, the Sister of Lies, and the Apparition or Illusion.

Too tenuously constructed for a full-length play, overly sentimental, and, to some, philosophically naive, the work nevertheless "looked through sordid material to universal values with a good deal of artistic unity," in Brooks Atkinson's view. Joseph Wood Krutch reasoned that "It is subduedly melodramatic and tastefully bawdy, but not any the better for that, since . . . it is merely sentimental and feeble." Many were seriously disturbed when the District Attorney's office decided to shut down the play in the midst of its run because of its allegedly prurient subject matter. Henceforth, announced the D.A., no play treating of a prostitute would be allowed a production. The critics mocked this ruling by pointing to the numerous classics with such characters, and it was not long before producers ignored the ban when mounting new works.

MAYFAIR [Comedy/Politics/Marriage/Sex/British] A/D: Laurence Eyre; P: Richard Herndon; T: Belmont Theatre; 3/17/30 (8)

Rosamund, Lady Clarges (Chrystal Herne), is married to a British foreign service diplomat (Frederick Worlock) who is more interested in being transferred to an important post in Rome than in maintaining her fidelity. He would arrange for her to have an affair with the right person if his career could be furthered. She has her eye instead on her spouse's young attache (Derek Glynne), who rejects her offer of elopement in favor of his own career objectives; she thus begins an affair with yet another diplomat (Arthur Hohl), who knows how to play both ends against the middle. He departs with her and sends her husband and the attache to Peru.

This epigrammatic boudoir comedy of manners proved a horrible bore. *Time* explained that "The heroine's feelings are almost as difficult to follow as Mr. Eyre's labyrinthine plot."

MAYFLOWERS [Musical/Romance/Period] B/LY: Clifford Grey; M: Edward Kunneke; SC: Arthur Richman's play *Not So Long Ago*; D: William J. Wilson and Joseph Santley; S: Watson Barratt; P: Messrs. Shubert; T: Forrest Theatre; 11/24/25 (81)

Mayflowers opened the new Forrest Theatre on West Forty-ninth Street and remained on its premises for nearly three months. In later years the theatre was known as the Coronet and from 1959 as the Eugene O'Neill.

Mayflowers was an operetta of New York in the 1860s, produced with "daintiness and charm" (Burns Mantle); it was "gently sentimental, completely romantic and filled to the brim with the adjuncts of real musical enjoyment" (Alan Dale). Its source was a popular 1920 play that had starred Eva Le Gallienne; its film version had recently been seen starring Betty Bronson. Much of the delight in the show came from its old-fashioned women's costumes with bustles, an unusual sight in this era of Broadway's infatuation with near-naked female bodies on the musical stage.

There were skilled and personable performances by leads Ivy Sawyer and Joseph Santley in this piece about wealthy Billy Ballard's love for seamstress Elsie Dover, despite his mother's objections. Billy Ballard is the name Elsie accidentally offers to her father (David Higgins) when she is asked the name of her boyfriend, at that time only an imaginary figure in her life. Learning of the seamstress's remarks, Billy plays along, and the consequence is romance.

ME [Drama/Illness/Romance/Crime/Mental Illness/Western/Rural] A: Henry Myers; D: Edward Clark Lilley; P: Arthur Kober; T: Princess Theatre; 11/23/25 (32)

A bizarre play with Pirandellian overtones set in a Rocky Mountains cabin where Donald Hood (Gerald Cornell), sick with consumption, has gone to regain his health. When he left his girlfriend Kate (Norma Millay), her mind went blank. Seven years pass and a tramp comes by, kills Donald, and assumes his clothes, manners, and personality—in fact, becomes him. The same day Kate's friends come to ask Donald to return to Kate in hopes that seeing him will restore her sanity. The ruse works, and the tramp passes into the girl's life as if he were her late lover.

Ward Morehouse thought *Me* "a brave fling at metaphysical melodrama—morbid melodrama, at that. It's an imaginative play and a sometimes interesting one, but one that you feel should be better." Alison Smith said, "It is obscure and halting and confused, and it necessitates that even the more rational characters should appear just a trifle half-witted."

MEANEST MAN IN THE WORLD, THE [Comedy/Business/Romance/Small Town] A: Augustin MacHugh; SC: a vaudeville sketch by Everett Ruskay; D: John Meehan; P: George M. Cohan; T: Hudson Theatre; 10/12/20 (204)

George M. Cohan not only produced this piece, he stepped in at the last minute to play its leading role; he also did a good deal of doctoring of the script, itself based on an old vaudeville bit. "The new play," advised Alexander Woollcott, "is a refreshingly unambitious comedy of a conventional but never-fail school—a pleasantly moral little play of the kind generally called wholesome."

Cohan gave one of his patented performances as lawyer Richard Clarke who, having failed at his profession, determines, on a friend's advice, to succeed by being what the title indicates. Set on collecting an overdue bill from a small-town concern, he discovers that the proprietor is a charming young lady (Marion Coakley); he sticks around to protect her interests from swindlers, promote a local oil boom, and marry the maid, with a future prosperity all but sewn up for good. Ludwig Lewisohn said Cohan gave "a finished and extraordinarily intelligent characterization which survives the feeble folly of the plot."

MECCA [Musical/Period/Africa/Politics/Romance/British] B: Oscar Asche; M: Percy E. Fletcher; D: E. Lyall Swete; CH: Michel Fokine; S: Joseph and Philip Harker; C: Percy Anderson, Leon Bakst; P: F. Ray Comstock and Morris Gest; T: Century Theatre; 10/4/20 (130)

A $400,000 Arabian Nights musical-melodramatic extravaganza, seen in New York before being given in it's author's native England. It was a visual feast to some, such as Charles Darnton, who called it "the marvel of the century." Pagan costumes, thrilling processions, Oriental ballets, half-nude dancers, exotic music, and melodramatic events conspired to fill the stage to memorable effect.

It followed the adventures of the young Sultan (Orville R. Caldwell), who dresses in rags so that he may go amongst his people in search of a suitable bride, and whose throne is the goal of wicked would-be usurpers. When he finds his future wife (Hannah Toback), the Prince (Herbert Grimwood) leading the enemy faction kidnaps her but is ultimately slain and the girl returned to her rightful owner.

The play palled by comparison with the splendor of its staging. "Of literary distinction ... there is nothing," lamented Arthur Hornblow. Michel Fokine choreographed several exquisite ballets, especially a wild bacchanal.

MEEK MOSE [Comedy-Drama/Religion/Small Town/Blacks/Southern] A: Frank Wilson; D: George MacEntee; S: Albert Bliss; P: Lester A. Walton; T: Princess Theatre; 2/6/28 (32)

Black actor Frank Wilson (then playing the title role in *Porgy*) authored this play about the black residents of a Texas town who are led by a reverent old man, Mose (Charles H. Moore), who believes in Jesus's prophecy that the meek will inherit the earth. When the whites force the blacks to move to a low-lying, swampy section of town, Mose advises passive resistance. Suffering and rebellion ensue, but all is happily resolved when oil is discovered on the property.

Wilson's play seemed to Alexander Woollcott "an awkward and artless contraption," poorly acted, and incompetently directed. Brooks Atkinson judged it "a childishly naive endeavor, full of sepia tint John Golden and depicting life only in slightly shop-worn terms of the theatre." Only the singing of several spirituals directed by Alston Burleigh pleased most critics.

Because the production was the first in a planned black repertory theatre, partly sponsored by financier Otto Kahn, various dignitaries, black and white, attended the opening, and Mayor Walker gave a speech vindicating "the progress of American government" in its handling of racial equality.

A 1934 manifestation of the piece was called *Brother Mose*.

MEET THE PRINCE [Comedy/Marriage/British] A: A. A. Milne; D: Basil Sydney; S: Jo Mielziner; P: Frobisher, Inc.; T: Lyceum Theatre; 2/25/29 (96)

Married players Basil Sydney and Mary Ellis starred as former spouses in Milne's "supremely unimportant bit of charming nonsense" (Richard Dana Skinner). After years of separation they meet once again at a dinner party thrown by the delightfully eccentric Simon Battersby (Moffat Johnston) at his home in London's suburbs. There among the sharply characterized guests, it evolves that he, the guest of honor, has been masquerading as the Prince of Neo-Slavonia, a fictional locale, and she as an important general's wife. They keep up their pretenses for everyone else's benefit as the action gradually brings them together again.

Deft characterizations and witty banter amused audiences greatly. However, many thought, as did Robert Littell, that "When Milne is thin, nothing is thinner." The play's London title had been *To Have the Honor*.

MEET THE WIFE [Comedy/Literature/Family/Romance] A: Lynn Starling; D: Bert French; S: Gertrude Lennox and Sheldon K. Viele; P: Rosalie Stewart and Bert French; T: Klaw Theatre; 11/26/23 (261)

"An original, witty, expert farce, played with refreshing gusto and humor by a wholly capable and appealing cast," was Arthur Hornblow's verdict about this play written by young actor Lynn Starling. The *Times* critic called him a "more than promising playwright" and declared his comedy "enormously enriched and at times lifted to the skies" by Mary Boland's performance as a society hostess with a penchant for celebrities. Her newest guest (Ernest Lawford) turns out to be her first husband, who was assumed dead in the San Francisco earthquake but who feigned death and disappeared to become a famous novelist. In a subplot, the hostess's daughter (Patricia Calvert) is pursued by two suitors (Humphrey Bogart and Clifton Webb).

H.H.

MEI LAN-FANG [One-Acts/Chinese/Chinese Language] P: F. C. Coppieus i/ a/w the China Institute in America; T: Forty-ninth Street Theatre; 2/17/30 (41)

The name of China's greatest actor was used to advertise the classical repertory he starred in during his highly influential world tour of 1930. This was the first visit to the West of the Peking (Beijin) or Chinese Opera, the musical-dramatic-acrobatic form of theatre that represents the classical Chinese theatre at its most sophisticated level. Mei Lan-Fang was the most successful star in its history (he was said to be earning about $750,000 a year); he was a delicately featured thirty-two-year-old gentleman who specialized in female roles, or what the Chinese call the *tan* classification. His plays employed a performance style dependent upon sparse settings, a highly elaborate code of symbolic movements and gestures, formalized vocal techniques, lavish costumes, and stylized makeups, as well as what seemed extremely uneuphonious music to Western ears. Symbolism (Mei preferred the word "patternism") prevailed in every facet of the ritual-like performance. Actors were trained under rigorous conditions from early childhood on, Mei himself beginning at age seven.

Mei's visit gave excited New Yorkers six brief selections from his 400-play repertoire. They were "The Suspected Slipper," "The End of the 'Tiger General,' " "The Ruse of the Empty City," "The King's Party with His Favorite," and the duel scene from "Green Stone Mountain." So well was Mei received that his plans for a two-week limited engagement were extended to five weeks. On March 10 he gave an invitational performance at the National Theatre in which he presented four other pieces.

Time declared of Mei's art: "he seemed like a painting of Hui Tsung miraculously come to elastic, undulating life. His dances with swords and wands possessed an extraordinarily feline continuity of movement. His falsetto was harsh but expressive. Watching his gait, his play with hands and voluminous sleeves, his tender coquetry, you could understand why Chinese poets have written panegyrics about his eye, smile, shoulder, even his waist." Some critics dared not offer any analytical impression, because they realized how difficult it would be to discuss intelligently an art so unfamiliar; Joseph Wood Krutch described the task as comparable to reading Homer with a dictionary. The presentation was made somewhat more understandable by a perfectly spoken mistress of ceremonies, Miss Soo Ying, who explained each scene and what the audience was to look for in the performance.

MELODY MAN, THE [Comedy/Music/Romance] A: Herbert Richard Lorenz; D: Lawrence Marston and Alexander Leftwich; T: Ritz Theatre; 5/13/24 (61)

Lew Fields returned to Broadway as Franz Henkel, a symphony composer forced to flee Germany because of a murder charge resulting from his wife's flirtation with an officer. In America Henkel's melodies are stolen by a ragtime publisher (Donald Gallaher), but everyone is happy after the publisher bribes authorities to clear Henkel's record, splits the ragtime royalties with him, marries his daughter (Betty Weston), and leaves Henkel free to write classical music.

The pseudonymous author of this play, which John Corbin dismissed as "pretty poor stuff," was actually a threesome, the as-yet-little-known Herbert Fields, Richard Rodgers, and Lorenz Hart, who would soon help shape musical theatre history. It was originally called *The Jazz King*, and Rodgers and Hart added to it a pair of songs designed to suggest the usual sort of tunes associated with Tin Pan Alley. Q.M. may have judged the piece "tremendously funny," but most agreed that, Lew Fields's performance aside, the show was second-rate.

H.H.

MENACE [Drama/Japan/Romance/Sex/Crime] A: Arthur M. Brilant; D: Arthur Hurley; S: Cleon Throckmorton; P: James E. Kennedy; T: Forty-ninth Street Theatre; 3/14/27 (24)

The motive for a good man killing someone in many twenties melodramas was to avenge the death of some girl who had been seduced and abandoned to have her child without benefit of marriage. Such was the case with Lattimer (Jack Roseleigh), who escaped from prison on the day of his execution to hide out on a secluded Japanese island where samurai Princess Setsu (Eve Casanova), a Smith College graduate, loves and ministers to him. Tracked down by the warden's daughter (Pauline MacLean), he falls for her, brazens it out with Setsu's local protectors, and is released by the Nipponese so that he may escape in one piece. Setsu contemplates *hara kiri.*

"The author of *Menace* appears to have studied life from an orchestra chair, acquiring knowledge of its major details from such authorities as *Madama Butterfly*, *East is West*, *Chicago* and the works of Willard Mack," jeered Arthur Hornblow.

MENDEL, INC. [Comedy/Jews/Family] A: David Freedman; SC: David Freedman's novel *Mendel Marantz*; D/P: Lew Cantor; T: Sam H. Harris Theatre; 11/25/29 (216)

Alexander Carr, of *Potash and Perlmutter* fame, was the centerpiece of this Jewish family comedy about an East Side plumber, Mendel Marantz, whose preoccupation with inventing a device to unburden housekeepers of their chores causes people to label him a loafer and drives his family to poverty and his wife (Lisa Silbert) to work, until the riches begin to pour in when his invention makes it big.

The usual stereotypes of New York Jewish immigrants were involved to excellent effect in this very funny piece. Carr's excellent work was seconded by vaudevillians Smith and Dale as the characters Bernard Shnaps and Charles

Shtrudel. The *Times* wrote that "There is no indication that Mr. Freedman was interested in anything but Mendel himself, a portrait drawn with obviously affectionate care.''

MERCENARY MARY [Musical/Legacy/Marriage] B: William B. Friedlander and Isabel Leighton; M/LY: William B. Friedlander and Con Conrad; SC: the farce *What's Your Wife Doing?* by E. Nyitray and H. H. Winslow; D: William B. Friedlander; CH: William Seabury; P: L. Lawrence Weber; T: Longacre Theatre; 4/13/25 (136)

Seven shows opened on April 13, 1925; this was one of the three that were musicals. It was based on a farce that had been seen on Broadway as recently as 1923. The story, hacked to shreds for musical purposes, was about a couple (Louis Simon and Winnie Baldwin), whose marriage threatens to have them dumped from the will of the husband's grandfather; they arrange with a friend (Allen Kearns) to act as corespondent in a situation that will allow them grounds for a divorce, thereby getting them back in the will. The grandfather (Sam Hearn) eventually relents before things go too far, and all ends happily.

Mercenary Mary was later a successful London show, but it did only moderately well on Broadway. Its chief virtues were an attractively rowdy chorus of sixteen lovelies and a plethora of uptempo terpsichore. Each girl had a solo showing off her specialty. The *Times* gave the show a rave, pointing to "its Spring finery, cobweb parasols, painted veils, bathing silks and a stageful of legs to stand on.''

(1) MERCHANT OF VENICE, THE [Dramatic Revival/Yiddish Language] A: William Shakespeare; D: Rudolph Schildkraut; P: Maurice Schwartz; T: Yiddish Art Theatre (OB); 11/11/20

A Yiddish-language presentation starring European actor Rudolph Schildkraut was the decade's first presentation of the Shakespearean play due to receive more revivals during the period than any other. The *Times* considered this version a superbly modern one that made the role of Shylock vividly true to life and completely credible. Playing the part in sympathetic and tragic terms, Schildkraut's portrayal "admits to an amazing degree the variety and contradictions, the incompletions and dissonances which today are recognized as the symphony of human character. This is a Shylock, flexible and casual, colloquial and, strange to say, unctuous. That is what makes the strange bargain possible. It is as Schildkraut plays it, really a jest that only subsequent events . . . endow with a sinister turn.'' As Ludwig Lewisohn saw it, "His Shylock is hoarse and far from voluble—a fat, graceless, old man. But in that figure vibrates a terrifying force. He asks for no sympathy; he wrenches it from you.'' Otherwise the production was pallid and employed a poor prose translation that did the author little justice.

(2) D/P: John E. Kellard; T: Manhattan Opera House (OB); 12/2/20 (4)

An insignificant production headed by John E. Kellard with a company including the young Ian Keith, given as part of a five-play Shakespeare repertory; the critics ignored the series.

(3) D/P: Fritz Leiber; T: Lexington Theatre (OB); 12/29/20 (2)

Fritz Leiber, diligent Shakespearean, brought a troupe to town with a seven-play Shakespeare repertory in which he played all the central roles and directed all of the plays. Formerly with Robert Mantell's company, he was a well-trained player and made, according to Alexander Woollcott, "an interesting, forceful and unfamiliarly youthful Shylock." The production was effective, with a funny Launcelot Gobbo (Robert Strauss) and a fine Portia (Irby Marshall). The troupe returned with the play on 12/31/21 for one showing.

(4) D/P: Edward Vroom; T: Cort Theatre; 4/1/21

Veteran Edward Vroom, who had acted with Edwin Booth, offered his version, "with a singularly heterogeneous company and with the most moth-eaten investiture this city has witnessed in many and many a day. . . . Mr. Vroom proved to be a pompous and incorrigibly operatic Shylock," Woollcott wrote. The critic likened his technique to that of a comic-opera actor: "He sang every line." Harry Wagstaff Gribble was Lorenzo, Leonard Mudie was Bassanio and the respected Adrienne Morrison was a Portia "of real spirit and distinction" (Woollcott). The play was heavily cut "to leave plenty of Vroom at the top."

(5) D/P: Edward Waldmonn; T: Longacre Theatre; 4/6/21 (6)

An unimportant revival headed by Edward Waldmonn, who took over the Longacre for a series of Shakespeare and Ibsen matinees in the spring of 1921. The critics ignored them.

(6) D/P: Walter Hampden; DS: Claude Bragdon; T: Broadhurst Theatre; 5/13/21 (7)

The 1920–1921 season's final production of the play was that for which Walter Hampden was responsible, during a season of Shakespearean repertory with his own company. This was his first showing of his Shylock in Manhattan; Alexander Woollcott judged it "a senile, dirty and singularly malignant Shylock, but one that is vital and convincing from first to last." This was a notably unsympathetic portrayal. Mary Hall made "a substantial and robustious Portia who reads always with clarity and humor" but who lacked a sense of Portia's dignity. The ensemble was notably effective.

(7) D/P: Julia Marlowe and E. H. Sothern; T: Century Theatre; 11/2/21 (8)

Julia Marlowe and E. H. Sothern's touring repertory of four Shakespeare classics came again to New York in 1921. Their production of *The Merchant of Venice* moved swiftly without long scene-shift waits, was simply mounted, and attained a "dignity and directness," according to Alexander Woollcott. Arthur Hornblow thought it was "the most delightful of all" of their stagings. Marlowe's Portia was a fine example of clear diction and thoughtful interpretation and gave the revival whatever eclat it attained. She added "to all the attributes of form, feature, charm and manner, the touches of zest and spontaneity that make the perfection of artistry," said Hornblow. Less successful was Sothern's Shylock, played as a cruel and vengeful man. "He leaves the scene of the trial with his shoulders back and a sneer for the mocking of Gratiano," wrote Woollcott.

The couple returned to New York with this production in tow on 11/5/23 for seven performances at the Fifty-ninth Street Theatre. The *Times* critic found the work a gorgeous one pictorially: "Settings of softened hues, rich brocades, colors from Morocco no less than from Venice, street corners with contrast of light and shadow—all pleased the eye whilst poetry had an honest reading." He noted how much the interpretation succeeded in evincing the show's humor and said of Marlowe's Portia, "It is not indifferent, never dull, but rather a pleasant symmetry of gayety in love-making, in law-making and at length in love-mocking."

(8) D/P: David Belasco; S: Ernest Gros; T: Lyceum Theatre; 12/21/22 (92)

One of five major Shakespearean revivals that came to Broadway in the 1922–1923 season, this was a heavily realistic, expensively produced production in the manner of nineteenth-century pictorialism. The critical response was mixed but tending toward the skeptical.

David Belasco tampered seriously with the play, cutting lines, rearranging scenes, transposing dialogue, and adding long passages of pantomimic action. This disturbed some more than others. One of the director's devices that proved particularly irksome was his combining most of the Shylock scenes into a single act and the Portia scenes into another. This threw the playwright's careful alternation of effects into the discard.

Controversy surrounded Belasco's extensive efforts in providing scenic realism (at a cost of nearly a quarter of a million dollars). "He gives us Italy of the sixteenth century," commented Ludwig Lewisohn; "he gives us Venice, the Venice of Titian and Veronese. . . . The scenes and costumes are at once correct and splendid," filling the stage with the teeming life of the city. Stark Young, however, observed inaccuracies of architecture, coloration, and costume and decried the absence of any truly "Venetian quality at all."

Slightly less controversial than Belasco's staging was the Shylock of David Warfield; it was a highly detailed, skillful, and touching impersonation that evoked sympathy for a pathetic, if necessarily vindictive Jew, but it met with many annoyed reactions. Lewisohn described it as fitting into the production's veristic depiction of Jewish customs, exclusive of their place in the Shakespearean scheme, with which they seemed to clash. Within this atmosphere of synagogues and mezuzzahs, Shylock was "a frail and intrepid figure, intense to the point of neurasthenia. The man has been rasped until there is no protective covering over his nerves. He has little or nothing in common with Shakespeare's magnifico. . . . His ferocity is never natural. It has been wrung from him by blows, slights, insults, cruelties, defamations." In the trial scene, according to John

Corbin, the actor failed to realize the tragic potentials of the role, opting instead for pathos ''to the last degree.'' This lack of tragic stature seems to have been Warfield's greatest weakness.

The supporting company was capable and well balanced. Philip Merivale as Bassanio, manly, noble, and attractive, came off best, with Mary Servoss's Portia a close second.

(9) (Le Marchand du Venise) [French Language] AD: Lucien Népoty; D: Firmin Gémier; T: Jolson's Fifty-ninth Street Theatre; 11/17/24 (5)

French ''*homme du théâtre*'' Firmin Gémier presented his *Merchant of Venice* in French as part of his company's New York repertory in 1924. It was a decidedly unconventional production for its day and attracted both boos and applause. The text was as adapted by Lucien Népoty, who ''cut, transposed and added to it at his own free will and so transmogrified . . . some of the characters that they are scarcely recognizable'' (John Ranken Towse). The staging was in the expansive Reinhardtian vein, using spectacular pictorial effects, with a considerable amount of mob activity in the theatre's aisles. Towse said, ''He has provided a picturesque, animated and interesting, if curious, show, but has delayed the action without adding to its coherence.'' Gilbert W. Gabriel thought they had ''made food for opera and ballet of it,'' and to George Jean Nathan it was a freakish *tour de force*, a stunt more than an organically developed concept.

The scene that commanded the most attention was the trial, which had opposing factions for and against Shylock surge down the aisles shouting at one another and continuing to demonstrate their hostility toward one another on stage, mirroring the shifting fortunes of the antagonists in the courtroom. As Shylock (Gémier) suffered defeat, his fellow Jews expressed his grief through the gradual bending of their backs, reflecting his own bowed posture. Another directorial interpolation was the bringing on of Shylock during the last act's scene of romantic comedy to cast a pall over the happy lovers by his ghostly, monk-like presence in a hooded cassock.

Gémier's Shylock was variously considered. A. G. Spiers wrote that he was an embodiment of the Jew's need to stand up to and seek justice from those Christians who ill use members of his faith; yet Gilbert W. Gabriel did not believe Gémier's was a pro-Jewish approach. He seemed, said the critic, ''an inhuman fiend, a monument to Hate.'' Gabriel described the method as ''entirely cerebral, a glittering, unaffecting parade of subtlest details he has gathered in its defense.''

(10) D/P: Walter Hampden; DS: Claude Bragdon; T: Hampden's Theatre; 12/26/25 (56)

Walter Hampden, who had been seen locally as Shylock earlier in the decade, returned with a new production of *The Merchant*, his Portia now being Ethel Barrymore, who recently had played Ophelia to his Hamlet. Claude Bragdon designed sets that were in the ''stale tradition'' (*Times*) of Shakespearean scenery, with literal Venetian backgrounds only occasionally relieved by neutral curtains before which some scenes were played.

The literalness of the sets was to a degree reflected in Hampden's unimpassioned acting. *Time* described his performance as "straightforward, stately without elocutionary claptrap." Percy Hammond noted that "This Shylock makes few roccoco gestures and mutters few incomprehensible sounds. . . . He does not rend his garments, and when in the courtroom he is forced to hit the ceiling he does so quietly and without gymnastics." But Alan Dale accused Hampden of being theatrical, old-fashioned, and stagey.

As Portia, Barrymore was more effective, especially in her brilliant court scene, for which she wore a robe of fiery crimson. Brooks Atkinson found that she adorned the revival "not only personally with beauty and charm, but she also illuminates its various moods by sheer force of intelligence and histrionic skill." Her diction seemed nearly flawless, and her characterization was of a mature and realistic woman. But Alan Dale thought "She played Portia just as she played Juliet and Ophelia—with the self-same plaintive monotone and the self-same suppressed sweetness."

(11) D/P: Winthrop Ames; S: Woodman Thompson; T: Broadhurst Theatre; 1/16/28 (72)

Winthrop Ames's thoroughly careful, meticulously worked out, and skillfully staged revival starring George Arliss and Peggy Wood was "lifeless," said Brooks Atkinson, and *Time* bemoaned its being "not always blood spotted with despair or dreamily alive with the enchantment of the poet's songs of love." The realistically mounted production suffered largely from Arliss's scrupulously refined gentleman of a money lender; for whatever Shylock gained in dignity by this approach, he lost in emotional power. "What we miss . . . is the range of the part—the full quantity of the hatred, bitterness, pathos and tragedy," wrote Atkinson. George Jean Nathan thought that he played the part "like an Episcopalian prelate in an English drawing-room comedy." Peggy Woods's "simple and unaffected diction and her arch sense of comedy" (Richard Dana Skinner) contributed to a charming Portia, although Atkinson thought she lacked "caprice" and the vocal "witchery" he anticipated. The most remarked on performance was Romney Brent's as Launcelot Gobbo, "because it moved and breathed and spoke with a life that was woefully lacking elsewhere" (John Mason Brown).

(12) D: Fritz Leiber; S: Herman Rosse; C: William Henry Matthews; P: Chicago Civic Shakespeare Society; T: Shubert Theatre; 3/27/30 (3)

Fritz Leiber revived the work during his nine-play Shakespeare season at the head of a new company from Chicago. John Hutchens said his interpretation of it made it "a buoyant love story unshadowed by venom." The *Times* valued it as "a competent, rounded production, gay, amusing and sometimes meditative. . . . His Shylock is throaty, powerful and often moving, but not venomous. . . . [W]hat comes out of the play is rather the charm of a love story than the dread of a fierce fight."

The speedily paced mounting featured Vera Allen as Portia, Hart Jenks as Bassanio, and Robert Strauss as Launcelot.

MERCHANTS OF GLORY (Les Marchands de gloire) [Comedy/Family/ War/Politics/French] A: Marcel Pagnol and Paul Nivoix; TR: Ralph Roeder; D: Philip Moeller; S: Ben Webster; P: Theatre Guild; T: Guild Theatre; 12/14/25 (41)

A French satire on war profiteering that struck home at those who used the noble deeds of men who fought in the war to further their own selfish ambitions. Its chief character, Bachelet (Augustin Duncan), is a simpleminded paterfamilias whose son (Jose Ruben) is reported killed in action. On the strength of his position as the father of a deceased war hero, Bachelet is exploited by political glory profiteers and is elected to various offices; he is on the verge of election to a major post when the son returns, having never been killed at all and only just having recovered from amnesia. At the urging of the party, he agrees to keep his existence secret, and the father wins the election.

The play had a telling effect as propaganda and drama for some. "There is bite to this play's irony," commented Burns Mantle, "and a sting in its exposures." But John Mason Brown thought the fine satirical idea was poorly managed and called the work "as wasteful and irritating a piece of playwriting as the season has seen."

MERCHANTS OF VENUS [Comedy/Romance] A: Alan Brooks; SC: Alan Brooks's sketch "Dollars and Sense"; D: Bertram Harrison and Alan Brooks; P: Richard Lambert; T: Punch and Judy Theatre; 9/27/20 (65)

Merchants of Venus served to bring Alan Brooks out of vaudeville, where he was well known as a popular writer of sketches. His play was based on such a sketch, which he turned into an overly epigrammatic but otherwise interesting study of the "utility or futility of marrying for money" (*Independent*).

Jack Bainbridge (Brooks) is in love with a mercenary debutante, Helen Davenport (Vivian Rushmore). She marries Billy Hasbrouck (Robert Kelly), the wealthier of her suitors. Jack tries to prevent the nuptials and also attempts to stop Verna Cromwell (Carroll McComas), the girl who loves him, from marrying the wrong guy. In the end, all is worked out to everyone's benefit.

Aside from an interesting last act in which lighting was made to illuminate three sections of the stage in alternation, the piece was not worth the effort. Poor direction and uneven writing were its chief faults. "Although undeniably possessed of its moments, it is a somewhat curious blend of satire, comedy and serious purpose, with the three ingredients so mixed that one is presently floundering and wondering what to make of it all," said the *Times*.

M.M.-C.

MERRY ANDREW [Comedy/Old Age/Family/Small Town] A: Lewis Beach; D: John Hayden and Lewis Beach; P: Laurence Rivers, Inc.; T: Henry Miller's Theatre; 1/21/29 (24)

Andrew Aiken (Walter Connolly), sixty-year-old small-town workaholic druggist, follows his wife's (Effie Shannon) advice to retire, but the idea turns sour when his restlessness upsets the entire household; by the end, Mrs. Aiken is plying her wiles at getting Andrew back in his old shop.

Ernest Boyd said this was "A comedy in the best *Saturday Evening Post* tradition," but Robert Littell thought that after a good start "it sinks into improbability and loses itself in the twists of plot and sub-plot."

MERRY MALONES, THE [Musical/Mystery/Romance/Family] B/M/LY/P: George M. Cohan; D: Edward Royce; CH: Jack Mason and Edward Royce; T: Erlanger's Theatre; 9/26/27 (216)

Four other hits opened on the same night as this one; the occasion also marked the inauguration of the new Erlanger Theatre on Forty-fourth Street. *The Merry Malones* was a familiar Cohanesque diversion dealing with the Cinderella love affair of a millionaire's son (Alan Edwards) for an Irish lass (Polly Walker) from the Bronx. "There were bands blaring from the stage, flags were waved at the slightest opportunity, there were lingering ballads detailing the charms of Molly Malone and recording the indisputable fact that God is good to the Irish," reported the *Times*. Cohan wrote the whole show, and when Arthur Deagon in the role of Molly's dad died before the opening, he took that part himself.

There was not much originality in the work. Its story, about the rich boy willing to give up his legacy to marry the poor girl but bamboozled when his father (Robinson Newbold) turns over his money to the bride, was strictly conventional. A comic mystery subplot was also included. Richard Dana Skinner thought the show was nothing more than an improved and expanded version of *Little Nellie Kelly*. It proved to be the last Cohan musical in which the popular star appeared.

MERRY, MERRY [Musical/Show Business/Romance] B/LY/D: Harlan Thompson; M: Harry Archer; S: P. Dodd Ackerman; P: Lyle D. Andrews; T: Vanderbilt Theatre; 9/24/25 (197)

Good reviews were the blessing that boosted this musical comedy to a substantial run. It had a not-particularly-novel story about Eve Walters (Marie Saxon), who comes to New York to make it as a chorus girl, meets and falls for Adam Winslow (Harry Puck) in a subway station, grows disillusioned when her roommate Sadi LaSalle (Sascha Beaumont) gets her involved as a witness in a law suit against a man Sadi is trying to extort for money, and gives up the theatre for a quiet married life.

Because the show dealt with chorus girls, the introduction of that musical-comedy element was made convincing. The music charmed critics' ears, especially "It Must Be Love," and the show's ingenious and numerous dance numbers kept the piece going at a fast and exhilarating pace. Arthur Hornblow said the show's assets were "pretty and lively girls, good dancing, tuneful song numbers, quite a bit of humor and much speed."

MERRY WIDOW, THE (Die Lustige Witwe) [Musical Revival] M: Franz Lehar; LY: Adrian Ross; D: George Marion; S: Joseph Urban; P: Henry W. Savage; T: Knickerbocker Theatre; 9/5/21 (56)

This "sumptuous and generally able revival" (Alexander Woollcott) of Franz Lehar's enormously popular 1905 Viennese operetta was "a rare treat for jazz-tired music lovers" (*Independent*); it established itself surely as the greatest of its genre, said Woollcott, and was "likely to remain so." Its book was unacceptable, but its lush melodies were as thrilling as ever. "Maxims'," "Women," "Vilya," and "A Dutiful Wife," were still memorable numbers, and the show's famous Act Two waltz number was again a show stopper.

The resplendent musical performances of Dutch singer Reginald Pasch as Prince Danilo and the Russian singer Lydia Lipkowska as Sonia, the Merry Widow, led a talented troupe.

(2) D: Milton Aborn; P: Jolson Theatre Musical Comedy Company; T: Jolson's Fifty-ninth Street Theatre; 12/2/29 (16)

The often-revived operetta was produced during a 1929–1930 series of operetta resuscitations directed by Milton Aborn. It "seemed lovelier and more melodious than ever" (Euphemia Van Rensselaer Wyatt) with Beppie De Vries, a Dutch prima donna, in the title part. *Time* said she "sings Franz Lehar's score considerably better than the rest of the cast and wheels through the famed waltz with the requisite abandon." Prince Danilo was well played by Evan Thomas.

MERRY WIVES OF WINDSOR, THE [Dramatic Revival] A: William Shakespeare; D/P: Harrison Grey Fiske; CH: Esther Gustafson; S: Gates and Morange; C: Henry Dreyfuss; T: Knickerbocker Theatre; 3/19/28 (24)

The lure to this revival of Shakespeare's "somewhat threadbare little comedy" (Perriton Maxwell) was the presence of Otis Skinner as Falstaff, Henrietta Crosman as Mistress Ford, and Mrs. Fiske as Mistress Page. Their efforts could only turn it into "a sprightly, if rather humorless and disjointed, romp," sighed Brooks Atkinson. He did, however, enjoy the basket scene and that in which Ford (Lawrence H. Cecil) tosses the dirty clothes around the set. The production was old fashionedly representational, had long waits between the scenes, and cut the text considerably. But Richard Dana Skinner appreciated it for its "simplicity and directness." Otis Skinner was witty and jovial but lacked the fat knight's coarseness, Crosman "looked as coy and magnetic as the old English bard ever hoped to find her" (Maxwell), and Mrs. Fiske was spirited, if somewhat loud, and played many of her lines straight to the audience.

MERRY WORLD, THE (Passions of 1926) [Revue/British] M: Maurie Rubens, J. Fred Coots, Herman Hupfeld, and Sam Timberg; LY: Clifford Grey; D:

J. C. Huffman; CH: Larry Ceballos; P: Messrs. Shubert i/a/w Albert de Courville; T: Imperial Theatre; 6/8/26 (87)

An English import that had equal amounts of comedy acting and lavish spectacle. The British ability at underplaying was appropriately employed in the sketches, especially those featuring Morris Harvey; his best bit was one in which he impersonated a Frenchman and spoke in a clever gibberish sounding just like French, but without using one word from that language. Clown Dezso Retter caused hysterics when he enacted a man engaged in a violent wrestling bout with himself.

The visual pleasures of the show came from a nicely costumed group of chorus girls who figured in numbers such as "Golden Gates," "Enchanted Forest," and "Jabberwalky." One scene, "Ceinture de chastete," proved especially distasteful to Brooks Atkinson, who had kind words for the remainder of the revue.

Solo performers of note in the show included Grace Hayes, Dorothy Whitmore, and Evelyn Herbert, all singers, and Emil Bereo, pianist-comedian. During the run, the show changed its title to *Passions of 1926*.

MERRY-GO-ROUND, THE [Revue] B/LY: Morrie Ryskind and Howard Dietz; M: Henry Souvaine and Jay Gorney; D: Allan Dinehart; CH: Walt Kuhn and Raymond Midgley; P: Richard Herndon; T: Klaw Theatre; 5/31/27 (135)

An exuberant intimate revue that received mixed notices and underwent some revisions during its first month of life. Brooks Atkinson thought it was "an uneven medley of fresh ideas and the hackneyed folderol of the night clubs," but Richard Dana Skinner dubbed it an "unusually sympathetic and delightful entertainment."

There were, among the funnier sketches, ones such as that about a firm of ambulance chasers, Mockowitz, Gogelich, Babblekroit, and Svonk, in which Philip Loeb as Svonk stood out; monologues by veterans William Collier and Marie Cahill; energetic dancing by Evelyn Bennett; Libby Holman's singing of "Hogan's Alley"; the black minstrelsy of the Pan-American Quartet; and so forth.

A number of revisions were introduced to allow for a second edition on 6/4/27. Included was a take off on *The Spider* and a burlesque of an old-time D. W. Griffith-type film.

MERTON OF THE MOVIES [Comedy/Films/Romance] A: George S. Kaufman and Marc Connelly; SC: a story by Harry Leon Wilson; D: Hugh Ford; P: George C. Tyler and Hugh Ford; T: Cort Theatre; 11/13/22 (398)

Kaufman and Connelly were on a fabulous roll when they followed up their hit plays, *Dulcy* and *To the Ladies*, with this extremely popular send-up of Hollywood based on a widely read *Saturday Evening Post* serial. Everything seemed to click in this production, from the script to the staging to the actors. The adaptation was unusually adept, and most thought it was a vast improvement on the original. The tale, observed F.W., "survived the ordeal with colors flying.... It emerged ... a merrier, brighter, shrewder thing." But "the touch of humanity," claimed Heywood Broun, "does not prevent it from being as savage a satire as has ever been directed against the motion pictures."

Glenn Hunter became a star in the title role of the midwestern grocery clerk who dreams only of being a movie star, travels to Hollywood, and is disillusioned when he discovers that most of what he believed from reading fan magazines is untrue; he is helped by the girl he loves (Florence Nash) to break into films and becomes an actor. His desire to be recognized as a serious artist is crushed when the film he makes fails as a work of depth but is a hit when released as a comedy; he has to learn to accept that his is a gift for comic, not dramatic, acting.

Hunter's "technical skill is extraordinary," wrote Arthur Hornblow, "which added to a personality that includes both charm and humor, produces a very creditable young actor."

MESSIN' AROUND [Revue/Blacks] B/D/P: Louis Isquith; M: Jimmy Johnson; LY: Perry Bradford; CH: Eddie Rector; T: Hudson Theatre; 4/22/29 (33)

Because it had a plot of sorts, this show hovered uncertainly between being regarded as either a musical or a revue. What story it contained followed the meanderings of comics Billy McLaurin and James Thompson from Harlem to the South and back again to a night club in their original neighborhood. Fast dancing, heavy rhythm, and passable but unmemorable comedy were its principal contributions. "*Messin' Around*," claimed Perriton Maxwell, "lived up to its title with startling accuracy."

Its most unique feature was a boxing match between two women billed as "champions" in which they bashed "each other with seemingly unfeigned zeal" (*Time*). Cora La Redd, eccentric dancer, was the outstanding performer in the revue.

METEOR [Comedy-Drama/Marriage/Business] A: S. N. Behrman; D: Philip Moeller; S: Raymond Sovey; P: Theatre Guild; T: Guild Theatre; 12/23/29 (92)

The Theatre Guild presented the Lunts in Behrman's "remarkable study of a self-infatuated soul with boundless ambition" (Euphemia Van Rensselaer Wyatt), one Raphael Lord, a Napoleonic man gifted with exceptional foresight whose meteoric success the play encompasses. *Meteor*, for all of its values, had too many failings to make it popular. Perriton Maxwell, for one, thought that Lord's character was simply too unsympathetic to appeal and that this had ruined the work.

Alfred Lunt gave a compelling and fiery performance as the superegotist Lord, whose rise from a college student with unusual prescience to a place as a king of Wall Street five years later is documented. His ruthless nature leads him to almost pathological behavior; his friends drop away, and when he finally makes a disastrous error, he casts aside his wife (Lynn Fontanne) who offers herself as a humble helpmeet to outride this adversity; he resolves to marshall his willpower and master the storms alone.

S. N. Behrman had been required to make extensive revisions in the script before its ultimate showing. There is an anecdote in Roy S. Waldau's *Vintage Years of the Theatre Guild* that concerns the playwright's response to the Guild's Lawrence Langner when the latter asked for improved scenes of conflict and tenderness; Behrman handed Langner several pages of rewritten script and said, "Here, Lawrence, are six pages of conflict, and here are three pages of tenderness." Behrman had to cut down a four-act script to three and had not completed the process by the dress rehearsal. He and director Moeller got into a spate, and both flew out of the theatre in a rage, leaving the actors without an ending. When the play approached the final curtain on opening night out of town, Alfred Lunt had to conclude with a long scene on the phone for which he had no dialogue. He told George Freedley (as reported in *The Lunts*), "I said to the stage manager, believe it or not, that when I said the word 'schlemiel,' he was to take the curtain down. That is the way we played it in Boston, but we got it fixed up by the time we got to New York."

Playwright Behrman later recalled that Alfred Lunt modeled his characterization of Lord on volatile producer Jed Harris and was made up to look like him. Harris inspired other actors as well, among them Laurence Olivier, whose famous Richard III in the movie of that name had features purposely resembling those of the producer. Behrman himself had worked for Harris and it is clear that the chief reason for Lunt's interpretation of the role is that the playwright had based the character on Harris.

MICHAEL AND MARY [Comedy/Marriage/British] A: A. A. Milne; D/P: Charles Hopkins; S: Thomas Farrer; T: Charles Hopkins Theatre; 12/13/29 (246)

A. A. Milne's comedy, set in London, and covering the years from 1905 to 1929, was a Best Play of the Year. It originally was conceived as a flashback drama, but Milne decided at last to write it in chronological sequence. It premiered locally nearly two months before being seen in London with Edna Best and Herbert Marshall.

Threads of sentiment, laughter, and melodrama ran through the fabric of this popular piece (originally titled *This Flower* after a line in Shakespeare). To some it bore a thesis, phrased by Perriton Maxwell as "the notion that we are never safe from the consequences of what society may call a crime, however white it may appear." The story supporting this idea depicted Mary (Edith Barratt) in 1905, deserted by her rat of a spouse for places unknown, marrying Michael (Henry Hull) on the chance that the first husband will never return. Their happily bigamous marriage is momentarily disrupted when the husband (Vernon Kelso) does return thirteen years later to blackmail them; a fatal heart attack prevents him from following through. However, at the very end, their illegal arrangement is once more on the brink of discovery.

Michael and Mary had an occasional cloying moment, but the *Times* reckoned

it "a constantly engrossing play with considerable charm and ingenious surprises." John Hutchens was particularly fond of how Michael and Mary were
"rendered into warm, human people by talk that is fluent, elliptical, full of small
humors and intimate shades."

MICHEL AUCLAIR [Comedy-Drama/Romance/French] A: Charles Vildrac;
D/DS: Robert Edmond Jones; P: Provincetown Players; T: Provincetown Playhouse (OB); 3/4/25 (20)

An importation from France that met with mingled reactions, this Vildrac
work centered on the naive village idealist named in the title (Edgar Stehli) who
loves Suzanne, but who leaves her for a year while he studies in Paris so that
he may return to found a bookstore. When he comes back, Suzanne has married
the soldier Armand (Walter Abel), a gambling n'er do well. The warm-hearted
Michel then strives to help the couple out, lending them money, and helping to
set Armand up in business.

The piece was seen as having a lovely first act but as bogging down afterwards
in Pollyanna optimism and cloying sentimentality. "It was like breaking in upon
a mellow twilight with a fireworks display for the sweetness of adversity,"
according to John Anderson.

MIDDLE WATCH, THE [Comedy/Sea/Romance/British] A: Ian Hay (John
Hay Beith) and Stephen King-Hall; D: Ian Hay; P: Arch Selwyn and Charles B.
Cochran; T: Times Square Theatre; 10/16/29 (29)

The H.M.S. *Falcon*, a British marine cruiser, served as setting for this bedroom
farce imported following a London success. "It is neither subtle nor suave. It
is candidly silly," wrote the *Times*.

A couple of young women, Fay Eaton (Dodo Watts) and her American pal
Mary Carlton (Ruth Abbott), dining aboard the ship with the Captain (Robert
Mawdesly), to whom the former is engaged, find themselves stuck on board
when the launch's engine fails, the ship is ordered out to sea, and the grumpy
Admiral (Fred Kerr) comes aboard. The fun comes from the efforts to keep this
gentleman from learning of the ladies' presence.

Every effort was made to captivate the audience with a nautical atmosphere,
including having them enter the playhouse on a gangplank and dressing the
ushers in sailor uniforms.

MIDSUMMER NIGHT'S DREAM, A [Dramatic Revival/German Language]
A: William Shakespeare; M: Felix Mendelssohn; D: Max Reinhardt; S: Oscar
Strnad; C: Ernest de Weerth; P: Gilbert Miller; T: Century Theatre; 11/17/27
(23)

Max Reinhardt, the German-speaking-world's most famous regisseur, brought
his actors from Berlin's Deutsches Theatre and Vienna's Josefstadt Theatre to
New York for a repertory season in which this revival figured importantly. Staged
in many variations by Reinhardt throughout his career, this version of the magical

comedy did not equally impress local critics. The once-daring innovations (he had first staged the play in 1905) now seemed somewhat tame, but the spectacular beauties still claimed respect. Some complained that the play was swallowed by all of the pageantry, but most agreed that, as an example of how the resources of the theatre could contrive to be blended into a unity of stunning effect, the work was exemplary. Stark Young, indeed, considered it superior to the director's world-famed *The Miracle*.

Given an atmosphere distinctly Teutonic, this *Dream* was staged on a masterly circular setting of steps, slopes, and levels, allowing for more than thirty entrance areas and backed by an "open space where great stars hung and sometimes the crescent moon" (Young). The exquisitely theatrical costumes were much re-marked upon, among them the choice of giving Lysander and Demetrius "the exalted and plumed abstractions of an Eighteenth Century Ballet" (John Mason Brown). Joseph Wood Krutch wrote, "Reinhardt is content with nothing less than a complete realization of every all-but-impossible suggestion of the text. The enchanted wood must actually be filled with incredibly magic lights and shadows, fairies, appearing from nowhere, must dance with an agility hitherto existing only in Shakespeare's imagination; and, in short, the whole poem must be translated into visual terms." The actors, exclaimed Krutch, had "heroic voices and the agility of acrobats."

The great Alexander Moissi played Oberon, Vladimir Sokoloff was the un-forgettable Puck, Hans and Hermann Thimig were Lysander and Demetrius, American actress Rosamond Pinchot played Helena, Maria Solveg was Hermia, Lili Darvas acted Titania, and Otto Wallburg clowned as Bottom.

(1) MIKADO, THE [Musical Revival] B/LY: William S. Gilbert; M: Arthur Sullivan; D: Milton Aborn; P: Messrs. Shubert; T: Forty-fourth Street Theatre; 4/11/25 (65)

Two Gilbert and Sullivan works were revived on Broadway in the same week, *The Mikado* and *Princess Ida*, and both received excellent notices. *The Mikado* was a grandiose production; "It's mounted with all the wholesaledness of a circus, exults in choruses of staggering size and volume, an overflowing or-chestra, principals taken ad-lib. from opera and extravaganza," reported Gilbert W. Gabriel.

The revival had controversial elements in it, but most agreed that it was exceptionally well sung. William Danforth's Mikado was strongly praised for his traditional rendering, and Tom Burke's Nanki-Poo and Marguerite Namara's Yum-Yum were effective. The most debated performance was that of vaude-villian Lupino Lane as Ko-Ko, whose acrobatic dexterity made the character more of a comic gymnast than a singing clown.

(2) D: Winthrop Ames; S: Raymond Sovey; CH: Michio Ito; P: Winthrop Ames's Gilbert and Sullivan Opera Company; T: Royale Theatre; 9/17/27 (110)

The third successful Gilbert and Sullivan revival staged by Winthrop Ames in the midtwenties, *The Mikado* eventually played for a time in repertory with the others, *Iolanthe* and *The Pirates of Penzance*. Purists were perturbed by some libretto liberties and directorial divagations, but others found this "an extraordinarily beautiful production, instinct with grace and loveliness, gloriously sung and lavishly staged," as Brooks Atkinson phrased it. Some of the acting, especially the broad comic parts, was middling, though. William Williams as Nanki-Poo, Lois Bennett as Yum-Yum, and John Barclay as the Mikado were almost able to compensate for lesser choices in the casting.

Ames's thoroughly detailed and well-drilled ensemble productions were marvels of the day. *Time* described some of the staging ideas: "Mr. Ames sees to it that the stage keeps moving. His Mikado skips over huddles of prostrate subjects. His sonorous aristocrat, Pooh-Bah, is tantalized by lively, romping girls. The color combinations change and move, too, so vividly that the performance could fascinate a deaf-mute."

MIKE ANGELO [Comedy/Art/Romance] A: Edward Locke; D: Clifford Brooke; P: Oliver Morosco; T: Morosco Theatre; 1/8/23 (48)

Leo Carrillo's light comic touch in the role of an aspiring Italian artist whose ancestry includes Michaelangelo validated this otherwise "simple little . . . tame and . . . unexciting" play of "little wit and less invention" (Q.M.).

Edward Locke's sentimental comedy presented Carrillo as Mike Angelo, who wants to be a painter badly enough to endure any petty chores around the studios that will allow him to absorb the techniques of the pros. In love with the daughter of a studio maestro, apparently also the beloved of Russian painter Smirnoff (Robert Strange), he enters a painting competition but selflessly switches his picture with that of his rival so the latter can win and get the girl. As such plots would have it, though, Smirnoff is a bounder, and he too sneaks into the gallery, but his aim is to smudge the painting he believes is Mike's. In the end the truth appears, and Mike is on his way to artistic and romantic success.

MILESTONES and "THE LITTLE FATHER OF THE WILDERNESS"
DS: Eric Pape; P: Players' Club; T: Empire Theatre; 6/2/30 (8)
Milestones [Dramatic Revival] A: Arnold Bennett and Edward Knoblock; D: Henry Stillman; "The Little Father of the Wilderness" [Drama/Period/One-Act/France] A/D: Austin Strong

A revival of the sentimental 1912 British chronicle play given as the annual production of the Players Club, whose "all-star" replications were normally of old classics. *Milestones* examined the business and personal activities of the Rhead family's members over three generations, from 1860 to 1885 to 1912.

Richard Dana Skinner maintained that no stars in the "name above the title" sense were to be found here, but that they were all respected "feature" players doing their utmost to provide a valid experience: "Such perfection of ensemble is rarely to be found on any stage." A play he remembered as "solemn" and "artful" now seemed to have "taken on glow, warmth and color." Dorothy

Stickney as Rose, Tom Powers as John Rhead, Beulah Bondi as Gertrude Rhead, Ernest Cossart as Ned Pym, and Selena Royle as Emily were lauded for their acting.

A one-act curtain raiser with a cast of forty-one, "The Little Father of the Wilderness" was a period piece set in France during the reign of Louis XV (Frederick Lewis) and concerned an incident in the life of Canadian missionary Pére Marlotte (Francis Wilson). Walter Hampden, Gene Lockhart, Margalo Gillmore, and Augustin Duncan were key figures in the presentation.

MILGRIM'S PROGRESS [Comedy/Small Town/Jews/Family/Romance/Business] A: B. Harrison Orkow; D: Louis Mann and Edwin Maxwell; P: J. M. Welch; T: Wallack's Theatre; 12/22/24 (66)

The *Times* noted with a sigh that *Milgrim's Progress* was "nothing more than a shell to cover the familiar theatrical endeavors of Louis Mann" in one of his conventional Jewish dialect roles. He acted the part of David Milgrim, a toymaker residing in a small Connecticut town, who earns a sudden fortune by the invention of a dyeing process, and is pressured by his educated son (Robert Williams) and daughter (Jeanne Greene) to move to New York City. He is uncomfortable there amid the city's blandishments and becomes even more so when he sees the baleful influence of urban mores on his family. In the end, he moves back to Connecticut, and his family returns there with him. Among the subplots was one concerning the planned marriage of the son to a Gentile girl (Mildred Wayne) who dances in the *Follies*, a marriage that parental interference will not affect.

The *Times* claimed that the plot was "shamelessly cheap," and Q.M. argued that "it does not make a very good play."

MIMA (A vörös malom) [Drama/Fantasy/Religion/Romance/Sex/Hungarian] A: Ferenc Molnar; AD/D/P: David Belasco; M: Edwin Ludwig; S: Joseph Wickes; T: Belasco Theatre; 12/12/28 (180)

Spectacular sets, lighting, and special effects overwhelmed the critics attending this Molnar fantasy (actually, an adaptation of his play *The Red Mill*). Belasco had made an outlay of $325,000 to alter the theatre to accommodate the extensive machinery required; the orchestra pit was removed and the proscenium arch taken apart, the boxes covered in metal sheets, and elevators installed on the stage proper. The result was a triumph of showmanship disguising a paltry piece of overblown dramaturgy. George Jean Nathan sniffed, "He has simply taken most of the scenic devices of the old Christmas pantomimes and, by the expenditure of a lot of money, dolled them up."

The play was a modern morality set in Hades, where Magister (A. E. Anson), an aide to Satan (Reginald Carrington), demonstrates for the latter his new invention, the Red Mill, designed to doom decent men to perdition in sixty minutes. Janos (Sidney Blackmer) is chosen as the guinea pig; under the influence of the machine in its guise as the temptress Mima (Lenore Ulric) he becomes almost completely corrupted, but before that is achieved weeps a tear for his old mother and thereby destroys the machine.

Perriton Maxwell sneered at *Mima* as "a trite and banal sermon on the persistence of virtue in its contest with sin."

MIMIC WORLD OF 1921, THE [Revue] B/LY: Harold Atteridge, James Hussey, and Owen Murphy; M: Jean Schwartz, Lew Pollock, and Owen Murphy; D/CH: Allan K. Foster; P: Messrs. Shubert; T: Century Promenade; 8/15/21 (27)

An extravagantly produced revue that opened a new space, the Century Promenade, atop the roof of the Century Theatre. Basically, the show was a series of twenty-six vaudeville acts, lacking continuity of theme or style. Elaborate showgirl scenes mixed with farcical sketches and specialty bits. An unusual musical routine, "Shakespeare's Garden of Love," introduced the Bard and various of his famous characters, all of them singing a jazz number. Mae West made her first Broadway visit of the decade in this routine, appearing as a sexy Cleopatra doing a bump and grind as she crossed the stage. Marc Connelly, remembering the moment over half a century later, declared, "Her grind was very, very graphic and very interesting. Caught the true spirit of Egypt" (quoted in George Eels and Stanley Musgrove's *Mae West: A Biography*). West was also seen as Shifty Liz in a "Times Square after Midnight" sketch, a French vamp in a Cafe de Paris scene, and a black-wigged Alla Nazimova in yet another bit.

The show was not particularly imaginative, and the *Times* called it "dreary." When headliner Jimmy Hussey failed to appear because of a backstage tiff, popular comic dancer James Barton was recruited following the final curtain of his show downstairs, *The Last Waltz*.

MINICK [Comedy/Family/Old Age] A: George S. Kaufman and Edna Ferber; SC: "Old Man Minick," a short story by Edna Ferber; D/P: Winthrop Ames; S: Woodman Thompson; T: Booth Theatre; 9/24/24 (154)

Constructed from a story so simple the critics thought of it as plotless, this successful Edna Ferber-George S. Kaufman collaboration was reducible to the following situation: an independent-minded old man, Minick (O. P. Heggie), takes up residence in Chicago with his son (Frederic Burt) and daughter-in-law (Phyllis Povah), who patiently put up with all of his crochets and eccentricities. When he disrupts a ladies' civic club meeting in the house, a scene of hilarity ensues as the daughter-in-law's frustration boils over. Having become friendly with the inhabitants of a nearby old-folks home, Minick eventually opts for retirement to that abode, realizing that he is better off among those of his own generation and interests.

Although the generation gap theme was familiar, this pleasant comedy based on a Ferber story had a decidedly original flavor to its treatment. A few hailed *Minick* as a major new work; others recognized its excellence, yet turned it down for various reasons. To Arthur Hornblow, *Minick* was "full of quiet sentiment and kindly humor,'' with finely drawn characters. Those who concluded that the play's blessings were mixed included *Time*, which said *Minick* had overshot ''the mark by a too tenacious realism. The characters are types rather than individuals.''

A month after it opened *Minick* moved into the smaller Bijou, where it ran out its days.

MIRACLE, THE (Das Mirakel) [Pantomime/Period/Religion/Fantasy/German] A: Karl Vollmoeller; M: Engelbert Humperdinck; D: Max Reinhardt; DS: Norman Bel Geddes; P: F. Ray Comstock and Morris Gest; T: Century Theatre; 1/16/24 (300)

Hoopla surrounding the American presentation of famed German director Max Reinhardt's religious spectacle led George Jean Nathan to grumble that ''art and dignity should have something in common.'' Karl Vollmoeller's dramatization of an old legend in which a young nun drawn to worldly pleasures endures much suffering and returns to the church to find that the Virgin Mother's statue had come to life and performed her sisterly duties while she was away, played in pantomime to music by Engelbert Humperdinck, was staged anew after a London run some twelve years before. Norman Bel Geddes was hired to design the production and turned the Century Theater into the interior of a Gothic cathedral.

The *Times* devoted one article to statistics about the show—how many props, how much lamp black, how many workers—for which the weekly preproduction payroll exceeded $40,000. Then there was the battle of the virgins: Reinhardt was unable to break a contract with his London Madonna, Maria Carmi, married to Vollmoeller during the British run but since become Princess Matchabelli. However, he seized an opportunity to engage Lady Diana Manners, a duke's daughter considered by many the most beautiful woman in the world, and producer Morris Gest hit upon ways to ease Carmi out. Lady Diana and the Princess were to alternate performances, but in a lot drawing stacked in her favor, Lady Diana won for the opening night. When the Princess was playing the Madonna, Gest had Lady Diana act the Nun. The Princess bowed out, and Lady Diana alternated the Madonna with opera star Mary Garden, and the Nun with Rosamond Pinchot. Other notables in the cast included Werner Kraus of *The Cabinet of Dr. Caligari* film fame as the Piper and Rudolph Schildkraut as the Emperor; there were some 700 extras. The principal players and Bel Geddes's designs won lavish praise from most critics.

Percy Hammond described what happened as the audience entered. They heard sacred music, were ushered by women in nun's wimples to seats that were pews, and heard the distant sound of church bells. Bel Geddes's cathedral featured ''vaulted ceilings, columns, chimes and pipe-organs, stained-glass windows and organs.'' When the pantomime began, choirs sang, organs pealed, and the widened aisles filled with worshipers. Nuns flooded the scene in hundreds, and as light lifted upon the altar the Madonna was seen ''motionless in her niche, with all the sorrows of the Lady of Tears in her eloquent eyes.''

John Corbin was as entranced, praising all of the elements and concluding: "But in it all and through it all was the masterly magic of Reinhardt's manipulation of crowds.... Everywhere the scene was multitudinously animated, vitalized, by the sweep of Reinhardt's imagination and his marvelous sense of detail." Both Corbin and Heywood Broun compared the production favorably with the Moscow Art Theatre's repertoire, Broun noting that not even the Russian troupe "has made man in the mass more completely alive." He praised "an extraordinary event in the history of the American stage. Max Reinhardt has brought into the theatre more beauty than we have ever seen there before. And combined with this beauty there is a mad, terrifying excitement."

H.H.

MIRAGE, THE [Drama/Sex/Romance] A/D: Edgar Selwyn; P: Selwyns; T: Times Square Theatre; 9/30/20 (190)

The opening of the new Times Square Theatre was marked by this expensively produced kept-woman melodrama that bore a resemblance to Eugene Walter's *The Easiest Way*. The shopworn story was that of small-town girl Irene Martin (Florence Reed), who, failing to make a successful career in New York, becomes the mistress of a local tycoon (Malcolm Williams); after seven years, when her old boyfriend (Allan Dinehart) is willing to take her back, she refuses to go until she can become truly worthy of him.

Alexander Woollcott criticized the author for making the basically affecting story "garish and bedizened," replete with purple lines like that the girl tells her mother when the truth about her is revealed: "You are my mother and I love you even if I am what the world calls (sob) a bad woman." Ludwig Lewisohn thought the play's "undoing" was the dramatist's assumption that the heroine was wicked, having taken "all moral attitudes at their public and advertised value."

MIRRORS [Drama/Sex/Marriage/Youth/Family] A: Milton Herbert Gropper; D/P: Albert Lewis; S: Nicholas Yellenti; T: Forrest Theatre; 1/18/28 (13)

The potentially provocative subject matter of this play was not geared toward placating critics with strictly moral sensibilities. It told of hanky panky in the suburbs, where the Nortons (Hale Hamilton and Marie Nordstrom), a middle-aged couple, and their neighbors are so into mate-swapping parties and living it up that their teenage kids begin to mirror their example. Only one upright daughter (Sylvia Sidney) resists the temptations; her standards temporarily alarm the Nortons. She wins the banker's son she wanted without having to compromise herself.

"If the play had got anywhere," criticized Perriton Maxwell, "there might have been a reason for it. But it was only a mirror reflecting the dirty, bad taste of a slimy night before."

MISANTHROPE, LE (The Misanthrope) [Dramatic Revival/French Language] A: Moliere; P: Messrs. Shubert; T: Thirty-ninth Street Theatre; 11/21/22 (2)

Moliere's dark comedy was revived in French by the visiting troup of Comédie Française sociétaire Cecile Sorel, with Albert Lambert in the role of Alceste and Sorel as Celimene. Alceste was made up to resemble the playwright himself. Sorel wore costumes of lavish design, but their period was indeterminate. Lambert had some line trouble but was otherwise admirable, according to the *Times*.

Sorel returned to New York with a new company in 1926 and brought *Le Misanthrope* as part of her repertory. She again essayed Celimene, but her Alceste this time was Louis Ravet. The play failed to interest, the *Times* noting the "yards and yards of monotonous, if clever rhyming and rhetoric." Sorel was expert, but it was wondered why she bothered with the old classic. It was years before a suitable presentation was given locally. The production was offered at the Cosmopolitan Theatre from 12/9/26 for four performances.

MISMATES [Drama/Marriage/Crime/Romance] A/P: Myron C. Fagan; D: Rollo Lloyd; T: Times Square Theatre; 4/13/25 (72)

Gilbert W. Gabriel reported, "Something called *Mismates*...proved to be frank, hard-breathing melodrama of the Bronx category. Take it or leave it. Even if you take it, you will probably leave early."

The most original feature of this poorly welcomed drama of marital squabbling was the presence onstage for about a minute at the show's start of an infant, about eighteen months old. The baby played the child of a mismatched couple, Judy (Clara Joel) and Jim (C. Henry Gordon), who come from different social backgrounds, and whose lives together lead to bitter wrangling over their lack of understanding of each other. Judy eventually goes to jail for a murder her brother committed, and her husband, thinking her dead, remarries. Only the intervention of a friend who loves her (Minor Watson) prevents her from killing Jim when she escapes from jail.

The baby was soon fired from the cast when a local child-protection agency protested about its presence to the producers.

MISS LULU BETT [Comedy/Small Town/Family/Marriage/Romance] A: Zona Gale; SC: Gale's novel of the same name; D/P: Brock Pemberton; T: Belmont Theatre; 12/27/20 (201)

The 1920–1921 Pulitzer Prize-winning play was, strange to say, not one of the Ten Best chosen by Burns Mantle for his annual compilation. It was based on Zona Gale's own best-seller, which she dramatized in a mere eight days.

Gale's Cinderella story concerns the thirty-four-year-old title character Lulu (Carroll McComas), a spinster who works as a drudge in the home of her self-satisfied sister Ina (Catherine Calhoun Doucet) and brother-in-law Dwight (William E. Holden), from whom she receives her room and board as payment. Dwight's friendly brother Ninian (Brigham Royce) shows up and a mock marriage ceremony between him and Lulu is jokingly arranged by Dwight, who then announces that the nuptials are binding, given his position as village magistrate. The couple depart only for Ninian to inform Lulu that he already is wed but believes his wife to be dead. Lulu leaves him and returns home, where her relatives now fear for their reputations. As originally produced, the ending had the first wife turn out to be alive, leading Lulu to contemplate the proposal of a local admirer; as revised shortly after the opening, the play concluded happily by offering proof that Ninian was indeed a widower.

Miss Lulu Bett actually premiered at Sing-Sing in a performance for the inmates the night before it came to Broadway. It appealed for the veracity and humor of its small-town characterizations, which Alan Dale called Dickensian, but it did not meet with the sort of potent response one would have expected from a Pulitzer Prize play. Many thought it an inferior adaptation of the novel. "All of Miss Gale's amusing satire and her truthful observation of American middle life were in the play, just as they had been in the novel. But they were projected through a medium to which they had not been adjusted," wrote the *Herald*.

Gale defended her revision of the ending on the basis of popular opinion having been opposed to the original situation in which Lulu was left alone to contemplate her future. There were those, like Ludwig Lewisohn, however, who had staunchly defended the work and who insisted that the revision was a betrayal of the plot's inevitability and that Lulu's "act of liberation is thus stultified and with it the significance and strength of the dramatic action sacrificed at one blow."

MR. FAUST [Drama/Verse/Religion] A: Arthur Davison Ficke; D/P: Ellen Van Volkenburg; S: Cleon Throckmorton; T: Provincetown Playhouse (OB); 1/30/22 (15)

A contemporary blank verse retelling of the great Faust story about an ultra-individualist, Mr. Faust (Maurice Browne). It was given an impressively skilled production, with excellent designs by Cleon Throckmorton, but stirred little more than passing interest. The *Times* dismissed the effort, by a minor poet of the day, as a "not very important..., somewhat hollow though high-sounding inquiry into the meaning of life.... The play is repetitious, undramatic, and only very occasionally interesting."

Ficke's version of the legend depicts Mr. Faust as a disaffected young New Yorker, world weary at the meaninglessness of life, to whom Nicholas Satan (Moroni Olsen) appears and offers a place in paradise if only the man will become his ally. Faust finds solace in neither an Indian temple nor a cathedral. Finally, a fanatical acquaintance kills the heart-sore young man.

MISTER MALATESTA (Papa Joe) [Comedy-Drama/Family/Romance] A: William Ricciardi; P: R. G. Kemmet; T: Princess Theatre; 2/26/23 (96)

A sort of "Guisseppi's Irish Mary" (B.F.), this picture of the domestic ups and downs in a Bronx Italian stevedore's family (first produced in London) was a sentimental piece overlaid with melodrama, enjoyed by a few, and reviled by many.

Joe Malatesta (William Ricciardi), married to a woman of Irish extraction (Ida Fitzhugh), is a well-to-do fellow with a lawyer son and a foster daughter (Rhys Derby), with whom the son has had an affair and to whom Joe makes his son get married. All ends happily when the son reveals that he has loved the girl all along.

Laurence Stallings said, "It is not a good play; it is a very bad play." Alison Smith termed it "a naive and preposterous little drama."

During the run, its title was changed to *Papa Joe*.

MR. MONEYPENNY [Comedy/Family/Fantasy] A/P: Channing Pollock; D: Richard Boleslavsky; DS: Robert Edmond Jones; T: Liberty Theatre; 10/16/28 (62)

More than fifty characters figured in this "verbal cartoon" of a Faustian morality play about timid, middle-aged bank clerk John Jones (Donald Meek); a Mephistophelian figure, Mr. Moneypenny (Hale Hamilton), makes it possible for him to have whatever he wants in a material way. But despite the delights that Jones now experiences, he fails to find true happiness. Realizing the obvious point that money is the root of all evil, he returns to his family's welcome embrace.

The critics disliked the allegorical play's overt didacticism and platitudinousness. Its manner was extravagantly expressionistic, with fragmented, telegraphic scenes, jazz music, and imaginative scenery. Staging aside, it failed to attract interest. Robert Littel said that "for all its attempts in the way of half-mad symbolical jumble, for all its use of the grammar of distortion. . . [it] is as prosaic as noonday glare."

Channing Pollock considered this his finest play; disillusioned by its negative reception, he wrote only one more play for Broadway before retiring from the theatre. As producer of the play (his only experience in this regard) he attempted to institute what he believed the necessary reform of low admission prices. However, the $100,000 production costs with weekly expenses of more than $14,000 (it had a company of 112 and used two orchestras) proved too much with seats at a two dollar top. Pollock's disheartening experiences with the play are provided in his memoir *Harvest of My Years*.

(1) MR. PIM PASSES BY [Comedy/Family/British/Romance] A: A. A. Milne; D: Philip Moeller; S: Lee Simonson; P: Theatre Guild; T: GarrickTheatre; 2/28/ 21 (210)

Kenneth Macgowan recorded that "The Theatre Guild scored a popular success and furnished also an evening of intelligent amusement in its production of *Mr. Pim Passes By*." Into a well-mannered Buckinghamshire country house ventures the mild, absent-minded, little old Australian visitor Carraway Pim (Erskine

Sanford); because of his confusion over names, he gives the house's owners, George and Olivia Marden (Dudley Digges and Laura Hope Crews), reason to believe that he recently met a man they assume to be Mrs. Marden's first husband, presumed dead. The plot hinges on their belief that they are bigamists and on the wife's getting her spouse, once they learn from Pim that the original husband has just died, to agree both to her niece's (Phyllis Povah) marriage and to her own new home decorations as conditions before she will marry him in the manner he now deems proper. It is discovered, after all, that Pim had the whole thing confused and had never met the man he said he had.

"The consequences of [Mr. Pim's] news—the revelation to the wife of attitudes in her husband that she had somehow never suspected, and the humorous and satiric exposition of character which this entails—are all the more amusing because of the unreality of the cause from which they spring," commented Macgowan. John Ranken Towse thought it was all a bit uneven but said, "it is written throughout in the true vein of comedy and well furnished with natural and amusing incidents and clever sketches of character."

(2) [Dramatic Revival] D: Philip Moeller; S: Kate Lawrence; P: Theatre Guild; T: Guild Theatre; 4/18/27 (36)

Laura Hope Crews, Erskine Sanford, and Dudley Digges returned to their original roles in this Theatre Guild revival at the Garrick. The play was very warmly applauded for its excellent ensemble and still-appealing substance. Few plays done during the six years between the original staging and this one, declared the *Times*, "have provoked more quiet, reflective enjoyment."

MISTER PITT [Drama/Small Town/Marriage/Family] A: Zona Gale; SC: Zona Gale's novel of the same name; D/P: Brock Pemberton; S: Herman Rosse; T: Thirty-ninth Street Theatre; 1/22/24 (87)

George Jean Nathan observed, "The trouble with Zona Gale is perfectly clear. She looks down upon the theatre. To her, the stage is the place where good novels go when they die." Heywood Broun found her play "a moving and appealing study of inarticulate man" but then paid a second visit and revised his opinion to consider it the study of a Nora-like woman in a situation of marital incompatability.

Marshall Pitt (Walter Huston), canned-goods salesman, marries Barbara Ellsworth (Minna Gombell) when she appreciates the sympathy he expresses upon her father's death. Within a year Barbara is fed up with him and runs off with a jazz musician. Marshall leaves for the Klondike, where he strikes it rich, but when he finally returns, his teenage son rejects him.

John Corbin had mixed feelings about the play but agreed with other commentators that Walter Huston was impressive in his legitimate Broadway debut after a vaudeville career. "[H]e endowed Mr. Pitt with a simplicity and translucency of goodness, a native modesty and a power of abiding affection," Corbin noted.

H.H.

MISTER ROMEO [Comedy/Sex/Marriage/Romance/Show Business] A: Harry Wagstaff Gribble and Wallace A. Manheimer; D: Edward Eliscu; P: Murray Phillips; T: Wallack's Theatre; 9/5/27 (16)

A "routine and only sporadically entertaining" (*Times*) comedy about a timid middle-aged gent (J. C. Nugent) whose sex drive steers him to the flat of burlesque performers Maisie Clark (Jane Meredith) and Helen Hughes (Sheila Trent), but whose spouse (Thais Lawton) conspires with the women to teach him a lesson and cure him of his roaming ways. Meanwhile a subplot about the bumpy romance between Helen and burlesque manager Buck Edwards (G. Pat Collins) is happily resolved.

MRS. BUMPSTEAD-LEIGH [Dramatic Revival] A: Harry James Smith; D/P: George C. Tyler; S: Gates and Morange; T: Klaw Theatre; 4/1/29 (72)

Mrs. Fiske brought back to town this comedy in which she had starred with some success in 1911; once again she was Della Sales, the Iowa social climber who calls herself Mrs. Bumpstead-Leigh in an effort to break into Long Island high society, only to be recognized by her small-town boyfriend (Sidney Toler). "As drama *Mrs. Bumpstead-Leigh* dates back to the dusting parlormaid period," noted Euphemia Van Rensselaer Wyatt. Mrs. Fiske's mannerisms were suited to the dated comedy, especially in her triumphant second-act scene when she must counter her old beau's suspicions. Trying to define Mrs. Fiske's success in such scenes, Richard Dana Skinner wrote that it could best be attributed to her timing; "[W]ith Mrs. Fiske the precise timing comes as spontaneously and joyously as the measures of a waltz."

MRS. DANE'S DEFENSE [Dramatic Revival] A: Henry Arthur Jones; D: Clifford Brooke; P: Chamberlain Brown; T: Cosmopolitan Theatre; 2/6/28 (16)

Henry Arthur Jones's 1900 drama of Victorian morality, about a stern judge (Robert Warwick) who separates his son (Horace Braham) from the woman (Violet Heming) he cherishes because the lady had once been involved in a serious scandal, was revived in a capable version that nevertheless failed miserably because of the script's outdatedness. As *Time* observed, "Older theatregoers remembered the sex dialectics of their youth. Younger ones were mystified by a creed of elaborate duplicity."

MRS. PARTRIDGE PRESENTS [Comedy/Family/Romance] A: Mary Kennedy and Ruth Hawthorne; D/P: Guthrie McClintic; T: Belmont Theatre; 1/5/25 (146)

"[A]n American comedy, humorous and skilfully done" (Louis Bromfield), that was found largely effective, because, said Arthur Hornblow, "Its dialogue is the genuine conversation exchanged between real human beings. The problems which arise are those of men and women harassed by the same trials which confront all of us." The play was chosen by Burns Mantle as one of the Best Plays of 1924–1925.

A generation-gap comedy that was often genuinely risible, *Mrs. Partridge Presents* starred veteran Blanche Bates as a wealthy widow who seeks to make her son (Edward Emery, Jr.) and daughter (Sylvia Field) enter careers she has chosen for them. She wants the boy to be an artist, the girl an actress, but the young people are perfectly content with the mediocrity of their lives and rebel against her dictates.

The play started quietly, noted E. W. Osborn, but before one knew it, "It just reached right over the footlights and took hold, and it never let go for an instant."

In the role of a young, slow-drawling family friend, Ruth Gordon attracted most attention. "One ought. . .to be a little subdued and shaken by anything so perfect," asserted Heywood Broun.

In his autobiography *Me and Kit*, Guthrie McClintic fondly remembered his experience working with the grand star, Blanche Bates, who came out of retirement to do this play. "Miss Bates was real theatre—age hadn't withered nor custom staled her attitude or enthusiasm. . . .There was never a moment when any of [her younger co-stars] was made to feel any less important to the play than she." Referring to Bates's sense of humor, McClintic recalled a time during rehearsals when Ruth Gordon arrived late, apologizing profusely. When McClintic noticed that the veteran had changed her usual place to sit next to Gordon and he asked her her reason, she responded, "I thought it might give me courage."

MRS. WARREN'S PROFESSION [Dramatic Revival] A: George Bernard Shaw; D/P: Mary Shaw; T: Punch and Judy Theatre; 2/22/22 (25)

Mary Shaw, who had been among those arrested when Shaw's once-controversial 1894 play was first staged in America, and who had appeared in many subsequent revivals of it, gave her last performance of Mrs. Warren in this production, which she staged along with Ibsen's *Ghosts*. In the role of the Victorian-era woman who parlayed her business instincts into a chain of thriving brothels, Shaw, said the *Tribune*, "leaves nothing to be desired." However, the Playgoer claimed that the piece was ill rehearsed and raggedly acted. "Every player went more or less 'on his own,' and the performance resolved itself into a memory test in which. . .the actor with the smallest part scored the highest mark."

MIXED DOUBLES [Comedy/Marriage/British] A: Frank Stayton; D: C. Aubrey Smith; S: Watson Barratt; P: Messrs. Shubert; T: Bijou Theatre; 4/26/27 (12)

A British marital farce of such confusing plot complexity that the actors as well as the audience seemed benumbed by it all. Set among members of the upper classes, it dealt with mixups regarding two married couples whom the action contrives to make believe they are not wed. Complications keep mushrooming until all is happily resolved. "Perhaps Mr. Stayton's piece is so bad because it is too good," suggested Brooks Atkinson, "because he has stirred up the plot so superingeniously." Thurston Hall, Margaret Lawrence, Eric Blore, Marion Coakley, and John Williams were among the actors who got less than two weeks work in it.

MIXED MARRIAGE [Dramatic Revival] A: St. John Ervine; S: Rollo Peters; T: Bramhall Playhouse (OB); 12/14/20 (107)

Irish dramatist and critic St. John Ervine's first produced work, originally staged in Ireland in 1911 and soon after seen briefly in New York, was a tragedy about religious bigotry among Irish Catholics and Protestants. Based on an actual incident, it dramatized the outcome of a situation in which an Orangeman, John Rainey (Augustin Duncan), is brought in by fellow workmen as a peacemaking force to a labor dispute, and who abandons his own professed liberalism when his son's (Rollo Peters) fiancée turns out to be Catholic; the girl (Angela McCahill) is killed in the riots he helps stir up.

Produced by a band of outstanding players, including Margaret Wycherly and Barry McCollum, the play stood forth as "an absorbingly interesting work, its last act conspicuously strained and awkward...but its first three adroitly and wisely and humorously written," according to Alexander Woollcott. Ludwig Lewisohn insisted on the pertinence of the theme that suggested how "accidental divisions keep men tragically weak in the face of real and common dangers."

MOB, THE [Drama/War/British] A: John Galsworthy; DS: Warren Dahler; P: Neighborhood Playhouse; T: Neighborhood Playhouse (OB); 10/9/20 (95)

Galsworthy's drama, produced in England in 1914, proved "a thoughtful and humorless play" (Alexander Woollcott) about a British statesman (Ian Maclaren) who tries without avail to prevent his country from engaging in a fateful war. He is publicly ridiculed for his pacificism and loses his wife (Deirdre Doyle) in the process but does not stop his campaigns until he is killed by a rampaging mob that invades his home. In an epilogue set years in the future, a statue dedicated to his idealism is revealed. The drama's subject was ostensibly the Boer War, which was vastly unpopular in England. Prepared for a 1914 staging in New York, it was withdrawn by the author so as not to draw comparisons with the most recent conflagration.

Ludwig Lewisohn wrote that Galsworthy's "moral courage was impaired by a touch of sentiment and a fear of impropriety. The consequence is that he sacrificed a great deal to an artifical lucidity and balance which give the play a structure...calculatedly geometrical." The play's ideas, in the face of World War I, seemed too lightweight an attack on the evils of imperialism, the critic noted. Kenneth Macgowan saw the work as an attack on the mob and not on imperialism, and this he found to be imperfectly expressed: "Mobs solidify wars once they are started, and are venomous in their patriotism. But mobs do not begin wars."

MOLLY DARLING [Musical/Romance/Show Business] B: Otto Harbach and William Cary Duncan; M: Tom Johnstone; LY: Phil Cook; D/CH: Julian Mitchell; P: Moore and Megley; T: Liberty Theatre; 9/1/22 (101)

"A so-so, routine musical comedy" (Alexander Woollcott) that provided a modicum of entertainment for tired businessmen, particularly via the comedic dancing skills of the versatile Jack Donahue.

The Cinderella story concerned Molly Ricardo (Mary Milburn), a poor, young woman whose father (Albert Roccardi), a destitute violin maker, is threatened with the loss of his lease. Through the help of her lawyer boyfriend (Clarence Nordstrom) and her skill at song writing, she manages to sell a song—"jazzed up" for popular appeal by comedian "Chic" Jiggs (Donahue)—that nets her $75,000 and saves the situation with plenty of cash to spare.

This formula show had nothing of extra dynamic or show-stopping uniqueness, but its "story is bearable, the tunes easy to remember, the dances superior, the comedians funny and the chorus rather human," declared Percy Hammond.

MONEY BUSINESS [Comedy/Business/Marriage/Family/Jews] A: Oscar M. Carter; D: Lawrence Marston; P: Carter-Arkatov Productions, Inc.; T: National Theatre; 1/20/26 (13)

Dialect comedian Lew Fields starred in this flop in which he played a Lower East Side delicatessan owner who moves with his family into a fancy uptown apartment and gives up the store when his wife (Pola Carter) steals his savings and gives them to their boarder (A. J. Herbert) to invest in Wall Street. The boarder turns out to be a bond thief, the family loses all of their money and returns to the old business downtown.

Fields and company acted the piece as low comedy, and, as such, it served him very well with his "drolleries, grimaces and threatening sallies" (*Times*). His Jewish character mannerisms were highly effective, and jokes that would have gone over big with a Jewish population were larded through the dialogue. Much of the humor came from the discomforts of the poor family trying to make themselves at ease in their posh new surroundings. However, audiences weren't interested, and the play died young.

MONEY FROM HOME [Comedy/Small Town/Legacy/Romance/Medicine] A/ D: Frank Craven; P: A. L. Erlanger; T: Fulton Theatre; 2/28/27 (32)

Author, director, and star Frank Craven brought this homey piece of hokum to Broadway after touring with it under the title *Coal-Oil Jennie*. Superficial in conception, wobbly in plot, implausible in situation, and stereotyped in character, "It proved merely routine entertainment and stock sentiment," in Gilbert W.

Gabriel's estimation. Arthur Hornblow deemed it "a safe, sane but rather dull play."

Several thousand dollars have fallen into small-town waitress and powder-mill worker Jennie Patrick's (Shirley Warde) lap as the result of a legacy. She goes to New York intending to have a fling with the cash and there meets a former M.D. turned con artist (Craven), whose income derives from fleecing the rubes. Thinking the only way to get what he believes to be Jennie's riches is to marry her, he does but then learns the truth. An explosion at the powder mill forces him to call on his medical training, which leads to a renewed purpose in his life and affection for his bride.

MONEY LENDER, THE [Comedy/Religion/Legacy/Jews/Romance/Family/British] A: Roy Horniman; D: Edward Clark Lilley; S: Robert Edmond Jones; P: Ned Jakobs; T: Ambassador Theatre; 8/27/28 (16)

An *Abie's Irish Rose*-like situation comedy about a British Christian money lender's (Charles Esdale) will, which requires that his 200,000 pounds be left to his daughter Lillian (Katherine Alexander) if his Jewish partner's son Samuel (Herbert Clark) refuses to marry her or to Samuel if Lillian rejects him. The young couple, already in love with others, agree, however, to these conditions, but difficulties arise such as the determination of their children's religious faith; eventually, they decide to stick with their first romances and forgo the inheritance.

Various commentators liked the play's handling of the mixed-marriage theme, because it lacked the preachment of Anne Nichol's far more successful work. *Time* wrote that "Though the play be shot with abortive aphorism, it is entertaining." But the *Times* found that the "play never succeeds in being very positive or, in quality, better than so-so." In England it was called *Love in Pawn*.

MONGOLIA [Drama/China/Military/Sex/Adventure] A: Conrad Westervelt; D: Edwin R. Wolfe; S: Louis Kennel and Entwistle; P: George H. Brennan; T: Greenwich Village Theatre (OB); 12/26/27 (48)

"Trite dialogue and exaggerated situations lessened the effectiveness of" this florid melodrama set in Northern China in 1919, said the *Times*. A Russian White Army general (Frederic Burt) seeks to convey to safety in Paris the five-year-old (Warren McCollum) descendent of the Romanoffs, who is also his nephew. After subjecting an American couple (Mildred Florence and Thomas Carrigan) to tests of their integrity, he consigns the child to their care. The plot contained scenes of the wife's attempted seduction by the military overlord (Harry Nelson) and the killing of one (Boyd Agin) who tries to abduct the boy. To Perriton Maxwell it was "one of the dramatic high points of this busy . . . season," but he was generally alone in this view.

MONGREL, THE (Der Querulant) [Comedy-Drama/Law/Crime/Austrian] A: Herman Bahr; TR: Frances C. Fay; AD: Elmer L. Rice; D: Winifred Lenihan; S: Lee Simonson; P: Warren P. Munsell; T: Longacre Theatre; 12/15/24 (34)

This 1914 Austrian drama had been an European success, but its English adaptation, produced as a vehicle for Rudolph Schildkraut, proved vastly disappointing. "[S]omething disconcerting has happened to it this side of the three-mile limit," commented Q.M. With its uneven development, uninteresting debates on justice, and clumsy ending, the play had little to offer. "*The Mongrel*'s bite seems considerably worse than his bark," opined John Anderson.

Schildkraut's role, which he had played during the war in Vienna and Berlin, was of an old road mender, Mathias, whose dog is killed by a forester (Carl Anthony) and who refuses to accept the money the Justice (Maurice Colborne) has ordered paid in recompense. Blind vengeance is his motif, and he seeks to strangle the forester's daughter (Ernita Lascelles) in his anger. When his mind clears he gives himself up, but no charges are pressed and the old man resumes his peaceful ways.

Schildkraut brought great pathos and realism to his portrayal.

MONKEY TALKS, THE (Singe qui parle) [Comedy-Drama/Romance/Circus/French] A: René Fauchois; AD: Gladys Unger; D: Frank Reicher; S: John Wenger; P: Arch Selwyn; T: Sam H. Harris Theatre; 12/28/25 (98)

A melodramatic novelty from Paris, this implausible but atmospheric play of circus life was interesting mainly for the title character as it was remarkably interpreted by actor-mime Jacques Lerner. Lerner played a stunted circus performer who, together with a nobleman (Philip Merivale) cut off from his family, creates a sensational act in which he performs as Faho, an intelligent chimp who is nearly able to talk. The plot engages against him a wicked master (Eugene Weber), who kidnaps him and forces him to do his act for the master's gain but is publicly denounced by the ape even though it means an end to his act's secret. There is also the sad love story of the monkey-actor and the slack-wire artist whose heart belongs to the nobleman.

The play was filled with many bits and pieces of circus fun, and one act set at the Folies Bergere displayed such awesome feats as a stilt dancer doing a gravity-defying Charleston. "The whole idea [of the play] would be utterly preposterous," wrote Richard Dana Skinner, "if it were not for the fact that Jacques Lerner does succeed so amazingly well...that for a moment you are almost ready to say, 'yes, it could happen.' "

MONSIEUR BRONTONNEAU [Comedy/Sex/Romance/Marriage/French/French Language] A: G. A. de Caillavet and Robert de Flers; P: Wendell Phillips Dodge; T: Fulton Theatre; 3/12/24 (4)

John Corbin deemed this offering of Maurice de Féraudy's Comédie Française troupe "a comedy light in texture but brimming with the kindly humor and deft, antiseptic satire which made its authors admired and loved throughout the world."

M. Brontenneau (de Féraudy), a bank teller, is a model husband to a shrewish wife who has a lover. He elopes with a stenographer and is happy with her until his spouse asks for a second chance. He attempts a *ménage à trois* with the younger woman living in the same building, but his wife's old temperament returns, and the scandalized neighbors force him to send the stenographer away.

De Féraudy's acting, said Corbin, was "one of those achievements so perfect that they defy analysis."

H.H.

MONSTER, THE [Drama/Mystery/Crime/Romance/Medicine] A: Crane Wilbur; D: Lawrence Marston; S: J.H.M. Dudley; P: Joseph M. Gaites; T: Thirty-ninth Street Theatre; 8/9/22 (112)

A strenuous attempt at raising the hair of Broadway audiences by means of a story of the innocent souls who wander into a mad doctor's reputedly haunted house. Enough critics were sufficiently traumatized by the goings on to induce a decent run for the thriller.

Taking refuge from a storm at the home of Dr. Gustav Ziska (Wilton Lackaye) are three disparate persons, a reporter (McKay Morris), a tramp (Frank McCormack), and a woman (Marguerite Risser). They are warned by the doctor that the house is home to spirits. During the night of their occupancy weird occurences abound. In the final act, Dr. Ziska plans to vivisect the girl, while the reporter is restrained in an electric chair. Heroic events transpire, the doctor is himself juiced in the chair, and his monstrous aides are put out of commission. Love dawns on the girl and the reporter, and the tramp is revealed as a detective.

The Monster was well produced with many unique effects. "Divans opened and shut mysteriously, secret panels swallowed whole actors, doors were opened by everything but human agency, candles went out, [and] apparatus appeared in mirrors," noted the *Times*.

MONTH IN THE COUNTRY, A (Mesyats v derevne) [Dramatic Revival] A: Ivan Turgenev; TR: M. S. Mandell; AD/D: Rouben Mamoulian; S: M. S. Dobuzinsky (as reproduced by Raymond Sovey); P: Theatre Guild; T: Guild Theatre; 3/17/30 (72)

The Theatre Guild gave Turgenev's 1850 Russian comedy its premiere American performance (it was the first Turgenev play done here in English), and it led to the play's gradually being recognized as a minor classic. In Russia it had had to wait twenty-two years before being produced. *A Month in the Country* is a play of penetrating psychological insights into its various persons; its dependence on internal states rather than external action established it as a harbinger of the style that would bring Chekhov his renown.

Treating of life and love on a country estate, its plot peruses the affairs of Natalia Petrovna (Alla Nazimova), whose husband Islaev (Douglas Dumbrille) has hired for their pretty daughter Viera (Eunice Stoddard) a charming young tutor, Alexsei (Alexander Kirkland). Her husband's friend, the ineffectual Rakitin

(Elliott Cabot), loves Natalia, but the latter loves the tutor who is also loved by Viera, although his affections, which he dare not reveal, are really for Natalia. Thinking Rakitin is the cause of the emotional troubles in his home, Islaev has him depart, a path taken also by Aleksei, while Viera escapes the house by marrying a neighbor.

Positive opinion about the play was far from universal. Brooks Atkinson denied that it had "force of character" and thought it was dull and dated by modern standards. Perriton Maxwell appreciated the play's naturalism but dismissed it as thin and empty. But Richard Dana Skinner considered it a "well-drawn portrait of a neurotic woman." The Guild's production was superlative in every way.

MONTMARTRE [Drama/Romance/Sex/French] A: Pierre Frondaile; TR: Benjamin Glazer; D: Clarke Silvernail; P: Players' Assembly; T: Belmont Theatre; 2/13/22 (112)

In *Montmartre* audiences were presented with "The old, old story which French playwrights never tire of telling. . . . The story of the woman of the Paris underworld who undertakes to step out of her native surroundings but who cannot. . .quite make the grade" (*Post*). The grisette was Marie-Claire (Galina Kopernak), a Montmartrois who leaves her composer-lover (Arthur Hohl) to be kept by a wealthy older man (Frank Doane); when she finally decides to return to the composer, she finds it is too late. She ends up amongst her dissolute companions at the Moulin Rouge.

Although it was a hit in Paris where Polaire played Marie-Claire, the play's most compelling feature in New York was the debut of blonde Russian newcomer Galina Kopernak, whose accent was too thick for Broadway ears to cut through. The *Herald* claimed that the translation (mistakenly credited to A. E. Thomas) was "stilted" and that the work was completely without surprises.

MOON IS A GONG, THE [Drama/Theatre/Politics/Romance] A: John Dos Passos; D: Edward Massey; S: Mordecai Gorelik; P: Juliet Barrett Rublee; T: Cherry Lane Theatre (OB); 3/12/26 (19)

Promising novelist John Dos Passos offered this "spotty and spasmodic affair" (Henry Longan Stuart) but failed to incite much zeal. His program note described it as "a protest against the machinery and automatism of modern life." The play was a kaleidoscopic expressionist phantasmagoria with barely any plot, revealing in disconnected scenes accompanied by a jazz band the state of contemporary American life. It viewed the fortunes of a young couple, Tom (Allyn Joslyn) and Jane (Helen Chandler), through a series of imagistic scenes descriptive of the chaos surrounding them. The heart of the action followed Jane to the peak of success as an actress coupled with her descent into the depravity of the life around her, followed by the salvation she is brought by Tom, himself an outcast, but one seeking to achieve the goal of beating the moon like a gong.

The piece was momentarily interesting but was too humorless and confused. Brooks Atkinson said, "Loud and shrill,. . . picturesque, it is novel and arresting.'' To John Mason Brown it was hazy and lumbering. The play was also known by the title *The Garbage Man* after the figure of such a character who, like the refuse collectors of Tennessee Williams's *Camino Real*, is meant to symbolize death.

MOON-FLOWER, THE (Az utolsó csók) [Comedy/Romance/Hungarian] A: Lajos Biro; AD: Zoë Akins; D: David Burton; P: Charles L. Wagner; T: Astor Theatre; 2/25/24 (48)

Playing a Budapest lawyer's clerk who spends his modest inheritance wooing a duke's mistress in Monte Carlo, Sidney Blackmer lost not only the girl but most critics' esteem. They found him dull and unromantic. Elsie Ferguson as the mercenary mistress who loves the boy but luxury more received mixed reviews. John Corbin thought she was gorgeous as the moon-flower—the clerk's one-night bloomer—but cold.

Opinions of the comedy varied from Woollcott's ''engaging and glamorous romance'' to Percy Hammond's ''histrionic lullabye...a bit languid and discursive.''

H.H.

MOONLIGHT [Musical/Gambling/Romance] B: William Le Baron; M: Con Conrad; LY/D: William B. Friedlander; SC: William Le Baron's farce *I Love You*; CH: Larry Ceballos; S: Joseph Urban; C: Mabel Johnston; P: L. Lawrence Weber; T: Longacre Theatre; 1/30/24 (174)

Based upon his 1919 farce *I Love You*, William Le Baron's book involved the unexpected working-out of a $5,000 bet between two society blades (Louis Cohen and Glen Dale) that anyone can be made to fall in love in the right atmosphere. Of the sixteen songs, ''On Such a Night'' lived beyond the show, for which the chorus got the best reviews.

''The play has a little fun to it,'' noted Q.M., but the comic business is not very well disseminated.'' The *Times* declared, ''Conrad's music is tuneful..., Mr. Friedlander's lyrics are adequate, Mr. Ceballos's chorus direction is in the latest, most whirlwindish fashion, and Mr. Weber has been more than lavish in his costuming and scenic investiture.''

H.H.

MORALS (Morale) [Dramatic Revival] A: Ludwig Thoma; TR: Charles Recht; REV: Sidney Howard; D: Dudley Digges; S: Donald Oenslager; P: Actors' Theatre; T: Comedy Theatre; 11/30/25 (41)

Ludwig Thoma's Moliere-like satire, first staged in German in 1908, had been seen at the Irving Place Theatre in 1914 in the German original. In revival it seemed a funny, risque, and interesting piece. ''*Morals*,'' insisted the *Sun*, ''remains a pattern of social satire, an utterly unsentimental, thrashing derision of the public ways and private means of the past generation.''

Its plot concerned the results of a raid on a brothel frequented by not only the

President of the Society for the Suppression of Vice but the Crown Prince himself. The *Times* was concerned with its verbosity and the naughtiness of the bawdy-house details, and Larry Barretto found it repetitious and obvious. George Jean Nathan explained that its once fresh notions had been stolen by others since it was first written.

MORNING AFTER, THE [Comedy/Romance/Crime] A: Len D. Hollister and Leona Stephens; D: Lester Lonergan; P: L. M. Simmons; T: Hudson Theatre; 7/27/25 (24)

A typical time passer for the dog days of summer was this farce set at a Maine house party with a suitably assorted gang of guests and a stereotyped black servant played in blackface (Emma Wise). During the proceedings the host (A. H. Van Buren) discovers that his valuable gas patent has been filched, and numerous complications thereby arise before the thief is discovered. During these activities, various romantic alliances are formed and reformed with a happy future in store at the end for several joyful couples.

Although nicely played, the piece had little to offer. The *Times* said it had "many moments that are dull, some that are mildly amusing and at the best one or two that are genuinely provocative of genuine laughter."

MORPHIA [Drama/Drugs/Sex/Romance/Austrian] A: Duncan McNab and Ludwig Herzer; D: Lowell Sherman; T: Eltinge Theatre; 3/6/23 (57)

A morbid Austrian drama given a Scottish setting in its English version. It was a sensationalistic treatment of drug addiction, a subject touched on by not a few plays of the era.

The *Sun* declared this "a gripping drama," but many others disagreed. It involved Julian Wade (Lowell Sherman), a writer driven by unrequited love to morphine highs on a regular three-hour basis, who is confronted by an old love (Olive Tell), an actress disguised as a nurse to get into his private quarters. She wants to help him break his habit and thus gives herself to him sexually as a means of getting him to stop; this fails to work, and he only really throws away his needle when she convinces him that, to make him happy, she too will become an addict.

Several critics, notably Laurence Stallings, tore their hair at so technically preposterous a situation: "it incenses any person with even an elementary knowledge of narcotics." Arthur Hornblow picked on the "exceptionally stilted English" of "this somewhat pointless piece" and had little good to say of the performances.

MOST IMMORAL LADY, A [Comedy-Drama/Marriage/Romance/Crime/France] A: Townsend Martin; D: Dwight Deere Wiman and Townsend Martin; S: Jo Mielziner; P: William A. Brady, Jr., and Dwight Deere Wiman; T: Cort Theatre; 11/26/28 (160)

A competent piece of work made tasty by Alice Brady's excellent acting.

Unfortunately, said Joseph Wood Krutch, its very interesting first two acts were capped in the third by "a highly conventional and rather pointless conclusion." Euphemia Van Rensselaer Wyatt had even less respect for it: "The lines, aping smartness, possess neither the honesty of humor nor the intelligence of wit."

The story concerned a married pair, Laura (Brady) and Humphrey (Austin Fairman), who earn their money by practicing the badger game on unwitting men. Laura falls for one of her victims (Guido Nadzo), and the plot eventually concludes in Paris, where she goes to divorce Humphrey.

MOUNTAIN FURY [Drama/Rural/Romance/Family/Crime] A: David Davidson, Jr.; D: E. J. Blunkall; S: P. Dodd Ackerman; P: Ack-Rud Enterprises, Inc.; T: President Theatre; 9/25/29 (13)

A hillbilly melodrama with a Romeo and Juliet theme; its locale was the Pennsylvania Alleghenies, and it concerned a feud between an upland family and one from the vales. The lowland sheriff's (Carleton Macy) son Paul (Herbert Ashton, Jr.) and the hillbilly's daughter Myra (Mary Miner) fall in love and incite their father's ire. Her parents want her to marry the unpleasant Bill (Frederick B. Manatt), but Fenicle (Barry Macollum), the village idiot, who also loves Myra, kills the unwanted suitor and then jumps off a cliff.

This was "a noisy and excitable melodrama" (*Times*) replete with "baying hounds, tempests, a forest fire, murder, suicide, theft, and the bemused mumblings of a woodland lunatic" (*Time*).

MOUNTEBANK, THE [Drama/France/War/Circus/Romance/Military] A: W. J. Locke and Ernest Denny; SC: W. J. Locke's novel of the same name; D: David Burton; P: Charles Frohman, Inc.; T: Lyceum Theatre; 5/7/23 (32)

"[A]n agreeable if leisurely entertainment, abounding in quiet sentiment and gentle humor," was John Corbin's judgment on this piece, but the *Herald*'s critic thought that "some of [W. J. Locke's] glamorous human interest seems to have been lost in the search for material that would provide enough situations to trick out each act."

It was about an English circus clown, Petit Patou (Norman Trevor), who works in a French circus with a French girl (Gabrielle Ravine) as his partner. During the war he joins up with England and becomes a brigadier general and hero. He would like to wed the aristocratic Lady Auriol (Lillian Kemble Cooper), but loyalty to his ex-partner draws him back to her, and it is only when the French girl runs off with his old friend (Lennox Pawle) that the clown-soldier feels free to marry his true love.

MOVE ON [Comedy/Journalism/Romance] A: Charles Bamfield Hoyt; D: Augustin Duncan; P: Edward A. Miller; T: Daly's Theatre; 1/18/26 (8)

The first thing the critics noticed about this inept newspaper comedy was the genteel tone of the city room of the Topeka *Daily Press*, the tabloid in whose offices part of the action takes place. It was intended as a comedy-melodrama designed to set off the character of the eccentric tramp printer Muscogee (Claude Cooper), a whiskey-guzzling creature who gets a job as a reporter with the paper and helps save the Governor's daughter (Hope Drown), who is being held for ransom in a speakeasy. He gives credit for the scoop to a cub reporter in love with the daughter and moves on down the line, seeking one more handout, one more drink.

Claude Cooper provided a richly detailed portrayal, but the play did "not differ radically from most pieces of stage carpentry for the old-time strolling players," according to Brooks Atkinson.

(1) **MOZART** [Musical/Period/Musical-Biographical/French] B/LY: Sacha Guitry; AD: Ashley Dukes; M: Reynaldo Hahn; D: William H. Gilmore and Norman Loring; P: E. Ray Goetz; T: Music Box Theatre; 11/22/26 (33)

Sacha Guitry's piece about the great Austrian composer's life had been written with an actress in mind for the role of Mozart. Guitry's wife, Yvonne Printemps, had played it in its hit Paris incarnation, and Irene Bordoni embodied it on Broadway. A month after the work opened, the Guitrys made their American premieres in a limited engagement of *Mozart*. The work was a musical but with original melodies composed for it. Bordoni, best known as a singer, was captivating during her songs but did not satisfy critical expectations regarding her acting.

The dramatic portion of the work focused on Mozart's six months in Paris at the age of twenty-two during which time he was patronized by the Baron von Grimm (Frank Cellier), made a stalwart attempt to gain acclaim for his music, had several notorious romances, and was then forced by his patron to leave France.

Mozart in English seemed an ill-baked proposition, despite its excellent mounting and fragile charm. It soon became "thin and attenuated," to the *Times*, and Robert Coleman thought that the author had "failed to catch the spark, the genius that was Mozart's."

(2) [and Act Two of *Deburau*] [Musical Revival/French Language] D: Sacha Guitry; P: A. H. Woods; T: Chanin's Forty-sixth Street Theatre; 12/27/26 (32)

The Guitry production, with Guitry as Baron von Grimm and Yvonne Printemps as Mozart, was markedly more effective than the above version. The Guitrys were among the great European stars of their day, and few could match their technical and personal accomplishments, especially in material designed expressly for them. The tenuousness of their vehicle ("a medley of speaking, singing and dancing"—Brooks Atkinson) seemed not so noticeable because of their performances. E. W. Osborn expostulated about Printemps: "The boyish charm of twenty-two, the graceful awkwardness of adolescence finding itself out, the stumbling speech and the easily flowing song...are all with this fascinating impersonator, and all reinforced by her own charms of person and voice.'' Guitry was warmly toasted: ''No American production has ever glistened with such perfection of detail,'' was Richard Dana Skinner's claim.

As curtain raiser, an act of Guitry's *Deburau*, seen several years earlier in an acclaimed David Belasco staging, was introduced. Atkinson called it ''amiable without distinction'' and noted that Guitry, in the title role, showed a technique that was ''supple and relaxed; his gestures have extraordinary grace and versatility.''

(1) MUCH ADO ABOUT NOTHING [Dramatic Revival] A: William Shakespeare; M: Douglas Moore; D: Richard Boleslavsky; C: Lilian Gaertner; P: American Laboratory Theatre; T: American Laboratory Theatre (OB); 11/18/27 (25)

The American Laboratory Theatre began its 1927–1928 season with this play in its new 299-seat theatre on East Fifty-fourth Street between Second and Third Avenues. The play had last been seen locally in 1913. George Macready played Benedict, and Blanche Tancock was Beatrice in the new mounting, which was ''a stylized presentation, done on a miniature scale in everything but the acting,'' according to the *Times*, which censured the performances for being ''exceptionally loud and florid.'' Nothing could have contrasted more obviously with the magnificence of Reinhardt's *Midsummer Night's Dream*, seen the night before. Richard Boleslavsky attained some nice touches in his staging, but the cast simply was not up to suggesting the author's humor. ''As the diction of Mr. Boleslavsky's players is distressingly inept,'' chastised John Mason Brown, ''and as their characters are but sketchily indicated, they make but few comic points.'' The interesting scenic background was based on the illuminated manuscript of *Roman de la Rose*, as evoked by a gold checkerboard drop, with blue, red, white, and black panels shown to suggest locales.

(2) D: Ben Greet and Peter Dearing; C: Doreen Erroll; P: Ben Greet and the Ben Greet Players; T: McMillin Academic Theatre (OB); 11/16/29 (1)

The second revival of the play in the decade was offered by England's roving Ben Greet Players, led by the British actor-manager, then aged seventy-two, who was knighted the same year this staging was seen locally. It was also Greet's jubilee year in the theatre. Much of his prewar career had been spent in New York, but after he returned to London in 1914 he helped found the Old Vic and did twenty-four Shakespeare plays there between 1915 and 1918. On the present occasion he staged *Much Ado* for only a single performance at a school auditorium and gave *Everyman* as his other presentation. *Much Ado* was treated, said Brooks Atkinson, ''as one of the minor frolics of a versatile Elizabethan play-scribbler, formal in its invention, conventional in the symmetry of its plot, labored and passing dull in its opening scenes, but ultimately waxing humorous and romantic amid a 'fantastical bouquet' of words.'' Scenery was nil, props reduced to the barest minimum, a forestage employed, and nary a gimmick or trick to be seen. The acting was all, and the play thusly came alive. The lines were completely comprehensible, whether spoken by lead or minor role. Thea Holme was Beatrice, Russell Thorndike was Benedict, Greet was Dogberry, Alison Pickard was Hero, and Arnold Walsh was Claudio.

MUD [Comedy/Youth/Business] A: Katherine Browning Miller; T: Cherry Lane Theatre (OB); 7/3/24 (6)

A terrible piece about a college student who gets involved in a promotional scheme designed to sell a mud treatment for skin beauty; the *Times* reported that it was "The dark horse entrant for the nomination for the worst play of the season."

MUD TURTLE, THE [Drama/Rural/Sex/Marriage/Family] A: Elliott Lester; D: Willard Mack; P: A. E. and R. R. Riskin; T: Bijou Theatre; 8/20/25 (52)

A serious, determined effort to provide a drama of elemental passions as exemplified by the French-Canadian residents of a large midwestern wheat farm. Reminiscent of the far superior *Desire under the Elms* and *They Knew What They Wanted*, it was concerned with the marriage of Lem Tustine (Buford Armitage) to Minneapolis waitress Kate (Helen MacKellar); she is reviled by Lem's domineering father (David Landau) and resolves to gain revenge and get her husband to stand up to the old man. She promises a farm worker sex if he will destroy the reaper, but the playwright keeps her pure, and a reconciliation with the humbled father is effected.

George Jean Nathan thought the author had taken a well-worn theme and given it "only a crudescence of melodrama." He assailed the stiff dialogue, awkward construction, and stenciled characters.

MULBERRY BUSH, THE [Comedy/Marriage/Sex/France] A: Edward Knoblock; D: Clifford Brooke; S: August Vimnera; P: Charles Dillingham and A. H. Woods; T: Republic Theatre; 10/26/27 (29)

One more in a succession of Al Woods bedroom-farce productions, *The Mulberry Bush* offered the inducement of James Rennie and Claudette Colbert playing Harry and Sylvia Bainbridge, a couple whose marriage is in a state of suspension owing to an English interlocutory law that requires a three-month separation before a divorce can be finalized. Each has romantic attachments that promise new mates, but Harry has two; one (Isobel Elsom), realizing she may not get Harry after all, locks the still-married couple in a bedroom for a night, thus arming her with proof she can bring to court guaranteeing that a reconciliation has taken place. But revenge is not so sweet since Harry and Sylvia decide to stay together, and the other woman ends up telling them to go to hell.

The mildly naughty farce, set in a French villa, was "short on wit, humor and suspense, and...chiefly long on pajamas," joked Stark Young.

MURDER ON THE SECOND FLOOR [Comedy-Drama/Crime/Mystery/Theatre/Drugs/British] A: Frank Vosper; D: Eilliam Mollison; S: P. Dodd Ackerman; P: A. H. Woods; T: Eltinge Theatre; 9/11/29 (45)

This British import, complete with a London cast, marked the first time Laurence Olivier's name appeared on a New York playbill. Brooks Atkinson said the drama "hardly seemed worth the labors of importation, and the vexations of a customs inspection." It was a stunt play with what Atkinson called "a parody prologue and epilogue" and featured the twenty-two-year-old future star in the role of playwright Hugh Bromilow, played in London by dramatist Frank Vosper himself. Bromilow is residing at a Bloomsbury boarding house, where his landlady's daughter prompts him to prove that he can write a suspense play as good as any, leading him to take her aside and watch the play he is going to write. His imaginary characters, all based on boarders at the house, come to life in nonillusionistic make-believe form involving a drug ring, murders, and the police. At the end all is explained as being the very same material included in the writer's play that premiered the night before.

Perriton Maxwell called it "an evening of amusing if not wildly exciting entertainment" and said that Olivier showed "an energetic seriousness which is highly infectious"; Atkinson remarked that he acted "with an alarming suggestion now and then of Alfred Lunt."

MURRAY ANDERSON'S ALMANAC [Revue] B: Noël Coward, John McGowan, Peter Arno, Paul Gerard Smith, Fred G. Cooper, Rube Goldberg, and Harry Ruskin; M: Milton Ager and Henry Sullivan; LY: Jack Yellen, John Murray Anderson, and Edward Eliscu; D: John Murray Anderson; CH: William Holbrook; S: Clark Robinson; C: Charles Le Maire, Robert Locher, Peter Arno, Louis Pinkney, Wynn, and Jacques Darcy; P: John Murray Anderson and Gil Boag; T: Erlanger's Theatre; 8/14/29 (69)

John Murray Anderson, having dropped his *Greenwich Village Follies* series, began another in this show, labeled "a revusical of yesterday, today, tomorrow," but it had only one edition, aside from a 1953 show using the same title. It failed to do business, despite a novel magazine format covering the half-century from 1880 to 1930. Numerous top talents contributed to its writing and design, and one musical perennial is indebted to its having been showcased here; this was Ager and Sullivan's "I May Be Wrong," introduced by Jimmy Savo and Trixie Friganza. A Reginald Marsh show curtain highlighted theatre history during the theme period; vaudeville clown Savo shot into prominence as a comic to be reckoned with; comedienne Eleanor Shaler with her Bea Lillie-like humor had not enough to do; Jack Powell did a first-rate blackface routine making music with a pair of drumsticks on various objects; magician Fred Keating was a clever M.C.; an Oscar Wilde story, "The Happy Prince," was represented as a Ballet Ballad; and a variety of other sketches and numbers scored. Still it all failed to coalesce. "[S]omehow," decided Brooks Atkinson, "its mixture of the good with the mediocre leaves you lacking a little in enthusiasm for it."

MURRAY HILL [Comedy/Family/Legacy/Romance/Alcoholism] A/D: Leslie Howard; S: Rollo Wayne; P: Messrs. Shubert; T: Bijou Theatre; 9/29/27 (28)

The first playwriting effort of English-born actor Leslie Howard was this unsuccessful farce, which the critics agreed was not funny enough to make the grade but did show evidence of writing talent. It was about a trio of prim maiden aunts (Alice May Tuck, Florence Edney, and Gaby Fay) who live with their pretty niece Amelia (Genevieve Tobin) in a Murray Hill townhouse and who expect their nephew Worthington Smythe (Glenn Anders) to arrive for an aunt's funeral and his inheritance of $100,000. A situation of mistaken identity is developed when the charming young Wrigley (Howard) substitutes for the bibulous nephew as a way of pursuing an attraction for the niece. Things get effectively ironed out, and Wrigley marries Amelia.

Howard's direction was inefficient, but his playing was excellent. As for the play, Alexander Woollcott was typical when he said, "the scenes of floundering mendacity hold the stage long past their due time and stage drunks weave interminably and fan the air."

(1) MUSIC BOX REVUE [Revue] B: Frances Nordstrom, Willie Collier, George V. Hobart, and T. J. Gray; M/LY: Irving Berlin; D: Hassard Short; CH: Bert French; S: Clark Robinson; C: Ralph Mulligan, Cora McGeachey, and Alice O'Neill; P: Sam H. Harris; T: Music Box Theatre; 9/22/21 (440)

Dignified ushers in white satin knickers escorted patrons to their seats for this revue that opened Sam H. Harris and Irving Berlin's exquisite Music Box Theatre in West Forty-fifth Street. The theatre's premiere show was a resplendent package of goodies that bowled over critics such as Arthur Hornblow who was stunned by "such ravishingly beautiful tableaux, such gorgeous costuming, such a wealth of comedy and spectacular freshness, such a piling up of Pelion on Ossa of everything that's decorative, dazzling, harmonious, intoxicatingly beautiful in the theatre." Alexander Woollcott had no difficulty picking Berlin's "Say It with Music," sung by Paul Frawley and Wilda Bennett, as the song hit of the event (the tune, introduced several months before the opening, became the official anthem of the four Music Box Revues). Another well-liked Berlin number in the twelve-song score was the ragtime "Everybody Step," sung by the Brox Sisters.

Hassard Short did an exceptional job of staging the $188,000 extravaganza, which attained smash-hit proportions. Leading comics Willie Collier and Sam Bernard convulsed the audiences as did comedienne Florence Moore. Their satirical sketches included "Under the Bed," in which Moore spoofed the bedroom-farce genre, and "Nothing but Cuts," which had Collier advising Bernard on the principles of playwriting. A tableau called "The Fan" had a "striking background of black silk and flashing jet" (Arthur Hornblow).

(2) [1922 Edition] B: Frances Nordstrom, George V. Hobart, Walter Catlett, and Paul Gerard Smith; M/LY: Irving Berlin; D: Hassard Short; CH: William

Seabury Stowitts; S: Clark Robinson; C: Ralph Mulligan and Gilbert Adrian; P: Sam H. Harris; T: Music Box Theatre; 10/23/22 (330)

The second *Music Box Revue* was a lavish show in the tradition established by the first. The *Times* announced, "Given a song, Hassard Short does something more than simply stage it. He dramatizes it; long after you think it is over, new golden curtains unfold to reveal new stage depths, new stairs, and new figures in towering costumes."

With Berlin's music and lyrics providing the rhythmic, melodic, and witty orchestral underpinnings, this edition made its mark by featuring performers such as the comedic duo Clark and McCullough, long-limbed dancing comedienne Charlotte Greenwood, opera singer Grace La Rue, actor William Gaxton, the Fairbanks twins, and many others. Bobby Clark of Clark and McCullough remained a major star for several decades.

The show's most lasting songs were "Lady of the Evening" (a favorite of the composer's), "Pack Up Your Sins and Go to the Devil," and "Crinoline Days," offered by La Rue in a scene of visual splendor showing her rising on an elevator that gradually allowed her hoop skirts to cover the full stage width.

(3) [1923 Edition] M/LY: Irving Berlin; D: Hassard Short; CH: Sammy Lee; S: Clark Robinson; C: Charles Le Maire and Ralph Mulligan; P: Sam H. Harris; T: Music Box Theatre; 9/22/23 (277)

Two sketches from the third *Music Box Revue* have since thrived on their own—George S. Kaufman's "If Men Played Cards as Women Do" (called "wildly hilarious" in the *Times*) and Robert Benchley's "Treasurer's Report," performed by Benchley himself (a sketch that Arthur Hornblow thought too sophomoric for a Broadway audience, remarking "at $5 a seat—phew!"). Grace Moore's singing of "The Waltz of Long Ago" and "What'll I Do" were highly rated, although generally the Irving Berlin score was judged as so-so.

Among outstanding sketches mentioned by reviewers were "Maid of Mesh," a dazzling display of dresses of gold and silver mesh; "Yes, We Have No Bananas," done grand-opera style; "The Fisherman's Dream," featuring Florence O'Denishawn dancing as a Star Fish caught by the bait of a diamond necklace; and "An Orange Grove in California," in which the audience was sprayed with orange perfume.

H.H.

(4) [1924 Edition] M/LY: Irving Berlin; D: John Murray Anderson; S: Clark Robinson; C: James Reynolds; P: Sam H. Harris; T: Music Box Theatre; 12/1/24 (184)

The fourth and last of the series was staged by John Murray Anderson. He "displayed his usual taste in line and color" (Heywood Broun), and the show was beautiful to behold, if somewhat simpler in effect than earlier editions. Woollcott called this "the best revue which these senses have experienced in ten years of playgoing along Broadway."

Berlin's songs were extraordinarily well delivered by the exquisite and lady-like Grace Moore and the handsome Oscar Shaw, as well as by the Brox Sisters. There were twenty songs, none of them gaining immortality. The one hit was an interpolation, the already popular "All Alone," sung at lighted phones by Shaw and Moore.

In "Bandanna Ball" the all-white chorus was turned instantaneously by a special lighting effect into an all-black chorus on a levee. Also of special interest was "In the Shade of the Sheltering Tree," in which the chorus used large, green, ostrich-plume fans on which electric fans blew to create a magical tree outlined against a black velour background. Humor and wistful charm came across in the "Ballet Dancers at Home" sequence, featuring Ula Sharon and Carl Randall going through their domestic routines as famous ballet melodies accompanied them.

On board were comic greats such as Bobby Clark and Fannie Brice. Clark had them rolling with his bit as a hapless boxer, Brice made them howl in her "Don't Send Me Back to Petrograd" routine. The clowns shared the stage for "I Want to Be a Ballet Dancer."

The entire show was framed within the concept of a Rip Van Winkle (Joseph McCauley) fable.

MUSIC IN MAY [Musical/Romance/Period/Austrian] B: Heinz Merley and Kurt Breuer; AD: Fanny Todd Mitchell; M: Emile Berte and Maurie Rubens; LY: J. Kiern Brennan; D: Lou Morton and Stanley Logan; CH: Chester Hale; S: Watson Barratt; P: Messrs. Shubert; T: Casino Theatre; 4/1/29 (80)

No one accused this operetta of originality or undue cleverness. It was based on a Viennese work, but much of its original score had been replaced by the melodies of Maurie Rubens. *The Student Prince* and *Blossom Time* echoed in its story of a Central European prince (Bartlett Simmons), a student who falls in love with a merchant's daughter (Gertrude Lang) at his university town and can only wed her by raising her from commoner status to that of a baroness.

The book was set in an early nineteenth-century setting and one of its characters was the historical figure of Metternich (Joseph Lertora), who warbled a ditty about having "put Napoleon on the skids." "Most of the situations are familiar," pronounced the *Times*, "but here and there it rose a bit above the commonplaces with the aid of some good voices and sensuoues [sic] Viennese Waltzes."

MY AUNT FROM YPSILANTI (Ma tante d'Honfleur) [Dramatic Revival] A: Paul Gavault; P: Henry Baron; T: Earl Carroll Theatre; 5/1/23 (7)

A flat French farce that had been produced in a different adaptation in 1915 called *She's in Again*. In the present version the action was transposed to Greenwich Village and Virginia, while the earlier work moved the story from the Village to Lakewood, New Jersey. It told of a pair of wealthy bachelors (Paul Gordon and Richard Sterling) and of the arrival of a meddling though benificent aunt (Alice Fischer) from the midwest during a rendezvous between her nephew and a masked lady he has invited to his apartment.

The *World* put it this way: "When bad farce collides with a clumsy company, the proceedings are a matter of autopsy rather than criticism."

MY COUNTRY [Comedy/Race/Romance/Family/Marriage/Jews] A: William J. Perlman; D: Charles Judels; P: Independent Producing Company; T: Chanin's Forty-sixth Street Theatre; 8/9/26 (49)

This play was assailed as a glaring attempt to imitate the revenue-producing ingredients of *Abie's Irish Rose*; its principal subject was ethnic prejudice, the groups involved being Jews, Irish, Italians, and WASPs. They were represented, said Brooks Atkinson, as the conventional "false racial symbols" of the stage. Arthur Hornblow condemned it as "a rather flabby play of the order which the Germans call 'Volksstuck.'...There is no invention and no plot to the thing."

The story pictured the animosities and reconciliations that evolve when a snooty seventh-generation descendent of Dutch settlers (Frederick Burton) is so offended by the impending marriages of his daughter (Marguerite Mosier) to a Jew (Roy R. Bucklee) and his son (Earl House) to an Italian (Erin O'Brien-Moore) that his own silver wedding anniversary is imperiled. An Irishman (Eddie O'Connor) helps to patch things up.

MY GIRL [Musical/Prohibition/Marriage] B/LY: Harlan Thompson; M: Harry Archer; P: Lyle D. Andrews; T: Vanderbilt Theatre; 11/24/24 (201)

In Arthur Hornblow's eyes, *My Girl* was "a tuneful and speedy musical farce which is entertaining almost every minute of the time." There were huzzahs for the generally well-written book, excellent tunes and lyrics, high-stepping and good-looking chorus, outstanding jazz orchestra, abundant comedy, and energetic principals.

The plot, which a few thought an improvement over the usual musical-comedy fare, was about the Whites (Jane Taylor and Russell Mack), an Omaha couple living in the East, who want to join the exclusive Rainbow Club and succeed only when a party they give to promote themselves for admission is enlivened by the introduction of fourteen cases of whiskey that a bootlegger (Roger Gray) wants to hide from the tax men.

MY GIRL FRIDAY [Comedy/Show Business/Sex] A/D: William A. Grew; P: Schnebbe-Bacon, Inc.; T: Republic Theatre; 2/12/29 (253)

The cast of this risque comedy was hauled off to court one night during its first week's run for appearing in an obscene show, but that did not stop the piece from continuing as a sensational hit. Its title on the road had been *Undressed Kid*. A typical review held that "The play is so thoroughly and pointlessly vulgar that the least we say about it the better" (Perriton Maxwell).

A trio of chorus lovelies (Lucile Mendez, Alice Weaver, and Esther Muir) are forced to entertain the gents at the home of their backer (William A. Grew);

there they arrange to make the men (two married and one bachelor) believe they have seduced them while drunk. The consequent confusion brought on by wives and girlfriends leads to the backer's making comfortable amends to the members of the abused chorus girl's profession.

MY MAGNOLIA [Musical/Blacks] B/D: Alex C. Rogers and Eddie Hunter; M: C. Luckyeth Roberts; LY: Alex C. Rogers; CH: Charles Davis; P: Walter Campbell; T: Mansfield Theatre; 7/12/26 (4)

A "lopsided and ambling" (*Times*) black musical that tried to tell a story but ended up seeming like an ill-conceived revue. As often is the case in these shows, the dynamic dance routines received the greatest praise. The *Times* said "the chorus of men and women, individually and collectively, seemed to look upon dancing as the breath of life. They performed Charlestons, taps and other convulsions with frenzied expertness."

Eddie Hunter, Adelaide Hall, and Lionel Monagas were among the featured performers.

MY MARYLAND [Musical/War/Military/Period/Southern/Romance] B/LY: Dorothy Donnelly; M: Sigmund Romberg; SC: Clyde Fitch's play *Barbara Frietchie*; D: J. C. Huffman; S: Watson Barratt; P: Messrs. Shubert; T: Jolson's Fifty-ninth Street Theatre; 9/12/27 (312)

The legend of Barbara Frietchie, made famous in Whittier's poem, had been turned into a successful play by Clyde Fitch in 1899; this in turn was the source for *My Maryland*. Set in the period of the Civil War, the plot unfolds the tale of young Barbara (Evelyn Herbert; the real-life Barbara was actually ninety-six at the time of the events depicted), a southerner who loves northern officer Captain Trumbull (Nathaniel Wagner); Barbara defiantly waves the Union flag in the path of rebel General Stonewall Jackson (James Ellis), although the Captain lies wounded in her own bedroom. Moved by her bravery, Jackson commands his men to "March on."

Despite its stirring premise, the book (Dorothy Donnelly's last before she died) was no more than a hokey heart thumper, and the *Times* said it was "notable rather for theatrical competence than for wit or taste." *Time* declared that "the melodramatics are so naive that a rousing march song by Sigmund Romberg, accompanied by stagy gestures, failed of the usual operatic magic." Actually, Romberg's score was the show's saving component, and the songs "Won't You Marry Me," "Silver Moon," "Mother," and, especially, "Your Land and My Land" were accorded thunderous approbation.

MY PRINCESS [Musical/Marriage/Romance] B/LY: Dorothy Donnelly and Edward Sheldon; M: Sigmund Romberg; SC: an unproduced play by Edward Sheldon, *Proud Princess*; D: Sam Forrest; CH: David Bennett and Albertina Rasch; S: P. Dodd Ackerman; P: Alfred A. Aarons; T: Shubert Theatre; 10/6/27 (20)

Former screen-star Hope Hampton primed herself with voice lessons before venturing forth as a musical-comedy leading lady in this show. The results were acceptable, but the show, apart from Sigmund Romberg's score, was a failure. It was an unfunny work about a young woman (Hampton) who attempts to join the ranks of high society by inducing an Italian organ grinder (Leonard Ceeley) to pose as her princely consort. She marries the man, has to live with him in his Little Italy flat, really falls in love with him, and then learns that he truly is a nobleman.

Romberg's versatility was applauded. "Male choruses of *The Vagabond King* school, lilting waltzes, sentimental lyrics, music box tinklings, pastoral serenades, a passionate tympany dance and plain jazz" (*Times*) were among his contributions.

During the run of this show its colibrettist, Dorothy Donnelly, lay dying in a New York hospital.

MY SON [Drama/Sea/Small Town/Romance/Crime/Family] A: Martha Stanley; D/P: Gustav Blum; T: Princess Theatre; 9/17/24 (275)

There were some pleased, if not excited, reviews for this well-done drama but none that would have led one to believe that it would run for nearly nine months. Taking place in the shop and living quarters of a Portuguese widow (Joan Gordon) living on Cape Cod with her son Brauglio (Herbert Clark), it depicted the widow's being wooed by the sheriff (George McQuarrie) and a Portuguese friend (E. L. Fernandez). The chief situation concerned the son, who, tempted by a flapper (Martha Madison) making her annual summer visit to the Cape, steals the girl's mother's necklace to finance an elopement to the big city. The theft is discovered, and the boy's mother arranges to send him away for two years on a whaling ship to help reform his character.

Stark Young declared the play somewhat old-fashioned and not terribly dramatic, but he thought that it was saved by the lifelikeness of the characters "and the warm glow of the Portuguese atmosphere."

MYRTIE [Drama/Religion/Romance] A: Willis Maxwell Goodhue; P: Oliver Morosco for Mitchell Productions Company, Inc.; T: Fifty-second Street Theatre; 2/4/24 (24)

Plaudits were largely reserved for the theatre and its amenities rather than its premiere production. Oliver Morosco took over the management of the Berkeley Theatre, renamed it the Fifty-second Street Theatre, and redecorated it in what the *Herald* critic called "the early Byzantine style of the movies." Q.M. thought that the play, which starred the producer's wife Selma Haley in the title role, "cannot be recommended as good drama."

Myrtie's father drags her to the rectory of a handsome young priest and his sister, complaining that she wants to be a prostitute. Myrtie mocks him and runs away with a wealthy man with bad intentions when the priest rejects her love for him.

The *Times* commented that the play was "so bad that at times it brings forth peals of laughter for its burlesque values."

H.H.

MYSTERY MAN, THE [Drama/Crime/Mystery] A: Morris Ankrum and Vincent Duffey; D/P: Gustav Blum; S: Nicholas Yellenti; T: Nora Bayes Theatre; 1/26/28 (100)

Robert Wheeler (Weldon Heyburn) returns to his Park Avenue apartment, somewhat the worse for drinking, and discovers an unknown corpse on his living room sofa. For three acts he and the police endeavor to determine whom he is and who bumped him off. Comedy is injected by Togo (Reo Suga) and Yogo (Sizuo Kowata), the Japanese servants. Suspicion falls on several men and a woman, and then another victim joins the first. At last the perpetrator is revealed as Mrs. Wells (Marjorie Dalton), who shot the dastard because he threatened to reveal publicly that she was not merely the maid of Wheeler's fiancée (Gail De Hart) but her mother.

"Nothing sensational in the technique of melodrama excited the sensibilities of the audience; nothing extraordinary happened all evening," observed the *Times*.

MYSTERY SHIP, THE [Drama/Sea/Mystery/Crime] A: Edgar M. Schoenberg and Milton Silver; D/P: Gustav Blum; S: Nicholas Yellenti; T: Garrick Theatre; 3/14/27 (121)

A murder melodrama set aboard an ocean liner bound from New York to Southhampton with a killing that occurs at the rise of the curtain and a plot that takes three acts to uncover the culprit. The play "sets sail with a favoring breeze," declared Larry Barretto, "but thereafter it runs into a dead calm which holds it stagnant to the end." Filled with all of the hokum devices of the genre, the play raised few hairs. An ill-assembled and trained cast made it seem even worse.

The plot concerned the efforts of criminologist Arthur Langdon (Wallace Erskine), sailing on the ship with his daughter (Marian Swayne), to find out the murderer, and then discovering that no one actually had been killed but that the man thought dead was only faking as part of a scam against an insurance company.

MYSTERY SQUARE [Drama/Mystery/Crime/Adventure] A: Hugh A. Anderson and George Bamman; SC: Robert Louis Stevenson's stories "Suicide Club" and "The Rajah's Diamonds"; D/P: Murray Phillips; S: Cleon Throckmorton; T: Longacre Theatre; 4/4/29 (44)

A suitable source, two short stories by Stevenson, was not well employed by this melodrama's collaborators in turning out a piece with the appropriate values of horror and suspense. "The play has its moments of tension. . . but they are followed by other moments that are so taken up with telling an interpolated love story or with establishing a fact of no great pertinence that the effect of what has gone before is lost,'' stated the *Times*. Particularly ineffective was the blend of Stevenson's language with that of the authors, which made for stuffy, anti-quated-sounding dialogue.

The story told of Prince Florizel (Gavin Muir), a role based on the former Prince of Wales, who joins the notorious Suicide Club, where cards are dealt determining who will die and who will be his killer. In the midst of these proceedings is a plot by a villainous trio to steal the Rajah's diamond, in the Prince's possession. The arrival of the police saves the threatened nobleman and secures the arrest of the blackguards.